PENGUIN CLASSICS

THE DECAMERON

GIOVANNI BOCCACCIO was born in 1313, either in Florence or Certaldo, a town in Florentine territory. His father, a prosperous merchant banker with the Compagnia dei Bardi, moved to Naples in 1327 as general manager of the bank's Neapolitan branch, taking the adolescent Boccaccio with him. He entertained notions of his son following in his footsteps, and apprenticed him to the trade, but when he realized that Boccaccio had no vocation for banking he arranged for him to study canon law. This was equally unsuccessful, and after a few years Boccaccio gave up his legal studies and devoted his time to literature and scholarship. At this period Naples, under King Robert of Anjou, was one of the major intellectual and cultural centres in Europe. To judge from references in his Latin epistles, Boccaccio considered his sojourn in Naples as the happiest period in his life. For political and economic reasons he was forced to return to Florence in 1341. His experiences during what is now known as the Black Death (1347-9) are recorded in the introduction to the *Decameron*'s First Day, and when he met Petrarch in 1350 he had probably begun work on his great narrative masterpiece. He had already gained a reputation in Florence as an eloquent and persuasive man of letters, and the government entrusted him with several official missions. In 1354 and 1365 he was sent to the Papal Court at Avignon, and in 1367 to Rome in order to congratulate Urban V on the temporary return of the papacy from its so-called Babylonian Captivity. He revisited Naples three times, in 1355, 1362 and 1370. He had moved to Certaldo after the second of these visits and spent most of the last thirteen years of his life there, dying in 1375, just over a year after Petrarch. Boccaccio wrote several other works, including the *Elegia di Madonna Fiammetta*, which has been described as 'the first modern psychological novel', and the narrative poem *Filostrato*, on which Chaucer's *Troilus and Criseyde* is based.

G. H. McWILLIAM, a former Fellow of Trinity College, Dublin, was Professor Emeritus of Italian in the University of Leicester. His publications include studies of Dante, Boccaccio, Verga, Pirandello, Ugo Betti, Italian literature in Ireland, Shakespeare's Italy, and the pronunciation of Italian in the sixteenth century. He translated plays by Italo Svevo, Pirandello and Betti, and poems by Salvatore Quasimodo. His translation of Verga's *Cavalleria rusticana and Other Stories* was published by Penguin Classics in 1999. He held the Italian Government's silver medal for services to Italian culture. He died in January 2001.

Giovanni Boccaccio

THE DECAMERON

TRANSLATED
WITH AN INTRODUCTION AND NOTES BY
G. H. McWILLIAM

Second Edition

PENGUIN BOOKS

PENGUIN BOOKS

Published by the Penguin Group
Penguin Books Ltd, 80 Strand, London, WC2R ORL, England
Penguin Putnam Inc., 375 Hudson Street, New York, New York 10014, USA
Penguin Books Australia Ltd, 250 Camberwell Road, Camberwell, Victoria 3124, Australia
Penguin Books Canada Ltd, 10 Alcorn Avenue, Toronto, Ontario, Canada M4V 3B2
Penguin Books India (P) Ltd, 11 Community Centre, Panchsheel Park, New Delhi – 110 017, India
Penguin Books (NZ) Ltd, Cnr Rosedale and Airborne Roads, Albany, Auckland, New Zealand
Penguin Books (South Africa) (Pty) Ltd, 24 Sturdee Avenue, Rosebank 2196, South Africa

Penguin Books Ltd, Registered Offices: 80 Strand, London, WC2R ORL, England

www.penguin.com

This translation first published 1972
Second edition, with new introduction, bibliography, maps and notes, published 1995
Reprinted 2003
018

Filmset by Datix International Limited, Bungay, Suffolk
Printed in England by Clays Ltd, St Ives plc
Set in 10/12pt Monophoto Bembo

ISBN-13: 978-0-140-44930-3

www.greenpenguin.co.uk

ALWAYS LEARNING   **PEARSON**

To Vittore Branca

Primus studiorum dux

CONTENTS

THE DECAMERON

FIRST DAY

SECOND DAY

THIRD DAY

FOURTH DAY

FIFTH DAY

SIXTH DAY

SEVENTH DAY

EIGHTH DAY

NINTH DAY

A great furore then ensues, and the wife, realizing her mistake, gets into her daughter's bed, whence with a timely explanation she restores the peace.

TENTH DAY

he realizes who it is, he is filled with shame, and thenceforth
becomes Nathan's friend.

skill in training hawks brings him to the notice of the Sultan, who recognizes him, reminds him of their previous encounter, and entertains him most lavishly. And when Messer Torello falls ill, he is conveyed by magic in the space of a single night to Pavia, where his wife's second marriage is about to be solemnized. But he is recognized by his wife at the wedding-feast, whence he returns with her to his house.

PREFACE TO THE SECOND EDITION

First published in 1972, the present translation of the *Decameron* has been several times reprinted since that date, with occasional emendations of a distinctly minor complexion. Meanwhile, two further complete English translations of Boccaccio's master work have appeared, the first by Peter Bondanella and Mark Musa in 1982, the second by Guido Waldman in 1993. My translation for Penguin Classics was compared with the Bondanella–Musa version some years ago by the American scholar Christopher Kleinhenz, who concluded that both 'furnish texts that are remarkably close to Boccaccio's original in meaning, tone, and nuance' and that 'moreover, they provide most enjoyable reading, and that is, after all, one of the principal reasons why Boccaccio wrote the *Decameron*.'[1]

Naturally, I would not wish to dissent from either of those conclusions, but for some little time I have felt that something was lacking in the Penguin *Decameron*. The translation itself still seems in my not altogether impartial judgement to read surprisingly well, and a hand more dextrous than my own would be required to improve it to any significant degree. I have however taken this opportunity to make certain minor changes, one of them being the proverb that concludes the story of Alatiel (II, 7), where a slightly stilted and prosaic wording is replaced by something that is closer in spirit and cadence to Boccaccio's original.

If the translation requires only marginal adjustment, my introduction to the first edition is now overdue for substantial revision. It provided the reader with a minimum of information about Boccaccio's life and work, or about the reasons why the *Decameron* occupies so important a place in the history of western literature. Its original justification lay in its provision of a brief history of earlier attempts to translate the *Decameron* into English, highlighting their virtues and deficiencies, and hence showing why yet another translation was required. One or two of its more interesting points are preserved in the new introduction and in the notes to this second edition, but the main emphasis is now switched so as to focus in

1 See 'The Art of Translation: Boccaccio's *Decameron*', *Yearbook of Comparative and General Literature* 36 (1987), p. 111.

greater detail on Boccaccio himself rather than the shortcomings (and occasional merits) of his numerous anglicizers.

For the monoglot, non-specialist English reader, as indeed for many students of Italian, the range of information available about Boccaccio and the *Decameron* is remarkably limited. The over-literal and often inaccurate American translation of Vittore Branca's *Profilo biografico* and sections of his *Boccaccio medievale,* flamboyantly entitled *Giovanni Boccaccio: The Man and His Works* (New York, 1976), falls some way short of delivering what it promises,[2] and Thomas G. Bergin's *Boccaccio* (New York, 1981) remains the clearest and most informative summary in English of the writer's life and literary output. Of the numerous publications by American scholars in recent years, nearly all are devoted to a detailed and sometimes abstruse or esoteric analysis of a particular aspect of Boccaccio's master work. The more lucid analysts, such as Aldo Scaglione, Marga Cottino-Jones, Robert Hollander, Victoria Kirkham, Giuseppe Mazzotta, Millicent Marcus and Janet Levarie Smarr, have little to offer to the general reader, whilst investigators of the *Decameron*'s framework, like Lucia Marino and Joy Hambuechen Potter, construct theses that even the specialist has some difficulty in deciphering. Other, more accessible American writers on the subject, apart from Cottino-Jones in her analysis of the *Decameron*'s structure, *Order from Chaos* (1982), are Janet Serafini-Sauli and David Wallace. But their books, too, have their limitations, the first because of a certain lack of critical depth and the second for its author's over-readiness to engage in speculative historical reasoning.

When one turns to look at what is available in English from publishers on this side of the Atlantic, the prospect, though rather less cluttered, is only slightly better focused on the central issues.

---

2 The book is a rich mine of connoisseurs of translators' English. On p. 21, Branca is reported as saying: 'While such spectacles prompted those gallant nostalgias in the late Gothic taste, which endured so long in the Florentine middle class and in Boccaccio the writer himself, the gay life of a refined society found softer and more Epicurean rhythms in sojourns along the delightful Parthenopean shores.' There are countless other unfortunate renderings of Branca's prose, of which one more must here suffice: 'Boccaccio must have heeded and followed Andalò del Negro, best known for his endless and confused studies, more than heretofore has been realized' (p. 34).

Kathleen Speight's edition for the Manchester University Press of twenty of the *novelle* has a brief introduction containing a succinct account of Boccaccio's life and of his influential role in the history of European literature. Aimed at the student of Italian, it also has a bibliography and a series of notes clarifying some of the complexities of Boccaccio's style and language. Also from the Manchester school, there is Robert Hastings' elegant series of short essays on *Nature and Reason in the 'Decameron'*. Then we have Guido Almansi's slightly flawed but brilliantly perceptive and entertaining analysis of a dozen of the *novelle*, with sundry characteristic glosses on a great many more, in his *The Writer as Liar*. Cormac Ó Cuilleanáin's *Religion and the Clergy in Boccaccio's 'Decameron'* is an excellent survey of one of the work's most important ingredients, showing how Boccaccio exploits the Church, its institutions and its iconography for his own narrative purposes. Finally, as in America so over here, there are numerous articles in learned journals on both general and particular aspects of the work, those by Jonathan Usher being among the most perceptive and thought-provoking examples of the genre.

Without necessarily provoking a superabundance of thought, what the new introduction to the Penguin Classics *Decameron* attempts to provide is a fairly detailed and informative account of Boccaccio's life and literary output, special attention naturally being paid to those lesser works of his that seem to have a direct bearing on the eventual formation of the *Decameron* itself.

As to the critical method of the new introduction, the approach is unashamedly neo-positivist. In the section outlining Boccaccio's life, the unreliability of autobiographical motifs in the Prologue (*Proemio*), the Introduction to the Fourth Day and the Author's Epilogue (*Conclusione dell'autore*) is explained for the benefit of those readers who are unacquainted with the conventions of medieval literature. Due prominence is given to such matters as Boccaccio's lifelong attachment to his *primus studiorum dux*, in other words to Dante, and to the importance of the *Divine Comedy* as a structural model for his own secular epic. Emphasis is also placed upon the relevance of Boccaccio's close association in his earlier years with Neapolitan courtly and commercial circles, the influence of French culture at the Angevin court, and the contacts he established in Naples with

eminent figures in the spheres of poetry and scholarship. The events
of Boccaccio's later post-Decameronian life, including his friendship
with Petrarch, his diplomatic missions and other travels, and his
retirement to Certaldo, are sketched in with economy, their bearing
on the composition of the *Decameron* being no more than marginal.

The account of Boccaccio's life and work takes up about a fifth
of the new introduction, the rest being devoted to an analysis of the
Decameron itself, beginning with a survey of its antecedents. There is
some discussion of previous collections of *novelle*, such as John of
Capua's re-working of the *Panchatantra* in his *Directorium Vitae
Humanae*, the *Libro dei sette savi* and the *Novellino*. The significance
of the phrase used by Boccaccio in the Prologue to describe his own
collection of tales ('a hundred stories or fables or parables or
histories') is underlined by pointing out its curiously exact corre-
spondence with their known sources in French *fabliaux*, medieval
Latin *exempla* and fourteenth-century Italian chronicles respectively.
The possible influence of antecedents on the actual form taken by
the *Decameron* is briefly examined before the conclusion is reached
that 'no amount of source-hunting can obscure the fact that the
frame of the *Decameron* is a unique and original creation, the
product of a fertile and imaginative intellect which had already
supplied the impetus for several of the more important genres of
western literature.'

In analysing the work's structure, a deaf ear is turned to the siren
songs of Joy Hambuechen Potter in her *Five Frames for the 'Decameron'*, so that only three separate levels of reality are identified:
author, narrators and narratives. The authorial viewpoint of the
Prologue, Introduction to the Fourth Day and Author's Epilogue is
treated with the required degree of scepticism, and an attempt is
made to uncover the real motives for Boccaccio's interventions, the
main one being identified as a determination to defend the hitherto
neglected or despised poetic genre of narrative prose fiction. As far
as the narrators are concerned, I take it to be inconceivable that the
ten members of the *lieta brigata* do not have an allegorical function,
even though, contrary to Boccaccio's practice in his earlier works,
none whatsoever is specified. So the pre-lapsarian world of the
narrators is seen as a refined and extended version of the *locus*

amœnus, peopled (in accordance with the scheme suggested by Victoria Kirkham) on the one hand by female figures embodying the seven virtues, and on the other by male figures representing the tripartite division of the soul into the baser human emotions of Anger and Lust and the nobler, intellectual power of Reason. The narratives themselves are analysed under the traditional thematic headings of Love, Intelligence and Fortune, with major emphasis on the first and the second.

Apart from the revised and expanded introduction, a major innovation in the new Penguin Classics *Decameron* is the provision of copious explanatory notes to the individual stories. For a long time, it has seemed to me unreasonable that a text judged to require 600 pages of commentary in Vittore Branca's incomparable edition for the Classici Mondadori has no version in English that makes any serious attempt to answer the many questions that may arise in the mind of the monoglot English reader. In compiling the notes, my debt to Branca is freely acknowledged, but I do not necessarily agree with all of his conclusions and interpretations. Where it was felt to be appropriate, the notes include indications of sources, both known and presumptive. Comparisons are drawn, also, with some of the more obvious analogues, especially those of English writers such as Chaucer, Shakespeare and Keats. In addition, the notes hazard interpretations of some of the more enigmatic words or phrases in Boccaccio's text, one example being his own gloss on the name of the main character of the opening tale, where he writes that

> ... the French, who did not know the meaning of the word Cepperello, thinking that it signified *chapel*, which in their language means 'garland', and because as we have said he was a little man, used to call him, not Ciappello, but Ciappelletto.

Would it really have affected the Burgundians' assessment of Cepperello's character if they had known that his name was suggestive of a log rather than a garland? Is it not more likely that the name Cepperello ('little log' or 'little stump') had some pejorative or possibly obscene connotation in popular fourteenth-century Florentine speech? Another name that requires a word of explanation is that of Monna Belcolore's husband, Bentivegna del Mazzo (VIII, 2). Branca merely tells us that Bentivegna was a very common name, and that a Bentivegna, probably from Certaldo, was a colleague of Boccaccio's in the Compagnia dei Bardi. But that is to overlook the sexual associations of the name, literally 'May good come to you of the rod', for which a near-equivalent in modern colloquial English is 'Get stuffed!'

As already pointed out, the explanatory notes appended to this second edition of my translation owe much to Branca's masterly commentary to his own edition of Boccaccio's text. But even Branca's scholarly and comprehensive notes are occasionally in need of revision. Who, for instance, was the King of England with the transvestite daughter who elected to dress up as an abbot (II, 3)? Branca plumps for Henry II, on the grounds that the 'unexpected war' referred to at one point in the narrative is possibly the rebellion against Henry II led by his sons, Henry and Richard, in 1173. True, the action of the narrative takes place some time after the 'unexpected war', but in 1173 the King of Scotland was William I, still only thirty years old, who would hardly fit the pseudo-Abbot's description of him as 'a very old man'. Other features of the tale, such as the reference to barons and their castles, suggest that the tale is set in a period closer to Boccaccio's own day, possibly during the turbulent reign (1307–27) of Edward II, which was marked by an endless series of conflicts including his defeat at Bannockburn in 1314. A more plausible candidate as the princess's prospective husband would therefore be Robert the Bruce, who by 1327 was in his early fifties and suffering from the terminal illness, possibly leprosy, which led to his death in 1329.

In addition to the explanatory notes, a further innovatory feature of this second edition of the Penguin Classics *Decameron* is a select bibliography, listing works both in English and Italian that will serve as an aid to further study of Boccaccio and his literary work. The maps of Florence and Tuscany, Italy, the Mediterranean, and north-west Europe will, it is hoped, help to clarify the precise location of the surprisingly large number of places named by Boccaccio in the text of the *Decameron*. The indexes at the end of the volume include references to proper nouns both in the translation itself and in my introduction and notes.

The observant reader will perhaps note that translated passages in the introduction do not always conform to the wording in the actual text of the translation. This is because a word-for-word translation was sometimes thought preferable in order to illustrate more clearly a particular argument. With the exception of one quotation from Christopher Ryan's English version of Dante's *Convivio*, the remaining translations of excerpts from Italian or Latin texts that appear in the introduction and notes are my own.

In conclusion, I take the opportunity to express my grateful thanks to those without whose help and support, whether in the distant past or in more recent times, it would not have been possible for me to complete this present undertaking. It was my earliest teacher of Italian, Professor Gwyn Griffith, who suggested to the then editor of Penguin Classics, Robert Baldick, that I might be a suitable recruit to the ranks of his translators. To Professor Peter Brand I owe a special debt of gratitude for his long and patient encouragement of my research in the area of Boccaccio studies. Like all serious Boccaccio scholars, I have taken advantage of the formidable amount of research undertaken and published by Professor Vittore Branca, whose lectures I first had the privilege of attending over forty years ago at the University for Foreigners in Perugia, and whose edition of the *Decameron* is the main text on which my translation is based. I remember with particular affection the many lively conversations I had in Canterbury in the late 1960s on possible interpretations of Boccaccio's narratives with Professor Guido Almansi. To Mr Peter Hainsworth I am grateful for his agreeing to read through the text of the translation in its original form, and for granting it his *imprimatur*. More recently, Professor John Woodhouse kindly read my new introduction and notes, and made several valuable suggestions for their emendation, many of which I have acted upon. My first wife, Jennifer, not only encouraged me against my better judgement to undertake the translation of a text that I believed to be untranslatable, but also gave me useful advice on English prosody when I was translating the *canzoni* that are sung towards the end of the company's proceedings on each of the ten days. My present wife, Elizabeth, read the new introduction and notes, encouraged me with a flattering assessment of their worth, and suggested how they might be improved upon. To both, I put on record my profound appreciation for their infinite patience and understanding during half a lifetime spent in the pursuit of my Boccaccio translation and research. I must thank Paul Keegan, chief editor of Penguin Classics, for his generous response to my several requests concerning this new edition. Thanks are also owed to my text editor, Richard Duguid, to my cartographer, Reg Piggott, who displayed Griselda-like patience in complying with my numerous suggested additions and amendments to his maps, and to David Bowron, who prepared the indexes. It is perhaps needless to add that for any errors, infelicities or omissions, whether in the translation itself or in the introduction, bibliography, notes, maps or indexes, I myself accept full responsibility.

G. H. McWilliam
Lewins, Chalfont St Peter
1995

TRANSLATOR'S INTRODUCTION

I. THE WORLD OF THE AUTHOR

The brief and elegant prologue with which Boccaccio introduces the *Decameron* to his readers should not be interpreted too literally. In it, he claims that his motives in writing the hundred tales were humanitarian, and expresses the hope that they will not only exert a healing effect upon the lovelorn ladies to whom the work is ostensibly addressed, but also provide them with useful instruction and advice. Few people would take seriously his contention that the *Decameron* is an improving work of literature specifically designed to assist young ladies in the throes of love. The gentle irony underlying the outwardly serious declaration of his aims is obvious to all but the most casual of readers. Yet when he alluded at an earlier point in the prologue to that most lofty and noble love by which he had been inflamed since his earliest youth, the temptation to interpret the passage as referring to a personal experience was one which many of his biographers were unable to resist, especially when read in conjunction with various 'autobiographical' motifs that keep on appearing in most of his other literary works. Thus arose the traditional portrait of Boccaccio as a bourgeois youth of humble beginnings who succeeded in winning the love of a royal princess, by whom he was ultimately rejected. But this fanciful account of the writer's life, based as it was upon an over-literal interpretation of incidents recounted in works of fiction by an author deeply versed in the allegorical conventions of medieval literature, has now been superseded.

The circumstances of the author's birth, in the summer of 1313, are obscure. What is certain is that he was illegitimate, the product of a liaison between a Florentine banking official, Boccaccio di Chellino, whose family had moved to Florence from Certaldo at the turn of the century, and a lady of whom nothing whatever is definitely known. The fact that his father's business took him on occasion to Paris, and that one of the writer's early biographers describes his mother as a Parisian, gave currency to the belief that he was born in the French capital, whence a proud and doting father brought him back to Italy in his infancy. But this romantic account of his origins is almost certainly false. It is now generally accepted that he was born in Tuscany, probably in Florence but possibly in his father's native town of Certaldo, where Boccaccio was to spend the last thirteen years of his life.

It was at any rate in Florence that Boccaccio spent his childhood. Contemporary records indicate that his infancy coincides with the period when his father was making his mark with the famous Florentine banking house known as the Compagnia dei Bardi. At some time before 1320, his father married Margherita de' Mardoli, whose family could proudly boast an ancestral connection with Beatrice Portinari, the inspiring force of Dante's *Commedia*. From early childhood, therefore, he was ideally placed to acquire the rudiments of that veneration of Dante which is evident in the whole of his work from his earliest compositions to the lengthy but unfinished commentaries on Dante's poem that constitute his last major literary labour. One of the companions of his childhood and adolescence was Zanobi da Strada, who like Boccaccio was destined to become a poet and to establish himself in Neapolitan society. And it was Zanobi's father, Giovanni Mazzuoli, acting as tutor to both, who encouraged his pupils to study and admire the work of the poet of the *Commedia*. Boccaccio's reverence for Dante was similar in its intensity to that of Dante himself for Virgil. Just as Dante's poetry is interspersed with echoes and reminiscences of the *Aeneid*, so Boccaccio's work is consistently studded with fragments from the medieval epic of his Florentine predecessor. Boccaccio's description of Dante, in a letter to Petrarch of 1359, as the first guide of his studies (*primus studiorum dux*) recalls the terminology used by Dante in the *Commedia* to describe the great Latin poet.

At the age of thirteen, or thereabouts, Boccaccio moved from Florence to Naples, where his father had been appointed to a high-ranking position in the Neapolitan branch of the Bardi bank, which, like the other leading Florentine banking houses, the Peruzzi and the Acciaiuoli, had for many years been the financial mainstay of the kingdom's Angevin rulers. Even before reaching adolescence, the young Boccaccio had himself been apprenticed by his father to a career in banking, for which he had no natural inclination whatsoever. After what he later described as 'six wasted years', he persuaded his father to allow him to take up the study of canon law at the Neapolitan *Studium*, a Dominican institution established in 1269, which had close links with the university, founded in 1224 by Emperor Frederick II. Although his formal course of studies there was little more congenial to him than the career he had abandoned, it enabled him not only to begin assembling the vast store of erudition that underpins all of his literary work, but also to establish influential contacts in the fields of scholarship and culture in general.

Naples was at that time a flourishing intellectual centre, attracting poets, philosophers, artists and men of letters from all over Europe, especially from France and northern Italy. King Robert the Wise, who occupied the throne from 1309 to 1343, was the most powerful ruler in the Italy of his day, and an enlightened patron and practitioner of the arts. Dante had expressed a poor opinion of the Angevin monarch in the early years of his reign, dubbing him the king who was fit only for writing sermons. But Boccaccio was later to describe him as a second Solomon, and one of the leading Florentine chroniclers of the period, Giovanni Villani, wrote that he was 'the wisest of the Christians of the last five hundred years'. The language of Robert's court being French, the influence of French culture was all-pervasive.

The 'six wasted years' of Boccaccio's apprenticeship as a minor banking official were wasted only in the sense that they temporarily prevented him from pursuing the career as a scholar and poet for which he had always considered himself instinctively suited from early childhood. The Neapolitan branch of the Bardi bank was situated in the Ruga Cambiorum ('Exchange Street'), in a quarter of the city that offered him the opportunity of daily contact with various aspects and personalities of a dynamic business and commercial world that is reflected in much of his later writing, in particular in many of the stories of the *Decameron*. His duties would have taken him regularly, for instance, through those areas of the city that he describes in such graphic detail in the famous story of Andreuccio of Perugia (II, 5). As a bank teller and bank messenger, he had regular dealings with a broad cross-section of the trading and seafaring classes that constituted the core of a thriving commercial society in what was regarded as one of the most important centres of economic activity in medieval Europe.

At the same time, because of his father's high standing with the Angevin court, the young Boccaccio was enabled to mix freely with the Neapolitan nobility. Many years afterwards, in a letter written to a friend in 1363, he recalled with deep nostalgia this period of his life when he had entertained in splendid style and with true Florentine hospitality the sons of the aristocracy, who 'were not ashamed to come and visit me in my house'. He was thus familiar with the life-style of a sophisticated courtly society, and his keen observation of the refined manners and sentiments of that milieu is reflected in many of his writings. The world of the storytellers in the *Decameron*, for all its heightened, 'literary' and deliberately unreal quality, is an idealized image of a society in which Boccaccio himself participated, albeit as a foreigner and an outsider, during the formative years of his life in Naples.

Even more important from the point of view of his future development as a writer were the numerous contacts he established in those years with the outstanding scholars and men of letters who had been attracted to Naples by the renown of its learned sovereign and patron of literature and the arts. Among those who guided and encouraged Boccaccio in his innate vocation for the study and practice of poetry was Paolo da Perugia, the curator of the Royal Library, with its rich collection of material in the areas of philosophy, mythology, medicine and theology. Paolo's encyclopaedic compendium of ancient myths, the *Collectiones*, was specifically acknowledged by Boccaccio as the inspiring force for his own immensely influential Latin work on the same subject, *Genealogia deorum gentilium* (*Genealogy of the Gentile Gods*), composed towards the end of his life. In an affectionate tribute to Paolo in the latter work, he describes him as a scholar, advanced in years, who would take enormous pains to track down references whenever the king sought his help and advice. In the same passage, Boccaccio regrets that on

Paolo's death his shrewish wife destroyed his *Collectiones* along with other works of his, thus making Boccaccio's own task all the more difficult. He concludes by claiming that Paolo had no equal in such studies.

Other outstanding representatives of learning and the arts with whom Boccaccio came into contact during his sojourn in Naples were the astronomer Andalò da Negro, the theologian and rhetorician Dionigi da Borgo San Sepolcro, and the two leading figures of early Neapolitan humanism, Barbato da Sulmona and Giovanni Barrili. All of these scholars, especially Paolo and Dionigi, had a considerable influence on Boccaccio's development as a writer, both in the broadening of his literary knowledge and in the formation and refinement of his style and technique. A further important figure in this respect was Cino da Pistoia, the poet whose work marks the transition between the *dolce stil novo* and the poetry of Petrarch. Cino was in Naples pursuing his profession as one of Italy's leading academic lawyers, and Boccaccio is known to have attended the lectures on jurisprudence that he gave in the university there. Evidence of his regard for Cino may be seen in the affectionate reference to him that occurs in the Introduction to the Fourth Day of the *Decameron*. Boccaccio may also have attended lectures given by another famous lawyer of the period, Luca da Penne, who had written an important commentary on the Justinian Code which reveals him as a scholar of impressive erudition.

All of the influences to which reference has been made are apparent in the works Boccaccio wrote during his 'Neapolitan' period, from *La caccia di Diana* (*Diana's Hunt*), a brief but immensely complex mythological poem listing the young women of all the more important Neapolitan families of the day, to the beautifully measured narrative in octave rhyme, *Filostrato*, the ultimate source for Chaucer's *Troilus and Criseyde*. The remaining two major works of this period were *Filocolo*, a prolix, rambling prose version of the well-known French medieval romance narrating the adventures of two young lovers, Flore and Blanchefleur, and the narrative poem *Teseida*, intended by its author as the first Italian martial epic, from which Chaucer was to derive the material for his *Knight's Tale*.

In writing the *Filocolo*, Boccaccio's indebtedness to French literary models is seen not only in the narrative itself, but also in his handling of the *amour courtois* material of the Provençal troubadours, in particular the literary device known as the Court of Love, a kind of debating chamber for deciding affairs of the heart. A typical case submitted to the Court's judgement concerned a lady who listened to one admirer whilst squeezing the hand of another and touching with her toe the foot of a third. Which of her three admirers was the one she favoured most? Although no such question arises in the pages of the *Decameron*, the *Filocolo* is of special interest for the lengthy episode in Book IV where the hero, Florio, delayed in Naples by a storm during his sea-voyage in search of his beloved Biancofiore, attends a *festa* held in his honour. There he is invited to join a company of four ladies and nine gentlemen, who in turn propose and discuss thirteen *questioni d'amore*, or questions concerning love. The structure of the episode is makeshift and rudimentary by comparison with the elaborate 'frame' of the *Decameron*. The *locus amœnus* where the discussions take place is very briefly described. The oldest of the men who are present, Ascalion, is unanimously elected King of the company. But Ascalion, claiming to have spent his life in the service of Mars rather than of Venus, declines the honour and bestows it instead on Fiammetta, whom he crowns with a garland of laurel. The initial suggestion that the company should spend the hotter part of the day in discussing various questions of love comes from Fiammetta, using much the same argument as the one Pampinea will use in the *Decameron* to persuade her companions to engage in storytelling. In each case, the object of the exercise is to gain profit and amusement from time that would otherwise be spent in idle pursuits. Likewise, the formulas used to introduce the *questioni* in the *Filocolo* are often similar to those that preface the *novelle* in the *Decameron*. Two of the thirteen *questioni* involve the recounting of stories that Boccaccio later refines and inserts into the *Decameron* itself (X, 4 and X, 5). But whereas the *Decameron* is distinctively Florentine, the background to the *Filocolo* is decidedly Neapolitan, or Parthenopean, as the author, in his determination to classicize his text, prefers to describe it.

The available information about Boccaccio's sojourn in Naples – by common consent the most crucial period of his career – is in fact remarkably sparse compared to the wealth of accessible documentary material relating to his later life in Florence and elsewhere. Opinions differ concerning the precise date of his return from Naples to Florence, but in all probability it was during the winter of 1340–41. This is because on the one hand he declares in his commentary on Dante's *Commedia* that he was not in Florence during the plague of 1340, whilst on the other hand he does not seem to have been in Naples during the early spring of 1341, when Petrarch visited the city *en route* to Rome, in April of that year, for his coronation as poet laureate. Boccaccio's return to Florence was at all events dictated by a combination of political and economic factors. The traditional ties of friendship between the Florentine commune and the Angevin monarchy had come under considerable strain, partly because of King Robert's refusal to support the Florentines in their protracted wars against Lucca, and partly, also, because the dependence of the Angevins on Florentine bankers had by that time dwindled to comparative insignificance. Boccaccio's father had already left Naples after breaking off his connection with the Bardi company in or around October 1338, and some of Boccaccio's biographers have suggested, without any real evidence, that his own return to Florence was an inevitable consequence of his father's bankruptcy. A more probable explanation is that far-reaching changes in Neapolitan foreign and economic policy had impaired his social links with the Angevin court and raised the spectre of insecurity, though there may well have been some more pressing reason for his reluctant departure.

That his departure from Naples was indeed reluctant is attested by a letter he wrote from Florence on 28 August 1341 to the friend and companion of his Neapolitan youth, Niccola Acciaiuoli, now a powerful and influential figure in the Angevin court. Acciaiuoli, three years older than Boccaccio, was a fellow Florentine who had gone to Naples in 1331. According to the chronicler Giovanni Villani, his meteoric rise to fame and fortune was not unconnected with his having become the lover of Catherine of Valois, sister-in-law to King Robert and Empress of Constantinople. It was Acciaiuoli who had been instrumental in introducing Boccaccio to the ranks of Neapolitan high society, and in the letter of August

1341 Boccaccio tells him of his dissatisfaction with life in Florence,[1] at the same time strongly hinting that his former friend could perhaps bring about a change in his fortunes, presumably by finding him a sinecure at court. But his plea, like others he addressed to Acciaiuoli on later occasions, fell upon deaf ears.

In a work Boccaccio wrote some two or three years after his return to Florence, the *Elegy of Madonna Fiammetta*, there is a passage which to some extent clarifies his motives for leaving Naples, at the same time confirming the distaste for life in Florence of which he had written to Acciaiuoli. In Book II, the Neapolitan heroine is remonstrating with her young Florentine lover, Panfilo, concerning his decision to abandon her and return to the distant city of his birth. It is mid-winter, a detail that accords with the hypothesis that Boccaccio's own return took place in the winter of 1340–41. Although, as stated earlier, such 'autobiographical' passages require to be treated with caution, it seems reasonable to assume that Panfilo, whose name will later be given to one of the three male storytellers of the *Decameron*, is an idealized self-portrait. It is perhaps revealing that Panfilo explains his decision to abandon Fiammetta as being due to the love he bears towards his father, who is now an elderly widower, bereft of all his remaining children and kinsfolk. Filial piety was of course a popular literary topos, and one that the author had already exploited in his *Filocolo*, in an episode where the hero is attempting to dissuade his father from sending him abroad. But it happens that Panfilo's description in the *Fiammetta* of his father's circumstances corresponds more or less exactly with the known facts about Boccaccio's own father at the time in question. His wife, Margherita de' Mardoli, was now dead, and so too were the children of that marriage, so that his natural son would indeed have seemed the sole remaining comfort of his declining years.

In another passage from the *Fiammetta*, the Neapolitan heroine reminds her Florentine lover of his own description of his native city:

---

1 At one point in the letter, B. writes: 'Of my being in Florence against my will, there is nothing for me to write, because that would need to be shown in tears rather than in ink.'

... as you once told me yourself, your city is full of pompous talk and cowardly deeds, the servant not of a thousand laws, but of as many opinions as there are people in it, bristling with arms, at war both at home and abroad, teeming with greedy, proud, and envious people, and full of countless anxieties: all of which things are ill-suited to your own temperament. As for the city you are preparing to leave, I know that you acknowledge it to be contented, peaceful, flourishing, liberal, and subject to a single ruler: and these things, if I know you at all, are greatly to your liking.[2]

Despite its studied rhetorical structure and its possible literary antecedents, such as Dante's contemptuous description of his native Florence in canto XV of *Inferno*, the passage could well reflect the author's private thoughts and feelings in the years immediately following his return to Tuscany. Living in the house of his widowed father, in a city far more deeply engrossed in commerce and high finance than the pursuit of culture and scholarship, a city torn by internal disputes and at war with the neighbouring state of Lucca, he must indeed have looked back with nostalgia to the refined, tranquil and orderly aristocratic milieu in which he had spent the thirteen years of his adolescence and early manhood.

His discontent with life in Florence may be glimpsed, also, in the closing paragraph of the first of Boccaccio's 'Florentine' works, *Comedía delle ninfe fiorentine*, popularly known as the *Ameto* from the name of its main character. It probably dates from 1341–2, and in the last paragraph the author dedicates the book to a friend of long standing, Niccolò di Bartolo del Buono, asking him to accept 'this rose, born amid the thorns of my adversity, which the beauty of Florence plucked by force from the unyielding brambles as I lay in the depths of despondency'.[3] The *Comedía delle ninfe fiorentine* is a

2 '... sì come tu medesimo già dicesti, la tua città è piena di voci pompose e di pusillanimi fatti, serva non a mille leggi, ma a tanti pareri quanti v'ha uomini, e tutta in arme, e in guerra, così cittadina come forestiera, fremisce, di superba, avara e invidiosa gente fornita, e piena di innumerabili sollecitudini: cose tutte male all'animo tuo conformi. E quella che di lasciare t'apparecchi so che conosci lieta, pacifica, abondevole, magnifica, e sotto ad un solo re: le quali cose, se io alcuna conoscenza ho di te, assai ti sono gradevoli.' (Elegia di Madonna Fiammetta, II, 18)

3 '... questa rosa, tra le spine della mia avversità nata, la quale a forza fuori de' rigidi pruni tirò la fiorentina bellezza, me nell'infimo stante delle tristezze .. ' (Comedía delle ninfe fiorentine, 50).

prose narrative interspersed with a number of poems, and in the last
of these the author complains about 'the dark, silent, melancholy
house' which harbours him against his will. What saddens him most
of all, he continues, is 'the coarse and horrible sight of a miserly old
man, cold and churlish' – perhaps a reference to his widowed father,
but more probably a metaphor for the prospect of senility in a
general sense. If a reference to his father was what he really
intended, he was being unkind. Boccaccio senior could hardly have
been as wizened and lifeless as he was painted if, some two years
later, he was to pass to a second marriage with Bice de' Bostichi,
who was to present him with a son, Iacopo.

Apart from the *Comedía delle ninfe fiorentine* and the *Fiammetta*
(1343–4), already briefly referred to above, the years immediately
following the author's return to Florence also saw the completion
of the *Amorosa visione* (1342), a complicated allegorical poem consisting of fifty cantos of *terza rima* in which the influence of the
Commedia looms even larger than in any of his earlier compositions.
There is also a lengthy pastoral poem, the *Ninfale fiesolano*, of which
the dating (and indeed the authorship) have been subject to some
dispute. Assuming that he was indeed the author, the maturity of its
style and the directness of its narrative-line would lend support to
Branca's tentative placing of its composition in the years 1344–6.
Although the poem is relatively free of the overt 'autobiographical'
material of most of his earlier writings, the delicate presentation in
one of its episodes of the affection of grandparents for their illegitimate grandson may well owe a part of its immediacy to his direct
personal experience, during those years, of the sentiments it so
charmingly depicts. Mario and Giulio, the first two of five children
he fathered, all illegitimate, were already approaching adolescence,
whilst the third, Violante, for whom he displays deep fatherly
affection in one of his later Latin eclogues, was born either in
Florence or Ravenna in the mid 1340s. More significantly, perhaps,
the house where he lived with his elderly father and second stepmother was gladdened by the birth of their child, Iacopo, in or
around 1344. Positivist critics used to make a connection between
the love-child of Mensola, the heroine of the *Ninfale*, with the
circumstances of Boccaccio's own illegitimate birth in 1313. It has

even been suggested that the story is a literary re-working of a scandalous love-affair, imperfectly documented, between the author and a Benedictine nun from the convent of San Martino a Mensola, where a farm belonging to his father was located.

Speculative tales of the sort doubtless arose in part from the dearth of reliable documentary evidence about Boccaccio in the years immediately preceding the advent of the Black Death in Florence in 1348. They were years of extreme political and economic uncertainty throughout the peninsula, especially in Florence and Naples, a city to which he had still not abandoned hope of returning under the patronage of his erstwhile friend Niccola Acciaiuoli. In Florence, the autocratic rule of the Duke of Athens (Walter of Brienne), nephew of King Robert of Naples, was brought to an end in 1343, to be replaced by the provisional government of the lesser guilds and merchants, the *popolo minuto*, whose reforms had severely diminished the influence and wealth of the prosperous merchant classes to which Boccaccio's family belonged. The collapse of the Bardi and Peruzzi banking houses in 1345, largely brought about by Edward III of England's repudiation of heavy debts he had contracted for his wars in France, aggravated the already serious decline in Florentine fortunes. In that same year, 1345, the Kingdom of Naples was thrown into confusion by the assassination of the husband of Queen Joanna, Andrew of Hungary, an event which two years later led to the punitive expedition into Italy of King Louis of Hungary. Joanna, along with her new husband, Luigi of Taranto, and their counsellor, Niccola Acciaiuoli, took refuge in Provence, and consequently Boccaccio's already slender prospects of returning to the Neapolitan court were for the time being extinguished. The turbulent events in Florence had in any case already prompted him to seek patronage elsewhere, and by 1346 he was living in Ravenna, a city with strong Florentine connections. Dante had died there in exile in 1321, and his daughter, Suor Beatrice, still lived there in the convent of San Stefano dell'Uliva. A few years later, in the autumn of 1350, Boccaccio returned to Ravenna on an official mission on behalf of the Florentine commune, in the course of which he presented ten gold ducats to Suor Beatrice, a symbolic gift from the Compagnia di Or San Michele in tardy recognition of her father's unique contribution to Florentine culture.

Meanwhile, in 1348, Italy had been ravaged by the most disastrous plague in European history, graphically described by Boccaccio in the Introduction to the First Day of the *Decameron*, where it serves both as a pretext for the assembly and the flight from Florence of the ten young people, the *lieta brigata* ('happy band'), to whom the telling of the hundred stories will be fictively entrusted. It also acts as the sombre and frightening prelude which medieval rhetoricians regarded as an essential component of the genre of comedy to which the *Decameron*, like Dante's great poem, was intended to belong. Both works, in fact, despite their obvious differences in form and subject-matter, respect the definition of comedy formulated for instance by Uguccione da Pisa in his *Derivationes*: '*a principio horribilis et fetidus, in fine prosperus desiderabilis et gratus*' ('foul and horrible at the beginning, in the end felicitous, desirable and pleasing'). It is to this feature of the work that the author alludes in the opening paragraph of the First Day, where he forewarns his readers of its grave and troublesome beginning, and encourages them not to be deterred on this account from proceeding to the book's remaining and more substantial portion, where they will encounter something more pleasing and entertaining. Boccaccio's evident desire to place the book squarely within a specific rhetorical genre is further underlined by the progression from the tales of vice in the First Day to the tales of virtue in the Tenth, from the embodiment of villainy in the opening story to the embodiment of saintliness in the concluding tale. That sequence has led many critics to classify the *Decameron* as the 'Human Comedy', complementing the *Divine Comedy* of his illustrious predecessor. The two works, outwardly so dissimilar, have many other features in common, not least the fact that both are set '*nel mezzo del cammin di nostra vita*' ('halfway along the path of our life').[4] For in 1348, the year of the great plague, Boccaccio had arrived, like Dante in 1300, at the halfway stage in the ideal biblical life span of three score years and ten.

In all probability, Boccaccio gave definitive shape to the *Decam-*

4 The opening line of Dante's *Commedia*.

eron between the years 1349 and 1352. At least three of the hundred tales had already appeared in different forms in his earlier works, two in the *Filocolo* and one in the *Comedia delle ninfe fiorentine*, and it seems inconceivable that he had not drafted the outlines of a large number of others, at intervals, during the course of his by now fairly lengthy literary career. The idea of assembling a collection of stories had probably rooted itself in his mind long before the year of the great plague, and there are various indications in the text of the *Decameron* that he had originally intended it to have a septenary structure, in other words that it should contain seventy rather than 100 stories. By refining and elaborating a scheme he had adopted in an episode from the *Comedia delle ninfe fiorentine*, where seven nymphs tell their life-stories, the seventy tales would be told by a company of seven young ladies. But once he had conceived the ingenious idea of setting his tales against the terrible events of 1348, it was inevitable, for reasons clearly set forth in the Introduction to the First Day, that the company of storytellers should be expanded by the inclusion of three young men, and that consequently an additional thirty stories should be inserted. This arrangement had the incidental advantage of giving the *Decameron* a structure comparable in some respects to that of the *Commedia*, which contains a hundred cantos and is divided into three sections. Some years earlier, when composing his martial epic, the *Teseida*, Boccaccio had been so sensitive to his main classical antecedent, the *Aeneid*, as to give it precisely the same number of lines as are contained in Virgil's poem, and there can be little doubt that in setting about the composition of his own distinctive 'comedy' the example of Dante loomed large in his planning of the work's structure. Significant in this connection are the two lengthy interludes in the flow of the *Decameron*'s narratives, strategically placed immediately after the numerically significant Third and Sixth Days, which have the effect of dividing the work into three *cantiche*, to use the term applied to the three sections of Dante's poem.

Whether, as the author claims at two different points in his Introduction, he was himself present in Florence during the plague of 1348, which is estimated by historians to have claimed the lives of two thirds to three quarters of the city's 100,000 inhabitants, it is difficult to judge. His description of the plague is heavily dependent on literary antecedents, especially that of the eighth-century historian of the Lombards, Paul the Deacon, and there is no external evidence to support Boccaccio's contention that he was an eye-witness to the terrible suffering to which the Florentines were subjected. If, as seems possible, he was not in Florence at that time, but still in Ravenna or (more probably) in Forlí, where he is known to have been at the end of 1347 and the beginning of 1348, at the court of Francesco Ordelaffi, many of the particulars of the plague's ruinous effect on Florentine daily life could well have been communicated to him by his father. As the Florentine Minister of Supply (*Ufficiale dell'Abbondanza*), his father was in fact actively engaged in implementing the emergency measures decreed by the Florentine government to combat such pressing problems as shortage of food and inattention to customary standards of hygiene.

Among its numerous victims, the plague accounted for many of Boccaccio's closest friends and literary acquaintances, as well as his second stepmother, Bice, who died in 1348. Not long afterwards his father also died, leaving Boccaccio, as the eldest son, to assume responsibilities as head of the family in the most trying circumstances it is possible to imagine. Perhaps there is more than a grain of truth in Branca's suggestion that, in this unaccustomed role, Boccaccio was forced into contact with a broader range of people and confronted with problems that in his sedentary life as a scholar had previously escaped his close attention. The varied experience he thereby acquired of the practical everyday world was bound to some extent to be reflected in the pages of the *Decameron*, the writing of which coincided with the years immediately following the death of his father.

The story of Boccaccio's life from about 1350 until his death in 1375 is the story of a steadily increasing involvement in humanistic culture combined with the growth of the reputation for diplomacy and eloquence he had already achieved among his Florentine fellow citizens. The first of numerous official missions was undertaken in the autumn of 1350, when he was sent to the Romagna for purposes difficult to determine. But it was after his return from the Romagna, in the early part of October 1350, that he was deputed to welcome the foremost man of letters in fourteenth-century Europe at the gates of the city, and offer him the traditional gift of a ring. Francesco Petrarca was on his way to Rome for the Jubilee, and during his stay in Florence he was a guest in Boccaccio's house in the San Felicita quarter of the city. From that moment there began a friendship between Petrarch and Boccaccio which was to endure for the rest of their lives, and which was one of the most influential meetings of minds in the history of European culture. Their relationship was not one of equals, however, for Boccaccio, nine years younger and still comparatively unknown beyond the borders of Florence and Naples, consistently referred to Petrarch as his *magister* until the latter's death in 1374, whilst Petrarch was well content to accept Boccaccio's over-modest assessment of his own role as *discipulus*. In a letter written in 1372 to Niccolò Orsini, he refers to Petrarch as 'my famous teacher . . . to whom I owe all that I am worth' ('*inclitus preceptor meus . . . cui quantum valeo debeo*').

In March 1351, five months after their initial meeting in Florence, the two men met again, this time in Padua. Boccaccio had been sent there as bearer of official letters setting aside a decree of 1302 which had exiled Petrarch's father and confiscated his property. The letters invited Petrarch not only to return to his native Tuscany but to accept a professorial chair at the *Studium*, or university of Florence. Boccaccio's mission was unsuccessful, much to the annoyance of the Signory, which revoked its decision. (Petrarch shortly afterwards accepted a similar offer from the Visconti lord of Milan, and took up a chair at the nearby University of Pavia.) One of Boccaccio's Latin epistles describes with unusual warmth and affection the lengthy discussions that he and Petrarch engaged in during his visit. It was probably on that occasion that he formulated the views on poetry he later set down in the last two books of his *Genealogia deorum gentilium* (*Genealogy of the Gentile Gods*), a work he had already begun at some time before 1350.

The first draft of the *Genealogia*, which was to become a standard work of reference on classical mythology for the next 500 years, was completed around 1360, and it was revised and enlarged at frequent intervals up to the year of the author's death, as indeed were most of his other encyclopaedic Latin works and some of his earlier, vernacular writings. The *Genealogia* is in essence a compendium of the knowledge concerning the myths of the ancient classical world accumulated by Boccaccio during a lifetime of intensive study. Critical attention tends nowadays to be focused, however, upon the two concluding books (there were fifteen in all), where the author's poetic creed, newly formulated in the wake of his discussions with Petrarch, is expounded with polemical vigour and intense inner conviction. In Book XIV, Boccaccio defends the art of poetry against its many detractors, asserting that it was a rare and precious accomplishment of an élite whose work was distinguished by Truth composed under a veil of Beauty. In a similar vein, he also describes the true poet's distinctive quality as 'a certain fervour for exquisitely discovering and saying, or writing, what you have discovered' (*fervor quidem exquisite inveniendi atque dicendi, seu scribendi, quod inveneris*'). As for the art of storytelling, he stresses its didactic function by saying that narratives should 'at one and the same reading instruct and entertain' ('*fabulae . . . una et eadem lectione proficiunt et delectant*'). In the concluding book (XV) Boccaccio proceeds to defend himself against those who have charged him with frivolity. There are echoes here of the *Decameron*, especially of his replies to his critics in the Introduction to the Fourth Day and in the Author's Epilogue, but in the *Genealogia* strong emphasis is placed upon the poet's moral and didactic function. The work ends with the significant claim, addressed to God, that poetry brings glory, not to its earthly creator, but to the name of the Lord: '*Non nobis, Domine, non nobis, sed nomini tuo dat gloriam.*'

Boccaccio's conversations with Petrarch in Padua, in the spring of 1351, coincide more or less exactly with a change of direction as well as of emphasis in his literary interests. At that time, he was almost certainly working on the latter part of the *Decameron*. It would be hazardous to suggest that the edifying tales of the Tenth Day, culminating in the story of Griselda's extraordinary forbearance (a story which Petrarch admired so greatly that he eventually translated it into Latin), were in any sense motivated by the older poet's moralizing counsels. It is certainly true, however, that after completing the *Decameron* Boccaccio wrote no other substantial piece of imaginative literature, and that the major part of his subsequent output was composed, not in Italian, but in Latin. The main exceptions to this second general rule (though not to the first) were the *Corbaccio*, one or two letters including the *Consolatoria a Pino de' Rossi*, a treatise in praise of Dante (*Trattatello in laude di Dante*), and his commentaries on the first seventeen cantos of Dante's *Inferno* (*Esposizioni sopra la Comedía di Dante*). All of these are markedly diverse in character, but they share one element in common, in that they all, in their separate ways, look back to the past instead of pointing resolutely forward (as most of the earlier vernacular works had done) to the future. The treatise on Dante is without question the most appealing of all these works, consisting as it does of an affectionate, anecdotal biography of Boccaccio's favourite poet, who is presented as the embodiment of the principles he sets forth in his Defence of Poetry in the last two books of the *Genealogia deorum gentilium*. The *Trattatello*, begun around 1357, underwent at least two revisions, and eventually acquired an imposing Latin title: *De origine vita studiis et moribus viri clarissimi Dantis Aligerii florentini poetae illustris et de operibus compositis ab eodem.*[5]

The *Corbaccio*, written, according to Giorgio Padoan, in or around 1365, but attributed more convincingly by Natalino Sapegno and others to a much earlier date (1355), is at once the most enigmatic and least attractive of Boccaccio's works. The very title is mysterious, being almost an anagram of the author's name and signifying a bird traditionally associated with omens of misfortune. The 'ugly crow' of the title can hardly refer to Boccaccio himself, and it is possible that all he intended it to suggest was the unceasing mockery (*il corbacchiare*) characterizing the work as a whole, which is a bitter invective against women. It therefore forms part of a tradition of misogynistic writing stretching back to Juvenal and to St Jerome. But although he had made one or two earlier excursions into this equivocal poetic terrain, for instance in an episode in the *Filocolo* and more especially in the story of the scholar and the widow (*Decameron*, VIII, 7), the sheer intensity and ferocity of the *Corbaccio*'s anti-feminism will astonish those who are accustomed to accept

---

5 'Concerning the origin, life, erudition and character of the illustrious Florentine poet, the celebrated Dante Alighieri, and the works that he composed'.

Boccaccio's own self-portrait in the *Decameron* as the champion of the gentle sex (see the Prologue and the Introduction to the Fourth Day). The *Corbaccio* is in fact the work which documents in most convincing fashion Boccaccio's conversion to the kind of literary asceticism to which he became increasingly committed after his encounter with Petrarch. As Sapegno has shrewdly observed, whereas the Muses in the *Decameron* had been compared to women (IV, *Intro.*), in the *Corbaccio* the '*Ninfe Castalidi*' ('Castalian nymphs', a circumlocution for the Muses) are contrasted with *wicked* women ('*malvagie femmine*').

The *Epistola consolatoria a Pino de' Rossi*, written in the winter of 1361–2 following the banishment from Florence of the addressee, is not only an attempt to offer encouragement to a close friend at a time of profound personal misfortune, but also an elegant and eloquent exercise in a literary genre with strong classical antecedents, a document that bears witness to the author's continuing and ever more intensive commitment to humanistic culture. The exile of Rossi had coincided with the execution of that same Niccolò di Bartolo del Buono to whom Boccaccio had dedicated his *Comedía delle ninfe fiorentine*, and in fact several of the author's close acquaintances fell victim to the purge carried out by the Florentine Signory after the abortive *coup d'état* of 1361, with the aims of which he had not, presumably, been entirely out of sympathy. It is perhaps significant that very soon afterwards, in that same year in fact, he handed over the family house in the San Felicita quarter to his stepbrother Iacopo, who was now of age, and retired to Certaldo, the town of his paternal forebears.

His withdrawal to Certaldo signalled a pause in his involvement in Florentine diplomatic affairs, which had lasted for more than a decade and had taken him at least three times to the Romagna (in 1350, 1353 and 1357), once to the court of Ludwig of Brandenburg in the South Tyrol to explore the reasons for his intervention in Milanese affairs (in December 1351/January 1352), and once as leading spokesman of an apparently very successful legation to Pope Innocent VI at Avignon (in May–June 1354). There was also his diplomatically abortive mission to Petrarch in Padua during the spring of 1351. Other journeys he undertook during the decade preceding his move to Certaldo included a visit in September 1355 to Naples, during which he worked briefly in the great library at Monte Cassino, and a further visit in March 1359 to Petrarch, who was now established in Milan. Boccaccio had long admired Petrarch's clerical garb, which by this time he had probably himself adopted, for there is a decree of Innocent VI dated 2 November 1360 granting certain dispensations and privileges to Boccaccio, which would suggest that he had taken holy orders some little time before it was issued. The decade was notable also, from Boccaccio's point of view, for the fleeting visit to Florence in 1355 of Niccola Acciaiuoli, by now universally known as the Grand Seneschal. It seems that during his visit, Acciaiuoli referred disparagingly to Boccaccio as *Iohannes tranquillitatum*, a label implying that he was a fair-weather friend whose support was not to be counted upon in times of political adversity such as Acciaiuoli had experienced during his exile from Naples to Avignon some years before.

Far from being discouraged by this outward token of Acciaiuoli's lack of esteem for the friend of his youth, Boccaccio continued to court his patronage almost up to the time of Acciaiuoli's death on 8 November 1365, though his attitude to the Grand Seneschal was by no means always one of fawning subservience. In the eighth of the sixteen Latin eclogues that comprise, under the title of *Buccolicum carmen*, Boccaccio's own contribution to that arcane and allusive genre of Latin poetry which both Dante and Petrarch had sought without success to revive, he complains of the indifference of Acciaiuoli during his Neapolitan journey of 1355. But it was only after yet another fruitless expedition to Naples that began in October 1362 and ended five months later that the full force of his invective was released, in a letter to Francesco Nelli. Having been expressly invited by Acciaiuoli to make his home in Naples, he had set off with his stepbrother Iacopo from Tuscany, in high hopes and with all of his books, only to discover upon his arrival that the lodging to which he had been allocated was quite unfit for human habitation. The shortcomings of the place are described in minute detail in the letter to Nelli, a fellow Florentine who occupied a prominent position at the Angevin court. The letter was probably never sent, however, for there is no record of any response in the correspond-ence of either Nelli or Acciaiuoli.

Meanwhile, in 1359–60, Boccaccio had given a significant new impetus to humanistic studies by persuading the Florentine *Studium* to establish the first chair of Greek in non-Byzantine Europe, and to invite Leontius Pilatus to occupy it. Leontius had been a pupil of the celebrated Greek scholar Barlaam of Calabria, whom Boccaccio had known in Naples, once describing him as 'tiny of body but very great in knowledge', and who had attempted in vain to teach the rudiments of Greek to Petrarch in Avignon. During his brief tenure of the Florentine chair, Leontius, whose unkempt appearance and barbaric manners are described in a passage of the *Genealogia deorum gentilium*, was a guest in Boccaccio's house, and it was Boccaccio who prodded him into completing the first, rudimentary translations into Latin of Homer's *Iliad* and *Odyssey*, as well as some of the works of Euripides and Aristotle. As for his lectures at the *Studium*, they aroused much adverse comment, not only because of the man's extraordinary boorishness, but because the instruction he provided was not sufficiently practical for those young Florentines preparing for a mercantile or diplomatic career in the eastern Mediterranean. All the same, Boccaccio prided himself with good reason on the role he had played in ensuring that the study of ancient Greek literature should take its place alongside the almost exclusively Latin-based researches of the fourteenth-century Italian humanists.

Shortly after his conversations with Petrarch in Padua in 1351, Boccaccio had begun to compile a notebook in which he copied out various texts to form a kind of anthology. This work, known nowadays as the *Zibaldone Magliabechiano*, belongs, probably, to the period 1351–6, and it in turn gave rise to two Latin works which were widely disseminated and translated in Europe during the succeeding two centuries: *De casibus virorum illustrium*, begun by Boccaccio around 1355, and *De mulieribus claris*, probably begun in the summer of 1361. The first draft of *De casibus* was completed around 1360, but the definitive enlarged version belongs to 1373–4, and is dedicated to Mainardo de' Cavalcanti, chancellor of the Duchy of Amalfi, who, during Boccaccio's Neapolitan journey of 1362–3, had entertained and lodged the author in a fashion more appropriate to a man of his standing than the miserly manner in which he had been received by Acciaiuoli. *De casibus* consists of a series of cautionary biographies, distributed over nine books, of famous men selected from biblical, Roman and contemporary history, from Adam to the tyrannical ruler of mid-fourteenth-century Florence, the Duke of Athens. With few exceptions, what the subjects of these biographical tales have in common is that they all rose to a position of eminence from which they were toppled by divine Providence through an excess of pride or folly, or a combination of both. The didacticism of the work is what chiefly distinguishes these tales, based upon biblical or historical figures, from several such tales in the pages of the *Decameron*, especially the stories of the Second Day, which are for the most part based on fictional figures. The theme of Fortune was one to which Boccaccio, like many other writers before and since, was strongly attracted. But whereas in the *Decameron* Fortune is seen on the whole as a benevolent force, in *De casibus* she is perceived from a moralistic viewpoint as a chastiser of men for their iniquities. *De casibus* thus reflects the new moral perspective that assumes increasing importance in the author's later, humanistic writings. Much the same could be said of *De mulieribus claris*, probably begun in the summer of 1361 and revised no fewer than nine times, the last revision belonging to 1375. *De mulieribus* is dedicated to Andrea Acciaiuoli, sister of the Grand Seneschal and later to become the wife of Mainardo de' Cavalcanti, and it contains 104 biographies of famous women, from Eve to Queen Joanna of Naples. Petrarch had written a similar volume about famous men, *De viris illustribus*, and it is possible that Boccaccio's work was intended as a companion volume, at the same time forming the tribute of a *discipulus* to his *magister*.

Whilst it is proper to emphasize Boccaccio's new sense of didactic purpose after the immensely important encounter with Petrarch in 1351, it would be misleading to convey the impression, as several of his biographers have done, that his involvement in humanistic studies led him to reject his earlier writings in the vernacular, in particular the *Decameron*. In this connection there is a story, better described as threadbare than well-worn, concerning a vision he is said to have experienced in 1362, when a mysterious messenger, originally nameless but referred to in later versions of the episode as

Gioacchino Ciani, a Carthusian monk of Siena, warned him on behalf of one Pietro Petroni, recently deceased in the odour of sanctity, that his life was approaching its end and that the time had come for him to repent the foolishness of his ways. In consequence of this vision, Boccaccio is said to have resolved to destroy all of his writings that could be construed as profane, including of course his masterpiece. But the truth of the matter is that Boccaccio, even if he experienced any such vision, never took such a resolution. The sole source for the legend of the mysterious messenger is a letter of Petrarch's (*Seniles*, I, 5) dated 28 May 1362, in which the older poet refers to a letter he claims to have received from Boccaccio describing the strange visitation and expressing concern over the prospect of imminent death. Petrarch takes great pains to reassure his friend, and adduces numerous examples from classical and biblical times to dispose of the argument that *both* of them (not just Boccaccio alone) were devoting too much of their time to the study and practice of literature and poetry. The question is discussed within the context of the debate about the relative merits of literary studies on the one hand and devotional practices on the other, a debate which had been going on at least since the age of Dante, and which in its simplest form could be expressed as Poetry *vs* Theology. It is at the end of this same letter, incidentally, that Petrarch suggests that they should pool their respective libraries (Boccaccio had apparently suggested that he should sell his own library to his *magister*), and live together under one roof.

Whether or not he took seriously Petrarch's suggestion that he should come and live with him, one cannot be certain. It is possible that he felt that such close propinquity to the *magister* would in some way damage what had up to that time been a fruitful relationship. But it is also possible that it was with precisely this invitation in mind that he abruptly departed from Naples in March 1363 after the crumbling of his hopes for a permanent lodging in the Angevin kingdom, for he proceeded directly to Padua and thence to Venice, where Petrarch received him in the splendid house he had been given on the Riva degli Schiavoni in return for a promise to bequeath his library, after his death, to the Venetian republic. Five months later, in August 1363, Boccaccio was back once more in Certaldo, where he continued with the task of correcting and revising his Latin writings, including perhaps his dictionary of geographical allusions in both classical and more recent literature, a work he had begun at some time between 1355 and 1357, and to which he gave the all-embracing title *De montibus, silvis, fontibus, lacubus, fluminibus, stagnis seu paludibus et de nominibus maris liber*.[6] It was Petrarch who had suggested that Boccaccio should compile such a work, and who directed his pupil to the main sources, in Pliny and various ancient geographers, for much of the material it contains. With the exception of *De mulieribus*, it was the last of Boccaccio's encyclopaedic Latin works, and it received its final revision in 1374, the year before he died.

Meanwhile, by August 1365, by which time the failed *coup d'état* of four years before had faded in the public memory, Boccaccio had returned to favour with the Florentine government, to the extent of being dispatched on an important mission to the papal court at Avignon. The purpose of his mission was to assure Urban V of Florence's support and goodwill in the event of the papacy's return to Italy, which in fact took place some two years later, on 9 June 1367. The Florentines had a reputation in papal circles for combining a surfeit of fine words with a disinclination to translate them into action, and it was part of Boccaccio's mission to dispel the Pope's understandable mistrust by offering a binding undertaking to provide five armed galleys and 500 helmeted soldiers as an escort for his journey from Avignon to Rome. So successfully did he accomplish his mission that when Urban V did return to Rome on 16 October 1367, after a temporary stay of four months in Viterbo, it was Boccaccio himself who, in November, was sent to convey Florence's congratulations on his safe deliverance from what historians would thenceforth refer to as the papacy's 'Babylonian Captivity', the term originally used to describe the seventy years that the Jews were captives in Babylon. Urban in fact returned in September 1370 to Avignon, where shortly afterwards he died, and it was left to his successor, Gregory XI, to effect the definitive end to the 'Babylonian

6 'Book concerning the mountains, woods, springs, lakes, rivers, swamps or marshes, and concerning the names of the sea'.

Captivity' with his transfer of the papal court to Rome in January
1377. In addition to his two official missions to Urban V, Boccaccio
undertook several other journeys in the last decade or so of his life.
In the winter of 1361–2 he had returned for the last time to
Ravenna under the shadow of some kind of personal misfortune,
the nature of which is unknown. In March 1367 he set out from
Florence for Venice in the hope of a further encounter with
Petrarch, but the two men never met, as Petrarch was detained by
illness in Pavia. Although Boccaccio was warmly received by the
poet's daughter, Francesca, who invited him to stay in her father's
house on the Riva degli Schiavoni, he lodged in fact with a
Florentine acquaintance, Francesco Allegri, returning to Tuscany
towards the end of June 1367. During the following winter he
supervised preparations in Florence for the defence of the city
against a threatened invasion by the Holy Roman Emperor, Charles
IV, which never materialized. In July 1368 he met Petrarch for
what was to be the last time, in Padua, whence he paid a further
visit to Venice before returning to Tuscany in the early part of
November of that year. In the winter of 1370–71 Boccaccio was
once again, and for the last time, in the Kingdom of Naples, where
he was more warmly received and entertained than at any time
since his youthful sojourn there had come to an end in 1341. Of the
numerous invitations he received to make his permanent home in
Naples, none can have given him greater cause for satisfaction than
the one he received from Queen Joanna herself. But he refused
them all, on the grounds that he had already declined Petrarch's
pressing invitation to settle in Venice. Petrarch had now retired to
the restful solitude of the Euganean hills, and it was with his
example in mind that Boccaccio returned to Certaldo in the spring
of 1371. There he carried out his final revisions of several of his
Latin works, having already completed his sixteen Latin eclogues,
Buccolicum carmen, between 1367 and 1369. And at some time during
the years 1370–71 he had carefully revised and re-copied the text of
the *Decameron* itself. The resulting manuscript, tampered with by
other hands over the intervening centuries, has come down to us in
the so-called Hamilton autograph 90, which is lodged in the Staats-
bibliothek of Berlin.

On 13 August 1373 Boccaccio was invited by the Florentine Signory to give a series of public lectures on Dante in the church of Santo Stefano di Badia. The first of these *lecturae Dantis* was given on Sunday 23 October 1373, and their substance is contained in what was to be Boccaccio's last major literary labour, the *Esposizioni sopra la Comedía di Dante*, an erudite commentary on the first seventeen cantos of the *Inferno* containing a mass of anecdotal detail, much of it superfluous.

On the night of 18–19 July 1374, Petrarch died in Arquà, and when, three months later, the news of his death reached Certaldo, Boccaccio wrote a commemorative sonnet, thus rounding off his own comparatively undistinguished collection of shorter poems, the *Rime*, with a final tribute to one whom he rightly acknowledged as his master in vernacular lyric poetry. The earlier poems constituting Boccaccio's *Rime* had been strongly derivative from the *dolce stil novo* and the *rime petrose* of Dante; the later ones took their cue from Petrarch. In the sixteenth century, the great Florentine linguist Lionardo Salviati was to assert that Boccaccio '*non fece mai verso che avesse verso nel verso*', by which he implied that his lyrical poetry was neither lyrical nor poetic. And whilst that is much too severe an assessment of Boccaccio's skills as a lyric poet, it is certainly true that in the *Rime* he fell far short of the heights he scaled in the art of narrative, whether in verse or in prose. Generally speaking, the *Rime* form the least original part of the output of a writer whose work, whatever its shortcomings, was seldom lacking in originality.

During the last few years of his life, Boccaccio was troubled by a succession of physical disorders, and suffered from severe obesity. This was probably the chief contributory factor to his final illness, leading to his death in Certaldo on 21 December 1375.

II. THE WORLD OF THE NARRATORS

The idea of assembling a substantial number of tales within a single work was doubtless one that Boccaccio had been contemplating for many years before he brought it to fruition. The *questioni* episode in the *Filocolo* and the nymphs' accounts of their amorous exploits in the *Comedía delle ninfe fiorentine* are the two most obvious tokens in his earlier writings of the path he was eventually to follow. Those two extended episodes may be regarded as trial runs for a project of far more ambitious proportions, for which he must already have begun to gather the formidable amount of narrative raw material he would require, some of it being pressed into service in two of the *questioni*, as well as in another episode of the *Filocolo*.

As for the actual design of the *Decameron*, there are many other significant pointers in the earlier works. One instance is the passage in the *Fiammetta* in which the narrator/protagonist reminisces nostalgically about excursions undertaken with her young Neapolitan fellow-patricians to Baiae, a location with strong classical associations where the remains of the ancient Roman Baths of Venus, the Terme di Venere, are still in evidence. There the hotter part of the day would be devoted, by the ladies themselves or in the company of young men (*o le donne per sé, o mescolate co' giovani*), to amorous discussions (*amorosi ragionamenti*), with music and dancing and singing as their other diversions. And similar scenes are portrayed, both in the *Amorosa visione* and in one of the author's best-known sonnets, beginning

> Intorn'ad una fonte, in un pratello
> di verdi erbette pieno e di bei fiori,
> sedeano tre angliolette, i loro amori
> forse narrando.[7]

The choice of verb here (*narrando*) would seem to be significant, but more importantly the passage is a good example of a recurrent leitmotif in Boccaccio's work: the *locus amœnus* inhabited by nymph-like maidens who talk of love. And it was perhaps inevitable that just such a setting should eventually form the backdrop to the hundred tales. All that was lacking was a suitable pretext to lend an air of realism to the circumstances in which the stories were claimed to have been told and, from this point of view, the public calamity of 1348 was for Boccaccio an event that had a positive aspect. For it

---

7 'Around a fountain, in a meadow filled with green grasses and lovely flowers, sat three angelic ladies, perhaps telling stories of their loves.'

enabled him not only to make it seem entirely natural that the stories were told in the way he pretends, but to apply his considerable descriptive and rhetorical skills to the structurally vital account of the plague and the ruinous social upheaval it produced, both in Florence and elsewhere in Europe.

Following the practice he had adopted earlier in the *Filocolo*, the *Filostrato* and the *Teseida*, Boccaccio gave his collection of tales a Greek title, meaning 'Ten Days' and referring to the ten separate days within a period of two weeks during which the stories were supposed to have been told. The tradition of hellenizing titles, which originated with Virgil, is associated with the epic, and the *Decameron* is often characterized as the epic of the Florentine merchant class, which, by the middle of the fourteenth century, had asserted itself as the dominant social force of medieval Italy. But more specifically, the title of Boccaccio's vernacular masterpiece is modelled upon a work of a very different kind, written a thousand years earlier by St Ambrose: the series of commentaries on Old Testament narratives known as the *Hexaemeron*. The contrast in subject matter between the two works could hardly be more pronounced, and it lends to the title of Boccaccio's book a subtle irony, almost certainly intentional in origin.

As for the storytelling, it is represented as having begun on a Wednesday in the early summer of 1348 and ended on a Tuesday two weeks later, no tales having been told on Fridays or Saturdays for reasons both religious and practical, which are carefully spelt out by the newly appointed queen, Neifile, at the end of the Second Day. Those two days, she says, are rather tedious, because they are days given over to prayer and fasting, Friday to commemorate the Passion of Our Lord, and Saturday out of reverence to His Mother, and also because the ladies are wont to wash their hair on Saturdays, so as to remove the dust and grime of the week's endeavours. One other reason Neifile gives for desisting from storytelling on Saturday afternoons is that the approach of Sunday should be honoured by resting from one's labours.

So much for the title of the work and its significance. When one comes to consider its precise form, numerous antecedents for collections of tales may be found, as well as for the literary device whereby such compilations are inserted within a frame-narrative, known to generations of Italians as the *cornice* ('frame'), a term which critics of the present day, after seemingly endless debate, tend to regard as misleading because it suggests that its purpose is merely decorative. Before the *Decameron*, the most important collection of tales in Italian was the anonymous *Novellino*, composed probably towards the end of the thirteenth century and consisting of a hundred anecdotes, for the most part very brief and narrated in a manner that is simple to the point, sometimes, of crudity. Some of the stories of the *Decameron*, for instance the tale of the three rings (I, 3), draw the substance of their narrative from the *Novellino*, but Boccaccio made more extensive use of other material. One of his most fertile sources was the collection of narratives in French verse known as *fabliaux*, notable for their brevity, humour and impropriety, to which he would have had ready access in the French-speaking milieu where his literary apprenticeship was served. Equally fruitful as a source of narrative material were the moralizing collections of *exempla*, generally written in Latin, whose primary purpose was to furnish edifying anecdotes for embellishment in church sermons. One of the most popular and influential of these collections was the *Disciplina clericalis* compiled by Peter Alphonsi, born in 1062, an erudite scholar and physician to King Alphonso I of Aragon. Boccaccio's sources also included medieval chronicles, both in Latin and Italian, and occasionally his stories have their origin in classical Latin literature, in particular the works of his favourite Latin authors, Ovid and Apuleius. It was from the latter, in fact, that he borrowed, whether directly or through an intermediate medieval Latin text, the broad outlines of the tales concerning the sodomitical husband, Pietro di Vinciolo (V, 10), and Peronella and the tub (VII, 2). The second of these stories contains whole phrases translated literally from Apuleius, whilst the fact that Boccaccio was well acquainted with Ovid's *Metamorphoses* is attested by his having transcribed it, in a manuscript still preserved in the Florentine Biblioteca Laurenziana, at around the time when he was working on the *Decameron*.

From a structural viewpoint, however, the most obvious of the *Decameron*'s antecedents were the collections of stories that had originated in the East during the early Middle Ages and were circulating, in translation, throughout western Europe in Boccaccio's own lifetime. One such collection was the *Panchatantra*, literally *The Five Heads*, originally written in Sanskrit at some time before AD 500, which, like the *Decameron*, takes the form of a frame-story containing several other stories. Occasionally, this basic design is further complicated by the insertion of yet another story within the story being told, so that the structure resembles that of a Chinese box, with its succession of interior spaces. Traces of this procedure may be glimpsed, also, in the *Decameron*, where the author sometimes makes his fictive storytellers preface their tales with an account of how or by whom the tale was originally told. The most obvious instance of this distancing device is the story of Federigo degli Alberighi and his precious falcon (V, 9), where the narrator, Fiammetta, attributes the tale she is about to relate to one Coppo di Borghese Domenichi, to whom she devotes a fulsome tribute in her opening remarks.

If, as seems likely, Boccaccio knew the *Panchatantra*, it was probably in the considerably modified Latin version of the work, *Liber Kelilae et Dimnae*, otherwise known as the *Directorium humanae vitae*, which John of Capua produced around 1270. John's version was based, by way of a Hebrew translation, upon the eighth-century Arabic version of the text, *Kalilah wa Dimna*, which in turn was based upon a sixth-century Pahlavi, or Old Persian, translation from the original Sanskrit. The names Kalilah and Dimnah were those of two jackals in the first of the *Panchatantra*'s five books, which, designed originally as a Mirror for Princes, or *Fürstenspiegel*, uses the Aesopian device of narrating animal fables in order to impart a moral – in this case, that guile and cunning are essential in the management of human affairs. In view of the prominence accorded to the role of intelligence in the *Decameron*, it could be argued that the affinity between Boccaccio's collection of tales and these oriental fables is not only structural but also thematic.

The *Panchatantra*, also known as *The Fables of Bidpai* (or *Pilpay*), from the word *bidbah*, which was the name given to the chief scholar at the court of an Indian prince, was not the sole oriental antecedent for a collection of tales boxed within a frame-story.

Another compendium, perhaps still more germane to an understanding of the genesis of the *Decameron*, was the collection of eastern
tales which entered western literature by way of Greek, Latin and
French versions, commonly known as *The Seven Wise Masters*. This
recounts the story of an emperor whose son is alleged by his
stepmother to have attempted to seduce her, whereupon the son is
sentenced to death. (There is an evident parallel between this
narrative and the tale of the Count of Antwerp and the Queen of
France which forms the subject of the eighth novella of the *Decameron*'s Second Day.) The son is unable to refute his stepmother's
allegation because she has caused him to lose the power of speech
for a period of seven days, during which time the emperor's seven
advisers, who represent the seven liberal arts, in turn supply the
emperor with a story that reveals the cunning of women and the evils
of summary jurisdiction. Their advice is nullified by the wicked
queen, who each night relates a tale to the emperor designed to
strengthen his resolve to carry out the sentence. When the seven
days have elapsed, the young prince, having regained the use of his
tongue, tells his father a tale which embodies the whole truth, thus
exposing the malice of the queen, who gets her deserts (by prevailing
oriental standards) by being burned at the stake.

As in the case of the *Panchatantra*, so with *The Seven Wise Masters*
(in Italian, *Il libro dei sette savi*), the work's affinity to the *Decameron*
is not just a question of external structure, for of Boccaccio's fictive
narrators the seven female members of the so-called 'happy band'
(*lieta brigata*) all possess in full measure the quality of wisdom
(*saviezza*) that distinguishes the storytellers in the earlier work. Each
of the seven young ladies is described from the start as being wise
(*savia ciascuna*), whereas the three young men are introduced merely
as being very agreeable and gently bred (*assai piacevole e costumato
ciascuno*).

It is with the structural analogy, however, that one is here more
closely concerned, and in this connection one should note that both
in *The Seven Wise Masters* (otherwise known, incidentally, as the
Dolopathos) and in the *Decameron*, the telling of stories is the means
whereby the spectre of imminent death is held at a manageable
distance, in the one case death by execution, in the other, death

from bubonic plague. The classic example of this sort of structural scheme is *The Thousand and One Nights*, but it may also be seen in the eighth and ninth books of the *Metamorphoses*, or *Golden Ass*, of Apuleius, some of whose stories are, as already noted, the ultimate source for tales found in the *Decameron*.

In devising the frame of his narrative masterpiece, Boccaccio doubtless took account of many other precedents, for instance the dialogues of Cicero and the *Saturnalia* of Macrobius, a work that seems to have influenced the scheme of the questioni episode in the *Filocolo*. But no amount of source hunting can obscure the fact that the frame of the *Decameron* is a unique and original creation, the product of a fertile and imaginative intellect which had already supplied the impetus for several of the more important genres of western literature.

In view of what has already been said about the *Decameron*'s oriental antecedents, in particular about the occasional complexity of their boxed structure, it is of interest to note that what is usually referred to as the *cornice* (i.e. the world of the storytellers) is in reality a frame-within-a-frame. Much critical attention has been focused in recent years on the *Decameron*'s structure, and many elaborate and ingenious theories about it have been given an airing, but in essence what the reader is presented with is a threefold structural scheme. The three levels on which the *Decameron* works could be defined, for the sake of clarity, as the world of the author, the world of the narrators, and the world of the narratives. The reader is introduced to the first of these worlds in the Prologue, on the surface autobiographical but in reality reflecting a widely used literary convention resorted to by the author in several of his earlier writings. Thus the world of the author, like the other two worlds, is itself a literary fiction, for in the Prologue he claims to be pursuing a natural human instinct by displaying compassion for the sufferings of others, in particular the sufferings caused by unrequited love, and he pretends that this is the sole *raison d'être* of the entire work. Having himself undergone and recovered from such an experience, Boccaccio writes, he is well qualified to prescribe a form of solace, which he intends to offer to ladies rather than to men, as the latter have many alternative ways of diverting their thoughts from the cause of their afflictions. For the sake, then, of ladies in the throes of love, he proposes

> to tell a hundred tales, or fables or parables or histories, call them what you will, told in ten days by a worthy group of seven ladies and three young men formed in the recent season of deadly pestilence, along with certain songs that were sung by the ladies for their pleasure.[8]

Boccaccio's alternative designation of his tales as 'fables or parables or histories' reflects with curious precision the three main sources of his narrative material: the French *fabliaux*, the Latin *exempla* and the Italian and Latin medieval chronicles. But why he should have attributed the *canzonette* to the ladies alone in this passage, rather than to all ten members of the *brigata*, which was the scheme he was eventually to adopt, is not at once apparent. The explanation tentatively offered by Vittore Branca is that the author originally intended that all ten songs should be sung by the ladies. But this is merely the first of several points in the work where Boccaccio seems to overlook the presence and participation, within the world of the narrators, of the three young men. It is therefore more likely that he at first envisaged his collection of tales as having a septenary structure, a thesis which has been persuasively argued by Giorgio Padoan.[9] The fact that already, in the pages of the *Comedía delle ninfe fiorentine*, he had employed in rudimentary outline just such a structural scheme, and that the seven young nymphs of the earlier work were explicitly presented as embodying the seven virtues, seems significant in this connection, implying as it does that he had similar allegorical intentions in planning the structure of his major work. The Prologue is the first of three passages in the *Decameron* in which the author explicitly addresses his readers concerning his aims and intentions, the others being the Introduction to the Fourth Day and the author's concluding remarks (*Conclusione dell'autore*). All three of these passages are characterized by an ambivalent, tongue-in-cheek

---

8 '. . . di raccontare cento novelle, o favole o parabole o istorie che dire le vogliamo, raccontate in diece giorni da una onesta brigata di sette donne e di tre giovani nel pistilenzioso tempo della passata mortalità fatta, e alcune canzonette dalle predette donne cantate al lor diletto.'
9 See G. Padoan, *Il Boccaccio, le Muse, il Parnaso e l'Arno*, Florence, 1978.

intonation, and it would be unwise to interpret them too literally, but the theories they embody concerning the function of literature provide some sort of insight into Boccaccio's view of art and society.

In all three passages, the impression is studiously fostered that the *Decameron* is written exclusively for ladies suffering from the pangs of unrequited love, and the author claims to be offering them his comfort and advice. But if one probes below the surface of this outward declaration of his intentions, it is very soon apparent that he is addressing himself to a much wider readership, and that the three passages in question, especially the second and third, have a very different object. Their purpose, in fact, is to establish the aesthetic validity of the literary genre, narrative prose fiction, to which the *Decameron* belongs. Before Boccaccio, no one in western Europe had ever considered prose fiction to be worthy of serious study, and for more than a century after his death it continued to be regarded as a frivolous literary pursuit. One of his most distinguished successors in this branch of literature, Franco Sacchetti (1335–1400), author of the collection of stories known as the *Trecentonovelle*, describes himself as a *'uomo discolo e grosso'* ('a crude, unlearned man'), though in fact he was nothing of the sort. The note of self-deprecation is found in the Prologue to his collection, where a handsome tribute to Boccaccio is qualified by a phrase suggesting that, in some respects, his predecessor's outstanding genius had been misapplied.

No such doubts can ever have assailed Boccaccio, who seems intent, in the three passages he addresses to the reader, on proving the worthiness of the task to which he has committed himself. The Prologue, with its fictive explanation of the origins and the objectives of the *Decameron*, is marked by a tone of extreme self-assurance and, from a technical viewpoint, by a virtuoso display of several of the most admired procedures of medieval rhetoric, the so-called *ars dictandi*. The opening words conform to the widely accepted practice of beginning with a proverb, in this case that it is human to take pity on people in distress (*umana cosa è aver compassione degli afflitti*). A similar opening statement is found in the *Fiammetta*,[10] but in the

10 '*Suole a' miseri crescere di dolersi vaghezza, quando di sé discernon o sentono compassione in alcuno.*' ('Those who are suffering tend to experience greater pain when they sense or notice another's compassion.')

earlier work it was much more elaborate and carried far less impact. Here it is pithy and direct, and rounded off by a rhetorical feature that occurs again and again in the Prologue, and partly accounts for its distinctive tone of high seriousness: the metrical sequence known as the *cursus planus*, consisting of a dactyl followed by a spondee (e.g. *dégli afflítti*). Another rhetorical feature woven into the opening, and reminiscent of the initial sonnet of Petrarch's *Canzoniere*, is the nostalgic evocation of an all-consuming love. But whereas in Petrarch, and for that matter in the *stilnovisti*, where this poetic motif is most extensively explored and elaborated upon, the love is platonic or unrequited or both, in Boccaccio there is a strong suggestion of reciprocity. The reason it caused him so much suffering, he is careful to stress, was not the cruelty of his lady-love, but the immoderate passion engendered within his mind by a craving that was ill-restrained.[11]

However, it is in the second *ad lectorem* passage, the Introduction to the Fourth Day, that the polemical intention of these authorial interventions (i.e. to establish the credentials of the genre in which Boccaccio was writing) can best be observed. It begins with a paragraph on Envy, which is likened to a fiery and impetuous wind whose effects, as the author disingenuously explains in an image borrowed from Dante, are normally felt in the highest of high places. Why then should the stories he has so far written, and which are already in circulation, have attracted so much hostile comment? After all, they are no more than *novellette* ('little tales') which bear no title and are written, not only in the Florentine vernacular and in prose, but in the most homely, unassuming style that anyone could imagine. Whatever the meaning of the phrase *senza titolo* (and it possibly connotes no more than 'unpretentious', though Boccaccio used the same phrase elsewhere to describe Ovid's *Amores*, in order to indicate the discontinuity of its material), it is obvious that he is here adopting an extreme defensive posture and that heavy irony is his chosen weapon. For the tales of the first three days, already circulating, are written in a style that is elegant to a fault, and more

---

11 '. . . *certo non per crudeltà della donna amata, ma per soverchio fuoco nella mente concetto da poco regolato appetito.*'

than worthy of stylistic comparison to any vernacular prose works (including those of Dante) which had preceded them. The false modesty of his description of the tales so far written is of course an example of a conventional medieval literary posture, seen also in several of his earlier works and in those of other writers such as Petrarch, who referred to his great series of vernacular poems, the *Canzoniere*, as *nugellae*, or mere trifles, and who was well aware of their exceptional worth, even if he did regard his costive Latin epic, the *Africa*, as the work by which posterity would measure his poetic stature. In spite of Dante's magnificent example, vernacular writing continued to be treated with distrust, and it was evidently for this reason, among others, that Boccaccio felt the need to justify his choice of linguistic medium for his prose masterpiece. As for the self-effacing phrase he uses to describe his style (*istilo umilissimo e rimesso*), it should be noted that his commentary on the first seventeen cantos of *Inferno* (*Esposizioni sopra la Comedía di Dante*) includes a very similar phrase to refer to the 'comic' style of Dante's poem (*lo stilo comico è umile e rimesso*).

Having thus neatly disposed of objections to his style and language, the author goes on to list five specific criticisms that he claims have been directed at him, concerning the thirty stories so far written. First, he says, he is accused of being a womanizer, who takes an unseemly delight in consoling and entertaining the ladies and in singing their praises.[12] The second criticism follows on from the first, and centres on the disparity in age between himself and his young female readers. No man of Boccaccio's age, say his critics, should be discussing the ways of women and providing for their pleasure.[13] But since Boccaccio was about thirty-five years old when he wrote these words, one is inclined to ask how seriously they were meant to be taken, and a similar question mark hangs over the third of the alleged criticisms of his tales. This consists of the simple proposition that he would be acting more sensibly if he were to

12 '. . . *hanno detto che voi mi piacete troppo e che onesta cosa non è che io tanto diletto prenda di piacervi e di consolarvi e . . . di commendarvi, come io fo.*'
13 '. . . *hanno detto che alla mia età non sta bene . . . a ragionar di donne o a compiacer loro.*'

spend his time in the company, not of young women, but of the Muses in Parnassus.[14] He then goes on to claim that there are others, who, far from advising him to practise the art of poetry, would prefer that he applied himself to the business of earning his daily bread.[15] And finally, he writes, there are those who try to belittle his efforts by claiming that his versions of the stories he has told are not consistent with the facts.[16]

Of the five charges supposed to have been levelled against him by his critics, this last is the most disingenuous of all, yet it is entirely consistent with the tone of the whole passage, which is more a series of mirthful observations than a chronicle of his alleged shortcomings. Only the most naïve of his readers could ever have supposed that his stories were faithful accounts of real historical events. But this is an impression he seeks to foster elsewhere, most notably in the Introduction to the First Day, but also in the preambles or postscripts to individual tales, for instance in the concluding paragraph of the story of Gianni Lotteringhi and the werewolf (VII, 1), where he solemnly presents alternative versions of the story he has just told, plumping for the one he claims to have greater historical accuracy. The quest for verisimilitude is one that Boccaccio never abandons, whether in telling a highly implausible tale or, as in the Introduction to the Fourth Day, in purporting to list the complaints of his critics.

Whatever his motives may have been for pausing to address his readers at the beginning of the Fourth Day (and, as we have sought to indicate, they probably had more to do with his awareness of the humble status of vernacular prose fiction and his determination to see that it was raised than with the five specific charges he mentions), Boccaccio exploits the occasion for a further display, if any were needed, of his mastery of the storyteller's craft. Employing the tools of the narrator to refute the charges of his critics, he recounts the tale of one Filippo Balducci, prematurely widowed, who retreats

14 '. . . dicono che io farei più saviamente a starmi con le Muse in Parnaso che . . . mescolarmi tra voi'.
15 '. . . hanno detto che io farei più discretamente a pensare donde io dovessi aver del pane.'
16 'E certi altri in altra guisa essere state le cose da me raccontatevi che come io le vi porgo s'ingegnano in detrimento della mia fatica di dimostrare.'

with his two-year-old son to a cave on the slopes of Monte Asinaio, or 'Mount Donkeyman', a pun on Monte Senario, where Florentine hermits traditionally sought refuge from the cares of the secular world. The boy grows up to manhood in blissful ignorance of the world and its vanities, but one day persuades his father to take him on one of his periodic trips to obtain essential supplies from the charitable people of Florence. The young man marvels at the palaces, houses, churches, and other urban features of interest, but what arouses his curiosity to fever pitch is the spectacle of some fair young ladies, elegantly dressed, who are coming away from a wedding, or as Boccaccio playfully describes it, seizing on the word's plurality, *'un paio di nozze'* ('a couple of nuptials'). In vain does the father insist that these attractive creatures are evil, and attempt to divert his son's attention away from them, being forced in the end to supply the young man with a name for them, *papere*, (literally 'goslings', though 'birds' would perhaps convey the sense better in present-day colloquial English). To his son's earnest plea that they should take one of these creatures home with them, so that he could give it something to fill its beak, the father replies: *'Io non voglio; tu non sai donde elle s'imbeccano!'* ('I won't do it; you don't know whereabouts they do their pecking!').

The tale of Filippo Balducci, sometimes referred to as the 101st story of the *Decameron*, is often thought of as unfinished, perhaps because Boccaccio himself tells us so:

> But before replying to any of my critics, I should like to strengthen
> my case by recounting, not a complete story (. . .), but a part of one,
> so that its very incompleteness will set it apart from the others.[17]

Although it may lack intentional finality, in which respect it differs not at all from several of the other tales, the story of Balducci is in fact complete, and has served its purpose, if indeed it was designed to demonstrate, as the author claims, that there is nothing remotely unnatural in taking a lively interest in the opposite sex. But is that the real purpose of the story, for which incidentally there are scores

17 'Ma avanti che io venga a far la risposta a alcuno, mi piace in favor di me raccontare, non una novella intera (. . .), ma parte d'una, acciò che il suo difetto stesso sé mostri non esser di quelle.'

of antecedents in oriental and western literature, though none so finely wrought as this? Is it not more likely that it is pressed into service at this juncture to sustain the initial fiction that the *Decameron* was written as consolatory material for ladies in the throes of love? In contrast to the mood of most of the stories to which it acts as preamble, the overall tone of this opening sequence to the Fourth Day is extremely light-hearted, interspersed as it is with puns, double meanings and lively banter. Yet beneath the outwardly nonchalant air one detects a deep inner seriousness, which is nowhere more apparent than in the author's rebuttal of the charge that he has abandoned the Muses. The passage not only offers a good example of the ambivalent tone of the whole, it also confirms the desire to place this genre of writing fairly and squarely within the realm of poetry:

> That I should stay with the Muses in Parnassus, I declare to be good advice, but all the same we can no more abide with the Muses than they can abide with us. If, on leaving them behind, a man delights in seeing what resembles them, that is not something worthy of blame: the Muses are ladies, and albeit the ladies are not worth as much as the Muses, yet at first sight they resemble them, so that, even if they pleased me for no other reason, they should please me for this; besides, ladies caused me to compose a thousand lines of verse, whereas Muses never caused me to write any. They helped me, certainly, and showed me how to write those thousand lines; and perhaps in writing these things, no matter how humble they are, they have come to stay with me more than once, perhaps to serve and to honour the resemblance the ladies bear to themselves: wherefore, in weaving these tales, I am straying less distant from Mount Parnassus and from the Muses than many may venture to think.[18]

18 'Che io con le Muse in Parnaso mi debbia stare, affermo che è buon consiglio, ma tuttavia né noi possiamo dimorar con le Muse né esse con esso noi. Se quando avviene che l'uomo da lor si parte, dilettasi di veder cosa che le somigli, questo non è cosa da biasimare: le Muse son donne, e benché le donne quel che le Muse vagliono non vagliano, pure esse hanno nel primo aspetto simiglianza di quelle, sí che, quando per altro non mi piacessero, per quello mi dovrebber piacere; senza che le donne già mi fur cagione di comporre mille versi, dove le Muse mai non mi furono di farne alcun cagione. Aiutaronmi elle bene e mostraronmi comporre que' mille; e forse a queste cose scrivere, quantunque sieno umilissime, si sono elle venute parecchie volte a starsi meco, in servigio forse e in onore della simiglianza che le donne hanno a esse; per che, queste cose tessendo, né dal monte Parnaso né dalle Muse non mi allontano quanto molti per avventura s'avisano.'

The outward display of nonchalance here conceals a firm belief in the seriousness of the task to which Boccaccio has committed himself and a deep conviction of its poetic worth and lasting significance. And this same blend of surface frivolity and inner seriousness characterizes, too, the third and last of the *ad lectorem* passages, the Epilogue or *Conclusione dell'autore*, where he briefly replies to certain objections which may perhaps have arisen in the minds, not so much of his critics, as of his readers in general.

The brevity of the Epilogue is deceptive, in that a number of important questions are addressed, such as the style and language of the *Decameron*, its 'truth to life' and the propriety of its subject-matter. Each of these questions elicits from Boccaccio a viewpoint that is at the same time rationally argued and vigorously expressed. When, for instance, he asks whether ladies who are truly virtuous should have narrated or listened to some of the stories told in the body of the work, he supplements the stock response of medieval rhetoricians to such questions (i.e. that no story is so improper as to prevent its being told, provided it is told in language that itself remains within the bounds of propriety) with a string of observations that are both witty and full of good sense. In the first place, he says, the nature of the story dictates the manner of its telling, so that what might seem to be lack of restraint on the part of the author is really a reflection of the lack of restraint implicit within the narrative, which could not have been told in any other way without distorting it beyond recognition. In making this point, he presumably had in mind such tales as those of Rustico and Alibech (III, 10) and of Caterina and the nightingale (V, 4), each of which demands explicitness in the telling. Secondly, however, there is the question of lexical improprieties, as exemplified in words in common use that may carry sexual overtones, words like *foro* ('hole'), *caviglia* ('rod'), *mortaio* ('mortar') and *pestello* ('pestle'). Here Boccaccio would seem to be treading on treacherous ground, for there are scores of examples in the *Decameron* of his exploiting the double meaning of words in this category, not to mention one conspicuous instance in the penultimate paragraph of the Epilogue itself, where he writes of the sweetness of his tongue (*lingua*), to which he claims that a lady who is a neighbour of his will readily bear full witness.

Incorrigible punster that he is, Boccaccio turns to the visual arts for his defence, observing that the points of saintly swords (those of St Michael and St George) are often depicted slaying serpents and dragons, whilst the feet of Our Lord are fixed to the cross with at least one nail, a word that in the Italian (*chiovo*) carries strong sexual overtones. Boccaccio's exuberant wit boils over at this point into something very close to blasphemy, but his most telling line of defence against the lexically prudish, reminiscent in its imagery of a passage from Guinizzelli's *canzone* beginning '*Al cor gentil repara sempre Amore*', is his statement that

> No corrupted mind ever construed a word wholesomely: and just as seemly words leave no impression on a mind that is corrupt, so words that are not so seemly cannot contaminate a mind that is well ordered, any more than mud contaminates the rays of the sun, or earthly filth the beauties of heaven.[19]

Two other features of note in the Epilogue are the author's final, ironic comment concerning the fiction that the work is intended only for ladies with time on their hands, and the explanation he supplies for the headings with which each of the stories is presented to the reader. As to the first, Boccaccio reminds those who complain of the excessive length of some of the tales that he had presented them from the outset '*all'oziose e non all'altre*', or to no ladies other than those who had nothing to do. If his readers have other ways of spending their time, he says, it would be foolish of them to waste it in reading his tales, no matter how briefly they were told. The mock dismissive tone is heightened still further by a reference to the major centres of learning in the ancient world (Athens) and modern world (Bologna and Paris) respectively. None of his fair readers, he asserts, will have studied in places of that kind, where reading-matter must of necessity be brief if students are to make good use of their time.

Considering the overall tone of these authorial interventions, which is one of exuberant irony, this last assertion could be taken as the final token of an ever-present feature of the *Decameron*: its solid

---

19 '*Niuna corrotta mente intese mai sanamente parola: e così come le oneste a quella non giovano, così quelle che tanto oneste non sono la ben disposta non posson contaminare, se non come il loto i solari raggi o le terrene brutture le bellezze del cielo.*'

connection with the practical, everyday world of fourteenth-century bourgeois society, and its distrust of the intellectualism fostered by the academies, here expressed in the notion that academic scholarship concerns itself with the examination of minutiae to the exclusion of material that, whilst taking longer to produce its impact, might conceivably bring greater mental refreshment. And a further instance of this regard for the practical aspects of literary consumption is the explanation he offers for the headings to the stories. These, he says, are supplied specifically for the purpose of allowing the reader to select the stories that will please, and ignore the ones that are liable to 'sting':

> But whoever goes reading among these should leave alone the ones that sting and read the ones that please: so as not to deceive anyone, each bears the mark on its brow of what lies hidden in its bosom.[20]

In the Epilogue, the author also reminds his readers of the circumstances in which the tales were supposed to have been told. They were told by young people, neither in a church nor in the schools of philosophers, but in gardens, in a place designed for pleasure. The wheel has come full circle, and the reader is given a final reminder of the Elysian world of the storytellers.

★ ★ ★

For all the dramatic intensity of its opening account of the plague, what strikes one most forcibly about the *Decameron*'s second plane of reality, the world of the *lieta brigata*, is its literariness, its artificiality, its sense of unworldliness. Poetically real, it is a very different world from the tangible world of the stories themselves. The coded implications of the world of the storytellers are at once apparent from the choice of their initial meeting place. They do not meet in the cathedral, or in one of Florence's more centrally situated churches, but in the church of Santa Maria Novella, which had only recently been incorporated within the walls of the city. The choice of assembly place is an early pointer to the author's delight in

20 '*Tuttavia chi va tra queste leggendo, lasci star quelle che pungono e quelle che dilettano legga: elle, per non ingannare alcuna persona, tutte nella fronte portan segnato quello che esse dentro dal loro seno nascose tengono.*'

wordplay, since its very name foreshadows the imminent participation of the young people who forgather in Santa Maria Novella in the telling of *novelle*.

But it is when Boccaccio introduces the various members of the group to his reader that the allusive implications begin to flow in earnest. In an effort to preserve the illusion of historical objectivity that has been studiously fostered in his description of the plague and its effects, he claims that he could tell us their actual names, but will refrain from doing so in order to protect them from possible future embarrassment. The embarrassment of which he writes is that which would result from the stories that will follow, all of which they either listened to or recounted themselves.

The protective pseudonyms supplied by Boccaccio for the ten members of the *lieta brigata* have given rise to much speculation. Confining ourselves to the facts, we may note that all of the names carry literary or mythological overtones and that several of them had already appeared as the names of characters in one or more of Boccaccio's earlier vernacular writings. Pampinea, literally 'full of vigour', is a name that had already appeared in the *Comedía delle ninfe fiorentine*. Fiammetta, 'little flame', was the name of the female protagonist and narrator of the *Elegia*, as well as that of the presiding figure in the *questioni d'amore* sequence in the *Filocolo*. Filomena, 'the beloved' or 'the lover of song', was the dedicatee of the *Filostrato*, whilst Emilia, 'she who allures', was the object of the intense rivalry of Palamon and Arcite in the *Teseida*. Of the other three ladies' names, Elissa is a variant on the original name of Virgil's Dido, Neifile ('newly enamoured') probably represents, according to Branca, the poetry of the *dolce stil novo* and of Dante himself, whilst Lauretta is the diminutive form of Petrarch's Laura. Thus these last three are associated with the poets (Virgil, Dante and Petrarch) whose work Boccaccio most greatly admired.

The names of the three young men have similar associations. Panfilo, 'all loving', was the young Florentine whose desertion of the Neapolitan Fiammetta gave rise to her outpourings of sorrow in the *Elegia*. Filostrato, 'defeated by love', was the name given by Boccaccio to his narrative poem on the love of Troilus for the faithless Cressida. The name of the most lively of all the storytellers,

Dioneo, is based on the legend, reported by Homer in the *Iliad*, that the goddess of Love, Aphrodite, was the daughter of Dione by Zeus, hence Dioneo's propensity for the telling of erotic tales, and his prescribing of the topic for the tales of adulterous wives in the Seventh Day.

The ten members of the *lieta brigata* clearly have allegorical and symbolic overtones, but opinions differ over what exactly they are supposed to represent. One of the most convincing and well argued theories of recent years has been that of the American scholar Victoria Kirkham, who detects in the frame of the *Decameron* an allegorically resonant structure that derives key features from Aristotelian–Thomistic ethics.[21] The ten narrators participate in a drama of the human soul, a drama which 'pits the rational appetite against the lower irascible and concupiscible appetites, a trio of forces personified by the three male narrators'. Reason ultimately dominates Anger and Lust, with the assistance of the seven virtues, represented by the seven young ladies. The tripartite division of the soul into the nobler, intellectual power of reason and the baser human emotions of anger and lust was a long-standing concept whose roots may be traced back from the *Summae* of the medieval scholastic philosophers through the patristic writings of Augustine and Jerome to the dialogues of Plato.

In the frame of the *Decameron*, the representative of Reason is Panfilo, who introduces the storytelling with his tale (I, 1) of the arch-villain Ciappelletto, a tale sandwiched between pious and outwardly sincere declarations concerning the loving-kindness and all-seeing wisdom of God. Panfilo also presides over the Tenth Day, with its series of uplifting tales on the subject of liberal and munificent deeds. On receiving the crown at the end of the Ninth Day, he had been told by his predecessor, Emilia, that it would be his task to compensate for the failings of herself and the others who had already filled the office he is about to assume. 'Her charge,' as Kirkham shrewdly remarks, 'suggests the corrective capacity of reason.' The member of the company associated with the concupis-

---

21 See V. Kirkham, 'An Allegorically Tempered *Decameron*', in *Italica*, 62, 1, Madison, 1985.

cible appetite, or Lust, is easy to identify. Dioneo is the narrator of
the first 'improper' tale of the *Decameron*, concerning the sexual
frolickings of the monk and the abbot (I, 4), and it is he who secures
for himself the privilege, for the remaining nine days, of always
being the last contributor to the day's storytelling. With the exception of the tale of Friar Cipolla (VI, 10) and of the patient Griselda
(X, 10), all of his stories are concerned with sexual gratification, and
it is Dioneo who shrugs aside the objections of his female companions and persists in prescribing the topic for the string of salacious
tales that are told on the Seventh Day. Kirkham makes a characteristically wry comment on the musical instrument played by Tindaro
to accompany the dancing at the end of the day:

> It is appropriate that only Dioneo's day evokes the bagpipes. An instru-
> ment that Chaucer's earthy miller could also well 'blow and sowne', the
> evocatively shaped cornemuse, was an established Priapic symbol.

The third member of the male trio, representing the irascible
appetite, is Filostrato, who prescribes the topic for the tragic tales of
the Fourth Day, and whose reign is marked by frequent displays of
irritability. His own story on that day describes how the fraternal
love of Guillaume de Roussillon and Guillaume de Cabestanh is
transformed into murderous hatred.

That the seven young ladies represent the seven virtues is the
obvious conclusion to be drawn from the fact that their prototypal
counterparts, the seven nymphs of the *Comedía delle ninfe fiorentine*,
are specifically said by the author to fulfil that symbolic function. In
the *Decameron*, Boccaccio offers no such direct indication of their
figurative role, but that is not surprising in view of his initial
presentation of the ladies as actual people whose true identity he
will conceal by providing them with pseudonyms. It is therefore
left to the reader to deduce what each of them represents, through
careful analysis of the textual evidence. Of the four cardinal virtues,
Prudence could be represented by more than one of the ladies, but
the prime candidate is clearly Pampinea, whose eloquent reasoning
persuades her companions to take the prudent course of retiring to
the countryside. Temperance and Fortitude are represented, according to Kirkham's analysis, by Fiammetta and Filomena respectively,

because, following the rule of the attraction of opposites, the first is matched with the concupiscible Dioneo, whilst the second is loved by the irascible Filostrato. Justice, the fourth of the cardinal virtues, can be assumed to be represented, through a process of deduction and elimination, by Lauretta, who, like the three already mentioned (and unlike the remaining three), is accompanied on her excursion to the countryside by a maidservant.

We are thus left with Neifile, Elissa and Emilia as representing the three theological virtues, and it can hardly be coincidental that these three are elected sovereign for the Third, Sixth and Ninth Days respectively. Triadically placed in the order of their presentation in the *Comedía delle ninfe fiorentine*, Charity is represented by Neifile, Hope by Elissa, and Faith by Emilia.

It remains an open question whether this kind of tentative clarification of the allegorical implications of the frame sheds any light on the work as a whole or on the intentions of its author. At most, it shows that the connection between the *Decameron* and earlier, explicitly allegorical works such as the *Caccia di Diana*, the *Teseida*, the *Comedía delle ninfe fiorentine* and the *Amorosa visione* is closer than used to be supposed. It also supports the now fashionable view that the author of the *Decameron*, by according a decisive role to Reason in the person of Panfilo as against the appetites of Anger and Lust as represented by Filostrato and Dioneo, was more attached to orthodox Christian values than his earlier reputation would suggest. But perhaps the most important contribution it makes is in revealing one aspect of the extreme care with which the structural foundations of his prose masterpiece were laid.

Another noteworthy aspect of Boccaccio's concern with the work's structure is his handling of the popular medieval topos of the *locus amœnus*. The three locations where according to the author the stories of the *Decameron* were told have certain elements in common, but there are also one or two striking contrasts. The first *locus amœnus* is described in the Introduction to the First Day, and it sets the scene and creates the atmosphere for the storytelling of the first two days. Although its isolation is stressed ('the spot in question lay some distance away from any road'), it is in fact situated no more than two miles from Florence, presumably in the area of

Fiesole, for it is a palace perched on the summit of a hill. The description of the place occupies a single paragraph, brief but surprisingly full of detail. Not only does the reader obtain a clear picture of the interior of the palace, with its spacious courtyard, its loggias and its richly decorated apartments, but the surrounding gardens and meadows are also sketched in, and there are references to wells of cool, refreshing water and cellars of precious wines. Finally, the pristine orderliness of the palace interior is given emphasis, with references to its speckless appearance, its neatly made-up beds, its profusion of freshly cut flowers, and its floors carpeted with rushes.

The image conjured up by this first *locus amœnus* is in fact that of an aristocratic country residence characterized by its extreme sense of order and purity, features that contrast markedly with the conditions, described earlier in such vivid detail, which the members of the *lieta brigata* have left behind them in Florence. There is no very obvious hint, as yet, of the symbolic connotations of the world of the storytellers, but simply a straightforward, realistic account of a patrician rural retreat. Even the lush green meadow where the young people assemble later in the day to begin their storytelling is economically described: its resemblance to an earthly paradise, or Garden of Eden, is at best only marginal. We are still moving within the realm of the historically possible.

The second *locus amœnus* occurs at the beginning of the Third Day. The change of location has been decreed by Neifile, who on being elected Queen at the end of the Second Day has advised her companions that they should desist from telling stories on the next day, a Friday, out of respect for Our Lord who was crucified on that day. Nor should they tell stories on the Saturday, this being the day on which young ladies are wont to wash their hair and rinse away the week's grime from their persons, and to refrain from all further activities out of respect for the approaching sabbath. And she decrees that on the Sunday they should move on to their second rural retreat, in order to avoid the possibility of being joined by others.

Many of the particulars in the passages describing the *brigata*'s transfer to their two rural retreats are identical. In both, the distance travelled is no more than two miles, whilst the palace itself, with its spacious courtyards, its loggias, its deep well providing a supply of cool water, its richly stocked wine cellars and its seasonable flowers, is set on a small hill. The similarities between the two locations should alert one to the fact that they exist only in the mind of the author, but that has not prevented commentators, from Renaissance times down to our own, from identifying them as actual places, the first on the hill known as Poggio Gherardi, near Fiesole, and the second as the Villa Schifanoia, at Camerata. Theories of that sort, still perpetuated by the modern tourist industry, may safely be discounted.

What distinguishes the second *locus amœnus* from the first is the elaborate description of a walled garden. Its air of orderliness and its numerous sensual delights are dwelt upon at considerable length, conveying the impression of a place that is set beyond the boundaries of common human experience. The prominence accorded to gardens in medieval literature dates roughly from the year 1240, when Guillaume de Lorris, in the first section of the French poem in octosyllabic couplets, *Roman de la Rose*, had composed a dream allegory recounting the wooing of a girl, symbolized by a rosebud, in a garden representing courtly society. It was the second, much longer section of the poem, written by Jean de Meung around 1280, with its mass of encyclopaedic detail, that accounted for the remarkable popularity of the poem among other medieval poets. Chaucer, who translated roughly a third of the poem into Middle English (*The Romaunt of the Rose*), was one of several writers who came strongly under its spell, and so too, many years before, did Boccaccio. Descriptions of marvellous gardens similar to that of Guillaume de Lorris had appeared in several of Boccaccio's earlier works, notably the *Amorosa visione*, but here in the Third Day of the *Decameron* his intention is made unmistakably clear by the company's unanimous assertion that 'if Paradise were constructed on earth, it was inconceivable that it could take any other form.' The topos of the *paradiso terrestre*, the Earthly Paradise or Garden of Eden, was one that appealed strongly to medieval writers, especially after Dante's visionary treatment of the theme in the concluding cantos of his *Purgatorio*, where the Garden of Eden is envisaged as a wooded region surrounded by Lethe, the stream of forgetfulness. But whereas Dante locates the Earthly Paradise in the afterlife, at the summit of the mountain of Purgatory, rising in sheer and awe-inspiring majesty from the waters of the southern hemisphere, Boccaccio characteristically implies that it is still accessible to those determined to escape from their literally (as well as symbolically) plague-ridden life on earth.

Woods and streams are a prominent feature of the *Decameron*'s third *locus amœnus*, the so-called Valley of the Ladies, described in the concluding section of the Sixth Day. The valley is perfectly circular in shape, and surrounded by six hills, each with a castle-like palace perched on its summit. A waterfall issues forth from a gorge between two of the hills, forming a clear stream on reaching the floor of the valley. The stream in turn forms a lake in the valley's centre, and from the lower end of the lake a second stream makes its way to the narrow defile that provides the valley's only means of access. This last particular offers a clue (if any were needed) to the valley's significance, recalling as it does the passage from St Matthew's gospel giving notice that 'strait is the gate, and narrow is the way, which leadeth unto life, and few there be that find it.' Apart, however, from its obvious paradisal connotations, the Valley of the Ladies has been seen as the culminating point of a highly complex allegory, in which the *cornice* is viewed as representing Art or Poetry, without which society is meaningless.[22] If that is so, the six castles dominating the valley could be taken to represent the six days of storytelling in the *Decameron* already in place, while the crystal-clear lake at its centre could signify the font of artistic inspiration to which the storytellers are led in preparation for the remainder of their narrative endeavours. When the seven young ladies (and later on, the three young men) discard their clothes and bathe in the waters of the lake, they are in effect renewing their commitment to the artistic process on which they had embarked at Pampinea's bidding on the first day of their spiritual and aesthetic retreat.

There is one final point to note about the *Decameron*'s second plane of reality – the world of the narrators – and that is the passage in the introductory section to the Ninth Day, where the ten young people, returning from their morning walk, are described in terms

22 See L. Marino, *The Decameron 'Cornice': Allusion, Allegory, and Iconology*, Ravenna, 1979.

that almost seem to foreshadow the figures as well as the spirit of a
Botticelli painting of the Renaissance:

> They were all wreathed in fronds of oak, and their hands were full of
> fragrant herbs or flowers, so that if anyone had encountered them, he
> would only have been able to say: 'either these people will not be
> vanquished by death, or they will welcome it with joy.'[23]

What is implied here is that in their pastoral retreat, the band of
storytellers figure forth a state of pre-lapsarian innocence, at one
with the paradisal world they inhabit. That impression is reinforced
at numerous other points in the frame, where the author is at pains
to stress the absolute propriety of their proceedings and relationships,
whatever may be said about the material of their narratives. Like all
good allegories, the world of Boccaccio's ten narrators can be
interpreted in many different ways, but its dominant characteristics
are its pristine candour and absence of guile.

III. THE WORLD OF THE NARRATIVES

In the popular imagination the *Decameron* is regarded first and
foremost as a collection of tales concerned mainly with the ingenious
stratagems adopted by wives and the religious to achieve the
gratification of their sexual desires. In both cases, an act of infidelity
is involved, on the one hand to matrimonial vows, on the other to
the vow of celibacy. The hypocrisy of the clergy and the wantonness
of women were the two favourite targets of the medieval satirist,
and it is not therefore surprising that these two themes should
occupy a prominent position in a work which, however strongly it
anticipates the ethos and spirit of the Renaissance, is rooted so
firmly in medieval culture. Yet when one considers the *Decameron*
as a whole, one cannot fail to be impressed by the extraordinary
range of its subject matter, and by the consequent impossibility of
fitting it into any single descriptive category. Whilst it is true that it

---

23 'Essi eran tutti di frondi di quercia inghirlandati, con le man piene o d'erbe odorifere o di
fiori; e chi scontrati gli avesse, niuna altra cosa avrebbe potuto dire se non: "O costor non
saranno dalla morte vinti o ella gli ucciderà lieti."'

is well stocked with tales of adulterous wives, and in fact one whole day, the seventh, is devoted exclusively to variations on that topic, there is also a large number of stories in which the virtues of conjugal fidelity are prominently displayed and roundly extolled, a good example being the tale of Messer Torello and his wife, Adalieta (X, 9). That is not to say that Boccaccio was more attached to conventional Christian morality than is popularly thought, as recent criticism, especially in America, has tended to assert, or that some kind of apologia is required for his apparent condoning of sexual promiscuity. Circumstances alter cases, and if any explanation is needed for the loose interpretation of the Seventh Commandment common to many of Boccaccio's characters, it may be found in the tragic story (IV, 1) which opens the proceedings on the Fourth Day.

In that famous tale, concerning Ghismonda's ill-fated love for Guiscardo, there is a phrase which neatly encapsulates the naturalistic attitude to human relationships that Boccaccio consistently adopts, especially in his handling of amatory material. The phrase is spoken by Guiscardo, and is all the more memorable because he says nothing else in a narrative conspicuous for the lengthy speeches of its two other leading characters. Guiscardo has been arrested on the orders of his master, Tancredi, whilst on his way to the bedchamber of Tancredi's daughter, Ghismonda. When Tancredi charges him with disloyalty to a benevolent master, Guiscardo tersely replies that '*Amor può troppo più che né voi né io possiamo*' ('The power of Love is greater than your power or mine'). The words are reminiscent of Virgil's '*Omnia vincit Amor; et nos cedamus Amori*,' ('Love conquers all; let us then yield to Love!').[24] But they also recall Francesca's celebrated justification of her love for Paolo in the fifth canto of Dante's *Inferno*, where she pleads that Love compels a loved one to love in return ('*Amor, che a nullo amato amar perdona . . .*'). Whereas Dante, however, intends that his reader shall reject this superficially attractive and plausible defence of the surrender to sexual passion, Boccaccio both in the story of Ghismonda and elsewhere in the *Decameron* seems intent upon showing its validity. Not only that, he implies that any attempt to interfere with the natural progression of

24 *Eclogues*, x, 69.

instinctive forces is doomed to failure, sometimes with disastrous results for the parties concerned.

The story of Ghismonda is a clear illustration of this principle, which finds expression on the theoretical plane in the author's warmly argued reply to his critics in the Introduction to the Fourth Day. There, as was seen earlier, Boccaccio lists the various objections that have been raised, or so at least he claims, to the tales already told, the first of these objections being that he is altogether too fond of the ladies, and that it is unseemly for him to take so much pleasure in entertaining them, consoling them and singing their praises. In answering this charge, Boccaccio characteristically employs the tools of his own craft, narrating the tale of a young man who, brought up from early childhood by a pious widowed father in total isolation, visits Florence for the first time, and no sooner catches his first glimpse of a group of young women than all his desires, all his curiosity, all the leanings of his affection are centred upon them, and them alone. The moral of the tale is self-evident, but in case anyone has failed to apprehend it, the author spells it out in a passage which, with its emphasis upon the strength and pleasures of natural affection, offers some indication of his essentially naturalistic philosophy. Ostensibly addressing his lady readers, Boccaccio writes:

> When you consider that even an apprentice hermit, a witless youth who was more of a wild animal than a human being, liked you better than anything he had ever seen, it is perfectly clear that those who criticize me on these grounds are people who, being ignorant of the strength and the pleasures of natural affection, neither love you nor desire your love, and they are not worth bothering about. [25]

But it is towards the end of his vigorous reply to the strictures of his critics that one finds the fullest confirmation of his respect for natural laws, for he declares that to love a woman is to do what is natural, and that in order to oppose the laws of nature, one has to possess exceptional powers. Even if a man possesses such powers, he

---

25 '. . . e spezialmente guardando che voi prima che altro piaceste a un romitello, a un giovinetto senza sentimento, anzi a uno animal salvatico? Per certo chi non v'ama e da voi non disidera d'essere amato, sí come persona che i piaceri né la vertú della naturale affezione né sente né conosce, cosí mi ripiglia; e io poco me ne curo.'

will often use them, not only in vain, but to his own serious harm. For himself, he confesses that he does not have such powers at his disposal, and that even if he did, he would sooner pass them on to others than use them himself.

In the story of Ghismonda, Tancredi opposes the laws of nature, not only by neglecting to find a second husband for his beautiful and intelligent widowed daughter, but also by severing with savage ferocity the liaison she has formed with Guiscardo. Both of these ill-considered actions stem from his own paternal love for Ghismonda which, as Boccaccio makes abundantly clear in the preamble to the narrative, as well as through his account of Tancredi's reactions to the events of the story itself, is so excessive as to border upon the incestuous. There are other stories in the *Decameron* where a father is outraged upon discovering that his daughter is, without his knowledge, actively and willingly involved in a sexual relationship, but it is only in the tale of Ghismonda that the sense of outrage is attributed, by implication, to the father's repressed incestuous feelings. In most other instances, it arises from the father's conviction that the young man with whom his daughter has formed a relationship is her social inferior, and it is instructive to note that once he has been reassured that this is not the case, the liaison is formalized by marriage and allowed to flourish. The point can best be illustrated by a comparison between the tragic outcome of Ghismonda's love for Guiscardo, and the joyous resolution of Caterina's love for Ricciardo, in the celebrated story of the song of the nightingale (V, 4). There is an obvious resemblance between these two narratives, in that both are concerned with the ingenious means through which a beautiful and resourceful young woman evades a watchful father and brings her lover to her bed, where the father eventually discovers them together. But whereas Tancredi, having restrained his initial impulse to vent his anger upon them, holds his peace and remains hidden so that he can pursue what he mistakenly considers a more prudent course of action that will do less damage to his honour, the father of Caterina, Messer Lizio, rouses his wife and conducts her to her daughter's bed, where she 'saw for herself exactly how her daughter had taken and seized hold of the nightingale, whose song she had so much yearned to hear'.

The mother's first impulse is to waken Ricciardo and shower him with abuse, but she is ordered by her husband to hold her tongue, for he has already devised a more sensible solution to their parental dilemma. Since Ricciardo is rich, and comes of noble stock, the problem can be resolved to the satisfaction of all four parties (father, mother, daughter and impetuous young lover) by compelling the youth to marry the girl at once, before being allowed to leave the house. When Ricciardo wakes up, he is presented by Messer Lizio with a simple choice: either take Caterina as his lawful wedded wife or prepare to meet his Maker. Ricciardo, with Caterina's ready approval, chooses the first alternative, whereupon Messer Lizio borrows one of his wife's rings, and Ricciardo marries Caterina there and then without moving from the spot, her parents bearing witness to the event. Once the relationship has been formalized in this manner, and his daughter's honour (and by extension his own) is no longer compromised, Messer Lizio withdraws with his wife, leaving the newly wedded pair to recommence their amorous sport:

> As soon as her parents had departed, the two young people fell once more into each other's arms, and since they had only passed a half-dozen milestones in the course of the night, they added another couple to the total before getting up. And for the first day they left it at that.[26]

The ethos of the *Decameron* is generally regarded, with good reason, as a faithful barometer of the enormous and far-reaching changes which had gradually come about in the thirteenth and fourteenth centuries in the structure of Italian society, largely as a result of the decline of the feudal aristocracy and the ever-increasing vitality of the bourgeoisie, especially in the spheres of banking and commerce. Boccaccio's own family had typified, through successive generations, this fundamental shift from a feudal society to one based largely upon the enterprise of the new merchant classes. As already seen earlier, his father, originally a smallholder in the Florentine *contado*, had moved at an early age to Florence itself,

26 'Partiti costoro, i giovani si rabbracciarono insieme, e non essendo più che sei miglia camminati la notte, altre due anzi che si levassero ne camminarono e fecer fine alla prima giornata.'

where he gradually achieved a position of importance in the city's banking fraternity. The practical, common-sense, hard-headed values of the prosperous bourgeois society in which Boccaccio was raised are everywhere apparent in the *Decameron*, which in turn exerted its greatest appeal upon those who shared and practised those values, hence the classifying of the *Decameron* as 'the epic of the bourgeoisie'. The account of Messer Lizio's sensible resolution of the problem created within his household by his wayward daughter's premature consummation of her love for Ricciardo may be construed as typifying the scale of values by which the fourteenth-century Italian bourgeoisie regulated their lives, and to which Boccaccio himself wholeheartedly subscribed.

But underlying the bourgeois values that the *Decameron* so clearly represents, there is also a noticeable regard for the code of conduct associated with the old feudal aristocracy, for whom the concept of honour was not so much a question of keeping up appearances as of strict adherence to a generally recognized series of rules governing polite behaviour, which set the nobility apart from their social inferiors. The tragic outcome of Ghismonda's love for Guiscardo is as much due to the collision between these two diverse ethical codes as to any incestuous overtones of Tancredi's affection for his daughter. In the brief but stupendous description of Tancredi's reaction to his witnessing of the passionate sexual encounter between Ghismonda and Guiscardo, the reader suddenly becomes aware of the full implications of the preamble to the novella, where Tancredi had been described as 'a most benevolent ruler, and kindly of disposition, except that in his old age he sullied his hands with the blood of passion', and where it had been pointed out that he had 'but a single child, a daughter', of whom he was 'as passionately fond . . . as any father who has ever lived'. His sense of outrage on waking to discover the two lovers locked together in amorous embrace is thus fully understandable as the natural reaction of one who has been deceived in the object of his deep affection. And likewise his over-reaction to the discovery – the brutal murder of Guiscardo and his sending of the young man's heart to his daughter in a golden chalice – is explicable in purely psychological terms. But in the lengthy central episode of the novella, reporting the heated exchanges between Tancredi and Ghismonda concerning the propriety of her love for Guiscardo, it is the clash between the old feudal values and the new bourgeois ethic that holds centre stage, and there is little doubt that Ghismonda, representing the latter, has the better of the argument. Tancredi reproaches his daughter on two grounds: firstly, that she has given herself to a man who was not her husband, and secondly, that she has chosen to bestow her favours upon one whose rank was inferior to her own. In answering the first of these charges, Ghismonda in effect enlarges with convincing eloquence upon the simple statement that Guiscardo has already uttered: '*Amor può troppo più che né voi né io possiamo.*' She is made of flesh and blood, not of stone or iron, she is still a young woman, subject to the laws of youth and full of amorous longings, intensified by her brief marriage, which had enabled her 'to discover the marvellous joy that comes from their fulfilment'. It is only natural that a woman in her condition should have sought a lover. Nor did she choose a lover at random, as many another woman would have done, but she consciously and deliberately selected a man who, notwithstanding his humble origins, displayed all the qualities associated with true nobility. If Tancredi would abandon the notion that a man's nobility is measured by the quality of his ancestry, and compare impartially the lives, customs and manners of each of his nobles with those of Guiscardo, he would be forced to conclude that Guiscardo alone is a patrician whilst all of his nobles are plebeians.

The concept of nobility expounded here so lucidly by Ghismonda is not of course an invention of Boccaccio's own, for it had been adumbrated in the thirteenth century by Guido Guinizzelli, the poet acknowledged by Dante as founder of the *dolce stil novo*, and thereafter it became a staple theme of the Italian lyric until well into the following century. For the *stilnovisti*, nobility of lineage counted less than what they termed nobility of the heart. The term '*gentil core*' ('noble heart') became a recurrent feature of the poetic vocabulary of the period. The songs with which Boccaccio brings each of the ten days of the *Decameron* to a close are the last significant specimens of that great poetic tradition which stretches back, via Cino da Pistoia, Dante and Guido Cavalcanti, to Guido Guinizzelli. But whereas in the poetry of the *stilnovisti* the sophisticated definitions of love and nobility had assumed the character of a refined intellectual exercise, Boccaccio appears to accept their validity, and he proceeds to examine their practical implications within a series of carefully delineated contexts.

It is above all in the story of Cimon and Iphigenia (V, 1) that Boccaccio makes his most brilliant and original contribution to that tradition, by incorporating one of its principal themes (the ennobling power of feminine beauty) within the framework of a prose narrative. The story tells of Cimon, the uncouth and witless son of a noble and prosperous Cypriot gentleman, who is a source of so much affliction to his despairing father that he is sent away to live in the country, where the rusticity of his manners will attract less attention. One afternoon as he is shambling doltishly through a wood on one of his father's estates, he comes upon a clearing surrounded by very tall trees, in a corner of which there is a lovely cool fountain. A beautiful girl is lying asleep beside it, and her dress is so flimsy that scarcely an inch of her fair white body is concealed from Cimon's admiring gaze. The effect of such wondrous beauty upon the boorish youth is electrifying. Not only does he fall deeply in love with the girl, Iphigenia, but in order to win her hand in marriage he totally abandons all his former habits and becomes, within the space of four years, the most graceful, refined and versatile young man in the island of Cyprus.

The violent manner in which Cimon eventually succeeds in his ambition to marry the fair Iphigenia carries distinct echoes of the myth of Pholus, the centaur named by Dante in *Inferno* (XII), who, at the wedding of Pirithous and Hippodamia, got drunk and attempted to rape the bride and other women present. In similar fashion, Cimon recruits an armed band to storm Iphigenia's wedding banquet and carry her off after slaughtering all those, including her prospective bridegroom, who attempt to get in his way. The violence is paralleled in several of the stories of the Fourth Day. Apart from the tale of Tancredi and Ghismonda, two other stories (IV, 5 and IV, 9) owe their tragic conclusions to the blind and unthinking adherence to an outmoded concept of honour, the first within a bourgeois setting and the second in a context that is feudal and aristocratic. All three stories share one other element in common, namely the inclusion within the narrative of an incident or episode that is peculiarly horrifying and macabre. In the Ghismonda story, there is the structurally vital episode of the golden chalice containing the heart of her lover, over which she weeps copious tears that, mingled with a poisonous fluid, she eventually imbibes in the presence of her bewildered ladies-in-waiting. She then arranges herself decorously on her bed, holds the heart of her dead lover close to her own, and silently waits for death to release her from her suffering. The whole of this episode is so macabre that in the hands of a less shrewd and sensitive writer it would seriously have risked emerging as farce. But so skilfully does Boccaccio arrange his material, so carefully does he construct an atmosphere of ritual, that the tone of high seriousness is never unduly disturbed, and the final impression is one of poignant tragedy and mysterious grandeur.

Boccaccio's handling of the improbable tale of Lisabetta da Messina (IV, 5) is no less secure, and the tragic fate of the heroine is if anything even more compelling. The story is familiar to English readers from Keats's romanticization of its details in a famous poem.[27] Boccaccio's version is altogether more sinewy and straightforward, and the motives of the various characters are more clearly defined. Lisabetta, the unmarried sister of three young and wealthy merchants, falls in love with the handsome young manager of their commercial enterprises, Lorenzo, who, after his amorous liaison with the girl has been discovered, is lured into the countryside by her three brothers and murdered in cold blood, his body being interred in a shallow grave. He appears to her in a dream, tells her how he was murdered, and describes the place where her brothers have buried his body. She goes to the spot with a maidservant, uncovers the young man's body, and, 'seeing that it was impossible for her to take away the whole body (as she would dearly have wished), she laid it to rest in a more appropriate spot, then severed the head from the shoulders as best she could and wrapped it in a

---

27 Jane Carlyle is reported to have said of Keats's 'Isabella' that the poem 'might have been written of a seamstress who had eaten too much for supper and slept upon her back'. (See William Allingham, *A Diary*, ed. H. Allingham and D. Radford, 1907, p. 310.)

towel.' Like Ghismonda, she drenches her gruesome treasure with copious tears, then she buries it in a pot, 'in which she planted several sprigs of the finest Salerno basil, and never watered them except with the essence of roses or orange-blossom, or with her own teardrops'. Once again, therefore, the macabre element of the narrative assumes strong ritualistic overtones which lend it an aura of high seriousness, and the tale proceeds ineluctably to its tragic albeit grotesque conclusion when, deprived by her brothers of her pot of basil, Lisabetta ultimately cries herself to death.

In the third tale (IV, 9) of this 'trilogy of horror', a Provençal knight, Guillaume de Roussillon, murders his best friend, Guillaume de Cabestanh, after his discovery of his wife's adulterous liaison with the latter. Having torn the heart from Cabestanh's breast, he hands it over to his cook, telling him it is the heart of a wild boar, and ordering him to use it in preparing the finest and most succulent dish he can devise. Boccaccio's subsequent description of the cook's labours comes perilously close to being interpreted as black humour:

> The cook took away the heart, minced it and added a goodly quantity of fine spices, employing all his skill and loving care to turn it into a dish that was too exquisite for words.[28]

But, having almost allowed his tragic tale to degenerate into farce, Boccaccio instantly reverts to a serious narrative tone with his description of the supper *à deux* during which the lady devours the dish to the last morsel. There follows an account of the ensuing conversation between husband and wife, when Roussillon tells her what she has eaten, whereupon she delivers a noble and dignified speech before flinging herself to her death from a lofty casement.

The deliberate placing of these three stories at the beginning (Ghismonda and Tancredi), the middle (Lisabetta), and the end (Roussillon and Cabestanh) of the tragedy-oriented Fourth Day is indicative of Boccaccio's overall conception of what constitutes good tragedy, at the same time offering further confirmation of the

---

28 '*Il cuoco, presolo e postavi tutta l'arte e tutta la sollecitudine sua, minuzzatolo e messevi di buone spezie assai, ne fece un manicaretto troppo buono.*'

extreme care he exercised in the disposition of his tales within the total narrative framework. In his regard for symmetry, and his manifest preoccupation with structural patterns based upon numbers that possessed mystical associations, the author reveals the extent to which, from the strictly formal point of view, he is influenced by medieval models, in particular of course by the *Commedia*. As for his conception of tragedy, it is clearly one that is based upon Latin rather than Greek models, and especially on the tragedies of Seneca, whose emphasis upon horror, cruelty and violence was to find favour with so many Renaissance playwrights, both in Italy and in England.

There were also, nevertheless, a number of possible medieval precedents for Boccaccio's 'trilogy of horror'. One has only to think of certain episodes in the *Commedia* such as the gruesome tale of Ugolino's death in the tower of hunger (*torre della fame*), itself gruesomely introduced and terminated by the description of Ugolino's eager champing at the nape of his adversary's neck.[29] But the specifically Senecan connotations of Boccaccio's concept of tragedy are undeniably present, both in his systematic recourse, in all three of his major tragic *novelle*, to the macabre as a generator of tragic sentiment, and in the close parallels between the story of Roussillon and Cabestanh (IV, 9) and Seneca's *Thyestes*. As one Boccaccio scholar puts it, a shade contentiously perhaps, 'the final section of this tragedy is conspicuous for a series of macabre conceits and amphibologies based on erotic/gastronomic *doubles entendres*. There is a constant play on love for one's family and love for the flesh of one's family; on possession by physical embrace and possession by incorporation in the digestive tract.'[30]

Whatever the force of Seneca's influence on Boccaccio's concept of tragedy, the three tales we have here been considering are all concerned with the satisfaction of honour, and it is significant that in two of them the murder of the transgressor brings such opprobrium upon the perpetrators of the deed that they are forced to flee for their lives, whilst in the third (IV, 1), the protagonist makes tardy repentance for his cruelty and sees that the remains of the two

29 Dante, *Inferno*, XXXIII.
30 G. Almansi, *The Writer as Liar*, London and Boston, 1975, pp. 144–5.

young lovers are honourably interred together in a single grave.
Likewise, in the concluding lines of the tale of Roussillon and
Cabestanh, it is reported that 'people were sent out from the castles
of the lady's family and of Guillaume de Cabestanh to gather up the
two bodies, which were later placed in a single tomb in the chapel
of the lady's own castle amid widespread grief and mourning.'

The inference is reasonably clear. In all three stories, the author,
by directing his reader's sympathy towards the lovers, and condemning the actions of those who cruelly severed their respective liaisons,
is proclaiming the supremacy of natural laws over any rigidly constructed and strictly interpreted code of ethical conduct. It is as though
Francesca's prophecy in the fifth canto of *Inferno* of her husband's
ultimate fate, '*Caina attende chi a vita ci spense*' ('Caina [the lowest part
of Hell] awaits the one who extinguished our lives'), which Dante
almost certainly intended as a pointer to her calculating vindictiveness,
is interpreted literally and validated through the analysis of three
sets of circumstances that are not dissimilar from her own. Where
Dante would have us condemn, Boccaccio commends. The difference in attitude is to some extent explained by a difference in
temperament. Where Dante, the arch-conservative, looks back to a
rigidly formalized code of behaviour that is characteristic of a feudal,
hierarchical society, Boccaccio's liberal, forward-looking instincts
lead him firmly in the direction of a form of morality that allows
for the unhindered interplay of natural passions and emotions.

This new moral attitude, which reflects the ascendancy of the
bourgeoisie and the decline of feudalism, and which incidentally
foreshadows the spirit of the Renaissance, is seen over and over
again in Boccaccio's treatment of amatory material. We find it
vigorously expressed, for instance, in the exciting and humorous
tale (III, 2), pointedly set in the age of feudalism, of the groom at
King Agilulf's court who, having fallen deeply in love with Agilulf's
consort, cleverly achieves the gratification of his desires and returns
unscathed to his normal, lowly duties. The story is really concerned
with honour, and how it may best be preserved. All cats are grey in
the dark, and the groom brings his desires to fruition by impersonating the king so as to gain admittance, at dead of night, to the lady's
bedchamber. But no sooner has he completed his amorous mission

and departed the scene than the king himself turns up in the darkened room and enters his wife's bed with the same object in view, only to discover from his wife's solicitous concern for his health that someone has been there before him. It is at this point in the narrative that Boccaccio inserts the first of two revealing authorial asides. Throughout the story, the cleverness of the groom and the wisdom of the king are repeatedly stressed, and when Agilulf correctly deduces that his wife has been taken in by an outward resemblance to his own physique and manner, he wisely decides, since neither the queen nor anyone else appears to have noticed the deception, to keep his own counsel and beat a tactful retreat. Boccaccio, through his narrator Pampinea, comments as follows:

> Many a stupid man would have reacted differently, and exclaimed: 'It was not I. Who was the man who was here? What happened? Who was it who came?' But this would only have led to complications, upsetting the lady when she was blameless and sowing the seeds of a desire, on her part, to repeat the experience. And besides, by holding his tongue his honour remained unimpaired, whereas if he were to talk he would make himself look ridiculous.[31]

The idea that honour, in certain circumstances, is best preserved by keeping up appearances, and suppressing painful realities, is one that would exercise a particular appeal upon the practical minds of the merchants, traders and entrepreneurs who constituted the author's ideal readership. And the steps which Agilulf takes to track down the seducer of his unwitting queen would also commend themselves, for their logic and ingenuity, to an audience schooled in the intricacies and subterfuges of a highly competitive commercial world. What Agilulf does, in fact, is to proceed at once to the sleeping-quarters of his servants, where he tests the heartbeats of each of the sleeping forms until he eventually reaches the groom, discovers that his heart is pounding, and rightly concludes that this

---

31 '. . . il che molti sciocchi non avrebbon fatto ma avrebbon detto: "Io non ci fui io: chi fu colui che ci fu? come andò? chi ci venne?" Di che molte cose nate sarebbono, per le quali egli avrebbe a torto contristato la donna e datale materia di disiderare altra volta quello che già sentito avea: e quello che tacendo niuna vergogna gli poteva tornare, parlando s'arebbe vitupero recato.'

man is the culprit. He then shears away a portion of the hair on one side of the groom's head, using a pair of scissors that he had brought along for the purpose, the better to identify him when he summons a general assembly of the household the following morning. The groom's resourcefulness is equal to the occasion, and he shears the hair of all his sleeping fellow-servants in exactly similar fashion, so that the identity parade next morning concludes with no more than a stern word of warning from the king to show the culprit that his deed has not passed undetected:

> 'Whoever it was that did it,' he said, addressing the whole assembly, 'had better not do it again. And now, be off with you.'[32]

There then follows the second of Boccaccio's authorial interventions in this particular novella, when, through Pampinea, he declares:

> Many another man would have wanted all of them strung up, tortured, examined and interrogated. But in so doing, he would have brought into the open a thing that people should always try their utmost to conceal. And even if, by displaying his hand, he had secured the fullest possible revenge, he would not have lessened his shame but greatly increased it, as well as besmirching the fame of his lady.[33]

The story of Agilulf and the groom is an excellent example of the author's ability to transform an improbable series of events into a superficially convincing realistic narrative. The conversion of fantasy into the realm of the possible is what constitutes the *Decameron*'s peculiar dynamic. But granted that Boccaccio's main purpose is storytelling, this is not to deny the relevance of his occasional asides, which in this instance are especially revealing in that they show the clear-headed, practical common sense that he brings to bear upon the highly emotive question of marital honour. His vindication of Agilulf's low-key response, first to the discovery that his marriage-bed has been violated by a stranger and then to the thwarting of his scheme to identify the culprit, is reminiscent for its clarity and

32 '. . . e a tutti rivolto disse: "Chi 'l fece nol faccia mai più, e andatevi con Dio." '
33 'Un altro gli avrebbe voluti far collare, martoriare, essaminare e domandare; e ciò faccendo avrebbe scoperto quello che ciascun dee andar cercando di ricoprire, e essendosi scoperto, ancora che intera vendetta n'avesse presa, non iscemata ma molto cresciuta n'avrebbe la sua vergogna e contaminata l'onestà della donna sua.'

persuasiveness of that section of his earliest major narrative work, the *Filocolo*, where the thirteen *questioni d'amore* are debated. Indeed, it would not be unduly fanciful to suggest that Boccaccio, in constructing several of the *novelle* in the *Decameron* that treat of love and honour, for example Bernabò and Zinevra (II, 9), Gilette of Narbonne (III, 9), Gentile de' Carisendi (X, 4), Messer Ansaldo (X, 5), King Charles the Old (X, 6) and Titus and Gisippus (X, 8), was drawing upon the experience he had acquired, in composing the *questioni d'amore* sequence in the earlier work, of debating the finer points of a topic that had engaged the minds and sensibilities of many of his medieval predecessors. The fact that two of these stories (those of Gentile de' Carisendi and Messer Ansaldo) were first narrated by Boccaccio in the relevant episode of the *Filocolo* tends to confirm the view that not only the overall structure of the *Decameron* but also the mode of presentation of several of the individual tales are ultimately traceable to the youthful exercises in casuistry that fill the fourth book of the earlier work. Like many other tales in the *Decameron*, the story of Agilulf and the groom summons from its reader the proverbial response '*Se non è vero è ben trovato*' ('If it is not true, it is a happy invention'). If one considers the plot objectively, many of its vital particulars (the facility with which the groom gains access to the queen's bedchamber, the coincidence of the king's arrival on the scene immediately after the groom's departure, the failure of any of the servants to wake up during the king's protracted investigation in their sleeping-quarters, and likewise their failure to notice the shearing of their hair, and so on) are seriously lacking in verisimilitude. In this respect, the tale conforms to the Johnsonian dictum that the essence of comedy consists in 'the fictitiousness of the transactions'. Hence it is possible to view the story as a *questione d'amore* in which the subject for discussion is whether a husband who finds that his wife has unwittingly committed adultery should communicate his discovery to others (including his wife) or maintain a façade of ignorance. In his authorial asides, Boccaccio strongly advocates the latter alternative, giving as his reason that only in this way will the husband's honour (to say nothing of the lady's reputation) remain unimpaired. But one should note in passing that with his customary playful malice, the

author offers, almost by way of an afterthought, the secondary
reason that if the wife were made aware of what had happened, she
would begin to desire a repetition of the experience. It is at such
moments as this (and the *Decameron* contains many other similar
observations) that the conventional view of Boccaccio as the champion of the gentle sex appears to require revision, and that the
misogynistic outpourings of the *Corbaccio* begin to look a little less
atypical of the writer than is generally thought.

The overt misogyny of the *Corbaccio* springs from a deeply
rooted conviction (possibly implanted by some painful personal
experience) of woman's faithlessness, a theme that the author had
already explored in considerable depth in his version of the story of
Troilus and Cressida, the *Filostrato*. But whereas the *Filostrato* chronicles the delusion and bewilderment of the youthful and inexperi-
enced idealist, the *Corbaccio* reflects the spleen and vindictiveness of
one whose mature awareness of the instability of sexual relationships
has conducted him to the wildest extremities of cynicism. In the
Decameron, on the other hand, Boccaccio adopts a relatively objective posture towards the question of the effect upon human relationships of instinctive sexual forces. His mood may in fact be likened
to that which prompted Shakespeare to declare that

> When my love swears that she is made of truth,
> I do believe her, though I know she lies.[34]

The verbal ambiguity ('Though I know she lies') would have
appealed to Boccaccio, and he would also have appreciated the
consummate irony of Byron's classic description of the surrender to
sexual passion:

> A little still she strove, and much repented,
> And whispering 'I will ne'er consent' – consented.[35]

Byron's couplet comes repeatedly to mind when reading Boccaccio's account of the successive couplings of Alatiel (II, 7), the
Egyptian princess who, having been sent by her father to marry his
wartime ally, the King of Algarve, is shipwrecked off the coast of
Majorca and then passes through the hands of nine different men

34 *Sonnets*, 138.
35 *Don Juan*, cxvii.

before being restored to her father, whom she convinces of her virginity before setting off once more to become the King of Algarve's wife. Virginity, like honour, resides in appearances, as the author stresses in the proverbial sally with which he concludes this extraordinary narrative:

> A kissed mouth doesn't lose its freshness: like the moon it turns up new again.[36]

It is beside the point to inquire whether one can describe Alatiel as a virgin without some risk of terminological inexactitude. What matters is that she is able to play the part with conviction, and thus ensure a long and contented marriage for herself and her husband.

But of course the fascination of the story lies, not so much in its paradoxical, fairy-tale conclusion, as in its vivid account of Alatiel's adventures, in which the disparity between resolution and deed, so often a feature of irregular sexual relationships, is a continual source of refined, ironic humour. When the princess is shipwrecked, she implores the three surviving members of her female retinue to preserve their chastity, 'declaring her own determination to submit to no man's pleasure except her husband's – a sentiment that was greeted with approval by the three women, who said they would do their utmost to follow her instructions'. But it takes no more than an abundance of good food and precious wines to destroy such pious sentiments and bring her to bed with Pericone, the first of her lovers. Boccaccio's mischievous comment at this point nicely highlights the impotence of good resolutions in the face of the unremitting demands of the flesh:

> She had no conception of the kind of horn that men do their butting with, and when she felt what was happening, it was almost as though she regretted having turned a deaf ear to Pericone's flattery. And without waiting to be bidden before spending her nights so agreeably, often it was she herself who issued the invitation, not so much with words, since she could not make herself understood, as with deeds.[37]

36 'Bocca basciata non perde ventura, anzi rinnuova come fa la luna.'
37 'Il che poi che ella ebbe sentito, non avendo mai davanti saputo con che corno gli uomini cozzano, quasi pentuta del non avere alle lusinghe di Pericone assentito, senza attendere d'essere a così dolci notti invitata, spesse volte se stessa invitava non con le parole, ché non si sapea fare intendere, ma co' fatti . . .'

Of Alatiel's nine separate lovers, three (Pericone, Marato and the Prince of Morea) are violently done to death by men who, fascinated by her beauty, are seized by an all-consuming desire to possess her; a fourth is seriously mutilated in a murderous duel with his brother arising from an argument over who is to have precedence in the enjoyment of her favours; a fifth (the Duke of Athens) is last reported defending his territory against an invading army that has been assembled to avenge the murder of her previous lover; a sixth (Constant) is taken prisoner by the Turks, who have learned that he is leading a dissolute life with his stolen mistress on the island of Chios, leaving himself wide open to attack; a seventh (Uzbek) is killed by a punitive expedition sent to avenge his treatment of Constant; an eighth (Antioco) dies peacefully is his bed, partly, one is encouraged to assume, because of his amorous exertions; whilst the ninth and last (the unnamed Cypriot merchant) is deprived of his mistress whilst away on a trading expedition in Armenia. Alatiel's four-year progress is thus for the most part attended by death and destruction, by internecine strife occasioned by the accident of her quite extraordinary beauty. It could be argued that Boccaccio is here presenting a latter-day version of the legend of Helen of Troy, but those critics, like Branca, who assert that the central theme of the novella is 'beauty as the cause of misfortune' are attributing too much importance to the tragic elements of the story and minimizing the tone of light-hearted banter in which even its most blood-curdling episodes are recounted. Had Boccaccio wished to tell a tale of suffering and woe, he would surely have told it differently, and located it among the stories of the Fourth Day.

The heroine's name, Alatiel, itself provides a clue to the lines along which the tale should be interpreted, for it is an anagram of 'La Lieta', or The Contented Lady. Here one should bear in mind the cabalistic science or superstition known as onomancy, based on the oracular principle of the *nomen omen*, meaning that a name conceals a prophecy. According to this 'science', with which Boccaccio was certainly familiar, the anagram of a proper name, a surname, or a forename may reveal the natural gifts or the destiny of a person or an institution. What the author seems to be suggesting is that the vicissitudes of Alatiel, far from arousing the emotions of pity and terror associated with tragedy, will evoke a kind of vicarious, voyeuristic pleasure, and possibly even envy, especially amongst his lady-readers. This at any rate is the clear implication of his description, at the beginning of the following tale, of the reaction of the lady members of the company to the chronicle of Alatiel's adventures:

> The ladies heaved many a sigh over the fair lady's several adventures: but who knows what their motives may have been? Perhaps some of them were sighing, not so much because they felt sorry for her, but because they longed to be married no less often than she had been.[38]

In his scattered references to the lady-members of the *lieta brigata*, the author consistently emphasizes the strength of their moral character and their adherence to Christian precepts, and thus his suggestion that their reaction to the tale of Alatiel may possibly be attributed to envy rather than to pity neatly highlights the ambivalence commonly to be found in attitudes towards sexual relationships. What he is intimating, in fact, is that the desire for a variety of sexual experiences is a natural one, even among the most upright and God-fearing of Christians, and in recounting the story of Alatiel's adventures he gives form and consistency to the unspoken sexual fantasies of his readership. That capacity for converting fantasy into apparent reality is one of the reasons for the *Decameron*'s enduring popularity, for its timeless relevance to the human condition. But Boccaccio's marginal comment on the ladies' reaction to the tale of Alatiel has to be read in conjunction with the story's lengthy preamble, one of the longest in the whole of the *Decameron*, where the narrator, Panfilo, presents an elegant disquisition on the subject of happiness, thus foreshadowing the anagrammatic relevance of the name of the heroine.

The burden of his argument is that men and women should rest content with whatever has been granted to them by 'the One who alone knows what we need and has the power to provide it for us'. From this it follows that those ladies who go to extraordinary lengths to improve the attractions bestowed on them by Nature are courting, if not disaster, at all events a state of unhappiness. Physical beauty can be a source of suffering, and the story of Alatiel, which

---

38 'Sospirava fu molto dalle donne per li varii casi della bella donna: ma chi sa che cagione moveva que' sospiri? Forse v'eran di quelle che non meno per vaghezza di cosí spesse nozze che per pietà di colei sospiravano.'

follows, is represented by Panfilo as a cautionary tale. This no doubt is the reason why Branca and others see the vicissitudes of Alatiel as a demonstration of the misfortune that physical beauty inevitably brings to its possessor. But as the author makes abundantly clear, the misfortunes of Alatiel are of brief duration. Whenever she is bereft of one of her lovers, she is very quickly 'consoled' by his successor, and she herself is almost totally unaffected by the trail of death and destruction that, by the accident of her beauty, she leaves in the wake of her amorous peregrinations. One commentator has likened her to a queen-bee, interpreting her various adventures as a kind of repeated copulative ritual leading ineluctably to the death of her successive partners:

> The story's impact hardly resides in Alatiel's anguished consciousness of her disastrous beauty (an allure that drags her to misfortune and her numerous lovers to their death), but rather in the very superlativeness of the beauty and therefore of the pleasure which she offers the male world. This 'maraviglioso piacere' poetically justifies her lovers' deaths. They seem to be repeating the zoological phenomenon of the male-bees who burn up their existence in a fatal coitus with the queen-bee.[39]

But this too seems an over-simplification of the events of the narrative. Whilst it is certainly true that the tale is concerned with the instinctive, elemental forces of sexual attraction, the correlation between copulation and death is insufficiently consistent to support such a thesis. (Only four of Alatiel's nine lovers in fact are destroyed as a direct result of their involvement with her.) The fascination of the story of Alatiel resides primarily in its convincing and dramatic enactment, in realistic terms, of a preposterous sexual odyssey, in the course of which such cherished concepts as purity, chastity and virginity are subjected to a fierce and sometimes taunting scrutiny. Panfilo's high-minded introductory discourse, together with his dire warnings of the consequences of artificially enhancing one's natural accomplishments, elegantly synthesizes the conventional, puritanical precepts relating to the pursuit of happiness. But the theory he expounds is to a large extent belied by the ensuing narrative, as well as by the postscript, which, as we have seen, underlines the

39 Almansi, *The Writer as Liar*, p. 125.

ambivalence of his listeners' response to the account of the heroine's adventures.

Boccaccio's reappraisal of conventional wisdom in regard to sexual morals, implicit in the tale of Alatiel, finds much more forcible expression in the stories of Nastagio degli Onesti (V, 8) and Madonna Filippa of Prato (VI, 7). The first of these tells of a wealthy young nobleman of Ravenna, who impoverishes himself in a series of futile attempts to win the love of a beautiful girl of the Traversari family, 'of far more noble lineage than his own'. He retires in despair to the solitude of a nearby pinewood, where one Friday morning he witnesses the extraordinary scene of a naked girl being pursued and killed by a horseman, and devoured by a brace of hounds. He attempts to intervene on her behalf, but desists on being informed by the mysterious horseman that he and his victim are both in Hell, himself for having committed suicide through his unrequited love for the girl, and she for failing to respond to his amorous entreaties. Their punishment consists in their enacting, over and over again, the horrifying scene to which Nastagio is the reluctant witness. Nastagio turns the situation to his advantage. On the following Friday he invites his kinsfolk and the lady he loves to a banquet in the selfsame clearing in the woods, where, to the consternation of his guests, the gruesome scene is enacted all over again. Being terrified at the prospect of suffering a similar fate, the lady repents of her haughty indifference towards Nastagio and places herself entirely at his disposal. His intentions towards her being impeccable, he proposes marriage, to which the girl promptly agrees, and they settle down to a long and happy life together.

The message of the story seems to be that no woman should unreasonably withhold her consent to the advances of an ardent wooer, for by behaving like a saint she may discover she is a sinner, and consequently suffer the torments of Hell for her cruel inflexibility. Although parts of the tale have antecedents in medieval literature, the manner of its telling and the conclusion to which it leads are very far removed from anything to be found, for instance, in the *Commedia*, of which one is constantly reminded by the unusually large number of Dantesque allusions that are woven into the fabric of this novella. There is, for instance, a clear link between the names of the two protagonists and a passage where Dante regrets the decline and extinction of the Traversari and Anastagi families of Ravenna, who once embodied all that was best and most noble in the medieval tradition of love and courtesy:

> . . . la casa Traversara e li Anastagi
> (e l'una gente e l'altra gente è diretata),
> le donne e' cavalier, li affanni e li agi
> che ne 'nvogliava amore e cortesia . . .[40]

Then again, the pinewood at Classe, near Ravenna, where the pitiless hunt is enacted in Boccaccio's tale, serves as the terrestrial point of comparison in Dante's description (*Purgatorio*, XXVIII) of the wood constituting his vision of the Earthly Paradise. The description of the fleeing damsel and of the two fierce mastiffs tearing at her flesh is clearly modelled on a famous passage from canto XIII of *Inferno*, where Dante recounts the gruesome punishments meted out, in the Wood of the Suicides, to one of a pair of *scialacquatori*, or profligates. And the story contains numerous other verbal borrowings from well-known passages in Dante's poem. But the use Boccaccio makes of his borrowings from Dante is arresting inasmuch as it frequently involves the deliberate distortion or even reversal of the semantic values of what has been borrowed.[41] By no stretch of the imagination would it be possible to conceive that Dante would so manipulate the elements of a macabre infernal vision as to reach the conclusion presented by Boccaccio in the tale of Nastagio degli Onesti, where the traditional conception of the afterworld is set upon its head.

If, in the story of Nastagio degli Onesti, the author remains within the bounds of Christian morality by allowing his hero to consummate his love only after marrying the woman who is the

---

40 '. . . the House of Traversaro and the Anastagi (both families now extinct), the ladies and the lords, the labours and the comforts, which love and courtesy inspired in us . . .' (*Purgatorio*, xiv, 107–10).

41 The subject of Boccaccio's borrowings from Dante has been widely discussed, among others by J. H. Whitfield, who concludes his lecture on 'Dante in Boccaccio' by remarking that 'in those places where Boccaccio echoes in seeming admiration the very words of Dante, where therefore they seem to come together, there also most they fall apart' (*The Barlow Lectures on Dante, 1959*, Cambridge, 1959, p. 32).

object of his deep affection, no such deference to conventional ethics is paid in the tale of Madonna Filippa (VI, 7), which on the contrary depends for its narrative force, like so many of the stories of the *Decameron*, especially those of the Seventh Day, on the proposition that the Seventh Commandment places an unreasonable restraint upon the freedom of the individual. The novella is set in Prato, where an ancient statute requires that any woman taken in adultery should be burnt alive. It is this statute that Madonna Filippa's husband invokes upon discovering her in the arms of her handsome young lover. Filippa, a beautiful woman, 'exceedingly passionate by nature', and full of spirit, is brought before the magistrate, to whom she makes a full and frank confession of her guilt. But she calls into question the validity of the statute, pointing out that it applies only to women, who are much better able than men to bestow their favours liberally and who, when the statute was framed, were not even consulted on the matter. If it is accepted that all individuals are equal before the law, then the statute is bad law. But the clinching argument in her defence comes when, having persuaded her husband to testify that she has always granted him whatever he required in the way of bodily gratification, she turns to the magistrate and asks:

> . . . if he has always taken as much of me as he needed and as much as he chose to take . . . what am I to do with the surplus? Throw it to the dogs? Is it not far better that I should present it to a gentleman who loves me more dearly than himself, rather than allow it to turn bad or go to waste?[42]

The logic of her novel argument is unanswerable, Madonna Filippa is freed, and the statute is amended so that it applies in future only to those wives who commit adultery for monetary gain, a class of women for whom the author registers his profound contempt in the story of Gulfardo and Guasparruolo (VIII, 1), where, as in Chaucer's *Shipman's Tale*, a wife's ill-gotten gains turn out to have been borrowed in advance from her husband, in whose presence she is later forced to acknowledge that the debt has been fully settled.

42 '. . . *se egli ha sempre di me preso quello che gli è bisognato e piaciuto, io che doveva fare o debbo di quel che gli avanza? Debbolo io gittare a' cani? Non è egli molto meglio servirne un gentile uomo che piú che sé m'ama, che lasciarlo perdere o guastare?*'

Madonna Filippa's outrageous but ostensibly rational defence of her wayward behaviour has been used to illustrate the thesis that for Boccaccio love consists in the gratification of instinctive sexual desires, whether within marriage or outside it. Such a view draws some support from several other stories in the *Decameron*, for instance the tales of Paganino of Monaco (II, 10), of the anonymous lady who uses a priest as her unwitting go-between (III, 3), of Zima and the wife of Francesco Vergellesi (III, 5), of Ricciardo Minutolo and Catella Sighinolfo (III, 6), of Teodoro and Violante (V, 7), and of the wife of Pietro di Vinciolo (V, 10). Other stories that are relevant in this connection are the tales of the Seventh Day in general, the tale of the three beds (IX, 6), and the prolix account of the remarkable friendship of Titus and Gisippus (X, 8). In several of these stories, the Christian view of marriage is questioned just as vigorously and outrageously as in Madonna Filippa's spirited defence of her adultery.

In the tale of Paganino, the Monegasque pirate, for instance, the beautiful young wife of a senile Pisan judge, who with the aid of a calendar of Saints has accustomed her to a frugal sexual regime matching his own limited physical powers, is seized by a dashing young pirate who wastes no time in supplying her with a more wholesome diet. The judge discovers where she is living, and goes to fetch her home, but she refuses to return with him, treating him to a torrent of vulgar abuse for his failure to satisfy her natural needs. When he appeals to her sense of honour, she replies that she will defend what remains of her honour as jealously as anyone, adding that she wishes that her parents had shown an equal regard for her honour when they bestowed her in marriage on an impotent and elderly husband.

The allusion to honour is interesting, for it triggers a powerful attack on the hypocrisy of a society in which the institution of marriage has been reduced to the status of a commercial transaction, no attention being paid to the natural inclinations or aspirations of the prospective bride. This of course is the standard way of justifying adulterous relationships in such a society. But it is also worth noting that Boccaccio is sufficiently sensitive towards generally accepted social conventions as to conclude his tale, as in the resolution of the story of Nastagio degli Onesti, with a reference to the marriage of the two protagonists, an outcome made possible in this case by the death of the disillusioned *senex*.

In most, but not all, of Boccaccio's stories of adulterous love (and it should be noticed incidentally that, contrary to popular belief, they account for only about a quarter of the hundred *novelle*) the senility of the husband is a major contributory factor. But the exceptions to this general rule should place us on our guard against concluding too readily that the author's object is purely the polemical one of calling into question the morality of the arranged marriages that were a common feature of the society in which he lived. This was no doubt a part of his intention, but it must never be forgotten that Boccaccio's main purpose is aesthetic. What he is chiefly concerned with is the communication, in as elegant and articulate a form as he can devise, of a series of interesting narratives, which, albeit for the most part inherently improbable, are rendered plausible by the manner of the telling.

With this important reservation in mind, it is none the less possible to detect where the author stands in relation to certain issues. So far as marriage is concerned, the institution is one that he respects, provided that it is based upon the mutual love and trust of the husband and wife. It is when this condition is not fulfilled that the kinds of irregularities which provide the raw material of Boccaccio's adulterous tales are most likely to occur. In the story of Pietro di Vinciolo (V, 10), for instance, the reader is told of a buxom young woman with red hair and a passionate disposition who finds herself wedded to a pederast. With the assistance of an old bawd, she takes steps to provide herself with what her husband has denied her, until one evening, as she is entertaining a handsome young man to supper, her husband returns home unexpectedly. The young man conceals himself beneath a chicken-coop, whence he involuntarily reveals his presence when he yells with pain as his projecting hand is trampled on by an ass. But all is satisfactorily resolved when the husband sees what a pretty young fellow his wife has been consorting with. As the narrator phrases it, in the concluding paragraph of the tale:

> How exactly Pietro arranged matters, after supper, to the mutual satisfaction of all three parties, I no longer remember. But I do know

that the young man was found next morning wandering about the piazza, not exactly certain with which of the pair he had spent the greater portion of the night, the wife or the husband.[43]

This outrageous but tidy resolution of the dilemma of the characters is in keeping with the novella's overall tone, which is engagingly frank and direct *vis-à-vis* the problem with which the wife of the sodomitical husband is initially confronted. Her musings upon her predicament, together with the old bawd's lengthy discourse on the role of women, who in a world dominated by men should make the most of the opportunities that fall in their path, are reminiscent of the harangue to which the wife subjects the impotent Pisan judge in the story of Paganino, already referred to above. In both of these stories, it is strongly implied that the satisfaction of sexual needs is a necessary prerequisite for successful conjugal relationships, and that, in the absence of such a condition, a wife is fully justified in seeking her pleasures elsewhere. Boccaccio, be it noted, draws no fine distinction between love and lust, in the manner of the Christian moralist, and in this respect he stands decisively apart from his medieval predecessors and contemporaries. Or, as one critic has observed, one of the most original features of Boccaccio's work is that 'in the world of the *Decameron* there is no immorality perceived as such, but rather the feeling that man is a part of nature, which is not governed by moral laws or principles, but answers only to instincts and impulses and biological phenomena that fall outside the scope of ethics'.[44]

---

43 '*Dopo la cena quello che Pietro si divisasse a sodisfacimento di tutti e tre m'è uscito di mente; so io ben cotanto, che la mattina vegnente infino in su la Piazza fu il giovane, non assai certo qual piú stato si fosse la notte o moglie o marito, accompagnato.*'

44 '*È questo uno degli aspetti piú originali del Boccaccio; non v'è nel mondo del Decameron l'immoralità avvertita come tale, ma piuttosto il senso che l'uomo fa parte della natura la quale non è governata da principî o leggi morali, ma risponde solo ad istinti ed impulsi e fenomeni biologici per i quali non esiste identificazione etica,*' (Azzurra B. Givens, *La dottrina d'amore nel Boccaccio*, Messina-Florence, 1968, p. 207). For an extended analysis of this whole subject, see also A. D. Scaglione, *Nature and Love in the Late Middle Ages*, Berkeley, 1963, and E. Auerbach, *Mimesis: the Representation of Reality in Western Literature*, translated by Willard R. Trask, Princeton, 1953, where it is asserted (p. 227) that 'The *Decameron* develops a distinct, thoroughly practical and secular ethical code rooted in the right to love . . .'

No analysis of Boccaccio's handling of amatory material in the *Decameron* would be complete without some reference to the concept of courtly love (*amour courtois*), which originated with the Provençal troubadours, and which occupied so prominent a position in both the lyric poetry and the prose romances of the later Middle Ages. In classical times, amorous relationships in high places had been described in some detail by Ovid in his *Ars amatoria*, at the cost of his banishment for life from Rome to the Black Sea by Emperor Augustus, and it was Ovid's poem that initially inspired the codification of the doctrine of courtly love by medieval theorists. Of these latter, the most notable was Andreas Capellanus, whose *Liber de arte honeste amandi et reprobatione inhonesti amoris* (*Book on the Art of Loving Honourably and the Reproof of Dishonourable Love*), written towards the end of the twelfth century, was enormously influential in shaping the attitudes of later writers, including Boccaccio, towards this particular topic. For Andreas, the business of the courtly lover was to serve his lady with absolute fidelity, no matter what obstacles (such as the fact that she was already married to another) were placed in his path. By a strange paradox, adulterous love thus acquired an exalted status.

Several of the stories in the *Decameron* reflect this aspect of the manners and ideals of the feudal society of an earlier age, and some contain traces of the actual terminology used by the love theorists. One instance is the story (VII, 7) of Lodovico and his successful wooing of the Bolognese married woman, Madonna Beatrice, the fame of whose beauty has spread to the corners of the earth. The preliminaries to the tale pointedly present Lodovico as the son of a Florentine nobleman who, living in Paris, is obliged by his straitened circumstances to become a merchant. After making a huge fortune, he secures a place for his son in the French royal household, 'where he was brought up with other young nobles and acquired the manners and attributes of a gentleman'. Having thus established the link in Lodovico's upbringing between his father's mercantile concerns and the feudal values of the French court, Boccaccio goes on to relate how Lodovico learns of the extraordinary beauty of Madonna Beatrice from a knight who has recently returned from the Holy Sepulchre. The earliest practitioners of the poetry of *amour courtois* are in fact thought to have been inspired by a knowledge of the mystical philosophy of the Islamic world brought to western Europe by the Crusaders. But what gives Boccaccio's tale a more specific connection with the troubadours is the idea of *amor de lonh* ('distant love') that is associated with the poetry of Jaufré Rudel of Blaye. When Lodovico, having changed his name to Anichino, arrives in Bologna from Paris, he finds that the lady is even more beautiful than he had been led to suppose, and secures a place in her husband's household. A further echo of the story's French antecedents is the way he reveals his love to Beatrice through allowing her to beat him at chess, a stratagem commonly used by aspiring lovers in the medieval romances. The game of chess is the foreplay, the first of the four stages commended to the lover by Andreas Capellanus for achieving the object of his desires. There follow the kiss as pledge (*arra*) of ultimate reward, the embrace, and the fulfilment. Not content with the ingredients from the French literary tradition he has already inserted freely into his story, Boccaccio rounds it off with an account of the delight experienced by the lover in administering a sound thrashing to the husband, for which precedents are found in the French *fabliaux*.

The standard metaphors and terminology of the medieval love theorists are found in many of Boccaccio's other narratives. Introducing her story of Ricciardo Minutolo's seduction of the virtuous wife of Filippello Sighinolfo (III, 6), Fiammetta says she will show how the lady was led 'to taste the fruits of love before she even noticed they had blossomed'. Elissa concludes her tragic account of Gerbino's *amor de lonh* for the daughter of the King of Tunis (IV, 4) by observing that 'the two young lovers met a violent end without ever having tasted the fruits of their love.' In the bawdy tale of the nun and the abbess (IX, 2), we are told that for some little time the nun and her handsome young admirer 'sustained without fruit'[45] their love for one another. A similar image is found near the end of the story of King Charles the Old (X, 6), who 'married off the girl he loved without having taken or gathered a single leaf, flower or fruit from his love'. In the story that follows, King Peter of Aragon learns (from a troubadour's song) that an

---

45 A word-for-word translation of Boccaccio's '*senza frutto sostennero*'.

apothecary's daughter is dying of her love for him after witnessing his feats of valour in a jousting contest. He effects a cure by paying her a visit, then bestows her in marriage to one of his young courtiers, providing them with a rich dowry, and saying: 'Now we desire to take the fruit of your love which is our due.' Then, holding her head between his hands, he implants a kiss on the young woman's brow. This tale of literal *amour courtois* is sealed with the comment that the king 'always styled himself her loyal knight for as long as he lived, and never entered the lists without displaying the favour she had sent him'.

Other common features of *amour courtois* are the lover's sighs and the lover's tears, both of which Boccaccio exploits to good effect in many of the tales. The account of Lodovico's *amor de lonh* for Madonna Beatrice (VII, 7) includes an episode where Lodovico, having allowed Beatrice to defeat him in a game of chess, heaves an enormous sigh as a prelude to revealing his love for her, after which she too begins to sigh. In the story of Zima's adulterous love for the wife of Francesco Vergellesi (III, 5), the lady's 'barely perceptible sighs' are the only means she has of responding to the amorous outpourings of her admirer, for she has been forbidden by her husband to utter a word during the meeting he has arranged between them for purposes of his own.[46] Although the tale is set in fourteenth-century Pistoia, its connection with the literature of Provence is observable in a seemingly anachronistic reference to Zima's tilting at the jousts and his troubadour-like skills in the composition of *aubades*. But even more indicative of its *amour courtois* antecedents is the lengthy monologue addressed by Zima to the lady, so fulsome in its protestations of love as to leave the impression that Boccaccio is engaged, as in the story of Titus and Gisippus (X, 8), in a deliberate parody of his literary models.

As for the lover's tears, the prime example of a story incorporating this and various other motifs of *amour courtois* is the famous account of Federigo and his prize falcon (V, 9), which the narrator claims to be offering to her lady hearers in order 'to acquaint you with the power of your beauty over men of noble spirit'. The aristocratic life-style of a bygone age is nostalgically recalled in the initial

46 He allows Zima to speak to his wife in exchange for a magnificent palfrey.

description of Federigo, who 'for his deeds of chivalry and courtly manners was more highly spoken of than any other squire in Tuscany'. The object of his love is a married lady, Monna Giovanna, whose attention he seeks to capture by riding at the ring, tilting, giving sumptuous banquets, and distributing largesse on so liberal a scale that he reduces himself to a state of poverty. In the best tradition of the courtly lover, he continues to serve his lady with unswerving fidelity. When, now widowed, she calls at his humble dwelling, he wrings the neck of his precious falcon without a second thought, so as to ensure that his unexpected guest is fed in as fitting a manner as his straitened circumstances will allow. The tears he sheds on learning the reason for her visit[47] are at first misinterpreted by the lady. Though he attributes them to the hostility of Fortune, they serve to convince the lady of the strength of his devotion. When her brothers urge her to take a second husband, she insists that she will marry no other man except Federigo, explaining that she prefers a gentleman without riches to riches without a gentleman. What began as an adulterous passion ends with the formalization of the relationship in a Christian marriage. Courtly love (*amour courtois*) is transmuted into married love (*amor conjugalis*).

The story of Federigo shares with all the other stories of the Fifth Day (except the last) a narrative line that ends in a happy marriage. One or two modern observers have taken this, along with evidence drawn from his other writings, to support the view that the author of the *Decameron*, far from encouraging adulterous liaisons, was a deeply committed moralist opposed to any departures from the norm of legitimate conjugal love.[48] Significant in this connection is the ending of the tale of Nastagio degli Onesti (V, 8), where (as already noted) the lover, having succeeded in transforming a young woman's enmity into love, insists first on marrying her to preserve her good name. The virtues of conjugal love are celebrated in many of the other stories, for instance in the tales of the Marchioness of Montferrat (I, 5), of Bernabò and Zinevra (II, 9), and of Messer Torello (X, 9). This last, one of the most touching narratives in the

47 She has called on him to ask for his falcon in a desperate attempt to save the life of her child.
48 See, for example, Robert Hollander, *Boccaccio's Two Venuses*, Columbia University Press, 1977.

whole of the *Decameron*, presents *amor conjugalis* in a particularly attractive light, focusing as it does not only on the bond of affection between husband and wife, but also on their nuclear family as a whole. But, as in so many other respects, it is impossible to construct a coherent theory about the overall moral tone of the *Decameron* on the basis of the tales just cited. There are at least as many stories, including the tale of Tedaldo degli Elisei (III, 7), which point to a contrary conclusion. The ambivalence of the authorial stance accounts in large measure for the work's endless fascination. Its morality is open-ended.

The theme of Love in the *Decameron* is one that defies exhaustive analysis. Perhaps the best way to summarize this whole question is by quoting Filomena's words in the preamble to her story of Madonna Francesca (IX, 1):

> In the course of our conversation, dear ladies, we have repeatedly seen how great and mighty are the forces of Love. Yet I do not think we have fully exhausted the subject, nor would we do so if we were to talk of nothing else for a whole year.[49]

★   ★   ★

The *Decameron* has been called '*il poema dell'intelligenza*',[50] or the epic of human intelligence, and this designation of the work seems so appropriate that it comes as something of a surprise to discover that neither the noun (*intelligenza*) nor the adjective (*intelligente*) appears anywhere in Boccaccio's text. The reasons for this are mainly etymological. Although both words were current in the author's day, their present-day meanings were almost invariably conveyed by other linguistic forms. Boccaccio in fact employs a wide range of terms connoting various kinds and manifestations of human intelligence, and attempts have been made to show that he chose his alternatives with care, according to the particular type of intelli-

---

49 '*Molte volte s'è, o vezzose donne, ne' nostri ragionamenti mostrato quante e quali sieno le forze d'amore; né però credo che pienamente se ne sia detto né sarebbe ancora, se di qui a uno anno d'altro che di ciò non parlassimo.*'

50 The phrase was coined by Umberto Bosco, one of the most assiduous and perceptive of Boccaccio's editors and commentators.

gence with which he was dealing in specific contexts.[51] Theories
of this sort, whilst directing our attention to the subtle semantic
nuances of particular words, are not entirely convincing, and more
often than not Boccaccio's choice between words of similar meaning
is dictated by considerations of rhythm and euphony rather than by
any doctrinaire obsession with semantic precision. In what follows,
the temptation to differentiate between the various aspects of the
theme of intelligence by close scrutiny of Boccaccio's terminology
will be eschewed, attention being directed instead to the overall
theme as it presents itself, both in the framework and in certain
individual tales or groups of tales.

The first allusion to intelligence (in this case *senno* or 'wisdom')
occurs in the Prologue, where it is accompanied, interestingly enough,
by a reference to another of the *Decameron*'s major themes, that of Fortune. The author is elaborating upon his reasons for composing the
work, claiming that it stems in large measure from the sense of gratitude he feels in having been released from the bonds of love. In order
not to appear ungrateful for his deliverance, he has resolved to employ
his talents in making restitution for what he has received. He will offer
solace to those who stand in need of it, or in other words to people
who remain enmeshed in the toils of love. Those friends and acquaintances who rendered him assistance in his own timely escape may
derive little benefit from all this, for their good sense (*senno*) or good
fortune (*buona fortuna*) will possibly render such a gift superfluous.

Thus, right from the outset of the *Decameron*, the author juxta-
poses the work's three central themes (Love, Intelligence and Fortune), and suggests that the trials and tribulations attending the first
can be assuaged or avoided by the application of the second or the

---

51 See, for example, Robert Hastings, *Nature and Reason in the 'Decameron'*, Manchester, 1975, p. 74n: '*Ragione* designates the use of the intellect, or rational faculty
in general, to control natural instinct. *Ingegno* and *senno* usually refer to active,
operative intelligence, resourcefulness and ingenuity . . . *Sapere* indicates 'know-how',
ability, expertise. *Sagacità* indicates care, caution, circumspection and deliberation.
Saviezza usually means reflective wisdom . . . *Discrezione* signifies discretion, but also
discernment, perspicacity. *Avvedimento* may mean a number of things: shrewdness,
perspicacity and discernment; resourcefulness and ingenuity; or an expedient, ruse or
stratagem.' See also Lino Pertile, 'Dante, Boccaccio e l'intelligenza', in *Italian
Studies*, 43 (1988), pp. 60–74, where it is argued that key words like *onestà* and
discrezione underline the importance Boccaccio attaches to appearances.

intervention of the third. This, in essence, is what the *Decameron* is about. As its sub-title (*Prencipe Galeotto*) implies, it is a work that shares with medieval romance, more specifically of the Arthurian variety, an abiding concern with the operation of profane love, Galeotto being the medieval archetype of the Pandar figure. The Dantesque associations of the sub-title should not be overlooked, for it will be remembered that Dante's allusion to Galeotto occurs in that episode of the *Commedia*, illustrating the sin of lust, where Francesca da Rimini claims that the mainspring of her adulterous liaison with Paolo Malatesta was their reading together of an Arthurian romance with that very title: 'The book was Galahalt, and he the one who wrote it.'[52] By deliberately choosing this name as the alternative title of his own collection of tales, the author is rejecting Dante's implicit condemnation of the literature of profane love, the genre of which Boccaccio had made himself a leading exponent long before he addressed himself to the writing of his master work. Whereas Dante had suggested that literature concerned with profane love was inherently harmful, Boccaccio polemically stresses its didactic value, at the same time pointing out that for those people blessed with intelligence or good fortune its usefulness is strictly limited. They, presumably, will read it, if they read it at all, for the pleasure they derive from whatever aesthetic values it may possess.[53]

---

52 '*Galeotto fu il libro, e chi lo scrisse*' (*Inferno*, V, 137).
53 The alternative title given by Boccaccio to the work has generated a great deal of critical discussion, especially, in recent years, among American scholars, some of whom would vigorously reject the interpretation offered here. Robert Hollander, for instance, who has expended considerable ingenuity in attempting to prove that Boccaccio is a great Christian moralist, asserts that such an interpretation implies that Boccaccio was 'a relatively mindless reader of Dante's texts' (see his essay, 'Boccaccio's Dante', in *Italica*, 63 (1986), pp. 278–89). Other contributors to the debate include Robert M. Durling ('Boccaccio on Interpretation: Guido's Escape (*Decameron* VI, 9)' in *Dante, Petrarch, Boccaccio: Studies in the Italian Trecento in Honor of Charles S. Singleton*, edited by A. Bernardo and A. Pellegrini, Binghamton, 1983, pp. 273–304), G. Mazzotta, *The World at Play in Boccaccio's 'Decameron'*, Princeton, 1986, and M. R. Menocal, *Writing in Dante's Cult of Truth: From Borges to Boccaccio*, Durham and London, 1991. Menocal challengingly asserts that in choosing *Prencipe Galeotto* as the *Decameron*'s alternative title, 'Boccaccio is confronting the reader with the dual and inseparable problems of the nature of the text and the nature of its interpretation' (p. 182), before expressing her contempt for an exegetical tradition that would have us believe that Boccaccio 'not only accepts Francesca's damning judgement at face value but is willing to apply it unambiguously to himself and his text' (p. 184).

That Boccaccio is adopting a polemical stance in relation to the literature of profane love – a position, moreover, that is diametrically opposed to that of Dante, whose poetry he greatly admired – cannot seriously be doubted. His passionate, eloquent, and occasionally mischievous defence of the *Decameron* in the Introduction to the Fourth Day, as well as the remarks he appends in the work's concluding pages, are indicative of the need he experienced to defend the genre within which he was working. And it is characteristic of Boccaccio's realistic view of the human condition that he should have seized upon the possibilities afforded by the great natural calamity of the Black Death to furnish his stories (many of which were doubtless already written before 1348) with a plausible *raison d'être*. The framework of the *Decameron*, and the circumstances in which the hundred tales are alleged to have been told, have already been discussed in some detail. What needs to be emphasized at this juncture is that the description of the plague, and of the moral and social upheaval to which it gave rise, is first and foremost a powerful instrument for ensuring that a hitherto neglected or despised literary genre will attract due recognition. Boccaccio's defensive posture is at once apparent in the opening paragraph of the Introduction to the First Day, where, referring to his description of the plague, he apologizes to his readers in advance for the work's irksome and ponderous opening (*grave e noioso principio*), and assures them that they will be affected no differently by this grim beginning than hikers confronted by a steep and rugged hill beyond which there lies a fair and delectable plain. The delectable plain is of course the main body of the work, the hundred stories themselves, but so aware is Boccaccio of the possible opprobrium that may accrue to him from his narration of the tales that he constructs an elaborate justificatory framework within which the stories are told, in a particular set of historical circumstances, by a group of ten fictitious narrators. By using this ingenious device, which, as already noted above, is not original to Boccaccio, but is rather a sophisticated form of a technique used by compilers of earlier collections of tales, not only does he distance himself from his material, but he also provides it with a valid aesthetic and historical *raison d'être*.

The chief impression conveyed by Boccaccio's horrendous account of the plague and its disastrous effects is one of chaos and disorder brought about by the decay of hallowed traditions and the sudden breakdown of long-established social institutions. Initially, it is asserted that against so massive and capricious a natural calamity all the wisdom and ingenuity of man are powerless. As Boccaccio reports, 'large quantities of refuse were cleared out of the city by officials specially appointed for the purpose, all sick persons were forbidden entry, and numerous instructions were issued for safeguarding the people's health, but all to no avail.' But it is interesting to observe that wisdom and ingenuity are precisely the qualities that ultimately accomplish the return to order and harmony, as represented by the paradisal world that the members of the *lieta brigata* construct for themselves. In introducing the seven young ladies to his readers, the author gives pride of place to the quality of their intellect (*savia*, or 'wise', is the adjective he applies to them), before going on to enumerate their other distinguishing features, which are their gentle breeding, their physical beauty, their graciousness, and their charming sense of decorum (*leggiadra onestà*). Pampinea's lengthy address to her companions, in which she carefully analyses their common predicament and advances cogent arguments in support of her proposal that they should retire to one of their country estates, offers an apt illustration of the first of the qualities to which the author had referred. The brief discussion that ensues, concerning the desirability on practical grounds of enlisting male support for their enterprise, carries strong traces of anti-feminism, for it is asserted that women, when left to themselves, are not the most rational of creatures, that they are by nature fickle, quarrelsome, suspicious, cowardly and easily frightened, and that, without a man to guide them, it rarely happens that any enterprise of theirs is brought to a worthy conclusion. But emphasis is once more laid upon the young ladies' powers of judgement, one of their number, Filomena, being described as *discretissima*, by way of indicating her exceptional prudence.

As with the seven young ladies, a key attribute of the three young men whose company they enlist is their intelligence, as seen in Pampinea's remarks on first catching sight of the trio: 'See how Fortune favours us right from the beginning, in setting before us three young men of courage and intelligence [*discreti giovani e valorosi*], who will readily act as our guides and servants if we are not too proud to accept them.' The reference to Fortune is

significant, coming immediately after the initial description of the
three young men, in which the author lays special emphasis on
the strength of their affection for three of the ladies present. Implicit
within this description is the concept, central to the poetry of the
dolce stil novo, of the ennobling effects of love, for the trio are
characterized as young men in whom neither the horrors of the
times nor the loss of friends or relatives nor concern for their own
safety has dampened the flames of love, much less extinguished
them completely. Thus, as in the Prologue, we once again find the
deliberate juxtaposition of the *Decameron*'s three central themes:
Love, Fortune, Intelligence.

In the course of his harrowing description of the plague and its
disastrous effects on the traditions and institutions of Florentine
society,[54] Boccaccio repeatedly directs attention to the chaos and
disorder brought by the Black Death to the city he nostalgically
recalls as the most noble of any in Italy ('*oltre ad ogni altra italica
nobilissima*'), and he deplores the breakdown of those moral and legal
restraints which had contributed to the city's cultural and social
pre-eminence. He stresses that in the face of the misery and affliction occasioned by the plague all respect for the laws of God and
of man had broken down and been extinguished, and that consequently everyone was free to behave as he pleased. The departure from generally accepted rules and standards of behaviour
is graphically illustrated in two passages referring to women. In the
first, Boccaccio writes that whenever a woman was taken ill, she
raised no objection, no matter how gracious or beautiful or gently
bred she might be, to being attended by a male servant, and that she
had no scruples about showing him every part of her body as freely
as she would have displayed it to a woman. This practice, he goes
on to suggest in a slightly flippant aside, was responsible for a
subsequent decline in the sexual morals of those women who were
fortunate enough to recover. But if chastity waned, so too did the
compassion ordinarily associated with the feminine ideal. In a

---

54 The description has strong lexical and stylistic affinities with a passage portraying
a similar calamity in the *Historia gentis Langobardorum* by the eighth-century historian
Paul the Deacon. It should not, therefore, be read as an eye-witness account, despite
the author's protestations to the contrary.

passage describing Florentine burial customs, and the role that had traditionally been played in them by the womenfolk of the dead, it is pointed out that these customs had been abandoned, and that not only did people die without having many women about them, but they also died with few people if any to mourn them, or even to witness their passing. Indeed, with the overturning of normal values that accompanied the plague, bereavement became the signal for black humour – laughter, witticisms, and general jollification – the practice of which, as the author ruefully adds, women had learned to perfection.

In all of this there is of course a remnant of the anti-feminism which is observable in much of the literature of the Middle Ages, and which surfaces at several points in the *Decameron*, despite Boccaccio's dedication of the work to the ladies and his frequent avowals of devotion to their well-being. But the overriding impression conveyed by his account of the plague is of a previously well-ordered and civilized society that has been precipitated into chaos and anarchy by the reversal of those values and standards of behaviour on which it depended for its survival, and to which the exercise of the traditional womanly virtues of modesty and compassion had made a decisive contribution. It is thus significant that in his fictive account of the return to a decorous and civilized mode of existence, as represented by the sealed-off world of the *lieta brigata*, Boccaccio not only attributes its generative impulse to a group of young ladies, but he stresses over and over again their strict adherence to rules of womanly conduct which in the outside world had fallen into disuse. Their sustained sense of decorum stands in marked contrast to the moral anarchy which has overtaken their contemporaries in the plague-ridden city. Pointed reference is made to the correctness of their behaviour, not only in the Introduction but in the interludes between one bout of storytelling and the next. And in the concluding pages of the Tenth Day, Panfilo claims that neither in word nor in deed nor in any other respect have he and his companions been deserving of censure.

The return to order, harmony, and self-discipline is effected by the application of wisdom, the quality to which the author gives pride of place in his description of the seven young ladies, and which is embodied to its fullest extent in Pampinea. It is she who not only supplies a graphic account of the indignation that she and her companions experience in their daily lives because of the collapse of traditional civilized values but also indicates how their dilemma may be resolved. Her eloquent address to her companions is faintly reminiscent of the harangue delivered to his crew by another, much more famous representative of human intelligence, Dante's Ulysses, who in a well-known passage from the twenty-sixth canto of *Inferno* impresses upon his shipmates that they were not born to live like animals, but to pursue virtue and knowledge.[55] So, too, Pampinea implants in her companions the desire to escape from a brute-like existence and pursue the virtue and knowledge which will inevitably flow from their active participation in the well-ordered, civilized mode of living she prescribes for their own brief odyssey. Like the quest of Dante's Ulysses, it has as its objective the attainment of a mythical state of well-being, associated in the medieval consciousness with the notion of the earthly paradise. The fate of Dante's Ulysses is a warning to those who pursue the spirit of inquiry beyond reasonable bounds, symbolically represented by the pillars of Hercules that stand at the extremity of the known terrestrial world. For Dante, the earthly paradise is located at the summit of the mountain of Purgatory, at the antipodes of the world as he and his contemporaries knew it. But no sooner do Ulysses and his companions, spurred on by their desire for knowledge, chance upon the mountain in their mortal state than they are caught up in a whirlwind and destroyed. In contrast, what Boccaccio seems to be suggesting is that, through human initiative allied to wisdom, mortals may indeed attain to a condition of terrestrial bliss.

To achieve that condition, the main prerequisites are a meticulous regard for order and a constant sense of propriety, and these are the attributes which figure most prominently in Pampinea's elaborate proposals for the withdrawal of the company to their pastoral refuge. In broaching her design to her companions, she stresses the

55   *'fatti non foste a viver come bruti,*
         ma per seguir virtute e canoscenza.'
         (*Inferno*, XXVI, 119–20)

need to observe certain standards of behaviour ('We could go and stay together on one of our country estates, shunning at all costs the lewd practices of our fellow citizens and feasting and merrymaking as best we may without in any way overstepping the bounds of what is reasonable'), and this same concern for propriety is seen in her spirited declaration that 'it is no more unseemly for us to go away and preserve our honour [*l'onestamente andare*] than it is for most other women to remain and forfeit theirs [*lo star disonestamente*].' When one of her companions, Neifile, objects that their retreat to the country in young men's company will bring disgrace and censure upon them all, she is promptly told (by Filomena this time) that if a woman lives honestly and with a clear conscience, then people may say whatever they like, for God and Truth will defend her.

These are noble sentiments, totally in keeping with the aristocratic ethos which informs the world of the *lieta brigata*, whose impeccable and carefully regulated mode of existence, with its leisurely, civilized daily routine of bodily and spiritual refreshment, its country walks, its noontide siestas, its games and pastimes, its polite conversations, its singing, dancing, and decorous merrymaking, above all its delight in beauty, whether natural or created by man, reflects the Golden Age, the first and best age of the world, in which the poets of antiquity envisaged mankind in a state of ideal prosperity and happiness. Such an ideal world, the attractions of which are greatly enhanced by the circumstances of its creation in direct antithesis to the barbaric and anarchic urban life described by Boccaccio in the opening pages of the Introduction, can exist only in the imagination of the author and his readers, so tenuous is its connection with everyday reality. It is above all for this reason that none of the individual members of the *lieta brigata*, not even Dioneo with his penchant for non-conformity and mischievous humour, acquires credibility as a fully formed individual composed of flesh and blood.

When one turns to the stories themselves, the unreality or artificiality of the frame becomes even more apparent. For although they, too, are exquisitely constructed literary artefacts, their events unfold within the orbit of common human experience, and they positively swarm with individuals who, however extraordinary or outrageous the situations in which they may have their being, are almost always convincing in purely psychological terms. This palpable contrast between the characters of the frame and the characters of the stories is only marginally due to differences (which in any case are relatively slight) in the manner of their presentation. The chief reason for the contrast lies elsewhere, in the fact that the *lieta brigata* inhabits an unreal world, the world of the artist as distinct from the world of man, and its members are, collectively, the personified abstractions of certain cherished ideals, doubtless associated in the mind of the author with the courtly Neapolitan society in which he had spent the years of his adolescence and early manhood, and to which in later life he was wont to look back with a profound sense of nostalgia.

Whatever the frame's personal overtones, it is clear that the society it depicts is aristocratic and élitist, and that the culture and refinement it embodies are far removed from the practical, workaday world with which Boccaccio is largely concerned in the *novelle*. This tonal antithesis between the world of the storytellers and the world of the narratives serves to highlight their separate, contrasting realities. But what the two worlds have in common is their persistent emphasis on the role of intelligence in human affairs. Of the eight days to which a single narrative topic is assigned, three are devoted specifically to stories concerned with quickness of wit or resourcefulness. The topic for the Sixth Day is 'those who, on being provoked by some verbal pleasantry, have returned like for like, or who, by a prompt retort or shrewd manoeuvre, have avoided danger, discomfort or ridicule'. The tricks played by women upon their husbands form the subject-matter of the Seventh Day, whilst the Eighth Day is given over to tales about 'tricks that people in general, men and women alike, are forever playing upon one another'. This last topic is one which could cover a large number of the remaining stories in the *Decameron*, and tales of verbal pleasantries are by no means confined to the Sixth Day, so that, viewed in its entirety, the *Decameron* is abundantly stocked with illustrations of human ingenuity.

There is nothing unusual in this. Other collections of short stories, like the anonymous *Novellino* that preceded the *Decameron* and Franco Sacchetti's *Trecentonovelle* that followed it, could be described in similar terms, and indeed it would be a dull series of narratives that did not accord an important role to the workings of people's intelligence. What is interesting about Boccaccio's treatment of the theme is his elevation of intelligence to a position in the scale of human values which places it on a par with the highest of the traditional virtues. This celebration of intelligence for its own sake is largely responsible for the ambiguous moral tone of the *Decameron*, a feature which forms a notorious stumbling-block for those critics and commentators who seek to extract from the work a coherent and consistent system of ethics.[56]

The tone of moral ambiguity is established in the very first of the hundred tales, which concerns the arch-villain Ser Cepperello, who by making a false confession to a holy friar on his death-bed is reputed to be a saint, and is thereafter revered as Saint Ciappelletto. Cepperello is hired by a rich Italian merchant to recover certain loans in Burgundy, a province notorious for the lawlessness of its inhabitants, but shortly after his arrival there he falls mortally ill in the house of two Florentine money-lenders, with whom he has taken up lodging. His hosts are faced with an awkward dilemma. Knowing of his thoroughly evil past, they are certain that no priest will give him absolution, and that his body will be refused burial in consecrated ground, in which case, being already unpopular because of their profession, they will incur the open hostility of the locals, possibly forfeiting their property and their lives. If on the other hand they turn a dying man out of the house, their prospects will be no less bleak, for Cepperello, prior to his illness, had done nothing to offend the Burgundians, on the contrary issuing his first demands 'in a gentle and amiable fashion that ran contrary to his nature'. Their conversation is overheard by their guest, who, as Boccaccio puts it in a characteristically acute psychological aside, 'was sharp of hearing, as invalids invariably are'. He persuades them to send for the holiest and ablest friar they can find, to whom he makes a death-bed confession which convinces the friar that he has led an extraordinarily devout and blameless life, with the result that he not

56 See, for example, R. Hastings, *Nature and Reason in the 'Decameron'*, Manchester, 1975, and his more recent article, 'To Teach or Not to Teach: The Moral Dimension of the *Decameron* Reconsidered', in *Italian Studies*, XLIV (1989), pp. 19–40.

only receives Extreme Unction, but his body is carried in solemn procession to the nearby monastery, where it is buried with pomp and ceremony in a marble tomb, thereafter being held in such veneration by the Burgundians that he is known as Saint Ciappelletto. What is more, Boccaccio adds, it is claimed that through his intercession God has wrought many miracles, and that He continues to work them for the benefit of anyone who commends himself devoutly to this particular Saint.

There are those who detect in the story of Ciappelletto a desire on Boccaccio's part to ridicule the Church and religious practices in general, especially the cult of saints and the belief in miracles. But although an element of scepticism is undoubtedly woven into the narrative, at no point does it assume the vigorous polemical overtones observable elsewhere in the *Decameron*, for instance in the story of Tedaldo (III, 7) or of Friar Rinaldo (VII, 3), and the holy friar who receives Ciappelletto's confession is presented in a more sympathetic light than most of the numerous friars, abbots, monks and priests of Boccaccio's other *novelle*. In fact, as Erich Auerbach somewhat disapprovingly notes, Boccaccio adopts a completely neutral position *vis-à-vis* the singular events he describes, neither condemning nor approving the penitent's sneering contempt for confession in the hour of death.[57] It is true that the tale is prefaced and rounded off with a series of pious observations on the infinite and all-seeing mercy of God, but these are no more than deliberate set-pieces, designed it seems to avert the charge of irreligiousness which a bare recital of the narrative would otherwise certainly have provoked. Nor does the remarkable catalogue of Ciappelletto's nefarious practices, concluding with the statement that 'he was perhaps the worst man ever born', imply, as Branca suggests,[58] that Boccaccio is adopting a disapproving attitude towards the character. On the contrary, in the remainder of the tale Ciappelletto controls the situation so masterfully as to arouse the reader's sneaking admiration.

The lengthy description of Ciappelletto, establishing him as a

57 E. R. Auerbach, *Mimesis: The Representation of Reality in Western Literature*, translated by W. R. Trask, Princeton, 1953, pp. 229–30.
58 Vittore Branca, *Boccaccio medievale* (7th edn), Sansoni, Florence, 1990, p. 28n.

forger, a liar, a hypocrite, a promoter of discord, a sadist, a psychopath, a blasphemer, an alcoholic, a pederast, a glutton, a gambler and a swindler is from the stylistic point of view quite unique in the *Decameron*, with the possible exception of the portrait of Gucci in the story of Friar Cipolla (VI, 10). The method normally used by Boccaccio to introduce his characters involves the communication of an absolute minimum of information, and the characters acquire depth and consistency through their participation in the narrative, rather than through what the author tells us about them. In departing from his normal practice for the tale of Ciappelletto, the author clearly had in mind the peculiar requirements of this particular narrative, which depends for its effect upon establishing from the very beginning that Ciappelletto is the personification of evil, that he is in fact 'the worst man ever born'. Only then is it possible to savour to the full the crescendo of effrontery that marks Ciappelletto's subsequent confession and that provides the story with its *raison d'être*. Unless the reader is made aware of the penitent's grossly iniquitous past, the motivation for the false confession is non-existent and the narrative becomes meaningless. Hence the lengthy portrait of Ciappelletto is no more and no less than a narrative device, quite insusceptible to a moralistic reading. In other words, it tells the reader everything he needs to know about Ciappelletto, and nothing at all about Boccaccio except that he was a shrewd craftsman, aware of the need to adapt his technique to the demands of a particular story.

What the tale of Ciappelletto, viewed as a whole, does tell us about Boccaccio is that he was alive to the paradoxes and inconsistencies of the established social order, and that he took a mischievous delight in directing attention towards them. There is no mistaking the tone of gleeful admiration in which he recounts Ciappelletto's stage-by-stage deception of the saintly, unsuspecting friar, a process involving the creation of a fictitious persona completely antithetical to Ciappelletto's true character. This contrast between appearance and reality, between seeming and being, is the fulcrum on which the opening tale of the *Decameron* is delicately balanced, and it would be possible to argue that it is one of the most prominent recurrent motifs of the work as a whole, that it is in fact the mainspring of the narrative process in the majority of the hundred tales.

Another of the *Decameron*'s recurrent motifs, and one which has been analysed in some detail by Branca,[59] is the entrepreneurial spirit that was so important a factor in establishing the economic prosperity of fourteenth-century Florence, and that seems to motivate a number of the characters in Boccaccio's stories, or at least to form part of the background to many of the narratives. The more obvious examples of this are to be found in the Second Day, where the topic for discussion ('those who after suffering a series of misfortunes are brought to a state of unexpected happiness') is itself conducive to the telling of stories set in the business and mercantile world, with its attendant hazards and opportunities, its see-saw movements between the extremes of ruinous loss and prodigious profit. But the motif of commercial enterprise (in Branca's phrase, the *ragion di mercatura*, which he sees as the dominant force of fourteenth-century Italy, as distinct from the *ragion di stato* of the Renaissance) is by no means confined to the stories of the Second Day. It is an important element in at least a score of the other *novelle*, and the *Decameron* as a whole, including the framework, reflects the *mores* and aspirations of the enterprising and industrious Florentine middle class which succeeded the feudal aristocracy of medieval Italy, and to which the author himself decidedly belonged.

The *ragion di mercatura* provides a sort of key to the interpretation of many of the stories, but it requires to be used with discretion. In the case of Ciappelletto, for example, it has been suggested, by Branca, that Boccaccio is here expressing his distaste for the inhumane and unscrupulous practices through which vast private fortunes were frequently accumulated,[60] or, to use a modern expression, what the author is doing is condemning the unacceptable face of capitalism. But an interpretation along these lines can be valid only if the narrator's prefatory and concluding remarks are read as reliable pointers to the writer's own opinion of Ciappelletto (instead of as the tongue-in-cheek declarations of piety that they patently

59 Branca, *Boccaccio medievale*, in the chapter headed 'L'epopea dei mercatanti', pp. 134–64.
60 Branca, *Boccaccio medievale*, p. 158.

are), and if moral as distinct from narrative significance is attached to certain passages, such as the one describing the main character as 'perhaps the worst man ever born' and the quite literally rhetorical question of the two money-lenders:

> 'What manner of man is this, whom neither old age nor illness, nor fear of the death which he sees so close at hand, nor even the fear of God, before whose judgement he knows he must shortly appear, have managed to turn away from his evil ways, or persuade to die any differently from the way he has lived?'[61]

The answer to their question is simply that Ciappelletto, unlike the majority of Boccaccio's contemporaries, is an unbeliever, that he is supremely indifferent to the possibility of eternal damnation, a possibility which is non-existent so far as he is concerned. When the narrator, Panfilo, declares in his concluding remarks that Ciappelletto 'should rather be in Hell, in the hands of the Devil, than in Paradise', he is doing no more than expressing the sentiments of Boccaccio's average reader, which do not necessarily coincide with those of the author himself. It is therefore at the very least dubious whether the author intended that the account of Ciappelletto's death-bed confession should be read as a kind of cautionary tale against the dire consequences of shedding one's scruples in the pursuit of the materialist goals of the *ragion di mercatura*.

A much more fruitful way of applying the interpretative key of the *ragion di mercatura* is that suggested by Giovanni Getto,[62] who uses it to rebut the view, first formulated by Croce,[63] that Ciappelletto's confession is the logical culminating *tour de force* in the career of a master-artist in the craft of deception, that it is motivated by no more than the desire to die in the manner in which he had lived. Nero's dying words, *'Qualis artifex pereo'* ('What an artist dies with me!'), correspond exactly, in the view of Croce and others,[64] with

61 '"Che uomo è costui, il quale né vecchiezza né infermità né paura di morte, alla quale si vede vicino, né ancora di Dio, dinanzi al giudicio del quale di qui a picciola ora s'aspetta di dovere essere, dalla sua malvagità l'hanno potuto rimuovere, né far che egli cosí non voglia morire come egli è vivuto?"'

62 Giovanni Getto, *Vita di forme e forme di vita nel 'Decameron'*, Turin, 1958, pp. 52–3.

63 Benedetto Croce, *Poesia popolare e poesia d'arte*, Bari, 1967, pp. 86–8.

64 See, e.g., Luigi Russo, *Letture critiche del 'Decameron'*, Bari, 1956, pp. 51–68.

the dying sentiments of Ciappelletto. But as Getto points out, Ciappelletto's offer to assist his hosts in resolving their dilemma is motivated by stronger and more deeply inbred sentiments than these. When, having eavesdropped on the anxious conversation of the two money-lenders, he attempts to reassure them ('I don't want you to worry in the slightest on my account, nor to fear that I will cause you to suffer any harm. I heard what you were saying about me and I agree entirely that what you predict will actually come to pass, if matters take the course you anticipate; but they will do nothing of the kind'), he is in effect displaying the same kind of hard-headed business sense that had originally prompted his employer to commission his services as a debt-collector, and that the money-lenders themselves presumably possess. His instinctive adherence to the *ragion di mercatura* is seen in the fellow-feeling (or as Getto engagingly suggests, the *omertà*) he displays towards the usurers, and in his total agreement with their assessment of the problem confronting them.

Like the tale of Ciappelletto, all of the stories of the First Day without exception are concerned in one way or another with the operation of human intelligence. The second story is about Abraham the Parisian Jew, who is converted to Christianity after visiting Rome. Whilst he is there, he observes the depravity of the leaders of the Church, and concludes that any religion that can survive and prosper with so much corruption at its head must of necessity be the one true faith. The conclusion of the story paradoxically illustrates the theme of intelligence at the same time as it drives home its anti-clerical polemic. Abraham, a hard-headed man of business, reaches his decision to convert to Christianity through the application of his experience and his assessment of observable facts. In the next story (I, 3), another Jew, Melchizedek, ingeniously avoids falling into a trap laid for him by Saladin (who has demanded to know which of the three main religions is the one true faith) by telling a story about three precious rings, all indistinguishable from one another, of which only one is authentic. The tale's purpose is to illustrate the impossibility of choosing between established faiths. All are equally valid to the unprejudiced observer.

The fiercely anti-clerical tone of the second story is tempered in the fourth, where a monk and his abbot, each caught in turn by the other in amorous dalliance with a comely wench smuggled into his cell by the former of the two, reach a gentleman's agreement on their future handling of a delicate situation. From the concupiscence of the religious, Boccaccio next turns to a story (I, 5) involving the concupiscence of a king, and of how it was held at bay by the resourcefulness of a young gentlewoman, the Marchioness of Montferrat, whose husband was away on a Crusade. The stratagem of the chicken banquet leads in turn to a story (I, 6) concerning food of an altogether different quality, where a man accused by an inquisitor of blasphemy humiliates his persecutor with a witty remark concerning the watery soup doled out to the poor by the inquisitor and his fellow Franciscans.

The shaming of a parsimonious benefactor forms the subject, also, of the tale that follows (I, 7), but this time it is brought about by the elaborate telling of a story within a story by one Bergamino, described as 'a faster and more brilliant talker than anyone could ever imagine' (*'oltre al credere di chi non l'udí presto parlatore e ornato'*). The target of Bergamino's timely parable is Can Grande della Scala, whose sudden fit of meanness towards his guest is totally out of character, whereas the protagonist of the following tale (I, 8), Ermino Grimaldi, is not only the richest man in Italy but also so much of a miser that his name has become synonymous with avarice. The transformation of his character is effected by the sharp riposte ('Let Generosity be painted there') of a distinguished courtier, Guiglielmo Borsiere, to his request for a suitable topic for a new picture he intends to commission for the main hall of his house in Genoa.

Admonitory wit effects a comparable transformation in the next story (I, 9), recounting the way in which a gentlewoman of Gascony, travelling through Cyprus, having suffered a brutal assault from a pack of ruffians, converts the king, a cowardly weakling, into the implacable scourge of all wrongdoers. And the First Day ends with yet another admonitory tale (I, 10), this time featuring a brilliant physician, Master Alberto of Bologna, now 'an old man approaching seventy', who reproaches a young gentlewoman and her companions for mocking his amatory feelings towards her, by his witty and delightfully allusive account of the way young ladies go about the eating of leeks.

No specific topic is prescribed for the stories of the First Day, but all are concerned with various forms of human weakness, and all involve the application of the intellectual faculties to correct or modify their harmful effects. Intelligence is thus established as the initial theme of the work as a whole, whilst in the stories of the Second Day the theme of Fortune occupies a dominant position. Boccaccio's third major theme is Love, which figures prominently in the stories of the following three days, although in several of the stories narrated on those days, especially on the Third Day, Intelligence is an important ancillary theme. As already noted, the protagonists of the story of King Agilulf and the groom (III, 2) embody the qualities of wisdom and ingenuity respectively in their reactions to the events of the narrative. Ingenuity is also the distinguishing feature of the anonymous Florentine noblewoman (III, 3) who hoodwinks a solemn friar into unwittingly acting as pander between herself and the young man on whom she has fixed her amorous longings. The initial description of the lady is significant, stressing as it does the strength of her intellectual character. According to the narrator, Filomena, she was:

> a noblewoman of striking beauty and impeccable breeding, who was endowed by Nature with as lofty a temperament and shrewd an intellect as could be found in any other woman of her time.[65]

The narrative, carefully structured and brilliantly told, includes a smattering of anti-clerical polemic and, by way of justification for the lady's adulterous quest, a disapproving commentary on arranged marriages (her husband being an immensely rich woollen-draper, incapable of anything more than 'distinguishing wool from cotton, supervising the setting up of a loom, or debating the virtues of a particular yarn with a spinner-woman'), but the novella's strength derives from the high degree of sophistication with which the lady pursues and eventually achieves her objective.

65 '. . . una gentile donna di bellezze ornata e di costumi, d'altezza d'animo e di sottili avvedimenti quanto alcuna altra dalla natura dotata . . .'

The exercise of intelligence in the pursuit of an objective, generally amatory in scope, is seen in most of the other stories of the Third Day, from the initial account of Masetto's heroic exertions in the convent (III, 1) to the tale, appropriated by Shakespeare in *All's Well that Ends Well*, of Gilette of Narbonne's successful fulfilment of the seemingly impossible conditions imposed by a reluctant husband for the consummation of their marriage (III, 9).

A variant on the same theme (intelligence as the spur in the cause of love) is found in the story of Cimon (V, 1), where the boorish hero, having miraculously acquired wisdom through his chance discovery in a woodland clearing of the sleeping form of the beautiful Iphigenia, employs all his resources of guile and physical strength to secure her as his bride. Whether he is deserving of such a prize, which he obtains through murder and abduction, depends on how much importance one attributes to the underlying intent to echo the myth of Pholus the centaur. The tale that immediately follows (V, 2) is a love story of quite a different kind, and includes an episode where Martuccio Gomito, having been captured and imprisoned by the Saracens, wins his freedom and the grateful esteem of the King of Tunis by providing him with some ingenious advice on how to win a war against a powerful invader.

The form of intelligence displayed in the narratives of the Sixth Day is verbal wit, of which several examples have already appeared in the course of the First Day's proceedings. The tale of Madonna Oretta (VI, 1) is of special interest, since her clever response to her admirer's persistent but clumsy attempts at storytelling is preceded by a catalogue of his shortcomings. Like the scene in which Hamlet advises the players on what to avoid in the art of acting, the passage reveals by implication the qualities that Boccaccio considered essential to the art of the storyteller: variety of phrasing, avoidance of repetition, clarity of exposition, and a delivery suited to the characters and incidents being described. Many recent commentators regard the story of Oretta as a *metanovella*, an extended metaphor on how *not* to tell a story, and some have sought to argue that its placing at the centre of the work – it being the fifty-first of the hundred stories – is a pointer to the importance Boccaccio attached to it as a key to the art of storytelling.

In her preliminary remarks to the tale of Oretta, Filomena describes shafts of verbal wit as an adornment to graceful manners and polite conversation, comparing them to stars bedecking the sky on cloudless nights. She asserts that the *bon mot* is better suited to women than to men, it being unseemly for women to go on talking at inordinate length. Her remarks echo almost exactly those of Pampinea in introducing the story of Master Alberto (I, 10). Both Pampinea and Filoména complain about the disuse into which the practice has fallen amongst their women contemporaries, most of whom are incapable not only of producing a witticism at the right moment, but also of recognizing one when they hear it. The point, distinctly anti-feminist, is driven home in the story of Cesca (VI, 8), whose failure to comprehend her uncle's glaringly obvious piece of advice induces the narrator to compare her to a *montone*, or a ram, synonymous for Italians with a mutton-head.

Notwithstanding the remarks of Pampinea and Filomena on the subject, in only three of the stories of the Sixth Day is the *bon mot* delivered by a woman. Apart from the tale of Oretta, the others are the accounts of Monna Nonna de' Pulci's biting retort to the banter of the Bishop of Florence (VI, 3) and of Madonna Filippa's spirited defence of women's rights (VI, 7), to which reference was made earlier in discussing the question of adulterous love.

Florentines prided themselves on their sharpness of wit, and all the stories of the Sixth Day are set either in Florence itself or in its immediate neighbourhood. The social backgrounds of the protagonists of these tales are remarkably wide, ranging from the most lowly to the professional middle classes and the political élite. In the tales of Cisti the baker (VI, 2) and of Chichibio (VI, 4), both extremes of the social spectrum are represented, but whereas Cisti displays throughout a refined sense of propriety that belies his humble calling, Chichibio's uncharacteristic *bon mot* is forced from his lips 'mysteriously' by his terror of a master's wrath. The professional and artistic world of early fourteenth-century Florence is evoked in the account (VI, 5) of Forese da Rabatta and Giotto returning on a summer evening astride emaciated old hacks through a heavy rainstorm from their country retreats. Of special interest in this brief tale is Boccaccio's eulogy of Giotto and his assessment of his innovatory genius in the art of painting. Whilst Giotto's realism represents a marked contrast with the Byzantine formalism of his predecessors, the exact reproduction of reality is not a quality one normally associates with the great Florentine painter. But that in effect is what Boccaccio claims to be his outstanding achievement, in a passage claiming that Giotto's fidelity to Nature was such as to persuade the onlooker to mistake a picture of his for the real thing.

In his fulsome praise of Giotto, Boccaccio takes his cue from Dante, who in a passage from *Purgatorio* concerning the transitory nature of earthly fame had reminded his readers that Giotto's reputation had now placed that of Cimabue in the shade.[66] Dante comes to mind, also, in the story Boccaccio tells (VI, 9) of Dante's friend and fellow poet Guido Cavalcanti, where he attributes to Guido the reputation for atheism that had prompted Dante to place the soul of Guido's father, Cavalcante de' Cavalcanti, in the circle of the flaming tombs reserved for heretics.[67] The tombs in Boccaccio's account were a well-known landmark in the centre of Florence near the church of San Giovanni, and what is interesting about the tale is not so much the prompt retort delivered by Guido to the young bloods on horseback who are tormenting him, as the picture it evokes of Florence and Florentine society in the early fourteenth century. No less evocative of the contemporary Florentine social scene is the story (VI, 6) in which Michele Scalza ingeniously proves to the satisfaction of his young companions that the Baronci are the most noble family, not only in Florence, but in the whole wide world.

In narrating the final story of the Sixth Day (VI, 10), Dioneo for the first and only time, unless one takes seriously his curious claim that the Griselda story (X, 10) exemplifies munificence in the person of her husband, conforms to the prescribed topic by portraying a character, Friar Cipolla, who displays verbal ingenuity of a very high order indeed. The remarkable dexterity shown by Cipolla in turning an awkward situation to his advantage represents the apotheosis of the day's talking point, which covers those who have 'avoided danger, discomfiture or ridicule' through resorting to a

---

66 See *Purgatorio*, XI, 94–6.
67 See *Inferno*, X, 52–72.

'prompt retort or shrewd manoeuvre'. Cipolla's capacity for thinking and talking on his feet, comparable, according to the narrator,
to the oratorical skills of Cicero and Quintilian, is not the result of a
refined upbringing and education, but is simply an inborn and
natural gift which he exploits to the full in persuading a not very
discerning audience that his flights of fancy are nothing less than
gospel truth. In his handling of the provincials who flock to hear his
annual sermon, he displays all the qualities associated with a market
salesman and many more besides. His triumphant escape from a
precarious position, sealed by his daubing of black crosses on the
clothes of his hearers, is made possible only because of the lack
of sophistication of an audience whose lives 'still conformed to
the honest precepts of an earlier age'. As in the case of the holy
friar who is taken in by Ciappelletto's confession (I, 1), there is
no real criticism, either open or implied, of the victims of the
deception, but rather a sneaking admiration for the ingenuity of its
perpetrator.

Quickness of wit is the distinguishing quality, also, of most of the
adulterous wives whose escapades are recounted in the stories of the
Seventh Day. Although several of the narratives are traceable to
other literatures, notably the French *fabliaux*, Boccaccio's elaborate
re-working of his source materials renders them distinctively Italian
in tone and atmosphere. With the exception of the ninth story, a
version of a medieval Latin text, which Boccaccio sets in ancient
Greece, the locations of these tales are representative of the flourishing commercial life and prosperous bourgeoisie of fourteenth-
century Italy: Florence, Naples, Siena, Arezzo, Rimini, Bologna.
One recent commentator has argued that the stories of the Seventh
Day reflect the 'battle for the control of domestic space'[68] that
inevitably arose in a society where arranged marriages were the
norm and where a woman's only way of preserving the status she
had brought to the marriage with her dowry (which passed at once
into the hands of the husband) was to establish herself as mistress of
her own household.

The battle for the control of domestic space is vividly illustrated

68 David Wallace, *Giovanni Boccaccio: Decameron*, Cambridge, 1991, p. 78.

in the story (VII, 4) of the wife who, having put her husband to bed thinking him drunk and incapable, finds herself locked out of the house on returning in pitch darkness from an assignation with her young lover. The husband, who on this occasion has merely pretended to be drunk so as to discover his wife's reasons for packing him off to bed, tells her to go away, and threatens to make an example of her in front of her neighbours and kinsfolk. Having pleaded in vain to be let into the house, the woman, who 'had all her wits about her', picks up an enormous stone and flings it down a nearby well, giving her husband the impression that she is committing suicide. He rushes from the house to rescue her, whereupon she seizes her opportunity to dash into the house, bolt the door, and subject him to such a torrent of abuse about his drinking habits that she arouses all the neighbours. When word of the incident reaches the ears of her kinsfolk, they hasten to the scene and give the husband a severe hiding before taking away his wife and all of her belongings. He is able to retrieve her only by surrendering total control of domestic space, giving his wife leave to amuse herself at will, provided that she does it discreetly and without his knowledge.

The woman is described as *semplicetta*, or not unduly intelligent, her ingenious stratagem for regaining entry to the house being attributed to the power of Love. Intelligence is not in fact a quality that is always admired in the women characters of the *Decameron*, as can be seen from the narrator's portrayal of Ghismonda (IV, I) as one who 'possessed rather more intelligence than a woman needs'.[69] But in the story of the werewolf (VII, I), Lotteringhi's wife is described as a woman 'of great intelligence and perspicacity' ('*savia e avveduta molto*'), qualities that she exhibits to the full in her hour of need, not only by inventing a plausible tale to allay her husband's suspicions, but by extemporizing a rhyming prayer to 'exorcize' the nocturnal visitor. The resourcefulness shown by Monna Sismonda (VII, 8), when her husband discovers the length of string that she uses to communicate with her lover, is no less impressive. The story is one that highlights incidentally the tensions that arose from

---

69 She is described as '*savia piú che a donna per avventura non si richiedea*'.

mixed marriages between the daughters of older patrician families and representatives of the newer Florentine social order, the affluent merchant class. The husband is presented as one who 'foolishly decided to marry into the aristocracy, and took to wife a young gentlewoman, quite unsuited to him', and towards the end of the story he is subjected to a barrage of violent and vulgar abuse by his mother-in-law, who roundly expresses her contempt for his origins and social pretensions.

Further examples of the celebration of intelligence in the *Decameron* may be seen in several of the stories of the last three days, but in the tenth and last day the theme is developed in such a way as to provide a grandiose, uplifting climax to the work as a whole. These tales of liberal or munificent deeds, prompted by the exercise of intelligence, have led some of Boccaccio's modern commentators to argue that his celebration of that quality is a pointer to the work's underlying morality, in that they show how the application of reason is the key to a virtuous and responsible way of life.[70] This may well be true of the edenic, unreal world of the storytellers, and also of some of the least plausible tales of the Tenth Day, such as the one recounting Nathan's deliberate placing of his life at risk (X, 3) as a token of his unworldly munificence. But as we have seen, the morality of the *Decameron* is open-ended. The stories are for the most part set firmly in the real world of fourteenth-century Italy. In his countless variations on the theme of intelligence, what Boccaccio is really celebrating is the triumph of the entrepreneurial spirit.

★   ★   ★

Fortune, the third of the *Decameron*'s main themes, is a dominant force in the stories of the Second Day, where the subject for discussion is 'those who after suffering a series of misfortunes are

70 See, for example, R. Hastings, *Nature and Reason in the Decameron*, p. 76, where it is stated that 'The more important reason for the celebration of intelligence in the *Decameron* is that virtue itself cannot exist without it. For not only is intelligence able to secure the satisfaction of natural desires, it is in addition the only thing that makes possible the rational control of natural instinct, the regulation of violent passion, and the education and refinement of instinct and impulse that are the basis of all virtuous and responsible conduct, as we see from those tales where the right use of intelligence leads directly to virtuous behaviour.'

brought to a state of unexpected happiness'. Like other major writers of classical, medieval and Renaissance times, Boccaccio was strongly attracted to this topic, which he explored in varying degrees of detail, reaching such varied conclusions that it is difficult to attribute to him any single, consistent theoretical viewpoint. In one of his stories (X, 1), he actually tells of a character, Ruggieri de' Figiovanni, who is persistently dogged by *ill* fortune. A twentieth-century counterpart to Ruggieri is the American blues singer Pleasant Joseph, who complains in one of his lyrics that 'Bad luck's been in my family, ever since I began to crawl,' and that 'If it wasn't for bad luck, I wouldn't have no luck at all.'[71]

If one considers his literary work as a whole, Boccaccio's views on Fortune may be seen, broadly speaking, to have evolved from a purely fatalistic conception such as that which he expressed in the prologues of both the *Filostrato* and the *Teseida* to the idea of Fortune as an instrument of Divine Providence — a position he adopts in several of his later works such as the *Amorosa visione* and *De casibus virorum illustrium*.

The idea of Fortune as a divinely created force is seen in a well-known passage from Dante's *Inferno*, where Fortune is defined as a 'general minister and guide' (*general ministra e duce*)[72] of men's destinies, created by God at the same time that He created the angels who guide and control the heavenly spheres. Dante's conception of Fortune as a divine force corresponds in its essentials with that of another famous exile, Ovid, who in one of his letters had written of Fortune as the unstable goddess (*dea non stabilis*).[73] It is probably because the ancients thought of Fortune as a deity that Dante, with his habitual inclination to subsume pagan beliefs into the Christian vision of the universe which he sets before us in the *Commedia*, expounds a theory of Fortune that stresses her divine origin. Nor is it accidental that the spokesman for this theory, as in many other instances where the philosophy of the classical period is modified and made compatible with Christian beliefs, should be

71 *Bad Luck Blues*, lyrics by Pleasant Joseph and Sammy Price. Sammy Price (piano), Danny Barker (guitar), Pops Foster (bass) and Kenny Clarke (drums). The recording, originally made in 1947, was reissued in 1959.
72 *Inferno*, VII, 78.
73 *Epistulae ex Ponto*, IV, 37.

Virgil, the poet whom Dante thought of as the bridge between the old world and the new. For Dante, Fortune transfers earthly possessions in her own good time from nation to nation and from family to family, in a way that defies all human understanding. Using a simile borrowed from Virgil, he describes her workings as 'hidden, like a snake in the grass'.[74]

Faint echoes of Dante's conception of Fortune are heard in the prefatory remarks to Boccaccio's tale of Alessandro and the abbot (II, 3). The narrator is Pampinea, who states that Fortune controls all human affairs, arranging and rearranging them in her own inscrutable fashion. She shifts them, now one way, then another, then back again, without pursuing any discernible pattern. A more obvious reminder of the passage from Dante occurs in the introduction to the story of Cisti the baker (VI, 2). Once again the narrator is Pampinea, who after claiming that Fortune, far from being blind, has a thousand eyes, uses Dante's terminology in depicting Fortune, along with Nature, as the two ministers of the world (*le due ministre del mondo*).

Boccaccio's conception of Fortune is distinctly medieval. There is no trace in the pages of the *Decameron* of the Renaissance idea that Fortune is capable of being controlled by the application of wisdom and forethought, a view most famously propounded by Machiavelli in the penultimate chapter of his treatise on monarchy. Writing in the early sixteenth century, Machiavelli compared Fortune to a river, which will cause enormous damage when it is in flood unless precautions have been taken to contain it by constructing high banks and overflow channels during the dry season. In a memorable and typically provocative phrase, he also compared Fortune to a woman, explaining that one needs to beat and shake it into submission.[75] An obvious point of comparison in the *Decameron* is the tale (IX, 9) of the young man with the shrewish wife who seeks advice from King Solomon, but Boccaccio's tale contains no reference to Fortune, being simply one of several that reflect the misogynistic sentiments of medieval literature.

In all of the stories of the Second Day except the last, Fortune is

74 *Inferno*, VII, 84.
75 '. . . *la fortuna è donna: ed è necessario, volendola tenere sotto, batterla e urtarla*' (N. Machiavelli, *Il principe*, c. 25).

an impersonal and capricious force, against whose operations the individual is incapable of any response other than an attitude of stoical indifference. A second common feature of these stories is their connection with the world of commerce, which assumes prominence in each of the first five stories as well as in the tales of Alatiel (II, 7) and of Bernabò and Zinevra (II, 9). The vicissitudes of Fortune are equated in most of these stories with the ups and downs of characters whose lives are dedicated to commercial enterprise, a typical example being the tale of Landolfo Rufolo (II, 4). Rufolo is a merchant who, determined to multiply his already considerable wealth, sails for Cyprus with a mixed cargo, only to find on his arrival that large quantities of goods similar to his own have already been landed there, forcing him to sell at a loss. He turns to piracy, accumulates a vast fortune, and sails contentedly for home. His ship is seized by heavily armed Genoese traders who take him prisoner, and when his captors are shipwrecked, he manages to survive by clinging for dear life to a chest that is floating on the surface of the sea. He is washed up more dead than alive on the island of Corfu, where he discovers that the chest is full of precious jewels. With these he eventually returns home, having succeeded in his original purpose of vastly increasing his wealth.

The story of Landolfo Rufolo is the first in the *Decameron* to be set in the south, and there is no mistaking the tone of nostalgic affection with which Boccaccio describes the Amalfi coast in its opening paragraph. There is also more than a hint of admiration for the spirit of enterprise that has brought prosperity to the numerous merchants who settled in a region familiar to the writer from the days of his youth. The story contains only two characters, Landolfo and the peasant woman who restores him to health after dragging him from the sea off the shore of Corfu. Like most of Boccaccio's characters, neither is developed in any great psychological depth, their personalities emerging fully formed from the events of the narrative. The distinguishing feature of Landolfo is his acquisitiveness, the motivating force behind all of his actions. The narrator focuses attention on the vicissitudes of the chief character, for which the sea is a sort of emblematic leitmotif. The sea is in fact the most important recurrent image in the narratives of the Second Day, playing a prominent role not only in the tale of Landolfo, but also in those of Beritola (II, 6), Alatiel (II, 7) and Paganino (II, 10). It also features briefly in the stories of Andreuccio (II, 5), the Count of Antwerp (II, 8) and Bernabò and Zinevra (II, 9). The image of the sea, ideal for representing the vicissitudes of Fortune, acts as a link between the main theme of the Second Day and the world of commerce that is depicted in so many of the stories.

The sea has other associations. In most, though not all, of the stories containing nautical episodes, the sea forms a conspicuous backdrop to an account of passionate love. This is especially true of the story of Alatiel (II, 7), whose erotic odyssey begins with a shipwreck and proceeds by a series of voyages arranged by six of her nine different lovers to seize for themselves the object of their passionate desires, often with fatal results. The second of her lovers, Marato, is flung overboard by the ship's two Genoese masters who aspire to take his place in her bed. They then engage in a knife duel, in which one is killed and the other severely injured before the ship reaches its port of call. Murderous violence at sea in pursuit of a woman's love is also recorded in the tales of Gerbino (IV, 4) and Cimon (V, 1). Elsewhere, as in the tales of Bartolomea (II, 10) and Gostanza (V, 2), the sea functions as the calm and benign agent for the successful attainment of the heroine's secret ambitions. The depth of Gianni da Procida's love for Restituta (V, 6) is underscored by an oblique reference to the classical myth of Hero and Leander in the introduction to the story, where we are told that Gianni would swim across the stretch of water separating Procida from Ischia if only to gaze ecstatically upon the walls of the house that sheltered his beloved.

In addition to their exploration of the theme of Fortune, their associations with the world of commerce and their abundance of maritime episodes, the stories of the Second Day of the *Decameron* illustrate an aspect of Boccaccio's narrative procedure that has engaged the attention of an outstanding storyteller of more recent times, Alberto Moravia.[76] According to Moravia, a delight in

76 See his essay on Boccaccio in *Man as an End – A Defence of Humanism: Literary, Social and Political Essays*, London, 1965.

weaving tales filled with realistic accounts of adventurous deeds, or
what he calls '*l'estetica dell'avventura*' ('the aesthetics of adventure'), is
the mark of a writer whose personal experience of such matters
derives from the breadth of his reading and the powers of his
imagination. Whether or not one accepts Moravia's characterization
of the author of the *Decameron* as the scholar and man of letters
absorbed at his desk in the vicarious fulfilment of his own desire for
adventure, it is certainly true that Boccaccio explores in unusual
detail the possible twists and turns of a narrative that is so uncompli-
cated in its essentials as to be capable of brief summary in the story's
heading. The account of Alatiel's multiple couplings is a particularly
good example. Another is the famous story of Andreuccio of
Perugia (II, 5), where in the course of a single night the hero is the
unwilling participant in a quite extraordinary series of perilous
adventures. And all the other stories of the Second Day reflect this
feature of Boccaccio's narrative technique, to which some commentators have applied the phrase *ars combinatoria*.

In this connection it is instructive to contrast Boccaccio's treatment of a particular set of circumstances with the way that the same
narrative material is handled by others. The story of the three beds
(IX, 6), retold by Chaucer in *The Reeve's Tale*, is one that had
earlier appeared in at least two of the French *fabliaux*. What
distinguishes Boccaccio's version from the others is the advantage he
takes of one further permutation of the story's basic elements: three
beds and a cot in a darkened room, where at different times during
the night a husband and wife, their nubile daughter, and two young
male lodgers all share their bed by accident or design with more
than one of the others. In Chaucer's version, the tale ends chaotically
with the beating and humiliation of the host, a crooked miller, and
his awareness that his daughter has been seduced. Boccaccio on the
other hand resolves the story to everyone's satisfaction by having
the wife move swiftly into her daughter's bed, from which she
declares that the girl's honour has remained unimpaired, being
supported in her claim by the second lodger's pretence that his
companion has been dreaming.

A classic instance of Boccaccio's delight in telling a complicated,
vivid and dramatic narrative is the story of Pietro Boccamazza and

Agnolella (V, 3), which incidentally mirrors and documents the lawlessness and factional strife prevalent in the Roman countryside during the 'Babylonian Captivity' of the papacy in Avignon. From the initial description of the runaway lovers departing from Rome on horseback to the final account of their marriage and return to the city, the story proceeds via a series of exciting episodes in a manner that foreshadows in rudimentary form the technique adopted by the outstanding narrative poet of the Italian Renaissance, Ludovico Ariosto, in the *Orlando furioso*. Ariosto so arranges the several strands of the narrative as to lead the reader to a climax in one episode, then switching to another, likewise taking that to a moment of crisis, and so on before he eventually returns to an earlier episode to describe what happened next. In the same way, Boccaccio's story proceeds alternately from crisis to crisis in the fortunes of the two main characters. When the lovers take a wrong turning, leading to their being set upon by an armed band, Agnolella escapes into a forest, whilst Pietro is seized and about to be hanged from a tree when his captors are in turn attacked by a second armed band. Pietro flees into the forest, where he spends the whole day in a fruitless search for his beloved before tethering his horse to an oak tree and climbing into its upper branches to preserve himself from being attacked by wild beasts and to await the dawn. The scene switches to the cottage of an elderly couple where Agnolella has taken refuge, but the cottage is invaded by yet another armed band. She hides under a pile of straw, narrowly avoiding death from a spear thrown carelessly into the straw by one of the brigands. Once they have left, she is led to safety in a nearby castle. The narrator then returns to the plight of Pietro, still perched in the branches of the oak, from which he witnesses the horrifying spectacle of his horse being devoured by a pack of wolves. Finally he too makes his way to the castle, where the couple are reunited and married before returning to Rome.

The tales of adventure are frequently spiced with humour, sometimes in the manner of the telling, at other times in the narrative itself. In the account of Landolfo Rufolo's ordeal in the sea, he is described as 'having nothing to eat and far more to drink than he would have wished', and by the following day he 'had almost turned into a sponge'. The story of Andreuccio (II, 5), set in Naples, includes two splendid comic vignettes of minor characters, to which attention was drawn by Benedetto Croce, himself a Neapolitan, in a well-known essay.[77] The first occurs when the hapless Andreuccio, having fallen from an upper storey of the courtesan's house in the middle of the night into an open sewer, repeatedly hammers on her door to be re-admitted. Various neighbours, awakened by the noise, fling open their windows and advise him to go away, whereupon the woman's bully sticks out his head and asks who is there 'in a low, fierce, spine-chilling growl'. Andreuccio looks up and catches sight of a face which

> . . . clearly belonged to some mighty man or other, who had a thick black beard and was yawning and rubbing his eyes as though he had just been roused from a deep sleep.[78]

Andreuccio's attempt to explain his presence there is cut short by the fearsome-looking newcomer, who showers him with abuse:

> 'I don't know what restrains me from coming down there and giving you the biggest pasting you've ever had in your life, you miserable drunken idiot, making all this racket in the middle of the night and keeping everyone awake.'[79]

Later in the same story, when Andreuccio finds himself imprisoned in a deep tomb with the corpse of a recently dead archbishop, a gang of grave robbers opens the tomb and props up its massive lid. An argument ensues over who should enter the tomb to steal the archbishop's ruby ring, then a priest steps forward, saying

> 'What are you afraid of? Do you think he is going to devour you? Dead men don't eat the living. I will go in myself.'[80]

77 B. Croce, 'La novella di Andreuccio di Perugia', in *Storie e leggende napoletane*, Bari, 1926.

78 '. . . *mostrava di dovere essere un gran bacalare, con una barba nera e folta al volto, e come se del letto e da alto sonno si levasse sbadigliava e stropicciavasi gli occhi.*'

79 '"*Io non so a che io mi tegno che io non vegno là giú, e deati tante bastonate quanto io ti vegga muovere, asino fastidioso e ebriaco che tu dei essere, che questa notte non ci lascerai dormire persona.*"'

80 '"*Che paura avete voi? Credete voi che egli vi manuchi? Li morti non mangian gli uomini: io v'entrerò dentro io.*"'

Fortune traditionally favours the brave, but not in this instance. When the priest lays the upper part of his body on the edge of the tomb and swivels round, ready to descend, Andreuccio stands up and grabs one of his legs, giving the priest the impression that he is about to be dragged inside by the corpse. The priest

> ... no sooner felt this happening than he let out an ear-splitting yell and hurled himself bodily out of the tomb. The rest of the gang were terrified by this turn of events, and, leaving the tomb open, they all started running away as though they were being pursued by ten thousand devils.[81]

The *Decameron*'s rich vein of comic invention, as seen in the story of Andreuccio, is of course one of the reasons for the work's timeless appeal. What is impressive is the breadth and variety of its humorous elements. Not only does Boccaccio invent a host of original comic characters, but he presents them in a broad range of situations, frequently using his mastery of comical discourse to heighten his effects. His outstanding comic creation is the naïve and gullible Florentine painter Calandrino, who appears in no fewer than four separate stories, and whose name has become co-terminous in the Italian language with a simpleton. In VIII, 3, Calandrino is deceived into thinking that he has rendered himself invisible by picking up a magic stone, the heliotrope. In an episode that borders on farce, Calandrino's greedy desire to keep his discovery to himself causes him to remain silent, leaping this way and that in agony as his companions, Bruno and Buffalmacco, pretend that he has left them in the lurch and pelt him with jagged rocks. In VIII, 6, he suffers another indignity, with equally amusing results, by under-going a lie-detector test staged by Bruno and Buffalmacco to prove that he has stolen his own pig. In IX, 3, he is persuaded by his two companions that he is pregnant, and attributes his condition to his wife's fondness for lying on top of him during their lovemaking. In IX, 5, he falls in love with his employer's pretty young mistress, who connives with Bruno and Buffalmacco to land him in a

---

81 'La qual cosa sentendo il prete mise uno strido grandissimo e presto dell'arca si gittò fuori; della qual cosa tutti gli altri spaventati, lasciata l'arca aperta, non altramente a fuggir cominciarono che se da centomila diavoli fosser perseguitati.'

compromising situation where he is discovered and severely beaten by his outraged wife, Monna Tessa.

Boccaccio's Calandrino was the prototype for many of the simpleton characters of Italian Renaissance comedy. It is sometimes claimed that in the *Decameron* he figures in more of the stories than any of the other characters, but that distinction belongs to Calandrino's two companions, Bruno and Buffalmacco, who appear in all four stories involving Calandrino and also in a fifth, the hoodwinking of the gullible physician, Master Simone (VIII, 9). Almost Rabelaisian in tone, the story is unique in the *Decameron* for its constant stream of scatological references, culminating in the dumping of the unfortunate Simone at dead of night in a cesspit. Boccaccio's delight in wordplay, a prominent aspect of the tale's humour, poses serious problems for the translator, especially in Bruno's outrageous catalogue of the exotic, high-born ladies with whom he claims acquaintance, and in Buffalmacco's equally outrageous list of the nobles who form part of the retinue of *la contessa di Civillari,* or the Countess of Cesspool.

The distinctively Florentine flavour of the five stories involving Bruno and Buffalmacco stems mainly from their being placed within specifically Florentine contexts, no opportunity being missed to pinpoint the exact location of particular narrative episodes. By contrast, there is one story, that of Monna Belcolore and the priest of Varlungo (VIII, 2), where the setting in the Florentine countryside (*contado*) is secondary in importance to its dazzling display of Florentine verbal wit. The wordplay here is a vital component of the narrative itself, which moves swiftly along by way of a series of lively and intricately assembled effusions of verbal humour, from the initial description of Monna Belcolore to the equivocal final paragraph, with its account of her eventual conversion to the priest's way of thinking. Florentinisms and double meanings pour forth in a constant stream, and even the names of the characters contribute to the tale's overall comic effect. Apart from Belcolore herself and her slow-witted husband, Bentivegna del Mazzo, the narrative includes a whole gallery of other characters whose sole *raison d'être* is to heighten the humorous effect by the very sound of their odd and at times equivocal Florentine names. And similar considerations apply to the various references to rustic pursuits, such as Belcolore's flair for singing and dancing and the priest's gardening skills that account for the curious presents he sends to the object of his lustful passion. No translation can convey the uniquely Florentine rustic tone of the original text, which is one of the most brilliant examples of humorous writing in medieval literature.

Wordplay of a different order is to be found in the story of Friar Alberto (IV, 2), set in Venice, where the vain and foolish Donna Lisetta is variously referred to, by antonomasia, as *Donna mestola*, *Donna zucca al vento*, *Madama baderla*, and *Donna pocofila*. The conversion of such titles into fairly close English equivalents presents no great difficulty: Lady Numbskull, Lady Bighead, Lady Noodle, Lady Birdbrain. But Boccaccio confronts his translators with the most serious problems of all in the tale of Friar Cipolla (VI, 10), whose lengthy and ingenious sermon is shot through from beginning to end with puns and double meanings. Most of Boccaccio's Italian editors maintain, with some reason, that the catalogue of far-flung places which Cipolla claims to have visited is mainly a list of localities in and around Florence, to which the writer has added a few of his own, such as *Truffia* ('Swindleland'), *Buffia* ('Prankland') and *terra di Menzogna* ('Spoofland'). The present translation dispenses with the possible Florentine associations of the passage. *Truffia* and *Buffia* are converted into Funland and Laughland, and *terra di Menzogna* into Liarland, thus hinting at a possible extension of the friar's globetrotting to include the Baltic region and the Celtic fringe. With further adjustments to Cipolla's exotic place-names, Boccaccio's surrealistic verbal fantasy is to some extent preserved:

> 'So away I went, and after setting out from Venison, I visited the Greek Calends, then rode at a brisk pace through the Kingdom of Algebra and through Bordello, eventually reaching Bedlam, and not long afterwards, almost dying of thirst, I arrived in Sardintinia . . . After crossing the Straits of Penury, I found myself passing through Funland and Laughland, . . . Then I went on to Liarland . . .'[82]

82 'Per la qual cosa messom'io in cammino, di Vinegia partendomi e andandomene per lo Borgo de' Greci e di quindi per lo reame del Garbo cavalcando e per Baldacca, pervenni in Parione, donde, non senza sete, dopo alquanto pervenni in Sardigna . . . Io capitai, passato il Braccio di San Giorgio, in Truffia e in Buffia, . . . e di quindi pervenni in terra di Menzogna . . .'

Difficult as it is to find English equivalents for Cipolla's nonsensical place-names, his account of his dealings with the Patriarch of Jerusalem, Besokindas Tocursemenot (*Nonmiblasmete Sevoipiace*), and the list of sacred relics he claims to have acquired from that venerable dignitary of the Church, place even greater obstacles in the path of Boccaccio's translators. To take a single instance, the relic described by Cipolla as *'una delle coste del Verbum-caro fatti alle finestre'* assumes more curious forms in some of the earlier English translations than the author himself can ever have imagined in his wildest fantasies. The gross error committed by his earliest English translator in the version first published in 1620 ('one of the ribbes of the Verbum Caro, fastened to one of the Windowes') was repeated with monotonous regularity by later translators and editors. In his elegant but archaically worded translation published in 1886, John Payne supplied an absolutely literal translation of Cipolla's relic ('one of the ribs of the Verbum Caro Get-thee-to-the-windows'), but a more recent translator, whether through ignorance, perverseness, or subtle design, calls it, in a version first published in 1930 that is cluttered with similar curiosities, 'a rib of the Verbum Caro made at the factory'.

★　★　★

Apart from Dante's *Commedia,* no work by any Italian writer has been translated so often, either wholly or in part, as the *Decameron.* Quite apart from the twelve separate English or American versions that have been published, there are so many English translations or adaptations of individual stories, or groups of stories, that their total defies accurate computation. And no other Italian writer has supplied English literature with so rich a store of narrative material.

The reasons for Boccaccio's perennial appeal to the English translator or reader are not far to seek, although it is clear that the aura of equivocation surrounding the name of Boccaccio is by no means the most important factor. His earliest translators directed their attention to those tales that remained strictly within the bounds of propriety and afforded the maximum amount of moral uplift to their hearers. The sixteen tales from the *Decameron* included in Painter's *The Palace of Pleasure*, first published in 1566, are carefully selected, and judiciously doctored, to present Boccaccio as a rigid moralist, and it was not until the nineteenth century was drawing to a close that the English reader was first made acquainted with the full range of Boccaccio's narrative versatility. Before the appearance in 1886 of John Payne's magniloquent English version, Boccaccio's taste for the erotic and the profane had been consistently glossed over or toned down in varying degrees by his English translators, so that it would be quite wrong to attribute his enduring popularity to this particular aspect of his work. Boccaccio's gifts as a storyteller, his phenomenal and absolute mastery in a genre of which there are few if any outstanding examples in English literature (a genre which nourishes and sustains other forms of literature such as the drama and narrative poetry), provide a more plausible explanation of his extraordinary *fortuna* in the Anglo-Saxon world.

Nevertheless, when one considers the problems which the *Decameron* poses for the would-be translator, it is perhaps surprising that the task has been attempted so often. On the one hand, there are those long, elaborate, beautifully balanced sentences, with their trailing clusters of dependent clauses, often arranged so as to reproduce the characteristic hendecasyllabic rhythms of Italian classical poetry, and employing all the stylistic devices of medieval rhetoric. On the other hand, one has a whole range of vivid and racy colloquialisms, found more especially in the tales that are set in the more humble milieux of medieval Italy. The variations and complexities of Boccaccio's style and language are limitless, and no translator can ever hope to do them full justice. But because, like Everest, the *Decameron* is there, and because it is inconceivable that a truly satisfactory English translation of this great European prose masterpiece will ever be produced, there will always be someone who is foolhardy enough to attempt the task, even if he is familiar with Dante's sombre warning that 'nothing that is harmonized by the bond of the Muse can be transformed from its own language into another without upsetting all its sweetness and harmony'.[83]

83 '. . . *nulla cosa per legame musaico armonizzata si può dalla sua loquela in altra trasmutare senza rompere tutta la sua dolcezza e armonia*' (*Convivio*, I, vii).

SELECT BIBLIOGRAPHY

The bibliography consists for the most part of books and articles cited in the Introduction and Notes to the present volume. It also includes several additional items that are relevant to further study of Boccaccio and the *Decameron*. For more detailed bibliographical data, the reader is referred to Joseph P. Consoli's splendidly comprehensive and informative *Giovanni Boccaccio: an Annotated Bibliography* (New York, 1992).

A WORKS BY BOCCACCIO

Amorosa visione, bilingual edition, translated by R. Hollander, T. Hampton and M. Frankel, with introduction by V. Branca (Hanover, New Hampshire and London, 1986).

Caccia di Diana, Filocolo, a cura di V. Branca e A. E. Quaglio, in *Tutte le opere*, í (Milan, 1967).

Comedía delle ninfe fiorentine, a cura di A. E. Quaglio, in *Tutte le opere*, II (Milan, 1964).

Corbaccio, a cura di T. Nurmela (Helsinki, 1968).

De casibus virorum illustrium, a cura di P. G. Ricci e V. Zaccaria, in *Tutte le opere*, IX (Milan, 1983).

De mulieribus claris, a cura di V. Zaccaria, in *Tutte le opere*, X (Milan, 1967).

Decameron, a cura di V. Branca, in *Tutte le opere*, IV (Milan, 1976). But see also the edition published in the series Nuova Universale Einaudi (Turin, 1980, 3rd edition 1987), containing updated notes, bibliography and indexes, as well as introductory essays on the *Decameron* and on B.'s life and works.

Elegia di madonna Fiammetta, a cura di C. Salinari e N. Sapegno. In Boccaccio, G., *Decameron, Filocolo, Ameto, Fiammetta*, a cura di E. Bianchi, C. Salinari e N. Sapegno (Milan and Naples, 1952).

Esposizioni sopra la Comedía di Dante, a cura di G. Padoan, in *Tutte le opere*, VI (Milan, 1965).

Filocolo, a cura di A. E. Quaglio, in *Tutte le opere*, I (Milan, 1967)

Filostrato, a cura di V. Branca, in *Tutte le opere*, II (Milan, 1964).

Genealogia deorum gentilium libri, a cura di V. Romano (Bari, 1951).

Ninfale fiesolano, a cura di A. Balduino, in *Tutte le opere*, III (Milan, 1974).

Rime, Caccia di Diana, a cura di V. Branca (Padua, 1958).

Teseida delle nozze di Emilia, a cura di A. Limentani, in *Tutte le opere*, II (Milan, 1964).

Trattatello in laude di Dante, a cura di P. G. Ricci, in *Tutte le opere*, III (Milan, 1974).

B ENGLISH TRANSLATIONS

Ameto (Comedía delle ninfe fiorentine), translated by Judith Serafini–Sauli (New York and London, 1985).

Concerning Famous Women, translated by Guido A. Guarino (reprint, London, 1964) (New Jersey, 1963).

The Corbaccio, translated and edited by Anthony K. Cassell (Urbana and London, 1975).

Diana's Hunt (Caccia di Diana), Boccaccio's First Fiction, translated and edited by A. K. Cassell and V. Kirkham (Philadelphia, 1991).

Eclogues, Latin text with translation by J. L. Smarr (New York and London, 1987).

The Elegy of Madonna Fiammetta, translated by Mariangela Causa-Steindler and Thomas Mauch (Chicago and London, 1990).

Filocolo, translated by David Cheaney and Thomas G. Bergin (New York, 1985).

Havely, Nicholas R., *Chaucer's Boccaccio: Sources of Troilus and the Knight's and Franklin's Tales* (Cambridge, 1980). Contains Havely's prose translation of the *Filostrato*.

Osgood, Charles (editor), *Boccaccio on Poetry, Being the Preface and the Fourteenth and Fifteenth Books of Boccaccio's 'Genealogia Deorum Gentilium'* (reprint, Indianapolis, 1956) (Princeton, 1930).

C BOOKS IN ITALIAN

Almansi, Guido, *Il ciclo della scommessa dal 'Decameron' al 'Cymbeline' di Shakespeare* (Rome, 1976).

Baratto, Mario, *Realtà e stile nel 'Decameron'* (Venice, 1970).

Barbina, Alfredo (editor), *Concordanze del 'Decameron'*, sotto la direzione di Umberto Bosco (2 vols.) (Florence, 1969).

Billanovich, Giuseppe, *Restauri boccacceschi* (Rome, 1947).

Bonomo, Giuseppe, *Scongiuri del popolo siciliano* (Palermo, 1953).

Bosco, Umberto, *Il 'Decameron': Saggio* (Rome, 1929). Of special interest is chapter VIII, 'Il poeta dell'intelligenza', pp. 190–95.

Branca, Vittore, *Boccaccio medievale* (revised edition, Florence, 1996).

Branca, Vittore, *Giovanni Boccaccio, profilo biografico* (Florence, 1977).

Branca, Vittore, *Tradizione delle opere di Giovanni Boccaccio, I, Un primo elenco dei codici e tre studi* (Rome, 1958).

Bruni, Francesco, *Boccaccio, l'invenzione della letteratura mezzana* (Bologna, 1990).

Cavallini, Giorgio, *La decima giornata del 'Decameron'* (Rome, 1980).

Curato, Baldo, *Introduzione al Boccaccio* (Cremona, 1961).

Di Pino, Guido, *La polemica del Boccaccio* (Florence, 1953).

Fido, Franco, *Il regime delle simmetrie imperfette: Studi sul 'Decameron'* (Milan, 1988).

Galletti, Salvatore, *Patologia al 'Decameron'* (Palermo, 1969).

Getto, Giovanni, *Vita di forme e forme di vita nel 'Decameron'* (Turin, 1958).

Giacalone, Giuseppe, *Boccaccio minore e maggiore* (Rome, 1959).

Givens, Azzurra B., *La dottrina d'amore nel Boccaccio* (Messina and Florence, 1968).

Grabher, Carlo, *Boccaccio* (Turin, 1945).

Leone, Giuseppe, *Johannes Utilitatum: Saggio sul 'Decameron'* (second edition, Bologna, 1967).

Moravia, Alberto, *L'uomo come fine e altri saggi* (fifth edition, Milan, 1976).

Muscetta, Carlo, *Boccaccio* (Bari, 1972).

Padoan, Giorgio, *Il Boccaccio, le Muse, il Parnaso e l'Arno* (Florence, 1978).

Russo, Luigi, *Ritratti e disegni storici, serie III* (Bari, 1951).

Sabatini, Francesco, *Napoli angioina: Cultura e società* (Naples, 1975).

Sapegno, Natalino, *Il Trecento* (Milan, 1960).

Trasselli, C., *Sicilia, Levante e Tunisia nei secoli XIV e XV* (Trapani, 1952).

D BOOKS IN ENGLISH

Almansi, Guido, *The Writer as Liar: Narrative Technique in the 'Decameron'* (London and Boston, 1975).

Auerbach, Erich R., *Mimesis: The Representation of Reality in Western Literature*, translated by W. R. Trask (Princeton, 1953). See in particular chapter 9, *Frate Alberto*.

Bergin, Thomas G., *Boccaccio* (New York, 1981).

Caporello-Szykman, Corradina, *The Boccaccian Novella, The Creation and Waning of a Genre* (New York, Bern, Frankfurt-am-Main and Paris, 1990).

Cottino-Jones, Marga, *An Anatomy of Boccaccio's Style* (Naples, 1968).

Cottino-Jones, Marga, *Order From Chaos: Social and Aesthetic Harmonies in Boccaccio's 'Decameron'* (Washington DC, 1982).

Curtius, Ernst Robert, *European Literature and the Latin Middle Ages*, translated by W. R. Trask (Princeton, 1973).

Dombroski, Robert S. (editor), *Critical Perspectives on the 'Decameron'* (London, 1976).

Fisher, J. H. (editor), *The Medieval Literature of Western Europe* (New York, 1966).

Forni, Pier Massimo, *Adventures in Speech: Rhetoric and Narration in Boccaccio's 'Decameron'* (Philadelphia, 1996).

Hastings, Robert, *Nature and Reason in the 'Decameron'* (Manchester, 1975).

Hollander, Robert, *Boccaccio's Two Venuses* (New York, 1977).

Huizinga, Johan, *The Waning of the Middle Ages*, translated by F. Hopman (Harmondsworth, 1955).

Kirkham, Victoria, *The Sign of Reason in Boccaccio's Fiction* (Florence, 1993).

Lee, Arthur Collingwood, *The 'Decameron': Its Sources and Analogues* (reprint, New York, 1967) (London, 1909).

Marcus, Millicent Joy, *An Allegory of Form: Literary Self-consciousness in the 'Decameron'* (Saratoga, California, 1979).

Marino, Lucia, *The 'Decameron' Cornice: Allusion, Allegory, and Iconology* (Ravenna, 1979).

Mazzotta, Giuseppe, *The World at Play in Boccaccio's 'Decameron'* (Princeton, 1986).

Menocal, María Rosa, *Writing in Dante's Cult of Truth: from Borges to Boccaccio* (London, 1991).

Ó Cuilleanáin, Cormac, *Religion and the Clergy in Boccaccio's 'Decameron'* (Rome, 1984).

Olson, G., *Literature as Recreation in the Later Middle Ages* (Ithaca and London, 1982).

Potter, Joy Hambuechen, *Five Frames for the 'Decameron'* (Princeton, 1982).

Scaglione, Aldo D., *Nature and Love in the Late Middle Ages: an Essay on the Cultural Context of the 'Decameron'* (Berkeley and Los Angeles, 1963).

Serafini–Sauli, Judith Powers, *Giovanni Boccaccio* (Boston, 1982).

Smarr, Janet Levarie, *Boccaccio and Fiammetta: the Narrator as Lover* (Urbana, Illinois, 1986).

Tournay, G. (editor), *Boccaccio in Europe* (Proceedings of the Boccaccio Conference, Louvain, December 1975) (Leiden, 1977).

Wallace, David, *Giovanni Boccaccio: 'Decameron'* (Cambridge, 1991).

Watson, Paul F., *The Garden of Love in Tuscan Art of the Early Renaissance* (Philadelphia, 1979).

Whitfield, John Humphreys, *The Barlow Lectures on Dante, 1959* (Cambridge, 1959).

E ARTICLES IN ENGLISH

Blackbourn, B. L., 'The Eighth Story of the Tenth Day of Boccaccio's *Decameron*. An Example of Rhetoric or a Rhetorical Example?', *Italian Quarterly*, XXVII (1986), 5–13.

Cottino-Jones, Marga, 'Magic and Superstition in Boccaccio's *Decameron*', *Italian Quarterly* (Spring, 1975), 5–32.

Durling, Robert M., 'Boccaccio on Interpretation: Guido's Escape (*Decameron*, VI, 9)', in *Dante, Petrarch and Boccaccio: Studies in the Italian Trecento in Honor of Charles S. Singleton*, edited by A. S. Bernardo and A. L. Pellegrini (Binghamton, New York, 1983), 273–304.

Hastings, R., 'To Teach or not to Teach: the Moral Dimension of the *Decameron* Reconsidered', *Italian Studies*, XLIV (1989), 19–40.

Kern, Edith G., 'The Gardens in the *Decameron* Cornice', *PMLA*, LXVI (June, 1951).

Kirkham, Victoria, 'An Allegorically Tempered *Decameron*', *Italica*, 62, 1 (1985), 1–23.

Kirkham, Victoria, 'Boccaccio's Dedication to Women in Love', in *Renaissance Studies in Honor of Craig Hugh Smyth*, edited by A. Morrow, F. Superbi Gioffredi, P. Morselli and E. Borsook (2 vols.) (Florence, 1985), I, 333–43.

Kirkpatrick, Robin, 'Giovanni Boccaccio: the *Decameron*', in *Medieval Literature: The European Inheritance* (New Pelican Guide to English Literature, Vol. 1, Part 2), edited by Boris Ford (Harmondsworth, 1983), 287–300.

McWilliam, G. H., 'On Translating the *Decameron*', in *Essays in Honour of John Humphreys Whitfield*, edited by H. C. Davis, D. G. Rees, J. M. Hatwell and G. W. Slowey (London, 1975), 71–83.

Marcus, Millicent Joy, 'The Sweet New Style Reconsidered: a Gloss on the Tale of Cimone (*Decameron*, V, 1)', *Italian Quarterly*, 81 (1980), 5–16.

Marcus, Millicent Joy, 'Misogyny as Misreading: a Gloss on *Decameron* VIII, 7', *Stanford Italian Review*, 4, 1 (1984), 23–40.

Thrall, W. F., '*Cymbeline*, Boccaccio, and the Wager Story in England', *Studies in Philology*, XXVIII, October (1931), 107–19.

Usher, J., 'Simona and Pasquino: "Cur moriatur homo cui salvia crescit in horto?"', *Modern Language Notes*, 106, 1–14.

Usher, J., 'Boccaccio's "Ars moriendi" in the *Decameron*', *Modern Language Review*, 81 (1986), 621–32.

Usher, J., 'The Fortune of "Fortuna" in Salviati's "rassettura" of the *Decameron*', in *Renaissance and Other Studies: Essays Presented to Peter M. Brown*, edited by Eileen D. Millar (Glasgow, 1988), 210–22.

Usher, J., 'Rhetorical and Narrative Strategies in Boccaccio's Translation of the *Comœdia Lydiae*', *Modern Language Review*, 84, 2 (April 1989), 337–44.

Usher, J., 'Frame and Novella Gardens in Boccaccio's *Decameron*', *Medium Aevum*, 58, 2 (1989), 274–85.

Usher, J., 'Frate Cipolla's *Ars praedicandi* or a "récit du discours" in Boccaccio', *Modern Language Review*, 88, 2 (April 1993), 321–36.

Watson, Paul F., 'On Seeing Guido Cavalcanti and the Houses of the Dead', *Studi sul Boccaccio*, XVIII (1989), 301–18.

F ARTICLES IN ITALIAN

Balduino, Armando, 'Divagazioni sulla ballata di Mico da Siena (*Decameron*, X 7)', *Studi sul Boccaccio*, 12 (1980), 47–69.

Barbi, Michelle, 'Il "sabato inglese" nell'antica Firenze', *Pan*, III, 8 (1 agosto 1935), 598–602.

Carrai, Stefano, 'Un musico del tardo Duecento (Mino d'Arezzo, in Nicolò de' Rossi e nel Boccaccio', *Studi sul Boccaccio*, 12 (1980), 39–46.

Chiecchi, G., Review of F. Bruni: *Boccaccio: L'invenzione della letteratura mezzana*, *Lettere italiane*, 43 (1991), 116–21.

Croce, Benedetto, 'La novella di Andreuccio di Perugia', in *Storie e leggende napoletane* (Bari, 1926).

Ferreri, R., 'Rito battesimale e comparatico nelle novelle senesi della vii giornata', *Studi sul Boccaccio*, 16 (1987), 307–14.

Grassi, C., 'Di Lippo Topo presunto pittore', *Storia della letteratura italiana*, 168 (1991), 271–3.

Levi, G. A., 'Sconcezze quattrocentesche nel Trecento', *La Nuova Italia*, IV (1933).

Mazzarino, A., 'Il basilico di Lisabetta', *Nuovi Annali della Facoltà di Magistero di Messina*, II, (1984).

Pertile, L., 'Dante, Boccaccio e l'intelligenza', *Italian Studies*, 43 (1988), 60–74.

G OTHER RELEVANT WORKS

Anon., *Gesta Romanorum: or, Entertaining Moral Stories*, translated by the

Rev. Charles Swan, revised and corrected by Wynnard Hooper (London, 1891). Swan's translation was originally published in London in 1824.

The Panchatantra, translated from the Sanskrit by Arthur W. Ryder (Chicago, 1964).

Ambrose, Saint, *Hexameron, Paradise, and Cain and Abel*, translated by John J. Savage (New York, 1961).

Andreas Capellanus, *The Art of Courtly Love*, introduced and translated by John Jay Parry (reprint, New York, 1970) (New York, 1941).

Apuleius, Lucius, *The Golden Ass*, translated by W. Adlington, revised by S. Gaselee (reprint, Cambridge, Massachusetts and London, 1947) (New York, 1915).

Bidpai, *Kalila and Dimna*, selected tales retold by Ramsay Wood, illustrated by Margaret Kilrenny (New York, 1980).

Chaucer, Geoffrey, *The Works of Geoffrey Chaucer*, edited by Fred N. Robinson (Boston, 1957).

Dante Alighieri, *La divina commedia* (3 vols.) a cura di N. Sapegno (Florence, 1955).

Dante Alighieri, *The Banquet*, translated with an introduction and notes by Christopher Ryan (Saratoga, California, 1989).

Jean de Meung and Guillaume de Lorris, *Le Roman de la Rose* (5 vols.) (Paris, 1914–24).

Kalidasa, *Sakuntala*, translated by Michael Coulson, in *Three Sanskrit Plays* (Harmondsworth, 1981).

Novellino e Conti del Duecento, a cura di Sebastiano Lo Nigro (Turin, 1963).

Ovid (Publius Ovidius Naso), *The Art of Love and Other Poems*, edited and translated by J. H. Mozley (Cambridge, Massachusetts and London, 1962).

Petrarca Francesco, *Petrarch's Lyric Poems*, translated and edited by Robert M. Durling (Italian text of the *Canzoniere* and *Rime sparse*, with facing English translation) (Cambridge, Massachusetts, 1976).

Sacchetti, Franco, *Il trecentonovelle*, in *Opere*, a cura di Aldo Borlenghi (Milan, 1957).

The Travels of Marco Polo, translated by Ronald Latham (Harmondsworth, 1958).

Villani, Giovanni, *Cronica di Giovanni Villani a miglior lezione ridotta* (3 vols.) (reprint, Rome, 1980) (Florence, 1823).

Here begins the book called Decameron,[1] *otherwise known as Prince Galahalt, wherein are contained a hundred stories, told in ten days by seven ladies and three young men.*

PROLOGUE

To take pity[2] on people in distress is a human quality which every man and woman should possess, but it is especially requisite in those who have once needed comfort, and found it in others. I number myself as one of these, because if ever anyone required or appreciated comfort, or indeed derived pleasure therefrom, I was that person. For from my earliest youth until the present day, I have been inflamed beyond measure with a most lofty and noble love,[3] far loftier and nobler than might perhaps be thought proper, were I to describe it, in a person of my humble condition. And although people of good judgement, to whose notice it had come, praised me for it and rated me much higher in their esteem, nevertheless it was exceedingly difficult for me to endure. The reason, I hasten to add, was not the cruelty of my lady-love, but the immoderate passion engendered within my mind by a craving that was ill-restrained. This, since it would allow me no proper respite, often caused me an inordinate amount of distress. But in my anguish I have on occasion derived much relief from the agreeable conversation and the admirable expressions of sympathy offered by friends, without which I am firmly convinced that I should have perished. However, the One who is infinite decreed by immutable law that all earthly things should come to an end. And it pleased Him that this love of mine, whose warmth exceeded all others, and which had stood firm and unyielding against all the pressures of good intention, helpful advice, and the risk of danger and open scandal, should in the course of time diminish of its own accord. So that now, all that is left of it in my mind is the delectable feeling which Love habitually reserves for those who refrain from venturing too far upon its deepest waters. And thus what was once a source of pain has now become, having shed all discomfort, an abiding sensation of pleasure.

But though the pain has ceased, I still preserve a clear recollection of the kindnesses I received in the past from people who, prompted by feelings of goodwill towards me, showed a concern for my sufferings. This memory will never, I think, fade for as long as I live. And since it is my conviction that gratitude, of all the virtues, is most highly to be commended and its opposite condemned, I have resolved, in order not to appear ungrateful, to employ what modest talents I possess in making restitution for what I have received. Thus, now that I can claim to have achieved my freedom, I intend to offer some solace, if not to those who assisted me (since their good sense or good fortune will perhaps render such a gift superfluous), at least to those who stand in need of it. And even though my support, or if you prefer, my encouragement, may seem very slight (as indeed it is) to the people concerned, I feel none the less that it should for preference be directed where it seems to be most needed, because that is the quarter in which it will be more effective and, at the same time, more readily welcomed.

And who will deny that such encouragement, however small, should much rather be offered to the charming ladies than to the men? For the ladies, out of fear or shame, conceal the flames of passion within their fragile breasts, and a hidden love is far more potent than one which is worn on the sleeve, as everyone knows who has had experience of these matters. Moreover they are forced to follow the whims, fancies and dictates of their fathers, mothers, brothers and husbands, so that they spend most of their time cooped up within the narrow confines of their rooms, where they sit in apparent idleness, wishing one thing and at the same time wishing its opposite, and reflecting on various matters, which cannot possibly always be pleasant to contemplate. And if, in the course of their meditations, their minds should be invaded by melancholy arising out of the flames of longing, it will inevitably take root there and make them suffer greatly, unless it be dislodged by new interests. Besides which, their powers of endurance are considerably weaker than those that men possess.

When men are in love, they are not affected in this way, as we can see quite plainly. They, whenever they are weighed down by melancholy or ponderous thoughts, have many ways of relieving or expelling them. For if they wish, they can always walk abroad, see and hear many things, go fowling, hunting, fishing, riding and gambling, or attend to their business affairs. Each of these pursuits has the power of engaging men's minds, either wholly or in part, and diverting them from their gloomy meditations, at least for a certain period: after which, some form of consolation will ensue, or the affliction will grow less intense.

So in order that I may to some extent repair the omissions of Fortune, which (as we may see in the case of the more delicate sex) was always more sparing of support wherever natural strength was more deficient, I intend to provide succour and diversion for the ladies, but only for those who are in love, since the others can make do with their needles, their reels and their spindles. I shall narrate a hundred stories or fables or parables or histories[4] or whatever you choose to call them, recited in ten days by a worthy band of seven ladies and three young men, who assembled together during the plague which recently took such heavy toll of life. And I shall also include some songs, which these seven ladies sang for their mutual amusement.

In these tales will be found a variety of love adventures, bitter as well as pleasing, and other exciting incidents, which took place in both ancient and modern times. In reading them, the aforesaid ladies will be able to derive, not only pleasure from the entertaining matters therein set forth, but also some useful advice. For they will learn to recognize what should be avoided and likewise what should be pursued, and these things can only lead, in my opinion, to the removal of their affliction. If this should happen (and may God grant that it should), let them give thanks to Love, which, in freeing me from its bonds, has granted me the power of making provision for their pleasures.

FIRST DAY

Here begins the First Day of the Decameron, *wherein first of all the author explains the circumstances in which certain persons, who presently make their appearance, were induced to meet for the purpose of conversing together, after which, under the rule of* Pampinea, *each of them speaks on the subject they find most congenial.*

Whenever, fairest ladies, I pause to consider how compassionate you all are by nature, I invariably become aware that the present work will seem to you to possess an irksome and ponderous opening. For it carries at its head the painful memory of the deadly havoc wrought by the recent plague, which brought so much heartache and misery to those who witnessed, or had experience of it. But I do not want you to be deterred, for this reason, from reading any further, on the assumption that you are to be subjected, as you read, to an endless torrent of tears and sobbing. You will be affected no differently by this grim beginning than walkers confronted by a steep and rugged hill, beyond which there lies a beautiful and delectable plain. The degree of pleasure they derive from the latter will correspond directly to the difficulty of the climb and the descent. And just as the end of mirth is heaviness,[1] so sorrows are dispersed by the advent of joy.

This brief unpleasantness (I call it brief, inasmuch as it is contained within few words) is quickly followed by the sweetness and the pleasure which I have already promised you, and which, unless you were told in advance, you would not perhaps be expecting to find after such a beginning as this. Believe me, if I could decently have taken you whither I desire by some other route, rather than along a path so difficult as this, I would gladly have done so. But since it is impossible without this memoir to show the origin of the events you will read about later, I really have no alternative but to address myself to its composition.

I say, then, that the sum of thirteen hundred and forty-eight years had elapsed since the fruitful Incarnation of the Son of God, when the noble city of Florence, which for its great beauty excels all others in Italy, was visited by the deadly pestilence.[2] Some say that it descended upon the human race through the influence of the heavenly bodies, others that it was a punishment signifying God's righteous anger at our iniquitous way of life. But whatever its cause, it had originated some years earlier in the East, where it had claimed countless lives before it unhappily spread westward, growing in strength as it swept relentlessly on from one place to the next.

In the face of its onrush, all the wisdom and ingenuity of man were unavailing. Large quantities of refuse were cleared out of the city by officials specially appointed for the purpose, all sick persons were forbidden entry, and numerous instructions were issued for safeguarding the people's health, but all to no avail. Nor were the countless petitions humbly directed to God by the pious, whether by means of formal processions or in all other ways, any less ineffectual. For in the early spring of the year we have mentioned, the plague began, in a terrifying and extraordinary manner, to make its disastrous effects apparent. It did not take the form it had assumed in the East, where if anyone bled from the nose it was an obvious portent of certain death. On the contrary, its earliest symptom, in men and women alike, was the appearance of certain swellings in the groin or the armpit, some of which were egg-shaped whilst others were roughly the size of the common apple. Sometimes the swellings were large, sometimes not so large, and they were referred to by the populace as *gavòccioli*. From the two areas already mentioned, this deadly *gavòcciolo* would begin to spread, and within a short time it would appear at random all over the body. Later on, the symptoms of the disease changed, and many people began to find dark blotches and bruises on their arms, thighs, and other parts of the body, sometimes large and few in number, at other times tiny and closely spaced. These, to anyone unfortunate enough to contract them, were just as infallible a sign that he would die as the *gavòcciolo* had been earlier, and as indeed it still was.

Against these maladies, it seemed that all the advice of physicians and all the power of medicine were profitless and unavailing.

Perhaps the nature of the illness was such that it allowed no remedy: or perhaps those people who were treating the illness (whose numbers had increased enormously because the ranks of the qualified were invaded by people, both men and women, who had never received any training in medicine), being ignorant of its causes, were not prescribing the appropriate cure. At all events, few of those who caught it ever recovered, and in most cases death occurred within three days from the appearance of the symptoms we have described, some people dying more rapidly than others, the majority without any fever or other complications.

But what made this pestilence even more severe was that whenever those suffering from it mixed with people who were still unaffected, it would rush upon these with the speed of a fire racing through dry or oily substances that happened to come within its reach. Nor was this the full extent of its evil, for not only did it infect healthy persons who conversed or had any dealings with the sick, making them ill or visiting an equally horrible death upon them, but it also seemed to transfer the sickness to anyone touching the clothes or other objects which had been handled or used by its victims.

It is a remarkable story that I have to relate. And were it not for the fact that I am one of many people who saw it with their own eyes, I would scarcely dare to believe it, let alone commit it to paper, even though I had heard it from a person whose word I could trust. The plague I have been describing was of so contagious a nature that very often it visibly did more than simply pass from one person to another. In other words, whenever an animal other than a human being touched anything belonging to a person who had been stricken or exterminated by the disease, it not only caught the sickness, but died from it almost at once. To all of this, as I have just said, my own eyes bore witness on more than one occasion. One day, for instance, the rags of a pauper who had died from the disease were thrown into the street, where they attracted the attention of two pigs. In their wonted fashion, the pigs first of all gave the rags a thorough mauling with their snouts, after which they took them between their teeth and shook them against their cheeks. And within a short time they began to writhe as though they had been poisoned, then they both dropped dead to the ground, spread-eagled upon the rags that had brought about their undoing.

These things, and many others of a similar or even worse nature, caused various fears and fantasies to take root in the minds of those who were still alive and well. And almost without exception, they took a single and very inhuman precaution, namely to avoid or run away from the sick and their belongings, by which means they all thought that their own health would be preserved.

Some people were of the opinion that a sober and abstemious mode of living considerably reduced the risk of infection. They therefore formed themselves into groups and lived in isolation from everyone else. Having withdrawn to a comfortable abode where there were no sick persons, they locked themselves in and settled down to a peaceable existence, consuming modest quantities of delicate foods and precious wines and avoiding all excesses. They refrained from speaking to outsiders, refused to receive news of the dead or the sick, and entertained themselves with music and whatever other amusements they were able to devise.

Others took the opposite view, and maintained that an infallible way of warding off this appalling evil was to drink heavily, enjoy life to the full, go round singing and merrymaking, gratify all of one's cravings whenever the opportunity offered, and shrug the whole thing off as one enormous joke. Moreover, they practised what they preached to the best of their ability, for they would visit one tavern after another, drinking all day and night to immoderate excess; or alternatively (and this was their more frequent custom), they would do their drinking in various private houses, but only in the ones where the conversation was restricted to subjects that were pleasant or entertaining. Such places were easy to find, for people behaved as though their days were numbered, and treated their belongings and their own persons with equal abandon. Hence most houses had become common property, and any passing stranger could make himself at home as naturally as though he were the rightful owner. But for all their riotous manner of living, these people always took good care to avoid any contact with the sick.

In the face of so much affliction and misery, all respect for the laws of God and man had virtually broken down and been extinguished in our city. For like everybody else, those ministers and executors of the laws who were not either dead or ill were left with so few subordinates that they were unable to discharge any of their duties. Hence everyone was free to behave as he pleased.

There were many other people who steered a middle course between the two already mentioned, neither restricting their diet to the same degree as the first group, nor indulging so freely as the second in drinking and other forms of wantonness, but simply doing no more than satisfy their appetite. Instead of incarcerating themselves, these people moved about freely, holding in their hands a posy of flowers, or fragrant herbs, or one of a wide range of spices, which they applied at frequent intervals to their nostrils, thinking it an excellent idea to fortify the brain with smells of that particular sort; for the stench of dead bodies, sickness, and medicines seemed to fill and pollute the whole of the atmosphere.

Some people, pursuing what was possibly the safer alternative, callously maintained that there was no better or more efficacious remedy against a plague than to run away from it. Swayed by this argument, and sparing no thought for anyone but themselves, large numbers of men and women abandoned their city, their homes, their relatives, their estates and their belongings, and headed for the countryside, either in Florentine territory or, better still, abroad. It was as though they imagined that the wrath of God would not unleash this plague against men for their iniquities irrespective of where they happened to be, but would only be aroused against those who found themselves within the city walls; or possibly they assumed that the whole of the population would be exterminated and that the city's last hour had come.

Of the people who held these various opinions, not all of them died. Nor, however, did they all survive. On the contrary, many of each different persuasion fell ill here, there, and everywhere, and having themselves, when they were fit and well, set an example to those who were as yet unaffected, they languished away with virtually no one to nurse them. It was not merely a question of one citizen avoiding another, and of people almost invariably neglecting their neighbours and rarely or never visiting their relatives, addressing them only from a distance; this scourge had implanted so great a terror in the hearts of men and women that brothers abandoned brothers, uncles their nephews, sisters their brothers, and in many cases wives deserted their husbands. But even worse, and almost incredible, was the fact that fathers and mothers refused to nurse and assist their own children, as though they did not belong to them.

Hence the countless numbers of people who fell ill, both male and female, were entirely dependent upon either the charity of friends (who were few and far between) or the greed of servants, who remained in short supply despite the attraction of high wages out of all proportion to the services they performed. Furthermore, these latter were men and women of coarse intellect and the majority were unused to such duties, and they did little more than hand things to the invalid when asked to do so and watch over him when he was dying. And in performing this kind of service, they frequently lost their lives as well as their earnings.

As a result of this wholesale desertion of the sick by neighbours, relatives and friends, and in view of the scarcity of servants, there grew up a practice almost never previously heard of, whereby when a woman fell ill, no matter how gracious or beautiful or gently bred she might be, she raised no objection to being attended by a male servant, whether he was young or not. Nor did she have any scruples about showing him every part of her body as freely as she would have displayed it to a woman, provided that the nature of her infirmity required her to do so; and this explains why those women who recovered were possibly less chaste in the period that followed.

Moreover a great many people died who would perhaps have survived had they received some assistance. And hence, what with the lack of appropriate means for tending the sick, and the virulence of the plague, the number of deaths reported in the city whether by day or by night was so enormous that it astonished all who heard tell of it, to say nothing of the people who actually witnessed the carnage. And it was perhaps inevitable that among the citizens who survived there arose certain customs that were quite contrary to established tradition.

It had once been customary, as it is again nowadays, for the women relatives and neighbours of a dead man to assemble in his house in order to mourn in the company of the women who had been closest to him; moreover his kinsfolk would forgather in front of his house along with his neighbours and various other citizens, and there would be a contingent of priests, whose numbers varied according to the quality of the deceased; his body would be taken thence to the church in which he had wanted to be buried, being borne on the shoulders of his peers amidst the funeral pomp of candles and dirges. But as the ferocity of the plague began to mount, this practice all but disappeared entirely and was replaced by different customs. For not only did people die without having many women about them, but a great number departed this life without anyone at all to witness their going. Few indeed were those to whom the lamentations and bitter tears of their relatives were accorded; on the contrary, more often than not bereavement was the signal for laughter and witticisms and general jollification – the art of which the women, having for the most part suppressed their feminine concern for the salvation of the souls of the dead, had learned to perfection. Moreover it was rare for the bodies of the dead to be accompanied by more than ten or twelve neighbours to the church, nor were they borne on the shoulders of worthy and honest citizens, but by a kind of gravedigging fraternity, newly come into being and drawn from the lower orders of society. These people assumed the title of sexton, and demanded a fat fee for their services, which consisted in taking up the coffin and hauling it swiftly away, not to the church specified by the dead man in his will, but usually to the nearest at hand. They would be preceded by a group of four or six clerics, who between them carried one or two candles at most, and sometimes none at all. Nor did the priests go to the trouble of pronouncing solemn and lengthy funeral rites, but, with the aid of these so-called sextons, they hastily lowered the body into the nearest empty grave they could find.

As for the common people and a large proportion of the bourgeoisie, they presented a much more pathetic spectacle, for the majority of them were constrained, either by their poverty or the hope of survival, to remain in their houses. Being confined to their own parts of the city, they fell ill daily in their thousands, and since they had no one to assist them or attend to their needs, they inevitably perished almost without exception. Many dropped dead in the open streets, both by day and by night, whilst a great many others, though dying in their own houses, drew their neighbours' attention to the fact more by the smell of their rotting corpses than by any other means. And what with these, and the others who were dying all over the city, bodies were here, there and everywhere.

Whenever people died, their neighbours nearly always followed a single, set routine, prompted as much by their fear of being contaminated by the decaying corpse as by any charitable feelings they may have entertained towards the deceased. Either on their own, or with the assistance of bearers whenever these were to be had, they extracted the bodies of the dead from their houses and left them lying outside their front doors, where anyone going about the streets, especially in the early morning, could have observed countless numbers of them. Funeral biers would then be sent for, upon which the dead were taken away, though there were some who, for lack of biers, were carried off on plain boards. It was by no means rare for more than one of these biers to be seen with two or three bodies upon it at a time; on the contrary, many were seen to contain a husband and wife, two or three brothers and sisters, a father and son, or some other pair of close relatives. And times without number it happened that two priests would be on their way to bury someone, holding a cross before them, only to find that bearers carrying three or four additional biers would fall in behind them; so that whereas the priests had thought they had only one burial to attend to, they in fact had six or seven, and sometimes more. Even in these circumstances, however, there were no tears or candles or mourners to honour the dead; in fact, no more respect was accorded to dead people than would nowadays be shown towards dead goats. For it was quite apparent that the one thing which, in normal times, no wise man had ever learned to accept with patient resignation (even though it struck so seldom and unobtrusively), had now been brought home to the feeble-minded as well, but the scale of the calamity caused them to regard it with indifference.

Such was the multitude of corpses (of which further consignments

were arriving every day and almost by the hour at each of the
churches), that there was not sufficient consecrated ground for them
to be buried in, especially if each was to have its own plot in
accordance with long-established custom. So when all the graves
were full, huge trenches were excavated in the churchyards, into
which new arrivals were placed in their hundreds, stowed tier upon
tier like ships' cargo, each layer of corpses being covered over with
a thin layer of soil till the trench was filled to the top.

But rather than describe in elaborate detail the calamities we
experienced in the city at that time, I must mention that, whilst an
ill wind was blowing through Florence itself, the surrounding
region was no less badly affected. In the fortified towns, conditions
were similar to those in the city itself on a minor scale; but in the
scattered hamlets and the countryside proper, the poor unfortunate
peasants and their families had no physicians or servants whatever to
assist them, and collapsed by the wayside, in their fields, and in their
cottages at all hours of the day and night, dying more like animals
than human beings. Like the townspeople, they too grew apathetic
in their ways, disregarded their affairs, and neglected their possessions. Moreover they all behaved as though each day was to be their
last, and far from making provision for the future by tilling their
lands, tending their flocks, and adding to their previous labours,
they tried in every way they could think of to squander the assets
already in their possession. Thus it came about that oxen, asses,
sheep, goats, pigs, chickens, and even dogs (for all their deep fidelity
to man) were driven away and allowed to roam freely through the
fields, where the crops lay abandoned and had not even been
reaped, let alone gathered in. And after a whole day's feasting,
many of these animals, as though possessing the power of reason,
would return glutted in the evening to their own quarters, without
any shepherd to guide them.

But let us leave the countryside and return to the city. What
more remains to be said, except that the cruelty of heaven (and
possibly, in some measure, also that of man) was so immense and so
devastating that between March and July of the year in question,
what with the fury of the pestilence and the fact that so many of the
sick were inadequately cared for or abandoned in their hour of need

because the healthy were too terrified to approach them, it is reliably thought that over a hundred thousand human lives were extinguished within the walls of the city of Florence? Yet before this lethal catastrophe fell upon the city, it is doubtful whether anyone would have guessed it contained so many inhabitants.

Ah, how great a number of splendid palaces, fine houses, and noble dwellings, once filled with retainers, with lords and with ladies, were bereft of all who had lived there, down to the tiniest child! How numerous were the famous families, the vast estates, the notable fortunes, that were seen to be left without a rightful successor! How many gallant gentlemen, fair ladies, and sprightly youths, who would have been judged hale and hearty by Galen, Hippocrates and Aesculapius[3] (to say nothing of others), having breakfasted in the morning with their kinsfolk, acquaintances and friends, supped that same evening with their ancestors in the next world!

The more I reflect upon all this misery, the deeper my sense of personal sorrow; hence I shall refrain from describing those aspects which can suitably be omitted, and proceed to inform you that these were the conditions prevailing in our city, which was by now almost emptied of its inhabitants, when one Tuesday morning (or so I was told by a person whose word can be trusted) seven young ladies[4] were to be found in the venerable church of Santa Maria Novella,[5] which was otherwise almost deserted. They had been attending divine service, and were dressed in mournful attire appropriate to the times. Each was a friend, a neighbour, or a relative of the other six, none was older than twenty-seven or younger than eighteen, and all were intelligent, gently bred, fair to look upon, graceful in bearing, and charmingly unaffected. I could tell you their actual names, but refrain from doing so for a good reason, namely that I would not want any of them to feel embarrassed, at any time in the future, on account of the ensuing stories, all of which they either listened to or narrated themselves. For nowadays, laws relating to pleasure are somewhat restrictive, whereas at that time, for the reasons indicated above, they were exceptionally lax, not only for ladies of their own age but also for much older women. Besides, I have no wish to supply envious tongues, ever ready to censure a laudable way of life, with a chance to besmirch the good name of these worthy ladies with their lewd and filthy gossip. And therefore, so that we may perceive distinctly what each of them had to say, I propose to refer to them by names which are either wholly or partially appropriate to the qualities of each. The first of them, who was also the eldest, we shall call Pampinea, the second Fiammetta, Filomena the third, and the fourth Emilia; then we shall name the fifth Lauretta, and the sixth Neifile, whilst to the last, not without reason, we shall give the name of Elissa.

Without prior agreement but simply by chance, these seven ladies found themselves sitting, more or less in a circle, in one part of the church, reciting their paternosters. Eventually, they left off and heaved a great many sighs, after which they began to talk among themselves on various different aspects of the times through which they were passing. But after a little while, they all fell silent except for Pampinea, who said:

'Dear ladies, you will often have heard it affirmed, as I have, that no man does injury to another in exercising his lawful rights. Every person born into this world has a natural right to sustain, preserve, and defend his own life to the best of his ability – a right so freely acknowledged that men have sometimes killed others in self-defence, and no blame whatever has attached to their actions. Now, if this is permitted by the laws, upon whose prompt application all mortal creatures depend for their well-being, how can it possibly be wrong, seeing that it harms no one, for us or anyone else to do all in our power to preserve our lives? If I pause to consider what we have been doing this morning, and what we have done on several mornings in the past, if I reflect on the nature and subject of our conversation, I realize, just as you also must realize, that each of us is apprehensive on her own account. This does not surprise me in the least, but what does greatly surprise me (seeing that each of us has the natural feelings of a woman) is that we do nothing to requite ourselves against the thing of which we are all so justly afraid.

'Here we linger for no other purpose, or so it seems to me, than to count the number of corpses being taken to burial, or to hear whether the friars of the church, very few of whom are left, chant their offices at the appropriate hours, or to exhibit the quality and quantity of our sorrows, by means of the clothes we are wearing, to all those whom we meet in this place. And if we go outside, we shall see the dead and the sick being carried hither and thither, or we shall see people, once condemned to exile by the courts for their misdeeds, careering wildly about the streets in open defiance of the law, well knowing that those appointed to enforce it are either dead or dying; or else we shall find ourselves at the mercy of the scum of our city who, having scented our blood, call themselves sextons and go prancing and bustling all over the place, singing bawdy songs that add insult to our injuries. Moreover, all we ever hear is "So-and-so's dead" and "So-and-so's dying"; and if there were anyone left to mourn, the whole place would be filled with sounds of weeping and wailing.

'And if we return to our homes, what happens? I know not whether your own experience is similar to mine, but my house was once full of servants, and now that there is no one left apart from my maid and myself, I am filled with foreboding and feel as if every hair of my head is standing on end. Wherever I go in the house, wherever I pause to rest, I seem to be haunted by the shades of the departed, whose faces no longer appear as I remember them but with strange and horribly twisted expressions that frighten me out of my senses.

'Accordingly, whether I am here in church or out in the streets or sitting at home, I always feel ill at ease, the more so because it seems to me that no one possessing private means and a place to retreat to is left here apart from ourselves. But even if such people are still to be found, they draw no distinction, as I have frequently heard and seen for myself, between what is honest and what is dishonest; and provided only that they are prompted by their appetites, they will do whatever affords them the greatest pleasure, whether by day or by night, alone or in company. It is not only of lay people that I speak, but also of those enclosed in monasteries, who, having convinced themselves that such behaviour is suitable for them and is only unbecoming in others, have broken the rules of obedience and given themselves over to carnal pleasures, thereby thinking to escape, and have turned lascivious and dissolute.

'If this be so (and we plainly perceive that it is), what are we doing here? What are we waiting for? What are we dreaming about? Why do we lag so far behind all the rest of the citizens in providing for our safety? Do we rate ourselves lower than all other women? Or do we suppose that our own lives, unlike those of others, are bound to our bodies by such strong chains that we may ignore all those things which have the power to harm them? In that case we are deluded and mistaken. We have only to recall the names and the condition of the young men and women who have fallen victim to this cruel pestilence, in order to realize clearly the foolishness of such notions.

'And so, lest by pretending to be above such things or by becoming complacent we should succumb to that which we might possibly avoid if we so desired, I would think it an excellent idea (though I do not know whether you would agree with me) for us all to get away from this city, just as many others have done before us, and as indeed they are doing still. We could go and stay together on one of our various country estates, shunning at all costs the lewd practices of our fellow citizens and feasting and merrymaking as best we may without in any way overstepping the bounds of what is reasonable.

'There we shall hear the birds singing, we shall see fresh green hills and plains, fields of corn undulating like the sea, and trees of at least a thousand different species; and we shall have a clearer view of the heavens, which, troubled though they are, do not however deny us their eternal beauties, so much more fair to look upon than the desolate walls of our city. Moreover the country air is much more refreshing, the necessities of life in such a time as this are more abundant, and there are fewer obstacles to contend with. For although the farmworkers are dying there in the same way as the townspeople here in Florence, the spectacle is less harrowing inasmuch as the houses and people are more widely scattered. Besides, unless I am mistaken we shall not be abandoning anyone by going away from here; on the contrary, we may fairly claim that we are the ones who have been abandoned, for our kinsfolk are either dead or fled, and have left us to fend for ourselves in the midst of all this affliction, as though disowning us completely.

'Hence no one can reproach us for taking the course I have

advocated, whereas if we do nothing we shall inevitably be confronted with distress and mourning, and possibly forfeit our lives into the bargain. Let us therefore do as I suggest, taking our maidservants with us and seeing to the dispatch of all the things we shall need. We can move from place to place, spending one day here and another there, pursuing whatever pleasures and entertainments the present times will afford. In this way of life we shall continue until such time as we discover (provided we are spared from early death) the end decreed by Heaven for these terrible events. You must remember, after all, that it is no more unseemly for us to go away and thus preserve our own honour than it is for most other women to remain here and forfeit theirs.'

Having listened to Pampinea's suggestion, the other ladies not only applauded it but were so eager to carry it into effect that they had already begun to work out the details amongst themselves, as though they wanted to rise from their pews and set off without further ado. But Filomena, being more prudent than the others, said:

'Pampinea's arguments, ladies, are most convincing, but we should not follow her advice as hastily as you appear to wish. You must remember that we are all women, and every one of us is sufficiently adult to acknowledge that women, when left to themselves, are not the most rational of creatures, and that without the supervision of some man or other their capacity for getting things done is somewhat restricted. We are fickle, quarrelsome, suspicious, cowardly, and easily frightened; and hence I greatly fear that if we have none but ourselves to guide us, our little band will break up much more swiftly, and with far less credit to ourselves, than would otherwise be the case. We would be well advised to resolve this problem before we depart.'

Then Elissa said:

'It is certainly true that man is the head of woman,[6] and that without a man to guide us it rarely happens that any enterprise of ours is brought to a worthy conclusion. But where are we to find these men? As we all know, most of our own menfolk are dead, and those few that are still alive are fleeing in scattered little groups from that which we too are intent upon avoiding. Yet we cannot very well go away with total strangers, for if self-preservation is our aim, we must so arrange our affairs that wherever we go for our pleasure and repose, no trouble or scandal should come of it.'

Whilst the talk of the ladies was proceeding along these lines, there came into the church three young men,[7] in whom neither the horrors of the times nor the loss of friends or relatives nor concern for their own safety had dampened the flames of love, much less extinguished them completely. I have called them young, but none in fact was less than twenty-five years of age, and the first was called Panfilo, the second Filostrato, and the last Dioneo. Each of them was most agreeable and gently bred, and by way of sweetest solace amid all this turmoil they were seeking to catch a glimpse of their lady-loves, all three of whom, as it happened, were among the seven we have mentioned, whilst some of the remaining four were closely related to one or other of the three. No sooner did they espy the young ladies than they too were espied, whereupon Pampinea smiled and said:

'See how Fortune favours us right from the beginning, in setting before us three young men of courage and intelligence, who will readily act as our guides and servants if we are not too proud to accept them for such duties.'

Then Neifile, whose face had turned all scarlet with confusion since she was the object of one of the youth's affections, said:

'For goodness' sake do take care, Pampinea, of what you are saying! To my certain knowledge, nothing but good can be said of any one of them, and I consider them more than competent to fulfil the office of which we were speaking. I also think they would be good, honest company, not only for us, but for ladies much finer and fairer than ourselves. But since it is perfectly obvious that they are in love with certain of the ladies here present, I am apprehensive lest, by taking them with us, through no fault either of theirs or of our own, we should bring disgrace and censure on ourselves.'

'That is quite beside the point,' said Filomena. 'If I live honestly and my conscience is clear, then people may say whatever they like; God and Truth will take up arms in my defence. Now, if only they were prepared to accompany us, we should truly be able to claim, as Pampinea has said, that Fortune favours our enterprise.'

Filomena's words reassured the other ladies, who not only withdrew their objections but unanimously agreed to call the young men over, explain their intentions, and inquire whether they would be willing to join their expedition. And so, without any further discussion, Pampinea, who was a blood relation to one of the young men, got up and walked towards them. They were standing there gazing at the young ladies, and Pampinea, having offered them a cheerful greeting, told them what they were planning to do, and asked them on behalf of all her companions whether they would be prepared to join them in a spirit of chaste and brotherly affection.

The young men thought at first that she was making mock of them, but when they realized she was speaking in earnest, they gladly agreed to place themselves at the young ladies' disposal. So that there should be no delay in putting the plan into effect, they made provision there and then for the various matters that would have to be attended to before their departure. Meticulous care was taken to see that all necessary preparations were put in hand, supplies were sent on in advance to the place at which they intended to stay, and as dawn was breaking on the morning of the next day, which was a Wednesday, the ladies and the three young men, accompanied by one or two of the maids and all three manservants, set out from the city. And scarcely had they travelled two miles from Florence before they reached the place at which they had agreed to stay.

The spot in question[8] was some distance away from any road, on a small hill that was agreeable to behold for its abundance of shrubs and trees, all bedecked in green leaves. Perched on its summit was a palace, built round a fine, spacious courtyard, and containing loggias, halls, and sleeping apartments, which were not only excellently proportioned but richly embellished with paintings depicting scenes of gaiety. Delectable gardens and meadows lay all around, and there were wells of cool, refreshing water. The cellars were stocked with precious wines, more suited to the palates of connoisseurs than to sedate and respectable ladies. And on their arrival the company discovered, to their no small pleasure, that the place had been cleaned from top to bottom, the beds in the rooms were made up, the whole house was adorned with seasonable flowers of every description, and the floors had been carpeted with rushes.

Soon after reaching the palace, they all sat down, and Dioneo, a youth of matchless charm and readiness of wit, said:

'It is not our foresight, ladies, but rather your own good sense, that has led us to this spot. I know not what you intend to do with your troubles; my own I left inside the city gates when I departed thence a short while ago in your company. Hence you may either prepare to join with me in as much laughter, song and merriment as your sense of decorum will allow, or else you may give me leave to go back for my troubles and live in the afflicted city.'

Pampinea, as though she too had driven away all her troubles, answered him in the same carefree vein.

'There is much sense in what you say, Dioneo,' she replied. 'A merry life should be our aim, since it was for no other reason that we were prompted to run away from the sorrows of the city. However, nothing will last for very long unless it possesses a definite form. And since it was I who led the discussions from which this fair company has come into being, I have given some thought to the continuance of our happiness, and consider it necessary for us to choose a leader, drawn from our own ranks, whom we would honour and obey as our superior, and whose sole concern will be that of devising the means whereby we may pass our time agreeably. But so that none of us will complain that he or she has had no opportunity to experience the burden of responsibility and the pleasure of command associated with sovereign power, I propose that the burden and the honour should be assigned to each of us in turn for a single day. It will be for all of us to decide who is to be our first ruler, after which it will be up to each ruler, when the hour of vespers approaches, to elect his or her successor from among the ladies and gentlemen present. The person chosen to govern will be at liberty to make whatever arrangements he likes for the period covered by his rule, and to prescribe the place and the manner in which we are to live.'

Pampinea's proposal was greatly to everyone's liking, and they unanimously elected her as their queen for the first day, whereupon Filomena quickly ran over to a laurel bush, for she had frequently heard it said that laurel leaves were especially worthy of veneration and that they conferred great honour upon those people of merit who were crowned with them. Having plucked a few of its shoots, she fashioned them into a splendid and venerable garland, which she set upon Pampinea's brow, and which thenceforth became the outward symbol of sovereign power and authority to all the members of the company, for as long as they remained together.

Upon her election as their queen, Pampinea summoned the servants of the three young men to appear before her together with their own maidservants, who were four in number. And having called upon everyone to be silent, she said:

'So that I may begin by setting you all a good example, through which, proceeding from good to better, our company will be enabled to live an ordered and agreeable existence for as long as we choose to remain together, I first of all appoint Dioneo's manservant, Parmeno,[9] as my steward, and to him I commit the management and care of our household, together with all that appertains to the service of the hall. I desire that Panfilo's servant, Sirisco, should act as our buyer and treasurer, and carry out the instructions of Parmeno. As well as attending to the needs of Filostrato, Tindaro will look after the other two gentlemen in their rooms whenever their own manservants are prevented by their offices from performing such duties. My own maidservant, Misia, will be employed full-time in the kitchen along with Filomena's maidservant, Licisca, and they will prepare with diligence whatever dishes are prescribed by Parmeno. Chimera and Stratilia, the servants of Lauretta and Fiammetta, are required to act as chambermaids to all the ladies, as well as seeing that the places we frequent are neatly and tidily maintained. And unless they wish to incur our royal displeasure, we desire and command that each and every one of the servants should take good care, no matter what they should hear or observe in their comings and goings, to bring us no tidings of the world outside these walls unless they are tidings of happiness.'

Her orders thus summarily given, and commended by all her companions, she rose gaily to her feet, and said:

'There are gardens here, and meadows, and other places of great charm and beauty, through which we may now wander in search of our amusement, each of us being free to do whatever he pleases. But on the stroke of tierce,[10] let us all return to this spot, so that we may breakfast together in the shade.'

The merry company having thus been dismissed by their newly elected queen, the young men and their fair companions sauntered slowly through a garden, conversing on pleasant topics, weaving fair garlands for each other from the leaves of various trees, and singing songs of love.

After spending as much time there as the queen had allotted them, they returned to the house to find that Parmeno had made a zealous beginning to his duties, for as they entered the hall on the ground floor, they saw the tables ready laid, with pure white tablecloths and with goblets shining bright as silver, whilst the whole room was decorated with broom blossom. At the queen's behest, they rinsed their hands in water, then seated themselves in the places to which Parmeno had assigned them.

Dishes, daintily prepared, were brought in, excellent wines were at hand, and without a sound the three manservants promptly began to wait upon them. Everyone was delighted that these things had been so charmingly and efficiently arranged, and during the meal there was pleasant talk and merry laughter from all sides. Afterwards, the tables were cleared, and the queen sent for musical instruments so that one or two of their number, well versed in music, could play and sing, whilst the rest, ladies and gentlemen alike, could dance a *carole*. At the queen's request, Dioneo took a lute and Fiammetta a viol, and they struck up a melodious tune, whereupon the queen, having sent the servants off to eat, formed a ring with the other ladies and the two young men, and sedately began to dance. And when the dance was over, they sang a number of gay and charming little songs.

In this fashion they continued until the queen decided that the time had come for them to retire to rest, whereupon she dismissed the whole company. The young men went away to their rooms, which were separated from those of the ladies, and found that, like the hall, they too were full of flowers, and that their beds were neatly made. The ladies made a similar discovery in theirs, and, having undressed, they lay down to rest.

The queen rose shortly after nones,[11] and caused the other ladies to be roused, as also the young men, declaring it was harmful to sleep too much during the day. They therefore betook themselves to a meadow, where the grass, being protected from the heat of the sun, grew thick and green, and where, perceiving that a gentle breeze was stirring, the queen suggested that they should all sit on the green grass in a circle. And when they were seated, she addressed them as follows:

'As you can see, the sun is high in the sky, it is very hot, and all is silent except for the cicadas in the olive-trees. For the moment, it would surely be foolish of us to venture abroad, this being such a cool and pleasant spot in which to linger. Besides, as you will observe, there are chessboards and other games here, and so we are free to amuse ourselves in whatever way we please. But if you were to follow my advice, this hotter part of the day would be spent, not in playing games (which inevitably bring anxiety to one of the players, without offering very much pleasure either to his opponent or to the spectators), but in telling stories – an activity that may afford some amusement both to the narrator and to the company at large. By the time each one of you has narrated a little tale of his own or her own, the sun will be setting, the heat will have abated, and we shall be able to go and amuse ourselves wherever you choose. Let us, then, if the idea appeals to you, carry this proposal of mine into effect. But I am willing to follow your own wishes in this matter, and if you disagree with my suggestion, let us all go and occupy our time in whatever way we please until the hour of vespers.'

The whole company, ladies and gentlemen alike, were in favour of telling stories.

'Then if it is agreeable to you,' said the queen, 'I desire that on this first day each of us should be free to speak upon whatever topic he prefers.'

And turning to Panfilo, who was seated on her right, she graciously asked him to introduce the proceedings with one of his stories. No sooner did he receive this invitation than Panfilo began as follows, with everyone listening intently:

FIRST STORY

Ser Cepperello deceives a holy friar with a false confession, then he dies; and although in life he was a most wicked man, in death he is reputed to be a Saint, and is called Saint Ciappelletto.

It is proper, dearest ladies, that everything made by man should begin with the sacred and admirable name of Him that was maker of all things. And therefore, since I am the first and must make a beginning to our storytelling, I propose to begin by telling you of one of His marvellous works, so that, when we have heard it out, our hopes will rest in Him as in something immutable, and we shall forever praise His name. It is obvious that since all temporal things are transient and mortal, so they are filled and surrounded by troubles, trials and tribulations, and fraught with infinite dangers which we, who live with them and are part of them, could without a shadow of a doubt neither endure, nor defend ourselves against, if God's special grace did not lend us strength and discernment. Nor should we suppose that His grace descends upon and within us through any merit of our own, for it is set in motion by His own loving-kindness, and is obtained by the pleas of people who like ourselves were mortal, and who, by firmly doing His pleasure whilst they were in this life, have now joined Him in eternal blessedness. To these, as to advocates made aware, through experience, of our frailty (perhaps because we have not the courage to submit our pleas personally in the presence of so great a judge) we present whatever we think is relevant to our cause. And our regard for Him, who is so compassionate and generous towards us, is all the greater when, the human eye being quite unable to penetrate the secrets of divine intelligence, common opinion deceives us and perhaps we appoint as our advocate in His majestic presence one who has been cast by Him into eternal exile. Yet He from whom nothing is hidden, paying more attention to the purity of the supplicant's motives than to his ignorance or to the banishment of the intercessor, answers those who pray to Him exactly as if the advocate were blessed in His sight. All of which can clearly be seen in the tale I propose to relate; and I say clearly because it is concerned, not with the judgement of God, but with that of men.

It is said, then, that Musciatto Franzesi,[1] having become a fine gentleman after acquiring enormous wealth and fame as a merchant in France, was obliged to come to Tuscany with the brother of the French king, the Lord Charles Lackland, who had been urged and encouraged to come by Pope Boniface. But finding that his affairs, as is usually the case with merchants, were entangled here, there, and everywhere, and being unable quickly or easily to unravel them, he decided to place them in the hands of a number of different people. All this he succeeded in arranging, except that he was left with the problem of finding someone capable of recovering certain loans which he had made to various people in Burgundy. The reason for his dilemma was that he had been told the Burgundians were a quarrelsome, thoroughly bad and unprincipled set of people; and he was quite unable to think of anyone he could trust, who was at the same time sufficiently villainous to match the villainy of the Burgundians. After devoting much thought to this problem, he suddenly recalled a man known as Ser Cepperello, of Prato, who had been a frequent visitor to his house in Paris. This man was short in stature and used to dress very neatly, and the French, who did not know the meaning of the word Cepperello, thinking that it signified *chapel*, which in their language means 'garland', and because as we have said he was a little man, used to call him, not Ciappello, but Ciappelletto: and everywhere in that part of the world, where few people knew him as Ser Cepperello, he was known as Ciappelletto.[2]

This Ciappelletto was a man of the following sort: a notary by profession, he would have taken it as a slight upon his honour if one of his legal deeds (and he drew up very few of them) were discovered to be other than false. In fact, he would have drawn up free of charge as many false documents as were requested of him, and done it more willingly than one who was highly paid for his services. He would take great delight in giving false testimony, whether asked for it or not. In those days, great reliance was placed in France upon sworn declarations, and since he had no scruples about swearing falsely, he used to win, by these nefarious means, every case in which he was required to swear upon his faith to tell the truth. He would take particular pleasure, and a great amount of trouble, in stirring up enmity, discord and bad blood between friends, relatives and anybody else; and the more calamities that ensued, the greater would be his rapture. If he were invited to witness a murder or any other criminal act, he would never refuse, but willingly go along; and he often found himself cheerfully assaulting or killing people with his own hands. He was a mighty blasphemer of God and His Saints, losing his temper on the tiniest pretext, as if he were the most hot-blooded man alive. He never went to church, and he would use foul language to pour scorn on all of her sacraments, declaring them repugnant. On the other hand, he would make a point of visiting taverns and other places of ill repute, and supplying them with his custom. Of women he was as fond as dogs are fond of a good stout stick; in their opposite, he took greater pleasure than the most depraved man on earth. He would rob and pilfer as conscientiously as if he were a saintly man making an offering. He was such a prize glutton and heavy drinker, that he would occasionally suffer for his over-indulgence in a manner that was most unseemly. He was a gambler and a card-sharper of the first order. But why do I lavish so many words upon him? He was perhaps the worst man ever born. Yet for all his villainy, he had long been protected by the power and influence of Messer Musciatto, on whose account he was many a time treated with respect, both by private individuals, whom he frequently abused, and by the courts of law, which he was forever abusing.

So that when Musciatto, who was well acquainted with his way of living, called this Ser Ciappelletto to mind, he judged him to be the very man that the perverseness of the Burgundians required. He therefore sent for him and addressed him as follows:

'Ser Ciappelletto, as you know, I am about to go away from here altogether, but I have some business to settle, amongst others with the Burgundians. These people are full of tricks, and I know of no one better fitted than yourself to recover what they owe me. And so, since you are not otherwise engaged at present, if you will attend to this matter I propose to obtain favours for you at court, and allow you a reasonable portion of the money you recover.'

Ser Ciappelletto, who was out of a job at the time and ill-supplied with worldly goods, seeing that the man who had long been his prop and stay was about to depart, made up his mind without delay and said (for he really had no alternative) that he would do it willingly. So that when they had agreed on terms, Ser Ciappelletto received powers of attorney from Musciatto and letters of introduction from the King, and after Musciatto's departure he went to Burgundy, where scarcely anybody knew him. And there, in a gentle and amiable fashion that ran contrary to his nature, as though he were holding his anger in reserve as a last resort, he issued his first demands and began to do what he had gone there to do. Before long, however, while lodging in the house of two Florentine brothers who ran a money-lending business there and did him great honour out of their respect for Musciatto, he happened to fall ill; whereupon the two brothers promptly summoned doctors and servants to attend him, and provided him with everything he needed to recover his health. But all their assistance was unavailing, because the good man, who was already advanced in years and had lived a disordered existence, was reported by his doctors to be going each day from bad to worse, like one who was suffering from a fatal illness. The two brothers were filled with alarm, and one day, alongside the room in which Ser Ciappelletto was lying, they began talking together.

'What are we to do about the fellow?' said one to the other. 'We've landed ourselves in a fine mess on his account, because to turn him away from our house in his present condition would arouse a lot of adverse comment and show us to be seriously lacking in common sense. What would people say if they suddenly saw us evicting a dying man after giving him hospitality in the first place, and taking so much trouble to have him nursed and waited upon, when he couldn't possibly have done anything to offend us? On the other hand, he has led such a wicked life that he will never be willing to make his confession or receive the sacraments of the Church; and if he dies unconfessed, no church will want to accept his body and he'll be flung into the moat like a dog.[3] But even if he makes his confession, his sins are so many and so appalling that the same thing will happen, because there will be neither friar nor priest who is either willing or able to give him absolution; in which case, since he will not have been absolved, he will be flung into the moat just the same. And when the townspeople see what has happened, they'll create a commotion, not only because of our profession which they consider iniquitous and never cease to condemn, but also because they long to get their hands on our money, and they will go about shouting: "Away with these Lombard dogs[4] that the Church refuses to accept"; and they'll come running to our lodgings and perhaps, not content with stealing our goods, they'll take away our lives into the bargain. So we shall be in a pretty fix either way, if this fellow dies.'

Ser Ciappelletto, who as we have said was lying near the place where they were talking, heard everything they were saying about him, for he was sharp of hearing, as invalids invariably are. So he called them in to him, and said:

'I don't want you to worry in the slightest on my account, nor to fear that I will cause you to suffer any harm. I heard what you were saying about me and I agree entirely that what you predict will actually come to pass, if matters take the course you anticipate; but they will do nothing of the kind. I have done our good Lord so many injuries whilst I lived, that to do Him another now that I am dying will be neither here nor there. So go and bring me the holiest and ablest friar you can find, if there is such a one, and leave everything to me, for I shall set your affairs and my own neatly in order, so that all will be well and you'll have nothing to complain of.'

Whilst deriving little comfort from all this, the two brothers nevertheless went off to a friary and asked for a wise and holy man to come and hear the confession of a Lombard who was lying ill in their house. They were given an ancient friar of good and holy ways who was an expert in the Scriptures and a most venerable man, towards whom all the townspeople were greatly and specially devoted, and they conducted him to their house.

On reaching the room where Ser Ciappelletto was lying, he sat down at his bedside, and first he began to comfort him with kindly words, then he asked him how long it was since he had last been to confession. Whereupon Ser Ciappelletto, who had never been to confession in his life, replied:

'Father, it has always been my custom to go to confession at least once every week, except that there are many weeks in which I go more often. But to tell the truth, since I fell ill, nearly a week ago, my illness has caused me so much discomfort that I haven't been to confession at all.'

'My son,' said the friar, 'you have done well, and you should persevere in this habit of yours. Since you go so often to confession, I can see that there will be little for me to hear or to ask.'

'Master friar,' said Ser Ciappelletto, 'do not speak thus, for however frequently or regularly I confess, it is always my wish that I should make a general confession of all the sins I can remember committing from the day I was born till the day of my confession. I therefore beg you, good father, to question me about everything, just as closely as if I had never been confessed. Do not spare me because I happen to be ill, for I would much rather mortify this flesh of mine than that, by treating it with lenience, I should do anything that could lead to the perdition of my soul, which my Saviour redeemed with His precious blood.'

These words were greatly pleasing to the holy friar, and seemed to him proof of a well-disposed mind. Having warmly commended Ser Ciappelletto for this practice of his, he began by asking him whether he had ever committed the sin of lust with any woman. To which, heaving a sigh, Ser Ciappelletto replied:

'Father, I am loath to tell you the truth on this matter, in case I should sin by way of vainglory.'

To which the holy friar replied:

'Speak out freely, for no man ever sinned by telling the truth, either in confession or otherwise.'

'Since you assure me that this is so,' said Ser Ciappelletto, 'I will tell you. I am a virgin as pure as on the day I came forth from my mother's womb.'

'Oh, may God give you His blessing!' said the friar. 'How nobly you have lived! And your restraint is all the more deserving of praise in that, had you wished, you would have had greater liberty

to do the opposite than those who, like ourselves, are expressly
forbidden by rule.'

Next he asked him whether he had displeased God by committing
the sin of gluttony; to which, fetching a deep sigh, Ser Ciappelletto
replied that he had, and on many occasions. For although, apart
from the periods of fasting normally observed in the course of the
year by the devout, he was accustomed to fasting on bread and
water for at least three days every week, he had drunk the water as
pleasurably and avidly (especially when he had been fatigued from
praying or going on a pilgrimage) as any great bibber of wine; he
had often experienced a craving for those dainty little wild herb
salads that women eat when they go away to the country; and
sometimes the thought of food had been more attractive to him
than he considered proper in one who, like himself, was fasting out
of piety. Whereupon the friar said:

'My son, these sins are natural and they are very trivial, and
therefore I would not have you burden your conscience with them
more than necessary. No matter how holy a man may be, he will
be attracted by the thought of food after a long spell of fasting, and
by the thought of drink when he is fatigued.'

'Oh!' said Ser Ciappelletto. 'Do not tell me this to console me,
father. As you are aware, I know that things done in the service of
God must all be done honestly and without any grudge; and if anyone should do otherwise, he is committing a sin.'

The friar, delighted, said to him:

'I am contented to see you taking such a view, and it pleases me
greatly that you should have such a good and pure conscience in
this matter. But tell me, have you ever been guilty of avarice, by
desiring to have more than was proper, or keeping what you should
not have kept?'

To which Ser Ciappelletto replied:

'Father, I would not wish you to judge me ill because I am in the
house of these money-lenders. I have nothing to do with their
business; indeed I had come here with the express intention of
warning and reproaching them, and dissuading them from this
abominable form of money-making; and I think I would have
succeeded, if God had not stricken me in this manner. However, I

would have you know that my father left me a wealthy man, and when he was dead, I gave the greater part of his fortune to charity. Since then, in order to support myself and enable me to assist the Christian poor, I have done a small amount of trading, in the course of which I have desired to gain, and I have always shared what I have gained with the poor, allocating one half to my own needs and giving the other half to them. And in this I have had so much help from my Creator that I have continually gone from strength to strength in the management of my affairs.'

'You have done well,' said the friar, 'but tell me, how often have you lost your temper?'

'Oh!' said Ser Ciappelletto, 'I can assure you I have done that very often. But who is there who could restrain himself, when the whole day long he sees men doing disgusting things, and failing to observe God's commandments, or to fear His terrible wrath? There have been many times in the space of a single day when I would rather have been dead than alive, looking about me and seeing young people frittering away their time, telling lies, going drinking in taverns, failing to go to church, and following the ways of the world rather than those of God.'

'My son,' said the friar, 'this kind of anger is justified, and for my part I could not require you to do penance for it. But has it ever happened that your anger has led you to commit murder or to pour abuse on anyone or do them any other form of injury?'

To which Ser Ciappelletto replied:

'Oh, sir, however could you, that appear to be a man of God, say such a thing? If I had thought for a single moment of doing any of the things you mention, do you suppose I imagine that God would have treated me so generously? Those things are the business of cut-throats and evildoers, and whenever I have chanced upon one of their number, I have always sent him packing, and offered up a prayer for his conversion!'

'May God give you His blessing,' said the friar, 'but now, tell me, my son: have you ever borne false witness against any man, or spoken ill of people, or taken what belonged to others without seeking their permission?'

'Never, sir, except on one occasion,' replied Ser Ciappelletto, 'when I spoke ill of someone. For I once had a neighbour who, without the slightest cause, was forever beating his wife, so that on this one occasion I spoke ill of him to his wife's kinsfolk, for I felt extremely sorry for that unfortunate woman. Whenever the fellow had had too much to drink, God alone could tell you how he battered her.'

Then the friar said:

'Let me see now, you tell me you were a merchant. Did you ever deceive anyone, as merchants do?'

'Faith, sir, I did,' said Ser Ciappelletto. 'But all I know about him is that he was a man who brought me some money that he owed me for a length of cloth I had sold him. I put the money away in a box without counting it, and a whole month passed before I discovered there were four pennies more than there should have been. I kept them for a year with the intention of giving them back, but I never saw him again, so I gave them away to a beggar.'

'That was a trivial matter,' said the friar, 'and you did well to dispose of the money as you did.'

The holy friar questioned him on many other matters, but always he answered in similar vein, and hence the friar was ready to proceed without further ado to give him absolution. But Ser Ciappelletto said:

'Sir, I still have one or two sins I have not yet told you about.'

The friar asked him what they were, and he said:

'I recall that I once failed to show a proper respect for the Holy Sabbath, by making one of my servants sweep the house after nones on a Saturday.'

'Oh!' said the friar. 'This, my son, is a trifling matter.'

'No, father,' said Ser Ciappelletto, 'you must not call it trifling, for the Sabbath has to be greatly honoured, seeing that this was the day on which our Lord rose from the dead.'

Then the friar said:

'Have you done anything else?'

'Yes, sir,' replied Ser Ciappelletto, 'for I once, without thinking what I was doing, spat in the house of God.'

The friar began to smile, and said:

'My son, this is not a thing to worry about. We members of religious orders spit there continually.'

'That is very wicked of you,' said Ser Ciappelletto, 'for nothing should be kept more clean than the holy temple in which sacrifice is offered up to God.'

In brief, he told the friar many things of this sort, and finally he began to sigh, and then to wail loudly, as he was well able to do whenever he pleased.

'My son,' said the holy friar. 'What is the matter?'

'Oh alas, sir,' replied Ser Ciappelletto, 'I have one sin left to which I have never confessed, so great is my shame in having to reveal it; and whenever I remember it, I cry as you see me doing now, and feel quite certain that God will never have mercy on me for this terrible sin.'

'Come now, my son,' said the holy friar, 'what are you saying? If all the sins that were ever committed by the whole of mankind, together with those that men will yet commit till the end of the world, were concentrated in one single man, and he was as truly repentant and contrite as I see you to be, God is so benign and merciful that He would freely remit them on their being confessed to Him; and therefore you may safely reveal it.'

Then Ser Ciappelletto said, still weeping loudly:

'Alas, father, my sin is too great, and I can scarcely believe that God will ever forgive me for it, unless you intercede with your prayers.'

To which the friar replied:

'You may safely reveal it, for I promise that I will pray to God on your behalf.'

Ser Ciappelletto went on weeping, without saying anything, and the friar kept encouraging him to speak. But after Ser Ciappelletto, by weeping in this manner, had kept the friar for a very long time on tenterhooks, he heaved a great sigh, and said:

'Father, since you promise that you will pray to God for me, I will tell you. You are to know then that once, when I was a little boy, I cursed my mother.' And having said this, he began to weep loudly all over again.

'There now, my son,' said the friar, 'does this seem so great a sin to you? Why, people curse God the whole day long, and yet He willingly forgives those who repent for having cursed Him. Why then should you suppose He will not forgive you for this? Take heart and do not weep, for even if you had been one of those who set Him on the cross, I can see that you have so much contrition that He would certainly forgive you.'

'Oh alas, father,' said Ser Ciappelletto, 'what are you saying? My dear, sweet mother, who carried me day and night for nine months in her body, and held me more than a hundred times in her arms! It was too wicked of me to curse her, and the sin is too great; and if you do not pray to God for me, it will never be forgiven me.'

Perceiving that Ser Ciappelletto had nothing more to say, the friar absolved him and gave him his blessing. He took him for a very saintly man indeed, being fully convinced that what Ser Ciappelletto had said was true; but then, who is there who would not have been convinced, on hearing a dying man talk in this fashion? Finally, when all this was done, he said to him:

'Ser Ciappelletto, with God's help you will soon be well again. But in case it were to happen that God should summon your blessed and well-disposed soul to His presence, are you willing for your body to be buried in our convent?'

To which Ser Ciappelletto replied:

'Yes, father. In fact, I would not wish to be elsewhere, since you have promised that you will pray to God for me. Besides, I have always been especially devoted to your Order. So when you return to your convent, I beg you to see that I am sent that true body of Christ which you consecrate every morning on the altar. For although I am unworthy of it, I intend with your permission to take it, and afterwards to receive the holy Extreme Unction, so that, having lived as a sinner, I shall at least die as a Christian.'

The holy man said that he was greatly pleased, that the words were well spoken, and that he would see it was brought to him at once; and so it was.

The two brothers, who strongly suspected that Ser Ciappelletto was going to deceive them, had posted themselves behind a wooden partition which separated the room where Ser Ciappelletto was lying from another, and as they stood there listening they could easily follow what Ser Ciappelletto was saying to the friar. When they heard the things he confessed to having done, they were so amused that every so often they nearly exploded with mirth, and they said to each other:

'What manner of man is this, whom neither old age nor illness, nor fear of the death which he sees so close at hand, nor even the fear of God, before whose judgement he knows he must shortly appear, have managed to turn from his evil ways, or persuade to die any differently from the way he has lived?'

Seeing, however, that he had said all the right things to be received for burial in a church, they cared nothing for the rest.

Shortly thereafter Ser Ciappelletto made his communion, and, failing rapidly, he received Extreme Unction. Soon after vespers[5] on the very day that he had made his fine confession, he died. Whereupon the two brothers made all necessary arrangements, using his own money to see that he had an honourable funeral, and sending news of his death to the friars and asking them to come that evening to observe the customary vigil, and the following morning to take away the body.

On hearing that he had passed away, the holy friar who had received his confession arranged with the prior for the chapter-house bell to be rung, and to the assembled friars he showed that Ser Ciappelletto had been a saintly man, as his confession had amply proved. He expressed the hope that through him the Lord God would work many miracles, and persuaded them that his body should be received with the utmost reverence and loving care. Credulous to a man, the prior and the other friars agreed to do so, and that evening they went to the place where Ser Ciappelletto's body lay, and celebrated a great and solemn vigil over it; and in the morning, dressed in albs and copes, carrying books in their hands and bearing crosses before them, singing as they went, they all came for the body, which they then carried back to their church with tremendous pomp and ceremony, followed by nearly all the people of the town, men and women alike. And when it had been set down in the church, the holy friar who had confessed him climbed into the pulpit and began to preach marvellous things about Ser Ciappelletto's life, his fasts, his virginity, his simplicity and innocence and saintliness, relating among other things what he had tearfully confessed to him as his greatest sin, and describing how he had barely been able to convince him that God would forgive him, at which point he turned to reprimand his audience, saying:

'And yet you miserable sinners have only to catch your feet in a wisp of straw for you to curse God and the Virgin and all the Saints in heaven.'

Apart from this, he said much else about his loyalty and his purity of heart. And in brief, with a torrent of words that the people of the town believed implicitly, he fixed Ser Ciappelletto so firmly in the minds and affections of all those present that when the service was over, everyone thronged round the body to kiss his feet and his hands, all the clothes were torn from his back, and those who succeeded in grabbing so much as a tiny fragment felt they were in Paradise itself. He had to be kept lying there all day, so that everyone could come and gaze upon him, and on that same night he was buried with honour in a marble tomb in one of the chapels. From the next day forth, people began to go there to light candles and pray to him, and later they began to make votive offerings and to decorate the chapel with figures made of wax, in fulfilment of promises they had given.

The fame of his saintliness, and of the veneration in which he was held, grew to such proportions that there was hardly anyone who did not pray for his assistance in time of trouble, and they called him, and call him still, Saint Ciappelletto. Moreover it is claimed that through him God has wrought many miracles, and that He continues to work them on behalf of whoever commends himself devoutly to this particular Saint.

It was thus, then, that Ser Cepperello of Prato lived and died, becoming a Saint in the way you have heard. Nor would I wish to deny that perhaps God has blessed and admitted him to His presence. For albeit he led a wicked, sinful life, it is possible that at the eleventh hour he was so sincerely repentant that God had mercy upon him and received him into His kingdom. But since this is hidden from us, I speak only with regard to the outward appearance, and I say that the fellow should rather be in Hell, in the hands of the devil, than in Paradise. And if this is the case, we may recognize how very great is God's loving-kindness towards us, in that it takes account, not of our error, but of the purity of our faith, and grants our prayers even when we appoint as our emissary one who is His enemy, thinking him to be His friend, as though we were appealing to one who was truly holy as our intercessor for His favour. And therefore, so that we, the members of this joyful company, may be guided safely and securely by His grace through these present adversities, let us praise the name of Him with whom we began our storytelling, let us hold Him in reverence, and let us commend ourselves to Him in the hour of our need, in the certain knowledge that we shall be heard.

And there the narrator fell silent.

SECOND STORY

A Jew called Abraham, his curiosity being aroused by Jehannot de Chevigny, goes to the court of Rome; and when he sees the depravity of the clergy, he returns to Paris and becomes a Christian.

The ladies were full of praise for Panfilo's story, parts of which they had found highly amusing. Everyone had listened closely, and when it came to an end Neifile, sitting next to Panfilo, was asked by the queen to continue the proceedings with a story of her own. Neifile, whose manners were no less striking than her beauty, replied with a smile that she would gladly do so, and began in this fashion:

Panfilo has shown us in his tale that God's loving-kindness is unaffected by our errors, when they proceed from some cause which it is impossible for us to detect; and I in mine propose to demonstrate to you how this same loving-kindness, by patiently enduring the shortcomings of those who in word and deed ought to be its living witness and yet behave in a precisely contrary fashion, gives us the proof of its unerring rightness; my purpose being that of strengthening our conviction in what we believe.

As I was once informed, fair ladies, there lived in Paris a great merchant, a worthy man called Jehannot de Chevigny, who was extremely honest and upright and ran a flourishing textile business. He was particularly friendly with an enormously rich Jew called Abraham, who was himself a merchant and an extremely upright and honest man. In view of Abraham's honesty and integrity, Jehannot began to have serious regrets that the soul of so worthy, good and wise a man should go to its perdition because it was lacking in proper faith. So he began in an amiable manner to urge him to abandon the erroneous ways of Judaism and embrace the true Christian faith, which being sound and holy was, as he could see for himself, steadily growing and prospering; whereas in contrast his own religion was manifestly declining and coming to nought.

The Jew replied that he considered no faith to be sound and holy except the Jewish, and that he had been born into that one, and meant to live and die in it; nor was there anything that would shift him from his resolve. This reply did not however deter Jehannot, a few days later, from renewing his appeal and showing him, in the sort of homespun language for which most merchants have a natural bent, on what grounds our faith was superior to the Jewish. And although Abraham was very learned in Jewish doctrine, nevertheless, either because of his great friendship for Jehannot or possibly because he was stirred by the words which the Holy Ghost put into the mouth of this ignoramus, he began to be highly entertained by Jehannot's explanations. But his belief was unshaken, and he would not allow himself to be converted.

The more stubbornly he resisted, the more Jehannot continued to pester him, until finally the Jew, overcome by such incessant importunity, said:

'Now listen, Jehannot, you would like me to become a Christian, and I am prepared to do so on one condition: that first of all I should go to Rome, and there observe the man whom you call the vicar of God on earth, and examine his life and habits together with those of his fellow cardinals; and if they seem to me such that, added to your own arguments, they lead me to the conclusion that your faith is superior to mine, as you have taken such pains to show me, then I shall do as I have promised; but if things should turn out differently, I shall remain a Jew as I am at present.'

When Jehannot heard this, he was thrown into a fit of gloom, and said to himself: 'I have wasted my energies, which I felt I had used to good effect, thinking I had converted the man; for if he goes to the court of Rome and sees what foul and wicked lives the clergy lead, not only will he not become a Christian, but, if he had already turned Christian, he would become a Jew again without fail.' And turning to Abraham, he said:

'Come now, my friend, why should you want to put yourself to the endless trouble and expense involved in going all the way from here to Rome? Besides, for a rich man like yourself, the journey both by sea and land is full of dangers. Do you suppose you will not find anyone here to baptize you? If by chance you have any doubts concerning the faith as I have outlined it to you, where else except in Paris will you find greater and more learned exponents of Christian doctrine, capable of answering your questions and resolving your difficulties?[1] Hence in my opinion this journey of yours is quite unnecessary. You must remember that the Church dignitaries in Rome are no different from the ones you have seen and can still see here, except that they are the better for being closer to the chief shepherd. And so if you will take my advice, you will save your energy for a pilgrimage on some later occasion, when perhaps I will keep you company.'

'Jehannot,' replied the Jew, 'I believe it to be just as you say it is, but to put the matter in a nutshell, if you really want me to do as you have urged me with so much insistence, I am fully prepared to go there. Otherwise, I shall do nothing about it.'

'Go then, and good luck to you,' said Jehannot, seeing that the Jew had made up his mind. He was quite certain that Abraham would never become a Christian, once he had seen the court of Rome; but since it would make no difference, he did not insist any further.

The Jew mounted a horse, and rode off with all possible speed to the court of Rome, where on his arrival he was warmly welcomed by his Jewish friends. And there he settled down, without telling anybody why he had come, and cautiously began to observe the behaviour of the Pope, the cardinals, the other Church dignitaries, and all the courtiers. Being a very perceptive person, he discovered, by adding the evidence of his own eyes to information given him by others, that practically all of them from the highest to the lowest were flagrantly given to the sin of lust, not only of the natural variety, but also of the sodomitic, without the slightest display of shame or remorse, to the extent that the power of prostitutes and young men to obtain the most enormous favours was virtually unlimited. In addition to this, he clearly saw that they were all gluttons, winebibbers, and drunkards without exception, and that next to their lust they would rather attend to their bellies than to anything else, as though they were a pack of animals.

Moreover, on closer inspection he saw that they were such a collection of rapacious money-grubbers that they were as ready to buy and sell human, that is to say, Christian blood as they were to trade for profit in any kind of divine object, whether in the way of sacraments or of church livings. In this activity, they had a bigger turnover and more brokers than you could find on any of the Paris markets including that of the textile trade. They had applied the name of 'procuration' to their unconcealed simony, and that of 'sustentation' to their gluttony, as if (to say nothing of the meaning of the words) God were ignorant of the intentions of their wicked minds and would allow Himself to be deceived, as men are, by the mere names of things.

All this, together with many other things of which it is more prudent to remain silent, was highly distasteful to the Jew, who was a sober and respectable man. And so, feeling he had seen enough, he decided to return to Paris, which he did. On hearing of his arrival, Jehannot, thinking nothing to be less likely than that his friend should have turned Christian, came to his house, where they made a great fuss of each other. And after Abraham had rested for a few days, Jehannot asked him what sort of an opinion he had formed about the Holy Father and the cardinals and the other members of the papal court. Whereupon the Jew promptly replied:

'A bad one, and may God deal harshly with the whole lot of them. And my reason for telling you so is that, unless I formed the wrong impression, nobody there who was connected with the Church seemed to me to display the slightest sign of holiness, piety, charity, moral rectitude or any other virtue. On the contrary, it seemed to me that they were all so steeped in lust, greed, avarice, fraud, envy, pride, and other like sins and worse (if indeed that is possible), that I regard the place as a hotbed for diabolical rather than devotional activities. As far as I can judge, it seems to me that your pontiff, and all of the others too, are doing their level best to reduce the Christian religion to nought and drive it from the face of the earth, whereas they are the very people who should be its foundation and support.

'But since it is evident to me that their attempts are unavailing, and that your religion continues to grow in popularity, and become more splendid and illustrious, I can only conclude that, being a more holy and genuine religion than any of the others, it deservedly has the Holy Ghost as its foundation and support. So whereas earlier I stood firm and unyielding against your entreaties and refused to turn Christian, I now tell you quite plainly that nothing in the world could prevent me from becoming a Christian.[2] Let us therefore go to the church where, in accordance with the traditional rite of your holy faith, you shall have me baptized.'

When Jehannot, who was expecting precisely the opposite conclusion, heard him saying this, he was the happiest man that ever lived. And he went with him to Nôtre Dame de Paris,[3] and asked the clergy there to baptize Abraham. This they did, as soon as they heard that he himself desired it: Jehannot stood as his sponsor, and gave him the name of John. And afterwards he engaged the most learned teachers to instruct him thoroughly in our religion, which he quickly mastered, thereafter becoming a good and worthy man, holy in all his ways.

THIRD STORY

Melchizedek[1] the Jew, with a story about three rings, avoids a most dangerous trap laid for him by Saladin.[2]

Neifile's story was well received by all the company, and when she fell silent, Filomena began at the queen's behest to address them as follows:

The story told by Neifile reminds me of the parlous state in which a Jew once found himself. Now that we have heard such fine things said concerning God and the truth of our religion, it will not seem inappropriate to descend at this juncture to the deeds and adventures of men. So I shall tell you a story which, when you have heard it, will possibly make you more cautious in answering questions addressed to you. It is a fact, my sweet companions, that just as folly often destroys men's happiness and casts them into deepest misery, so prudence extricates the wise from dreadful perils and guides them firmly to safety. So clearly may we perceive that folly leads men from contentment to misery, that we shall not even bother for the present to consider the matter further, since countless examples spring readily to mind. But that prudence may bring its reward, I shall, as I have promised, prove to you briefly by means of the following little tale:

Saladin, whose worth was so great that it raised him from humble beginnings to the sultanate of Egypt and brought him many victories over Saracen and Christian kings, had expended the whole of his treasure in various wars and extraordinary acts of munificence, when a certain situation arose for which he required a vast sum of money. Not being able to see any way of obtaining what he needed at such short notice, he happened to recall a rich Jew, Melchizedek by name, who ran a money-lending business in Alexandria, and would certainly, he thought, have enough for his purposes, if only he could be persuaded to part with it. But this Melchizedek was such a miserly fellow that he would never hand it over of his own free will, and the Sultan was not prepared to take it away from him by force. However, as his need became more pressing, having racked his brains to discover some way of compelling the Jew to assist him, he resolved to use force in the guise of reason. So he sent for the Jew, gave him a cordial reception, invited him to sit down beside him, and said:

'O man of excellent worth, many men have told me of your great wisdom and your superior knowledge of the ways of God. Hence I would be glad if you would tell me which of the three laws, whether the Jewish, the Saracen, or the Christian, you deem to be truly authentic.'

The Jew, who was indeed a wise man, realized all too well that Saladin was aiming to trip him up with the intention of picking a quarrel with him, and that if he were to praise any of the three more than the others, the Sultan would achieve his object. He therefore had need of a reply that would save him from falling into the trap, and having sharpened his wits, in no time at all he was ready with his answer.

'My lord,' he said, 'your question is a very good one, and in order to explain my views on the subject, I must ask you to listen to the following little story:

'Unless I am mistaken, I recall having frequently heard that there was once a great and wealthy man who, apart from the other fine jewels contained in his treasury, possessed a most precious and beautiful ring. Because of its value and beauty, he wanted to do it the honour of leaving it in perpetuity to his descendants, and so he announced that he would bequeath the ring to one of his sons, and that whichever of them should be found to have it in his keeping, this man was to be looked upon as his heir, and the others were to honour and respect him as the head of the family.

'The man to whom he left the ring, having made a similar provision regarding his own descendants, followed the example set by his predecessor. To cut a long story short, the ring was handed down through many generations till it finally came to rest in the hands of a man who had three most splendid and virtuous sons who were very obedient to their father, and he loved all three of them equally. Each of the three young men, being aware of the tradition concerning the ring, was eager to take precedence over the others, and they all did their utmost to persuade the father, who was now an old man, to leave them the ring when he died.

'The good man, who loved all three and was unable to decide which of them should inherit the ring, resolved, having promised it to each, to try and please them all. So he secretly commissioned a master-craftsman to make two more rings, which were so like the first that even the man who had made them could barely distinguish them from the original. And when he was dying, he took each of his sons aside in turn, and gave one ring to each.

'After their father's death, they all desired to succeed to his title and estate, and each man denied the claims of the others, producing his ring to prove his case. But finding that the rings were so alike that it was impossible to tell them apart, the question of which of the sons was the true and rightful heir remained in abeyance, and has never been settled.

'And I say to you, my lord, that the same applies to the three laws which God the Father granted to His three peoples, and which formed the subject of your inquiry. Each of them considers itself the legitimate heir to His estate, each believes it possesses His one true law and observes His commandments. But as with the rings, the question as to which of them is right remains in abeyance.'

Saladin perceived that the fellow had ingeniously side-stepped the trap he had set before him, and he therefore decided to make a clean breast of his needs, and see if the Jew would come to his assistance. This he did, freely admitting what he had intended to do, but for the fact that the Jew had answered him so discreetly.

Melchizedek gladly provided the Sultan with the money he required. The Sultan later paid him back in full, in addition to which he showered magnificent gifts upon him, made him his lifelong friend, and maintained him at his court in a state of importance and honour.

FOURTH STORY

A monk, having committed a sin deserving of very severe punishment, escapes the consequences by politely reproaching his abbot with the very same fault.

No sooner did Filomena stop talking, having reached the end of her tale, than Dioneo,[1] who was sitting next to her and already knew it was his turn to address them because of the order in which they were speaking, began in the following manner without awaiting further instructions from the queen:

Sweet ladies, if I have properly understood your unanimous intention, we are here in order to bring pleasure to each other with our storytelling. I therefore contend that each must be allowed (as our queen agreed just now that we might) to tell whatever story we think most likely to amuse. So having heard how Abraham's soul was saved through the good advice of Jehannot de Chevigny, and how Melchizedek employed his wisdom in defending his riches from the wily manoeuvres of Saladin, I intend, without fear of your disapproval, to give you a brief account of the clever way in which a monk saved his body from very severe punishment.

In Lunigiana,[2] which is not all that far from where we are now, there is a monastery that once had a greater supply of monks and of saintliness than it nowadays has, and in it there was a young monk whose freshness and vitality neither fasts nor vigils could impair. One day, about noon, when all the other monks were asleep, he chanced to be taking a solitary stroll round the walls of the monastery, which lay in a very lonely spot, when his eyes came to rest on a strikingly beautiful girl, perhaps some local farmhand's daughter, who was going about the fields collecting wild herbs. No sooner did he see her, than he was fiercely assailed by carnal desire.

He went up to her and engaged her in conversation, passing from subject to subject till he came to an understanding with her and took her back to his cell, making sure that no one was watching. But being carried away by the vigour of his passion, he threw all caution to the winds, and whilst he was cavorting with the girl, the Abbot, who happened to have risen from his siesta and was quietly walking past the monk's cell, heard the racket that the pair were creating. So that he might recognize the voices, he crept softly up to the door of the cell, stood there listening, and came to the definite conclusion that one of the voices was a woman's. His first impulse was to order the door to be opened, but he then decided to deal with the matter differently and returned to his room, where he waited for the monk to come out.

The monk, albeit he had taken the greatest of pleasure and delight in the young woman's company, suspected none the less that something was amiss, for it had seemed to him that he could hear the shuffling of feet in the corridor. He had therefore applied his eye to a tiny aperture, from which he had obtained an excellent view of the Abbot, standing there listening. He was thus well aware that the Abbot had had the opportunity of knowing that the girl was in his cell, and consequently he was very worried, for he knew he would be punished severely on account of all this. But without betraying his anxiety to the girl, he quickly ran his mind over various expedients to see if he could chance upon one that might do him some good, and hit upon a novel piece of mischief, which would have precisely the effect he was seeking. Pretending to the girl that he thought they had spent sufficient time together, he said to her:

'I am just going to find a way of letting you out of here without your being seen. So stay here and make no sound till I return.'

He then emerged from his cell and, having locked the door, went straight to the Abbot's room and handed him his key, this being the usual practice whenever any monk was going out. Then without so much as batting an eyelid, he said:

'Sir, this morning I was not able to bring in all the faggots that were cut for me, so with your permission I should like to go to the wood and have them brought in.'

The Abbot, thinking that the monk knew nothing of the fact that he had seen him, was glad of the chance to find out more about the offence he had committed, and he gladly accepted the key and gave him his ready permission. After watching the monk go away, he began to consider whether it would be better for him to open the man's cell in the presence of all the monks and let them bear witness to his disgrace, so that they would have no reason to complain against him later when he punished the fellow, or first to hear the girl's account of the affair. On reflecting that she might be a respectable woman or the daughter of some man of influence, not wishing to make the mistake of putting such a lady to shame by displaying her to all of the monks, he decided he would first go and see who she was and then make up his mind. So he quietly made his way to the cell, opened the door, entered, and locked the door behind him.

When she saw the Abbot coming in, the girl was terrified out of her wits, and began to weep for shame. Master Abbot, having looked her up and down, saw that she was a nice, comely wench, and despite his years he was promptly filled with fleshly cravings, no less intense than those his young monk had experienced. And he began to say to himself: 'Well, well! Why not enjoy myself a little, when I have the opportunity? After all, I can have my fill of sorrow and afflictions whenever I like. This is a fine-looking wench, and not a living soul knows that she is here. If I can persuade her to play my game, I see no reason why I shouldn't do it. Who is there to know? No one will ever find out, and a sin that's hidden is half forgiven. I may never get another chance as good as this. It's always a good idea, in my opinion, to accept any gift that the Good Lord places in our path.' Having said all this to himself, and completely reversed his original intention in going there, he went up to the girl and gently began to console her and tell her not to cry. One subject led to another, and eventually he came round to explaining what he had in mind.

The girl, who was not exactly made of iron or of flint, fell in very readily with the Abbot's wishes. He took her in his arms and kissed her a few times, then lowered himself on to the monk's little bed. But out of regard, perhaps, for the weight of his reverend person and the tender age of the girl, and not wishing to do her any injury, he settled down beneath her instead of lying on top, and in this way he sported with her at considerable length.

Meanwhile the monk, who had only pretended to go to the wood, had hidden himself in the corridor, and when he saw the Abbot entering the cell by himself, he felt quite reassured, being convinced that everything was proceeding according to plan. And when he perceived that the Abbot had locked himself in, he was left in no doubt whatsoever. Emerging from his hiding-place, he quietly crept up to a chink in the wall, through which he saw and heard all that the Abbot was doing and saying.

The Abbot, deciding he had spent enough time with the girl, locked her in the cell and returned to his room. And after a while, hearing the monk and supposing he had just returned from the wood, he determined to give him a jolly good scolding and have him locked up, so that he alone would possess the prize they had captured. So he sent for the monk, put on a stern face, reprimanded him most severely, and ordered him to be locked in the punishment-cell.

Without hesitating for a moment, the monk replied:

'Sir, I have not yet been long enough in the Order of Saint Benedict to have had a chance of acquainting myself with all its special features, and you had failed until just now to show me that monks have women to support, as well as fasts and vigils. But now that you have pointed this out, I promise that if you will forgive me just this once, I will never again commit the same error. On the contrary, I shall always follow your good example.'

The Abbot, who was no fool, quickly realized that the monk had outwitted him and, moreover, seen what he had done. Being tarred with the same brush, he was loath to inflict upon the monk a punishment of which he himself was no less deserving. So he pardoned the monk and swore him to secrecy concerning what he had seen, then they slipped the girl out unobtrusively, and we can only assume that they afterwards brought her back at regular intervals.

FIFTH STORY

The Marchioness of Montferrat, with the aid of a chicken banquet and a few well-chosen words, restrains the extravagant passion of the King of France.

As they listened to Dioneo's story, the ladies at first felt some embarrassment, which showed itself in the modest blushes that appeared on all their faces. Then, glancing at one another and barely managing to restrain their laughter, they giggled as they listened. When it came to an end, however, they gently rebuked him with a few well-chosen words, in order to show that stories of that kind should not be told when ladies were present. Then the queen turned to Fiammetta, who was sitting on the grass next to him, and indicated that it was her turn to continue. Whereupon, with a cheerful smile towards the queen, she gracefully began:

Whereas men, if they are very wise, will always seek to love ladies of higher station than their own, women, if they are very discerning, will know how to guard against accepting the advances of a man who is of more exalted rank. For which reason, and also because of the pleasure I feel at our having, through our stories, begun to demonstrate the power of good repartee, I have been prompted to show you, fair ladies, in the story that I have to tell, how through her words and actions a gentlewoman avoided this pitfall and guided her suitor clear of its dangers.

The Marquis of Montferrat[1] was a man of outstanding worth, who had sailed as Gonfalonier of the Church with a Christian host on a Crusade to the Holy Land.[2] And one day, during a conversation about his merits at the court of King Philippe Le Borgne,[3] who was also preparing to leave France to join the Crusade, a courtier observed that there was not a wedded couple under the sun to compare with the Marquis and his lady; for just as the Marquis was a paragon of all the knightly virtues, so the lady was more beautiful and worthy of esteem than any other woman in the world.

These words left such a deep impression on the French king's mind, that without having ever seen the lady, he at once became fervently enamoured of her, and decided that under no circumstances would he embark for the Crusade at any other port but Genoa, so that, by travelling overland, he would have a plausible pretext for paying the Marchioness a visit. In this way he thought he would succeed, since the Marquis would be absent, in bringing his desires to fruition.

He lost no time in putting his deep-laid scheme into effect. Having sent all his men on ahead, he set out with a small retinue of nobles, and as they approached the territory of the Marquis, he sent word to the lady, a day in advance, that she was to expect him for breakfast on the following morning. Being an intelligent and judicious woman, she sent back a message to say that she was glad to have been singled out for this uniquely great favour, and that the King would be very welcome. She then began to wonder why such a great king should be calling upon her in her husband's absence. Nor was she wrong in the conclusion that she reached, namely, that he was being drawn thither by the fame of her beauty. Nevertheless, with her habitual nobility of spirit she made ready to entertain him; and after summoning all the few remaining gentlemen of rank, acting upon their advice she issued instructions for the necessary preparations to be made, at the same time insisting that she alone would arrange the banquet and devise its menu. Without a moment's delay, she collected together all the hens that could be found in the neighbourhood, and ordered her cooks to prepare a series of dishes, using these alone, for the royal banquet.

The King arrived on the day he had appointed, and was warmly and honourably received by the lady. On meeting her for the first time, he was greatly amazed to find that she was even more beautiful, intelligent and gentle-mannered than he had been led to expect from the words of the courtier, and he was lavish with his compliments, for he had become all the more inflamed with passion on finding that the lady exceeded his expectations. After he had rested for a while in rooms that had been richly appointed with all the furnishings appropriate to the reception of so great a king, it was time for the banquet, and the King sat with the Marchioness at one table, whilst the remaining guests were entertained at other tables according to their rank and quality.

The King, being served with many dishes one after another and with choice and precious wines, and gazing contentedly from time to time at the beautiful Marchioness, was filled with intense pleasure. But as one dish was followed by the next, he began to feel somewhat perplexed, for he could not help noticing that although the courses were different, each and every one of them consisted solely of chicken. He was well enough acquainted with that particular region to know that it should be well stocked with a variety of game, and by sending the lady advance notice of his arrival he had given her ample time to organize a hunt. But although he was greatly surprised by all this, he had no desire to give her any cause for embarrassment, except for putting in a word about her chickens. So smiling broadly, he turned towards her and said:

'Madam, is it only hens that flourish in these parts, and not a single cock?'

The Marchioness, who understood his question perfectly, saw this as exactly the kind of Heaven-sent opportunity she had hoped for in order to make clear her intentions. On hearing the King's inquiry, she turned boldly towards him and replied:

'No, my lord, but our women, whilst they may differ slightly from each other in their rank and the style of their dress, are made no differently here than they are elsewhere.'

On hearing this, the King saw clearly the reason for the banquet of chickens, and the virtue that lay concealed beneath her little homily. He realized that honeyed words would be wasted on a lady of this sort, and that force was out of the question. And thus, in the same way that he had foolishly become inflamed, so now he wisely decided that he was honour-bound to extinguish the ill-conceived fires of his passion. Fearing her replies, he teased her no further, but applied himself to his meal, by now convinced that all hope was lost. And as soon as he had finished eating, in order to compensate for his dishonourable coming by his swift departure, he thanked her for her generous hospitality and departed for Genoa, with the lady wishing him God-speed.

SIXTH STORY

With a clever remark, an honest man exposes the wicked hypocrisy of the religious.

All the ladies applauded the courage of the Marchioness and the eloquent rebuff she had given to the King of France. Then in deference to the wishes of the queen, Emilia, who was seated next to Fiammetta, started boldly to speak:

I likewise will describe a stinging rebuke, but one which was administered by an honest layman to a grasping friar, with a gibe no less amusing than it was laudable.

Not long ago then, dear young ladies, there was in our city a Franciscan, an inquisitor[1] on the look-out for filthy heretics, who whilst trying very hard, as they all do, to preserve an appearance of saintly and tender devotion to the Christian faith, was no less expert at tracking down people with bulging purses than at seeking out those whom he deemed to be lacking in faith. His diligence chanced to put him on the trail of a certain law-abiding citizen, endowed with far more money than common sense, who one day, not from any lack of faith but simply in the course of an innocent conversation with his friends, came out with the remark that he had a wine of such a quality that Christ himself would have drunk it.

The worthy soul had been drinking too much perhaps, or possibly he was over-excited, but unfortunately his words were reported to the inquisitor, who on hearing that the man had large estates and a tidy sum of money, hastily proceeded *cum gladiis et fustibus*[2] to draw up serious charges against him. This, he thought, would have the effect, not so much of lessening his victim's impiety, as of lining his own pockets with florins, which was what in fact happened. Having issued a summons, he asked the man whether the charges against him were correct. The good man admitted that they were, and explained the circumstances, whereupon this devout and venerable inquisitor of Saint John Golden-Mouth[3] said:

'So you turned Christ into a drinker, did you, and a connoisseur of choice wines, as if he were some tosspot or drunken tavern-crawler like one of yourselves? And now you eat humble-pie, and try to pass the whole thing off as something very trifling. But that is where you are mistaken. The fire is what you deserve when we come to take action against you, as indeed we must.'

The friar addressed these words to him, and a great many more, with a menacing look all over his features, as though the fellow were an Epicurean[4] denying the immortality of the soul. In brief, he struck such terror into him, that the poor man arranged for certain go-betweens to grease the friar's palm with a goodly amount of Saint John Golden-Mouth's ointment (a highly effective remedy against the disease of galloping greed common among the clergy, and especially among Franciscans, who look upon money with distaste), so that the inquisitor would deal leniently with him.

The ointment he used is highly efficacious (though it is not mentioned by Galen in any of his treatises on medicine), and he applied it so liberally and effectively that the fire with which he had been threatened was graciously commuted to the wearing of a cross, which made him look as if he were about to set off on a Crusade. In order to make his badge more attractive, the friar stipulated that the cross should be yellow on a black ground. And apart from this, having pocketed the money, he kept him for several days under open arrest, ordering him by way of penance to attend mass every morning in Santa Croce and report to him every day at the hour of breakfast, after which he was free to do as he pleased for the rest of the day.

The man carried out his instructions to the letter, and one morning at mass he happened to be listening to the Gospel when he heard these words being sung: 'For every one you shall receive an hundredfold, and shall inherit everlasting life.' He committed the words firmly to memory, and at the usual hour he presented himself as instructed before the inquisitor, whom he found already at table. The inquisitor asked him whether he had listened to mass that morning, and he promptly replied that he had. Whereupon the inquisitor said:

'Do you have any doubts, or questions you wish to ask, about anything you heard during the service?'

'To be sure,' the good man replied, 'I have no doubts about any of the things I heard, indeed I firmly believe them all to be true. But one of the things I heard made me feel very sorry for you and your fellow friars, and I still feel very sorry when I think what an awful time you are all going to have in the life to come.'

'And what was it,' asked the inquisitor, 'which caused you to feel so sorry for us?'

'Sir,' the good man replied, 'it was that passage from the Gospel which says that for every one you shall receive an hundred-fold.'[5]

'That is true,' said the inquisitor. 'But why should this have perturbed you so?'

'Sir,' replied the good man, 'I will tell you. Every day since I started coming here, I have seen a crowd of poor people standing outside and being given one and sometimes two huge cauldrons of vegetable-water which, being surplus to your needs, is taken away from you and the other friars here in the convent. So if you are

going to receive a hundred in the next world for every one you
have given, you will have so much of the stuff that you will all
drown in it.'

The other friars sitting at the inquisitor's table all burst out
laughing, but the inquisitor himself, on hearing their guzzling
hypocrisy exposed in this fashion, flew into a towering rage. And
but for the fact that the affair had already brought him discredit, he
would have laid further charges against the man for the way his
amusing remark had held both him and the other lazy rogues up to
ridicule. So he angrily told him to go about his business, and not to
show his face there again.

SEVENTH STORY

*Bergamino, with the help of a story about Primas and the Abbot of Cluny,
tellingly chides Can Grande della Scala for a sudden fit of parsimony.*

Emilia's story, and the vivacious manner of its telling, provoked the
laughter of the whole company, including the queen, and everybody
applauded the crusader's novel interpretation of the gospel. When the
laughter subsided and they were all quiet again, Filostrato, whose turn it
was to tell a story, began to speak as follows:

Excellent ladies, it is a fine thing to strike a sitting target. But when
an archer takes sudden aim, and hits an unusual object that has
suddenly appeared from nowhere, his achievement is well-nigh
miraculous. It is not unduly difficult, for anyone so inclined, to
discuss, criticize and admonish the clergy for their foul and corrupt
way of life, which in many ways resembles a sitting target of evil.
And although our honest man did well to pierce the self-esteem of
the inquisitor by pointing out the hypocrisy of friars who offer in
alms to the poor what they should be giving to the pigs or
throwing down the drain, I feel that the hero of my story (for
which I have taken my cue from the previous tale) is the more
worthy of praise; for this man censured a great prince, Can Grande
della Scala,[1] for a quite unwonted and sudden fit of miserliness, by
telling a charming tale in which he represented, through others,

what he wanted to say about himself and Can Grande. My story runs as follows:

It is a matter of very common knowledge throughout the greater part of the world that Can Grande della Scala, upon whom Fortune smiled in so many of his deeds, was one of the most outstanding and munificent princes that Italy has known since the Emperor Frederick the Second.[2] He once arranged to hold a splendid and marvellous festival at Verona to which many people would be coming from all over the place, in particular court-entertainers of various kinds. But for reasons of his own, he suddenly changed his mind about it, offered token presents to those who had come, and sent them all packing. The only person to receive neither present nor *congé* was a certain Bergamino, a conversationalist of quite extraordinary wit and brilliance, who lingered on in the hope that it would eventually turn out to his advantage. But Can Grande had the fixed idea that whatever he gave to this man would be more surely wasted than if he had thrown it into the fire. He did not, however, say anything personally to Bergamino about this, nor did he have him told by others.

Several days went by, and Bergamino, receiving neither a summons to the Duke's table nor any request for his professional services, began to feel the crippling expense of staying at the inn with his servants and horses, and fell into a state of melancholy. But he waited just the same, thinking it would be unwise of him to leave. In his luggage he had three fine rich robes, which had been given to him by other noble lords, so that he would cut a graceful figure at the festivities. And since the innkeeper was demanding payment, he first gave him one of these, and then, after staying a while longer, he was compelled to give him the second, since otherwise he would have had to leave the inn altogether. Then he began to live off the third, having decided to stay until he had seen how long it would last, and then go away.

Now while he was living off this third robe, he happened one day to be standing with a very gloomy expression on his face, in front of the table where Can Grande was dining. More out of a desire to tease him than to be entertained by any of his witticisms, Can Grande looked towards him and said:

'Bergamino, what is the matter? You are looking so sad! Say something to us.'

Without a moment's reflection, yet with all the fluency of a speech prepared long in advance, Bergamino suddenly came out with a story relevant to his own case, which ran as follows:

'My lord, I must begin by telling you that Primas³ was a very great grammarian and had no equal as a quick and gifted versifier. These two qualities made him so famous and respected, that even though he was not known everywhere by sight, his name and reputation were such that there was hardly anybody who did not know who Primas was.

'Now it happened that once, while living in Paris in a state of poverty (which was the way he mostly lived, for his abilities were little appreciated by those who were rich enough to help him), he heard mention of a certain abbot of Cluny,⁴ who was believed to have a higher revenue from his estates than any other prelate in God's Church, with the exception of the Pope. He heard people saying wonderful and magnificent things about this Abbot, for instance that he always held open court and that nobody who called upon him was ever refused food and drink, provided only that he asked for it while the Abbot was at table. When Primas heard this, he decided, being a man who enjoyed seeing gentlemen and princes, that he would go and discover for himself how splendidly the Abbot lived, and he inquired how far it was from Paris to his residence. On being told it was a distance of about six miles, Primas calculated that by setting out early in the morning he could reach the place in time for breakfast.

'He ascertained which road he should take, but since nobody else appeared to be going there, he was afraid that he might be unlucky enough to lose his way, and arrive at some spot where a meal would not be so easy to come by. So in order to be on the safe side, he decided, by way of insuring himself against total lack of sustenance, to take along three loaves, reflecting at the same time that he would always be able to find water to drink, although this commodity was not much to his taste. And so he set out, with the loaves stuffed inside his tunic, and made such excellent progress that he arrived before breakfast at the place where the Abbot was living. Once inside, he took a good look round, and saw that a great number of tables had been set, the kitchen was a hive of activity, and various other dining arrangements had been put in hand, whereupon he thought to himself: "This man is truly as excellent as people say." He spent a little more time surveying the scene, and then, since the meal was now ready, the Abbot's steward ordered in the water for them to wash their hands, after which he seated them all at table. By a pure coincidence, the place where Primas was seated happened to be directly opposite the door of the room from which the Abbot would emerge as he came into the hall to dine.

'It was a custom of the house that neither wine nor bread nor any other food or drink was ever placed on the tables till the Abbot came and occupied his seat. So when the steward had got everybody settled, he sent word to the Abbot that the meal was ready and they were awaiting his pleasure.

'The Abbot ordered a servant to open the door of his room so that he could proceed into the hall, but as he was on his way in, he looked straight ahead, and the first man he happened to catch sight of was Primas, who was very scruffily dressed and unknown to him by sight. No sooner did the Abbot see him, than a malicious thought suddenly crossed his mind, of a sort he had never entertained before, and he said to himself: "Why should I give my hospitality to the likes of this fellow?" And turning on his heel, he ordered the door of his room to be shut, and asked his attendants whether any of them knew the identity of the uncouth fellow who was seated at table opposite the door of his room. But nobody knew who he was.

'Primas had worked up an appetite from his walk and was not in the habit of going without food, so after waiting for a while and seeing no sign of the Abbot's return, he took out one of the three loaves he had brought with him, and started to eat. Meanwhile the Abbot ordered one of his servants to go and see whether the man was still there.

'"Yes, sir," replied the servant. "What is more, he is eating a loaf of bread, which he must have brought with him."

'"Then let him eat his own food, if he has some," said the Abbot, "for he shall eat none of ours today."

'The Abbot would have preferred that Primas should go away of his own accord, for he felt it would be discourteous to order him to leave. Having eaten the first loaf, there being still no sign of the Abbot, Primas began to eat the second. This fact also was reported to the Abbot, who had sent to see whether he was still there.

'Finally, since the Abbot showed no sign of coming, Primas, having finished the second loaf, started to eat the third. This too was reported to the Abbot, who began to ponder the matter and say to himself: "Now what on earth has got into me today? Why have I suddenly become such a miser? Why should I feel so much contempt for this unknown visitor? For years I have provided food for any man who cared to eat it, without inquiring whether he was a peasant or a gentleman, poor or rich, merchant or swindler. With my own eyes, I have seen any number of rogues devouring my food, and I have never felt as I do today about this fellow. No ordinary man can have caused me to be afflicted with such meanness. This fellow I regard as a knave must be someone important, for me to have set my heart so firmly against offering him my hospitality."

'Having said this to himself, he was anxious to know who the man might be. And when he discovered it was Primas, who had come there to see if the tales of his generosity were true, the Abbot felt thoroughly ashamed, for he had long been aware of the reputation Primas enjoyed as a man of excellent worth. Being desirous of making amends, he went out of his way to do him honour. After having fed him in a manner appropriate to his renown, he saw that he was richly clothed, provided him with money and a saddle-horse, and offered him the freedom of his household. Well satisfied, Primas thanked the Abbot as heartily as he could, before returning on horseback to Paris, whence he had set out on foot.'

Can Grande, being a man of some intelligence, had no need to hear any more in order to see exactly what Bergamino was driving at. And with a broad smile, he said to him:

'Bergamino, you have given an apt demonstration of the wrongs you have suffered. You have shown us your worth, my meanness, and what it is that you want from me. To tell you the truth, I was never seized before with the meanness I have lately felt on your account. But I shall drive it away with the stock that you yourself have furnished.'

Can Grande saw that the innkeeper's account was settled, then dressed Bergamino most sumptuously in one of his own robes, provided him with money and a saddle-horse, and offered him the freedom of his household for the rest of his stay.

EIGHTH STORY

With a few prettily spoken words, Guiglielmo Borsiere punctures the avarice of Ermino de' Grimaldi.

Next to Filostrato was sitting Lauretta, who, knowing that she was expected to speak, without waiting to be bidden allowed the applause for Bergamino's cleverness to subside, then gracefully began as follows:

The previous story, dear friends, implants in me a desire to tell you how, in similar fashion and not without fruitful effects, a worthy courtier derided the covetous habits of a very rich merchant. Although the burden of my tale is similar to the last, that is no reason for you to find it less agreeable, when you consider how much good eventually came of it.

In Genoa, then, a long time ago, there lived a gentleman called Ermino de' Grimaldi,[1] who was generally acknowledged, on account of his vast wealth and huge estates, to be by far the richest citizen in the Italy of his day. Not only was he richer than any man in Italy, he was incomparably greedier and more tight-fisted than every other grasper or miser in the whole wide world. For he would entertain on a shoestring, and in contrast to the normal habits of the Genoese (who are wont to dress in the height of fashion), he would sooner go about in rags than spend any money on his personal appearance. Nor was his attitude to food and drink any different. It was therefore not surprising that he had lost the surname of Grimaldi and was simply known to one and all as Ermino Skinflint.

Now, it so happened that whilst this fellow, by spending not a penny, was busily increasing his fortune, there arrived in Genoa a worthy courtier, Guiglielmo Borsiere[2] by name, who was refined of manner and eloquent of tongue, altogether different from the courtiers of today. For to the eternal shame of those who nowadays lay claim, despite their corrupt and disgraceful habits, to the title and distinction of lords and gentlemen, our modern courtiers are better described as asses, brought up, not in any court, but on the dungheap of all the scum of the earth's iniquities. In former times, their function usually consisted, and all their efforts were expended, in making peace whenever disputes or conflicts arose between two nobles, negotiating treaties of marriage, friendship or alliance, restoring tired minds and amusing the courts with fine and graceful witticisms, and censuring the failings of miscreants with pungent, fatherly strictures, all of which they would do for the slenderest of rewards. Whereas nowadays they spend the whole of their time in exchanging scandal with each other, sowing discord, describing acts of lewdness and ribaldry, or worse still, practising them in the presence of gentlemen. Or else they will justly or falsely accuse one another of wicked, disgusting and disreputable conduct, and entice noble spirits with false endearments to do what is evil and sinful. And the man who is held in the greatest esteem, who is most highly honoured and richly rewarded by our base and wretched nobles, is the one whose speech and actions are the most reprehensible. All of which is greatly and culpably to the shame of the modern world, and proves very clearly that the present generation has been stripped of all the virtues, and left to wallow abjectly in a cesspit of vices.

But to return to what I had begun to say before my righteous anger carried me somewhat further astray than I had intended, the aforesaid Guiglielmo received a warm and ready welcome from all the best families in Genoa. And after he had spent a number of days in the city, and listened to several accounts of Ermino's greed and miserliness, he was eager to see what manner of man he was.

Ermino had already been told what an excellent fellow Guiglielmo Borsiere was, and since, for all his meanness, he still preserved a glimmer of civility, he received him very sociably, with cheerful countenance, and began to converse with him on various different topics. As they talked, he conveyed him, along with certain other Genoese who were present, to a splendid house he had recently caused to be built for his use. And having shown him all over the building, he said:

'Well now, Guiglielmo, as one who has seen and heard many things in his time, could you perhaps suggest a thing that no man has ever seen, which I could commission to be painted in the main hall of this house of mine?'

To which Guiglielmo, on hearing him talk in this unseemly fashion, replied:

'Sir, I do not think I could suggest a thing that no man has ever seen, unless it were a fit of the sneezes or something of that sort. But if you like, I can certainly suggest a thing I do not believe that you yourself have ever seen.'

'Ah,' said Ermino, who was not expecting the answer he was about to be given, 'then I beg you to tell me what it is.'

Whereupon Guiglielmo promptly replied:

'Let Generosity be painted there.'

When Ermino heard this word, he was so overcome with shame, that his character was suddenly and almost totally transformed.

'Guiglielmo,' he said, 'I shall have it painted there in such a way that neither you nor anyone else will ever again have cause to tell me that I have not seen and known it.'

Guiglielmo's remark had such a potent effect upon Ermino that from that day forth he became the most courteous and generous gentleman in the Genoa of his time, and was respected above all others, not only by his fellow-citizens, but by visitors to the city.

NINTH STORY

The King of Cyprus is transformed, on receiving a sharp rebuke from a lady of Gascony, from a weakling into a man of courage.

The queen's final word of command was reserved for Elissa, who, without pausing to hear it, began all merrily as follows:

It has frequently come about, young ladies, that a single word, uttered more often by chance than with studied intent, has sufficed to cure a person of something against which various strictures and

any number of punishments have proved ineffectual. This fact
is very well brought out in the story told by Lauretta, and I
too propose to show it to you in another tale, which shall be
very brief. For good stories may always come in useful, and
you should lend them an attentive ear, no matter who does the
telling.

I say, then, that during the reign of the first king of Cyprus,[1] after
the conquest of the Holy Land by Godfrey of Bouillon, it happened
that a gentlewoman of Gascony made a pilgrimage to the Sepulchre,
and having arrived in Cyprus on her return journey, she was
brutally assaulted by a pack of ruffians. Her sorrow at this deed was
inconsolable, and she resolved to go and lay a complaint before the
King. But she was told that she would be wasting her time, for the
King was of such a weak and craven disposition, that not only
would he allow others' wrongs to go unpunished by the law, but
like a despicable coward he would suffer all manner of insults
offered to his own royal person. So much so, indeed, that whenever
anybody had an axe to grind, he would relieve his feelings by
shaming or insulting the King.

On hearing this, the woman lost all hope of being revenged, but
she decided, as some small compensation for her woes, to taunt this
king with his faint-heartedness. So she presented herself in tears
before him, and said:

'My lord, I do not come before you in the expectation of any
redress for the wrong inflicted upon me. But by way of repara-
tion for my injury, I beg you to instruct me how you manage
to endure the wrongs which, as I am led to understand, are
inflicted upon you, so that I might learn from you to bear my
own with patience. God knows that, if I could, I would willingly
make you a present of it, since you find these things so easy to
support.'

The King, who until that moment had been so slow and passive,
reacted as though he had been roused from sleep. Beginning with the
injury done to this lady, which he avenged most harshly, he
thenceforth became the implacable scourge of all those who did
anything to impugn the honour of his crown.

TENTH STORY

Master Alberto of Bologna neatly turns the tables on a lady who was intent upon making him blush for being in love with her.

Once Elissa was silent, only the tale of the queen remained to be told, and she began with womanly grace to address them as follows:

Just as the sky, worthy young ladies, is bejewelled with stars on cloudless nights, and the verdant fields are embellished with flowers in the spring, so good manners and pleasant converse are enriched by shafts of wit. These, being brief, are much better suited to women than to men, as it is more unseemly for a woman to speak at inordinate length, when this can be avoided, than it is for a man. Yet nowadays, to the universal shame of ourselves and all living women, few or none of the women who are left can recognize a shaft of wit when they hear one, or reply to it even if they recognize it. For this special skill, which once resided in a woman's very soul, has been replaced in our modern women by the adornment of the body. She who sees herself tricked out in the most elaborate finery, with the largest number of gaudy stripes and speckles, believes that she should be much more highly respected and more greatly honoured than other women, forgetting that if someone were to dress an ass in the same clothes or simply load them on its back, it could still carry a great deal more than she could, nor would this be any reason for paying it greater respect than you would normally accord to an ass.

I am ashamed to say it, since in condemning others I condemn myself: but these over-dressed, heavily made-up, excessively ornamented females either stand around like marble statues in an attitude of dumb indifference, or else, on being asked a question, they give such stupid replies that they would have been far better advised to remain silent. And they delude themselves into thinking that their inability to converse in the company of gentlemen and ladies proceeds from their purity of mind. They give the name of honesty to their dull-wittedness, as though the only honest women are those who speak to no one except their maids, their washerwomen, or their pastrycooks. Whereas if, as they fondly imagine, this had been Nature's intention, she would have devised some other means for restricting their prattle.

In this as in other things one must, it is true, take account of the time and the place and the person with whom one is speaking. For it sometimes happens that men or women, thinking to make a person blush through uttering some little pleasantry, and having underestimated the other person's powers, find the blush intended for their opponent recoiling upon themselves. Wherefore, in order that you may learn to be on your guard, and also in order that people should not associate you with the proverb commonly heard on everyone's lips, namely that women are always worsted in any argument, I desire that the tale which it falls to me to relate, and which completes our storytelling for today, should be one which will make you conversant with these matters. Thus you will be able to show that you are different from other women, not only for the noble qualities of your minds, but also for the excellence of your manners.

Not many years ago, there lived in Bologna a brilliant physician of almost universal renown, and perhaps he is alive to this day, whose name was Master Alberto.[1] Although he was an old man approaching seventy, and the natural warmth had almost entirely departed from his body, his heart was so noble that he was not averse to welcoming the flames of love. One day, whilst attending a feast, he had seen a strikingly beautiful woman, a widow whose name, according to some accounts, was Malgherida de' Ghisolieri. He was mightily attracted by the lady, and, no differently than if he had been in the prime of his youth, he felt those flames so keenly in his mature old breast, that he never seemed able to sleep at night, unless in the course of the day he had seen the fair lady's fine and delectable features. Hence he began to pass regularly up and down in front of the lady's house, sometimes on foot and sometimes on horseback, depending on his mood. And accordingly both she and several other ladies quickly divined his motive, and often jested with one another to see a man of such great age and wisdom caught in the toils of love. For the good ladies seemed to suppose that the delightful sensations of love could take root and thrive in no other place than the frivolous hearts of the young.

Master Alberto continued to pass up and down, and one Sunday, whilst the lady happened to be seated outside her front door with a number of other ladies, they caught sight of him in the distance, coming in their direction. Whereupon they all resolved, with the lady's agreement, to receive him and do him honour, and then make fun of him over this great passion of his. And that was precisely what they did. For they all stood up and invited him to accompany them into a cool walled garden, where they plied him with excellent wines and sweetmeats, and eventually they asked him, charmingly and with good grace, how it came about that he had fallen in love with this fair lady, when he was well aware that she was being courted by many a handsome, well-bred and sprightly young admirer. On hearing himself chided so politely, the doctor replied, smiling broadly:

'My lady, the fact that I am enamoured should not excite the wonder of anyone who is wise, and especially not your own, because you are worthy of my love. For albeit old men are naturally deficient in the powers required for lovemaking, they do not necessarily lack a ready will, or a just appreciation of what should be loved. On the contrary, in this respect their longer experience gives them an advantage over the young. The hope which sustains an old man like myself in loving one who is loved, as you are, by many young men, is founded on what I have often observed in places where I have seen ladies eating lupines and leeks whilst taking a meal out of doors. For although no part of the leek is good, yet the part which is less objectionable and more pleasing to the palate is the root, which you ladies are generally drawn by some aberration of the appetite to hold in the hand while you eat the leaves, which are not only worthless, but have an unpleasant taste. How am I to know, my lady, whether you are not equally eccentric in choosing your lovers? For if this were so, I should be the one you would choose, and the others would be cast aside.'

The gentlewoman, who along with the others was feeling some-what abashed, replied:

'Master Alberto, you have given us a charming and very sound reproof for our presumptuousness. Your love is none the less precious to me, since it proceeds from so patently wise and excellent a man. And therefore, saving my honour, you are free to ask of me what you will, and regard it as yours.'

The doctor stood up with his companions, thanked the lady, took his leave of her amid much laughter and merriment, and departed.

Thus the lady, thinking she would score a victory, underestimated the object of her raillery and was herself defeated. And if you ladies are wise, you will guard against following her example.

★   ★   ★

Already the sun was dipping towards the west, and the heat of the day had largely abated, when the stories told by the seven young ladies and the three young men were found to be at an end. Accordingly their queen addressed them, in gracious tones, as follows:

'For the present day, dear friends, my reign is complete except for giving you another queen, who shall decide for herself how her time and ours should be spent in seemly pleasures on the morrow. And albeit some little time still appears to be left until nightfall, I believe this to be the most suitable hour at which to begin all the days that ensue, since preparations can thus be made for whatever the new queen considers appropriate with regard to the following day. For we are unlikely to make proper provision for the future unless some thought is devoted beforehand to the matter. And therefore, with due reverence to the One who gives life to all things, and with an eye to our common good, I decree that on this coming day the queen who will govern our realm shall be Filomena, a young lady of excellent judgement.'

Having spoken these words, she rose to her feet and removed her laurel garland, which she reverently placed upon Filomena; after which, first she herself, then all the other maidens, and the young men too, hailed Filomena as their queen and pledged themselves with good grace to her sovereignty.

Filomena blushed a little for modesty on finding that she had been crowned as their queen. But recalling the words so recently uttered by Pampinea, and not wishing to appear obtuse, she plucked up courage, and first of all she confirmed the appointments made by Pampinea, and gave instructions as to what should be done for the following morning, as well as for supper that evening, due account being taken of the place in which they were staying. Then she began to address the company as follows:

'Dearest companions, albeit Pampinea, more out of kindness of heart than for any merit of my own, has made me your queen, I do not intend, in shaping the manner in which we should comport ourselves, merely to follow my personal judgement, but rather to blend my judgement with yours. In order that you may know what I have in mind, and thus be at liberty to suggest additions or curtailments to my programme, I propose to expound it to you briefly. Unless I am mistaken, I would say that the formalities observed today by Pampinea were both laudable and pleasing. And so, until such time as we should find them wearisome, whether through constant repetition or for some other reason, I consider they ought to remain unaltered.

'Having thus confirmed the procedure for the activities upon which we have now embarked, we can rise from this place, and go off in search of our amusement. And when the sun is about to set, we shall sup out of doors, and then we shall have a few songs and other entertainments, after which it will be time to go to bed. Tomorrow morning we shall rise early, whilst it is yet cool, and once more we shall go off somewhere and engage in whatever pastime each of us may prefer. In due course we shall return, as we did today, in order to breakfast together. We shall then dance for a while, and when we have risen from our siesta, we shall return and resume our storytelling, from which I consider that a great deal of pleasure and of profit is derived.

'I do however wish to initiate a practice which Pampinea, because she was elected late as our queen, was unable to introduce: namely, to restrict the matter of our storytelling[1] within some fixed limit which will be defined for you in advance, so that each of us will have time to prepare a good story on the subject prescribed.

'Ever since the world began, men have been subject to various tricks of Fortune, and it will ever be thus until the end. Let each of us, then, if you have no objection, make it our purpose to take as our theme *those who after suffering a series of misfortunes are brought to a state of unexpected happiness.*'

This rule was commended by all the company, gentlemen and ladies alike, and they agreed to be bound by it. But Dioneo said, when the rest had finished talking:

'My lady, like all the others, I too say that the rule you have given us is highly attractive and laudable. But I would ask you to grant me a special privilege, which I wish to have conferred upon me for as long as our company shall last, namely, that whenever I feel so inclined, I may be exempted from this law obliging us to conform to the subject agreed, and tell whatever story I please. But so that none shall think I desire this favour because I have but a poor supply of stories, I will say at once that I am willing always to be the last person to speak.'

The queen, knowing what a jovial and entertaining fellow he was, and clearly perceiving that he was only asking this favour so that, if the company should grow weary of hearing people talk, he could enliven the proceedings with some story that would move them to laughter, cheerfully granted his request, having first obtained the consent of the others. She then stood up, and they all sauntered off towards a stream of crystal-clear water, which descended the side of a hill and flowed through the shade of a thickly wooded valley, its banks lined with smooth round stones and verdant grasses. On reaching the stream, they stepped barefoot and with naked arms into the water and began to engage in various games with each other. But when it was nearly time for supper, they made their way back to the house, and there they supped merrily together.

After supper, instruments were sent for, and the queen decreed that a dance should begin, which Lauretta was to lead whilst Emilia was to sing a song, accompanied on the lute by Dioneo. No sooner did she hear the queen's command than Lauretta promptly began to dance, and she was joined by the others, whilst Emilia sang the following song in amorous tones:

'In mine own beauty take I such delight
That to no other love could I
My fond affections plight.

'Since in my looking-glass each hour I spy
Beauty enough to satisfy the mind,
Why seek out past delights, or new ones try
When all content within my glass I find?
What other sight so pleasing to mine eyes
Is there that I might see
Which further I could prize?

'My sweet reflection never fades away;
My consolation ever is
To see it every day.
It lies beyond the tongue's expressing
To celebrate a joy so fine;
None understands this bliss who has not burned
With a delight like mine.

'The longer I reflect upon those same
Eyes that stare from mine own face back to me,
The fiercer burns the flame.
I yield it all my heart, it renders back
All that I gave; I taste the bliss
It promised me; and hope yet more to have.
Ah, who has loved like this!'

Albeit the words of this little song caused not a few to ponder its meaning, they all joined cheerfully in the choruses. When it was over, they danced and sang some other short pieces, and then, as the night was short and much of it already spent, the queen was pleased to bring the first day to an end. Having called for torches to be lit, she ordered her companions to retire to rest till the following morning, and this command, returning to their several rooms, they duly obeyed.

Here ends the First Day of the Decameron

SECOND DAY

Here begins the Second Day, wherein, under the rule of Filomena, *the discussion turns upon those who after suffering a series of misfortunes are brought to a state of unexpected happiness.*

The sun, having already ushered in the new day, was casting its light into every corner, and the birds singing gaily among the green boughs were announcing its presence to the ear, when the seven ladies and the three young men rose with one accord from their slumbers. Entering the gardens, they went from one part to another, and amused themselves for a long time by wandering unhurriedly over the dew-flecked lawns and weaving pretty garlands of flowers. And as they had done on the previous day, so they did on this. Having breakfasted in the open air, they danced a little and then retired to rest. Rising in the afternoon at about the hour of nones, as their queen had requested, they came to the little green meadow, where they seated themselves in a circle around her. She, looking most shapely and attractive, sat there with her laurel crown on her head, gazing in turn at each of her companions, and eventually she requested Neifile to open the day's proceedings by telling the first story. Whereupon, without awaiting further encouragement, Neifile cheerfully began in the following manner:

FIRST STORY

Martellino, having pretended to be paralysed, gives the impression that he has been cured by being placed on the body of Saint Arrigo.[1] When his deception is discovered, he is beaten, arrested, and very nearly hanged: but in the end he saves his skin.

It has often happened, dearest ladies, that a man who has attempted to hold people up to ridicule, especially in matters worthy of reverence, has merely found himself humiliated, sometimes suffering injury into the bargain. Hence, in deference to the queen's wishes, and by way of introduction to our theme, I propose in this story of mine to tell you what happened to a fellow citizen of ours who, after running into serious trouble, escaped far more lightly than he had anticipated.

Not long ago there lived in Treviso a German, whose name was Arrigo. He was just a poor fellow who carried people's heavy goods for hire, yet everyone regarded him as a man of honest and very saintly ways. Whether it is true or not I cannot say, but the Trevisans claim that when he died, all the bells of the cathedral in Treviso began to ring of their own accord. This was taken as a miracle, and everyone said that Arrigo must be a Saint. The whole of the populace therefore converged on the house in which his corpse was lying, and from there they conveyed it to the cathedral, treating it as though it were indeed the body of a Saint. People who were lame or blind or paralysed were taken to the church, along with others suffering from any kind of illness or infirmity, in the belief that they would all be cured by contact with Arrigo's body.

In the middle of all this turmoil, with people rushing hither and thither, three fellow citizens of ours, whose names were Stecchi, Martellino, and Marchese, happened to arrive in Treviso. These three used to do the rounds of the various courts, where they would entertain their audiences by putting on disguises and making all manner of gestures, by means of which they could impersonate anyone they pleased. They had never been to Treviso before, and were surprised to find so much commotion. But when they heard the reason, they immediately wanted to go and see for themselves. After calling at an inn, where they left their belongings, Marchese said:

'We ought to go and inspect this Saint. But I can't see how we are to reach him, because from what I have heard, the square is swarming with Germans,[2] to say nothing of the armed men stationed there by the ruler to prevent disturbances. And in any case, the church itself is said to be crammed with so many people, that it can hardly take another living soul.'

'Don't be put off by a little thing like that,' said Martellino, who was eager to see what was going on. 'I shall certainly find a way of reaching the Saint's body.'

'How?' said Marchese.

'Like this,' Martellino replied. 'I'll disguise myself as a paralytic, and pretend I can't walk. Then with you propping me up on one side and Stecchi on the other, you will both go along giving the impression that you're taking me to be healed by the Saint. When they see us coming, everyone will step aside and let us through.'

Marchese and Stecchi thought this a splendid idea, so all three of them promptly left the inn and went to a lonely spot, where Martellino contorted not only his hands, fingers, arms and legs, but also his mouth, his eyes and the whole of his face, becoming such a horrifying spectacle that no one would have taken him for anything other than a genuine case of hopeless and total bodily paralysis. In this state he was taken up by Marchese and Stecchi, and they headed for the church, with pity written all over their faces, humbly beseeching all those blocking their path to make way, for the love of God. They persuaded people to move without any trouble, and in brief, to the accompaniment of almost continuous cries of 'Make way! Make way!', and with all eyes turned in their direction, they arrived at the place where the body of Saint Arrigo was lying. There were some gentlemen standing round the body, and they quickly took hold of Martellino and laid him across it, so that it might help him regain the use of his limbs.

Martellino lay there motionless for a while, with all eyes fixed upon him to see what would happen. Then, like the skilled performer that he was, he began to go through the motions of straightening out one of his fingers, then a hand, then an arm, and so on until he had unwound himself completely. When the people saw this, they applauded Saint Arrigo so rowdily that a roll of thunder would have passed unnoticed.

Now it happened that there was a Florentine standing nearby, and although he was very well acquainted with Martellino, he had failed to recognize him when he was first led in, because of the grotesqueness of his appearance. But when he saw him standing up straight, he knew at once who it was, and he burst out laughing and said:

'God damn the fellow! Who would have thought, to see him arriving, that he was not really paralysed at all!'

'What?' exclaimed a number of Trevisans, who had overheard the Florentine's words. 'Do you mean to say he was not paralysed?'

'Heaven forbid!' the Florentine replied. 'He has always stood as straight as the rest of us. But as you could see just now, he has this extraordinary knack of disguising himself in any manner he chooses.'

There was no need to say any more, for on hearing this they forced their way to the front, and began to shout:

'Take hold of that blaspheming swindler! He comes here pretending to be a cripple, poking fun at our Saint and making fools of us when he wasn't really crippled at all!'

And so saying, they seized him and dragged him away; then they took him by the hair, tore every stitch of clothing from his back, and started to punch and to kick him. In fact, everybody within sight was bearing down upon him, or so it seemed to Martellino.

'Mercy, for the love of God!' he cried, defending himself as best he could. But it was of no use, for more and more people were piling on top of him every minute.

When Marchese and Stecchi saw what was happening, they began to have serious misgivings. Fearing for their own safety, they dared not go to Martellino's assistance, but on the contrary they yelled 'Kill him!' as loudly as anybody else, at the same time trying to devise some way of rescuing him from the hands of the mob.

And he would certainly have been killed but for a quick piece of thinking on the part of Marchese, who made his way as swiftly as possible to the captain in charge of the watch, drawn up in strength outside the church, and said to him:

'For God's sake, come quickly! There's a villain over here who has cut my purse, and robbed me of a hundred gold florins at the very least. Arrest him! Please don't let him run off with my money!'

On hearing this, a dozen or more of the officers rushed over to the place where poor Martellino was having his brains beaten out, and after forcing their way through the crowd with enormous difficulty, they removed him all bruised and battered from their clutches, and hauled him off to the magistrate's palace.

A number of people followed him all the way, still angry with him for hoodwinking them, and when they heard he had been arrested as a cutpurse, they too began to claim that he had stolen their purses, thinking this as fair a way as any of making life unpleasant for him. The magistrate, who was of a harsh disposition, no sooner heard these accusations than he took him aside and began to interrogate him on the matter. But Martellino gave him facetious answers, as though quite unconcerned at his arrest. This upset the judge, who had him fastened to the strappado, and ordered him to be given a series of good hard blows, with the intention of extracting a confession from him before having him hanged. When they let him down, and the judge asked him whether the accusations brought against him were true, he replied, since a straight denial would have been useless:

'Sir, I am ready to confess the truth. But make each of my accusers say when and where I cut his purse, and I will tell you whether or not I did it.'

'A good idea!' said the judge, and he ordered several of them to be summoned. One of them claimed that his purse had been stolen a week before, another said six days, another four, and some of them said they had been robbed that very day. Whereupon Martellino retorted:

'Sir, they are all a lot of bare-faced liars, and I can prove it to you, because I only arrived in this city for the first time a couple of hours ago. I wish to God I had never set foot in it at all! As soon as I arrived, I went to have a look at the body of this Saint, where I had the ill-luck to be given a good drubbing, as you can see for yourself. Ask the customs officer at the city gates, consult his register, ask my landlord, and they will all bear out what I have told you. And if you find I am telling the truth, I beg you to listen no further to these vicious perjurers. Please don't let me be tortured and put to death.'

Meanwhile, with the matter proceeding along these lines, word had reached Marchese and Stecchi that the judge was giving him a rough handling and had already put him on the strappado. 'We have made a fine mess of things,' they said, shaking with fright. 'We have taken him out of the frying-pan, and dropped him straight in the fire.'[3] Being determined to leave no stone unturned, they tracked down their landlord, and explained to him what had happened. The landlord, who was highly amused at their tale, took them to see a man called Sandro Agolanti, a Florentine living in Treviso who had considerable influence with the ruler of the city. Having acquainted him with all the facts, the landlord joined the other two in pleading with him to intervene on Martellino's behalf.

Sandro laughed heartily, then he went off to see the prince, and persuaded him to send for Martellino. The men who were sent to fetch him found him still standing in front of the judge, wearing nothing but a shirt, and trembling all over with fear and dismay because the judge would not listen to anything that was said in his defence. Indeed, since he happened to have some sort of grudge against Florentines, he was quite determined to have him hanged, and stubbornly refused to hand him over until he was compelled to do so. When Martellino came before the ruler, he gave him a full account of what had happened, and begged him as a supreme favour to let him go about his business; for until he was safely back in Florence, he would always feel that he had a noose round his neck. The ruler went into fits of laughter to hear of such remarkable goings on and ordered each of them to be provided with a new suit of clothes. Thus all three emerged from this dreadful ordeal better than they ever expected, and returned home safe and sound.

SECOND STORY

Rinaldo d'Asti is robbed, turns up at Castel Guiglielmo, and is provided with hospitality by a widow. Then, having recovered his belongings, he returns home safe and sound.

Neifile's account of Martellino's adventures brought gales of laughter from the ladies and the young men, especially Filostrato, who, being seated next to Neifile, was bidden by the queen to tell the next story. He began straightway, as follows:

Fair ladies, the story that takes my fancy is one that contains a judicious mixture of piety, calamity and love. Possibly it has no more to recommend it than its usefulness, but it will be especially helpful to people wandering through the uncertain territories of love, where those who have not made a regular habit of saying Saint Julian's paternoster,[1] even though they have good beds, may find themselves uncomfortably lodged.

During the reign of the Marquis Azzo of Ferrara, a merchant whose name was Rinaldo d'Asti was returning home after dispatching certain business in Bologna. He had already passed through Ferrara, and was riding towards Verona, when he fell in with three men who, though they had the appearance of merchants, were in fact brigands of a particularly desperate and disreputable sort. With these he struck up conversation, and rashly agreed to ride along in their company.

On seeing that he was a merchant, who was probably carrying a certain amount of money with him, these men resolved to rob him at the earliest opportunity. But in order not to arouse his suspicions, they assumed an air of simplicity and respectability, restricting their conversation to the subject of loyalty and other polite topics, and went out of their way to appear humble and obliging towards him. He consequently thought himself very fortunate to have met them, for he was travelling alone except for a single servant on horseback. As they went along, with the conversation passing as usual from one thing to another, they got on to the subject of the prayers that people address to God, and one of the bandits turned to Rinaldo and said:

'What about you, sir? What prayer do you generally say when you are travelling?'

'To tell the truth,' Rinaldo replied, 'in matters of this kind I am rather simple and down-to-earth. I am one of the old-fashioned sort who likes to call a spade a spade, and I don't know many prayers. All the same, when I am travelling it is my custom never to leave the inn of a morning without reciting an Our Father and a Hail Mary for the souls of Saint Julian's father and mother, after which I pray to God and the Saint to give me a good lodging for the night to come. On many a day, in the course of my travels, I have met with great dangers, only to survive them all and find myself at nightfall in a safe place and a comfortable lodging. Now I firmly believe this favour to have been obtained for me from God by Saint Julian, in whose honour I recite my prayer; and if on any morning I neglected to say it, I would feel I could do nothing right the whole day, and would come to some harm before the evening.'

'Did you say it this morning?' said the man who had asked him the question.

'I did indeed,' replied Rinaldo.

The man, who by this time knew what was going to happen, said to himself: 'A fat lot of good it will do you, for I reckon you are going to have a poor night's lodging if all goes according to plan.' Then he turned to Rinaldo and said:

'I too have travelled a great deal, and although I have heard many people speak highly of this Saint, I have never prayed to him myself. Nevertheless, I have always managed to find good quarters. Perhaps we shall see this evening which of us is the better lodged: you, who have said the prayer, or I, who have not said it. Mind you, I *do* use another one instead, either the *Dirupisti* or the *Intemerata* or the *De Profundis*, all of which are extremely effective, or so my old grandmother used to tell me.'

And so they went along, talking of this and that, with the three men biding their time and waiting for a suitable place to carry their villainous plan into effect. The day was drawing to a close when, at a concealed and deserted river-crossing on the far side of the fortress-town called Castel Guiglielmo, the three bandits took advantage of the lateness of the hour to launch their attack and rob him of everything he possessed, including his horse. Before leaving, they turned to him as he stood there in nothing but his shirt, and called out:

'Now see whether the prayer you said to Saint Julian will give you as good a night's lodging as our own saint will provide for us.' They then crossed the river, and rode off.

Rinaldo's wretch of a servant did nothing to assist his master on seeing him attacked, but turned his horse round and galloped all the way to Castel Guiglielmo without stopping. It was already dark by the time he entered the town, so he conveniently forgot the whole business, and put up for the night at an inn.

Rinaldo, bare-footed and wearing only a shirt, was at his wits' end, for the weather was very cold, it was snowing hard the whole time, and it was getting darker every minute. Shivering all over, his teeth chattering, he began to look round for a sheltered spot where he could spend the night without freezing to death. But since there had been a war in the countryside[2] a short time previously and everything had been burnt to the ground, there was no shelter to be seen anywhere, and so he set off for Castel Guiglielmo, walking at a brisk pace on account of the cold. He had no idea whether his servant had fled to the fortress or to some other town, but he thought that, once inside the walls, God would surely send him some sort of relief.

He still had over a mile to go when night came on with a vengeance, and when he finally arrived it was so late that the gates were locked, the drawbridges were up, and he was unable to gain admittance. Feeling depressed and miserable, he looked round with tears in his eyes to see whether there was a place where he would at least find some protection from the snow, and he happened to catch sight of a house that jutted out appreciably from the top of the castle walls, so he decided to go and take refuge beneath it till daybreak. When he reached the spot, he discovered there was a postern underneath the overhang, and although the door was locked, at its base he heaped a quantity of straw which was lying nearby, and settled down upon it. He was thoroughly fed up, and complained at regular intervals to Saint Julian, saying that this was no way to treat one of his faithful devotees. Saint Julian had not lost sight of him, however, and before very long he was to see that Rinaldo was comfortably settled.

In the castle there was a widow, lovelier of body than any other woman in the world, with whom the Marquis Azzo was madly in love. He had set her up there as his mistress, and she was living in the very house beneath which Rinaldo had taken refuge. As it happened, the Marquis had arrived at the castle on that very day with the intention of spending the night with her, and had made secret arrangements to have a sumptuous supper prepared, and to take a bath in the lady's house beforehand. Everything was ready, and she was only waiting for the Marquis to turn up, when a servant happened to arrive at the gate, bringing the Marquis a message requiring him to leave immediately. So he sent word to the lady that he would not be coming, then hastily mounted his horse and rode away. The lady, feeling rather disconsolate and not knowing what to do with herself, decided she would have the bath which had been prepared for the Marquis, after which she would sup and go to bed. And so into the bath she went.

As she lay there in the bath, which was near the postern on the other side of which our unfortunate hero had taken shelter, she could hear the wails and moans being uttered by Rinaldo, who sounded from the way his teeth were chattering as if he had been turned into a stork.[3] She therefore summoned her maid, and said:

'Go upstairs, look over the wall, and see who it is on the other side of this door. Find out who he is and what he is doing there.'

The maid went up, and by the light of the stars she saw him sitting there just as we have described him, bare-footed and wearing only his shirt, and quivering all over like a jelly. She asked him who he was, and Rinaldo, who was shaking so much that he could hardly articulate, told her his name and explained as briefly as possible how and why he came to be there. He then implored her, in an agonized voice, to do whatever she could to prevent his being left there all night slowly freezing to death.

The maid, feeling very sorry for him, returned to her mistress and told her the whole story. The lady too was filled with pity, and, remembering that she had a key for that particular door, which the Marquis occasionally used for his clandestine visits, she said to the maid:

'Go and let him in, but do it quietly. We have this supper here, and no one to eat it. And we can easily put him up, for there's plenty of room.'

The maid warmly commended her mistress's charity, then she went and opened the door and let him in. Perceiving that he was almost frozen stiff, the lady of the house said to him:

'Quickly, good sir, step into that bath whilst it is still warm.'

He willingly obeyed, without waiting to be bidden twice. His whole body was refreshed by its warmth, and he felt as if he were returning from death to life. The lady had him supplied with clothes that had once belonged to her husband, who had died quite recently, and when he put them on they fitted him to perfection. As he awaited further instructions from the lady, he fell to thanking God and Saint Julian for rescuing him from the cruel night he had been expecting, and leading him to what appeared a good lodging.

Meanwhile the lady had taken a brief rest, having first ordered a huge fire to be lit in one of the rooms, to which she presently came, asking what had become of the gentleman.

'He's dressed, ma'am,' replied the maid, 'and he's ever so handsome, and seems a very decent and respectable person.'

'Then go and call him,' said the woman, 'and tell him to come here by the fire and have some supper, for I know he has not had anything to eat.'

On entering the room, Rinaldo, judging from her appearance that she was a lady of quality, greeted her with due reverence and thanked her with all the eloquence at his command for the kindness she had done him. When she saw him and heard him speak, the lady concluded that her maid had been right, and she welcomed him cordially, installed him in a comfortable chair beside her own in front of the fire, and asked him what had happened and how he came to be there, whereupon Rinaldo told her the whole story in detail.

The lady had already heard bits of the story after the arrival of Rinaldo's servant at the castle, and so she fully believed everything he told her. She in turn told him what she knew about his servant, adding that it would be easy enough to find him next morning. But by now the table was laid for supper, and Rinaldo, after washing his hands with the lady, accepted her invitation to sit down and eat at her side.

He was a fine, tall, handsome fellow in the prime of manhood, with impeccably good manners, and the lady cast many an appreciative glance in his direction. As she had been expecting to sleep with the Marquis, her carnal instincts were already aroused, and after supper she got up from the table and consulted with her maid to find out whether she thought it a good idea, since the Marquis had let her down, to make use of this unexpected gift of Fortune. The maid, knowing what her mistress had in mind, encouraged her for all she was worth, with the result that the lady returned to Rinaldo, whom she had left standing alone by the fire, and began to ogle him, saying:

'Come, Rinaldo, why are you looking so unhappy? What's the good of worrying about the loss of a horse and a few clothes? Do relax and cheer up. I want you to feel completely at home here. In fact, I will go so far as to say that seeing you in those clothes, I keep thinking you are my late husband, and I've been wanting to take you in my arms and kiss you the whole evening. I would certainly have done so, but I was afraid you might take it amiss.'

On hearing these words and perceiving the gleam in the lady's eyes, Rinaldo, who was no fool, advanced towards her with open arms, saying:

'My lady, I shall always have you to thank for the fact that I am alive, and when I consider the fate from which you delivered me, it would be highly discourteous of me if I did not attempt to further your inclinations to the best of my ability. Kiss and embrace me, therefore, to your heart's content, and I shall be more than happy to return the compliment.'

There was no need for any further preliminaries. The lady, who was all aflame with amorous desire, promptly rushed into his arms. Clasping him to her bosom, she smothered him with a thousand eager kisses and received as many in return, then they both retired into her bedroom, where they lost no time in getting into bed, and before the night was over they satisfied their longings repeatedly and in full measure.

They arose as soon as dawn began to break, for the lady was anxious not to give cause for scandal. Having provided him with some very old clothes and filled his purse with money, she then explained which road he must take on entering the fortress in order to find his servant, and finally she let him out by the postern through which he had entered, imploring him to keep their encounter a secret.

As soon as it was broad day and the gates were opened, he entered the castle, giving the impression he was arriving from a distance, and rooted out his servant. Having changed into the clothes that were in his portmanteau, he was about to mount his servant's horse, when as if by some divine miracle the three brigands were brought into the castle, after being arrested for another crime they had committed shortly after robbing him on the previous evening. They had made a voluntary confession, and consequently Rinaldo's horse, clothing and money were restored to him, and all he lost was a pair of garters, which the robbers were unable to account for.

Thus it was that Rinaldo, giving thanks to God and Saint Julian, mounted his horse and returned home safe and sound, whilst the three robbers went next day to dangle their heels in the north wind.

THIRD STORY

Three young men squander their fortunes, reducing themselves to penury. A nephew of theirs, left penniless, is on his way home when he falls in with an abbot, whom he discovers to be the daughter of the King of England. She later marries him and makes good all the losses suffered by his uncles, restoring them to positions of honour.

The whole company, men and ladies alike, listened with admiration to the adventures of Rinaldo d'Asti, commending his piety and giving thanks to God and Saint Julian, who had come to his rescue in the hour of his greatest need. Nor, moreover, was the lady considered to have acted foolishly (even though nobody openly said so) for the way she had accepted the blessing that God had left on her doorstep. And while everyone was busy talking, with half-suppressed mirth, about the pleasant night the lady had spent, Pampinea, finding herself next to Filostrato and realizing rightly that it would be her turn to speak next, collected her thoughts together and started planning what to say. And upon receiving the queen's command, she began, in a manner no less confident than it was lively, to speak as follows:

Excellent ladies, if the ways of Fortune are carefully examined, it will be seen that the more one discusses her actions, the more remains to be said. Nor is this surprising, when you pause to consider that she controls all the affairs we unthinkingly call our own, and that consequently it is she who arranges and rearranges them after her own inscrutable fashion, constantly moving them now in one direction, now in another, then back again, without following any discernible plan. The truth of this assertion is clearly illustrated by everything that happens in the space of a single day, as well as being borne out by some of the previous stories. Nevertheless, since our queen has decreed that we should speak on this particular theme, I shall add to the tales already told a story of my own, from which my listeners will possibly derive some profit, and which in my opinion ought to prove entertaining.

In our city there once lived a nobleman named Messer Tebaldo, who according to some people belonged to the Lamberti family, whilst others maintain he was an Agolanti,[1] perhaps for the simple reason that Tebaldo's son later followed a profession with which the Agolanti family has always been associated and which it practises to this day. But leaving aside the question to which of the two families he belonged, I can tell you that he was one of the wealthiest nobles of his time, and that he had three sons, of whom the first was called Lamberto, the second Tebaldo, and the third Agolante. These three had grown into fine and mettlesome youths, the eldest being not yet eighteen, when Messer Tebaldo died very rich, and they inherited all of his lands, houses and movables.

Finding they had come into a vast amount of money and

possessions, they began to indulge in a reckless orgy of spending, heedless of everything except their own pleasure. They employed a veritable army of servants, kept large numbers of thoroughbred horses, hounds and hawks, entertained continuously, gave presents, and entered the lists at jousts and tournaments. They engaged, not only in all the activities befitting a gentleman, but also in any others falling within the range of their youthful inclinations. However, they had not been leading this sort of life for long when the fortune left to them by their father dwindled to nothing, and since their income was inadequate to meet their commitments, they began to pawn and sell their possessions. So busily were they occupied in selling one thing after another, that they were scarcely aware of being almost bankrupt, until one day their eyes, which had been kept closed by riches, were opened by poverty.

Lamberto therefore called the others together and pointed to the contrast between their father's splendour and their own sorry condition. He reminded them how rich they had been, and how they had fallen into poverty on account of their extravagance. And he encouraged them, with all the strength at his command, to join with him in selling what little they still possessed and to go away, before their destitution became even more apparent. They agreed to do so, and without the slightest attempt at leave-taking or any other ceremony, they set out from Florence and travelled without pause until they arrived in England. There they took a small house in London, and, reducing their spending to an absolute minimum, they began to lend money at a high rate of interest, and their business prospered so well that within a few years they amassed a huge fortune.

In consequence they were able to return one by one to Florence, where they re-purchased a large part of their possessions, buying many other things in addition, and they all married. Since they were still lending money in England, they sent a young nephew of theirs, called Alessandro, to manage the business there, whilst they themselves remained in Florence. Having forgotten the parlous condition to which they had previously been reduced by their recklessness, and despite the fact that they now had families to support, they spent with less restraint than ever, borrowing large

sums of money, and piling up huge debts with every merchant in
Florence. For a few years they managed to meet their expenses with
the help of the money remitted to them by Alessandro, who had
opened up an extremely profitable line of business by offering
mortgages to barons on their castles and other properties.

The three brothers spent lavishly, and, since they could always
count on England, they borrowed money whenever they ran short.
But suddenly, a totally unexpected war broke out in England
between the King and one of his sons,[2] splitting the whole of the
island into two rival factions, as a result of which the castles of the
barons were taken out of Alessandro's control, and all his other
assets were frozen. But he remained in the island in the hope that
son and father would make peace at any moment, in which case he
might recover not only all his capital, but the outstanding interest as
well. Meanwhile, in Florence, the three brothers made no attempt
whatever to curb their enormous expenditure, but borrowed more
and more each day.

But as the years went by one after another, and their expectations
were seen to be bearing no fruit, the three brothers lost their sources
of credit, and immediately afterwards, since their creditors were
demanding payment, they were thrown into prison. Their assets
were realized to meet their debts, but the amount they raised was
insufficient, and so they remained in prison, leaving their wives and
little children to wander off in rags, some taking to the country,
some going to one place, some to another, with nothing but a
lifetime of poverty ahead of them.

Alessandro, after waiting several years in England for a peace that
never came, thought it not only pointless but positively dangerous
to stay there any longer, and decided to return to Italy. He set out
all alone on his journey, but as he was leaving Bruges[3] he happened
to see, also leaving the city, an abbot dressed in white, who was
attended by many monks and preceded by a large number of
retainers and a substantial baggage train. Bringing up the rear were
two worthy knights, relatives of the King, with whom Alessandro
was personally acquainted. And so, having made his presence
known, they readily received him as one of their company.

As he jogged along beside the two knights, Alessandro made

polite inquiries concerning the identity of the monks who were riding ahead with this large retinue of servants, and asked where they were all going.

'The person riding up front,' replied one of the knights, 'is a young relative of ours who has just been appointed Abbot of one of the largest abbeys in England. But because he is below the minimum age prescribed by law for this great office, we are going with him to Rome in order to ask the Holy Father to give him dispensation for his excessive youth and confirm him in office. But we wish to keep the matter a secret.'

The new abbot rode on, sometimes going ahead, sometimes falling back behind his retinue, in the style regularly to be observed in gentlemen of quality when they are travelling, until eventually he found himself level with Alessandro, who was very young, exceedingly good-looking and well-built, and the most well-mannered, agreeable and finely spoken person you can imagine. The Abbot's first glimpse of Alessandro gave him more genuine pleasure than anything he had ever seen in his life. Calling him to his side, he began to converse amicably with him, asking who he was, whence he had come, and whither he was bound. Alessandro answered all his questions, frankly revealing the exact state of his affairs and placing himself at the Abbot's entire disposal for whatever small service he might be able to render.

The Abbot, on hearing his fine, precise way of talking and observing his manners more closely, judged him to be a gentleman despite the lowly nature of his past occupation, and became even more enraptured with him. Being filled with compassion by the tale of Alessandro's misfortunes, he began to console him in tones of deep affection, telling him not to lose hope; for if he kept his courage, God would not only restore him to the position from which he had been toppled by Fortune, but set him even higher. The Abbot then said that he too was making for Tuscany, and invited Alessandro to join his party. Alessandro thanked him for his kind words, and declared his readiness to do whatever he was asked.

So the Abbot rode on, becoming more and more fascinated by what he saw of Alessandro. And after a few days, they arrived at a small town, not very richly endowed with inns, where the Abbot wished to put up for the night. Alessandro persuaded the Abbot to dismount at a place run by a very good friend of his, and saw that he was given a room in the most comfortable part of the house. By this time, Alessandro, being a very experienced traveller, had become a sort of major-domo to the Abbot, and he searched high and low to find accommodation in the town for the whole of the Abbot's retinue, lodging some in one place, some in another. By the time he returned to the inn, the Abbot had supped, the hour was very late, and everyone had gone off to bed. He asked the landlord where he could sleep, and the landlord replied:

'I really don't know. As you can see, the place is completely full, and my family and I are having to sleep on benches. But in the Abbot's room there are some cupboards for storing grain. If you like, I'll show you where they are and fix you up some sort of bed in there to sleep the night on as best you can.'

'How am I to squeeze into the Abbot's room?' said Alessandro. 'You know how tiny it is. There wasn't even any space in there for a single one of his monks to lie on the floor. If only I had noticed those cupboards when the Abbot's bed-curtains were drawn! His monks could have slept in those, and I could have lodged where the monks are staying.'

'Well, that's how matters stand,' said the landlord. 'Once you resign yourself to it, you'll sleep like a top in there. The Abbot is asleep, and the curtains are drawn in front of his bed. I'll slip in quietly, and put down a nice mattress for you to sleep on.'

When he saw that it could all be arranged without disturbing the Abbot, Alessandro fell in with the scheme, and, making as little noise as possible, he bedded down where the landlord had suggested.

The Abbot, far from being asleep, was locked in meditation on the subject of certain newly aroused longings of his. He had overheard the conversation between Alessandro and the landlord, and was listening, too, when Alessandro turned in for the night.

'God has answered my prayers,' said the Abbot delightedly to himself. 'If I do not seize this opportunity, it may be a long time before another comes my way.' Having firmly made up his mind, he waited for complete silence to descend on the inn, then he called out to Alessandro in a low voice, and, firmly brushing aside the latter's numerous excuses, persuaded him to undress and lie down at his side. The Abbot placed one of his hands on Alessandro's chest, and then, to Alessandro's great astonishment, began to caress him in the manner of a young girl fondling her lover, causing Alessandro to suspect, since there seemed to be no other explanation for his extraordinary behaviour, that the youth was possibly in the grip of some impure passion. But either by intuition, or because of some movement on Alessandro's part, the Abbot understood at once what he was thinking, and began to smile. Then, hastily tearing off the shirt he was wearing, he took Alessandro's hand and placed it on his bosom, saying:

'Drive those silly thoughts out of your head, Alessandro. Lay your hand here, and see what I am hiding.'

And placing his hand on the Abbot's bosom, Alessandro discovered a pair of sweet little rounded breasts, as firm and finely shaped as if they were made of ivory. It dawned on him at once that this was a woman, and without awaiting further invitation he immediately took her in his arms. But just as he was about to kiss her, she said:

'Wait! Before you come any closer, there is something I want to tell you. As you can gather, I am not a man, but a woman. I am also a virgin, and I set out from home in order to obtain the Pope's permission for my marriage. I know not whether to call it your good fortune or my misfortune, but from the moment I saw you, the other day, I burned with a love deeper than woman has ever experienced for any man. Hence I am resolved to have you as my husband rather than any other. But if you do not want to marry me, you must leave me at once and return to your own place.'

Alessandro had no idea who she was, but in view of the size of her retinue he judged her to be a rich noblewoman, and could see for himself that she was very beautiful. So without wasting too much time in thought, he replied that if this was what she desired, he was only too ready to oblige.

She then sat up in bed, handed him a ring, and made him plight her his troth beneath a small picture of Our Lord, after which they fell into each other's arms, and for the rest of the night they disported themselves to their great and mutual pleasure. They decided carefully what they should do, and when it was daybreak,

Alessandro arose and, retracing his steps, stole away from the room without anyone realizing where he had passed the night. Then, reeling with happiness, he set out once more with the Abbot and her retinue, and several days later they arrived in Rome.

They had been staying in the city for only a few days when the Abbot, attended by Alessandro and the two knights, was received in audience by the Pope. Having paid him their respects in the appropriate fashion, the Abbot began:

'As you, Holy Father, must know better than all others, whoever desires to live a good and honest life is obliged to shun as best he may every possible motive for behaving otherwise. I myself, being one who desires to live a thoroughly honest life, have come all this way in the clothes you see me wearing, ostensibly to seek Your Holiness's blessing for my marriage. But in reality, I have fled, taking with me a considerable part of the treasures belonging to my father, the King of England, for he was planning to marry me to the King of Scotland, who is a very old man whereas I myself am a young girl, as you can see. What caused me to run away, was not so much the King of Scotland's age, as the fear that, once married to him, my youthful frailty might tempt me into contravening God's laws and staining the honour of my royal-blooded father.

'In this frame of mind, I was on my way hither when God, who alone knows best how to measure our needs, being stirred as I believe by His compassion, set before my eyes the person He decreed should be my husband. The one I refer to is the young man' – and she pointed to Alessandro – 'whom you see standing here at my side. It may well be that he is less pure-blooded than a person of royal birth, but both in bearing and in character he is a worthy match for any great lady. He, therefore, is the man I have taken; it is him alone that I want, and no matter what my father or anyone else may have to say on the subject, I will never accept any other. The ostensible aim of my journey has thus been removed. But I desired to complete it, for two reasons: firstly, to meet Your Holiness and visit the venerable and sacred places in which this city abounds; and secondly, so that through your good offices I could make public, before you and the whole world, the marriage that Alessandro and I have contracted with God as our only witness.

What is pleasing to God and to me should not be disagreeable to you, and I therefore beg you in all humility to give us your blessing, armed with which, since you are God's vicar, we should be more certain of His entire approval. And thus we may live our lives together, till death us do part, to the greater glory not only of God but also of yourself.'

On hearing that his wife was the daughter of the King of England, Alessandro could scarcely contain his astonishment and happiness. But the two knights were even more astonished, and they were so furious that they would have done Alessandro an injury, and possibly the lady as well, if they had been anywhere else but in the Pope's presence. The Pope, for his part, was greatly astonished both by the lady's attire and by her choice of a husband. But he realized there was no turning back, and decided to grant her request. He could see, however, that the knights were seething with rage, and so first of all he pacified them and reconciled them with Alessandro and the lady, then he gave orders for what was to be done.

For the appointed day, the Pope arranged a magnificent ceremony to which he had invited all the cardinals and a large number of other great nobles, and he summoned the couple into their presence. The lady, dressed in regal robes and looking very gracious and beautiful, was greeted with unanimous and well-deserved praise, as also was Alessandro, who carried his fine clothes with such a natural and dignified air that, honourably attended by the two knights, he looked more like a royal prince than a young man who had once been engaged in money-lending. Without further ado, the Pope had them taken solemnly through the marriage ceremony from the beginning, then a sumptuous wedding-feast was held, after which he dismissed them with his blessing.

On leaving Rome, it was the wish of both Alessandro and his bride that they should make for Florence, where their story had already been noised abroad. There the townspeople received them with all possible honour, and the three brothers were released from prison on the petition of the lady, who had seen that all their creditors were paid. She then settled the brothers and their wives once more in their estates, after which Alessandro and his wife took their leave of all concerned, and, taking Agolante with them, they set out from Florence for Paris, where they were honourably received by the King. From Paris, the two knights went on ahead to England, where they worked on the King to such good effect that he pardoned the princess and gave a magnificent welcome both to her and to his son-in-law, on whom, with great pomp and ceremony, he shortly afterwards conferred a knighthood, creating him Earl of Cornwall[4] for good measure.

Being a very astute and capable man, Alessandro brought great benefit to the island by reconciling father and son, consequently winning the affection and gratitude of the entire population. At the same time, Agolante recovered all their money down to the last penny, and returned to Florence immensely rich, having first been given a knighthood by Earl Alessandro. As for the Earl, he lived a life of great renown with his lady. Indeed, there are those who maintain that, partly through his own ability and intelligence, and partly with the help of his father-in-law, he later conquered Scotland[5] and was crowned her king.

FOURTH STORY

Landolfo Rufolo is ruined and turns to piracy; he is captured by the Genoese and shipwrecked, but survives by clinging to a chest, full of very precious jewels; finally, having been succoured by a woman on Corfu, he returns home rich.

When she saw that Pampinea had brought her story to its triumphant close, Lauretta, who was seated next to her, took up her cue without a pause and began to speak as follows:

Fairest ladies, it is in my opinion impossible to envisage a more striking act of Fortune than the spectacle of a person being raised from the depths of poverty to regal status, which is what happened, as we have been shown by Pampinea's story, in the case of her Alessandro. And since, from now on, nobody telling a story on the prescribed subject can possibly exceed those limits, I shall not blush to narrate a tale which, whilst it contains greater misfortunes, does not however possess so magnificent an ending. I realize of course,

when I think of the previous story, that my own will be followed
less attentively. But since it is the best I can manage, I trust that I
shall be forgiven.

Few parts of Italy, if any, are reckoned to be more delightful than
the sea-coast between Reggio and Gaeta. In this region, not far
from Salerno, there is a strip of land overlooking the sea, known to
the inhabitants as the Amalfi coast,[1] which is dotted with small
towns, gardens and fountains, and swarming with as wealthy and
enterprising a set of merchants as you will find anywhere. In one of
these little towns, called Ravello,[2] there once lived a certain Landolfo
Rufolo, and although Ravello still has its quota of rich men, this
Rufolo was a very rich man indeed. But being dissatisfied with his
fortune, he sought to double it, and as a result he nearly lost every
penny he possessed, and his life too.

This Rufolo, then, having made the sort of preliminary calculations that merchants normally make, purchased a very large ship,
loaded it with a mixed cargo of goods paid for entirely out of his
own pocket, and sailed with them to Cyprus. But on his arrival, he
discovered that several other ships had docked there, carrying
precisely the same kind of goods as those he had brought over
himself. And for this reason, not only did he have to sell his cargo at
bargain prices, but in order to complete his business he was practically forced to give the stuff away, thus being brought to the verge
of ruin.

Being extremely distressed about all this, not knowing what to
do, and finding himself reduced overnight from great wealth to
semi-poverty, he decided he would make good his losses by privat-
eering, or die in the attempt. At all events, having set out a rich
man, he was determined not to return home in poverty. And so,
having found a buyer for his merchantman, he combined the
proceeds with the money he had raised on his cargo, and purchased
a light pirate-vessel, which he armed and fitted out, choosing only
the equipment best suited for the ship's purpose. He then applied
himself to the systematic looting of other people's property, especially that of the Turks.

In his new role, he met with far more success than he had

encountered in his trading activities. Within the space of about a year, he raided and seized so many Turkish ships that, quite apart from having regained what he had lost in trading, he discovered that he was considerably more than twice as wealthy as before. He thus had enough, he now realized, to avoid the risk of repeating his former mistake, and once he had persuaded himself to rest content with what he had, he made up his mind to call it a day and return home with the loot. Being wary of commercial ventures, he did not bother to invest his money, but simply steered a homeward course, at breakneck speed, in the tiny ship with which he had collected his spoils. He had come as far as the Archipelago,[3] when he found himself sailing one evening directly into the teeth of a southerly gale, and his frail craft was barely able to cope with the mountainous seas. So he put into a cove on the leeward side of a small island, with the intention of waiting for more favourable winds. He had not been there long, however, when two large Genoese carracks,[4] homeward-bound from Constantinople, struggled into the bay to escape the same storm from which Landolfo had taken shelter. The crews of the Genoese ships recognized Landolfo's vessel, which they already knew from various rumours to be loaded with booty. And being by nature a rapacious, money-grubbing set of people, they blocked his way of escape and made their preparations for seizing the prize. First they put ashore a party of well-armed men with crossbows, who were strategically placed so that no one was able to leave Landolfo's vessel without running into a barrage of arrows. Then they launched cutters, by means of which, aided by the current, they drew themselves towards Landolfo's little ship. This they captured without losing a man, after a brief and half-hearted struggle, and they took her crew prisoner. Landolfo was left wearing nothing but a threadbare old doublet and taken aboard one of their ships, and after everything of value had been removed from his vessel, they sent it to the bottom.

The next day, the wind changed quarter, and the two ships hoisted their sails and set a westerly course. For the whole of that day they made good progress, but in the evening a gale began to blow, producing very heavy seas and separating the two carracks from each other. By a stroke of ill-luck, the ship in which the

wretched, destitute Landolfo was travelling was driven by the force
of the gale on to the coast of the island of Cephalonia, where she ran
aground with a tremendous crash, split wide open, and like a piece
of glass being flung against a wall, was smashed to smithereens. As is
usually the case when this happens, the sea was rapidly littered with an
assortment of floating planks, chests and merchandise. And although
it was pitch dark and there was a heavy swell, the poor wretches
who had survived the wreck, or those of them who could swim, began
to cling to whatever object happened to float across their path.

One of their number was poor Landolfo, who had in fact been
calling out all day for death to come and take him, for he felt he
would rather die than return home poverty-stricken. But now that
he was staring death in the face, he was frightened by the prospect,
and like the others he too clung to the first spar that came within his
reach, in the hope that by remaining afloat for a little longer, God
might somehow come to his rescue.

Settling himself astride the spar as best he could, he clung on till
daybreak, meanwhile being tossed hither and thither by sea and
wind. When dawn came, he cast his eyes around him, but all he
could see was clouds and water, and a chest floating on the sea's
surface. To his great consternation, this chest floated every so often
into his vicinity, causing him to fear lest it should collide into him
and do him an injury. So whenever it came too near, he summoned
up the meagre strength he still possessed, and pushed it away as best
he could with his hands.

But as luck would have it, the sea was struck by a sudden squall,
which sent the chest hurtling into Landolfo's spar, upending it and
inevitably causing Landolfo to lose his grip and go under. When he
re-surfaced, he found that he was some distance away from the spar,
and was afraid that he would never reach it, for he was exhausted
and only his panic was keeping him afloat. He therefore made for
the chest, which was quite close at hand, and dragging himself up
on its lid, he sprawled across it and held it steady with his arms.
And in this fashion, buffeted this way and that by the sea, with
nothing to eat and far more to drink than he would have wished,
not knowing where he was and seeing nothing but water, he
survived for the whole of that day and the following night.

By the next day, Landolfo had almost turned into a sponge when, either through the will of God or the power of the wind, he arrived off the coast of the island of Corfu. Clinging grimly to the edges of the chest with both hands, just as we see a man in danger of drowning attaching himself firmly to anything within reach, he was sighted by a peasant woman, who happened to be scouring and polishing her pots and pans in the sand and salt-water.

At first, being unable to make out what creature it was that was approaching the shore, she started back with a cry of alarm. He said nothing to her, for he was quite unable to speak and scarcely able to see. But as the current bore him closer to the shore, she could make out the shape of the chest, and, peering more intently, she first of all recognized a pair of arms stretched across its lid, after which she picked out the face and realized it was a human being. Prompted by compassion, she waded some distance out into the sea, which was now quite calm, took him by the hair and dragged him to the shore, chest and all. There, with an effort, she unhooked his hands from the chest, which she placed on the head of her young daughter who was with her, whilst she herself carried Landolfo away like a baby and put him into a hot bath. She rubbed away so vigorously at him and poured so much hot water over him, that eventually he began to thaw out and recover some of his lost strength. And when she judged it to be the right moment, she took him from the bath and refreshed him with a quantity of good wine and nourishing food. After she had nursed him to the best of her ability for several days, his recovery was complete and he took stock of his surroundings. The good woman therefore decided it was time to hand over his chest, which she had been keeping for him, and to tell him that from now on he must fend for himself. And this she did.

He could remember nothing about any chest, but he nevertheless accepted it when the good woman offered it to him, for he thought it could hardly be so valueless that it would not keep him going for a few days. His hopes were severely jolted when he discovered how light it was, but all the same, when the woman was out of the house, he forced it open to see what was inside, and discovered that it contained a number of precious stones, some of them loose and others mounted. Being quite knowledgeable on the subject of jewels, he realized from the moment he saw them that they were extremely valuable, and his spirits rose higher than ever. He praised God for once again coming to his rescue, but since Fortune had dealt him two cruel blows in rapid succession, and might conceivably deal him a third, he decided he would have to proceed with great caution if he wanted to convey these things safely home. So he wrapped them up as carefully as he could in some old rags, told the woman that if she liked, she could keep the chest, since he no longer had any use for it, and asked her to let him have a sack in exchange.

The good woman gladly complied with his request, and after he had thanked her profusely for the assistance she had rendered, he slung his sack over his shoulder and went on his way, first taking a boat to Brindisi and then making his way gradually up the coast as far as Trani, where he met some cloth-merchants who hailed from his native town. Without mentioning the chest, he gave them an account of all his adventures, and they felt so sorry for him that they fitted him out with new clothes, lent him a horse, and sent him back with company to Ravello, whither he was intent on returning at all costs.

Secure at last in Ravello, he gave thanks to God for leading him safely home, untied his little sack, and made what was virtually his first real inspection of its contents. The stones he possessed were, he discovered, so valuable and numerous, that even if he sold them at less than their market value, he would be twice as rich as when he had set out. So that, having taken steps to dispose of his gems, he sent, by way of payment for services received, a tidy sum of money to the good woman of Corfu who had fished him out of the sea. And likewise, he sent a further sum to the people at Trani who had given him the new clothes. He was no longer interested in commerce, so he kept the remainder of the money and lived in splendour for the rest of his days.

FIFTH STORY

Andreuccio of Perugia comes to buy horses in Naples, where in the course of a single night he is overtaken by three serious misfortunes, all of which he survives, and he returns home with a ruby.

The stones found by Landolfo – began Fiammetta, whose turn it was to tell the next story – have put me in mind of a tale almost as full of perils as the one narrated by Lauretta. But it differs from hers in that its dangers arose in the space of a single night, as you shall hear, whereas in Lauretta's story they were perhaps spread over several years.

I was once informed that there lived in Perugia a young man whose name was Andreuccio di Pietro, a horsedealer, who, having heard good reports of the Neapolitan horse-trade, stuffed five hundred gold florins in his purse and, though he had never left home before, set out for Naples with one or two other merchants. He arrived one Sunday evening as darkness was falling, and the next morning, having been told by his innkeeper how to get there, he went to the market. He saw a great many horses, to a number of which he took a liking, and he made offers for several of them without however being able to strike a single bargain. But in order to indicate his willingness to buy, he kept pulling out his purse bulging with florins, and waving it about in full view of all the passers-by, thus displaying a lack of both caution and experience.

While he was conducting his business in this manner and holding out his money for inspection, it happened that a young Sicilian woman passed by, without attracting his attention. She was not only very beautiful, but willing to do any man's bidding for a modest fee, and when she saw the purse she immediately fell to thinking how contented she would be if she could lay her hands on the money. However, she walked straight on.

She was accompanied by an old woman, also Sicilian, who on seeing Andreuccio allowed her companion to go on ahead, whilst she herself rushed over to him and threw her arms around him in

a display of affection. On seeing this, the young woman said nothing, but held herself aloof from the proceedings and waited for
the other woman to catch her up. Andreuccio, having turned
round and recognized the old woman, made a great fuss of her and
extracted a promise that she would call and see him at his inn. After
conversing briefly with him, she then went away, and Andreuccio
returned to business, without however purchasing anything that
morning.

The young woman, having spied Andreuccio's purse and noted
how well her companion was acquainted with him, was determined
to see if she could find some way of relieving him of the whole or a
part of his cash. So she began to put out feelers, asking the older
woman who he was, where he came from, what he was doing in
Naples, and how it came about that she knew him. Andreuccio
himself could hardly have furnished her with a more particular
account of his affairs than the one given her by the old woman, for
she had lived with Andreuccio's father over a long period in Sicily,
and later in Perugia. Moreover she was also able to reveal where he
was staying and why he had come to Naples.

Now that she was fully informed about his family and the names
of his various relatives, the young woman devised an ingenious plan
for achieving her object. On arriving home, she gave the old
woman enough work to occupy her for the rest of the day, so that
she could not keep her appointment with Andreuccio. Then she
took aside a maidservant of hers, to whom she had given a thorough
grounding in affairs of this sort, and towards evening she sent
her to the inn where Andreuccio was staying. On arriving at the
door of the inn, she happened to run across our hero, who was
by himself, and she asked him where she could find Andreuccio.
When he told her that he was the very man, she drew him aside and
said:

'Sir, there is a gentlewoman of this city who would be glad of a
few words with you, if you have no objection.'

When he heard this, Andreuccio immediately assumed, on looking himself up and down and thinking what a handsome fellow he
was, that the woman must have fallen in love with him, as though
he were the only good-looking youth at that time to be found in

Naples. So he readily agreed, and asked where and when the lady would like to see him.

'You may come whenever you wish, sir,' said the maid. 'She is waiting for you at her house.'

'Lead the way then,' Andreuccio promptly replied. 'I'll follow you.' And without leaving any message at the inn, off he went.

The maid conveyed him to the lady's house, which was situated in a quarter called The Fleshpots,[1] the mere name of which shows how honest a district it was. But Andreuccio neither knew nor suspected anything of all this, being of the opinion that he was on his way to see a gentlewoman in a perfectly respectable part of the city. Eventually, with the maid leading the way, they arrived at the lady's house, and Andreuccio went boldly in. The maid had already hailed her mistress with the words 'Andreuccio's here!', and as he mounted the stairs he saw the lady coming out on the landing to receive him.

She was still very young, tall in stature, with a very beautiful face, and her clothes and jewellery were a model of good taste. Just before Andreuccio reached her, she opened her arms wide and descended three steps to meet him. Then she clasped him round the neck and remained for some time without speaking, as though hindered by a surge of powerful emotion. Finally, her eyes filling with tears, she kissed his brow and said, in a somewhat faltering voice:

'Oh, Andreuccio my dear, how delighted I am to see you.'

Not knowing what to make of this barrage of affection, he replied, in tones of deep astonishment:

'My lady, the pleasure is mine.'

Then she took him by the hand, and led him up to the main room of her house, from whence, without another word, she passed with him into her bedroom, which was all fragrant with roses, orange-blossom and other pleasant odours. There he saw an exquisite curtained bed, a large number of dresses hanging from pegs, as is the custom in those parts, and other very beautiful, expensive-looking objects. He had never seen such finery before, and was firmly convinced that the lady must be nothing less than a genuine aristocrat.

Having made him sit by her side on a chest at the foot of the bed, she began to address him as follows:

'Andreuccio, I am quite sure you must be astonished at me for embracing you like this and bursting into tears, for you do not know me and it may be that you have never even heard of me before. But you are now to hear something that will possibly increase your astonishment, for the fact is that I am your sister. I have always longed to meet all of my brothers, and now that God has been good enough to allow me to see one of them, I shall no longer die disconsolate when the time comes for me to depart this life. But in case you know nothing of this, I will tell you all about it.

'Pietro, who is my father as well as yours, lived for many years in Palermo, as I suppose you may have heard. Being a good and amiable man, he was greatly loved there, and he is still loved there to this day by those who knew him. But of all his profound admirers, none loved him more than my mother, who was a widowed lady of gentle birth. Indeed, she loved Pietro so deeply, that she abandoned all fear of her father, her brothers and her good name, and their friendship became so intimate that it led to the birth of the person you see here now, sitting beside you.

'When I was still a little girl, Pietro's business called him away from Palermo and he returned to Perugia, leaving my mother and me to fend for ourselves, and as far as I have been able to discover, he never gave either of us another thought. For this reason, but for the fact that he was my father, I would be inclined to reproach him bitterly, considering (to say nothing of the affection he should have had for me, his own daughter, born neither of a serving-wench nor of any low-class woman) the ingratitude he displayed towards my mother. For she, prompted by her unswerving devotion, surrendered herself body and soul to this man, without so much as knowing who he was.

'But never mind about all that. Wrongs committed in the distant past are far easier to condemn than to rectify. At all events, the fact is that he abandoned me when I was still a tiny child in Palermo, where I eventually grew up, and my mother, being a wealthy woman, married me off to a worthy nobleman from Girgenti, who out of affection for my mother and myself came to live in Palermo.

Being a staunch supporter of the Guelphs, he began to intrigue on behalf of King Charles of Naples. But before the plot could be sprung, it reached the ears of King Frederick,[2] and we had to flee from Sicily just as I was about to become the greatest lady in the island. Of our huge store of possessions, we took away only those few things we were able to carry with us, and leaving behind our lands and palaces, we came as refugees to this country, where we found King Charles so well-disposed towards us that he made good some of the losses we had suffered on his account. He gave us estates and houses, and as you will see for yourself, he makes generous and regular provision for my husband, or in other words your brother-in-law. And that, my dear sweet brother, is how I came to be in Naples, where, thanks more to God than to yourself, I have met you at last.' And having said all this, sobbing with affection, she embraced him a second time and kissed him once again on the forehead.

She had told her tale very glibly and with great self-assurance, neither stammering at any point nor swallowing any of her words. For his part, Andreuccio remembered that his father really had been in Palermo, and he knew from his own experience how lightly young men are apt to regard the love of a woman. So what with her tears of affection, her fond embraces and her chaste kisses, he was more than satisfied that she was telling the truth. And when she had finished, he replied:

'I beg you not to take my amazement too much to heart, madam, for to tell you the truth I have never had the slightest knowledge of your existence. For some reason or other, my father never spoke of you and your mother, or if he did I never came to hear of it. But I am all the more delighted to find my sister in Naples, because I was feeling rather lonely here and the discovery was so unexpected. I myself am merely a small trader, but I know of no man, however exalted his station, who would not be equally delighted upon finding such a sister. There is one thing, though, that I would like you to explain: how did you know I was here?'

To which she replied:

'I learned about it this morning from a poor old woman, who often comes to see me because she spent a long time with our father in Palermo and Perugia; or at least she tells me she did. And if it weren't for the fact that I thought it more decorous for you to come to my own house than for me to visit you in another's, I would have called to see you hours ago.'

After saying this, she began to inquire about all of his relatives, naming each one individually, and Andreuccio, allowing himself to be led even further up the garden path, told her how they all were.

As it was a very hot evening, and they had been talking together for some little time, she sent for Greek wine[3] and sweetmeats and saw that Andreuccio was given something to drink, after which he got up to go, saying it was time for supper. She refused to allow him to do any such thing: on the contrary, pretending to be deeply hurt, she flung her arms round his neck, saying:

'Alas, now I am quite certain how little you care for me! What else am I to think, when you are with a sister you have never seen before, in her own house, where you should have stayed from the moment you arrived, and now you want to leave me to go and have supper at some inn! Really! You are going to sup with me. My husband is not at home, for which I am very sorry, but though I am merely a woman, I am quite capable of supplying you with a little hospitality.'

Andreuccio, not knowing how else to reply, said:

'I care for you just as much as any man should care for his sister, but if I don't go back they will be waiting for me all evening to turn up for supper, and I shall cut a bad figure.'

Whereupon she said:

'Good heavens, as if I didn't have anyone in the house who could be sent to tell them not to expect you! But you would be doing a much greater kindness, and no more than your duty, if you were to send word to your companions that they should come and have supper here. And then afterwards, if you still insist on leaving, you could all go back to the inn together.'

Andreuccio replied that he would rather do without his companions that evening, and that he would place himself entirely at her disposal, if this was what she really wanted. She accordingly went through the motions of sending word to the inn that they should not expect him for supper. Then after a lot of further talk, they sat down to a splendid supper, consisting of several courses, which she cunningly prolonged until darkness had completely fallen. When they got up from table, Andreuccio said he would have to go, but she refused to hear of it under any circumstances, telling him that Naples was no place to wander about in at night, especially if one was a stranger, and that when she had sent word to the inn not to expect him for supper, she had told them he would not be sleeping there either.

He swallowed all this, and since, being taken in by appearances, he was enjoying her company, he stayed where he was. After supper, she engaged him, not without her reasons, in a protracted conversation about this and that, and when the night was well advanced she left Andreuccio to sleep in her room, with a page-boy to show him where to find anything he needed, whilst she herself retired into another room with her maidservants.

The heat was stifling, and so, on finding himself alone, Andreuccio stripped to his doublet and removed his hose and breeches, and laid them under his bolster. Nature demanded that he should relieve his belly, which was inordinately full, so he asked the page where he could do it, and the boy showed him a door in one of the corners of the room, saying:

'Go through there.'

Andreuccio passed jauntily through, and chanced to step on to a plank, which came away at its other end from the beam on which it was resting, so that it flew up in the air and fell into the lower regions, taking Andreuccio with it. Although he had fallen from a goodly height, he mercifully suffered no injury; but he got himself daubed from head to foot in the filthy mess with which the place was literally swimming.

Now in order to give you a clearer picture of what has preceded and what follows, I shall describe the sort of place it was. In a narrow alleyway, such as we often see between two houses, some boards, and a place to sit, had been rigged up on two beams, running across from one house to the next; and it was one of these boards that had collapsed under Andreuccio's weight.

So finding himself down there in the alley, Andreuccio, cursing his bad luck, began calling out to the boy. But as soon as he had heard him falling, the boy had hurried off to tell his mistress, who rushed into her room and made a rapid search for Andreuccio's clothes. These she found, together with his money, which being a doubting sort of fellow he stupidly carried with him wherever he went. And so it was that this woman of Palermo, this self-styled sister of a Perugian, obtained the prize for which she had laid her trap. Being no longer interested in Andreuccio, she quickly went and locked the door through which he had passed just before he fell.

Receiving no answer from the boy, Andreuccio began to call more loudly, but it was of no use. His suspicions being already aroused, he began, now that it was too late, to see how he had been hoodwinked, and having climbed a low wall dividing the alleyway from the road, he scrambled down into the street and went up to the front-door, which he was easily able to identify. He stood there for ages, vainly calling out, and shaking and beating the door for all he was worth. Finally, plainly perceiving the predicament he was in, he burst into tears and said to himself:

'Oh, poor me! What a sudden way to lose five hundred florins and a sister!'

He said a lot more besides, then began to shout and to pummel on the door all over again, creating such a disturbance that he woke a number of the people living nearby, who got up out of bed as they could not endure the racket. One of the woman's maids came to the window, all bleary-eyed, and said in tones of annoyance:

'Who is knocking down there?'

'Oh,' said Andreuccio, 'don't you recognize me? I am Andreuccio, the brother of Madonna Fiordaliso.'⁴

'My good man,' she replied, 'if you have had too much to drink, go and sleep it off and come back in the morning. I don't know any Andreuccio; you are talking nonsense. Be off with you, for goodness' sake, and let us sleep.'

'What!' said Andreuccio. 'Talking nonsense, am I? You know very well I'm not. But if it's really true that Sicilians make a habit of discovering blood-relatives and then forgetting all about them, at least give me back the clothes I left there, and I'll go away gladly.'

'My good man,' she said, hardly able to contain her laughter, 'you must be dreaming.'

As she said this, she simultaneously withdrew her head and closed the window, whereupon Andreuccio, who no longer had the slightest doubt that he had lost everything, grew so distressed, that whereas he was very angry to begin with, he now became almost frantic with rage. Deciding that force was a more effective weapon than words for retrieving his belongings, he picked up a large stone and started all over again to rain blows on the door like a madman, this time with much greater energy.

Taking exception to his hammering, many of the neighbours previously roused from their beds now appeared at their windows, and regarding him as some troublemaker who had invented the things he was saying in order to make this good woman's life a misery, they began to shout in unison, like all the dogs in one particular district howling at a stray.

'This is a fine way to carry on,' they shouted, 'coming round here at this hour and knocking up honest women with your ridiculous tall stories. For heaven's sake clear off, man, and please let us get some sleep. If you have any business with the lady, leave it till the morning and stop annoying us like this in the middle of the night.'

Being, perhaps, encouraged by this chorus of abuse, a man concealed inside the house, who was the good woman's bully, and whom Andreuccio had as yet neither seen nor heard, came to the window and said, in a low, fierce, spine-chilling growl:

'Who's that down there?'

Andreuccio raised his head towards the point from which the growl was coming, and caught sight of a face which, so far as he could judge, clearly belonged to some mighty man or other, who had a thick black beard and was yawning and rubbing his eyes as though he had just been roused from a deep sleep.

'It's me,' replied Andreuccio, not without marked trepidation. 'The brother of the lady who lives here.'

The man did not wait for Andreuccio to finish, but adopting an even more threatening tone, he exclaimed:

'I don't know what restrains me from coming down there and giving you the biggest pasting you've ever had in your life, you miserable drunken idiot, making all this racket in the middle of the night and keeping everyone awake.' He then retired from view, and bolted the window.

Being better informed than Andreuccio about the sort of person he was, some of the neighbours addressed Andreuccio in hushed, compassionate tones, saying:

'For God's sake, be a good chap and take yourself off, unless you want to be killed down there tonight. Do go away for your own good.'

So Andreuccio, terrified out of his wits by the man's voice and appearance, and urged on by the advice of these people, whose words seemed to him to be prompted by Christian charity, set off with the intention of returning to the inn. He had no idea where he was, so he simply struck out in the direction from which, following in the maidservant's footsteps, he had come on the previous day. All he felt certain of was that he would never see his money again and that he was the most wretched man alive.

However, he had not progressed very far when he became uncomfortably aware of the odour emanating from his person, and, deciding he had better make for the sea in order to have a wash, he turned off to the left and started to walk along a street known as the Ruga Catalana.[5] As he was approaching the upper part of the city, he happened to see two people coming towards him carrying a lantern, and fearing lest they might turn out to be officers of the watch or a pair of cut-throats, he decided to avoid them by slipping quietly into a nearby hut. But the two men also came into the same hut, as though it were the very place they had been heading for. Once inside, one of them put down some iron tools he had been carrying over his shoulder, and they both began to inspect these and pass various comments about them. Presently, the first man said:

'What can be causing this unholy stench? I reckon it's the worst I've ever smelt.'

As he said this, they raised their lantern a little, and catching sight of poor Andreuccio, they let out a gasp of astonishment and demanded to know who he was.

Andreuccio at first said nothing, but when they took the light nearer to him and asked him what he was doing there, covered with filth in this manner, he told them the whole story of his adventures. The two men, who could well imagine where all this had taken place, said to each other:

'It must have happened round at Butch Belchfire's[6] place.'

Then one of them said, addressing Andreuccio:

'Listen, friend, you may have lost your money, but you can thank God that you happened to fall and couldn't get back into the house. Because if you hadn't fallen, you can rest assured that as soon as you were asleep you would have been done in, and in that case you'd have lost your life as well as your money. What's the use of crying over spilt milk? You've about as much chance of plucking stars from the heavens as you have of recovering a single penny. But you may very well have your throat cut, if you ever breathe a word about it and he finds out.'

The two men then conferred briefly together, after which they said to him:

'Look, we're feeling sorry for you, and since we were on our way to do a little job, if you'd like to join us we can almost guarantee that your share of the proceeds will more than make up for what you've lost.' And as he was feeling desperate, Andreuccio agreed to go with them.

Now, just a few hours earlier, the burial had taken place of an archbishop whose name was Messer Filippo Minutolo.[7] He was the Archbishop of Naples, and he had been buried with some very valuable regalia and wearing a ruby on his finger, worth more than five hundred gold florins, which these two fellows were on their way to plunder. They disclosed their intentions to Andreuccio, and being more covetous than well-advised, he set off in their company. As they were on their way to the cathedral, with Andreuccio still putting forth a powerful odour, one of them said:

'Couldn't we find some place or other where this fellow could be washed, so that he didn't stink so appallingly?'

'Certainly,' said the other. 'Not far from here, there's a well, which always used to have a pulley and a big bucket at the top. Let's go there and give him a quick wash.'

On reaching the well, they found that the rope was still there, but the bucket had been removed. So they hit on the idea of tying him to the rope and lowering him into the well so that he could wash himself down below. When he had finished washing, he was to give the rope a tug, and they would haul him up again.

Shortly after they had lowered him into the well, some officers of the watch, feeling thirsty on account of the heat and also because they had been chasing somebody, happened to come to the well for a drink. When the other two saw them coming, they immediately took to their heels, making good their escape without being spotted by the officers.

Meanwhile Andreuccio, having completed his ablutions at the bottom of the well, gave a tug on the rope. The officers had taken off their surcoats and laid them on the ground beside their bucklers and pikestaffs, and they now began to haul away at the rope, thinking it had a bucket full of water attached to it.

When Andreuccio saw that he had nearly reached the top of the well, he let go the rope and threw himself on to the rim, clinging to it with both hands. On seeing this apparition, the officers were filled with sudden panic, and without a word they dropped the rope and began to run as fast as their legs would carry them. Andreuccio stared at them in blank amazement, and if he hadn't held on tightly, he would have fallen to the bottom, perhaps being killed or doing himself serious injury. However, he clambered out, and when he saw these weapons, he grew even more perplexed, for he knew they had not been left there by his companions. Bewailing his misfortune, and fearing lest anything worse should befall him, he decided to leave all these things where they were and clear off. So away he went without having the slightest idea where he was going.

As he was walking along, he came across his two companions, who were on their way back to the well to haul him out. They could hardly believe their eyes when they saw him coming, and they asked him who had helped him out. Andreuccio said he didn't know and gave them a detailed account of how it had happened, describing what he had found lying beside the well. Putting two and two together, they had a good laugh and told him why they had run away, and explained who it was that had hauled him out of the well. And without wasting any more words, the night already being half spent, they made their way to the cathedral, which they entered without any difficulty. On reaching the tomb, which was very big and made of marble, they got out their tools and lifted the enormously heavy lid, propping it up so that there was just enough room for a man to squeeze his way inside. When this operation was complete, one of them said:

'Who's going in?'

'I'm not,' said the other.

'And I'm not, either,' said the first. 'How about Andreuccio?'

'I won't do it,' said Andreuccio, whereupon both the others rounded on him saying:

'What do you mean, you won't do it? If you don't damned well get in there quickly, we'll give you such a hammering over the pate with these iron bars that we'll kill you stone dead.'

Shaking with fear, Andreuccio crawled into the tomb, thinking to himself as he did so: 'These two are making me go inside so as to leave me in the lurch. Once I've handed everything out, they'll go about their business while I'm still struggling my way out of the tomb, and I shall be left empty-handed.' He therefore decided that before doing anything else, he would make certain of his own share of the plunder. Remembering what they had said about the precious ring, as soon as he reached the floor of the vault he took the ring from the archbishop's finger and put it on his own, then he handed out the crosier, the mitre and the gloves, and having stripped the body down to the shift and handed everything out, he told them there was nothing left.

The others insisted that the ring should be there, and told him to make a thorough search. But he replied that he was unable to find it, and kept them waiting for some little time, pretending to look for it. And since, for their part, they were just as sharp-witted as Andreuccio, they told him to go on looking, and as soon as they got the chance they took away the prop supporting the lid. Then they made off, leaving Andreuccio imprisoned inside the tomb.

You can easily imagine the effect that all of this had upon Andreuccio. He tried again and again, using first his head and then his shoulders, to see if he could raise the lid, but he was merely wasting his energies, and in the end, in the depths of despair, he fainted and collapsed on the archbishop's corpse. If anyone could have seen them at that moment, he would have had a job to tell which of the two, the archbishop or Andreuccio, was the cadaver. But when Andreuccio came to his senses, he burst into copious tears, for he realized beyond any doubt that there were only two possible ends in store for him: either he would die of hunger and the noxious odours inside the tomb, covered all over in maggots from the dead body; or if someone were to come and find him there, he would be hanged as a thief.

Whilst these unpleasant thoughts were running through his mind, feeling thoroughly down in the dumps, he heard a number of people talking and moving about in the cathedral, and quickly realized that they had come to carry out the work already completed by himself and his companions, whereupon he became considerably more alarmed. But having opened the tomb and propped up the lid, they began to argue about who should go inside, and no one was willing to do it. However, after much heated discussion, a priest came forward, saying:

'What are you afraid of? Do you think he is going to devour you? Dead men don't eat the living. I will go in myself.'

Having said this, he laid his chest on the edge of the tomb and swivelled round, thrusting his legs inside preparatory to descending, and with only his head sticking out.

When Andreuccio saw this, he stood up and grasped the priest by one of his legs, giving the priest the impression that he was about to be dragged down into the tomb. The priest no sooner felt this happening than he let out an ear-splitting yell and hurled himself bodily out of the tomb. The rest of the gang were terrified by this turn of events, and, leaving the tomb open, they all started running away as though they were being pursued by ten thousand devils.

When Andreuccio perceived what had happened, he was contented beyond his wildest hopes, and, clambering hastily out, he left the cathedral by the way he had come. By now it was almost daybreak, and as he was wandering aimlessly along with the ring on his finger, he eventually came to the waterfront. Shortly thereafter he stumbled across his inn, where he found that his companions and the innkeeper had been up all night, wondering what on earth had become of him. After telling them what had happened, he was

urged by the innkeeper to leave Naples at once. He promptly
followed the innkeeper's advice, and returned to Perugia, having
invested, in a ring, the money with which he had set out to
purchase horses.

SIXTH STORY

*Madonna Beritola, having lost her two sons, is found on an island with
two roebucks and taken to Lunigiana, where one of her sons, having
entered the service of her lord and master, makes love to the daughter of the
house and is thrown into prison. After the Sicilian rebellion against King
Charles, the son is recognized by his mother, he marries his master's
daughter, he is reunited with his brother, and they are all restored to
positions of great honour.*

The whole company, ladies and young men alike, rocked with
laughter over Fiammetta's account of Andreuccio's misfortunes, and
then Emilia, on seeing that the story was finished and receiving a
signal from the queen, began as follows:

The erratic course pursued by Fortune frequently leads to pain
and irritation. But since our mental faculties, which are easily lulled
to sleep by her blandishments, are aroused as often as a subject is
openly discussed, I consider that nobody, whether he be happy or
miserable, should ever object to hearing an account of her eccentricities, in that the first man will be placed on his guard and the second
will receive some consolation. Accordingly, I propose to tell you a
story, no less true than touching, on this same topic upon which
such splendid things have already been said. And whilst my tale has
a happy ending, the suffering contained therein was so intense and
protracted, that I can scarcely believe it was ever entirely assuaged
by the happiness that ensued.

You are to know, dear ladies, that Manfred,[1] who was crowned
King of Sicily after the death of the Emperor Frederick II, held few
of his courtiers in higher esteem than a gentleman of Naples called
Arrighetto Capece, who had a beautiful and noble wife, also

Neapolitan, called Madonna Beritola Caracciolo.² Arrighetto was in fact governing the island, when news reached him that King Charles I had defeated and killed Manfred at Benevento, and that the whole kingdom had gone over to the conqueror. Knowing that the Sicilians could never be trusted for long, and not wishing to become a subject of his master's enemy, he prepared to flee. But his plans were discovered by the Sicilians, who promptly took him prisoner and delivered him over to King Charles along with many other friends and servants of King Manfred. And shortly afterwards, the island itself was surrendered.

In the face of all this upheaval, not knowing what had become of Arrighetto, frightened by what had happened and fearing a possible attempt on her own honour, Madonna Beritola abandoned everything she possessed, and though pregnant and reduced to poverty, she fled by ship to Lipari with her son, Giusfredi, who was about eight years old. There she gave birth to a second son, whom she called The Outcast, and having hired a nurse, she embarked with all three on a tiny ship bound for Naples, with the intention of rejoining her family. But her plans misfired, for the ship was driven by strong winds to the island of Ponza,³ where they put in to a little bay and began to await more favourable weather for their voyage.

Like the others, Madonna Beritola went ashore there, and she sought out a deserted and remote spot on the island where, in complete solitude, she could give vent to her sorrow for the loss of her husband. This became a daily ritual of hers, until one day, as she was busy sorrowing, it happened that a pirate-galley arrived, taking the crew and everyone else unawares, and departed again after capturing the ship and all hands.

Having completed her daily lament, Madonna Beritola, following her usual practice, returned to the shore to look for her children. On finding nobody in sight she was at first perplexed, and then, suddenly suspecting what had happened, she cast her eyes seaward and saw the galley, not yet very far distant, with the little ship in tow. Realizing all too clearly that she had now lost her children as well as her husband, and finding herself abandoned there, alone and destitute, without the slightest notion of how she was going to find them again, she fell in a dead faint on to the sand with the names of her husband and children on her lips.

There was nobody at hand to revive her with cold water or other remedies, and hence it was some time before she came to her senses. When, eventually, the strength returned to her poor exhausted body, bringing with it further tears and lamentations, she called out over and over again to her children and searched high and low for them in every cavern she could find. But when she saw that her efforts were useless and that the night was approaching, she began, prompted by an instinctive feeling that all was not entirely lost, to devote some attention to her own predicament. And, leaving the shore, she returned to the cave where she was in the habit of giving vent to her tears and sorrow.

She had had nothing to eat since midday, and a little after tierce on the following morning, having spent the night in great fear and incredible anguish, she was compelled to start eating grass in order to appease her hunger. Having fed herself to the best of her ability, she then started brooding, tearfully, about what was to become of her. And whilst in the midst of these various reflections, she caught sight of a doe, which came towards her and disappeared into a nearby cave, emerging shortly afterwards and then running away into the woods. Getting up from where she was sitting, she entered the cave from which the doe had emerged, and inside she saw two newly born roebucks, no more than a few hours old, which seemed to her the sweetest and most charming sight it was possible to imagine. And since her own milk was not yet dry after her recent confinement, she picked them up tenderly and applied them to her breast. They showed no sign of refusing this favour, but took suck from her as though she were their own mother; and from then on they made no distinction between their mother and herself. Thus the lady felt she had found some company on this deserted island, and having become just as familiar with the doe as with the two roebucks, she resolved to remain there for the rest of her days on a diet of grass and water, bursting into tears whenever she remembered her past life with her husband and children.

As a result of leading this sort of life, the gentle woman had turned quite wild when, a few months later, a small Pisan ship

happened to be driven in by a storm, casting anchor in the same little
bay where she herself had arrived, and lying there for several days.

Now, aboard this ship there was a gentleman of the Malespina
family called Currado,[4] who was returning home from a pilgrimage
with his worthy and devout lady after visiting all the holy places in
the Kingdom of Apulia. One day, in order to relieve the monotony
of the delay, he went ashore with his wife, some of his servants, and
his dogs, and started exploring the island. And not very far from
the place where Madonna Beritola was, Currado's dogs began
giving chase to the two roebucks, which had now grown quite big
and were out grazing. Pursued by the dogs, the two roebucks ran to
the very cave where Madonna Beritola was sheltering.

Seeing what was happening, she got up, took hold of a stick, and
drove the dogs back. Shortly afterwards, Currado and his lady,
who had been following the dogs, arrived on the scene; and when
they saw her standing there, all bronzed and emaciated, with long
and unkempt hair, their astonishment, though much less than her
own, was very great indeed. However, after Currado had complied
with her entreaties to call off his dogs, they persuaded her, with a
good deal of coaxing, to tell them who she was and what she was
doing there, and she gave them a full account of her past life and all
her misfortunes, ending by revealing her fierce determination to
stay on the island. On hearing this, Currado, who had been very
well acquainted with Arrighetto Capece, wept with compassion,
and attempted to talk her out of her proud decision, offering to take
her back to her home, or alternatively, to honour her as a sister and
keep her in his own family, where she could stay until such time as
God granted her a kindlier fate. However, she would have nothing
to do with his proposals, and so he left her with his wife, bidding
her to arrange for food to be brought, and, since the woman was all
in rags, to let her have some of her own clothes to wear. But most
important, she was to do all she could to bring her back to the ship.

On being left alone with Beritola, Currado's wife shed countless
tears over the lady's misfortunes, then she gave instructions for food
and clothes to be brought, which she had the greatest difficulty in
persuading her to accept. And finally, after a stream of entreaties,
with Madonna Beritola asserting that on no account would she go

to any place in which she was known, she persuaded her to accompany them to Lunigiana, bringing with her the doe and the two roebucks. The doe had meanwhile, in fact, returned, and, to the no small astonishment of Currado's wife, it had greeted Beritola with a display of affection.

And so, once the weather had improved, Madonna Beritola embarked on the ship with Currado and his lady, taking with her the doe and the two roebucks, a circumstance which, since few people knew her real name, led to her being referred to as Cavriuola.[5] The winds were favourable, and they soon reached the mouth of the River Magra, where they left the ship and proceeded to Currado's estates in the hills.

After her arrival at the castle, Madonna Beritola, dressed in widow's weeds, began to live a humble, secluded and obedient life as a maid of honour to Currado's lady, at the same time continuing to treat her roebucks with affection and ensuring that they were properly fed.

Meanwhile, the pirates who had unwittingly abandoned Madonna Beritola at Ponza and seized the ship on which she had been travelling, had arrived at Genoa with all their captives. When the spoils were divided between the owners of the galley, it turned out that Madonna Beritola's nurse and the two children were assigned, along with a quantity of goods, to a certain Messer Guasparrino d'Oria,[6] who sent the woman and the two boys to his house with the intention of employing them as slaves on household duties.

Being exceedingly distressed by the loss of her mistress and by the sorry state to which she saw herself and the two children reduced, the nurse wept over and over again. But she was a sensible and prudent woman despite her lowly station in life, and once she had realized that her tears were not going to help in freeing them all from slavery, she did all she could to comfort the children. Considering where they were, she thought it quite possible that the two boys would be molested if their identity were discovered. And moreover, she was hoping that sooner or later their luck would change, in which case, provided they were still alive, the children might regain the positions of honour they had lost. So she resolved not to tell anybody who they were until a suitable occasion presented itself, and meanwhile, whenever she was questioned on the matter, she would claim that the children were her own. Renaming the older boy Giannotto di Procida instead of Giusfredi and leaving the younger boy's name unaltered, she explained very carefully to Giusfredi why she had changed his name and how dangerous it might be for him if he were recognized. And she drummed this into him so often and with so much persistence, that, being an intelligent boy, he followed the instructions of his wise nurse to the letter.

And so the two boys and their nurse, badly clothed and worse shod, continued for many years in Messer Guasparrino's house, patiently performing all the most menial tasks it is possible to imagine. But Giannotto was made of sterner stuff than slaves are made of, and by the time he was sixteen the baseness of a servile existence had become so repugnant to him that he abandoned Messer Guasparrino's household and enlisted as a seaman on galleys plying between Genoa and Alexandria, after which he travelled far and wide without however finding a single opportunity for advancement.

Finally, when he had almost lost hope of a change of fortune, his wanderings led him to Lunigiana, where he chanced to enter the service of Currado Malespina, whom he attended, to the latter's no small satisfaction, with considerable efficiency. It was now some three or four years since his departure from Messer Guasparrino's and he had grown into a well-built, handsome young man. He had meanwhile heard that his father, whom he had supposed to be dead, was still alive, but languishing under heavy guard in one of King Charles's dungeons. And whilst he occasionally saw his mother, who was in attendance on Currado's lady, he never recognized her, nor she him, for they had both changed a great deal in the period that had elapsed since they had last seen one another.

Now, whilst Giannotto was in Currado's service, it happened that a daughter of Currado's, whose name was Spina, was left a widow by a certain Niccolò da Grignano, and returned to her father's house. Being a beautiful and very graceful girl of little more than sixteen, she began to take an interest in Giannotto, and he in her, with the result that they fell madly in love with one another. Their love was soon consummated, and since it continued for several months undetected, they became excessively confident and were less cautious than they should have been. And one day, while out walking in a fine, thickly wooded forest, Giannotto and the girl, forging on ahead of their companions, came to a delectable spot all covered with grass and flowers and surrounded by trees, and, thinking they had left the others far behind, they began to make love.

So great was their enjoyment that they lost all track of time, and they had been together for ages when the girl's mother arrived on the scene, to be followed a moment later by Currado. Dismayed beyond measure by what he saw,[7] he ordered three of his servants, without giving any reasons, to seize the pair of them, bind them, and march them off to one of his castles. Then he stalked away, seething with distress and anger, and intent on having them ignominiously put to death.

The girl's mother was extremely upset, and regarded no punishment as too severe for her daughter's lapse. But she could not stand passively aside and allow them to suffer the kind of fate which, on piecing together certain of Currado's remarks, she realized he was intending to inflict on the culprits. So she hurried to catch up with her irate husband, and began pleading with him not to ruin his old age by killing his own daughter in a sudden fit of frenzy and soiling his hands with the blood of one of his servants. He could, she insisted, find some other way of placating his anger, such as having them incarcerated, so that, as they languished in prison, they would have a chance of repenting in full for their sinful behaviour. The saintly woman pressed these views and many others upon him with so much urgency, that she dissuaded him from killing them. And he ordered each of them to be imprisoned in different places, where they were to be closely guarded, receive a minimum of food, and suffer the maximum of discomfort, until such time as he decided otherwise. These instructions were promptly carried out, and I leave you to imagine the sort of life they led in their captivity, weeping incessantly and almost starving to death.

Now, when Giannotto and Spina had been languishing in these wretched conditions for more than twelve months, and Currado had dismissed them from his thoughts, it came about that King Peter of Aragon, with the aid of a subversive movement led by

Messer Gian di Procida, stirred up a rebellion in Sicily[8] and wrested the island from King Charles. Currado, being a Ghibelline, was overjoyed at the news, and when Giannotto heard about it from one of his gaolers, he heaved a deep sigh, and said:

'Oh, alas! for fourteen long years I have travelled the world in continual hardship, waiting only for this to happen! And now that it has come about, just to prove the vanity of all my hopes, I find myself here in this prison-cell, without the slightest prospect of being released until the day I die.'

'What are you talking about?' said the gaoler. 'Surely the affairs of mighty monarchs are no concern of yours? What was your business in Sicily?'

'It almost breaks my heart,' replied Giannotto, 'when I recall the business of my father. For although I was still a small boy when I fled from the island, yet I remember seeing him as its governor, when King Manfred was alive.'

'And who was this father of yours?' asked the gaoler.

'My father's name,' said Giannotto, 'can now be safely revealed, since I no longer have anything to fear from its disclosure. He was called (and if he is still alive he is still called) Arrighetto Capece, and my own name is not Giannotto but Giusfredi. Furthermore, I have not the slightest doubt that if I were a free man, I could return to Sicily and occupy, even now, a position of the highest importance.'

The good man asked no more questions, but at the first opportunity he referred the whole matter to Currado. And although, as he listened, Currado put on a show of indifference for the gaoler's benefit, he went straight to Madonna Beritola and asked her in a pleasant manner whether she and Arrighetto had ever had a son called Giusfredi. Bursting into tears the woman replied that if the older of her two sons was still alive, this indeed would be his name, and that he would now be twenty-two years old.

On hearing this, Currado concluded that the young man must be telling the truth, and it occurred to him that, in this case, he was in a position to perform an act of clemency that would repair both his own and his daughter's honour, namely to offer her to him in marriage. He therefore arranged a secret interview with Giannotto, in the course of which he interrogated him in detail on the whole of his past life. And having confirmed beyond any doubt that he was indeed Giusfredi, the son of Arrighetto Capece, he said:

'Giannotto, you are aware how great an injury you have done to me in the person of my own daughter. I treated you as a friend, and it was your duty as my servant never to do anything that would undermine my honour, or that of my family. Many another man, in my place, would have had you ignominiously put to death, but I could not bring myself to do such a thing. Now, since what you say is true, and you are a man of gentle birth, I desire with your consent to put an end to your suffering and release you from your wretched, captive existence, at the same time restoring both your own reputation and mine. As you are aware, my daughter Spina, for whom you formed so loving but improper an attachment, is a widow, and she has a good, large dowry. You are acquainted with her ways, and with her father and mother; of your own present condition, I say nothing. Therefore, if you are agreeable, I am willing to convert a dishonourable friendship into an honourable marriage, and allow you to live with her here in my house for as long as you wish to remain, as though you were my own son.'

Giannotto's fine physique had been wasted away by his imprisonment, but the innate nobility of his spirit was in no way impaired, and he still loved his lady as wholeheartedly as ever. So that, although he found himself in the other man's power, and wished for nothing better than what Currado was proposing, he had not the slightest hesitation in following the promptings of his noble heart.

'Currado,' he replied, 'neither the lust for power nor the desire for riches nor any other motive has ever led me to harbour treacherous designs against your person or property. I loved your daughter, I love her still, and I shall always love her, because I consider her a worthy object of my love. And if, in wooing her, I was acting in a manner that would commonly be regarded as dishonourable, the fault I committed was one which is inseparable from youth. In order to eradicate it, one would have to do away with youth altogether. Besides, it would not be considered half so serious as you and many others maintain, if old men would remember that they were once young, and if they would measure other people's shortcomings against their own and vice versa. I committed this fault, not as your enemy, but as your friend. It has always been my wish to do what you are now proposing, and if I had thought your consent would be forthcoming, I would have asked you long ago for your daughter's hand. Coming at this moment, when my expectations were at such a low ebb, your consent is all the more gratifying to me. But if your intentions do not match your words, please do not feed me with vain hopes. Send me back to my prison-cell and have me treated as cruelly as you like. Whatever you do to me, I shall always love Spina, and for her sake I shall always love and respect her father.'

Currado listened in amazement to Giannotto's words, which convinced him of both his courage and the warmth of his love, increasing his esteem for the young man. He therefore rose to his feet, embraced and kissed him, and gave orders without further ado for Spina to be brought there in secret.

She had turned all pale, thin and weak in prison, and like Giannotto, she almost seemed another person as, in Currado's presence and by mutual consent, they took the marriage vows according to our custom.

A few days later, having kept the whole matter secret and provided them with everything they could possibly need or desire, he decided it was time to break the glad tidings to their respective mothers, and summoning his lady and Cavriuola, he turned to the latter and said:

'What would you say, my lady, if I were to arrange for your elder son to be restored to you, as the husband of one of my daughters?'

'The only thing I could say,' replied Cavriuola, 'would be that if it were possible for me to be more obliged to you than I am already, then inasmuch as you would be giving me something I value more than my own life, my debt would be correspondingly large. And by restoring him to me in the way you describe, you would in some measure be rekindling my lost hopes.'

She then stopped and burst into tears, and Currado turned to his lady, saying:

'And what would you say, my dear, if I were to present you with such a son-in-law?'

'If it were pleasing to you,' the lady replied, 'I would not object to a vagrant for a son-in-law, let alone a man who is of noble birth.'

'Within a few days,' said Currado, 'I hope to have good news for you both.'

Meanwhile, the two young people were gradually putting flesh on their bones, and when Currado saw that they had quite recovered, he had them dressed in fine clothes, and turned to Giusfredi, saying:

'Would it not add greatly to your happiness to see your mother in this place?'

'My mother suffered such appalling misfortunes,' replied Giusfredi, 'that I cannot believe she has survived them. But if she has, I would be very glad indeed to see her, for with her advice I believe I could largely repair my fortunes in Sicily.'

Currado then summoned the two ladies, and they both smothered the new bride with affection, at the same time wondering what had happened to soften Currado's heart to the extent of uniting her in wedlock with Giannotto.

With Currado's words fresh in her memory, Madonna Beritola had meanwhile begun to stare intently at the young man. Suddenly, some occult force stirred within her, causing her to recollect the boyish features of her son's face. And without awaiting further proof of his identity, she rushed towards him and flung her arms about his neck. Her feelings of maternal joy and affection were so intense that she was unable to utter a word: on the contrary, she lost all the power of her five senses and collapsed in the arms of her son as though she were dead. Giannotto, for his part, was filled with amazement, for he could remember having seen her on many previous occasions in that same castle without ever having recognized her. Nevertheless, he now knew instinctively that she was his mother, and, bursting into tears and reproaching himself for his former indifference, he received her in his arms and kissed her with tenderness. Shortly afterwards, with the loving assistance of Spina and Currado's lady, who applied cold water and other remedies, Madonna Beritola recovered her senses and embraced her son all over again, weeping copiously and uttering a stream of gentle endearments. And, giving vent to her maternal affection, she kissed him a thousand times or more whilst he held her in his arms and gazed at her in awe and reverence.

When the chaste and joyful greetings had been repeated three or four times[9] to the no small pleasure and approval of the onlookers, and mother and son had exchanged the story of their adventures, Giusfredi turned to Currado, who, having already informed his friends about the marriage and received their delighted approval, had given orders for a sumptuous and splendid banquet, and he said:

'Currado, you have bestowed many favours upon me and you have long sheltered my mother under your roof. But so that we may use your good offices to the full, I now want to ask you to gladden my mother, my wedding-feast and myself by sending for my brother. As I have told you already, he and I were seized by pirates acting for Messer Guasparrino d'Oria, who is detaining him in his house in the role of a servant. And I would also like you to send somebody to Sicily who can bring us a clear picture of conditions there, and tell us whether my father, Arrighetto, is alive or dead, and whether, if he is alive, he is in good health.'

Giusfredi's request was well received by Currado, who immediately sent experienced couriers to Genoa and Sicily. The one who went to Genoa called on Messer Guasparrino and earnestly entreated him on Currado's behalf to send him The Outcast and his nurse, giving him a concise account of what Currado had done for Giusfredi and his mother.

'It is true,' said Messer Guasparrino, who was greatly astonished by this tale, 'that I would do anything in my power to please Currado. And for the past fourteen years, the boy you mention, and his mother, have certainly been under my roof. I will gladly send them to him, but you are to warn him from me not to pay too much attention to the tall stories of Giannotto, who now masquerades, if I understand you aright, under the name of Giusfredi. That young man is much more cunning than Currado seems to realize.'

He said no more, but having attended to the good man's lodging he secretly sent for the nurse and questioned her closely on the subject. She had already heard about the rebellion in Sicily, and on learning that Arrighetto was alive, she abandoned her former fear and told him the whole story, explaining her reasons for the action she had taken.

On finding that the nurse's account corresponded exactly with that of Currado's emissary, Messer Guasparrino began to take her story seriously. Being a very astute man, he took various steps to have it thoroughly checked, becoming more and more convinced of its veracity with every scrap of new evidence he discovered. Ashamed at having treated the boy so contemptuously, he made amends by bestowing a wife on him in the person of his pretty little eleven-year-old daughter, together with a huge dowry, for he was well aware of Arrighetto's past and present fame. After celebrating the event in great style, he embarked, along with the youth, his daughter, Currado's emissary, and the nurse, on a well-armed galliot, and sailed for Lerici,[10] where he was met by Currado. Then, with the whole of his company, he proceeded to one of Currado's castles, not very far from there, where the great wedding-feast was about to be held.

The general rejoicing, whether that of the mother on seeing her son again, or that of the two brothers, or that with which all three greeted the faithful nurse, or that displayed by everyone towards Messer Guasparrino and his daughter and vice versa, or that of the whole company in the presence of Currado, his lady, his children and his friends, would be impossible to describe in words. And thus I leave it, ladies, to your imagination. But to crown it all, the Lord God, whose generosity knows no bounds once it is set in motion, arranged things so that news should arrive that Arrighetto was alive and in good health.

For amid the great rejoicing, when the guests, men and women, were still seated round the tables, having proceeded no further than the first course, Currado's other emissary returned from Sicily. Amongst other things, he narrated how Arrighetto had been held prisoner in Catania on the orders of King Charles, and how, after the country's insurrection against the King, the people had stormed the prison, killing his gaolers and setting him free. Since he was King Charles's bitterest opponent, they had then elected him their leader and joined him in pursuing and killing the French. For this reason, he had achieved a high reputation in the eyes of King Peter, who had reinstated him in all his possessions and titles. And so he now enjoyed a position of great honour and authority.

The messenger added that Arrighetto had welcomed him very warmly, being overjoyed beyond description to hear about his wife and son, of whom he had received no news since the time of his capture. He was in fact sending a brigantine with some gentlemen aboard, to come and fetch them, and they were due to arrive at any moment.

The envoy's announcement was greeted with prolonged cheering and rejoicing, and Currado promptly went out with some of his friends to meet the gentlemen who were coming to fetch Madonna Beritola and Giusfredi; and after giving them a hearty welcome, he took them in to his banquet, less than half of which had so far been served.

Such was the delight of Beritola, Giusfredi and all the others on seeing them that they almost raised the roof with their greeting. But before sitting down to eat, the Sicilians conveyed Arrighetto's warmest greeting and deepest thanks to Currado and his lady for the hospitality they had offered to his wife and son, and pledged his readiness to assist them in any way within his power. They then turned to Messer Guasparrino, whose courteous action had taken them by surprise, and said they were quite certain that when Arrighetto came to know of the generous settlement he had made on The Outcast he would be just as grateful to him as he was to Currado, or possibly even more. Then without further ado, they turned with great gusto to the business of feasting the two brides and their respective bridegrooms.

Currado's entertainment of his son-in-law and his other friends and relatives was not confined to that day alone, but extended over many of the days that followed. When the feasting was over, and Madonna Beritola, Giusfredi and the others felt that the time had come for their departure, they went aboard the brig, taking Spina with them, and to the accompaniment of copious tears they took their leave of Currado, his wife, and Messer Guasparrino. The winds being favourable, they soon reached Sicily, and on their arrival at Palermo they were all, the two sons and their womenfolk alike, greeted by Arrighetto with a warmth that beggars description. There it is believed that they all lived long and happily, at peace with the Almighty and grateful for the blessings He had bestowed upon them.

SEVENTH STORY

The Sultan of Babylon sends his daughter off to marry the King of Algarve. Owing to a series of mishaps, she passes through the hands of nine men in various places within the space of four years. Finally, having been restored to her father as a virgin, she sets off, as before, to become the King of Algarve's wife.

The young ladies, who were feeling very sorry for Madonna Beritola, would possibly have dissolved into tears if Emilia's recital of the lady's woes had continued for very much longer. When, finally, the tale was finished, it was the queen's wish that Panfilo should take up the storytelling, and being very obedient he began forthwith as follows:

Delectable ladies, it is no easy matter for a man to decide what is in his best interests. For as we have often had occasion to observe, there are many who have considered that only their poverty stood between themselves and a secure, trouble-free life, and they have not only prayed to God for riches, but sought deliberately to acquire them, sparing themselves neither effort nor danger in the process. And no sooner have they succeeded, than the prospect of a substantial legacy has frequently caused them to be murdered by people who, before they had become rich, had never dreamed of doing them any harm. Others have risen from low estate to the dizzy heights of kingship through a thousand dangerous battles, spilling the blood of their nearest and dearest as they went along, thinking sovereign power represented the peak of happiness. But as they could have seen and heard for themselves, it was a happiness fraught with endless fear and worry, and at the cost of their lives they came to realize that the chalice at a royal table may sometimes be poisoned, even though it is made of gold. Again, there have been many people who have ardently yearned for bodily strength and beauty, whilst others have longed with equal intensity for bodily ornaments, only to discover too late that the very things they so unwisely desired were the cause of their death or unhappiness.

But in order not to become involved in a detailed review embracing the whole range of human desires, I will merely affirm that no man can, with complete confidence, elect any one of them as being wholly immune from the accidents of Fortune. For if we were to proceed at all times in a correct manner, we would have to resign ourselves to the acquisition and possession of whatever has been granted to us by the One who alone knows what we need and has the power to provide it for us. However, there are many ways in which people sin through their desires, and you, gracious ladies, sin above all in one particular way, which is in your desiring to be beautiful, inasmuch as, being dissatisfied with the attractions bestowed upon you by Nature, you go to extraordinary lengths in trying to improve them. And therefore I would like to tell you a story about a Saracen girl's ill-starred beauty, which in the space of about four years caused her to be newly married on nine separate occasions.

A long time ago, Babylon was ruled by a sultan called Beminedab,[1] during whose reign it was unusual for anything to happen that was contrary to his wishes. Apart from numerous other children, both male and female, this man possessed a daughter called Alatiel,[2] who, at that period, according to everybody who had set eyes on her, was the most beautiful woman to be found anywhere on earth. Now, the Sultan had recently been attacked by a great horde of Arabs, and inflicted a major defeat on his aggressors, receiving timely assistance from the King of Algarve,[3] who asked the Sultan, as a special favour, to give him Alatiel as his wife. The Sultan agreed, and having seen her aboard a well-armed and well-appointed ship with a retinue of noblemen and noblewomen and a large quantity of elegant and precious accoutrements, he bade her a fond farewell.

Finding the weather favourable, the ship's crew put on full sail, and for several days after leaving Alexandria the voyage was prosperous. But one day, when they had passed Sardinia and were looking forward to journey's end, they ran into a series of sudden squalls, each of which was exceptionally violent, and these gave the ship such a terrible buffeting that passengers and crew were convinced time and again that the end had come. But they had plenty of spirit, and by exerting all their skill and energy they survived the onslaught of the mountainous seas for two whole days. However, as night approached for the third time since the beginning of the storm, which showed no sign of relenting but on the contrary was increasing in fury, they felt the ship foundering. Though in fact they were not far from the coast of Majorca, they had no idea where they were, because it was a dark night and the sky was covered with thick black clouds, and hence it was impossible to estimate their position either with the ship's instruments or with the naked eye.

It now became a case of every man for himself, and there was nothing for it but to launch a longboat, into which the ship's officers leapt, preferring to put their trust in that rather than in the crippled vessel. But they had no sooner abandoned ship than every man aboard followed their example and leapt into the longboat, undeterred by the fact that the earlier arrivals were fighting them off with knives in their hands. Thus, in trying to save their lives, they did the exact opposite; for the longboat was not built for holding so many people in weather of this sort and it sank, taking everybody with it.

Meanwhile, the ship itself, though torn open and almost water-logged, was driven swiftly along by powerful winds until eventually it ran aground on a beach on the island of Majorca. By this time, the only people still aboard were the lady and her female attendants, and they were all lying there like dead creatures, paralysed with terror by the raging tempest. The ship's impetus was so great that it thrust its way firmly into the sand before coming to rest a mere stone's throw from the shore, and since the wind was no longer able to move it, there it remained for the rest of the night, to be pounded by the sea.

By the time it was broad daylight, the storm had abated considerably, and the lady, who was feeling practically half-dead, raised her head and began, weak as she was, to call out to her servants one after another. But it was all to no purpose, because they were too far away to hear. On receiving no response and seeing nobody about, she wondered what on earth had happened, and began to be filled with considerable alarm. She staggered to her feet to discover that her maids of honour and the other women were lying about all over the ship, and she attempted to rouse each of them in turn by calling to them at the top of her voice. But few of them showed any signs of life because they had all been laid low by their terror and the heavings of their stomachs, and her own fears were accordingly increased. Nevertheless, since she was all alone and possessed no idea of her whereabouts, she felt in need of someone to talk to, and so she went round prodding the ones who were still alive and forced them to their feet, only to discover that none of them had any idea what had happened to all the men aboard. And when they saw that the ship was aground and full of water, they all started crying as though they would burst.

It was not until mid-afternoon that they were able to make their plight apparent to anybody on the shore or elsewhere in the vicinity who would come to their assistance. Halfway through the afternoon, in fact, a nobleman whose name was Pericone da Visalgo happened to pass that way as he was returning from one of his estates. He was riding along on horseback with several of his men, and when he saw the ship he immediately guessed what had happened. So he ordered one of his servants to try and clamber aboard without further delay and bring him a report on how matters stood. The servant had quite a struggle, but eventually he boarded the ship, where he found the young gentlewoman, frightened out of her senses, hiding with her handful of companions in the forepeak. On seeing him, the women burst into tears and repeatedly pleaded for mercy, but when they perceived that neither he nor they could understand what the other party was saying,[4] they tried to explain their predicament by means of gestures.

Having sized up the situation to the best of his ability, the servant reported his findings to Pericone, who promptly arranged for the women to be brought ashore along with the most valuable of those items on the ship that could be salvaged, and escorted them all to his castle, where he restored the women's spirits by arranging for them to be fed and rested. He could see, from the richness of their apparel, that he had stumbled across some great lady of quality, and he quickly gathered which of them she must be because she was the sole centre of the other women's attention. The lady was pallid and extremely dishevelled-looking as a result of her exhausting experiences at sea, but it seemed to Pericone that she possessed very fine features, and for this reason he resolved there and then that if she had no husband he would marry her, and that, if marriage proved to be out of the question, he would make her his mistress.

Pericone, who was a very powerful, vigorous-looking fellow, caused the lady to be waited upon hand and foot, and when, after a few days, she had fully recovered, he found that she was even more beautiful than he had ever thought possible. He was greatly pained by the fact that they were unable to communicate with each other, and that he could not therefore discover who she was. Nevertheless, being immensely taken with her beauty, he behaved lovingly and agreeably towards her in an endeavour to persuade her to do his pleasure without a struggle. But it was no use: she refused to have anything to do with him; and meanwhile Pericone's ardour continued to increase.

The lady had no idea where she was, but she quickly gathered from their mode of living that the people she was staying with were Christians, and she could see little purpose, even if she had known her whereabouts, in revealing her identity. From the way Pericone was behaving, she knew that sooner or later, whether she liked it or not, she would be compelled to let him have his way with her, but meanwhile she was proudly resolved to turn a blind eye to her sorrowful predicament. To the three surviving members of her female retinue, she gave instructions that they should never disclose their identity to anyone until such time as they were in a position that offered them a clear prospect of freedom. Furthermore, she implored them to preserve their chastity, declaring her own determination to submit to no man's pleasure except her husband's – a sentiment that was greeted with approval by the three women, who said they would do their utmost to follow her instructions.

As the days passed, and Pericone came into closer proximity with the object of his desires, his advances were more firmly rejected, and the flames of his passion raged correspondingly fiercer. Realizing that his flattery was getting him nowhere, he decided to fall back on ingenuity and subterfuge, holding brute strength in reserve as a last resort. He had noticed more than once that the lady liked the taste of wine, which, since it is prohibited by her religion, she was unaccustomed to drinking, and by using this in the service of Venus, he thought it possible that she would yield to him. And so one evening, having feigned indifference concerning the matter for which she had paraded so much distaste, he held a splendid banquet with all the trappings of a great festive occasion, at which the lady was present. The meal was notable for its abundance of good food, and Pericone arranged with the steward who was serving the lady to keep her well supplied with a succession of different wines. The steward carried out his instructions to the letter, and the lady, being caught off her guard and carried away by the agreeable taste of the wines, drank more than was consistent with her decorum. Forgetting all the misfortunes she had experienced, she became positively merry, and when she saw some women dancing in the Majorcan manner, she herself danced Alexandrian fashion.[5]

On seeing this, Pericone felt that he would soon obtain what he wanted, and calling for further large quantities of food and drink, he caused the banquet to continue until the small hours of the morning. Finally, when the guests had departed, he accompanied the lady, alone, into her room. Without the least show of embarrassment, being rather more flushed with wine than tempered by virtue. she then undressed in Pericone's presence as though he were one of her maidservants, and got into bed. Pericone lost no time in following her example. Having snuffed out all the lights, he quickly scrambled in from the other side and lay down beside her, and taking her into his arms without meeting any resistance on her part, he began making amorous sport with her. She had no conception of the kind of horn that men do their butting with, and when she felt what was happening, it was almost as though she regretted having turned a deaf ear to Pericone's flattery, and could not see why she had waited for an invitation before spending her nights so agreeably. For it was she herself who was now issuing the invitation, and she did so several times over, not in so many words, since she was unable to make herself understood, but by way of her gestures.

Great indeed was their mutual delight. But Fortune, not content with converting her from a king's bride into a baron's mistress, thrust a more terrible friendship upon her.

Pericone had a twenty-five-year-old brother, fair and fresh as a garden rose, whose name was Marato. He had already seen the lady and taken an enormous liking to her, and as far as he could judge from her reactions, she seemed to be very fond of him also. Thus the only thing that appeared to be standing between him and the conquest he desired to make of her was the strict watch maintained by Pericone. He therefore devised a nefarious scheme which he lost no time in pursuing to its dreadful conclusion.

In the port of the town, there happened at that time to be a ship commanded by two young Genoese, with a full cargo for Corinth in the Peloponnese.[6] She was already under canvas, ready to put to sea with the first favourable wind, and Marato made an arrangement with her masters for himself and the lady to be taken aboard the following night. This done, he decided how he would have to proceed, and when it was dark he wandered unobtrusively into his brother's house, to which he had open access, and concealed himself inside.

He had meanwhile enlisted the aid of some trusted companions for his enterprise, and in the dead of night, having let them into the house, he led them to the place where Pericone and the woman were sleeping. Entering the room, they killed Pericone in his sleep and seized the lady, who woke up and started to cry, threatening her with death if she made any noise. Then, taking with them a considerable quantity of Pericone's most precious possessions, they departed without being heard and made their way to the quayside, where Marato boarded the ship with the lady, leaving his companions to go their separate ways.

The ship's crew, taking advantage of a strong and favourable wind, cast off and sailed swiftly away.

The lady was sorely distressed by this second catastrophe, coming as it did so soon after the first. But Marato, with the Heaven-sent assistance of Saint Stiffen-in-the-Hand,[7] began consoling her to such good effect that she soon returned his affection and forgot all about Pericone. She had hardly begun to feel settled, however, before Fortune, not content, it seemed, with her previous handiwork, engineered yet another calamity. As we have almost grown tired of repeating, the woman had the body of an angel and a temperament to match, and the two young masters of the vessel fell so violently in love with her that they could concentrate on nothing else except how best they might make themselves useful and agreeable to her, at the same time taking care not to let Marato see what they were up to.

On discovering that they were both in love with the same woman, they talked the matter over in secret and agreed to make the lady's conquest a mutual affair, as though love were capable of being shared out like merchandise or profits. For some time their plans were thwarted because they found that Marato kept a close watch on her. But one day, when the ship was sailing along like the wind and Marato was standing on the stern facing seaward without the least suspicion of their intentions, they both crept up on him, seized him quickly from behind, and hurled him into the sea. By the time anybody so much as noticed that Marato had fallen overboard, they had already sailed on for over a mile, and the lady, hearing what had happened and seeing no way of going to his rescue, began to fill the whole ship with the sounds of her latest affliction.

The two gallants immediately rushed to her assistance, and with the aid of honeyed words and extravagant promises, few of which she understood, they attempted to pacify her. What she was bemoaning was not so much the loss of Marato as her own sorry plight, and so after she had listened to a stream of fine talk, repeated twice over, she seemed considerably less distraught. The two brothers then got down to a private discussion to decide which of them was to take her off to bed. Each man claimed priority over the other, and having failed to reach any agreement on the matter they began to argue fiercely between themselves. Nor did their quarrel stop with the exchange of verbal abuse. Losing their tempers, they reached for their knives and hurled themselves furiously upon one another, and before the ship's crew could separate the pair, they had both inflicted a number of stab-wounds, from which one man died instantly whilst the other emerged with serious injuries to various parts of his body. The lady was sorely distressed by all this, for she could see that she was now alone on the ship with nobody to turn to for help or advice, and she was greatly afraid lest the relatives and companions of the two men should vent their rage upon her. However, partly because of the injured man's pleas on her behalf, partly because they soon arrived at Corinth, the danger to her person was short-lived. On their arrival, she disembarked with the injured man, and went to live with him at an inn, whence the story of her great beauty spread rapidly through the city, eventually reaching the ears of the Prince of Morea,[8] who was living in Corinth at that time. He therefore demanded to see her, and on discovering her to be more beautiful than she had been reported, he immediately fell so ardently in love with her that he could think of nothing else.

When he learnt about the circumstances of her arrival in the city, he saw no reason why he should not be able to have her. And indeed, once the wounded man's relatives discovered that the Prince was putting out inquiries, they promptly sent her off to him without asking any questions. The Prince was highly delighted, but so also was the lady, who considered that she had now escaped from a most dangerous situation. On finding that she was endowed with stately manners as well as beauty, the Prince calculated, since he could obtain no other clue to her identity, that she must be a woman of gentle birth, and his love for her was accordingly redoubled. And not only did he keep her in splendid style, but he treated her as though she were his wife rather than his mistress.

On comparing her present circumstances with the awful experiences through which she had passed, the lady considered herself very fortunately placed. Now that she was contented and completely recovered, her beauty flourished to such a degree that the whole of the eastern empire seemed to talk of nothing else. And so it was that the Duke of Athens,[9] a handsome, powerfully proportioned youth who was a friend and relative of the Prince, was smitten with a desire to see her, and under the pretext of paying the Prince one of his customary visits, he came with a splendid and noble retinue to Corinth, where he was received with honour amid great rejoicing.

A few days later, the two men fell to conversing about this

woman's beauty, and the Duke asked whether she was so marvellous an object as people claimed.

'Far more so,' replied the Prince. 'But instead of accepting my word for it, I would rather that you judged with your own eyes.'

Thereupon the Prince invited the Duke to follow him, and they made their way to the lady's apartments. Having been warned of their approach, she received them with great civility, her face radiant with happiness. She seated herself between the two men, but the pleasure of conversing with her was denied them because she understood little or nothing of their language. And so each man stared in fascination upon her, in particular the Duke, who could scarcely believe that she was a creature of this earth. Little realizing, as he gazed at her, that he was imbibing the poison of love through the medium of his eyes, and fondly believing that he could satisfy his pleasure merely by looking at her, he was completely bowled over by her beauty and fell violently in love with her.

When he and the Prince had taken their leave of her, and he had an opportunity to indulge in a little quiet reflection, he came to the conclusion that the Prince must be the happiest man on earth, in possessing so beautiful a plaything. Many and varied were the thoughts that passed through his mind until eventually, his blazing passion gaining the upper hand over his sense of honour, he decided that whatever the consequences, he would remove this pleasure-giving object from the Prince and do all in his power to make it serve his own happiness.

Being determined to move swiftly, he thrust aside all regard for reason and fair play, and concentrated solely on cunning. And one day, in the furtherance of his evil designs, he made arrangements with one of the Prince's most trusted servants, Ciuriaci by name, to have all his horses and luggage placed secretly in readiness for a sudden departure. During the night, he and a companion, both fully armed, were silently admitted by the aforesaid Ciuriaci into the Prince's bedroom. It was a very hot night, and although the woman was asleep, the Prince was standing completely naked at a window overlooking the sea, taking advantage of a breeze that was blowing from that quarter. The Duke, having told his companion beforehand what he had to do, stole quietly across the room as far as the window, drove a dagger into the Prince's back with so much force that it passed right through his body, and catching him quickly in his arms he hurled him out of the window.

Now the palace stood very high above sea-level, and the window at which the Prince had been standing overlooked a cluster of houses that had been laid in ruins by the violence of the sea. It was but rarely, if ever, that anybody went there, and consequently, as the Duke had already foreseen, no one's attention was attracted by the body of the Prince as it fell.

On seeing this deed accomplished, the Duke's companion quickly produced a noose that he had brought along for the purpose, and pretending to embrace Ciuriaci, he threw it round his neck, and drew it tight so that Ciuriaci could not make any noise. He was then joined by the Duke, and they strangled the man before hurling him out to join his master. This done, they satisfied themselves that neither the lady nor anybody else had heard them, and then the Duke picked up a lantern, carried it over to the bed, and silently uncovered the woman, who was sleeping soundly. Having exposed her whole body, he gazed upon her in rapt fascination, and although he had admired her when she was clothed, now that she was naked his admiration was greater beyond all comparison. The flames of his desire burned correspondingly fiercer, and, unperturbed by the crime he had just committed, he lay down at her side, his hands still dripping with blood, and made love to the woman, who was half-asleep and believed him to be the Prince.

Eventually, after spending some time with her, he rose giddily to his feet and summoned a few of his men, whom he commanded to hold the lady in such a way that she could not make any noise. Then he conducted her through the secret door by way of which he had entered, and, having settled her on horseback with a minimum of noise, he set out with all his men in the direction of Athens. Since he was already married, however, it was not in Athens itself that he deposited this unhappiest of women, but at a very beautiful palace of his, not far from the city, overlooking the sea. Here he established her in secluded splendour, and saw that she was provided with everything she needed.

On the following day, the Prince's courtiers had waited until the late afternoon for their master to rise from his bed. But when they still heard no sound, they pushed open his bedroom doors, which were not locked, and found the room deserted. They thereupon assumed that he had gone away somewhere in secret in order to spend a few days in the delightful company of this fair mistress of his, and they gave no further thought to the matter.

It was thus that matters stood, when on the very next day a local idiot, who had strayed into the ruins where the bodies of the Prince and Ciuriaci were lying, dragged Ciuriaci forth by the rope round his neck and started pulling him through the streets. On recognizing who it was, the people were greatly astonished, and talked the idiot into leading them to the place from which he had dragged the body, where, to the enormous grief of the whole city, they also found the body of the Prince. After burying him with full honours, they took steps to discover who was responsible for this unspeakable crime, and on finding that the Duke of Athens had departed secretly and was nowhere to be found, they rightly concluded that he must be the culprit and that he must have carried off the lady as well. So that, having hastily elected their dead ruler's brother as their new prince, they urged him with all the eloquence at their command to take his revenge. And when further evidence came to light, proving that their suspicions were correct, the Prince summoned friends, kinsfolk and servants from various places to come to his support and he quickly assembled a huge and powerful army, with which he set out to make war on the Duke of Athens.

When the Duke received word of the operations, he too mobilized all his armed forces for his defence, and many powerful outsiders came to his assistance, including two who were sent by the Emperor of Constantinople, namely his son, Constant, and his nephew, Manuel. These latter, arriving at the head of large and well-drilled contingents, received a warm welcome from the Duke. But the welcome they received from the Duchess was even warmer, because she was Constant's sister.

With the prospect of war becoming daily more imminent, the Duchess chose a convenient moment to invite the two men to her room, where, talking without stopping amid floods of tears, she told them the whole story, explaining the reasons for the war and exposing the wrong practised upon her by the Duke on account of this woman, of whose existence he imagined her to be ignorant. Bewailing her lot in no uncertain terms, she begged them, for the sake of the Duke's honour and her own happiness, to take whatever measures they could devise for setting matters to rights.

The young men were already fully informed about the whole business, and so without asking too many questions they consoled her to the best of their ability and gave her every ground for optimism. Then, having discovered from the Duchess where the lady was staying, they took their leave of her. Since they had often heard glowing accounts of this woman's marvellous beauty, they were naturally anxious to see her, and they therefore asked the Duke if he would introduce her to them. The Duke agreed to do so, forgetting the fate which had befallen the Prince after granting a similar favour. And the following morning, having ordered a magnificent banquet to be prepared in a beautiful garden on the estate where the lady was living, he took the two men and a handful of other friends to dine with her.

On sitting down in her company, Constant began to stare at her in blank amazement, vowing to himself that he had never seen anything so beautiful, and that no one could possibly reproach the Duke, or anybody else, for resorting to treachery and other dishonest means in order to gain possession of so fair an object. Moreover, his admiration increased with every look he cast in her direction, so that eventually the same thing happened to him as had previously happened to the Duke. And when the time came for him to leave, he was so much in love with her that he dismissed the war completely from his mind and concentrated his thoughts on planning a way of abducting her, at the same time taking good care not to reveal his love to anyone.

But whilst he was struggling with his passion, the time arrived for marching against the Prince, who by now had almost reached the Duke's territories. Accordingly, at a given signal, the Duke set out from Athens with Constant and all the others, and they took up combat positions along certain stretches of the frontier so as to halt the Prince's advance. Constant's thoughts and sentiments continued to focus on the woman, and now that the Duke was no longer near her, he fancied that he had an excellent opportunity for obtaining what he wanted. And so a few days after their arrival at the frontier, he pretended to be seriously ill so that he would have a pretext for returning to Athens. He then handed over all his powers to Manuel, and with the Duke's permission he returned to Athens to stay with his sister. A few days later, having steered the conversation round to the sense of injury under which she was labouring on account of the Duke's mistress, he told her that if she so desired he could be of considerable assistance to her in this affair, in that he could have the woman removed from where she was staying and taken elsewhere.

Thinking that Constant was motivated by brotherly love and not by his love for the woman, the Duchess said that she would be only too pleased, provided it could be carried out in such a way that the Duke never discovered that she had given her consent to the scheme. Constant reassured her completely on this point, and accordingly the Duchess gave him permission to proceed in whatever way he considered best.

The first thing he did was to fit out a fast boat in secret, which one evening, having informed his men on board what they were to do, he sent to a spot near the garden of the place where the lady was living. Then he went there with another group of his men, to be amicably received by her retainers as well as by the lady herself, who, at her visitor's suggestion, accompanied Constant and his companions into the garden, whilst her servants trailed along behind. As though he wished to impart some message from the Duke, he then led her off alone in the direction of a gate, overlooking the sea, which had already been unlocked by one of his accomplices. At a given signal, the boat nosed her way inshore, and having had the lady seized and bundled quickly aboard, he turned to her servants, saying:

'Unless you want to be killed, don't move or make any sound. It is not my intention to steal the Duke's mistress, but to remove the injury he does to my sister.'

Since nobody dared offer any reply, Constant embarked with his men, settled himself next to the lady, who was crying, and ordered them to cast off and start rowing. And they plied their oars to such good effect that just before dawn on the following day they arrived at Aegina.[10]

Going ashore there in order to rest, Constant amused himself in the company of the lady, who was bitterly bewailing her ill-starred beauty. Then they boarded the ship once again, and a few days later they arrived at Chios,[11] where Constant decided to remain, for he thought he would be safe there from his father's strictures and from the possibility of having to surrender the stolen woman. For several days, the fair lady bemoaned her misfortune. Eventually, however, she responded to Constant's efforts at consoling her, and began, as on previous occasions, to derive pleasure from the fate to which Fortune had consigned her.

And this was how matters stood when Uzbek,[12] who was at that time the King of the Turks and who was constantly at war with the Emperor, happened to pass through Smyrna, where he learned that Constant was leading a dissolute life on Chios with some stolen mistress of his, leaving himself wide open to attack. Arriving by night with a squadron of light warships, Uzbek quietly entered the town with his men, took numerous people captive from their beds before they were aware of their enemies' arrival, and slaughtered those who had woken up in time to seize their arms. The invaders then set the whole town on fire, and having loaded their booty and prisoners on to the ships, they returned to Smyrna.

On reviewing the spoils of the expedition immediately after their return, Uzbek, who was a young man, was delighted to discover the fair lady, whom he recognized as the one who had been taken, along with Constant, as she was lying asleep in her bed. So he promptly married her, and after celebrating the nuptials he happily devoted himself, for the next few months, to the pleasures of the marriage-bed.

Now, during the period immediately preceding these happenings, the Emperor had been negotiating a pact with the King of Cappadocia, Basano,[13] whereby the latter was to descend with his forces on Uzbek from one direction whilst the Emperor attacked him with his own troops from the other. He had not yet been able to bring the negotiations to a successful conclusion, however, because of his unwillingness to concede some of the more outrageous of Basano's demands. But on hearing what had happened to his son, he was so incensed that he immediately agreed to the King of Cappadocia's terms, and urged him to attack Uzbek as soon as he possibly could, meanwhile making his own preparations for marching against him from the opposite direction.

When he heard about this, rather than allow himself to be sandwiched between two mighty rulers, Uzbek assembled his army and marched against the King of Cappadocia, leaving his fair lady at Smyrna under the close supervision of a faithful retainer and friend. Some time later, he confronted and engaged the King of Cappadocia, and in the ensuing battle he was killed, whilst his army was defeated and put to flight. Flushed with victory, Basano began to advance unopposed on Smyrna, and all the people on his route did homage to him as their conqueror.

Meanwhile, the retainer in whose care Uzbek had left his fair lady, Antioco by name, had been so overwhelmed by her beauty that he had betrayed the trust of his friend and master, and although he was getting on in years, he had fallen in love with her. He was familiar with her language, and this pleased her immensely because for several years she had been more or less forced to lead the life of a deaf-mute as she could neither understand what anybody was saying nor make herself understood. With love spurring him on, Antioco began in the first few days to take so many liberties with her that before long they ceased to care about their lord and master who had gone off soldiering to the wars, and not only did they become good friends, they also became lovers. And as they lay between the sheets, they had a very happy time of it together.

But when they heard that Uzbek had been defeated and killed, and that Basano was on his way there, carrying all before him, they decided with one accord not to await his arrival. Taking with them a substantial quantity of Uzbek's most valuable possessions, they fled together in secret and came to Rhodes. But they had not been living there for very long when Antioco became mortally ill. With him at the time there happened to be staying a Cypriot merchant, a bosom friend of his whom he loved dearly, and realizing that his life was drawing to its close, he decided to bequeath his property to him, along with his beloved mistress. And so, shortly before he died, he summoned them both to his bedside, and said:

'I see quite plainly that my strength is failing, which saddens me greatly because life has never been sweeter to me than of late. There is one thing, however, that reconciles me to my fate, for I shall find myself dying – if die I must – in the arms of the two people I love best in the whole world: yours, my dear dear friend, and those of this woman whom I have loved more deeply than I love myself, from the earliest days of our acquaintance. All the same, it worries me to think that when I am gone, she might be left here alone in a strange place, with nobody to turn to for help or advice. And I should be all the more worried if it were not for the knowledge of your own presence, for I believe that you will cherish her, for my sake, as tenderly as you would cherish me. In the event of my death, therefore, I commit her and all my property to your charge, and with all my power I entreat you to handle them both in whatever way you think most likely to console my immortal spirit. And I beseech you, dear sweet lady, not to forget me when I am dead, so that in the next world I can claim to be loved in this world by the fairest woman ever fashioned by Nature. Promise me faithfully that you will carry out these two requests of mine, and I shall undoubtedly die contented.'

As they listened to these words, both the lady and his merchant friend shed many a tear. When he had finished speaking, they soothed him and gave him their word of honour that in the event of his death they would do as he had asked. Very soon afterwards he passed away, and they saw that he was given an honourable funeral.

A few days later, having completed all his business in Rhodes and being desirous of taking ship on a Catalan carrack that was about to sail for Cyprus, the Cypriot merchant inquired of the fair lady what she was proposing to do, telling her that for his part, he was compelled to return to Cyprus. The lady said that if he had no objection, she would gladly accompany him, because she had hoped that out of his affection for Antioco, he would treat and regard her as a sister. The merchant assured her of his willingness to do whatever she asked, and with the object of protecting her from any harm that might befall her before they reached Cyprus, he passed her off as his wife. Having embarked on the ship, therefore, they were assigned to a small cabin on the poop-deck, and in order to maintain appearances, he bedded down with her in the same narrow little bunk. What happened next was something that neither of them had bargained for when leaving Rhodes, because what with the darkness, the enforced idleness, and the warmth of the bed, all of which are powerful stimulants, they were each consumed with an almost equally intense longing, and without sparing a thought for the love and friendship they owed to the dead Antioco, they began to excite each other, with the result that by the time they reached the Cypriot's home-port of Paphos, they had become husband and wife in good earnest. And for some time after their arrival in Paphos, they lived together in the merchant's house.

Now it so happened that there came to Paphos, on some business or other, a gentleman called Antigono, who was old in years and even older in wisdom. He was not a very rich man, because although he had undertaken numerous commissions in the service of the King of Cyprus, Fortune had never been particularly kind to him. One day, as he was walking past the house where the fair lady was living, at a time when the Cypriot merchant was away on a trading mission in Armenia, this Antigono happened to catch sight of the lady at one of the windows. Since she was very beautiful, he began to stare at her, and it occurred to him that he had seen her on some previous occasion, but try as he would he could not remember where.

For a long time now, the fair lady had been a plaything in the hands of Fortune, but the moment was approaching when her trials would be over. When she espied Antigono, she recalled having seen him in Alexandria, where he once occupied a position of some importance in her father's service. Knowing that her merchant was away, and being suddenly filled with the hope that there might be some possibility of returning once more to her regal status with the help of this man's advice, she sent for him at the earliest opportunity. When he called upon her, she shyly asked whether she was right in thinking him to be Antigono of Famagusta. Antigono said that he was, adding:

'I have an idea, ma'am, that I have seen you before, but I cannot for the life of me remember where. Pray be good enough, therefore, if you have no objection, to remind me who you are.'

On hearing that this was indeed the man she had assumed him to be, the lady burst into tears and threw her arms round his neck, and presently she asked her highly astonished visitor whether he had ever seen her in Alexandria. No sooner had she put the question than Antigono recognized her as the Sultan's daughter Alatiel, whom everybody believed to be drowned at sea, and he prepared to make her the ceremonial bow that was her due. But she would not allow this and asked him instead to come and sit down with her for a while. Complying, Antigono asked her in reverential tones how, when and whence she had come to Cyprus, and told her that the whole Egyptian nation had been convinced, for many years, that she had been drowned at sea.

'I wish to goodness they were right,' said the lady, 'and I think my father would share my opinion if he were ever to discover the sort of life I have led.' And so saying, she started crying prodigiously all over again, whereupon Antigono said to her:

'My lady, it is too soon for you to go upsetting yourself like this. Tell me about your misfortunes, if you like, and about the life you have been living. Possibly we shall find that the point has been reached where we shall be able, with God's help, to devise some happy outcome to your dilemma.'

'Antigono,' the fair lady replied, 'the other day, when I first saw you, it was as if I was seeing my own father. Prompted by the love and tenderness that I have an obligation to bear him, I revealed my presence to you, when I could have remained concealed. Yours is the first familiar face I have encountered for many years, and there are few people I could possibly be so contented to see. To you, therefore, as though you were my father, I shall reveal the story of my appalling misfortunes, which I have never related to anyone before. If, when you have heard what I have to say, you see any possibility of restoring me to my former state, I beseech you to explore it; if not, I must ask you never to tell a living soul that you have either seen me or heard anything about me.'

And so saying, never ceasing to weep, she told him about

everything that had happened to her since the day on which she was shipwrecked off Majorca, whereupon Antigono too began to weep with compassion, and after considering the matter at some length, he said:

'My lady, since your identity has remained a secret throughout the course of your misadventures, I shall have no difficulty in restoring you to a higher place than ever in your father's affection, and you will then go to marry the King of Algarve, as originally arranged.'

When she inquired how it was to be managed, he explained to her in detail what she was to do. And to avoid all further delay and any further complications, Antigono returned at once to Famagusta and went to see the King, addressing him thus:

'My lord, if it pleases you, you can at the same time cover yourself with glory and render a most valuable service to one who has grown poor while acting on your behalf. I refer of course to myself.'

The King asked him to explain, and Antigono replied:

'The fair young daughter of the Sultan, who was long reputed to have been drowned at sea, has arrived in Paphos. For many years, she has endured extreme hardship in the struggle to preserve her honour, she has been reduced to comparative poverty, and she wishes to return to her father. If you were to send her back to the Sultan under my escort, it would redound greatly to your credit, and I would be sure of a rich reward. It is unlikely, moreover, that the Sultan will ever forget your charitable deed.'

His regal magnanimity having been stirred, the King readily gave his consent, and he dispatched a guard of honour to accompany the lady to Famagusta, where he and the Queen welcomed her amid scenes of indescribable rejoicing and magnificent pomp and splendour. And when she was asked by the King and Queen to tell them about her adventures, she replied exactly as she had been instructed by Antigono.

A few days later, at her own request, the King sent her back to the Sultan under the guardianship of Antigono, providing her with a distinguished retinue of fine gentlemen and ladies-in-waiting, and needless to say, the Sultan gave her a tremendous welcome, which he extended also to Antigono and the whole of her retinue. After she had rested for a while, the Sultan demanded to know how it came about that she was still alive, where she had been living all this time, and why she had never sent word of what she was doing.

Remembering Antigono's instructions to the tiniest detail, the lady then addressed her father as follows:

'Father, some twenty days after my departure, our ship was disabled by a raging tempest, and ran aground at night on the shores of the western Mediterranean, near a place called Aigues-mortes.[14] I never discovered what happened to all the men who were in the ship. All I can remember is that when the dawn arrived, I truly felt as if I was rising from the dead. The local people had already espied the wreck, and they came running from miles around in order to plunder it. I was put ashore with two of my maidservants, who were instantly snatched by young men and carried off in different directions, and that was the last I saw or heard of them. I myself, after putting up stout resistance, was overpowered by two young men and hauled away by my tresses, weeping bitterly all the time. But just as they were crossing a road in order to drag me into a thick forest, four men happened to pass that way on horseback, and when my captors saw them coming, they instantly let me go and took to their heels.

'On seeing this, the four men, who to judge from their appearance seemed to hold positions of authority, rode swiftly up and asked me a lot of questions, to which I gave as many answers. But it was impossible to make ourselves understood. After talking together for some little while, they took me up on one of their horses and conducted me to a convent of nuns who practised these men's religion. I do not know what it was that they said to the nuns, but at any rate I was kindly received by everybody, and I was always treated with great respect. Whilst there, I joined them in the reverent worship of Saint Stiffen-in-the-Hollows, to whom the women of that country are deeply devoted. But after staying with them for some time, and acquiring a discreet knowledge of their language, I was asked who I was and where I had come from. Knowing where I was, I feared to tell them the truth lest they should expel me as an enemy of their religion, and so I replied that I was the daughter of a fine nobleman of Cyprus, who was sending me to be married in Crete when we were driven by a storm on to those shores and shipwrecked.

'For fear of meeting a worse fate, I imitated their customs regularly, in various ways. Eventually, I was asked by the oldest of these women, whom the others refer to as the Abbess, whether I wished to return to Cyprus, and I replied that there was nothing I desired more. However, being concerned for my honour, she was unwilling to entrust me to anyone coming to Cyprus until about two months ago, when certain French gentlemen, some of them related to the Abbess, arrived there with their wives. And when she heard that they were going to Jerusalem to visit the Sepulchre, where the man they look upon as God was buried after being killed by the Jews, she placed me under their care and asked them to hand me over to my father on reaching Cyprus.

'It would take too long to describe how greatly I was honoured and how warmly I was welcomed by these noblemen and their wives. Suffice it to say that we all took ship, and that several days later we reached Paphos, where I found myself facing a dilemma, because there was nobody there who knew me and I had no idea what to say to these gentlemen, who were anxious to carry out the venerable lady's instructions and hand me over to my father.

'However, it was the will of Allah, who was possibly feeling sorry for me, that just as we stepped ashore at Paphos Antigono should be standing on the quayside. I promptly called out to him, and using our own language so that neither the gentlemen nor their wives would follow what I was saying, I told him to welcome me as his daughter. He promptly complied, made a tremendous fuss of me, and strained his modest resources to the limit in ensuring that those noblemen and their ladies were suitably entertained. He afterwards conveyed me to the King of Cyprus, and I could never adequately describe how honourably I was received or how much trouble the King took in returning me to you here in Alexandria. And now, if there is anything else that remains to be said, let it be told by Antigono, to whom I have recounted the story of my adventures over and over again.'

'My lord,' said Antigono, turning to the Sultan, 'her story

corresponds in every detail with the account she has given me on many occasions, as well as with the assurances I received from the noblemen in whose company she came to Cyprus. One thing only she has refrained from mentioning because it would not have been appropriate for her to do so, and I shall tell you what it is. Those good people who brought her to Cyprus paid glowing tribute to the honest life she had led while living with the nuns, they were full of praise for her virtue and her excellent character, and when the time came for them to commit her to my charge and bid her a fond farewell, they all, gentlemen and ladies alike, burst into floods of tears. Were I to provide you with a full account of what they said to me on this particular subject, I could go on talking all day and all night without coming to the end of it. I trust, however, that these few remarks will suffice to convince you that, as their words showed and as I have been able to observe for myself, no other living monarch can claim to possess such a beautiful, virtuous and courageous daughter.'

The Sultan was absolutely delighted to hear these tidings, and prayed repeatedly that Allah would grant him an opportunity to make proper restitution to those who had done honour to his daughter, in particular the King of Cyprus who had restored her to him in such splendid style. A few days later, having ordered sumptuous presents to be prepared for Antigono, he gave him leave to return to Cyprus, at the same time dispatching letters and special envoys to convey his heartfelt thanks to the King for the favours he had bestowed upon his daughter.

Then finally, since it was his wish to make an end of what was begun, or in other words that she should become the King of Algarve's wife, he wrote informing him of all that had happened, adding that, if he still desired to marry her, he should send his envoys to fetch her. The King of Algarve was delighted with these tidings, sent a suitably distinguished party to act as her escort, and upon her arrival he gave her a joyous welcome. And so, despite the fact that eight separate men had made love to her on thousands of different occasions, she entered his bed as a virgin and convinced him that it was really so. And for many years afterwards she lived a contented life as his queen. Hence the proverbial saying: 'A kissed

mouth doesn't lose its freshness: like the moon it turns up new
again.'[15]

EIGHTH STORY

*The Count of Antwerp, being falsely accused, goes into exile and leaves
his two children in different parts of England. Unknown to them, he
returns from Ireland to find them comfortably placed. Then he serves as a
groom in the army of the King of France, and having established his
innocence, is restored to his former rank.*

The ladies heaved many a sigh over the fair lady's several adventures:
but who knows what their motives may have been? Perhaps some
of them were sighing, not so much because they felt sorry for
Alatiel, but because they longed to be married no less often than she
was. However, leaving this question aside, when they had all
finished laughing at Panfilo's final words, from which the queen
assumed his tale to be finished, she turned to Elissa and enjoined her
to continue the proceedings with a story of her own. Being only
too pleased to oblige, Elissa began as follows:

The field through which we are roaming today is exceedingly
broad, and it would be very easy for anyone to try his skill there,
not only once but a dozen times, since Fortune has stocked it so
abundantly with her marvels and afflictions. But to choose a single
story from among the infinite number that could be narrated, I shall
begin by telling you that when the Roman imperial authority[1]
passed from French into German hands, the two nations became
sworn enemies and made bitter and continuous war upon one
another. Accordingly, in order to defend their own country and
attack the other, the King of France and his son mobilized all their
kingdom's resources, including those of their friends and kinsfolk,
and assembled a huge army to march against their enemies. But
before proceeding any further, not wishing to leave their country
ungoverned, and knowing that Walter, Count of Antwerp, was a
noble, intelligent man and a most loyal friend and servant to their

cause, and thinking, moreover, that although he was well skilled in the art of war, his talents would be even better employed in the subtleties of state government, they left him to rule over the whole of the kingdom of France as their viceroy, and went upon their way.

And so it was that Walter settled down to the wise and orderly performance of his duties, always consulting the Queen and her daughter-in-law on all matters of importance, for although they had been left under his custody and jurisdiction, he treated them as far as possible with the same degree of deference that he would have displayed towards his rulers and superiors. This Walter was about forty years old, physically very handsome, and as agreeable and courteous a nobleman as you could ever imagine. Moreover, apart from being the most elegantly dressed, he was more refined and graceful in bearing than any other knight of his times.

Now, it so happened that while the King of France and his son were away at the wars we have mentioned, Walter's wife died, leaving him a widower with two small children, a boy and a girl. And whilst he was continuing to hold court with the aforesaid ladies, frequently sounding out their opinions on weighty matters of state, the wife of the King's son cast her eyes upon him, and being hugely taken with his handsome looks and agreeable manners, she fell violently and secretly in love. Considering her own unspoilt, youthful appearance and the fact that he was not tied to any woman, she thought it would be an easy matter to obtain what she wanted, and since only her shame seemed to be standing in her way, she decided to be rid of it and lay her cards on the table. So one day, finding herself alone and feeling the time to be ripe, she summoned him to her room under the pretext of discussing affairs of state.

Being quite unprepared for what was to follow, the Count answered her summons without the slightest delay. Having entered the room, he found himself alone with the lady, and at her request he sat down beside her on a sofa. He then asked her, twice, why she had summoned him, but each time the lady remained silent. Finally, driven on by her passion, she blushed a deep crimson and, almost on the point of tears, trembling from head to toe, she started hesitantly to speak:

'Sweet friend and master, dearest one of all, since you are wise you will readily acknowledge that men and women are remarkably frail, and that, for a variety of reasons, some are frailer than others. It is therefore right and proper that before an impartial judge, people of different social rank should not be punished equally for committing an identical sin. For nobody would, I think, deny that if a member of the poorer classes, obliged to earn a living through manual toil, were to surrender blindly to the promptings of love, he or she would be far more culpable than a rich and leisured lady who lacked none of the necessary means to gratify her tiniest whim.

'I consider, then, that circumstances such as these must go a long way towards excusing any woman who allows herself to be enmeshed in the toils of love; and if, in addition, she has chosen a judicious and valiant lover on whom to bestow her affection, she no longer needs any justification whatever. Now, since it is my opinion that both of these prerequisites are present in my own case, and since, moreover, I possess additional incentives for loving, such as my youth and my husband's absence, they must inevitably operate in my favour and elicit your sympathy for my impetuous passion. And if they carry as much influence as they ought to carry with a man of your experience, I appeal to you for your advice and assistance.

'The fact is that I am unable, in my husband's absence, to withstand the promptings of the flesh and the powers of Love, which are so irresistible that even the strongest of men, not to mention frail women like myself, have often succumbed to them in the past and will always continue to do so. Living in the lap of luxury as I do, with nothing to occupy me, I have allowed my thoughts to dwell upon the pleasures of the senses, and fallen hopelessly in love. I realize of course that if this were to become known, it would be regarded as highly improper; but if it is kept secret I can't really see any harm in it, especially since the God of Love has seen fit not to deprive me of my good judgement in the business of choosing a lover. On the contrary, he has greatly enhanced it by showing me that you, my lord, are worthy in all respects to be loved by a lady of my condition. For unless I am greatly deceived, you are the most handsome, agreeable, elegant and judicious knight to be found anywhere in the Kingdom of France; and just as I can claim to be without a husband, you for your part are without a wife. In the name, therefore, of the immense love that I bear you, I entreat you not to deny me your own, but to take pity on my youth, which I assure you is melting away for you like ice beside a fire.'

These last words brought such a spate of tears in their train, that although she had intended to entreat him still further, she was bereft of the power of speech. And lowering her eyes, she allowed her head to fall upon his breast, weeping incessantly and very nearly swooning with emotion.

Being a knight of unimpeachable loyalty, the Count began to take her severely to task for this insane passion and to repulse the lady, who was already on the point of throwing her arms about his neck. With many an oath, he declared that he would sooner allow himself to be quartered than permit any such harm to be done to his master's honour, whether by himself or anyone else.

No sooner did the lady hear this than she forgot all about loving him and flew into a savage temper.

'So!' she said. 'Am I to be spurned in this fashion by an upstart knight? It seems you want to break my heart, but I shall break yours, so help me God, or have you hounded off the face of the earth.'

Whereupon she ran her hands through her hair, leaving it all rumpled and dishevelled, after which she tore open the front of her dress, at the same time calling out in a loud voice:

'Help! Help! The Count of Antwerp is trying to ravish me!'

When he saw what was happening, the Count was far more concerned about the envious proclivities of the courtiers than reassured by his own clear conscience in the matter; and for this reason he feared that the lady's wicked lies would carry greater conviction than his own protestations of innocence. He therefore hurried out of the room, got quickly away from the palace, and fled to his own house, whence, without pausing for further reflection, he took horse with his children and set off at breakneck speed in the direction of Calais.

The lady's caterwauling brought several people running, and
when they saw her and heard what she was shouting about, they
were convinced she was telling the truth, more especially because
they now assumed that the Count had long been exploiting his
charm and his elegant ways for no other purpose. There followed a
wild rush to the Count's residence, with the intention of placing
him under arrest. But on finding that he was not at home, they
ransacked the whole of the premises and then razed them to the
ground.

When the story, embroidered with various obscenities, reached
the King and his son in the field, they were greatly distressed, and
condemned the Count and his descendants to perpetual exile, promising huge rewards for his capture, dead or alive.

Meanwhile the Count, full of misgivings for having turned his
innocence into apparent guilt by his hurried departure, arrived at
Calais with his children, having succeeded in concealing his identity
and escaping recognition. He then crossed rapidly to England, and
proceeded, raggedly dressed, towards London. But before entering
the city, he talked at great length with the two little children, laying
great stress on two points in particular: first, that they must patiently
support the state of poverty into which, through no fault of their
own, Fortune had cast them along with their father; and second,
that if they valued their lives, they must always be on their guard
against telling anyone where they had come from or who their
father was.

The boy, who was called Louis, was about nine years old, whilst
the girl, whose name was Violante,[2] was about seven, and considering their tender age, they paid the closest possible attention to their
father's instructions, as they were later to prove. In order to make
their task easier, the Count decided it would be necessary to change
their names, and this he did, calling the boy Perrot and the girl
Jeannette. And on arriving, poorly dressed, in London, they began
to go round begging for alms, in the manner of the French vagrants
that we see here in Italy.

And it was when they were begging outside a church one
morning, that a great lady, the wife of one of the King of England's
marshals, happened to catch sight of the Count and his two children

as she was coming away from her devotions. On asking where he came from and whether the two children were his, he replied that he was from Picardy and that he was indeed their father. But he had been compelled to leave home with the children and lead a vagabond existence because of a crime that an elder son of his had committed.

The lady, who was of a kindly nature, ran her eyes over the girl and took a great liking to her, for she was a pretty little thing and had an air of gentility about her.

'Good sir,' said the lady. 'If you would like to leave this little girl with me, I will gladly look after her, for she is a pretty-looking child. And if she turns out as well as she promises, when the time comes I shall arrange a good marriage for her.'

This request greatly pleased the Count, who promptly gave his consent, and with tears in his eyes he handed over his daughter, warmly commending her to the lady's care. He was well aware of the lady's identity, and now that he had found a good home for the child, he decided not to remain there any longer. And so, begging as he went, he made his way with Perrot to the other side of the island, finding the journey very tiring as he was unused to travelling on foot. Eventually he arrived in Wales, where there was another of the King's marshals, a man who lived in great style and kept a large number of servants, and to this man's castle the Count, either by himself or with his son, would frequently go in order to obtain something to eat.

There were several children at the castle, of whom some belonged to the Marshal himself and others were the sons of the local gentry, and whilst they were competing with each other in children's sports, like running and jumping, Perrot began to mix with them, performing equally as well or better than any of the others in every game they played. His prowess attracted the attention of the Marshal, who, taking a great liking to the child's manner and general behaviour, demanded to know who he was.

On being told that he was the son of a pauper who sometimes came into the castle begging for alms, the Marshal sent someone to ask whether he could keep him; and although it distressed him to part with the child, the Count, who was praying that such a thing might happen, willingly handed him over.

Now that both his son and his daughter were well bestowed, the Count decided to tarry no longer in England. So he crossed the sea to Ireland as best he could and eventually arrived at Strangford,[3] where he entered the service of one of the feudatories of a rural baron, performing all the usual tasks of a groom or a servant. And there he remained for many years, unrecognized by anyone, and compelled to endure great hardship and discomfort.

Meanwhile, Violante, who was now called Jeannette, was being brought up by the gentlewoman in London, becoming a great favourite, not only of the lady and her husband, but of everyone else in the house and indeed of all those who knew her, and as she grew up she became so beautiful that she was a marvel to behold. Nor could anyone deny, on observing how impeccably she comported herself, that she deserved all the honour and blessings that her future might bring. Since receiving the girl from her father, the gentlewoman had never succeeded in discovering anything about him apart from what he had told her, and she now decided that the time had come for her to estimate the girl's rank as best she could, and find her a suitable husband.

But knowing her to be a woman of gentle birth, doing penance for another's sin through no fault of her own, the Lord above, who rewards all according to their deserts, arranged matters otherwise. One must in fact conclude that He alone, out of His loving kindness, made possible the train of events which followed, in order to prevent this nobly-born maiden from falling into the hands of a commoner.

The lady with whom Jeannette was living possessed an only son, who was dearly loved by both his parents, not only because he was their son but also because, being an outstandingly well-bred, talented, courageous and fine-bodied youth, he was eminently worthy of their affection. He was some six years older than Jeannette, and when he noticed how exceedingly beautiful and graceful she was becoming, he fell so deeply in love with her that he had eyes for no one else. But because he supposed her to be of low estate, he dared not ask his parents to allow him to marry her. Moreover, since he was afraid of being reproached with falling in love with a commoner, he did all he could to keep his love a secret, and thus he was afflicted with sharper pangs than any he would have suffered had he brought it into the open.

Eventually, his suffering became so acute that he fell very seriously ill. A number of physicians were summoned in turn to his bedside, but in spite of carrying out test after test on one thing after another, they were unable to diagnose his ailment, and all of them despaired of finding a cure. The boy's father and mother were so weighed down with grief and worry that they almost collapsed under the strain. They begged him over and over again, in tones of deep affection, to tell them what was the matter, but by way of answer he would merely sigh deeply or tell them that he felt himself burning all over.

One day, he was being attended by a doctor who, though very young, was also very clever. The doctor was holding him by the wrist, taking his pulse, when Jeannette, who waited hand and foot on the invalid for his mother's sake, entered the room in which the youth was lying. When he saw her coming in, the flames of passion flared up in the young man's breast, and although he neither spoke nor moved, his pulse began to beat more strongly. The doctor noted this at once, but concealing his surprise he remained silent, waiting to see how long his pulse would continue to beat so rapidly.

As soon as Jeannette left the room, the young man's pulse returned to normal, whereupon the doctor concluded that he was halfway towards solving the mystery of the youth's illness. He waited for a while, and then, still holding his patient by the wrist, he sent for Jeannette, pretending that he wanted to ask her a question. She came at once, and no sooner did she enter the room than the youth's pulse began to race all over again: and when she departed, it subsided.

The doctor was therefore fully confirmed in his suspicions, and having risen to his feet, he took the youth's parents aside, saying:

'Your son's health cannot be restored by any doctor, for it rests in the hands of Jeannette. As I have discovered through certain unmistakable symptoms, the young man is ardently in love with her, though as far as I can tell, she herself is unaware of the fact. But you will now know what measures to apply if you want him to recover.'

On hearing this, the nobleman and his lady were greatly relieved, for at least there was now a possibility that he could be cured. But they were very disturbed at the prospect, however remote it might seem, of being forced to accept Jeannette as their daughter-in-law. So when the doctor had left, they made their way to the invalid's bedside.

'My son,' said the lady, 'I would never have imagined you capable of desiring something and not telling your mother, especially when you could see that your health was suffering through not having what you wanted. You may be quite sure, indeed you should have known all along, that I would do anything to make you happy, even if it meant stretching the rules a little. However, since you have refused to take me into your confidence, Our Heavenly Father has seen fit to intervene on your behalf, thus displaying more pity towards you than you were prepared to concede to yourself. And, so that you would not die from your malady, He has shown me the reason for this illness of yours, which turns out to be nothing more than the excessive love you bear towards some young woman or other. It was really quite unnecessary for you to feel ashamed about revealing it, for this sort of thing is perfectly natural in someone of your age. Indeed, if you were not in love, I would think very poorly of you. Do not hide things from me, my son, but acquaint me freely with all your wishes. Get rid of all the sadness and anxiety that are causing your illness, and look on the bright side of things. You can be quite certain that I will move Heaven and earth to see that you have whatever you need to make you happy, for your happiness means more to me than anything else in the world. Cast aside all your shame and your fear, and tell me what I can do to make this love of yours prosper. And if I don't put heart and soul into it and arrange matters to your liking, you can consider me the cruellest mother that ever brought a son into the world.'

On first hearing these words, the young man was thrown into a state of confusion, but after reflecting that nobody was in a better position than his mother to procure his happiness, he conquered his embarrassment, and said:

'If I kept my love a secret, madam, that was only because I have noticed that most people, after reaching a certain age, try to forget that they were ever young. But now that I can see what a tolerant mother you are, not only will I not deny what you claim to have noticed, but I will tell you who the girl is, on condition that you do everything in your power to keep your promise and thus make it possible for me to recover.'

The lady, being over-confident in her ability to arrange things in a way she should never have even considered, willingly replied that he should feel quite free to take her fully into his confidence. For she would take immediate steps to ensure that he obtained what he wanted.

'Madam,' said the youth, 'you find me in my present condition because of the excellent beauty and impeccable manners of our Jeannette, or rather owing to my inability to make her notice, still less reciprocate, my feelings for her, and because I never dared reveal them to a living soul. And unless you can find some means of making good the promise you have given me, you may rest assured that my days are numbered.'

'My poor boy,' said the lady, thinking it preferable to encourage rather than reproach him. 'What a thing to become so upset about! Now calm yourself and leave everything to me, because you are going to recover.'

Being filled with new hope, the youth very quickly showed signs of making a splendid recovery, to the immense satisfaction of his mother, who decided she would now attempt to make good her promise. So one day she took Jeannette aside, and adopting a light-hearted tone, asked her very tactfully whether she had a lover.

'Oh, my lady,' replied Jeannette, blushing all over. 'It would not be at all proper for a poor girl like me, exiled from her home and living in another's service, to indulge in such a luxury as love.'

'Well,' said the lady, 'if you don't possess a lover, we are going to give you one, so that you can lead a merry life and enjoy your beauty to the full. It isn't right for a lovely girl like you to be without a lover.'

'My lady,' answered Jeannette, 'ever since the day you took me from my father, you have brought me up as your own daughter, and therefore I ought never to oppose any of your wishes. But I can't possibly agree to do this, and I think I am right to refuse. I intend to love no man unless he be my lawful spouse, and if you wish to present me with a husband, well and good. Since my sole remaining family heirloom is my honour, I am determined to safeguard and preserve it for as long as I live.'

Jeannette's reply seemed to present a serious obstacle to the plans the lady had devised for keeping her promise to her son, though in her heart of hearts, being a sensible woman, she greatly admired the girl's sentiments.

'Come now, Jeannette,' she said. 'Supposing His Royal Highness the King of England, who is a dashing young nobleman, wished to enjoy the love of an exquisitely beautiful girl like yourself, would you deny it to him?'

To which Jeannette promptly replied:

'The King could take me by force, but I would never consent freely unless his intentions were honourable.'

The lady, realizing how strong a character the girl possessed, pressed the matter no further, but decided to put her to the test. And so she informed her son that as soon as he was better, she would lock them in a room together so that he could try and bend her to his will, adding that it seemed undignified for her to go bowing and scraping on her son's behalf, as though she were a procuress, to one of her own ladies-in-waiting.

The young man was not at all pleased with this idea, and his condition immediately took a severe turn for the worse. On seeing this, the lady took Jeannette into her confidence, only to find that she was more adamant than ever. So she acquainted her husband with what she had done, and although both of them thought it a grave step to take, they mutually decided to let him marry her, preferring their son to be alive with an unsuitable wife than dead without any wife at all. And after a great deal of further heart-searching, they announced their consent.

This made Jeannette very happy, and she thanked God from the depths of her devout heart for not deserting her; nor, despite everything, did she once reveal that she was anyone other than a Picard's daughter.

The young man recovered, married the girl thinking himself the happiest of men, and proceeded to enjoy her to his heart's content.

Meanwhile, Perrot, who had remained in Wales in the household of the King of England's Marshal, had likewise become a favourite of his lord and master. He was an outstandingly handsome and fearless youth, and there was no one in the island who could match his skill at jousts, tournaments and other contests of arms. Everybody called him Perrot the Picard, and his fame resounded through the length and breadth of the country.

And just as God had not forgotten his sister, so too He showed that He had not lost sight of Perrot. For a great plague descended on that region, carrying off half the population and causing a large number of the remainder to take refuge in other parts, so that the country appeared to be totally deserted. The victims of the plague included Perrot's master and mistress, their son, and several of his master's brothers, grandchildren and other relatives, so that only a daughter of marriageable age survived, together with some members of the household, among them Perrot. Once the plague had abated somewhat, the young woman, knowing Perrot to be strong and capable, and having received encouragement and advice from her few surviving neighbours, made him her husband and proclaimed him master of all the goods and property she had inherited. Nor was it long before the King of England, having heard of the Marshal's death and knowing the worth of Perrot the Picard, appointed him his marshal in the dead man's place.

And that, in brief, was what happened to the two innocent children of the Count of Antwerp after he was forced to abandon them.

More than eighteen years had elapsed since his hurried departure from Paris when the Count, who was now an old man and still living in Ireland, having led a truly wretched life and endured all manner of hardships, was seized by a longing to discover what had become of his children. His physical appearance, as he could see for himself, had changed beyond all recognition, but because of the years he had spent in manual toil he felt much fitter now than when he was young and living a life of leisure. And so, very poor and badly dressed, he left the person in whose household he had served

for all those years, returned to England,[4] and made for the place
where he had left Perrot. Much to his delight and amazement, he
discovered that his son was now a marshal and a great lord, and that
he was a vigorous, fine-looking fellow. But he did not want to
reveal himself before learning what had become of Jeannette.

He therefore set out once more, and never stopped until he
arrived in London, where he made discreet inquiries about the lady
with whom he had left his daughter and the life she was now
leading. On discovering that Jeannette was married to the lady's
son, he almost wept for joy. And now that he had traced both his
children and found them so comfortably established, he forgot
about all of his earlier misfortunes. Being anxious to see her, he
began to loiter near her house in the guise of a pauper, until one day
he was noticed by Jeannette's husband, whose name, by the way,
was Jacques Lamiens. Seeing how poor and decrepit he looked,
Jacques took pity on the old man and ordered one of his servants
to bring him into the house and provide him with something to eat
for charity's sake, which the servant readily did.

Jeannette had already presented Jacques with several children, of
whom the eldest was no more than eight, and they were the
prettiest and most delightful infants imaginable. When they saw the
Count at his meal, they all gathered round and made a fuss of him,
as though impelled by some mysterious instinct which told them
that this was their grandfather. Knowing them to be his grandchildren, the old man began to show them his affection and fondle
them, with the result that the children were unwilling to come
away, however much their tutor cajoled and threatened them.
Hearing the commotion, Jeannette left the room she was in, came
to where the Count was sitting, and spoke sharply to the children,
threatening to chastise them if they did not obey their tutor's
instructions. The children began to cry, protesting that they wanted
to stay with this worthy fellow who loved them more than their
tutor, whereupon the lady and the Count smiled broadly at one
another.

The Count had risen to his feet, not in the manner of a father
greeting his daughter but rather in the role of a pauper paying his
respects to a fine lady, and as soon as he set eyes upon her, his heart

was filled with a marvellous joy. But she never suspected for a moment who he was, either then or later, for he was thin and elderly-looking, and what with his beard, his greying hair and his dark complexion, he no longer seemed the same person. But on seeing how reluctant the children were to be parted from the old man, and how dismally they wailed whenever any attempt was made to dislodge them, the lady told their tutor to leave them for the present where they were.

It was while the children were playing with this worthy fellow that Jacques' father, who now loathed Jeannette, happened to return home and hear the whole story from their tutor.

'Let them stay where they are,' he said, 'and to hell with them. It's obvious which side of the family they take after, for they are descended from a vagrant on their mother's side, and it's hardly surprising if they feel at home in a vagrant's company.'

The Count overheard these words, and was deeply wounded. But he simply shrugged his shoulders, and suffered the insult as patiently as he had borne countless others.

Although Jacques was displeased when he heard the children making such a fuss of the worthy fellow, or in other words the Count, he was nevertheless so fond of them that, rather than see them cry, he gave instructions that if the man was willing to stay, he should be offered some job or other in the household. The Count gladly agreed to stay, but pointed out that the only thing he was good at was looking after horses, which he had been accustomed to handling all his life. A horse was therefore allotted to him, and when he had finished grooming it, he would occupy himself in keeping the children amused.

Whilst Fortune was treating the Count of Antwerp and his children in the manner we have just described, it happened that the King of France died, and was succeeded by the son whose wife had been responsible for the Count's exile. The old King had negotiated a series of truces with the Germans, and now that the last of these had expired, the new King reopened hostilities[5] with a vengeance. The King of England, having recently become a relative of his, offered him assistance in the form of a large expeditionary force under the command of his marshal, Perrot, and Jacques Lamiens, the son of the second marshal. Our worthy fellow, or the Count, was a member of Jacques' contingent, for a long time serving in the army as a groom without ever being recognized; and being an able man, he made himself extremely useful by giving timely advice and performing various tasks over and above his normal duties.

During the war, the Queen of France happened to fall seriously ill, and realizing instinctively that she was about to die, she repented of all her sins, making a devout confession before the Archbishop of Rouen, who was famous for his excellence and saintliness. Among her other sins, she told him of the great wrong that had been perpetrated on the Count of Antwerp at her own instigation. Nor was she content solely with telling the Archbishop, but she gave a true account of the whole affair in the presence of many other gentlemen, requesting them to use their good offices with the King in order to secure the rehabilitation of the Count if he was still alive, or if he was dead, of his children. Not long afterwards she died, and was buried with full regal honours.

When the King was told about her confession, he heaved many an anguished sigh over the wrongs to which this excellent man had been so unjustly subjected. He then issued an edict, which was published far and wide, both throughout the army and elsewhere, to the effect that he would pay substantial rewards to anyone bringing him information concerning the whereabouts of the Count of Antwerp or any of his children. Because of the Queen's confession – so the edict continued – the King held him to be innocent of the charges which had led to his exile, and it was his intention, not only to restore him to his former position, but to grant him still higher honours. Rumours of the announcement reached the ears of the Count, who was still working as a groom, and when he had confirmed them he went at once to Jacques and asked him to arrange a meeting with Perrot so that he could show them what the King was looking for.

When all three of them had come together, the Count said to Perrot, who was already thinking of announcing his identity:

'Perrot, Jacques here is married to your sister, and never received any dowry from her. In order, therefore, that your sister should not remain without a dowry, I propose that he alone should claim these huge rewards that the King is offering. This he will do by declaring you to be the Count of Antwerp's son, his wife to be your sister Violante, and myself to be your father, the Count of Antwerp.'

On hearing this, Perrot looked intently at the old man, and it dawned upon him that this was indeed his father. Dissolving into tears, he threw himself at the Count's feet and embraced him, saying:

'Father, what a joy it is to see you!'

Jacques, having listened to the Count's words and witnessed Perrot's response, was so delighted and astonished that he hardly knew where to put himself. But being convinced that it was all true, and bitterly ashamed for occasionally having spoken harshly to the groom or Count, he too burst into tears and sank to his knees at the old man's feet, humbly begging his pardon for all the wrongs he had done him. Whereupon the Count, having first of all persuaded him to stand up again, assured him very graciously that he was forgiven.

When the three of them had finished telling one another about their adventures, weeping and laughing endlessly together, Perrot and Jacques offered to supply the Count with new clothes, but he could in no way be persuaded to accept them. On the contrary, he was determined that Jacques, once he had claimed the promised reward, should present him exactly as he was, in his groom's clothing, so that the King would feel all the more ashamed for what had happened.

Jacques therefore presented himself to the King along with the Count and Perrot, and offered to produce the Count and his children if and when, in accordance with the terms of the edict, the reward was forthcoming. The King promptly ordered all three portions to be displayed, making Jacques' eyes pop out with astonishment, and told him he could take away the reward whenever he had made good his offer to show him the Count and his children.

Jacques then turned and made way for his groom and Perrot.

'My lord,' he said. 'Here are the father and son. The daughter, who is my wife, is not here at present, but God willing you will see her soon.'

On hearing this, the King stared at the Count, and although his features were greatly altered, after surveying him at length he none the less knew him again. Restraining his tears with an effort, he raised the Count from his knees to his feet, and kissed and embraced him. And after having warmly greeted Perrot, he ordered that the Count should instantly be provided with all the clothes, servants, horses and accoutrements that were proper to his noble rank. This was no sooner said than done, and moreover the King did much honour also to Perrot and insisted on hearing a full account of his past adventures.

When Jacques accepted the three enormous rewards for locating the Count and his children, the Count said to him:

'Take away these gifts so generously endowed by His Royal Highness, and remember to tell your father that your children, who are his grandchildren as well as mine, are not descended from a vagrant on their mother's side.'

Jacques took away the treasure, and arranged for his wife and his mother to come to Paris. Perrot's wife came too, and they all stayed with the Count, who entertained them on a truly lavish scale, having been reinstated in all his lands and property, and granted higher rank than he had ever had before. Then they all obtained the Count's leave to return to their respective homes, whilst he remained to the end of his days in Paris, covering himself with ever greater glory.

NINTH STORY

Bernabò of Genoa is tricked by Ambrogiuolo, loses his money, and orders his innocent wife to be killed. She escapes, however, and, disguising herself as a man, enters the service of the Sultan. Having traced the swindler, she lures her husband to Alexandria, where Ambrogiuolo is punished and she abandons her disguise, after which she and Bernabò return to Genoa, laden with riches.

Elissa's touching tale being at an end and her duty done, their queen, the tall and lovely Filomena, than whom none possessed more pleasing and cheerful a countenance, composed herself and said:

'The contract we made with Dioneo must be honoured, and since only he and I are left to speak, I shall tell my story first, and Dioneo, who laid special claim to that privilege, will be the last to address us.' And having said this, she began as follows:

There is a certain proverb, frequently to be heard on the lips of the people, to the effect that a dupe will outwit his deceiver – a saying which would seem impossible to prove but for the fact that it is borne out by actual cases. And therefore, dearest ladies, I would like, without overstepping the limits of our theme, to show you that the proverb is indeed true. Nor should you find my story unpalatable, for it will teach you to be on your guard against deceivers.

A number of very prosperous Italian merchants were once staying at the same inn in Paris, a city which people of their sort frequently have cause to visit for one reason or another. One evening, after they had all dined merrily together, they began talking about this and that, one subject led to another, and they eventually came round to discussing the womenfolk they had left behind in Italy.

'I don't know what my wife gets up to,' laughed one of them, 'but I do know this, that whenever I meet a girl here in Paris who takes my fancy, I have as much fun with her as I can manage, and forget about my wife.'

'I do the same,' said the second man, 'because whether or not I believe my wife is behaving herself, she will be making the most of her opportunities. So it's a case of tit for tat. Do as you would be done by, that's my motto.'

The third man was of more or less similar opinion. And indeed, it looked as though they were unanimous in agreeing that the women they had left behind would not be allowing the grass to grow under their feet.

Only one of them, a Genoese called Bernabò Lomellin, took a different line, maintaining that he, on the contrary, was blessed with a wife who was possibly without equal in the whole of Italy, for not only was she endowed with all the qualities of the ideal woman, but she also possessed many of the accomplishments to be found in a knight or esquire. She was extremely good looking and still very young, she was lithe and lissom, and there was no womanly pursuit, such as silk embroidery and the like, in which she did not outshine all other members of her sex. Furthermore, he claimed it was impossible to find a page or servant who waited better or more efficiently at a gentleman's table, for she was a paragon of intelligence and good manners, and the very soul of discretion. He then turned to her other accomplishments, praising her skill at horse-riding, falconry, reading, writing and book-keeping, at all of which she was superior to the average merchant. And finally, after a series of further eulogies, he came round to the subject they were discussing, stoutly maintaining that she was the most chaste and honest woman to be found anywhere on earth. Consequently, even if he stayed away for ten years or the rest of his life, he felt quite certain that she would never play fast and loose in another man's company.

Among the people present at this discussion, there was a young merchant from Piacenza called Ambrogiuolo, who, on hearing the last of Bernabò's laudatory assertions about his lady, began roaring with laughter and jokingly asked him whether it was the Emperor himself who had granted him this unique privilege.

Faintly annoyed, Bernabò replied that this favour had been conceded to him, not by the Emperor, but by God, who was a little more powerful than the Emperor.

Then Ambrogiuolo said:

'Bernabò, I do not doubt for a moment that you believe what you say to be true. But as far as I can judge, you have not devoted much attention to the study of human nature. For if you had, you surely possess enough intelligence to have discovered certain things that would cause you to think twice before making such confident assertions. When the rest of us spoke so freely about our womenfolk, we were merely facing facts, and so as not to let you run away with the idea that we suppose our wives to be any different from yours, I would like to pursue this subject a little further with you.

'I have always been told that man is the most noble of God's mortal creatures, and that woman comes second. Moreover, man is generally considered the more perfect, and the evidence of his works confirms that this is so. Being more perfect, it inevitably follows that he has a stronger will, and this too is confirmed by the fact that women are invariably more fickle, the reasons for which are to be found in certain physical factors which I do not propose to dwell upon.

'Man, then, has the stronger will. Yet quite apart from being unable to resist any woman who makes advances to him, he desires any woman he finds attractive, and not only does he desire her, but he will do everything in his power to possess her. And this is how he carries on, not just once a month, but a thousand times a day. What chance then do you think a woman, fickle by nature, can have against all the entreaties, the blandishments, the presents, and the thousand other expedients to which any intelligent lover will resort? Do you think she is going to resist him? Of course not, and you know it, no matter what you claim to the contrary. Why, you told us yourself that your wife is a woman, made of flesh and blood like the rest, in which case her desires are no different from any other woman's, and her power to resist these natural cravings cannot be any greater. So that, however virtuous she may be, it's quite possible that she acts like all the others. And whenever a thing is possible, one should not discount it prematurely or affirm its opposite, as you are doing.'

Bernabò's reply was brief and to the point.

'I am a merchant, not a philosopher,' he said, 'and I shall give you a merchant's answer. I am well aware that the sort of thing you describe can happen in the case of foolish women who are without any sense of shame. But the more judicious ones are so eager to safeguard their honour that they become stronger than men, who are indifferent to such matters. And my wife is one of these.'

'If, of course,' said Ambrogiuolo, 'a horn, bearing witness to their doings, were to sprout from their heads whenever they were unfaithful, then I think that the number of unfaithful women would be small. Not only do they not grow any horns, however, but the judicious ones leave no visible trace of their activities. There can't be any shame or loss of honour without clear evidence, and so if they can keep it a secret, either they get on with it or they desist because they are weak in the head. You can rest assured that the only chaste woman is either one who never received an improper proposal or one whose own proposals were always rejected. Even though I know that there are cogent and logical arguments to support this assertion, I would not be spelling it out with so much confidence were it not for the fact that I have often had occasion to prove it for myself with any number of women. And I will tell you this, that if I were any-where near this ever-so-saintly lady of yours, I shouldn't think it would take me long to lead her where I have led others in the past.'

'We could go on arguing like this indefinitely,' said Bernabò, who was by this time thoroughly incensed. 'You would say one thing, I would say another, and in the end we would get precisely nowhere. But since you claim that they are all so compliant and that you are so clever, I am prepared, in order to convince you of my lady's integrity, to place my head on the block if you ever persuade her to meet your wishes in this respect. And if you don't succeed, all I want you to lose is a thousand gold florins.'

'Bernabò,' replied Ambrogiuolo, who was warming to his sub-ject, 'I wouldn't know what to do with your head, if I were to win. But if you really want to see proof of what I have been saying, you can put up five thousand florins of your own, which is less than you'd pay for a new head, against my thousand. And whereas you did not fix any term, I will undertake to go to Genoa and have my way with this lady of yours within three months from the day I leave Paris. By way of proof, I shall return with some of her most intimate possessions, and I shall furnish you with so many relevant particulars that you will be forced to admit the truth of it with your own lips. I make one condition, however, and that is that you promise me on your word of honour neither to come to Genoa during this period nor to give her any hint in your letters of what is afoot.'

Bernabò declared himself to be quite satisfied with these terms, and however much the other merchants present, knowing that the affair could have serious repercussions, tried to prevent it from going any further, the passions of the two men were so strongly aroused that, contrary to the wishes of the others, they drew up a form of contract[1] with their own hands which was binding on both parties.

When the bond was sealed, Bernabò remained in Paris whilst Ambrogiuolo came by the quickest possible route to Genoa. Having discovered where the lady lived, he spent the first few days after his arrival in making discreet inquiries about her way of life, and since the information he gathered more than confirmed the description he had been given by Bernabò, he began to feel he was on a fool's errand. However, he became friendly with a poor woman, who regularly visited the house and enjoyed the lady's deep affection. Being unable to persuade her to assist him in any other way, he bribed her to have him taken into the house inside a chest, made according to his own specifications, which found its way not only into the house but into the lady's very bedroom. Following Ambrogiuolo's instructions, the good woman pretended that it was on its way to some other place, and obtained the lady's permission to leave it for a day or two in her room for safe keeping.

When night had descended, and Ambrogiuolo was satisfied that the lady was asleep, he prised the chest open with certain tools of his and stepped silently forth into the room, where a single lamp was burning. He then began, by the light of the lamp, to inspect the arrangement of the furniture, the paintings, and everything else of note that the room contained, and committed it all to memory.

Next, having approached the bed and found the lady with a little girl beside her, both soundly asleep, he uncovered her from head to toe and saw that she was every bit as beautiful without any clothes as when she was fully dressed. But her body contained no unusual mark of any description except for the fact that below her left breast there was a mole, surrounded by a few strands of fine, golden hair.[2] Having noted this, he silently covered her up again, although on seeing how beautiful she was he was sorely tempted to hazard his life and lie down beside her. However, having heard tales of her unbending strictness and her violent distaste for that sort of thing, he decided not to risk it. Roaming about the room at his leisure for most of the night, he removed a purse and a long cloak from a strong-box, together with some rings and one or two ornamental belts, all of which he stowed away in the chest before retiring into it himself and clamping down the lid again from the inside. And in this way he spent two whole nights there without the lady noticing that anything was amiss.

The good woman, following his instructions, returned on the morning of the third day for her chest, and had it taken back to its original place. Ambrogiuolo let himself out, and having paid the woman the sum he had promised her, he hurried back to Paris with his ill-gotten gains, arriving well within the agreed time-limit. He then called together the merchants who had been at the discussion when the bets were placed, and in Bernabò's presence he announced that since he had made good his boast he had won the wager. By way of proof, he began by describing the shape of the bedroom and the pictures it contained, then he showed them the things he had brought back with him, claiming that they had been given to him by the lady herself.

Bernabò conceded that his description of the room was correct, and furthermore he admitted that he did indeed recognize the exhibits as having once belonged to his lady. But he pointed out that Ambrogiuolo could have learnt about the arrangement of the room from one of the servants, and obtained these objects in similar fashion. So that, unless further evidence was forthcoming, he did not feel that the claim was substantiated.

'In all conscience, this should have been quite sufficient,' Ambrogiuolo retorted. 'But since you want me to provide further evidence, I will do so. And I will tell you that just below her left breast, your wife Zinevra has a sizeable little mole surrounded by about half-a-dozen fine golden hairs.'

When Bernabò heard this, he felt as though he had been stabbed through the heart, such was the pain that assailed him. His whole face changed, so that even if he had not uttered a word, it would have been quite obvious that what Ambrogiuolo had said was true.

'Gentlemen,' he said, after a long pause. 'What Ambrogiuolo says is true, and therefore, since he has won the wager, he may come whenever he likes in order to collect his due.' And the next day, Ambrogiuolo was paid in full.

Bernabò left Paris, and came hurrying back to Genoa with murder in his heart. But as he was approaching his destination, he decided to go no further, halting instead at an estate of his some twenty miles from the city. He then sent a retainer of his whom he greatly trusted to Genoa, with two horses and a letter telling his wife he had returned, and asking her to come and join him under this man's escort. And he secretly instructed the servant that on reaching the most suitable place, he was to kill her without showing any mercy and return to him alone.

When the retainer reached Genoa, he handed over the letter and delivered his master's message, being welcomed by the lady with great rejoicing; and next morning, they mounted their horses and set out for Bernabò's estate in the country. As they were riding along together, conversing on various topics, they came to a very deep ravine, a lonely spot with precipitous crags and trees all round it, which seemed to the retainer the ideal place to carry out his master's orders without any risk of detection. He therefore drew his dagger and seized the lady's arm, saying:

'Commend your soul to God, my lady, for this is the place where you must die.'

On seeing the dagger and hearing these words, the lady was completely terror-stricken.

'For God's sake, have mercy!' she cried. 'Before putting me to death, tell me what I ever did to you, that you should want to kill me.'

'My lady,' he replied. 'To me you have never done anything; but you must have done something or other to your husband, for he ordered me to kill you without mercy in the course of our journey. And if I fail to carry out his instructions, he has threatened to have me hanged by the neck. You know very well how much I depend upon him, and how impossible it would be for me to disobey him. God knows I feel sorry for you, but I have no alternative.'

The lady began to weep.

'Oh, for the love of God, have mercy!' she said. 'Don't allow yourself to murder someone who never did you any harm, just for the sake of obeying an order. As God is my witness, I have never given my husband the slightest cause for taking my life. But leaving that aside, you have it within your power to satisfy your master without offending God or laying a finger upon me. All you have to do is to take these outer garments I am wearing and leave me a cloak and a doublet. You can then return to our lord and master with the clothes and tell him you have killed me. And I swear to you, upon the life you will have granted me, that I will disappear and go away somewhere so that neither he nor you nor the people of these parts will ever hear of me again.'

The retainer was by no means eager to kill her, and was easily moved to compassion. And so, having taken the clothes, he gave her a tattered old doublet of his and a cloak to put on, left her some money she was carrying, and begged her to disappear entirely from those parts. He then abandoned her in the valley on foot and returned to his master, informing him that not only had his orders been carried out, but he had left her dead body surrounded by a pack of wolves.

Some time afterwards, Bernabò returned to Genoa, but once the story had leaked out, he never succeeded in living it down.

The lady, abandoned and forlorn, disguised herself as best she could, and when it was dark she went to a nearby cottage, where she obtained some things from an old woman and altered the doublet, shortening it to make it fit. She also converted her shift into a pair of knee-length breeches, cut her hair, and having transformed her appearance completely so that she now looked like a sailor, she made her way down to the coast, where she happened to encounter the master of a ship lying some distance offshore, a Catalan gentleman called Señor En Cararch, who had come ashore at Albenga³ to take on supplies of fresh water. Engaging him in conversation, she persuaded him to sign her on as his cabin-boy, calling herself Sicurano da Finale, and once they had gone aboard, the gentleman supplied her with some smarter clothes to wear. And she served him so well and so efficiently that he grew very attached to her.

Now it so happened that not long afterwards, the Catalan docked in Alexandria with a cargo which included some peregrine falcons that he was taking to the Sultan. These he duly delivered, after which he was occasionally invited to dine at the royal table, and the Sultan, on observing the ways of Sicurano, who was still in attendance upon him, was greatly impressed with the youth and asked the Catalan if he would allow him to keep him. Although he was loath to let him go, the Catalan gave his consent, and it was not very long before Sicurano's able performance of his duties had earned him the same degree of favour and affection from the Sultan that he had enjoyed with his previous master.

Now, at a certain season of the year, it was the custom to hold a trade-fair within the Sultan's domain at Acre, where merchants, both Christian and Saracen, used to congregate in large numbers. And in order to protect the merchants and their merchandise, the Sultan always used to send, in addition to his other officials, one of his court dignitaries with a contingent of guardsmen. And so it was that when the time for the fair drew near, the Sultan thought that he would send Sicurano to discharge this function, as he already had an excellent knowledge of the language; and this he did.

Sicurano duly arrived in Acre, therefore, as captain in charge of the special guard whose duties were to protect the merchants and their merchandise. And as he went round on tours of inspection, discharging his functions with diligence and skill, he came across a number of merchants from Sicily, Pisa, Genoa, Venice and other parts of Italy, with whom he readily made friends out of a nostalgic feeling for the country of his birth.

Now, it so happened that on one of these occasions, having dismounted at the stall of some Venetian merchants, in the midst of various other valuable objects he caught sight of a purse and an ornamental belt, which he promptly recognized as his own former belongings. Concealing his astonishment, he politely asked who owned them and whether they were for sale.

One of the merchants attending the fair was Ambrogiuolo of Piacenza, who had arrived there on a Venetian ship with a large quantity of goods, and on hearing that the captain of the guard was asking who owned the articles in question, he stepped forward, grinning all over his face.

'Sir,' he said, 'these things belong to me, and they are not for sale. But if you like them, I will gladly make you a present of them.'

When Sicurano saw him laughing, he suspected that the fellow had somehow seen through his disguise, but keeping a straight face, he asked:

'Why do you laugh? Is it because you see me, a soldier, inquiring about these female commodities?'

'No, sir,' replied Ambrogiuolo. 'That is not the reason. I am laughing about the way I acquired them.'

'Oh,' said Sicurano. 'Then perhaps, if the explanation is not too improper, you will be good enough to tell us about it.'

'Sir,' replied Ambrogiuolo. 'These things were given to me, along with various others, by a gentlewoman of Genoa called Donna Zinevra, the wife of Bernabò Lomellin. It was after I had slept with her for the night, and she asked me to keep them as a token of her love. And I was laughing just now because I was reminded of the foolishness of her husband, who was insane enough to wager five thousand gold florins against a thousand that I would not succeed in seducing his lady. I won the wager of course, and I am given to understand that the husband, who should have punished himself for his stupidity instead of punishing his wife for doing what all other women do, returned from Paris to Genoa and had her put to death.'

On hearing these words, Sicurano understood at once why Bernabò had been so enraged with her, and realized that this was the fellow who was responsible for all her woes. And she vowed to herself that he would not remain unpunished.

Sicurano therefore pretended to be greatly amused by his story and skilfully cultivated his friendship, so that when the fair was over, Ambrogiuolo packed up all his goods and at Sicurano's invitation went with him to Alexandria, where Sicurano had a warehouse built for him and placed a large sum of money at his disposal. And Ambrogiuolo, seeing that it was greatly to his profit, was only too ready to stay there.

Being anxious to offer Bernabò clear proof of his wife's innocence, Sicurano never rested until, with the assistance of one or two influential Genoese merchants in the city and a variety of ingenious pretexts, he had enticed him to come to Alexandria. Bernabò was by now in a state of poverty, and Sicurano secretly commissioned some of his friends to shelter him and keep him out of the way until such time as he felt he could put his plans into effect.

Sicurano had already persuaded Ambrogiuolo to repeat his story in front of the Sultan, who had greatly relished it. But now that Bernabò had arrived, he wanted to see the business through as quickly as possible, and took the earliest opportunity to induce the Sultan to summon Ambrogiuolo and Bernabò to his presence, so that, in Bernabò's hearing, Ambrogiuolo could be coerced by fair means or foul to confess the truth concerning his boast with regard to Bernabò's wife.

So Ambrogiuolo and Bernabò duly appeared before the Sultan, who glared fiercely at Ambrogiuolo and ordered him to tell the truth about the manner in which he had won the five thousand gold florins from Bernabò. Among the many people present was Sicurano, whom Ambrogiuolo trusted more than anybody, but Sicurano glared even more fiercely at him and threatened him with dire tortures if he refused to speak out. Ambrogiuolo was therefore terrified whichever way he looked, and after being subjected to a little further persuasion, not anticipating any punishment other than the restitution of the five thousand gold florins and the articles he had stolen, he described in detail to Bernabò and all the others present exactly what had happened.

No sooner had he finished speaking than Sicurano, acting as though he were the Sultan's public prosecutor, rounded on Bernabò.

'And you?' he said. 'What was your reaction to these falsehoods concerning your lady?'

'I was overcome with rage at the loss of my money,' replied Bernabò, 'and also with shame at the damage to my honour that I thought my wife had committed. And so I had her killed by one of my retainers, and according to his own account, she was immediately devoured by a pack of wolves.'

Sicurano then addressed the Sultan, who, though he had been listening carefully and taking it all in, was still in the dark about Sicurano's motives in requesting and arranging this meeting.

'My lord,' he said. 'It will be quite obvious to you what a fine swain and a fine husband that good lady was blessed with. For the swain deprives her of her honour by besmirching her good name with lies, at the same time ruining her husband. And the husband, paying more attention to another man's falsehoods than to the truth that years of experience should have taught him, has her killed and eaten by wolves. Moreover, both the suitor and the husband love and respect her so deeply that they are able to spend a long time in her company without even recognizing her. But in order that you shall be left in no possible doubt concerning the merits of these two gentlemen, I am ready, provided that you will grant me the special favour of pardoning the dupe and punishing the deceiver, to make the lady appear, here and now, before your very eyes.'

The Sultan, who was prepared to allow Sicurano a completely free hand in this affair, gave his consent and told him to produce the lady. Bernabò, being firmly convinced that she was dead, was unable to believe his ears, whilst Ambrogiuolo, for whom things were beginning to look desperate, was afraid in any case that he was going to have more than a sum of money to pay, and could not see that it would affect him either one way or the other if the lady really were to turn up. But if anything he was even more astonished than Bernabò.

No sooner had the Sultan agreed to Sicurano's request than Sicurano burst into tears and threw himself on his knees at the Sultan's feet, at the same time losing his manly voice and the desire to persist in his masculine role.

'My lord,' he said, 'I myself am the poor unfortunate Zinevra, who for six long years has toiled her way through the world disguised as a man, a victim of the false and wicked calumnies of this traitor Ambrogiuolo and of the iniquitous cruelty of this man who handed her over to be killed by one of his servants and eaten by wolves.'

Tearing open the front of her dress and displaying her bosom, she made it clear to the Sultan and to everyone else that she was indeed a woman. Then she rounded on Ambrogiuolo, haughtily demanding to know when he had ever slept with her, as he had claimed. But Ambrogiuolo, seeing who it was, simply stood there and said nothing, as though he were too ashamed to open his mouth.

The Sultan, who had always believed her to be a man, was so astonished on seeing and hearing all this, that he kept thinking that he must be dreaming and that his eyes and ears were deceiving him. But once he had recovered from his astonishment and realized that it was true, he lauded Zinevra to the skies for her virtuous way of life, her constancy, and her strength of character. And having ordered women's clothes of the finest quality to be brought, and provided her with a retinue of ladies, he complied with her earlier request and spared Bernabò from the death he assuredly deserved. On recognizing his wife, Bernabò threw himself in tears at her feet asking her forgiveness, and although he merited no such favour, she graciously conceded it and helped him up again, clasping him in a fond and wifely embrace.

The Sultan next commanded that Ambrogiuolo should instantly be taken to some upper part of the city, tied to a pole in the sun, smeared with honey, and left there until he fell of his own accord; and this was done. He then decreed that all of Ambrogiuolo's possessions, which amounted in value to more than ten thousand doubloons, should be handed over to the lady. And for his own part, he put on a splendid feast, at which Bernabò, being Lady Zinevra's husband, and the most excellent Lady Zinevra herself were the guests of honour. And in addition he presented her with jewels, gold and silver plate, and money, all of which came to a further ten thousand doubloons in value.

He meanwhile commissioned a ship to be specially fitted out for their use, and once the feast held in their honour was concluded, he gave them leave to return to Genoa whenever it suited their purpose. And when they sailed into Genoa, weak with joy and laden with riches, a magnificent welcome awaited them, especially Lady Zinevra, whom everyone had thought to be dead. And thereafter, for as long as she lived, she was held in high esteem and regarded as a paragon of virtue.

As for Ambrogiuolo, on the very day that he was tied to the pole and smeared with honey, he was subjected to excruciating torments by the mosquitoes, wasps and horseflies which abound in that country, and not only was he slain, but every morsel of his flesh was devoured. Hanging by their sinews, his whitened bones remained there for ages without being moved, an eloquent testimony of his wickedness to all who beheld them. And thus it was that the dupe outwitted his deceiver.

TENTH STORY

Paganino of Monaco steals the wife of Messer Ricciardo di Chinzica, who, on learning where she is, goes and makes friends with Paganino. He asks Paganino to restore her to him, and Paganino agrees on condition that he obtains her consent. She refuses to go back with Messer Ricciardo, and after his death becomes Paganino's wife.

Every member of the worthy company complimented the queen most warmly for telling so excellent a story, especially Dioneo, who was the sole remaining speaker of the day. And when he had finished singing its praises, he addressed them as follows:

Fair ladies, there was one feature of the queen's story which has caused me to substitute another tale for the one I was intending to relate. I refer to the stupidity of Bernabò, and of all other men who are given to thinking, as he apparently was, that while they are gadding about in various parts of the world with one woman after another, the wives they left behind are simply twiddling their thumbs. I will grant you that things turned out nicely for Bernabò, but we, who spend our lives in the company of women from the cradle upwards, know perfectly well what they enjoy doing most. In telling you this story, I shall demonstrate the foolishness of such people as Bernabò. And at the same time, I shall show the even greater foolishness of those who, overestimating their natural powers, resort to specious reasoning to persuade themselves that they can do the impossible, and who attempt to mould other people in their own image, thus flying in the face of Nature.

There once lived, in Pisa, a very wealthy judge called Messer Ricciardo di Chinzica, who had rather more brain than brawn, and who, thinking perhaps he could satisfy a wife with those same talents that he brought to his studies, went to a great deal of trouble to find himself a wife who was both young and beautiful; whereas, had he been capable of giving himself such good advice as he gave to others, he should have avoided marrying anyone with either of the attributes in question. He succeeded in his quest, however, for Messer Lotto Gualandi agreed to let him marry a daughter of his called Bartolomea, who was one of the prettiest and most charming young ladies in Pisa, a city where most of the women look as ugly as sin.[1] The judge brought her home with an air of great festivity, and although the wedding was celebrated in truly magnificent style, on the first night he only managed to come at her once in order to consummate the marriage, and even then he very nearly fell out of the game before it was over. And next morning, being a skinny and a withered and a spineless sort of fellow, he had to swallow down *vernaccia,*[2] energy-tablets and various other restoratives to pull himself round.

Now, this judge fellow, having thus obtained a better notion of his powers, began to teach her a calendar which schoolchildren are apt to consult, of the sort that was once in use at Ravenna.[3] For he made it clear to her that there was not a single day that was not the feast of one or more Saints, out of respect for whom, as he would demonstrate by devious arguments, man and woman should abstain from sexual union. To the foregoing, he added holidays of obligation, the four Ember weeks,[4] the eves of the Apostles and a numerous array of subsidiary Saints, Fridays and Saturdays, the sabbath, the whole of Lent, certain phases of the moon, and various special occasions, possibly because he was under the impression that one had to take vacations from bedding a woman, in the same way that he sometimes took vacations from summing up in the law-courts. For a long time (much to the chagrin of his lady, whose turn came round once a month at the most) he abided by this régime, always keeping a close watch on her lest anyone else should teach her as good a knowledge of the working-days as he had taught her of the holidays.

One summer, during a heat-wave, Messer Ricciardo happened to be seized by a longing to go and relax in the fresh air at a very fine villa of his near Montenero,[5] and he took his fair lady with him. And during their stay, in order to provide her with a little recreation, he arranged a day's fishing, he and the fishermen taking out one boat whilst she and some other ladies went along to watch from a second. But as he became absorbed in what he was doing, they drifted several miles out to sea almost before they realized what was happening.

While their concentration was at its peak, a small galley came upon the scene commanded by Paganino da Mare, a notorious pirate of the time, who having caught sight of the two boats came sailing towards them. They turned and fled, but before they could reach safety, Paganino overtook the boat containing the women, and on catching sight of the fair lady, he disregarded everything else and took her aboard his galley before making off again under the very eyes of Messer Ricciardo, who had meanwhile reached the shore. Needless to say, our friend the judge was extremely distressed on seeing all this, for he was jealous of the very air that she breathed. And all he could do now was to wander about Pisa and other places, bemoaning the wickedness of the pirates, without having any idea who it was that had kidnapped his wife or where she had been taken.

Paganino reckoned himself very fortunate when he saw how beautiful she was, and since he was unmarried, he made up his mind to keep her. But she was weeping bitterly, and so he poured out a stream of endearments in an attempt to console her, and when night descended, having come to the conclusion that he had been wasting his time all day with words, he turned to comforting her with deeds, for he was not the sort of man to pay any heed to calendars, and he had long since forgotten about feasts and holy days. So effective were the consolations he provided, that before they had reached Monaco,[6] the judge and his laws had faded from the lady's memory, and life with Paganino was a positive joy. And after he had brought her to Monaco, in addition to consoling her continuously night and day, Paganino treated her with all the respect due to a wife.

When, some time afterwards, information reached Messer Ricciardo of his lady's whereabouts, he was passionately resolved to go and fetch her in person, being convinced that he alone could handle the affair with the necessary tact. He was quite prepared to pay whatever ransom was demanded, and took ship for Monaco, where he caught sight of her soon after his arrival. But she had seen him, too, and that same evening she warned Paganino and informed him of her husband's intentions.

Next morning, Messer Ricciardo saw Paganino and engaged him in conversation, losing no time in getting on friendly and familiar terms with him, while Paganino, pretending not to know who he was, waited to see what he was proposing to do. At the earliest opportunity, Messer Ricciardo disclosed the purpose of his visit as concisely and politely as he could, then asked Paganino to hand the lady over, naming whatever sum he required by way of ransom.

'Welcome to Monaco, sir,' replied Paganino, smiling broadly. 'And as to your request, I will answer you briefly, as follows. It is true that I have a young lady in my house, but I couldn't say whether she is your wife or some other man's wife, for I do not know you, and all I know about the lady is that she has been living with me for some time. I have taken a liking to you, however, and since you appear to be honest, I will take you to see her, and if you are indeed her husband, as you claim to be, she will no doubt recognize you. If she confirms your story and wants to go with you, you are such an amiable sort of fellow that I am content to leave the amount of the ransom to your own good judgement. But if your story isn't true, it would be dishonest of you to try and deprive me of her, for I am a young man and no less entitled than anyone else to keep a woman, especially this one, for she is the nicest I ever saw.'

'Of course she is my wife,' said Messer Ricciardo. 'You will soon be convinced when you take me to see her, for she will fling her arms round my neck immediately. I could ask for nothing better than the arrangement you suggest.'

'In that case,' said Paganino, 'let us proceed.'

And so off they went to Paganino's house, where they entered a large room and Paganino sent for the lady, who came in from another room, composed in appearance and neatly dressed, and walked over to where the two men were standing. But she took no more notice of Messer Ricciardo than if he were some total stranger coming into the house as Paganino's guest. On seeing this, the judge was greatly astonished, for he had been expecting her to greet him with a display of frenzied rejoicing. 'Perhaps,' he thought, 'the melancholy and prolonged suffering to which I have been subjected, ever since I lost her, have wrought such a change in my appearance that she no longer knows who I am.' He therefore addressed her as follows:

'Madam, it was a costly idea of mine to take you fishing with me, for nobody ever experienced so much sorrow as I have endured from the day I lost you, and now it appears, from the coldness of your greeting, that you do not even recognize me. Don't you see that I am your Messer Ricciardo? Don't you understand that I came to Monaco fully prepared to offer this gentleman whatever ransom he required, so that I could have you back again and take you away from this house? And are you perhaps unaware that he has been good enough to tell me that he'll hand you over for whatever sum I choose to pay?'

The lady turned towards him, with the faintest suggestion of a smile on her lips.

'Are you addressing me, sir?' she asked. 'You must surely be mistaking me for someone else, for as far as I can recall, I have never seen you before in my life.'

'Oh, come now,' said Messer Ricciardo. 'Take a good look at me, and if you choose to remember properly, you will soon see that I am your husband, Ricciardo di Chinzica.'

'You will forgive me for saying so, sir,' said the lady, 'but it is not so proper as you imagine for me to stare at you. And in any case, I have already looked at you sufficiently to know that I have never seen you before.'

Messer Ricciardo supposed her to be doing this because she was afraid of Paganino, in whose presence she was perhaps reluctant to admit that she recognized him. And so, after a while, he asked Paganino if he would kindly allow him to speak with her alone in her room. Paganino agreed, on condition that he made no attempt to kiss her against her will, and he told the lady to go with Messer Ricciardo into her room, listen to what he had to say, and reply as freely as she pleased.

Thus the lady and Messer Ricciardo went into her room, closed the door behind them, and sat down.

'Oh, my dearest,' said Messer Ricciardo, 'my dear, sweet darling, my treasure, now do you remember your Ricciardo who loves you more than life itself? No? How is this possible? Can I have changed so much? Oh, my pretty one, do take another little look at me.'

The lady, who had begun to laugh, interrupted his babbling, saying:

'You are well aware that I possess a sufficiently good memory to know that you are my husband, Messer Ricciardo di Chinzica. But you showed very little sign of knowing *me*, when I was living with you, because if, either then or now, you were as wise as you wish to pretend, you should certainly have had the gumption to realize that a fresh and vigorous young woman like myself needs something more than food and clothes, even if modesty forbids her to say so. And you know how little of that you provided.

'If you were more interested in studying the law than in keeping a wife, you should never have married in the first place. Not that you ever seemed to me to be a judge. On the contrary, you had such an expert knowledge of feasts and festivals, to say nothing of fasts and vigils, that I thought you must be a town-crier. And I can tell you this, that if you had given as many holidays to the workers on your estates as you gave to the one whose job it was to tend my little field, you would never have harvested a single ear of corn. But by the merciful will of God, who took pity on my youth, I chanced

upon the man with whom I share this room, where holy days – the
ones you used to celebrate so religiously, being more devoted to
pious works than to the service of the ladies – have never been
heard of. And not only has that door remained firmly shut against
sabbaths, Fridays, vigils, Ember Days and Lent (which is such a
long-drawn-out affair), but work goes on all the time here day and
night, so that the place is a positive hive of activity. Why, this very
morning, the bell for matins had barely stopped ringing before he
was up and about, and I can't begin to tell you how busy we were.
Hence I intend to remain with him, and work while I am still
young, and save up all those fasts and holy days so that I can turn to
them, along with pilgrimages, when I am an old woman. As for
you, be so good as to clear off as soon as you can, and have as many
holidays as you like, but not with me.'

As he listened to these words, Messer Ricciardo suffered the
agonies of the damned, and when he saw that she had finished, he
said:

'Oh, my dearest, how can you say such things? Have you lost all
regard for your honour and that of your parents? Do you mean to
say you prefer to stay on here, living in mortal sin as this man's
strumpet, rather than to live in Pisa as my wife? When this fellow
grows tired of you, he will turn you out and make you an object of
ridicule, whereas I will always cherish you, and you will always be
the mistress of my house whatever happens. Do you mean to cast
aside your honour and forsake one who loves you more than life
itself, simply because of this immoderate and unseemly appetite of
yours? Oh, my treasure, don't say these things any more, come
away with me. Now that I know what you want, I'll make a special
effort in the future. Do change your mind, my precious, and come
back to me, for my life has been sheer misery ever since the day you
were taken away from me.'

'As to my honour,' the lady replied, 'I mean to defend what
remains of it as jealously as anyone. I only wish my parents had
displayed an equal regard for it when they handed me over to you!
But since they were so unconcerned about my honour then, I do
not intend to worry about their honour now. And if I am living in
mortar sin, it can be pestle sin[7] too for all I care, so stop making

such a song and dance about it. And let me tell you this, that I feel as though I am Paganino's wife here. It was in Pisa that I felt like a strumpet, considering all that rigmarole about the moon's phases and all those geometrical calculations that were needed before we could bring the planets into conjunction, whereas here Paganino holds me in his arms the whole night long and squeezes and bites me, and as God is my witness, he never leaves me alone.

'You say you will make an effort. But how? By doing things in three easy stages, and springing to attention with a blow from a cudgel? I've noticed, of course, what a fine, strong fellow you've become since I saw you last. Be off with you, and put your efforts into staying alive, for it seems to me that you won't survive much longer, you have such a sickly and emaciated look about you. Oh, and another thing. Even if Paganino leaves me (and he seems to have no such intention, provided I want to stay), I would never come back to you in any case, because if you were to be squeezed from head to toe there wouldn't be a thimbleful of sauce to show for it. Life with you was all loss and no gain as far as I was concerned, so if there were to be a next time, I would be trying my luck elsewhere. Once and for all, then, I repeat that I intend to stay here, where there are no holy days and no vigils. And if you don't clear off quickly I shall scream for help and claim you were trying to molest me.'

On seeing that the situation was hopeless, and realizing for the first time how foolish he had been to take a young wife when he was so impotent, Messer Ricciardo walked out of the room, feeling all sad and forlorn, and although he had a long talk with Paganino, it made no difference whatever. And so finally, having achieved precisely nothing, he left the lady there and returned to Pisa, where his grief threw him into such a state of lunacy that whenever people met him in the street and put any question to him, the only answer they got was: 'There's never any rest for the bar.'[8] Shortly afterwards he died, and when the news reached Paganino, knowing how deeply the lady loved him, he made her his legitimate wife. And without paying any heed to holy days or vigils or observing Lent, they worked their fingers to the bone and thoroughly enjoyed themselves. So it seems to me, dear ladies, that our friend Bernabò, by taking the course he pursued with Ambrogiuolo, was riding on the edge of a precipice.

★   ★   ★

This story threw the whole company into such fits of laughter that there was none of them whose jaws were not aching, and the ladies unanimously agreed that Dioneo was right and that Bernabò had been an ass. But now that the tale was ended, the queen waited for the laughter to subside, and then, seeing that it was late and everyone had told a story, and realizing that her reign had come to an end, she removed the garland from her own head in the usual way, and, placing it on Neifile's, she said to her with a laugh:

'Dear sister, I do hereby pronounce you sovereign of our tiny nation.' And then she returned to her place.

Neifile blushed a little on receiving this honour, so that her face was like the rose that blooms at dawn in early summer, whilst her eyes, which she had lowered slightly, glittered and shone like the morning star. There followed a round of respectful applause, in token of the joy and goodwill of her companions, and when the clapping had subsided and she had recovered her composure, she seated herself in a slightly more elevated position, and said to them:

'I have no wish to depart from the excellent ways of my predecessors, of whose government you have shown your approval by your obedience. But since I really am your queen, I shall acquaint you briefly with my own proposals, and if they meet with your consent we shall carry them into effect.

'As you know, tomorrow is Friday and the next day is Saturday,[1] both of which, because of the food we normally eat on those two days, are generally thought of as being rather tedious. Moreover, Friday is worthy of special reverence because that was the day of the Passion of Our Lord, who died that we might live, and I would therefore regard it as perfectly right and proper that we should all do honour to God by devoting that day to prayer rather than storytelling. As for Saturday, it is customary on that day for the ladies to wash their hair and rinse away the dust and grime that may have settled on their persons in the course of their week's endeavours.

Besides, in deference to the Virgin Mother of the Son of God, they are wont to fast on Saturdays, and to refrain from all activities for the rest of the day, as a mark of respect for the approaching sabbath. Since, therefore, it would be impossible on a Saturday to profit to the full from the routine upon which we have embarked, I think we would be well advised to abstain from telling stories on that day also.

'It will then be four days since we came to stay here, and in order to avoid being joined by others,[2] I think it advisable for us to move elsewhere. I have already thought of a place for us to go, and made the necessary arrangements.

'Our discourse today has taken place within very broad limits. But by the time we assemble after our siesta on Sunday afternoon at our new abode, you will have had more time for reflection, and I have therefore decided, since it will be all the more interesting if we restrict the subject-matter of our stories to a single aspect of the many facets of Fortune, that our theme should be the following: *People who by dint of their own efforts have achieved an object they greatly desired or recovered a thing previously lost.* Let each of us, therefore, think of something useful, or at least amusing, to say to the company on this topic, due allowance being made for Dioneo's privilege.'

The queen's speech met with general approval, and her proposal was unanimously adopted. She then summoned her steward, and having explained where he should place the tables for that evening, instructed him fully concerning his duties for the remainder of her reign. This done, she rose to her feet, her companions followed her example, and she gave them leave to amuse themselves in whatever way they pleased.

And so the ladies made their way with the three young men to a miniature garden, where they whiled away their time agreeably before supper. They then had supper, in the course of which there was much laughter and merriment, and when they had risen from table, at the queen's request Emilia began to dance whilst Pampinea sang the following song, the others joining in the chorus:

'If 'twere not I, what woman would sing,
Who am content in everything?

'Come, Love, the cause of all my joy,
Of all my hope and happiness,
Come let us sing together:
Not of love's sighs and agony
But only of its jocundness
And its clear-burning ardour
In which I revel, joyfully,
As if thou wert a god to me.

'Love, the first day I felt thy fire
Thou sett'st before mine eyes a youth
Of such accomplishment
Whose able strength and keen desire
And bravery could none, in truth,
Find any complement.
With thee I sing, Lord Love, of this,
So much in him lies all my bliss.

'And this my greatest pleasure is:
That he loves me with equal fire,
Cupid, all thanks to thee;
Within this world I have my bliss
And I may in the next, entire,
I love so faithfully,
If God who sees us from above
Will grant this boon upon our love.'

When this song was finished, they sang a number of others, danced many dances and played several tunes. But eventually the queen decided it was time for them to go to bed, and they all retired to their respective rooms, carrying torches to light them on their way. For the next two days, they attended to those matters about which the queen had spoken earlier, and looked forward eagerly to Sunday.

Here ends the Second Day of the Decameron

THIRD DAY

Here begins the Third Day, wherein, under the rule of Neifile, *the discussion turns upon people who by dint of their own efforts have achieved an object they greatly desired, or recovered a thing previously lost.*

On the following Sunday, when already the dawn was beginning to change from vermilion to orange with the approach of the sun, the queen arose and summoned all her companions. Some time earlier, the steward had dispatched most of the things they required to their new quarters, together with servants to make all necessary preparations for their arrival. And once the queen herself had set out, he promptly saw that everything else was loaded on to the baggage train, as though he were striking camp, and then departed with the rest of the servants who had remained behind with the ladies and gentlemen.

Meanwhile the queen, accompanied and followed by her ladies and the three young men, and guided by the song of perhaps a score of nightingales and other birds, struck out westward at a leisurely pace along a little-used path carpeted with grass and flowers, whose petals were gradually opening to greet the morning sun. After walking no more than two miles, she brought them, long before tierce was half spent,[1] to a most beautiful and ornate palace,[2] which was situated on a slight eminence above the plain. Entering the palace, they explored it from end to end, and were filled with admiration for its spacious halls and well-kept, elegant rooms, which were equipped with everything they could possibly need, and they came to the conclusion that only a gentleman of the highest rank could have owned it. And when they descended to inspect the huge, sunlit courtyard, the cellars stocked with excellent wines, and the well containing abundant supplies of fresh, ice-cold water, they praised it even more. The whole place was decked with seasonable flowers and cuttings, and by way of repose they seated themselves on a loggia overlooking the central court. Here they were met by the steward, who had thoughtfully laid on a supply of delectable sweetmeats and precious wines for their refreshment.

After this, they were shown into a walled garden alongside the palace, and since it seemed at first glance to be a thing of wondrous beauty, they began to explore it in detail. The garden was surrounded and criss-crossed by paths of unusual width, all as straight as arrows and overhung by pergolas of vines, which showed every sign of yielding an abundant crop of grapes later in the year. The vines were all in flower, drenching the garden with their aroma, which, mingled with that of many other fragrant plants and herbs, gave them the feeling that they were in the midst of all the spices ever grown in the East. The paths along the edges of the garden were almost entirely hemmed in by white and red roses and jasmine, so that not only in the morning but even when the sun was at its apex one could walk in pleasant, sweet-smelling shade, without ever being touched by the sun's rays. It would take a long time to describe how numerous and varied were the shrubs growing there, or how neatly they were set out: but all the ones that have aught to commend them and flourish in our climate were represented in full measure. In the central part of the garden (not the least, but by far the most admirable of its features), there was a lawn of exceedingly fine grass, of so deep a green as to almost seem black, dotted all over with possibly a thousand different kinds of gaily-coloured flowers, and surrounded by a line of flourishing, bright green orange- and lemon-trees, which, with their mature and unripe fruit and lingering shreds of blossom, offered agreeable shade to the eyes and a delightful aroma to the nostrils. In the middle of this lawn there stood a fountain of pure white marble, covered with marvellous bas-reliefs. From a figure standing on a column in the centre of the fountain, a jet of water, whether natural or artificial I know not, but sufficiently powerful to drive a mill with ease, gushed high into the sky before cascading downwards and falling with a delectable plash into the crystal-clear pool below. And from this pool, which was lapping the rim of the fountain, the water passed through a hidden culvert and then emerged into finely constructed artificial channels surrounding the lawn on all sides.

Thence it flowed along similar channels through almost the whole of the beautiful garden, eventually gathering at a single place from which it issued forth from the garden and descended towards the plain as a pure clear stream, furnishing ample power to two separate mills on its downward course, to the no small advantage of the owner of the palace.

The sight of this garden, and the perfection of its arrangement, with its shrubs, its streamlets, and the fountain from which they originated, gave so much pleasure to each of the ladies and the three young men that they all began to maintain that if Paradise were constructed on earth, it was inconceivable that it could take any other form, nor could they imagine any way in which the garden's beauty could possibly be enhanced. And as they wandered contentedly through it, making magnificent garlands for themselves from the leaves of the various trees, their ears constantly filled with the sound of some twenty different kinds of birds, all singing as though they were vying with one another, they became aware of yet another delightful feature, which, being so overwhelmed by the others, they had so far failed to notice. For they found that the garden was liberally stocked with as many as a hundred different varieties of perfectly charming animals, to which they all started drawing each other's attention. Here were some rabbits emerging from a warren, over there hares were running, elsewhere they could observe some deer lying on the ground, whilst in yet another place young fawns were grazing. And apart from these, they saw numerous harmless creatures of many other kinds, roaming about at leisure as though they were quite tame, all of which added greatly to their already considerable delight.

When, however, they had wandered about the garden for some little time, sampling its various attractions, they instructed the servants to arrange the tables round the fountain, and then they sang half-a-dozen canzonets and danced several dances, after which, at the queen's command, they all sat down to breakfast. Choice and dainty dishes, exquisitely prepared, were set before them in unhurried succession, and when they rose from table, merrier than when they had started, they turned once more to music, songs and dancing. Eventually, however, as the hottest part of the day was approaching, the queen decided that those who felt so inclined should take their siesta. Some of them accordingly retired, but the rest were so overwhelmed by the beauty of their surroundings that they remained where they were and whiled away their time in reading romances or playing chess or throwing dice whilst the others slept.

But a little after nones, they all went and refreshed their faces in cool water before assembling, at the queen's request, on the lawn near the fountain, where, having seated themselves in the customary manner, they began to await their turn to tell a story on the topic the queen had proposed. The first of their number to whom she entrusted this office was Filostrato, who began as follows:

FIRST STORY

Masetto of Lamporecchio pretends to be dumb, and becomes a gardener at a convent, where all the nuns combine forces to take him off to bed with them.

Fairest ladies, there are a great many men and women who are so dense as to be firmly convinced that when a girl takes the white veil and dons the black cowl, she ceases to be a woman or to experience feminine longings, as though the very act of making her a nun had caused her to turn into stone. And if they should happen to hear of anything to suggest that their conviction is ill-founded, they become quite distressed, as though some enormous and diabolical evil had been perpetrated against Nature. It never enters their heads for a moment, possibly because they have no wish to face facts, that they themselves are continually dissatisfied even though they enjoy full liberty to do as they please, or that idleness and solitude are such powerful stimulants. Again, there are likewise many people who are firmly convinced that digging and hoeing and coarse food and hardy living remove all lustful desires from those who work on the land, and greatly impair their intelligence and powers of perception. But, since the queen has bidden me to speak, I would like to tell you a little tale, relevant to the topic she has prescribed, which will show you quite clearly that all these people are sadly mistaken in their convictions.

In this rural region of ours, there was and still is a nunnery, greatly renowned for its holiness, which I shall refrain from naming for fear of doing the slightest harm to its reputation. At this convent, not long ago, at a time when it housed no more than eight nuns and an abbess, all of them young, there was a worthy little man whose job it was to look after a very beautiful garden of theirs. And one day, being dissatisfied with his remuneration, he settled up with the nuns' steward and returned to his native village of Lamporecchio.

On his return, he was warmly welcomed by several of the villagers, among them a young labourer, a big, strong fellow called Masetto, who, considering that he was of peasant stock, possessed a remarkably handsome physique and agreeable features. Since the good man, whose name was Nuto, had been away from the village for some little time, Masetto wanted to know where he had been, and when he learned that Nuto had been living at a convent, he questioned him about his duties there.

'I tended a fine, big garden of theirs,' Nuto replied, 'in addition to which, I sometimes used to go and collect firewood, or I would fetch water and do various other little jobs of that sort. But the nuns gave me such a paltry wage that it was barely sufficient to pay for my shoe-leather. Besides, they are all young and they seem to me to have the devil in them, because whatever you do, it is impossible to please them. Sometimes, in fact, I would be working in the garden when one of them would order me to do one thing, another would tell me to do something else, and yet another would snatch the very hoe from my hands, and tell me I was doing things the wrong way. They used to pester me to such an extent that occasionally I would down tools and march straight out of the garden. So that eventually, what with one thing and another, I decided I'd had enough of the place and came away altogether. Just as I was leaving, their steward asked me whether I knew of anyone who could take the job on, and I promised to send somebody along, provided I could find the right man, but you won't catch me sending him anybody, not unless God has provided the fellow with the strength and patience of an ox.'

As he listened, Masetto experienced such a longing to go and stay with these nuns that his whole body tingled with excitement, for it was clear from what he had heard that he should be able to achieve what he had in mind. Realizing, however, that he would get nowhere by revealing his intentions to Nuto, he replied:

'How right you were to come away from the place! What sort of a life can any man lead when he's surrounded by a lot of women? He might as well be living with a pack of devils. Why, six times out of seven they don't even know their own minds.'

But when they had finished talking, Masetto began to consider what steps he ought to take so that he could go and stay with them. Knowing himself to be perfectly capable of carrying out the duties mentioned by Nuto, he had no worries about losing the job on that particular score, but he was afraid lest he should be turned down because of his youth and his unusually attractive appearance. And so, having rejected a number of other possible expedients, he eventually thought to himself: 'The convent is a long way off, and there's nobody there who knows me. If I can pretend to be dumb, they'll take me on for sure.' Clinging firmly to this conjecture, he therefore dressed himself in pauper's rags and slung an axe over his shoulder,[1] and without telling anyone where he was going, he set out for the convent. On his arrival, he wandered into the courtyard, where as luck would have it he came across the steward, and with the aid of gestures such as dumb people use, he conveyed the impression that he was begging for something to eat, in return for which he would attend to any wood-chopping that needed to be done.

The steward gladly provided him with something to eat, after which he presented him with a pile of logs that Nuto had been unable to chop. Being very powerful, Masetto made short work of the whole consignment, and then the steward, who was on his way to the wood, took Masetto with him and got him to fell some timber. He then provided Masetto with an ass, and gave him to understand by the use of sign-language that he was to take the timber back to the convent.

The fellow carried out his instructions so efficiently that the steward retained his services for a few more days, getting him to tackle various jobs that needed to be done about the place. One day, the Abbess herself happened to catch sight of him, and she asked the steward who he was.

'The man is a poor deaf-mute, ma'am, who came here one day begging for alms,' said the steward. 'I saw to it that he was well fed, and set him to work on various tasks that needed to be done. If he turns out to be good at gardening, and wants to stay, I reckon we would do well out of it, because we certainly need a gardener, and this is a strong fellow who will always do as he's told. Besides, you wouldn't need to worry about his giving any cheek to these young ladies of yours.'

'I do believe you're right,' said the Abbess. 'Find out whether he knows what to do, and make every effort to hold on to him. Provide him with a pair of shoes and an old hood, wheedle him, pay him a few compliments, and give him plenty to eat.'

The steward agreed to carry out her instructions, but Masetto was not far away, pretending to sweep the courtyard, and he had overheard their whole conversation. 'Once you put me inside that garden of yours,' he said to himself, gleefully, 'I'll tend it better than it's ever been tended before.'

Now, when the steward had discovered what an excellent gardener he was, he gestured to Masetto, asking him whether he would like to stay there, and the latter made signs to indicate that he was willing to do whatever the steward wanted. The steward therefore took him on to the staff, ordered him to look after the garden, and showed him what he was to do, after which he went away in order to attend to the other affairs of the convent, leaving him there by himself. Gradually, as the days passed and Masetto worked steadily away, the nuns started teasing and annoying him, which is the way people frequently behave with deaf-mutes, and they came out with the foulest language imaginable, thinking that he was unable to hear them. Moreover, the Abbess, who was possibly under the impression that he had lost his tail as well as his tongue, took little or no notice of all this.

Now one day, when Masetto happened to be taking a rest after a

spell of strenuous work, he was approached by two very young
nuns who were out walking in the garden. Since he gave them the
impression that he was asleep, they began to stare at him, and the
bolder of the two said to her companion:

'If I could be sure that you would keep it a secret, I would tell
you about an idea that has often crossed my mind, and one that
might well work out to our mutual benefit.'

'Do tell me,' replied the other. 'You can be quite certain that I
shan't talk about it to anyone.'

The bold one began to speak more plainly.

'I wonder,' she said, 'whether you have ever considered what a
strict life we have to lead, and how the only men who ever dare set
foot in this place are the steward, who is elderly, and this dumb
gardener of ours. Yet I have often heard it said, by several of the
ladies who have come to visit us, that all other pleasures in the
world are mere trifles by comparison with the one experienced by a
woman when she goes with a man. I have thus been thinking, since
I have nobody else to hand, that I would like to discover with the
aid of this dumb fellow whether they are telling the truth. As it
happens, there couldn't be a better man for the purpose, because
even if he wanted to let the cat out of the bag, he wouldn't be able
to. He wouldn't even know how to explain, for you can see for
yourself what a mentally retarded, dim-witted hulk of a youth the
fellow is. I would be glad to know what you think of the idea.'

'Dear me!' said the other. 'Don't you realize that we have
promised God to preserve our virginity?'

'Pah!' she said. 'We are constantly making Him promises that
we never keep! What does it matter if we fail to keep this one?
He can always find other girls to preserve their virginity for
Him.'

'But what if we become pregnant?' said her companion. 'What's
going to happen then?'

'You're beginning to worry about things before they've even
happened. We can cross that bridge if and when we come to it.
There'll be scores of different ways to keep it a secret, provided we
control our own tongues.'

'Very well, then,' said the other, who was already more eager than the first to discover what sort of stuff a man was made of. 'How do we set about it?'

'As you see,' she replied, 'it is getting on for nones, and I expect all our companions are asleep. Let's make sure there's nobody else in the garden. And then, if the coast is clear, all we have to do is to take him by the hand and steer him across to that hut over there, where he shelters from the rain. Then one of us can go inside with him while the other keeps watch. He's such a born idiot that he'll do whatever we suggest.'

Masetto heard the whole of this conversation, and since he was quite willing to obey, the only thing he was waiting for now was for one of them to come and fetch him. The two nuns had a good look round, and having made certain that they could not be observed, the one who had done all the talking went over to Masetto and woke him up, whereupon he sprang instantly to his feet. She then took him by the hand, making alluring gestures to which he responded with big broad, imbecilic grins, and led him into the hut, where Masetto needed very little coaxing to do her bidding. Having got what she wanted, she loyally made way for her companion, and Masetto, continuing to act the simpleton, did as he was asked. Before the time came for them to leave, they had each made repeated trials of the dumb fellow's riding ability, and later on, when they were busily swapping tales about it all, they agreed that it was every bit as pleasant an experience as they had been led to believe, indeed more so. And from then on, whenever the opportunity arose, they whiled away many a pleasant hour in the dumb fellow's arms.

One day, however, a companion of theirs happened to look out from the window of her cell, saw the goings-on, and drew the attention of two others to what was afoot. Having talked the matter over between themselves, they at first decided to report the pair to the Abbess. But then they changed their minds, and by common agreement with the other two, they took up shares in Masetto's holding. And because of various indiscretions, these five were subsequently joined by the remaining three, one after the other.

Finally, the Abbess, who was still unaware of all this, was taking a stroll one very hot day in the garden, all by herself, when she came across Masetto stretched out fast asleep in the shade of an almond-tree. Too much riding by night had left him with very little strength for the day's labours, and so there he lay, with his clothes ruffled up in front by the wind, leaving him all exposed. Finding herself alone, the lady stood with her eyes riveted to this spectacle, and she was seized by the same craving to which her young charges had already succumbed. So, having roused Masetto, she led him away to her room, where she kept him for several days, thus provoking bitter complaints from the nuns over the fact that the handyman had suspended work in the garden. Before sending him back to his own quarters, she repeatedly savoured the one pleasure for which she had always reserved her most fierce disapproval, and from then on she demanded regular supplementary allocations, amounting to considerably more than her fair share.

Eventually, Masetto, being unable to cope with all their demands, decided that by continuing to be dumb any longer he might do himself some serious injury. And so one night, when he was with the Abbess, he untied his tongue and began to talk.

'I have always been given to understand, ma'am,' he said, 'that whereas a single cock is quite sufficient for ten hens, ten men are hard put to satisfy one woman, and yet here am I with nine of them on my plate. I can't endure it any longer, not at any price, and as a matter of fact I've been on the go so much that I'm no longer capable of delivering the goods. So you'll either have to bid me farewell or come to some sort of an arrangement.'

When she heard him speak, the lady was utterly amazed, for she had always believed him to be dumb.

'What is all this?' she said. 'I thought you were supposed to be dumb.'

'That's right, ma'am, I was,' said Masetto, 'but I wasn't born dumb. It was owing to an illness that I lost the power of speech, and, praise be to God, I've recovered it this very night.'

The lady believed him implicitly, and asked him what he had meant when he had talked about having nine on his plate. Masetto explained how things stood, and when the Abbess heard, she realized that every single one of the nuns possessed sharper wits than her own. Being of a tactful disposition, she decided there and then that rather than allow Masetto to go away and spread tales concerning the convent, she would come to some arrangement with her nuns in regard to the matter.

Their old steward had died a few days previously. And so, with Masetto's consent, they unanimously decided, now that they all knew what the others had been doing, to persuade the people living in the neighbourhood that after a prolonged period of speechlessness, his ability to talk had been miraculously restored by the nuns' prayers and the virtues of the saint after whom the convent was named, and they appointed him their new steward. They divided up his various functions among themselves in such a way that he was able to do them all justice. And although he fathered quite a number of nunlets and monklets, it was all arranged so discreetly that nothing leaked out until after the death of the Abbess, by which time Masetto was getting on in years and simply wanted to retire to his village on a fat pension. Once his wishes became known, they were readily granted.

Thus it was that Masetto, now an elderly and prosperous father who was spared the bother of feeding his children and the expense of their upbringing, returned to the place from which he had set out with an axe on his shoulder, having had the sense to employ his youth to good advantage. And this, he maintained, was the way that Christ treated anyone who set a pair of horns on His crown.

SECOND STORY

A groom makes love to King Agilulf's wife. Agilulf finds out, keeps quiet about it, tracks down the culprit, and shears his hair. The shorn man shears all the others, thus avoiding an unpleasant fate.

There were some parts of Filostrato's tale that caused the ladies to blush, others that provoked their laughter, and as soon as it had come to an end, the queen requested Pampinea to take up the storytelling. She accordingly began as follows, laughing all over her face:

Some people, having discovered or heard a thing of which they were better left in ignorance, are so foolishly anxious to publish the fact that sometimes, in censuring the inadvertent failings of others with the object of lessening their own dishonour, they increase it out of all proportion. And I now propose, fair ladies, to illustrate the truth of this assertion by describing a contrary state of affairs, wherein the wisdom of a mighty monarch was matched by the guile[1] of a man whose social standing was possibly inferior to that of Masetto.

When Agilulf[2] became King of the Lombards, he followed the example set by his predecessors and chose the city of Pavia, in Lombardy, as the seat of his kingdom. He had meanwhile married Theodelinda, who was the beautiful widow of the former Lombard king, Authari, and although she was a very intelligent and virtuous woman, she once had a most unfortunate experience with a suitor of hers. For during a period when the affairs of Lombardy, owing to the wise and resolute rule of this King Agilulf, were relatively calm and prosperous, one of the Queen's grooms, a man of exceedingly low birth, gifted out of all proportion to his very humble calling, who was as tall and handsome as the King himself, happened to fall hopelessly in love with his royal mistress.

Since his low station in life had not blinded him to the fact that this passion of his was thoroughly improper, he had the good sense not to breathe a word about it to anyone, nor did he even dare to cast tell-tale glances in the lady's direction. But although he was quite resigned to the fact that he would never win her favour, he could at least claim that his thoughts were directed towards a lofty goal. And being scorched all over by the flames of love, he outshone every one of his companions by the zealous manner in which he performed any trifling service that might conceivably bring pleasure to the Queen. Thus it came about that whenever the Queen was obliged to go out on horseback, she preferred to ride the palfrey that was under his care, rather than any of the others. On these occasions, the fellow considered himself to be in his seventh heaven, and he would remain close beside her stirrup, almost swooning with joy whenever he was able simply to brush against the lady's clothes.

However, one frequently finds in affairs of this sort that the weakening of expectation goes hand in hand with a strengthening of the initial passion, and that is exactly what happened in the case of this poor groom. So much so, in fact, that having no glimmer of hope to sustain him, he found it increasingly difficult to keep his secret yearnings under control, and since he was unable to rid himself of his passion, he kept telling himself that he would have to die. In reflecting on the ways and the means, he was determined to die in such a manner that his motive, in other words his love for the Queen, would be inferred from the circumstances leading up to his death. And at the same time, he resolved that these circumstances should offer him an opportunity of trying his luck and seeing whether he could bring his desires either wholly or partially to fruition. Knowing that it would be quite futile to start either confiding in the Queen or writing letters to acquaint her with his love, he thought he would explore the possibility of entering her bed by means of a stratagem. He had already discovered that the King was not in the habit of invariably sleeping with her, and hence the one and only stratagem that might conceivably succeed was for him to find some way of impersonating the King so that he could approach her quarters and gain admittance to her bedchamber.

Accordingly, with the aim of discovering how the King was dressed and what procedure he followed when paying the Queen a visit, the groom concealed himself for several nights running in the King's palace, in a spacious hall situated between the respective royal bedchambers. And during one of these nocturnal vigils, he saw the King emerge from his room in an enormous cloak, with a flaming torch in one hand and a stick in the other.[3] Walking over to the Queen's room, the King knocked once or twice on the door with his stick, whereupon he was instantly admitted and the torch was removed from his hand. Some time later, the King retired in like fashion to his own quarters, and the groom, who had been keeping a careful watch, decided that he too would have to adopt this same ritual. He therefore procured a torch and a stick, and a cloak similar to the one he had seen the King wearing, and having soaked himself thoroughly in a hot bath so that there should be no possibility of his giving offence to the Queen or arousing her suspicions by smelling of the stable, he transported these articles to the great hall and concealed himself in his usual place.

When he sensed that everyone was asleep, and that the time had finally come for him to gratify his longing or perish nobly in the attempt, he kindled a small flame with the aid of a flint and steel that he had brought along for the purpose, lit his torch, and, wrapping himself carefully up in the folds of the cloak, walked over to the door of the bedchamber and knocked twice with his stick. The door was opened by a chambermaid, still half asleep, who took the light and put it aside, whereupon without uttering a sound he stepped inside the curtain, divested himself of his cloak, and clambered into the bed where the Queen was sleeping. Knowing that the King, whenever he was angry about anything, was in the habit of refusing all discourse, he drew the Queen lustfully into his arms with a show of gruff impatience, and without a single word passing between them, he repeatedly made her carnal acquaintance. He was most reluctant to depart, but nevertheless he eventually arose, fearing lest by over-staying his welcome the delight he had experienced should be turned into sorrow, and having donned his cloak and retrieved his torch, he stole wordlessly away and returned as swiftly as possible to his own bed.

He could hardly have reached his destination when, to the Queen's utter amazement, the King himself turned up in her room, climbed into bed, and offered her a cheerful greeting.

'Heavens!' she said, emboldened to speak by his affable manner. 'Whatever has come over you tonight, my lord? You no sooner leave me, after enjoying me more passionately than usual, than you come back and start all over again! Do take care of your health!'

On hearing these words, the King immediately came to the conclusion that the Queen had been taken in by an outward resemblance to his own physique and manner. But he was a wise man, and since neither the Queen nor anybody else appeared to have noticed the deception, he had no hesitation in deciding to keep his own counsel. Many a stupid man would have reacted differently, and exclaimed: 'It was not I. Who was the man who was here? What happened? Who was it who came?' But this would only have led to complications, upsetting the lady when she was blameless and sowing the seeds of a desire, on her part, to repeat the experience. And besides, by holding his tongue his honour remained unimpaired, whereas if he were to talk he would make himself look ridiculous.

And so, showing little sign of his turbulent inner feelings either in his speech or in his facial expression, the King answered her as follows:

'Do you think, my dear, that I am incapable of returning to you a second time after being here once already?'

'Oh no, my lord,' the lady replied. 'But all the same, I beg you not to overdo it.'

'Your advice is sound, and I intend to follow it,' said the King. 'I shall go away again, and bother you no further tonight.'

And so, boiling with anger and indignation because of the trick that had clearly been played upon him, he put on his cloak again and departed, bent upon tracking the culprit quietly down, for the King supposed that he must be a member of the household, in which case, no matter who the fellow was, he would still be within the palace walls.

Accordingly, having equipped himself with a small lantern shedding very little light, he made his way to a dormitory above the palace-stables containing a long row of beds, where nearly all of his servants slept. And since he calculated that the author of the deed to which the lady had referred would not yet have had time to recover a normal pulse and heartbeat after his exertions, the King began at one end of the dormitory and went silently along the row, placing his hand on each man's chest in order to discover whether his heart was still pounding.

Although all the others were sleeping soundly, the one who had been with the Queen was still awake. And when he saw the King approaching, he realized what he was looking for and grew very frightened, with the result that the pounding of his heart, already considerable because of his recent labours, was magnified by his fear. He was convinced that the King would have him instantly put to death if he were to notice the way his heart was racing, and reflected on various possible courses of action. Eventually, however, on observing that the King was unarmed, he decided he would pretend to be asleep and wait for the King to make the first move.

Having examined a large number of the sleepers without finding the man he was looking for, the King came eventually to the groom, and on discovering that his heart was beating strongly, he said to himself: 'This is the one.' Since, however, he had no wish to broadcast his intentions, all he did was to shear away a portion of the hair on one side of the man's head, using a pair of scissors that he had brought along for the purpose. In those days, men wore their hair very long, and the King left this mark so that he could identify him by it next morning. He then departed from the scene, and returned to his own room.

The groom had witnessed the whole episode, and being of a sharp disposition, he realized all too clearly why he had been marked in this particular fashion. He therefore leapt out of bed without a moment's delay, and having laid his hands on one of several pairs of shears that happened to be kept in the stable for grooming the horses, he silently made the rounds of all the sleeping forms in the dormitory and cut everybody's hair in precisely the same way as his own, just above the ear. Having completed his mission without being detected, he crept back to bed and went to sleep.

When he arose the next morning, the King gave orders for the palace gates to remain closed until his whole household had appeared before him, and they duly assembled in his presence, all of them bare-headed. The King then began to inspect them with the intention of picking out the man whose hair he had shorn, only to discover, to his amazement, that the hair on most of their heads had been cut in exactly similar fashion.

'This fellow I'm looking for may be low-born,' he said to himself, 'but he clearly has all his wits about him.'

Then, realizing that he could not achieve his aim without raising a clamour, and not wishing to bring enormous shame upon himself for the sake of a trifling act of revenge, he decided to deal with the culprit by issuing a stern word of warning and showing him that his deed had not passed undetected.

'Whoever it was who did it,' he said, addressing himself to the whole assembly, 'he'd better not do it again. And now, be off with you.'

Many another man would have wanted to have all of them strung up, tortured, examined and interrogated. But in so doing, he would have brought into the open a thing that people should always try their utmost to conceal. And even if, by displaying his hand, he had secured the fullest possible revenge, he would not have lessened his shame but greatly increased it, as well as besmirching the fame of his lady.

Not unnaturally, the King's little speech caused quite a stir amongst his listeners, and a long time subsequently elapsed before they grew tired of discussing between themselves what it could have meant. But nobody divined its import except the one man for whom it was intended, and he was far too shrewd ever to throw any light on the subject while the King was still alive, nor did he ever risk his life again in performing any deed of a similar nature.

THIRD STORY

Under the pretext of going to confession and being very pure-minded, a lady who is enamoured of a young man induces a solemn friar to pave the way unwittingly for the total fulfilment of her desires.

Pampinea was now silent, and the bravery and prudence of the groom were praised by most of her listeners, who likewise applauded the wisdom of the King. Then the queen turned to Filomena, enjoining her to continue, whereupon Filomena began to speak, gracefully, as follows:

The story I propose to relate, concerning the manner in which a sanctimonious friar was well and truly hoodwinked by a pretty woman, should prove all the more agreeable to a lay audience inasmuch as the priesthood consists for the most part of extremely stupid men, inscrutable in their ways, who consider themselves in all respects more worthy and knowledgeable than other people, whereas they are decidedly inferior. They resemble pigs, in fact, for they are too feeble-minded to earn an honest living like everybody else, and so they install themselves wherever they can fill their stomachs.

It is not only in obedience to the command I have received, dear ladies, that I shall tell you this story. I also wish to impress upon you that even the clergy, to whom we women pay far too much heed on account of our excessive credulity, are capable of being smartly deceived, as indeed they sometimes are, both by men and by one or two of ourselves.

A few short years ago, in our native city, where fraud and cunning prosper more than love or loyalty, there was a noblewoman of striking beauty and impeccable breeding, who was endowed by Nature with as lofty a temperament and shrewd an intellect as could be found in any other woman of her time. Although I could disclose her name, along with those of the other persons involved in this story, I have no intention of doing so, for if I did, certain people still living would be made to look utterly contemptible, whereas the whole matter should really be passed off as a huge joke.

This lady, being of gentle birth and finding herself married off to a master woollen-draper because he happened to be very rich, was unable to stifle her heartfelt contempt, for she was firmly of the opinion that no man of low condition, however wealthy, was deserving of a noble wife. And on discovering that all he was capable of, despite his massive wealth, was distinguishing wool from cotton, supervising the setting up of a loom, or debating the virtues of a particular yarn with a spinner-woman, she resolved that as far as it lay within her power she would have nothing whatsoever to do with his beastly caresses. Moreover she was determined to seek her pleasure elsewhere, in the company of one who seemed more worthy of her affection, and so it was that she fell deeply in love with an extremely eligible man in his middle thirties. And whenever a day passed without her having set eyes upon him, she was restless for the whole of the following night.

However, the gentleman suspected nothing of all this, and took no notice of her; and for her part, being very cautious, she would not venture to declare her love by dispatching a maidservant or writing him a letter, for fear of the dangers that this might entail.

But having perceived that he was on very friendly terms with a certain priest, a rotund, uncouth individual who was nevertheless regarded as an outstandingly able friar on account of his very saintly way of life, she calculated that this fellow would serve as an ideal go-between for her and the man she loved. And so, after reflecting on the strategy she would adopt, she paid a visit, at an appropriate hour of the day, to the church where he was to be found, and having sought him out, she asked him whether he would agree to confess her.

Since he could tell at a glance that she was a lady of quality, the friar gladly heard her confession, and when she had got to the end of it, she continued as follows:

'Father, as I shall explain to you presently, there is a certain matter about which I am compelled to seek your advice and assistance. Having already told you my name, I feel sure you will know my family and my husband. He loves me more dearly than life itself, and since he is enormously rich, he never has the slightest difficulty or hesitation in supplying me with every single object for which I display a yearning. Consequently, my love for him is quite unbounded, and if my mere thoughts, to say nothing of my actual behaviour, were to run contrary to his wishes and his honour, I would be more deserving of hellfire than the wickedest woman who ever lived.

'Now, there is a certain person, of respectable outward appearance, who unless I am mistaken is a close acquaintance of yours. I really couldn't say what his name is, but he is tall and handsome, his clothes are brown and elegantly cut, and, possibly because he is unaware of my resolute nature, he appears to have laid siege to me. He turns up infallibly whenever I either look out of a window or stand at the front door or leave the house, and I am surprised, in fact, that he is not here now. Needless to say, I am very upset about all this, because his sort of conduct frequently gives an honest woman a bad name, even though she is quite innocent.

'I have made up my mind on several occasions to inform my brothers about him. But then it has occurred to me that men are apt to be tactless in their handling of these matters, and when they receive a dusty answer they start bandying words with one another

and eventually somebody gets hurt. So in order to avoid unpleasantness and scandal, I have always held my tongue. Since, however,
you appear to be a friend of his, I decided I would break my silence,
for after all it is perfectly proper for you to censure people for this
kind of behaviour, no matter whether they are your friends or total
strangers. For the love of God, therefore, I implore you to speak to
him severely and persuade him to refrain from his importunities.
There are plenty of other women who doubtless find this sort of
thing amusing, and who will enjoy being ogled and spied upon by
him, but I personally have no inclination for it whatsoever, and I
find his behaviour exceedingly disagreeable.'

And having reached the end of her speech, the lady bowed her
head as though she were going to burst into tears.

The reverend friar realized immediately who it was to whom she
was referring, and having warmly commended her purity of mind
(for he firmly believed she was telling the truth), he promised to
take all necessary steps to ensure that the fellow ceased to annoy her.
Moreover, knowing her to be very rich, he expounded the advan-
tages of charitable deeds and almsgiving, and told her all about his
needy condition, whereupon the lady said:

'Please do restrain him, for the love of God; and if he should
deny it, by all means tell him who it was who informed you and
complained to you about it.'

Then, having completed her confession and received her penance,
suddenly remembering the friar's injunctions to her on the subject
of almsgiving, she casually stuffed his palm with money and requested him to say a few masses for the souls of her departed ones,
after which she got up from where she was kneeling at his feet, and
made her way home.

Shortly afterwards, the gentleman in question paid one of his
regular visits to the reverend friar, and after they had conversed
together for a while on general topics, the friar drew him to one
side and reproached him in a very kindly sort of way for the
amorous glances which, as the lady had given him to understand, he
believed him to be casting in her direction.

Not unnaturally, the gentleman was amazed, for he had never so
much as looked at the lady and it was very seldom that he passed by

her house. But when he started to protest his innocence, the friar interrupted him.

'Now it's no use pretending to be shocked,' he said, 'or wasting your breath denying it, because you simply haven't a leg to stand on. This is no piece of idle gossip that I picked up from her neighbours. I had it from the lady's own lips, when she came here complaining bitterly about your behaviour. And apart from the fact that a man of your age ought to know better than to engage in such frivolous activities, I might inform you that I have never come across any woman possessing a more violent distaste for irresponsible conduct of that sort. So, out of regard for your own reputation and the lady's peace of mind, be so good as to desist and leave her in peace.'

The gentleman, being rather more perceptive than the reverend friar, was not exactly slow to appreciate the lady's cleverness, and putting on a somewhat sheepish expression, he promised not to bother her any more. But after leaving the friar, he made his way towards the house of the lady, who was keeping continuous vigil at a tiny little window so that she would see him if he happened to pass by. When she saw him coming, she smiled at him so prettily that he was able to conclude beyond all doubt that his interpretation of the friar's words was correct. And from that day forward, proceeding with the maximum of prudence and conveying the impression that he was engaged in some other business entirely, he became a regular visitor to the neighbourhood, thereby deriving much pleasure and affording the lady considerable delight and satisfaction. It was not long, however, before the lady, having by now ascertained that her fondness for him was reciprocated, became eager to stimulate his passion and demonstrate how deeply she loved him. At the first available opportunity, therefore, she returned to the reverend friar, and, kneeling in the church at his feet, she burst into tears.

On seeing this, the friar asked her in soothing tones what new affliction was troubling her.

'Father,' replied the lady, 'my new affliction is none other than that accursed friend of yours, of whom I complained to you the other day. I honestly believe he was born to tempt me into doing something that I shall regret for the rest of my days. And, in that case, I shall never have the courage to kneel before you again.'

'What!' said the friar. 'Do you mean to say he is still annoying you?'

'He certainly is,' said the lady. 'Indeed, he appears to have taken exception to my complaining to you about him, and ever since, as though out of pure malice, he has been turning up seven times more often than he did before. Would to God that he was satisfied with parading up and down and staring at me, but yesterday he had the bare-faced impertinence to send a maidservant to me, in my own house, with his nonsensical prattle, and he sent me a belt and a purse, as though I didn't have enough belts and purses already. It made me absolutely furious, indeed it still does, and if I had not been afraid of committing a sin and hence incurring your displeasure, I would have stirred up a scandal there and then. So far, however, I have managed to restrain myself, because I did not wish to do or say anything without informing you first.

'As for the belt and the purse, I immediately handed them back to the woman who brought them, telling her to return them to her employer, and sent her off with a flea in her ear. But then it occurred to me that she might keep them for herself and tell him I had accepted them, and so I called her back and snatched them out of her hands in a blazing temper. I decided to bring them along to you instead, so that you could hand them back and tell him I have no need of his goods, because thanks both to God and to my husband, I possess so many belts and purses that I could bury myself under them. And I am sorry to have to say it, father, but if he doesn't stop pestering me after this, I shall tell my husband and brothers, come what may. For if needs be, I would much rather have him take a severe hiding than allow him to besmirch my good name. And that's all there is to it, father.'

She was still sobbing uncontrollably when, having come to the end of her speech, she extracted a very splendid, expensive-looking purse from beneath her cloak together with a gorgeous little belt, and hurled them into the lap of the friar, who, being fully taken in by her story, was feeling exceedingly distressed and accepted them without any question.

'Daughter,' he said, 'I am not surprised that you are so upset by what has happened, and I certainly cannot blame you. On the contrary, I am full of admiration for the way you have followed my advice in this affair. He has obviously failed to keep the promise he gave me the other day, when I first took him to task. Nevertheless, I believe that this latest outrage of his, following in the wake of his earlier misdemeanours, will enable me to give him such a severe scolding that he will not trouble you any further. In the meantime, you must with God's blessing contain your anger and refrain from informing any of your relatives, because that could bring him altogether too heavy a punishment. Never fear that this will harm your good name, for I shall always be here to bear unwavering witness, whether before God or before men, to your virtuous nature.'

The lady gave the appearance of being somewhat mollified, and then, knowing how covetous he and his fellow friars were, she moved on to another subject.

'Father,' she said, 'for the past few nights I have been dreaming about various departed relatives of mine, and they all appear to be suffering dreadful torments and continually asking for alms, especially my mother, who seems to be in such a state of affliction and misery that it would break your heart to see her. I think she is suffering abominably at seeing me persecuted like this by that enemy of God, and hence I should like you to pray for their souls and say the forty masses of Saint Gregory,[1] so that God may release them from this scourging fire.' And so saying, she slipped a florin into his hand.

The reverend friar gleefully pocketed the money, and having poured out a torrent of fine words and pious tales to reinforce her godliness, he gave her his blessing and let her go.

Unaware that he had been hoodwinked, the friar watched her depart and then summoned his friend, who realized as soon as he arrived, from the friar's agitated appearance, that he was about to receive some news from the lady, and waited to hear what the friar had to say. The latter repeated all that he had said to him previously, and for the second time, angrily and without mincing his words, gave him a severe scolding for what the lady alleged he had done.

Being as yet unsure of which way the friar was going to jump, the gentleman denied having sent the purse and the belt, speaking without much conviction so as not to undermine the friar's belief in the story, just in case he had heard it from the lady herself.

The friar practically exploded with rage.

'What!' he said. 'Can you really have the effrontery to deny it, you scoundrel? Here, take a look at them – she brought them to me herself, with her eyes full of tears – and tell me whether or not you recognize them!'

The gentleman put on a display of acute embarrassment.

'Yes, indeed I do,' he said. 'I admit that it was wrong of me, and now that I fully appreciate her inclinations, I guarantee that you won't be troubled again.'

The words now started to flow in good earnest, and eventually the blockhead of a friar handed over the purse and the belt to his friend. Finally, after preaching him a lengthy sermon and getting him to promise that he would call a halt to his importunities, he sent him about his business.

The gentleman was feeling absolutely delighted, for not only did it appear quite certain that the lady loved him, but he had also received a handsome present. On leaving the friar, he went and stood in a sheltered place from which he showed his lady that both of the items were now in his possession, all of which made her very happy, the more so because her scheme appeared to be working better and better. All that she was waiting for now, in order to bring her work to a successful conclusion, was for her husband to go away somewhere, and not long afterwards it so happened that he was indeed called away on business to Genoa.

The next morning, after he had ridden off on horseback, the lady paid yet another visit to the reverend friar, filling his ears with sobs and lamentations.

'Father,' she said. 'I simply cannot bear it any longer. However, since I did promise you the other day that I wouldn't do anything without telling you first, I have come now to offer you my apologies in advance. And lest you should imagine that my tears and complaints are unjustified, I want to tell you what that friend of yours, or rather, that devil incarnate, did to me early this morning, a little before matins.

'I don't know what unfortunate accident led him to discover that my husband went away to Genoa yesterday morning, but during the night, at the hour I mentioned, he forced his way into the grounds and climbed up a tree to my bedroom-window, which overlooks the garden. He had already opened the window and was about to enter the room, when I awoke with a start, leapt out of bed, and began to scream. And I would have continued to scream but for the fact that he announced who he was and implored me to stop for your sake and for the love of God. Not wishing to cause you any distress, I stopped screaming, and since he was not yet inside, I rushed to the window, naked as on the day I was born, and slammed it in his face, after which I think the rogue must have taken himself off, because I heard no more of him. Now, I leave you to judge whether this sort of thing is either pleasant or permissible, but I personally have no intention of allowing him to get away with it any longer. In fact, I've already put up with more than enough of his antics for your sake.'

The lady's story threw the friar into such a state of turmoil that all he could do by way of reply was to ask her, over and over again, whether she was quite sure that it had not been some other man.

'Merciful God!' she replied. 'I ought to know the man by now! It was he, I tell you, and if he denies it, don't you believe him.'

'Daughter,' replied the friar, 'all I can say is that he has taken an unpardonable liberty and carried things beyond all reasonable bounds, and you took the proper course in sending him off as you did. But I would implore you, since God has protected you from dishonour, that just as you have followed my advice on the two previous occasions, you should do so again this time. Do not, in other words, complain to any of your kinsfolk, but leave things to me, and I shall see whether I can restrain this headstrong devil, whom I had always thought of as such a saintly person. If I can succeed in taming the beast that possesses him, all well and good. If I can't, then you have my blessing and my permission to follow your instinct and take whatever measures you consider most appropriate.'

'Very well, then,' said the lady. 'I have no wish to upset you, and therefore I shall follow your instructions just once more. But you'd better see that he takes care not to pester me again, because I promise you that if there's any more of it, I shan't be coming back to you.' And without saying another word, she turned her back on the friar and strode away.

She had hardly left the church when the gentleman arrived and was summoned by the friar, who drew him aside and gave him the fiercest scolding anyone ever had, calling him a disloyal traitor and a perjurer.

Having twice previously had occasion to observe the eventual drift of these reprimands, the man was careful not to commit himself, but simply tried to wheedle an explanation out of the friar by interpolating ambiguous comments, his first words being:

'Why are you creating such a fuss? Anyone would think I had crucified Christ.'

'For shame, you villain!' exclaimed the friar. 'Just listen to the man! He talks for all the world as if a year or two had passed, blotting out the memory of his wickedness and depravity. Can you have forgotten the offence you perpetrated in the short time that has elapsed since matins? Where were you this morning, a little before dawn?'

'I don't recall where I was,' replied the gentleman. 'But it didn't take you long to find out.'

'It certainly did not,' said the friar. 'I presume you were under the impression, since the husband was away, that the good lady would promptly welcome you into her arms. By heavens, sir, you're a fine gentleman! No mistake about it. A nocturnal prowler, a garden invader, and a tree climber, all rolled into one! Do you think you're going to conquer this lady's integrity through sheer impudence, clambering up trees to windows in the small hours? There's nothing in the world that she loathes more profoundly than these importunities of yours, and yet you still persist with them. Even supposing, however, that she had not made her attitude perfectly plain, you appear to have taken a fat lot of notice of my admonitions. Now, just listen to me. It isn't because she loves you that she has refrained, so far, from telling anyone about your importunities, but merely because I pleaded with her not to speak out. But she will not hold her peace any longer. I have given her my permission, if you annoy her just once more, to take whatever action she thinks best. What are you going to do if she informs her brothers?'

Having gathered all the information he needed, the gentleman pacified the friar to the best of his ability with a string of specious promises, and went about his business. Next morning, at the hour of matins, having broken into the garden, scaled the tree, and found the window open, he entered the bedroom, and before you could say knife he was lying in the arms of his fair mistress. And as she had been awaiting his arrival with intense longing, she gave him a rapturous welcome.

'A thousand thanks to our friend the friar,' she said, 'for instructing you so impeccably how to get here.'

Then, each enjoying the other to the accompaniment of many a hilarious comment about the stupid friar's naïveté, and random jibes about such draperly concerns as slubbing and combing and carding, they gambolled and frolicked until they very nearly died of bliss. After this first encounter, having devoted some little thought to the subject, they arranged matters in such a way that, without having further recourse to their friend the friar, they slept together no less pleasurably on many later occasions. And I pray to God that in the bountifulness of His mercy He may very soon conduct me, along with all other like-minded Christian souls, to a similar fate.

FOURTH STORY

Dom Felice teaches Friar Puccio how to attain blessedness by carrying out a certain penance, and whilst Friar Puccio is following his instructions, Dom Felice has a high old time with the penitent's wife.

When, having reached the end of her story, Filomena lapsed into silence, Dioneo added a few well-turned phrases of his own, warmly commending both the anonymous lady and the prayer with which Filomena had rounded off her narrative. Then the queen, laughing, looked towards Panfilo and said:

'Now, Panfilo, let us have some agreeable trifle to add to our enjoyment.'

Having promptly expressed his willingness to comply with her command, Panfilo began as follows:

Madam, many are those who, whilst they are busy making strenuous efforts to get to Paradise, unwittingly send some other person there in their stead; and not very long ago, as you are now about to hear, this happy fate befell a lady living in our city.

Close beside the Church of San Pancrazio, or so I have been told, there once lived a prosperous, law-abiding citizen called Puccio di Rinieri, who was totally absorbed in affairs of the spirit, and on reaching a certain age, became a tertiary in the Franciscan Order,[1] assuming the name of Friar Puccio. In pursuit of these spiritual interests of his, since the other members of his household consisted solely of a wife and maidservant, which relieved him of the necessity of practising a profession, he attended church with unfailing regularity. Being a simple, well-intentioned soul, he recited his paternosters, attended sermons, went to mass, and turned up infallibly whenever lauds were being sung by the lay-members. Moreover, he practised fasting and other forms of self-discipline, and it was rumoured that he was a member of the flagellants.

His wife, who was called Monna Isabetta, was still a young woman of about twenty-eight to thirty, and she was as shapely, fair and fresh-complexioned as a round, rosy apple, but because of her husband's godliness and possibly on account of his age, she was continually having to diet, so to speak, for much longer periods than she would have wished. Thus it frequently happened, that when she was in the mood for going to bed, or, in other words, playing games with him, he would treat her to an account of the life of Our Lord, following this up with the sermons of Brother Anastasius or the Plaint of the Magdalen[2] or other pieces in a similar vein.

And that was how matters stood when a certain Dom Felice, a handsomely built young man who was one of the conventual monks at San Pancrazio, returned from a sojourn in Paris. This Dom Felice was a man of acute intelligence and profound learning, and Friar Puccio assiduously cultivated his friendship. And because, in addition to being very good at resolving all of Friar Puccio's spiritual problems, Dom Felice went out of his way, knowing the sort of person he was, to give him the impression that he was exceedingly saintly, Friar Puccio formed the habit of taking him home and offering him lunch, or supper, according to the time of day. And in order to please her husband, Monna Isabetta became equally friendly with him and did all she possibly could to make him feel at home.

In the course of his regular visits to Friar Puccio's house, the monk therefore had every opportunity to observe this shapely little wife, blooming with vitality, and being quick to realize what it was that she lacked most, he decided, in order to spare Friar Puccio the trouble, that he would do his level best to supply it. And so, taking good care not to arouse the Friar's suspicions, he began to cast meaningful glances in her direction, with the result that he kindled in her breast a yearning that corresponded to his own. On perceiving her response to his advances, the monk seized the earliest opportunity to acquaint her verbally with his intentions. But although he found her very willing to give effect to his proposals, it was impossible to do so because she would not risk an assignation with the monk in any other place except her own house, and her own house was ruled out because Friar Puccio never went away from the town, all of which made the monk very disconsolate.

However, after devoting a great deal of thought to the subject, he lighted upon a foolproof method for keeping company with the lady in her own house, even though Friar Puccio happened to be under the same roof. And one day, when Friar Puccio called round to see him, he spoke to him as follows:

'It has been obvious to me for some time, Friar Puccio, that your one overriding ambition in life is to achieve saintliness, but you appear to be approaching it in a roundabout way, whereas there is a much more direct route which is known to the Pope and his chief prelates, who, although they use it themselves, have no desire to publicize its existence. For if the secret were to leak out, the clergy, who live for the most part on the proceeds of charity, would immediately disintegrate, because the lay public would no longer give them their support, whether by way of almsgiving or in any other form. However, you are a friend of mine and you have been very good to me, and if I could be certain that you would not reveal it to another living soul, and that you wanted to give it a trial, I would tell you how it is done.'

Being anxious to learn all about it, Friar Puccio began by earnestly begging Dom Felice to teach him the secret, then he swore that he would never, without Dom Felice's express permission, breathe a word about it to anyone, at the same time declaring that provided it was the sort of thing he could manage, he would apply himself to it with a will.

'Since you have given me your promise,' said the monk, 'I will let you in on the secret. There is one thing, though, that I must emphasize. True, the doctors of the Church maintain that any person who wishes to attain blessedness should perform the penance I am about to describe. But listen carefully. I do not say that after doing the penance you will automatically cease to be a sinner. What will happen is this, that all the sins you have committed up to the moment of doing the penance will be purged and remitted as a result. And as for those you commit afterwards, they will never be counted as deadly sins, but on the contrary they will be erased by holy water, as happens already in the case of the venial ones.

'Now, let us proceed. It is necessary, first and foremost, for the penitent to confess his sins with very great thoroughness immediately before beginning the penance; and next, he must start to fast and practise a most rigorous form of abstinence, this to continue for forty days, during which you must abstain, not only from the company of other women, but even from touching your own wife. In addition, it is necessary to have some place in your own house from which you can look up at the heavens after night has fallen, and to which you will proceed at compline,[3] having first positioned a very broad plank there in such a way that you can stand with your back resting against it, and, keeping your feet on the floor, extend your arms outwards in an attitude of crucifixion; and by the way, if you want to support them on a couple of wall-pegs, that'll be perfectly all right. With your eyes fixed on the heavens, you must maintain this same posture, without moving a muscle, until matins. If you happened to be a scholar, you would, during the course of the night, be obliged to recite certain special prayers which I would give you to learn; but since you are not, you will have to say three hundred paternosters and three hundred Hail Marys in honour of the Trinity. As you gaze towards Heaven, you must constantly bear in mind that God created Heaven and earth. And at the same time, you must concentrate on the Passion of Christ, for you will be re-enacting His own condition on the cross.

'As soon as you hear the bell ringing for matins, you may, if you wish, proceed to your bed and lie down, fully dressed, for a short sleep. Later in the morning you must go to church, listen to at least three masses, and say fifty paternosters followed by the same number of Hail Marys. Then you must attend unobtrusively to your business, if you have any, after which you will take lunch, and report at the church just before vespers in order to recite certain prayers, of which I shall provide you with written copies. (These are absolutely vital, if you want the thing to work.) Finally, at compline, you return to the beginning, and follow the same procedure all over again. I once did all this myself, and I assure you that there is every prospect, if you follow these instructions and put plenty of devotion into it, that before your penance comes to an end you will be experiencing a wonderful sensation of eternal blessedness.'

'This is not too heavy a task,' said Friar Puccio, 'nor does it last very long. It should be quite possible to get the thing done, and I therefore propose, God willing, to make a start this coming Sunday.'

After leaving Dom Felice he went straight home, where, having obtained the monk's permission beforehand, he explained everything to his wife in minute detail.

The lady grasped the monk's intentions all too clearly, particularly when she heard about the business of standing still without moving a muscle until matins. Thinking it an excellent arrangement, she told her husband that she heartily approved of the idea, and also of any other measures he took for the good of his soul, adding that in order to persuade God to make his penance profitable she would join him in fasting, but there she would draw the line.

Thus the whole thing was settled, and on the following Sunday Friar Puccio began his long penance, during which Master Monk, by prior arrangement with the lady, came to supper with her nearly every evening at an hour when he could enter the house unobserved, always bringing with him large quantities of food and drink. Then, after supper, he would sleep with her all night until matins, when he would get up and leave, and Friar Puccio would return to bed.

The place where Friar Puccio had elected to do his penance was adjacent to the room where the lady slept, from which it was separated only by a very thin wall. And one night, when Master Monk was cutting too merry a caper with the lady and she with him, Friar Puccio thought he could detect a certain amount of vibration in the floorboards. When, therefore, he had recited a hundred of his paternosters, he came to a stop, and without leaving his post, he called out to his wife and demanded to know what she was doing.

His wife, who had a talent for repartee, and who at that moment was possibly riding bareback astride the nag of Saint Benedict or Saint John Gualbert,[4] replied:

'Heaven help me, dear husband, I am shaking like mad.'

'Shaking?' said Friar Puccio. 'What is the meaning of all this shaking?'

His wife shrieked with laughter, for she was a lively, energetic sort of woman, and besides, she was probably laughing for a good reason.

'What?' she replied. 'You don't know its meaning? Haven't I heard you saying, hundreds of times: "He that supper doth not take, in his bed all night will shake"?'

Since she had already given him the impression that she was fasting, Friar Puccio readily assumed this to be the cause of her sleeplessness, which in turn accounted for the way she was tossing and turning in bed.

'Wife,' he replied, in all innocence, 'I told you not to fast, but you would insist. Try not to think about it. Try and go to sleep. You're tossing about so violently in the bed that you're shaking the whole building.'

'Don't worry about me,' said his wife. 'I know what I'm doing. Just you keep up the good work, and I'll try and do the same.'

So Friar Puccio said no more, but turned his attention once again to his paternosters. From that night onward, Master Monk and the lady made up a bed in another part of the house, in which they cavorted to their hearts' content until the time came for the monk to leave, when the lady would return to her usual bed, being joined there shortly afterwards by Friar Puccio as he staggered in from his penance.

Thus, while the Friar carried on with his penance, his wife carried on with the monk, pausing now and then to deliver the same merry quip:

'You make Friar Puccio do penance, but we are the ones who go to Paradise.'

The lady was of the opinion that she had never felt better in her life, and having been compelled to diet by her husband for so long, she acquired such a taste for the monk's victuals that when Friar Puccio reached the end of his long penance, she found a way of banqueting with the monk elsewhere. And for a long time thereafter, she continued discreetly to enjoy such repasts.

To return to my opening remarks then, this was how it came about that Friar Puccio did penance with the intention of reaching Paradise, to which on the contrary he sent both the monk, who had shown him how to get there quickly, and his wife, who shared his house but lived in dire need of something which Master Monk, being a charitable soul, supplied her with in great abundance.

FIFTH STORY

Zima presents a palfrey to Messer Francesco Vergellesi, who responds by granting him permission to converse with his wife. She is unable to speak, but Zima answers on her behalf, and in due course his reply comes true.

The ladies shook with laughter over Panfilo's story of Friar Puccio, and when he had finished, the queen, with womanly grace, called upon Elissa to continue. Whereupon, speaking rather haughtily, not from affectation but from habit long established, Elissa began to address them as follows: .

Many people imagine, because they know a great deal, that other people know nothing; and it frequently happens that when they think they are hoodwinking others, they later discover that they have themselves been outwitted by their intended victims. Consequently I consider it is quite insane for anyone to put another person's powers of intelligence to the test when he has no need to do so. But since, possibly, there are those who would not share my opinion, I should like, without straying from the topic of our discussion, to tell you what happened once to a certain nobleman of Pistoia.

The nobleman in question was called Messer Francesco, and belonged to the Vergellesi family of Pistoia.[1] He was a very wealthy and judicious man, and he was also shrewd, but at the same time he was exceedingly mean. On being appointed Governor of Milan, he laid in all the paraphernalia appropriate to his new rank before setting out for that city, but was unable however to find a palfrey handsome enough to suit his requirements, and this caused him no small concern.

Now, in Pistoia at that time there was a very rich young man of humble birth called Ricciardo, who because of his well-groomed, elegant appearance was generally referred to by all the townspeople as Zima, or in other words, the Dandy. For a long time he had loved and wooed, without success, the exceedingly beautiful and virtuous wife of Messer Francesco, and it so happened that this man owned one of the finest palfreys in Tuscany, to which he was deeply attached because of its beauty. And since it was common knowledge that he was madly fond of Messer Francesco's wife, someone told Messer Francesco that if he asked for the palfrey he was bound to get it on account of Zima's devotion to his lady.

Spurred on by his greed, Messer Francesco sent for Zima and asked him to sell him the palfrey, in the expectation that Zima would hand it over for nothing.

'Sir,' replied Zima, liking the sound of the nobleman's request, 'if you were to offer me everything you possess in the world you could not buy my palfrey: but you could certainly have it as a gift, whenever you liked, on this one condition, that before you take possession of it, you allow me, in your presence, to address a few words to your good lady in sufficient privacy for my words to be heard by her and by nobody else.'

Prompted by his avarice, and hoping to make a fool of the other fellow, the nobleman agreed to Zima's proposal, adding that he could talk to her for as long as he liked. And having left him to wait in the great hall of his palace, he went to his wife's room, explained to her how easy it would be to win the palfrey, and obliged her to come and listen to Zima; but she was to be very careful not to utter so much as a single word in reply to anything he said.

Although she strongly resented being involved in this arrangement, nevertheless, since she was obliged to do her husband's bidding, the lady agreed and followed him into the great hall in order to hear what Zima; had to say. Zima took the nobleman aside to confirm the terms of their agreement, then went to sit with the lady in a corner of the hall that was well beyond everyone else's hearing.

'Illustrious lady,' he began, 'since you are not imperceptive, you will undoubtedly have become well aware, long before now, that I am deeply in love with you, not only because of your beauty, which without any question surpasses that of every other woman I ever saw, but also on account of your laudable manners and singular virtues, any one of which would be sufficient to capture the heart of the noblest man alive. It is thus unnecessary for me to offer you a long-winded account of my love for you. Suffice it to say that no man ever loved any woman more deeply or more ardently, and that I shall continue to do so unfailingly for as long as life sustains this poor, suffering body of mine, and longer still; for if, in the life hereafter, people love as they do on earth, I shall love you for ever. Consequently, you may rest assured that there is nothing you possess, be it precious or trifling, that you can regard as so peculiarly your own or count upon so infallibly under all circumstances as my humble self, and the same applies to all my worldly goods. But so that you may be fully persuaded that this is so, I assure you that I would deem it a greater privilege to be commissioned by you to perform some service that was pleasing to you,

than to have the whole world under my own command and ready
to obey me.

'Since, as you perceive, I belong to you unreservedly, it is not
without reason that I will venture to address my pleas to your noble
heart, which is the one true source of all my peace, all my
contentment, and all my well-being. Dearest beloved, since I am
yours and you alone have the power to fortify my soul with some
vestige of hope as I languish in the fiery flames of love, I beseech
you, as your most humble servant, to show me some mercy and
mitigate the harshness you have been wont to display towards me
in the past. Your compassion will console me, enabling me to claim
that it is to your beauty that I owe, not only my love, but also my
very life, which will assuredly fail unless your proud spirit yields to
my entreaties, and then indeed people will be able to say that you
have killed me. Now, leaving aside the fact that my death would
not enhance your reputation, I believe, also, that your conscience
would occasionally trouble you and you would be sorry for having
been the cause of it, and sometimes, when you were even more
favourably disposed, you would say to yourself: "Alas, how wrong
it was of me not to take pity on my poor Zima!" But this
repentance of yours, coming too late, would only serve to heighten
your distress.

'Therefore, in order to forestall so regrettable an outcome, instead
of allowing me to die, take pity on me whilst there is still time, for
in you alone lies the power of making me the happiest or the most
wretched man alive. It is my hope and my belief that you will not
be so unkind as to allow death to be my reward for such passionate
devotion, and that you will gladly consent to my humble entreaty,
thus restoring my failing spirits, which have turned quite faint with
awe in your gracious presence.'

At this point, his words trailed off into silence and he began to
heave enormous sighs, after which his eyes shed a certain number of
tears and he settled back into his chair to await the noble lady's
answer.

Though she had previously remained unmoved by Zima's protracted courtship, his tilting at the jousts, his *aubades*, and all the
other ways in which he had demonstrated his devotion, the lady

was certainly stirred now by the tender words of affection addressed to her by this passionate suitor, so that, for the first time in her life, she began to understand what it meant to be in love. And despite the fact that, in obedience to her husband's instructions, she said nothing, she was unable to restrain herself from uttering one or two barely perceptible sighs, thus betraying what she would willingly have made clear to Zima, had she been able to reply.

Having waited for some time, only to discover that no answer was forthcoming, Zima was at first perplexed, but gradually began to realize how cleverly the nobleman had played his hand. Even so, as he continued to gaze upon her face, he noticed that every so often her eyes would dart a gleam in his direction, and this, together with the fact that she was obviously having some difficulty in restraining her sighs, filled him with hope and inspired him to improvise a second line of approach. And thus, mimicking the lady's voice whilst she sat and listened, he began to answer his own plea, speaking as follows:

'My poor, dear Zima, you may rest assured that I have been aware for some time of the depth and completeness of your devotion, and what you have just said has made it all the more obvious to me. I am glad of your love, as is only natural, and I would not wish you to suppose, because I have seemed harsh and cruel, that my outward appearance reflected my true feelings towards you. On the contrary, I have always loved you and held you higher than any other man in my affection, but I was obliged to behave as I did for fear both of my husband and of damaging my good name. However, the time is now approaching when I shall be able to show you clearly how much I love you, at the same time offering you some reward for your past and present devotion towards me. Take heart, then, and be of good cheer, for Messer Francesco will leave within the next few days to become Governor of Milan, a fact of which you, who have given him your handsome palfrey for my sake, are already aware. And in the name of the true love I bear you, I give you my solemn promise that within a few days of his departure you will be able to come to me, and we shall bring our love to its total and pleasurable consummation.

'However, since there will be no further opportunity for us to discuss the matter, I must explain without further ado that one day in the near future you will see two towels hanging in the window of my room, which overlooks the garden. On that same evening, after darkness has fallen, you are to come to me, entering by way of the garden-gate and taking good care not to let anyone see you. There you will find me waiting for you, and we shall spend the whole night having all the joy and pleasure of one another that we desire.'

Having impersonated the lady whilst he said all this, Zima now began to speak on his own behalf.

'My dearest,' he answered, 'your kind reply has filled all of my faculties with such a surfeit of happiness that I am scarcely able to express my gratitude. But even if I could go on talking for as long as I wished, it would still be impossible for me to thank you as fully as my feelings dictate and your kindness deserves. I will therefore leave it to your own excellent judgement to imagine what I vainly long to put into words, merely pausing to assure you that I will carry out your instructions to the letter. I will then perhaps be better placed to appreciate the full extent of your generosity towards me, and I will spare no effort to show you all the gratitude of which I am capable. For the present, then, there is nothing further that remains to be said; and hence I will bid you farewell, my dearest, and may God grant you all those joys and blessings that you most eagerly desire.'

The lady never uttered a single word from beginning to end of this interview, and when it was over, Zima got up and began to return in the direction of the nobleman, who, seeing Zima on his feet, walked towards him laughing.

'Well?' he said. 'Don't you agree that I kept my promise?'

'I do not, sir,' Zima replied, 'for you promised that you would allow me to talk to your good lady and you have had me talking to a marble statue.'

This reply greatly pleased the nobleman, who, whilst he had always had a high opinion of the lady, now thought even better of her.

'From now on,' he said, 'that palfrey you owned belongs to me.'

'Quite so,' Zima replied. 'And for all the good it did me to insist on this favour of yours, I might as well have presented it to you without conditions in the first place. Indeed, I wish to God I had, because now you have bought the palfrey and I have got nothing to show for it.'

The nobleman was highly amused by all this, and now that he was supplied with a palfrey, he set out a few days later on the road to Milan and his governorship.

Left at home to her own devices, the lady recalled Zima's words, reflecting how deeply he loved her and how, for her sake, he had given away his palfrey; and on observing him from the house as he passed regularly up and down, she said to herself: 'What am I doing? Why am I throwing away my youth? This husband of mine has gone off to Milan and won't be returning for six whole months. When is he ever going to make up for lost time? When I'm an old woman? Besides, when will I ever find such a lover as Zima? I'm all by myself, and there's nobody to be afraid of. I don't see why I shouldn't enjoy myself whilst I have the chance. I won't always have such a good opportunity as I have at present. Nobody will ever know about it, and even if he were to find out, it's better to do a thing and repent of it than do nothing and regret it.'

The outcome of all this soul-searching was that one day she hung two towels in the window overlooking the garden, in the way Zima had indicated. Zima was overjoyed to see them, and after nightfall he cautiously made his way, unaccompanied, to the lady's garden-gate, which he found unlocked. Thence he proceeded to a second door, leading into the house itself, where he found the gentlewoman waiting for him.

When she saw him coming, she rose to meet him, and welcomed him with open arms. Embracing her and kissing her a hundred thousand times, he followed her up the stairs and they went directly to bed, where they tasted love's ultimate joys. And although this was the first time, it was by no means the last, for not only during the nobleman's absence in Milan but also after his return Zima visited the house again on numerous other occasions, to the exquisite pleasure of both parties.

SIXTH STORY

Ricciardo Minutolo loves the wife of Filippello Sighinolfo, and on hearing of her jealous disposition he tricks her into believing that Filippello has arranged to meet his own wife on the following day at a bagnio and persuades her to go there and see for herself. Later she learns that she has been with Ricciardo, when all the time she thought she was with her husband.

Elissa had nothing further to add, and after they had praised the skill of Zima, the queen called upon Fiammetta to proceed with the next story.

'Willingly, my lady,' replied Fiammetta, laughing gaily; and so she began:

I should like to move away a little from our own city (which is no less fertile in stories for all occasions than in everything else), and tell you something, as Elissa has done already, of events in the world outside. Let us therefore proceed to Naples, and I shall describe how one of those prudes,[1] who profess such a loathing for love, was led by her lover's ingenuity to taste the fruits of love before she even noticed they had blossomed. You will thus, at one and the same time, be forearmed against things that could happen, and entertained by those that actually did.

In the ancient city of Naples, which is perhaps as delectable a city as any to be found in Italy, there once lived a young patrician, immensely rich and blue-blooded, whose name was Ricciardo Minutolo.[2] Although he was married to a charming and very lovely young wife, he fell in love with a lady who by common consent was far more beautiful than any other woman in Naples. A paragon of virtue, she was called Catella, and was married to a young nobleman called Filippello Sighinolfo, whom she loved and cherished more dearly than anything else in the world.

So although Ricciardo Minutolo was in love with this Catella and did all the right things for winning a lady's favour and affection, he was unable to make the slightest impression upon her, and had almost reached the end of his tether. Even if he had known how to free himself from the bonds of love, he was quite incapable of doing so, and yet he could neither die nor see any point in living. And one day, as he languished away in this manner, it happened that certain kinswomen of his urged him very strongly to call a halt to his philandering, pointing out that he was wasting his energies because Catella loved no man except Filippello, towards whom she was so jealously devoted that she suspected the very birds flying through the air, lest they should whisk him away from her.

On learning of Catella's jealousy, Ricciardo suddenly thought of a possible way to gratify his longings. He began to pretend that, having abandoned all hope of winning Catella's affection, he had fallen in love with another lady, and that it was now for her sake that he tilted and jousted and did all the things he had formerly done for Catella. Nor did it take him very long before he convinced nearly everyone in Naples, including Catella, that he was madly in love with this other lady. And so successful was he in sustaining this pretence, that Catella herself, not to mention various other people who had previously snubbed him on account of the attentions he was paying her, began to offer him the same civil, neighbourly greeting, whenever she met him, that she accorded to others.

Now it so happened that one day, during a spell of hot weather, several parties of the Neapolitan nobility, in accordance with local custom, set off for an outing along the sea-coast, where they would lunch and sup before returning home. And on discovering that Catella had gone there with a party of ladies, Ricciardo got together a little group of his own and made for the same place, which he no sooner reached than he received an invitation to join Catella's party. This he accepted after a certain show of reluctance, as though he were not at all anxious to press himself on their company. The ladies then began, with Catella joining in the fun, to pull Ricciardo's leg on the subject of his latest lady-love, whereupon he pretended to take violent offence, thus supplying them with further food for gossip. Eventually, as is the custom on such occasions, several of the ladies wandered off one by one in different directions, until only a handful of them, including Catella, were left behind with Ricciardo, who at a certain point threw off a casual reference to some affair that her husband was supposed to be having. Catella was promptly seized by an attack of jealousy, and her whole body began to throb with a burning desire to know what Ricciardo was talking about. She sat and brooded for a while, but in the end, unable to contain her feelings any longer, she implored Ricciardo, in the name of the lady he loved above all others, to be so good as to explain his remark about Filippello.

'Since you have implored me for *her* sake,' he told her, 'I dare not refuse you anything, no matter what it may be. I am therefore prepared to tell you about it, but you must promise me never to breathe a word of it either to your husband or to anyone else until you have confirmed the truth of my story. This you can do quite easily, and if you like, I will show you how.'

The lady took him up on this offer, which convinced her all the more that he was telling the truth, and swore to him that her lips would remain sealed. They then drew aside from the others so that they would not be overheard.

'Madam,' Ricciardo began, 'if I were still in love with you, as I once was, I would not have the heart to tell you anything that might possibly bring you distress; but since my love for you is now a thing of the past, I shall have fewer misgivings in disclosing exactly what is afoot. I do not know whether Filippello ever took offence at my being in love with you, or whether he mistakenly thought that you reciprocated my love; at all events, he never gave me any such impression. But now, having waited perhaps until such time as he thought me least likely to suspect, he appears to be intent on doing me the same service as he doubtless fears I have done to him: in other words, he is having an affair with my wife. From what I have been able to discover, he has been courting her for some time with the utmost secrecy, sending her a number of messages, all of which she has referred to me; and she has been replying in accordance with my instructions.

'But this very morning, before setting out from home to come here, I found my wife engaged in earnest conversation with some woman whom I instantly recognized for what she was, and so I called my wife and asked her what this person wanted. "It's that brute of a Filippello," she said. "By sending him replies and raising his hopes, you have encouraged him to pester me, and now he says he must know at all costs what I am proposing to do. He tells me that he could make arrangements for us to meet in secret at a bagnio³ in the city, and he refuses to take no for an answer. If it weren't for the fact that you have forced me to lead him on in this way, for reasons best known to yourself, I would have taught him so painful a lesson that he would never have had the courage to look in my direction again." When I heard this, I felt that the fellow was going too far and was no longer to be tolerated, and it seemed to me that I should inform you about it, so that you might know how he rewards that unswerving fidelity of yours which once was almost the death of me.

'Lest you were to imagine, however, that this was all a fairy story, and so as to let you see the whole thing for yourself if you so desired, I prevailed upon my wife to tell the woman, who was still waiting for her answer, that she would present herself at the bagnio tomorrow afternoon around nones, when everyone is asleep. And the woman went away, looking very pleased with herself.

'Now, I don't suppose you imagine I was going to send her to the bagnio. But if I were you, I would see to it that he found *you* there instead of the lady he was expecting; and after playing him on the hook for a while, I would let him perceive who it was he had been consorting with, and regale him with all the abuse he deserved. If you do as I suggest, it is my belief that he will be put to so much shame that we shall both be avenged for his evil designs at a single blow.'

As is usually the way with people who suffer from jealousy, Catella immediately swallowed the whole story without bothering to consider the kind of person who was telling it or whether he could be deceiving her, and began to connect this tale of Ricciardo's with certain things that had happened in the past. Flying into a sudden rage, she said that she would certainly do as he suggested, because after all, it would cost so little effort on her part. And if Filippello really were to turn up, she was determined to make him feel so ashamed of himself that he would never look at another woman again without being stricken with guilt.

Ricciardo was pleased with her reaction, and, feeling that he was making good progress with his scheme, he added a number of other details to reinforce her belief in his story, at the same time extracting a faithful promise that she would never reveal the source of her information.

Next morning, Ricciardo presented his compliments to the good woman who supervised the bagnio that he had mentioned to Catella, explained his intentions, and asked her to give him all the assistance she could. And since she was greatly beholden to him, she willingly agreed to cooperate, and arranged with Ricciardo what she was to do and say.

In the building where the bagnio was situated, the woman had one room that was extremely dark, there being no window to let in the light. And following Ricciardo's instructions, she prepared this room for him and caused it to be furnished with her most comfortable bed, upon which, after he had lunched, Ricciardo lay down and began to wait for Catella to arrive.

Meanwhile, on the previous evening, the lady in question had returned home in high dudgeon after hearing Ricciardo's tale, by which she had allowed herself to be much too easily convinced. Shortly afterwards, Filippello also returned home, and being preoccupied with other matters, he treated her with rather less than his customary affection. This made her considerably more suspicious, and she began saying to herself: 'He's obviously thinking of the woman he is planning to have fun and games with tomorrow, but he's in for a big disappointment.' And this reflection, together with the thought of what she would say to him after their assignation, kept her awake for most of the night.

But to cut a long story short, when it was nones Catella collected her personal maid and proceeded, without a second thought, to the bagnio which Ricciardo had told her about.

On her arrival, she chanced upon the good woman in charge of the establishment, and asked her whether Filippello had been there during the course of the day, to which the woman replied, as instructed by Ricciardo:

'Are you the lady who was to come and speak with him?'

'I am,' Catella replied.

'Then go straight in,' said the woman. 'He's waiting for you.'

Catella, heavily veiled, and hotly in pursuit of something she would not have wished to find, got the woman to take her to the room where Ricciardo was waiting, and locked the door from the inside. On seeing her coming, Ricciardo rose joyfully to his feet, took her in his arms, and whispered:

'Welcome, my dearest.'

In her anxiety to prove that she really was the person he was expecting, Catella kissed and hugged and made a great fuss of him, at the same time refraining from speaking in case he should recognize her voice.

The room was exceedingly dark, a circumstance which suited both parties, and it was impossible, even after staying there for any length of time, to make things out with any degree of clarity. Ricciardo quickly guided her to the bed, however, and there they remained for a very long time to their immense and mutual pleasure and delight, though neither ventured to utter a word for fear of being recognized.

But eventually, Catella felt that the time had come to release her pent up indignation, and blazing with passionate anger she exclaimed:

'Ah! how wretched is the lot of women, and how misplaced the love that many of them bear their husbands! Alas, woe is me! For eight years I have loved you more than my very life, and now I find that you are totally absorbed in a passionate attachment to some other woman. Oh, you unspeakable villain! Who do you think you have just been cavorting with? You have been with the woman who has been lying beside you for the past eight years, the woman you have been deceiving for God knows how long with your false endearments, pretending to love her when all the time you were in love with another.

'You faithless scoundrel, I am not Ricciardo's wife, but Catella; listen to my voice, and you'll soon realize who I really am. Oh, how I long to be back again in the light of day, so that I can put you to the shame you so richly deserve, you filthy, loathsome beast. Alas! who have I been loving devotedly for all these years? A faithless cur, who thinks he has a strange woman in his arms, and lavishes more caresses and amorous attention upon me in the brief time I have spent with him here than in the whole of the rest of our married life.

'You unprincipled lout, I must say you have given a splendid display of manly vigour here today, in contrast with the feeble, worn-out, lack-lustre manner that you always adopt in your own house. But thanks be to God, it was your own land you were tilling and not some other man's, as you fondly imagined. It is no wonder that you kept me at a distance last night: you were planning to disburden yourself elsewhere, and you wanted to arrive fresh and strong at the jousting. But with God's help, I saw to it that the stream took its natural course.

'Why do you not answer me, you villain? Why don't you say something? Have my words deprived you of the power of speech? In God's name, I don't know how I manage to refrain from plucking your eyes out. You thought you were going to conceal your infidelity very cunningly, didn't you? But you didn't succeed, by God, because I'm just as clever as you are, and I've had better hounds on your tail than you bargained for.'

Ricciardo was inwardly relishing this sermon, and without offering any reply he embraced and kissed her, and caressed her more passionately than ever, whereupon she began to harangue him afresh.

'Oh, yes! Now you think you are going to get round me with your false caresses, you disgusting beast. But if you think you can pacify and console me, you're very much mistaken. I shall never be consoled for this outrage until I have denounced you to every single one of our friends, neighbours and relatives.

'Well now, villain, am I not as beautiful as Ricciardo Minutolo's wife? Am I not as nobly bred as she? Why don't you answer me, you foul beast? What has she got that I haven't? Stay away from me, keep your filthy hands to yourself; you have done quite enough tilting for one day. Oh, I am well aware that you could impose your will on me by brute force, now that you know who I am; but with God's grace I shall see that you go hungry. Indeed, I cannot understand what prevents me from sending for Ricciardo, who loved me more dearly than his very life, and yet was never able to claim that I so much as looked at him once. I see no reason why I shouldn't, because after all, you thought you had his wife here, and it would have been all the same to you if you really had. So if I were to have him, you could hardly hold it against me.'

Now, the words flowed thick and fast, and the lady's sense of grievance was very great. But in the end, Ricciardo, on reflecting how much trouble might ensue if he let her go away without undeceiving her, decided to disclose who he was. He therefore took her in his arms, holding her tightly so that she could not escape, and said:

'Sweet my soul, do not upset yourself so. What I was unable to achieve by mere wooing, Love has taught me to obtain by deception. I am your Ricciardo.'

No sooner did Catella hear these words and recognize his voice than she tried to leap out of bed, only to find that she was unable to move. She then prepared to scream, but Ricciardo placed a hand over her mouth, saying:

'My lady, it is impossible now to undo what has happened, even if you were to scream for the rest of your life. Besides, if you scream, or if you ever make this known to anyone, two things will ensue. The first (which ought to cause you no small concern) is that your honour and good name will be laid in ruins, because no matter how much you insist that I tricked you into coming here, I shall say that you are lying. Indeed, I shall maintain that I induced you to come by promising you money and presents, and that the reason you are making such a song and dance about it is simply that you were annoyed because your gains fell short of your expectations. I need hardly remind you that people are more inclined to believe in bad intentions than in good ones, and hence my account will carry no less conviction than yours. In the second place, your husband and I will become mortal enemies, and it could just as easily happen that he is killed by me as I by him, in which case you would inevitably spend the rest of your days in grief and mourning.

'Light of my life, do not at one and the same time bring dishonour upon yourself and jeopardize the lives of your husband and me by setting us at each other's throats. You are not the first woman to have been deceived, nor will you be the last, and in any case I had no intention of depriving you of anything. I was impelled to do it by excess of love, and indeed I am prepared to love you and serve you in all humility for the rest of my days. For a long time past, I and everything I possess have been yours, and all my power and influence have been at your disposal; but henceforth I intend to place them more completely than ever at your command. You are a wise woman, and I am certain that you will act now with that same good sense that you are wont to display in other matters.'

Catella wept bitterly while Ricciardo was speaking, and though she was exceedingly annoyed and upset, she was none the less able to see that he was right, and realized that events could easily follow the course he predicted.

'Ricciardo,' she said. 'I do not know how God can ever provide me with sufficient strength to bear the wicked deception you have practised upon me. I have no wish to raise a clamour in this place, to which I was led by my own simplicity and excessive jealousy. But you may rest assured that I shall never be happy until I see myself avenged in some way or other for the wrong you have done me. Now let me go, and get out of here! You have had what you wanted, you have tortured me to your heart's content, and now you can go. For heaven's sake, go!'

On seeing that she was still far from mollified, Ricciardo, who was determined not to leave her until she had recovered her equanimity, set about the task of appeasing her with a stream of honeyed endearments. And he exhorted and cajoled and beseeched her to such good effect that she eventually succumbed and forgave him, after which, by mutual consent, they tarried together at some length to their inordinate delight.

And so it was that from that day forward, the lady abandoned the stony attitude she had previously displayed to Ricciardo, and began to love him with all the tenderness in the world. And by proceeding with the greatest of discretion, they enjoyed their love together on many a later occasion. May God grant that we enjoy ours likewise.

SEVENTH STORY

Tedaldo, exasperated with his mistress, goes away from Florence. Return-
ing after a long absence disguised as a pilgrim, he talks to the lady, induces
her to acknowledge her error, and liberates her husband, who has been
convicted of murdering Tedaldo and is about to be executed. He then effects
a reconciliation between the husband and his own brothers; and thereafter he
discreetly enjoys the company of his mistress.

On lapsing into silence, Fiammetta was congratulated by all present,
and the queen, being anxious not to lose any time, promptly called
upon Emilia to tell her story. So Emilia began:

For my own part, I intend to return to our own city, from which
the last two speakers chose to depart, and show you how a citizen
of ours regained his lost mistress.

In Florence, then, there once lived a noble youth named Tedaldo
degli Elisei, who, having fallen passionately in love with the wife of
a certain Aldobrandino Palermini,[1] a lady of impeccable breeding
called Monna Ermellina, duly earned the reward of his persistent
devotion. But Fortune, the enemy of those who prosper, undermined his happiness, inasmuch as the lady, having already begun to
grant her favours to Tedaldo, suddenly decided for no apparent
reason to withhold them from him entirely. Not only would she
not listen to any of the messages he caused her to receive, but she
absolutely refused to acknowledge his existence, thus casting him
into a state of profound and excruciating melancholy. Since, however, he had carefully concealed this love-affair of his, no one
guessed the reason for his sorrow.

Feeling that he had lost the lady's favours through no fault of his
own, he tried in every possible way to retrieve them, only to
discover that all his efforts were unavailing. And because he had no
wish to allow her the satisfaction of seeing him suffer on her
account, he resolved to vanish from the scene. Having scraped
together all the money he could obtain, he departed in secret
without informing any of his friends or relatives except for one

companion of his who knew all about the affair, and went to Ancona, assuming the name of Filippo di Sanlodeccio. In Ancona, he made the acquaintance of a wealthy merchant with whom he obtained employment, travelling with him to Cyprus on one of his ships, and the merchant was so impressed by his character and abilities that he not only paid him a handsome salary but gave him a share in the business and placed him in charge of a sizeable portion of his affairs. To these, he devoted so much skill and diligence that within a few years he had made a name for himself as an able and prosperous merchant. And whilst his thoughts frequently returned to his cruel mistress and he still experienced sharp pangs of love and longed to see her again, he was so strong-willed that for seven years he succeeded in conquering his feelings.

But one day, in Cyprus, he happened to hear someone singing a song that he himself had composed, recounting the love that he bore to his mistress, her love for him, and the pleasure he had of her. And thinking it impossible that she should have forgotten him, he was stricken with such a burning desire to see her again that he could endure it no longer, and decided to return to Florence. Having wound up his affairs, he travelled with a servant as far as Ancona, where he waited for all his belongings to arrive and then shipped them to Florence, to a friend of his partner in Ancona, after which he himself followed with his servant, disguised as a pilgrim returning from the Holy Sepulchre; and when they arrived in Florence, they put up at a small inn run by two brothers, which was not far away from the lady's house. The first thing he did was to hurry over to her house in the hope of seeing her, but he found that all the windows and doors were barred and bolted, which led him to fear that she might be dead, or that she had moved elsewhere.

Deeply perturbed, he walked on until he reached the house of his kinsfolk, in front of which he saw four of his brothers, all of whom, to his great astonishment, were dressed in black. And knowing that he would not easily be recognized, on account of the marked changes in his clothing and physical appearance, he walked boldly up to the local shoemaker and asked him why these men were wearing black.

'They are wearing black,' replied the shoemaker, 'because within the past fortnight a brother of theirs called Tedaldo, who disappeared from the neighbourhood many years ago, was found murdered. As far as I can gather, they have proved in court that his murderer was a certain Aldobrandino Palermini, who has now been arrested. It seems that the murdered man was in love with Palermini's wife, and had returned here in disguise to be with her.'

Tedaldo was greatly astonished that anyone could resemble him so closely as to be mistaken for his own person, whilst the news of Aldobrandino's plight distressed him deeply. On making further inquiries he discovered that the lady was alive and well, and since it was now dark, he returned to the inn, his mind in a positive whirl. After dining in the company of his servant, he was shown up to his sleeping quarters, which were situated almost at the very top of the building. But because his mind was so active and his bed so uncomfortable, and also perhaps because of the meagreness of his supper, Tedaldo was unable to drop off to sleep. He was still wide awake when, halfway through the night, he thought he could hear people entering the building by way of the roof; and shortly afterwards, through the cracks in the bedroom door, a glimmer of light could be seen.

He therefore crept silently across to the door and began to peep through the crack in order to discover what was happening, and caught sight of a very pretty girl carrying the light and being met by three men who had descended from the roof. They all exchanged certain greetings, then one of the men addressed the girl as follows:

'We've nothing more to fear, thank God, because we've learnt for certain that Tedaldo Elisei's brothers have proved he was killed by Aldobrandino Palermini, who has made a confession. The sentence has already been signed, but all the same we'll have to keep this thing quiet, because if it ever leaks out that we did it, we'll be in the same sorry plight as Aldobrandino.'

This announcement was greeted by the woman with evident relief, and they all retired to bed in the lower part of the house.

Having overheard the whole of this, Tedaldo began to reflect how fatally easy it was for people to cram their heads with totally erroneous notions. His thoughts turned first of all to his brothers, who had gone into mourning and buried some stranger in his own stead, after which they had been impelled by their false suspicions to accuse this innocent man and fabricate evidence so as to have him brought under sentence of death. This in turn led him to reflect upon the blind severity of the law and its administrators, who in order to convey the impression that they are zealously seeking the truth, often have recourse to cruelty and cause falsehood to be accepted as proven fact, hence demonstrating, for all their proud claim to be the ministers of God's justice, that their true allegiance is to the devil and his iniquities. Finally, Tedaldo turned his thoughts to the question of how he could save Aldobrandino, and decided upon the course of action he would have to adopt.

When he got up next morning, he left his servant behind and made his way, at what seemed a suitable hour, to the house of his former mistress. Since the door happened to be open, he went in, and there, sitting on the floor in a little room downstairs, he found his lady-love, all tearful and forlorn. Scarcely able to restrain himself from crying at this piteous spectacle, he walked over to where she was sitting.

'Madam,' he said, 'do not torment yourself: your troubles will soon be over.'

On hearing his voice, the lady looked up at him and sobbed, saying:

'Good sir, you appear to be a pilgrim and a stranger; how can you know anything of my troubles and torments?'

'Madam,' replied the pilgrim, 'I come from Constantinople and I have just arrived in this city, to which I was sent by God to convert your tears into joy and deliver your husband from death.'

'But if you come from Constantinople,' said the woman, 'and if you have only just arrived, how can you know anything of me or my husband?'

Starting from the beginning, the pilgrim provided a full account of Aldobrandino's predicament and told her exactly who she was, how long she had been married, and many other things that he knew concerning her private affairs. This recital greatly astonished the lady, who took him to be some kind of prophet and knelt down at his feet, beseeching him in God's name, if he really had come to save Aldobrandino, to do so quickly before it was too late.

'Stand up, my lady,' said the pilgrim, assuming a very saintly air, 'and cry no more. Listen closely to what I am about to say, and take good care never to repeat it to anyone. God has revealed to me that your tribulation arises from a certain sin you once committed, which He intends that you should purge, partially at any rate, by means of this present affliction. He is very anxious that you should make amends for it, because otherwise you would assuredly be plunged into much greater suffering.'

'I have committed many sins, sir,' said the lady, 'and I do not know which particular one it is that the Lord God desires me to atone for out of all the rest. So if you know which one it is, please tell me, and I shall do whatever I can to make amends for it.'

'I know very well what it is, madam,' said the pilgrim. 'And I shall now ask you a few questions about it, not for my own benefit, but merely to enable you to acknowledge the sin of your own free will, and repent more fully. But let us come to the point. Tell me, do you remember whether you ever had a lover?'

On hearing this question, the lady fetched a deep sigh and was greatly amazed, for she was under the impression that nobody had ever discovered her secret, albeit there had been a certain amount of gossip since the murder of the man who had been buried for Tedaldo, because of certain things which had been said, rather unwisely, by the friend in whom Tedaldo had confided.

'It is obvious,' she replied, 'that God reveals all of men's secrets to you, and I therefore see no reason for attempting to conceal my own. In my younger days, I was indeed deeply in love with the unfortunate young man whose death has been imputed to my husband. I was enormously grieved to hear that he was dead, and I have wept countless tears over him, for although I assumed an air of haughty indifference towards him before he went away, neither his departure nor his long absence nor even his unfortunate death has been able to dislodge him from my heart.'

'You were never in love with this hapless youth who has died,' said the pilgrim, 'but with Tedaldo Elisei. However, tell me: what reason did you have for snubbing him? Did he ever offend you?'

'Oh, no!' replied the lady. 'He certainly never offended me. My aloofness was prompted by the words of an accursed friar, to whom I once went for confession. When I told him how much I loved this man and described the intimacy of our relationship, he gave me such a severe scolding that I have never recovered from the shock to this day, for he told me that unless I mended my ways I would be consigned to the devil's mouth at the bottom of the abyss² and exposed to the torments of hellfire. I was so frightened by all this that I firmly made up my mind never to have anything more to do with him. So as to remove all temptation, I refused from then on to accept any of his letters or messages. I suppose he eventually gave up and went away in despair. But if he had persevered a little longer, I am sure I would have relented, for I could see that he was wasting away like snow in the rays of the sun, and I was longing to break my resolve.'

'Madam,' said the pilgrim, 'it is this sin alone which lies at the root of all your suffering. I know for a fact that Tedaldo never coerced you in the slightest. When you fell in love with him, you did so of your own accord because you found him attractive. It was with your full consent that he began to visit you and enjoy your intimate favours, and your delight in him was so obvious from your words and deeds that, though he already loved you before, you intensified his love a thousandfold. And if this was so (as I know it was), what possible reason could prompt you to withdraw yourself so inflexibly from him? You should have thought about all these things beforehand, and if you felt it was wrong, if you felt you were going to have to repent, you should not have had anything to do with him in the first place. The point is this, that when he became yours, so you became his. Inasmuch as he belonged to you, you were perfectly free to discard him whenever you wished. But since, at the same time, you belonged to him, it was quite improper of you, indeed it was robbery on your part, to remove yourself from him against his will.

'Now, I would have you know that I myself am a friar. I am therefore familiar with all their ways, and it is not unfitting for me, as it would be for a layman, to express myself somewhat freely about them for your benefit. I do this, and I do it willingly, so that you will know them better in the future than you appear to have done in the past.

'There was once a time³ when friars were very saintly and worthy men, but those who lay claim nowadays to the title and reputation of friar have nothing of the friar about them except the habits they wear. Even these are not genuine friars' habits, because whereas the people who invented friars decreed that the habit should be close-fitting, coarse, and shabby, and that, by clothing the body in humble apparel, it should symbolize the mind's disdain for all the things of this world, your present-day friars prefer ample habits, generously cut and smooth of texture, and made from the finest of fabrics. Indeed, they now have elegant and pontifical habits, in which they strut like peacocks through the churches and the city squares without compunction, just as though they were members of the laity showing off their robes. And like the fisherman who tries to take a number of fish from the river with a single throw of his casting-net, so these fellows, as they wrap themselves in the capacious folds of their habits, endeavour to take in many an over-pious lady, many a widow, and many another simpleton of either sex, this being their one overriding concern. It would therefore be more exact for me to say that these fellows do not wear friars' habits, but merely the colours of their habits.

'Moreover, whereas their predecessors desired the salvation of men, the friars of today desire riches and women. They have taken great pains, and still do, to strike terror into simple people's hearts with their loud harangues and specious parables, and to show that sins may be purged through almsgiving and mass-offerings. In this way, having taken refuge in the priesthood more out of cowardice than piety and in order to escape hard work, they are supplied with bread by one man and wine by another, whilst a third is persuaded to part with donations for the souls of his departed ones.

'It is of course true that prayers and almsgiving purge sins. But if only the donors were familiar with the sort of people to whom they were handing over their money, they would either keep it for themselves or cast it before a herd of swine. These so-called friars are well aware that the fewer the people who share a great treasure, the better off they are, and so each of them strives by blustering and intimidation to exclude others from whatever he is anxious to retain for his own exclusive use. They denounce men's lust, so that when the denounced are out of the way, their women will be left to the denouncers. They condemn usury and ill-gotten gains, so that people will entrust them with their restitution, and this enables them to make their habits more capacious and procure bishoprics and the other major offices of the Church, using the very money which, according to them, would have led its owners to perdition.

'Whenever anyone reproaches them with these and countless other wicked ways of theirs, they consider themselves acquitted from every charge, however serious, simply by replying: "Do as we say, not as we do." To hear them talk, one would think it was easier for the sheep to be strong-willed and law-abiding than it is for the shepherds. But this specious answer of theirs does not fool everyone by any means, and a great many of them know it.

'The friars of today want you to do as they say, or in other words fill their purses with money, confide your secrets to them, remain chaste, practise patience, forgive all wrongs, and take care to speak no evil, all of which are good, seemly and edifying goals to pursue. But why? Simply so that they can do the things they will be prevented from doing if they are done by the laity. Who will deny that laziness cannot survive without money to support it? If we were to spend our money on our own pleasures, the friar would no longer be able to idle away his time in the cloisters; if we were to go pursuing the ladies, the friars would be put out of business; if we failed to practise patience and forgive all wrongs, the friar would no longer have the effrontery to call upon us in our own homes and corrupt our families. But why should I elaborate every point in detail? Every time they come out with that hoary old excuse of theirs, they condemn themselves in the eyes of all intelligent men and women. Why do they not choose to remain within their own walls, if they feel themselves unable to behave in a chaste and godly manner? Or if they really must rub shoulders with the laity, why do they not follow that other holy text from the Gospel: "Then Christ began to act and to teach"? Let them set an example, before they start preaching to the rest of us. In my time I've seen a thousand of them laying siege, paying visits and making love, not only to ordinary women but to nuns in convents; and some of them were the ones who ranted loudest from the pulpit. Are these, then, the people whose advice we should follow? Anyone is free to do so if he likes, but God knows whether he will be acting wisely.

'However, even supposing we granted that the friar who censured you was right in this instance, and that to break one's marriage vows is a very grave offence, is it not far worse to steal? Is it not far worse to murder a man or send him wandering through the world in exile? Everyone will agree that it is, because after all, for a woman to have intimate relations with a man is a natural sin, but to rob him or to kill him or expel him is to act from evil intention.

'That you did indeed rob Tedaldo I have already proved to you just now, for you removed yourself from him when you belonged to him of your own free will. Secondly, I would suggest that you did your utmost to murder him, for it would not have been surprising, in view of the cruel way you treated him, if he had taken his own life; and in the eyes of the law, the accessory to a crime is as guilty as the person who actually commits it. Finally, it cannot be denied that you were responsible for condemning him to wander through the world for seven whole years in exile. So that on any one of the three articles to which I have referred, you committed a far greater sin than by your intimacy with him. But let us consider the matter more closely. Could it be that Tedaldo deserved all he received? He certainly did not, as you yourself have already conceded; and besides, I know that he loves you more dearly than his very life.

'Nothing was ever so warmly revered, so greatly extolled, or so highly exalted as you were by him above all other women, whenever he could speak of you without giving rise to suspicion. To you alone he entrusted the whole of his well-being, the whole of his honour, the whole of his freedom. Was he not a noble youth? Was he not as handsome as any of his fellow citizens? Was he not outstanding in those activities and accomplishments that pertain to the young? Was he not loved, esteemed, and given a ready welcome by all who met him? This, too, you will be willing to concede.

'What possible reason could you have had, then, for heeding the insane ravings of a stupid, envious little friar and deciding to treat him so cruelly? Why is it, I wonder, that certain women make the mistake of holding themselves aloof from men and looking down upon them? If they would only consider their own natures, and stop to think of how much more nobility God has conceded to man than to any of the other animals, they would undoubtedly be proud of a man's love and hold him in the highest esteem, and do everything in their power to please him, so that he would never grow tired of loving them. Did you do all this? No, because you allowed yourself to be swayed by the words of a friar who must without a doubt have been some soup-guzzling pie-muncher, and who in all probability intended to install himself in the place from which he was intent on dislodging another.

'This, then, was the sin which divine justice, all of whose dealings are perfectly balanced, would not allow to remain unpunished. You tried without good reason to remove yourself from Tedaldo; and likewise your husband's life, without good reason, has been placed in jeopardy and remains in jeopardy on Tedaldo's account, whilst you yourself have been cast into sorrow. If you want to release yourself from this affliction, here is what you must promise, or rather, what you must do: if it were ever to happen that Tedaldo returned here from his lengthy exile, you must restore to him your favour, your love, your goodwill and intimate friendship, and reinstate him in the position he occupied before you so foolishly heeded that lunatic friar.'

Here the pilgrim finished speaking, and meanwhile the lady had listened in rapt attention to every word he had uttered, for she felt his arguments to be very sound and was convinced, having heard him say so, that her affliction really stemmed from that one sin of hers.

'Friend of God,' she said, 'I know full well that what you say is true, and you have taught me a great deal about friars, all of whom I have hitherto regarded as saints. I can see that I undoubtedly committed a serious error in behaving as I did towards Tedaldo, and if it lay within my power I would willingly make amends in the way you suggest. But how is this to be done? Tedaldo cannot ever return here again; he is dead. So what is the point of my giving you a pledge that I cannot keep?'

'Madam,' said the pilgrim, 'God has revealed to me that Tedaldo is not dead at all, but alive and well, and if only he enjoyed your favour he would also be happy.'

'But you must surely be mistaken,' said the lady. 'I saw him lying dead from a number of stab-wounds on my own doorstep, and held him in these arms and shed countless tears on his poor dead face, which possibly accounts for the malicious gossip that has been put about.'

'No matter what you may say, madam,' said the pilgrim, 'I assure you that Tedaldo is alive. And provided that you give me the pledge and intend to keep it, there is every hope of your seeing him soon.'

'I will do it, and willingly,' said the lady. 'Nothing would bring me greater joy than to see my husband released unharmed and Tedaldo alive.'

Tedaldo now decided that the time had come to make himself known to the lady and reassure her about her husband.

'Madam,' he said, 'in order to set your mind at rest about your husband, I shall have to tell you an important secret, which you must take care never to reveal for as long as you live.'

Since they were alone in a very remote part of the house (the lady being quite disarmed by the pilgrim's appearance of saintliness), Tedaldo drew forth a ring which he had religiously preserved and which the lady had given him on their last night together, and held it out for her to see, saying:

'Do you know this ring, madam?'

The lady recognized it at once.

'I do indeed, sir,' she replied. 'I gave it long ago to Tedaldo.'

The pilgrim thereupon stood up straight, and having thrown off his cloak and removed his hood, he addressed her in a Florentine accent, saying:

'And do you know me, too?'

When the lady saw that it was Tedaldo, she was utterly astonished, and began to tremble with fright, as though she were seeing a ghost. Far from rushing forward to welcome a Tedaldo who had returned from Cyprus, she shrank back in terror from a Tedaldo who had seemingly risen from the grave.

'Do not be afraid, my lady,' he said. 'I really am your Tedaldo. I am alive and well, and whatever you and my brothers may believe, I never died and was never murdered.'

Somewhat reassured by the sound of his voice, the lady looked at him more closely, and having convinced herself that he really was Tedaldo, she burst into tears, flung her arms about his neck, and kissed him, saying:

'Tedaldo, my sweet Tedaldo, you are welcome!'

'My lady,' said Tedaldo, after embracing and kissing her, 'there is no time now to exchange more intimate greetings. I must go and arrange for Aldobrandino to be restored to you safe and sound, and trust that you will hear good news of my endeavours before tomorrow evening. Indeed, I fully expect by tonight to hear that he is safe, in which case I should like to come and tell you all about it in a more leisurely way than I have time for at present.'

Donning once again his pilgrim's cloak and hood, he kissed the lady a second time, assured her that everything would be all right, and left her. He then proceeded to the place where Aldobrandino, more preoccupied with the dread of his impending doom than with the hope of his future release, was being held prisoner. And having been admitted to Aldobrandino's cell by the prison-warders, who assumed that he had come to minister to the condemned man, he sat down beside him, saying:

'Aldobrandino, I am a friend, sent here to save you by God, who has been moved to pity by your innocence. If, therefore, out of reverence to Him you will grant me the trifling favour that I am about to ask of you, it is certain that by tomorrow evening, instead of languishing here under sentence of death, you will hear the news of your acquittal.'

'Good sir,' Aldobrandino replied, 'I neither know you nor recall ever having seen you before, but since you show concern for my safety, you must indeed be a friend. It is perfectly true that I did not commit the crime for which it is said that I must be condemned to death, even though I have sinned in many other ways, which possibly explains my present predicament. In all reverence to God, however, I can tell you this: that if He were to have mercy on me now, there is nothing, whether great or small, that I would not do, and do willingly, let alone promise. Ask of me what you please, then, for you may be quite certain that if I should happen to be released I shall honour my word to the letter.'

'All I want you to do,' replied the pilgrim, 'is to pardon Tedaldo's four brothers for landing you in this plight in the mistaken belief that you murdered their brother, and, provided that they ask you to forgive them, to treat them as your own kith and kin.'

'Only the person who has been wronged,' replied Aldobrandino, 'knows how sweet and how intense is the desire for revenge. But in order that God may take thought for my salvation, I shall willingly forgive them; indeed, I do forgive them, here and now. And if I ever emerge from this place with my life and liberty, I shall act in a way that will certainly meet with your approval.'

This reply satisfied the pilgrim, and without enlightening him any further he departed, strongly urging him to be of good cheer and assuring him that before the next day was over he would hear the news of his deliverance.

After leaving Aldobrandino, he made his way to the law-courts and obtained a private interview with the most senior official.

'Sir,' he began, 'no man, especially in your position, should ever shrink from the task of uncovering the truth, so that, when a crime is committed, punishment may be inflicted on the guilty and not on the innocent. So as to ensure that this is done, thus bringing credit to yourself and retribution to those who have earned it, I have been prompted to call upon you. As you know, you have brought Aldobrandino Palermini to trial, you think you have discovered convincing proof that he is the man who murdered Tedaldo Elisei, and you are about to pronounce sentence upon him. But the evidence is false beyond any shadow of a doubt, and I believe I can prove it to you between now and midnight by handing over the young man's real murderers.'

The worthy official was already feeling sorry for Aldobrandino, and gladly gave ear to the words of the pilgrim, who furnished him with such a wealth of corroborative detail that he had the two inn-keeping brothers and their servant arrested, without a struggle, shortly after they had retired to bed. Being determined to get at the truth of the matter, he would have put them to the torture, but they broke down and made a full confession, individually at first and then all together, saying that they were the people who had murdered Tedaldo Elisei, who was a complete stranger to them. On being asked the reason, they said it was because he had been pestering one of their wives whilst they were away from the inn, and that he had tried to ravish her.

Having heard about their confession, the pilgrim took his leave of the official and made his way back to the house of Monna Ermellina, which he entered unobserved. All the servants had gone to bed, and he found her waiting up alone for him, equally desirous of hearing good news about her husband and of being fully reunited with Tedaldo. He went up to her, smiling happily, and said:

'My darling mistress, be of good cheer, for it is certain that Aldobrandino will be restored to you here tomorrow, safe and sound.' And in order to prove to her that it was so, he told her of all he had done.

Monna Ermellina was the happiest woman who ever lived, for twice in quick succession the impossible had happened: in the first place she had got Tedaldo back again, alive and well, after genuinely thinking she had mourned him as dead, and in the second she had seen Aldobrandino delivered from danger when she thought that within a few days she would be having to mourn his death also. And so, passionately hugging Tedaldo and smothering him with kisses, she retired with him to bed, where, to their mutual and delectable joy, they gladly and graciously made their peace with one another.

A little before daybreak, Tedaldo arose, having apprised the lady of his intentions and repeated his plea that she should keep everything secret, and putting on his pilgrim's garb, he left the house, so as to be ready at a moment's notice to act on Aldobrandino's behalf.

As soon as dawn arrived, the magistrates, confident that all the relevant facts were now in their possession, set Aldobrandino at liberty; and a few days later they had the delinquents beheaded at the scene of the murder. Aldobrandino was overjoyed to find

himself at liberty, and so too were his wife and all his friends and
relatives. Knowing full well that the whole thing was due to the
efforts of the pilgrim, they offered him their hospitality for as long
as he chose to remain in the city. And having brought him to their
house, they fêted and feasted him without being able to stop,
especially the lady, since she alone knew who it was she was
honouring. But before very long, having learned that his brothers
were being held up to ridicule on account of Aldobrandino's release
and that they had armed themselves in fear and trembling, he
decided that the time had come to reconcile the two sides, and
reminded Aldobrandino of his promise. Aldobrandino readily
agreed to carry it out, and the pilgrim persuaded him to arrange a
sumptuous banquet for the following day, to which he was to
invite not only his own relatives and womenfolk but also the four
brothers and their wives. Moreover, the pilgrim offered to call on
the four brothers in person and invite them to the reunion and
banquet on Aldobrandino's behalf.

Aldobrandino gave his consent, whereupon the pilgrim immediately went to call upon the four brothers, and having told them as
much as they needed to know, he eventually persuaded them
without difficulty, using impeccable arguments, to ask Aldobrandino's forgiveness and patch up their differences with him. He
then invited them to take their wives along to Aldobrandino's
banquet on the following morning, and the brothers, being convinced of his good faith, gladly agreed to do so.

Next morning, therefore, at the hour of breakfast, Tedaldo's four
brothers, still dressed in black and accompanied by some friends of
theirs, presented themselves at the house of Aldobrandino, who was
waiting to greet them. And in the presence of all the people who
had been invited by Aldobrandino to join them in the festivities,
they laid their weapons on the ground and threw themselves on
Aldobrandino's mercy, asking him to forgive them for the way
they had treated him. Aldobrandino received them with affection,
his eyes full of tears, and having kissed each one of them on the
mouth, he quickly said what he had to say and pardoned them for
the wrongs he had suffered. They then made way for their wives
and sisters, who were all dressed in mourning, and were given a

gracious welcome by Monna Ermellina and the other ladies. Then all the guests, gentlemen and ladies alike, sat down to a splendid meal, excellent in every respect save for the general air of reticence engendered by the recent bereavement which Tedaldo's kinsfolk had suffered, and which was made more apparent by the sombre clothes they were wearing. For this very reason, in fact, some people had condemned the pilgrim's scheme for holding the banquet, and Tedaldo, who was well aware of their objections, felt that the time had now come to spring his surprise and disperse the mists of melancholy. He therefore rose to his feet while the others were still eating their dessert, and said:

'All that this banquet requires to bring it to life is the presence of Tedaldo. He has been here all the time, as it happens, but since you have failed to notice him, I want to point him out.'

Then, throwing off his cloak and all his pilgrim's clothing, he stood before them wearing a tunic of green taffeta, to be inspected and scrutinized at great length, and with no small display of astonishment, before anyone ventured to believe that he really was Tedaldo. Seeing how incredulous they looked, Tedaldo identified the families to which they belonged, told them about various things that had happened to them, and described his own adventures, whereupon his brothers and the other men rushed to embrace him, all weeping with joy, and the ladies followed their example, kinsfolk and others alike, with the sole exception of Monna Ermellina.

'Ermellina!' exclaimed Aldobrandino. 'What is this that I see? Why are you not greeting Tedaldo, like the other ladies?'

'I would greet him more willingly,' she replied, in everyone's hearing, 'than any of the ladies who have done so already, because it was thanks to him that you have been restored to me, and thus my debt to him is greater than anyone's. But I refrain because of the mischievous things that were said when we were mourning the man we mistook for Tedaldo.'

'Away with you!' said Aldobrandino. 'Do you suppose I pay any attention to gossip-mongers? He has amply proved that the stories were untrue by securing my release, and I never believed them in the first place. Up you get, quickly; go and embrace him.'

The lady could desire nothing better, and was not slow to obey her husband's instructions. Rising from her place, she threw her arms about his neck, as the other ladies had done, and gave him an ecstatic welcome.

Tedaldo's brothers were delighted by Aldobrandino's magnanimous gesture, as were all the other gentlemen and ladies who were present; and so it was that every trace of the doubts implanted in certain people's minds by the rumours was expelled.

Now that everyone had given Tedaldo a handsome welcome, he himself stripped his brothers of their mourning, tore asunder the sombre dresses that their wives and sisters were wearing, and ordered different clothes to be brought. And when all were newly attired, they made merry with a number of songs, dances and other entertainments, so that in contrast to its subdued beginning the banquet had a noisy ending. Nor was this all, for they immediately made their way to Tedaldo's house, singing and dancing as they went, and dined there that evening. And without varying the order of their festivities, they kept the party going for several days in succession.

For some time, the Florentines thought of Tedaldo as a man who had miraculously risen from the grave. Many people, including his own brothers, were left with a faint suspicion in their minds that he was not really Tedaldo at all. Even now, in fact, they were not entirely convinced, and they would possibly have remained unconvinced for a long time afterwards, but for the fact that some days later they accidentally discovered who the murdered man was.

It happened like this. One day, a group of soldiers from Lunigiana were passing the house, and when they caught sight of Tedaldo they rushed towards him, exclaiming:

'Good old Faziuolo!'

Tedaldo informed them, in the presence of his brothers, that they were mistaking him for another, and as soon as they heard his voice they became embarrassed and gave him their apologies.

'God's truth!' they said. 'You are the living image of a mate of ours called Faziuolo da Pontremoli, who came here about a fortnight or so ago and has never been heard of since. It's no wonder we were surprised by the clothes you're wearing, because he was just a common soldier like ourselves.'

On hearing this, Tedaldo's eldest brother interrupted to ask what sort of clothes this Faziuolo of theirs had been wearing. Their description fitted the facts so precisely, that what with this and other indications, it became quite obvious that the murdered man was not Tedaldo, but Faziuolo; and thenceforth, neither Tedaldo's brothers nor anyone else harboured any further doubts about him.

Tedaldo, who had made a fortune during his absence, remained constant in his love, whilst for her part his mistress never rebuffed him again. And by proceeding with discretion, they long enjoyed their love together. May God grant that we enjoy ours likewise.

EIGHTH STORY

Ferondo, having consumed a special powder, is buried for dead. The Abbot who is cavorting with his wife removes him from his tomb, imprisons him, and makes him believe he is in Purgatory. He is later resurrected, and raises as his own a child begotten on his wife by the Abbot.

Emilia had thus reached the end of her story, which in spite of its length was not unfavourably received. On the contrary, they all maintained that it had been briefly told, considering the number and variety of the incidents it had touched upon. And now the queen, making her wishes evident by a brief nod in the direction of Lauretta, induced her to begin:

Dearest ladies, I find myself confronted by a true story, demanding to be told, which sounds far more fictitious than was actually the case, and of which I was reminded when I heard of the man who was buried and mourned in mistake for another. My story, then, is about a living man who was buried for dead, and who later, on emerging from his tomb, was convinced that he had truly died and been resurrected − a belief that was shared by many other people, who consequently venerated him as a Saint when they should have been condemning him as a fool.

★

In Tuscany, then, there was and still is a certain abbey, situated, as so many of them are, a little off the beaten track. Its newly appointed abbot was a former monk who was a veritable saint of a man in all his ways except for his womanizing, a hobby that he pursued so discreetly that very few people suspected, let alone knew about it, and hence he was considered to be very saintly and upright in every respect.

Now, this abbot happened to become closely acquainted with a very wealthy yeoman called Ferondo, an exceedingly coarse and unimaginative fellow whose company he suffered only because Ferondo's simple ways were sometimes a source of amusement. From associating with Ferondo, the Abbot made the discovery that he was married to a very beautiful woman, and he fell so ardently in love with her that she occupied his thoughts day and night, and he could concentrate on nothing else. But when he further discovered that Ferondo, for all his fatuousness and stupidity in every other respect, was extremely sensible in his devotion to this wife of his, and kept a careful watch upon her, the Abbot was driven to the brink of despair. Nevertheless, being very shrewd, he managed on occasion to persuade Ferondo to bring her to the abbey, when they would all go for a pleasant stroll together in the grounds and the Abbot would converse with them in a highly polite and articulate manner about the blessedness of the life eternal and the saintly deeds of various men and women of the past. Because of this, the lady was seized with the desire of going to him for confession, and she asked and obtained Ferondo's permission to do so.

And thus, much to the delight of the Abbot, the lady came to him in order to be confessed. First of all, however, having seated herself at his feet,[1] she addressed him as follows:

'Sir, if God had given me a real husband, or no husband at all, perhaps it would be easy for me to set out under your guidance along the path you were telling us about, which leads to the life eternal. Considering the sort of man Ferondo is, and the moronic way he behaves, I am no better off than a widow. Yet I am a married woman, inasmuch as, while he lives, I cannot have any other husband except this half-witted oaf who for no reason whatever guards me with such extraordinary and excessive jealousy that my life with him is one long torment and misery. And so, before going any further with my confession, I humbly beseech you, with all my heart, to advise me what to do about it. For unless I take this as the starting point of my endeavours to lead a better life, no amount of confessing or of other pious deeds will do me any good.'

These sentiments were very much to the liking of the Abbot, who felt that Fortune had placed his greatest desire within sight of fulfilment.

'My daughter,' he said, 'I consider it a great affliction for a beautiful and sensitive woman like yourself to have a half-witted husband, but I consider it an even greater affliction to have a husband who is jealous; and since you are saddled with both, I can well believe what you say about your torment and misery. Without going into too many details, there is only one piece of advice, only one remedy, that I can suggest: namely, that Ferondo must be cured of his jealousy. What is more, I am able to provide him with the very medicine he needs, if only you have the necessary will to keep what I tell you a secret.'

'Have no fear on that account, Father,' said the lady, 'for I would sooner die than repeat anything you had asked me to keep to myself. But how is this cure to be effected?'

'If we want him to recover,' replied the Abbot, 'then obviously he will have to go to Purgatory.'

'But how can he go there if he's still alive?'

'He will have to die, that is how he will go there. And when he has had enough punishment to purge him of this jealousy of his, we shall recite certain prayers asking God to bring him back to life, and God will attend to it.'

'Am I to be left a widow, then?'

'Yes, for a while. But you must take good care not to remarry, because if you did, God would take it amiss. And besides, you would have to go back to Ferondo when he returned from Purgatory, and he would be more jealous than ever.'

'It sounds all right to me, provided it cures this malady of his, so that I no longer have to spend my whole life under lock and key. Do whatever you think best.'

'Right you are,' said the Abbot. 'But what reward are you prepared to offer me for rendering you so useful a service?'

'Whatever you ask, Father, provided I have it to give,' she replied. 'But what possible reward could a mere woman like myself offer to a man in your position?'

'Madam,' said the Abbot, 'you can do as much for me as I am about to do for you. Just as I am making preparations for your welfare and happiness, so you can do something that will lead to my freedom and salvation.'

'In that case,' said the lady, 'I am quite willing to do it.'

'All you need to do,' said the Abbot, 'is to give me your love and let me enjoy you. I am burning all over; I am pining for you.'

'Oh, Father!' exclaimed the lady, who was hardly able to believe her ears. 'Whatever are you asking me to do? I always took you for a saint. Is this the sort of request a saintly man should be making to a lady who goes to him for advice?'

'Do not be so astonished, my treasure,' said the Abbot. 'No loss of saintliness is involved,[2] for saintliness resides in the soul, and what I am asking of you is merely a sin of the body. But be that as it may, your beauty is so overpowering that love compels me to speak out. And what I say is this, that when you consider that your beauty is admired by a Saint, you have more reason to be proud of it than other women, because Saints are accustomed to seeing the beauties of Heaven. Furthermore, even though I am an Abbot, I am a man like the others, and as you can see I am still quite young. It should not be too difficult for you to comply with my request; on the contrary, you ought to welcome it, because whilst Ferondo is away in Purgatory, I will come and keep you company every night and provide you with all the solace that he should be giving you. Nobody will suspect us, because my reputation stands at least as high with everyone else as it formerly did with you. Do not cast aside this special favour which is sent to you by God, for you can have something that countless women yearn for, and if you are sensible enough to accept my advice, it will be yours. Moreover, I possess some fine, precious jewels, and I intend that you alone should have them. Do not therefore refuse, my dearest, to do me a service that I will do for you with the greatest of pleasure.'

Not knowing how to refuse him, yet feeling it was wrong to grant his request, the lady fixed her gaze upon the ground. The Abbot knew that she had heard him, and when he saw her at a loss for an answer, he felt she was already half-converted. He therefore followed up his previous arguments with a torrent of new ones, and by the time he had finished talking, he had convinced her that it was all for the best. And so in bashful tones she placed herself entirely at his disposal, adding that she could do nothing until Ferondo had gone to Purgatory.

'In that case,' said the Abbot, beaming with joy, 'we shall see that he goes there at once. Send him along to see me tomorrow, or the following day.'

Whereupon he furtively slipped a magnificent ring into her hand, and sent her away. The lady was delighted with her present, and looked forward to receiving others. And having rejoined her companions, she regaled them with marvellous accounts of the Abbot's saintliness as they made their way home together.

A few days later, Ferondo called at the abbey, and no sooner did the Abbot see him than he decided to pack him off to Purgatory. So he sought out a wondrous powder which had been given him in the East by a mighty prince, who maintained that it was the one used by the Old Man of the Mountain[3] whenever he wanted to send people to his paradise in their sleep or bring them back again. The prince had further assured him that by varying the dose, one could render people unconscious for longer or shorter periods, during which they slept so profoundly that nobody would ever guess that they were still alive. Without letting Ferondo see what he was doing, the Abbot measured out a quantity sufficient to put him to sleep for three days, poured it into a glass of somewhat cloudy wine, and gave it to him to drink whilst they were still in his cell. He then led him off to the cloister, where he and several of his monks began to amuse themselves at Ferondo's expense and make fun of his imbecilities. Before very long, however, the powder began to take effect, and Ferondo, being suddenly overcome by a powerful sensation of drowsiness, fell asleep where he was standing and collapsed to the ground unconscious.

The Abbot, feigning consternation at this occurrence, got someone to loosen his clothing, sent for cold water and had it sprinkled over Ferondo's face, and ordered various other remedies to be applied, as though he were intent on restoring the life and feeling of which he had been deprived by his stomach-wind or whatever else it was that had felled him. But on seeing that he failed to come round despite all their efforts, and on testing his pulse and finding it had stopped, the Abbot and his monks unanimously concluded that he must be dead. So somebody was sent to inform his wife and kinsfolk, and they all came rushing to the scene. And when his wife and kinswomen had finished weeping, the Abbot caused him to be laid to rest in a tomb, in the clothes he was wearing.

Ferondo and his wife had a little boy, and when she returned home, she told the child that she intended to stay there for the rest of her days. Thus she remained in Ferondo's house, and applied herself to the task of looking after the child and administering the fortune left behind by her husband.

Meanwhile, the Abbot quietly rose from his bed in the middle of the night, and with the assistance of a Bolognese monk whom he trusted implicitly and who had arrived that same day from Bologna, he dragged Ferondo from the tomb and moved him into a vault, totally devoid of any light, which served as a place of confinement for monks who had broken their vows. Having removed the clothes Ferondo was wearing and dressed him in a monastic habit, they left him lying on a bundle of straw until such time as he should come to his senses. And in the meantime, unbeknown to anyone else, the Bolognese monk waited for Ferondo to come round, having been told what to do by the Abbot.

Next day, the Abbot, accompanied by one or two of his monks, called on the lady to pay her his respects, and found her dressed in black and full of woe. After offering her a few words of comfort, he quietly reminded her of her promise, and the lady, having caught sight of another fine ring on the Abbot's finger, and realizing that she was now a free agent, unhindered by Ferondo or anyone else, told him that she was ready to honour it and arranged for him to call there after dark that evening.

After dark, therefore, the Abbot decked himself out in Ferondo's clothes and set off for her house accompanied by his monk. Having spent the whole night in her arms with enormous pleasure and delight, he returned a little before matins to the abbey, and from then on he went regularly. back and forth on the same errand. It occasionally happened that people would chance upon the Abbot as he wended his way to and fro, and they concluded that it must be Ferondo's ghost, wandering through the district doing penance. So that, in the course of time, various strange legends grew up among the simple countryfolk, and some of these reached the ears of Ferondo's wife, who was not mystified in the slightest.

When Ferondo recovered his senses, without having the faintest idea where he was, the Bolognese monk burst in upon him brandishing a bunch of sticks; and with a terrifying roar, he seized hold of him and gave him a severe thrashing. Weeping and howling, Ferondo kept repeating the same question:

'Where am I?'

'You are in Purgatory,' replied the monk.

'What?' said Ferondo. 'Do you mean to say I am dead, then?'

'You certainly are,' said the monk; whereupon Ferondo started bemoaning his fate and weeping over the plight of his wife and child, coming out with the most extraordinary statements imaginable.

The monk then brought him some food and drink, and Ferondo gasped with astonishment, saying:

'Do dead people eat?'

'Yes,' said the monk. 'As a matter of fact, the food I am giving you was sent this morning to the church by the woman who was your wife, with a request that masses should be said for your soul. And it is God's wish that you should have it here and now.'

'God bless her little heart!' exclaimed Ferondo. 'I did love her a lot of course, before I died. Why, I used to hold her in my arms all night, and I never stopped kissing her. And when the mood took me, I did more besides.'

His appetite being enormous, he then began to eat and drink, but the wine was not entirely to his liking.

'God damn the woman!' he exclaimed. 'This wine she's given to the priest didn't come from the cask alongside the wall.'

He continued with his meal, however, and when he had finished, the monk brandished his bunch of sticks once again, seized him a second time, and gave him another severe hiding.

'Hey!' yelled Ferondo, making the dickens of a protest. 'What are you doing this to me for?'

'Because the Almighty has given strict orders that you are to be beaten twice every day.'

'For what reason?'

'Because you were jealous of your wife, who was the finest woman in the whole district.'

'Alas, how right you are,' said Ferondo. 'She was also the sweetest; aye, sweeter than a sugar-plum. But I would never have been jealous if I had known I was giving offence to the Almighty.'

'You should have thought of that while you were still on the other side,' said the monk. 'You should have mended your ways before it was too late. And if you ever happen to return, be very careful to remember what I am doing now, and never be jealous again.'

'Eh? But surely the dead don't ever return, do they?'

'Some do, if God so wills it.'

'Well, I'm blessed!' said Ferondo. 'If I ever go back, I shall be the best husband in the world. I'll never beat her, nor scold her either, except about the wine she sent this morning. Which reminds me: she didn't send a single candle, and I was forced to eat in the dark.'

'She did send some,' said the monk, 'but they were used up during the masses.'

'Ah, yes,' said Ferondo, 'that'll be what has happened. Anyway, if I go back, I shall definitely allow her to do as she pleases. But tell me, why should *you* be doing this to me? Who are you?'

'I also am dead,' replied the monk. 'I lived in Sardinia, and because I lauded my master to the skies for his jealousy, God has decreed that I should be punished by supplying you with food and drink and these thrashings until He decides what to do with us next.'

'Is there anybody else here, apart from ourselves?' asked Ferondo.

'Yes, thousands,' said the monk. 'But you cannot see or hear them, any more than they can see or hear you.'

'And how far are we away from home?'

'Oho! Far more miles than one of our turds would travel.'

'Crikey! that's a fair distance. I should think we must have left the earth behind entirely.'

This kind of gibberish,[4] together with his food rations and his regular beatings, kept Ferondo going for ten whole months during which the Abbot was highly assiduous and enterprising in his visits to the fair lady, with whom he had the jolliest time imaginable. But accidents will happen, and the lady eventually became pregnant, promptly told the Abbot about it, and they both agreed that Ferondo must be recalled at once from Purgatory and reunited with his wife, who undertook to convince him that it was he who had got her with child.

So the following night, the Abbot went to Ferondo's cell, and disguising his voice, he called to him and said:

'Ferondo, be of good cheer, for God has decreed that you should go back to earth, where, after your return, your wife will present you with a son.[5] See that the child is christened Benedict, for it is in answer to the prayers of your reverend Abbot and your wife, and because of His love for Saint Benedict, that God has done you this favour.'

This announcement was received by Ferondo with great glee.

'I am very glad to hear it,' he said. 'God bless Mister Almighty and the Abbot and Saint Benedict and my cheesy-weesy, honey-bunny, sweetie-weetie wife.'

Having put sufficient powder in Ferondo's wine to send him to sleep for about four hours, the Abbot dressed him in his proper clothes again and quietly restored him, with the aid of his monk, to the tomb in which he had originally been laid to rest.

A little after dawn next morning, Ferondo came to his senses and noticed a chink of light coming through a crack in the side of the tomb. Not having seen any light for ten whole months, he concluded that he must be alive, and started to shout:

'Open up! Open up!'

At the same time, he began to press his head firmly against the lid of the tomb, and not being very secure, it yielded and he started to push it aside. Meanwhile the monks, who had just finished reciting their matins, hurried to the scene, and when they recognized Ferondo's voice and saw him emerging from the tomb, they were all terrified by the novelty of the occurrence and ran off to inform the Abbot.

The Abbot pretended to be rising from prayer.

'My sons,' he said, 'be not afraid. Take up the cross and the holy water and follow me. Let us go and see what God's omnipotence has in store for us.' And away he strode.

Ferondo, who was as white as a sheet on account of his prolonged incarceration in total darkness, had meanwhile emerged from the tomb, and on seeing the Abbot approaching, he hurled himself at his feet, saying:

'Father, I have been rescued from the torments of Purgatory and restored to life, and it was revealed to me that my release was brought about by your prayers, together with those of my wife and Saint Benedict. God bless you, therefore, and make you prosper, now and forever more!'

'God be praised for His omnipotence!' exclaimed the Abbot. 'Now that He has sent you back again, just you run along, my son, and comfort your good lady, for she has done nothing but weep since the day you departed this life. And take good care, from now on, to serve God and hold on to His friendship.'

'That's good advice, sir, and no mistake,' said Ferondo. 'Leave things to me. I love her so much that I'll give her a great big kiss the moment I find her.'

The Abbot pretended to marvel greatly over what had happened, and as soon as he was alone with his monks, he had them all devoutly chanting the *Miserere*.

When Ferondo returned to his village, everyone he met ran away from him in horror, and his wife was no less frightened of him than the rest, but he called them all back, assuring them that he had been restored to life. And once they recovered from the initial shock and saw that he really was alive, they bombarded him with questions, to all of which he replied as though he had been transformed into some kind of soothsayer, providing them with information about the souls of their kinsfolk and inventing all manner of marvellous tales about what went on in Purgatory. Moreover, he supplied the assembled populace with an account of the revelation he had received, before his return, from the Arse-angel Bagriel's own lips.[6]

Having returned home with his wife and retaken possession of his property, he got her with child, or so he thought at any rate. He had been recalled not a moment too soon, for after a pregnancy that happened to be long enough to confirm the vulgar error which supposes that women carry their babies for exactly nine months, his wife gave birth to a son, which was christened Benedetto Ferondi.

Since nearly everyone was convinced that he really had been brought back from the dead, Ferondo's return and his tall stories immeasurably enhanced the Abbot's reputation for saintliness. And for his own part, because of the countless hidings he had received on account of his jealousy, Ferondo stopped being jealous and became a reformed character, so that the expectations held out to the lady by the Abbot were fulfilled to the letter. Of this she was very glad, and thereafter she lived no less chastely with her husband than she had in the past, except that, whenever the occasion arose, she gladly renewed her intimacy with the Abbot, who had ministered to her greatest needs with such unfailing skill and diligence.

NINTH STORY

Gilette of Narbonne,[1] having cured the King of France of a fistula,[2] asks him for the hand of Bertrand of Roussillon in marriage. Bertrand marries her against his will, then goes off in high dudgeon to Florence, where he pays court to a young woman whom Gilette impersonates, sleeping with him and presenting him with two children. In this way, he finally comes to love her and acknowledge her as his wife.

When Lauretta's tale had ended, the queen, not wishing to revoke Dioneo's privilege, and realizing that she herself was the only person left to speak, began without waiting to be urged. And with all her considerable charm she addressed her companions as follows:

How is anyone to tell a better story than the one we have just heard from Lauretta? It was certainly fortunate for us that hers was not the first, for otherwise we would have derived little pleasure from the ones that followed, which is what I fear will happen with the last two stories of today. However, for what it is worth, I am going to tell you a story on the topic we proposed.

★

In the kingdom of France, there once lived a nobleman who was called Isnard, Count of Roussillon, and who, being something of an invalid, always kept a doctor, named Master Gerard of Narbonne, at his beck and call. The Count had only one child, a little boy of exceedingly handsome and pleasing appearance called Bertrand, who was brought up with other children of his own age, among them the daughter of the doctor I have mentioned, whose name was Gilette. Gilette was head over heels in love with this Bertrand, being more passionately attached to him than was strictly proper in a girl of so tender an age, so that when, on the death of the Count, Bertrand was committed to the guardianship of the King and had to go away to Paris, she was driven to the brink of despair. Shortly afterwards, her own father died, and if she could have found a plausible excuse, she would gladly have gone to Paris in order to visit Bertrand. But she could see no way of doing it without causing a scandal, for she had inherited the whole of her father's fortune, and was kept under constant surveillance.

Even after reaching marriageable age, she still could not forget Bertrand, and without offering any explanation she rejected numerous suitors whom her kinsfolk had urged her to marry.

Now, because she had heard that Bertrand had become an exceedingly handsome young man, the flames of her love were raging more fiercely than ever when she happened to hear that the King of France had been suffering from a chest-tumour, which, because it had been treated maladroitly, had left him with a fistula that was causing him endless trouble and discomfort. Numerous doctors had been consulted, but he had not yet succeeded in finding a single one who was able to cure him. On the contrary, they had merely made matters worse, with the result that the King had abandoned all hope of recovery, and was refusing to accept further advice or treatment from anyone.

The girl was filled with joy to hear these tidings, for she realized that not only did they give her a legitimate reason for going to Paris, but, if the illness of the King was what she thought it was, she would have little difficulty in obtaining Bertrand's hand in marriage. Using the knowledge she had acquired in the past from her father, she proceeded to make up a powder from certain herbs that were good for the ailment she had diagnosed, then she rode off to Paris. Before doing anything else, she contrived to see Bertrand, after which she obtained an audience of the King and asked his permission to examine his malady. Not knowing how to refuse a young woman of such evident charm and beauty, the King allowed her to do so, and she knew at once that she could make him recover.

'Sire,' she said, 'if you are willing, with God's help I can cure you of this malady within the space of a week, without causing you any bother or discomfort.'

The King refused to take her seriously, saying to himself: 'How could a young woman succeed in doing something that has defeated the skill and knowledge of the world's greatest physicians?' He therefore thanked her for her good intentions, adding that he had resolved to decline all further medical advice.

'Sire,' said the girl, 'you are sceptical of my powers because I am young and because I am a woman; but I would have you know that my powers of healing do not depend so much upon my knowledge as upon the assistance of God and the expertise of my late father, Master Gerard of Narbonne, who in his day was a famous physician.'

'Who knows?' thought the King to himself. 'Perhaps this woman has been sent to me by God. Why not find out what she can do? After all, she claims she can cure me in next to no time without causing me any discomfort.' And by reasoning thus, he persuaded himself that he should put her claims to the test.

'Young woman,' he said. 'Suppose we were to break our resolve, only to find that you fail to effect a cure? What penalty would you consider appropriate?'

'Sire,' replied the girl. 'Keep me under guard, and if I do not cure you within a week, order me to be burned. But what reward shall I have if I make you recover?'

'If you do that,' replied the King, 'then since you appear to be unmarried, we shall provide you with a fine and noble husband.'

'Sire,' said the girl, 'I would certainly like you to give me a husband, but only the one I shall ask for, and you may rest assured that I shall not ask you for one of your sons or any other royal personage.'

The King gave her his promise forthwith, and the girl began to apply her remedy, restoring him to health with time to spare. Whereupon the King, feeling he had quite recovered, said to her:

'Young woman, you have clearly won yourself a husband.'

'In that case, sire,' she replied, 'I have won Bertrand of Roussillon, with whom I have been deeply in love since the days of my childhood.'

It was no laughing matter to the King that he should be obliged to give her Bertrand. But not wishing to break the promise he had given her, he sent for him and said:

'Bertrand, you are now fully trained and mature, and it is our pleasure that you should return to govern your lands, taking with you the young lady whom we have decided you should marry.'

'And who, my lord, may this young lady be?' asked Bertrand.

'She is the one who has restored our health with her physic,' replied the King.

Bertrand knew the girl, and had thought her very beautiful on seeing her again. But knowing that her lineage was in no way suited to his own noble ancestry, he was highly indignant, and said:

'But surely, sire, you would not want to marry me to a she-doctor. Heaven forbid that I should ever accept a woman of that sort for a wife.'

'The young lady has demanded your hand in marriage as her reward for restoring our health,' said the King. 'Surely you would not want us to break the promise we have given her.'

'Sire,' said Bertrand, 'you have the power to take away everything I possess, and hand me over to anyone you may choose, for I am merely your humble vassal. But I can assure you that I shall never rest content with such a match.'

'Of course you will,' said the King, 'for she is beautiful, intelligent, and deeply in love with you. Hence we are confident that you will be much happier with her than you would ever have been with a lady of loftier birth.'

Bertrand said no more, and the King gave orders for a splendid wedding feast to be arranged. And so, much against his will, on the appointed day and in the presence of the King, Bertrand married the girl who loved him more dearly than her very life. Having already made up his mind what he should do, as soon as the wedding was over he sought the King's permission to depart, saying that he wished to return to his own estates and consummate his marriage there. So he duly set out on horseback, but instead of going to his estates he came to Tuscany, where he learned that the Florentines were waging war against the Sienese,[3] and resolved to offer them his assistance. The Florentines welcomed him with open arms and placed him in command of a sizeable body of men, paying him a good stipend, and for a long time thereafter he remained in their service.

His bride was far from happy with the turn events had taken, and in the hope of persuading him to return to his estates by her wise administration, she went to Roussillon, where all the people received her as their rightful mistress. Since there had been no Count to govern the territory for some little time, she was faced on her arrival with nothing but confusion and chaos. But being a capable woman, she applied herself with great diligence to the task in hand, and soon had everything restored to order, thus winning the profound respect and devotion of her subjects, who were enormously pleased by her endeavours and strongly critical of the Count because of his indifference towards her.

Having fully restored the Count's domain to order, the lady communicated this fact to her husband by way of two knights, beseeching him to inform her whether it was on her account that he was deserting his lands, in which case she would go away in order to please him. He answered them very brusquely, saying:

'She may do whatever she likes. For my own part, I shall go back to live with her when she wears this ring upon her finger, and when she is carrying a child of mine in her arms.'

The ring was very dear to him, and he never let it stray from his finger on account of certain magical powers which he had been told that it possessed.

The knights realized that it was virtually impossible for the lady to comply with either of these harsh conditions, but no amount of reasoning on their part could shift him from his resolve, and they therefore returned to their mistress to acquaint her with his answer. Their tidings filled her with dismay, but after giving some thought to the matter she decided to try and find out how and where these two things might be accomplished, thus enabling her to win back her husband. Having carefully considered what she must do, she called together a group of the leading notables of those parts, gave them a highly succinct and moving description of all she had done out of her love for the Count, and pointed out the results of her endeavours. Then she told them that she had no intention of protracting her stay if this entailed the Count's continued exile; on the contrary, she meant to spend the rest of her days in making pilgrimages and performing works of charity for the good of her soul. Finally, she asked them to take over the defence and administration of the territory, and to inform the Count that she had left him its exclusive and unencumbered title; then she vanished from the scene, having resolved never to set foot in Roussillon again.

As she spoke, her worthy hearers shed countless tears and pleaded with her over and over again to change her mind and stay with them, but all to no avail. Having bidden them farewell, she set out with one of her maidservants and a man who was her cousin, both of whom were dressed, like herself, in pilgrim's garb, and taking with her a goodly quantity of money and precious jewels. She had told no one where she was going, but in fact she made straight for Florence without pausing to rest. On her arrival, she chanced upon a little inn that was kept by a kindly widow, and there she quietly took up her abode in the guise of a poor pilgrim, eager for news of her husband.

It so happened that on the very next day, she saw Bertrand go riding past the inn on horseback with his men, and although she recognized him quite distinctly, she none the less inquired who he was from the good lady of the inn.

'He is a foreign nobleman,' replied the hostess. 'His name is Count Bertrand, he is a great favourite with the Florentines because of his affable and gentlemanly nature, and he is head over heels in love with a young lady living nearby, who is nobly bred but poor. The fact is that she is a most virtuous girl, who has not yet married on account of her poverty, but lives with her mother, a lady of great wisdom and probity. Indeed, but for this mother of hers, it is quite possible that the Count would already have had his way with the girl.'

The Countess committed everything to memory, and after giving further thought to each of the things she had heard and building a mental picture of the affair as a whole, she decided on her course of action. And one day, having discovered the name and address of the lady and this daughter of hers who was loved by the Count, she made her way unobtrusively to their house, wearing her pilgrim's habit. The poverty of the two women was immediately apparent to the Countess, who greeted them and asked the lady if she could talk to her in private.

The gentlewoman rose to her feet, assuring her that she was ready to listen, and led her into another room, where they sat down.

'Madam,' said the Countess, 'you and your daughter would appear to have fallen on hard times, and I too am dogged by ill luck. But if you so desired, you could perhaps repair your fortunes as well as my own at one and the same time.'

The lady replied that nothing would please her better than to repair her fortunes without compromising her honour.

'It is essential that I should be able to trust you,' continued the Countess, 'because if you were to betray my confidence, you would ruin everything, for all three of us.'

'You may confide in me as much as you like,' said the gentlewoman, 'for you may rest assured that I shall never betray you.'

The Countess then disclosed her true identity and related the whole history of her love from its earliest beginnings, telling her tale so touchingly that the gentlewoman, who had already gleaned some knowledge of the matter from elsewhere, was convinced that she was telling the truth and began to take pity on her. Having told her all the facts, the Countess continued:

'This, then, is the tale of my misfortunes. As you have heard, there are two things I must obtain if I am to have my husband. And I know of no one who can help me to obtain them except yourself, if it is true, as I have been led to believe, that my husband the Count is deeply in love with your daughter.'

'I know not, madam, whether the Count is in love with my

daughter,' replied the gentlewoman. 'He claims to be, certainly, but how will this make it easier for me to assist you?'

'I will tell you,' said the Countess, 'but first of all I want to explain how I intend to repay your assistance. I see that your daughter is beautiful and of marriageable age, but it seems, both from what I have been told and from the evidence of my own eyes, that the impossibility of making a good marriage for her compels you to keep her at home. I therefore propose to reward your services by promptly supplying her, from my own resources, with whatever dowry you think she needs for an honourable marriage.'

The lady, being destitute, was attracted by this offer. But she was also proud of spirit, and she replied:

'Pray explain to me, madam, in what way I can assist you. If it is honourable for me to further your plans, I shall be glad to do so, and afterwards you may reward me in whatever way you please.'

Whereupon the Countess said:

'What I require you to do is to send some trustworthy person to inform my husband, the Count, that your daughter is prepared to place herself entirely at his disposal, but only on condition that he proves to her that his love is as deep and genuine as he claims; this she will never believe until he sends her the ring which he wears upon his hand and to which she understands that he is deeply attached. If he sends her the ring, you will hand it over to me, and then you will send him a message to the effect that your daughter is ready to do his bidding, and you will cause him to come here in secret and, all unsuspecting, lie with me instead of your daughter. Perhaps by the grace of God I shall become pregnant, and later on, with my husband's ring on my finger and my husband's child in my arms, I will regain his love and live with him as a wife should live with a husband. And it will all be thanks to you.'

In the eyes of the gentlewoman, this was no trivial request, for she was afraid lest her daughter's name be brought into disrepute. But after due reflection, she came to the conclusion that it was right and proper for her to assist the good lady to retrieve her husband, for she would be acting in pursuit of a worthy objective. And therefore, placing her trust in the transparent goodness and honesty of the Countess, she not only promised to do what was required, but within the space of a few days, proceeding with all necessary secrecy and caution, she had obtained possession of the ring from the Count (who was somewhat reluctant to part with it), and achieved the remarkable feat of putting the Countess to bed with him in place of her own daughter.

In the course of their earliest embraces, to which the Count devoted considerable ardour, God so willed that the lady should conceive two sons, as became manifest when the time arrived for her to bring them forth. This was not the only occasion, however, on which the gentlewoman arranged for the Countess to enjoy her husband's love, for she devised many other such encounters, proceeding with so much secrecy that nobody ever came to know about them. The Count went on believing that he had been consorting, not with his wife, but with the girl he loved; and before leaving her in the morning, he would present her with beautiful and precious jewels, all of which the Countess took special care to preserve.

Once she perceived that she was pregnant, the Countess no longer desired to trouble the gentlewoman any further, and said to her:

'By the grace of God, my lady, and thanks to your assistance, I now have what I wanted, and hence it is time for me to do whatever you want me to do, so that I may take my leave.'

The gentlewoman insisted that so long as the Countess was contented with what she had achieved, then she too was satisfied, and that she had not assisted her in the hope of obtaining any reward, but merely because she had felt it her duty to support so worthy a cause.

'I fully understand,' said the Countess. 'And for my own part, I have no intention of granting you any reward. I shall give you whatever you ask of me because the cause is worthy and I feel obliged to support it.'

The gentlewoman was sorely embarrassed, but her needs were great, and she asked for a hundred pounds so that she could marry her daughter. On hearing her ask for so modest a sum, the Countess, sensing her embarrassment, gave her five hundred pounds, together with a quantity of fine and precious jewels that probably amounted in value to the same sum again. The gentlewoman, quite overcome, thanked the Countess as warmly as she could, after which the Countess took her leave of her and returned to the inn.

So that Bertrand should have no further reason for sending messages or paying visits to her house, the gentlewoman took her daughter away with her to live with relatives in the country. And shortly afterwards, Bertrand was recalled by his nobles and returned home, having been assured that the Countess had gone away.

On hearing that he had left Florence and returned to his estates, the Countess was overjoyed. She herself remained in Florence until the time came for her confinement, when she gave birth to twin sons who were the image of their father. She took special care to have them properly nursed, and when she considered the time to be ripe, she set out with the children and succeeded in reaching Montpelier[4] without being recognized. There she rested for a few days, making inquiries concerning the Count and his whereabouts, and on learning that he would be holding a magnificent feast for his lords and ladies on All Saints' Day in Roussillon, she too made her way there, still attired in the pilgrim's garb to which she had by now become accustomed.

Arriving at the Count's palace, she heard all the lords and ladies talking together prior to sitting at table, and so she made her way up to the hall, still wearing the same clothes and carrying the two infants in her arms, and threaded her way through the guests until, catching sight of the Count, she flung herself at his feet and burst into tears, saying:

'My lord, behold your unfortunate bride, who has suffered the pangs of a long and bitter exile so that you could return and settle in your ancestral home. I now beseech you, in God's name, to observe the conditions you imposed upon me through the agency of those two knights I sent to you. Here in my arms I carry, not merely one of your children, but two; and here is your ring. So the time has come for you to honour your promise and accept me as your wife.'

The Count could scarcely believe his ears, yet had to admit that the ring was his and that the children, since they resembled him so exactly, must also be his. All he could find to say was:

'How can this have happened?'

To the utter astonishment of the Count and all the others present, the Countess then related the whole of her story from beginning to end. Well knowing that she was telling the truth, and seeing what a handsome pair of children her remarkable persistence and intelligence had produced, the Count could no longer feel hostile towards her, and he not only honoured his promise but endeared himself to his lords and ladies (who were all entreating him to accept and welcome her as his lawful spouse) by helping the Countess to her feet, smothering her with kisses and embraces, and recognizing her as his lawful wife, at the same time acknowledging the children to be his. And having caused her to change into robes befitting her rank, he gave up the rest of the day to feasting and merrymaking, to the no small pleasure of those present and all of his vassals who came to hear of it. The festivities continued for several days, and from that time forth, never failing to honour the Countess as his lawful wedded wife, he loved her and held her in the greatest esteem.

TENTH STORY

Alibech becomes a recluse, and after being taught by the monk, Rustico, to put the devil back in Hell, she is eventually taken away to become the wife of Neerbal.

Dioneo had been following the queen's story closely, and on perceiving that it was finished, knowing that he was the only speaker left, he smiled and began without waiting to be bidden:

Gracious ladies, you have possibly never heard how the devil is put back into Hell, and hence, without unduly straying from the theme of your discussions for today, I should like to tell you about it. By learning how it is done, there may yet be time perhaps for you to save our souls from perdition, and you will also discover that, even though Love is more inclined to take up his abode in a gay palace and a dainty bedchamber than in a wretched hovel, there is no denying that he sometimes makes his powers felt among pathless woods, on rugged mountains, and in desert caves; nor is this surprising, since all living things are subject to his sway.

★

Now, to come to the point, there once lived in the town of Gafsa,[1] in Barbary, a very rich man who had numerous children, among them a lovely and graceful young daughter called Alibech. She was not herself a Christian, but there were many Christians in the town, and one day, having on occasion heard them extol the Christian faith and the service of God, she asked one of them for his opinion on the best and easiest way for a person to 'serve God', as they put it. He answered her by saying that the ones who served God best were those who put the greatest distance between themselves and earthly goods, as happened in the case of people who had gone to live in the remoter parts of the Sahara.[2]

She said no more about it to anyone, but next morning, being a very simple-natured creature of fourteen or thereabouts, Alibech set out all alone, in secret, and made her way towards the desert, prompted by nothing more logical than a strong adolescent impulse. A few days later, exhausted from fatigue and hunger, she arrived in the heart of the wilderness, where, catching sight of a small hut in the distance, she stumbled towards it, and in the doorway she found a holy man, who was astonished to see her in those parts and asked her what she was doing there. She told him that she had been inspired by God, and that she was trying, not only to serve Him, but also to find someone who could teach her how she should go about it.

On observing how young and exceedingly pretty she was, the good man was afraid to take her under his wing lest the devil should catch him unawares. So he praised her for her good intentions, and having given her a quantity of herb-roots, wild apples and dates to eat, and some water to drink, he said to her:

'My daughter, not very far from here there is a holy man who is much more capable than I of teaching you what you want to know. Go along to him.' And he sent her upon her way.

When she came to this second man, she was told precisely the same thing, and so she went on until she arrived at the cell of a young hermit, a very devout and kindly fellow called Rustico, to whom she put the same inquiry as she had addressed to the others. Being anxious to prove to himself that he possessed a will of iron, he did not, like the others, send her away or direct her elsewhere, but kept her with him in his cell, in a corner of which, when night descended, he prepared a makeshift bed out of palm-leaves, upon which he invited her to lie down and rest.

Once he had taken this step, very little time elapsed before temptation went to war against his willpower, and after the first few assaults, finding himself outmanoeuvred on all fronts, he laid down his arms and surrendered. Casting aside pious thoughts, prayers, and penitential exercises, he began to concentrate his mental faculties upon the youth and beauty of the girl, and to devise suitable ways and means for approaching her in such a fashion that she should not think it lewd of him to make the sort of proposal he had in mind. By putting certain questions to her, he soon discovered that she had never been intimate with the opposite sex and was every bit as innocent as she seemed; and he therefore thought of a possible way to persuade her, with the pretext of serving God, to grant his desires. He began by delivering a long speech in which he showed her how powerful an enemy the devil was to the Lord God, and followed this up by impressing upon her that of all the ways of serving God, the one that He most appreciated consisted in putting the devil back in Hell, to which the Almighty had consigned him in the first place.

The girl asked him how this was done, and Rustico replied:

'You will soon find out, but just do whatever you see me doing for the present.' And so saying, he began to divest himself of the few clothes he was wearing, leaving himself completely naked. The girl followed his example, and he sank to his knees as though he were about to pray, getting her to kneel directly opposite.

In this posture, the girl's beauty was displayed to Rustico in all its glory, and his longings blazed more fiercely than ever, bringing about the resurrection of the flesh.[3] Alibech stared at this in amazement, and said:

'Rustico, what is that thing I see sticking out in front of you, which I do not possess?'

'Oh, my daughter,' said Rustico, 'this is the devil I was telling you about. Do you see what he's doing? He's hurting me so much that I can hardly endure it.'

'Oh, praise be to God,' said the girl, 'I can see that I am better off than you are, for I have no such devil to contend with.'

'You're right there,' said Rustico. 'But you have something else instead, that I haven't.'

'Oh?' said Alibech. 'And what's that?'

'You have Hell,' said Rustico. 'And I honestly believe that God has sent you here for the salvation of my soul, because if this devil continues to plague the life out of me, and if you are prepared to take sufficient pity upon me to let me put him back into Hell, you will be giving me marvellous relief, as well as rendering incalculable service and pleasure to God, which is what you say you came here for in the first place.'

'Oh, Father,' replied the girl in all innocence, 'if I really do have a Hell, let's do as you suggest just as soon as you are ready.'

'God bless you, my daughter,' said Rustico. 'Let us go and put him back, and then perhaps he'll leave me alone.'

At which point he conveyed the girl to one of their beds, where he instructed her in the art of incarcerating that accursed fiend.

Never having put a single devil into Hell before, the girl found the first experience a little painful, and she said to Rustico:

'This devil must certainly be a bad lot, Father, and a true enemy of God, for as well as plaguing mankind, he even hurts Hell when he's driven back inside it.'

'Daughter,' said Rustico, 'it will not always be like that.' And in order to ensure that it wouldn't, before moving from the bed they put him back half a dozen times, curbing his arrogance to such good effect that he was positively glad to keep still for the rest of the day.

During the next few days, however, the devil's pride frequently reared its head again, and the girl, ever ready to obey the call to duty and bring him under control, happened to develop a taste for the sport, and began saying to Rustico:

'I can certainly see what those worthy men in Gafsa meant when they said that serving God was so agreeable. I don't honestly recall ever having done anything that gave me so much pleasure and satisfaction as I get from putting the devil back in Hell. To my way of thinking, anyone who devotes his energies to anything but the service of God is a complete blockhead.'

She thus developed the habit of going to Rustico at frequent intervals, and saying to him:

'Father, I came here to serve God, not to idle away my time. Let's go and put the devil back in Hell.'

And sometimes, in the middle of their labours, she would say:

'What puzzles me, Rustico, is that the devil should ever want to escape from Hell. Because if he liked being there as much as Hell enjoys receiving him and keeping him inside, he would never go away at all.'

By inviting Rustico to play the game too often, continually urging him on in the service of God, the girl took so much stuffing out of him that he eventually began to turn cold where another man would have been bathed in sweat. So he told her that the devil should only be punished and put back in Hell when he reared his head with pride, adding that by the grace of Heaven, they had tamed him so effectively that he was pleading with God to be left in peace. In this way, he managed to keep the girl quiet for a while, but one day, having begun to notice that Rustico was no longer asking for the devil to be put back in Hell, she said:

'Look here, Rustico. Even though your devil has been punished and pesters you no longer, my Hell simply refuses to leave me alone. Now that I have helped you with my Hell to subdue the pride of your devil, the least you can do is to get your devil to help me tame the fury of my Hell.'

Rustico, who was living on a diet of herb-roots and water, was quite incapable of supplying her requirements, and told her that the taming of her Hell would require an awful lot of devils, but promised to do what he could. Sometimes, therefore, he responded to the call, but this happened so infrequently that it was rather like chucking a bean into the mouth of a lion, with the result that the girl, who felt that she was not serving God as diligently as she would have liked, was found complaining more often than not.

But at the height of this dispute between Alibech's Hell and Rustico's devil, brought about by a surplus of desire on the one hand and a shortage of power on the other, a fire broke out in Gafsa, and Alibech's father was burnt to death in his own house along with all his children and every other member of his household, so that Alibech inherited the whole of his property. Because of this a young man called Neerbal who had spent the whole of his substance in sumptuous living, having heard that she was still alive, set out to look for her, and before the authorities were able to appropriate her late father's fortune on the grounds that there was no heir, he succeeded in tracing her whereabouts. To the great relief of Rustico, but against her own wishes, he took her back to Gafsa and married her, thus inheriting a half-share in her father's enormous fortune.

Before Neerbal had actually slept with her, she was questioned by the women of Gafsa about how she had served God in the desert, and she replied that she had served Him by putting the devil back in Hell, and that Neerbal had committed a terrible sin by stopping her from performing so worthy a service.

'How do you put the devil back in Hell?' asked the women.

Partly in words and partly through gestures, the girl showed them how it was done, whereupon the women laughed so much that they are laughing yet; and they said:

'Don't let it worry you, my dear. People do the job every bit as well here in Gafsa, and Neerbal will give you plenty of help in serving the Lord.'

The story was repeated throughout the town, being passed from one woman to the next, and they coined a proverbial saying there to the effect that the most agreeable way of serving God was to put the devil back in Hell. The dictum later crossed the sea to Italy, where it survives to this day.

And so, young ladies, if you stand in need of God's grace, see that you learn to put the devil back in Hell, for it is greatly to His liking and pleasurable to the parties concerned, and a great deal of good can arise and flow in the process.

★   ★   ★

So aptly and cleverly worded did Dioneo's tale appear to the virtuous ladies, that they shook with mirth a thousand times or more. And when he had brought it to a close, the queen, acknowledging the end of her sovereignty, removed the laurel from her head and placed it very gracefully on Filostrato's, saying:

'Now we shall discover whether the wolf can fare any better at leading the sheep than the sheep have fared in leading the wolves.'

On hearing this, Filostrato laughed and said: 'Had you listened to me, the wolves would have taught the sheep by now to put the devil back in Hell, no less skilfully than Rustico taught Alibech. But you have not exactly been behaving like sheep, and therefore you must not describe us as wolves. However, you have placed the kingdom in my hands, and I shall govern it as well as I am able.'

'Allow me to tell you, Filostrato,' replied Neifile, 'that if you men had tried to teach us anything of the sort, you might have learned some sense from us, as Masetto did from the nuns, and retrieved the use of your tongues when your bones were rattling from exhaustion.'

On perceiving that the ladies had as many scythes as he had arrows, Filostrato abandoned his jesting and turned to the business of ruling his kingdom. Summoning the steward, he asked him to explain how matters stood, after which he discreetly gave him his instructions, consisting of what he thought would be appropriate and agreeable to the company as a whole. He then turned to the ladies, saying:

'Charming ladies, ever since I was able to distinguish good from evil, it has been my unhappy lot, owing to the beauty of one of your number, to find myself perpetually enslaved to Love. I have humbly and obediently followed all of his rules to the very best of my ability, only to find that I have invariably been forsaken to make way for another. Things have gone from bad to worse for me, and I do not suppose they will improve to my dying day. I therefore decree that the subject of our discussions for the morrow should be none other than the one which applies most closely to myself, namely, *those whose love ended unhappily.* For my part, I expect my own love to have a thoroughly unhappy ending, nor was it for any other reason that I was given (by one who knew what he was talking about) the name by which you address me.'[1] And having uttered these words, he rose to his feet and dismissed them all till suppertime.

The garden was so lovely and delectable, that none of them chose to stray beyond its confines in search of greater pleasure in other parts. On the contrary, once the sun was now much cooler and no longer made hunting a chore, some of the ladies set off in pursuit of the hares and roebucks and other animals in the garden, that had been startling them by leaping a hundred times or more into their midst as they sat and talked. Dioneo and Fiammetta began to sing a song about Messer Guiglielmo and the Lady of Vergiú,[2] whilst Filomena and Panfilo settled down to a game of chess. So intently were they all engaged upon their several activities, that the time passed by unnoticed, and when the hour of supper came, it caught them unawares. The tables were then placed round the edge of the beautiful fountain, and there, to their immense delight, they supped in the cool of the evening.

No sooner had the tables been removed than Filostrato, wishing to follow the same path that the ladies crowned before him had taken, called upon Lauretta to dance and sing them a song.

'My lord,' she said, 'the only songs I know are the ones I have composed myself, and of those I remember, none is especially apt for so merry a gathering as this. But if you would like me to sing you one, I will gladly oblige.'

'Nothing of yours could be other than pleasing and beautiful,' replied the king. 'Sing it, therefore, exactly as you wrote it.'

And so, in mellifluous but somewhat plaintive tones, Lauretta began as follows, and the other ladies repeated the refrain after each verse:

'None has need for lamentation
More than have I
Who, alas, all sick for love
In vain do sigh.

'He who moves the stars and heavens[3]
Decreed me at my birth
Light, lovely, graceful, fair to see,
To show men here on earth
Some sign of that eternal grace
That shines for ever in His face.

But I went all unprized
Because of men's unknowing
And mortal imperfection
Spurned and despised!

'One man once loved me dearly.
In his embrace
He held me, and in all his thoughts
I held high place.
My eyes with love inflamed him
And all my time I spent,
Which flew by all so lightly,
In tender blandishment.
    But now I am forsaken;
    From me, alas, he's taken.

'And now there came before me
A youth all proud and vain
Though noble reputation
Gave him a valiant name.
He took me, and false fancies,
Alas for me!
Made him a jealous gaoler:
Gone liberty!
    And I, who came to earth
    To bring mankind delight
    Learned to despair, almost,
    Gone all my mirth!

'I curse my wretched fate
When I agreed
To change to wedding clothes
From widow's weeds.
Though they were dark, perhaps,
My life was fair; but now
I live a weary life,
With far less honour, too.
    Oh cursed wedding-tie!
    Before I took those vows
    That brought me to this pass
    Would God had let me die!

'Oh, sweetest love, with whom
I once was so content!
From where you stand, with Him
To whom our souls are sent,
Ah, spare some pity for me
For I cannot remove
Your memory which burns me
With all the pain of love!
   Ah, pray that I may soon return
   To those sweet climes for which I yearn!'

Here Lauretta ended her song, to which all had listened raptly and construed in different ways. There were those who took it, in the Milanese fashion,[4] to imply that a good fat pig was better than a comely wench. But others gave it a loftier, more subtle and truer meaning, which this is not the moment to expound.

The king then called for lighted torches to be set at regular intervals amongst the lawns and flowerbeds, and at his behest, Lauretta's song was followed by many others until every star that had risen was beginning its descent, when, thinking it time for them all to retire, he bade them goodnight and sent them away to their various rooms.

Here ends the Third Day of the Decameron

FOURTH DAY

Here begins the Fourth Day, wherein, under the rule of Filo-strato, *the discussion turns upon those whose love ended unhappily.*

Dearest ladies, both from what I have heard on the lips of the wise, and from what I have frequently read and observed for myself, I always assumed that only lofty towers and the highest summits of trees could be assailed by Envy's fiery and impetuous blast;[1] but I find that I was mistaken. In the course of my lifelong efforts to escape the fierce onslaught of those turbulent winds, I have always made a point of going quietly and unseen about my affairs, not only keeping to the lowlands but occasionally directing my steps through the deepest of deep valleys. This can very easily be confirmed by anyone casting an eye over these little stories of mine, which bear no title[2] and which I have written, not only in the Florentine vernacular and in prose, but in the most homely and unassuming style[3] it is possible to imagine. Yet in spite of all this, I have been unable to avoid being violently shaken and almost uprooted by those very winds, and was nearly torn to pieces by envy. And thus I can most readily appreciate the truth of the wise men's saying, that in the affairs of this world, poverty alone is without envy.[4]

Judicious ladies, there are those who have said, after reading these tales, that I am altogether too fond of you, that it is unseemly for me to take so much delight in entertaining and consoling you, and, what is apparently worse, in singing your praises as I do. Others, laying claim to greater profundity, have said that it is not good for a man of my age to engage in such pursuits as discussing the ways of women and providing for their pleasure. And others, showing deep concern for my renown, say that I would be better advised to remain with the Muses in Parnassus, than to fritter away my time in your company.

Moreover, there are those who, prompted more by spitefulness than common sense, have said that I would be better employed in earning myself a good meal than in going hungry for the sake of producing nonsense of this sort. And finally there are those who, in order to belittle my efforts, endeavour to prove that my versions of the stories I have told are not consistent with the facts.

By gusts of such a kind as these, then, by teeth thus sharp and cruel, distinguished ladies, am I buffeted, battered, and pierced to the very quick whilst I soldier on in your service. As God is my witness, I take it all calmly and coolly; and though I need no one but you to defend me, I do not intend, all the same, to spare my own energies. On the contrary, without replying as fully as I ought, I shall proceed forthwith to offer a simple answer to these allegations. For I have not yet completed a third of my task, and since my critics are already so numerous and presumptuous, I can only suppose that unless they are discredited now, they could multiply so alarmingly before I reached the end that the tiniest effort on their part would be sufficient to demolish me. And your own influence, considerable though it may be, would be powerless to prevent them.

But before replying to any of my critics, I should like to strengthen my case by recounting, not a complete story[5] (for otherwise it might appear that I was attempting to equate my own tales with those of that select company I have been telling you about), but a part of one, so that its very incompleteness will set it apart from the others. For the benefit of my assailants, then, I say that some time ago, there lived in our city a man called Filippo Balducci,[6] who despite his lowly condition was as prosperous, knowledgeable, and capable a fellow as you could ever wish to meet. He was deeply in love with the lady who was his wife, and since she fully reciprocated his love, their marriage was peaceful, and they went out of their way to make each other's lives completely happy.

Now it so happened, as it happens to us all eventually, that the good lady departed this life, leaving nothing of herself to Filippo but their only son, who was then about two years old.

No man was ever more sorely distressed by the loss of the thing he loved than Filippo by the death of his wife. On finding himself

bereft of the companion he adored, he firmly resolved to withdraw
from the world and devote his life to the service of God, taking his
little son with him. He therefore gave all he possessed to charity,
and made his way forthwith to the slopes of Mount Asinaio,[7] where
he installed himself in a tiny little cave with his son, fasting and
praying and living on alms. At all times, he took very great care not
to let him see any worldly things, or even to mention their
existence, lest they should distract him from his devotions. On the
contrary, he was forever telling him about the glory of the life
eternal, of God, and of the Saints, and all he taught him was to pray
devoutly. He kept this up for a number of years, never permitting
the boy to leave the cave or to see any living thing except for his
father.

Every so often, the good man came to Florence, where various
kindly people supplied him with things he needed, and then he
returned to his cave. But one day, his son, who by this time was
eighteen years old, happened to ask Filippo, who had reached a ripe
old age, where he was going. Filippo told him that he was going to
Florence, whereupon the youth said:

'Father, you are an old man now, and not as strong as you used
to be. Why not take me with you on one of your excursions to
Florence, introduce me to those charitable and devout people, and
let me meet your friends? I am young, and stronger than you are,
and if you do as I suggest, in future you'll be able to send me to
Florence whenever we need anything, and you can stay here.'

On reflecting that this son of his was now grown up and no
longer likely to be attracted to worldly things because he was so
inured to the service of God, the worthy man said to himself: 'The
fellow's talking sense.' And since he had to go to Florence anyway,
he took him with him.

When the young man saw the palaces, the houses, the churches
and all the other things that meet the eye in such profusion
throughout the city, he could not recall ever having seen such
objects before and was filled with amazement. He questioned his
father about many of them and asked him what they were called.

Once his father had answered one of his questions, his curiosity
was satisfied and he went on to ask about something else. And so

they went along, with the son asking questions and the father replying, until they chanced upon a party of elegantly dressed and beautiful young ladies, who were coming away from a wedding; and no sooner did the young man see them, than he asked his father what they were.

'My son,' replied his father, 'keep your eyes fixed on the ground and don't look at them, for they are evil.'

'But what are they called, father?' inquired his son.

Not wishing to arouse any idle longings in the young man's breast, his father avoided calling them by their real name, and instead of telling him that they were women, he said:

'They are called goslings.'[8]

Now, the extraordinary thing about it was that the young man, who had never set eyes on one of these objects before, took no further interest in the palaces, the oxen, the horses, the asses, the money, or any of the other things he had encountered, and promptly replied:

'Oh, father, do please get me one of those goslings.'

'Alas, my son, hold your tongue,' said his father. 'I tell you they are evil.'

'Do you mean to say evil looks like this?'

'Yes.'

'You can say what you like, father, but I don't see anything evil about them. As far as I am concerned, I don't think I have ever in my whole life seen anything so pretty or attractive. They are more beautiful than the painted angels that you have taken me to see so often. O alas! if you have any concern for my welfare, do make it possible for us to take one of these goslings back with us, and I will pop things into its bill.'

'Certainly not,' said his father. 'Their bills are not where you think, and require a special sort of diet.' But no sooner had he spoken than he realized that his wits were no match for Nature, and regretted having brought the boy to Florence in the first place.

But I have no desire to carry this tale any further, and I shall now direct my attention to the people for whose ears it was intended.

As you will recall, young ladies, some of my critics claim that it is wrong of me to take so much trouble to please you, and that I am altogether too fond of you. To these charges I openly plead guilty: it is quite true that I am fond of you and that I strive to please you. But what, may I ask, do they find so surprising about it, when you consider that a young man who had been nurtured and reared within the confines of a tiny cave on a bleak and lonely mountainside, with no other companion except his father, no sooner caught sight of you than all his desires, all his curiosity, all the leanings of his affection were centred upon you, and you alone? Nor, delectable ladies, was he yet aware of the amorous kisses, the sweet caresses, and the blissful embraces that you so often bestow upon us, for a man has merely to fix his eyes upon you to be captivated by your graceful elegance, your endearing charm, and your enchanting beauty, to say nothing of your womanly decorum.

Am I to be abused by these people, then, am I to be mauled and mangled for liking you and striving to please you, when Heaven has given me a body with which to love you and when my soul has been pledged to you since childhood because of the light that gleams in your eyes, the honeyed sounds that issue from your lips, and the flames that are kindled by your sighs of tender compassion? When you consider that even an apprentice hermit, a witless youth who was more of a wild animal than a human being, liked you better than anything he had ever seen, it is perfectly clear that those who criticize me on these grounds are people who, being ignorant of the strength and pleasure of natural affection, neither love you nor desire your love, and they are not worth bothering about.

As for those who keep harping on about my age, they are clearly unaware of the fact that although the leek's head[9] is white, it has a green tail. But joking apart, all I would say to them is that even if I live to be a hundred, I shall never feel any compunction in striving to please the ones who were so greatly honoured, and whose beauty was so much admired, by Guido Cavalcanti and Dante Alighieri in their old age, and by Cino da Pistoia[10] in his dotage. And but for the fact that I would be transgressing the normal bounds of polite debate, I would invoke the aid of history-books and show they are filled with examples from antiquity of outstanding men, who, in their declining years, strove with might and main to give pleasure to the ladies. If my critics are ignorant of this, let them go and repair the gaps in their knowledge.

As for my staying with the Muses in Parnassus, I fully concede the soundness of this advice, but all the same one cannot actually live with the Muses, any more than they can live with us. And if, when he strays from their company, a man takes pleasure in seeing that which resembles them, this is no reason for reproaching him. The Muses are ladies, and although ladies do not rank as highly as Muses, nevertheless they resemble them at first sight, and hence it is natural, if only for this reason, that I should be fond of them. Moreover, ladies have caused me to compose a thousand lines of poetry in the course of my life, whereas the Muses never caused me to write any at all. It is true that they have helped me, and shown me *how* to write; and it is possible that they have been looking over my shoulder several times in the writing of these tales, however unassuming they may be, perhaps because they acknowledge and respect the affinity between the ladies and themselves. And so, in composing these stories, I am not straying as far from Mount Parnassus or from the Muses as many people might be led to believe.

But what are we to say to those who are moved so deeply by my hunger that they advise me to procure myself a good meal? All I know is this, that whenever I ask myself what their answer would be if I had to beg a meal from them, I conclude that they would tell me to go and sing for it. And indeed, the poets have always found more to sustain them in their songs, than many a rich man has found in his treasures. The pursuit of poetry has helped many a man to live to a ripe old age, whereas countless others have died young by seeking more to eat than they really needed. All that remains to be said, then, is that these people are perfectly free to turn me away if I should ever come asking them for anything. Thank God, I am not yet starving in any case; and even if I were, I know, in the words of the Apostle, both how to abound and to suffer need.[11] Let them attend to their own business, then, and I shall attend to mine.

Finally, I would be greatly obliged to the people who claim that these accounts are inaccurate if they would produce the original versions, and if these turn out to be different from my own, I will grant their reproach to be just, and endeavour to mend my ways. But so long as they have nothing but words to offer, I shall leave them to their opinions, stick to my own, and say the same things about them as they are saying about me.

And there, gentle ladies, I will rest my case for the moment. Being confident that God and you yourselves will assist me, I shall proceed patiently on my way, turning my back on these winds and letting them blow as hard as they like. For whatever happens, my fate can be no worse than that of the fine-grained dust, which, when a gale blows, either stays on the ground or is carried aloft, in which case it is frequently deposited upon the heads of men, upon the crowns of kings and emperors, and even upon high palaces and lofty towers, whence, if it should fall, it cannot sink lower than the place from which it was raised.

Moreover, whilst I have always striven to please you with all my might, henceforth I shall redouble my efforts towards that end, secure in the knowledge that no reasonable person will deny that I and other men who love you are simply doing what is natural. And in order to oppose the laws of Nature, one has to possess exceptional powers, which often turn out to have been used, not only in vain, but to the serious harm of those who employ them.

I for one confess that I do not have such powers at my disposal, nor do I desire them; and even if I were to possess them, I would sooner transfer them to others than use them myself. So let the critics hold their tongues, and if they are unable to radiate any warmth, let them freeze, let them pursue the pleasures that appeal to their jaded palates, and leave me to enjoy my own in the brief life that we are given.

But we have digressed considerably, fair ladies, and now it is time for us to return whence we departed, and proceed on our established course.

Already the sun had extinguished every star in the heavens and expelled night's humid shadows from the earth, when Filostrato got up and caused his companions to be roused. Betaking themselves to the garden, they resumed their various pastimes, and in due course they breakfasted in the place where they had supped the night before. Whilst the sun was at its zenith they took their siesta, and, after they had risen, they seated themselves beside the beautiful fountain as usual. Filostrato then instructed Fiammetta to tell the first story of the day; and without waiting to be bidden twice, she began, in tones of womanly grace, to speak as follows:

FIRST STORY

Tancredi, Prince of Salerno,[1] kills his daughter's lover and sends her his heart in a golden chalice; she besprinkles the heart with a poisonous liquid, which she then drinks, and so dies.

Cruel indeed is the topic for discussion assigned to us today by our king, especially when you consider that, having come here to fortify our spirits, we are obliged to recount people's woes, the telling of which cannot fail to arouse compassion in speaker and listener alike. Perhaps he has done it in order to temper in some degree the gaiety of the previous days; but whatever his motive, it is not for me to alter his decree, and I shall therefore relate an occurrence that was not only pitiful, but calamitous, and fully worthy of our tears.

Tancredi, Prince of Salerno, was a most benevolent ruler, and kindly of disposition, except for the fact that in his old age he sullied his hands with the blood of passion. In all his life he had but a single child, a daughter, and it would have been better for him if he had never had any at all.

He was as passionately fond of this daughter as any father who has ever lived, and being unable to bring himself to part with her, he refused to marry her off, even when she was several years older than the usual age for taking a husband.[2] Eventually, he gave her to a son of the Duke of Capua, but shortly after her marriage she was left a widow and returned to her father. In physique and facial appearance, she was as beautiful a creature as there ever was; she was youthful and vivacious, and she possessed rather more intelligence than a woman needs. In the house of her doting father she led the life of a great lady, surrounded by comforts of every description. But realizing that her father was so devoted to her that he was in no hurry to make her a second marriage, and feeling that it would be shameless to approach him on the subject, she decided to see whether she could find herself a secret lover who was worthy of her affections.

In her father's court, she encountered many people of the kind to be found in any princely household, of whom some were nobly bred and others not. Having studied the conduct and manners of several of these, she was attracted to one above all the rest – a young valet of her father's called Guiscardo, who was a man of exceedingly humble birth, but noble in character and bearing. By dint of seeing him often, before very long she fell madly and secretly in love with him, and her admiration of his ways grew steadily more profound. As for the young man himself, not being slow to take a hint, from the moment he perceived her interest in him he lost his heart to her so completely that he could think of virtually nothing else.

And so they were secretly in love with each other. The young woman was longing to be with him, and being unwilling to confide in anyone on the subject of her love, she thought of a novel idea for informing him how they could meet. Having written him a letter, explaining what he was to do in order to be with her on the following day, she inserted it into a length of reed, which later on she handed to Guiscardo, saying as though for the fun of it:

'Turn it into a bellows-pipe for your serving-wench, so that she can use it to kindle the fire this evening.'

Guiscardo took it and went about his business, reflecting that she could hardly have given it to him or spoken as she had without some special motive. As soon as he returned home, he examined the reed, saw that it was split, opened it, and found her letter inside. And when he had read it and taken careful note of what he was to do, he was the happiest man that ever lived, and set about making his preparations for going to see her in the way she had suggested.

Inside the mountain on which the Prince's palace stood, there was a cavern, formed at some remote period of the past, which was partially lit from above through a shaft driven into the hillside. But since the cavern was no longer used, the mouth of the shaft was almost entirely covered over by weeds and brambles. There was a secret staircase leading to the cavern from a room occupied by the lady, on the ground-floor of the palace, but the way was barred by a massive door. So many years had passed since the staircase had last been used, that hardly anybody remembered it was still there; but Love, to whose eyes nothing remains concealed, had reminded the enamoured lady of its existence.

For several days, she had been struggling to open this door by herself, using certain implements of her own as picklocks so that no one should perceive what was afoot. Having finally got it open, she had descended alone into the cavern, seen the shaft, and written to Guiscardo, giving him a rough idea of the distance between the top of the shaft and the floor of the cavern, and telling him to try and use the shaft as his means of access. With this object in view, Guiscardo promptly got hold of a suitable length of rope, tied various knots and loops in it to allow him to climb up and down, and the following night, without breathing a word to anyone, he made his way to the shaft, wearing a suit of leather to protect himself from the brambles. Firmly tying one end of the rope to a stout bush that had taken root at the mouth of the opening, he lowered himself into the cavern and waited for the lady to come.

In the course of the following day, the princess dismissed her ladies-in-waiting on the pretext of wanting to sleep, and having locked herself in her chamber, she opened the door and descended into the cavern, where she found Guiscardo waiting. After giving each other a rapturous greeting, they made their way into her chamber, where they spent a goodly portion of the day in transports of bliss. Before parting, they agreed on the wisest way of pursuing their lovemaking in future so that it should remain a secret, and then Guiscardo returned to the cavern, whilst the princess, having bolted the door behind him, came forth to rejoin her ladies-in-waiting.

During the night, Guiscardo climbed back up the rope, made his way out through the aperture by which he had entered, and returned home. And now that he was conversant with the route, he began to make regular use of it.

But their pleasure, being so immense and so continuous, attracted the envy of Fortune, who brought about a calamity, turning the joy of the two lovers into tears and sorrow.

From time to time, Prince Tancredi was in the habit of going alone to visit his daughter, with whom he would stay and converse for a while in her chamber and then go away. And one day, after breakfast, he came down to see her, entering her room without anyone hearing or noticing, only to discover that the princess (whose name was Ghismonda) had gone into her garden with all her ladies-in-waiting. Not wishing to disturb her whilst she was enjoying her walk in the garden, he sat down to wait for her on a low stool at a corner of her bed. The windows of the room were closed, and the bed-curtains had been drawn aside, and Tancredi rested his head against the side of the bed, drew the curtain round his body as though to conceal himself there on purpose, and fell asleep.

Whilst he was asleep, Ghismonda, who unfortunately had made an appointment with Guiscardo for that very day, left her attendants in the garden and stole quietly into the room, locking herself in without perceiving that anyone was there. Having opened the door for Guiscardo, who was waiting for her, they then went to bed in the usual way; but whilst they were playing and cavorting together, Tancredi chanced to wake up, and heard and saw what Guiscardo and his daughter were doing. The sight filled him with dismay, and at first he wanted to cry out to them, but then he decided to hold his peace and, if possible, remain hidden, so that he could carry out, with greater prudence and less detriment to his honour, the plan of action that had already taken shape in his mind.

The two lovers remained together for a considerable time, as was their custom, without noticing Tancredi; and when they felt it was time for them to part, they got up from the bed and Guiscardo returned to the cavern. Ghismonda too left the room, and Tancredi, though he was getting on in years, clambered through a window and lowered himself into the garden without being seen, returning thence in deep distress to his own apartment.

On Tancredi's orders, Guiscardo was taken prisoner by two guards soon after dark that very night, just as he was emerging, hindered by the suit of leather he was wearing, from the hole in the ground. He was then conducted in secret to Tancredi, who almost burst into tears on seeing him, and said:

'Guiscardo, my benevolence towards you deserved a better reward than the shameful deed I saw you committing today, with my own eyes, against that which belongs to me.'

By way of reply, all that Guiscardo said was:

'Neither you nor I can resist the power of Love.'³

Tancredi then ordered him to be placed under secret guard in one of the inner rooms, and this was done.

Ghismonda knew nothing of this, and after breakfast on the next day, Tancredi, who had been thinking all manner of strange and terrible thoughts, paid his usual call upon his daughter in her chamber. And having locked the door behind him, his eyes filled with tears, and he said to her:

'Never having doubted your virtue and honesty, Ghismonda, it would never have occurred to me, whatever people might have said, that you would ever so much as think of yielding to a man who was not your husband. But now I have actually seen you doing it with my own eyes, and the memory of it will always torment me during what little remains of my old age.

'Moreover, since you felt bound to bring so much dishonour upon yourself, in God's name you might at least have chosen someone whose rank was suited to your own. But of all the people who frequent my court, you have to choose Guiscardo, a youth of exceedingly base condition, whom we took into our court and raised from early childhood mainly out of charity. Your conduct has faced me with an appalling dilemma, inasmuch as I have no idea how I am to deal with you. I have already come to a decision about Guiscardo, who is under lock and key, having been arrested last night on my orders as he was emerging from the cavern; but God knows what I am to do with you. I am drawn in one direction by the love I have always borne you, deeper by far than that of any other father for a daughter; but on the other hand I seethe with all the indignation that the folly of your actions demands. My love prompts me to forgive you; my indignation demands that I should punish you without mercy, though it would be against my nature to do so. But before I reach any decision, I should like to hear what you have to say for yourself on the subject.' And so saying, he lowered his gaze and began to wail as though he were a child who had been soundly beaten.

Realizing, from what her father had said, that not only had her secret been discovered but Guiscardo was captured, Ghismonda was utterly overcome with sorrow, and needed all the self-control she possessed to prevent herself from screaming and sobbing as most other women would have done. But her proudness of heart more than made up for her shattered spirits, and by a miraculous effort of will, she remained impassive, and rather than make excuses for herself, she resolved to live no longer, being convinced that her Guiscardo was already dead.

She therefore allowed no trace of contrition or womanly distress to cloud her features, but addressed her father in a firm, unworried voice, staring him straight in the face without a single tear in her eyes.

'Tancredi,' she said, 'I am resolved neither to contradict you nor to implore your forgiveness, because denial would be pointless and I want none of your clemency. Nor do I have the slightest intention of appealing either to your better nature or to your affection. On the contrary, I propose to tell you the whole truth, setting forth convincing arguments in defence of my good name, and afterwards I shall act unflinchingly in accordance with the promptings of my noble heart. It is true that I loved Guiscardo, and that I love him still. I shall continue to love him until I die, which I expect to do very soon. And if people love each other beyond the grave, I shall never cease to love him. I was prompted to act as I did, not so much by my womanly frailty as by your lack of concern to marry me, together with his own outstanding worth. You are made of flesh and blood, Tancredi, and it should have been obvious to you that the daughter you fathered was also made of flesh and blood, and not of stone or iron. Although you are now an old man, you should have remembered, indeed you should still remember, the nature and power of the laws of youth. And although much of your own youth was spent in pursuit of military glory, you should none the less have realized how the old and the young are alike affected by living in comfort and idleness.

'As I have said, since you were the person who fathered me, I am made of flesh and blood like yourself. Moreover, I am still a young woman. And for both of these reasons, I am full of amorous longings, intensified beyond belief by my marriage, which enabled me to discover the marvellous joy that comes from their fulfilment. As I was incapable of resisting these forces, I made up my mind, being a woman in the prime of life, to follow the path along which they were leading, and I fell in love. But though I was prepared to commit a natural sin, I was determined to spare no effort to ensure that neither your good name nor mine should suffer any harm. To this end, I was assisted by compassionate Love and benign Fortune, who taught me the means whereby I could secretly achieve the fulfilment of my desires. No matter who told you about my secret, no matter how you came to discover it, I do not deny that the thing has happened.

'I did not take a lover at random, as many women do, but deliberately chose Guiscardo in preference to any other, only conceding my love to him after careful reflection; and through the patience and good judgement of us both, I have long been enjoying the gratification of my desires. It seems, however, that you prefer to accept a common fallacy rather than the truth, for you reproach me more bitterly, not for committing the crime of loving a man, but for consorting with a person of lowly rank, thus implying that if I had selected a nobleman for the purpose, you would not have had anything to worry about. You clearly fail to realize that in this respect, your strictures should be aimed, not at me, but at Fortune, who frequently raises the unworthy to positions of eminence and leaves the worthiest in low estate.

'But leaving this aside, consider for a moment the principles of things, and you will see that we are all of one flesh and that our souls were created by a single Maker, who gave the same capacities and powers and faculties to each. We were all born equal, and still are, but merit first set us apart, and those who had more of it, and used it the most, acquired the name of nobles to distinguish them from the rest. Since then, this law has been obscured by a contrary practice, but nature and good manners ensure that its force still remains unimpaired; hence any man whose conduct is virtuous proclaims himself a noble, and those who call him by any other name are in error.

'Consider each of your nobles in turn, compare their lives, their customs and their manners with those of Guiscardo, and if you judge the matter impartially, you will conclude that he alone is a patrician whilst all these nobles of yours are plebeians. Besides, it was not through hearsay that Guiscardo's merit and virtues came to my notice, but through your good opinion of him, together with the evidence of my own eyes. For was it not you yourself who sang his praises more loudly than any, claiming for him all the qualities by which one measures a man's excellence? Nor were you mistaken by any means, for unless my eyes have played me false, I have seen him practise the very virtues for which you commended him, in a manner more wonderful than your words could express. So that if I was deceived in my estimate of Guiscardo, it was you alone who deceived me.

'If, then, you maintain that I gave myself to a man of base condition, you are wrong. If, on the other hand, you were to describe him as poor, then perhaps you would be right, and you should hang your head in shame for the paltry rewards you bestowed on so excellent a servant. But in any case, a man's nobility is not affected by poverty, as it is by riches. Many kings, many great princes, were once poor; many a ploughman or shepherd, not only in the past but in the present, was once exceedingly wealthy.

'As for the last of your dilemmas, concerning how you are to deal with me, you can dismiss it from your thoughts entirely. If you are intent, in your extreme old age, upon behaving as you never behaved in your youth, and resorting to cruelty, then let your cruelty be aimed at me, for it was I who caused this so-called sin to be committed. I am resolved not to plead for clemency, and I swear that unless you do the same to me as you have already done, or intend to do, to Guiscardo, these hands of mine will do it for you.

'Now get you hence to shed your tears among the women, and if you think we have earned your cruelty, see that you slaughter us both at one and the same time.'

Although Tancredi knew that his daughter had a will of iron, he doubted her resolve to translate her words into action. So he went away and decided that whilst he would dismiss all thought of venting his rage on Ghismonda, he would cool her ardent passion by taking revenge on her lover. He therefore ordered the two men who were guarding Guiscardo to strangle him noiselessly that same night, after which they were to take out his heart and bring it to him; and they carried out his orders to the letter.

Early next day, the Prince called for a fine, big chalice made of gold, and having placed Guiscardo's heart inside it, he ordered one of his most trusted servants to take it to his daughter, bidding him utter these words as he handed it over: 'Your father sends you this to comfort you in the loss of your dearest possession, just as you have comforted him in the loss of his.'

After her father had left, Ghismonda, unflinching in her harsh resolve, had called for poisonous herbs and roots, which she then distilled and converted into a potion, so that, if things turned out as she feared, she would have it ready to hand. And when the servant came to her with her father's gift and recited the message, she accepted it with great composure and removed the lid, no sooner seeing the heart and hearing the servant's words than she knew for certain that this was the heart of Guiscardo.

So she looked up at the servant, and said to him:

'Nothing less splendid than a golden sepulchre would have suited so noble a heart; in this respect, my father has acted wisely.'

Having spoken these words, she raised it to her lips and kissed it, then continued:

'Throughout my life, which is now approaching its end, I have had constant reminders of my father's devoted love, but never so patent a token as this. And in thanking him for the last time, I bid you tell him how grateful I was for so priceless a gift.'

Then she turned to the chalice, which she was holding firmly in her two hands, and gazing down upon Guiscardo's heart, she said:

'Ah! dear, sweet vessel of all my joys, cursed be the cruelty of him who has compelled me to see you with the eyes of my body, when it was enough that I should keep you constantly in the eyes of my mind! Your life has run the brief course allotted to it by Fortune, you have reached the end to which all men hasten, and in leaving behind the trials and tribulations of our mortal life, you have received at the hands of your enemy a burial worthy of your excellence. Your funeral rites lacked nothing but the tears of the woman you loved so dearly; but so that you should not be without them, God impelled my pitiless father to send you to me, and I shall cry for you even though I had resolved to die with tearless eyes and features unclouded by fear. And the instant my tears are finished I shall see that my soul is united with that other soul which you kept in your loving care. How could I wish for a better or surer companion as I set forth towards the unknown? I feel certain that his soul still lingers here within you, waiting for mine and surveying the scenes of our mutual happiness, and that our love for one another is as deep and enduring as ever.'

She said no more, but leaned over the chalice, suppressing all sound of womanly grief, and began to cry in a fashion wondrous to behold, her tears gushing forth like water from a fountain; and she implanted countless kisses upon the lifeless heart.

Her ladies-in-waiting, by whom she was surrounded, were at a loss to know what heart this was, nor were they able to make any sense of her words, but they too began to cry in unison, being filled with compassion for their mistress. They pleaded with her to explain why she was weeping, but to no avail; and for all their strenuous efforts, they were unable to console her.

But when she had cried as much as she deemed sufficient, she raised her head from the chalice, and after drying her eyes, she said:

'Oh, heart that I love so dearly, now that I have fully discharged my duties towards you, all that remains to be done is to bring my soul and unite it with yours.'

Having pronounced these words, she called for the phial containing the potion she had prepared on the previous day, and, pouring it into the chalice, where the heart lay bathed in her own abundant tears, she raised the mixture to her lips without any show of fear and drank it. After which, still holding on to the chalice, she climbed on to her bed, arranged herself as decorously as she could, and placing the heart of her dead lover close to her own, she silently waited for death.

Her ladies-in-waiting had no idea what potion it was that she had drunk, but her speech and actions were so strange that they had sent to inform Tancredi of all that was happening, and he, fearing the worst, had hurried down at once to his daughter's chamber, arriving there just as she had settled herself upon the bed. On seeing the state she was in, he tried to console her with honeyed words, and burst into floods of tears, but the time for pity was past, and Ghismonda said to him:

'Save those tears of yours for a less coveted fate than this of mine, Tancredi, and shed them not for me, for I do not want them. Who ever heard of anyone, other than yourself, who wept on achieving his wishes? But if you still retain some tiny spark of your former love for me, grant me one final gift, and since it displeased you that I should live quietly with Guiscardo in secret, see that my body is publicly laid to rest beside his in whatever spot you chose to cast his remains.'

The vehemence of his sobbing prevented the Prince from offering any reply, and the young woman, sensing that she was about to breathe her last, clasped the dead heart tightly to her bosom, saying:

'God be with you all, for I now take my leave of you.'

Then her vision grew blurred, she lost the use of her senses, and she left this life of sorrow behind her.

Thus the love of Guiscardo and Ghismonda came to its sad conclusion, as you have now heard. And as for Tancredi, after shedding countless tears and making tardy repentance for his cruelty, he saw that they were honourably interred together in a single grave, amid the general mourning of all the people of Salerno.

SECOND STORY

Friar Alberto, having given a lady to understand that the Angel Gabriel is in love with her, assumes the Angel's form and goes regularly to bed with her, until, in terror of her kinsfolk, he leaps out of the window and takes shelter in the house of a pauper; the latter disguises him as a savage and takes him on the following day to the city square, where he is recognized and seized by his fellow friars, and placed under permanent lock and key.

Fiammetta's story had more than once brought tears to the eyes of the other ladies present, but the king seemed quite unmoved by it, for when it came to an end he looked at them sternly and said:

'I would think it a small price to pay if I were to give my life in exchange for one half of the bliss Ghismonda had with Guiscardo. Nor should any of you consider this surprising, because I die a thousand deaths in the course of every hour that I live, without being granted the tiniest portion of bliss in return. But leaving my affairs to take care of themselves for the moment, I will ask Pampinea to continue the proceedings by relating some gruesome tale that has a bearing on my own sorry state. And if she follows Fiammetta's example, I shall doubtless begin to feel one or two dewdrops descend on the fire that rages within me.'

On hearing herself singled out as the next speaker, Pampinea, knowing that her own feelings were a better guide than the king's words to the mood of her companions, was more inclined to amuse them than to satisfy the king in aught but his actual command; and so she decided that without straying from the agreed theme, she would narrate a story to make them laugh, and began thus:

There is a popular proverb which runs as follows: 'He who is wicked and held to be good, can cheat because no one imagines he would.' This saying offers me ample scope to tell you a story on the topic that has been prescribed, and it also enables me to illustrate the extraordinary and perverse hypocrisy of the members of religious orders. They go about in those long, flowing robes of theirs, and when they are asking for alms, they deliberately put on a forlorn expression and are all humility and sweetness; but when they are reproaching you with their own vices, or showing how the laity achieve salvation by almsgiving and the clerics by almsgrabbing, they positively deafen you with their loud and arrogant voices. To hear them talk, one would think they were excused, unlike the rest of us, from working their way to Heaven on their merits, for they behave as though they actually own and govern the place, assigning to every man who dies a position of greater or lesser magnificence there according to the quantity of money he has bequeathed to them in his will. Hence they are pulling a massive confidence trick, of which they themselves, if they really believe what they say, are the earliest victims; but the chief sufferers are the people who take these claims of theirs at their face value.

If only I were allowed to go into the necessary details, I would soon open many a simpleton's eyes to the sort of thing these fellows conceal beneath the ample folds of their habits. However, for the time being we must hope that God will punish their lies by granting to each and every one of them a fate similar to that which befell a certain Franciscan, by no means young in years, who was reputed in Venice to be one of the finest that Assisi had ever attracted to its cause. His story is one that I am especially pleased to relate, because you are all feeling saddened by hearing of Ghismonda's death, and perhaps I can restore your spirits a little by persuading you to laugh and be merry.

In the town of Imola, excellent ladies, there once lived a depraved and wicked fellow by the name of Berto della Massa. The townspeople learned from experience that his dealings were crooked, and he brought himself into so much disrepute that there was not a single person in the whole of Imola who was prepared to believe a word he uttered, no matter whether he was speaking the truth or telling a lie. He therefore perceived that Imola no longer afforded him any outlet for his roguery, and as a last resort he moved to Venice,[1] where the scum of the earth can always find a welcome. There he decided to go in for some different kind of fraud from those he had practised elsewhere, and from the moment of his arrival, as though conscience-stricken by the crimes he had committed in the past, he gave people the impression that he was a man of quite extraordinary humility. What was more, having transformed himself into the most Catholic man who ever lived, he went and became a Franciscan, and styled himself Friar Alberto of Imola. Having donned the habit of his Order, he gave every appearance of leading a harsh, frugal existence, began to preach the virtues of repentance and abstinence, and never allowed a morsel of meat or a drop of wine to pass his lips unless they came up to his exacting standards.

Nobody suspected for a moment that he had been a thief, pander, swindler and murderer before suddenly blossoming into a great preacher; nor had he abandoned any of these vices, for he was simply biding his time until an opportunity arose for him to practise them in secret. His crowning achievement was to get himself ordained as a priest, and whenever he was celebrating mass in the presence of a large congregation, he would shed copious tears for the Passion of the Saviour, being the sort of man who could weep as much as he pleased at little cost to himself.

In short, what with his sermons and shedding of tears, he managed to hoodwink the Venetians so successfully that hardly anyone there made a will without depositing it with him and making him the trustee. Many people handed over their money to him for safe keeping, and he became the father-confessor and confidential adviser to the vast majority of the men and women of the city. Having thus been transformed from a wolf into a shepherd, he acquired a reputation for saintliness far greater than any Saint Francis had ever enjoyed in Assisi.

Now it happened that a frivolous and scatterbrained young woman, whose name was Monna Lisetta da Ca' Quirino, the wife of a great merchant who had sailed away to Flanders aboard one of his galleys, came to be confessed by this holy friar of ours accompanied by a number of other ladies. Being a Venetian, and therefore capable of talking the hind leg off a donkey, she had only got through a fraction of her business, kneeling all the time at his feet, when Friar Alberto demanded to know whether she had a lover.

'What, Master Friar?' she exclaimed, giving him a withering look. 'Have you no eyes in your head? Does it seem to you that my charms are to be compared to those of these other women? I could have lovers to spare if I wanted them, but my charms are not at the service of every Tom, Dick or Harry who happens to fall in love with them. How often do you come across anyone as beautiful as I? Why, even if I were in Heaven itself, my charms would be thought exceptional.'

But this was only the beginning, and she droned on interminably, going into such raptures about this beauty of hers that it was painful to listen to her.

Friar Alberto had sensed immediately that she was something of a half-wit, and realizing that she was ripe for the picking, he fell passionately in love with her there and then. This was hardly the moment, however, for whispering sweet nothings in her ear, and in order to show her how godly he was, he got up on to his high horse, reproached her for being vainglorious and made her listen to a great deal more of his balderdash. The lady retorted by calling him an ignoramus, and asserting that he was incapable of distinguishing one woman's beauty from another's. And since he did not want to irritate her unduly, Friar Alberto, having heard the rest of her confession, allowed her to proceed on her way with the others.

After biding his time for a few days, he went with a trusted companion to call upon Monna Lisetta at her own house, and, having got her to take him into a room where nobody could see what he was doing, he threw himself on his knees before her, saying:

'Madam, in God's name I beseech you to forgive me for talking to you as I did on Sunday last, when you were telling me about your beauty. That same night, I was punished so severely for my insolence that I have been laid up in bed ever since, and was only able to rise again today for the first time.'

'Who was it who punished you, then?' asked Lady Numskull.

'I will tell you about it,' said Friar Alberto. 'When I was praying in my cell that night, as I invariably do, I suddenly saw a great pool of radiant light, and before I was able to turn round and discover its source, I caught sight of an incredibly handsome young man, standing over me with a heavy stick in his hand. He grabbed me by the scruff of the neck, dragged me to the floor at his feet, and beat me so severely that my body was an aching mass of weals and bruises. When I asked him why he had done it, he replied: "Because, earlier today, you had the infernal cheek to speak ill of Monna Lisetta's celestial charms, and apart from God himself there is no one I love so dearly." I then asked him who he was, and he told me that he was the Angel Gabriel. "Oh, sir," said I, "I beg you to forgive me." "Very well," said he, "I shall forgive you, but on this sole condition, that you pay a personal call on the lady at your earliest opportunity and offer her your apologies. And should she refuse to accept them, I shall come back here again and give you such a hiding that you will never recover from it." He then went on to tell me something else, but I dare not tell you what it was unless you forgive me first.'

Being somewhat feeble in the upper storey, Lady Bighead believed every word and felt positively giddy with joy. She paused a little, then said:

'You see, Friar Alberto? I told you my charms were celestial.

However, so help me God, I do feel sorry for you, and in order to spare you any further injury I shall pardon you forthwith, but only on condition that you tell me what it was that the Angel said next.'

'Since I am forgiven, madam, I will gladly tell you,' he replied. 'However, I must ask you to take great care never to repeat it to another living soul, because by so doing you will ruin everything and you will no longer be the luckiest woman alive, as you assuredly are at present.

'The Angel Gabriel asked me to tell you that he had taken such a liking to you that he would have come to spend the night with you on several occasions except for the fact that you might have been frightened. He now charges me to inform you that he would like to come to you on some night in the near future and spend a little time in your company. But since he is an angel and would not be able to touch you if he were to come in his own angelic form, he says that for your own pleasure he would prefer to come in the form of a man. He therefore desires that you should let him know when, and in whose form, you would like him to come, and he will carry out your instructions to the letter. Hence you have every reason to regard yourself as the most blessed woman on earth.'[2]

Lady Noodle said she was delighted to hear that the Angel Gabriel was in love with her, for she herself was greatly devoted to him and never failed to light a fourpenny candle in his honour whenever she came across a painting in which he was depicted. So far as she was concerned, he would be welcome to visit her whenever he pleased, but only if he promised not to desert her for the Virgin Mary, of whom it was said that he was a great admirer, as seemed to be borne out by the fact that in all the paintings she had seen of him, he was invariably shown kneeling in front of the Virgin. As for the form in which he should visit her, she would leave the choice entirely to him so long as he was careful not to give her a fright.

'You speak wisely, madam,' said Friar Alberto, 'and I shall certainly arrange for him to do as you suggest. But I want to ask you a great favour and one that will cost you nothing, namely, that you should instruct him to use this body of mine for the purpose of his visit. The reason is this, that when he enters my body, he will remove my soul and set it down in Heaven, where it will stay for the whole of the time he remains in your company.'

'What a good idea!' said Lady Birdbrain. 'It will make up for the blows he gave you on my account.'

'Very well, then,' said Friar Alberto. 'Now remember to leave your door unlocked for him tonight, because otherwise, since he will be arriving inside a human body, he will be unable to get in.'

The woman assured him that it would be done, and Friar Alberto took his leave of her. As soon as he had gone, she strutted up and down sticking her head so high in the air that her smock rose clear of her bottom, and thinking that the hour for the Angel Gabriel's visit would never come, so slowly did the time seem to pass.

Meanwhile, Friar Alberto, working on the assumption that his role would be that of a paladin rather than an angel during the night ahead, began to gorge himself on sweetmeats and various other delicacies so as to ensure that he would not be easily thrown from his mount. And as soon as darkness had fallen, having received permission to be absent, he departed with a companion and went to the house of a lady-friend which he had used as his base before when setting out to sow his wild oats. At what he judged a suitable hour, he made his way thence, suitably disguised, to Monna Lisetta's house; and having let himself in, he transfigured himself into an angel with the aid of certain gewgaws that he had brought along for the purpose. Then he climbed the stairs and strode into her bedroom.

When she saw this pure white object advancing towards her, the woman fell upon her knees before it. The Angel gave her his blessing, helped her to her feet, and motioned her to get into bed. This she promptly did, being only too ready to obey, and the Angel lay down at his votary's side.

Friar Alberto was a powerful, handsomely proportioned fellow at the peak of physical fitness, and his approach to the bedding of Monna Lisetta, who was all soft and fresh, was altogether different from the one employed by her husband; hence he flew without wings several times before the night was over, causing the lady to shriek with delight at his achievements, which he supplemented with a running commentary on the glories of Heaven. Then, shortly before dawn, having made arrangements to visit her again, he collected his trappings and returned to his companion, with whom the mistress of the house had generously bedded down for the night so that he would not be afraid of the dark.

After breakfast, the lady went with her maidservant to call upon Friar Alberto and brought him tidings of the Angel Gabriel, describing what he was like, repeating all the things he had told her about the glories of the Life Eternal, and filling out her account with wondrous inventions of her own.

'Madam,' said Friar Alberto, 'I know not how you fared with him. But I do know that when he came to see me last night and I gave him your message, he immediately took my soul and set it down amid a multitude of flowers and roses, more wonderful to behold than anything that was ever seen on earth. And there I remained until matins this morning, in one of the most delectable places ever created by God. As for my actual body, I haven't the slightest idea what became of it.'

'But that's exactly what I am telling you,' said the lady. 'Your body spent the whole night in my arms with the Angel Gabriel inside it. And if you don't believe me, take a look under your left breast, where I gave the Angel such an enormous kiss that it will leave its mark there for the best part of a week.'

'In that case,' said Friar Alberto, 'I shall undress myself later today – which is a thing I have not done for a very long time – in order to see whether you are telling the truth.'

The woman chattered away for a good while longer before returning once more to her own house, which from then on Friar Alberto visited regularly without encountering let or hindrance.

One day, however, Monna Lisetta was chatting with a neighbour of hers, and their conversation happened to touch upon the subject of physical beauty. She was determined to prove that no other woman was as beautiful as herself, and, being a prize blockhead, she remarked:

'You would soon cease to prattle about the beauty of other women if I were to tell you who has fallen for mine.'

At this, her neighbour's curiosity was thoroughly aroused, and, well knowing the sort of woman with whom she was dealing, she replied:

'You may well be right, my dear, but you can hardly expect to convince me unless I know who it is that you are talking about.'

'My good woman,' retorted Monna Lisetta, who was quick to take offence, 'I should not be telling you this, but my admirer is the Angel Gabriel, who loves me more than his very self. And he informs me that it is all because I am the most beautiful woman on the face of the earth, and the face of the water too.'

Her neighbour wanted to burst out laughing there and then, but being eager to draw Monna Lisetta out a little further on the subject, she continued to keep a straight face.

'God bless my soul!' she exclaimed. 'If your admirer is the Angel Gabriel, my dear, and if he tells you this, then it must be perfectly true. But I never imagined the angels did this sort of thing.'

'That is where you are mistaken,' said the lady. 'I swear to you by God's wounds that he does it better than my husband, and he informs me that they do it up there as well. But he has fallen in love with me because he thinks me more beautiful than any of the women in Heaven, and he is forever coming down to keep me company. So there!'

On leaving Monna Lisetta, her friend could scarcely contain her eagerness to repeat what she had heard, and at the earliest opportunity, whilst attending a party with a number of other ladies, she recounted the whole of the story from beginning to end. These ladies passed the tale on to their husbands and to various of their female acquaintances, and thus within forty-eight hours the news was all over Venice. Unfortunately, however, the brothers of Monna Lisetta's husband were among those to whose ears the story came, and they firmly made up their minds, without breathing a word to the lady herself, to run this angel to earth and discover whether he could fly. And for several nights running they lay in wait for his coming.

Some tiny hint of what had occurred chanced to reach the ears of Friar Alberto, who, having called upon the lady one night with the intention of giving her a scolding, had scarcely stripped off his clothes before her brothers-in-law, who had seen him arrive at the house, were hammering at the door and trying to force it open. Hearing the noise and guessing what it signified, Friar Alberto leapt out of bed, and seeing that there was nowhere to hide, he threw open a window overlooking the Grand Canal and took a flying leap into the water.

Friar Alberto was a good swimmer, and because the water was deep he came to no harm. Having swum across the canal, he dashed through the open door of a house on the other bank, and pleaded with its tenant, an honest-looking fellow, to save his life for the love of God, spinning him some yarn to account for his arrival there at such a late hour in a state of nudity.

The honest man took pity on him, and since he was in any case obliged to go and attend to certain affairs of his, he tucked the Friar up in his own bed and told him to stay there until he returned. And having locked him in, he went about his business.

On forcing their way into her room, the lady's in-laws discovered that the Angel Gabriel had flown, leaving his wings behind. They were feeling discountenanced, to say the least, and bombarded the woman with a torrent of violent abuse, after which they left her there, alone and disconsolate, and returned home with the Angel's bits and pieces.

Meanwhile, in the clear light of morning, the honest man happened to be passing through the Rialto district[3] when he heard people talking about how the Angel Gabriel, having gone to spend the night with Monna Lisetta, had been discovered there by her in-laws, whereupon he had hurled himself into the canal in a fit of terror, thereafter vanishing without trace. The man immediately realized that the person in question was none other than the one he was sheltering under his roof, and having returned to the house, he persuaded the Friar, after turning a deaf ear to a string of tall stories, to admit that this was indeed the case. The man then insisted on being paid fifty ducats in exchange for keeping the Friar's whereabouts secret from the lady's in-laws, and the two of them devised a way for the payment to be made.

Once the money had been handed over, Friar Alberto was anxious to get away from the place, and the honest man said to him:

'There is only one way of doing it, but it won't work unless you are willing to cooperate. Today we are holding a carnival, to which everyone has to bring a partner wearing some form of disguise, so that one man will be dressed up as a bear, another as a savage, and so on and so forth. To round off the festivities, there is to be a sort of fancy-dress hunt, or *caccia*, in Saint Mark's Square, after which all the people disperse, going off wherever they choose and taking their partners with them. Now if, instead of lying low here until someone gets wind of your whereabouts, you were to let me take you along in one of these disguises, after the ceremony I could leave you off wherever you wished. Apart from this, I can think of no other way for you to escape from here without being recognized, because the lady's in-laws have realized that you must have gone to ground somewhere in this part of the city, and their men are keeping watch over the whole neighbourhood, ready to seize hold of you the moment you appear.'

Although he baulked at the notion of going about the streets in a disguise of this sort, Friar Alberto was so terrified of the lady's in-laws that he allowed himself to be persuaded, and he told the fellow where he wanted to be taken, leaving him to work out the actual details.

The man applied a thick layer of honey to the Friar's body, after which he covered him with downy feathers from head to foot. He then tied a chain round his neck, put a mask over his face, and placed a club in one of his hands, whilst to the Friar's other hand he tethered two enormous dogs which he had collected earlier from the slaughterhouse. Meanwhile, he sent an accomplice to the Rialto to announce that anyone wishing to see the Angel Gabriel should hurry along to Saint Mark's Square – which goes to show how far you can trust a Venetian.

Once these preparations were complete, the man waited a little longer and brought the Friar forth, getting him to lead the way whilst he held on to him from behind by means of the chain. Eventually, having stirred up a great commotion along the route and provoked the question 'Whoever is it?' from all the people he met, he drove his captive into the square. And what with all the crowds following in his wake, and those who had flocked from the

Rialto after hearing the announcement, there were so many people in the square that it was impossible to count them. Upon his arrival, the man had tied his savage to a pillar in an elevated and conspicuous position, and was now pretending to wait for the mock-hunt, or *caccia*, to begin, whilst the Friar, since he was smeared with honey, was being pestered by hordes of gnats and gadflies.

When he saw that the square was more or less filled to capacity, the man stepped towards his savage as though to release him. But instead of setting him free, he tore the mask from Friar Alberto's face, proclaiming:

'Ladies and gentlemen, since the boar refuses to put in an appearance, there is not going to be any *caccia*. But so that you will not feel that your coming here was a waste of time, I want you to see the Angel Gabriel, who descends by night from Heaven to earth to amuse the women of Venice.'

As soon as his mask was removed, Friar Alberto was immediately recognized by all the onlookers, who jeered at him in unison, calling him by the foulest names and shouting the filthiest abuse ever to have been hurled at any scoundrel in history, at the same time pelting his face with all the nastiest things they could lay their hands upon. They kept this up without stopping, and would have gone on all night but for the fact that half-a-dozen or so of his fellow friars, having heard what was going on, made their way to the scene. The first thing they did on arriving was to throw a cape over his shoulders, after which they set him free and escorted him back, leaving a tremendous commotion in their wake, to their own quarters, where they placed him under lock and key. And there he is believed to have eked out the rest of his days in wretchedness and misery.

Thus it was that this arch-villain, whose wicked deeds went unnoticed because he was held to be good, had the audacity to transform himself into the Angel Gabriel. In the end, however, having been turned from an angel into a savage, he got the punishment he deserved, and repented in vain for the crimes he had committed. May it please God that a similar fate should befall each and every one of his fellows.

THIRD STORY

Three young men fall in love with three sisters and elope with them to Crete. The eldest sister kills her lover in a fit of jealousy; the second, by giving herself to the Duke of Crete, saves her sister's life but is in turn killed by her own lover, who flees with the eldest sister. The murder is imputed to the third lover and the third sister, who are arrested and forced to make a confession. Fearing execution, they bribe their gaolers and flee, impoverished, to Rhodes, where they die in penury.

On finding that Pampinea had reached the end of her story, Filostrato brooded for a while, then turned to her and said:

'The ending of your story was not without a modicum of merit, from which I drew a certain satisfaction. But there was far too much matter of a humorous kind in the part that preceded it, and this I would have preferred to do without.'

He then turned to Lauretta, and said:

'Madam, pray proceed with a better tale if possible.'

'You are being much too unkind toward lovers,' she replied, laughing, 'if all you demand is an unhappy ending to their adventures. However, for the sake of obedience I shall tell you a story about three lovers, all of whom met an unpleasant fate before they were able to enjoy their separate loves to the full.'

Then she began:

Young ladies, as you are perfectly well aware, all vices can bring enormous sorrow to those who practise them, and in many cases they also bring affliction to others. But it seems to me that the one that leads us into danger more swiftly than any other is the vice of anger. For anger is nothing more than a sudden, thoughtless impulse, which, set in motion by a feeling of resentment, expels all reason, plunges the mind's eye into darkness, and sets our hearts ablaze with raging fury. And although men are not immune from this particular vice, and some men are more prone to it than others, nevertheless it has been observed to produce its most catastrophic effects among the ladies, for they catch fire more easily, their anger burns more fiercely, and they are carried away by it without offering more than a token resistance.

Nor is this fact surprising, for if we examine the matter closely, we shall see that fire, by its very nature, is more likely to be kindled in those things which are light in weight and soft in texture than in harder and heavier objects. And if the gentlemen will forgive me for saying so, we are invariably more delicate than they are, as well as being much more capricious.

Bearing in mind, then, that we have a natural propensity to fly into a temper, that our cheerfulness and mildness of manner have a pleasing and very soothing effect upon our menfolk, and that anger and fury can bring about so much peril and anguish, I intend to strengthen our will to resist this vice by telling this story of mine, which, as I have already said, concerns the love of three young men and three young women, and which shows how, through the anger of one of these latter, their happiness was transformed into complete and utter misery.

Marseilles, as you know, is an ancient and illustrious city on the coast of Provence, and it used to boast a larger number of wealthy citizens and great merchants than appears to be the case nowadays. One of these was a certain N'Arnald Civada, who, despite his exceedingly humble origins, had built himself a firm reputation as an honest merchant and amassed a huge fortune, both in money and capital goods. His wife presented him with a number of children, of whom the eldest three were girls, whilst all the rest were boys. Two of the girls were fifteen-year-old twins, the third was fourteen, and marriages had been arranged for all three by their kinsfolk, who were simply waiting for the return of N'Arnald from Spain, whither he had gone with a consignment of merchandise. The names of the first two girls were Ninetta and Maddalena; the third was called Bertella.

Ninetta was loved, with the devotion of his entire being, by a young man called Restagnone, who was poor but of noble birth. The girl reciprocated his love, and they had managed to devise a way of consummating it without revealing the fact to a living soul. They had already been enjoying the fruits of their love for quite some time when two young men called Folco and Ughetto, who were mutual friends and whose fathers had died, leaving them very wealthy, happened to fall in love with Maddalena and Bertella respectively.

It was Ninetta who first drew Restagnone's attention to this, and having confirmed that it was so, he cudgelled his brains for a way of using the young men's loves to repair his own fortunes. Having struck up an acquaintance with them, he made a practice of taking them, sometimes individually and sometimes together, to visit the three young ladies. And one day, when he felt that he was on sufficiently friendly and familiar terms with the two young men, he invited them round to his house, and said to them:

'My dear young friends, we have now become well enough acquainted for you to perceive the strength of my affection towards you, and to realize that I would work no less zealously in the pursuit of your interests than I would in pursuing my own. Because of my deep affection for you, I am going to lay before you a certain proposal of mine, which you will be free to reject or act upon as you think proper. If you have been speaking the truth, and if I rightly interpret what I have observed of your conduct over a great many days and nights, you burn with passionate love for the two young ladies whose sister is the object of my own no less ardent devotion. Being firmly resolved to assuage these fiery torments of ours, I have concocted a very sweet and pleasant remedy, which, provided you give your consent, will assuredly do the trick. Allow me to explain. You young men are very rich and I am not. If you will give me a third share in your combined wealth, and decide whereabouts in the world you would like us to go and live happily with our ladies, I will undertake without fail to persuade the three sisters to come with us to the place we have chosen, bringing with them a substantial part of their father's fortune. Each of us will have his own lady, and we shall be able to live as three brothers, more contented than any other men on earth. That is my proposal, and now it is up to you to decide whether you are going to act upon it or turn it down.'

The two youths were exceedingly lovesick, and once they had heard that they were to have their ladies, they had no difficulty in making up their minds, telling Restagnone that if things turned out in the manner he had described, they were ready to do as he asked.

A few days after receiving this answer from the two young men, Restagnone found himself alone with Ninetta, with whom every so often he was able to consort, but only at great inconvenience. Having dallied with her for a while, he told her about the discussion he had had with the young men, and plied her with numerous arguments in an effort to win her over to his scheme. This, however, was a relatively easy matter, for she was even more anxious than he was that they should be able to meet freely, without the constant fear of being discovered. And after pledging him her full support and assuring him that her sisters would follow her advice, especially in this particular matter, she asked him to make all necessary preparations as quickly as possible. Restagnone returned to the two youths, who pressed him a great deal on the subject of their earlier discussion, and he told them that as far as their ladies were concerned the whole thing was settled. Having chosen Crete as the place to which they should go, they sold certain properties of theirs under the pretext of using the proceeds for a trading expedition, converted everything else they possessed into hard cash, purchased a brigantine, which they provisioned in secret on a lavish scale, and waited for the appointed day to come. For her part, Ninetta, who had a very clear notion of the wishes of her two sisters, described the scheme to them in such glowing colours and fired them with so much enthusiasm that they thought they would never live long enough to see it carried out. When the night finally arrived for them to go aboard the brigantine, the three sisters opened up a huge chest belonging to their father and took a large amount of money and jewellery from it, which they carried quietly away from the house according to plan. Their three lovers were waiting for them, and all six hurried aboard the brigantine, which immediately weighed anchor and put out to sea. After an unbroken voyage, they arrived next evening in Genoa, where the new lovers enjoyed the first delectable fruits of their love.

Having taken on all the fresh provisions they needed, they put to sea again, making their way unimpeded from one port to the next until, a week later, they arrived in Crete. There, not far from Candia,[1] they purchased vast and magnificent estates, upon which they built houses of great beauty and splendour. And what with their large retinue of servants, their dogs, their birds, and their horses, they began to live like lords, banqueting and merrymaking and rejoicing in the company of their ladies, the most contented men on God's earth.

This, then, was their way of life. But as we all know from experience, a surfeit of good things often leads to sorrow, and now that Restagnone, who had once been very much in love with Ninetta, was able to possess her whenever he liked without fear of discovery, he began to have second thoughts about her, with the result that his love began to wane. Furthermore, he was powerfully attracted to a beautiful and gently bred young woman of the neighbourhood whom he had glimpsed at a banquet, and he began to court her with the maximum of zeal, paying her extravagant compliments and putting on entertainments for her benefit. When Ninetta perceived what was happening, she was so distraught with jealousy that he was unable to make a move without her getting wind of it and pelting him with so much abuse and hostility that she made Restagnone's life a misery as well as her own.

In the same way, however, that a surfeit of good things generates distaste, so the withholding of a desired object sharpens the appetite, and Ninetta's resentment merely served to fan the flames of Restagnone's new-born love. Whether or not he eventually succeeded in possessing his beloved, we shall never know. But at all events somebody or other convinced Ninetta that he had, and she fell into a state of deep melancholy, which rapidly gave way to anger and finally to blazing fury. All her former love for Restagnone was transformed into bitter hatred, and in a paroxysm of rage she resolved to murder him and thus avenge the affront she believed him to have offered her. Having called in an old Greek woman who was expert in the preparation of poisons, she persuaded her by means of gifts and promises to concoct a lethal potion. And one evening, without giving the matter a second thought, she served this up to Restagnone, who was feeling thirsty because of the heat and was totally off his guard. The drink was so potent that it finished him off before matins, and the news of his death was sent to Folco, Ughetto, and their ladies. Without knowing that he had been poisoned, they joined their own bitter tears to those of Ninetta, and saw that he was given an honourable burial.

But a few days later, it happened that because of some other piece of villainy, the old woman who had concocted the poisonous potion for Ninetta was arrested. Under torture, she confessed to this particular crime along with the others she had committed, and supplied a full account of what had happened. The Duke of Crete said nothing about it to anyone, but one night he threw a cordon round Folco's palace, quietly arrested Ninetta, and took her away without a struggle. There was no need to resort to torture, for he very quickly learned from Ninetta everything he wanted to know about Restagnone's death.

Folco and Ughetto had been secretly informed by the Duke of the reason for Ninetta's arrest, and they in turn informed their ladies. All four were greatly distressed, and spared no effort to save Ninetta from being burnt at the stake, which was the punishment to which they realized she would be condemned, as she richly deserved. But the Duke was determined that justice should take its course, and it seemed that there was nothing they could do to make him change his mind.

Maddalena was a strikingly beautiful young woman, and for some little time she had been the object of the Duke's affection. She had never given him the slightest encouragement, but she now thought that by placating his desires she would be able to rescue her sister from the fire, and she informed him through a trusted messenger that she was ready to do his bidding on two conditions: first, that her sister should be returned to her unharmed; and secondly, that the whole matter should be kept secret. On receipt of the message, the sound of which was much to his liking, the Duke devoted a great deal of thought to it and in the end agreed to its terms, sending back word to that effect. And one evening, with the young woman's prior consent, he had Folco and Ughetto arrested on the pretext of hearing their version of the affair, and secretly went to spend the night with Maddalena. First, however, he had tied Ninetta up in a sack and made it appear that he intended to dump her in the sea, instead of which he took her with him and presented her to her sister by way of payment for his night of pleasure.

Next morning, before leaving, he begged Maddalena not to look upon this first night of their love as the last they would spend together, and implored her to send her guilty sister away so that he should not be taken to task and compelled to put her on trial all over again.

That same morning, Folco and Ughetto were released, having been told that Ninetta had been executed by drowning in the course of the night. Believing this to be true, they returned home to comfort their ladies in the death of their sister, and although Maddalena made every effort to conceal her from Folco, he nevertheless discovered, much to his astonishment, that she was there. His suspicions were immediately aroused, for he had already heard it said that the Duke was in love with Maddalena, and he demanded to know how it came about that Ninetta was in the house.

Maddalena spun him a long-winded tale in an effort to explain, but he was too shrewd to be taken in by much of what she was saying, and kept pressing her to tell him the truth. She talked and talked, but in the end she had to tell him. Folco was overcome with dismay, and in a fit of blazing fury he drew out his sword and killed her, turning a deaf ear to her pleas for mercy. Fearing the Duke's wrath and retribution, he left her dead body where it lay and went off in search of Ninetta, whom he greeted with a false show of gaiety, saying:

'Let us go at once to the place where your sister has decided that I should take you, so that you won't fall into the Duke's hands a second time.'

Ninetta, who trusted him implicitly, was a frightened woman, and was only too anxious to make good her escape. By now it was already dark, and without stopping to bid her sister farewell, she and Folco set out, taking with them all the money he could lay his hands upon, which did not amount to very much. On reaching the sea-coast they took to a boat, and that was the last that was ever heard of them.

Next morning, when Maddalena's body was discovered, the Duke was immediately informed of the murder by certain people who had long regarded Ughetto with hatred and envy. The Duke, who was deeply in love with Maddalena, rushed to the house breathing fire and slaughter, arrested Ughetto and his lady, and forced them (though they were as yet ignorant of what had happened) to confess that they were jointly responsible with Folco for Maddalena's death.

In view of this confession, they were afraid, not without reason, that they would be put to death, and so they very cleverly bribed the men appointed to guard them by handing over a certain sum of money which they always kept hidden in the house for whenever it might be needed. There was no time to lose, and leaving behind all their possessions, they boarded a ship with their gaolers and fled under cover of darkness to Rhodes, where shortly thereafter they ended their days in poverty and distress.

And so it was that Restagnone's reckless love and Ninetta's anger brought ruin, not only to themselves, but also to others.

FOURTH STORY

Gerbino, violating a pledge given by his grandfather King William, attacks a ship belonging to the King of Tunis with the object of abducting the latter's daughter. She is killed by those aboard the ship, he kills them, and afterwards he is beheaded.

Her story having come to an end, Lauretta was now silent whilst various members of the company turned to their neighbours, lamenting the fate of the lovers. Some of them blamed it all on Ninetta's anger, but opinion was divided on this point, and they were still debating the pros and cons among themselves when the king, who all this time had seemed rapt in meditation, looked up and gave Elissa a signal to proceed. And in tones of humility she began, as follows:

Winsome ladies, there are many who believe that Love looses his arrows only when kindled by the eyes, and who regard with contempt anyone who maintains that a person may fall in love on the strength of verbal report.[1] In this belief they are mistaken, as will be seen very clearly in a story I propose to relate, from which you will observe that hearsay not only caused two people to fall in love

without ever having seen one another, but also swept each of the
lovers to a tragic death.

According to the Sicilians, William the Second,[2] King of Sicily, had
two children: a son who was called Ruggieri, and a daughter whose
name was Gostanza. Ruggieri died before his father, leaving a son
named Gerbino, who, having been carefully reared by his grandfather, grew up to be a strikingly handsome young man and won
great renown for his daring and courtesy. His fame was not
confined to Sicily itself, but echoed round many other parts of the
world, flourishing above all in Barbary,[3] which at that time happened to be a tributary to the King of Sicily. The marvellous tales
that were told of Gerbino's courtesy and valour reached the ears of
a great many people, including a daughter of the King of Tunis – a
lady who, in the opinion of all who had seen her, was one of the
loveliest creatures ever fashioned by Nature, as well as being the
most gracious, and endowed with a truly noble heart. Being very
receptive to tales of gallant men, she lovingly treasured the various
accounts that filtered through to her on the subject of Gerbino's
valorous exploits, and was fascinated by them to such a degree that
she formed a mental picture of the sort of man he was, falling
passionately in love with him; and nothing gave her greater pleasure
than to talk about Gerbino and to listen whenever his name was
mentioned by others.

Conversely, astounding reports of her own beauty and excellence
had spread amongst other places to Sicily, where they came to the
notice of Gerbino, who, far from remaining indifferent, derived no
small pleasure from them and began to burn with a love the equal
of her own.

Though he longed to see her, he lacked a plausible reason for
seeking his grandfather's leave to visit Tunis, and he therefore
charged every friend of his who went there to do all he possibly
could in the way of drawing attention to his secret and devoted
love, and return with tidings of the lady. One of these friends
discharged his mission very skilfully, for by posing as a merchant
and taking her a quantity of jewels for her to look at, he succeeded
in apprising her fully of Gerbino's passionate devotion and in

placing him, together with everything he possessed, entirely at her service. The lady's eyes shone with pleasure as she received the envoy and listened to his message, and having assured him that her own regard for Gerbino was no less passionate than his for her, she sent him one of her most valuable jewels as a token of her burning affection. No precious object ever brought greater delight to the person to whom it was sent than this jewel she gave to Gerbino, who, using the same messenger, wrote her many letters and sent her the most marvellous presents. And it was understood between them that whenever Fortune offered them a suitable occasion, they would meet and become properly acquainted.

The affair had been dragging on in this fashion for somewhat longer than either of them would have wished, with the young lady pining away in Tunis and Gerbino doing the same in Sicily, when the King of Tunis suddenly announced his intention of marrying her to the King of Granada. This news distressed her enormously, for it meant that not only would a vast distance separate her from her lover but to all intents and purposes she would be kept entirely out of his reach; and if she had been able to devise any way of doing so, she would willingly have run away from her father to forestall such a calamity, and sailed across to Gerbino.

When Gerbino heard of the marriage, he too suffered the agonies of the damned, and vowed repeatedly to himself that if she were to travel to her husband by sea and a suitable opportunity arose, he would carry her off by main force.

Rumours of their love and of Gerbino's resolution came to the ears of the King of Tunis, who was apprehensive of the young man's determination and courage, and when the time for his daughter's departure approached he sent word of his intentions to King William, informing him that as soon as he had his assurance that neither Gerbino nor any of his associates would interfere with his plans, he would carry them into effect. King William, who was getting on in years, had no inkling of Gerbino's love for the lady, and never supposed for a moment that this was the reason why he was being asked for such an assurance. So he freely granted the King of Tunis's request, and sent him his glove[4] as a token of his royal word. Once he had received this pledge, the King of Tunis had a fine, big ship fitted out in the port of Carthage, saw that it was provisioned with everything that the people who were to sail in her would need, and made sure it was embellished and equipped in a suitable style for conveying his daughter to Granada, after which there was nothing left for him to do but sit back and wait for favourable weather.

On observing all this activity and knowing its purpose, the young lady had secretly dispatched one of her servants to Palermo and commissioned him to deliver her greetings to the gallant Gerbino, informing him that she was to leave within a few days for Granada. Thus it would now be seen whether he was as daring a man as people reported, and whether he loved her as deeply as he had so often claimed.

The man whom she entrusted with the embassy carried out her instructions to the letter and returned to Tunis. Gerbino, who had heard all about his grandfather's pledge to the King of Tunis, was at a loss to know how he should react to the lady's message; but under the promptings of his love, not wishing to appear a coward, he hurried off to Messina, where he took over a pair of light galleys and rapidly put them into fighting trim. He then signed on a crew of stout-hearted men for each of the vessels, and sailed to Sardinian waters, through which he calculated that the lady's ship would have to pass.

Nor were his calculations very wide of the mark, for within a few days of his arrival in those waters, the lady's ship came sailing up on a light breeze, not far distant from the place where he was waiting to intercept her. On catching sight of the ship, Gerbino turned to address his companions.

'Gentlemen,' he said. 'If you are as gallant as I conceive you to be, I doubt whether there is a single one of you who has never been in love. It is my conviction that no mortal being who is without experience of love can ever lay claim to true excellence. And if you are in love, or have ever been in love, it will not be difficult for you to understand what it is that I desire. For I am in love, gentlemen, and it was love that impelled me to engage you for the task that lies before us. The object of my love dwells out there upon that ship, which not only holds that which I desire above all else, but is crammed to the gunwales with treasure. If you are brave, and fight manfully, it will not be too difficult for us to take possession of these riches. My only claim upon the spoils of our victory is the lady for whose love I have taken up arms. Everything else I freely concede to you here and now. Let us set forth, then, and assail the ship whilst Fortune smiles upon us. God favours our enterprise, for He has stilled all breezes, and the ship is lying out there at our mercy.'

The dashing youth need not have wasted so many words, for the Messinese who were with him, being avid for plunder, already had visions of themselves performing the deed to which Gerbino was inciting them with his oratory. So that when he reached the end of his speech, they filled the air with a thunderous roar of approval, trumpets were sounded, and they all took up their weapons. Then they steered for the ship, plying their oars with gusto.

The ship was totally becalmed, and when the people aboard her saw the galleys approaching in the distance, they prepared to repel all boarders.

On reaching the ship, Gerbino called upon her officers to come aboard the galleys, unless they wanted a battle on their hands.

Having proclaimed who they were and discovered what it was that their attackers were demanding, the Saracens asserted that what they were doing was in breach of the royal pledge, the granting of which they confirmed by displaying King William's glove. At the same time, they made it perfectly clear that they would neither surrender nor give anything away without a fight. Gerbino, who had caught sight of the lady as she stood on the ship's poop, looking infinitely more beautiful than he had pictured her, grew more inflamed with passion than ever before, and when the glove was produced he retorted that since there were no falcons around at that particular moment, the glove was superfluous, adding that if they refused to hand over the lady, they had better look to their weapons. Hostilities commenced without further ado, each side raining arrows and stones upon the other, and in this manner they fought for a long time, doing one another a fair amount of damage. In the end, finding that he was making little headway, Gerbino lowered a small boat that they had picked up in Sardinia, set it on fire, and manoeuvred it into a position alongside the ship with the aid of both of his galleys. Perceiving this, and knowing they were faced with the alternative of being roasted alive or surrendering, the Saracens brought the King's daughter up on deck from her cabin, where she had been giving vent to copious tears, and led her to the ship's prow. And having called upon Gerbino to witness the deed, they slaughtered her before his very eyes, whilst all the time she was screaming for help and pleading for mercy. They then cast her body into the sea with the words:

'Take her thus, for we are left with no choice but to let you have her in the form your treachery deserves.'

Upon seeing this act of cruelty, Gerbino seemed to abandon every instinct of self-preservation and edged right alongside the ship, oblivious to stones or arrows. Clambering aboard in defiance of impossible odds, he started laying about him with his sword, cutting down Saracens without mercy on all sides, as though he were a starving lion falling upon a herd of young bullocks and tearing and ripping them apart one after another, intent on appeasing its anger rather than its hunger. By now the fire was spreading rapidly through the ship, and having dispatched a large number of his opponents, Gerbino got his seamen to salvage all they could in return for their services and then abandoned ship, having gained a victory that was anything but rewarding.

He then saw to the recovery from the sea of the fair lady's body, which he mourned over at length, shedding a great many tears. And on returning to Sicily he had it honourably buried on the tiny island of Ustica, which is almost opposite Trapani, whence he returned home sadder than any other man on earth.

When the King of Tunis learned what had happened, he sent ambassadors to King William, dressed in black robes, to protest against his failure to observe his pledge. They explained precisely how it had been broken, to the no small consternation of the King, who, seeing no way of denying them the justice they were demanding, ordered Gerbino to be arrested. And with his own lips, whilst every one of his barons endeavoured to dissuade him, he sentenced Gerbino to death and had him beheaded in his presence, preferring to lose his only grandson rather than gain the reputation of being a monarch whose word was not to be trusted.

Thus, therefore, in the tragic manner I have described and within the space of a few days, the two young lovers met a violent end without ever having tasted the fruits of their love.

FIFTH STORY

Lisabetta's brothers murder her lover. He appears to her in a dream and shows her where he is buried. She secretly disinters the head and places it in a pot of basil,[1] over which she weeps for a long time every day. In the end her brothers take it away from her, and shortly thereafter she dies of grief.

When Elissa's story came to an end, the king bestowed a few words of praise upon it and then called upon Filomena to speak next. Being quite overcome with compassion for the hapless Gerbino and his lady-love, she fetched a deep sigh, then began as follows:

This story of mine, fair ladies, will not be about people of so lofty a rank as those of whom Elissa has been speaking, but possibly it will prove to be no less touching, and I was reminded of it by the mention that has just been made of Messina, which was where it all happened.

In Messina, there once lived three brothers, all of them merchants who had been left very rich after the death of their father, whose native town was San Gimignano.[2] They had a sister called Lisabetta, but for some reason or other they had failed to bestow her in marriage, despite the fact that she was uncommonly gracious and beautiful.

In one of their trading establishments, the three brothers employed a young Pisan named Lorenzo, who planned and directed all their operations, and who, being rather dashing and handsomely proportioned, had often attracted the gaze of Lisabetta. Having noticed more than once that she had grown exceedingly fond of him, Lorenzo abandoned all his other amours and began in like fashion to set his own heart on winning Lisabetta. And since they were equally in love with each other, before very long they gratified their dearest wishes, taking care not to be discovered.

In this way, their love continued to prosper, much to their common enjoyment and pleasure. They did everything they could to keep the affair a secret, but one night, as Lisabetta was making her way to Lorenzo's sleeping-quarters, she was observed, without knowing it, by her eldest brother. The discovery greatly distressed him, but being a young man of some intelligence, and not wishing to do anything that would bring discredit upon his family, he neither spoke nor made a move, but spent the whole of the night applying his mind to various sides of the matter.

Next morning he described to his brothers what he had seen of Lisabetta and Lorenzo the night before, and the three of them talked the thing over at considerable length. Being determined that the affair should leave no stain upon the reputation either of themselves or of their sister, he decided that they must pass it over in silence and pretend to have neither seen nor heard anything until such time as it was safe and convenient for them to rid themselves of this ignominy before it got out of hand.

Abiding by this decision, the three brothers jested and chatted with Lorenzo in their usual manner, until one day they pretended they were all going off on a pleasure-trip to the country, and took Lorenzo with them. They bided their time, and on reaching a very remote and lonely spot, they took Lorenzo off his guard, murdered him, and buried his corpse. No one had witnessed the deed, and on their return to Messina they put it about that they had sent Lorenzo away on a trading assignment, being all the more readily believed as they had done this so often before.

Lorenzo's continued absence weighed heavily upon Lisabetta, who kept asking her brothers, in anxious tones, what had become of him, and eventually her questioning became so persistent that one of her brothers rounded on her, and said:

'What is the meaning of this? What business do you have with Lorenzo, that you should be asking so many questions about him? If you go on pestering us, we shall give you the answer you deserve.'

From then on, the young woman, who was sad and miserable and full of strange forebodings, refrained from asking questions. But at night she would repeatedly utter his name in a heart-rending voice and beseech him to come to her, and from time to time she would burst into tears because of his failure to return. Nothing would restore her spirits, and meanwhile she simply went on waiting.

One night, however, after crying so much over Lorenzo's absence that she eventually cried herself off to sleep, he appeared to her in a dream, pallid-looking and all dishevelled, his clothes tattered and decaying, and it seemed to her that he said:

'Ah, Lisabetta, you do nothing but call to me and bemoan my long absence, and you cruelly reprove me with your tears. Hence I must tell you that I can never return, because on the day that you saw me for the last time, I was murdered by your brothers.'

He then described the place where they had buried him, told her not to call to him or wait for him any longer, and disappeared.

Having woken up, believing that what she had seen was true, the young woman wept bitterly. And when she arose next morning, she resolved to go to the place and seek confirmation of what she had seen in her sleep. She dared not mention the apparition to her brothers, but obtained their permission to make a brief trip to the country for pleasure, taking with her a maidservant who had once acted as her go-between and was privy to all her affairs. She immediately set out, and on reaching the spot, swept aside some dead leaves and started to excavate a section of the ground that appeared to have been disturbed. Nor did she have to dig very deep before she uncovered her poor lover's body, which, showing no sign as yet of decomposition or decay, proved all too clearly that her vision had been true. She was the saddest woman alive, but knowing that this was no time for weeping, and seeing that it was impossible for her to take away his whole body (as she would dearly have wished), she laid it to rest in a more appropriate spot, then severed the head from the shoulders as best she could and enveloped it in a towel. This she handed into her maidservant's keeping whilst she covered over the remainder of the corpse with soil, and then they returned home, having completed the whole of their task unobserved.

Taking the head to her room, she locked herself in and cried bitterly, weeping so profusely that she saturated it with her tears, at the same time implanting a thousand kisses upon it. Then she wrapped the head in a piece of rich cloth, and laid it in a large and elegant pot, of the sort in which basil or marjoram is grown. She next covered it with soil, in which she planted several sprigs of the finest Salernitan basil,[3] and never watered them except with essence of roses or orange-blossom, or with her own teardrops. She took to sitting permanently beside this pot and gazing lovingly at it, concentrating the whole of her desire upon it because it was where her beloved Lorenzo lay concealed. And after gazing raptly for a long while upon it, she would bend over it and begin to cry, and her weeping never ceased until the whole of the basil was wet with her tears.

Because of the long and unceasing care that was lavished upon it, and also because the soil was enriched by the decomposing head inside the pot, the basil grew very thick and exceedingly fragrant. The young woman constantly followed this same routine, and from time to time she attracted the attention of her neighbours. And as they had heard her brothers expressing their concern at the decline in her good looks and the way in which her eyes appeared to have sunk into their sockets, they told them what they had seen, adding:

'We have noticed that she follows the same routine every day.'

The brothers discovered for themselves that this was so, and having reproached her once or twice without the slightest effect, they caused the pot to be secretly removed from her room. When she found that it was missing, she kept asking for it over and over again, and because they would not restore it to her she sobbed and cried without a pause until eventually she fell seriously ill. And from her bed of sickness she would call for nothing else except her pot of basil.

The young men were astonished by the persistence of her entreaties, and decided to examine its contents. Having shaken out the soil, they saw the cloth and found the decomposing head inside it, still sufficiently intact for them to recognize it as Lorenzo's from the curls of his hair. This discovery greatly amazed them, and they were afraid lest people should come to know what had happened. So they buried the head, and without breathing a word to anyone, having wound up their affairs in Messina, they left the city and went to live in Naples.

The girl went on weeping and demanding her pot of basil, until eventually she cried herself to death, thus bringing her ill-fated love to an end. But after due process of time, many people came to know of the affair, and one of them composed the song which can still be heard to this day:

> Whoever it was,
> Whoever the villain
> That stole my pot of herbs, etc.

SIXTH STORY

Andreuola loves Gabriotto. She tells him of a dream she has had, and he tells her of another. He dies suddenly in her arms, and whilst she and a maidservant of hers are carrying him back to his own house, they are arrested by the officers of the watch. She explains how matters stand, and the chief magistrate attempts to ravish her, but she wards him off. Her father is informed, her innocence is established, and he secures her release. Being determined not to go on living in the world, she enters a nunnery.

The story related by Filomena was much appreciated by the ladies, for they had heard this song on a number of occasions without ever succeeding, for all their inquiries, in discovering why it had been written. It was now Panfilo's turn, and as soon as the king had heard the concluding words of the previous tale, he instructed him to proceed. Panfilo therefore began:

The dream referred to in the last story offers me a pretext for narrating a tale in which two dreams are mentioned, both of them relating to a future event as distinct from something, as in Lisabetta's case, that had already taken place. Moreover, no sooner were they described by the people who had experienced them than both dreams came true. For the fact is, dear ladies, that every living being suffers from the common affliction of seeing various things in his sleep. And although whilst he is asleep they all seem absolutely real, and after waking up he judges some to be real, others possible, and a portion of them totally incredible, nevertheless you will find that many of them come true in the end.

This explains why a lot of people have just as much faith in their dreams as they would have in the things they see when they are wide awake, and why their dreams are sufficient of themselves to make them cheerful if they have seen something encouraging, or sorrowful if they have been frightened. At the other extreme there are those who refuse to believe in dreams until they discover that they have fallen into the very predicament of which they were forewarned. In my opinion, neither of these attitudes is commendable, because dreams are neither true every time nor always false. That they are not all true, each of us has frequently had occasion to discover; that they are not all false has been demonstrated a little while ago in Filomena's story, and, as I said earlier, I intend to show it in my own. For I maintain that if one conducts one's life virtuously, there is no reason to be afraid of any dream that encourages one to behave differently or to abandon one's good intentions because of it: and if one harbours perverse and wicked intentions, however much one's dreams appear favourable to these and encourage one to pursue them by presenting auspicious omens, none of them should be believed, whilst full credence should be given to those which predict the opposite. But let us turn now to the story.

In the city of Brescia there once lived a nobleman called Messer Negro da Pontecarraro. He had several children, including a daughter whose name was Andreuola, and although she was an exceedingly beautiful young woman, she was as yet unmarried. Andreuola chanced to fall in love with a neighbour of hers called Gabriotto, a man of low estate but full of admirable qualities, as well as being handsome and pleasing in appearance. Aided and abetted by her maidservant, the girl not only succeeded in apprising Gabriotto of her love but had him conveyed regularly into a beautiful garden in the grounds of her father's house, to the mutual joy of the two parties concerned. And so that this delectable love of theirs should never be torn asunder save by the hand of death, they secretly became husband and wife.

They continued to make love by this furtive means until one night, as she lay asleep, the girl had a dream in which she seemed to

see herself in the garden with Gabriotto, giving and getting intense
pleasure as she held him in her arms: and whilst they were thus
occupied, she seemed to see a dark and terrible thing issuing from
his body, the form of which she could not make out. The thing
appeared to take hold of Gabriotto, and, by exerting some miraculous force, to tear him away from her despite all she could do to
prevent it. It then vanished below ground, taking him with it, and
they never set eyes upon one another again. Her sorrow was so
intense that it woke her up, and although, now that she was awake,
she felt relieved that she had merely been imagining all this, she was
nevertheless filled with terror because of the dreadful things she had
dreamt about. And for this reason, knowing that Gabriotto was
anxious to visit her that evening, she did everything in her power to
ensure that he stayed away. The following night, however, seeing
that he was determined to come, she received him in the garden as
usual. The roses were in flower, and she plucked a large number,
some red and others white,[1] before going to join him at the edge of
a magnificent, crystal-clear fountain situated in the garden. There
they disported themselves merrily together for a long while, and
afterwards Gabriotto asked her why she had forbidden him to come
on the previous evening, whereupon the girl explained to him
about the dream she had experienced during the night before, and
told him about the forebodings it had aroused in her.

On hearing her explanation, Gabriotto burst out laughing and
told her that it was very silly to take any notice of dreams, since
they were caused either by overeating or undereating, and they
invariably turned out to be meaningless. Then he said:

'If I were the sort of person who takes dreams seriously, I would
not have come to see you, not so much because of your own dream
but because of one that I too experienced on the night before last. In
it, I seemed to be out hunting in a fine and pleasant wood, and I
captured the most beautiful and fetching little doe you ever saw. It
was whiter than the driven snow, and it quickly grew so attached to
me that it followed me about everywhere. For my part, I was
apparently so fond of the animal that I put a golden collar round its
neck and kept it on a golden chain to prevent it from straying.

'But then I dreamt that, whilst the doe was asleep, resting its head

upon my chest, a coal-black greyhound appeared as if from nowhere, starving with hunger and quite terrifying to look upon. It
advanced towards me, and I seemed powerless to resist, for it sank
its teeth into my left side and gnawed away until it reached my
heart, which it appeared to tear out and carry off in its jaws. The
pain of it was so excruciating that I came to my senses, and the first
thing I did on waking up was to run my hand over my left side just
to make sure that it was still intact; but on discovering that I had
come to no harm, I laughed at myself for being so credulous. But in
any case, what does it signify? I have had the same kind of dream
before, and much more terrifying ones, and they have never affected
my life in the slightest degree, either one way or the other. So let us
forget all about them and concentrate on enjoying ourselves.'

If the girl was already feeling frightened on account of her own
dream, her fears were magnified on learning about Gabriotto's. She
did her best to conceal them, however, for she did not wish to upset
him. Although she took some solace in returning his kisses and
caresses, she was filled with mysterious forebodings and kept looking
into his face more often than usual. And every so often she cast her
eyes round the garden to make sure that there was no sign of any
black thing approaching.

As they lingered there together, Gabriotto suddenly heaved a
tremendous sigh, enfolded her in his arms, and said:

'Alas, my dearest, comfort me, for I am dying.' And so saying,
he fell back to the ground and lay motionless upon the grass.

On seeing this, the girl drew her fallen lover to her bosom, and,
choking back her tears with an effort, she exclaimed:

'Oh, my precious husband! Alas! What is the matter?'

Gabriotto did not reply, but simply lay there gasping for breath
and perspiring all over, and shortly thereafter he gave up the ghost.

You can all imagine the girl's distress and agony, for she loved
him more dearly than her very self. Bursting into floods of tears,
she called out to him over and over again, but all to no avail;
and eventually, having run her fingers over the whole of his
body and discovered that he was completely cold, she was forced
to acknowledge that he was dead. Stricken with anguish, not
knowing what to do or say, her tears streaming down her cheeks,

she ran to fetch her maidservant, who knew about her affair with Gabriotto, and poured out all the sorrow and misery she was feeling.

The two women wept for some time, gazing down together upon Gabriotto's lifeless features, and then the girl said to her maidservant:

'Now that God has taken this man away from me, I shall live no longer. But before I proceed to kill myself, I want us to do all things necessary to preserve my good name, to keep our love a secret, and to ensure that his body, from which his noble spirit has departed, will receive a proper burial.'

'Do not talk of killing yourself, my daughter,' said the maidservant. 'For though you may have lost him in this life, if you kill yourself you will lose him in the next life as well, because you will end up in Hell, which is the last place I would expect to find the soul of so virtuous a youth as Gabriotto. It is far better that you should be of good cheer and give some thought to assisting his soul by means of prayers and other good works, just in case he needs them on account of some peccadillo he may have committed. As to burying his body, the quickest way would be to do it here and now in the garden. Nobody will ever find out, because nobody knows that he was ever here. But if you do not like this idea, let us carry him from the garden and leave him outside, where he will be found in the morning and taken to his own house to be buried by his kinsfolk.'

Though she was filled with despair and wept the whole time, the girl was not deaf to her maidservant's advice. Rejecting the first of her suggestions, she seized upon the second, saying:

'I am sure that God would not wish me to permit so precious a youth, a man whom I love so deeply and to whom I am married, to be buried like a dog or left lying in the street. I have given him my own tears, and I am determined that he shall have the tears of his kinsfolk. What is more, I am beginning to see how we can manage it.'

She promptly sent the maid to fetch a length of silk cloth which was kept in one of her strongboxes, and when she returned with it they spread it on the ground and placed Gabriotto's body upon it. Then, weeping continuously, she rested his head on a cushion,

closed his lips and his eyelids, made him a wreath out of roses, and
filled all the space around him with the other roses they had
gathered. And turning to her maidservant, she said:

'It is not far from here to his house, and so you and I are going to
carry him to his front-door and leave him there, just as we have
arranged him. Soon it will be day, and they will take him indoors.
It won't be any consolation to his family, but for me at least, in
whose arms he has died, it will bring some small pleasure.'

And so saying, she threw herself upon him once again, her tears
streaming freely down her cheeks. She lay there sobbing for a long
while until eventually, heeding her maidservant's repeated and
anxious reminders that the dawn was approaching, she dragged
herself to her feet. Then, removing from her finger the ring with
which Gabriotto had married her, she threaded it on to his, saying
through her tears:

'Dear husband, if your spirit is witness to my tears, and if there is
any consciousness or feeling left in the human body after its soul has
departed, receive fondly this final gift from the woman you loved
so greatly when you were living on earth.'

No sooner had she said this, than she swooned and fell yet again
upon his body. After a while she came to her senses and stood up,
and then she and the maidservant took up the piece of cloth upon
which his body was lying, went forth from the garden, and
proceeded in the direction of his house. But as they were making
their way along the street with his dead body, they had the
misfortune to be discovered and stopped by the officers of the
watch, who happened at that precise moment to be passing
through the district on their way to investigate some other
mishap.

After what had happened, Andreuola was more eager to die than
to go on living, and, on recognizing the officers of the watch, she
addressed them frankly and said:

'I know who you are, and realize that it would be futile for me
to try and escape. I am quite prepared to come with you and
explain all this before the magistrates. But if any of you should
venture to lay a finger on me, or to remove anything from this
man's body, you may rest assured that I shall denounce you.'

And so no hand was laid upon her, and she was led away with Gabriotto's body to the palace of the *podestà*.

The *podestà*, in other words the chief magistrate, having been roused from sleep, ordered her to be brought to his private quarters, where he questioned her about the circumstances of the case. He then got certain physicians to carry out a post mortem so as to ascertain that the good man had not been murdered, whether by poison or by any other means, and they unanimously confirmed that he had died a natural death from asphyxia, caused by the bursting of an abscess located in the region of his heart.

Feeling that the girl was not entirely blameless, despite the physicians' report, the magistrate made a pretence of offering her a favour that was not within his power to bestow, telling her that if she would yield to his pleasures, he would set her at liberty. On getting no response from her, he exceeded all the bounds of decorum and attempted to take her by force. But Andreuola, seething with indignation and summoning every ounce of her strength, defended herself vigorously and hurled him aside with a torrent of haughty abuse.

When it was broad day, the affair was reported to Messer Negro, who, sick with anxiety, set out with numerous friends for the palace of the *podestà*, where, having heard the whole story from the lips of the chief magistrate himself, he protested about the seizure of his daughter and demanded her release.

The chief magistrate, thinking it preferable to make a clean breast of his attempt on the girl rather than to wait for her to denounce him, began by praising her for her constancy, in proof of which he went on to describe how he had behaved towards her. On discovering how resolute she was, he had fallen deeply in love with her. And if it was agreeable to Messer Negro, who was her father, and also to the young lady herself, he would gladly take her for his wife, notwithstanding the fact that she had previously been married to a man of lowly condition.

Whilst they were talking in this fashion, Andreuola came into her father's presence, and, bursting into tears, threw herself on her knees before him.

'Father,' she cried, 'I suppose it is quite unnecessary for me to tell you about my reckless behaviour and about the tragedy that has befallen me, for I am sure you will already have been informed about these things. My sole request – and it is one that I make in all humility – is that you should pardon my transgression in taking as my husband, and without your knowledge, the man who was more pleasing to me than any other. Nor do I crave this forgiveness in order that my life shall be spared, but so that I may die as your daughter and not as your enemy.'

She thereupon collapsed in tears at his feet, and Messer Negro too began to cry, for he was by nature generous and affectionate, and he was getting on in years. And so, with tears in his eyes, he helped her tenderly to her feet, saying:

'My daughter, it was always my dearest wish that you should marry a man whom I considered worthy of you; and if you did indeed choose such a man, and he was pleasing to you, then I could have wished for nothing better. All the same, I am saddened to think that you did not trust me sufficiently to tell me about him, the more so on discovering that you have lost him even before I had any inkling of the matter. But still, since this is the way of it, I intend that he should be paid the same respect, now that he is dead, that I would willingly have paid to him for your sake if he were still alive; in other words, I intend to honour him as my son-in-law.' And, turning to his sons and kinsfolk, he instructed them to see that suitably splendid and honourable arrangements were put in hand for Gabriotto's funeral.

News of what had happened had meanwhile reached the ears of the young man's kinsfolk, who had now arrived upon the scene together with nearly all the men and women in the city. The body was therefore laid upon Andreuola's piece of silk cloth in the midst of all her roses and placed in the centre of the courtyard, where it publicly received the tears, not only of Andreuola and of Gabriotto's kinswomen, but of nearly all the women in the city and many of the men. And it was from the palace yard, in the style not of a plebeian but of a patrician, that his remains were taken with very great reverence to their burial, borne on the shoulders of the highest nobles in the land.

After the funeral, the chief magistrate repeated his previous offer and Messer Negro talked the matter over with his daughter, but she would have nothing to do with it. And within the space of a few days, it being her father's will that her own wishes should be scrupulously observed in this respect, she and her maidservant entered a convent of great renown for its sanctity, where they thenceforth lived long and virtuous lives as nuns.

SEVENTH STORY

Simona loves Pasquino; they are together in a garden; Pasquino rubs a sage-leaf against his teeth, and dies. Simona is arrested, and, with the intention of showing the judge how Pasquino met his death, she rubs one of the same leaves against her own teeth, and dies in identical fashion.

When Panfilo had dispatched his tale, the king, showing no trace of compassion for Andreuola, made it clear by looking towards Emilia that he wished her to add her tale to the ones already told; and without pausing in the least, she began:

My dear companions, having heard Panfilo's story I am impelled to narrate one that is dissimilar to his in every respect, except that, just as Andreuola lost her lover in a garden, so did the girl of whom I am obliged to speak. Like Andreuola, she too was arrested, but she freed herself from the arm of the law, not through physical strength or unwavering virtue, but by her untimely and unexpected death. As we have already had occasion to remark, whilst Love readily sets up house in the mansions of the aristocracy, this is no reason for concluding that he declines to govern the dwellings of the poor. On the contrary, he sometimes chooses such places for a display of strength no less awe-inspiring than that used by a mighty overlord to intimidate the richest of his subjects. Though the proof will not be conclusive, this assertion will in large measure be confirmed by my story, which offers me the pleasing prospect of returning to your fair city, whence, in the course of the present day, ranging widely over diverse subjects and directing our steps to various parts of the world, we have strayed so far afield.

★

Not so very long ago, then, there lived in Florence a young woman called Simona, a poor man's daughter,[1] who, due allowance being made for her social condition, was exceedingly gracious and beautiful. Although she was obliged to earn every morsel that passed her lips by working with her hands, and obtained her livelihood by spinning wool, she was not so faint-hearted as to close her mind to Love, which for some time had been showing every sign of wishing to enter her thoughts via the agreeable words and deeds of a youth no more highly placed than herself, who was employed by a wool-merchant to go round and distribute wool for spinning. Having thus admitted Love to her thoughts in the pleasing shape of this young man, whose name was Pasquino, she was filled with powerful yearnings but was too timid to do anything about them. And as she sat at her spinning and recalled who had given her the wool, she heaved a thousand sighs more torrid than fire for every yard of woollen thread that she wound round her spindle. For his part, Pasquino developed a special interest in seeing that his master's wool was properly spun, and, acting as though the finished cloth was to consist solely of the wool that Simona was spinning, and no other, he encouraged her far more assiduously than any of the other girls. The young woman responded well to Pasquino's encouragement. She cast aside a good deal of her accustomed modesty and reserve, whilst he acquired greater daring than was usual for him, so that eventually, to their mutual pleasure and delight, their physical union was achieved. This sport they found so much to their liking that neither waited to be asked to play it by the other, but it was rather a question whenever they met of who was going to be first to suggest it.

With their pleasure thus continuing from one day to the next and waxing more impassioned in the process, Pasquino chanced to say to Simona that he would dearly like her to contrive some way of meeting him in a certain garden, whither he was anxious for her to come so that they could feel more relaxed together and less apprehensive of discovery.

Simona agreed to do it, and one Sunday, immediately after lunch, having given her father to understand that she was going to the pardoning at San Gallo,[2] she made her way with a companion of hers called Lagina to the garden Pasquino had mentioned. When she got there, she found him with a friend of his whose name was Puccino, but who was better known as Stramba, or Dotty Joe. Stramba hit it off with Lagina from the very beginning, and so Simona and Pasquino left them together in one part of the garden and withdrew to another to pursue their own pleasures.

In that part of the garden to which Simona and Pasquino had retired, there was a splendid and very large clump of sage,³ at the foot of which they settled down to amuse themselves at their leisure. Some time later, having made frequent mention of a picnic they were intending to take, there in the garden, after they had rested from their exertions, Pasquino turned to the huge clump of sage and detached one of its leaves, with which he began to rub his teeth and gums, claiming that sage prevented food from sticking to the teeth after a meal.

After rubbing them thus for a while, he returned to the subject of the picnic about which he had been talking earlier. But before he had got very far, a radical change came over his features, and very soon afterwards he lost all power of sight and speech. A few minutes later he was dead, and Simona, having witnessed the whole episode, started crying and shrieking and calling out to Stramba and Lagina. They promptly rushed over to the spot, and when Stramba saw that not only was Pasquino dead, but his face and body were already covered with swellings and dark blotches, he exclaimed:

'Ah! you foul bitch, you've poisoned him!'

He made such a din that he was heard by several of the people living in the neighbourhood of the garden, and they rushed to see what it was all about. On finding this fellow lying there, dead and swollen, and hearing Stramba taking it out on Simona and accusing her of having tricked Pasquino into taking poison, whilst the girl herself, grief-stricken because of the sudden death of her lover, was so obviously at a loss for an explanation, they all concluded that Stramba's version of what had happened must be correct.

She was therefore seized and taken to the palace of the *podestà*, shedding copious tears all the way. Stramba had by this time been joined by two other friends of Pasquino, who were known as Atticciato and Malagevole, or in other words, Potbelly and Killjoy, and the three of them stirred up so much fuss that a judge was persuaded to interrogate her forthwith about the circumstances of Pasquino's death. But being unable to conceive how Simona could have practised any deceit, or how she could possibly be guilty, he insisted that she should accompany him to the site of the occurrence, so that, by getting her to show him the manner of it and seeing the dead body for himself, he could form a clearer impression of the matter than he had been able to obtain from her words alone.

Without creating any disturbance, he therefore had her conveyed to the spot where Pasquino's body lay, still swollen up like a barrel, and shortly afterwards he went there himself. Gazing at the body in astonishment, he asked her to show him precisely how it had happened, whereupon Simona walked over to the clump of sage, and, having told the judge what they had been doing together so as to place him fully in possession of the facts, she did as Pasquino had done, and rubbed one of the sage-leaves against her teeth.

Simona's actions were greeted with hoots of derision by Stramba, Atticciato, and Pasquino's other friends and acquaintances, who told the judge that they were pointless and frivolous, and denounced her wickedness with greater vehemence, at the same time demanding that she be burnt at the stake, since no lesser punishment would be appropriate for so terrible a crime. The poor creature was petrified, not only on account of her sorrow at losing her lover, but also because of her fear of suffering the punishment demanded by Stramba. But suddenly, as the result of having rubbed the sage-leaf against her teeth, she met the very same fate as the one that had befallen Pasquino, to the no small amazement of all those present.

Oh, happy souls, who within the space of a single day were granted release from your passionate love and your mortal existence! And happier still, if your destination was shared! And happy beyond description, if love is possible after death, and you love one another in the after-life as deeply as you did on earth! But happiest of all, so far as we, who have survived her, are able to judge, is the soul of Simona herself, since Fortune preserved her innocence against the testimony of Stramba and Atticciato and Malagevole – who were certainly worth no more than a trio of carders, and possibly even less – and, by causing her to die in the same way as her lover, found a more seemly way of ending her misery. For not only was she able to clear herself from their slanderous allegations, but she went to join the soul of her beloved Pasquino.

The judge, along with all the others present, was hardly able to believe his eyes, and remained rooted to the spot for some little time, not knowing what to say. But eventually, he recovered his wits, and said:

'The sage is evidently poisonous, which is rather unusual, to say the least. Before it should claim any further victims, let it be hacked down to its roots and set on fire.'

In the judge's presence, the man in charge of the garden proceeded to carry out these instructions, but he had no sooner felled the giant clump than the reason for the deaths of the two poor lovers became apparent.

Crouching beneath the clump of sage, there was an incredibly large toad, by whose venomous breath they realized that the bush must have been poisoned. Nobody dared to approach it, and so they surrounded it with a huge pyre, and cremated it alive together with the sage-bush. So ended the investigation of His Worship into the death of poor Pasquino, whose swollen body, together with that of his beloved Simona, was buried by Stramba and Atticciato and Guccio Imbratta[4] and Malagevole in the Church of Saint Paul, which happened to be the parish to which the two dead lovers belonged.

EIGHTH STORY

Girolamo loves Salvestra; he is prevailed upon by his mother to go to Paris, and on his return he finds Salvestra married. Having secretly entered her house, he lies down and dies at her side; his body is taken to a church, where Salvestra lies down beside him, and she too dies.

When Emilia's tale had wound to a close, Neifile, having been bidden to speak by the king, began as follows:

Excellent ladies, to my way of thinking there are those who

imagine that they know more than others when in fact they know less, and hence they presume to set up this wisdom of theirs against not only the counsels of their fellow men, but also the laws of Nature. No good has ever come of their presumption, and from time to time it has done an enormous amount of harm. Now, there is nothing in the whole of Nature that is less susceptible to advice or interference than Love, whose qualities are such that it is far more likely to burn itself out of its own free will than be quenched by deliberate pressure. And so it occurs to me that I should tell you a story about a lady who, in the belief that she could remove, from an enamoured heart, a love which had possibly been planted there by the stars, sought to be wiser than she actually was, and by flaunting her cleverness in a matter that was beyond her competence, succeeded at one and the same time in driving both Love and life from the body of her son.

According to the tales of our elders, there once lived in our city a very powerful and wealthy merchant whose name was Leonardo Sighieri, who had a son from his wife called Girolamo, and who, after the child was born, carefully put all his affairs in order and departed this life. The boy's interests were skilfully and scrupulously managed by his guardians, acting in conjunction with his mother. He grew up with the children of other families in the neighbourhood, and became very attached to a little girl of his own age, who was the daughter of a tailor. As they grew older, their friendship ripened into a love so great and passionate that Girolamo could not bear to let her out of his sight, and her own regard for him was certainly no less extreme. On perceiving this, the boy's mother took him to task several times, and even punished him for it. But on finding that he could not be deterred, she took the matter up with the boy's guardians, being convinced that because of her son's great wealth she could, as it were, turn a plum into an orange.[1]

'This boy of ours,' she told them, 'who has only just reached the age of fourteen, is so enamoured of a local tailor's daughter, Salvestra by name, that if we do not separate them we shall perhaps wake up one morning to find that he has married her without telling anyone about it, and I shall never be happy again. If on the other hand he sees her marrying another, he will pine away. And so it would seem to me that in order to nip the affair in the bud, you ought to pack him off to some distant part of the world in the service of the firm. For if he is prevented from seeing the girl over a long period, she will vanish from his thoughts and we shall then be able to marry him to some young lady of gentle breeding.'

The guardians agreed with the lady's point of view and assured her that they would do all in their power to carry out her proposal. And having sent for the boy at the firm's premises, one of them began talking to him in tones of great affection, saying:

'My boy, you are quite a big fellow now, and it would be a good thing for you to start attending to your own affairs. We would therefore be very happy if you were to go and stay for a while in Paris, where you will not only see how a sizeable part of your business is managed, but you will also, by mixing with all those lords and barons and nobles who abound in that part of the world, become a much better man, and acquire greater experience and refinement, than by remaining here. And then you can return to Florence.'

Having listened carefully, the lad gave them a short answer, saying that he would have none of it, since he considered he had as much right as anyone else to remain in Florence. His worthy mentors made several further attempts to persuade him, but being unable to extract any different answer, they reported back to the mother. She was livid with anger, and gave him a fierce scolding, not because he did not want to go to Paris but on account of his love for Salvestra. But then, soothing him with honeyed words, she began to pay him compliments and to coax him gently into following the advice of his guardians. And she played her cards so cleverly that in the end he agreed that he should go and stay there, but only for twelve months, and so it was arranged.

Still passionately in love, Girolamo went off to Paris, where he was detained by a series of delaying tactics for two whole years. On returning to Florence, more deeply in love than before, he was mortified to discover that his beloved Salvestra was married to a worthy young man who was by trade a tentmaker. Since there was nothing he could do about it, he tried to reconcile himself to the situation; and having inquired into where she was living, he began to walk up and down in the manner of a lovelorn youth outside her house, being convinced that she could not have forgotten him, any more than he had forgotten her. But this was not the case, for as the young man very soon perceived, to his no small sorrow, she no more remembered him than if she had never seen him before, and if she did indeed recollect anything at all, she certainly never showed it. Nevertheless the young man did everything he could to make her acknowledge him again; but feeling that he was getting nowhere, he resolved to speak to her in private, even if he were to die in the attempt.

Having inquired of a person living nearby regarding the disposition of the rooms, he secretly let himself in to the house one evening whilst she and her husband were attending a wake with some neighbours of theirs, and concealed himself behind some sheets of canvas that were stretched across a corner of her bedroom. There he waited until they had returned home and retired to bed, and when he was sure that her husband was asleep, he crept over to that part of the room where he had seen Salvestra lying down, placed his hand on her bosom, and said:

'Are you asleep already, my dearest?'

The girl, who was not asleep, was about to scream when the young man hastily added:

'For pity's sake, do not scream, for it is only your Girolamo.'

On hearing this, she trembled from head to toe, and said:

'Oh, merciful heavens, do go away Girolamo. We are no longer children, and the time has passed for proclaiming our love from the house-tops. As you can see, I am married, and therefore it is no longer proper for me to care for any other man but my husband. Hence I beseech you in God's name to get out of here. If my husband were to hear you, even supposing nothing more serious came of it, it would certainly follow that I could never live in peace with him again, whereas up to now he has loved me and we live calmly and contentedly together.'

To hear her talking like this, the young man was driven to the brink of despair. He reminded her of the times they had spent in each other's company and of the fact that his love for her had never diminished despite their separation. He poured out a stream of entreaties and promised her the moon. But he was unable to make the slightest impression.

All he wanted to do now was to die, and so finally, invoking the great love he bore her, he pleaded with her to let him lie down at her side so that he could get warm, pointing out that his limbs had turned numb with cold whilst he was waiting for her. He assured her that he would neither talk to her nor touch her, and promised to go away as soon as he had warmed himself up a little.

Feeling rather sorry for him, Salvestra agreed to let him do it, but only if he kept his promises. So the young man lay down at her side without attempting to touch her, and, concentrating his thoughts on his long love for her, on her present coldness towards him, and on the dashing of his hopes, he resolved not to go on living. Without uttering a word, he clenched his fists and held his breath until finally he expired at her side.

After a while, wondering what he was doing and fearing lest her husband should wake up, the girl made a move.

'Girolamo,' she whispered, 'it's time for you to be going.'

On receiving no answer, she assumed that he had fallen asleep. So she stretched out her hand to wake him up and began to prod him, but found to her great astonishment that he was as cold as ice to the touch. She then prodded him more vigorously but it had no effect, and after trying once more she realized that he was dead. The discovery filled her with dismay and for some time she lay there without the slightest notion what to do.

In the end she decided to put the case to her husband without saying who was involved, and ask his opinion about what the people concerned ought to do about it; and having woken him up, she described her own recent experience as though it had happened to someone else, then asked him what advice he would give supposing it had happened to her.

To this, the worthy soul replied that in his view, the fellow who was dead would have to be taken quietly back to his own house and left there, and that no resentment should be harboured against the woman, who did not appear to him to have done any wrong.

'In that case,' said the girl, 'we shall have to do likewise.' And taking his hand, she brought it into contact with the young man's body, whereupon he leapt to his feet in utter consternation, lighted a lamp, and, without entering into further discussion with his wife, dressed the body in its own clothes. And without further ado, he lifted it on to his shoulders and carried it, confident in his own innocence, to the door of Girolamo's house, where he put it down and left it.

Next morning, when the young man's corpse was discovered lying on the doorstep, a great commotion was raised, in particular by the mother. The body was carefully examined all over, but no trace of a wound or a blow could be found, and it was the general opinion of the physicians that he had died of grief, as indeed he had. His remains were taken into a church, to which the sorrowing mother came with numerous kinswomen and neighbours, and they all began to weep and keen over his body, as is customary in our part of the world.

Whilst the tears and lamentations were at their height, the worthy man in whose house Girolamo had died turned to Salvestra and said:

'Just cover your head in a mantle and go over to the church where Girolamo was taken. Mingle with the women, and listen to what they are saying about this business, and I will do the same among the men, so that we may find out whether anything is being said against us.'

The girl readily assented, for she was stirred to pity now that it was too late and was eager to gaze upon the dead features of the man who had been unable to persuade her, whilst he was still alive, to grant him so much as a single kiss. And so off she went to the church.

What a wonderful thing Love is, and how difficult it is to fathom its deep and powerful currents! The girl's heart, which had remained sealed to Girolamo for as long as he was smiled upon by Fortune, was unlocked by his far from fortunate death. The flames of her former love were rekindled, and no sooner did she catch sight of his dead face than they were all instantly transformed into so much compassion that she edged her way forward, wrapped in her mantle, through the cluster of women mourners, coming to a halt only when she was almost on top of the corpse itself. Then with a piercing scream, she flung herself upon the dead youth, and if she failed to drench his face with her tears, that was because, almost as soon as she touched him, she died, like the young man, from a surfeit of grief.

The women, who had thus far failed to recognize her, crowded round to console her and urge her to her feet, but since she did not respond they tried to lift her themselves, only to discover that she was quite still and rigid. And when they finally succeeded in raising her, they saw at one and the same time that it was Salvestra and that she was dead. The women now had double cause for weeping, and they all began wailing again much more loudly than before.

The news spread through the church to the men outside and reached the ears of her husband, who happened to be standing in their midst. Having burst into tears, he simply went on crying, oblivious to the efforts of various bystanders to console and comfort him; but eventually he told several of them about what had occurred the night before between this young man and his wife, thus clearing up the mystery of their deaths, and everyone was filled with enormous sorrow.

The dead girl was taken up and decked out in all the finery with which we are wont to adorn the bodies of the dead, then she was laid on the selfsame bier upon which the young man was already lying. For a long time they mourned her, and afterwards the two bodies were interred in a single tomb: and thus it was that those whom Love had failed to join together in life were inseparably linked to each other in death.

NINTH STORY

Guillaume de Roussillon causes his wife to eat the heart of her lover,
Guillaume de Cabestanh,[1] *whom he has secretly murdered. When she*
finds out, she kills herself by leaping from a lofty casement to the ground
below, and is subsequently buried with the man she loved.

The king had no intention of interfering with Dioneo's privilege,
and when, having planted no small degree of compassion in the
hearts of her companions, Neifile's story came to its conclusion,
there being no others left to speak, he began as follows:

Since you are so deeply moved, tender ladies, by the recital of
lovers' woes, the tale that presents itself to me must inevitably arouse
as much pity among you as the previous one, for the people whose
misfortunes I shall describe were of loftier rank, and their fate was
altogether more cruel.

You must know, then, that according to the Provençals, there once
lived in Provence two noble knights, each of whom owned several
castles and had a number of dependants. The name of the first was
Guillaume de Roussillon, whilst the other was called Guillaume de
Cabestanh. Since both men excelled in feats of daring, they were
bosom friends and made a point of accompanying one another to
jousts and tournaments and other armed contests, each bearing the
same device.

Although the castles in which they lived were some ten miles
apart, Guillaume de Cabestanh chanced to fall hopelessly in love
with the charming and very beautiful wife of Guillaume de Roussillon,
and, notwithstanding the bonds of friendship and brotherhood that
united the two men, he managed in various subtle ways to bring his
love to the lady's notice. The lady, knowing him to be a most gallant
knight, was deeply flattered, and began to regard him with so much
affection that there was nothing she loved or desired more deeply.
All that remained for him to do was to approach her directly,
which he very soon did, and from then on they met at frequent
intervals for the purpose of making passionate love to one another.

One day, however, they were incautious enough to be espied by the lady's husband, who was so incensed by the spectacle that his great love for Cabestanh was transformed into mortal hatred. He firmly resolved to do away with him, but concealed his intentions far more successfully than the lovers had been able to conceal their love.

His mind being thus made up, Roussillon happened to hear of a great tournament that was to be held in France. He promptly sent word of it to Cabestanh and asked him whether he would care to call upon him, so that they could talk it over together and decide whether or not to go and how they were to get there. Cabestanh was delighted to hear of it, and sent back word to say that he would come and sup with him next day without fail.

On receiving Cabestanh's message, Roussillon judged this to be his opportunity for killing him. Next day, he armed himself, took horse with a few of his men, and lay in ambush about a mile away from his castle, in a wood through which Cabestanh was bound to pass. After a long wait, he saw him approaching, unarmed, and followed by two of his men, who were likewise unarmed, for he never suspected for a moment that he was running into danger. Roussillon waited until Cabestanh was at close range, then he rushed out at him with murder and destruction in his heart, brandishing a lance above his head and shouting: 'Traitor, you are dead!' And before the words were out of his mouth he had driven the lance through Cabestanh's breast.

Cabestanh was powerless to defend himself, or even to utter a word, and on being run through by the lance he fell to the ground. A moment later he was dead, and his men, without stopping to see who had perpetrated the deed, turned the heads of their horses and galloped away as fast as they could in the direction of their master's castle.

Dismounting from his horse, Roussillon cut open Cabestanh's chest with a knife, tore out the heart with his own hands, and, wrapping it up in a banderole, told one of his men to take it away. Having given strict orders that no one was to breathe a word about what had happened, he then remounted and rode back to his castle, by which time it was already dark.

The lady had heard that Cabestanh was to be there that evening for supper and was eagerly waiting for him to arrive. When she saw her husband arriving without him she was greatly surprised, and said to him:

'And how is it, my lord, that Cabestanh has not come?'

To which her husband replied:

'Madam, I have received word from him that he cannot be here until tomorrow.'

Roussillon left her standing there, feeling somewhat perturbed, and when he had dismounted, he summoned the cook and said to him:

'You are to take this boar's heart and see to it that you prepare the finest and most succulent dish you can devise. When I am seated at table, send it in to me in a silver tureen.'

The cook took the heart away, minced it, and added a goodly quantity of fine spices, employing all his skill and loving care and turning it into a dish that was too exquisite for words.

When it was time for dinner, Roussillon sat down at the table with his lady. Food was brought in, but he was unable to do more than nibble at it because his mind was dwelling upon the terrible deed he had committed. Then the cook sent in his special dish, which Roussillon told them to set before his lady, saying that he had no appetite that evening.

He remarked on how delicious it looked, and the lady, whose appetite was excellent, began to eat it, finding it so tasty a dish that she ate every scrap of it.

On observing that his lady had finished it down to the last morsel, the knight said:

'What did you think of that, madam?'

'In good faith, my lord,' replied the lady, 'I liked it very much.'

'So help me God,' exclaimed the knight, 'I do believe you did. But I am not surprised to find that you liked it dead, because when it was alive you liked it better than anything else in the whole world.'

On hearing this, the lady was silent for a while; then she said:

'How say you? What is this that you have caused me to eat?'

'That which you have eaten,' replied the knight, 'was in fact the heart of Guillaume de Cabestanh, with whom you, faithless woman that you are, were so infatuated. And you may rest assured that it was truly his, because I tore it from his breast myself, with these very hands, a little before I returned home.'

You can all imagine the anguish suffered by the lady on hearing such tidings of Cabestanh, whom she loved more dearly than anything else in the world. But after a while, she said:

'This can only have been the work of an evil and treacherous knight, for if, of my own free will, I abused you by making him the master of my love, it was not he but I that should have paid the penalty for it. But God forbid that any other food should pass my lips now that I have partaken of such excellent fare as the heart of so gallant and courteous a knight as Guillaume de Cabestanh.'

And rising to her feet, she retreated a few steps to an open window, through which without a second thought she allowed herself to fall.

The window was situated high above the ground, so that the lady was not only killed by her fall but almost completely disfigured.

The spectacle of his wife's fall threw Roussillon into a panic and made him repent the wickedness of his deed. And fearing the wrath of the local people and of the Count of Provence, he had his horses saddled and rode away.

By next morning the circumstances of the affair had become common knowledge throughout the whole of the district, and people were sent out from the castles of the lady's family and of Guillaume de Cabestanh to gather up the two bodies, which were later placed in a single tomb in the chapel of the lady's own castle amid widespread grief and mourning. And the tombstone bore an inscription, in verse, to indicate who was buried there and the manner and the cause of their deaths.

TENTH STORY

The wife of a physician, mistakenly assuming her lover, who has taken an opiate, to be dead, deposits him in a trunk, which is carried off to their house by two money-lenders with the man still inside it. On coming to his senses, he is seized as a thief, but the lady's maidservant tells the judge that it was she who put him in the trunk, thereby saving him from the gallows, whilst the usurers are sentenced to pay a fine for making off with the trunk.

Now that the king had finished, only Dioneo was left to address the company. Knowing this to be so, and having already been asked by the king to proceed, he began as follows:

These sorrowful accounts of ill-starred loves have brought so much affliction to my eyes and heart (to say nothing of yours, dear ladies) that I have been longing for them to come to an end. Unless I were to add another sorry tale to this gruesome collection (and Heaven forbid that I should), they are now, thank God, over and done with. And instead of lingering any longer on so agonizing a topic, I shall make a start on a better and rather more agreeable theme, which will possibly offer some sort of guide to the subject we ought to discuss on the morrow.

Fairest maidens, I will have you know that in the comparatively recent past there lived in Salerno a very great surgeon called Doctor Mazzeo della Montagna,[1] who, having reached a ripe old age, married a beautiful and gently bred young lady of that same city. No other woman in Salerno was kept so lavishly supplied as Mazzeo's wife with expensive and elegant dresses, jewellery, and all the other things a woman covets; but the fact is that for most of the time she felt chilly, because the surgeon failed to keep her properly covered over in bed.

Now, you may remember my telling you about Messer Ricciardo di Chinzica, and of the way he taught his wife to observe the feasts of the various Saints. This old surgeon did much the same thing, for he pointed out to the girl that you needed heaven knows how many days to recover after making love to a woman, and spouted a lot of similar nonsense, all of which made her wretchedly unhappy. But as she was a woman of considerable spirit and intelligence, she resolved to put the family jewels in cotton wool and wear out some other man's gems. Having gone out into the streets, she cast a critical eye over a number of young bloods, eventually finding one who was exactly to her liking, and she made him the sole custodian of her hopes, heart, and happiness. On perceiving her interest in him, the young man was powerfully smitten, and wholeheartedly reciprocated her love.

His name was Ruggieri d'Aieroli, and he was of noble birth. But he led such a disreputable life, and mixed with so many undesirable characters, that he had alienated all his friends and relatives, none of whom wished him any good or wanted anything to do with him. He was notorious throughout Salerno for his acts of larceny and for other highly unsavoury activities, about which the lady was more or less indifferent because she liked him for other reasons. Using a maidservant as a go-between, she so arranged matters that she and her lover were united, but after they had been making love together for a while she began to censure his way of life and to entreat him for her sake to reform his ways. And in order to make it worth his while to do so, she furnished him from time to time with various sums of money.

Taking good care not to be discovered, they had been meeting in this fashion for some time when it happened that a man with a diseased leg was placed under the doctor's care. Having examined the ailment, the doctor informed the man's kinsfolk that unless he removed a gangrenous bone in the patient's leg, it would have to be amputated altogether, otherwise he would die. At the same time, whilst the removal of the bone offered every chance of a cure, there was no guarantee that the operation would be successful. The man's family accepted the surgeon's advice along with the reservations he had expressed, and handed the patient into his keeping.

The operation was to be performed towards evening, and that same morning, realizing that the invalid would be unable to withstand the pain unless he were doped beforehand, the doctor issued a special prescription providing for the distillation of a certain liquid which he intended to administer to the patient in order to put him to sleep for as long as the pain and the operation were likely to last. And having had it delivered to his house, he put it down on a window-ledge in his bedroom without bothering to tell anyone what it was.

That evening, just as the surgeon was about to go to his patient, a messenger arrived from some very close friends of his in Amalfi,[2] telling him that he was to abandon everything and go there at once because of a serious brawl in which a number of people had suffered injury.

Postponing the operation on the leg until the following morning, the surgeon got into a boat and went to Amalfi, whereupon the lady, knowing that he would be away from home for the rest of the night, secretly sent for Ruggieri in her usual way and showed him into her bedroom, locking him inside until certain other people in the house had retired for the night.

Whether because of having had a tiring day or because he had eaten food containing a lot of salt or because of some peculiarity of his constitution, Ruggieri, whilst he was waiting in the bedroom for his mistress, suddenly felt enormously thirsty. And catching sight of the bottle of medicine which the doctor had left on the window-ledge, he mistook it for drinking water, raised it to his lips, and drank it down to the last drop. Almost at once he was filled with a feeling of great drowsiness, and shortly afterwards he fell fast asleep.

At the earliest opportunity, the lady came up to the bedroom, and on finding Ruggieri asleep she began to prod him and whisper to him to get up. But it was no use; he neither answered nor moved a muscle. And so the lady, growing somewhat impatient, gave him a more violent shove, saying:

'Get up, lazybones. If you wanted to sleep, you should have gone to your own house to do it instead of coming round here.'

The lady's shove toppled Ruggieri from the chest on which he was lying, and he fell to the floor, showing no more sign of life than if he were a corpse. The lady was rather frightened, and she began to try and raise him, then shook him more vigorously and

tweaked his nose and pulled his beard. But it was all to no purpose:
he was sleeping like a log.

The lady now began to fear that he was dead, and in her panic
she started pinching him viciously and holding a lighted candle
against his skin, but it was no use. And hence, being no physician
herself even though she was married to one, she was quite convinced
that he must be dead. Since there was nothing in the world that she
loved so much, her distress can readily be imagined. Not daring to
make any noise, she began to weep in silence over his body and
lament her ghastly misfortune.

After a while, however, being afraid that she might lose her
reputation on top of losing her lover, the lady saw that she must
immediately devise some means for getting his body out of the
house. Having no idea how she should go about it, she called out
softly to her maid, showed her the dilemma she was in, and asked
her what they ought to do. The maid was greatly astonished, and
she too began shaking and pinching him, but when she saw that
he was without any feeling, she agreed with her mistress that he
really was dead, and said that he would have to be put out of the
house.

'But where on earth can we leave him,' inquired the lady, 'so as
to prevent people suspecting, when he is discovered in the morning,
that this was the house from which he was taken?'

'Ma'am,' replied the maid, 'late this evening I caught sight of a
trunk standing outside the shop of our neighbour, the carpenter. It
was not a very large trunk, but if it is still there it will come in nice
and handy, because we can put the body inside, stab him two or
three times with a dagger, and leave him there. No matter who
finds him in the trunk, they will have no reason for supposing that
he came from here rather than from somewhere else. In fact, since
he was such an unruly sort of youth, they will think that he was
murdered by one of his enemies as he was about to commit some
crime or other, and then stuffed inside the trunk.'

The lady said that no power on earth would persuade her to stab
him, but that otherwise the maid's proposal seemed to her a good
one, and she sent her to see whether the trunk was still in the same
place. Having confirmed that it was, the maid, who was a sturdy

young woman, lifted Ruggieri on to her shoulders with the help of
her mistress. And with the lady walking on ahead to make sure no
one was coming, they got him to the trunk, put him inside, closed
the lid, and left him there.

Now, a few days earlier, two young men had moved into a house
a little further along the street. They were money-lenders, always
on the lookout for ways of making pots of money and saving a few
coppers, and since they were short of furniture and had noticed the
trunk lying there the previous day, they had agreed that if it was
still there after dark, they would carry it off to their own house.

In the dead of night they came out of their house, found the
trunk, and without stopping to examine it closely (though it did
seem a little heavy), they carried it quickly back to their house and
dumped it in the first convenient place, which happened to be
immediately beside a room where their womenfolk were sleeping.
And without bothering to see that it was in a secure position, they
left it there and went off to bed.

Ruggieri slept for a very long time, but eventually he digested
the potion, its effects wore off, and just before matins he woke up.
But although he had emerged from sleep and recovered the use of
his senses, his mind was still blurred, and in fact it was some days
before he shook off his state of bewilderment. On opening his eyes
and finding that he could not see anything, he groped about with
his hands and discovered that he was inside this trunk, whereupon
he began to ponder and mutter to himself, saying: 'What's all this?
Where am I? Am I asleep, or awake? I have a clear recollection of
entering my lady's bedchamber this evening, and now I appear to
be inside some sort of chest. What does it mean? Can it be that the
doctor returned home, or that something equally unexpected happened, causing my mistress to conceal me here whilst I was asleep?
Why of course, that's the explanation, that's it exactly.'

And so he kept quiet and listened to see whether he could hear
anything. But after remaining stock-still for some considerable
time, feeling rather uncomfortable inside the trunk, which was none
too big, and getting a pain in the side on which he was lying, he
decided to turn over. This operation he performed with such a
degree of skill that in pressing his back against one of the sides of

the trunk, which had not been placed on an even keel, he caused it to topple over and fall with a resounding crash, waking up the women who were asleep in the adjoining room and giving them such a fright that they hardly dared to breathe, let alone open their mouths.

Ruggieri received quite a shock when the trunk toppled over, but on finding that it had burst open in falling, he preferred to clamber out rather than stay where he was, just in case anything worse was about to happen to him. Being at his wits' end, and not knowing where he was, he began to fumble his way round the premises in order to see whether he could find a door or a staircase that would offer him a means of escape.

The women heard these fumbling sounds as they lay there awake, and they began calling out: 'Who's there?' Being unable to recognize their voices, Ruggieri offered no reply, and so the women started calling to the two young men, who, because they had gone to bed so late, were soundly asleep and had heard nothing of all the racket.

Feeling more frightened than ever, the women got out of bed and ran to the windows, shouting: 'Burglars! Burglars!' And so several of their neighbours rushed into the house from various directions, some by way of the roof, some by the front-door, and others by the entrance at the rear. And the noise reached such a pitch that even the young men woke up and scrambled out of bed.

On finding himself in the midst of all this commotion, Ruggieri very nearly collapsed with astonishment. He was in no condition to make a dash for it, and in any case he could see that escape was impossible; so he was seized and handed over to the chief magistrate's officers, who had meanwhile rushed to the scene, having been attracted by all the noise. He was then taken before the chief magistrate, and since he had a very bad reputation he was immediately put to the torture and forced to confess that he had broken into the money-lenders' house with intent to rob, whereupon the magistrate resolved to have him hanged by the neck at the earliest opportunity.

During the course of the morning, the news that Ruggieri had been caught red-handed burgling the money-lenders' house spread

like wildfire through the whole of Salerno. And when the lady and
her maid came to hear of it, they were so bewildered and astonished
that they almost began to think that instead of actually doing what
they had done the night before they had merely been dreaming.
What was more, the lady was nearly out of her mind with anxiety
at the thought of the danger that Ruggieri was in.

Halfway through the morning, the doctor returned from Amalfi
and sent someone to fetch his potion so that he could operate on his
patient, and when the bottle was found to be empty he made a
great commotion and protested that he could not leave anything in
his own house without people interfering with it.

The lady, who had troubles of her own to think about, lost her
temper with him and said:

'I wonder what you would say if something really terrible had
happened, when you create so much fuss over a spilled bottle of
water? Isn't there plenty more of it about?'

'My dear,' said the surgeon, 'you seem to think that it was
ordinary water, but that is not the case. On the contrary, it was a
potion specially prepared for putting people to sleep.'

He then told her what he needed it for, and it immediately
dawned upon the lady that Ruggieri must have drunk the potion,
which explained why they had thought he was dead.

'We knew nothing of all that,' she said. 'You'll have to make
yourself some more of it.'

Seeing that he had no alternative, the surgeon sent out for a
second bottle of the stuff, and shortly afterwards the maid, who on
the lady's instructions had gone out to discover what people were
saying about Ruggieri, returned to her mistress, saying:

'Everyone is saying awful things about him, ma'am, and as far as
I was able to discover, there is not one of his friends or relatives
who has lifted a finger to save him or has any intention of doing so.
Everyone is quite convinced that the judge will have him hanged
tomorrow. But there's another thing I want to tell you, and that is
that I think I have discovered how he came to be in the money-
lenders' house. Just listen, and I'll tell you. You know the carpenter,
don't you, in front of whose shop we found the trunk to put
Ruggieri in? Well, he was having a heated argument just now with

a man to whom it appears that the trunk belonged. The man was demanding to be paid for his trunk, and the carpenter was denying he had sold it, saying that on the contrary it had been stolen from him during the night. And the man said: "It's not true. You sold it to the two young money-lenders. They told me so themselves, for I spotted the trunk on going into their house early this morning, when Ruggieri was being arrested." "They are lying," said the carpenter, "for I never sold it to them. They must have stolen it from me last night. Let us go round and see them." So off they went by mutual agreement to the money-lenders' house, and I came back here. As you can see, I think this explains how Ruggieri was taken to the place where he was discovered. But I still can't make out how he came to life again.'

The lady now understood exactly what had happened. She told the maid about her conversation with the doctor, and begged her to help in freeing Ruggieri, telling her that she was in a position, if she so wished, to save Ruggieri and preserve the reputation of her mistress at one and the same time.

'Tell me what I have to do, ma'am,' said the maid, 'and I'll do it gladly, no matter what it involves.'

The lady, who saw that there was no time to lose, quickly improvised a plan of campaign and expounded it carefully to the maid, who first of all went straight to the doctor and, bursting into tears, said to him:

'Sir, I have done you a serious wrong, and I must ask you to forgive me.'

'And what may that be?' asked the surgeon.

'Sir,' replied the maid, continuing to weep, 'it concerns Ruggieri d'Aieroli. You know what a headstrong lad he is? Well, he took a fancy to me, and what with my fear of him on the one hand and my love for him on the other, a month or two ago I was obliged to become his mistress. When he discovered you were not going to be here last night, he talked me into allowing him into your house to sleep with me in my room. He said he was thirsty, but I hadn't a drop of wine or water to offer him. I couldn't go downstairs without being seen by your good lady, who was in the drawing-room, but I remembered having seen a bottle of water in your bedroom, and so I ran to fetch it, gave it him to drink, and put the bottle back again where I had found it. They tell me you've been playing merry hell about it, and I freely confess that it was wrong of me to do it, but then everybody makes a blunder occasionally. I can only say that I am very sorry, not only for doing what I did, but also for Ruggieri's sake, because he is about to lose his life over it. I therefore beseech you with all my heart to forgive me and let me go and see what I can do to help Ruggieri.'

Angry though he was to hear what she had done, the doctor had difficulty in keeping a straight face.

'You have been hoist with your own petard,' he replied. 'For you thought you had a young man who would shake your skin-coat well and truly last night, instead of which you had a slug-abed. Now go and see about saving your lover, and take good care in future not to bring him into the house again, otherwise I shall make you pay for it twice over.'

Feeling that she had emerged with flying colours from the first of her engagements, the maid hurried round as quickly as possible to the prison and wheedled the gaoler into letting her speak to Ruggieri. And after telling him what he was to say to the judge if he wanted to be saved, she actually succeeded in getting the judge himself to grant her a hearing.

The judge saw that she was a tasty-looking dish, and thought he would have just one little nibble before listening to what she had to say. Knowing that she would obtain a better hearing, the girl did not object in the slightest, and when the snack was finished she picked herself up and said:

'Sir, you are holding Ruggieri d'Aieroli here on a charge of theft, but you've arrested the wrong man.'

She then told him the whole story from beginning to end, explaining how she, who was his mistress, had let him into the doctor's house, and how she had unwittingly given him the opiate to drink, and how she had stuffed him inside the trunk thinking him to be dead. After this she told him about the conversation she had overheard between the master-carpenter and the trunk's owner, thus showing him how Ruggieri had ended up in the house of the money-lenders.

Seeing that it was an easy matter to verify her story, the judge first of all inquired of the surgeon whether what she had said about the potion was true, and discovered that it was. He then summoned the carpenter, the owner of the trunk, and the money-lenders, and after listening to a string of tall stories from the money-lenders, he found that they had stolen the trunk during the night and brought it into their house. Finally he sent for Ruggieri and asked him where he had lodged the previous evening. Ruggieri replied that he had no idea where he had lodged, but that he clearly remembered going to lodge with Doctor Mazzeo's maid, in whose bedroom he had drunk some water because he was very thirsty; what happened to him after that he was unable to say, except that he had woken up in the money-lenders' house to find himself inside a trunk.

The judge was greatly entertained by what he had heard, and made Ruggieri and the maid and the carpenter and the money-lenders repeat their stories several times over. In the end, pronouncing Ruggieri innocent, he ordered the money-lenders to pay a fine of ten gold florins, and set Ruggieri at liberty. You can all imagine what a relief this was for Ruggieri, and of course his mistress was absolutely delighted. She later celebrated his release in the company of Ruggieri himself, and along with the dear maid who had wanted to stick him with a knife, they had many a good laugh about it together. Their love continued to flourish, affording them greater and greater pleasure – which is what I should like to happen to me, except that I would not want to be stuffed inside a trunk.

★   ★   ★

If the earlier stories had saddened the fair ladies' hearts, this last one of Dioneo's caused so much merriment, especially the bit about the judge and his little nibble, that it drove away the melancholy engendered by the others.

But perceiving that the sun was beginning to turn yellow and that his reign had come to a close, the king offered the fair ladies a most handsome apology for having foisted so disagreeable a theme as the misfortunes of lovers upon them. Having made his excuses, he stood

up and removed the laurel wreath from his head. All the ladies
wondered to which of them it would be given, and eventually he
set it down with a flourish upon the fine blonde head of Fiammetta,
saying:

'I now bequeath you this crown, knowing that you are better
able than any other to restore the spirits of our fair companions
tomorrow after the rigours of the present day's proceedings.'

Fiammetta, who had long, golden curls that cascaded down over
delicate, pure white shoulders, a softly rounded face that glowed
with the authentic hues of white lilies and crimson roses, a pair of
eyes in her head that gleamed like a falcon's, and a sweet little
mouth with lips like rubies, answered Filostrato with a smile, saying:

'I accept it with pleasure, Filostrato; and so that you may the
more keenly appreciate the error of your ways, I desire and decree
forthwith that each of us should be ready on the morrow to recount
*the adventures of lovers who survived calamities or misfortunes and
attained a state of happiness.*'

Fiammetta's proposal met with general approval, and after summoning the steward and making appropriate arrangements, she
rose to her feet and gaily dismissed the whole company till suppertime.

So they all wandered off to amuse themselves until supper in
whatever way they pleased, some of them remaining in the garden,
of whose beauties one did not easily tire, whilst others ventured
beyond its confines and made for the windmills, whose sails were
turning in the evening breeze.

When it was time for supper, they forgathered as usual beside the
beautiful fountain, and partook of a most delicious meal, excellently
served. Then, having risen from table, they devoted themselves to
singing and dancing in their customary fashion, with Filomena
leading the revels, and the queen said:

'Filostrato, it is not my intention to depart from the ways of my
predecessors. Like them, I too intend to command that a song
should be sung, and since I am sure that your songs will be no less
gloomy than your stories, I desire that you should choose one and
sing it to us now, so that no day other than this will be blighted by
your woes.'

Filostrato replied that he would be only too willing to obey, and launched immediately into a song, the words of which ran as follows:

'With fitting tears, I show
The mourning heart bereaved,
Its faith in Love deceived.

'Love, who first fixed into my heart
She for whom now I sigh in vain,
You showed me her so full of grace
That I held light each bitter pain
    Which came to torment me
    So everlastingly.
    I know my error now;
    Not without grief, I vow.

'I comprehend that false deceit
And see how, while I thought that she
Seemed to allow my love, she'd found
Another servant, spurning me.
    Ah, then I could not see
    My future misery!
    But she the other took
    And me for him forsook.

'A mournful song swelled through my heart
When I perceived that I was spurned,
That dwells there still; and oft I curse
Faith, hope, love and the hour I learned
    Her noble beauteousness
    Whose radiance doth oppress
    My dying soul, which yet
    Cannot those charms forget.

'Bereft of every comfort now,
Oh, Lord of love, to you I cry;
  I burn with such a torment here
  That for a less I'd crave to die.
    Come Death, then, end my life
    With all its cruel strife;
    Strike down my misery!
    I shall the better be.

'No other way nor other ease
Remains to soothe my grief but death.
Grant me this, Love, and end my woes;
Take from me now my wretched breath.
    All joy is gone from me,
    No pleasure's left for me;
    Make then my death content her
    As the new love you sent her.

'My song, if none should learn to sing
Thee over, I take little care;
No one can sing thee as I can.
Only, to Love one message bear:
    Beg him, since life was all
    Loathsome to me, and vile,
    To safer haven take
    Me for his honour's sake.'

Filostrato's mood, and the reason, were made abundantly clear by the words of his song. And perhaps the face of one of the ladies dancing[1] would have clarified the matter still further if the shades of darkness, which had meanwhile descended, had not concealed the blush which spread across her cheeks as he was singing.

Many other songs followed, until finally it was time for them to go to bed, whereupon, by the queen's command, they all retired to their rooms.

Here ends the Fourth Day of the Decameron

FIFTH DAY

Here begins the Fifth Day, wherein, under the rule of Fiammetta, *are discussed the adventures of lovers who survived calamities or misfortunes and attained a state of happiness.*

The whole of the East was already suffused with white, and the heavens of our western world were shot through by the rays of the rising sun, when Fiammetta was roused from sleep by the melodious songs of the birds in the trees, chanting their joyous greetings to the dawn. She arose and sent for all the other ladies and the three young men, then sauntered down with her companions to the fields, where, walking over the dew of the broad and grassy plain, she conversed agreeably with the others upon this and that, till the sun had climbed well into the sky. But as the heat of the sun's rays grew more intense, she retraced her steps, and on reaching the house she saw that her companions were refreshed from the gentle exertions of their walk with excellent wines and sweetmeats, after which they whiled away their time till breakfast in the delectable garden. No detail had been overlooked by their resourceful steward in the preparation of the meal, to which in due course, at the bidding of the queen, after singing some canzonets and one or two *ballades*, they gaily addressed themselves. One by one, they disposed of the various dishes with relish, and when the meal was over, mindful of the practice already established, they danced and sang to the music of instruments. The queen then dismissed them till after the siesta hour, whereat some of them went away to sleep, whilst the others remained in the garden to savour its pleasures.

But shortly after nones,[1] at the queen's command, they all forgathered as usual beside the fountain. And having seated herself in a position of honour, the queen fixed her gaze upon Panfilo, smiled, and bade him tell the first of the day's stories, all of which were to end happily. Panfilo readily agreed, and began as follows:

FIRST STORY

Cimon[1] acquires wisdom through falling in love with Iphigenia, whom he later abducts on the high seas. After being imprisoned at Rhodes, he is released by Lysimachus, with whom he abducts both Iphigenia and Cassandra whilst they are celebrating their nuptials. They then flee with their ladies to Crete, whence after marrying them they are summoned back with their wives to their respective homes.

Delectable ladies, I can think of many stories with which I could aptly make a beginning to so joyful a day as this. But there is one in particular that strikes me as specially pleasing, for not only will it enable you to perceive the happy goal to which our discussions will from now on be directed, but it will also allow you to appreciate the sacredness, the power, and the beneficial effects of the forces of Love, which so many people, ignorant of what they are saying, mistakenly treat with contempt and abuse. All of which, unless I am mistaken, you will find most agreeable, for I take it that you are yourselves in love.

In the chronicles of the ancient Cypriots, then, we read that there once lived in the island of Cyprus a very noble gentleman, Aristippus by name, who was richer in worldly possessions than any other man in the country. And if Fortune had not presented him with one particular source of affliction, he would have accounted himself the happiest man alive. This consisted in the fact that one of his children, a youth of outstandingly handsome appearance and perfect physique, was to all intents and purposes an imbecile, whose case was regarded as hopeless. His true name was Galesus, but since the sum total of his tutor's persistent efforts, his father's cajolings and beatings, and all the ingenuity of various others, had failed to drum a scrap of learning or good manners into his head, on the contrary leaving him coarsely inarticulate and with the manners rather of a wild beast than a human being, he had earned himself the unflattering nickname of Cimon, which in their language has the same sort of meaning as 'simpleton' in ours. His hopeless condition was a

matter of very grave concern to his father, who, despairing of any
improvement and not wishing to have the source of his affliction
constantly before him, ordered him to go and live with his farm-
workers in the country. Cimon was only too pleased to obey, for
to his way of thinking the customs and practices of country yokels
were far more congenial than life in the city.

So Cimon went away to the country, where one afternoon,
whilst going about his rustic business on one of his father's estates,
with a stick on his shoulder, he chanced to enter a wood, renowned
in those parts for its beauty, the trees of which were thickly leaved
as it happened to be the month of May.[2] As he was walking
through the wood, guided as it were by Fortune, he came upon a
clearing surrounded by very tall trees, in a corner of which there
was a lovely cool fountain. Beside the fountain, lying asleep on the
grass, he saw a most beautiful girl, attired in so flimsy a dress that
scarcely an inch of her fair white body was concealed. From the
waist downwards she was draped in a pure white quilt, no less
diaphanous than the rest of her attire, and at her feet, also fast
asleep, lay two women and a man, who were the young lady's
attendants.

On catching sight of this vision, Cimon stopped dead in his
tracks, and, leaning on his stick, began to stare at her, rapt in silent
admiration, as though he had never before set eyes upon the female
form. And deep within his uncouth breast, which despite a thousand
promptings had remained stubbornly closed to every vestige of
refined sentiment, he sensed the awakening of a certain feeling
which told his crude, uncultured mind that this girl was the
loveliest object that any mortal being had ever seen. He now began
to consider each of her features in turn, admiring her hair, which he
judged to be made of gold, her brow, nose and mouth, her neck
and arms; and especially her bosom, which was not yet very
pronounced. Having suddenly been transformed from a country
bumpkin into a connoisseur of beauty, he longed to be able to see
her eyes, but they were closed in heavy slumber, from which the
girl gave no apparent sign of awakening. Several times he was on
the point of rousing her so that he might observe them, but as she
seemed far more beautiful than any woman he had ever seen, he

supposed that she might be a goddess, and he had sufficient mother wit to appreciate that divine things require more respect than those pertaining to earth. He therefore refrained, and waited for her to wake up of her own accord; and though he grew tired of waiting, he was filled with such strange sensations of pleasure that he was unable to tear himself away.

A long time elapsed before the girl, whose name was Iphigenia, raised her head and opened her eyes. Her attendants were still asleep, and on catching sight of Cimon standing before her, leaning on his stick, she was greatly astonished. She recognized him at once, for Cimon was known to almost everyone in those parts, not only because of the contrast between his handsome appearance and boorish manner, but also on account of his father's rank and riches.

'Cimon!' she exclaimed. 'What brings you here to the woods at this time of day?'

Cimon made no reply, but stood there gazing into her eyes, which seemed to shine with a gentleness that filled him with a feeling of joy such as he had never known before. When she saw him staring at her, Iphigenia was afraid that his rusticity might impel him to act in a way that would bring dishonour upon her, and having awakened her maidservants, she rose to her feet, saying:

'Cimon, I bid you good day.'

'I shall come with you,' Cimon replied.

Still feeling somewhat apprehensive, the girl refused his company, but did not succeed in shaking him off till he had escorted her all the way to her door. He then proceeded to his father's house, where he declared that he would on no account return to the country. His father and family were greatly displeased about this, but allowed him to stay in the hope of discovering what had caused him to change his mind.

Now that Cimon's heart, which no amount of schooling had been able to penetrate, was pierced by Love's arrow through the medium of Iphigenia's beauty, he suddenly began to display a lively interest in one thing after another, to the amazement of his father, his whole family, and everyone else who knew him. He first of all asked his father's permission to wear the same sort of clothes as his brothers, including all the frills with which they were in the habit of adorning themselves, and to this his father very readily agreed. He then began to associate with young men of excellence, observing the manners befitting a gentleman, more especially those of a gentleman in love, and within a very short space of time, to everyone's enormous stupefaction, he not only acquired the rudiments of learning but became a paragon of intelligence and wit. Furthermore (and this again was a consequence of his love for Iphigenia), he abandoned his coarse and rustic accent, adopting a manner of speech that was more seemly and civilized, and even became an accomplished singer and musician, whilst in horse-riding and in martial prowess, whether on sea or land, he distinguished himself by his skill and daring.

In short, (without going into further detail about his various accomplishments), in the space of four years from the day he had fallen in love, he turned out to be the most graceful, refined, and versatile young man in the island of Cyprus.

What, then, are we to say, fair ladies, of this young man? Surely, all we need say is that the lofty virtues instilled by Heaven in Cimon's valiant spirit were chained together and locked away by envious Fortune in a very small section of his heart, and that her mighty bonds had been shattered and torn apart by a much more powerful force, in other words that of Love. Being a rouser of sleeping talents, Love had rescued those virtues from the darkness in which they had lain so cruelly hidden, and forced them into the light, clearly displaying whence he draws, and whither he leads, those creatures who are subject to his rule and illumined by his radiance.

Although, in common with many another young man in love, Cimon was inclined in some ways to carry his love for Iphigenia to extremes, nevertheless Aristippus, on reflecting that Love had turned his son from an ass into a man, not only treated him with patience and tolerance but encouraged him to go further, and taste Love's pleasures to the full. But Cimon (who refused to be called Galesus because he recalled that Iphigenia had addressed him by his nickname) was determined to achieve the object of his yearning by honourable means, and made several attempts to persuade Iphigenia's father, Cypsehus, to grant him her hand in marriage, only to be told on each occasion that Cypsehus had already promised her to Pasimondas, a young nobleman of Rhodes, and had no intention of breaking his word.

When the time came for Iphigenia's marriage contract to be honoured, and her husband sent to fetch her, Cimon said to himself: 'Ah, Iphigenia! Now is the time for me to prove how deeply I love you! Through you I have achieved manhood, and if I succeed in winning you, beyond doubt I shall achieve greater glory than any of the gods. And win you I certainly shall, or I shall perish.' Being thus resolved, he furtively enlisted the help of certain young nobles who were friends of his, made secret arrangements to fit out a ship with everything one needed for a naval battle, and put out to sea, where he hove to and waited for the vessel which was to convey Iphigenia to her husband in Rhodes. And after her husband's friends had been sumptuously entertained by her father, they escorted her aboard, pointed the ship's prow in the direction of Rhodes, and departed.

On the following day, Cimon, who was very much on the alert, caught up with them in his own vessel, and standing on the prow, he hailed the crew of Iphigenia's ship in a loud voice:

'Lower your sails and heave to, or prepare to be overwhelmed and sunk!'

Cimon's opponents had brought up weapons from below and were making ready to defend themselves, so he followed up his words by seizing a grappling-iron and hurling it on to the stern of the Rhodian ship as it was pulling swiftly away, thus bringing his bows hard up against the enemy's poop. Without waiting to be joined by his comrades, he leapt aboard the Rhodians' ship like a raging lion as though contemptuous of all opposition. Spurred on by his love, he set about his adversaries with astonishing vigour, striking them down with his cutlass, one after another, like so many sheep. On seeing this the Rhodians laid down their arms, and more or less in chorus gave themselves up as his prisoners.

Then Cimon said to them:

'Young men, it was not the desire for plunder, nor any hatred towards you personally, that impelled me to leave Cyprus and subject you to armed attack on the high seas. My motive was the acquisition of something which I value most highly, and which it is very easy for you to surrender to me peaceably. I refer to Iphigenia, whom I love more than anything else in the world. Since I was unable to obtain her from her father by friendly and peaceable means, Love has compelled me to seize her from you in this hostile fashion, by force of arms. And now I intend to be to her such as your master, Pasimondas, was to have been. Give her to me, then, and proceed with God's grace on your voyage.'

The young men, more from necessity than the kindness of their hearts, handed over the weeping Iphigenia to her captor.

'Noble lady,' said Cimon, on perceiving her tears, 'do not distress yourself. It is your Cimon that you see before you. The constant love I have borne you gives me far more right to possess you than the plighted troth of Pasimondas.'

Having seen that Iphigenia was taken aboard, he returned to his own ship and allowed the Rhodians to go with all their possessions intact.

The winning of so precious a prize made Cimon the happiest man on earth. After spending some time consoling his tearful mistress, he persuaded his companions that they should not return to Cyprus for the present, and they all agreed to steer their ship towards Crete, where Cimon and most of the others had family ties, both recently made and long established, as well as numerous friends and acquaintances. And for this very reason they thought it safe to go there with Iphigenia.

They had reckoned without the fickleness of Fortune, however, for no sooner had she handed the lady into Cimon's keeping, than she converted the boundless joy of the enamoured youth into sad and bitter weeping.

Scarcely four hours had elapsed since Cimon and the Rhodians had parted company, when, with the approach of night, to which Cimon was looking forward with a keener pleasure than any he had ever experienced, an exceptionally violent storm arose, filling the sky with dark clouds and turning the sea into a raging cauldron. It thus became impossible for those aboard to see what they were doing or steer a proper course, or to keep their balance sufficiently long to perform their duties.

Needless to say, Cimon was greatly aggrieved by all this. The gods had granted his desire, but only, it seemed, to fill him with dread at the prospect of dying, which without Iphigenia he would have faced with cheerful indifference. His companions were equally woebegone, but the saddest one of all was Iphigenia, who was shedding copious tears and trembled with fear at every buffeting of the waves. Between her tears she bitterly cursed Cimon's love and censured his temerity, declaring that this alone had brought about the raging tempest, though it could also have arisen because Cimon's desire to marry her was contrary to the will of the gods, who were determined, not only to deny him the fruits of his presumptuous longing, but to make him witness her demise before he, too, died a miserable death.

These laments she continued to pour forth, along with others of still greater vehemence, until, with the wind blowing fiercer all the time, the seamen at their wits' end, and everyone ignorant of the course they were steering, they arrived off the island of Rhodes. Not realizing where they were, they did everything in their power to make a good landfall, and thus prevent loss of life.

Fortune was kindly to their endeavours, and guided them into a tiny bay, to which the Rhodians released by Cimon on the previous day had brought their own vessel a little while before. Dawn was breaking as they entered the bay, turning the sky a little brighter, and no sooner did they become aware that they were at the island of Rhodes than they perceived the very ship from which they had parted company, lying no more than a stone's throw away from their own. Cimon was dismayed beyond measure by this discovery, and fearing just such a fate as eventually overtook him, he called upon his crew to spare no effort in getting away from there and allowing Fortune to carry them wherever she pleased, since she could hardly choose a worse place than the one they were in. They strove with might and main to make good their escape, but without success, for a fierce gale was blowing directly against them, which not only prevented them from leaving the bay but drove them of necessity to the shore.

They eventually ran aground and were recognized by the

Rhodian sailors, who by now were already ashore. One of these hurried off to inform the young Rhodian nobles, who had meanwhile made their way to a nearby town, that the ship carrying Cimon and Iphigenia had, like their own, been driven into the bay by the storm.

Overjoyed by these tidings, the young Rhodians assembled a large number of the townspeople and instantly returned to the shore. Cimon and his companions had meanwhile disembarked, intending to seek refuge in some neighbouring woods, but before they could do so they were all seized, along with Iphigenia, and led away to the town. Here they were held until Lysimachus, the chief magistrate of Rhodes in that particular year, came from the city and marched them all off to prison under a specially heavy armed escort, as arranged by Pasimondas, who had lodged a complaint with the Senate of Rhodes as soon as the news had reached him.

And so it came about that the hapless Cimon lost his beloved Iphigenia almost as soon as he had won her, with nothing to show for his pains except one or two kisses. As for Iphigenia, she was given hospitality by various noble ladies of Rhodes, who restored her spirits from the shock of her abduction and the fatigue she had suffered in the tempest; and she remained with them until the day appointed for her wedding.

Pasimondas urged with all his eloquence that Cimon and his companions should be put to death, but their lives were spared on account of having set the young Rhodians at liberty on the previous day, and they were condemned to spend the rest of their lives in prison. And there, as may readily be imagined, they led a wretched existence, and despaired of ever knowing happiness again.

It was whilst Pasimondas was pressing zealously ahead with the preparations for his forthcoming marriage that Fortune, as though to make amends for the sudden blow she had dealt to Cimon's hopes, devised a novel way of procuring him his liberty. Pasimondas had a brother, younger but no less eligible than himself, whose name was Ormisdas, and who for some time had been seeking to marry a beautiful young noblewoman of the city called Cassandra, with whom Lysimachus, the chief magistrate, was very deeply in love. But the marriage had been several times postponed because of some unexpected turn of events.

Now, seeing that he was about to hold a huge reception to celebrate his own wedding, Pasimondas thought it would be an excellent idea to arrange for Ormisdas to be married at the same time, thus avoiding a second round of spending and feasting. He therefore re-opened discussions with Cassandra's kinsfolk and brought them to a successful conclusion, all the parties agreeing that on the day that Pasimondas married Iphigenia, Ormisdas should marry Cassandra.

Lysimachus, having heard of this arrangement, was greatly distressed, for it now appeared that all his hopes of marrying Cassandra, provided that Ormisdas did not marry her first, had suddenly vanished. He was wise enough, however, to conceal the agony he was suffering, and began to study various ways and means of preventing the marriage from taking place, eventually concluding that the only possible solution was to abduct her.

This seemed a feasible proposition because of the office he held, although if he had held no office at all he would have thought it a far less dishonourable course to take. But in short, after lengthy reflection his sense of honour gave way to his love, and he resolved, come what may, to carry Cassandra off. On giving thought to the sort of companions he would need for effecting his design, and planning the strategy he should adopt, he remembered that he was holding Cimon prisoner, together with all his men, and it occurred to him that for an enterprise such as this it would be impossible to find a better or more loyal accomplice.

So during the night he had Cimon secretly conveyed to his chamber, and introduced the subject in this fashion:

'Not only, Cimon, do the gods most freely and generously distribute their largesse amongst men, they also have exceedingly subtle ways of putting our merits to the test. And those whom they discover to be firm and constant in all circumstances, since they are the worthiest, are singled out for the highest rewards. The gods desired surer proofs of your excellence than you were able to display when living in the house of your father, whom I know to be immensely rich. And having first of all transformed you (or so I have been told) from an insensate beast into a man through the keen stimulus of Love, they are now intent upon seeing whether, after a severe ordeal and the discomforts of imprisonment, you are any less resolute than when you briefly enjoyed the spoils of victory. Nothing they have previously granted you, however, can have brought you so much joy and happiness as the thing which, if your courage has not deserted you, they are preparing to offer to you now. And in order to restore your strength, and put fresh heart into you, I intend to explain what it is.

'Pasimondas, who gloats over your undoing and fervently advocates your death, is making every effort to bring forward the celebration of his nuptials to your beloved Iphigenia, and thus enjoy the prize which Fortune had no sooner been content to bestow upon you than she angrily snatched away from you again. If he should succeed, and if you are as deeply in love as I suspect, I can readily imagine the pain you will suffer, for on that same day his brother, Ormisdas, is proposing to do the same to me by marrying Cassandra, whom I love more dearly than anything else in the world. If we are to prevent Fortune from dealing us so heavy and calamitous a blow, it seems to me that she has left us with no other recourse except the stoutness of our hearts and the strength of our right hands, with which we must seize our swords and fight our way to our ladies, you to carry off Iphigenia for the second time and I to carry off Cassandra for the first. If, therefore, you value the prospect of recovering your lady (not to mention your liberty, which must in any case mean little to you without Iphigenia), the gods have placed the means within your reach, provided you will join me in my enterprise.'

These words restored Cimon's depleted spirits to the full, and his answer was quickly forthcoming.

'Lysimachus,' he said, 'if this scheme of yours procures me the reward of which you have spoken, you could not have chosen a more resolute or loyal comrade. Therefore entrust me with whatever task you desire me to perform, and you will marvel at the energy I devote to your cause.'

'Two days hence,' said Lysimachus, 'the brides will cross their husbands' threshold for the first time. As dusk is falling, we shall go to the house, you with your companions and I with some of mine whom I trust implicitly, and make our way inside by armed force. We shall then seize the ladies from the midst of the assembled guests, and carry them off to a ship which I have caused to be fitted out in secret, killing anyone who should have the temerity to stand in our way.'

Cimon agreed to the plan, and lay quietly in prison until the appointed time.

When the wedding-day arrived, it was marked by magnificent pomp and splendour, and the house of the two brothers was filled throughout with sounds of revelry and rejoicing. Lysimachus, having completed all his preparations, handed out weapons to Cimon and his companions, as well as to his own friends, and these they concealed beneath their robes. He then delivered a lengthy harangue to fire them with enthusiasm for his plan, and when he judged the time to be ripe, he divided them into three separate groups, one of which he prudently dispatched to the harbour so that no one could prevent them from embarking when the time came for them to leave. Having led the other two parties to the house of Pasimondas, he posted one of them at the main entrance to frustrate any attempt to lock them inside or bar their retreat, whilst with the other, including Cimon, he charged up the stairs. On reaching the hall, where the two brides were already seated and about to dine along with numerous other ladies, they marched boldly forward and hurled the tables to the floor. Then each of the two men seized his lady and handed her over to his companions, instructing them to carry them off at once to the waiting ship.

The brides began to cry and scream, the other ladies and the servants followed suit, and the whole place was filled in an instant with uproar and wailing. But Cimon and Lysimachus and their companions, having drawn their swords, made their way unopposed to the head of the staircase, everyone standing aside to let them pass. As they were descending the stairs, they were met by Pasimondas, who had been attracted by all the noise and came up wielding a heavy stick; but he was struck such a fierce blow over the head by Cimon that a good half of it was severed from his body, and he dropped dead at the feet of his assailant. In rushing to his brother's assistance, the hapless Ormisdas was likewise slain by one of Cimon's lusty blows, whilst a handful of others who ventured to approach were set upon and beaten back by the rest of the invaders.

Leaving the house full of blood, tumult, tears, and sadness, they made their way unimpeded to the ship, keeping close together and carrying their spoils before them. Having handed the ladies aboard, Cimon and Lysimachus followed with their comrades just as the shore began to fill with armed men who were coming to the rescue of the two ladies. But they plied their oars with a will, and made good their escape.

On arriving in Crete they were given a joyous welcome by a large number of their friends and relatives, and after they had married their ladies and held a great wedding-feast, they gaily enjoyed the spoils of their endeavours.

In Rhodes and in Cyprus their deeds gave rise to great commotion and uproar, which took some time to subside. But in the fullness of time, their friends and relatives interceded on their behalf in both these places, and made it possible for Cimon and Lysimachus, after a period of exile, to return to Cyprus and Rhodes with Iphigenia and Cassandra respectively. And each lived happily ever after with his lady in the land of his birth.

SECOND STORY

Gostanza, in love with Martuccio Gomito, hears that he has died, and in her despair she puts to sea alone in a small boat, which is carried by the wind to Susa; she finds him, alive and well, in Tunis, and makes herself known to him, whereupon Martuccio, who stands high in the King's esteem on account of certain advice he had offered him, marries her and brings her back with a rich fortune to Lipari.[1]

Perceiving that Panfilo's story was at an end, the queen, having warmly commended it, directed Emilia to proceed with one of hers, and Emilia began as follows:

It is only natural that we should rejoice on seeing an enterprise crowned with rewards appropriate to the sentiments that inspired it. And since it is proper for true love to be rewarded in the long run with joy rather than suffering, it gives me far greater pleasure to obey the queen, and speak upon the present topic, than it gave me yesterday to address myself to the one prescribed for us by the king.

You are to know then, dainty ladies, that near Sicily there is a small island called Lipari, on which, not very long ago, there lived a most beautiful girl, Gostanza by name, who belonged to one of the noblest families on the island. With this girl, a young man called Martuccio Gomito, who also lived on the island, and who, apart from being an outstanding craftsman, was exceedingly handsome and well-mannered, fell in love. And Gostanza reciprocated his love so wholeheartedly that she was never happy when he was out of her sight. Desiring to make her his wife, Martuccio requested her father's consent, but was told that since he was too poor he couldn't have her.

Martuccio, indignant at seeing himself rejected on the grounds of his poverty, commissioned a small sailing-ship with certain friends and relatives of his, and vowed never to return to Lipari until he was a rich man. Having put to sea, he began to play the pirate along the Barbary coast, plundering every vessel that was weaker than his own. He had all the luck that was going for as long as he kept his ambition within reasonable bounds. But it was not enough that Martuccio and his companions should have quickly amassed a small fortune for themselves; their appetite for riches was enormous, and in trying to assuage it they encountered a flotilla of Saracen ships, by which, after lengthy resistance, they were captured and plundered. Most of Martuccio's men were dumped into the sea, and their ship was sunk, but Martuccio himself was hauled off to Tunis, where he was left to languish in a prison-cell.

Word was meanwhile brought to Lipari, not merely by one or two but by several different people, that Martuccio and all the men aboard his ship had drowned.

When she heard that Martuccio and his companions were dead, the girl, who had been distressed beyond measure by his departure,

wept incessantly and resolved to put an end to her life. Lacking
the courage to do herself violently to death, she hit upon a novel
but no less certain way of killing herself; and one night, she secretly
left her father's house and made her way to the harbour, where she
chanced upon a tiny fishing-boat, lying some distance away from
the other vessels. Its owners having gone ashore just a little while
earlier, the boat was still equipped with its mast, its sail, and its oars.
And since, like most of the women on the island, she had learnt the
rudiments of seamanship, she stepped promptly aboard, rowed a
little way out to sea, and hoisted the sail, after which she threw the
oars and rudder overboard and placed herself entirely at the mercy
of the wind. She calculated that one of two things would inevitably
happen: either the boat, being without ballast or rudder, would
capsize in the wind, or it would be driven aground somewhere and
smashed to pieces. In either case she was certain to drown, for she
would be unable to save herself even if she wanted to. So having
wrapped a cloak round her head, she lay down, weeping, on the
floor of the boat.

But her calculations proved quite wrong, for the wind blew so
gently from the north that the sea was barely disturbed, the boat
maintained an even keel, and towards evening on the following day
she drifted ashore near a town called Susa,² a hundred miles or so
beyond Tunis.

The girl was not aware that she was more ashore than afloat, for
she had not raised her head once from the position in which it was
lying, nor had she any intention of doing so, whatever happened.

As luck would have it, when the boat ran aground there was a
poor woman on the shore, taking in nets that had been left in the
sun by the fishermen for whom she worked. On seeing the boat,
she wondered how the fishermen aboard could have let it run
aground under full sail, and assumed that they must be asleep. So
she went up to the boat, but the only person she could see was this
young woman, lying there fast asleep. Having called to her several
times, she eventually got her to wake up, and since she could see
that the girl was a Christian from the clothes she was wearing, she
asked her in Italian how it came about that she had landed in that
particular spot, and in that particular boat, all by herself.

Hearing herself addressed in Italian, the girl wondered whether she had been driven back to Lipari by a change of wind. She started to her feet and looked around, and on seeing that she was grounded on a coastline that was totally unfamiliar to her, she asked the good woman where she was.

'You are near Susa, in Barbary, my daughter,' the woman replied.

On learning where she was, the girl, dismayed that God had denied her the death she was seeking, was afraid lest worse should befall her. Not knowing what to do, she sat down beside the keel of the boat and burst into tears. On seeing this, the good woman took pity on her and persuaded her, after a good deal of coaxing, to go with her to her little cottage, where she treated her so kindly that Gostanza told her how she came to be there. The woman realized that she must be hungry, and so she placed some dry bread, water, and a quantity of fish before her, and with much difficulty persuaded her to eat a little.

Then Gostanza asked her who she was, and how she came to speak such fluent Italian, whereupon the good woman told her that she was from Trapani, that her name was Carapresa, and that she was employed by some fishermen, who were Christians.

The girl was feeling very sorry for herself, but on hearing the name Carapresa (which means 'precious gain'), without knowing why, she took it as a good omen. For some strange reason she began to feel more hopeful, and was no longer so anxious to put an end to herself. Without disclosing who she was or whence she came, she earnestly entreated the good woman, in God's name, to have mercy on her youth and advise her how to save herself from coming to any harm.

The woman was a kindly soul, and after leaving her for a while in the cottage whilst she quickly gathered up her nets, she returned and wrapped her from head to foot in her own cloak, then took her with her to Susa. And on arriving in the town, she said:

'Gostanza, I am going to take you to the house of a very kind Saracen lady, who employs me regularly on various errands. She is elderly and tender-hearted: I shall commend you to her as warmly as I possibly can, and I am quite certain that she will gladly take you in and treat you as a daughter. Once you are under her roof, you are to serve her as loyally as you can, so as to win and retain her favour until such time as God may send you better fortune.'

Carapresa was as good as her word. When the lady, who was getting on in years, had heard her story, she looked into Gostanza's eyes, burst into tears, gathered her in her arms and kissed her on the forehead. Then she led her by the hand into the house, where she lived with certain other women, isolated from all male company. The women worked with their hands in various ways, producing a number of different objects made of silk, palm, and leather, and within a few days, the girl, having learned to make some of these objects, was sharing the work with the others. Her benefactress and the other ladies were remarkably kind and affectionate towards her, and before very long they had taught her to speak their language.

Now, whilst the girl was living in Susa, having long been given up as dead by her family, it happened that the King of Tunis, whose name was Mulay Abd Allah, was threatened by a powerful young grandee, who came from Granada, and who claimed that the kingdom of Tunis belonged to him. And having assembled an enormous army, he marched against the King to drive him from the realm.

Tidings of these events came to the ears of Martuccio Gomito as he lay in prison, and as he was well versed in the language of the Saracens, on learning that the King of Tunis was making strenuous efforts to defend himself, he said to one of the men who were guarding him and his companions:

'If I could speak to the King, I am sure I could advise him how to win this war of his.'

The gaoler reported Martuccio's words to his superior, who immediately passed them on to the King. The King therefore ordered Martuccio to be brought before him, and asked him what advice he had in mind.

'My lord,' replied Martuccio, 'years ago I spent some time in this country of yours, and if I rightly observed the tactics you employ in battle, it seems that you leave the brunt of the fighting to your archers. If, therefore, one could devise a way of cutting off the enemy's supply of arrows whilst leaving your own men with arrows to spare, I reckon that your battle would be won.'

'If this could be done,' replied the King, 'without a doubt I should be confident of winning.'

'My lord,' said Martuccio, 'it can certainly be done if you have a mind to do it. Listen, and I shall tell you how. You must see that the bows of your archers are fitted with much finer string than that which is normally used. You must then have arrows specially made, the notches of which will only take this finer string. All of this must be done in great secrecy so that the enemy knows nothing about it, otherwise he would take suitable counter-measures. The reason for my advice is this: as you know, when your enemy's archers have fired all their arrows, and your own men have fired theirs, each side will have to gather up the other's arrows for the battle to continue. But the arrows fired by your archers will be useless to the enemy because their bow-strings will be too thick to fit into the small notches, whereas your own men will have no difficulty at all in using the enemy's arrows because a fine string goes perfectly well into a wide notch. Thus your own men will have an abundant supply of arrows, and the others will have none at all.'

Being a man of some intelligence, the King approved of Martuccio's plan and carried it out to the letter, thereby winning the war. Martuccio was therefore raised to a high position in the King's favour, and consequently grew rich and powerful.

Tidings of these events spread throughout the country, and when it was reported to Gostanza that Martuccio Gomito, whom she had long supposed to be dead, was in fact alive, her love for him, which by now was beginning to fade from her heart, was suddenly rekindled, blazing more fiercely than ever, and all her lost hopes were revived. She therefore recounted all her vicissitudes to the good lady with whom she was living, and told her that she desired to go to Tunis, so that she might feast her eyes upon that which her ears had made them eager to behold. Her request was warmly approved by the lady, who, treating her as a daughter, took her by sea to Tunis, where she and Gostanza were honourably received in the house of one of the lady's kinswomen.

They had brought Carapresa with them, and the lady sent her to find out all she could about Martuccio. When she returned with the news that Martuccio was alive and of high estate, the lady resolved to go in person to Martuccio and inform him of the arrival of his beloved Gostanza. And so one day, she called upon Martuccio, and said to him:

'Martuccio, a servant of yours from Lipari has turned up at my house, and desires to talk to you there in private. Since he did not wish me to entrust his mission to others, I have come to inform you in person.'

Martuccio thanked the lady, and followed her back to her house.

The girl was so delighted to see him that she nearly died. Carried away by her feelings, she ran up to him and flung her arms round his neck; then she burst into tears, unable to speak because of her joy and the bitter memory of her past misfortunes.

When he saw who it was, Martuccio was at first struck dumb with astonishment, but then he began to sigh, and said:

'Oh, Gostanza, can it really be you? I was told, long ago, that you had vanished from Lipari, never to be heard of again.' And this was all he could say before he, too, burst into tears, took her tenderly in his arms, and kissed her.

Gostanza described to him all that had happened to her, and told him of the honour paid to her by the noble lady with whom she had been staying. Martuccio spent some time conversing with her, after which he left her and went to the King, his master, to whom he gave a full account, not only of his own vicissitudes but also those of the girl, adding that he intended, by the King's leave, to marry her according to the Christian rite.

The King, who was filled with amazement, summoned the girl to his presence; and having heard her confirm Martuccio's story with her own lips, he said:

'Then you have certainly earned the right to marry him.'

He then called for sumptuous and splendid gifts to be brought, and divided them between Gostanza and Martuccio, granting them leave to arrange matters between themselves in whatever way they pleased.

The gentlewoman with whom Gostanza had been staying was

nobly entertained by Martuccio, who thanked her for all she had done to assist Gostanza, gave her such presents as were suitable to a person of her rank, and commended her to God, after which she and Gostanza took their leave of one another, shedding many tears. By the King's leave, they then embarked on a small sailing-ship, taking Carapresa with them, and with the aid of a prosperous wind they came once more to Lipari, where there was such great rejoicing that no words could ever describe it.

There, Martuccio and Gostanza were married, celebrating their nuptials in great pomp and splendour; and they spent the rest of their lives in the tranquil and restful enjoyment of the love they bore one another.

THIRD STORY

Pietro Boccamazza flees with Agnolella; they encounter some brigands; the girl takes refuge in a forest, and is conducted to a castle; Pietro is captured by the brigands, but escapes from their clutches, and after one or two further adventures, he reaches the castle where Agnolella is, marries her, and returns with her to Rome.

There was not one member of the company who failed to applaud Emilia's story, which the queen no sooner discovered to be at an end than she turned to Elissa and bade her to continue. Elissa was only too eager to obey, and began as follows:

The tale that presents itself to me, gracious ladies, concerns a calamitous night that was once experienced by two young people slightly lacking in good sense; but since it was followed by many a day of happiness, hence falling within our terms of reference, I should like to tell you about it.

Not long ago, in the city of Rome – which was once the head and is now the rump of the civilized world[1] – there lived a young man called Pietro Boccamazza, belonging to an illustrious Roman family, who fell in love with a charming and very beautiful girl called Agnolella, the daughter of a certain Gigliuozzo Saullo, who, though a plebeian, was much respected by his fellow-citizens. So skilfully did he press his suit that the girl soon came to love him in equal measure. Spurred on by the intensity of his love, and no longer willing to endure the pangs of his desire, Pietro asked for her hand in marriage. But when his kinsfolk discovered what he was proposing to do, they all descended on him and took him severely to task, at the same time letting it be known to Gigliuozzo Saullo that he should on no account take Pietro seriously, otherwise they would never acknowledge him as their friend or kinsman.

Having thus been prevented from attaining his desire by the only means he could think of, Pietro all but died of grief. If he could only have secured Gigliuozzo's consent, he would have defied every one of his relatives and married the girl whether they liked it or not. But in any case he was determined, provided he had her support, to see this affair through to the end; and having learned through the medium of a third party that her approval was forthcoming, he arranged with her that they should elope from Rome together. So one morning, having made all necessary preparations, Pietro got up very early, saddled a pair of horses, and rode away with her in the direction of Anagni,² where there were certain friends of his whom he trusted implicitly. Since they were afraid that they might be pursued, they had no time to stop and celebrate their nuptials, so they simply murmured sweet nothings to one another as they rode along, and exchanged an occasional kiss.

Now, the route they were taking was not very familiar to Pietro, and when they were about eight miles away from Rome, instead of turning right, they turned off along a road to the left. Scarcely had they ridden for two miles along this road when they found themselves close to a castle, from which, as soon as they were sighted, a dozen soldiers emerged. Just as they were about to be intercepted by the soldiers, the girl saw them coming and let out a shriek, saying:

'Quickly, Pietro, let's fly; they are coming for us.'

Employing all her strength, she pulled her nag's head sharply round in the direction of a huge forest; and clinging to the saddle for dear life, she dug her spurs into the animal's sides, whereupon the nag, being thus goaded, carried her off into the forest at a brisk gallop.

Pietro, who had been busy gazing into the girl's eyes instead of watching where he was going, was slower than she to catch sight of the soldiers, and he was still looking about him to discover from which direction they were coming when he was fallen upon, caught, and forced to dismount. They asked him who he was, and when he told them, they began to confer among themselves, saying: 'This fellow's a friend of the Orsini,[3] our enemies. What better way to show them our contempt than to take away his clothes and his nag, and string him up from one of these oak trees.' This idea commanded their unanimous approval, and they ordered Pietro to strip.

As he was undressing, knowing only too well what was in store for him, it happened that a company of soldiers, at least two dozen strong, descended on them with shouts of 'Kill them! Kill them!' In their confusion, the others abandoned Pietro and looked to their defence; but on finding themselves greatly outnumbered, they took to their heels, with their assailants in full pursuit. When Pietro saw this, he promptly gathered up his belongings, leapt on to his steed, and galloped away as fast as he could along the path by which the girl had already fled.

But on finding no sign of a track through the forest, or even the imprint of a horse's hoof, he was overcome with despair, and as soon as he judged himself to be beyond the reach of his captors and their assailants, he burst into tears and began to meander through the forest, calling her name in all directions. But there was no reply, and, not daring to retrace his steps, he rode on without having the slightest notion of where he was going. To add to his misery, he was afraid, not only on his own account but also on the girl's, of all the wild beasts that are generally to be found lurking in forests, and in his mind's eye he constantly saw her being suffocated by bears or devoured by wolves.

And so our luckless Pietro careered all day long through the forest, shouting and calling, sometimes going round in circles when he thought he was proceeding in a straight line, until eventually, what with shouting and weeping and feeling afraid and not having eaten, he was so exhausted that he could go no further. Finding that darkness had fallen, and not knowing what else he could do, he dismounted from his nag, tethered it to a large oak, and then climbed the tree to avoid being devoured in the night by wild beasts. The night was clear, and before very long the moon had risen, but for fear of tumbling from his perch Pietro dared not fall asleep. This would in any case have been impossible because he was far too dejected and concerned for Agnolella's safety, and so his only alternative was to stay awake, groaning and cursing and bewailing his misfortune.

Meanwhile the girl, who as we have stated was fleeing with no destination in mind, simply let her nag carry her wherever it chose, and soon she had penetrated so far into the forest that she could no longer discern the way by which she had entered. So she spent the whole day just as Pietro had done, threading her way through the wildwood, pausing occasionally to rest, weeping and calling out incessantly, and bemoaning her terrible fate.

Finally, as dusk was falling and there was still no sign of Pietro, she stumbled upon a narrow path, along which her nag proceeded to trot, and after riding along it for over two miles, she saw a cottage ahead of her in the distance, to which she made her way as speedily as possible, there to find a kindly man of very ancient appearance, with a wife little younger than himself.

On seeing that she was by herself, they exclaimed:

'Alas, child, whatever are you doing in these parts, all alone, at this hour?'

Through her tears, the girl told them that she had lost her companion in the forest, and asked them how far it was to Anagni.

'This road doesn't lead to Anagni, my child,' the good man replied. 'It's a dozen miles or so from here to Anagni.'

Whereupon Agnolella said:

'Then is there a house nearby where I could spend the night?'

'None that you could reach before dark,' he answered.

To which the girl said:

'For the love of God, would you be so kind, since I cannot go elsewhere, to let me stay here for the night?'

'Young woman,' he replied, 'we should be happy for you to

spend the night with us, but at the same time we must warn you that these parts are infested, day and night, by bands of cut-throats who fight among themselves and every so often wreak damage and hardship upon us. If we had the misfortune to be invaded by one of these bands whilst you were here, on seeing what a pretty young woman you are they would affront and manhandle you, and we could not lift a finger to help. We want you to know about this so that if such a thing were to happen, you would harbour no resentment against us.'

The old man's words filled the girl with alarm, but seeing that the hour was so late, she replied:

'God willing, we shall all be spared from any such calamity, but even if such a fate were to befall me, it is a much lesser evil to be misused by men than to be torn to pieces by wild beasts in the forest.'

And so saying, she dismounted and went inside the poor man's dwelling, where she supped frugally with them on what little food they had in the house, after which, still fully clothed, she settled down exhausted with the others on their tiny little bed. And there she lay, sobbing the whole night long and bewailing the misfortunes of herself and Pietro, to whom she could only suppose that the worst must have happened.

A little before dawn, she heard a loud trampling of horses' hooves, so she got up and made her way into a spacious yard at the rear of the cottage. Along one of its sides, she saw a great pile of hay, in which she decided to hide, so that if these strangers came to the cottage, she would not be so easily found. No sooner had she finished concealing herself, than the horsemen, a large band of marauders, arrived at the door of the cottage. Having forced the old people to open the door, they pushed their way inside, where they found the girl's nag still fully saddled, and demanded to know who was there.

Seeing no sign of the girl, the good man replied:

'There is no one here apart from ourselves. But this nag, whoever it ran away from, turned up here yesterday evening, and we brought it into the house so that it would not be devoured by wolves.'

'In that case,' the gang's leader replied, 'since he doesn't belong to anyone we shall take him along with us.'

The bandits dispersed through the cottage, and some of them found their way into the yard, where they put off their lances and wooden shields. But one of their number, having nothing better to do, happened to hurl his lance into the hay, coming within an ace of killing the hidden girl, who all but gave herself away as the head of the lance skimmed her left breast, passing so close to her body that it tore through her clothes. She very nearly let out a great scream, fearing that she would come to serious harm, but remembered just in time where she was and kept quiet, trembling from head to foot.

The men roamed freely about the house in small groups, and having cooked themselves some goat's meat and one or two other things they had brought with them, they ate and drank to their hearts' content. They then went about their business, taking the girl's nag with them, and when they were at a safe distance from the cottage, the good man turned to his wife, and said:

'Whatever became of the young woman who came to us yesterday evening? I haven't set eyes on her from the time we got up.'

The good woman said she had no idea, and went off to look for her.

On realizing that the men had gone away, the girl clambered out of the hay. The old man was greatly relieved to discover that she had not fallen into their clutches, and since it was now growing light he said to her:

'Now that the day is breaking, we shall go with you, if you like, to a castle which is only five miles away, where you will find yourself in good hands. You'll have to walk, though, because that bunch of rogues who have just left took your nag away with them.'

Resigning herself to the loss of her nag, the girl begged them in God's name to conduct her to the castle; whereupon they set out, and arrived there when the hour of tierce was about half spent.

The castle belonged to a member of the Orsini family called Liello di Campo di Fiore, whose wife, a devout and exceedingly worthy woman, happened at that time to be staying there. On seeing Agnolella, she recognized her instantly and gave her a cordial welcome, and insisted on knowing precisely how she came to be there. The girl told her the whole story from start to finish.

The lady, who also knew Pietro because he was a friend of her husband, was greatly distressed to learn what had happened, and on hearing where he had been seized, she was convinced that he must be dead.

So she said to the girl:

'Since you have no idea what has become of Pietro, you must stay here with me until such time as I can send you safely back to Rome.'

Pietro had meanwhile stayed put in the branches of the oak, feeling as miserable as sin, and towards midnight he saw at least a score of wolves approaching. On seeing the nag, they crept up on him from all sides, but the nag heard them coming, and, tossing his head, broke loose from his tether and started to run away. Since he was surrounded, he could not get very far, so he set about the wolves with his teeth and his hooves, holding them at bay for quite some time till eventually they forced him to the ground, throttled the life out of him, and tore out his innards. They all began to gorge upon their prey, and having picked the carcase clean, they went away leaving nothing but the bones. Pietro was thrown into despair by this spectacle, for to him the nag was a sort of comrade, a prop and stay in his afflictions, and he began to think that he would never succeed in leaving the forest alive.

He continued to keep a lookout on all sides, however, and a little before dawn, when he was all but freezing to death up there in the oak, he caught sight of a huge fire, about a mile from where he was sheltering. So as soon as daylight had come he descended from his perch, feeling distinctly apprehensive, and made off in that direction. On reaching the spot he found a number of shepherds sitting and making merry round the fire, and they took pity on him and asked him to join them. When he had eaten and warmed himself at the fire, having given them an account of his misfortunes and explained how it was that he came to be wandering alone through the forest, he asked them whether there was any village or township thereabouts to which he might go.

The shepherds replied that some three miles away there was a castle belonging to Liello di Campo di Fiore, and that Liello's wife was at present living there. Overjoyed, Pietro asked whether any of the shepherds would guide him as far as the castle, and two of them volunteered to do so. On reaching the castle, Pietro met various people he knew, and whilst he was trying to arrange for them to go out and search for the girl in the forest, he was told that Liello's wife wanted to see him. He promptly answered her summons, and on finding that she had Agnolella with her, he was the happiest man that was ever born.

He was positively longing to take her in his arms, but was too embarrassed to do so in the presence of the lady. And if his own joy knew no bounds, the girl was no less delighted on seeing him.

The noble lady took him in and made him very welcome, and having heard the tale of his adventures from his own lips, she spoke to him severely for attempting to defy the wishes of his kinsfolk. But on seeing that he was quite unrepentant, and that the girl was eager to marry him, she said to herself: 'Why should I go to all this trouble? They are in love, they understand one another, both are friends of my husband, and their intentions are honourable. Besides, it seems to me that they have God's blessing, for one of them has been saved from being hanged, the other from being killed by a lance, and both of them from being devoured by wild beasts. So let them do as they wish.' She therefore turned to them, and said:

'If you have really set your hearts on becoming husband and wife, so be it; you shall have my blessing, the wedding can be celebrated here at Liello's expense, and after you are married you can safely leave it to me to make peace between you and your kinsfolk.'

So there they were married, and Pietro's enormous joy was only surpassed by that of Agnolella. The noble lady gave them as splendid a wedding as could possibly be arranged in her mountain retreat, and it was there that they tasted the first exquisite fruits of their love.

Some days later, guarded by a powerful escort, they returned with the lady on horseback to Rome, where, on finding that Pietro's kinsfolk were greatly angered by what he had done, she succeeded in restoring him to their good graces. And afterwards, he and Agnolella lived to a ripe old age in great peace and happiness.

FOURTH STORY

Ricciardo Manardi is discovered by Messer Lizio da Valbona with his daughter, whom he marries, and remains on good terms with her father.

Elissa, falling silent, listened as her companions lauded her tale, and the queen called upon Filostrato to tell his story. Laughing, he began as follows:

I have been teased so many times, and by so many of you, for obliging you to tell cruel stories and making you weep, that I feel obliged to make some slight amends for the sorrow I caused, and tell you something that will make you laugh a little. Hence I propose to tell you a very brief tale about a love which, apart from one or two sighs and a moment of fear not unmixed with embarrassment, ran a smooth course to its happy conclusion.

Not long ago then, excellent ladies, there lived in Romagna a most reputable and virtuous gentleman called Messer Lizio da Valbona,[1] who, on the threshold of old age, had the good fortune to be presented by his wife, Madonna Giacomina, with a baby daughter. When she grew up, she outshone all the other girls in those parts for her charm and beauty, and since she was the only daughter left to her father and mother, they loved and cherished her with all their heart, and guarded her with extraordinary care, for they had high hopes of bestowing her in marriage on the son of some great nobleman.

Now, to the house of Messer Lizio there regularly came a handsome and sprightly youth called Ricciardo de' Manardi da Brettinoro, with whom Messer Lizio spent a good deal of his time; and he and his wife would no more have thought of keeping him under surveillance than if he were their own son. Whenever he set eyes on the girl, Ricciardo was struck by her great beauty, her graceful bearing, her charming ways and impeccable manners, and, seeing that she was of marriageable age, he fell passionately in love with her. He took great pains to conceal his feelings, but the girl divined that he was in love with her, and far from being offended, to Ricciardo's great delight she began to love him with equal fervour. Though frequently seized with the longing to speak to her, he was always too timid to do so until one day, having chosen a suitable moment, he plucked up courage and said to her:

'Caterina, I implore you not to let me die of love for you.'

'Heaven grant,' she promptly replied, 'that you do not allow me to die first for love of you.'

Ricciardo was overjoyed by the girl's answer, and, feeling greatly encouraged, he said to her:

'Demand of me anything you please, and I shall do it. But you alone can devise the means of saving us both.'

Whereupon the girl said:

'Ricciardo, as you see, I am watched very closely, and for this reason I cannot think how you are to come to me. But if you are able to suggest anything I might do without bringing shame upon myself, tell me what it is, and I shall do it.'

Ricciardo turned over various schemes in his mind, then suddenly he said:

'My sweet Caterina, the only way I can suggest is for you to come to the balcony overlooking your father's garden, or better still, to sleep there. Although it is very high, if I knew that you were spending the night on the balcony, I would try without fail to climb up and reach you.'

'If you are daring enough to climb to the balcony,' Caterina replied, 'I am quite sure that I can arrange to sleep there.'

Ricciardo assured her that he was, whereupon they snatched a single kiss and went their separate ways.

It was already near the end of May, and on the morning after her conversation with Ricciardo, the girl began complaining to her mother that she had been unable to sleep on the previous night because of the heat.

'What are you talking about, child?' said her mother. 'It wasn't in the least hot.'

To which Caterina said:

'Mother, if you were to add "in my opinion", then perhaps you would be right. But you must remember that young girls feel the heat much more than older women.'

'That is so, my child,' said her mother, 'but what do you expect me to do about it? I can't make it hot or cold for you, just like that. You have to take the weather as it comes, according to the season. Perhaps tonight it will be cooler, and you will sleep better.'

'God grant that you are right,' said Caterina, 'but it is not usual for the nights to grow any cooler as the summer approaches.'

'Then what do you want us to do about it?' inquired the lady.

'If you and father were to consent,' replied Caterina, 'I should like to have a little bed made up for me on the balcony outside his room, overlooking the garden. I should have the nightingale to sing me off to sleep, it would be much cooler there, and I should be altogether better off than I am in your room.'

Whereupon her mother said:

'Cheer up, my child; I shall speak to your father about it, and we shall do whatever he decides.'

The lady reported their conversation to Messer Lizio, who, perhaps because of his age, was inclined to be short-tempered.

'What's all this about being lulled to sleep by the nightingale?' he exclaimed. 'She'll be sleeping to the song of the cicadas if I hear any more of her nonsense.'

Having heard what he had said, on the following night, more to spite her father than because she was feeling hot, Caterina not only stayed awake herself but, by complaining incessantly of the heat, also prevented her mother from sleeping.

So next morning, her mother went straight to Messer Lizio, and said:

'Sir, you cannot be very fond of this daughter of yours. What difference does it make to you whether she sleeps on the balcony or not? She didn't get a moment's rest all night because of the heat. Besides, what do you find so surprising about a young girl taking pleasure in the song of the nightingale? Young people are naturally drawn towards those things that reflect their own natures.'

'Oh, very well,' said Messer Lizio. 'Take whichever bed you

please, and set it up for her on the balcony with some curtains
round it. Then let her sleep there and hear the nightingale singing
to her heart's content.'

On hearing that her father had given his permission, the girl
promptly had a bed made up for herself on the balcony; and since it
was her intention to sleep there that same night, she waited for
Ricciardo to come to the house, and gave him a signal, already
agreed between them, by which he understood what was expected
of him.

As soon as he had heard his daughter getting into bed, Messer
Lizio locked the door leading from his own room to the balcony,
and then he too retired for the night.

When there was no longer any sound to be heard, Ricciardo
climbed over a wall with the aid of a ladder, then climbed up the
side of the house by clinging with great difficulty to a series of
stones projecting from the wall. At every moment of the ascent, he
was in serious danger of falling, but in the end he reached the
balcony unscathed, where he was silently received by the girl with
very great rejoicing. After exchanging many kisses, they lay down
together and for virtually the entire night they had delight and joy
of one another, causing the nightingale to sing at frequent
intervals.

Their pleasure was long, the night was brief, and though they
were unaware of the fact, it was almost dawn when they eventually
fell asleep without a stitch to cover them, exhausted as much by
their merry sport as by the nocturnal heat. Caterina had tucked her
right arm beneath Ricciardo's neck, whilst with her left hand she
was holding that part of his person which in mixed company you
ladies are too embarrassed to mention.

Dawn came, but failed to wake them, and they were still asleep
in the same posture when Messer Lizio got up out of bed. Remembering that his daughter was sleeping on the balcony, he quietly
opened the door, saying:

'I'll just go and see whether Caterina has slept any better with the
help of the nightingale.'

Stepping out on to the terrace, he gently raised the curtain
surrounding the bed and saw Ricciardo and Caterina, naked and

uncovered, lying there asleep in one another's arms, in the posture just described.

Having clearly recognized Ricciardo, he left them there and made his way to his wife's room, where he called to her and said:

'Be quick, woman, get up and come and see, for your daughter was so fascinated by the nightingale that she has succeeded in way-laying it, and is holding it in her hand.'

'What are you talking about?' said the lady.

'You'll see, if you come quickly,' said Messer Lizio.

The lady got dressed in a hurry, and quietly followed in Messer Lizio's footsteps until both of them were beside the bed. The curtain was then raised, and Madonna Giacomina saw for herself exactly how her daughter had taken and seized hold of the nightin-gale, whose song she had so much yearned to hear.

The lady, who considered that she had been seriously deceived in Ricciardo, was on the point of shouting and screaming abuse at him, but Messer Lizio restrained her, saying:

'Woman, if you value my love, hold your tongue! Now that she has taken him, she shall keep him. Ricciardo is a rich young man, and comes of noble stock. We could do a lot worse than have him as our son-in-law. If he wishes to leave this house unscathed, he will first have to marry our daughter, so that he will have put his nightingale into his own cage and into no other.'

The lady was reassured to see that her husband was not unduly perturbed by what had happened, and on reflecting that her daugh-ter had enjoyed a good night, was well-rested, and had caught the nightingale, she held her peace.

Nor did they have long to wait before Ricciardo woke up, and on seeing that it was broad daylight, he almost died of fright and called to Caterina, saying:

'Alas, my treasure, the day has come and caught me unawares! What is to happen to us?'

At these words, Messer Lizio stepped forward, raised the curtain, and replied:

'What you deserve.'

On seeing Messer Lizio, Ricciardo nearly leapt out of his skin and sat bolt upright in bed, saying:

'My lord, in God's name have mercy on me. I know that I deserve to die, for I have been wicked and disloyal, and hence you must deal with me as you choose. But I beseech you to spare my life, if that is possible. I implore you not to kill me.'

'Ricciardo,' said Messer Lizio, 'this deed was quite unworthy of the love I bore you and the firm trust I placed in you. But what is done cannot be undone, and since it was your youth that carried you into so grievous an error, in order that you may preserve not only your life but also my honour, you must, before you do anything else, take Caterina as your lawful wedded wife. And thus, not only will she have been yours for this night, but she will remain yours for as long as she lives. By this means alone will you secure your freedom and my forgiveness; otherwise you can prepare to meet your Maker.'

Whilst this conversation was taking place, Caterina let go of the nightingale, and having covered herself up, she burst into tears and implored her father to forgive Ricciardo, at the same time beseeching Ricciardo to do as Messer Lizio wished, so that they might long continue to enjoy such nights as this together in perfect safety.

All this pleading was quite superfluous, however, for what with the shame of his transgression and his urge to atone on the one hand, and his desire to escape with his life on the other (to say nothing of his yearning to possess the object of his ardent love), Ricciardo readily consented, without a moment's hesitation, to do what Messer Lizio was asking.

Messer Lizio therefore borrowed one of Madonna Giacomina's rings, and Ricciardo married Caterina there and then without moving from the spot, her parents bearing witness to the event.

This done, Messer Lizio and his wife withdrew, saying:

'Now go back to sleep, for you doubtless stand in greater need of resting than of getting up.'

As soon as Caterina's parents had departed, the two young people fell once more into each other's arms, and since they had only passed half-a-dozen milestones in the course of the night, they added another two to the total before getting up. And for the first day they left it at that.

After they had risen, Ricciardo discussed the matter in greater detail with Messer Lizio, and a few days later he and Caterina took appropriate steps to renew their marriage vows in the presence of their friends and kinsfolk. Then, amid great rejoicing, he brought her to his house, where the nuptials were celebrated with dignity and splendour. And for many years thereafter he lived with her in peace and happiness, caging nightingales by the score, day and night, to his heart's content.

FIFTH STORY

Before he dies, Guidotto da Cremona consigns to Giacomino da Pavia a young girl, who later on, in Faenza, is wooed by Giannole di Severino and Minghino di Mingole; these two come to blows, but when the girl is identified as Giannole's sister, she is given in marriage to Minghino.

In listening to the tale of the nightingale, all the ladies laughed so much that it was some time after Filostrato had finished before they managed to contain their mirth. But when their laughter had died away, the queen said:

'Without a doubt, Filostrato, though you plunged us all into sorrow yesterday, you have tickled our ribs so much today that we cannot hold it against you any longer.'

Then, turning to Neifile, she asked her to tell her story, and Neifile cheerfully began, as follows:

Since Filostrato crossed the borders of Romagna for the subject of his tale, I too shall take the liberty of roaming for a while in that part of the world.

In the town of Fano,[1] then, there once lived two Lombards, of whom the first was called Guidotto da Cremona and the second Giacomino da Pavia. No longer young, they had spent the greater part of their lives in warring and soldiering, and on his deathbed, Guidotto, who had no children of his own and trusted Giacomino more than any other friend or relative, committed to his comrade's care a little girl of his, who was about ten years of age. He also bequeathed him all his worldly possessions, and having talked to him at length about his affairs, he departed this life.

Now, around that period, the town of Faenza,[2] which for many years had been ravaged by war and other calamities, was restored to somewhat more stable conditions, and anyone wishing to return was freely permitted to do so. Hence Giacomino, who had once lived in Faenza and had grown attached to the place, returned there with all his belongings, taking with him the girl entrusted to him by Guidotto, whom he loved and treated as a daughter.

As she grew older, the girl became singularly beautiful, being better looking than any other young woman then living in Faenza; and with her beauty were united a virtuous disposition and graceful manners. She thus began to attract the gaze of various admirers, and in particular of two very handsome and well-connected young men, who fell so violently in love with her that their jealousy and hatred of each other surpassed all bounds. The first of these was called Giannole di Severino, the second Minghino di Mingole, and neither would have hesitated for a moment to marry the girl, who had now reached the age of fifteen, if the consent of his kinsfolk had been forthcoming. But since this was not the case, each of them resolved to seize possession of her by whatever means he could devise.

Giacomino had in his house an elderly maidservant and a serving-man called Crivello, a highly sociable and entertaining sort of fellow, with whom Giannole became very friendly. Choosing the right moment Giannole told Crivello all about his love for the girl, imploring him to assist him in attaining his desire, and promising to reward him handsomely in return.

'Now look,' said Crivello, 'there is only one possible way in which I could be of service to you, and that consists in waiting for Giacomino to dine away from home and then letting you in to the room where she happens to be. If I were to broach the subject to her orally, she would never stop to listen. If this plan appeals to you, I promise to see it through, and I shall be as good as my word, after which it will be up to you to make the most of your opportunities.'

Giannole assured him that this was all he desired, and there, for the time being, the matter rested.

For his part, Minghino had made friends with the maidservant, working upon her to such good effect that she had delivered several messages to the girl and almost fired her with Minghino's love. Moreover she had promised to convey him to her as soon as Giacomino chanced for any reason to be away from the house for the evening.

A few days after his conversation with Giannole, Crivello persuaded Giacomino to accept an invitation to supper at the house of one of his friends; and having passed the word to Giannole, he arranged that on receiving a certain signal Giannole was to come to the front door, which he would find unlocked. Meanwhile the maidservant, knowing nothing of all this, sent word to Minghino that Giacomino was going out to supper, and told him to stay near the house so that, when she gave him the signal, he could come and be let in.

Neither of the two lovers knew anything of the other's movements, and soon after dusk, each of them, being suspicious of his rival, set out with a number of armed companions so as to be certain of carrying off the prize. Since they were obliged to wait for the signal, Minghino and his men stationed themselves in a house nearby belonging to one of his friends, whilst Giannole bided his time with his companions some little distance away from the girl's house.

Once Giacomino was out of the way, Crivello and the maidservant made strenuous efforts to send each other packing.

'Why don't you go to bed?' said Crivello. 'What are you pottering about the house for at this hour?'

'What about you?' said the maidservant. 'Why not go and wait for your master? What are you hanging about here for, now that you've had your supper?'

Thus neither could persuade the other to go away, and Crivello, realizing that the hour agreed upon with Giannole had come, said to himself: 'Why should I worry about her? If she doesn't keep her mouth shut, so much the worse for her.'

And so, having given the prearranged signal, he went to open the door for Giannole, who promptly arrived with two of his companions and made his way inside. Finding the girl in the hall, they seized her in order to carry her off, but she began to struggle and scream at the top of her voice, and the maidservant followed her example. On hearing all the noise, Minghino rushed to the spot with his companions to find the girl already being dragged through the doorway; whereupon they all drew their swords, and with shouts of 'Ah, traitors, you are dead! You shan't get away with this! What's the meaning of this outrage?' they started raining blows on their opponents. Meanwhile a number of people from the neighbouring houses, having taken up lanterns and weapons, had rushed out into the street in order to see what the noise was about, and begun to hurl abuse at the girl's assailants. And with their assistance, Minghino managed after a long struggle to snatch the girl away from Giannole and put her back inside the house. The affray continued until the officers of the *podestà* arrived on the scene and arrested a large number of the combatants including Minghino, Giannole, and Crivello, all of whom were led away to prison.

By the time Giacomino returned home, peace had been restored. And though he was greatly perturbed by what had happened, on looking into the matter and discovering that the girl was in no way to blame, he was partially reassured. At the same time he resolved, so as to prevent the same thing happening all over again, to have the girl married at the earliest opportunity.

Next morning he received a deputation from the kinsfolk of the two parties concerned, who had apprised themselves of the facts and were well aware of the parlous situation in which the arrested youths would find themselves if Giacomino were to seek the retribution he had every right to demand. With honeyed words, they begged him to suit his actions, not so much to the injury he had received from the young men's thoughtlessness, as to the love and goodwill which they were convinced that he bore to themselves, his humble suppliants. Then they offered, on behalf not only of themselves but also of the young men who had perpetrated the deed, to make whatever amends Giacomino cared to specify.

Giacomino's answer was quickly given, for in the course of his life he had seen many worse things than this, and he was not the sort of man to harbour resentment.

'Gentlemen,' he said, 'even if I were in my native city, and not in yours, I count myself the sort of friend who would never do anything that was contrary to your wishes, either in the present instance or in any other. Besides, I am more than ever bound to respect your wishes in this matter inasmuch as you have wronged one of yourselves, for this young woman comes neither from Cremona nor Pavia, as many people may possibly have supposed, but from Faenza, though neither she nor I nor the person who entrusted her to my care ever discovered whose daughter she was. Hence I am fully prepared to do as you ask.'

The worthy men were surprised to learn that the girl was a native of Faenza, and having thanked Giacomino for taking so generous a view of the matter, they asked him to be so kind as to explain how she had come under his control, and how he knew that she was from Faenza.

Giacomino said to them:

'Guidotto da Cremona, who was a friend and comrade of mine, informed me on his deathbed that when this town was captured by the Emperor Frederick, and everything was being plundered, he and his companions entered a house and found it full of booty. All the inhabitants had fled except for this girl, who would be about two years old at the time, and as he was going up the stairs, she called him "father". He felt sorry for the child, and together with all the valuables from the house, he took her with him to Fano. And in Fano, as he lay dying, he appointed me her guardian and bequeathed to me everything he possessed, on the understanding that when she grew up I would see that she was married, handing over his fortune to her by way of dowry. She is now of marriageable age, but I have not yet succeeded in finding a suitable husband for her. The sooner I can do so the better, for I've no wish to suffer the things I suffered last night all over again.'

One of the people present was Guiglielmino da Medicina, who had been with Guidotto at the time of this escapade, and remembered quite clearly whose house Guidotto had plundered. Seeing the owner of the house standing there with the others, he went up to him and said:

'Bernabuccio, do you hear what Giacomino says?'

'Yes,' said Bernabuccio, 'and I was just thinking about it, because during those upheavals I lost a little girl of the age that Giacomino mentioned.'

'Then it must be the same girl,' said Guiglielmino, 'for I was once in a place where I heard Guidotto describing the house he had looted, and I recognized it as yours. Try and remember whether the child had any mark by which you could identify her, and get them to look for it. I am certain you will find that she is your daughter.'

Having pondered for a while, Bernabuccio remembered that she ought to have a small scar above her left ear in the shape of a cross – the remains of an abscess which he had had removed shortly before his house was looted. So without further ado he went up to Giacomino, who was still standing on his doorstep, and asked him to take him into the house and let him see the girl.

Giacomino readily took him inside, and introduced him to the girl. As soon as Bernabuccio set eyes on her, he could see that she was the living image of the child's mother, who was still a good-looking woman. Not content with this, however, he asked Giacomino if he would kindly allow him to lift the hair above the girl's left ear, and Giacomino told him to go ahead.

Bernabuccio went up to the girl, who was feeling rather embarrassed by all this, and having raised her hair with his right hand, he caught sight of the cross-shaped scar. Now that he knew for certain that she was his daughter, he burst into tears and enfolded her in a tender embrace, albeit the girl attempted to hold him at a distance; and turning to Giacomino he said:

'Brother, this is my daughter; it was my house that was plundered by Guidotto, and in the heat of the moment my wife, the child's mother, left her behind. Later that day, my house was set on fire, and we had always supposed until now that the child was burned to death.'

On hearing this the girl, having taken account of his age and the fact that his words rang true, was prompted by some mysterious impulse to relax in his arms and tenderly mingle her tears with his.

Bernabuccio instantly sent for her mother and for other women relatives, as well as for her brothers and sisters, and having presented her to each of them in turn and told them the story, he took her

back to his house amid great rejoicing and the exchange of a
thousand embraces, Giacomino being well content that he should
have her. Tidings of these events were brought to the *podestà*, an
excellent fellow, who, knowing that Giannole, whom he was
holding prisoner, was the son of Bernabuccio and the girl's blood-
brother, decided to deal with him leniently and overlook the
offence he had committed. What was more, he took a personal
interest in the affair, and in consultation with Bernabuccio and
Giacomino he induced Giannole and Minghino to make peace with
one another. Then, to the enormous satisfaction of Minghino's
kinsfolk, he announced that the girl, whose name was Agnesa, was
to be married to Minghino; and having set the two young men at
liberty, he also released Crivello and the others who had been
implicated in the matter.

Shortly afterwards Minghino, overjoyed, celebrated his nuptials
in truly magnificent style and conveyed his bride to his house,
thereafter living many years with her in peace and prosperity.

SIXTH STORY

*Gianni of Procida is found with the girl he loves, who had been handed
over to King Frederick. He and the girl are tied to a stake, and are about to
be burnt when he is recognized by Ruggieri de Loria. He is then set free,
and afterwards they are married.*

Neifile's story found much favour with the ladies, and when it
came to an end, the queen called on Pampinea to tell them one of
hers. Her face upraised and smiling, she forthwith began:

Mighty indeed, dear ladies, are the powers of Love, inducing
lovers, as they do, to endure great hardships and expose themselves
to extraordinary and incredible risks. Ample confirmation of this is
to be found in many of the stories already told, both today and on
other occasions, but nevertheless I should like to prove it once again
with this tale of a young lover's courage.

On Ischia, which is an island very near Naples, there once lived an

exceedingly charming and beautiful girl called Restituta, the daughter of Marin Bòlgaro,[1] a nobleman of the island. She was loved to
the point of distraction by a young man from Procida, a small
island close to Ischia, whose name was Gianni, and she in turn was
in love with him. Not content with going from Procida to Ischia
every day to catch a glimpse of his beloved, Gianni would frequently
make the crossing by night, swimming there and back[2] if no boat
was available, so that, even if he could see nothing else, he could at
least gaze upon the walls of her house.

Thus they were deeply in love with each other, but one summer's
day, as the girl was wandering by herself along the shore, prising
sea-shells from the rocks with a small knife, she chanced upon a tiny
cove, hemmed in by cliffs, where a number of young Sicilians, on
their way from Naples, had landed from their frigate in order to
relax in the shade and take fresh water from a nearby spring.

The girl failed to notice them, and when they perceived how
beautiful she was, seeing that she was all alone, the youths resolved
to seize her and carry her off. Nor did they waste any time in
giving effect to their resolve, but promptly took hold of the girl,
and, though she screamed and shouted, bundled her aboard their
ship. They then sailed away, but on arriving in Calabria, they fell to
arguing among themselves over which of them was to take possession of the girl, each of them wanting her for himself. Being unable
to reach any sort of agreement, they decided, rather than make
matters worse and bring ruin upon themselves for the sake of a girl,
to give her to King Frederick of Sicily,[3] who was then a young
man, much addicted to pretty things of that sort. And this they did
on reaching Palermo.

The girl was greatly prized by the King on account of her
beauty, but as he was feeling somewhat indisposed, he ordered that
until such time as he recovered she should be lodged with a retinue in
a sumptuous villa in one of his gardens, known as La Cuba;[4] and
these instructions were carried out.

The girl's abduction gave rise to a great furore in Ischia, but the
worst part about it was that they had no idea who it was that had
carried her off. Gianni, who was the person most deeply affected by
her disappearance, knew better than to hang about waiting for news

in Ischia, and, having ascertained the direction taken by her captors, he hired a frigate of his own, in which, as swiftly as possible, he scoured the whole of the coast from Cape Minerva to Scalea[5] in Calabria, making inquiries about the girl wherever he went. Finally, at Scalea, he was told she had been taken by Sicilian sailors to Palermo, and thither he made his way as speedily as he could. On discovering, after searching high and low for her, that she had been given to the King and was being kept by him in La Cuba, he was greatly perturbed and not only despaired of retrieving her but almost gave up hope of ever seeing her again.

Nevertheless, sustained by Love, he sent away the frigate and remained in Palermo, for it was clear that nobody in those parts knew who he was. He frequently walked past La Cuba, and one day, to the great joy both of himself and the girl, they caught sight of each other as she was standing at a window. Seeing that the street was deserted, Gianni got as near to her as he could manage, spoke to her, and was told by the girl of the means he would have to adopt if he wanted to talk to her in greater privacy. He then went away, having first surveyed with care the surrounding area. Biding his time till long after darkness had fallen, he returned to the spot, and by climbing over a wall that would not have afforded a perch to a woodpecker, he made his way into the garden. There he found a long pole, and having, in accordance with the girl's instructions, propped it against a window, he hauled himself up to it without any trouble.

Feeling that her honour was by now as good as lost, the girl, who in the past had treated him rather cruelly in her determination to preserve it, had made up her mind to gratify his every desire, for she could think of no man who had a greater right to possess her, and moreover she was hopeful of persuading him to effect her release; she had therefore left the window open, to ensure that he had immediate access to her.

Finding the window open, Gianni clambered silently into the room and lay down beside the girl, who was not asleep by any means. Before they did anything else, the girl apprised him fully of her intentions, imploring him with all her heart to release her from captivity and take her away. Gianni assured her that nothing would

give him greater pleasure, and that, on taking his leave of her, he
would without fail make such arrangements as would enable him,
on his next visit, to convey her to safety.

They then enfolded one another in a blissful embrace, and
partook of the greatest pleasure that Love can supply, repeating the
experience several times over until they unwittingly fell asleep in
each other's arms.

Shortly before daybreak, the King, who had taken an instant
liking to the girl and was now feeling better, called her to mind,
and resolved, despite the lateness of the hour, to go and spend some
time in her company; so he quietly made his way to La Cuba with
one of his retainers. On entering the building, he went straight to
the room where he knew the girl to be sleeping and got the servants
to open the door without making a sound. Preceded by a huge,
blazing torch,[6] he walked into the room, only to discover, on
looking at the bed, that Gianni and the girl were lying there asleep
and naked in one another's arms. This spectacle rendered him
speechless with horror and distress, and he was so enraged that he
could scarcely forbear from drawing a dagger from his belt and
killing them where they lay. But on reflecting that it would be a
most cowardly deed for any man, let alone a king, to kill two
people lying naked and asleep, he held himself in check, and
resolved instead to have them publicly burnt at the stake. Turning
to the single companion who was with him, he said:

'What think you of this shameless hussy, in whom I once reposed
my hopes?'

He then inquired of his companion whether he could recognize
this young man, who had had the impudence to come and perpe-
trate such an outrage on the King in his own house, and the man
replied that he could not recall having ever set eyes on the
youth.

So the King stormed out of the room, and ordered that the two
lovers, naked as they were, should be seized and tied up; and as soon
as daylight came, they were to be brought to the main square in
Palermo and bound, back to back, to a stake, there to remain till the
hour of tierce, so that they could be seen by the whole of the
populace, after which they were to be burnt alive in accordance

with their deserts. These instructions given, he returned to Palermo
and retired in high dudgeon to his room.

As soon as the King had left, several men burst in on the two
lovers, and not only woke them up, but swiftly seized and bound
them without any pity. As may readily be imagined, on seeing
what was happening to them the two young people were greatly
alarmed, and, fearing they would be put to death, they burst into
tears and bitterly reproached themselves. In accordance with the
King's command, they were taken to Palermo and tied to a stake in
the square; and before their eyes faggots were stacked in readiness
for them to be burnt alive at the hour the King had decreed.

All the men and women of Palermo immediately hurried to the
square in order to see the two lovers: and whilst the men stood and
gazed at the girl, unanimously praising her shapeliness and beauty,
so the women were all clustering round the youth, expressing their
warm approval of his fine figure and handsome features. But the
pair of hapless lovers hung their heads in shame and bewailed their
misfortune, expecting at any moment to be cruelly consumed by
the fire.

Whilst they were thus being held until the hour fixed for their
execution, news of their offence was bruited abroad and reached the
ears of Ruggieri de Loria, a man of inestimable worth, who at that
time was the Admiral of the Royal Fleet. Curious to see who they
were, he made his way towards the place where they stood bound
to the stake, and, on reaching the spot, he looked at the girl and
found her exceedingly beautiful. He then directed his gaze at the
youth, whom he recognized without too much trouble, and moving
a little nearer he asked him whether he was Gianni of Procida.

Gianni raised his eyes, and, recognizing the Admiral, he replied:

'My lord, I was indeed the man of whom you speak, but I am
about to be that person no longer.'

Whereupon the Admiral asked what had brought him to such a
pass, and Gianni replied:

'Love, and the wrath of the King.'

The Admiral persuaded him to elaborate, and having heard the
whole story from Gianni's own lips, he turned to go. But Gianni
called him back, and said:

'Alas, my lord, procure me a favour, if this be possible, from the person who set me here.'

Ruggieri asked what favour he had in mind, and Gianni said:

'I see that I must die, and very soon. Wherefore, seeing that I have been set here back to back with this young woman, whom I loved more dearly than life itself, being loved no less deeply in return, I should like us to be turned face to face, so that I may have the consolation of gazing into her eyes as I depart.'

'With pleasure!' exclaimed Ruggieri, with a laugh. 'And if I have my way, you shall see so much of her that before you die you'll be sorry you ever asked such a favour.'

Leaving Gianni, he spoke to the men charged with carrying out the sentence, and ordered them not to proceed any further without new instructions from the King, to whom he forthwith made his way. And although he could see that the King was extremely distraught, he was not to be deterred from speaking his mind.

'My lord,' he said, 'what injury have you suffered from the two young people you have sentenced to be burnt down there in the square?'

The King told him, and Ruggieri continued:

'They have done wrong, and well deserve to be punished, but not by you; for although wrongdoing requires a punishment, good deeds require a reward, to say nothing of pardon and clemency. Do you realize who these people are that you are so eager to put to death at the stake?'

The King replied that he did not know them, whereupon Ruggieri said:

'Then I shall make it my business to tell you, so that you will see how unwise it is for you to let yourself be carried away by your anger. The young man is the son of Landolfo of Procida, blood-brother to Messer Gianni of Procida, through whose efforts you became King and master of this island. The girl is the daughter of Marin Bòlgaro, without whose power and influence Ischia would be lost to you tomorrow.[7] What is more, these two youngsters have long been in love with one another, and it was not out of any disrespect towards your royal highness, but rather through being constrained by their love, that they committed this sin of theirs – if sin is a suitable word to describe the things young people do in the cause of love. Why, then, should you wish to have them put to death, when you ought to be entertaining them right royally and bestowing precious gifts upon them?'

On realizing that Ruggieri must be speaking the truth, the King was not only filled with horror over what he was proposing to do, but bitterly regretted the action he had already taken. So he promptly sent word that the two young lovers were to be released from the stake and brought into his presence. These orders were carried out, and after inquiring fully into their condition, the King decided that he must make amends, through largesse and hospitality, for the indignity he had caused them to suffer. He therefore had them newly clothed in courtly attire, and arranged, by their mutual consent, for Gianni and the girl to be married. And finally he sent them back, well content and laden with magnificent presents, to the place from which they had come. There they were received with tremendous rejoicing, and long thereafter lived in joy and happiness together.

SEVENTH STORY

Teodoro falls in love with Violante, the daughter of his master, Messer Amerigo. He gets her with child, and is sentenced to die on the gallows. But whilst he is being whipped along the road to his execution, he is recognized by his father and set at liberty, after which he and Violante become husband and wife.

All the ladies were on tenterhooks, anxiously wondering whether the two lovers would be burnt, and on learning that they had escaped, they all rejoiced and offered thanks to God. Then, having heard the end of the story, the queen entrusted the telling of the next to Lauretta, who cheerfully began as follows:

Fairest ladies, there once lived in the island of Sicily, during the reign of good King William,[1] a nobleman called Messer Amerigo

Abate of Trapani,[2] who was blessed with many possessions, including a large number of children. He was therefore in need of servants,
and when certain galleys arrived from the Levant belonging to
Genoese pirates,[3] who had captured a great many children along the
Armenian coast, he purchased a number of them, believing them to
be Turkish. For the most part they appeared to be of rustic,
shepherd stock, but there was one, Teodoro by name, who seemed
gently bred and better looking than any of the others.

Though he was treated as a servant, Teodoro was brought up in
the house along with Messer Amerigo's children, and as he grew
older, being prompted by his innate good breeding rather than by
the accident of his menial status, he acquired so much poise and so
agreeable a manner that Messer Amerigo granted him his freedom.
Supposing him to be a Turk,[4] Messer Amerigo had him baptized
and re-named Pietro, and placed him in charge of his business
affairs, taking him deeply into his confidence.

Side-by-side with Messer Amerigo's other children, there grew
up a daughter of his called Violante,[5] a dainty young beauty who,
as her father was not in a hurry to marry her off, chanced to fall in
love with Pietro. But whilst she loved him, and held his conduct
and achievements in high esteem, she was too shy to tell him so
directly. Love spared her this trouble, however, for Pietro, having
cast many a furtive glance in her direction, fell so violently in love
with her that he felt unhappy whenever she was out of his sight.
Since he could not help feeling that what he was doing was wrong,
he was greatly afraid lest anyone should discover his secret; but the
girl, who was by no means averse to his company, divined his
feelings towards her, and, in order to bolster his confidence, she let
it appear that she was delighted, as indeed she was. And on this
footing their relationship rested for some considerable time, neither
of them venturing to say anything to the other, much as they
mutually desired to do so. Consumed by the flames of love, they
longed for one another with equal ardour till Fortune, as though
deciding that they should be united, found a way for them to dispel
the fears and apprehensions by which they were impeded.

About a mile away from Trapani itself, Messer Amerigo kept a
very charming property, to which his wife, with their daughter and

various other ladies and maidservants, frequently went by way of recreation. Having gone there one day when the weather was very hot, taking Pietro with them, they suddenly found that the sky had become overcast with thick dark clouds, such as we occasionally observe in the course of the summer. And so the lady, not wishing to be caught there by the storm, set off with her companions along the road leading back to Trapani, making all the haste they could. But Pietro and Violante, being young and fit, soon found themselves well ahead of the girl's mother and the other ladies, perhaps because they were prompted no less by their love than by fear of the weather. And when they had drawn so far ahead of the others that they were almost out of sight, there was a series of thunderclaps,[6] immediately followed by a very heavy hailstorm, from which the lady and her companions took shelter in the house of a farm-labourer.

Pietro and the girl, having nowhere more convenient to take refuge, entered an old, abandoned cottage that was almost totally in ruins; and, having both squeezed in beneath the fragment of roof that still remained intact, they were forced by the inadequacy of their shelter to huddle up close to one another. The contact of their bodies made them pluck up the courage to disclose their amorous yearnings, Pietro being the first to broach the subject by saying:

'Would to God that this hailstorm would never come to an end, so that I could remain here for ever!'

'That would suit me very well,' said the girl.

Having uttered these words, they went on to hold and squeeze one another's hands, after which they proceeded to embrace and then to exchange kisses, while the hailstorm continued.

But to cut a long story short, by the time the weather improved they had tasted Love's ultimate delights and arranged to meet again in secret for their mutual pleasure.

The cottage was not far from the city gate, and once the storm was over they went and waited there for the lady, and returned with her to the house. Every so often, employing the maximum of secrecy and discretion, they would meet again, to their considerable enjoyment, in the same place as before. But what happened in the end was that the girl became pregnant, much to the dismay of both parties, whereupon she took various measures to frustrate the course of nature and miscarry, but all to no effect.

Pietro, in fear of his life, made up his mind to flee, and told her so. But on hearing this, the girl said:

'If you go away, I shall kill myself without fail!'

To which Pietro, who was deeply in love with her, replied:

'But, my lady, how can you possibly want me to remain here? Our offence will be brought to light by your pregnancy. And whereas you will be readily forgiven, I shall be the poor wretch who has to suffer the penalty for your sin and my own.'

'My sin will be only too obvious, Pietro,' she replied, 'but rest assured that your own will never be discovered unless you reveal it yourself.'

Whereupon Pietro said:

'Since you have given me this promise, I shall stay; but take good care not to break it.'

The girl did all she possibly could to conceal her condition, but one day, seeing that she could hide it no longer on account of the swelling of her body, she went to her mother in floods of tears and made a full confession, imploring her to rescue her from harm.

The lady was utterly appalled, and admonished her severely, demanding to know how it had come about. So as to protect Pietro, the girl invented a tale containing a garbled version of the facts, which the lady believed, and in order to conceal her daughter's transgression she sent her away to a property of theirs in the country. Messer Amerigo very rarely set foot in this particular place, and her mother never thought for a moment that he would be going there, but just as the time came for the girl to be delivered, it so happened that on his way back from a hawking expedition he was passing directly beside the room where his daughter was in labour. Much to his astonishment, he heard the girl shrieking, as women are wont to do at such times, and he therefore walked straight in to inquire what was going on.

On seeing her husband arrive, the lady rose to her feet in dismay and explained what had happened to their daughter. But being less credulous than his wife, he maintained it was not possible for the girl to be ignorant of who had got her with child, and said he would ferret out the facts, come what may. Let her tell him the truth, therefore, and she would be restored to his favour; otherwise, she could expect to be put to death without mercy.

The lady did her utmost to persuade her husband to rest content with the story which she herself had accepted, but it was no use. Brandishing his sword, he rushed over in a towering rage to the bedside of his daughter, who meanwhile, as her mother was conversing with her father, had given birth to a son, and he said:

'Either you reveal the name of this child's father, or you shall die forthwith.'

Fearing she would be killed, the girl broke her promise to Pietro and made a clean breast of everything that had passed between them, whereupon the knight raved and stormed like a madman, and barely managed to restrain himself from putting her to death. However, after speaking his mind in no uncertain terms, he remounted his horse and rode off to Trapani, where he lodged a complaint with the Viceroy,[7] a certain Messer Currado, about the injury Pietro had done him. Since he was unprepared for this turn of events, Pietro was promptly taken into custody, and on being put to the torture, he made a full confession.

A few days later the Viceroy sentenced him to be whipped through the town and then hanged by the neck. And in order to ensure that the two lovers and their child should all perish at the same time, Messer Amerigo, whose anger was by no means appeased by the destruction of Pietro, mixed some poison with wine in a goblet and handed it to one of his servants together with an unsheathed dagger, saying:

'Go with this goblet and this dagger to Violante, and tell her in my name that she is to die forthwith by whichever of the two means she prefers, the poison or the steel. Tell her she is to do it at once, otherwise I shall see that she is burnt alive, as she deserves, in the presence of every man and woman in the town. This done, you are to take the child which was born to her the other day, dash its head against a wall, and cast it away to be devoured by the dogs.'

As soon as the cruel father had passed this savage sentence on his daughter and grandchild, the servant, who was more disposed to evil than to good, took his leave.

Meanwhile Pietro, having been condemned to die, was being whipped along to the gallows by a troop of soldiers, when the leaders of the procession took it into their heads to pass in front of an inn where three Armenian noblemen were staying. These latter were ambassadors from the King of Armenia,[8] on their way to Rome in order to negotiate with the Pope on very important matters connected with a crusade that was about to be launched. Having broken their journey at Trapani for a few days' rest and relaxation, they had been lavishly entertained by the noblemen of the town, and by Messer Amerigo in particular. And on hearing Pietro's escort passing the inn, they came to a window and peered out.

One of the three ambassadors, an elderly gentleman who wielded great authority and whose name was Phineas, fixed his gaze on Pietro, who was stripped to the waist with his hands tied behind his back, and perceived that on his chest there was a large red spot, which was not painted on the skin but imprinted there by Nature, being what the women in this part of the world describe as a strawberry mark. On seeing this, he was at once reminded of a son of his who had been abducted by pirates from the shore at Lajazzo[9] some fifteen years earlier and had never been heard of since. Having made a mental estimate of the age of the poor wretch who was being scourged, he calculated that his son, if he were still alive, would be roughly the same age. Hence, because of the mark on the youth's chest, he began to suspect that this was his own son; and he thought to himself that if this were indeed the case, the youth would still remember his name and that of his father, as well as one or two words of the Armenian language.

So when the youth came within earshot, Phineas called out:
'Theodor!'

As soon as he heard this cry, Pietro raised his head, whereupon Phineas addressed him in Armenian, saying:

'Where do you come from? Whose son are you?'

The soldiers escorting him halted in deference to the great man, allowing Pietro to reply:

'I am from Armenia, my father's name was Phineas, and I was brought here as a child by strangers.'

On hearing these words, Phineas knew for certain that this was the son he had lost. With tears in his eyes, he descended with his companions and ran through the ranks of the soldiers to embrace him. He then removed the exquisite silken cloak he was wearing, threw it over the young man's shoulders, and asked the leader of the execution-party to be good enough to wait there until he received the order to proceed. The man readily agreed to do so.

Phineas was already aware of the reason for which the young man was being led away to his death, for it had been bruited all over the town, and he therefore hurried off with his companions and their retinue to Messer Currado, whom he addressed as follows:

'Sir, this fellow whom you are sending to die as a slave is my own son, a freeman, and he is prepared to plight his troth to the girl he is alleged to have robbed of her virginity. I beg you therefore to postpone the execution until it is known whether she will have him as her husband, for otherwise you may find that you have acted illegally.'

On hearing that the youth was the son of Phineas, Messer Currado was filled with astonishment. Having uttered one or two apologetic phrases concerning the waywardness of Fortune, he agreed that Phineas had proved his case, and got him to return forthwith to the inn. He then sent for Messer Amerigo and told him what had happened.

Believing his daughter and grandchild to be already dead, Messer Amerigo was the most repentant man on earth, for he realized full well that if only she were still alive, it would be possible to set the whole affair to rights. However, just in case his instructions had not been carried out, and he was still in time to countermand them, he sent a message post-haste to the place where his daughter was.

The messenger found that the servant who had been sent by Messer Amerigo, having set the knife and poison in front of the girl, was bombarding her with abuse for taking so long to make up her mind, and trying to coerce her into choosing between the two. But on hearing his master's latest command, he stopped tormenting her, returned to Messer Amerigo, and told him how matters stood. Feeling greatly relieved, Messer Amerigo made his way to the place

where Phineas was staying, and, choking back his tears, he apolo-
gized as best he could for what had happened, declaring that if
Theodor wished to marry his daughter, he would be delighted to
let him have her.

Phineas gladly accepted his apologies, and replied:

'I intend that my son should marry your daughter. And if he
should raise any objection to doing so, let the sentence passed upon
him be carried out.'

Being thus in agreement, Phineas and Messer Amerigo went to
Pietro, who, though delighted at having found his father again, was
still in great fear of being put to death, and they inquired into his
own wishes on the subject.

On hearing that Violante would marry him if he so wished,
Theodor was filled with such transports of joy that he had the
sensation of passing from Hell into Heaven at a single bound; and
he said that if this was what the two fathers were proposing, he
could only regard it as the greatest of favours.

They therefore sent someone to ascertain the wishes of the
girl herself, who after some time, having learned what had happened
to Theodor and what was being proposed, ceased to be the
saddest woman alive, awaiting only death to put an end to
her misery. Giving some credence to the messenger's words,
she began to take a slightly rosier view of her circumstances,
and replied that if she were to follow her own inclinations
in the matter, nothing would make her happier than to marry
Theodor; but at all events she would do whatever her father
ordered.

By mutual consent, therefore, the girl's betrothal was announced
and a very great feast was held, to the immense pleasure of all the
townspeople. Putting her infant son out to nurse, the girl recovered
her strength, and before very long she appeared more lovely than
ever. On rising from her confinement, she presented herself to
Phineas, whose return from Rome everyone had meanwhile been
awaiting, and greeted him with all the reverence due to a father.
Phineas, delighted to have acquired so beautiful a daughter-in-law,
saw to it that their nuptials were celebrated in the grand manner,
with much feasting and merrymaking, and from then on he always

looked upon Violante as his daughter. A few days after the nuptials, he took ship with her, his son, and his infant grandson, and sailed away with them to Lajazzo, where the two lovers lived in comfort and happiness for the rest of their days.

EIGHTH STORY

In his love for a young lady of the Traversari family, Nastagio degli Onesti squanders his wealth without being loved in return. He is entreated by his friends to leave the city, and goes away to Classe, where he sees a girl being hunted down and killed by a horseman, and devoured by a brace of hounds. He then invites his kinsfolk and the lady he loves to a banquet, where this same girl is torn to pieces before the eyes of his beloved, who, fearing a similar fate, accepts Nastagio as her husband.

No sooner did Lauretta fall silent, than at the bidding of the queen Filomena began as follows:

Adorable ladies, just as our pity is commended, so is our cruelty severely punished by divine justice. And in order to prove this to you, as well as to give you an incentive for banishing all cruelty from your hearts, I should like to tell you a story as delightful as it is full of pathos.

In Ravenna,[1] a city of great antiquity in Romagna, there once used to live a great many nobles and men of property, among them a young man called Nastagio degli Onesti, who had inherited an incredibly large fortune on the deaths of his father and one of his uncles. Being as yet unmarried, he fell in love, as is the way with young men, with a daughter of Messer Paolo Traversari, a girl of far more noble lineage than his own, whose love he hoped to win by dint of his accomplishments. But though these were very considerable, and splendid, and laudable, far from promoting his cause they appeared to damage it, inasmuch as the girl he loved was persistently cruel, harsh and unfriendly towards him. And on account possibly of her singular beauty, or perhaps because of her exalted rank, she became so haughty and contemptuous of him that she positively loathed him and everything he stood for.

All of this was so difficult for Nastagio to bear that he was frequently seized, after much weeping and gnashing of teeth, with the longing to kill himself out of sheer despair. But, having stayed his hand, he would then decide that he must give her up altogether, or learn if possible to hate her as she hated him. All such resolutions were unavailing, however, for the more his hopes dwindled, the greater his love seemed to grow.

As the young man persisted in wooing the girl and spending money like water, certain of his friends and relatives began to feel that he was in danger of exhausting both himself and his inheritance. They therefore implored and advised him to leave Ravenna and go to live for a while in some other place, with the object of curtailing both his wooing and his spending. Nastagio rejected this advice as often as it was offered, but they eventually pressed him so hard that he could not refuse them any longer, and agreed to do as they suggested. Having mustered an enormous baggage-train, as though he were intending to go to France or Spain or some other remote part of the world, he mounted his horse, rode forth from Ravenna with several of his friends, and repaired to a place which is known as Classe, some three miles distant from the city. Having sent for a number of tents and pavilions, he told his companions that this was where he intended to stay, and that they could all go back to Ravenna. So Nastagio pitched his camp in this place, and began to live in as fine and lordly a fashion as any man ever born, from time to time inviting various groups of friends to dine or breakfast with him, as had always been his custom.

Now, it so happened that one Friday morning towards the beginning of May,[2] the weather being very fine, Nastagio fell to thinking about his cruel mistress. Having ordered his servants to leave him to his own devices so that he could meditate at greater leisure, he sauntered off, lost in thought, and his steps led him straight into the pinewoods. The fifth hour of the day was already spent, and he had advanced at least half a mile into the woods, oblivious of food and everything else, when suddenly he seemed to hear a woman giving vent to dreadful wailing and ear-splitting screams. His pleasant reverie being thus interrupted, he raised his head to investigate the cause, and discovered to his surprise that he was in the pinewoods. Furthermore, on looking straight ahead he caught sight of a naked woman, young and very beautiful, who was running through a dense thicket of shrubs and briars towards the very spot where he was standing. The woman's hair was dishevelled, her flesh was all torn by the briars and brambles, and she was sobbing and screaming for mercy. Nor was this all, for a pair of big, fierce mastiffs were running at the girl's heels, one on either side, and every so often they caught up with her and savaged her. Finally, bringing up the rear he saw a swarthy-looking knight, his face contorted with anger, who was riding a jet-black steed and brandishing a rapier, and who, in terms no less abusive than terrifying, was threatening to kill her.

This spectacle struck both terror and amazement into Nastagio's breast, to say nothing of compassion for the hapless woman, a sentiment that in its turn engendered the desire to rescue her from such agony and save her life, if this were possible. But on finding that he was unarmed, he hastily took up a branch of a tree to serve as a cudgel, and prepared to ward off the dogs and do battle with the knight. When the latter saw what he was doing, he shouted to him from a distance:

'Keep out of this, Nastagio! Leave me and the dogs to give this wicked sinner her deserts!'

He had no sooner spoken than the dogs seized the girl firmly by the haunches and brought her to a halt. When the knight reached the spot he dismounted from his horse, and Nastagio went up to him saying:

'I do not know who you are, or how you come to know my name; but I can tell you that it is a gross outrage for an armed knight to try and kill a naked woman, and to set dogs upon her as though she were a savage beast. I shall do all in my power to defend her, of that you may be sure.'

Whereupon the knight said:

'I was a fellow citizen of yours, Nastagio, my name was Guido degli Anastagi, and you were still a little child when I fell in love with this woman. I loved her far more deeply than you love that

Traversari girl of yours, but her pride and cruelty led me to such a pass that, one day, I killed myself in sheer despair with this rapier that you see in my hand, and thus I am condemned to eternal punishment. My death pleased her beyond measure, but shortly thereafter she too died, and because she had sinned by her cruelty and by gloating over my sufferings, and was quite unrepentant, being convinced that she was more of a saint than a sinner, she too was condemned to the pains of Hell. No sooner was she cast into Hell than we were both given a special punishment, which consisted in her case of fleeing before me, and in my own of pursuing her as though she were my mortal enemy rather than the woman with whom I was once so deeply in love. Every time I catch up with her, I kill her with this same rapier by which I took my own life; then I slit her back open, and (as you will now observe for yourself) I tear from her body that hard, cold heart to which neither love nor pity could ever gain access, and together with the rest of her entrails I cast it to these dogs to feed upon.

'Within a short space of time, as ordained by the power and justice of God, she springs to her feet as though she had not been dead at all, and her agonizing flight begins all over again, with the dogs and myself in pursuit. Every Friday at this hour I overtake her in this part of the woods, and slaughter her in the manner you are about to observe; but you must not imagine that we are idle for the rest of the week, because on the remaining days I hunt her down in other places where she was cruel to me in thought and deed. As you can see for yourself, I am no longer her lover but her enemy, and in this guise I am obliged to pursue her for the same number of years as the months of her cruelty towards me. Stand aside, therefore, and let me carry out the judgement of God. Do not try to oppose what you cannot prevent.'

On hearing these words, Nastagio was shaken to the core, there was scarcely a single hair on his head that was not standing on end, and he stepped back to fix his gaze on the unfortunate girl, waiting in fear and trembling to see what the knight would do to her. This latter, having finished speaking, pounced like a mad dog, rapier in hand, upon the girl, who was kneeling before him, held by the two mastiffs, and screaming for mercy at the top of her voice. Applying all his strength, the knight plunged his rapier into the middle of her breast and out again at the other side, whereupon the girl fell on her face, still sobbing and screaming, whilst the knight, having laid hold of a dagger, slashed open her back, extracted her heart and everything else around it, and hurled it to the two mastiffs, who devoured it greedily on the instant. But before very long the girl rose suddenly to her feet as though none of these things had happened, and sped off in the direction of the sea, being pursued by the dogs, who kept tearing away at her flesh as she ran. Remounting his horse, and seizing his rapier, the knight too began to give chase, and within a short space of time they were so far away that Nastagio could no longer see them.

For some time after bearing witness to these events, Nastagio stood rooted to the spot out of fear and compassion, but after a while it occurred to him that since this scene was enacted every Friday, it ought to prove very useful to him. So he marked the place and returned to his servants; and when the time seemed ripe, he sent for his friends and kinsfolk, and said to them:

'For some little time you have been urging me to desist from wooing this hostile mistress of mine and place a curb on my extravagance, and I am willing to do so on condition that you obtain for me a single favour, which is this: that on Friday next you arrange for Messer Paolo Traversari and his wife and daughter and all their womenfolk, together with any other lady you care to invite, to join me in this place for breakfast. My reason for wanting this will become apparent to you on the day itself.'

They thought this a very trifling commission for them to undertake, and promised him they would do it. On their return to Ravenna, they invited all the people he had specified. And although they had a hard job, when the time came, in persuading Nastagio's beloved to go, she nevertheless went there along with the others.

Nastagio saw to it that a magnificent banquet was prepared, and had the tables placed beneath the pine-trees in such a way as to surround the place where he had witnessed the massacre of the cruel lady. Moreover, in seating the ladies and gentlemen at table, he so arranged matters that the girl he loved sat directly facing the spot where the scene would be enacted.

The last course had already been served, when they all began to hear the agonized yells of the fugitive girl. Everyone was greatly astonished and wanted to know what it was, but nobody was able to say. So they all stood up to see if they could find out what was going on, and caught sight of the wailing girl, together with the knight and the dogs. And shortly thereafter they came into the very midst of the company.

Everyone began shouting and bawling at the dogs and the knight, and several people rushed forward to the girl's assistance; but the knight, by repeating to them the story he had related to Nastagio, not only caused them to retreat but filled them all with terror and amazement. And when he dealt with the girl in the same way as before, all the ladies present (many of whom, being related either to the suffering girl or to the knight, still remembered his great love and the manner of his death) wept as plaintively as though what they had witnessed had been done to themselves.

When the spectacle was at an end, and the knight and the lady had gone, they all began to talk about what they had seen. But none was stricken with so much terror as the cruel maiden loved by Nastagio, for she had heard and seen everything distinctly and realized that these matters had more to do with herself than with any of the other guests, in view of the harshness she had always displayed towards Nastagio; consequently, she already had the sensation of fleeing before her enraged suitor, with the mastiffs tearing away at her haunches.

So great was the fear engendered within her by this episode, that in order to avoid a similar fate she converted her enmity into love; and, seizing the earliest opportunity (which came to her that very evening), she privily sent a trusted maidservant to Nastagio, requesting him to be good enough to call upon her, as she was ready to do anything he desired. Nastagio was overjoyed, and told her so in his reply, but added that if she had no objection he preferred to combine his pleasure with the preservation of her good name, by making her his lawful wedded wife.

Knowing that she alone was to blame for the fact that she and Nastagio were not already married, the girl readily sent him her consent. And so, acting as her own intermediary, she announced to her father and mother, to their enormous satisfaction, that she would be pleased to become Nastagio's wife. On the following Sunday Nastagio married her, and after celebrating their nuptials they settled down to a long and happy life together.

Their marriage was by no means the only good effect to be produced by this horrible apparition, for from that day forth the ladies of Ravenna in general were so frightened by it that they became much more tractable to men's pleasures than they had ever been in the past.

NINTH STORY

In courting a lady who does not return his love, Federigo degli Alberighi spends the whole of his substance, being left with nothing but a falcon, which, since his larder is bare, he offers to his lady to eat when she calls to see him at his house. On discovering the truth of the matter, she has a change of heart, accepts him as her husband, and makes a rich man of him.

Once Filomena had finished, the queen, finding that there was no one left to speak apart from herself (Dioneo being excluded from the reckoning because of his privilege), smiled cheerfully and said:

It is now my own turn to address you, and I shall gladly do so, dearest ladies, with a story similar in some respects to the one we have just heard. This I have chosen, not only to acquaint you with the power of your beauty over men of noble spirit, but so that you may learn to choose for yourselves, whenever necessary, the persons on whom to bestow your largesse, instead of always leaving these matters to be decided for you by Fortune, who, as it happens, nearly always scatters her gifts with more abundance than discretion.

You are to know, then, that Coppo di Borghese Domenichi,[1] who once used to live in our city and possibly lives there still, one of the most highly respected men of our century, a person worthy of eternal fame, who achieved his position of pre-eminence by dint of his character and abilities rather than by his noble lineage, frequently took pleasure during his declining years in discussing incidents from the past with his neighbours and other folk. In this pastime he excelled all others, for he was more coherent, possessed a superior memory, and spoke with greater eloquence. He had a fine repertoire, including a tale he frequently told concerning a young Florentine called Federigo, the son of Messer Filippo Alberighi,[2] who for his deeds of chivalry and courtly manners was more highly spoken of than any other squire in Tuscany. In the manner of most young men of gentle breeding, Federigo lost his heart to a noble lady, whose name was Monna Giovanna, and who in her time was considered one of the loveliest and most adorable women to be found in Florence. And with the object of winning her love, he rode at the ring, tilted, gave sumptuous banquets, and distributed a large number of gifts, spending money without any restraint whatsoever. But since she was no less chaste than she was fair, the lady took no notice, either of the things that were done in her honour, or of the person who did them.

In this way, spending far more than he could afford and deriving no profit in return, Federigo lost his entire fortune (as can easily happen) and reduced himself to poverty, being left with nothing other than a tiny little farm, which produced an income just sufficient for him to live very frugally, and one falcon of the finest breed in the whole world. Since he was as deeply in love as ever, and felt unable to go on living the sort of life in Florence to which he aspired, he moved out to Campi,[3] where his little farm happened to be situated. Having settled in the country, he went hunting as often as possible with his falcon, and, without seeking assistance from anyone, he patiently resigned himself to a life of poverty.

Now one day, while Federigo was living in these straitened circumstances, the husband of Monna Giovanna happened to fall ill, and, realizing that he was about to die, he drew up his will. He was a very rich man, and in his will he left everything to his son, who was just growing up, further stipulating that, if his son should die without legitimate issue, his estate should go to Monna Giovanna, to whom he had always been deeply devoted.

Shortly afterwards he died, leaving Monna Giovanna a widow, and every summer, in accordance with Florentine custom, she went away with her son to a country estate of theirs, which was very near Federigo's farm. Consequently this young lad of hers happened to become friendly with Federigo, acquiring a passion for birds and dogs; and, having often seen Federigo's falcon in flight, he became fascinated by it and longed to own it, but since he could see that Federigo was deeply attached to the bird, he never ventured to ask him for it.

And there the matter rested, when, to the consternation of his mother, the boy happened to be taken ill. Being her only child, he was the apple of his mother's eye, and she sat beside his bed the whole day long, never ceasing to comfort him. Every so often she asked him whether there was anything he wanted, imploring him to tell her what it was, because if it was possible to acquire it, she would move heaven and earth to obtain it for him.

After hearing this offer repeated for the umpteenth time, the boy said:

'Mother, if you could arrange for me to have Federigo's falcon, I believe I should soon get better.'

On hearing this request, the lady was somewhat taken aback, and began to consider what she could do about it. Knowing that Federigo had been in love with her for a long time, and that she had never deigned to cast so much as a single glance in his direction, she said to herself: 'How can I possibly go to him, or even send anyone, to ask him for this falcon, which to judge from all I have heard is the finest that ever flew, as well as being the only thing that keeps him alive? And how can I be so heartless as to deprive so noble a man of his one remaining pleasure?'

Her mind filled with reflections of this sort, she remained silent, not knowing what answer to make to her son's request, even though she was quite certain that the falcon was hers for the asking.

At length, however, her maternal instincts gained the upper hand, and she resolved, come what may, to satisfy the child by going in person to Federigo to collect the bird and bring it back to him. And so she replied:

'Bear up, my son, and see whether you can start feeling any better. I give you my word that I shall go and fetch it for you first thing tomorrow morning.'

Next morning, taking another lady with her for company, his mother left the house as though intending to go for a walk, made her way to Federigo's little cottage, and asked to see him. For several days, the weather had been unsuitable for hawking, so Federigo was attending to one or two little jobs in his garden, and when he heard, to his utter astonishment, that Monna Giovanna was at the front-door and wished to speak to him, he happily rushed there to greet her.

When she saw him coming, she advanced with womanly grace to meet him. Federigo received her with a deep bow, whereupon she said:

'Greetings, Federigo!' Then she continued: 'I have come to make amends for the harm you have suffered on my account, by loving me more than you ought to have done. As a token of my esteem, I should like to take breakfast with you this morning, together with my companion here, but you must not put yourself to any trouble.'

'My lady,' replied Federigo in all humility, 'I cannot recall ever having suffered any harm on your account. On the contrary I have gained so much that if ever I attained any kind of excellence, it was entirely because of your own great worth and the love I bore you. Moreover I can assure you that this visit which you have been generous enough to pay me is worth more to me than all the money I ever possessed, though I fear that my hospitality will not amount to very much.'

So saying, he led her unassumingly into the house, and thence into his garden, where, since there was no one else he could call upon to chaperon her, he said:

'My lady, as there is nobody else available, this good woman, who is the wife of the farmer here, will keep you company whilst I go and see about setting the table.'

Though his poverty was acute, the extent to which he had squandered his wealth had not yet been fully borne home to

Federigo; but on this particular morning, finding that he had nothing to set before the lady for whose love he had entertained so lavishly in the past, his eyes were well and truly opened to the fact. Distressed beyond all measure, he silently cursed his bad luck and rushed all over the house like one possessed, but could find no trace of either money or valuables. By now the morning was well advanced, he was still determined to entertain the gentlewoman to some sort of meal, and, not wishing to beg assistance from his own farmer (or from anyone else, for that matter), his gaze alighted on his precious falcon, which was sitting on its perch in the little room where it was kept. And having discovered, on picking it up, that it was nice and plump, he decided that since he had nowhere else to turn, it would make a worthy dish for such a lady as this. So without thinking twice about it he wrung the bird's neck and promptly handed it over to his housekeeper to be plucked, dressed, and roasted carefully on a spit. Then he covered the table with spotless linen, of which he still had a certain amount in his possession, and returned in high spirits to the garden, where he announced to his lady that the meal, such as he had been able to prepare, was now ready.

The lady and her companion rose from where they were sitting and made their way to the table. And together with Federigo, who waited on them with the utmost deference, they made a meal of the prize falcon without knowing what they were eating.

On leaving the table they engaged their host in pleasant conversation for a while, and when the lady thought it time to broach the subject she had gone there to discuss, she turned to Federigo and addressed him affably as follows:

'I do not doubt for a moment, Federigo, that you will be astonished at my impertinence when you discover my principal reason for coming here, especially when you recall your former mode of living and my virtue, which you possibly mistook for harshness and cruelty. But if you had ever had any children to make you appreciate the power of parental love, I should think it certain that you would to some extent forgive me.

'However, the fact that you have no children of your own does not exempt me, a mother, from the laws common to all other mothers. And being bound to obey those laws, I am forced, contrary to my own wishes and to all the rules of decorum and propriety, to ask you for something to which I know you are very deeply attached – which is only natural, seeing that it is the only consolation, the only pleasure, the only recreation remaining to you in your present extremity of fortune. The gift I am seeking is your falcon, to which my son has taken so powerful a liking, that if I fail to take it to him I fear he will succumb to the illness from which he is suffering, and consequently I shall lose him. In imploring you to give me this falcon, I appeal, not to your love, for you are under no obligation to me on that account, but rather to your noble heart, whereby you have proved yourself superior to all others in the practice of courtesy. Do me this favour, then, so that I may claim that through your generosity I have saved my son's life, thus placing him forever in your debt.'

When he heard what it was that she wanted, and realized that he could not oblige her because he had given her the falcon to eat, Federigo burst into tears in her presence before being able to utter a single word in reply. At first the lady thought his tears stemmed more from his grief at having to part with his fine falcon than from any other motive, and was on the point of telling him that she would prefer not to have it. But on second thoughts she said nothing, and waited for Federigo to stop crying and give her his answer, which eventually he did.

'My lady,' he said, 'ever since God decreed that you should become the object of my love, I have repeatedly had cause to complain of Fortune's hostility towards me. But all her previous blows were slight by comparison with the one she has dealt me now. Nor shall I ever be able to forgive her, when I reflect that you have come to my poor dwelling, which you never deigned to visit when it was rich, and that you desire from me a trifling favour which she has made it impossible for me to concede. The reason is simple, and I shall explain it in few words.

'When you did me the kindness of telling me that you wished to breakfast with me, I considered it right and proper, having regard to your excellence and merit, to do everything within my power to prepare a more sumptuous dish than those I would offer to any ordinary guest. My thoughts therefore turned to the falcon you have asked me for and, knowing its quality, I reputed it a worthy dish to set before you. So I had it roasted and served to you on the trencher this morning, and I could not have wished for a better way of disposing of it. But now that I discover that you wanted it in a different form, I am so distressed by my inability to grant your request that I shall never forgive myself for as long as I live.'

In confirmation of his words, Federigo caused the feathers, talons and beak to be cast on the table before her. On seeing and hearing all this, the lady reproached him at first for killing so fine a falcon, and serving it up for a woman to eat; but then she became lost in admiration for his magnanimity of spirit, which no amount of poverty had managed to diminish, nor ever would. But now that her hopes of obtaining the falcon had vanished she began to feel seriously concerned for the health of her son, and after thanking Federigo for his hospitality and good intentions, she took her leave of him, looking all despondent, and returned to the child. And to his mother's indescribable sorrow, within the space of a few days, whether through his disappointment in not being able to have the falcon, or because he was in any case suffering from a mortal illness, the child passed from this life.

After a period of bitter mourning and continued weeping, the lady was repeatedly urged by her brothers to remarry, since not only had she been left a vast fortune but she was still a young woman. And though she would have preferred to remain a widow, they gave her so little peace that in the end, recalling Federigo's high merits and his latest act of generosity, namely to have killed such a fine falcon in her honour, she said to her brothers:

'If only it were pleasing to you, I should willingly remain as I am; but since you are so eager for me to take a husband, you may be certain that I shall never marry any other man except Federigo degli Alberighi.'

Her brothers made fun of her, saying:

'Silly girl, don't talk such nonsense! How can you marry a man who hasn't a penny with which to bless himself?'

'My brothers,' she replied, 'I am well aware of that. But I would sooner have a gentleman without riches, than riches without a gentleman.'

Seeing that her mind was made up, and knowing Federigo to be a gentleman of great merit even though he was poor, her brothers fell in with her wishes and handed her over to him, along with her immense fortune. Thenceforth, finding himself married to this great lady with whom he was so deeply in love, and very rich into the bargain, Federigo managed his affairs more prudently, and lived with her in happiness to the end of his days.

TENTH STORY

Pietro di Vinciolo goes out to sup with Ercolano, and his wife lets a young man in to keep her company. Pietro returns, and she conceals the youth beneath a chicken coop. Pietro tells her that a young man has been discovered in Ercolano's house, having been concealed there by Ercolano's wife, whose conduct she severely censures. As ill luck would have it, an ass steps on the fingers of the fellow hiding beneath the coop, causing him to yell with pain. Pietro rushes to the spot and sees him, thus discovering his wife's deception. But in the end, by reason of his own depravity, he arrives at an understanding with her.

When the queen's tale had reached its conclusion, they all praised God for having given Federigo so fitting a reward, and then Dioneo, who was not in the habit of waiting to be asked, began straightway as follows:

Whether it is an accidental failing, stemming from our debased morals, or simply an innate attribute of men and women, I am unable to say; but the fact remains that we are more inclined to laugh at scandalous behaviour than virtuous deeds, especially when we ourselves are not directly involved. And since, as on previous occasions, the task I am about to perform has no other object than to dispel your melancholy, enamoured ladies, and provide you with laughter and merriment, I shall tell you the ensuing tale, for it may well afford enjoyment even though its subject matter is not altogether seemly. As you listen, do as you would when you enter a garden, and stretch forth your tender hands to pluck the roses, leaving the thorns where they are. This you will succeed in doing if you leave the knavish husband to his ill deserts and his iniquities, whilst you laugh gaily at the amorous intrigues of his wife, pausing where occasion warrants to commiserate with the woes of her lover.

Not so very long ago, there lived in Perugia[1] a rich man called Pietro di Vinciolo, who, perhaps to pull the wool over the eyes of his fellow-citizens or to improve the low opinion they had of him, rather than because of any real wish to marry, took to himself a wife. But the unfortunate part about it, considering his own proclivities, was that he chose to marry a buxom young woman with red hair and a passionate nature, who would cheerfully have taken on a pair of husbands, let alone one, and now found herself wedded to a man whose heart was anywhere but in the right place.

Having in due course discovered how matters stood, his wife, seeing that she was a fair and lusty wench, blooming with health and vitality, was greatly upset about it, and every so often she gave him a piece of her mind, calling him the foulest names imaginable. She was miserable practically the whole time, but one day, realizing that if she went on like this her days might well be ended before her husband's ways were mended, she said to herself: 'Since this miserable sinner deserts me to go clogging through the dry,[2] I'll get someone else to come aboard for the wet. I married the wretch, and brought him a good big dowry, because I knew he was a man and thought he was fond of the kind of thing that other men like, as is right and proper that they should. If I hadn't thought he was a man, I should never have married him. And if he found women so repugnant, why did he marry me in the first place, knowing me to be a woman? I'm not going to stand for it any longer, I have no desire to turn my back on the world, nor have I ever wanted to, otherwise I'd have gone into a nunnery; but if I have to rely on this fellow for my fun and games, the chances are that I'll go on waiting until I'm an old woman. And what good will it do me then, in my old age, to look back and complain about the way I wasted my youth, which this husband of mine teaches me all too well how to enjoy? He has shown me how to lead a pleasurable life, but whereas in his case the pleasure can only be condemned, in my own it will commend itself to all, for I shall simply be breaking the laws of marriage, whereas he is breaking those of Nature as well.'

These, then, were the wife's ideas, to which she doubtless gave further thought on other occasions, and in order to put them into effect, she made the acquaintance of an old bawd who to all outward appearances was as innocent as Saint Verdiana feeding the serpents,[3] for she made a point of attending all the religious services clutching her rosary, and never stopped talking about the lives of the Fathers of the Church and the wounds of St Francis, so that nearly everyone regarded her as a saint. Choosing the right moment, the wife took her fully into her confidence, whereupon the old woman said:

'The Lord above, my daughter, who is omniscient, knows that you are very well advised, if only because you should never waste a moment of your youth, and the same goes for all other women. To anyone who's had experience of such matters, there's no sorrow to compare with that of having wasted your opportunities. After all, what the devil are we women fit for in our old age except to sit round the fire and stare at the ashes? No woman can know this better than I, or prove it to you more convincingly. Now that I am old, my heart bleeds when I look back and consider the opportunities I allowed to go to waste. Mind you, I didn't waste all of them – I wouldn't want you to think I was a half-wit – but all the same I didn't do as much as I should have done. And God knows what agony it is to see myself reduced now to this sorry state, and realize that if I wanted to light a fire, I couldn't find anyone to lend me a poker.

'With men it is different: they are born with a thousand other talents apart from this, and older men do a far better job than younger ones as a rule; but women exist for no other purpose[4] than to do this and to bear children, which is why they are cherished and admired. If you doubt my words, there's one thing that ought to convince you, and that is that a woman's always ready for a man, but not vice-versa. What's more, one woman could exhaust many men, whereas many men can't exhaust one woman. And since this is the purpose for which we are born, I repeat that you are very well advised to pay your husband in his own coin, so that when you're an old woman your heart will have no cause for complaint against your flesh.

'You must help yourself to whatever you can grab in this world, especially if you're a woman. It's far more important for women than for men to make the most of their opportunities, because when we're old, as you can see for yourself, neither our husbands nor any other man can bear the sight of us, and they bundle us off into the kitchen to tell stories to the cat, and count the pots and pans. And what's worse, they make up rhymes about us, such as "When she's twenty give her plenty. When she's a gammer, give her the hammer," and a lot of other sayings in the same strain.

'But I won't detain you any longer with my chit-chat. You've told me what you have in mind, and I can assure you right away that you couldn't have spoken to anyone in the world who was better able to help. There's no man so refined as to deter me from telling him what's required of him, nor is there any so raw and uncouth as to prevent me from softening him up and bending him to my will. So just point out the one you would like, and leave the rest to me. But one thing I would ask you to remember, my child, and that is to offer me some token of your esteem, for I'm a poor old woman, and from now on I want you to have a share in my indulgences and all the paternosters I recite, so that God may look with favour on the souls of your departed ones.'

Having said her piece, she came to an understanding with the young lady that if she should come across a certain young man who frequently passed through that part of the city, and of whom she was given a very full description, she would take all necessary steps. The young woman then handed over a joint of salted meat, and they took their leave of one another.

Within the space of a few days, the youth designated by the lady was ushered secretly into her apartments by the beldam, and thereafter, at frequent intervals, several others who had taken the young woman's fancy were similarly introduced to her. And although she was in constant fear of being discovered by her husband, she made the fullest possible use of her opportunities.

One evening, however, her husband having been invited to supper by a friend of his called Ercolano, the young woman commissioned the beldam to fetch her one of the prettiest and most agreeable youths in Perugia, and her instructions were duly carried out. But no sooner were she and the youth seated at the supper-table than her husband, Pietro, started clamouring at the door to be let in.

The woman was convinced, on hearing this, that her final hour had come. But all the same she wanted to conceal the youth if possible, and not having the presence of mind to hide him in some other part of the house, she persuaded him to crawl beneath a chicken-coop in the lean-to adjoining the room where they were dining, and threw a large sack over the top of it, which she had emptied of its contents earlier in the day. This done, she quickly let in her husband, to whom she said as he entered the house:

'You soon gobbled down that supper of yours.'

'We never ate a crumb of it,' replied Pietro.

'And why was that?' said his wife.

'I'll tell you why it was,' said Pietro. 'No sooner had Ercolano, his wife and myself taken our places at table than we heard someone sneezing, close beside where we were sitting. We took no notice the first time it happened, or the second, but when the sneezing was repeated for the third, fourth and fifth times, and a good many more besides, we were all struck dumb with astonishment. Ercolano was in a bad mood anyway because his wife had kept us waiting for ages before opening the door to let us in, and he rounded on her almost choking with fury, saying: "What's the meaning of this? Who's doing all that sneezing?" He then got up from the table, and walked over to the stairs, beneath which there was an alcove boarded in with timber, such as people very often use for storing away bits and pieces when they're tidying up the house.

'As this was the place from which Ercolano thought the sneezes were coming, he opened a little door in the wainscoting, whereupon the whole room was suddenly filled with the most appalling smell of sulphur, though a little while before, when we caught a whiff of sulphur and complained about it, Ercolano's wife said: "It's because I was using sulphur earlier in the day to bleach my veils. I sprinkled it into a large bowl so that they would absorb the fumes, then placed it in the cupboard under the stairs, and it's still giving off a faint smell." After opening the little door and waiting for the fumes to die down a little, Ercolano peered inside and caught sight of the fellow who'd been doing all the sneezing, and was still sneezing his head off because of the sulphur. But if he'd stayed there much longer he would never have sneezed again, nor would he have done anything else for that matter.

'When he saw the man sitting there in the cupboard, Ercolano turned to his wife and shouted: "Now I see, woman, why you kept us waiting so long at the door just now, without letting us in; but I'll make you pay for it, if it's the last thing I do." On hearing this, since it was perfectly obvious what she had been doing, his wife got up from the table without a word of explanation and took to her heels, and what became of her I have no idea. Not having noticed that his wife had fled, Ercolano called repeatedly on the man who was sneezing to come out, but the fellow was already on his last legs and couldn't be persuaded to budge. So Ercolano grabbed him by one of his feet, dragged him out, and ran for a knife in order to kill him, at which point, since I was afraid we would all be arrested, myself included, I leapt to my feet and saved him from being killed or coming to any harm. As I was defending him from Ercolano, · my shouts brought several of the neighbours running to the scene, and they picked up the youth, who was no longer conscious, and carried him out of the house, but I've no idea where they took him. All this commotion put paid to our supper, so that, as I said, not only did I not gobble it down, but I never ate a crumb of it.'

On hearing this tale, his wife perceived that other women, even though their plans occasionally miscarried, were no less shrewd than herself, and she was strongly tempted to speak up in defence of Ercolano's wife. But thinking that by censuring another's misconduct she would cover up her own more successfully, she said:

'What a nice way to behave! What a fine, God-fearing specimen of womanhood! What a loyal and respectable spouse! Why, she had such an air of saintliness that she looked as if butter wouldn't melt in her mouth! But the worst part about it is that anyone as old as she is should be setting the young so fine an example. A curse upon the hour she was born! May the Devil take the wicked and deceitful hussy, for allowing herself to become the general butt and laughing-stock of all the women of this city! Not only has she thrown away her own good name, broken her marriage vows, and forfeited the respect of society, but she's had the audacity, after all he has done for her, to involve an excellent husband and venerable citizen in her disgrace, and all for the sake of some other man. So help me God, women of her kind should be shown no mercy; they ought to be done away with; they ought to be burnt alive and reduced to ashes.'

But at this point, recollecting that her lover was concealed beneath the chicken-coop in the very next room, she started coaxing Pietro to go to bed, saying it was getting late, whereupon Pietro, who had a greater urge to eat than to sleep, asked her whether there was any supper left over.

'Supper?' she replied. 'What would I be doing cooking supper, when you're not at home to eat it? Do you take me for the wife of Ercolano? Be off with you to bed, and give your stomach a rest, just for this once.'

Now, earlier that same evening, some of the labourers from Pietro's farm in the country had turned up at the house with a load of provisions, and had tethered their asses in a small stable adjoining the lean-to without bothering to water them. Being frantic with thirst, one of the asses, having broken its tether, had strayed from the stable and was roaming freely about the premises, sniffing in every nook and cranny to see if it could find any water. And in the course of its wanderings, it came and stood immediately beside the coop under which the young man lay hidden.

Since the young man was having to crouch on all fours, one of his hands was sticking out slightly from underneath the coop, and as luck would have it (or rather, to his great misfortune) the ass brought one of its hooves to rest on his fingers, causing him so much pain that he started to shriek at the top of his voice. Pietro, hearing this, was filled with astonishment, and, realizing that the noise was coming from somewhere inside the house, he rushed from the room to investigate. The youth was still howling, for the ass had not yet shifted its hoof from his fingers and was pressing firmly down upon him all the time. 'Who's there?' yelled Pietro as he ran to the coop, lifting it up to reveal the young man, who, apart from suffering considerable pain from having his fingers crushed beneath the hoof of the ass, was trembling with fear from head to foot in case Pietro should do him some serious injury.

Pietro recognized the young man as one he had long been pursuing for his own wicked ends, and demanded to know what he was doing there. But instead of answering his question, the youth pleaded with him for the love of God not to do him any harm.

'Get up,' said Pietro. 'There's no need to worry, I shan't do you any harm. Just tell me what you're doing here, and how you got in.'

The young man made a clean breast of the whole thing, and Pietro, who was no less pleased with his discovery than his wife was filled with despair, took him by the hand and led him back into the room, where the woman was waiting for him in a state of indescribable terror. Pietro sat down, looked her squarely in the face, and said:

'When you were heaping abuse on Ercolano's wife just now, and saying that she ought to be burnt alive, and that she was giving women a bad name, why didn't you say the same things about yourself? And if you wanted to keep yourself out of it, what possessed you to say such things about her, when you knew full well that you were tarred with the same brush? The only reason you did it, of course, was because all you women are alike. You go out of your way to criticize other people's failings so as to cover up your own. Oh, how I wish that a fire would descend from Heaven and burn the whole revolting lot of you to ashes!'

On finding that all she had to contend with, in the first flush of his anger, was a string of verbal abuse, and noting how delighted he seemed to be holding such a good-looking boy by the hand, the wife plucked up courage and said:

'It doesn't surprise me in the least that you want a fire to descend from Heaven and burn us all to ashes, seeing that you're as fond of women as a dog is fond of a hiding, but by the Holy Cross of Jesus you'll not have your wish granted. However, now that you've raised the subject, I'd like to know what you're grumbling about. It's all very well for you to compare me to Ercolano's wife, but at least he gives that sanctimonious old trollop whatever she wants, and treats her as a wife should be treated, which is more than can be said for you. I grant you that you keep me well supplied with clothes and shoes, but you know very well how I fare for anything else, and how long it is since you last slept with me. And I'd rather go barefoot and dressed in rags, and have you treat me properly in bed, than have all those things to wear and a husband who never comes near me. For the plain truth is, Pietro, that I'm no different from other women, and I want the same that they are having. And if you won't let me have it, you can hardly blame me if I go and get it elsewhere. At least I do you the honour not to consort with stable-boys and riff-raff.'

Pietro saw that she could go on talking all night, and since he was not unduly interested in his wife, he said:

'Hold your tongue now, woman, and leave everything to me. Be so good as to see that we're supplied with something to eat. This young man looks as though he's had no more supper this evening than I have.'

'Of course he hasn't had any supper,' said his wife. 'We were no sooner seated at table than you had to come knocking at the door.'

'Run along, then,' said Pietro, 'and get us some supper, after which I'll arrange matters so that you won't have any further cause for complaint.'

On perceiving that her husband was so contented, the wife sprang to her feet and quickly relaid the table. And when the supper she had prepared was brought in, she and the youth and her degenerate husband made a merry meal of it together.

How exactly Pietro arranged matters, after supper, to the mutual satisfaction of all three parties, I no longer remember. But I do know that the young man was found next morning wandering about the piazza, not exactly certain with which of the pair he had spent the greater part of the night, the wife or the husband. So my advice to you, dear ladies, is this, that you should always give back as much as you receive; and if you can't do it at once, bear it in mind till you can, so that what you lose on the swings, you gain on the roundabouts.

★   ★   ★

Dioneo's story was thus concluded, and if the ladies' laughter was restrained, this was more out of modesty than because it had failed to amuse them. But now the queen, perceiving that her sovereignty had come to an end, rose to her feet; and transferring the laurel crown from her own head to that of Elissa, she said to her:

'Madam, it is now for you to command us.'

Elissa, having accepted the honour, proceeded as before, first of all arranging with the steward about what was to be done during her term of office, and then, to the general satisfaction of the company, she addressed them as follows:

'Already we have heard many times how various people, with some clever remark or ready retort, or some quick piece of thinking, have been able, by striking at the right moment, to draw the teeth of their antagonists or avert impending dangers. This being so splendid a topic, and one which may also be useful, I desire that with God's help our discussion on the morrow should confine itself to the following: *those who, on being provoked by some verbal pleasantry, have returned like for like, or who, by a prompt retort or shrewd manoeuvre, have avoided danger, discomfiture or ridicule.*'

This proposal was warmly approved by one and all, and so the queen, having risen to her feet, dismissed the whole company till suppertime.

On seeing that the queen had risen, the honourable company did likewise; then all of them turned their attention, in the usual way, to whatever pleased them most. But when the cicadas' song was no longer to be heard, everyone was called back, and they all sat down to supper. Of this they partook in a gay and festive spirit, and when the meal was over they proceeded to sing and make music. Emilia having begun to dance, Dioneo was called upon to sing them a song, and he promptly came out with: 'Monna Aldruda, lift up your tail, for marvellous tidings I bring.'[1] Whereupon all the ladies began to laugh, especially the queen, who ordered him to stop and sing them another.

'My lady,' said Dioneo, 'if I had a drum, I'd sing you "Skirts up, Monna Lapa", or "The grass beneath the privet grows", or, if you preferred, "The waves of the sea are my torment". But I haven't a drum, so take your pick from among these others. Would you like "Out you come to wither away, like to the flower that blossoms in May"?'

'No,' said the queen, 'sing us something else.'

'In that case,' said Dioneo, 'I'll sing you "Monna Simona, put wine in your cask. Not till October, sir, she said".'

'Oh, confound you,' said the queen, with a laugh, 'if you're going to sing, choose something nice. We don't want to hear that one.'

'Come, my lady,' said Dioneo, 'don't take offence. Which do you like best? I know a thousand of them, at least. Would you like "I never have enough of my little bit of stuff", or "Ah! be gentle, husband dear", or "I bought myself a cock for a hundred pounds"?'

All the ladies laughed except the queen, who was beginning to grow impatient with him.

'No more of your nonsense, Dioneo,' she said. 'Sing us something pleasant, or you'll learn what it means to provoke my anger.'

Dioneo, hearing these words, curtailed his idle chatter and promptly began to sing the following song:

> 'Cupid, the beauteous light
> That shines forth from my mistress' eyne
> Has made me both her slave and thine.

> 'Moved by the splendour of those lovely eyes
> Which first thy flame did kindle in my heart,
> Their gaze transfixing mine,
> I understood what lofty virtue lies
> In thee, for her fair countenance hath art
> In my esteem to shine,
> So that no virtue known can with her vie,
> Which gives me all the more a cause to sigh.

'Therefore, my dear Lord, I have lately grown
One of thy servants, and obedient wait
Clemency from thy might.
Yet I know not if my whole state is known –
That high desire thou didst initiate
And, too, that faith so bright
In her, that doth my mind so utterly possess
That this apart I crave no other happiness.

'And so I pray thee, gentle Lord of mine,
That thou wilt show her this, and let her feel
Some inkling of thy power
To do me some small service, since I pine
Consumed with love, and in its torments reel,
And wither hour by hour;
I beg thee, when thou canst, do this for me,
And when thou goest, would I might come with thee!'

When, by his silence, Dioneo showed them that his song was
finished, the queen, having warmly commended it, called for many
others to be sung. But it was now very late, and the queen,
perceiving that the cool of the night had banished the warmth of
the day, bade them all go and sleep to their hearts' content till the
morning.

Here ends the Fifth Day of the Decameron

SIXTH DAY

Here begins the Sixth Day, wherein, under the rule of Elissa, *the discussion turns upon those who, on being provoked by some verbal pleasantry, have returned like for like, or who, by a prompt retort or shrewd manoeuvre, have avoided danger, discomfiture or ridicule.*

The moon, poised in the centre of the heavens, had lost her radiance, and the whole of our hemisphere was already suffused with the fresh light of dawn, when the queen arose and summoned her companions. Leaving their fair abode, they sauntered over the dew, conversing together on one subject after another, and discussing the merits and demerits of the stories so far narrated, at the same time laughing anew over the various adventures therein related, until, as the sun rose higher and the air grew warmer, they decided with one accord to retrace their steps, whereupon they turned about and came back to the house.

The tables being already laid, with fragrant herbs and lovely flowers strewn all around, they followed the queen's bidding and addressed themselves to their breakfast before the heat of the day should become too oppressive. And after making a merry meal of it, they first of all sang some gay and charming songs, after which some of their number retired to sleep, whilst others played chess or threw dice. And Dioneo, along with Lauretta, began to sing a song about Troilus and Cressida.[1]

When the time came for them to reassemble, the queen saw that they were all summoned in the usual way, and they seated themselves round the fountain. But just as the queen was about to call for the first story, something happened which had never happened before, namely, that she and her companions heard a great commotion,[2] issuing from the kitchen, among the maids and menservants. So the steward was summoned, and, on being asked who was shouting and what the quarrel was about, he replied that it was some dispute between Licisca and Tindaro. He was unable to explain its cause, as he had no sooner arrived on the scene to restore order than he had been called away by the queen. She therefore ordered him to fetch Licisca and Tindaro to her at once, and when they came before her, she demanded to know what they were quarrelling about.

Tindaro was about to reply, when Licisca, who was no fledgeling and liked to give herself airs, rounded on him with a withering look, spoiling for an argument, and said:

'See here, you ignorant lout, how can you dare to speak first, when I am present? Hold your tongue and let me tell the story.'

She then turned back to the queen, and said:

'Madam, this fellow thinks he knows Sicofante's[3] wife better than I do. I've known her for years, and yet he has the audacity to try and convince me that on the first night Sicofante slept with her, John Thomas had to force an entry into Castle Dusk, shedding blood in the process; but I say it is not true, on the contrary he made his way in with the greatest of ease, to the general pleasure of the garrison. The man is such a natural idiot that he firmly believes young girls are foolish enough to squander their opportunities whilst they are waiting for their fathers and brothers to marry them off, which in nine cases out of ten takes them three or four years longer than it should. God in Heaven, they'd be in a pretty plight if they waited all that long! I swear to Christ (which means that I know what I'm saying) that not a single one of the girls from my district went to her husband a virgin; and as for the married ones, I could tell you a thing or two about the clever tricks they play upon their husbands. Yet this great oaf tries to teach me about women, as though I were born yesterday.'

While Licisca was talking, the ladies were laughing so heartily that you could have pulled all their teeth out. Six times at least the queen had told her to stop, but all to no avail: she was determined to have her say. And when she had come to the end of her piece, the queen turned, laughing, to Dioneo, and said:

'This is a dispute for you to settle, Dioneo. Be so good, therefore, when we come to the end of our storytelling, to pronounce the last word on the subject.'

'Madam,' Dioneo swiftly replied, 'the last word has already been spoken. In my opinion, Licisca is right. I believe it is just as she says; and Tindaro is a fool.'

Hearing this, Licisca burst out laughing, and, turning back to Tindaro, she said:

'There! What did I tell you? Now get along, and stop thinking you know more than I do, when you're hardly out of your cradle. Thanks be to God, I haven't lived for nothing, believe you me!'

But for the fact that the queen sternly commanded her to be silent, told her not to shout or argue any more unless she wanted to be whipped, and sent her back to the kitchen with Tindaro, there would have been nothing else to do for the rest of the day but listen to her prattle. And when they had withdrawn, the queen enjoined Filomena to tell the first story, whereupon Filomena gaily began, as follows:

FIRST STORY

A knight offers to take Madonna Oretta riding through the realm of narrative, but makes such a poor job of it that she begs him to put her down.

Tender ladies, as stars bedeck the heavens on cloudless nights, and in the spring the green meadows are adorned with flowers, and hillsides with saplings newly come into leaf, so likewise are graceful manners and polite discourse enriched by shafts of wit. These, being brief, are much better suited to women than to men, since it is more unseemly for a woman to make long speeches than it is for a man.

But for some reason or other, whether because we are lacking in intelligence or because all the women of our generation were born under an unlucky star, few if any women now remain who can produce a witticism at the right moment, or who, on hearing a witticism uttered, can understand its meaning. Since Pampinea has already spoken at some length on this subject,[1] I do not propose to elaborate further upon it. But in order to show you how exquisite these sayings can be if proffered at the right moment, I should like to tell you about the courteous way in which a lady imposed silence upon a certain knight.

★

As many of you will know, either through direct personal acquaintance or through hearsay, a little while ago there lived in our city a lady of silver tongue and gentle breeding, whose excellence was such that she deserves to be mentioned by name. She was called Madonna Oretta, and she was the wife of Messer Geri Spina. One day, finding herself in the countryside like ourselves, and proceeding from place to place, by way of recreation, with a party of knights and ladies whom she had entertained to a meal in her house earlier in the day, one of the knights turned to her, and, perhaps because they were having to travel a long way, on foot, to the place they all desired to reach, he said:

'Madonna Oretta, if you like I shall take you riding along a goodly stretch of our journey by telling you one of the finest tales in the world.'

'Sir,' replied the lady, 'I beseech you most earnestly to do so, and I shall look upon it as a great favour.'

Whereupon this worthy knight, whose swordplay was doubtless on a par with his storytelling, began to recite his tale, which in itself was indeed excellent. But by constantly repeating the same phrases, and recapitulating sections of the plot, and every so often declaring that he had 'made a mess of that bit', and regularly confusing the names of the characters, he ruined it completely.[2] Moreover, his mode of delivery was totally out of keeping with the characters and the incidents he was describing, so that it was painful for Madonna Oretta to listen to him. She began to perspire freely, and her heart missed several beats, as though she had fallen ill and was about to give up the ghost. And in the end, when she could endure it no longer, having perceived that the knight had tied himself inextricably in knots, she said to him, in affable tones:

'Sir, you have taken me riding on a horse that trots very jerkily. Pray be good enough to set me down.'

The knight, who was apparently far more capable of taking a hint than of telling a tale, saw the joke and took it in the cheerfullest of spirits. Leaving aside the story he had begun and so ineptly handled, he turned his attention to telling her tales of quite another sort.

SECOND STORY

By means of a single phrase, Cisti the Baker shows Messer Geri Spina that he is being unreasonable.

Madonna Oretta's timely remark was warmly commended by all the men and ladies present, and then the queen ordered Pampinea to continue in the same vein. Pampinea therefore began, as follows:

Fair ladies, I cannot myself decide whether Nature is more at fault in furnishing a noble spirit with an inferior body, or Fortune in allotting an inferior calling to a body endowed with a noble spirit, as happened in the case of Cisti, our fellow citizen, and many other people of our own acquaintance. This Cisti was a man of exceedingly lofty spirit, and yet Fortune made him a baker.

I would assuredly curse Nature and Fortune alike, if I did not know for a fact that Nature is very discerning, and that Fortune has a thousand eyes, even though fools represent her as blind. Indeed, it is my conviction that Nature and Fortune, being very shrewd, follow the practice so common among mortals, who, uncertain of what the future will bring, make provision for emergencies by burying their most precious possessions in the least imposing (and therefore least suspect) part of their houses, whence they bring them forth in the hour of their greatest need, their treasure having been more securely preserved in a humble hiding place than if it had been kept in a sumptuous chamber. In the same way, the two fair arbiters of the world's affairs frequently hide their greatest treasure beneath the shadow of the humblest of trades, so that when the need arises for it to be brought forth, its splendour will be all the more apparent. This is amply borne out by a brief anecdote I should now like to relate, concerning an episode, in itself of no great importance, in which Cisti the Baker opened the eyes of Messer Geri Spina[1] to the truth, and of which I was reminded by the tale we have just heard about Madonna Oretta, who was Messer Geri's wife.

I say, then, that when Pope Boniface,[2] who held Messer Geri in the highest esteem, sent a delegation of his courtiers to Florence on urgent papal affairs, they took lodging under Messer Geri's roof; and almost every morning, for one reason or another, it so happened that Messer Geri and the Pope's emissaries were obliged by the nature of their business to walk past the Church of Santa Maria Ughi,[3] beside which Cisti had his bakery, where he practised his calling in person.

Though Fortune had allotted to Cisti a very humble calling, she had treated him so bountifully that he had become exceedingly rich; but it would never have occurred to him to exchange this occupation for any other, for he lived like a lord, and in addition to numerous other splendid possessions, he kept the finest cellar of wines, both red and white, to be found anywhere in Florence or the surrounding region. On noticing that Messer Geri passed by his door every morning with the Pope's emissaries, it occurred to Cisti that since the season was very hot he might as well do them the kindness of offering them some of his delicious white wine. But, being sensible of the difference in rank between himself and Messer Geri, he considered it would be presumptuous of him to issue an invitation and resolved to arrange matters in such a way that Messer Geri would come of his own accord.

And so every morning, wearing a gleaming white doublet and a freshly laundered apron, which made him look more like a miller than a baker, Cisti appeared in his doorway at the hour in which Messer Geri and the emissaries were due to pass by, and called for a shiny metal pail of fresh water and a brand new little Bolognese flagon containing a quantity of his best white wine, together with a pair of wineglasses, that gleamed as brightly as if they were made of silver. He then seated himself in the doorway, and just as they were passing, he cleared his throat a couple of times and began to drink this wine of his with so much relish that he would have brought a thirst to the lips of a corpse.

Messer Geri, having witnessed this charade on two successive mornings, turned to him on the third, and said:

'How does it taste, Cisti? Is it good?'

'Indeed it is, sir,' Cisti replied, springing to his feet, 'but how am I to prove how exquisite it tastes, unless you sample it for yourself?'

Now, whether because of the heat, or as a result of expending more energy than usual, or through observing Cisti drinking with so much gusto, Messer Geri had conceived such a keen thirst that he turned, smiling, to the emissaries, and said:

'My lords, we would do well to test the quality of this gentleman's wine; perhaps it will be such as to give us no cause for regret.'

He thereupon led them over to Cisti, who promptly arranged for a handsome bench to be brought out from his bakery and invited them to sit down. Their servants then stepped forward to wash the wineglasses, but Cisti said:

'Stand aside, my friends, and leave this office to me, for I am no less skilled at serving wine than at baking bread. And if you are expecting to taste so much as a single drop, you are going to be disappointed.'

And so saying, he washed four handsome new glasses with his own hands, called for a small flagon of his best wine, and, taking meticulous care, filled the glasses for Messer Geri and his companions, none of whom had tasted such an exquisite wine for years. Messer Geri affirmed that the wine was excellent, and for the remainder of the emissaries' stay in Florence, he called there nearly every morning with them to sample it afresh.

When their mission was completed and the emissaries were about to depart, Messer Geri held a magnificent banquet, to which he invited a number of the most distinguished citizens of Florence. He also sent an invitation to Cisti, who could by no means be persuaded to accept. So he ordered one of his servants to take a flask, ask Cisti to fill it with wine, and serve half a glass of it to each of the guests during the first course.

The servant, who was possibly feeling somewhat annoyed that he had never been allowed to sample the wine, took along a huge flask, and when Cisti saw it, he said:

'Messer Geri has not sent you to me, my lad.'

The servant kept assuring him that he had, but could obtain no other answer. So he returned to Messer Geri and told him what Cisti had said.

'Go back to him,' said Messer Geri, 'and tell him that I *am* sending you to him; and if he gives you the same answer, ask him to whom I am sending you.'

The servant returned to Cisti, and said:

'I can assure you, Cisti, that it is to you that Messer Geri sends me.'

'And I can assure you, my lad,' Cisti replied, 'that you are wrong.'

'To whom is he sending me then?' asked the servant.

'To the Arno,'[4] replied Cisti.

When the servant reported this conversation to Messer Geri, his eyes were immediately opened to the truth, and he asked the servant to show him the flask. On being shown the flask, he said:

'Cisti is perfectly right.' And having given the servant a severe scolding, he ordered him to return with a flask of more modest proportions.

On seeing this second flask, Cisti said:

'Now I know that he has sent you to me.' And he filled it up for him contentedly.

Later that same day, Cisti filled a small cask with wine of the same vintage and had it tenderly conveyed to Messer Geri's house, after which he called on Messer Geri in person, and said:

'Sir, I would not want you to suppose that I was taken aback on seeing the large flask this morning. But since you appeared to have forgotten what I have shown you with the aid of my small flagons during these past few days, namely, that this is not a wine for servants, I thought I would refresh your memory. However, since I have no intention of storing it for you any longer, I have now sent you every single drop of it, and henceforth you may dispose of it as you please.'

Messer Geri set great store by Cisti's gift, and thanked him as profusely as the occasion seemed to warrant. And from that day forth he held him in high esteem and regarded him as a friend of his for life.

THIRD STORY

With a quick retort, Monna Nonna de' Pulci puts a stop to the unseemly banter of the Bishop of Florence.

When Pampinea came to the end of her story, Cisti's reply was warmly applauded by all those present, and so too was his generosity, after which the queen was pleased to call upon Lauretta, who gaily began to speak, as follows:

Lovesome ladies, there is much truth in what both Pampinea and Filomena have been saying about the beauty of repartee and our own lack of skill in its use. It is unnecessary to repeat their arguments, but I should like to remind you that apart from what has already been said on this subject, the nature of wit is such that its bite must be like that of a sheep rather than a dog, for if it were to bite the listener like a dog, it would no longer be wit but abuse. The remark made by Madonna Oretta, and Cisti's retort, were excellent examples of the genre.

It is of course true, in the case of repartee, that when someone bites like a dog after having, so to speak, been bitten by a dog in the first place, his reaction does not seem as reprehensible as it would have been had he not been provoked; and one therefore has to be careful over how, when, on whom, and likewise where one exercises one's wit. To these matters, one of our prelates paid so little attention on one occasion, that he received no less painful a bite than he administered; and I should now like to tell you, in a few words, how this came about.

While Messer Antonio d'Orso,[1] a wise and worthy prelate, was Bishop of Florence, there came to the city a Catalan nobleman called Messer Dego della Ratta,[2] who was Marshal to King Robert of Naples. Being a fine figure of a man, and inordinately fond of women, Messer Dego pursued a number of the Florentine ladies, for one of whom, a ravishing beauty, he conceived a particular liking, and she happened to be the niece of the Bishop's brother.

Having learnt that the lady's husband, though he came of a good family, was very greedy and corrupt, he came to an arrangement with him whereby he would give him five hundred gold florins for allowing him to sleep for one night with his wife. But what he actually did was to gild five hundred coins of silver, called *popolini*, which were in everyday use at that period, and, having slept with the man's wife against her will, he handed these over to the husband. Subsequently the story became common knowledge, so that the scoundrelly husband was not only cheated but held up to ridicule. And the Bishop, being a wise man, feigned complete ignorance of the whole affair.

The Bishop and the Marshal were frequently to be seen in one another's company, and one day, it being the feast of St John,[3] they happened to be riding side by side down the street along which the *palio*[4] is run, casting an eye over the ladies, when the Bishop spotted a young woman (now, alas, no longer with us, having died in middle age during this present epidemic), whose name was Monna Nonna de' Pulci. You all know the person I mean – she was the cousin of Messer Alesso Rinucci, and at the time of which I am speaking she was a fine-looking girl in the flower of youth, well spoken and full of spirit, who had recently been married and set up house in the Porta San Piero quarter. The Bishop pointed her out to the Marshal, then he rode up beside her, clapped his hand on the Marshal's shoulder, and said:

'How do you like this fellow, Nonna? Do you think you could make a conquest of him?'

It seemed to Monna Nonna that the Bishop's words made her out to be less than virtuous, or that they were bound to damage her reputation in the eyes of those people, by no means few in number, in whose hearing they were spoken. So that, less intent upon vindicating her honour than upon returning blow for blow, she swiftly retorted:

'In the unlikely event, my lord, of his making a conquest of me, I should want to be paid in good coin.'

These words stung both the Marshal and the Bishop to the quick, the former as the author of the dishonest deed involving the niece of the Bishop's brother, and the latter as its victim, inasmuch as she was one of his own relatives. And without so much as looking at

one another, they rode away silent and shamefaced, and said no
more to Monna Nonna on that day.

In this case, therefore, since the girl was bitten first, it was not
inappropriate that she should make an equally biting retort.

FOURTH STORY

*Currado Gianfigliazzi's cook, Chichibio, converts his master's anger into
laughter with a quick word in the nick of time, and saves himself from the
unpleasant fate with which Currado had threatened him.*

When Lauretta was silent, and they had all paid glowing tribute to
Monna Nonna, the queen called upon Neifile to tell the next story,
whereupon Neifile began:

Amorous ladies, whilst a ready wit will often bring a swift
phrase, apposite and neatly turned, to the lips of the speaker, it
sometimes happens that Fortune herself will come to the aid of
people in distress by suddenly putting words into their mouths that
they would never have been capable of formulating when their
minds were at ease; which is what I propose to show you with this
story of mine.

As all of you will have heard· and seen for yourselves, Currado
Gianfigliazzi[1] has always played a notable part in the affairs of our
city. Generous and hospitable, he lived the life of a true gentleman,
and, to say nothing for the moment of his more important activities, he
took a constant delight in hunting and hawking. One day, having
killed a crane with one of his falcons in the vicinity of Peretola,[2]
finding that it was young and plump, he sent it to an excellent
Venetian cook of his, whose name was Chichibio,[3] telling him to
roast it for supper and to see that it was well prepared and seasoned.

Chichibio, who was no less scatterbrained than he looked, plucked
the crane, stuffed it, set it over the fire, and began to cook it with
great care. But when it was nearly done, and giving off a most
appetizing smell, there came into the kitchen a fair young country
wench called Brunetta, who was the apple of Chichibio's eye. And

on sniffing the smell of cooking and seeing the crane roasting on the spit, she coaxed and pleaded with him to give her one of the legs. By way of reply, Chichibio burst into song:

'I won't let you have it, Donna Brunetta, I won't let you have it, so there!'

This put Donna Brunetta's back up, and she said:

'I swear to God that if you don't let me have it, you'll never have another thing out of me!' In short, they had quite a lengthy set-to, and in the end, not wishing to anger his girl, Chichibio cut off one of the crane's legs and gave it to her.

A little later, the crane was set before Currado and his guests, and much to his surprise, Currado found that one of the legs was missing. So he sent for Chichibio and asked him what had happened to it. Being a Venetian, and hence a good liar,[4] Chichibio promptly replied:

'My lord, cranes have only the one leg.'

Whereupon Currado flew into a rage, and said:

'What the devil do you mean, cranes have only the one leg? Do you think I've never seen a crane before?'

'What I mean, sir,' continued Chichibio, 'is that they have only the one leg. We'll go and see some live ones, if you like, and I'll show you.'

Not wishing to embarrass his visitors, Currado decided not to pursue the matter, but said:

'I've never seen a one-legged crane before, nor have I ever heard of one. But since you have offered to show me, you can do so tomorrow morning, and then I shall be satisfied. But I swear to you by the body of Christ that if you fail to prove it, I shall see that you are given such a hiding that you will never forget my name for as long as you live.'

There the matter rested for that evening, but next morning, as soon as it was light, Currado, whom a night's sleep had done nothing to pacify, leapt out of bed, still seething with anger, and ordered his horses to be saddled. And, having obliged Chichibio to mount an old jade, he led the way to a river bank where cranes were usually to be seen in the early morning, saying:

'We shall soon see which of us was lying last night.'

On perceiving that Currado was still as angry as ever, and that he would now have to prove what he had said, Chichibio, who had no idea how he was going to do it, rode along behind Currado in a state of positive terror. If he could have run away he would gladly have done so, but since that was out of the question, he kept gazing ahead of him, behind him, and to each side, and wherever he looked he imagined he could see cranes standing on two legs.

However, just as they were approaching the river, Chichibio caught sight of well over a dozen cranes, all standing on one leg on the river bank, which is their normal posture when they are asleep. So he quickly pointed them out to Currado, saying:

'Now you can see quite plainly, sir, that I was telling you the truth last night when I said that cranes have only the one leg. Take a look at the ones over there.'

'Wait a bit,' said Currado, 'and I'll show you they have two.' And moving a little closer to them, he yelled: 'Oho!' whereupon the cranes lowered their other leg, and after taking a few strides, they all began to fly away. Currado then turned to Chichibio, saying:

'What do you say to that, you knave? Do they have two legs, or do they not?'

Chichibio was almost at his wits' end, but in some mysterious way he suddenly thought of an answer.

'They do indeed, sir,' he said, 'but you never shouted "Oho!" to the one you had last night, otherwise it would have shoved its second leg out, like these others.'

Currado was so delighted with this answer that all his anger was converted into jollity and laughter.

'You're right, Chichibio,' he said. 'Of course, I should have shouted.'

This then, was how Chichibio, with his prompt and amusing reply, avoided an unpleasant fate and made his peace with his master.

FIFTH STORY

Messer Forese da Rabatta and Master Giotto, the painter, returning from Mugello, poke fun at one another's disreputable appearance.

The ladies were highly amused by Chichibio's reply, and in deference to the queen's wishes, as soon as Neifile had stopped, Panfilo began:

Dearest ladies, whilst it is true that Fortune occasionally conceals abundant treasures of native wit in those who practise a humble trade, as was demonstrated just now by Pampinea, it is equally true that Nature has frequently planted astonishing genius in men of monstrously ugly appearance.

This was plainly to be observed in two citizens of ours, about whom I now propose to say a few words. The first, who was called Messer Forese da Rabatta,[1] being deformed and dwarf-like in appearance, with a plain snub-nosed face that would have seemed loathsome alongside the ugliest Baronci[2] who ever lived, was a jurist of such great distinction that many scholars regarded him as a walking encyclopaedia of civil law. The second, whose name was Giotto,[3] was a man of such outstanding genius that there was nothing in the whole of creation that he could not depict with his stylus, pen, or brush. And so faithful did he remain to Nature (who is the mother and the motive force of all created things, via the constant rotation of the heavens), that whatever he depicted had the appearance, not of a reproduction, but of the thing itself, so that one very often finds, with the works of Giotto, that people's eyes are deceived and they mistake the picture for the real thing.

Hence, by virtue of the fact that he brought back to light an art which had been buried for centuries beneath the blunders of those who, in their paintings, aimed to bring visual delight to the ignorant rather than intellectual satisfaction to the wise, his work may justly be regarded as a shining monument to the glory of Florence. And all the more so, inasmuch as he set an example to others by wearing his celebrity with the utmost modesty, and always refused to be called a master, even though such a title befitted him all the more resplendently in proportion to the eagerness with which it was sought and usurped by those who knew less than himself or by his own pupils. But for all the greatness of his art, neither physically nor facially was he any more handsome than Messer Forese.

Turning now to our story, I should first point out that both Messer Forese and Giotto owned properties in the region of Mugello.[4] And one summer, when the law courts were closed for the vacation, Messer Forese had gone to visit this property of his, and was returning to Florence astride an emaciated old hack, when whom should he meet up with along the road but the aforementioned Giotto, who was likewise returning from a visit to his property. Giotto was no better accoutred than himself, his mount was just as decrepit, and, since they were both getting on in years and travelling at a snail's pace, they rode along together.

However, they happened to be caught in a sudden downpour such as we often experience in summer, and they took shelter as soon as they could in the house of a peasant, who was known to both men and was in fact a friend of theirs. But after a while, since the rain showed no sign of stopping and they wanted to reach Florence by nightfall, they borrowed a pair of shabby old woollen capes from the peasant, along with a couple of hats that were falling to bits from old age, these being the best he could provide, and resumed their journey.

After they had travelled some distance, by which time they were soaked to the skin and bespattered all over by the steady spray of mud that hacks kick up with their hooves (none of which is calculated to improve anyone's appearance), the weather cleared up a little, and the two men, having ridden for a long time in silence, began to converse with one another.

As Messer Forese was riding along listening to Giotto, who was a very fine talker, he turned to inspect him, shifting his gaze from Giotto's flank to his head and then to the rest of his person, and on perceiving how thoroughly unkempt and disreputable he looked, giving no thought to his own appearance he burst out laughing, and said:

'Giotto, supposing we were to meet some stranger who had never seen you before, do you think he would believe that you were the greatest painter in the world?'

To which Giotto swiftly replied:

'Sir, I think he would believe it if, after taking a look at you, he gave you credit for knowing your ABC.'

On hearing this, Messer Forese recognized his error, and perceived that he was hoist with his own petard.

SIXTH STORY

Michele Scalza proves to certain young men that the Baronci are the most noble family in the whole wide world, and wins a supper.

The ladies were still laughing over Giotto's swift and splendid retort when the queen called for the next story from Fiammetta, who began as follows:

Young ladies, Panfilo's mention of the Baronci, with whom, possibly, you are less well acquainted than he is, has reminded me of a story demonstrating their great nobility, and since it falls within the scope of our agreed topic, I should like to relate it to you.

In our city, not so very long ago, there was a young man called Michele Scalza, who was the most entertaining and agreeable fellow you could ever wish to meet, and he was always coming out with some new-fangled notion or other, so that the young men of Florence loved to have him with them when they were out on the spree together.

Now, one day, he was with some friends of his at Montughi,[1] and they happened to start an argument over which was the most ancient and noble family in Florence. Some maintained it was the Uberti, some the Lamberti,[2] and various other names were tossed into the discussion, more or less at random.

Scalza listened to them for a while, then he started grinning, and said:

'Get along with you, you ignorant fools, you don't know what you're talking about. The most ancient and noble family, not only in Florence but in the whole wide world, is the Baronci.[3] All the philosophers are agreed on this point, and anyone who knows the Baronci as well as I do will say the same thing. But in case you think I'm talking about some other family of that name, I mean the Baronci who live in our own parish of Santa Maria Maggiore.'

His companions, who had been expecting him to say something quite different, poured scorn on this idea, and said:

'You must be joking. We know the Baronci just as well as you do.'

'I'm not joking,' said Scalza. 'On the contrary I'm telling you the gospel truth. And if there's anyone present who would care to wager a supper to be given to the winner and six of his chosen companions, I'll gladly take him up on it. And just to make it easier for you, I'll abide by the decision of any judge you choose to nominate.'

Whereupon one of the young men, who was called Neri Mannini, said:

'I am ready to win this supper.' And having mutually agreed to appoint Piero di Fiorentino, in whose house they were spending the day, as the judge, they went off to find him, being followed by all the others, who were eager to see Scalza lose the wager so that they could pull his leg about it.

They told Piero what the argument was all about, and Piero, who was a sensible young man, listened first to what Neri had to say, after which he turned to Scalza, saying:

'And how do you propose to prove this claim you are making?'

'Prove it?' said Scalza. 'Why, I shall prove it by so conclusive an argument that not only you yourself, but this fellow who denies it, will have to admit that I am right. As you are aware, the older the family, the more noble it is, and everyone agreed just now that this was so. Since the Baronci are older than anyone else, they are *ipso facto* more noble; and if I can prove to you that they really are older than anybody else, I shall have won my case beyond any shadow of a doubt.

'The fact of the matter is that when the Lord God created the Baronci, He was still learning the rudiments of His craft, whereas He created the rest of mankind after He had mastered it. If you don't believe me, picture the Baronci to yourselves and compare them to other people; and you will see that whereas everybody else has a well-designed and correctly proportioned face, the Baronci sometimes have a face that is long and narrow, sometimes wide beyond all measure, some of them have very long noses, others have short ones, and there are one or two with chins that stick out and turn up at the end, and with enormous great jaws like those of an ass; moreover, some have one eye bigger than the other, whilst others have one eye lower than the other, so that taken by and large, their faces are just like the ones that are made by children when they are first learning to draw. Hence, as I've already said, it is quite obvious that the Lord God created them when He was still learning His craft. They are therefore older than anybody else, and so they are more noble.'

When Piero, the judge, and Neri, who had wagered the supper, and all the others, recalling what the Baronci looked like, had heard Scalza's ingenious argument, they all began to laugh and to declare that Scalza was right, that he had won the supper, and that without a doubt the Baronci were the most ancient and noble family, not only in Florence, but in the whole wide world.

And that is why Panfilo, in wanting to prove the ugliness of Messer Forese, aptly maintained that he would have looked loathsome alongside a Baronci.

SEVENTH STORY

Madonna Filippa is discovered by her husband with a lover and called before the magistrate, but by a prompt and ingenious answer she secures her acquittal and causes the statute to be amended.

Fiammetta had finished speaking, and everyone was still laughing over the novel argument used by Scalza to ennoble the Baronci above all other families, when the queen called upon Filostrato to tell them a story; and so he began:

Worthy ladies, a capacity for saying the right things in the right place is all very well, but to be able to say them in a moment of dire necessity is, in my opinion, a truly rare accomplishment. With this ability, a certain noblewoman of whom I propose to speak was so liberally endowed, that not only did she provide laughter and merriment to her listeners, but, as you shall presently hear, she disentangled herself from the meshes of an ignominious death.

In the city of Prato, there used to be a statute, no less reprehensible, to be sure, than it was severe, which without exception required that every woman taken in adultery by her husband should be burned alive, whether she was with a lover or simply doing it for money.

While this statute was in force, a case arose in which a certain noble lady, beautiful and exceedingly passionate by nature, whose name was Madonna Filippa, was discovered one night in her own bedchamber by her husband, Rinaldo de' Pugliesi,[1] in the arms of Lazzarino de' Guazzagliotri, a handsome young noble of that city, with whom she was very deeply in love, and who loved her in return. Rinaldo, seeing them together, was greatly dismayed, and could scarcely prevent himself from rushing upon them and killing them; and but for the fact that he feared the consequences to himself, he would have followed the promptings of his anger, and done them to death.

Having been restrained by his caution from taking precipitate action, he could not however be restrained from desiring the death of his wife, and since it would have been unlawful for him to kill her with his own hands, he was determined to invoke the city statute. And so, having more than sufficient evidence to prove her guilt, he denounced her on the very next morning without inquiring any further into the matter, and took out a summons.

Now, a woman who is genuinely in love is apt to be quite fearless, and Rinaldo's wife was no exception. And although many of her friends and relatives advised her against such a course, she firmly resolved to answer the summons, confess the truth, and die a courageous death, rather than run away like a coward, thus being forced to live in exile for defying the court, and proving herself unworthy of a lover such as the man in whose arms she had lain the night before. So that, attended by a numerous throng of men and women, all encouraging her to protest her innocence, she went before the *podestà*,[2] looked him squarely between the eyes, and asked him in a firm voice what it was that he required of her.

On gazing at this woman and observing that she was very beautiful and impeccably well-bred, to say nothing of the fortitude of spirit to which her words bore witness, the *podestà* was touched with compassion for her, being afraid lest she should confess and thus compel him, if he wished to preserve his authority, to have her put to death. Nevertheless, being unable to avoid questioning her about what she was alleged to have done, he said:

'Madam, as you see, Rinaldo your husband is here, and he has lodged a complaint against you, claiming that he has taken you in adultery. He is therefore demanding that I should punish you, as prescribed by one of our statutes, by having you put to death. But this I cannot do unless you confess, and therefore I must warn you to be very careful how you answer. Now tell me, is your husband's accusation true?'

Without flinching in the slightest, the lady replied in a most fetching sort of voice:

'Sir, it is true that Rinaldo is my husband, and that he found me last night in Lazzarino's arms, wherein, on account of the deep and perfect love I bear towards him, I have lain many times before; nor shall I ever deny it. However, as I am sure you will know, every man and woman should be equal before the law, and laws must have the consent of those who are affected by them. These conditions are not fulfilled in the present instance, because this law only applies to us poor women, who are much better able than men to bestow our favours liberally. Moreover, when this law was made, no woman gave her consent to it, nor was any woman even so much as consulted. It can therefore justly be described as a very bad law.

'If, however, to the detriment of my body and your soul, you wish to give effect to this law, that is your own affair. But before you proceed to pass any judgement, I beseech you to grant me a small favour, this being that you should ask my husband whether or not I have refused to concede my entire body to him, whenever and as often as he pleased.'

Without waiting for the *podestà* to put the question, Rinaldo promptly replied that beyond any doubt she had granted him whatever he required in the way of bodily gratification.

'Well then,' the lady promptly continued, 'if he has always taken as much of me as he needed and as much as he chose to take, I ask you, Messer Podestà, what am I to do with the surplus? Throw it to the dogs?³ Is it not far better that I should present it to a gentleman who loves me more dearly than himself, rather than allow it to turn bad or go to waste?'

The nature of the charge against the lady, coupled with the fact that she was such a well-known figure in society, had brought almost all the citizens of Prato flocking to the court, and when they heard the charming speech she made in her defence, they rocked with mirth and, as with a single voice, they all exclaimed that the lady was right and that it was well spoken. And at the *podestà*'s suggestion, before they left the court, they amended the harsh statute so that in future it would apply only to those wives who took payment for being unfaithful to their husbands.

After making such a fool of himself, Rinaldo departed from the scene feeling quite mortified; and his wife, now a free and contented woman, having, so to speak, been resurrected from the flames, returned to her house in triumph.

EIGHTH STORY

Fresco urges his niece not to look at herself in the glass, if, as she has claimed, she cannot bear the sight of horrid people.

As they listened to Filostrato's tale, the ladies at first felt a trifle embarrassed, and showed it by the blush of modesty that appeared on their cheeks; but then they began to exchange glances with one another, and, scarcely able to contain their laughter, they heard the rest of it with their faces wreathed in smiles. When it came to an end, the queen turned to Emilia and called upon her to speak next; and Emilia, heaving a sigh as though she had just been awakened from a pleasant dream, began as follows:

Fair young ladies, having been absorbed for a while in distant reverie, I shall now bestir myself to obey the queen's command, and recount a tale, much shorter perhaps than the one I would have told you if I had had all my wits about me, concerning the foolish error of a young woman, and how it was corrected by an amusing remark of her uncle's, though she was far too dense to appreciate its significance.

There was once a certain gentleman called Fresco da Celatico, and he had a niece whose pet-name was Cesca.[1] Whilst she had a good figure and a pretty face (though it was far from being one of those angelic faces that we not infrequently come across), she had such a high opinion of herself and gave herself so many airs that she fell into the habit of criticizing everything and everyone she ever set eyes upon, never thinking for a moment of her own defects, even though she was the most disagreeable, petulant, and insipid young woman imaginable, and nothing could be done to please her. Moreover, her pride was so enormous that even in a scion of the French royal family it would have been excessive. And whenever she walked along the street, she was continually wrinkling up her nose in disgust, as though a nasty smell was assailing her nostrils every time she saw or met anyone.

Now, leaving aside her many other tiresome and disagreeable mannerisms, and coming to the point, she happened one day to return from a walk, and, finding Fresco at home, she flounced into a chair at his side, simpering like a spoilt child, and fretting and fuming. Fresco cast her a quizzical look, and said:

'Cesca, why do you come home so early, when today is a feast day?'

'The truth is,' Cesca replied, affecting a thoroughly world-weary air, 'that I have come home early because I doubt whether I have ever seen such a tiresome and disagreeable set of people as the ones who are walking our streets today. Every man and woman that I meet is utterly repellent to me, and I don't believe there is a woman anywhere in the world who is so upset by the sight of horrid people as I am. So I came home early to spare myself the torment of looking at them.'

Whereupon Fresco, who found the fastidious airs of his niece highly distasteful, said to her:

'If you can't bear the sight of horrid people, my girl, I advise
you, for your own peace of mind, never to look at yourself in the
glass.'[2]

But the girl, whose head was emptier than a hollow reed even
though she imagined herself to be as wise as Solomon, might have
been a carcase of mutton for all she understood of Fresco's real
meaning, and she told him that she intended to look in the glass just
like any other woman. So she remained as witless as before, and she
is still the same to this day.

NINTH STORY

*With a barbed saying, Guido Cavalcanti politely delivers an insult to
certain Florentine gentlemen who had taken him by surprise.*

The queen, perceiving that Emilia had dashed off her story and that
she herself was the sole remaining speaker apart from the person
who was privileged to speak last of all, began to address the
company as follows:

Sweet ladies, although you have deprived me of at least two of
the stories that I had thought of telling you today, I still have
another in reserve, towards the end of which there occurs a *bon mot*
that is more subtle, perhaps, than any of the ones we have heard so
far.

I must first of all remind you that in days gone by, our city was
noted for certain excellent and commendable customs, all of which
have now disappeared, thanks to the avarice which, increasing as it
does with the growing prosperity of the city, has driven them all
away. One of these customs was that in various parts of Florence a
limited number of the gentlemen in each quarter of the city would
meet regularly together in one another's houses for their common
amusement. Only those people who could afford to entertain on a
suitably lavish scale were admitted to these coteries, and they took it
in turn to play the host to their companions, each of them being
allotted his own special day for the purpose. Distinguished visitors

to Florence were frequently invited to these gatherings, and so too were a number of the citizens. At least once every year they all wore the same kind of dress, whilst on all the more important anniversaries they rode together through the city, and sometimes they tilted together, especially on the principal feasts or when the news of some happy event had reached the city, such as a victory in the field.

Among these various companies, there was one that was led by Messer Betto Brunelleschi,[1] into whose ranks Messer Betto and his associates had striven might and main to attract Messer Cavalcante de' Cavalcanti's son, Guido.[2] And not without reason, for apart from the fact that he was one of the finest logicians in the world and an expert natural philosopher (to none of which Betto and his friends attributed very much importance), Guido was an exceedingly charming and sophisticated man, with a marked gift for conversation, and he outshone all of his contemporaries in every activity pertaining to a gentleman that he chose to undertake. But above and beyond all this he was extremely rich, and could entertain most sumptuously those people whom he happened to consider worthy of his hospitality.

However, Messer Betto had never succeeded in winning him over, and he and his companions thought this was because of his passion for speculative reasoning, which occasionally made him appear somewhat remote from his fellow beings. And since he tended to subscribe to the opinions of the Epicureans, it was said among the common herd that these speculations of his were exclusively concerned with whether it could be shown that God did not exist.

Now, one day, Guido had walked from Orsammichele along the Corso degli Adimari as far as San Giovanni, which was a favourite walk of his because it took him past those great marble tombs, now to be found in Santa Reparata,[3] and the numerous other graves that lie all around San Giovanni. As he was threading his way among the tombs, between the porphyry columns that stand in that spot and the door of San Giovanni, which was locked, Messer Betto and his friends came riding through the piazza of Santa Reparata, and on seeing Guido among all these tombs, they said:

'Let's go and torment him.'

And so, spurring their horses and making a mock charge, they were upon him almost before he had time to notice, and they began to taunt him, saying:

'Guido, you spurn our company; but supposing you find that God doesn't exist, what good will it do you?'

Finding himself surrounded, Guido promptly replied:

'Gentlemen, in your own house you may say whatever you like to me.'

Then, placing a hand on one of the tombstones, which were very tall,⁴ he vaulted over the top of it, being very light and nimble, and landed on the other side, whence, having escaped from their clutches, he proceeded on his way.

Betto and his companions were left staring at one another, then they began to declare that he was out of his mind, and that his remark was meaningless, because neither they themselves nor any of the other citizens, Guido included, owned the ground on which their horses were standing. But Messer Betto turned to them, and said:

'You're the ones who are out of your minds, if you can't see what he meant. In a few words he has neatly paid us the most back-handed compliment I ever heard, because when you come to consider it, these tombs are the houses of the dead, this being the place where the dead are laid to rest and where they take up their abode. By describing it as our house, he wanted to show us that, by comparison with himself and other men of learning, all men who are as uncouth and unlettered as ourselves are worse off than the dead. So that, being in a graveyard, we are in our own house.'

Now that Guido's meaning had been pointed out to them, they all felt suitably abashed, and they never taunted him again. And from that day forth, they looked upon Messer Betto as a paragon of shrewdness and intelligence.

TENTH STORY

Friar Cipolla promises a crowd of country folk that he will show them a feather of the Angel Gabriel, and on finding that some bits of coal have been put in its place, he proclaims that these were left over from the roasting of Saint Lawrence.

His nine companions having each told a story, Dioneo knew without waiting for any formal command that it was now his own turn to speak. He therefore silenced those of his companions who were praising Guido's clever retort, and began:

Charming ladies, although I have the privilege of speaking on any subject I may choose, I do not propose to depart from the topic on which all of you have spoken so appositely today. On the contrary, following in your footsteps, I intend to show you how one of the friars of Saint Anthony,[1] by a quick piece of thinking, neatly side-stepped a trap which had been laid for him by two young men. And if I speak at some length, so as to tell the whole story as it should be told, this ought not to disturb you unduly, for you will find, if you look up at the sun, that it is still in mid heaven.

Certaldo,[2] as you may possibly have heard, is a fortified town situated in the Val d'Elsa, in Florentine territory, and although it is small, the people living there were at one time prosperous and well-to-do. Since it was a place where rich pickings were to be had, one of the friars of Saint Anthony used to visit the town once every year to collect the alms which people were foolish enough to donate to his Order. He was called Friar Cipolla,[3] and he always received a warm welcome there, though this was doubtless due as much to his name as to the piety of the inhabitants, for the soil in those parts produces onions that are famous throughout the whole of Tuscany.

This Friar Cipolla was a little man, with red hair and a merry face, and he was the most sociable fellow in the world. He was quite illiterate, but he was such a lively and excellent speaker, that anyone hearing him for the first time would have concluded, not only that he was some great master of rhetoric, but that he was Cicero in person, or perhaps Quintilian.⁴ And there was scarcely a single man or woman in the whole of the district who did not regard him as a friend, familiar or well-wisher.

During one of his regular annual visits to Certaldo, on a Sunday morning in the month of August, when all the good folk from the neighbouring hamlets were gathered in the parish church for mass, Friar Cipolla, choosing a suitable moment, came forward and said:

'Ladies and gentlemen, as you know, every year it is your custom to send to the poor of the Lord Saint Anthony a portion of your wheat and oats, varying in amount from person to person according to his ability and devotion, so that the blessed Saint Anthony will protect your oxen, asses, pigs and sheep from harm. Moreover it is customary, in particular for those of you who are enrolled as members of our confraternity, to pay those modest sums which fall due every year at this time, and it is precisely to collect these contributions of yours that my superior, Master Abbot, has sent me among you. And so, with God's blessing, when you hear the bells ring after nones,⁵ you will assemble outside the church, where as usual I shall preach the sermon and you will kiss the cross. But in addition to this, since I know how deeply devoted you all are to the Lord Saint Anthony, I shall show you, by way of special favour, a most sacred and beautiful relic, which I myself brought back from a visit I once paid to the Holy Land across the sea; and this is one of the feathers of the Angel Gabriel, which was left behind in the bedchamber of the Virgin Mary when he came to annunciate her in Nazareth.'

And at this point he ended his homily and returned to the mass.

Now, among the large congregation present in the church when Friar Cipolla made this announcement, were a pair of very wily young fellows, one of whom was called Giovanni del Bragoniera and the other Biagio Pizzini. Having had a good laugh together over Friar Cipolla's relic, they decided, though they were his good friends and boon companions, to have a little fun with this feather at the Friar's expense. They knew that Friar Cipolla was to breakfast with a friend that morning in the citadel,⁶ and so they waited until he was safely seated at table, then made their way down into the street, whence they proceeded to the inn where the Friar was staying, their intention being that Biagio should engage Friar Cipolla's servant in conversation whilst Giovanni rummaged through the Friar's belongings and removed this feather, or whatever it was, so that later in the day they could see how he explained its disappearance to the populace.

Friar Cipolla had a servant, variously known as Guccio Balena, or Guccio Imbratta, or Guccio Porco,[7] who was such a coarse fellow that he could have given lessons in vulgarity to Lippo Topo[8] himself, and whom Friar Cipolla frequently used to make fun of in conversation with his cronies, saying:

'My servant has nine failings, any one of which, had it been found in Solomon or Aristotle or Seneca, would have sufficed to vitiate all the ingenuity, all the wisdom, and all the saintliness they ever possessed. So you can imagine what this fellow must be like, considering that he hasn't a scrap of ingenuity, wisdom or saintliness, and possesses all nine.'

Friar Cipolla had put these nine failings into rhyme, so that whenever he was asked what they were, he replied:

'I'll tell you: he's untruthful, distasteful and slothful; negligent, disobedient, and truculent; careless, witless and graceless. Apart from this, he has one or two other little foibles, that are best passed over in silence. But the funniest thing about him is that wherever he goes, he's always wanting to find himself a wife and rent a house; and because he has a big, black, greasy beard, he thinks he's very handsome and seductive, and that every woman he meets is desperately in love with him; and if he were left to his own devices, he'd be so busy chasing the girls that he could lose his breeches and be none the wiser. All the same I must confess that he's a great help to me, because he won't allow me to be burdened with anybody's secrets, but always insists on sharing them with me; and if anyone asks me a question, he's so afraid I won't be able to answer that he does it for me, putting in a quick "yes" or a quick "no" as the occasion appears to merit.'

This, then, was the man Friar Cipolla had left behind at the inn, with strict instructions not to allow anyone to touch his belongings, in particular his saddlebags, which contained his sacred bits and pieces.

But no nightingale was ever as happy on the branch of a tree as Guccio Imbratta in the kitchen of an inn, especially if there happened to be a serving-wench in the offing. And having caught a glimpse of a stocky little kitchen-maid, who was plump and coarse and bowlegged, with a pair of paps like a couple of dung-baskets and a face like a Baronci, her skin plastered in sweat, grease and soot, he left Friar Cipolla's things to take care of themselves, and, like a vulture descending on carrion, down he swooped. Although it was August, he took a seat beside the fire and struck up a conversation with the girl, whose name was Nuta, telling her that he was a gentleman by proxy, that he had more florins than anyone could count, not excluding the ones he had to pay out, which were even more in number, and that not even his master could do and say so many fine things as he. Moreover, paying no heed to the cowl he was wearing, which had enough grease on it to season the soup-cauldron of Altopascio,[9] or to his patched and tattered doublet, which was smeared with filth round the collar and under the armpits, and stained all over in more colours than a length of cloth from India or Tartary, or to his shoes, that were falling to bits, or to his hose, that were gaping at the seams, he told her, as though he were the Lord of Chatillon[10] himself, that he would buy her some fine new clothes, set her up in comfort, release her from her drudgery, and, whilst she wouldn't have much to call her own, give her something to look forward to at any rate. But all these promises, and a great many more, though uttered with a good deal of affection, were as insubstantial as the air itself, and like most of the projects he undertook, they came to nothing.

Finding Guccio Porco thus occupied with Nuta, the two young men were delighted, since it meant that half their job was already done. And so they made their way unhindered to Friar Cipolla's room, the door of which was unlocked; and having let themselves in, the very first thing they laid hands upon was the saddlebag containing the feather. On opening the bag, they found a small casket wrapped in a length of taffeta, and when they raised the lid, and found that it contained one of the tail feathers of a parrot, they concluded that this must be the one he had promised to display to the people of Certaldo.

And without a doubt he could easily have got away with it in those days, because the luxuries of Egypt had not yet infiltrated to any marked degree into Tuscany, as they were later to do on a very wide scale, to the ruination of the whole of Italy. A few people in Tuscany were aware that such things existed, but they were almost totally unknown in Certaldo, where, since the lives of the people still conformed to the honest precepts of an earlier age, not only had they never seen any parrots, but the vast majority had never even heard of them.

Delighted, then, with their discovery, the young men removed the feather from the casket, and in its place, so as not to leave the casket empty, they put a few pieces of coal, which they had found lying in a corner of the room. They then closed the lid, and, leaving everything just as they had found it, they made off, undetected, with the feather, chortling with glee, and waited to see what Friar Cipolla, on finding the coals instead of the feather, would have to say for himself.

When mass was over, the simple folk who were in the church, having heard that they would be seeing the feather of the Angel Gabriel after nones, had returned to their homes and passed the news on to all their friends and neighbours. And after they had eaten their midday meal, they thronged the citadel in such vast · numbers, all agog to see the feather, that they scarcely had sufficient room to move their limbs.

Having eaten a hearty breakfast and taken a short siesta, Friar Cipolla arose shortly after nones, and on perceiving that a great multitude of peasants had come to see the feather, he sent word to Guccio Imbratta that he was to come up to the citadel, bringing with him the bells and the saddle-bags. So Guccio tore himself away from the kitchen and from Nuta, and made his way up at a leisurely pace. His body was swollen up like a balloon with all the water he had been drinking, and so he arrived there puffing and panting; but having, in accordance with Friar Cipolla's instructions, taken up his stance in the church doorway, he began to ring the bells with great gusto.

When the entire populace was assembled in front of the church, Friar Cipolla began to preach his sermon, never suspecting for a moment that any of his things had been tampered with. He harangued his audience at great length, carefully stressing what was required of them, and on reaching the point where he was to display the Angel Gabriel's feather, he first recited the *Confiteor*[11] and caused two torches to be lit; then, throwing back the cowl from his head, he carefully unwound the taffeta and drew forth the casket, which, after a few words in praise and commendation of the Angel Gabriel and his relic, he proceeded to open. When he saw that it was full of coal, Guccio Balena was the last person he suspected of playing him such a trick, for he knew him to be incapable of rising to such heights of ingenuity. Nor did he even blame the man for being so careless as to allow others to do it, but inwardly cursed his own stupidity in entrusting his things to Guccio's care, knowing full well, as he did, that he was negligent, disobedient, careless and witless. Without changing colour in the slightest, however, he raised his eyes and hands to Heaven, and in a voice that could be heard by all the people present, he exclaimed:

'Almighty God, may Thy power be forever praised!'

Then, closing the casket and turning to the people, he said:

'Ladies and gentlemen, I must explain to you that when I was still very young, I was sent by my superior into those parts where the sun appears,[12] with express instructions to seek out the privileges of the Porcellana,[13] which, though they cost nothing to seal and deliver, bring far more profit to others than to ourselves.

'So away I went, and after setting out from Venison, I visited the Greek Calends, then rode at a brisk pace through the Kingdom of Algebra and through Bordello, eventually reaching Bedlam, and not long afterwards, almost dying of thirst, I arrived in Sardintinia. But why bother to mention every single country to which I was directed by my questing spirit? After crossing the Straits of Penury, I found myself passing through Funland and Laughland, both of which countries are thickly populated, besides containing a lot of people. Then I went on to Liarland, where I found a large number of friars belonging to various religious orders including my own, all of whom were forsaking a life of discomfort for the love of God, and paying little heed to the exertions of others so long as they led to their own profit. In all these countries, I coined a great many phrases, which turned out to be the only currency I needed.

'Next I came to the land of Abruzzi,[14] where all the men and women go climbing the hills in clogs, and clothe pigs in their own entrails;[15] and a little further on I found people carrying bread on staves, and wine in pouches, after which I arrived at the mountains of the Basques, where all the waters flow downwards.

'In short, my travels took me so far afield that I even went to Parsnipindia,[16] where I swear by this habit I am wearing that I saw the feathers flying – an incredible spectacle for anyone who has never witnessed it. And if any of you should doubt my words, Maso del Saggio[17] will bear me out on this point, for he has set up a thriving business in that part of the world, cracking nuts and selling the shells retail.

'But being unable to find what I was seeking, or to proceed any further except by water, I retraced my steps and came at length to the Holy Land, where in summertime the cold bread costs fourpence a loaf, and the hot is to be had for nothing. There I met the Reverend Father Besokindas Tocursemenot,[18] the most worshipful Patriarch of Jerusalem, who, out of deference to the habit of the Lord Saint Anthony, which I have always worn, desired that I should see all the holy relics[19] he had about him. These were so numerous, that if I were to give you a complete list, I would go on for miles without reaching the end of it. But so as not to disappoint the ladies, I shall mention just a few of them.

'First of all he showed me the finger of the Holy Ghost, as straight and firm as it ever was; then the forelock of the Seraph that appeared to Saint Francis; and a cherub's fingernail; and one of the side-bits of the Word-made-flash-in-the-pan; and an article or two of the Holy Catholic faith; and a few of the rays from the star that appeared to the three Magi in the East; and a phial of Saint Michael's sweat when he fought with the Devil; and the jawbone of Death visiting Saint Lazarus; and countless other things.

'And because I was able to place freely at his disposal certain portions of the *Rumpiad* in the vernacular, together with several extracts from Capretius,[20] which he had long been anxious to acquire, he gave

me a part-share in his holy relics, presenting me with one of the
holes from the Holy Cross, and a small phial containing some of the
sound from the bells of Solomon's temple, and the feather of the
Angel Gabriel that I was telling you about, and one of Saint
Gherardo da Villamagna's sandals,[21] which not long ago in Florence
I handed on to Gherardo di Bonsi, who holds him in the deepest
veneration; and finally, he gave me some of the coals over which
the blessed martyr Saint Lawrence was roasted. All these things I
devoutly brought away with me, and I have them to this day.

'True, my superior has never previously allowed me to exhibit
them, until such time as their authenticity was established. However,
by virtue of certain miracles they have wrought, and on account of
some letters he has received from the Patriarch, he has now become
convinced that they are genuine, and has granted me permission to
display them in public. But I am afraid to entrust them to others,
and I always take them with me wherever I go.

'Now, the fact is that I keep the feather of the Angel Gabriel in a
casket to prevent it being damaged, and in another casket I keep the
coals over which Saint Lawrence was roasted. But the two caskets
are so alike that I often pick up the wrong one, which is what has
happened today; for whereas I intended to bring along the one
containing the feather, I have brought the one with the coals. Nor
do I consider this a pure accident; on the contrary I am convinced
that it was the will of God, and that it was He who put the casket
of coals into my hands, for I have just remembered that the day
after tomorrow is the Feast of Saint Lawrence.[22] And since it was
God's intention that I should show you the coals over which he was
roasted, and thus rekindle the devotion which you should all feel
towards Saint Lawrence in your hearts, He arranged that I should
take up, not the feather which I had meant to show you, but the
blessed coals that were extinguished by the humours of that most
sacred body. You will therefore bare your heads, my blessed
children, and step up here in order to gaze devoutly upon them.

'But before you do so, I must tell you that all those who are
marked with the sign of the cross by these coals may rest assured
that for a whole year they will never be touched by fire without
getting burnt.'[23]

And so saying, he chanted a hymn in praise of Saint Lawrence, opened up the casket, and displayed the coals. For some little time, the foolish multitude gazed open-mouthed upon them in awe and wonderment, then they all pressed forward in a great throng round Friar Cipolla, and, giving him larger offerings than usual, they begged him one and all to touch them with the coals.

So Friar Cipolla took the coals between his fingers and began to scrawl the biggest crosses he could manage to inscribe on their white smocks and on their doublets and on the shawls of the women, declaring that however much the coals were worn down in making these crosses, they recovered their former shape when restored to the casket, as he had often had occasion to observe.

At considerable profit to himself, therefore, having daubed crosses on all the citizens of Certaldo, Friar Cipolla neatly turned the tables on the people who had sought to make a fool of him by taking away his feather. Having attended his sermon and observed the ingenious manner in which he had turned the situation to his advantage with his preposterous rigmarole, the two young men laughed until they thought their sides would split. And when the crowd had dispersed, they went up to him, shaking with mirth, and told him what they had done, at the same time handing back the feather, which proved the following year to be no less lucrative to him than the coals had been on this occasion.

*　*　*

The whole company was vastly pleased and entertained by Dioneo's tale, and they all laughed heartily over Friar Cipolla, especially at his pilgrimage and at the relics, both the ones he had seen and those he had brought back with him. On perceiving that it was finished, and that her reign, too, had come to an end, the queen stood up, and removing her crown, she placed it on Dioneo's head, saying with a laugh:

'The time has come, Dioneo, for you to discover what a burden it is to have ladies under your control and guidance. Be our king, therefore, and rule us wisely, so that when your reign is ended, we shall have cause to sing your praises.'

Dioneo accepted the crown, and replied, laughing:

'I daresay you have often seen kings whose worth is far greater than mine – on a chessboard, I mean. But without a doubt, if you were to obey me as a true king ought to be obeyed, I should see that you received a measure of that joy without which no entertainment is ever truly pleasurable and complete. But enough of this idle chatter. I shall rule as best I can.'

And having, in accordance with their usual practice, sent for the steward, he gave him clear instructions about the duties he was to perform during the remainder of his sovereignty, after which he said:

'Worthy ladies, our discussions have ranged so widely over the field of human endeavour, and touched upon such a variety of incidents, that if Mistress Licisca had not come here a short while ago and said something which offered me a subject for our deliberations on the morrow, I suspect I should have had a hard job to find a suitable theme. As you will have heard, she told us that none of the girls in her neighbourhood had gone to her husband a virgin; and she added that she knew all about the many clever tricks played by married women on their husbands. But leaving aside the first part, which even a child could have told you, I reckon that the second would make an agreeable subject for discussion; and hence, taking our cue from Mistress Licisca, I should like us to talk tomorrow about *the tricks which, either in the cause of love or for motives of self-preservation, women have played upon their husbands, irrespective of whether or not they were found out.*'

Some of the ladies felt that it would be unseemly for them to discuss a subject of this sort, and asked him to propose another, but the king replied:

'Ladies, I know as well as you do that the theme I have prescribed is a delicate one to handle; but I am not to be deterred by your objections, for I believe that the times we live in permit all subjects to be freely discussed, provided that men and women take care to do no wrong. Are you not aware that because of the chaos of the present age, the judges have deserted the courts, the laws of God and man are in abeyance, and everyone is given ample licence to preserve his life as best he may? This being so, if you go slightly beyond the bounds of decorum in your conversation, with the object, not of behaving improperly but of giving pleasure to yourselves and to others, I do not see how anyone in the future can have cause to condemn you for it.

'Besides, it seems to me that this company of ours has comported itself impeccably from the first day to this, despite all that we have heard, and with God's help it will continue to do so. Furthermore, everybody knows that you are all highly virtuous, and I doubt whether even the fear of dying could make you any less so, to say nothing of a little pleasurable discourse.

'But the real point is this, that if anyone were to discover that you had refrained at any time from discussing these little peccadilloes, he might well suspect that you had a guilty conscience[1] about them, and that this was why you were so reluctant to talk about them. Apart from which, you would be paying me a nice compliment if, having elected me as your king and law-giver, you were to refuse to speak on the subject I prescribe, especially when you consider how obedient I was to all of you. Set aside these scruples, then, which ill become such healthy minds as your own, and let each of you put her best foot forward and think of some entertaining story to relate.'

Having listened to Dioneo's arguments, the ladies agreed to fall in with his scheme, whereupon he gave permission to them all to occupy their time until supper in whatever way they pleased.

The sun was still very high, for the day's discussions had been relatively brief, and so Elissa, seeing that Dioneo had started a game of dice with the other young men, drew all the ladies aside, and said:

'Ever since we came here, I have been wanting to take you to a place where none of you, so far as I know, has ever been, called the Valley of the Ladies.[2] It is not far away from here, but this is the first opportunity I have had (the sun being still very high) of taking you to see it. So if you would all like to come, I am quite sure that once you are there you will not be in the least disappointed.'

The ladies agreed to go with her, and without saying anything to the young men, they sent for one of their maidservants, and set out; nor had they gone much more than a mile, when they came to the Valley of the Ladies. This they entered by way of a very narrow path, along one side of which there flowed a beautifully clear stream, and they found it to be as delectable and lovely a place, especially since the weather was so hot, as could possibly be imagined. And according to the description I was given later by one of their number, the floor of the valley was perfectly circular in shape, for all the world as if it had been made with compasses, though it seemed the work of Nature rather than of man. It was little more than half a mile in circumference, and surrounded by half-a-dozen hills, all comparatively low-lying, on each of whose summits one could discern a palace, built more or less in the form of a pretty little castle. The sides of the hills ranged downwards in a regular series of terraces, concentrically arranged like the tiers of an amphitheatre, their circles gradually diminishing in size from the topmost terrace to the lowest.

Of these slopes, the ones facing south were covered all over in vines, olives, almonds, cherries, figs, and many other species of fruit trees, whilst those which faced north were thickly wooded with young oaks, ashes, and various other trees, all as green and straight as you could imagine. The plain itself, to which there was no other means of access than the path by which the ladies had entered, was filled with firs, cypresses, bay-trees, and a number of pines, all of which were so neatly arranged and symmetrically disposed that they looked as if they had been planted by the finest practitioner of the forester's craft. And when the sun was overhead, few or none of its rays penetrated their foliage to the ground beneath, which was one continuous lawn of tiny blades of grass interspersed with flowers, many of them purple in colour.

But the thing that afforded them no less pleasure was a stream cascading down over the living rock of a gorge separating two of the surrounding hills, which produced a most delectable sound as it descended and looked from a distance as though it was issuing forth under pressure in a powdery spray of fine quicksilver. On reaching the floor of the valley, it flowed swiftly along a neat little channel to the centre of the plain, where it formed a tiny lake like one of those fishponds that prosperous townspeople occasionally construct in their gardens. The lake was not very deep, so that if a man were to stand in it, the water would have come up no further than his chest; and since it was free of all impurities, its bed showed up vividly as a stretch of very fine gravel, every fragment of which could have been counted by anyone with sufficient patience and nothing better to do. But apart from the bed of the lake, on looking into the water one could see a number of fishes darting in all directions, which were not only delightful but wondrous to behold. The lake had no other banks than the floor of the valley itself, and all around its edges the grass grew much more thickly through being so close to the water. And it was drained by a second little channel, through which the stream flowed out of the valley and so downwards to its lower reaches.

This, then, was the place to which the young ladies came; and after they had gazed all around and extolled its marvellous beauty, seeing the limpid pool shimmering there before them they made up their minds, since it was very hot and they were in no danger of being observed, to go for a swim. And having ordered their maid to go back and keep watch along the path by which they had entered the valley, and bring them warning if anyone should come, all seven of them undressed and took to the water, which concealed their chaste white bodies no better than a thin sheet of glass would conceal a pink rose. And when they were in the water, which remained as crystal-clear as before, they began as best they could to swim hither and thither in pursuit of the fishes, which had nowhere to hide, and tried to seize hold of them with their hands.

In this sport they persisted for a while, and after they had caught some of the fish, they emerged from the pool and put on their clothes again. And being unable to bestow higher praise upon the place than that which they had already accorded to it, feeling that it was time to make their way back again, they set forth at a gentle pace, talking all the while of its beauty. It was as yet quite early when they arrived at the palace, where they found the young men still playing dice in the place where they had left them, and Pampinea greeted them with a laugh, saying:

'We have stolen a march upon you today.'

'What?' said Dioneo. 'Do you mean to say you have begun to do these things even before you talk about them?'

'Yes, Your Majesty,' said Pampinea. And she gave him a lengthy description of the place from which they had come, telling him how far away it was, and what they had been doing there.

On hearing her account of the place's beauty, the king was anxious to see it for himself, and he straightway ordered supper to be served. This they all proceeded to eat with a great deal of relish, and when it was over, the three young men and their servants deserted the ladies and made their way to the Valley. None of them had been there before, and all things considered, they concluded admiringly that it was one of the loveliest sights in the world. And when they had bathed and dressed, since the hour was very late they went straight back home, where they found the ladies dancing a *carole*³ to an air being sung by Fiammetta. They joined them in the dance, and when it was finished, having taken up the subject of the Valley of the Ladies, they talked at length in praise of its beauty.

And so the king sent for the steward, and ordered him to see that things were set out for them next morning in that very place, and that beds were carried there in case anyone should want to sleep or lie down in the middle part of the day. Then he called for lights to be brought, together with wine and sweetmeats, and when they had taken a little refreshment, he ordered everyone to join in the dancing. At his request, Panfilo began the first dance, whereupon the king turned to Elissa and in pleasing tones he said:

'Fair lady, just as you honoured me today with the crown, so I wish to honour you this evening with the privilege of singing to us. Sing to us therefore, and let your song be about the one you prefer to all the rest.'

Elissa, with a smile, readily consented and began to sing in dulcet tones as follows:

'Love, if I ever from thy claws break free
I think no other hook will tangle me.

'I entered in thy war, a fair young maid,
Believing it was perfect peace benign,
And all my arms upon the ground I laid,
Thinking to find thy honour like to mine.
    But thou, disloyal tyrant,
    Leapt'st out at me instead
    In armour fiercely girded
    With talons cruel outspread.

'And now, all bound around with chains of thine,
To him who for my very death was born
Thou gav'st me prisoner; and now I pine
Within his grasp, and in distraction mourn.
  His lordship is so cruel
  That all my tears and cries
  Go unregarded, while, alas,
  I waste away with sighs.

'The wind has swept away my every prayer;
  E'en now, when my cruel torment grows so high,
None listens to them, none will give them ear;
My life is hateful, yet how may I die?
  Since I lie in thy bondage
  Have pity, Lord, on me,
  Do for me what I cannot
  And set my spirit free.

'But if thou canst not grant me this, alas,
Cut all those bonds of hope that bind me fast.
I pray thee, Lord, at least to grant me this,
For if thou dost, my faith is that at last
  I may regain that beauty
  That once I had by right
  And, sorrow banished, deck me
  With flowers of red and white.'[4]

When Elissa, fetching a most pathetic sigh, had brought her song to a close, albeit everyone puzzled over the words no one was able to say who it was that had caused her to sing such a song. The king, however, who was in good mettle, sent for Tindaro and ordered him to bring out his cornemuse,[5] to the strains of which he caused several reels to be danced. But when a goodly portion of the night was spent, he told them, one and all, to retire to bed.

Here ends the Sixth Day of the Decameron

SEVENTH DAY

Here begins the Seventh Day, wherein, under the rule of Dioneo, are discussed the tricks which, either in the cause of love or for motives of self-preservation, women have played upon their husbands, irrespective of whether or not they were found out.

Every star had vanished from the eastern heavens, excepting that alone which we call Lucifer,[1] which was still glowing in the whitening dawn, when the steward arose and made his way with a large baggage-train to the Valley of the Ladies, there to arrange everything in accordance with his master's orders and instructions. And after his departure it was not long before the king also arose, having been awakened by the noise of the servants loading the animals, and caused all the ladies and the other young men to be roused.

Nor were the sun's rays shining as yet in all their glory, when the whole company set forth; and it seemed to them that they had never heard the nightingales and other birds sing so gaily as they appeared to sing that morning. Their songs accompanied them all the way to the Valley of the Ladies, where they were greeted by a good many more, so that all the birds seemed to be rejoicing at their coming.

On roaming through the valley and surveying it for a second time, they thought it even more beautiful than on the day before, inasmuch as the hour showed off its loveliness to better advantage. And when they had broken their fast with good wine and delicate sweetmeats, so as not to be outdone by the birds they too burst into song, whereupon the valley joined forces with them, repeating every note that was uttered; and to these songs of theirs, sweet new notes were added by all the birds, as though they were determined not to be out-matched.

When it was time to eat, they took their places at the tables, which in deference to the king's wishes had been set beneath the leafy bay-trees and the other fine trees fringing the delectable pool, and as they ate they could see the fishes swimming about the lake in enormous shoals, which attracted not only their attention but also an occasional comment. At the end of the meal, the tables were cleared and taken away, and they began to sing even more merrily than before, then played upon their instruments and danced one or two *caroles*.

Their discreet steward had meanwhile made up several beds in different parts of the little valley, surrounding them with drapes of French cretonne and bedecking them with canopies, and the king gave leave to those who so desired to retire for their siesta; and those who had no desire to sleep were free to amuse themselves to their hearts' content in the various ways to which they were accustomed. In due course, when the time came for them to address themselves once more to their story telling, they all got up and proceeded to seat themselves on rugs which, in accordance with the king's instructions, had been laid upon the grass beside the lake, in a spot not far away from where they had breakfasted. Then the king ordered Emilia to open the proceedings, and with a broad smile, she gaily began to speak, as follows:

FIRST STORY

Gianni Lotteringhi hears a tapping at his door in the night; he awakens his wife, and she leads him to believe it is a werewolf, whereupon they go and exorcize it with a prayer, and the knocking stops.

My lord, I should have counted myself very fortunate if you had chosen some person other than myself to introduce so splendid a topic as the one on which we are called upon to speak; but since you desire me to set a reassuring example to the other ladies, I shall willingly do so. I shall endeavour, dearest ladies, to say something that might prove useful to you in the future, for if other women are no different from myself, we are easily frightened, and in particular by werewolves.[1] Heaven knows that I am unable to explain what these creatures might be, nor have I ever found any woman who could, but we are frightened of them just the same. However, if you should ever encounter one, you will henceforth be able to drive it away, for by listening carefully to my story you will learn a fine and godly prayer which is tailored to the purpose.

There once lived in Florence, in the quarter of San Pancrazio,[2] a master-weaver whose name was Gianni Lotteringhi, a man more successful in his calling than sensible in other matters, for although he was a simple sort of fellow, he was regularly elected as the leader of the laud-singers at Santa Maria Novella, and had to conduct their rehearsals, and he was often given other such trifling little duties, so that all in all he had a mighty high opinion of himself; yet the only reason these functions were entrusted to him was that, being comfortably off, he frequently used to supply the friars with a good meal.

These latter, since they often wrung a pair of hose or a cloak or a scapular out of him, taught him some good prayers and gave him copies of the Paternoster in the vernacular and the song of Saint Alexis[3] and the lament of Saint Bernard[4] and the laud of Lady Matilda[5] and a whole lot of other drivel, all of which he greatly prized, and preserved with the greatest of loving care for the good of his soul.

Now, this man had a most charming and beautiful wife, a woman of great intelligence and perspicacity, whose name was Monna Tessa, the daughter of Mannuccio dalla Cuculia.[6] Realizing that she had a nincompoop for a husband, she fell in love with Federigo di Neri Pegolotti, a handsome fellow in the full vigour of his youth, and he with her, and she made arrangements through one of her maidservants for Federigo to come and keep her company at a splendid villa belonging to her husband in Camerata,[7] where she used to spend the whole of the summer, and to which Gianni would occasionally come in the evening in order to sup with her and stay overnight before returning next morning to his place of business or sometimes to his laud-singers.

Federigo desired nothing better, and one day, when the coast was clear, he made his way up to the villa as prearranged, a little before vespers. Gianni was not expected that evening, so Federigo was thoroughly at his ease; and to his immense pleasure, he was able to sup there and spend the night with the lady, who lay in his arms and took him through a good half dozen of her husband's lauds before the night was over.

But neither she nor Federigo intended that this first time should also be the last, and since it was imprudent to send the maid to fetch him every time, they came to the following arrangement: that every day, on his way to or from a villa of his that stood a little further up the road, he should keep an eye on the vineyard alongside her house, where he would see the skull of an ass[8] perched on top of one of the stakes of the vines. If he saw that the face was turned in the direction of Florence, he would come to her after dark that evening without fail and in complete safety, and if the door was locked he would knock three times and she would come and let him in; but if he saw that the face of the skull was pointing towards Fiesole he would stay away, because it would mean that Gianni was at home. And by using this system they were able to meet together regularly.

But on one of these occasions when Federigo was due to come and take supper with Monna Tessa, and she had roasted a pair of fat capons in his honour, it so happened that, much to the lady's annoyance, Gianni turned up unexpectedly, very late in the evening. She and her husband supped on a small quantity of salted meat which she had cooked separately; and meanwhile she got her maid to wrap the two roast capons in a white tablecloth together with a quantity of new-laid eggs and a flask of choice wine, and carry them into her garden, which it was possible to reach without going through the house, and where every so often she and Federigo used to sup. And she told the maid to leave all these things at the foot of a peach-tree that stood at the edge of a neat little lawn.

But she was so enraged by what had happened that she forgot to tell the maid to wait until Federigo arrived, so as to inform him that Gianni was at home and that he was to take away the things from the garden. And so not long after she and Gianni had gone to bed, and the maid had also retired for the night, Federigo came and tapped gently at the door, which was so near to the bedroom that Gianni heard it immediately, and so did the lady. But so that Gianni could have no possible reason to suspect her, she pretended to be asleep.

Federigo waited a little, then knocked a second time, whereupon Gianni began to wonder what it was all about and gave his wife a little poke, saying:

'Tessa, do you hear what I hear? It sounds like someone tapping at our door.'

His wife, who had heard it much more clearly than he had, made a show of waking up, and murmured:

'Mm? What's that you say?'

'I said,' Gianni replied, 'that it sounds like someone tapping at our door.'

'Tapping?' she said. 'Oh, heavens, Gianni dear, d'you know what it'll be? It'll be the werewolf that's been frightening me out of my senses for these past few nights. I was so terrified that every time I heard it I stuck my head under the bedclothes and kept it there until it was broad daylight.'

'Come now, don't be afraid, my dear,' said Gianni. 'If that's all it is, there's no need to worry, because before we got into bed I recited the *Te lucis*[9] and the *Intemerata*[10] and various other excellent prayers, and I also made the sign of the cross from corner to corner of the bed in the name of the Father, the Son and the Holy Ghost, so no matter how powerful this werewolf may be, it can't do us any harm.'

In case Federigo should become suspicious of her and take offence, Monna Tessa decided that, come what may, she must get up out of bed and apprise him of the fact that Gianni was there, and so she said to her husband:

'That's all very well. You can spout as many words as you like, but as far as I'm concerned I shan't feel safe or secure until we exorcize it, and now that you are here we can do it.'

'Exorcize it?' said Gianni. 'How are we to do that?'

'I know exactly how to exorcize it,' said his wife, 'because the day before yesterday, when I went to the pardoning at Fiesole, I came across a hermitess, who as God is my witness, Gianni dear, is the most saintly woman you ever met, and when she saw how terrified I was of the werewolf, she taught me a fine and godly prayer, telling me that she had tried it many a time before becoming a recluse, and that it had always worked for her. Heaven knows that I would never have sufficient courage to try it out by myself, but now that you are here, I want us to go and exorcize it.'

Gianni thought this an excellent idea, and so they both got up out of bed and tiptoed over to the door, on the other side of which Federigo, his suspicions already aroused, was still waiting. On reaching the door, Gianni's wife said to him:

'As soon as I give you the word, have a good spit.'[11]

'Right you are,' said Gianni.

Then the lady began the exorcism, saying:

'Werewolf, werewolf, black as any crow, you came here with your tail erect, keep it up and go; go into the garden, and look beneath the peach, and there you'll find roast capons, and a score of eggs with each; raise the flask up to your lips, and take a swig of wine; then get you gone and hurt me not, nor even Gianni mine.' And so saying she turned to her husband, and said:

'Spit, Gianni.' And Gianni spat.

Federigo, who was standing outside and heard every syllable, had stopped feeling jealous, and despite all his frustration he had to hold his sides to prevent himself from bursting out laughing. And in a low murmur, as Gianni was doing his spitting, he groaned:

'The teeth!'

When Monna Tessa had exorcized the werewolf three times in this same fashion, she and her husband returned to bed.

Federigo had come with an empty stomach, for he had been expecting to sup with his mistress. But having clearly grasped the meaning of the words of the prayer, he made his way into the garden, where at the foot of the large peach-tree he found the two capons and the wine and the eggs, which he took back with him to his house, there to make a splendid and leisurely meal of it all. And on many a later occasion, when he was with his mistress, they had a good laugh together over this incantation of hers.

It is true that some people maintain that the lady had in fact turned the skull of the ass towards Fiesole, and that a farmhand, passing through the vineyard, had poked his stick inside it and given it a good twirl, so that it ended up facing towards Florence, hence causing Federigo to think that she wanted him to come. According to this second account,[12] the words of the lady's prayer went like this: 'Werewolf, werewolf, leave us be; the ass's head was turned, but not by me; I curse the one who did it, and I think you will agree; for I'm here with my dear Gianni, as anyone can see.' And so Federigo beat a hasty retreat, and lost his supper that evening as well as his lodging.

However, there is a neighbour of mine, a very old woman, who tells me that both accounts are correct if there is any truth in a story which she was told when she was still a child, and that the second version refers, not to Gianni Lotteringhi, but to a man from Porta San Piero called Gianni di Nello, who was just as great a dunderhead as Gianni Lotteringhi.

I therefore leave it to you, dear ladies, to choose the version you prefer, or perhaps you would like to accept both, for as you have heard, they are extremely effective in situations like the one I have described. Commit them to memory, then, for they may well stand you in good stead in times to come.

SECOND STORY

Peronella hides her lover in a tub when her husband returns home unexpectedly. Her husband has sold the tub, but she tells him that she herself has already sold it to a man who is inspecting it from the inside to see whether it is sound. Leaping forth from the tub, the man gets the husband to scrape it out and carry it back to his house for him.

Emilia's story was received with gales of laughter, and everyone agreed that the prayer was indeed a fine and godly one. When the tale was finished, the king ordered Filostrato to follow, and so he began:

Adorable ladies, so numerous are the tricks that men, and husbands in particular, play upon you, that whenever any woman happens to play one on her husband, you should not only be glad to hear about it but you should also pass it on to as many people as you can, so that men will come to realize that women are just as clever as their

husbands. All of which is bound to work out to your own advantage, for when a man knows that he has clever people to deal with,
he will think twice before attempting to deceive them.

Who can be in any doubt, therefore, that when husbands come
to learn of what we shall be saying today on this subject, they
will have every reason to refrain from trifling with you, knowing
that if you so desired you could do the same to them? And for this
reason, it is my intention to tell you about the trick which a young
woman, though she was of lowly condition, played on the
spur of the moment upon her husband, in order to save her own
skin.

Not so long ago, in Naples, a poor man took to wife a charming
and beautiful girl, whose name was Peronella.[1] He was a bricklayer
by trade, and earned a very low wage, but this, together with the
modest amount she earned from her spinning, was just about
sufficient for them to live on.

Now one day, Peronella caught the eye of a sprightly young
gallant, who, finding her exceedingly attractive, promptly fell in
love with her, and by using all his powers of persuasion, he
succeeded in gaining her acquaintance. So that they could be
together, they came to this arrangement: that since her husband got
up early every morning to go to work or to go and look for a job,
the young man should lie in wait until he saw him leaving the
house; and as the district where she lived, which was called Avorio,
was very out-of-the-way, as soon as the husband had left, he should
go in to her. And in this way they met very regularly.

But one particular morning, shortly after the good man had left
the house and Giannello Scrignario[2] (such was the young gallant's
name) had gone inside to join Peronella, the husband, who was
usually away for the whole day, returned home. Finding the door
locked on the inside, he knocked, and after he had knocked he said
to himself:

'May the Lord God be forever praised; for though He has willed
that I should be poor, at least He has given me the consolation of a
good, chaste girl for a wife. See how quick she was to lock the door
after I left, so that no one should come in and give her any trouble.'

Now, Peronella knew it was her husband from his way of knocking, and she said:

'O alas, Giannello my love, I'm done for! That's my husband, curse the fellow, who for some reason or other has come back home. I've never known him to return at this hour before; perhaps he saw you coming in. But whatever the reason, for God's sake hop into this tub over here while I go and let him in and find out what has brought him home so early in the day.'

Giannello promptly got into the tub, whereupon Peronella went and opened the door to her husband, and, pulling a long face, she said:

'What's got into you this morning, coming back home so early? It looks to me, seeing that you're carrying your tools, as if you've decided to take the day off, in which case what are we going to live on? How are we to buy anything to eat? Do you think I'm going to let you pawn my Sunday dress and my other little bits and pieces? Here I am, stuck in this house from morning till night and working my fingers to the bone, so that we shall at least have sufficient oil to keep our lamp alight! Oh, what a husband! I haven't a single neighbour who doesn't gape and laugh at me for slaving away as I do; and yet you come back here twiddling your thumbs when you ought to be out working.'

At this point she burst into tears, then started all over again, saying:

'O alas, woe is me, why was I ever born, what did I do to deserve such a husband! I could have had a decent, hard-working young fellow, and I turned him down to marry this worthless good-for-nothing, who doesn't appreciate what a good wife I am to him. All the other wives have a jolly good time: they have two or three lovers apiece, and they whoop it up under their husbands' noses, whereas for poor little me, just because I am a respectable woman and find that sort of thing distasteful, there's nothing but misery and ill luck. I just can't understand why I don't take one or two lovers, as other women do. It's time you realized, husband, that if I wanted to misbehave, I'd soon find someone to do it with, for there are plenty of sprightly young fellows who love and admire me, and who have offered me large sums of money, or dresses and jewels if I preferred, but not being the daughter of that kind of woman, I never had it in me to accept. And what is my reward? A husband who slopes back home when he ought to be out working.'

'Oh, for Heaven's sake, woman,' said her husband, 'stop making such a song and dance about it. I know how virtuous you are, and as a matter of fact I saw the proof of it this very morning. The fact is that I went to work, but what you don't seem to realize, and I didn't either, is that today is the feast of Saint Galeone[3] and everybody's on holiday, and that's the reason I came home so early. But even so I've made sure that we shall have enough food to last us for over a month. You know that tub that's been cluttering up the house for ages? Well, I've sold it for five silver ducats to this man waiting here on the doorstep.'

Whereupon Peronella said:

'That really does put the lid on it. One would think that since you are a man and get about a good deal, you ought to know the value of things; yet you sell a tub for five silver ducats, which I, a mere woman who hardly ever puts her nose outside the front door, seeing what a nuisance it was to have it in the house, have just sold to an honest fellow here for seven ducats. He's inside the tub now, as a matter of fact, seeing whether it is sound.'

When he heard this, her husband was delighted, and turning to the man who had come to collect the tub, he said:

'Run along now, there's a good fellow. You heard what my wife said. She's sold it for seven, and all you would offer me for it was five.'

'So be it,' said the good fellow, and away he went.

And Peronella said to her husband:

'Now that you are here, you'd better come up and settle this with him yourself.'

Giannello was listening with both ears to see whether there was anything he had to guard against or attend to, and on hearing Peronella's words, he leapt smartly out of the tub. And with a casual sort of air, as though he had heard nothing of the husband's return, he called out:

'Are you there, good woman?'

Whereupon the husband, who was just coming up, said:

'Here I am, what can I do for you?'

'Who the hell are you?' said Giannello. 'It's the woman who was selling me this tub that I wanted to speak to.'

'That's all right,' said the good man. 'You can deal with me: I'm her husband.'

So Giannello said:

'The tub seems to be in pretty good shape, but you appear to have left the lees of the wine in it, for it's coated all over with some hard substance or other that I can't even scrape off with my nails. I'm not going to take it unless it's cleaned out first.'

So Peronella said:

'We made a bargain, and we'll stick to it. My husband will clean it out.'

'But of course,' said the husband. And having put down his tools and rolled up his sleeves, he called for a lamp and a scraping tool, lowered himself into the tub, and began to scrape away. Peronella, as though curious to see what he was doing, leaned over the mouth of the tub, which was not very wide, and resting her head on her arm and shoulder, she issued a stream of instructions, such as: 'Rub it up there, that's it, and there again!' and 'See if you can reach that teeny-weeny bit left at the top.'

While she was busy instructing and directing her husband in this fashion, Giannello, who had not fully gratified his desires that morning before the husband arrived, seeing that he couldn't do it in the way he wished, contrived to bring it off as best he could. So he went up to Peronella, who was completely blocking up the mouth of the tub, and in the manner of a wild and hot-blooded stallion mounting a Parthian mare[4] in the open fields, he satisfied his young man's passion, which no sooner reached fulfilment than the scraping of the tub was completed, whereupon he stood back, Peronella withdrew her head from the tub, and the husband clambered out.

Then Peronella said to Giannello:

'Here, take this lamp, my good man, and see whether the job's been done to your satisfaction.'

Having taken a look inside the tub, Giannello told her everything was fine, and he was satisfied. He then handed seven silver ducats to the husband, and got him to carry it round to his house.

THIRD STORY

Friar Rinaldo goes to bed with his godchild's mother; her husband finds them together in the bedroom, and they give him to understand that the Friar was charming away the child's worms.

Filostrato's reference to the Parthian mare was not so abstruse as to prevent the alert young ladies from grasping its meaning and having a good laugh, albeit they pretended to be laughing for another reason. But when the king saw that the story was finished, he called upon Elissa to speak, and she promptly obeyed, beginning as follows:

Winsome ladies, Emilia's exorcizing of the werewolf has reminded me of a story about another incantation, and although it is not so fine a tale as hers, it is the only one I can think of for the moment that is relevant to our theme, and I shall therefore relate it to you.

You are to know that there once lived in Siena a dashing young man of respectable parentage, Rinaldo by name, who had fallen desperately in love with the very beautiful wife of a wealthy neighbour of his. Having convinced himself that if only he could find a way of conversing with her in private he would obtain all he wanted from her, he resolved, since the woman was pregnant and he could think of no other pretext, to offer himself as the child's godfather;[1] so having made friends with the woman's husband, he put this proposition to him in as tactful a way as he could manage, and it was all agreed.

Having thus strengthened his hand by becoming the godfather to Madonna Agnesa's child, which gave him a slightly more plausible excuse for conversing with her, he conveyed to her in so many words what had long been apparent to her from the gleam in his eyes. But his words made little impression on the lady, though she was not displeased to have heard them.

Not long afterwards, for reasons best known to himself, Rinaldo decided to become a friar, and there were clearly some good

pickings to be had, for he persevered in that profession. Although at
first he put aside his love for his neighbour's wife and gave up
one or two of his other vices, nevertheless in the course of time,
without abandoning the habit of his Order, he reverted to his former
ways; and he began to take a pride in his appearance, wear expensively
tailored cassocks, affect an air of sprightliness and elegance in
all his doings, compose canzonets and sonnets and *ballades*, sing
various songs, and engage in countless other activities of a similar
nature.

But why do I ramble on about this Friar Rinaldo of ours? Is there
a single one of these friars who behaves any differently? Ah, scandal
of this corrupt and wicked world! It doesn't worry them in the least
that they appear so fat and bloated, that a bright red glow suffuses
their cheeks, that their clothes are smooth as velvet, and that in all
their dealings they are so effeminate; yet they are anything but
dovelike, for they strut about like so many proud peacocks with all
their feathers on display. Furthermore, their cells are stuffed with
jars filled with unguents and electuaries, with boxes full of various
sweetmeats, with phials and bottles containing oils and liquid es-
sences, and with casks brimming over with Malmsey and Greek and
other precious wines, so that to any impartial observer they look
more like scent shops or grocery stores than the cells of friars. But
what is worse, they are not ashamed to admit that they suffer from
gout, as though it were not widely known and recognized that
regular fasting, a meagre and simple diet, and a sober way of life
make people lean and slender, and for the most part healthy. Or at
least, if they produce infirmity, this does not take the form of gout,
for which the remedy usually prescribed is continence and all the
other features of a humble friar's existence. Moreover, they think
we are too stupid to realize that a frugal life, lengthy vigils, prayer
and self-restraint ought to give to people a pale and drawn appearance, and that neither Saint Dominic nor Saint Francis had four
cloaks apiece, or swaggered about in habits that were elegantly
tailored and finely woven, but clad themselves in coarse woollen
garments of a natural colour, made to keep out the cold. However,
God will doubtless see that they, and the simple souls who keep
them supplied with all these things, receive their just deserts.

As I was saying, then, Friar Rinaldo was filled once more with all his earlier cravings, and began to pay regular visits to the mother of his godchild. And having become more self-confident, he entreated her to grant his wishes with greater persistence than ever.

One day, Friar Rinaldo importuned her so repeatedly that the good lady, finding herself under so much pressure and thinking him more handsome, perhaps, than he had seemed to her in the past, resorted to the expedient that all women fall back upon when they are itching to concede what is being asked of them, and said:

'Come now, Friar Rinaldo! Do you mean to say that friars indulge in that sort of thing?'

'Madam,' he replied, 'from the moment I am rid of this habit, which I can slip off with the greatest of ease, I shall no longer seem a friar to you, but a man who is made no differently from the rest.'

The lady puckered her lips in a smile, and said:

'Heaven help me, you are my child's godfather; how could you suggest such a thing? It would be awfully wicked; in fact I was always told it was one of the worst sins anyone could commit, otherwise I should be only too willing to do as you suggest.'

'If that's the only thing that deters you,' said Friar Rinaldo, 'then you're just being silly. I don't say it isn't a sin, but God forgives greater sins than this to those who repent. However, tell me this, to whom is this child of yours more closely related: myself, who held him at his baptism, or your husband, by whom he was begotten?'

'My husband, naturally,' she replied.

'Exactly,' said the friar, 'and doesn't your husband go to bed with you?'

'Of course he does,' the lady replied.

'Well then,' said the friar, 'since your husband's more closely akin to the child than I am, surely I can do the same.'

Since logic was not one of her strong points, and she needed little persuasion in any case, the lady either believed or pretended to believe that the friar was speaking the truth, and she replied:

'How could anyone refute so sensible an argument?'

After which, notwithstanding the fact that he was her child's godfather, she allowed him to have his will of her. And thereafter, having taken the first step, they forgathered very frequently, for his sponsorship of the child made it easy for him to come and go without arousing suspicion.

On one of these occasions, having called at the lady's house with one of his fellow friars, to discover that she was alone except for the child and a very pretty and attractive little maidservant, he packed his companion off to the attic to teach the wench the Lord's Prayer, whilst he and the lady, who was holding her little boy by the hand, made their way into her bedroom, locking the door behind them. And having settled down on a sofa, they began to have a merry time of it together.

But while they were carrying on in this fashion, the child's father happened to return home, and before anyone realized he was there, he was knocking at the door of the bedroom and calling for his wife.

Hearing his voice, Madonna Agnesa said:

'Oh my God, I'm done for, that's my husband. Now he's bound to discover why you and I are always so friendly.'

'That's true enough,' said Friar Rinaldo, who had nothing on except his vest, having discarded his habit and his hood. 'If only I had my clothes on, we could invent some explanation. But if you open the door and he sees me like this, no excuse can possibly do any good.'

Then the woman had a sudden inspiration. 'You get dressed,' she said, 'and as soon as you've got your clothes on, take your godson in your arms and listen carefully to what I shall say to him, so that you can back me up later. But in the meantime, leave everything to me.'

Scarcely had the good man finished knocking at the door, when his wife replied:

'All right, I'm coming.' And, getting up, she went and opened the bedroom door, looking a picture of innocence.

'Oh, husband,' she said, 'I tell you it was God who sent our neighbour Friar Rinaldo to us today, for if he hadn't come, we should certainly have lost our child.'

'What's this?' exclaimed the poor fool of a husband, turning white as a sheet.

'Oh, husband,' said the woman, 'a short while ago, the child fell into a sudden faint, and I thought he must be dead. I was so terrified that I could neither move nor speak, but just at that moment our neighbour Friar Rinaldo turned up. He took the child in his arms and said: "Neighbour, these are worms that he has in his body, and if they were to come any closer to his heart, they could easily be the death of him. But don't you worry, because I am going to cast a spell on them and kill them all off. And before I leave this house the child will be as fit and well as you have ever known him." He wanted you to recite some special prayers, but the maid couldn't find you, so he got a companion of his to recite them in the highest part of the house, while he and I came in here with the child. And since it is only the mother who can be of service in matters of this sort, we locked ourselves in so that we shouldn't be disturbed. He still has the child in his arms, and all he's waiting for now, I think, is to hear from his companion that the prayers have been said, and then the spell will be complete, for already the child is quite himself again.'

The simple soul believed all this nonsense, being so overwhelmed by his concern for the child that he never stopped to think that his wife could be deceiving him. And fetching a deep sigh, he said:

'I want to go and see him.'

'Don't go to him yet,' said the woman, 'or you'll ruin what's been done. Wait here while I go and see whether it's all right for you to come in, and I'll give you a call.'

Friar Rinaldo, who had overheard the entire conversation and put on his clothes with time to spare, took the child in his arms, and when he had arranged things to his liking, he called out:

'Is that the father's voice I can hear out there, my dear?'

'It is indeed,' our simple friend replied.

'In that case,' said Friar Rinaldo, 'come along in.'

The simpleton went in, and Friar Rinaldo said to him:

'Here, take this child, who has been restored to health by the grace of God, when at one time I never thought you would see him alive at vespers. I suggest that you commission a wax figure, the same size as the child, and have it placed to the glory of God in front of the statue of Saint Ambrose, through whose merits God has granted you this favour.'

On catching sight of its father, the boy ran up and made a great fuss of him, as small children do, whereupon the father took him in his arms, and, with tears flowing down his cheeks as though he were snatching him up from the grave, he began to rain kisses on the child and thank his neighbour for saving his life.

Friar Rinaldo's companion had meanwhile taught the pretty little maidservant not merely one Lord's Prayer but possibly as many as four, and had presented her with a white linen purse that had been given to him by a nun, thus making her his devotee. When he heard the simpleton calling to his wife at the door of her bedroom, he quietly went and stood in a place from which he could see and hear all that was going on; and on finding that everything was proceeding so smoothly, he came downstairs, entered the bedroom, and said:

'I've recited all four of those prayers that you asked me to say, Friar Rinaldo.'

'Brother,' said Friar Rinaldo, 'you've done an excellent job and I admire your stamina. I personally managed to recite only two before my neighbour turned up. But through our combined efforts the Lord God has granted our request, and the child is cured.'

Then the simpleton called for choice wines and sweetmeats, and regaled his neighbour and the other friar with exactly the sort of pick-me-up they needed, after which he accompanied them to the door and bade them a grateful farewell. And without any delay he had the waxen image made, and sent it to be hung with the others in front of the statue of Saint Ambrose, but not the one from Milan.[2]

FOURTH STORY

Tofano locks his wife out of the house one night, and his wife, having pleaded with him in vain to let her in, pretends to throw herself down a well, into which she hurls an enormous stone. Tofano emerges from the house and rushes to the well, whereupon she steals inside, bolts the door on her husband, and rains abuse upon him at the top of her voice.

No sooner did the king perceive that Elissa's story was at an end, than he turned towards Lauretta, indicating that he wanted her to speak next; and without hesitation she began as follows:

O Love, how manifold and mighty are your powers! How wise your counsels, how keen your insights! What philosopher, what artist could ever have conjured up all the arguments, all the subterfuges, all the explanations that you offer spontaneously to those who nail their colours to your mast? Every other doctrine is assuredly behindhand in comparison with yours, as may clearly be seen from the cases already brought to our notice. And to these, fond ladies, I shall now add yet another, by telling you of the expedient adopted by a woman of no great intelligence, who to my way of thinking could only have been motivated by Love.

In the city of Arezzo,[1] then, there once lived a man of means, Tofano by name, who, having taken to wife a woman of very great beauty, called Monna Ghita, promptly grew jealous of her without any reason. On perceiving how jealous he was, the lady took offence and repeatedly asked him to explain the reason, but since he could only reply in vague and illogical terms, she resolved to make him suffer in good earnest from the ill which hitherto he had feared without cause.

Having observed that a certain young man, a very agreeable sort of fellow to her way of thinking, was casting amorous glances in her direction, she secretly began to cultivate his acquaintance. And when she and the young man had carried the affair to the point where it only remained to translate words into deeds, she once again took the initiative and devised a way of doing it. She had already discovered that one of her husband's bad habits was a fondness for drink, and so she began not only to commend him for it, but to encourage him deliberately whenever she had the chance. With a little practice, she quickly acquired the knack of persuading him to drink himself into a stupor almost as often as she chose, and once she saw that he was blind drunk, she put him to bed and forgathered with her lover. This soon became a regular habit of theirs, and they met together in perfect safety. Indeed, the lady came to rely so completely on the fellow's talent for drinking himself unconscious that she made bold, not only to admit her lover to the premises, but on occasion to go and spend a goodly part of the night with him at his own house, which was no great distance away.

The amorous lady had been doing this for quite some time when her unfortunate husband happened to notice that although she encouraged him to drink, she herself never drank at all, which made him suspect (as was indeed the case) that his wife was making him drunk so that she could do as she pleased when he was asleep. In order to prove whether this was so, he returned home one evening, having refrained from drinking for the whole day, and pretended to be as drunk as a lord, scarcely able to speak or stand on his feet. Being taken in by all this, and concluding that he would sleep like a log without imbibing any more liquor, his wife quickly put him to bed, then left the house and made her way, as on previous occasions, to the house of her lover, where she stayed for half the night.

Hearing no sound from his wife, Tofano got up, went and bolted the door from the inside, and stationed himself at the window so that he would see her coming back and let her know that he had tumbled to her mischief; and there he remained until she returned. Great indeed was the woman's distress when she came home to find that she was locked out, and she began to apply all her strength in an effort to force the door open.

Tofano put up with this for a while, then he said:

'You're wasting your energies, woman. You can't possibly get in. Go back to wherever it is that you've been until this hour of the night, and rest assured that you won't return to this house till I've made an example of you in front of your kinsfolk and neighbours.'

Then his wife began to plead with him for the love of God to let her in, saying that she had not been doing anything wrong, as he supposed, but simply keeping vigil with a neighbour of hers, who could neither sleep the whole night because it was too long, nor keep vigil in the house by herself.

Her pleas were totally unavailing, for the silly ass was clearly determined that all the Aretines should learn about his dishonour, of which none of them had so far heard anything. And when she saw that it was no use pleading with him, the woman resorted to threats, and said:

'If you don't let me in, I shall make you the sorriest man on earth.'

To which Tofano replied:

'And how are you going to do that?'

The lady had all her wits about her, for Love was her counsellor, and she replied:

'Rather than face the dishonour which in spite of my innocence you threaten me with, I shall hurl myself into this well, and when they find me dead inside it, they will all think that it was you who threw me into it when you were drunk; and so either you will have to run away, lose everything you possess, and live in exile, or you will have your head chopped off for murdering your wife, which in effect is what you will have done.'

Having made up his stupid mind, Tofano was not affected in the slightest by these words, and so his wife said:

'Now look here, I won't let you torment me any longer: may God forgive you, I'll leave my distaff here, and you can put it back where it belongs.'

The night was so dark that you could scarcely see your hand in front of your face, and having uttered these words, the woman groped her way towards the well, picked up an enormous stone that was lying beside it, and with a cry of 'God forgive me!' she dropped it into the depths. The stone struck the water with a tremendous thump, and when Tofano heard this he was firmly convinced that she had thrown herself in. So he seized the pail and its rope, rushed headlong from the house, and ran to the well to assist her. His wife was lying in wait near the front door, and as soon as she saw him running to the well, she stepped inside the house, bolted the door, and went to the window, where she stood and shouted:

'You should water down your wine when you're drinking it, and not in the middle of the night.'

When he heard her voice, Tofano saw that he had been outwitted and made his way back to the house. And on finding that he couldn't open the door, he ordered her to let him in.

Whereas previously she had addressed him in little more than a whisper, his wife now began to shout almost at the top of her voice, saying:

'By the cross of God, you loathsome sot, you're not going to come in here tonight. I will not tolerate this conduct of yours any longer. It's time I showed people the sort of man you are and the hours you keep.'

Being very angry, Tofano too began to shout, pouring out a stream of abuse, so that the neighbours, men and women alike, hearing all this racket, got up out of bed and appeared at their windows, demanding to know what was going on.

The woman's eyes filled with tears, and she said: 'It's this villain of a man, who returns home drunk of an evening, or else he falls asleep in some tavern or other and then comes back at this hour. I've put up with it for God knows how long and remonstrated with him until I was blue in the face. But I can't put up with it any longer, and so I've decided to take him down a peg or two by locking him out, to see whether he will mend his ways.'

Tofano on the other hand, like the fool that he was, explained precisely what had happened, and came out with a whole lot of threats and abuse, whereupon his wife spoke up again, saying to the neighbours:

'You see the sort of man he is! What would you say if I were in the street and he was in the house, instead of the other way round? In God's faith I've no doubt you would believe what he was saying. So you can see what a crafty fellow he is. He accuses me of doing the very thing that he appears to have done himself. He thought he could frighten me by dropping something or other down the well; but I wish to God that he really had thrown himself in, and drowned himself at the same time, so that all the wine he's been drinking would have been well and truly diluted.'

The neighbours, men and women alike, all began to scold Tofano, putting the blame on him alone and reviling him for slandering his poor wife; and in brief, they created such an uproar that it eventually reached the ears of the woman's kinsfolk.

Her kinsfolk hurried to the scene, and having listened to the accounts of several of the neighbours, they took hold of Tofano and hammered him till he was black and blue. They then went into the house, collected all the woman's belongings, and took her back with them, threatening Tofano with worse to follow.

Seeing what a sorry plight he had landed himself in on account of his jealousy, Tofano, since he was really very fond of his wife, persuaded certain friends of his to intercede on his behalf with the lady's kinsfolk, with whom he succeeded in making his peace and arranging for her to come back to him. And not only did he promise her that he would never be jealous again, but he gave her permission to amuse herself to her heart's content, provided she was sensible enough not to let him catch her out. So, like the stupid peasant, he first was mad and then was pleasant. Long live love, therefore, and a plague on all skinflints!

FIFTH STORY

A jealous husband disguises himself as a priest and confesses his wife, by whom he is given to understand that she loves a priest who comes to her every night. And whilst the husband is secretly keeping watch for him at the front door, the wife admits her lover by way of the roof and passes the time in his arms.

Thus Lauretta brought her tale to an end, and after everyone had commended the lady for treating her reprobate husband as he deserved, the king, not wanting to waste any time, turned to Fiammetta and graciously entrusted her with the telling of the next story; and she therefore began, as follows:

Illustrious ladies, I too am prompted, after listening to the

previous tale, to tell you about a jealous husband, for in my estima-
tion they deserve all the suffering their wives may inflict upon them,
especially when they are jealous without reason. And if the law-
givers had taken all things into account, I consider that in this respect
the punishment they prescribed for wives should have been no
different from that which they prescribe for the person who attacks
another in self-defence. For no young wife is safe against the
machinations of a jealous husband, who will stop at nothing to
destroy her.

After being cooped up for the whole week looking after the
house and the family, like everyone else she yearns on Sundays for
peace and comfort, and wants to enjoy herself a little, just as farm-
labourers do, or the workers in the towns, or the magistrates on the
bench; just as God did, in fact, when on the seventh day He rested
from all His labours. And indeed, it is laid down in both canon and
civil law, which aim to promote the glory of God and the common
good of the people, that working days should be distinguished from
days of rest. But jealous husbands will have none of this: on the
contrary, when other women are enjoying their day of rest, their
own wives are more wretched and miserable than ever, for they are
kept more securely under lock and key; and only those poor
creatures who have had to put up with this sort of treatment can
describe how exhausting it all is. To sum up, therefore, no matter
what a wife may do to a husband who is jealous without cause, she
is surely to be commended rather than condemned.

But turning now to the story, there once lived in Rimini a very
rich merchant and landowner, who, having married an exceedingly
beautiful woman, became inordinately jealous of her. He had no
other reason for this except that, because he loved her a great deal
and thought her very beautiful and knew that she did everything
she could to please him, he concluded that every other man must feel
the same about her, and also that she would take just as much trouble
to please other men as she did in pleasing her husband. And in his
jealousy he kept such a constant watch upon her and guarded her so
closely, that I doubt whether many of those condemned to death
are guarded by their gaolers with the same degree of vigilance.

It wasn't just a question of her not being able to attend a party or a wedding, or go to church, or step outside her door for a single moment: he wouldn't even allow her to stand at the window or cast so much as a solitary glance outside the house. Her life thus became a complete misery, and her suffering was all the more difficult to bear in that she had done nothing to deserve it.

For her own amusement, finding herself persecuted so unfairly by her husband, the lady cast about her to see whether she could find any way of supplying him with a just and proper motive for his jealousy. Not being allowed to stand at the window, she was unable to offer signs of encouragement to any potential suitor who might be passing her way. But knowing there was a handsome and agreeable young man in the house next door, she calculated that if she could find a crack in the wall separating their two houses, she could keep on peering through it until an opportunity arose of speaking to the youth and offering him her love if he was prepared to accept it, after which, provided they could find some way of doing it, they could come together once in a while. And in this way she could keep body and soul together until her husband came to his senses.

So when her husband was not at home, she went from room to room carefully inspecting the wall, until eventually, in a very remote part of the house, she came across a place where it was cracked. She peered through to the other side, and although she could not make very much out, she could see enough to realize that it was a bedroom, and she said to herself: 'If this turned out to be the bedroom of Filippo' (the name of the youth next door) 'there wouldn't be much left for me to do.' So she got one of her maidservants, who was feeling rather sorry for her, to keep watch whenever there was nobody about, and discovered that it was indeed the young man's bedroom, and that he slept there all by himself. By paying regular visits to the crack in the wall, and dropping tiny pieces of stone and straw through the opening whenever she could hear the young man on the other side, she eventually succeeded in getting him to come and investigate. Then she called to him in a low whisper, and the young man, recognizing her voice, replied; whereupon, since there was no likelihood of her

being disturbed, she briefly told him what she had in mind. Overjoyed, the young man proceeded to widen the hole on his own side
of the wall, which he did in such a way that nobody would notice,
and from then on they would very often talk to each other there
and touch one another's hands, though it was impossible to do
more on account of the strict watch maintained by the jealous
husband.

Now, seeing that Christmas was approaching, the lady told her
husband that she would like, with his permission, to attend church
on Christmas morning and go to confession and Holy Communion
like any other Christian.

'And what sins have you committed,' said the jealous husband,
'that you want to go to confession?'

'Oh, really!' she exclaimed. 'Do you think I'm a saint, just
because you keep me locked up? You know very well that I have
my sins just as other people do, but I'm not going to reveal them to
you, because you're not a priest.'

Her words made the husband suspicious, and he decided to try
and find out what these sins were. So he granted her request, but
told her that she could only go to their own chapel and not to any
of the other churches. Moreover, she was to go there early in the
morning, and be confessed, either by their own chaplain or by the
priest whom the chaplain allotted to her, and not by anybody else,
after which she was to come straight back to the house. The lady
had a shrewd suspicion that it was some sort of trap, but asked no
questions and replied that she would do as he wished.

On the morning of Christmas Day, the lady got up at dawn, and
as soon as she was neatly dressed she went to the church her
husband had specified. Meanwhile he too had risen and made his
way to the same church, arriving there before she did. And having
explained to the chaplain what he was proposing to do, he disguised
himself in the robes of a priest, with a large hood that came down
over his cheeks, like the ones that are often worn by priests; this he
pulled forward a little, so as to conceal his features, then he seated
himself in one of the pews.

On arriving at the church, the lady asked to speak to the
chaplain. So the chaplain came, and when she told him that she

wanted to be confessed, he said he was too busy, but would send her one of his fellow priests. He then went away, and sent the jealous husband, unfortunately for him, to hear her confession. The husband walked solemnly up to her, and although the light was not very good and he had pulled the hood well down over his eyes, she knew immediately who it was, and said to herself: 'God be praised, the fellow's turned from a jealous husband into a priest; but never mind, I'll see that he gets what he's looking for.' And pretending not to recognize him, she seated herself at his feet.[1]

Master Jealous had stuffed a few bits of gravel in his mouth so as to impede his speech and prevent his wife from recognizing his voice, and he thought that his disguise was so perfect in all other respects that she was bound to be taken in by it.

But to come now to the confession, among the things which the lady told him, having first of all pointed out that she was married, was that she had fallen in love with a priest, who came to her every night and slept with her.

When he heard this, the jealous husband felt as though a knife had been driven into his heart; and but for the fact that he was eager to know more about it, he would have abandoned the confession there and then, and taken himself off. However, he stood his ground, and said to her:

'What's this I hear? Doesn't your husband sleep with you?'

'Oh yes, Father,' she replied.

'In that case,' said the husband, 'how can the priest sleep with you as well?'

'Father,' said the lady, 'it's a mystery to me how the priest manages to do it, but there isn't a door in the house that is so securely locked that it doesn't spring open the moment he touches it. He tells me that before opening the door of my bedroom, he recites a certain formula that sends my husband straight off to sleep, and as soon as he hears him snoring, he opens the door, comes into the bedroom, and lies down at my side. And the system never fails.'

'Madam,' he said, 'this is an evil business, and you must put a stop to it at all costs.'

'Father,' said the lady, 'I don't think I could ever do that, for I love him too dearly.'

'Then I cannot give you absolution,' he said.

'I am sorry about that,' said the lady. 'But I didn't come here to tell lies, and if I thought I could do as you are asking, I should tell you so.'

'I am truly sorry for you, madam,' he said, 'for I see that your soul will be lost if this is allowed to continue. But I will do you a favour, and go to the trouble of saying certain special prayers to God on your behalf, which may possibly assist you. I shall send one of my seminarists to call on you, and you are to tell him whether or not my prayers have had any effect. And if they achieve their object, we can go on from there.'

'Oh, Father,' she said, 'don't send anyone to the house, because if my husband were to hear about it, he is so madly jealous that nothing in the world could dissuade him from believing that some great evil was afoot, and he'd be impossible to live with for a whole year.'

'Don't worry about that,' he said, 'for I shall make sure that everything is so discreetly arranged that you won't hear a word out of him.'

'If you can manage to do that,' said the lady, 'then I have no objection.' And after reciting the *Confiteor* and receiving her penance, she got up from where she was kneeling at his feet and went off to listen to the mass.

Fuming with rage, the luckless husband went away, abandoned his priestly disguise, and returned home, determined to find a way of catching this priest and his wife together, so that he could bring the pair of them to book. When his wife came back from the church, she saw from the expression on her husband's face that she had spoilt his Christmas for him; but he tried as best he could to conceal what he had done and what he thought he had discovered.

After breakfast, having made up his mind to spend the following night lying in wait near the front door to see whether the priest would turn up, he said to his wife:

'I have to go out to supper this evening, and I won't be back till the morning, so take good care to lock the front door, the landing door, and the bedroom door, and go to bed when you feel like it.'

'Very well,' said the lady.

As soon as she had the chance, she went to the hole in the wall and gave the usual signal, which Filippo no sooner heard than he came to the spot. She then gave him an account of what she had done that morning, and told him what her husband had said to her after breakfast, then she said:

'I'm certain he won't leave the house: he's just going to keep watch at the front door. So climb up on to the roof tonight and find your way in here, so that we can be together.'

The young man was delighted with this turn of events, and said:

'My lady, leave everything to me.'

As soon as it was dark, the jealous husband crept into hiding, armed to the teeth, in one of the rooms on the ground floor, and his wife, having locked all the doors, in particular the one on the landing so that her husband could not come up, bided her time in her room. When the coast was clear, the young man picked his way carefully over the roof from his own room to hers, and they got into bed, where they had a blissful time and a merry one together until dawn next morning, when he returned to his own house.

The husband, supperless, aching all over, and freezing to death, waited practically the whole night beside the front door with his weapons at the ready, to see whether the priest would turn up; and just before daybreak, being unable to keep his eyes open any longer, he dropped off to sleep in the ground-floor room.

A little before tierce[2] he woke up to find the front door already unlocked, and pretending that he had just arrived home he went upstairs and had his breakfast. Shortly after breakfast he sent a young servant to his wife, disguised as the seminarist of the priest who had confessed her, to ask her whether 'that certain person' had called upon her again.

His wife, who recognized the messenger very easily, replied that he had failed to call for once, and that if he continued to absent himself she might very well forget all about him, although she would be sorry if this were to happen.

What more remains to be said? For night after night, the jealous husband lay in wait for the priest, and his wife lay in bed with her lover, till eventually, being unable to contain himself any longer, he flew into a tearing rage and demanded to know what his wife had said to the priest on the morning she had gone to confession. She told him that his question was neither fair nor proper, and refused to answer it, whereupon he exclaimed:

'Loathsome woman, whether you like it or not I know exactly what you said to him, and I absolutely insist on knowing the name of this priest with whom you're so infatuated and who uses magic spells to sleep with you every night, otherwise I shall slit your gullet.'

His wife told him it was untrue that she was infatuated with a priest.

'What!' he cried. 'Isn't that what you said to the priest who confessed you?'

'As a matter of fact I did,' said his wife. 'But I can't imagine how you came to be so well informed. You must have been eavesdropping.'

'Never mind about that,' said her husband. 'Just tell me who this priest is, and be quick about it.'

His wife began to smile, and said:

'It's an edifying sight, I must say, when a mere woman leads an intelligent man by the nose, as though she were leading a ram by its horns to the slaughter. Not that you are all that intelligent, nor ever have been since the day you allowed the evil spirit of jealousy to enter your heart, without any obvious reason. And the more thickheaded and stupid you are, the lesser my achievement.

'Do you suppose, dear husband, that my eyes are as defective as your reasoning? Because if so, you're greatly mistaken. I recognized my confessor from the moment I set eyes on him, I knew perfectly well it was you. I was determined to let you have what you were looking for, and I succeeded. But if you were as clever as you imagine, you would never have resorted to that sort of trick for discovering the secrets of your good little wife; nor would you have become a prey to idle suspicion, for you would have realized that she was confessing the truth to you without having sinned in the least.

'I told you I was in love with a priest: but is it not a fact that you, whom I am misguided enough to love, had turned into a priest? I told you he could open any door in the house when he wanted to come and sleep with me: but which of the doors in your own house has ever prevented you from coming to me, no matter where I happened to be? I told you the priest slept with me every night: but haven't you always slept with me? And as you know very well, every time you sent that seminarist of yours to me, you had slept elsewhere, and so I sent you word that the priest had not been with me. How could anybody, other than a man who had allowed himself to be blinded by his jealousy, have been witless enough not to understand all this? But in your case, what do you do? You spin me some yarn every evening about going out to supper and staying the night with friends, then hang about the house keeping an all-night vigil at the front door.

'Isn't it time that you took yourself in hand, started behaving like a man again, and stopped allowing yourself to be made such a fool of by someone who knows you as well as I do? Leave off keeping such a strict watch over me, because I swear to God that if I were to set my heart on making you a cuckold, I should have my fling and you'd be none the wiser.'

And so it was that the jealous wretch, having thought himself very clever in ferreting out his wife's secret, saw that he had made an ass of himself. Without saying anything by way of reply, he began to look upon his wife as a model of intelligence and virtue. And just as he had worn the mantle of the jealous husband when it was unnecessary, he cast it off completely now that his need for it was paramount. So his clever little wife, having, as it were, acquired a licence to enjoy herself, no longer admitted her lover by way of the roof as though he were some kind of cat, but showed him in at the front door. And from that day forth, by proceeding with caution, she spent many an entertaining and delightful hour in his arms.

SIXTH STORY

Whilst she is entertaining Leonetto, Madonna Isabella is visited by Messer Lambertuccio, who has fallen in love with her. Her husband returning unexpectedly, she sends Messer Lambertuccio running forth from the house with a dagger in his hand, and Leonetto is taken home a little later on by her husband.

Fiammetta's story was marvellously pleasing to the whole company, and everyone declared that the wife had taught the stupid man a salutary lesson. But now that this tale was concluded, the king enjoined Pampinea to tell the next, and she began:

Many are those who naïvely maintain that Love impairs the intellect[1] and that anyone falling in love is more or less turned into a fool. This, it seems to me, is a ridiculous assertion, as is amply proved by the stories we have heard so far, as well as by the one I now propose to relate.

In our fair city, where the good things of life are to be found in great abundance, there once lived a gently bred and exceedingly beautiful young woman, who was married to a nobleman of great worthiness and excellence. But just as it frequently happens that people grow tired of always eating the same food, and desire a change of diet, so this lady, being somewhat dissatisfied with her husband, fell in love with a young man called Leonetto, who, albeit his origins were humble, was extremely agreeable and accomplished. He too fell in love with her, and since it is unusual, as you know, for nothing to ensue when both of the parties are agreed, not much time elapsed before they consummated their love.

Now, because she was such a charming and beautiful woman, it happened that a gentleman called Messer Lambertuccio fell desperately in love with her, but as she thought him very tiresome and disagreeable, she could not be persuaded to love him on any account. The fellow kept pestering her with a stream of messages, however, and when these failed to have any effect, being a man of considerable influence, he threatened to ruin her if she refused to yield. Hence the lady was filled with fear and trembling, and knowing the sort of man he was, she brought herself to do his bidding. But having gone to stay, as we Florentines are apt to do in the summer, at her beautiful country villa, the lady, whose name was Madonna Isabella, sent word to Leonetto that he was to come and keep her company, since her husband had ridden off that morning, saying that he would be away for the next few days. Leonetto was overjoyed, and made his way to the villa post-haste.

Meanwhile, Messer Lambertuccio, hearing that the lady's husband was not at home, saddled his horse, rode unaccompanied to the villa, and knocked at the door.

The lady's maid, seeing who it was, immediately went to warn her mistress, who was in her bedroom with Leonetto, and having called her forth, she said:

'Messer Lambertuccio is downstairs, ma'am, and he's all alone.'

The lady was aggrieved beyond measure to hear of Lambertuccio's arrival, but as she was so afraid of him, she asked Leonetto if he would mind concealing himself for a while behind the curtains of the bed until such time as he should take his leave of her.

Leonetto, being no less terrified of the man than she was herself, hid behind the bed, and she told her maid to go and let Messer Lambertuccio in. This she did, and having ridden into the courtyard, he dismounted, tethered his palfrey to a ring, and came up the stairs. The lady came to meet him, smiling, at the head of the stairs, and having bidden him a cheerful welcome she asked him the nature of his business.

He embraced and kissed her, and said:

'My dearest, I heard that your husband was away, so I've come to keep you company for a while.' And without further preliminaries, they went into the bedroom, and Messer Lambertuccio, having locked the door, proceeded to bend her to his pleasure.

But whilst he was thus tarrying with the lady, to her utter amazement her husband happened to return. No sooner did the maid espy him approaching the villa, than she ran at once to her mistress's bedroom and said:

'It's the master, he's coming back, ma'am. He'll be down there in the yard by now, I should think.'

Finding herself with two men in the house, and knowing it was impossible to conceal the second because his horse was standing in the yard, the lady thought her hour had come. However, with extraordinary presence of mind she leapt out of bed and said to Messer Lambertuccio:

'Sir, if you love me in the slightest degree, and wish to save my life, do as I shall tell you. Take out your dagger, wave it about in your hand, and charge down the stairs like a madman, breathing fire and slaughter, and shouting: "I vow to God I'll catch up with him yet!" If my husband should try to stop you or ask you any questions, keep repeating these same words. And when you reach your horse, leap into the saddle and ride away without stopping for an instant.'

Messer Lambertuccio willingly agreed to do it, and having drawn his dagger, his face all flushed from his recent exertions, as well as from his anger at the husband's return, he carried out the lady's instructions to the letter. The husband, having already dismounted, was puzzling over the palfrey in the courtyard, and was just about to mount the stairs, when he saw Lambertuccio descending. And being taken aback by his words and the wild expression on his face, he said:

'What is the meaning of this, sir?'

But Messer Lambertuccio, having inserted his foot in the stirrup and vaulted into the saddle, uttered not a word, except: 'I swear to God I'll get him, wherever he may be!' And away he rode.

On mounting the staircase, the nobleman found his wife at the top, looking all distressed and terrified, and he said to her:

'What is going on? What has got into Messer Lambertuccio? For whom are these threats of his intended?'

Retreating towards the bedroom so that Leonetto would overhear, the lady replied:

'Oh husband, I've never had such a fright in all my life. Some young man or other came running into the house, with Messer Lambertuccio in pursuit, brandishing a dagger. He burst into my room, the door of which happened to be open, and trembling from head to foot, he said: "Madam, for God's sake save me from being killed and expiring in your arms." I stood up, and I was just about to ask him who he was and what it was all about when Messer Lambertuccio came charging up the stairs, shouting: "Blackguard, where are you?" I stood in the doorway to prevent him coming any further, and when he saw that I didn't want him to enter the room, he had the decency not to insist. And after a long rigmarole, he went rushing off down the stairs, as you saw for yourself.'

'You did the right thing, my dear,' said the husband. 'It would have been a very serious matter for us if anyone had been murdered under our own roof. And it was highly improper of Messer Lambertuccio to pursue a man who had taken refuge within these walls.'

He then asked what had become of the young man, and his wife replied:

'I have no idea where he can have hidden himself.'

So her husband called out:

'Where are you? Come on out, you're quite safe.'

Having overheard everything, Leonetto emerged from his hiding place with an expression of terror all over his features, which was not very surprising considering that he had indeed been frightened out of his wits, and the husband said to him:

'What is your business with Messer Lambertuccio?'

'Sir,' replied the young man, 'I have no business with him whatsoever, and that is why I firmly believe that he is out of his mind, or that he mistook me for somebody else, for no sooner did he see me, a little way down the road, than he drew his dagger and said: "Say your prayers, you blackguard." Without stopping to ask him the reason, I took to my heels and ran in here, where thanks to God and to this kind lady, I escaped from his clutches.'

Then the nobleman said:

'Come now, don't be afraid; I shall see you to your doorstep safe and sound, and then you can have some inquiries made, and discover what it is all about.'

After they had all had supper together, the husband conveyed the young man back to Florence on horseback, and saw him to his own front door. Later that evening, in accordance with instructions he had received from the lady, Leonetto spoke privately with Messer Lambertuccio, and so arranged matters that even though many more words were spoken on the subject, the nobleman never came to know of the trick that his wife had played upon him.

SEVENTH STORY

Lodovico discloses to Madonna Beatrice how deeply he loves her, where-upon she persuades her husband, Egano, to impersonate her in a garden, and goes to bed with Lodovico, who in due course gets up, goes into the garden, and gives Egano a hiding.

The stratagem adopted by Madonna Isabella, as recounted by Pampinea, drew gasps of astonishment from every member of the company. But the king now called upon Filomena to follow, and she said:

Lovesome ladies, unless I am much mistaken I think I can offer you no less splendid a story, which will not take long to relate.

You are to know, then, that in Paris there was once a Florentine nobleman, who on account of his straitened circumstances decided to become a merchant, in which capacity he was so successful that he made a huge fortune. His wife had borne him no more than a single child, to whom he had given the name of Lodovico, and because this child was more of a patrician's son than the son of a merchant, instead of launching him on a career in business the father had secured him a place in the French royal household, where he was brought up with other young nobles and acquired the manners and attributes of a gentleman.

One day, whilst Lodovico happened to be discussing with several other young men the rival merits of various beautiful ladies from France, England, and other parts of the world, they were joined by a number of knights who had recently returned from the Holy Sepulchre. And one of these latter began to maintain that of all the women he had ever seen in the numerous places he had visited, he had never encountered anyone so beautiful as Madonna Beatrice, the wife of Egano de' Galluzzi,[1] who lived in Bologna. Moreover, he claimed that those of his companions who, like himself, had seen the lady in Bologna, were entirely of the same opinion.

Having listened to this gentleman's words, Lodovico, who had never yet fallen in love, was inflamed with such a longing to see her that he could think of nothing else. And having firmly made up his mind to go to Bologna and see this lady, and to stay there for a while if she lived up to his expectations, he gave his father to understand that he wished to go to the Holy Sepulchre, and with the greatest of difficulty obtained his permission.

He therefore assumed the name of Anichino, and came to Bologna, where, as luck would have it, on the day following his arrival he saw the lady at a banquet, and discovered that her beauty was even greater than he had been led to believe. Hence he was swept completely off his feet, and resolved never to leave Bologna until he had won her love. Having given some thought to various possible ways of achieving this object, he discarded them one by one, and concluded that his only hope lay in finding employment with the lady's husband, who kept a large household of servants.

He therefore sold all his horses and arranged for his servants to be comfortably lodged, having ordered them to pretend not to know him; and having struck up an acquaintance with the landlord of his inn, he explained that he would like, if possible, to enter the service of some gentleman of standing, whereupon the landlord said:

'You are exactly the kind of attendant who would appeal to a nobleman, Egano by name, who lives in this city and keeps a great many servants. He makes a point of surrounding himself with good-looking fellows like yourself. I'll mention your name to him.'

The landlord was as good as his word, and by the time he had taken his leave of Egano, he had arranged for Anichino to enter his service, which suited Anichino down to the ground.

Now that he was living under Egano's roof, and frequently had occasion to see his lady, he began to serve his master so efficiently, and earned himself so high a place in his esteem, that Egano could do nothing without consulting him beforehand; and he placed not only his own person, but all of his affairs under Anichino's control.

Now one day Egano went out hawking, leaving Anichino at home, and Madonna Beatrice, who so far knew nothing of his love for her, albeit she had often had occasion to observe his ways and had formed a very good opinion of his character, invited him to play chess[2] with her. Anichino, wishing to make her happy, played his pieces very skilfully and allowed her to beat him, which sent the lady into transports of joy. And when the lady's attendants, who had been watching the game, had all drifted away and left them alone together, Anichino fetched an enormous sigh.

The lady looked at him, and said:

'What's the matter, Anichino? Does it hurt you so much to be beaten?'

'My lady,' Anichino replied, 'I sighed for a much stronger reason than that.'

So the lady said:

'Alas, if I hold any place in your affection, do tell me what it is.'

At the mention of the place she held in his affection, Anichino, who loved her above everything else in the whole world, heaved a second sigh, much deeper than the first, whereupon the lady pleaded with him once again to explain the reason.

'My lady,' said Anichino, 'I am greatly afraid that you might be offended, if I were to tell you; and for all I know you might repeat it to some other person.'

'I shall certainly not take it amiss,' said the lady, 'and you may rest assured that no matter what you tell me, I shan't repeat a word of it to anyone without your permission.'

So Anichino said:

'Since you give me this assurance, I shall tell you all about it.' And controlling his tears with an effort, he told her who he was, the things he had heard about her, how and where he had fallen in love with her, how he had come to Bologna, and why he had entered her husband's service. Then he humbly asked her whether she could bring herself to take pity on him, and grant him the secret desire that burned so fiercely in his heart. But if she was unwilling to do this, he begged her to be content that he should love her, and allow him to continue in her service.

Ah, how singularly sweet is the blood of Bologna![3] How admirably you rise to the occasion in moments such as these! Sighs and tears were never to your liking: entreaties have always moved you, and you were ever susceptible to a lover's yearnings. If only I could find words with which to commend you as you deserve, I should never grow tired of singing your praises!

Whilst Anichino was speaking, the gentlewoman fixed her gaze

upon him, and being fully convinced of his sincerity, she was so
overcome by his protestations of love that she, too, began to sigh.
And when her sighs had abated, she replied:

'Anichino, my dearest, be of good cheer; many are those that
have wooed me, and that woo me to this day, but neither gifts nor
promises nor fine words have ever succeeded in persuading me to
fall in love with a single one of my admirers, whether he was a
nobleman or a mighty lord or any other man; yet within the brief
space of these few words of yours, you have made me feel that I
belong far more to you than to myself. I consider that you have
well and truly earned my love. I therefore concede it to you, and
before the coming night is over, I promise that it will be yours to
enjoy. In order to bring this about, see that you come to my room
towards midnight. I shall leave the door open. You know the side of
the bed on which I sleep: come to me there, and if I should be
asleep, touch me so that I wake up, and then I shall give you the
solace that you have so long desired. So that you believe what I am
saying, I want to give you a kiss by way of pledge.' Whereupon,
throwing her arms round his neck, she gave him an amorous kiss,
and Anichino did the like to her.

There, for the time being, the matter rested, and Anichino, having
taken his leave of the lady, went off to attend to certain duties of his,
ecstatically looking forward to the coming of the night. Egano
returned home from his hawking, and as soon as he had supped, feeling .
weary, he retired to bed. The lady soon followed his example, and, as
she had promised, she left the door of the bedroom ajar.

Thither, at the appointed hour, Anichino came, and having crept
quietly into the room and bolted the door behind him, he made his
way to the side of the bed where the lady usually slept. Placing his
hand on her bosom, he found that she was not asleep, for she
promptly clasped his hand between both her own, and, holding it
tightly, she twisted and turned in the bed until she succeeded in
waking Egano, to whom she said:

'I didn't want to say anything of this last night, because you
seemed so tired; but tell me truthfully, of all the servants you have
in the house, which do you regard as the finest, the most loyal, and
the most deeply attached to his master?'

'My dear,' Egano replied, 'why do you ask such a question when you know very well that I have never had anyone I could trust so completely, or respect so profoundly, as I trust and respect Anichino?'

On learning that Egano had woken up, and hearing his own name being mentioned, Anichino made several attempts to withdraw his hand so that he could make good his escape, for he strongly suspected that the lady was going to give him away. But she was clasping his hand so firmly that it was impossible for him to retrieve it.

'I'll tell you why,' said the lady, in reply to Egano's question. 'My own opinion of Anichino was the same as yours; I too considered him the most faithful of your servants. But he has undeceived me, for yesterday, when you were out hawking and he stayed behind, he had the impudence, thinking it a good opportunity, to propose that I should minister to his pleasures. And so that I should have no difficulty in providing you with tangible and visible evidence of all this, I gave him my consent and told him that I would go into the garden, shortly after midnight, and wait for him at the foot of the pine-tree. I personally have no intention of going there, of course: but if you desire to know what a trustworthy servant he is, you can easily slip into one of my skirts, cover your head in a veil, and go down there to see whether he turns up, as I am certain he will.'

'I must certainly look into this,' said Egano. So he got out of bed, and, groping around in the darkness, he struggled into one of his wife's skirts as best he could and covered his head in a veil. Then he made his way down to the garden and stood at the foot of the pine-tree, waiting for Anichino to turn up.

As soon as she heard him leaving the bedroom, the lady got up and bolted the door from the inside.

After experiencing the biggest fright that he had ever had in his life, and struggling with all his might to free himself from the lady's grasp, and silently heaping a hundred thousand curses upon the lady and upon himself for loving her and trusting her, Anichino was positively overjoyed when, at the end of it all, he saw what she had done. As soon as the lady had returned to her bed, she urged him to strip off his clothes and get in beside her, and there they lay for quite some time together, to their mutual pleasure and delight.

When the lady thought it was time for Anichino to go, she persuaded him to get up and put on his clothes, saying:

'My darling treasure, find yourself a good stout stick and go down to the garden. Make it appear that you were putting my fidelity to the test, pretend to think that Egano is me, shower him with abuse, and give him a sound thrashing[4] with the stick. Just think of the wonderful joy and amusement it'll bring to us both!'

So Anichino got up and made his way to the garden with a switch of silver willow in his hand, and just as he was approaching the pine-tree, Egano, seeing him coming, stood up and came to meet him, as though with the intention of bidding him a most cordial welcome. But Anichino said:

'So you came after all, did you, you filthy little whore? You thought me capable of wronging my master, did you? A thousand curses upon you!' And raising his stick, he began to beat him.

On hearing this outburst and catching sight of the stick, Egano took to his heels without saying a word, being closely pursued by Anichino, who kept on saying:

'Take that, you shameless hussy, and may God punish you as you deserve! Mark my words, I shall tell Egano of this tomorrow!'

Bruised and battered all over, Egano returned as fast as he could to his bedroom, and his wife asked him whether Anichino had come to the garden.

'Would to God that he hadn't,' said Egano, 'for he mistook me for you, beat me black and blue with a cudgel, and addressed me by the foulest names that any wicked woman was ever called. I must say I thought it very strange that he should have spoken to you as he did with the intention of dishonouring me. But I see now that, finding you so gay and sociable, he simply wanted to put you to the test.'

Then the lady said:

'Thanks be to God that he tested me with words, and saved his deeds for you! At least it can be said that his words tried my patience less severely than his deeds tried yours. But since he is so loyal to you, we should do him honour and hold him high in our esteem.'

'I agree with you entirely,' said Egano.

In view of what had happened, Egano came to the conclusion

that he was blessed with the most faithful wife and the most loyal servant that any nobleman had ever possessed. And for this reason, whilst on many a future occasion they all three had a good laugh over the events of that particular night, at the same time it became far easier than it would otherwise have been for Anichino and the lady to do the thing that brought them pleasure and delight, at any rate for as long as Anichino chose to remain with Egano in Bologna.

EIGHTH STORY

A husband grows suspicious of his wife, and discovers that her lover comes to her at night, forewarning her of his arrival by means of a string attached to her toe. Whilst the husband is giving chase to the lover, his wife gets out of bed and puts another woman in her place, who receives a beating from the husband and has her tresses cut off. The husband then goes to fetch his wife's brothers, who, on discovering that his story is untrue, subject him to a torrent of abuse.

Filomena's listeners were all of the opinion that Madonna Beatrice had adopted a curiously subtle means of duping her husband, and everyone declared that Anichino must have had a terrible fright when the lady was holding him so tightly and he heard her saying that he had made advances to her. The king, however, seeing that Filomena had finished, turned to Neifile and said:

'Now it's your turn.'

Neifile smiled a little, then began:

Fair ladies, if I am to entertain you with a story as excellent as the ones with which you have been regaled by my predecessors, my task will indeed be difficult; but I hope, with God's aid, to give a good account of myself.

You are to know, then, that in our fair city there once lived a very rich merchant called Arriguccio Berlinghieri,[1] who, like many of his counterparts of the present day, foolishly decided to marry into the aristocracy, and took to wife a young gentlewoman, quite unsuited to him, whose name was Monna Sismonda. And since, as is commonly the way with merchants, he was always going out and about and rarely stayed at home with his wife, she fell in love with a young man called Ruberto, who had been courting her for some little time.

Having become his mistress, she took such a delight in his company that she possibly grew a little careless, for Arriguccio, either because he had got wind of the affair or for some other reason, suddenly became exceedingly jealous, and, having stopped going out and about, he left all his other affairs hanging in abeyance, and devoted almost the whole of his time to keeping her under close surveillance. Nor would he ever drop off to sleep until he saw that she was safely abed. Consequently the lady was utterly mortified, because it was now quite impossible for her to be with her Ruberto.

But having given a great deal of thought to devising some means of consorting with her lover, and being under constant pressure from Ruberto himself to find a way out of this impasse, she eventually hit upon the following expedient: since her bedroom overlooked the street, and she had frequently had occasion to observe that Arriguccio, once he was asleep, slept like a log, she would ask Ruberto to come to the front door towards midnight and she would go and let him in. In this way she could spend some time in his arms whilst her husband was soundly asleep. But so that she would know that he had come, she contrived, in such a way that nobody would notice, to dangle a length of string from the bedroom window with its end almost touching the ground; at its other end, the string ran along the floor of the room to the bed, finishing up under the bedclothes, and as soon as she was in bed, she tied it to her big toe.

Ruberto was duly informed beforehand, and she further directed him that, on arriving at the house, he was to give the string a tug, and if her husband was asleep, she would release it and go downstairs to let him in; but if her husband was still awake, she would hold on to the string and haul it in, to let him know that he was to go away. This arrangement suited Ruberto down to the ground, and he made regular use of it, sometimes being able to see her and sometimes not.

They continued to use this ingenious device until one night, when the lady was asleep, Arriguccio happened to stretch his leg down the bed and catch his foot in the string. Having groped for it with his hand and discovered that it was attached to the lady's toe, he said to himself: 'This must clearly be some devilish trick or other.' On observing that the string passed out by the window, he was quite convinced of it; so he gently detached it from the lady's toe, tied it to his own, and waited, alert and vigilant, to see what would happen.

Shortly afterwards, Ruberto came along and jerked the string as usual, giving Arriguccio a start. He had not tied it on properly, and so Ruberto, who had given it a good tug and was left with the string in his hands, assumed that he was to wait, which is what in fact he did.

Arriguccio, having leapt out of bed and buckled on his sword and dagger, rushed to the door to find out who this fellow was, and do him an injury. Now, for all that he was a merchant, Arriguccio was as strong and as fierce as a bull, and in opening the door he made a lot of noise, whereas his wife always opened it quietly. On hearing this, Ruberto, as he waited outside, rightly concluded that the person opening the door was Arriguccio, and so he promptly took to his heels, with Arriguccio in hot pursuit.

Eventually, after running for quite a while without shaking off his pursuer, Ruberto, who was also armed, drew his sword and faced about; and so they began to fight, with Arriguccio attacking and Ruberto defending himself.

Meanwhile, Arriguccio's wife, having woken up as he opened the door of the bedroom, had no sooner found that the string was missing than she realized that her stratagem had been discovered, and on hearing Arriguccio giving chase to Ruberto, she leapt out of bed. Foreseeing what was likely to happen, she summoned her maid, who knew all about the affair, and prevailed upon her to take her own place in the bed, at the same time entreating her to keep her identity a secret and patiently bear all the blows that Arriguccio might give her, for which service she would be so well rewarded that she would have no cause for complaint. And after extinguishing the light that was burning in the bedroom, she went away and concealed herself in another part of the house, and waited to see what would happen.

On hearing Arriguccio and Ruberto fighting with one another, the people living nearby rose from their beds and began to curse and swear at them; and so Arriguccio, for fear of being recognized, broke off the engagement and reluctantly made his way home, seething with anger, having failed either to identify the young man or to injure him in the slightest. And on reaching the bedroom, he began to shout and rave, saying:

'Where are you, strumpet? You thought you'd get away from me by putting out the light, did you? Well, you'd better think again!'

Then, going up to the bed, he took hold of the maidservant, thinking her to be his wife, and kicked and punched her with all the power he had in his feet and hands, until her face was black and blue all over, at the same time addressing her by the foulest names that an unchaste woman was ever called; and finally, he cut off her hair.

The maidservant wept bitterly, and with good reason, but although from time to time she cried out, saying 'Alas, for God's sake have mercy!' or 'Oh, please, no more!' her speech was so distorted by her sobbing, and Arriguccio was so demented with rage, that he failed to notice that the voice was not his wife's.

Having given her an unholy thrashing and cut off her hair, as we have already mentioned, he said:

'Vile hussy, I'll not soil my hands with you any further, but I shall go seek out your brothers and tell them about the fine way you behave. Furthermore, I shall tell them to come and deal with you as their honour requires, and take you away from here, because you're certainly not going to stay in this house any longer.' And having spoken these words, he stormed out of the room, bolted the door on the outside, and strode off, all alone, into the night.

Monna Sismonda had been listening the whole time, and as soon as she heard her husband leaving the house, she opened the bedroom door and re-lit the lamp, to discover her maidservant lying there, all bruised and battered, and crying her eyes out. Having consoled her as best she could, she led the girl back to her own room, where she covertly arranged for her to be nursed back to health and waited upon, and rewarded her so handsomely from Arriguccio's own coffers that the girl was more than contented.

No sooner was the maid safely bestowed in her room than Monna Sismonda returned, remade the bed, and tidied up the whole room so as to make it look as if no one had slept there. Having re-lit the main lamp, she dressed herself and combed her hair to give the impression that she had not yet gone to bed, then she lit another lamp, which she took out on to the landing with some of her sewing. She then sat down and began to sew, and waited to see how things would develop.

On leaving the house, Arriguccio had hurried round to his wife's brothers' house as fast as his legs would carry him, and hammered away at the door until someone came to let him in. Hearing that it was Arriguccio, the lady's three brothers and her mother got up out of bed, called for lights to be lit, and came down to ask him what had brought him to see them, all alone, at that hour of the night.

Arriguccio gave them a full account of all that he had found and all that he had done, beginning with his discovery of the string attached to Monna Sismonda's toe; and in order to prove his story beyond any shadow of a doubt, he handed over the hair which he had cut off (or so he thought) from his wife's head, adding that they were to come and fetch her and deal with her according to the dictates of their family honour, as he had no intention of permitting her to darken his doorstep again.

The lady's brothers, who believed every word of his story, were exceedingly angry, and, calling for torches to be lit, they set forth with Arriguccio and made their way to his house, determined to punish her severely. On seeing how incensed they were against her daughter, the mother burst into tears and began to follow them, pleading with each of them in turn not to be taken in so quickly by everything they heard without looking further into the matter. She pointed out that the husband might have some other reason for losing his temper and knocking her about, and that he might have trumped up these charges against her as a cover for his own misdeeds. Moreover, she was astonished that such a thing could have happened, knowing her daughter as she did, and having brought her up herself from her infancy. And she made a great many more observations, all of them in similar vein.

On arriving at Arriguccio's house, they all went inside and began to ascend the stairs, and Monna Sismonda, hearing them coming, called out:

'Who is it?'

Whereupon one of her brothers replied:

'You'll find out soon enough who it is, you brazen hussy.'

And so Monna Sismonda said:

'What can be the meaning of this? Good Lord, deliver us.' And rising to her feet, she added:

'Brothers, how nice to see you. But what can have brought the three of you here at this hour of the night?'

When they saw her sitting there with her sewing, and without a mark on her face albeit Arriguccio had claimed that he had beaten her black and blue all over, her brothers were somewhat taken aback, and the vehemence of their anger was diminished. But having recovered from the initial shock, they demanded an explanation of the complaint that Arriguccio had laid against her, threatening to deal with her severely if she told them any lies.

'I don't know what I'm supposed to tell you,' said the lady, 'nor do I know why Arriguccio should have complained to you about me.'

Arriguccio could do nothing but gape at her as though he had lost his wits, for he could remember having punched her times without number about the face, scratched it well and truly, and given her the biggest hiding imaginable, yet as far as he could tell she bore no trace whatever of all this.

But to cut a long story short, her brothers told her what Arriguccio had said, mentioning the string and the thrashing he had given her and all the other details, whereupon the lady turned to Arriguccio, saying:

'Heavens above, husband, what is this that I hear? Why bring so much shame upon yourself by making me out to be an adulteress, when I am nothing of the sort, and claiming to have done something cruel and wicked, when you haven't? You hadn't even set foot in the house tonight until just now, let alone come anywhere near me! When did you give me this beating? I have no recollection of it.'

'What!' exclaimed Arriguccio. 'Vile woman, did we not go to bed together this evening? Did I not return here, after giving chase to your lover? Did I not give you a hiding, and cut off your hair?'

To which his wife replied:

'You never went to bed in this house tonight. But let us leave that point aside, for I have only my own words to prove it, and take up what you said about giving me a hiding and cutting off my hair. You never gave me any hiding, as everybody here, including yourself, can see quite clearly by examining my person. Nor would I advise you ever to make so bold as to lay your hands on me, for, by the cross of God, I would deform your face for life. What's more, you never cut off my hair either, unless you did it without my noticing: let's just see now whether my hair has been cut off or not.'

And removing her veils, she displayed a fine head of hair, which showed no signs of having been trimmed.

When her brothers and her mother saw and heard all this, they rounded on Arriguccio, saying:

'What sort of a joke is this, Arriguccio? This doesn't correspond in the least to what you came and told us, and you're going to have a job to prove the rest of your story.'

Arriguccio stood transfixed, as if he were in a trance. Although he was bursting to speak, on seeing there was no truth in the very thing he thought he could prove, he made no attempt to say anything.

So the lady turned back to her brothers, and said:

'I see now, brothers, what his intentions were: he wanted me to tell you about the wicked and scoundrelly way he behaves, which is a subject I have never had any desire to discuss, but now I shall do so. I firmly believe that his story is true, that he did all the things he was telling you about, and that what happened was this:

'The worthy gentleman, to whom I had the misfortune to be given by you in marriage, who calls himself a merchant and wants people to think that he is more temperate than a monk and more chaste than a virgin (as indeed he should be) goes carousing nearly every night in the taverns, and consorting with one harlot after another; and meanwhile I have to sit here, as you found me when you arrived, and wait up half the night for him, and sometimes he never comes home at all until morning. It's my belief that he got himself blind drunk and bedded down with some strumpet or other, then woke up to find the string attached to her foot, after which he performed all those brave exploits he's been telling you about, and finally returned to his doxy, beat her up, and cut off her hair. Since he was still in his cups, he believed (as I'm sure he still does) that he'd done all this to me; and if you take a good look at his face, you'll see that he is still half drunk even now. But all the same, whatever he may have said about me, I would not want you to take it as anything other than the lunatic ravings of someone who is full of Dutch courage. And since I am prepared to forgive him, you must do the same.'

Having heard what her daughter had said, the mother now began to raise a clamour, saying:

'By the cross of God, daughter, we ought to do no such thing; on the contrary, this loathsome, ungrateful cur ought to be put to death. You were far too good for him in the first place. God in Heaven, you'd think he had picked you up out of the gutter! To hell with this small-time trader in horse manure, let him take his foul slander elsewhere! These country yokels, they move into town after serving as cut-throat to some petty rustic tyrant, and wander about the streets in rags and tatters, their trousers all askew, with a quill sticking out[2] from their backsides, and no sooner do they get a few pence in their pockets than they want the daughters of noble gentlemen and fine ladies for their wives. And they devise a coat of arms for themselves, and go about saying: "I belong to such-and-such a family" and "My people did so-and-so". If only my sons had followed my advice! They could easily have married you into the finest family in Florence, with no more than a hunk of bread for a dowry, instead of which they had to give you to this perfect jewel of a man, who has the impudence, when he's married to the most chaste and respectable girl in the city, to wake us up in the middle of the night and call you a strumpet, as if we didn't know you.

God's faith! if I had anything to do with it, he'd be given such a thrashing that he'd smart for the rest of his days.'

Then, turning to her sons, she said:

'Didn't I tell you all along that it couldn't be true? Have you heard how your poor sister is treated by this precious brother-in-law of yours? He's a tuppenny-ha'penny pedlar, that's what he is! If I were in your place, after hearing what he's said about her and what he's done to her, I'd never rest content till I'd scourged him from the face of the earth. And if I were a man, and not a woman, I wouldn't allow anyone to stop me. God punish the drunken villain! He ought to be ashamed of himself!'

Angered by what they had seen and heard, the young men turned on Arriguccio and called him all the names under the sun; and by way of conclusion, they said:

'We'll let you off lightly this time, seeing that you've had too much to drink. But as you value your life, take care never to disturb us again with your nonsensical stories, because if we hear any more from you, you can rest assured we shall pay you out twice over.' And with this dire warning they departed.

Arriguccio was left standing there, gazing into space like an idiot, and not knowing whether the things he had done were real or part of a dream. However, he said no more about it, but left his wife in peace, so that not only had she kept her wits about her and avoided the immediate danger, but she had also made it possible, from then on, to enjoy herself to her heart's content without any fear of her husband.

NINTH STORY

Lydia, wife of Nicostratos, falls in love with Pyrrhus, who sets her three tasks as a proof of her sincerity. She performs all three, in addition to which she makes love to Pyrrhus in her husband's presence, causing Nicostratos to believe that his eyes have been deceiving him.

Neifile's story was so much to their liking that the ladies could not be restrained from laughing and talking about it, even though the king, who had ordered Panfilo to narrate his own tale, called upon them several times to be silent. But as soon as they were quiet, Panfilo began as follows:

Venerable ladies, it is my conviction that there is no enterprise, however perilous or difficult it may be, that those who are fervently in love will not have the courage to undertake. And although this has been proved in many of the stories we have heard, nevertheless I believe that I can prove it better still with the one I now propose to relate, in which you will hear of a lady whose deeds were far more favoured by Fortune than tempered by common sense. Consequently I would not advise any of you to take the risk of following her example, seeing that Fortune is not always so kindly disposed, and that all men are not equally gullible.

In Argos,[1] that most ancient city of Greece, whose kings brought it universal renown out of all proportion to its size, there was once a noble lord, Nicostratos by name, upon whom, on the threshold of old age, Fortune bestowed a wife of great distinction, no less bold than she was beautiful, whose name was Lydia.[2]

Being a wealthy patrician, Nicostratos kept a large number of servants, hawks and hounds, and was passionately fond of hunting. One of his retainers, whose name was Pyrrhus, was a sprightly and elegant young man, handsomely proportioned, and skilled in every activity he chose to pursue, and Nicostratos loved and trusted him above all others.

With this young man, Lydia fell desperately in love, to such an

extent that her thoughts were fixed upon him alone at every hour of
the day and night. But Pyrrhus, either failing or not desiring to notice,
showed a total lack of interest in her love, which filled the lady's heart
with unspeakable sorrow. But being determined at all costs to acquaint
him with her feelings, she summoned a maid of hers, named Lusca,[3]
whom she was able to trust implicitly, and said to her:

'Lusca, the favours you have had from me in the past should have
sufficed to earn me your loyalty and obedience, and hence you must
take good care that nobody ever hears what I am about to tell you,
apart from the person to whom I shall ask you to repeat it. As you can
see, Lusca, I am young and vigorous, and I am well supplied with all
the things a woman could desire. In short, with one exception I have
nothing to complain about, and the exception is this: that my husband
is much older than myself, and consequently I am ill provided with the
one thing that gives young women their greatest pleasure. And
because I desire this thing no less than other women, I long ago
made up my mind that since Fortune has been so unkind as to give me
an elderly husband, I would repair her omissions myself, and devise
the means of winning solace and salvation through my own efforts.
So that my enjoyment therein should be no less complete than in other
matters, I have decided that our Pyrrhus, since he is more worthy of
my love than any other man, should supply my needs with his
embraces, and such is the love that I bear him, that I am never content
except when I am gazing or musing upon him. Unless I can forgather
with him very soon, I firmly believe that I shall die. And therefore, as
you value my life, you must acquaint him with my love in whatever
way you think best, and ask him on my behalf to favour me with his
company at such time as you shall go to fetch him.'

The maidservant willingly agreed to carry out her mistress's
instructions; and at the first opportunity, having taken Pyrrhus
aside, she conveyed the lady's message as best she could. Pyrrhus
was greatly astonished to hear it, for he had never had the slightest
inkling that the lady was in love with him, and suspected that she
had sent the message in order to test his loyalty. So without
mincing his words, he abruptly replied:

'Lusca, I cannot believe that these words have come from my lady,
so be careful of what you are saying. Even if they really did come

from her, I cannot believe that she meant me to take them seriously. But if she did, I should never dream of doing such an injury to my master, who already honours me more than I deserve. So take care never to speak to me of such matters again.'

Not to be deterred by the severity of his tone, Lusca replied:

'Pyrrhus, if my mistress commands me to speak to you of these or any other matters, I shall do so as often as she tells me, whether you like it or not, and all I can say is that you are an obstinate fool.'

Feeling somewhat galled by the answer that Pyrrhus had given her, she returned to her mistress, who, on hearing the result of her mission, simply wanted to lie down and die. However, a few days later she raised the subject once more with her maidservant, and said:

'Lusca, as you know, an oak is not felled by a single blow of the axe. So it seems to me that you should return to this man, who has such a curious way of proving his loyalty at my expense, and, choosing a suitable moment, make a full declaration of my passion and do everything you can to bring this affair to a happy conclusion. For if things are left in their present state, I shall pine away and he will think I was putting his fidelity to the test, so that, whereas I want him to love me, he will end up by hating me.'

The maidservant comforted her mistress, and when she found Pyrrhus in a cheerful and agreeable mood, she said to him:

'Pyrrhus, a few days ago I told you of the ardent flames of love with which my mistress is consumed on your account, and I now assure you for the second time that if you persist in treating her so cruelly, she cannot go on living for much longer. I therefore appeal to you to lay aside your scruples, and grant her the solace she desires. I have always thought you very sensible, but if you carry this stubbornness of yours any further, I shall begin to think you're a blockhead. What greater honour could you have than to be loved above all else by so noble and beautiful and wealthy a lady as this? Don't you realize how fortunate you are, to be offered so pleasant a remedy to the cravings of your youth, and so secure a refuge from all your material needs? Which of your equals will lead a more blissful life than your own, if only you will see reason? Which of them will you find so abundantly supplied with arms and horses, or with clothes and money, if only you will grant her your love?

'Open your heart to my appeals, and return to your senses. Remember how seldom it happens that Fortune greets the same man twice with smiling face and open arms! If such a man should fail to grasp her bounty with both hands, and later suffer poverty and distress, he will only have himself to blame, not Fortune. And another thing: the loyalty of servants to their masters is quite a different matter from the loyalty of friends and equals. In fact, so far as it lies within their power, servants should treat their masters no differently from the way their masters treat them. If you had a beautiful wife, or mother or daughter or sister, and Nicostratos took a liking to her, do you honestly think he would bother his head, as you are doing, with notions of loyalty? More fool you, if that is what you believe; for you can rest assured that if flattery and coaxing proved ineffectual, he would take her by force, and you'd be powerless to stop him. So let us treat them and their belongings as they would treat us and ours. Make the most of Fortune's blessings; don't spurn the lady, go out and meet her half-way, for you may be sure that if you fail to do so, not only will you bring about the certain death of your mistress, but you will reproach yourself so often for it that you too will want to die.'

Having already reflected at length on Lusca's original message, Pyrrhus had made up his mind that if she were to approach him again on the subject, his answer would be different, and he would do all in his power to please the lady, provided it could be proved that she was not simply putting his loyalty to the test. And so he replied as follows:

'Look here, Lusca, I agree with everything you say, but on the other hand I know my master to be very wise and very shrewd, and now that he has entrusted me with the conduct of all his affairs, I strongly suspect that Lydia is doing this with his advice and encouragement, so as to put me to the test. But if she will do three things to reassure me, she can count on me in future to do whatever she asks without a moment's hesitation. The three things I want her to do are these: first, she must kill Nicostratos' favourite sparrowhawk before his very eyes; second, she must send me a tuft of Nicostratos' beard; and lastly, she must send me one of the best teeth he has left in his jaw.'

These terms seemed harsh to Lusca and well nigh impossible to the lady. But Love, that great comforter and excellent teacher of guile, bolstered her resolve, and through her maidservant she sent him word that she would carry out all of his demands to the letter, and without undue delay. Moreover, since Pyrrhus seemed to think Nicostratos so intelligent, she informed him that she would make love to Pyrrhus under the old man's nose, and then persuade Nicostratos that he was suffering from hallucinations.

Pyrrhus therefore waited to see what the lady would do, and a few days later, when Nicostratos was entertaining certain gentlemen to a sumptuous banquet, this being a regular practice of his, the tables had no sooner been cleared away than Lydia issued forth from her chamber, wearing a dress of green velvet and a splendid array of jewels, and strode majestically into the hall where the gentlemen were. In full view of Pyrrhus and all the others, she then went up to the perch where the sparrowhawk, so greatly prized by Nicostratos, was standing, unhooked its chain as though intending to take it on her hand, and having seized it by the jesses, dashed its head against the wall and killed it.

Nicostratos yelled at her, saying: 'For pity's sake, woman, what have you done?' but she ignored him, and turning instead to the gentlemen with whom he had been dining, she said: 'Gentlemen, even if a king were to insult me, I should be hard put to avenge myself if I hadn't the courage to take my revenge on a sparrowhawk. I should like you to know that for some little time, this bird has been depriving me of all the attention that men should devote to their ladies' pleasure; for Nicostratos gets up every morning at the crack of dawn, mounts his horse, and with his sparrowhawk perched on his wrist, he rides away to the open plains in order to watch it fly, leaving me, such as you see me, alone and ill content in my bed. Hence I have often longed to do the thing I have done just now, and all I was waiting for was an opportunity to do it in the presence of men who would judge my cause impartially, as I trust you gentlemen will.'

Supposing that her affection for Nicostratos was no less profound than her words appeared to imply, all the gentlemen started to laugh. And turning to Nicostratos, who was flushed with anger, they said:

'Well, well! How right the lady was to avenge her wrongs by killing the sparrowhawk!' And by dint of various witty remarks on the subject (the lady having meanwhile returned to her chamber), they converted Nicostratos' rage into laughter.

Pyrrhus, who had witnessed the whole of this episode, said to himself: 'The lady has set my love on a firm and noble footing. God grant that she may persevere, and thus conduct it to a happy conclusion.'

Having killed the sparrowhawk, Lydia bided her time, and a few days later, being closeted in her chamber with Nicostratos, she began to caress him and tease him, and he took her playfully by the hair, giving it a gentle pull. This provided her with the chance to fulfil the second of Pyrrhus' demands, and she promptly took hold of a small tuft of his beard, and, laughing the whole time, jerked it with so much violence that it came away entirely from his chin. When Nicostratos began to protest, she interrupted him, saying:

'What's the matter? Why do you pull such a face just because I've plucked some half-dozen hairs from your beard? I can't possibly have hurt you as much as you hurt me, when you were tugging at my hair just now.'

And so they continued jesting and sporting with one another, and the lady, having carefully preserved the tuft she had removed from his beard, sent it that same day to her beloved.

The third demand presented a rather more difficult problem, but Love had greatly sharpened the lady's wits, and since she was no dullard in the first place, she had already thought of a way of fulfilling it.

Now, Nicostratos had two young boys in his household, who, since they came of noble stock, had been entrusted to his care by their fathers so that they might learn good manners, and when Nicostratos was at table, one of them carved his meat whilst the other poured out his drink. Having sent for these two boys, the lady gave them to understand that they suffered from bad breath, and instructed them that, whenever they were waiting upon Nicostratos, they should hold their heads as far to one side as possible; but they were not to mention this matter to anyone.

The boys believed her, and began to do as the lady had told

them, so that eventually she took Nicostratos aside, and said to him:

'Have you noticed what these boys do when they are waiting upon you?'

'I have indeed,' said Nicostratos, 'and in fact, I've been meaning to ask them why they do it.'

Whereupon the lady said:

'There's no need: I can tell you the reason. I've been keeping it to myself for ages as I didn't want to upset you, but now that others have begun to notice, it's time that you were told. All that's wrong is that you suffer from appallingly bad breath, and I've no idea why this should be, because you never used to have it. However, it is quite repulsive, and seeing that you have to consort with people of quality, we shall have to find some way of curing it.'

'What could be causing it, I wonder?' said Nicostratos. 'Can it be that one of my teeth is rotten?'

'That's quite possible,' said Lydia. Whereupon, having taken him over to a window, she got him to open his mouth, and after carefully inspecting both sides of his jaw, she exclaimed:

'Oh, Nicostratos, how can you have endured it for so long? There's a tooth over here, on this side of your mouth, that as far as I can see is not only decayed, but rotten to the very core, and if it stays there much longer it will certainly contaminate the ones on either side of it. I advise you to have it out, before the damage gets any worse.'

'If that is your advice, I shall act upon it,' said Nicostratos. 'Send at once for a surgeon to come and take it out.'

'Heaven forbid,' replied the lady, 'that we should bother with a surgeon in a trifling matter of this sort. I feel quite capable of taking it out for you myself. Besides, these surgeons are quite barbaric when it comes to extracting people's teeth, and I couldn't possibly bear to see you suffering under the hands of any one of them. No, I absolutely insist on doing it myself, and then at least, if you're in too much pain, I shall stop at once, whereas a surgeon would take no notice.'

So she sent for the necessary implements, and cleared everybody out of the room except Lusca. She then locked the door, persuaded

Nicostratos to lie down on a table, and, inserting the pincers in his mouth, clapped them to one of his teeth. And though he screamed with pain, one of the women held him firmly down whilst the other, employing all the manual strength she possessed, extracted the tooth, which she promptly hid away, replacing it with another, horribly decayed, that she had been holding in her hand. This she showed to Nicostratos, who was writhing in agony and very nearly half dead, saying:

'Just take a look at this tooth that you've been carrying around in your mouth for all this time.'

Nicostratos was completely taken in, and although the pain had been quite excruciating and he was rending the air with his plaints, nevertheless, now that the tooth was out, it seemed to him that he felt much better. And when they had soothed and mollified him, and the pain had abated, he got up and went away.

Taking up the tooth, the lady sent it forthwith to her lover, who, being by now convinced of her love, declared that he was ready to minister to all her pleasures. But the lady wished to reassure him still further, and albeit she could hardly wait for him to take her in his arms, she was determined to keep the promise she had given him. She therefore pretended to be ill, and one day, when Nicostratos came to visit her after breakfast, attended only by Pyrrhus, she asked him whether they would help her down to the garden so as to relieve the tedium of her sick-bed. So they conveyed her to the garden, Nicostratos supporting her on one side and Pyrrhus on the other, and set her down on a lawn at the foot of a beautiful pear-tree.[4] And after sitting there together for a while, she turned to Pyrrhus, to whom she had sent word beforehand of what he was to do, and said:

'Pyrrhus, I long to have one or two of those pears. Climb the tree and throw some of them down.'

Pyrrhus, having swiftly clambered up, began to throw down some of the pears, and as he was doing so, he called out to Nicostratos saying:

'For shame, sir, what are you doing? And you, my lady, how can you be so brazen as to allow it in my presence? Do you think I am blind? Until a moment ago you were very ill; how can you have recovered so rapidly? If you wanted to indulge in that sort of thing, you have plenty of fine bedrooms in the house – why don't you go and do it in one of those? It would surely be more seemly than doing it here in my presence.'

The lady turned to her husband, and said:

'What's Pyrrhus talking about? Is he quite mad?'

Whereupon Pyrrhus said:

'I'm not mad, my lady. Do you think I can't see you?'

Nicostratos gaped at him in blank astonishment, and said:

'Why, Pyrrhus, I think you must be dreaming.'

'No, my lord,' he replied, 'I am wide awake, and so are you, it appears. In fact, you're putting so much vigour into it that if this tree were to be given so hard a buffeting, there wouldn't be a single pear left on it.'

'What can this mean?' said the lady. 'Can he really be seeing what he professes to be seeing? Heaven help me, if only I were fit and strong, I should climb up there and see for myself what these marvels are that he claims to be witnessing.'

Meanwhile, Pyrrhus continued to pour forth a stream of similar remarks from his vantage-point in the pear-tree, until eventually Nicostratos ordered him to come down. And when he had reached the ground, Nicostratos said:

'What is it you claim to be seeing?'

'I do believe,' said Pyrrhus, 'that you take me for an idiot or a lunatic. Since you force me to speak, I saw you lying on top of your lady, and as soon as I started to descend, you got up and sat in the spot where you are sitting now.'

To which Nicostratos replied:

'You are certainly behaving like an idiot, for we haven't moved in the slightest since you climbed up the tree.'

'What's the use of arguing about it?' said Pyrrhus. 'I can only repeat that I saw you, and you were going to it merrily.'

Nicostratos grew visibly more astonished, until finally he said:

'I'm going to find out for myself whether this pear-tree is enchanted, and what kind of marvels you can see from its branches.' So up he climbed, and no sooner had he done so than Pyrrhus and his lady began to make love together, whereupon Nicostratos, seeing what they were about, shouted:

'Ah, vile strumpet, what are you doing? And you, Pyrrhus, after all the trust I placed in you!' And so saying, he began to climb down again.

'We are just sitting here quietly,' said Pyrrhus and the lady. But on seeing him descending, they returned to their former places. No sooner had Nicostratos descended and found them sitting where he had left them than he began to shower them with abuse.

'Why Nicostratos,' said Pyrrhus, 'I must confess that you were right after all, and that my eyes were deceiving me when I was up in the tree. My only reason for saying this is that I know for a fact that you too have had a similar illusion. If you think I am wrong, you have only to stop and reflect whether a woman of such honesty and intelligence as your good lady, even if she wished to stain your honour in this manner, would ever bring herself to do it before your very eyes. Of myself I say nothing, except that I would sooner allow myself to be drawn and quartered than even contemplate such an act, let alone do it in your presence. Hence it is quite obvious that whatever it is that is distorting our vision, it must emanate from the pear-tree. For nothing in the world would have dissuaded me from believing that you had lain here carnally with your lady, until I heard you claiming that I had apparently been doing something which I most certainly never did, nor even thought of doing for a moment.'

At this point, he was interrupted by the lady, who rose to her feet and said to her husband, in tones of considerable annoyance:

'The devil take you if you have such a low opinion of me as to suppose that, had I wanted to comport myself as scandalously as you claim to have seen, I should do it before your very eyes. You may rest assured that if I should ever feel the urge to do it, I shouldn't do it out here in the garden. On the contrary, I'd find myself a nice, comfortable bed, and arrange the whole thing so discreetly that if you ever got to know about it I should be very much surprised.'

Nicostratos now felt that they must both be speaking the truth, and that they could never have brought themselves to do such a thing in his presence. So he ceased his shouting and raving, and began to talk about the strangeness of the thing, and about the miraculous way in which a man's eyesight could be affected by climbing a tree.

But the lady pretended to be angry because of the aspersions that Nicostratos seemed to have cast on her character and intelligence, and she said:

'This pear-tree will certainly never bring shame upon me or any other woman again if I can help it. Run and fetch an axe, Pyrrhus, and, at one and the same time, avenge us both by chopping it down, though in point of fact it would be much better to cleave Nicostratos' skull with the axe for allowing the eyes of his intellect to be blinded so easily. For however much your eyes may have borne out what you were saying, Nicostratos, you should never have allowed your mind to accept it, or even to entertain the idea for a moment.'

So Pyrrhus very quickly went to fetch the axe, and chopped the pear-tree down. And no sooner was it felled than the lady turned to Nicostratos, saying:

'Now that I have seen the fall of my honour's adversary, all my anger has departed.'

Then, as Nicostratos was pleading with her to forgive him, she graciously consented to do so, bidding him never again to harbour such ignoble thoughts about his lady, who loved him more dearly than herself.

And so the poor deluded husband returned with her and her lover to the palace, within whose walls it thenceforth became easier for Pyrrhus and Lydia to meet, at regular intervals, for their common delight and pleasure. May God grant that we enjoy a similar fate!

TENTH STORY

Two Sienese fall in love with a woman of whose child one of them is the godfather. This man dies, returns to his companion from the afterworld in fulfilment of a promise he had given him, and describes what people do there.

All that now remained was for the king to tell his story, and as soon as he perceived that the ladies had stopped mourning over the fate of the innocent pear-tree, he began:

It goes without saying that a just king must be the first to observe those laws that he has himself prescribed, and that, if he fails to do so, he deserves rather to be punished as a slave than honoured as a king. And yet, almost of necessity, it now behoves me, as your king, to commit precisely this error and thus incur your censure. Yesterday evening, when I decreed the form that our discussions of today were to take, I fully intended to forgo my privilege for once, submit to the same rule as yourselves, and address myself to the theme upon which you have all been speaking. But the story I was proposing to relate has now been told; and moreover, the subject has been so extensively and admirably discussed, that for my own part, however much I cudgel my brains, I cannot think of anything to say on this topic that will stand comparison with the things already said. Since, therefore, being obliged to infringe the law which I myself have made, I am worthy of punishment, I shall straightway declare that I am ready to make whatever amends may be required of me, and fall back upon my customary privilege.

Taking my cue, dearest ladies, from Elissa's compelling account of the godfather and the mother of his godchild, as well as from the extraordinary simplicity of the Sienese,[1] I shall tell you a little tale about them, which has nothing to do with the tricks played by clever wives on their foolish husbands, but which, albeit much of it will strain your credulity, should nevertheless prove entertaining in parts.

There once lived, in the Porta Salaia district of Siena, two young men of the people, called Tingoccio Mini and Meuccio di Tura, who nearly always went about together and who, to all outward appearances, were quite devoted to one another. Being in the habit, like other folk, of going to church and listening to sermons, they had frequently heard about the glory and the suffering that awaited the souls of the dead, each according to his merits, in the world to come. But since they wanted to find out for certain about these matters, and could think of no other way of doing it, they promised one another that whichever of them died first would return, if possible, to the one who was still alive, and give him all the information he wanted; and they sealed this compact with a solemn oath.

Not long after making this promise, whilst the pair of them were still going about together in the way we have described, Tingoccio happened to become godfather to the infant son of a man called Ambruogio Anselmini, who lived with his wife, Monna Mita, in the district of Camporeggi.

Now, this Monna Mita was a woman of great beauty and attractiveness, and notwithstanding his sponsorship of the child, Tingoccio, who called to see her every now and then with Meuccio, fell in love with her. But he was not the only one, for Meuccio, having heard Tingoccio singing her praises and finding her very attractive, also fell in love with her. Neither man spoke to the other about his love for the lady, but each for a different reason. Tingoccio took care not to say anything to Meuccio because he had a guilty · conscience about falling in love with the mother of his godchild, and would have been ashamed to have anyone know about it. But Meuccio kept it to himself for quite another reason, namely, that he realized how fond Tingoccio was of her, and therefore said to himself: 'If I take him into my confidence, he will be jealous of me; and since he is her child's godfather, and can talk to her whenever he likes, he will do his best to turn her against me, with the result that I shall never get anywhere with her.'

Things remained much as we have described them, with the two young men pining away for Monna Mita, until Tingoccio, who was in a better position to open his heart to the lady, played his cards so skilfully that he obtained what he wanted from her – a circumstance that did not escape the notice of Meuccio, who was anything but pleased about it. However, since he was hoping that his own desires would one day find fulfilment, and was anxious not to provide Tingoccio with the slightest cause to ruin his chances or interfere in any way with his plans, he pretended to know nothing.

And there, for the time being, the matter rested, Tingoccio being luckier than his comrade in his love for the lady. But the richness of the soil in Monna Mita's garden inspired Tingoccio to dig it over with so much energy and zeal that he contracted a fever from his labours, which left him so enfeebled that within the space of a few days, being unable to shake it off, he departed this life.

On the night of the third day after his unfortunate demise (being unable, perhaps, to make it any sooner), he kept his promise and appeared to Meuccio, who was lying in bed fast asleep. Tingoccio called out to him, and Meuccio woke up with a start, saying:

'Who are you?'

'I am Tingoccio,' he replied, 'and I have returned, as I promised, to bring you tidings of the other world.'

Having recovered from the shock of seeing him, Meuccio said:

'My brother, you are welcome.'

He then asked him whether, as he put it, he was 'lost', and Tingoccio replied:

'Lost? If a thing is lost, it can't be found; so what on earth would I be doing here, if I was lost?'

'That's not what I mean,' said Meuccio. 'What I want to know is whether you're among the souls of the damned, in the scourging fires of Hell.'

'Not exactly,' replied Tingoccio. 'But I'm being severely punished just the same, because of the sins I committed, and it's all very painful.'

Then Meuccio questioned him in detail about the punishments that were meted out there for each of the sins committed on earth, and Tingoccio described them one by one. And when Meuccio went on to ask him whether there was anything he could do for him, Tingoccio replied in the affirmative, saying that he should arrange for prayers and masses to be recited on his behalf, and for alms to be given, since these things were highly beneficial to the souls of the dead. All of this Meuccio readily agreed to do.

Just as Tingoccio was leaving, Meuccio remembered about Monna Mita, and raising his head a little, he said:

'By the way, Tingoccio: what punishment have they given you for making love to the mother of your godchild?'

Whereupon Tingoccio replied:

'My brother, as soon as I arrived down there, I was met by one who seemed to know all of my sins by heart, and who ordered me to proceed to the place where I am being severely punished for my misdeeds. There I found a large company of souls condemned to the same punishment as myself, and as I stood in their midst, I suddenly remembered how I had carried on with my godchild's mother. And since I was expecting to have to pay a much heavier penalty for this than the one I had been given, I began, even though I was being roasted in a fierce and enormous fire, to tremble all over with fear. On noticing this, one of my fellow sinners said: "Why do you tremble so when standing in the fire? Have you done something worse than the rest of us?" "Oh, my friend," said I, "it fills me with terror when I think of the judgement that awaits me for a dreadful sin I have committed." He then asked me which sin I was referring to, and I said: "I made love to the mother of my godchild, and went to it so heartily that I shed my pelt in the process." He had a good laugh over this, and said: "Be off with you, you fool! There's nothing special down here about the mother of a godchild." I was so relieved to hear it that I could have wept.'

The dawn was now approaching, so Tingoccio said:

'Farewell, Meuccio, I can't stay here any longer.' And all of a sudden he was gone.

Having learnt that there was nothing special down there about the mother of a godchild, Meuccio began to laugh at his own stupidity for having in the past spared several such ladies from his attentions. From that day forth, having shed his ignorance, he was a much wiser man in dealing with such matters. And if only Friar Rinaldo had known as much as Meuccio, there would have been no need for him to make up syllogisms when persuading Madonna Agnesa to minister to his pleasures.

*   *   *

The sun was descending in the west and a gentle breeze had risen, when the king, having brought his story to an end, removed the crown of laurel from his brow, there being no one else left to speak, and placed it upon the head of Lauretta, saying:

'With this, your namesake,[1] madam, I crown you queen of our company. And now it is up to you, as our empress, to give such orders as you consider apt for our common entertainment and pleasure.'

He then returned to his place and sat down, and Lauretta, having become their queen, summoned the steward and ordered him to set the tables in the delectable valley at a somewhat earlier hour than usual, so that they could return at their leisure to the palace; and she also instructed him about the things he was to do during the rest of her reign.

This done, she turned to address the company, saying:

'Yesterday, Dioneo insisted that we should talk, today, about the tricks played upon husbands by their wives; and but for the fact that I do not wish it to be thought that I belong to that breed of snapping curs who immediately turn round and retaliate, I should oblige you, on the morrow, to talk about the tricks played on wives by their husbands. But instead of doing that, I should like each of you to think of a story about *the tricks that people in general, men and women alike, are forever playing upon one another*. This, I feel sure, will be no less agreeable a topic than the one to which we have today been addressing ourselves.'

Having spoken these words, she rose to her feet and dismissed the company until suppertime.

And so the whole company arose, gentlemen and ladies alike, and some of them began to wade, barefooted, in the limpid waters of the lake, whilst others went roaming off over the greensward to beguile the time amongst the tall, straight trees. Dioneo and Fiammetta sang a long duet about Palamon and Arcite.[2] And so, in their several different ways, they whiled away the time to their entire delight and joy until the hour of supper, when they seated themselves at table beside the tiny lake. There they supped in gay and leisurely fashion with never a fly to trouble them, fanned by a gentle breeze that came from the surrounding hills, with the dulcet songs of a thousand birds delighting their ears.

No more than half the vesperal hour had elapsed when the tables were cleared away, and at the queen's behest, they wandered for a while through the delectable valley before slowly retracing their steps towards their lodging. Jesting and laughing not only about the things they had been saying earlier in the day, but many others also, in due course they arrived at the goodly palace a little before dark. There they dispelled the fatigue of their brief journey with the coolest of wines and the daintiest of sweetmeats, and in no time at all they were dancing *caroles* beside the beautiful fountain, accompanied sometimes by Tindaro on the cornemuse and sometimes by the music of other instruments.

Finally, however, the queen ordered Filomena to sing a song, and she began as follows:

'Alas, my life is desolate!
For will I ne'er return
Whence I departed all disconsolate?

'Certain I know not, such is the desire
That burns within my breast
There to return, alas, where once I was.
Oh, my true love, who sets my heart afire,
My one, my only rest,
Tell me what I should do, my dearest lord;
I dare ask none, nor know to whom to go
To beg for hope and help except thyself,
My soul is wounded so.

'I cannot well relate how great the pleasure
Which so impassioned me
That neither day nor night could yield me rest.
My hearing, sight and touch, in strongest measure
Were so increased in me
That each sense lit new fires within my breast
Which burn and scorch me to the very core.
Save thee alone, no one can comfort me
Or my faint heart restore.

'Alas, come tell me when it is to be,
When will that time return
When I may come upon thee once again
And kiss those eyes which have so murdered me?

My love, for whom I yearn,
Tell me when thou wilt come, and tell me "soon",
And somewhat ease the pains Love made me bear.
Say thou wilt swiftly come, then linger here;
How long I do not care.

'If I perchance should hold thee once again,
I may not be the fool
That I have been before to let thee go.
My grasp this time I firmer will maintain;
Let Fate do what she will.
For I must satisfy my craving soul
With thy sweet lips: I have no more to say.
Therefore come quickly, come embrace me soon;
I sing to think you may!'

All of her companions surmised from this song that Filomena was engrossed in some new and exciting love; and since the words seemed to imply that she had gone beyond the mere exchange of amorous glances, some of those present, supposing her to have savoured the fruits of her love, were not a little envious. But when her song was finished, the queen, remembering that the following day was a Friday, graciously addressed the whole company as follows:

'Noble ladies, young gentlemen, tomorrow as you know is the day that is consecrated to the Passion of Our Lord, and you will doubtless recall that when Neifile was our queen,[3] we observed it devoutly, abstaining from our agreeable discussions, not only on that day, but on the ensuing Saturday. Wherefore, being desirous to follow the good example which Neifile has set us, I feel that for the next two days it would be seemly for us to suspend our pleasant storytelling, as we did last week, and meditate upon the things that were done on those two days for the salvation of our souls.'

The queen's devout words commanded general approval, and so, a goodly portion of the night being already spent, she dismissed the whole company and they all betook themselves to their rest.

Here ends the Seventh Day of the Decameron

EIGHTH DAY

Here begins the Eighth Day, wherein, under the rule of Lauretta, are discussed the tricks that people in general, men and women alike, are forever playing upon one another.

On the Sunday morning, the rays of the rising sun had already appeared among the highest mountain peaks, the shades of night had departed, and all things were plainly visible, when the queen and her companions rose from their beds; and after sauntering for a while upon the dew-flecked lawns, they made their way, the hour of tierce being nearly half spent, to a nearby chapel,[1] where they heard divine service. Returning to the palace, they breakfasted in gay and festive mood, and after they had sung and danced a little, they were dismissed by the queen, so that those who wished to go and rest were free to do so.

But in compliance with the wishes of the queen, once the sun was past its zenith they took their places beside the delectable fountain to proceed as usual with their storytelling, and at the queen's command Neifile began as follows:

FIRST STORY

Gulfardo borrows from Guasparruolo a sum of money equivalent to the amount he has agreed to pay the latter's wife in return for letting him sleep with her. He gives her the money, but later tells Guasparruolo, in her presence, that he has handed it back to his wife, and she has to admit it.

Since God has ordained that I should tell the first of our stories today, I am well content to do so. And since we have talked a great deal, fond ladies, of the tricks played by women upon men, I should like to tell you of one which was played by a man upon a woman, my intention being, not to censure the man for what he did or to claim that the woman was misused, but on the contrary to commend the man and censure the woman, and to show that men are just as capable of deceiving those who trust them, as of being deceived by those in whom they place their trust. Strictly speaking, however, the incident I am about to relate should not be termed a deception, but rather a reprisal. For a woman should act at all times with the greatest decorum, and guard her chastity with her life, on no account permitting herself to defile it; and although it is not always possible for us to observe this precept to the full on account of our frailty, nevertheless I declare that any woman who strays from the path of virtue for monetary gain deserves to be burnt alive, whereas the woman who yields to the forces of Love, knowing how powerful they are, deserves a lenient judge who will order her acquittal – which, as was pointed out to us the other day by Filostrato, is what happened to Madonna Filippa in Prato.

Now, in the city of Milan there was once a German soldier of fortune, a fearless fellow by the name of Gulfardo, who, unlike the majority of his countrymen, was extremely loyal to those in whose service he enrolled. And since he was always most scrupulous in repaying sums of money he had borrowed, he could find any number of merchants who were willing to lend him as much as he wanted, at a low rate of interest.

Since coming to live in Milan, he had fallen in love with a very beautiful woman called Madonna Ambruogia,[1] the wife of a wealthy merchant, Guasparruolo Cagastraccio by name, with whom he was on the most friendly and familiar of terms, but neither her husband nor anyone else was aware of his love for the lady, for he proceeded at all times with the utmost discretion. And one day, he sent her a message, imploring her to grant him the sweet reward of his devotion, and affirming that he, for his part, was prepared to do whatever she might ask of him.

After much humming and hawing, the lady made up her mind, and informed Gulfardo that she was prepared to comply with his request on two conditions: firstly, that he must never breathe a word of it to anyone; and secondly, that since he was well off and she wanted to buy something for herself, he was to give her two hundred gold florins, and then she would always be at his service.

On hearing of the woman's rapacity, Gulfardo, who had always thought of her as a perfect lady, was incensed by her lack of decorum, and his fervent love was transmuted into a feeling more akin to hatred. Being resolved to beat her at her own game, he sent word that he would be only too willing to meet her wishes, and do everything else in his power to make her happy. She was therefore to let him know when she would like him to come to her, and he would bring her the money. And she could rest assured that nobody would hear of the matter, except for a comrade of his whom he greatly trusted, who was privy to all his affairs.

The lady, or strumpet rather, was delighted with this reply, and sent back word that in a few days' time Guasparruolo, her husband, had to go to Genoa on business, and as soon as he was out of the way she would let Gulfardo know and invite him to call.

Having waited for the right moment, Gulfardo went to Guasparruolo and said:

'I'm about to drive a bargain, for which I require two hundred gold florins. Would it be possible for you to lend them to me, at the same rate of interest as usual?'

Guasparruolo willingly agreed to lend him the money, and counted it out for him right away.

A few days later, Guasparruolo went off to Genoa as his wife had predicted, and she therefore sent word to Gulfardo that he should come to her, bringing the two hundred gold florins. So Gulfardo, taking his friend with him, went to the lady's house, where he found her waiting for him, and the first thing he did was to hand over the two hundred gold florins in his comrade's presence, saying:

'Here, take this money, my lady, and give it to your husband when he returns.'

The lady took the money, thinking Gulfardo had used this form of words simply so that his comrade should not suspect he was giving it to her by way of payment. And she replied:

'I shall see that he gets it, of course, but first I should like to make sure that it is all here.' Whereupon she emptied the florins out on to a table, and on finding, to her great satisfaction, that they came to exactly two hundred, she put them away in a safe place. She then went back to Gulfardo and conveyed him to her bedroom, where, not only on that occasion but on many others before her husband's return from Genoa, she placed her person freely at his disposal.

No sooner did Guasparruolo return from Genoa than Gulfardo, having made certain that his wife would be with him, called upon him with his companion, and said to him in the lady's presence:

'Guasparruolo, those two hundred gold florins you lent me the other day were not needed after all, as I was unable to complete the transaction. So I brought them straight back and handed them over to your wife. Do remember to cancel my debt, won't you?'

Turning to his wife, Guasparruolo asked her whether she had received the money, and since she could hardly deny the fact when the witness was staring her in the face, she said:

'Yes, I did indeed receive the money, but forgot to tell you about it.'

'That settles it, then. Don't worry, Gulfardo, I shall make quite sure that it's entered up in the books.'

Having made a fool of the lady, Gulfardo took his leave, and she gave her husband the ill-gotten proceeds of her depravity; and thus the sagacious lover had enjoyed the favours of his rapacious lady free of charge.

SECOND STORY

The priest of Varlungo goes to bed with Monna Belcolore, leaving her his cloak by way of payment; then, having borrowed a mortar from her, he sends it back and asks her to return the cloak which he had left with her as a pledge. The good woman hands it over, and gives him a piece of her mind.

The gentlemen and ladies alike were still applauding Gulfardo's treatment of the covetous Milanese lady when the queen turned, smiling, to Panfilo, and enjoined him to follow; so Panfilo began:

Fair ladies, it behoves me to relate a little story against a class of persons who keep on offending us without our being able to retaliate. I am referring to the priests, who have proclaimed a crusade against our wives, and who seem to think, when they succeed in laying one of them on her back, that they have earned full remission of all their sins, as surely as if they had brought the Sultan back from Alexandria to Avignon[1] in chains. Whereas we poor dupes who belong to the laity cannot do the same to them, albeit we may vent our spleen against their mothers, sisters, mistresses and daughters with no less passion than the priests display when assailing our wives. But however that may be, I propose to tell you this tale of country love, more amusing for its ending than conspicuous for its length, from which you will be able to draw a useful moral, namely, that you shouldn't believe everything that a priest tells you.

I say then, that in Varlungo,[2] which as all of you know or will possibly have heard is a hamlet, no great distance from here, there once lived a worthy priest, robust and vigorous in the service of the ladies, who, albeit he was none too proficient at reading books, always had a rich stock of good and holy aphorisms with which to entertain his parishioners under the elm every Sunday. And whenever the men of the parish were away from their homes, he was far more assiduous in calling on their wives than any of his predecessors, bringing them fairings and holy water and a candle-end or two, and giving them his blessing.

Now, among the many women in his parish who had taken his fancy, there was one in particular for whom he had a very soft spot indeed. Her name was Monna Belcolore,[3] she was married to a farmworker called Bentivegna del Mazzo,[4] and without a doubt she was a vigorous and seductive-looking wench, buxom and brown as a berry, who seemed better versed in the grinder's art than any other girl in the village. When, moreover, she had occasion to play the tambourine, and sing 'A little of what you fancy does you good', and dance a reel or a jig, with a dainty little kerchief in her hand, she could knock spots off every single one of her neighbours. Master Priest was so enthralled by all these talents of hers that he was driven to distraction, and spent his whole time loitering about the village in the hope of seeing her. Whenever he caught sight of her in church on a Sunday morning, he would intone a *Kyrie* and a *Sanctus*, trying very hard to sound like a master cantor when in fact he was braying like an ass, whereas if she was nowhere to be seen he would hardly open his lips. But on the whole he managed to disguise his feelings, so that neither Bentivegna del Mazzo nor any of his neighbours noticed anything unusual in his behaviour.

With the object of getting to know Monna Belcolore better, every now and then he gave her presents, sometimes sending her a few cloves of fresh garlic, of which he grew the finest specimens thereabouts in his own garden, and sometimes a basket of beans, or a bunch of chives or shallots. If he met her in the street, he would look at her with a forlorn expression on his face, and whisper fond reproaches in her ear, but being a stubborn little thing, she pretended not to notice and passed him by with her nose in the air, so that Master Priest was getting precisely nowhere.

One day, however, while the priest was strolling aimlessly about the village, a little after noon, he happened to meet Bentivegna del Mazzo, who was driving a heavily laden ass before him. The priest hailed him and asked him where he was going, and Bentivegna replied:

'Faith, Father, to tell the honest truth I have some business to attend to in town, and I'm taking these things to the lawyer, Ser Bonaccorri da Ginestreto, so that he'll help me to answer this 'ere summings I've had from the tawny general to appear before the judge at the sizes.'

The priest was delighted.

'You do well, my son,' he said, 'Go now, with my blessing, and come back soon. And if you should happen to meet Lapuccio or Naldino, don't forget to ask them to bring me those leather thongs[5] for my flails.'

Bentivegna promised he would see about it, and continued on his way towards Florence, while the priest, having decided that the time had come for him to call upon Belcolore and try his luck, set off at a spanking pace, never slowing up for a moment until he had arrived on her doorstep. As he entered the house, he called out:

'God bless all here! Is anyone at home?'

Belcolore was upstairs, and on hearing his voice she called down to him:

'Oh, Father, you are welcome! But why go traipsing round the village in this awful heat?'

'By the grace of God,' replied the priest, 'I've come to keep you company for a while, for I met your husband on his way to town.'

Belcolore came downstairs, took a seat, and began to sift a heap of cabbage seed that her husband had gathered earlier in the day.

'Come now, Belcolore,' said the priest, 'must you always drive me to despair like this?'

Belcolore began to laugh, and said: 'What have I done to you?'

'Nothing,' replied the priest. 'But the trouble is that there's something I'd like to do to you, something ordained by God, and you won't let me do it.'

'Bless my soul!' said Belcolore. 'Priests don't do that sort of thing.'

'We certainly do,' replied the priest. 'Why on earth shouldn't we? What's more, we do a much better job of it than other men, and do you know why? It's because we do our grinding when the millpond's full. So if you want to make hay while the sun shines, hold your tongue and let me get on with it.'

'What sort of hay do you mean?' said Belcolore. 'You priests are all the same, you're as tight-fisted as the very devil.'

'You only have to tell me what you want,' said the priest, 'and you shall have it. Would you like a pretty little pair of shoes, or a silk head-scarf, or a fine woollen waistband, or what?'

'That's a splendid choice, I must say!' exclaimed Belcolore. 'I already have all those things. But if you're really so fond of me, why not do me a little favour, and then I would do whatever you want?'

'Tell me what the favour is, and I'll do it gladly,' said the priest.

So Belcolore said:

'I have to go to Florence on Saturday to deliver some wool that I have spun, and get my spinning wheel mended. And if you'll lend me five pounds, which a man like you can easily afford, I shall call at the pawnbroker's and collect my black skirt and the waistband I wear on Sundays. I wore it on my wedding-day, you understand, and ever since I pawned it I haven't been able to go to church or anywhere else. Do me this one favour, and I'll be yours for evermore.'

'So help me God,' said the priest, 'I haven't the money with me, or I'd gladly let you have it. But you may depend on me to see that you get it by Saturday.'

'Oh yes,' said Belcolore, 'you all make these fine promises, and then you fail to keep any of them. Do you think you're going to treat me as you treated Biliuzza, who went away empty-handed and ended up walking the streets because of what you did to her? God's faith, you'll not fool me so easily. If you haven't the money with you, you can go and fetch it.'

'Oh come!' said the priest. 'Don't make me go all the way back for it now, when you can see for yourself that I'm rearing to get on with the job. By the time I returned, there might be someone here to thwart our plans, and Lord knows when I shall be in such fine fettle again as I am at present.'

'That's your own lookout,' she said. 'If you want to go, go; if not, take your fettle elsewhere.'

Seeing that she was not prepared to do his bidding without a *quid pro quo*, and had turned down his suggestion of a *sine custodia*, the priest said:

'I'll tell you what I'll do. Since you won't trust me to send you the money, I'll leave you this fine blue cloak of mine by way of surety.'

Belcolore looked up at him and said:

'Will you now? And how much is the cloak worth?'

'How much is it worth?' said the priest. 'Why, I'll have you know that it's made of pure Douai,[6] not to say Trouai, and there are those in the parish who would claim that it's Quadrouai. I bought it less than a fortnight ago from Lotto, the old-clothes merchant, for exactly seven pounds, and according to Buglietto d'Alberto, who as you know is an expert in such matters, it would have been cheap at half the price.'

'Is that so?' said Belcolore. 'So help me God, I would never have believed it. But anyway, let's have a look at it.'

Master Priest, who was champing at the bit, took off his cloak and gave it to her. And when she had put it safely away, she said:

'Let's go into the barn, Father. Nobody ever comes near the place.'

So off they went to the barn, where he smothered her with luscious kisses and made her a kinswoman of the Lord God. And after spending some time in amorous sport with her, he made his way back to the church in his surplice, as though he'd been officiating at a wedding.

By the time he arrived there, it began to dawn on him that all the candle-ends he could muster from a whole year's offerings would scarcely amount to a half of five pounds in value, and he could have kicked himself for being so stupid as to leave her his cloak. So he began to consider how he might retrieve it without having to pay.

Being a crafty sort of fellow, he soon thought of a very good way of getting it back, and it worked to perfection. On the following day, which happened to be a feast day, he sent the child of one of his neighbours to Monna Belcolore's house, asking her whether she would kindly lend him her stone mortar, because Binguccio dal Poggio and Nuto Buglietti were due to breakfast with him later in the morning, and he wanted to prepare a sauce.

Belcolore sent him the mortar, and when it was nearly time for breakfast and the priest knew that Bentivegna del Mazzo and Belcolore would be about to sit at table, he called his sacristan and said:

'Take this mortar back to Monna Belcolore, and say to her: "Father says thank you very much, and would you mind sending back the cloak that the boy left with you by way of surety."'

So the sacristan took the mortar along to Belcolore's house, where he found her sitting at table with Bentivegna, having breakfast; and having put the mortar down on the table, he gave her the priest's message.

When she heard him asking for the cloak, Belcolore tried to speak, but Bentivegna rounded on her angrily, saying:

'What's all this about taking sureties from the priest? Jesus Christ, I've a good mind to thrash the hide off you. Pox take you, woman, go and get the cloak and hand it back, and be quick about it. And just you remember from now on: if the priest wants anything, he's to have it, no matter what it is, even if he asks for our ass.'

Belcolore got up, grumbling and muttering to herself, and went to fetch the cloak, which she had tucked away in a chest at the foot of the bed. And as she handed it over to the sacristan, she said:

'Give the priest this message from me: "Belcolore says that she swears to God you won't be grinding any more of your sauces in her mortar, after the shabby way you've treated her over this one."'

The sacristan took the cloak back to the priest and gave him Belcolore's message, whereupon he burst out laughing and said:

'Next time you see her, tell her that if she doesn't lend me her mortar, I shan't let her have my pestle. It's no use having one without the other.'

Bentivegna supposed his wife had spoken as she did because of the scolding he had given her, and thought no more about it. But Belcolore was infuriated with the priest for having made such a fool of her, and refused to speak to him for the rest of the summer until the grape-harvest, by which time he had scared the life out of her so successfully by threatening to see that she was consigned to the very centre of Hell, that she made her peace with him over a bottle of must and some roast chestnuts. From then on, they had many a good guzzle together, and instead of giving her the five pounds, the priest put a new skin on her tambourine and tricked it out with a pretty little bell, which made her very happy.

THIRD STORY

Calandrino, Bruno and Buffalmacco set off in search of the heliotrope along the banks of the Mugnone. Thinking he has found it, Calandrino staggers home carrying an enormous load of stones, and his wife gives him a piece of her mind, causing him to lose his temper and beat her up. Then finally, he tells his companions what they have known all along.

The ladies laughed so heartily over Panfilo's tale that they are laughing yet, and when it was over, the queen called upon Elissa to follow him. And so, still laughing, she thus began:

Charming ladies, I know not whether, with this little story of mine, which is no less true than entertaining, I shall succeed in making you laugh as much as Panfilo has done with his, but at any rate I shall do my best.

Not long ago, there lived in our city, where there has never been any lack of unusual customs and bizarre people, a painter called Calandrino,[1] a simple, unconventional sort of fellow, who was nearly always to be found in the company of two other painters, whose names were Bruno and Buffalmacco. These latter were a very jovial pair, but they were also shrewd and perceptive, and they went about with Calandrino because his simple-mindedness and the quaintness of his ways were an endless source of amusement to them.

Also in Florence at that time there was a most agreeable, astute, and successful young man called Maso del Saggio,[2] who, having heard one or two stories about Calandrino's simplicity, decided to have a little fun at his expense by playing some practical joke upon him, or putting some fantastic notion into his head.

So one day, happening to find him in the church of San Giovanni staring intently at the paintings and bas-reliefs of the canopy which had recently been erected above the high altar, he decided that this was the ideal time and place for doing what he had in mind. And having explained his intentions to a companion of his, they walked over to the place where Calandrino was sitting, and pretending not to notice him, they began to discuss the properties of various stones, of which Maso spoke with tremendous authority, as though he were a great and famous lapidary.

Hearing them talking together, Calandrino pricked up his ears, and after a while, seeing that their conversation was not intended to be private, he got up and joined them, much to the delight of Maso, who continued to hold forth until finally Calandrino asked him where these magical stones were to be found.

Maso replied that they were chiefly to be found in Nomansland, the territory of the Basques, in a region called Cornucopia, where the vines are tied up with sausages, and you could buy a goose for a penny, with a gosling thrown in for good measure. And in those parts there was a mountain made entirely of grated Parmesan cheese, on whose slopes there were people who spent their whole time making macaroni and ravioli, which they cooked in chicken broth and then cast it to the four winds, and the faster you could pick it up, the more you got of it. And not far away, there was a stream of Vernaccia wine, the finest that was ever drunk, without a single drop of water in it.'

'That's a marvellous place, by the sound of it,' said Calandrino, 'but tell me, what do they do with all the chickens they cook?'

'They are all eaten by the Basques,' Maso replied.

Then Calandrino asked him whether he had ever been there himself, and Maso replied:

'Been there myself? If I've been there once, I've been there a thousand times at least.'

Whereupon Calandrino asked:

'How many miles away is it?'

'More than a milling, that spends the whole night trilling,'³ said Maso.

'In that case,' said Calandrino, 'it must be further than the Abruzzi.'

'It is indeed,' Maso replied. 'Just a trifle.'

Seeing that Maso was saying this with a completely straight face, the simple-minded Calandrino took every word of it as gospel, and he said:

'It's too far away for me, then; but if it were nearer, I can assure you that one of these days I'd come with you, so as to see all that macaroni tumbling down, and feed my face on it. But do please tell me, are there none of these magical stones to be found in this part of the world?'

'Yes,' replied Maso. 'There are two kinds of stone that are very magical indeed. First of all we have the sandstones of Settignano and Montici, from which, when they are turned into millstones, we get all our flour; hence the popular saying, in the countries I was telling you about, that blessings come from God and millstones from Montici. But we have such a lot of these sandstones, that we think as little of them as they do of emeralds, of which they have whole mountains, higher than Monte Morello,⁴ that sparkle and glitter in the middle of the night, believe you me if they don't! And by the way, did you know that anyone who could master the art of setting millstones in rings, before a hole was bored in them, and who took them to the Sultan, could have anything he chose? Now, the second is a stone that we lapidaries call the heliotrope,[5] which has the miraculous power of making people invisible when they are out of sight, provided they are carrying it on their person.'

'Amazing!' said Calandrino. 'But this second stone, where is it to be found?'

Maso replied that one could usually find decent specimens in the valley of the Mugnone,[6] whereupon Calandrino said:

'How big are these stones? What colour are they?'

'The size varies,' Maso replied. 'Some of them are bigger and others smaller, but they are all very nearly black in colour.'

Having made a mental note of all that he had heard, Calandrino pretended that he had other things to attend to and took his leave of Maso, determined to go and look for one of these stones; but he decided that before doing so, he would have to inform Bruno and Buffalmacco, who were his bosom friends. He therefore went to look for them, so that they could all set forth at once in search of the stone before anyone else should come to hear about it, and he spent the whole of the rest of the morning trying to trace them.

Finally, in mid-afternoon, he suddenly remembered that they were working at the nunnery a little beyond the city gate on the road to Faenza, so he abandoned everything he was doing and proceeded to the nunnery, running nearly all the way in spite of the tremendous heat. And having called them away from their painting, he said to them:

'Pay attention to me, my friends, and we can become the richest men in Florence, for I have heard on good authority that along the Mugnone there's a certain kind of stone, and when you pick it up you become invisible. I reckon we ought to go there right away, before anyone else does. We'll find it without a doubt, because I know what it looks like; and once we've found it, all we have to do is to put it in our purses and go to the money-changers, whose counters, as you know, are always loaded with groats and florins, and help ourselves to as much as we want. No one will see us; and so we'll be able to get rich quick, without being forced to daub walls all the time like a lot of snails.'

When Bruno and Buffalmacco heard this, they had a good laugh to themselves, stared one another in the face pretending to be greatly astonished, and told Calandrino that they thought it a splendid idea. Then Buffalmacco asked him what the stone was called, but Calandrino, being rather dense, had already forgotten its name, and so he replied:

'Why should we bother about the name, when we know about its special powers? Let's not waste any more time, but go and look for it now.'

'Very well,' said Bruno, 'but what do these stones look like?'

'They come in various shapes and sizes,' said Calandrino, 'but they're all the same colour, which is very nearly black. So what we have to do is to collect all the black stones we happen to see, until we come across the right one. Come on, let's get going.'

'Wait a minute,' said Bruno. And turning to Buffalmacco, he said:

'Calandrino appears to be talking sense, but there's no point in going there at this time of day, because the sun is shining straight down on the Mugnone and it will have dried all the stones, so that the ones that seem black in the early morning, before the sun gets at them, will be just as white as the others. Besides, as it's the middle of the week there'll be a lot of people along the Mugnone, and if they were to see us they might guess what we were up to, in which case they might follow our example, and come across the stone before we do. We don't want to kill the goose that lays the golden egg. Wouldn't you agree, Buffalmacco, that we ought to do this job in the early morning, so that we can distinguish the black stones from the white ones, and that we should wait until the weekend, when nobody will see us?'

Since Bruno's advice was supported by Buffalmacco, Calandrino agreed to wait, and it was arranged that on the following Sunday morning they would all go and look for the magic stone. Meanwhile Calandrino pleaded with them not to breathe a word of this to anyone, as it had been revealed to him in strict confidence, and he then went on to tell them what he had heard about the land of Cornucopia, declaring with many an oath that he was speaking the gospel truth. And when he had taken his leave of them, they put their heads together and agreed on their plan of campaign.

Calandrino looked forward eagerly to Sunday morning, and when it came, he got up at crack of dawn and went round to call for his friends. Then they all proceeded to the Mugnone by way of the Porta San Gallo and began to work their way downstream, looking for the stone. Being the keenest of the trio, Calandrino went on ahead, darting this way and that, and whenever he caught sight of a black stone he leapt on it, picked it up, and stuffed it down his shirt, while the other two trailed along behind, occasionally picking up an odd stone here and there. Before he had gone very far, Calandrino found that there was no more room in his shirt, so he gathered up the hem of his skirt, which was not cut in the Hainaut style,[7] attached it securely to his waist all round, and turned it into a capacious bag, which took him no long time to fill, after which he made a second bag out of his cloak, which in no time at all he had likewise filled up with stones.

Now that Calandrino was fully laden and the hour of breakfast was approaching, Bruno turned to Buffalmacco, as they had prearranged, and said:

'Where's Calandrino got to?'

Buffalmacco, who could see him quite plainly, turned to gaze in every direction, and then replied:

'I've no idea. He was here a moment ago, just a little way ahead of us.'

'A moment ago, indeed! I'll bet you he's at home by now, tucking into his breakfast, after putting this crazy idea into our heads of searching for black stones along the Mugnone.'

'Well,' said Buffalmacco, 'I can't say I blame him for leaving us in the lurch like this, seeing that we were stupid enough to believe him in the first place. What a pair of blockheads we are! No one in his right mind would ever have believed all that talk about finding such a valuable stone in the Mugnone.'

Hearing them talk in this fashion, Calandrino concluded that he must have picked up the stone without knowing it, and that because of its special powers they were unable to see him, even though he was standing just a few yards away. He therefore decided, being delighted with his good fortune, to go back home; and without saying anything to the others, he turned about and started to return by the way he had come.

On seeing this, Buffalmacco turned to Bruno and said:

'What'll we do now? Why don't we go home, the same as he did?'

'Come on then,' Bruno replied. 'But I swear to God that I won't fall for any more of Calandrino's tricks. If he were as close to me now as he's been all morning, I'd give him such a rap on the heels with this pebble that he wouldn't forget this little hoax of his for the best part of a month.' No sooner were the words out of his mouth than he took aim and caught Calandrino squarely on the heel with the pebble, whereupon Calandrino, grimacing with pain, jerked his foot high in the air and began to puff and gasp for breath. But he none the less managed to hold his tongue, and continued on his way.

Then Buffalmacco took between his fingers one of the stones he had collected earlier, and said to Bruno:

'D'you see this nice sharp bit of flint? How I'd love to send it whizzing into Calandrino's back!' He then let it go, and it caught Calandrino a nasty blow in the small of the back. But to cut a long story short, they kept stoning Calandrino in this fashion, making various abusive remarks, all the way back along the Mugnone to the Porta San Gallo, where, having thrown away the rest of the stones they had collected, they paused to chat with the customs guards. These latter, having been let into the secret beforehand, had allowed Calandrino to pass unchallenged, and were splitting their sides with laughter.

Calandrino walked on without stopping until he reached his house, which was situated near the Canto alla Macina, and Fortune favoured the hoax to such an extent that at no point along his route, either beside the river or in the city streets, did anyone address a single word to him, though as a matter of fact he encountered very few people because nearly everyone was at breakfast.

Calandrino let himself into the house, staggering under his burden, but as luck would have it, his wife, a handsome-looking gentlewoman called Monna Tessa, was standing at the head of the stairs; and as she was somewhat annoyed with him for staying out so long, no sooner did she catch sight of him than she began to scold him, saying:

'A fine fellow you are, I must say, coming home to breakfast when everyone else has finished eating. Where the devil have you been?'

On realizing that she could see him, Calandrino was filled with anger and dismay, and began to shout:

'Blast you, woman, why did you have to be standing there? Now you've ruined everything, but I swear to God I'll make you pay for it.' And having ascended the stairs, he deposited his enormous collection of stones in one of the smaller rooms and rushed upon his wife like a madman. Catching her by the tresses, he hurled her to the ground at his feet and began to pummel her and kick her as hard as he could until she was bruised and battered all over from head to foot, whilst all the time she was pleading in vain for mercy and clasping her hands in a gesture of supplication.

Bruno and Buffalmacco, having tarried for a while at the city gate to have a good laugh with the watchmen, slowly set off to follow Calandrino at a distance, and when, on reaching his front door, they heard the sound of the terrible beating he was inflicting on his wife, they pretended they had only just returned, and called out to him. Calandrino appeared at the window, flushed, panting, and covered in sweat, and asked them to come up. So up the stairs they went, scowling all over their faces, to find the room cluttered up with stones and the woman huddled in a corner, her hair dishevelled, her clothes torn, and her face covered with scratches and bruises, crying her eyes out, whilst at the other side of the room Calandrino was sitting gasping for breath as though he were completely exhausted, his clothes in total disarray.

Having spent a little time surveying the scene, they said:

'What's all this, Calandrino? Are you planning to build a wall with all these stones we can see lying about?' And so as to add insult to injury, they continued:

'What's happened to Monna Tessa? It looks as though you've been giving her a beating. Whatever made you do that?'

What with the weight of all the stones he had carried, and the fury with which he had assailed his wife, and his despair over losing the fortune he had imagined to be within his grasp, Calandrino was so fatigued that he couldn't draw sufficient breath to utter a single word in reply. So Buffalmacco, having paused for a while, began all over again, saying:

'Look here, Calandrino, you had no right to play such a mean trick on us, just because you were feeling piqued about something or other. You talked us into going with you to look for this magic stone, and then, without so much as bidding us fare you well or fare you badly, you left us standing there along the Mugnone like a pair of boobies, and cleared off home. We're not exactly pleased with the way you've behaved: and you can rest assured that you'll never do this to us again.'

This was more than Calandrino could bear, so he summoned up all his energies and replied:

'Don't be angry, my friends, you're quite wrong about what happened. I actually found the stone, and if you don't believe me, I'll prove it. When you started asking one another where I was, I was standing less than ten yards away from you the whole time. And when I saw that you were making tracks for home and couldn't see me, I walked ahead of you. As a matter of fact, I was just a little way in front of you all the way back to the city gate.'

He then gave them an account of everything they had said and done from beginning to end, and showed them the marks made by the stones on his heels and his back, after which he said:

'And I'll tell you another thing: as I was coming in at the city gate, loaded up to the eyebrows with all these stones you see here, nobody said a word to me, and you know for yourselves what those customs men are like, with their tedious and offensive manner of demanding to see everything. Besides, I met various friends and neighbours as I was coming along the road, who are always in the habit of bidding me good morning and offering me a drink, yet none of them uttered so much as a syllable, and they passed me by as though they hadn't seen me. But when I finally arrived home, I was met by this blasted devil of a woman; and because, as you know, all things lose their virtue in the presence of a woman,[8] the spell was broken and she saw me. So instead of being the luckiest man in Florence, she's made me the unluckiest, which is why I beat her with all the strength I had in my hands. So help me God, I could slit the woman's throat for her. I curse the hour that I first set eyes on her, and the day she came into this house.'

And flying once more into a rage, he made as though to get up and give her another good thrashing.

As they listened to Calandrino's tale, Bruno and Buffalmacco feigned great astonishment, and nodded at regular intervals to confirm what he was saying, though it was all they could do to prevent themselves from bursting out laughing. But when they saw him rising furiously to his feet to beat his wife a second time, they rushed forward to restrain him, declaring that if anyone was to blame it was not the lady, but Calandrino himself, for he was well aware that women caused things to lose their virtue, and hadn't warned her beforehand not to show her face that day in his presence. Moreover it was God Himself, they argued, who had prevented him from taking this precaution, either because Calandrino was not destined to enjoy this singular piece of good fortune, or because he was intending to deceive his companions, to whom he should have revealed his discovery the moment he realized the stone was in his possession.

After a lot of palaver, they managed, with a great deal of effort, to conciliate the hapless lady and her husband, and they then departed, leaving him to sit and brood with his house full of stones.

FOURTH STORY

The Provost of Fiesole falls in love with a widow, but his love is not reciprocated. He goes to bed with her maid, thinking it to be the widow, and the lady's brothers cause him to be found there by his bishop.

When Elissa came to the end of her tale, which in the course of its telling had brought no small pleasure to the entire company, the queen turned to Emilia and indicated that she would like her to tell her own story next; so Emilia promptly began, as follows:

Worthy ladies, it has already been shown, as I recall, in several of the stories we have heard, that priests, friars, and clerics of all descriptions will stop at nothing to force themselves on our attention. But however much we may discuss this particular subject, more will remain to be said; and I therefore propose to tell you a story about a provost[1] who was determined, come what may, to obtain the favours of a certain widow, whether she wanted to grant them to him or not. But being highly intelligent, the lady, who was of gentle birth, treated him according to his deserts.

As you all know, Fiesole, which stands on top of a hill, clearly visible from where we are now, is a city of great antiquity,[2] and was once very large. Although it has now fallen into total ruin, it has never been without a bishop, and there is one living there to this day. Some years ago, a widow of gentle birth called Monna Piccarda had an estate there, not far from the principal church; and since she was not the wealthiest of women, she resided there for almost the entire year, in a house of modest proportions, together with her two brothers, a pair of very worthy and polite young gentlemen.

Now, this lady went regularly to the nearby church, and since she was still a very beautiful and charming young woman, its provost fell so passionately in love with her that she alone commanded the whole of his attention. And in the end he waxed so bold as to acquaint the lady with his wishes, imploring her to be content that he should love her, and to requite his ardent passion.

Though elderly in years, this provost had the mentality of a small child, being haughty and presumptuous, and possessing a mighty high opinion of himself. He was forever picking holes in people and making himself generally unpleasant, and was so pompous and tedious that he was disliked by everybody, but especially by this lady, who not only disliked but positively loathed him. But being an intelligent woman, as we have said, she replied:

'Sir, I am extremely flattered that you should love me. I am bound to love you in return, and I shall do so with all my heart, but there must never be anything unseemly about our love for one another. You are my spiritual father, you are a priest, and you are fast approaching your old age, all of which things require that you should lead a chaste and honourable life. Besides, I am no longer a young girl, able to take affairs of this sort in her stride, but a widow; and you know how essential it is that widows should follow the path of virtue. You must therefore excuse me, for I can never love you in the way you request, nor do I wish to be loved in this manner by you.'

Although he could obtain no other answer from her at this first encounter, the Provost was not the sort of man to be discouraged or defeated by a single rebuff, and with his habitual arrogance and effrontery he importuned her repeatedly by means of letters and messages, as well as by word of mouth whenever he saw her coming into church. And so the lady, finding that his attentions were becoming quite intolerable, resolved that she would teach him a salutary lesson, albeit she would do nothing without first consulting her brothers. She therefore told them all about the Provost's importunate behaviour, and explained what she was proposing to do about it. Having obtained their full consent, a few days later she went to the church as usual, and no sooner did the Provost catch sight of her than he came over to her and spoke to her in his customary, over-familiar manner.

When she saw him coming, the lady fixed her gaze upon him and gave him a cheerful smile. So the Provost led her to a secluded corner of the church, and plied her with his usual stream of endearments, whereupon the lady fetched a deep sigh and said:

'Sir, I have frequently heard it said that no fortress is sufficiently strong to withstand a perpetual siege, and I have now discovered, from my own experience, that this is perfectly true. For you have beleaguered me so completely with your tender words and countless acts of courtesy that you have forced me to break my former resolve. And seeing that you find me so much to your liking, I am willing to surrender.'

'Heaven be praised!' said the Provost, who could scarcely contain his joy. 'To tell you the truth, madam, I am amazed that you should have held out for so long, seeing that this has never happened to me with any woman before. And in fact, I have sometimes had

occasion to reflect, that if women were made of silver, you couldn't
turn them into coins, as they bend too easily. But no more of this:
when and where can we be together?'

'Sweet my lord,' replied the lady, 'we can meet whenever you
please, for I have no husband to whom I must give an account of
my nights. But as to where we are going to meet, I have no
idea.'

'Why not?' said the Provost. 'Why don't we meet in your house?'

'Sir,' replied the lady, 'as you know, I have two younger brothers,
who bring their friends to the house at all hours of the day and
night, and since my house is not very big, it would be quite
impossible for us to meet there unless we were to remain completely
silent, like deaf-mutes, without saying a word, and move about in
the dark, as though we were blind. In this case, it would be feasible,
for my brothers never invade my bedroom; but their own is
immediately next to mine, and one can't even whisper without
being heard.'

'That's no great problem,' said the Provost. 'Let's do as you
suggest for a night or two, until I can think of a place where we can
meet more freely.'

'I leave that to you, sir,' said the lady, 'but on one thing I must
insist: that the affair remains a secret, and you never breathe a word
of it to anyone.'

'Of that you may rest assured, madam,' replied the Provost. 'But
when are we to meet? Can you arrange it for tonight?'

'Why, of course,' said the lady. And having explained to him
how and when he was to come, she took her leave of him and
returned home.

Now, this lady had a maidservant, who was none too young and
had the ugliest and most misshapen face you ever saw. She had a
huge, flat nose, a wry mouth, thick lips, big teeth, which were
unevenly set, and a pronounced squint; moreover she was always
having trouble with her eyes, and her complexion was a sort of
yellowy green, so that she looked as though she had spent the
summer, not in Fiesole, but in Senigallia.[3] Apart from this, she was
hipshot on the right side, and walked with a slight limp. Her name
was Ciuta, but because she was so ugly to look at, everyone called

her Ciutazza.[4] And although her body was so misshapen, she was always prepared for a spot of mischief.

So the lady sent for her and said:

'Ciutazza, if you will do something for me tonight, I shall give you a fine new smock.'

At the mention of a smock, Ciutazza pricked up her ears and said:

'If you give me a smock, ma'am, I'll go through fire for you.'

'That's good,' said the lady. 'Now, what I want you to do is to sleep with a man tonight in my bed, and ply him with caresses. But you must take care not to utter a single word in case my brothers should hear you, for as you know, they sleep in the room next to mine. And tomorrow you shall have the new smock.'

'If need be,' said Ciutazza, 'I would sleep with half-a-dozen men, let alone one.'

After dark that evening, the Provost came to the house as arranged, and in accordance with the lady's plans, the two young men were in their own room, making a good deal of noise. The Provost entered the lady's bedroom without a sound, and groped his way through the dark, as instructed, to the bed, on which Ciutazza was already lying, having been carefully briefed by her mistress about what she was to do.

Master Provost, thinking it was the lady who was lying beside him, took Ciutazza in his arms and began to kiss her without saying a word, and Ciutazza returned the compliment. And so the Provost began to disport himself with her, taking possession of the prize he had so long been coveting.

Having thus brought the pair together, the lady directed her brothers to put the rest of her plan into effect. They therefore stole quietly out of their room and made their way towards the piazza; and Fortune was even kinder to their scheme than they had hoped, for since it was a very hot evening, the Bishop had been looking for the two young men and was already on his way to their house for a convivial chat and some liquid refreshment. As soon as he saw them coming, he told them what he had in mind, and they all returned to the house, where, to his no small pleasure, he sat with them in a cool little courtyard in which numerous lanterns had been lit, and drank some excellent wine of theirs.

When they had taken their fill, the young men said:

'Since you have been so kind as to honour us with your company in our humble little abode, to which we were just about to invite you, we should like you to take a look at something we are anxious to show you.'

The Bishop readily agreed, and so one of the young men seized a lighted torch and led the way, being followed by the Bishop and all the rest of the company, to the room where Master Provost was lying in bed with Ciutazza. In order to make up for lost time, the Provost had been riding at a furious pace, and already, by the time all these people arrived, he had covered at least three miles, so that, in spite of the heat, feeling a little weary, he had dropped off to sleep with Ciutazza in his arms.

So when the young man bearing the torch entered the room with the Bishop and all the others in their wake, the first thing they saw was the Provost lying there with Ciutazza in his arms. At that precise moment, the Provost woke up, and seeing all these people standing round him in the torchlight, he thrust his head under the bedclothes, feeling thoroughly ashamed and confused. But the Bishop, taking him severely to task, forced him to show his face and have a good look at the person with whom he had been sleeping.

What with his discovery of the lady's deception, and the disgrace that he felt he had suffered, the Provost was instantly transformed into the saddest man who ever lived. The Bishop ordered him to dress, and when he had done so, he was marched back to the church under heavy escort, there to suffer severe penance for the sin he had committed.

Before taking his leave of the lady's brothers, the Bishop asked them how it had come about that the Provost had gone to their house to sleep with Ciutazza, and the young men told him the whole story from beginning to end. On hearing what had happened, the Bishop warmly commended the lady and the two young men, who, not wishing to soil their hands with the blood of a priest, had treated the Provost as he deserved.

The Provost was forced by his bishop to do forty days' penance for his sin, but love and indignation prolonged his suffering to forty-nine days at the very least, to say nothing of the fact that for a long time afterwards, he was unable to walk down the street without being pointed at by small boys, who would taunt him with the words: 'There goes the man who went to bed with Ciutazza.' And this riled him so much that he was almost driven out of his mind.

This, then, was the way in which the worthy lady rid herself of the presumptuous Provost's insufferable attentions, and Ciutazza won herself a smock.

FIFTH STORY

Three young men pull down the breeches of a judge from the Marches whilst he is administering the law on the Florentine bench.

When Emilia had brought her story to an end, and the widow had been commended by all those present, the queen looked towards Filostrato, and said:

'Now it is your turn to speak.'

Filostrato promptly replied that he was ready to do so, and began as follows:

Delectable ladies, after hearing Elissa referring just now to the young man called Maso del Saggio, I have been prompted to discard the tale I was intending to relate in order to tell you one about Maso and some of his companions, which, though not improper, contains certain words that you ladies would hesitate to use. But since it is highly amusing, I am sure you would like to hear it.

As all of you will doubtless have heard, the chief magistrates of our city very often come from the Marches,[1] and tend as a rule to be mean-hearted men, who lead such a frugal and beggarly sort of life that anyone would think they hadn't a penny to bless themselves with. And because of their inborn miserliness and avarice, they

bring with them judges and notaries who seem to have been
brought up behind a plough or recruited from a cobbler's shop
rather than from any of the schools of law.

Now, one of these March-men came here once to take up his
appointment as *podestà*, and among the numerous judges he
brought with him, there was one called Messer Niccola da San
Lepidio, who looked more like a coppersmith than anything else,
and he was assigned to the panel of judges that tried criminal
cases.

Now it frequently happens that people go to the law-courts who
have no business to be there at all, and this was the case with Maso
del Saggio, who had gone there one morning to look for a friend.
His gaze being attracted to the place where this Messer Niccola was
sitting, he was struck by the man's curious and witless appearance,
and began to scrutinize him carefully. And amongst the many
strange features that he noted, unbecoming in any person of tidy
habits and gentle breeding, he saw that the fur of his judge's cap
was thick with grime, that he had a quill-case dangling from his
waist, and that his gown was longer than his robe. But the most
remarkable thing of all, to Maso's way of thinking, was a pair of
breeches, the crotch of which, when the judge was sitting down
and his clothes gaped open in front owing to their skimpiness,
appeared to come halfway down his legs.

Having seen all he wanted to see of the judge's breeches, he
abandoned the search for his friend and set off on a different quest,
this time for two companions of his called Ribi and Matteuzzo,
who were no less high-spirited than Maso himself. And when he
had tracked them down, he said to them:

'If my friendship means anything to you, come along with me to
the law-courts, and I'll show you the most priceless booby you ever
saw.'

So off he went with Ribi and Matteuzzo to the law-courts,
where he showed them the judge and his breeches. Viewing this
spectacle from the back of the court, they began to laugh, and on
coming closer to the platform on which Master Judge was seated,
they saw that it would be very easy for a person to conceal himself
underneath it. Moreover the plank on which the judge's feet were

resting had a large hole in it, through which a hand and an arm could be thrust with the greatest of ease.

Maso therefore turned to his companions, and said:

'Let's pull those breeches right down for the fellow. We can do it quite easily.'

The other two had already seen how it could be done, and having arranged with one another what they were to say and do, they returned there the following morning. Despite the fact that the courtroom was crowded, Matteuzzo managed to crawl into the space beneath the platform without being seen, and positioned himself exactly below the spot where the judge's feet were resting. Then Maso went up to the judge on one side and seized the hem of his robe, whilst Ribi approached him from the other side and did the same.

'Sir,' Maso began. 'O sir, I beseech you in God's name not to let this petty thief, who is standing at the other side of you, escape from this courtroom before you have made him give me back the pair of thigh-boots he has stolen from me. He claims he didn't do it, and yet I saw him, less than a month ago, having them re-soled.'

Then Ribi shouted in his other ear:

'Don't you believe him, sir; he's a lying rogue, and because he knows that I've come to lay a complaint against him for stealing a saddlebag of mine, he comes out with this story about the thigh-boots, which I've had in my house for donkey's years. If you don't believe me, I can call any number of witnesses, such as the woman next door, who runs the fruit stall, and Grassa the tripe-merchant, and a dustman from Santa Maria a Verzaia, who saw him on his way home from town.'

Maso for his part was not prepared to leave all the talking to Ribi, but he too began to shout, and Ribi shouted even louder. And as the judge stood up and edged closer to them in order to follow what they were saying, Matteuzzo seized his opportunity, thrust his hand through the hole in the plank, took a firm hold on the seat of the judge's breeches, and pulled hard. The breeches came down forthwith, for the judge was a scraggy fellow, and very lean in the buttocks. Being at a loss to understand how this had come about, the judge tried to cover himself up by drawing his clothes across the front of his body and sitting down, but Maso and Ribi were still holding on to them at either side and shouting their heads off, saying:

'It's monstrous, sir, that you should refuse me a hearing, and try to withdraw without giving your verdict. Surely you don't need written evidence to decide a trifling matter of this sort.' And whilst they were saying all this, they held on to his clothes sufficiently long for everyone in court to perceive that he had lost his breeches. Then finally, Matteuzzo, having clung to them for some little time, released his hold and made good his escape from the courtroom without being seen, whilst Ribi, deciding he had done quite enough, exclaimed:

'I swear to God I'll appeal to the Senate.'

At the same time, Maso let go the judge's robe on his side, saying:

'I shan't go to any Senate. I'll keep coming back here, sir, until I find you in less of a muddle than you seem to be in this morning.'

Then they both made off in opposite directions as fast as their legs would carry them.

It was only at this point that Master Judge, having pulled up his breeches before all those present, as though he were just getting up out of bed, became aware of the deception and demanded to know what had become of the two men who were arguing about the thigh-boots and the saddlebag. But when they couldn't be found, he began to swear by the bowels of God that somebody should tell him whether it was the custom in Florence for a judge to have his breeches removed whilst sitting on the bench of justice.

When the *podestà*, for his part, was told what had happened, he practically threw a fit. But when it was pointed out by his friends that this had only been done in order to show him that the Florentines knew he had brought fools with him instead of judges so as to save money, he thought it best to hold his tongue, and nothing more was said about the matter.

SIXTH STORY

Bruno and Buffalmacco steal a pig from Calandrino. Pretending to help him find it again, they persuade him to submit to a test using ginger sweets and Vernaccia wine. They give him two sweets, one after the other, consisting of dog ginger seasoned with aloes, so that it appears that he has stolen the pig himself. And finally they extract money from him, by threatening to tell his wife about it.

Filostrato had no sooner completed his story, which aroused a great deal of laughter, than the queen called on Filomena to follow, whereupon she began, saying:

Gracious ladies, just as Filostrato was prompted to tell you the previous tale by hearing the name of Maso, in precisely the same way I too have been prompted by hearing the names of Calandrino and his companions to tell you another, which I believe you will find to your liking.

It is unnecessary for me to explain to you who Calandrino, Bruno and Buffalmacco were, for you have heard enough on that score in the earlier tale. So I shall omit the preliminaries, and tell you that Calandrino had a little farm not far from Florence, which he had received from his wife by way of a dowry. Among the other things he acquired from this farm, every year he used to obtain a pig there, and it was his regular custom to go to the country in December with his wife, slaughter the pig, and have it salted.

Now, it so happened that one year, when Calandrino's wife was not feeling very well, he went to the farm by himself to slaughter the pig. And when Bruno and Buffalmacco heard about this, knowing that his wife was remaining behind, they went to stay for a few days with a priest, who was a very great friend of theirs and lived near Calandrino's farm.

Calandrino had slaughtered the pig on the morning of the very day they arrived, and on seeing them with the priest, he called out to them, saying:

'I bid you a hearty welcome, my friends. Come along inside, and I'll show you what an excellent farmer I am.' And having taken them into the farmhouse, he showed them the pig.

It was a very fine pig, as they could see for themselves, and when they learnt from Calandrino that he intended to salt it and take it back to his family, Bruno said:

'You must be out of your mind! Why not sell it, so that we can all have a good time on the proceeds? You can always tell your wife it's been stolen.'

'Not a chance,' said Calandrino. 'She wouldn't believe me, and she'd kick me out of the house. Now, stop pestering me, because I shall never do anything of the sort.'

They argued with him at great length, but it was no use. And after Calandrino had invited them to stay for supper with so reluctant an air that they decided not to accept, they all took their leave of him.

After leaving Calandrino, Bruno said to Buffalmacco:

'Why don't we steal that pig of his tonight?'

'But how are we to do that?' said Buffalmacco.

'I've already thought of a good way to do it,' said Bruno, 'provided that he doesn't move it to some other place.'

'In that case,' said Buffalmacco, 'let's do it. After all, why not? And when the deed is done, you and I, and our friend the priest here, will all make merry together.'

The priest was very much in favour of this idea, and so Bruno said:

'This thing calls for a certain amount of finesse. Now you know, Buffalmacco, don't you, that Calandrino is a mean sort of fellow, who's very fond of drinking when other people pay. So let's go and take him to the tavern, where the priest can pretend to play the host to the rest of us and pay for all the drinks. When he sees that he has nothing to pay, Calandrino will drink himself into a stupor, and then the rest will be plain sailing because there's no one else staying at the house.'

Everything turned out as Bruno had predicted. When Calandrino saw that the priest would not allow him to pay, he began to drink like a fish, and quaffed a great deal more than he needed to make him drunk. By the time he left the tavern, it was already very late, and not wishing to eat any supper, he staggered off home and went to bed, thinking he had bolted the door whereas in fact he had left it wide open.

Buffalmacco and Bruno went and had supper with the priest, and when the meal was over they stealthily made their way to Calandrino's house, taking with them certain implements so that they could break in at the spot that Bruno had decided on earlier in the day. On finding the door open, however, they walked in, collected the pig, and carted it off to the priest's house, where they stowed it away and went off to bed.

Next morning, having slept off the effects of the wine, Calandrino got up and went downstairs to find that his pig had gone and the door was open. So he went round asking various people whether they knew who had taken the pig, and being unable to find any trace of it, he began to make a great outcry, shouting: 'Alas! Woe is me! Somebody's stolen my pig!'

Meanwhile, Bruno and Buffalmacco got up and went round to Calandrino's to hear what he had to say about the pig. And no sooner did he catch sight of them than he called out to them, almost in tears, saying:

'Alas, my friends, somebody's stolen my pig.'

Bruno then went up to him, and, speaking out of the corner of his mouth, he said:

'Fancy that! So you've had a bit of sense at last, have you?'

'Pah!' exclaimed Calandrino. 'I'm telling you the gospel truth.'

'That's the way,' said Bruno. 'Go on shouting like that, so that people will think it's really happened.'

Whereupon Calandrino began to shout even louder, saying:

'God's body, man, I tell you it's been stolen, it really has.'

'Excellent, excellent,' said Bruno. 'Keep it up, give the thing plenty of voice and make yourself heard, so as to make it sound convincing.'

'You'll drive me to perdition in a minute,' said Calandrino. 'Do I have to hang myself by the neck before I can convince you that it really has been stolen?'

'Get away with you!' said Bruno. 'How can that be, when I saw it there myself only yesterday? Are you trying to make me believe it's flown away?'

'It's gone, I tell you,' said Calandrino.

'Go on,' said Bruno, 'you're joking.'

'I swear to you I'm telling the truth,' said Calandrino. 'What am I to do now? I can't go back home without the pig. My wife will never believe me, but even if she does, she'll make my life a misery for the next twelve months.'

'Upon my soul,' said Bruno, 'it's a serious business, if you're speaking the truth. But as you know, Calandrino, I was telling you only yesterday that you ought to say this. I wouldn't like to think that you were fooling your wife and us too at the same time.'

Calandrino protested loudly, saying:

'Ah! why are you so intent on driving me to despair and provoking me to curse God and all the Saints in Heaven? I tell you the pig was stolen from me during the night.'

'If that's the case,' said Buffalmacco, 'we'll have to see if we can find some way of getting it back.'

'How are we to do that?' asked Calandrino.

So Buffalmacco said:

'Whoever took your pig, we can be quite sure that he didn't come all the way from India to do it. It must have been one of your neighbours. So all you have to do is to bring them all together so that I can give them the bread and cheese test,[1] and we'll soon see who's got it.'

'Oh, yes,' said Bruno, 'your bread and cheese will work miracles, I'm sure, on some of the fine folk who live around here. It's quite obvious that one of them has the pig. They'd guess what we were up to, and stay away.'

'What's to be done, then?' asked Buffalmacco.

'What we ought to do,' Bruno replied, 'is to use the best ginger sweets we can get hold of, along with some fine Vernaccia wine, and invite them round for a drink. They wouldn't suspect anything, and they'd all turn up. And it's just as easy to bless ginger sweets as it is to bless bread and cheese.'

'You certainly have a point there,' said Buffalmacco. 'What do you say, Calandrino? Shall we give it a try?'

'Of course,' said Calandrino. 'Let's do that, for the love of God. If only I could find out who took it, I shouldn't feel half so miserable about it!'

'That's settled then,' said Bruno. 'Now I'd be quite willing to go to Florence and get these things for you, if you'll give me the money.'

Calandrino gave him all the money he had, which amounted to about forty pence, and so Bruno went to Florence and called on a friend of his, who was an apothecary. Having bought a pound of the best ginger sweets he had in stock, he got him to make two special ones, consisting of dog ginger² seasoned with fresh hepatic aloes; then he had these coated with sugar, like the rest, and so as not to lose them or confuse them with the others, he had a tiny mark put on them which enabled him to recognize them without any difficulty. And having bought a flask of fine Vernaccia, he returned to Calandrino's place in the country, and said to him:

'See to it that you invite all the people you suspect to come and drink with you tomorrow morning. It's a holiday, so they'll all come readily enough. Tonight, along with Buffalmacco, I shall cast a spell on the sweets, and bring them round to your house first thing tomorrow morning. I shall hand the sweets out myself, to save you the trouble, and I shall pronounce all the right words and do all the right things.'

Calandrino issued the invitations, and next morning a goodly crowd of people assembled round the elm in front of the church, of whom some were farmworkers and others were young Florentines who happened to be staying in the country. Then along came Bruno and Buffalmacco with the box of sweets and the flask of wine, and having got them to stand in a circle, Bruno made the following announcement:

'Gentlemen, I must explain to you why you are here, so that if you should take offence at anything that happens, you won't go and blame it on me. The night before last, Calandrino, who is here among us, was robbed of a fine fat pig, and he can't find out who has taken it. And since it could only have been taken by one of the people here, he wants to discover who it was by offering, to each of you in turn, one of these sweets to eat, together with a drink of this wine. I should explain to you right away that whoever has taken the pig will be unable to swallow the sweet – in fact, he will find it more bitter than poison, and spit it out. So before he is put to so much shame in the presence of all these people, perhaps it would be better for the person responsible to make a clean breast of it to the priest, and I can call the whole thing off.'

All of them were only too eager to eat one of the sweets, and so Bruno, having lined them up with Calandrino in the middle, started from one end and began to hand one out to each of them in turn. When he came to Calandrino, he picked up one of the sweets of the canine variety and placed it in the palm of his hand. Calandrino promptly tossed it into his mouth and began to chew on it, but no sooner did his tongue come into contact with the aloe than, finding the bitter taste quite intolerable, he spat it out again.

They were all keeping a close watch on one another to see who was going to spit out his sweet, and Bruno, who still had several more to distribute, carried on as though nothing had happened until he heard a voice behind him saying: 'Hey, Calandrino, what's the meaning of this?' Turning quickly round, and seeing that Calandrino had spat his out, he said:

'Wait a minute! Perhaps he spat it out for some other reason. Here, take another!' And picking up the second one, he thrust it into Calandrino's mouth before proceeding to hand out the ones he had left.

Bitter as Calandrino had found the first, the second seemed a great deal more so, but being ashamed to spit it out, he kept it in his mouth for a while. As he chewed away at it, tears as big as hazelnuts began to roll down his cheeks until eventually, being unable to bear it any longer, he spat it out like the first.

Buffalmacco was meanwhile handing out drinks all round, with the assistance of Bruno. And when, along with all the others, they observed what had happened, everyone declared that Calandrino had obviously stolen the pig himself, and there were one or two who gave him a severe scolding about it.

However, when the crowd had dispersed, leaving Bruno and Buffalmacco alone with Calandrino, Buffalmacco turned to him and said:

'I was convinced all along that you were the one who had taken it. You were just pretending to us that it had been stolen so that you wouldn't have to buy us a few drinks out of the proceeds.'

Calandrino, who still had the bitter taste of the aloe in his mouth, swore to them that he had not taken the pig, but Buffalmacco said:

'Own up, man, how much did it fetch? Six florins?'

Calandrino was by now on the brink of despair, but Bruno said:

'You might as well know, Calandrino, that one of the fellows we were drinking and eating with this morning told me that you had a girl up here, that you kept her for your pleasure and gave her all the little titbits that came your way, and that he was quite certain you had sent her this pig of yours. You've become quite an expert at fooling people, haven't you? Remember the time you took us along the Mugnone?[3] There we were, collecting those black stones, and as soon as you'd got us stranded up the creek without a paddle, you cleared off home, and then tried to make us believe that you'd found the thing. And now that you've given away the pig, or sold it rather, you think you can persuade us, by uttering a few oaths, that it's been stolen. But you can't fool us any more: we've cottoned on to these tricks of yours. As a matter of fact, that's why we took so much trouble with the spell we cast on the sweets; and unless you give us two brace of capons for our pains, we intend to tell Monna Tessa the whole story.'

Seeing that they refused to believe him, and thinking that he had enough trouble on his hands without letting himself in for a diatribe from his wife, Calandrino gave them the two brace of capons. And after they had salted the pig, they carried their spoils back to Florence with them, leaving Calandrino to scratch his head and rue his losses.

SEVENTH STORY

A scholar falls in love with a widow, who, being in love with someone else, causes him to spend a winter's night waiting for her in the snow. But on a later occasion, as a result of following his advice, she is forced to spend a whole day, in mid July, at the top of a tower, where, being completely naked, she is exposed to the flies and the gadflies and the rays of the sun.

Though the ladies shook with laughter over the hapless Calandrino, they would have laughed even more if the people who had stolen

his pig had not relieved him also of his capons, which made them
feel sorry for him. However, the story having come to an end, the
queen called upon Pampinea to tell hers, and she began forthwith,
as follows:

Dearest ladies, one cunning deed is often capped by another,
and hence it is unwise to take a delight in deceiving others.
Many of the stories already narrated have caused us to laugh a
great deal over tricks that people have played on each other, but
in no case have we heard of the victim avenging himself. I therefore propose to enlist your sympathy for an act of just retribution
that was dealt to a fellow townswoman of ours, who very nearly
lost her life when she was hoist with her own petard. Nor will it
be unprofitable for you to hear this tale, for it will teach you to
think twice before playing tricks on people, which is always a
sensible precaution.

Not many years ago, there lived in Florence a young woman called
Elena, who was fair of body, proud of spirit, very gently bred, and
reasonably well endowed with Fortune's blessings. When her husband died prematurely, leaving her a widow,[1] she made up her
mind that she would never remarry, having fallen in love with a
handsome and charming young man of her own choosing. And
now that she was free from all other cares, she succeeded, with the
assistance of a maidservant whom she greatly trusted, in passing
many a pleasant hour in his arms, to the wondrous delight of both
parties.

Now it happened that around that time, a young nobleman of
our city called Rinieri,[2] having spent some years studying in Paris
with the purpose, not of selling his knowledge for gain as many
people do, but of learning the reasons and causes of things (a most
fitting pursuit for any gentleman), returned from Paris to Florence.
There he was held in high esteem for his nobility and his learning,
and he led the life of a gentleman.

But it frequently happens that the more keen a man's awareness
of life's profundities, the more vulnerable he is to the forces of
Love, and so it was in the case of this Rinieri. For one day, being in
need of a little diversion, he went to a banquet, where his eyes came

to rest upon this young woman, Elena, who was dressed (as our widows usually are) in black, and seemed to him the loveliest and most fascinating woman he had ever seen. He thought to himself that the man to whom God should grant the favour of holding her naked in his arms could truly claim that he was in Paradise. And having stolen many a cautious glance at the lady, knowing that so great and precious a prize could not be won without considerable effort, he firmly resolved to devote all his care and attention to pleasing the lady, so that he might win her love and savour her manifest beauty to the full.

The young woman, who was her own greatest admirer, was not in the habit of keeping her eyes fixed upon the ground, but darted coy glances in every direction and swiftly singled out those men who were showing an interest in her. And on catching sight of Rinieri, she laughed to herself and thought: 'I shan't have wasted my time in coming here today, for unless I am mistaken, I'm about to lead a simpleton by the nose.' She then began to look at him every so often out of the corner of her eye, and did her utmost to make it appear that she took an interest in him, being of the opinion, in any case, that the more men she could entice and conquer with her charms, the more highly would her beauty be prized, especially by the young man on whom, along with her love, she had bestowed it.

The learned scholar, setting all philosophical meditations aside, filled his mind exclusively with thoughts of the lady; and thinking it would please her, he discovered where she lived and began to walk past her house at frequent intervals, inventing various pretexts for passing that way. For the reason already mentioned, this greatly encouraged the lady's vanity, and she pretended to be very flattered. And so at the first opportunity the scholar made friends with her maidservant, declared his love for the lady, and begged her to use her influence with her mistress so that he might win her favours.

The maid promised him the moon and reported their conversation to her mistress, who laughed so much that she nearly died. And she said:

'I wonder where he's left all that wisdom that he brought back with him from Paris? But never mind, let's give him what he's looking for. Next time he speaks to you, tell him that I love him far more than he loves me; but tell him that I have to protect my honour, so that I may hold up my head in the company of other women. And if he's as wise a man as they say he is, this ought to make him think more highly of me.'

Ah, what a poor, misguided wretch she must have been, dear ladies, to suppose that she could get the better of a scholar!

But to return to our narrative, the maid having delivered the lady's message, the scholar, overjoyed, proceeded to entreat her with greater warmth than before, writing letters to her and sending her presents, all of which she accepted. But the only answers he received were couched in the vaguest of terms; and in this fashion she toyed with him for some little time.

She meanwhile gave a full account of the affair to her lover, who took it rather amiss and displayed a certain amount of jealousy. And so at length, in order to show him that his jealousy was misconceived, she sent her maid to the scholar, who was bombarding her with entreaties, to tell him on her behalf that albeit since the day he had first declared his love, she had not had a single opportunity to grant his desires, she hoped it would be possible to forgather with him in the immediate future, during Christmastide. If, therefore, he would like to come to the courtyard of her house after dark on the evening of the day after Christmas, she would meet him there as soon as she conveniently could.

The scholar was the happiest man in Christendom, and having gone to her house at the time she had specified, he was taken by the maid to a courtyard, where he was locked in and began to wait for the lady.

Earlier that evening, the lady had invited her lover to the house, and after they had supped merrily together, she told him what she was proposing to do that night, adding:

'And you'll be able to see exactly how much I love this fellow, whom you were foolish enough to regard as your rival.'

These words brought great joy to the heart of her lover, who was impatient to see what the outcome would be.

Now, it so happened that earlier in the day there had been a heavy fall of snow, and it lay thick all over the place, so before the scholar had spent much time in the courtyard, he began to feel distinctly chilly. But since he was expecting relief at any moment, he suffered it all in patience.

After a while, the lady said to her lover:

'Let's go and spy on this precious rival of yours from the little window in the bedroom, and see what he has to say to the maid. I have just sent her down to have a few words with him.'

So off they went to the bedroom, from which they could look down on the courtyard without being seen, and they heard the maid addressing the scholar from another window.

'Rinieri,' she said, 'my mistress is positively at her wits' end, for one of her brothers called on her this evening and kept her talking for ages, after which he insisted on staying for supper, and he still hasn't left, though I think he'll be going quite soon. This explains why she hasn't been able to come to you; but she'll be down in a moment, and begs you not to be angry with her for having to wait so long.'

Thinking the maid's story was true, the scholar replied:

'Tell my lady that she is not to worry on my account until it is convenient for her to come. But tell her to come as soon as she can.'

The maid closed the window and retired to bed, whereupon the lady said to her lover:

'What do you say to that, my dearest? Do you think I'd keep him out there freezing to death if I cared for him, as you suspect?'

Her lover's doubts were by now almost totally dispelled, and she got into bed with him, where they disported themselves merrily and rapturously for hours on end, laughing and making fun of the hapless scholar.

The scholar was walking up and down the courtyard to keep himself warm, and since there was nowhere for him to sit down or take shelter, he kept cursing the lady's brother for tarrying so long with her. Whenever he heard a sound, he thought it must be the lady opening a door to let him in, but his hopes were dashed every time.

After cavorting with her lover till the early hours of the morning, the lady said:

'What do you think of this scholar, my darling? Which would you say was the greater: his wisdom, or my love for him? Will the cold I am causing him to suffer dispel the coldness that entered your heart when I spoke of him in jest to you the other day?'

'But of course, my precious,' replied the lover. 'Now I can see quite clearly that you care for me as deeply as I care for you, who are the true source of my well-being, my repose and my delight, and the haven of all my desires.'

'Then give me a thousand kisses at least,' said the lady, 'so that I may see whether you are telling me the truth.' Whereupon, clasping her firmly to his bosom, her lover kissed her, not a thousand times, but more than a hundred thousand. But after they had billed and cooed in this fashion for a while, the lady said:

'Come, let's get up and see whether those flames, in which this weird lover of mine was always claiming to be consumed, show any sign of abating.'

They accordingly got up and returned once more to the window, and on looking down into the yard, they saw the scholar performing a sort of eightsome reel in the snow, for which the sound of his chattering teeth provided the backing. And because of the extreme cold, he was moving his feet at such a furious pace that they had never seen a dance to compare with it.

'What do you say to that, my sweetheart?' said the lady. 'Don't you think it clever of me to make men dance without the aid of trumpets or bagpipes?'

'I do indeed, my darling,' replied her lover, shaking with laughter.

Then the lady said:

'Let's go down to the door leading into the courtyard. You keep quiet while I talk to him, and we'll hear what he has to say. Perhaps it will be just as funny as it is to stand here and watch him.'

And so, having tiptoed out of the bedroom, they crept downstairs to the courtyard-door, and without opening it by so much as a fraction of an inch, the lady called out to the scholar in a low voice, through a tiny crack in the door.

On hearing her summons, the scholar gave thanks to God,

wrongly concluding that she was about to let him in. And walking across to the door, he said:

'Here I am, my lady. Open up for the love of God, for I'm freezing to death.'

'Ah yes, you must be very cold,' said the lady. 'But can it really be so chilly as all that out there, simply because it's been snowing a little? It snows a great deal harder in Paris, or so I've been told. I can't let you in at present, because this accursed brother of mine, who came to supper with me yesterday evening, still hasn't gone. However, he'll be going soon, and when he does, I'll come and let you in right away. I had an awful job to tear myself away from him just now, so that I could come and encourage you not to take offence over having to wait.'

'But, madam,' said the scholar, 'I implore you for the love of God to let me in, so that I can take shelter, for there was never such a heavy fall of snow as this, and it's still coming down. Once you've let me in, I'll wait as long as you please.'

'Alas, my dearest, I can't do that,' said the lady. 'This door makes such a din when it's opened that my brother would be sure to hear it. But I'll see if I can persuade him to go away now, and then I'll come back to let you in.'

'Go quickly then,' said the scholar. 'And I beg you to make sure there's a nice big fire, so that I can warm myself up when I come in. I'm so cold that I scarcely have any feeling left in my body.'

'I don't see how that can be possible,' said the lady. 'You always claim in your letters that you are burning all over because of your love for me. But it's clear to me now that you must have been joking. However, I must go now. Wait here, and keep your fingers crossed.'

The lady's lover, having heard every syllable, was mightily pleased, and returned with his mistress to bed, where they slept very little, but spent virtually the entire night disporting themselves and making fun of the unfortunate scholar.

Perceiving that he had been duped, the scholar, whose teeth were chattering so vigorously that he seemed to have been turned into a stork,[3] tried the door several times to see whether it would open, and searched all round the courtyard for some other way out. But finding none, he paced to and fro like a lion in a cage, cursing the severity of the weather, the perfidy of the lady, the inordinate length of the night, and his own stupidity. So indignant did he feel about the way he had been treated by the lady that his fervent and longstanding love was transformed into savage and bitter hatred, and his mind dwelt on various elaborate schemes for securing his revenge, which he now desired far more ardently than he had formerly yearned to hold her in his arms.

It seemed to him that the night would never end, but eventually the dawn began to appear, and the maidservant, following the instructions of her mistress, came down to open the courtyard gate. Pretending to be very sorry for him, she said:

'A curse on that brother of hers for coming here yesterday evening. He's kept us in suspense the entire night, and frozen you to the marrow. But you know how it is! Don't be disheartened, try again some other night, and perhaps you'll have better luck. My mistress is heartbroken that this should have happened, she really is.'

Though seething with indignation, the scholar was wise enough to know that menaces simply forearm the person who is threatened, and so, swallowing all the resentment that was striving within him for an outlet, he said to her in a quiet voice, without betraying the slightest hint of his anger:

'To be honest, it was the worst night I have ever spent, but I could see that the lady was in no way to blame, for she was so concerned about me that she came down in person to apologize and offer me her sympathy. And as you say, perhaps I shall have better luck some other night. So fare you well, and commend me to your mistress.'

Paralysed in every limb and every joint, he returned as best he could to his own house, where, feeling utterly exhausted, he flung himself on to his bed and fell fast asleep. Some time later, he woke up to find that he could scarcely move his arms or his legs, and having sent for physicians and told them about the chilling he had suffered, he placed himself under their care.

Though the physicians applied the most prompt and efficient remedies they could devise, it was some little time before they managed to restore his circulation and straighten out his limbs, and but for his relative youth and the advent of milder weather, he would never have recovered at all. However, having regained his health and vigour, he suppressed his hatred of the widow and pretended to be far more enamoured of her than he had ever been before.

Now, after a certain amount of time had elapsed, Fortune supplied the scholar with a chance to gratify his longing for revenge. For the young man who was the object of the widow's affection, paying no heed whatever to the love that she bore him, fell in love with another woman and resolved to have nothing more to do with her, so that she pined away in tears and bitter lamentations. But her maid, feeling very sorry for her and finding no way of assuaging the grief that had seized her mistress in the loss of her lover, conceived the foolish idea that the young man might be persuaded to return to his former love by the application of some form of magic. And since she supposed that the scholar, whom she regularly caught sight of in the neighbourhood as he passed by the house in his usual fashion, must be a great expert in the art of magic, she broached the idea to her mistress.

The lady was not very intelligent, and it never occurred to her that if the scholar had known anything about magic he would have used it on his own behalf. She therefore took the maid's suggestion seriously, and told her to go and find out at once whether he would do it. And in return for his assistance, she would promise him faithfully to give him whatever he wanted.

The maid scrupulously delivered the message, on hearing which the scholar was overjoyed, and said to himself: 'Praise be to God, for with His assistance, the time has come for me to punish the wicked hussy for the wrong she did me in exchange for all the love I bore her.' And turning to the maid, he said:

'Tell my lady not to worry about this, for even if her lover were in India, I should make him return to her at once and ask her forgiveness for flouting her wishes. Tell her that she has only to fix a time and a place, and I shall explain to her what she must do in order to remedy matters. And do please give her my kindest regards.'

The maid took his answer to her mistress, and it was arranged that they should meet in the church of Santa Lucia, near the Prato gate.

So there they met, the lady and the scholar, and as they conversed alone together, quite forgetting that this was the man she had almost conveyed to his death, she freely poured out all her troubles, told him what she desired, and begged him to come to her rescue, whereupon the scholar said:

'Madam, it is perfectly true that magic was one of the subjects I studied in Paris. I can assure you that I learned all there is to know about it, but since it is most distasteful to God, I made a vow never to practise it, either for my own or anyone else's benefit. However, my love for you is so intense that I find it impossible to refuse you anything, so even if I were to be consigned to Hell for this alone, I am ready to do it, since that is what you want of me. Nevertheless, I must warn you that this is a more difficult thing to achieve than perhaps you imagine, especially when a woman wishes to regain the love of a man or vice versa, for it cannot be done except by the person most closely involved. Moreover it is essential for this person to be very brave, for the operation must be carried out at night in a lonely place, with no other people present, and I do not know whether you are ready to comply with these conditions.'

Being more a slave to her love than a model of common sense, the lady replied:

'So powerful are the promptings of Love that I would do anything to possess again the man who has so cruelly forsaken me. But tell me, why do I have to be brave?'

'Madam,' replied the scholar, with devilish cunning, 'it will be my job to make an image, in tin, of the man whose love you wish to regain, and this I shall send to you in due course. Holding the image in your hand, you must make your way all alone, in the dead of night, when the moon is well on the wane, to a flowing stream, in which you must immerse yourself seven times, completely naked, after which, still naked, you must climb up a tree or on to the roof of some deserted building. Facing towards the north, with the image still in your hand, you must repeat seven times in succession a certain formula which I shall write down for you, whereupon you will be approached by two young ladies, as fair as you have ever seen, who will greet you amicably and ask you what it is that you want to be done. See that you explain your wishes to them as clearly and as fully as you can, and make sure that you give them the name of the right person. Once you've done that, they will go away, and you'll be able to descend to the place where you left your clothes, put them on again, and return home. And without a shadow of a doubt, by the middle of the following night your lover will come to you in tears, asking you to forgive and take pity on him. Thenceforth, I can assure you that he will never again desert you for another woman.'

The lady, hanging on his every word, was already, in her mind's eye, holding her lover once again in her arms, and half her troubles seemed to be over.

'You may rest assured,' she replied, 'that I shall carry out your instructions to the letter, and I know the very place to do it, for I have a farm along the upper reaches of the Arno which is very close to the banks of the river, and since we are now in the month of July it will be a pleasure to go for a bathe. Moreover, I recall that not far from the river there is a small tower, which is totally abandoned except for the fact that every so often the shepherds climb up the wooden ladder to a platform at the top, in order to scan the countryside for their lost sheep. The place is very deserted and out-of-the-way, and by climbing to the top of the tower, I hope to be in an ideal spot to do all you require.'

The scholar knew exactly where the lady's property and the little tower were situated, and being pleased to find that things were working according to plan, he said:

'I was never in those parts, madam, and hence I know neither the farm nor the tower of which you speak. But if your description is correct, there couldn't be a better place in the whole world. When the time is ripe, therefore, I shall send you the image and the magic formula; but I do urge you to remember, once your wish has been granted and you realize how well I have served you, to keep the promise you have given me.'

The lady assured him that she would do so without fail, and having taken her leave of him she returned to her house.

Delighted at the prospect of what was about to happen, the scholar fashioned an image with certain hieroglyphics upon it, and wrote down some nonsense concocted by himself to serve as a

formula. These he sent in due course to the lady, bidding her to
wait no longer, but to act upon his instructions on the very next
night; then he secretly made his way with a servant to the house of
one of his friends, which was not far away from the tower, in order
to carry his plan into effect.

For her part, the lady set out with her maidservant and went to
the farm. As soon as night had fallen, pretending that she was about
to retire, she sent the maid off to bed, and in the dead of night, she
stole softly out of the house and made her way to the bank of the
Arno, near the tower of which she had spoken. Then, having
peered in every direction and listened carefully to make sure that no
one was about, she undressed, concealed her clothes under a bush,
and dipped herself seven times in the river, clutching the image in
her hand; after which, still holding the image, she made her way,
naked, towards the tower.

Near the tower there was a clump of willows and other trees
from which the scholar, having concealed himself there with his
manservant shortly after dark, had viewed the whole of these
proceedings. When the lady, in all her naked beauty, was passing
within an arm's length of where he lay hidden, he could see her
white form piercing the shades of the night, and as he gazed upon
her bosom and the other parts of her body, perceiving how lovely
they were and thinking to himself what was shortly to happen to
them, he could not help feeling sorry for her. Moreover, being
suddenly assailed by the desires of the flesh, which caused a recum-
bent part of his person to stand, he was strongly tempted to sally
forth from his hiding-place, seize her in his arms, and take his
pleasure of her. So that, what with his pity on the one hand and his
lust on the other, he very nearly gave himself away. But when he
remembered who he was, the wrong he had suffered, the reason for
it, and the person who had inflicted it upon him, his indignation
was rekindled, dispelling all his pity and fleshly desires, and, clinging
firmly to his resolve, he allowed her to proceed on her way.

Having climbed to the top of the tower, the lady turned to face
the north and began to recite the words given to her by the scholar,
who meanwhile, having followed her into the tower, had silently
dismantled piece by piece the ladder leading up to the platform on

which she was standing. And he was now waiting to see what she would say and do.

The lady repeated the formula seven times and began to await the arrival of the two fair maidens, but she had so long to wait that, apart from feeling far more chilly than she would have wished, she was still there when the dawn began to appear. Feeling somewhat aggrieved that things had not worked out as the scholar had told her, she said to herself: 'I strongly suspect he was trying to give me a night like the one I provided for him; but if that was his intention, he's chosen a feeble way of avenging himself, for the night he spent was at least three times as long, and the cold was far more severe.' But as she had no desire to be found up there in broad daylight, she now prepared to descend, only to discover that the ladder had gone.

She accordingly felt as though the world beneath her feet had suddenly been taken away, and fell in a dead faint on the platform of the tower, where she lay for some time before recovering her senses. On coming round, she began to weep and wail in a most heartrending fashion, and realizing all too well that this was the scholar's handiwork, she repented the wrong she had done, as well as the excessive trust she had placed in someone she had every reason to look upon as her enemy. And whilst she was thus reproaching herself, a considerable time elapsed.

Eventually she looked all around her in search of some way to descend, but being unable to find any, she burst once more into tears and thought, bitterly, to herself: 'Oh, hapless woman, what will your brothers, your kinsfolk, your neighbours, and Florentine people in general have to say, when it is known that you were found in this spot, completely naked? Your fair repute will be seen as merely an empty façade; and if you try to brazen it out by giving some spurious explanation or other, you will be exposed by this accursed scholar, who knows all about your private affairs. Ah, poor wretch, that at one and the same moment you should have lost not only the young man you were foolish enough to love, but your good name into the bargain!' And her anguish grew to such a pitch that she was almost on the point of hurling herself from the tower to the ground.

The sun having now arisen, however, she moved a little closer to the wall on one side of the tower, thinking she might see some youngster driving his sheep in her direction, whom she could send to fetch her maidservant. But as she peeped over the rim, she caught sight of the scholar, who had just woken up after sleeping for a while under a bush.

'Good morning, madam,' he said. 'Have the young ladies arrived yet?'

On hearing these words, the lady burst into tears yet again, and begged him to come inside the tower so that she could speak to him.

The scholar very politely granted her request, and the lady, lying face downwards on the floor of the roof in such a way that only her head appeared in the aperture, addressed him, weeping plaintively and saying:

'You have certainly paid me back, Rinieri, for the unpleasant night I caused you to spend, for although we are in the month of July, I was convinced, not having any clothes on, that I was going to freeze to death up here last night. But apart from this I've been crying so much over the trick I played on you and over being such a fool as to believe you, that it's a miracle I have any eyes left in my head. I therefore implore you, not for love of me, whom you have no reason to love, but for your own sake, as a gentleman, to let this suffice by way of revenge for the injury I did you, and bring me my clothes and let me down. Please don't deprive me of that which you could never restore to me even if you wished, in other words, my good name. For even if I did prevent you from spending one night with me, I can make amends for it whenever you like by letting you spend many another night with me in exchange for that one. Rest content with what you have done. Let it suffice you, as a gentleman, to have succeeded in avenging yourself and making me aware of the fact. Don't apply your strength against a mere woman: the eagle that conquers a dove has nothing to boast about. For the love of God and the sake of your honour, do have mercy on me.'

The scholar, indignantly reflecting on the injury she had done him, and perceiving her tears and her entreaties, was filled with pleasure and sorrow at one and the same time: the pleasure of that revenge which he had desired above all else, and the sorrow engendered by his compassionate nature at the sight of her distress. His compassion being unequal, however, to his craving for revenge, he replied:

'Madonna Elena, if by my entreaties (albeit I had not the power to flavour them with tears and honeyed words as you do your own) I had succeeded, on the night I spent freezing to death in that snow-filled courtyard of yours, in prevailing upon you to shelter me in any way at all, it would be an easy matter for me now to grant your request. But since you display so much more concern now for your good name than you ever showed in the past, and find it so unpleasant to stay up there in a state of nudity, why do you not direct these pleas of yours to the man in whose arms, as you well remember, you were pleased to spend that night, no less naked than you are now, listening to me as I tramped with chattering teeth through the snow in your yard? Why not ask him to assist you, why not ask him to bring you your clothes, why not ask him to set up the ladder for you to descend? Why not turn to him to protect this good name of yours, since it is for his sake that you have placed it in jeopardy, not only now but a thousand times before?

'Why do you not call to him to come and help you? What could be more appropriate, since you belong to him? If he refuses to help and protect you, whom will he ever help and protect? Go on, you silly woman, call to him, and see whether your love for him and your intelligence, combined with his own, can save you from my stupidity. After all, did you not ask him, when you were cavorting together, whether he considered my stupidity or your love for him to be the greater? As for the generous offer you made just now to grant me your favours, I no longer desire them, and you couldn't very well deny them to me if I did. Save your nights for your lover, if you should happen to escape from here alive; you and he are welcome to them. One night was quite enough for me, and I have no intention of being fooled a second time.

'What is more, by cunningly mincing your words, you attempt through flattery to soften my heart towards you, calling me a gentleman, and quietly trying to dissuade me from punishing you for your wickedness, by appealing to my better nature. But the eyes of my mind will not be clouded now by your blandishments, as once they were by your perfidious promises. I know myself better now than I did earlier, for you taught me more about my own character in a single night than I ever learned during the whole of my stay in Paris.

'But even supposing I were a charitable man, you are not the sort of woman who deserves to be treated with charity. For a savage beast of your sort, death is the only fit punishment, the only just revenge, though admittedly, had I been dealing with a human being, I should already have done enough. So whilst I am not an eagle, yet, knowing that you are not a dove, but a poisonous snake, I intend to harry you with all the hatred and all the strength of a man who is fighting his oldest enemy. To call it revenge, however, is a misuse of words, for it is rather a punishment, inasmuch as revenge must exceed the offence and this will fall short of it. For when I consider how nearly you came to causing my death, it would not suffice for me to take your life by way of revenge, nor a hundred others like it, since I should only be killing a foul and wicked strumpet.

'For how, in the name of Lucifer, do you differ from any other miserable little whore, apart from having a tolerably pretty face, which in any case a few years hence will be covered all over in wrinkles? Yet it was not for lack of trying that you failed to murder a gentleman (as you called me just now), who can bring more benefit to humanity in a single day than a hundred thousand women of your sort can bring to it for as long as the world shall last. By suffering as you do now, then, you will possibly learn what it means to trifle with a man's affections, and to hold a man of learning up to ridicule; and if you should escape with your life, you will have good cause never to stoop to such folly again.

'But if you are so anxious to descend, why do you not throw yourself over the parapet? With God's help, you would break your neck, and so release yourself from the pain you seem to be suffering, at the same time making me the happiest man alive. That is all I have to say to you for the present. Now that I have managed to put you up there, let's see whether you are as clever at finding your way down as you were at making me look such a fool.'

Whilst the scholar was speaking, the hapless woman wept without stopping, time was passing, and the sun was climbing higher in the sky. But now that he was silent, she said:

'Ah! how could any man be so cruel! If you suffered so much on that accursed night, and my fault seemed so unpardonable, that neither my youth, my beauty, my bitter tears, nor my humble entreaties can evoke the tiniest crumb of pity, at least you should be touched to some extent, and hence prepared to treat me less severely, by the fact that I eventually trusted in you and told you all my secrets, thus allowing you to show me the error of my ways. For if I had not confided in you, you would not have been able to avenge yourself upon me, as you appear so eagerly to have wished.

'Alas! set your anger aside now, and grant me your forgiveness. If you will only forgive me and allow me to descend, I am prepared to forsake that faithless youth entirely, and you alone will be my lover and my lord, even though you despise my beauty, showing it to be fleeting and of little worth. But whatever you may say about it, or indeed about the beauty of any other woman, I can at least tell you this: that our beauty should be prized, if for no other reason than because it brings sweetness, joy, and solace to a man's youth; and you yourself are not old, by any means. Furthermore, however cruelly you treat me, I cannot believe that you would wish to see me suffer so ignominious a death as to throw myself down like a desperate woman before your very eyes – those eyes to which, unless you lied then as you do now, the sight of me was once so pleasing. Ah! in the name of God, have mercy on me, for pity's sake! The sun is becoming unbearably hot, and just as I suffered from the intense cold during the night, so now does the heat begin to distress me exceedingly.'

'Madam,' replied the scholar, who was only too delighted to converse with her, 'it was not because you loved me that you took me into your confidence, but to recover the love that you had lost, and hence you deserve to be treated even more harshly. Moreover you are out of your mind if you suppose that this was the only way I had of obtaining the revenge that I coveted. I had a thousand others, and I had placed a thousand snares around your feet whilst pretending to love you, so that even if this one had failed, you would inevitably have stumbled into another before very long.

True, you could not have chosen to fall into a trap which would bring you greater shame and suffering than this, but then I laid it in this way, not in order to spare your pain, but to enhance my pleasure. And even supposing that all my little schemes had failed, I should still have had my pen, with which I should have lampooned you so mercilessly, and with so much eloquence, that when my writings came to your notice (as they certainly would), you would have wished, a thousand times a day, that you had never been born.

'The power of the pen is far greater than those people suppose who have not proved it by experience. I swear to God (and may He grant that my revenge will continue to be as sweet from now until its end as it has been in its beginning), that you yourself, to say nothing of others, would have been so mortified by the things I had written that you would have put out your eyes rather than look upon yourself ever again. It's no use reproaching the sea for having grown from a tiny stream.

'As for your love, or that you should belong to me, these are matters towards which, as I said before, I am utterly indifferent. Go on belonging, if you can, to the man you belonged to before, whom I now love as much as I formerly hated, considering the pretty pass to which you have been brought on his account. You women are always falling in love with younger men, and yearning for them to love you in return, because of their fresher complexions and darker beards, their jaunty gait, their dancing and their jousting; but when a man is properly mature, he has put such matters as these behind him, and knows a thing or two that these young fellows have yet to learn.

'Moreover, because a young man will cover more miles in a single day, he seems to you a better rider. But whereas I admit that he will shake your skin-coat[4] with greater vigour, the older man, being more experienced, has a better idea of where the fleas are lurking. Besides, a portion that is small, but delicately flavoured, is infinitely preferable to a larger one that has no taste at all. And a hard gallop will tire and weaken a man, however young, whilst a gentle trot, though it may bring him somewhat later to the inn, will at least ensure that he is still in good fettle on arrival.

'Senseless creatures that you are, you fail to perceive how much evil may lie concealed beneath their handsome outward appearance. A young man is never content with one woman, but desires as many as he sets his eyes upon, thinking himself worthy of them all; hence his love can never be stable, as you can now bear witness all too clearly for yourself. Besides, they feel they have a right to be pampered and worshipped by their women, and take an enormous pride in boasting of their conquests – a failing which has caused many a woman to land in the arms of the friars, who keep their lips sealed about such matters. When you claim that your maid and I are the only people who know of your secret love, you are sadly mistaken. You deceive yourself if that is what you believe, for the people of the district where he lives, as well as of your own, talk about nothing else; but the person most closely involved is invariably the last to hear of these things. And you should also remember that young men will steal from you, whereas older men will give you presents.

'And so, having made a bad choice, you may remain his to whom you gave yourself, and leave me, whom you spurned, to another; for I have found a lady who is far more worthy of my love, and understands me better than you ever did. It seems that you do not believe me when I tell you, here and now, that I long to see you dead: but if you want proof of my words in the life hereafter, why not throw yourself to the ground without any further ado, in which case your soul, which I truly believe to be nestling already in the arms of the Devil, will soon see whether or not your headlong fall has brought any tears to my eyes? But since you are unlikely to afford me so great a pleasure as this, I shall simply advise you, if you find yourself being scorched, to remember the freezing you gave me, and if you mix the hot with the cold, you will doubtless find the rays of the sun more bearable.'

On perceiving from the scholar's words that he was determined to wreak vengeance upon her, the hapless lady burst once more into tears, and said:

'Since nothing pertaining to me can move you to pity me, at least be moved by the love you bear this other lady, who is so much wiser than myself, and by whom you claim to be loved. Forgive me for her sake, fetch me my clothes so that I may dress, and let me come down.'

Whereupon the scholar burst out laughing, and observing that it was already well past the hour of tierce, he replied:

'Ah, how can I refuse your request, now that you have appealed to me in her name? Tell me where your clothes are, so that I can go and fetch them and arrange for you to descend.'

The lady took him seriously and, feeling somewhat reassured, described to him exactly where she had hidden her clothes, whereupon the scholar issued forth from the tower and ordered his servant not to move away from the spot, but to stay close to the tower and do his best to see that no one set foot inside it until he returned. And having given him these instructions, he made his way to his friend's house, where in due course, after eating a most leisurely meal, he retired for a siesta.

The lady continued to lie on the roof of the tower, foolishly entertaining some faint hope of a speedy end to her predicament, until, feeling exceedingly sore, she sat up and crawled over to that section of the parapet which afforded a little shade from the sun, where she settled down to wait with no other company than her own bitter thoughts. By turns brooding and weeping, now hoping and now despairing of the scholar's return with her clothes, her mind flitting from one doleful reflection to the next, she eventually succumbed to her grief, and since she had been awake for the whole of the previous night, she fell into a deep slumber.

The sun was positively blazing, and having reached its zenith, was beating freely down, with all its power, straight on to her soft and tender body and on to her unprotected head, so that not only did it scorch every part of her flesh that was exposed to its rays, but it caused her skin to split into countless tiny cracks and fissures. And so intense was the roasting she received that although she was soundly asleep, it forced her to wake up.

On finding she was being burnt, she attempted to move, whereupon she felt as if the whole of her scorched skin was being rent asunder like a piece of flaming parchment being stretched from both ends. Moreover (and this was not in the least surprising), she had such an excruciating pain in her head that she thought it would burst. The floor of the tower-roof was so hot that she could find nowhere to stand or sit down, and so she kept shifting her position the whole time, weeping incessantly. But apart from all this, there being not a breath of wind, the air was literally teeming with flies and gadflies, which, settling in the fissures of her flesh, stung her so ferociously that every sting was like a spear being thrust into her body. And hence she flailed her arms in all directions, heaping a constant stream of curses upon herself, her life, her lover, and the scholar.

Being thus goaded, tormented, and pierced to the very quick by the incalculable heat, the rays of the sun, the flies and gadflies, her hunger and above all her thirst, as well as by a thousand agonizing thoughts, she stood up straight and looked about her in the hope of seeing or hearing someone who could be summoned to her assistance, being by now prepared to do anything, come what may, to effect her release.

But here too she was dogged by ill luck. The peasants had all deserted the fields on account of the heat, and in any case nobody had been working near the tower that morning because they were staying at home to thresh the corn. So all she heard was the sound of cicadas, and the only moving thing in sight was the Arno, whose inviting waters did nothing to lessen her thirst, but only made it worse. And scattered about the countryside she could see houses and woods and shaded places, all of which played no less cruelly upon · her desires.

What more are we to say of this hapless widow? What with the sun beating down from above, the torrid heat of the floor beneath her feet, and the flies and gadflies piercing her flesh all over, she was in such a sorry state that her body, whose whiteness had dispelled the shades of night just a few hours before, had now turned red as madder, and being liberally flecked with blood, it would have seemed, to anyone who saw it, the ugliest thing in the world.

There, then, she remained, bereft of all counsel and all hope, expecting rather to die than survive, until late in the afternoon, when the scholar, having risen from his siesta, returned to the tower to see how his lady was faring, and told his servant, who had not yet eaten, to go and procure himself a meal. On hearing him talking to the servant, the lady painfully dragged her weak, tormented body to the aperture, where she sat down, burst into tears, and said:

'Surely your revenge has exceeded all the bounds of reason, Rinieri. For whereas I made you freeze by night in my courtyard, you have roasted me on this tower by day, or rather burnt me to a cinder, and caused me to die of hunger and thirst in the process. I therefore beg you in God's name to come up here, and, since I do not have the courage to take my own life, to kill me yourself, for death is the one thing I desire above all else, such is the torture I am suffering. But if you are unwilling to concede me this favour, let me at least have a beaker of water so that I may moisten my mouth, which is so parched and dry that my tears will not suffice to bathe it.'

From the sound of her voice, the scholar realized all too plainly that her strength was failing. Furthermore, from that part of her body which was visible to him, he could see that she must be burnt by the sun from head to toe. All of which, together with the humble tone of her entreaties, caused him to feel a modicum of pity for her; but nevertheless he replied:

'Vile strumpet that you are, you shall not perish by these hands of mine, but by your own, if you really want to die. You will have as much water from me to relieve you from the heat, as you gave me fire to restore me from the cold. My one great regret is that the illness I suffered on account of the cold had to be treated with the warmth of stinking dung, whereas your own injuries, occasioned by the heat, can be treated with fragrant rose-water. And whereas I practically lost my life as well as the use of my limbs, you will merely be flayed by this heat, and emerge with your beauty unimpaired, like a snake that has sloughed off its skin.'

'Ah! woe is me,' cried the lady. 'I pray to God that only my worst enemies should acquire beauty by such means as this! But how could you be so cruel as to torture me in this fashion? What greater punishment could you or anyone else have inflicted upon me, if I had caused your entire kith and kin to die a lingering death? Of this at least I am certain, that no traitor who had put a whole city to the slaughter could have been more barbarously treated than

I have, for not only do you cause me to be roasted in the sun and devoured by flies, but you refuse me a beaker of water, when even a condemned murderer on his way to the gallows will frequently be given wine to drink if only he asks for it. However, since I see you are determined to be quite ruthless, and my suffering cannot move you in the slightest, I shall now prepare to die with resignation, so that God may have mercy on my soul, and I pray that He will observe what you have done and judge you accordingly.'

Having uttered these words, she crawled in terrible agony, being convinced that she would never survive the intense heat, towards the centre of the platform, where, quite apart from her other torments, she felt that she would swoon from thirst at any moment. And all the time, she was wailing loudly and bemoaning her misfortunes.

Finally, however, with the approach of evening, the scholar, feeling he had done enough, sent for her clothes and wrapped them in his servant's cloak, after which he made his way to the hapless lady's house, where he found her maid sitting sadly and forlornly on the doorstep, not knowing what she should do.

'My good woman,' he said, 'tell me, what has become of your mistress?'

'Sir,' replied the maidservant, 'I cannot rightly say. I was convinced that I saw her going to bed last night, and thought I should find her there this morning. But she was nowhere to be seen, and I have no idea what has become of her. I am dreadfully worried about her, but perhaps you, sir, have brought me some news of her whereabouts?'

'Would to God,' replied the scholar, 'that I had been able to put you in the place where I have put your mistress, so that I could punish you for your sins as I have punished your mistress for hers! But I assure you that you shan't escape from my clutches until I have paid you back with so much interest that you'll never make a fool of any man again without remembering me first.'

Then, turning to his servant, he said:

'Give her these clothes and tell her to go and fetch her, if she wants to.'

The servant did as he was bidden, and the maid, having seized the clothes from his hands, and recognized them, turned pale with terror, strongly suspecting, in view of what she had been told, that they had murdered her. Scarcely able to prevent herself from screaming, she burst into tears, and, the scholar having now departed, she immediately set off at a run towards the tower, with the clothes under her arm.

That same afternoon, a swineherd from the lady's estate had had the misfortune to lose two of his pigs, and, searching all over for them, he arrived at the tower shortly after the scholar had left. Peering into every nook and cranny to see whether his pigs were anywhere to be found, he heard the unfortunate lady's despairing moans, and climbing as far up the tower as he could, he called out:

'Who is it that is crying up there?'

Recognizing the swineherd's voice, the lady called to him by name, and said:

'Alas! go fetch my maid and tell her to come up here.'

'Oh my God!' he exclaimed, seeing who it was. 'How ever did you get up there, ma'am? Your maid has been searching high and low for you the whole day. But who would have thought of looking for you here?'

Seizing the ladder by the two uprights, he set it in the proper position and began to tie on the rungs by means of withies. As he was doing this, the maidservant arrived on the scene, and on entering the tower, no longer able to hold herself in check, she clapped her palms to the sides of her head and cried out:

'My poor, sweet mistress, where are you?'

On hearing the maidservant's voice, the lady called to her with all her strength, saying:

'Here I am, my sister. Up here. Don't cry, but just bring me my clothes, and quickly.'

No sooner did she hear the voice of her mistress, than her fears were almost entirely dispelled, and climbing the ladder, which by this time was all but repaired, she succeeded with the swineherd's assistance in reaching the platform, where, finding her mistress lying naked on the floor, utterly broken and exhausted, looking more like a burnt log than a human form, she dug her nails into her face and burst into tears, as though she were gazing down upon a corpse. However, the lady implored her for God's sake to be silent and help her to dress. And having learnt from the maid that no one knew where she had been, except for the swineherd and those who had brought her clothes, she felt somewhat relieved, and begged them for God's sake never to breathe a word about it to anyone.

The lady could not descend by herself, and so, after some little discussion, the swineherd hoisted her on to his shoulders and carried her safely down the ladder and out of the tower, leaving the maidservant to make her own way down. But being in too much of a hurry, the poor maidservant missed her footing as she was descending the ladder, and fell to the ground, breaking her thigh in the process, whereupon she began to roar with agony like a wounded lion.

Having set the lady down on the grass, the swineherd returned to see what was wrong with the maidservant, and on finding she had broken her thigh, he brought her forth in the same fashion, setting her on the grass by the side of her mistress. When the lady saw that, on top of her other afflictions, the person on whose assistance she most depended had broken her thigh, she burst yet again into tears, weeping so bitterly that not only was the swineherd unable to console her, but he too started to cry.

But as the sun was by now beginning to set, and the hapless lady was anxious that they should be away from there before nightfall, she prevailed upon him to go back to his house, whence, having enlisted the aid of his wife and two of his brothers, he returned with a plank on which they placed the maidservant and conveyed her to the house. Meanwhile, the lady's spirits having been restored by a draught of cool water and a torrent of sympathy, the swineherd hoisted her once more on to his shoulders, and carried her home, setting her down in her own bedroom.

His wife prepared a bowl of gruel for the lady, after which she undressed her and put her to bed. Between them they arranged that both the lady and her maid should be taken to Florence later that same night, and this was duly done.

On returning to Florence, the lady, who was by no means deficient in guile, wove a completely fictitious account of how she and her maid had sustained their injuries, and persuaded her brothers, sisters, and everyone else that it had all come about through the machinations of evil spirits.

The physicians promptly set to work upon the lady, but since she shed the whole of her skin several times over because it kept sticking to the bedclothes, she suffered untold agony and torment before they succeeded in curing her of her raging fever and other infirmities. They also attended to the maidservant's thigh, which in due course mended itself.

In view of what she had been through, the lady gave no further thought to her lover, and from then on she wisely refrained from playing any more tricks or falling deeply in love with anyone. As for the scholar, when he heard that the maid had broken her thigh, he deemed his revenge sufficient, and went happily about his business and said no more about it.

This, then, was the foolish young lady's reward for supposing it was no more difficult to trifle with a scholar than with any other man, being unaware that scholars – not all of them, mind you, but the majority at any rate – know where the devil keeps his tail.

I advise you therefore to think twice, ladies, before you play such tricks, especially when you have a scholar to deal with.

EIGHTH STORY

A story concerning two close friends, of whom the first goes to bed with the wife of the second. The second man finds out, and compels his wife to lock the first man in a chest, on which he makes love to his friend's wife whilst he is trapped inside.

Grievous and painful as the recital of Elena's woes had been to the ladies, their compassion was restrained by the knowledge that she had partially brought them upon herself, though at the same time they considered the scholar to have been excessively severe and relentless, not to say downright cruel. However, now that Pampinea had come to the end of her story, the queen called next upon Fiammetta, who, all eager to obey, began as follows:

Charming ladies, since you appear to have been somewhat

stricken by the harshness of the offended scholar, I consider this a
suitable moment at which to soothe your outraged feelings with
something a little more entertaining; and I therefore propose to tell
you a brief story about a young man who took a more charitable
view of an injury he received, and devised a more harmless way of
avenging himself. You will thereby be enabled to apprehend, that
when a man seeks to avenge an injury, it should be quite sufficient
for him to render an eye for an eye and a tooth for a tooth, without
wanting to inflict a punishment out of all proportion to the original
offence.

You are to know, then, that there once lived in Siena (or so I have
heard) two highly prosperous young men of good plebeian families,
of whom the first was called Spinelloccio Tavena and the second
was called Zeppa di Mino,[1] and they lived next door to one another
in the district of Camollia. They always went about together, and
to all outward appearances were as deeply attached to one another
as if they were brothers. And both were married to very beautiful
women.

Now, it happened that Spinelloccio spent a great deal of his time
in Zeppa's house, and since Zeppa was not always at home, he
made such good friends with Zeppa's wife that they became lovers,
and it was a long time before anyone discovered their secret. One
day, however, when Zeppa was at home and his wife was unaware
of the fact, Spinelloccio called at his house, and, on being informed
by the wife that Zeppa was out, he swiftly went up to the parlour,
where, perceiving that she was all alone, he enfolded her in his arms
and began to kiss her, and she greeted him in the same way.
Although Zeppa saw all this happening, he held his tongue and
remained hidden, so that he could see where their little game was
going to end; and before long, to his utter dismay, he saw his wife
and Spinelloccio, still clinging to one another, make their way into
the bedroom and lock themselves in. Realizing, however, that
neither by creating an uproar nor by interfering in any way was he
going to reduce the extent of his injury, but that on the contrary his
dishonour would thereby be increased,[2] he applied his mind to
devising some form of revenge that would satisfy his wounded

pride without causing any scandal, and after pondering at some length, he thought he had discovered a way of doing it.

He remained in hiding for as long as Spinelloccio and his wife were together, but as soon as Spinelloccio had left, he walked into the bedroom, where he found his wife still putting the finishing touches to her headdress, which had fallen off whilst she was cavorting with her lover.

'Well, woman,' he said, 'and what may you be doing?'

'Can't you see?' she replied.

'Yes,' said Zeppa, 'I can see all right. And I've seen one or two other things that I would have preferred not to see at all.' He then took her to task over what she had been doing, and after making numerous excuses, she confessed in fear and trembling to those aspects of her relationship with Spinelloccio that she could not very well deny, then burst into tears and asked his forgiveness.

Whereupon Zeppa said to her:

'Now listen to me, woman. You've done wrong, and if you want me to forgive you, see that you do exactly as I am about to tell you. I want you to tell Spinelloccio that tomorrow morning, about the hour of tierce, he is to invent some excuse for quitting my company so that he can come back here to you. Once he is here, I shall return home, and as soon as you hear me coming, you are to make him hide in this chest and lock him in, after which I shall give you the rest of your instructions. There's no need whatever for you to worry about doing all this. I give you my word that I shan't do him any harm.'

In order to please him, his wife agreed to do it, and gave Spinelloccio the message.

The following morning, Zeppa and Spinelloccio were roaming the streets together, and when it was nearly tierce, Spinelloccio, who had promised Zeppa's wife that he would call on her at that hour, said to his companion:

'I have to breakfast with a friend this morning, and I don't want to keep him waiting, so I think I'll be getting along.'

'You can't go to breakfast at this hour,' said Zeppa. 'It's too early.'

'That doesn't matter,' said Spinelloccio. 'I also have one or two things to discuss with him, so I still have to arrive there in good time.'

Having, therefore, taken leave of Zeppa, Spinelloccio doubled back on his tracks and was soon under Zeppa's roof in the company of his wife. But they had scarcely set foot inside the bedroom before Zeppa returned home, and as soon as the woman heard him coming, she pretended to be frightened out of her senses and, having persuaded Spinelloccio to take cover in the chest to which her husband had referred, she locked him inside it and left the room.

Zeppa came upstairs and asked her whether it was time for breakfast, and on being told that it was, he said:

'Spinelloccio is taking breakfast with a friend of his this morning, and he's left his wife all alone in the house. Go and call out to her from the window, and tell her to come and have breakfast with us.'

Still feeling apprehensive on her own account, the woman was only too ready to obey him, and promptly did as she was told. And so, after a good deal of coaxing, Spinelloccio's wife, hearing that her husband would not be returning home for breakfast, was persuaded by Zeppa's wife to come and join them. As soon as she set foot inside the house, Zeppa made a great fuss of her and took her tenderly by the hand. Then, having ordered his wife, in a low whisper, to go along to the kitchen, he led the other woman off into the bedroom, and no sooner had they crossed the threshold than he turned round and locked the door on the inside.

When she saw him locking the door, the woman said:

'Come now, Zeppa, what is the meaning of this? Was this, then, your reason for inviting me here? I thought you loved Spinelloccio as a brother, I thought you were his loyal friend.'

Holding her firmly round the waist, Zeppa guided her closer to the chest in which her husband was confined, and said to her:

'Before you go complaining, my dear, listen to what I have to say to you. I loved Spinelloccio as a brother, and I still do, but yesterday I discovered, without his knowing it, that my trust in him had come to this, that he makes love just as freely to my wife as he does to you. Now, because I love him, the only revenge I propose to take is one that exactly matches the offence. He has possessed my wife, and I intend to possess you. If you refuse to cooperate, I shall certainly catch him out sooner or later, and since I have no intention of allowing his offence to go unpunished, I shall deal with him in such a way as to make both of your lives a perpetual misery.'

Having listened to Zeppa's story and questioned him closely about it, the woman was convinced that he was telling the truth, and she said:

'My dear Zeppa, if I have to bear the brunt of your revenge, so be it; but only if you will see that your wife harbours no resentment against me over this deed we are obliged to perform, just as I myself, in spite of what she has done to me, intend to harbour none against her.'

To which Zeppa replied:

'I shall certainly see to that; and what's more, I shall present you with as fair and precious a jewel as any you possess.' So saying, he took her in his arms and began to kiss her; and having laid her on the chest in which her husband was imprisoned, he sported with her upon it to his heart's content, and she with him.

Spinelloccio, who was inside the chest and had not only heard all that Zeppa had said but also his wife's reply and the fandango that shortly thereafter took place directly above his head, was torn with anguish, and felt at any moment he would die. But for his fear of Zeppa, he would have given his wife a severe scolding, even though he was under lock and key. In the end, however, recalling that he himself was to blame in the first place, that Zeppa was justified in doing this to him and that he had chosen a civil and comradely way of taking his revenge, Spinelloccio vowed that, if Zeppa was agreeable, they would thenceforth become greater friends than ever.

Having taken his fill of pleasure, Zeppa stepped down from the chest, and on being asked by the lady for the jewel he had promised, he opened the door and summoned his wife. The only words she uttered, on entering the room, were:

'My dear, you've paid me back in my own coin.' And as she said this, she laughed.

Then Zeppa said to her:

'Open up this chest.'

She duly obeyed, and turning to the lady, Zeppa pointed to the huddled figure of her husband, Spinelloccio, who was now revealed inside it.

It would be hard to decide which of the two was the more embarrassed: Spinelloccio, on seeing Zeppa standing over him and knowing that he knew what he had done; or the lady, on seeing her husband and realizing that he had heard and felt what she had been doing directly above his head.

However, Zeppa broke the silence, saying to the lady:

'Here's the jewel I promised to give you.'

Spinelloccio now emerged from the chest, and without making too much fuss, he said:

'Now we are quits, Zeppa. So let us remain friends, as you were saying just now to my wife. And since we have always shared everything in common except our wives, let us share them as well.'

Zeppa having consented to this proposal, all four breakfasted together in perfect amity. And from that day forth, each of the ladies had two husbands, and each of the men had two wives, nor did this arrangement ever give rise to any argument or dispute between them.

NINTH STORY

Being eager to 'go the course' with a company of revellers, Master Simone, a physician, is prevailed upon by Bruno and Buffalmacco to proceed by night to a certain spot, where he is thrown by Buffalmacco into a ditch and left to wallow in its filth.

When the ladies had quite finished commenting upon the two Sienese and their wife-sharing, the queen, who short of offending Dioneo was the only one left to address them, began as follows:

When you consider, fond ladies, how richly Spinelloccio deserved the trick played upon him by Zeppa, you will I think agree with what Pampinea was saying earlier, when she tried to show that one should not judge a person too harshly for playing a trick on another, if the victim is being hoist with his own petard, or if he is simply asking to be made a fool of. The case of Spinelloccio belongs to the first of these categories, and I now propose to tell you of a man who belonged to the second, for I consider that those who played the trick upon him are worthy rather of praise than of blame. The man to whom I refer was a physician, who came to Florence from Bologna, like the ass that he was, covered in vair[1] from head to tail.

We are constantly seeing fellow-citizens of ours returning from Bologna as judges or physicians or lawyers, tricked out in long flowing robes of scarlet and vair, looking very grand and impressive, but failing to live up to their splendid appearance. Master Simone da Villa was a man of this sort, for his patrimony was far more substantial than his learning, and when, a few years ago, he came to Florence dressed in scarlet robes with a fine-looking hood, and calling himself a doctor of medicine, he set up house in the street we now call Via del Cocomero.[2]

Being, as we have said, newly arrived in Florence, this Master Simone made it a practice, among his other eccentricities, to ask whoever he happened to be with at the time about all the people he saw passing down the street; and he duly noted and remembered everything he was told about them, as though this information was essential in prescribing the right medicine for his patients.

Among the people who aroused his greatest curiosity were the two painters already mentioned twice here today,[3] Bruno and Buffalmacco, who were neighbours of his and never out of one another's company. Since they seemed to him the jolliest and most carefree fellows in the world, as was indeed the case, he made various inquiries about their social condition, and everyone told him that these two men were painters, who hadn't a penny to bless themselves with. But as he was unable to conceive how they could possibly lead such merry lives without visible means of support, he came to the conclusion, having heard that they were very clever, that they must be drawing huge profits from a source that other people had no knowledge of. He therefore became eager to make friends with one of them at least, if not with both, and eventually succeeded in striking up an acquaintance with Bruno, who, realizing from the first that this physician was a blockhead, began to take a huge delight in the man's extraordinary simplicity, whilst the physician for his part found Bruno wondrously entertaining. Having invited Bruno to breakfast with him a few times, thereby assuming that he could treat him as a familiar, he told him how amazed he was that he and Buffalmacco, considering they were so poor, could lead such merry lives; and he pleaded with Bruno to explain to him how they did it. Taking the physician's words as yet another proof of his crass stupidity, Bruno burst out laughing, and on the principle that a silly question deserves a silly answer, he replied as follows:

'Master Simone, there are few people to whom I would reveal this secret of ours, but since you are a friend and I know you won't let it go any further, I shan't keep it all to myself. It's perfectly true that my comrade and I lead as full and contented a life as you suppose, and even more so. Yet if we had to rely on our painting, or on the income from our capital, we shouldn't have enough to pay the water-rates. Not that I want you to think that we live by stealing: no, we simply go the course, as the saying is, by which means we obtain all the pleasures and necessities of life without doing harm to anyone; and that is how, as you've noticed, we always manage to be so cheerful.'

The physician, hanging on his every word without knowing what he was talking about, was filled with amazement by all this, and promptly conceived a burning desire to discover what was meant by 'going the course'. So he begged and pleaded with him to explain it, declaring most emphatically that he would never tell another living soul.

'Good heavens, Master!' exclaimed Bruno. 'Do you realize what you are asking me to do? The secret you want me to reveal is so tremendous that if anyone were to find out I had told you, I could be ruined and driven from the face of the earth; I could even finish up in the jaws of the Lucifer at San Gallo.[4] However, such is my veneration for your truly distinguished ineptitude that I am obliged to grant your every wish, and therefore I shall let you into the secret, but only on condition that you swear by the cross of Montesone[5] to keep your promise, and never repeat it to anyone.'

The physician gave him the required assurance, and Bruno continued:

'Know then, my sweet Master, that not long ago there came to this city a great master in necromancy, whose name was Michael Scott,[6] for he was a native of Scotland. He was entertained in princely style by many Florentine nobles, of whom only a handful are still alive, and when the time came for him to depart, they persuaded him to leave behind him two able disciples, whom he charged with the duty of ministering promptly to the pleasures of these nobles who had done him so much honour.

'These two men freely assisted the aforesaid nobles in certain love-affairs and other little escapades of theirs, and after a while, having taken a liking to the city and the ways of its people, they decided to settle here permanently. They soon acquired a goodly number of intimate friends in the city, without caring whether they were rich or poor, patrician or plebeian, provided only that they were men whose interests coincided with their own. And in order to please these friends of theirs, they founded a society of about five-and-twenty members, who were to meet at least twice a month in whatever place the pair of them should decide. When they are all assembled, each of the members makes a wish, and the two magicians see that it is granted that same night.

'Now, because Buffalmacco and I are on the most friendly and intimate of terms with these two men, they enrolled us in this society of theirs, and we've belonged to it ever since. I assure you that whenever we hold one of our meetings, it's a wonderful thing to behold the tapestries all round the walls of the banqueting hall, and the tables set in regal style, and the noble array of handsome-looking servants, both male and female, who are at the beck and call of every member of the company, and the bowls and the jugs, the flasks and the goblets, and the rest of the vessels from which we either eat or drink, all made of silver or of gold; and no less marvellous than all this, the abundance and variety of the dishes that are set before us one after the other, each of them suited to our own particular tastes.

'I could never describe to you the range and multiplicity of the dulcet sounds from countless instruments, and the melodious songs, that descend upon our ears at these gatherings. Nor could I tell you how many candles we burn at these banquets, or estimate the number of sweetmeats we consume, or the value of the wines that we drink. Neither would I want you to imagine, my dear wiseacre, that we attend these meetings in the clothes you normally see us wearing; even the most beggarly of the people present looks like an emperor, for we are decked out, one and all, in sumptuous robes and other finery.

'But over and above all these other delights, there are the beautiful women who are brought to us there, the moment we ask for them, from every corner of the earth. Not only would you see the Begum of Barbanicky, the Queen of the Basques, and the Sultana of Egypt, but also the Empress of Uzbek, the Chitchatess of Norwake, the Semolina of Nomansland, and the Scalpedra of Narsia. But why bother to enumerate them all? You would see every queen in the world there, not even excluding the Skinkymurra of Prester John,[7] who has horns sticking out of his anus: now there's a pretty sight! And when they have wined and dined, these ladies trip the light fantastic for a little while, after which each of them retires to a bedroom with the man who asked for her to be brought.

'Now these rooms, mark you, are so glorious to behold that you'd swear you were in Paradise itself. Moreover they're as fragrant as the spice-jars in your dispensary when you're pounding the cumin,[8] and the beds on which we lie are every bit as splendid as the Doge's bed in Venice. I leave you to imagine how busily these ladies work the treadle, and how nimbly they pull the shuttle through, to weave a fine close fabric. But the people who have the best time of all, in my opinion, are Buffalmacco and myself, because Buffalmacco invariably sends for the Queen of France, and I send for the Queen of England, who when all's said and done are two of the handsomest women on God's earth. So you can work it out for yourself whether we have good reason to be happier than other men, considering that we enjoy the love of two such queens as these, not to mention the fact that when we have need of a couple of thousand florins, they hand them over to us right away.

And that's what we mean when we talk about going the course, for just as the corsair takes away other people's goods, we do the same; but whereas corsairs never restore their plunder, we give ours back as soon as we've put it to good use.

'Now that you've discovered what is meant, my precious Master, by going the course, you will see for yourself how important it is that you should keep it a secret; so there's no need for me to say any more on the subject.'

Master Simone, the extent of whose medical knowledge was sufficient, perhaps, to treat an infant for thrush, took everything Bruno had said as the gospel truth, and was inflamed with an intense longing to become a member of their society, as though this were the highest good to which any mortal being could possibly aspire. He accordingly told Bruno that he was no longer in the least surprised that they were always so cheerfully disposed; and it was with the greatest difficulty that he restrained himself from urging him to enrol him there and then, rather than waiting until he had plied him more generously with his hospitality, after which he could plead his cause with a better chance of success.

Having therefore held himself in check, he assiduously began to court Bruno's friendship, regularly inviting him to breakfast and supper, and displaying boundless affection towards him. And they spent so much time in one another's company that it began to look as though the physician was unable to exist without him.

Bruno counted his blessings, and in order not to appear ungrateful for the physician's lavish hospitality, he painted a Lenten mural for him on the wall of his dining-room and an *Agnus Dei* at the entrance to his bedroom and a chamber-pot over his front door,[9] so that those people who needed to consult him could distinguish his house from the rest. Moreover, he decorated the loggia with a painting of the battle between the cats and the mice, which in the eyes of the physician was something of a masterpiece.

One morning, after failing to turn up to supper the previous evening, Bruno said to the physician:

'I was with the company last night, but as I'm tiring a little of the Queen of England, I got them to fetch me the Gumedra of the Great Khan of Altarisi.'

'Gumedra?' said the physician. 'What does that signify? I don't understand these titles.'

'I'm not a bit surprised, my dear Master,' said Bruno, 'for I've heard that neither Watercress nor Avadinner say anything on the subject.'

'You mean Hippocras and Avicenna,'[10] said the physician.

'You may well be right,' said Bruno, 'for these names of yours mean about as much to me as mine do to you. However, the word Gumedra in the language of the Great Khan is equivalent to the word Empress in ours. And believe you me, she's really delicious! She'd soon make you forget all about your medicines and your pills and your poultices, I can tell you.'

From time to time, by recounting other tales of a similar kind, Bruno added further fuel to the flames of the physician's longings, until, very late one evening, when Bruno was busy painting the battle between the cats and the mice by the light of a lantern being held aloft by Master Simone, the physician decided that Bruno was by now sufficiently in his debt for him to bring his feelings into the open. And since they were alone in the house, he said:

'As God is my witness, Bruno, there isn't anyone on earth for whom I would do all the things I would do for you. Why, even if you were to ask me to go all the way from here to Peretola,[11] I almost believe I would do it. So I trust you will not take it amiss if I speak to you now as an intimate friend, and ask you a favour in strict confidence. As you know, you spoke to me not long ago about the doings of your merry company, and ever since that day, I've been positively dying to attend your meetings. I have good reason for wanting to come, as you'll see for yourself if I should happen to be invited, for I assure you here and now that if I don't get those magicians of yours to fetch the comeliest serving wench you've seen for many a long day, I deserve to be taken for an idiot. I fell passionately in love with the girl from the moment I clapped eyes on her, last year in Cacavincigli,[12] and I swear to God that I offered her ten Bolognese groats, but she turned them down. So I implore you, from the bottom of my heart, to tell me what I have to do to become a member, and I beg you to use all your power and influence to bring it about, for I can assure you that you could never have a better or more loyal comrade, nor one who would bring you greater credit. I don't suppose, for instance, that any of your members is a doctor of medicine, and you can see for yourself what a handsome fellow I am, with a fine pair of shanks and a face like a rose. Besides, I know lots of good stories and some excellent songs. Would you like to hear one?' And without waiting for an answer, he burst into song.

Bruno was so amused by all this that he had a job to keep a straight face; and when the song was finished, the Master said:

'Well, Bruno, what do you think of that?'

'It's fantastic,' said Bruno. 'With a cacophonous voice like that, you could charm the vultures out of the trees.'

'If you hadn't heard it with your own ears,' said the Master, 'you wouldn't have believed it possible, would you?'

'I certainly wouldn't,' said Bruno.

'I know lots of others,' said the Master, 'but let's forget about those for the moment. Such as you see me, my father was a nobleman, though he lived in the country, and on my mother's side I was born into a family from Vallecchio.[13] Furthermore, as you will have seen, I have a finer collection of books, and a more splendid wardrobe, than any other doctor in Florence. God's faith! I have a robe that cost me nearly a hundred pounds in farthings, all told, ten years ago at the very least. So I do implore you to have me enrolled in your company; and· if you get me in, God's faith! you can be as ill as you like, and I'll never charge you a penny for my services.'

Bruno was more than ever convinced, having listened to his prattle, that the man was a complete nincompoop, and said to him:

'Shed a little more light up here, Master, and just be patient till I've finished putting the tails on these mice, then I'll give you my answer.'

When he had finished off the tails, Bruno pretended to be very worried by the doctor's request, and said:

'I know about the great things you would do for me, Master, but nevertheless the favour you are asking, though it may seem trivial to a man of your rare intellect, is anything but simple to my way of thinking, and even if I were in a position to grant it, I know of no one in the world for whom I would do it, apart from yourself. And I would do it for you, not only because I love you as a brother, but because your words are seasoned with so much wisdom that they would startle a pious old lady out of her boots, let alone persuade me to change my mind; indeed, the more time I spend in your company, the wiser you appear. Besides, even if I had no other reason for loving you, I am bound to love you on seeing that you have lost your heart to such a beauty as the one you described. I must however point out that I am not as influential as you suppose in these matters, and it is not within my power to grant your request. But if you will give me your solemn pledge, as a gentleman and a moron, to keep my words a secret, I shall explain how you can achieve your aim without my assistance. And since you have all those fine books and the other things you were telling me about, I feel certain that your efforts will be crowned with success.'

'Have no fear, you may speak out,' said the Master. 'If you knew me a little better, you'd soon find out whether I can keep a secret or not. Why, when Messer Guasparruolo da Saliceto was on the magistrates' bench at Forlimpopoli,[14] he confided nearly all his secrets to me, knowing they would be in safe keeping. And if you want me to prove it, I was the first man he told that he was about to marry Bergamina. Now what do you think of that?'

'That settles it,' said Bruno. 'If a man of that sort confided in you, I can certainly do the same. Now what you have to do is this. In this company of ours we have a captain and two counsellors, all of whom hold office for six months, and we know for certain that from the beginning of next month, Buffalmacco is to be captain and I am to be one of the counsellors. Whenever there is any question of nominating and electing a new member, the captain's views carry a great deal of weight, so I advise you to go out of your way to make friends with Buffalmacco, and entertain him on a suitably lavish scale. Buffalmacco's the sort of man who will take a powerful liking to you from the moment he discovers how intelligent you are, and when you've softened him up a little with your sparkling wit and those priceless treasures of yours, you can put the question to him, and he won't know how to refuse. I've already had a word with him about you, and he's dying to make your acquaintance, so do as I've suggested, and then leave the rest to Buffalmacco and myself.'

'This plan of yours seems most excellent,' said the Master, 'for if Buffalmacco takes a delight in the company of the wise, he has only to converse with me for a little while, and I guarantee that he will never want to let me out of his sight. I have enough intelligence to supply a whole city, and still remain a paragon of wisdom.'

Having thus arranged matters with Master Simone, Bruno recounted the whole tale in all its particulars to Buffalmacco, who was so impatient to proceed to the task of supplying Master Simpleton with the object of his quest, that every hour that passed seemed more like a thousand.

Being inordinately eager to go the course, the physician never relaxed until he had made Buffalmacco his friend, which he easily succeeded in doing. He then began to treat him to the finest suppers and breakfasts you could possibly imagine, to which Bruno also was invited. For their part, Bruno and Buffalmacco assiduously courted his company, and on finding themselves regaled with precious wines and fat capons and an abundance of other excellent dishes at Master Simone's table, they stuffed themselves like princes, and turned up for a meal even when they were not invited, always giving him to understand that they would not have done this for anyone else.

Eventually however the Master made the same request to Buffalmacco that he had previously made to Bruno, whereupon Buffalmacco pretended to be very angry and subjected Bruno to a torrent of abuse, saying:

'By the great tall God of Passignano,[15] I swear I've a good mind to give you such a pasting over the face that your nose would end up in your boots, traitor that you are, for you alone can have revealed these secrets to the Master.'

But Bruno was stoutly defended by the physician, who swore and affirmed that he had heard about these things from another source, and eventually succeeded in mollifying Buffalmacco with a goodly quantity of his pearls of wisdom, after which Buffalmacco turned to him and said:

'It's quite plain that you've been at Bologna, my dear Master, and that you came back here with a pair of well-sealed lips. Moreover you obviously didn't learn your alphabet from a black-board, as many an ignoramus has done, but from a blackamoor; and unless I'm mistaken, you were christened on a Sunday.[16] Bruno tells me you were studying medicine up there in Bologna, but it seems to me that you studied how to capture men's minds, for what with your wisdom and your singular ways, you're a better exponent of that particular art than any other man I ever saw.'

But at this point he was interrupted by the physician, who turned to Bruno and said:

'What a thing it is to meet and converse with men of wisdom! Who but this worthy man would have been so prompt to read all my thoughts? You were not nearly so quick as Buffalmacco to appreciate my excellence; but you might at least tell him what I said to you when you told me he took a delight in the company of the wise: do you think I've been as good as my word?'

'Better,' said Bruno.

The Master then turned to Buffalmacco, saying:

'You'd have had a lot more to say if you'd seen me in Bologna, where there wasn't a single person, great or small, student or professor, who didn't worship the very ground beneath my feet, such was the pleasure I was able to give to each and every one of them with my wise and witty conversation. And I can tell you this, that whenever I opened my mouth, I made everybody laugh because I was so popular. When the time came for me to leave Bologna, they were all heartbroken and wanted me to stay. In fact they were so anxious to keep me there that they offered to let me do all the teaching in the faculty of medicine. But I declined the offer because I'd made up my mind to return to the huge estates that my family has always owned in this part of the world. And that was what I did.'

Whereupon Bruno said to Buffalmacco:

'There now, I told you so, but you wouldn't believe me. Holy Mother of Jesus! There's not a doctor in the land who knows more than he does about the urine of an ass, nor would you find his equal if you were to go all the way from here to the gates of Paris. Surely you'll agree to help him now.'

'Bruno is quite right,' said the physician, 'but people don't appreciate me here. You Florentines are not very bright on the whole; I only wish you could see me in my natural element, surrounded by my fellow doctors.'

So Buffalmacco said:

'I must confess, Master, that you have a much better head on your shoulders than I ever gave you credit for. So speaking with all the deference that is due to a man of your great wisdom, I give you my equivocal promise that without fail I shall see that you are enrolled in our company.'

Now that he had been given this assurance, the doctor positively lavished hospitality on the two men, who enjoyed themselves enormously, persuading him to swallow the most fantastic pieces of nonsense; and they promised that he should have as his mistress the Countess of Cesspool,[17] who was the finest thing to be found in the entire arse-gallery of the human race. When the doctor asked them who this Countess was, Buffalmacco replied:

'Ah! my pretty pumpkin, she's a very great lady, and there are few houses anywhere on earth in which she doesn't make her presence smelt; why, even the Franciscans pay their tributes to her on the big bass drum, to say nothing of the countless others she receives. And I can tell you this, that wherever she happens to be, she lets people know about it, even though she generally holds herself aloof. All the same, she swept past your front door the other night when she was on her way to the Arno to bathe her feet and get a breath of fresh air; but she spends most of her time in Laterina.[18] You can regularly see her footmen going the rounds, all carrying a rod in one hand and a bucket in the other as symbols of her authority; and wherever you look you'll find many of her nobles, such as Baron Ffouljakes, Lord Dung, Viscount Broom-handle, and the Earl of Loosefart, and others, with all of whom I believe you are acquainted, though perhaps you don't recall them just at present. This, then, if all goes according to plan, is the great lady in whose tender arms we shall place you, in which case you can forget about that girl from Cacavincigli.'

Having been born and bred in Bologna, the physician was unable to grasp the meaning of their words, and told them that the lady would suit him down to the ground. Nor did he have long to wait before the two painters brought him the news of his election to the company.

On the morning of the day appointed for the next meeting of the society, the Master invited the pair of them to breakfast, and after the meal he asked them how he was to get there, to which Buffalmacco replied:

'See here, Master, for reasons you are now about to hear, you will have to be very brave, otherwise you may run into trouble and make things very awkward for us. This evening, after dark, you must contrive to climb up on to one of the raised tombs[19] that were erected just recently outside Santa Maria Novella, wearing one of your most sumptuous robes, for not only does the company require you to be nobly dressed when you are presented for the first time, but since you are gently bred, the Countess is proposing (or so we have been told, for we have never actually met her) to make you a Knight of the Bath[20] at her own expense. And you are to remain on the tomb till we send for you.

'Now, so that you will know exactly what to expect, I should explain that we shall be sending a black creature with horns to come and fetch you, which, though not very large, will attempt to frighten you by parading up and down before you in the piazza, leaping high in the air, and making loud hissing noises. When it sees that you are not afraid, it will come silently towards you, and as soon as it has drawn near to where you are sitting, you must clamber boldly down from the tomb, and, without invoking God or any of the Saints, leap on to its back. Once you are seated firmly on its back, you must fold your arms across your chest and leave them there, for you mustn't touch the beast with your hands.

'It will then move slowly off, and convey you to the place where we are all assembled; but I must stress here and now that if you invoke God or any of the Saints, or if you display any fear, you could be thrown off or dashed against something, and then you really will be in a stinking mess. So unless you're quite sure that your courage won't desert you, I advise you not to come, for you would only do yourself an injury and bring no credit to ourselves.'

'You don't know me yet,' said the physician. 'Perhaps it's because

I wear gloves and long robes that you doubt my courage. But if I
were to tell you about some of my nocturnal escapades in Bologna,
when I used to go after the women with my companions, you'd be
lost in admiration. God's faith, I remember a night when there was
one girl (a scraggy little baggage, what's more, no bigger than a
midget) who refused to come with us, so after giving her a few
good punches I picked her up bodily and carried her very nearly a
stone's throw, and in the end I forced her to come. Then there was
the time when I was all by myself except for my servant, and
shortly after the Angelus I walked past the cemetery of the Franciscans, where a woman had been buried earlier in the day, and I
wasn't the least bit afraid. So you have no need to worry on that
score, because I'm as brave and as bold a man as you're ever likely
to meet. As to my being nobly dressed for the occasion, I can tell
you that I shall wear the scarlet robes in which I was commenced,[21]
and you'll soon discover whether the company will rejoice to see
me, and whether I'm not elected captain before very long. Just wait
till I arrive there this evening, and you'll see how things will go, for
this Countess has never set eyes on me yet, and she's already so
enamoured of me that she wants to make me a Knight of the Bath.
Perhaps you think a knighthood wouldn't suit me, and that I shan't
know what to do with it when I've got it; but leave it to me, and
I'll show you!'

'That's all very well,' said Buffalmacco, 'but see that you don't
let us down, either by not coming or by not being there when we
send for you. The reason I say this is that the weather is cold, and
you medical men are very sensitive to the cold.'

'Heaven forbid,' said the physician. 'I'm not one of your cold-
blooded creatures; I don't mind the cold. In fact, whenever I get up
in the night to relieve nature, as we all do at times, I very rarely
throw anything over my nightshirt other than a fur coat. So you
may rest assured that I shall be there.'

Bruno and Buffalmacco then departed, and when darkness was
beginning to fall, the Master invented some excuse for leaving his
wife, and having smuggled his splendid gown out of the house, he
duly put it on and made his way to one of the aforementioned
tombs, where, since it was a bitterly cold evening, he sat huddled

on the marble, and began to await the arrival of the mysterious beast.

Buffalmacco, who was tall in stature and sturdy as an ox, had procured one of the masks that people used to wear at those special festivals that are nowadays no longer held;[22] and having donned a coat of black fur, he got himself up to look exactly like a bear, except that his mask had the face of the devil and was furnished with horns. In this strange garb, with Bruno following at a safe distance in order to observe the proceedings, he made his way to the new piazza at Santa Maria Novella. And no sooner did he perceive that the learned doctor was there than he began to dance and leap all over the piazza, hissing, screaming and shrieking like one possessed.

When the Master saw and heard all this, every hair of his head stood on end and he began to tremble all over, just like a woman, except that he was far more frightened. He began to think he should have stayed at home, but now that he had come so far, he tried to put a bold face upon it, such was his eagerness to observe the marvels of which the two men had spoken.

After cavorting madly for some little time in the manner we have described, Buffalmacco appeared to calm down, and coming over to the tomb on which the Master was seated, he stopped and stood perfectly still. Being terrified out of his wits, the Master could not decide whether to mount the creature or remain where he was, but in the end, fearing lest the thing should attack him if he failed to climb on to its back, he chose the lesser of the two evils; and having clambered down from the tomb, he leapt on the creature's back, whispering 'God preserve me' as he did so. Once he was firmly seated, still trembling like a leaf, he folded his arms across his chest as instructed, whereupon Buffalmacco moved slowly off on all fours in the direction of Santa Maria della Scala, and carried him almost as far as the nunnery of Ripole.[23]

Now at that time there were some ditches in those parts into which the farmers used to pour the offerings of the Countess of Cesspool, to enrich their lands. And when Buffalmacco reached this spot, he ambled up to the edge of one of the ditches, and, choosing the right moment, grabbed one of the doctor's feet and heaved him smartly off his back, casting him head first into the ditch. He then began to snarl in a most terrifying manner, leaping frantically all over the place, and eventually made his way back past Santa Maria della Scala towards the meadow of Ognissanti, where he rejoined Bruno who had run away because he was unable to contain his laughter. And hugging one another with glee, they went and watched from a safe distance to see what the filth-bespattered doctor would do.

The worthy physician, finding himself in this unspeakably loathsome place, endeavoured to stand on his feet and grope his way out, but stumbled and fell in all directions before he finally succeeded in scrambling clear, sorrowing and forlorn, and covered in filth from head to toe, having parted company with his doctoral hood and swallowed several drams of the ditchwater. Then, scraping the stuff off with his hands as best he could, he made his way back to his house, not knowing what else he could do, and knocked at the door until his wife came down to let him in.

He was no sooner inside the house, reeking to high heaven, and the door had been closed behind him, than Bruno and Buffalmacco were listening at the keyhole to hear what sort of a reception the Master's wife would accord him. And as they stood there on the doorstep, all ears, they heard the lady giving him the biggest scolding that ever a poor devil received.

'God, what a fine state you are in!' she said. 'Went to see some other woman, and wanted to cut a dashing figure in your scarlet robe, I suppose? Were you not satisfied with me? Hell's bells, I could satisfy a whole parish, let alone you. I wish to Christ they had drowned you, instead of simply dumping you where you deserved. A splendid physician you are, I don't think, to abandon your wife and go chasing after other people's women at this time of night!'

To these reproaches she added countless others whilst the physician was giving himself a good wash, and never stopped tormenting him until well into the small hours.

Next morning, Bruno and Buffalmacco painted bruises on their torsoes to make it look as if they had been severely beaten, then made their way to the house of the physician, who was already up and about. A foul smell assailed their nostrils from the moment they set foot inside the house, for no amount of washing and scrubbing had been able to disperse all trace of it. When the doctor was told that they had called to see him, he advanced to meet them, bidding them good morning, but Bruno and Buffalmacco looked at him angrily, as they had prearranged, and replied:

'We shan't say the same to you. On the contrary, we pray to God that you'll have a terrible morning and end up with your throat cut, for you are the dirtiest traitor that ever lived. We put ourselves to endless trouble to see that you should be honoured and entertained, and what thanks do we get, apart from being practically slaughtered like a pair of dogs? Why, you could have driven an ass all the way to Rome with fewer blows than the ones we received last night on account of your treachery, not to mention the fact that we were very nearly expelled from the very company we'd arranged for you to join. And if you think we're making this up, take a look at our bodies.' At which point they bared their chests sufficiently long for him to catch a glimpse of the mass of bruises they had painted there, then instantly covered them up again.

The physician attempted to apologize, recounting the saga of his misfortunes and telling them how he had been thrown into the ditch, but Buffalmacco cut him short, saying:

'I wish he'd hurled you from the bridge into the Arno. Didn't we warn you beforehand not to mention God or any of the Saints?'

'I swear to God I did no such thing,' said the physician.

'Is that so?' said Buffalmacco. 'And I suppose you're going to tell us you weren't afraid, either. But our informant told us you were trembling like a leaf, and didn't know whether you were coming or going. You've led us right up the garden path, but we shan't allow anyone to impose on us again. And as for you, we shall see that you are treated with the contempt you deserve.'

The physician pleaded with them to forgive him, and strove to mollify them with all the eloquence at his command, imploring them not to bring disgrace upon him. And out of fear lest they should make a public laughing-stock of him, from that day forth he pampered and fêted them on a much more lavish scale than ever before.

So now you have heard how wisdom is imparted to anyone who has not acquired much of it in Bologna.

TENTH STORY

A Sicilian lady cleverly relieves a merchant of the goods he has brought to Palermo. He later returns there pretending to have brought a much more valuable cargo, and after having borrowed a sum of money from the lady, leaves her with nothing but a quantity of water and tow.

There is no need to inquire whether the ladies laughed heartily over certain of the passages from the queen's story: they laughed so much that the tears ran down their cheeks a dozen times at the very least. But when the tale was ended, Dioneo, knowing it was now his turn, addressed the company as follows:

Gracious ladies, it goes without saying that the more cunning a person is, the greater our satisfaction in seeing that person cunningly deceived. And hence, whilst the stories you have told have all been excellent, the one I propose to relate should afford you greater pleasure than any of the others, inasmuch as it concerns the duping of a lady who knew far more about the art of deception than any of the men or women who were beguiled in the tales we have heard so far.

In the seaports of all maritime countries, it used to be the practice, and possibly still is, that any merchant arriving there with merchandise, having discharged his cargo, takes it to a warehouse, which in many places is called the *dogana*[1] and is maintained by the commune or by the ruler of the state. After presenting a written description of the cargo and its value to the officers in charge, he is given a storeroom where his merchandise is placed under lock and key. The officers then record all the details in their register under the merchant's name, and whenever the merchant removes his goods from bond, either wholly or in part, they make him pay the appropriate dues. It is by consulting this register that brokers, more often than not, obtain their information about the amount and value of the goods stored at the *dogana*, together with the names of the merchants to whom they belong. And when a suitable opportunity presents itself, they approach the merchants and arrange to barter, exchange, sell, or otherwise dispose of their merchandise.

Among the many seaports where this system prevailed was Palermo, in Sicily, which was also notable, and still is, for the number of women, lovely of body but strangers to virtue, who to anyone unfamiliar with their ways are frequently mistaken for great ladies of impeccable honesty. Their sole aim in life consists, not so much in fleecing men, as in skinning them wholesale, and whenever they catch sight of a merchant from foreign parts, they find out from the *dogana* register what goods he has deposited there and how much he is worth; after which, using all their charms and amorous wiles, and whispering honeyed words into the ears of their unsuspecting victim, they attempt to ensnare him into falling in love with them. In this way they have enticed a large number of merchants to part with a substantial proportion of their goods, and a great many others to hand over the entire lot, whilst some of them have been known to forfeit not only their merchandise, but their ships as well, and even their flesh and their bones, so daintily has the lady-barber known how to wield her razor.

To Palermo, then, not so very long ago, there came one of our young Florentines, Niccolò da Cignano[2] by name, though he was generally known as Salabaetto, who had been sent there by his principals with a consignment of woollens, worth about five hundred gold florins, which were left over from the fair at Salerno. Having handed the invoice for these goods to the officers of the *dogana*, he put them into store, and without showing any great eagerness to dispose of them, he began to see what the city could offer him in the way of amusement.

Since he was a very handsome youth, of fair complexion, with blond hair and a most shapely figure, it was not long before one of these lady-barbers, who styled herself Madonna Jancofiore,[3] having gleaned some knowledge of his affairs, began to cast glances in his direction. The young man, perceiving this, and assuming her to be some fine lady who had fallen for his handsome looks, decided that he would have to be very careful in conducting this little amour, and without breathing a word about it to anyone, he took to walking past her house at frequent intervals. He was soon observed by the lady, who after kindling the flames of his passion for a few days by flashing her eyes at him and appearing as if she was pining away for his love, secretly sent one of her maidservants to call upon him. This woman, being well versed in the arts of the procuress, spun him a long rigmarole and then, almost bursting into tears, informed him that her mistress was so taken up with his handsome looks and agreeable manners that she was unable to rest by day or night; she therefore hoped that he would agree to meet her in secret at some bagnio, there being nothing she more ardently desired; and finally, taking a ring from her purse, she handed it over to him with the lady's compliments.

When he heard this, Salabaetto was the happiest man who ever lived, and taking the ring, he brushed it against his eyelids, kissed it, and put it on his finger, telling the good woman that Madonna Jancofiore's love was fully reciprocated, since he loved her more than his very life, and that he was ready to meet her wherever and whenever she pleased.

The go-between returned with this answer to her mistress, and soon afterwards Salabaetto was informed that he was to wait for her at a certain bagnio on the following day after vespers. Without giving the slightest hint to anyone about where he was going, Salabaetto swiftly made his way to the bagnio at the appointed hour, and found that it was reserved for the lady. He had not been there long before two slave-girls arrived, one of whom was carrying a fine big feather mattress on her head, whilst the other had a huge basket filled with this, that, and the other. And having laid the mattress on a bed in one of the rooms of the bagnio, they covered it with a pair of sheets, fine as gossamer and edged all round with silk, over which they placed a quilt of whitest Cyprian buckram, together with two exquisitely embroidered pillows. They then undressed, got into the bath, and washed and scrubbed it all over until it gleamed.

Nor was it long before the lady herself arrived at the bagnio, attended by two more slave-girls. She no sooner saw Salabaetto than she rushed ecstatically forward to greet him, flung her arms round his neck, and smothered him with kisses; and after heaving several deep sighs, she said:

'My fascinating Tuscan, I know of no other man who could have brought me to do this. My heart is all on fire because of you.'

She then undressed, bidding him do the same, and they both stepped naked into the bath, attended by two of the slave-girls. Nor would she allow either of the girls to lay a hand upon him, but she herself washed Salabaetto from head to toe with marvellous care, using soap that was steeped in musk and cloves; and finally, she had herself washed and rubbed down by the two slave-girls.

This operation completed, the slave-girls fetched two sheets, white as snow and very finely woven, from which there came the fragrant smell of roses, so powerful that it seemed the bagnio was filled with roses and nothing else. Having wrapped Salabaetto in one of these and their mistress in the other, the slave-girls took them up and conveyed them both to the bed, where, when they had ceased to perspire, the sheets enfolding them were removed and they found themselves lying naked between the sheets of the bed. Silver phials, exquisitely wrought, were then produced from the basket, some filled with rose-water, others with the water of orange flowers or jasmine blossom, with which their bodies were liberally sprinkled by the slave-girls, after which they refreshed themselves for a while with precious wines and sweetmeats.

Salabaetto thought he was in Paradise, and devoured the lady a thousand times over with his eyes, for she was assuredly a very beautiful woman. Every hour that passed seemed to him a hundred years as he waited for the slave-girls to depart so that he might find himself in her embrace. Eventually, however, at the lady's command, they withdrew from the room, leaving a lighted torch behind them, whereupon she and Salabaetto fell into one another's arms. And there they remained together for some little time, to the immense delight of Salabaetto, who imagined her to be wasting away out of her love for him.

At length the lady decided it was time for them to rise, so she summoned the slave-girls, who helped them to dress. They then took some further refreshment in the form of wine and sweetmeats, and washed their faces and hands in the flower-scented waters. And as they were on the point of leaving, the lady said to Salabaetto:

'If it pleases you, I should consider it a very great favour if you were to come to my house for supper this evening, and spend the night with me.'

Being thoroughly taken in by her beauty and her calculated charm, and firmly believing that she loved him to distraction, Salabaetto replied:

'Whatever pleases you, my lady, is infinitely pleasing to me. Ask of me what you will, therefore, whether this evening or at any other time, and I shall do it gladly.'

And so returning to her house, the lady arranged for an impressive array of her gowns and other paraphernalia to be put on display in her bedroom, and having given instructions for a magnificent supper to be prepared, she waited for Salabaetto to come. As soon as it was reasonably dark, he made his way to the house, where he received a rapturous welcome, and after a most convivial supper, impeccably served, she led him off into the bedroom. The air was heavy with the wondrous fragrance of eagle-wood, and looking round, he observed that the bed was profusely adorned with mechanical songbirds, and that masses of beautiful gowns were hanging from the walls on pegs. All these things together, and each in particular, led him to the firm conviction that she was a great and wealthy lady. For although he had heard one or two rumours portraying her in quite a different light, nothing in the world could persuade him that there was any truth in these reports; and even if the suspicion crossed his mind that she had beguiled men before, he could never imagine for a moment that the same thing would happen to him.

It would be impossible to describe his bliss as he lay all night in her arms, the flames of his love burning ever more fiercely; and when morning came, she fastened a dainty and beautiful little silver girdle round his waist, with a fine purse to go with it, and said to him:

'My darling Salabaetto, I implore you to remember that just as my person is yours to enjoy, so everything I have here is yours, and all that I can do is at your command.'

Salabaetto took her in his arms and kissed her, then walked jauntily forth from the house and made his way down to that part of the city where his fellow merchants forgathered. From then on he consorted with her regularly without spending so much as a farthing, becoming ever more deeply enamoured. And when, eventually, he disposed of his woollen goods for ready money at a substantial profit, the good lady was immediately informed, though not by Salabaetto himself.

On the following evening, Salabaetto called to see her, and she began to jest and frolic with him, kissing and hugging him with such a show of burning passion that it seemed she would die of love in his arms. And she kept asking him to accept a pair of exquisite silver goblets, which Salabaetto refused to take, having at one time and another had presents from her worth at least thirty gold florins, without ever managing to persuade her to take so much as a silver groat in return. At length, however, when she had worked him up into a frenzy of excitement with her display of passion and generosity, she was called away from the room by one of her slave-girls, acting upon instructions received beforehand from her mistress. After a brief absence she returned, her eyes full of tears, and hurling herself face downwards on the bed, she began to give vent to the most piteous wailings that ever issued from a woman's lips, much to the astonishment of Salabaetto, who took her in his arms, and mingling his own tears with hers, he said:

'Ah, dearest heart of my body, what has happened to you so suddenly? What is the cause of all this sorrow? Ah! do tell me, my darling.'

After allowing Salabaetto to coax and cajole her for some little time, the lady replied:

'Alas, my sweet master, I know not what to do nor what to say. I have just received a letter from my brother, who writes from Messina, telling me that unless I send him a thousand gold florins without fail within the next seven days, by selling and pawning everything I have in the house, he will lose his head on the block. I have no idea how I am to find so large a sum at such short notice. If only I had a fortnight at my disposal, I should be able to raise twice the amount by collecting a certain sum of money that is owed to me, or I could sell one of the family estates. But since this is out of the question, I wish I'd been struck dead before this dreadful news had ever reached my ears ...' At which point she broke off, appearing sorely distressed, and the tears rolled down her cheeks in a never-ending torrent.

Salabaetto, who in the heat of his amorous passion had mislaid a substantial part of his wits, thought that her tears were genuine, and her words even more so. And he replied:

'Be of good cheer, my lady, for though I couldn't supply you with a thousand, I could certainly let you have five hundred gold florins, if you are sure you can repay me within the next fortnight. Fortunately for you, I managed only yesterday to dispose of my cargo of woollens, otherwise I shouldn't have been able to lend you a groat.'

'Do you mean to say,' said the lady, 'that you have been short of money? Why on earth didn't you ask me for some? I don't have a thousand, but I could easily have given you a hundred, and possibly two. And now that you have told me all this, I simply wouldn't have the heart to accept your offer of assistance.'

Deeply touched by these sentiments, Salabaetto replied:

'That is no reason for you to refuse, my lady. If my own need had been as great as yours, I should certainly have asked for your help.'

'Oh, my Salabaetto!' exclaimed the lady. 'I plainly perceive that your love for me is true and perfect, when without waiting to be asked for such a large sum of money, you freely offer to help me in my hour of need. And though I was all yours without this token of your love, from now on I shall assuredly belong to you even more completely; nor shall I ever forget that you saved my brother's life. God knows that I am reluctant to accept your offer, knowing that you are a merchant, and merchants do all their business with money. But I shall accept the money all the same, for my need is very urgent and I am quite confident that I shall be able to repay you in the near future. And as to the remainder of the sum I require, if I cannot find any swifter way of raising it, I shall place all these belongings of mine in pawn.' Whereupon she flung herself in tears across the bed, and buried Salabaetto's head in her bosom.

Salabaetto then set about consoling her as best he could, and after spending the night with her, he proved his generosity and devotion towards her by bringing her five hundred sparkling gold florins without waiting to be asked. These she accepted with laughter in her heart and tears in her eyes, promising to repay them as soon as she could, which was all that Salabaetto required by way of bond.

Now that she had her hands on the money, it became a different story altogether; for whereas he had always had free access to the lady whenever he pleased, she now began to fob him off with various excuses, so that nine times out of ten he was turned away from the house, and even when he did get in to see her, she no longer greeted him with the smiling countenance, the caresses, or the lavish hospitality to which he had previously been accustomed.

Not only did the lady fail to repay Salabaetto by the date she had promised, but a further month went by, then another, and when he asked her for his money, all he could get out of her was a string of excuses. Salabaetto now realized how cleverly he had been taken in by her villainy, and knowing that he could prove nothing against her (for he had no written evidence of the transaction, and there was no independent witness), he was exceedingly distressed and reproached himself bitterly for his foolishness. Moreover, he was too ashamed to lodge a complaint with the authorities, because he had been warned of her character beforehand and had only himself to blame if he was made a laughing-stock for behaving so stupidly. And when he received several letters from his principals ordering him to change the money and forward it to them, fearing lest his lapse should be discovered if he remained in Palermo any longer without obeying their instructions, he decided to leave. So he boarded a small ship, and instead of sailing to Pisa as he should have done, he went to Naples.

Now, there happened at that time to be living in Naples a compatriot of ours, Pietro dello Canigiano,[4] who was treasurer to Her Highness the Empress of Constantinople[5] – a man of great intelligence and shrewdness, and a very close friend of Salabaetto and his family. Knowing him to be the very soul of discretion, Salabaetto took him into his confidence a few days after his arrival, told him about what he had done and about the sad fate which had befallen him, and requested his assistance and advice in finding some means of livelihood in Naples, declaring that he had no intention of ever returning to Florence.

Saddened by what he had heard, Canigiano replied:

'A fine state of affairs, I must say; a fine way to carry on; a fine sense of loyalty you have shown to your employers. No sooner do you lay your hands on a large sum of money, than you squander the lot in riotous living. But what's done is done, and now we must look to the remedy.'

Since he had a shrewd head on his shoulders, Canigiano quickly saw what was to be done, and explained his plan to Salabaetto, who, thinking it an excellent idea, set about putting it into effect. He still had a little money of his own, and supplementing this with a loan from Canigiano, he ordered a number of bales of merchandise to be packed and tightly corded up, and having purchased and filled about a score of oil-casks, he loaded the entire consignment aboard a ship and returned to Palermo. There he presented the invoice for the bales to the officers of the *dogana*, to whom he also declared the value of the casks, and having made sure that they had registered everything under his own name, he placed the goods in store, saying that he wished to leave them there until the arrival of a further consignment of merchandise he was expecting.

On learning of his return and hearing that the goods he had brought were worth two thousand gold florins at the very least, without counting the goods still to come, which were valued at more than three thousand, Madonna Jancofiore, thinking she had set her sights too low, decided to repay him the five hundred florins so that she could get her claws on the greater portion of the five thousand, and sent word that she would like to see him.

When Salabaetto called upon her, she pretended to know nothing of the merchandise he had brought and gave him the warmest of welcomes, saying:

'Listen, my love; in case you were angry with me for not paying you back that money of yours punctually . . .'

But Salabaetto, having profited from his earlier mistakes, laughed and said:

'To tell the truth, my lady, I was very little displeased, for I would pluck the very heart from my body and give it to you, if I thought it would make you happy. But I should like you to judge for yourself how angry I am with you. So great and so particular is the love I bear you, that I have sold the greater part of my possessions, and now I have brought with me to Palermo a consignment of goods worth over two thousand florins. Moreover, I am expecting a further consignment from the West worth more than three thousand, and I intend to start a business in Palermo and settle here for good, for I consider myself more fortunate in loving you than any other lover in the world.'

'I do assure you, Salabaetto,' said the lady, 'that any success of yours gives me enormous pleasure, since I love you more dearly than my very life; and I am delighted that you have returned here with the intention of staying, for I hope we shall still have many a good time together. But I owe you a little apology for all those occasions, before you went away, when you wanted to come here and I was unable to see you, as well as for the times when you came and you were not so well received as usual. And I must also ask you to forgive me for not repaying your money by the date I had promised.

'You must remember that I was terribly sad and distressed at that particular time, and whenever a woman is in this condition, no matter how much she may love anyone, she cannot be as unfailingly cheerful and attentive towards him as he would like her to be. Besides, as you can hardly fail to realize, it is no easy matter for a woman to scrape together a thousand gold florins. We are always being fobbed off with lies, and people fail to keep their promises to us, with the result that we ourselves are compelled to tell lies to others. It was for this reason alone, and not through any ulterior motive, that I failed to pay you back. However, I did obtain the money shortly after you went away, and had I known your address, you may be quite sure that I would have sent it on to you; but since I didn't know where you were, I put it away for you in a safe place.'

Then, having called for a purse that contained the very florins he had given her, she placed it in his hand, saying:

'Count them and make sure they come to five hundred.'

Salabaetto had never felt so happy in his whole life, and having counted the florins and confirmed that they amounted to exactly five hundred, he tucked them away, saying:

'I know that you are telling me the truth, my lady. Indeed, you have done more than enough to prove it, and because of this, as also because of the love I bear you, I assure you that whenever you are in need of money in the future, and it is within my power to supply it, you have only to ask and it shall be yours. Once I have set up my business here in Palermo, you will see for yourself that this is no idle promise.'

Having thus cemented his love for the lady by means of these verbal protestations, Salabaetto began once more to play the gallant with her, whilst for her part she entertained and solaced him for all she was worth, pretending to love him to the point of distraction. However, Salabaetto was determined that his own duplicity should punish hers, and one evening, having received an invitation from her earlier in the day to sup and spend the night with her, he turned up at her house looking so distraught and miserable that it seemed he was about to die at any moment. Jancofiore, hugging and kissing him, began to question him about the reasons for his sadness, and after allowing her to wheedle him for a while, he replied:

'I am utterly ruined, for the ship carrying the goods I was expecting has been seized by Monegasque pirates.[6] They are demanding a ransom of ten thousand gold florins, of which I have to pay a thousand, and I haven't a penny to my name, because as soon as you paid me back those five hundred florins, I sent them to Naples to be invested in a consignment of linen which is now on its way to Palermo. If I were to sell the goods I have in store here at the moment, I should lose half their true value, because it's the wrong time to sell. On the other hand, I can't find anyone here to lend me the money, because I am still not well enough known in the city. Hence I have no idea what to do or what to say; if I don't send the money soon, my merchandise will be shipped to Monaco and I shall never see it again.'

These tidings were highly irritating to the lady, for it seemed she was about to lose everything; but perceiving what she must do to prevent the goods going to Monaco, she said:

'God knows I love you so dearly that I am very sorry to hear of your misfortune. But what's the use of becoming so upset about it? If I had the money to lend you, God knows that I should let you have it here and now, but I haven't got it. It's true that I know of someone who might help – the person who lent me the remaining five hundred florins I needed the other month – but he charges a high rate of interest. You'd have to pay him at least thirty per cent if you were to borrow the money from him, and he would want something substantial by way of security. Now I personally would be prepared for your sake to offer him all I possess, myself included, as security for whatever sum he will lend, but how are you going to guarantee the rest of the loan?'

Salabaetto was delighted, for he knew exactly what was prompting her to do him this favour, and perceived that it was she herself who would be lending him the money. So after he had thanked her, he told her that he would not be deterred by the exorbitant rate of interest, as he needed the money very badly; and he then went on to explain that by way of surety he would place the merchandise he had at the *dogana* to the credit of the person who was to lend him the money. However, he wished to retain the key to the warehouse, so as to be able to display his merchandise if anyone should ask him to do so, and also to ensure that his goods were not interfered with or exchanged or moved elsewhere.

The lady agreed that this was a wise precaution, and declared that a surety of this kind would be more than adequate. Early next morning, she sent for a broker who was privy to most of her secrets, and having explained the situation to him, she gave him a thousand gold florins, which the broker lent to Salabaetto, having first ensured that all the goods that Salabaetto had at the *dogana* were transferred to his own name. Various documents were signed and countersigned by the two men, and when all was settled between them, they went their separate ways to attend to their other affairs.

At the earliest opportunity, Salabaetto took ship with his fifteen hundred gold florins, and returned to Pietro dello Canigiano in Naples, whence he made full remittance to his principals in Florence for the woollens with which they had originally sent him to

Palermo. And having paid Pietro and all his other creditors, he made merry with Canigiano over the trick he had played on the Sicilian woman, celebrating his success for several days on end. He then left Naples, and having decided to retire from commerce, made his way to Ferrara.

When Jancofiore learned that Salabaetto was no longer to be found in Palermo, her suspicions were aroused and she began to wonder what had become of him. After waiting for at least two months without seeing any sign of him, she got the broker to force a way into the warehouse. And having first of all tested the casks, which were supposed to be full of oil, she discovered that they were filled with sea-water, apart from about a firkin of oil that was floating at the top of each cask, near the bung-hole. Then, untying the bales, she found that all except two (which consisted of woollens) were filled with tow. And in fact, to cut a long story short, the whole consignment was worth no more than two hundred florins.

On perceiving that she had been outwitted, Jancofiore lamented long and bitterly over the five hundred florins she had repaid, and even more over the thousand she had lent, frequently repeating to herself the old saw: 'Honesty's the better line, when dealing with a Florentine.' And so it was that, having burnt her fingers and covered herself in ridicule, she discovered that some people are every bit as knowing as others.

*   *   *

No sooner had Dioneo reached the end of his story, than Lauretta, knowing that the time had come for her to abdicate, commended the advice given by Pietro dello Canigiano, which to judge by its effects had been very sound; and having also praised the sagacity of Salabaetto, who was no less worthy of commendation for translating Pietro's advice into practice, she removed the laurel crown from her head and placed it upon Emilia's, saying with womanly grace:

'I know not, madam, whether you will make an agreeable queen, but we shall certainly have a fair one. See to it, then, that your actions are in keeping with your beauty.'

Lauretta then resumed her seat, leaving Emilia feeling somewhat ill at ease, not so much in having been made their queen as in hearing herself praised in public for something to which ladies are wont to attach most importance, and her face turned the colour of fresh roses at dawn. But having lowered her gaze until her blushes had receded, she summoned the steward and made appropriate arrangements for their activities of the morrow, after which she addressed them as follows:

'Delectable ladies, we may readily observe that when oxen have laboured in chains beneath the yoke for a certain portion of the day, their yoke is removed and they are put out to grass, being allowed to roam freely through the woods wherever they please. Similarly, we may perceive that gardens stocked with numerous different trees are much more beautiful than forests consisting solely of oaks. And therefore, having regard to the number of days during which our deliberations have been confined within a predetermined scheme, I consider that it would be both appropriate and useful for us to wander at large for a while, and in so doing recover the strength for returning once again beneath the yoke.

'Accordingly, when we resume our storytelling on the morrow, I do not propose to confine you to any particular topic; on the contrary, I desire that each of us should speak on whatever subject he or she may choose,[1] it being my firm conviction that we shall find it no less rewarding to hear a variety of themes discussed than if we had restricted ourselves to one alone. Moreover, by doing as I have suggested, we shall all recruit our strength, and thus my successor will feel more justified in forcing us to observe our customary rule.'

The members of the company applauded the queen for proposing so sensible an arrangement; and rising from their places, they turned to various forms of relaxation, the ladies making garlands and otherwise amusing themselves whilst the young men sang songs and played games. In this way they whiled away their time until supper, to which in due course they gaily addressed themselves, sitting in a circle round the delectable fountain. And when supper was over they freely engaged in their usual pastimes of singing and dancing.

Finally the queen, out of deference to the ways of her predecessors, ordered Panfilo to sing a song, notwithstanding the fact that various

members of the company had already sung several of their own
accord. And so Panfilo promptly began, as follows:

> 'Love, I take such delight in thee,
> And find such joy and pleasure in thy name,
> That I am happy burning in thy flame.
>
> 'I feel such joy within my breast,
> Grown from the precious grace
> Which thou hast brought to me,
> So strong it cannot be suppressed
> But shines out from my face
> Declaring me to be
> Enamoured joyfully –
> Happy to stay and burn so nigh
> To one in place and name so high!
>
> 'I cannot sing aloud in song
> Or sketch forth with my hand
> The joy, Love, that I know;
> For to reveal it would be wrong,
> That I well understand.
> A torment it would grow;
> But I am happy so.
> All speech would be subdued and broken
> 'Ere one small part of it were spoken.
>
> 'Who is there who aright could guess
> My arms would find that place
> That they were clasped around?
> None would believe my happiness
> That I might bend my face
> Whither I did, and found
> Salvation sweet and grace.
> Hence I with burning joy conceal
> A rapture I may not reveal.'

Thus did Panfilo's song come to an end, and though everyone
had joined wholeheartedly in the refrain, there was not a single
person present who did not attend more carefully than usual to the
words, striving to guess what Panfilo had implied he was obliged to
conceal. And whilst several formed their own opinions as to his

meaning, they were all well wide of the mark. But in the end the queen, perceiving that Panfilo's song was finished and that the young ladies and the gentlemen were showing clear signs of fatigue, ordered them all to retire to bed.

Here ends the Eighth Day of the Decameron

NINTH DAY

Here begins the Ninth Day, wherein, under the rule of Emilia, it is left to all the members of the company to speak on whatever subject they choose.

The light whose radiance dispels the shades of night had already softened into pale celestial hues the deep azure of the eighth heaven,[1] and the flowerets in the meadows had begun to raise their drooping heads, when Emilia arose and caused the other young ladies to be called, and likewise the three young men. Answering her summons, they set off at a leisurely pace behind the queen, and made their way to a little wood, not very far from the palace. On entering the wood, they observed a number of roebucks, stags, and other wild creatures, which, as though sensing they were safe from the hunter on account of the plague, stood their ground as if they had been rendered tame and fearless. However, by approaching these creatures one after another as though intending to touch them, they caused them to run away and leap in the air; and in this way they amused themselves for some little time until, the sun being now in the ascendant, they thought it expedient to retrace their steps.

They were all wreathed in fronds of oak, and their hands were full of fragrant herbs or flowers, so that if anyone had encountered them, he would only have been able to say: 'Either these people will not be vanquished by death, or they will welcome it with joy.'

And so back they came, step by gradual step, singing, chattering, and jesting with one another as they walked along, and on reaching the palace they found everything neatly arranged and the servants all gay and festive. They then rested for a while, nor did they sit down at table before half-a-dozen canzonets, each of them more lively than the one preceding it, had been sung by the young men and the ladies; after which, having rinsed their hands in water, they were shown to their places at table by the steward, acting on instructions from the queen. The food was served, and they all ate merrily; and after rising from their meal, they danced and made music for a while until the queen gave permission, to those who so desired, to retire to rest.

At the customary hour, however, they were all seated in their usual places for the start of their discussions, and the queen, looking towards Filomena, bade her tell the first story of the day, whereupon Filomena smiled and began as follows:

FIRST STORY

Madonna Francesca is wooed by a certain Rinuccio and a certain Alessandro, but is not herself in love with either. She therefore induces the one to enter a tomb and pose as a corpse, and the other to go in and fetch him out, and since neither succeeds in completing his allotted task, she discreetly rids herself of both.

Since it is your wish, my lady, that I should be the first to sally forth into this broad and spacious arena to which we have been brought by your bounteous decree, I shall do so with the greatest of pleasure. And if I should acquit myself favourably therein, I daresay those who follow me will do as well as I, and even better.

In the course of our conversations, dear ladies, we have repeatedly seen how great and mighty are the forces of Love. Yet I do not think we have fully exhausted the subject, nor would we do so if we were to talk of nothing else for a whole year. And since Love not only leads lovers into divers situations fraught with mortal peril, but will even induce them to enter the houses of the dead in the guise of corpses, I should like to tell you a story on this very subject, by way of addition to those already told, from which you will not only comprehend the power of Love, but learn of the ingenious means employed by a worthy lady to rid herself of two unwanted admirers.

I say then that in the city of Pistoia, there was once a very beautiful widow, of whom, as chance would have it, two of our fellow-

Florentines, who were living in Pistoia after being banished from Florence, became deeply enamoured. Their names were Rinuccio Palermini and Alessandro Chiarmontesi,[1] and each of them, unknown to the other, was secretly doing his utmost to win the lady's love.

The gentlewoman, whose name was Madonna Francesca de' Lazzari,[2] was subjected to a steady stream of messages and entreaties from the two men, to which on occasion she had been incautious enough to lend a ready ear; and being unable to extricate herself, as she was prudent enough to wish, she conceived a plan[3] for ridding herself from their importunities. This consisted in asking them to do her a service which, though not impossible, she thought that no one would ever perform, so that when they failed to carry it out she would have plausible and legitimate grounds for rejecting their advances; and her plan was as follows.

On the day the idea came into her head, the death had occurred in Pistoia of a man who, despite the nobility of his lineage, was reputed to be the greatest rogue who had ever lived, not only in Pistoia but in the whole world. Moreover, he was so deformed of body and his features were so hideously distorted that any stranger, on seeing him for the first time, would have been terrified out of his wits. He had been buried in a tomb outside the church of the Franciscans, and the lady, seeing this as a good opportunity to further her intentions, summoned one of her maidservants and said:

'As you know, not a day passes without my being plagued and tormented from morning till night with the attentions of those two Florentines, Rinuccio and Alessandro. I have no intention of conceding my love to either of the two, and in order to be rid of them, I have made up my mind, since they are always so free with their promises, to test their sincerity by setting them both a task which I am certain they will fail to accomplish, and thus I shall put an end to their pestering.

'Now this is how I shall go about it. As you know, this morning at the convent of the Franciscans, the burial took place of Scannadio[4] (such was the name of the villain in question), the sight of whom was sufficient, when he was still alive, let alone now that he is dead, to frighten the bravest men in the land. So I want you first of all to go secretly to Alessandro, and say to him: "Madonna Francesca sends me to tell you that the time has come when you may have the love for which you have been craving, and that if you so desire you can go to her in the manner I shall now explain. For reasons you will be told about later, a kinsman of hers is obliged to convey to her house, tonight, the body of Scannadio, who was buried this morning. And since she is utterly repelled by the thought of harbouring this man's corpse under her own roof, she implores you to do her a great favour, namely that when darkness has fallen, you should enter Scannadio's tomb, put on his clothes, and lie there impersonating him till her kinsman comes to fetch you. Without saying a word or uttering any sound, you are to allow yourself to be taken from the tomb and brought to her house. She will be waiting there to receive you, and you will be able to stay with her for as long as you like, leaving everything else to her." If he agrees to do this, all well and good; but if he refuses, you are to tell him from me that I never want to set eyes on him again, and that if he values his life he will take good care not to send me any more of his messages or entreaties.

'You will then go to Rinuccio Palermini and say to him: "Madonna Francesca says she is ready to grant your every wish, provided you do her a great favour, namely that just before midnight tonight you go to the tomb where Scannadio was buried this morning, and without saying a word about anything you may see or hear, fetch his body gently forth and take it to her house. There you will discover why she wants you to do her this service, and you will have all you desire of her. But if you should refuse to do it, she charges you here and now never to send her any further messages or entreaties."'

The maidservant called on each of the men in turn and delivered the two messages exactly as instructed, in each case receiving the same answer, namely that they would venture into Hell itself, let alone a tomb, if she wanted them to do so. So the maid conveyed this answer to her mistress, who waited to see whether they were mad enough to carry out her request.

After dark, having waited until most people were asleep, Alessandro Chiarmontesi stripped down to his doublet and set forth from

his house in order to take Scannadio's place in the tomb. But as he
was on his way to the graveyard, he began to feel very frightened,
and to say to himself: 'Why should I be such a fool? Where do I
think I'm going? For all I know, her kinsfolk may have discovered
I'm in love with her. Perhaps they think I've seduced her, and have
forced her into this so that they can murder me inside the tomb. If
that's the case, I shan't stand a dog's chance, nobody will be any the
wiser, and they'll escape scot free. Or possibly, for all I know, it's a
trap prepared for me by some enemy of mine, who persuaded her
to do him this favour because she's in love with him.'

But then he thought: 'Let's suppose that neither of these things
will happen, and her kinsfolk really do have to take me to her
house. It's hardly likely they would want Scannadio's body in order
to embrace it or put it to bed with the lady. On the contrary, one
can only conclude that they want to wreak vengeance upon it in
return for some wrong he has done them. She tells me not to make
a sound, no matter what may happen; but what if they were to
gouge my eyes out, or wrench out my teeth, or cut off my hands,
or do me some other piece of mischief, where would I be then?
How could I keep quiet? And yet if I open my mouth, they will
recognize me and possibly give me a sound hiding. But even if they
don't, I shall have achieved precisely nothing, because they won't
leave me with the lady in any case. Besides, she will say that I have
disobeyed her instructions, and will never have anything to do with
me again.'

So powerfully did these reflections prey upon his mind that he
was on the point of turning round and going back home. But his
great love spurred him on, suggesting counter-arguments that were
so persuasive that they brought him at length to the tomb. Having
opened it up, he stepped inside, stripped the corpse, and donned
Scannadio's clothes. Then, shutting himself inside the tomb, he lay
down in the dead man's place, and his mind began to dwell on the
kind of man he had been, and upon the weird things that were said
to have happened at night in various quite ordinary places, not to
mention cemeteries. Every hair of his head stood on end, and he
was convinced that Scannadio would rise to his feet at any moment
and slit his throat on the spot. But drawing sustenance from his

fervent love, he subdued these as well as other gruesome thoughts, and, lying perfectly still as if he were the corpse, settled down to wait and see what would happen.

When midnight was approaching, Rinuccio set forth from his house to do the deed which his lady had commissioned him to perform. As he walked along, he was assailed by a multitude of thoughts on the various things that might happen to him, such as being caught red-handed by the watch with Scannadio's corpse on his shoulders, and being condemned to the stake as a sorcerer, or of incurring the hatred of Scannadio's kinsfolk if they should ever find out what he had done. And several other fears of a similar nature entered his head, by which he was all but deterred from going on.

But he took a firm grip on himself, saying: 'Here's a pretty state of affairs! Am I to say nay to the first request I receive from this noble lady, when I have loved her so deeply and still do, and when, moreover, she offers me her favours as my reward? No, I shall proceed to honour the promise I have given her, even if it means my certain death.' And so, putting his best foot forward, he came at length to the tomb, which he opened without any difficulty.

On hearing the tomb being opened, Alessandro was filled with terror, but managed none the less to remain perfectly still. Rinuccio clambered in, and thinking he was taking up the body of Scannadio, seized Alessandro by the feet, dragged him out, hoisted him on to his shoulders, and set off in the direction of the gentlewoman's · house. It was such a dark night that he couldn't really see where he was going, and being none too particular about his burden, he frequently banged Alessandro's body against the edges of certain benches that were set at intervals along the side of the street.

The gentlewoman, being eager to see whether Rinuccio would fetch Alessandro, was standing with her maidservant at the window, forearmed with a suitable pretext for sending them both packing. But just as Rinuccio came up to her front door, he was challenged by the officers of the watch, who happened to be lying in ambush for an outlaw in that very part of the city. On hearing the sound of Rinuccio's laboured tread, they promptly produced a lantern to see what was afoot, and seizing their shields and their lances, they called out:

'Who goes there?'

Rinuccio realized at once who it was, and not having time to stop and compose his thoughts, he dropped Alessandro like a sack of coal and ran off as fast as his legs would carry him. Meanwhile Alessandro scrambled quickly to his feet, and though he was encumbered by the dead man's garments, which were inordinately long, he too took to his heels.

By the light of the officers' lantern, the lady had plainly observed Rinuccio carrying Alessandro on his shoulders, dressed in Scannadio's clothes, and was greatly amazed by this evident proof of their courage. But for all her amazement, she was convulsed with laughter when she saw Alessandro being dropped, and when she saw them running away. Delighted at the turn which events had taken, and giving thanks to God for ridding her from their tiresome attentions, she withdrew from the window and retired to her room, declaring to her maidservant that her two suitors must without a doubt be very much in love with her, as it seemed they had followed her instructions to the letter.

Rinuccio was heartbroken over what had happened, and cursed his evil luck, but instead of going home, he waited till the officers had gone, and returned to the place where he had dumped Alessandro. He then began to grope about on hands and knees in search of the body so that he could carry out the rest of his assignment, but being unable to find it, he assumed it had been taken away by the officers, and sadly made his way back home.

Not knowing what else he could do, Alessandro likewise returned home without ever having discovered who had fetched him from the tomb, feeling bitterly disappointed that things should have turned out so disastrously.

Next morning, when Scannadio's tomb was found open and there was no sign of the corpse (Alessandro having rolled it down into the lower depths), the whole of Pistoia was alive with rumours as to what exactly had happened, the more simple-minded concluding that Scannadio had been spirited away by demons.

Each of the lady's suitors informed her what he had done and what had happened, and, apologizing on this account for not carrying out her instructions to the full, demanded her forgiveness and her love. But she pretended not to believe them, and by curtly replying that she wanted no more to do with either of them, as they had failed to carry out her bidding, she neatly rid herself of both.

SECOND STORY

An abbess rises hurriedly from her bed in the dark when it is reported to her that one of her nuns is abed with a lover. But being with a priest at the time, the Abbess claps his breeches on her head, mistaking them for her veil. On pointing this out to the Abbess, the accused nun is set at liberty, and thenceforth she is able to forgather with her lover at her leisure.

When Filomena was silent, the good sense shown by the lady in ridding herself of those she had no wish to love was praised by the whole of the company, who one and all described not as love but as folly the daring presumption of the lovers. Then Elissa was graciously asked by the queen to continue, and she promptly began as follows:

Dearest ladies, the manner in which Madonna Francesca released herself from her affliction was indeed very subtle; but I should now like to tell you of a young nun who, with the assistance of Fortune, freed herself by means of a timely remark from the danger with which she was threatened. As you all know, a great many people are foolish enough to instruct and condemn their fellow creatures, but from time to time, as you will observe from this story of mine, Fortune deservedly puts them to shame. And that is what happened to the Abbess who was the superior of the nun whose deeds I am now about to relate.

You are to know, then, that in Lombardy there was once a convent, widely renowned for its sanctity and religious fervour, which housed a certain number of nuns, one of them being a girl of gentle birth, endowed with wondrous beauty, whose name was Isabetta. One day, having come to the grating to converse with a kinsman of hers, she fell in love with a handsome young man who was with him; and the young man, observing that she was very beautiful, and divining her feelings through the language of the eyes, fell no less passionately in love with her.

For some little time, to the no small torment of each, their love remained unfulfilled; but eventually, their desire for one another being equally acute, the young man thought of a way for him and his nun to forgather in secret; and with her willing consent he visited her not only once but over and over again, to their intense and mutual delight. This went on for some considerable time until one night, unbeknown either to himself or to Isabetta, he was seen by one of the other nuns as he left her cell and proceeded on his way. The nun told several of her companions, who at first were inclined to report Isabetta to the Abbess, a lady called Madonna Usimbalda, whose goodness and piety were a byword among all the nuns and everyone else who knew her. But on second thoughts they decided, so that their story should admit of no denial, to try and arrange for the Abbess to catch her red-handed with the young man. So they kept it to themselves, and secretly took it in turns to keep her under close and constant watch in order to take her *in flagrante*.

Now Isabetta knew nothing of all this, and one night, taking no special care, she happened to arrange for her lover to come. This he no sooner did than he was espied by the nuns whose business it was to keep watch, and after biding their time until well into the night, the nuns formed themselves into two separate groups, the first mounting guard at the entrance to Isabetta's cell whilst the second hurried off to the chamber of the Abbess. Their knocking at the door was promptly acknowledged by the Abbess, and so they called out to her, saying:

'Get up, Mother Abbess, come quickly! We've discovered Isabetta has a young man with her in her cell!'

The Abbess was keeping company that night with a priest, whom she frequently smuggled into her room in a chest, and on hearing this clamour, fearing lest the nuns, in their undue haste and excess of zeal, should burst open the door of her chamber, she leapt out of bed as quick as lightning and dressed as best she could in the dark. Thinking, however, that she had taken up the folded veils which nuns wear on their heads and refer to as psalters,[1] she happened to seize hold of the priest's breeches. And she was in such a tearing hurry, that without noticing her mistake, she clapped these on to her head instead of her psalter and sallied forth, deftly locking the door behind her and exclaiming:

'Where is this damnable sinner?'

Then in company with the others, who were so agog with excitement and so anxious to catch Isabetta in the act that they failed to notice what the Abbess had on her head, she arrived at the door of the cell, which, with a concerted heave, they knocked completely off its hinges. On bursting into the cell, they found the two lovers, who were lying in bed in one another's arms, and who, stunned by this sudden invasion, not knowing what to do, remained perfectly still.

The girl was immediately seized by the other nuns, and led away to the chapter-house by command of the Abbess. The young man meanwhile stayed where he was, and having put on his clothes, he waited to see how the affair would turn out, being resolved, if his girl should come to any harm, to do a serious mischief to as many of them as he could lay hold of, and to take her away from the convent altogether.

The Abbess, having taken her seat in the chapter-house in the presence of all the nuns, who only had eyes for the delinquent, began to administer the most terrible scolding that any woman was ever given, telling her that by her foul and abominable conduct, if it ever leaked out, she had defiled the sanctity, the honour, and the good name of the convent; and by way of addition to this torrent of abuse, she threatened her with the direst of penalties.

Knowing herself to be at fault, the girl was at a loss for an answer, so she simply stood there looking shy and embarrassed without saying a word, with the result that the others began to feel sorry for her. But as the strictures of the Abbess continued to flow thick and fast, she happened to raise her eyes and perceive what the Abbess had on her head, with the braces dangling down on either side.

Realizing what the Abbess had been up to, she took heart and said:

'By the grace of God, Mother Abbess, tie up your bonnet, and then you may say whatever you like to me.'

The Abbess, having no idea what she meant by this, said to her:

'What bonnet, you little whore? Are you going to have the effrontery to stand there making witty remarks? Do you think it funny to have behaved in this disgraceful manner?'

And so, for the second time, the girl said:

'I would ask you once again, Mother Abbess, to tie up your bonnet, and then you may address me in whatever way you please.'

Accordingly, several of the nuns looked up at the Abbess, and the Abbess likewise raised her hands to the sides of her head, so that they all saw what Isabetta was driving at. Whereupon the Abbess, recognizing that she was equally culpable and that there was no way of concealing the fact from all the nuns, who were gazing at her with their eyes popping out of their heads, changed her tune and began to take a completely different line, arguing that it was impossible to defend oneself against the goadings of the flesh. And she told them that provided the thing was discreetly arranged, as it had been in the past, they were all at liberty to enjoy themselves whenever they pleased.

Isabetta was then set at liberty, and she and the Abbess returned to their beds, the latter with the priest and the former with her lover. She thenceforth arranged for him to visit her at frequent intervals, undeterred by the envy of those of her fellow nuns, without lovers, who consoled themselves in secret as best they could.

THIRD STORY

Egged on by Bruno and Buffalmacco and Nello, Master Simone persuades Calandrino that he is pregnant. Calandrino then supplies the three men with capons and money for obtaining a certain medicine, and recovers from his pregnancy without giving birth.

When Elissa had completed her story, and all the ladies had given thanks to God for safely conducting the young nun to so sweet a

haven after the buffeting she had received from her jealous companions, the queen called upon Filostrato to follow; and without
waiting to be asked twice, he began:

Lovely ladies, that uncouth fellow from the Marches, the judge
of whom I spoke to you yesterday, took from the tip of my tongue
a story I was on the point of telling you concerning Calandrino.
We have already heard a good deal about Calandrino and his
companions, but since anything we may say about him is bound to
enhance the gaiety of our proceedings, I shall now proceed to
recount the tale I intended to tell you yesterday.

We all retain a vivid picture, from our earlier discussions, of
Calandrino and the other people to whom I am obliged to refer in
this story, so without any further ado I shall tell you that an aunt of
Calandrino died, leaving him two hundred pounds in brass farthings.
He accordingly started to talk of wanting to purchase a farm, and,
acting as though he had ten thousand gold florins to spend, he
approached every broker in Florence and entered into negotiations,
all of which were abruptly broken off as soon as the price of the
property was mentioned.

When Bruno and Buffalmacco came to hear of this, they told
him again and again that he would do far better to spend the
money with them, having a riotous time, than to go buying land, as
if he needed it to make mud pies. But far from bringing Calandrino
round to their own point of view, they were unable to wring so
much as a solitary meal out of him.

One day, as they were grumbling to one another on the subject,
they were joined by a fellow-painter of theirs, whose name was
Nello,[1] and the three of them decided they must find some way of
stuffing themselves at Calandrino's expense. So without dilly-dally-
ing, having come to an agreement on the strategy to adopt, they lay
in wait next morning as Calandrino was leaving his house, and
before he had gone very far along the road, Nello came up to him
and said:

'Good morning, Calandrino.'

By way of answer, Calandrino said that he wished Nello a good
morning and good year too, after which Nello, stepping back a

little, began to look Calandrino intently in the face.

'What are you staring at?' said Calandrino.

'Has anything happened to you overnight?' said Nello. 'You look odd, somehow.'

Calandrino was immediately thrown into a panic, and said:

'Odd, you say? Lord! What do you think is the matter with me?'

'Oh, I don't say you're ill or anything,' said Nello. 'You look quite different, that's all. But perhaps it's merely my imagination.'

Nello then took his leave, and Calandrino, feeling very worried, but otherwise perfectly fit and well, proceeded on his way. However, Buffalmacco was lurking a little further along the road, and on seeing him leave Nello, he walked up to him, bade him good morning, and asked him whether he was feeling all right.

'I'm not exactly sure,' Calandrino replied. 'I was talking to Nello just now, and he said I looked quite different. I wonder if there's anything wrong with me?'

'Oh, it's nothing,' said Buffalmacco. 'You just look half dead, that's all.'

Calandrino was beginning to feel decidedly feverish, when all of a sudden Bruno appeared on the scene, and the first thing he said was:

'What on earth's the matter, Calandrino? You look just like a corpse. Are you feeling all right?'

When he heard both of them saying the same thing, Calandrino was quite certain he was ill, and asked them in tones of deep alarm:

'What am I to do?'

So Bruno said:

'I reckon you ought to return home, go straight to bed, keep yourself well covered up, and send a specimen of your water to Master Simone,² who as you know is a close friend of ours. He'll soon tell you what you have to do. We shall come with you, and if anything needs to be done, we'll attend to it.'

So together with Nello, who now came up and joined them, they returned with Calandrino to his house, where he made his way to his bedroom, feeling as though he were on his last legs, and said to his wife:

'Come and cover me up well; I'm feeling very poorly.'

He accordingly got into bed, and dispatched a servant-girl with a specimen of his water to Master Simone, whose surgery at that time was situated in the Mercato Vecchio, at the sign of the pumpkin.

Turning to his companions, Bruno said:

'You stay here with him, whilst I go and see what the doctor has to say, and fetch him back here if necessary.'

'Ah, yes, there's a good fellow!' said Calandrino. 'Go to him and find out for me how matters stand. Goodness knows what's going on inside my poor stomach. I feel awful.'

Bruno therefore set off for the doctor's, arriving there ahead of the girl carrying the specimen, and explained to Master Simone what they were up to. So that when the girl turned up with the specimen, Master Simone examined it and said to her:

'Go and tell Calandrino that he is to keep himself nice and warm. I shall be coming round straightway to tell him what's wrong with him, and explain what he has to do.'

The girl delivered the message, and shortly afterwards the Master arrived with Bruno, sat down at Calandrino's bedside, and proceeded to take his pulse. Then after a while, in the hearing of Calandrino's wife, who was present in the room, he said:

'Look here, Calandrino, speaking now as your friend, I'd say that the only thing wrong with you is that you are pregnant.'

When Calandrino heard this, he began to howl with dismay, and turning to his wife, he exclaimed:

'Ah, Tessa, this is your doing! You will insist on lying on top. I told you all along what would happen.'

When she heard him say this, Calandrino's wife, who was a very demure sort of person, turned crimson with embarrassment, and lowering her gaze, left the room without uttering a word.

Meanwhile Calandrino continued to wail and moan, saying:

'Ah, what a terrible fate! What am I to do? How am I to produce this infant? Where will it come out? This woman's going to be the death of me now, with her insatiable lust, I can see that. May God make her as miserable as I desire to be happy. I swear that if I were fit and strong, which is far from being the case, I should get up from this bed and break every bone in her body. It serves me right, though; I should never have allowed her to lie on top: but if I ever get out of this alive, she certainly won't do it again, even if she's dying of frustration.'

Bruno and Buffalmacco and Nello were so vastly amused by Calandrino's outburst that it was all they could do to keep a straight face, although Master Simone guffawed so heartily that all his teeth could have been pulled out one after another. At length, however, on being urged and entreated by Calandrino for advice and assistance, the doctor said:

'Now there's no cause for alarm, Calandrino. By the grace of God we've diagnosed the trouble early enough for me to cure you quite easily in a matter of a few days. But it's going to cost you a pretty penny.'

'Get on with it then, doctor, for the love of God,' said Calandrino. 'I have two hundred pounds here with which I was going to buy a farm, but you can take the whole lot if necessary, provided I don't have to bear this child. I simply don't know how I could manage it, when I think of the great hullabaloo women make when they are having babies, even though they have plenty of room for the purpose. If I had all that pain to contend with, I honestly think I should die before I ever produced any child.'

'Just leave everything to me,' said the doctor. 'I shall prescribe a certain medicine for you, a distilled liquid that is most effective in cases of this sort, and highly agreeable to the palate, which will clear everything up in three days and leave you feeling fit as a fiddle. But in future you must be more sensible and desist from these foolish antics. Now in order to prepare this medicine, we shall need three brace of good fat capons, and you must give five pounds in small change to Bruno and the others, so that they can purchase the remaining ingredients we require. See that everything is brought round to my surgery, and tomorrow morning I shall send you the distilled beverage, which you are to start drinking at once, a good big glassful at a time.'

'Whatever you say, doctor,' said Calandrino. And handing over five pounds to Bruno, together with the money for the three brace of capons, he asked him to purchase the things he needed, apologizing for putting him to so much trouble.

The doctor then went away, and concocted a harmless medicinal draught, which he duly sent round to Calandrino. As for Bruno, having purchased the capons and various other essential delicacies, he made a hearty meal of them in company with the doctor and his two companions.

Calandrino took the medicine for three mornings running, then the doctor called to see him along with his three friends, and having taken Calandrino's pulse, he said:

'You're cured, Calandrino, without a shadow of a doubt; so there's no need for you to stay at home any longer. It's quite safe now for you to get up and do whatever you have to.'

So Calandrino got up and went happily about his business, and whenever he fell into conversation with anyone he bestowed high praise on Master Simone for his miraculous cure, which in only three days had effected a painless miscarriage. Bruno, Buffalmacco, and Nello were delighted with themselves for getting round Calandrino's avarice so cleverly, but they had not deceived Monna Tessa, who muttered and moaned to her husband about it for a long time afterwards.

FOURTH STORY

Cecco Fortarrigo gambles away everything he possesses at Buonconvento, together with the money of Cecco Angiulieri. He then pursues Cecco Angiulieri in his shirt claiming that he has been robbed, causes him to be seized by peasants, dons his clothes, mounts his palfrey, and rides away leaving Angiulieri standing there in his shirt.

All the members of the company roared with laughter on hearing what Calandrino had said about his wife; but when Filostrato had finished speaking, Neifile began, at the queen's behest, as follows:

Worthy ladies, but for the fact that it is more difficult for people to display their wisdom and their virtues than it is to show their folly and their vices, it would be so much wasted effort for them to reflect carefully before opening their mouths to speak; all of which has been amply demonstrated by the stupidity of Calandrino, who was under no obligation whatever, in order to recover from the malady from which in his simplicity he believed himself to be suffering, to hold forth about the secret pleasures of his wife in public. But the story of Calandrino brings to mind a tale of a totally different sort, wherein one man's cunning defeats the wisdom of another, to the latter's extreme distress and embarrassment; and I should now like to tell you about it.

In Siena, not many years ago, there lived two young men, who had both come of age and were both called Cecco, the one being the son of Messer Angiulieri[1] and the other of Messer Fortarrigo.[2] And whilst they failed to see eye-to-eye with each other on several matters, there was one respect at least – namely, their hatred of their respective fathers[3] – in which they were in such total agreement that they became good friends and were often to be found in one another's company.

But Angiulieri, who was as handsome a man as he was courteous, feeling that he was leading a poor sort of life in Siena on the meagre allowance he was given by his father, and hearing that the new papal ambassador in the March of Ancona was a certain cardinal who was very well disposed towards him, resolved to make his way there in the belief that by doing this he would better his lot. And having spoken to his father on the subject, he came to an arrangement with him whereby he would receive six months' allowance in advance, so that he could purchase new clothes and a good horse, and go there looking reasonably respectable.

No sooner did he begin to look round for someone to take with him as his servant than his plans reached the ears of Fortarrigo, who immediately called on Angiulieri and begged him with all the eloquence at his command to take him with him, saying that he would be willing to act as his servant, his valet, and his general factotum without requiring any other payment than his food and lodging. But Angiulieri refused his offer, not because he had the slightest doubt of his ability to perform these duties, but because Fortarrigo was an inveterate gambler and furthermore he occasionally got very drunk. Fortarrigo assured him that he would

guard against both these weaknesses and swore repeatedly that
he would keep his promise, to which he added such a torrent
of entreaties that Angiulieri finally yielded and agreed to take
him.

So early one morning they set forth together, reaching Buonconvento[4] in time for breakfast. Since it was a very warm day,
after breakfast Angiulieri asked the innkeeper to prepare a bed
for him, and with Fortarrigo's assistance he got undressed and lay
down to rest, telling Fortarrigo to call him at the hour of
nones.[5]

As soon as Angiulieri was asleep, Fortarrigo went straight to the
tavern, where after a few drinks he started to gamble with one or
two other people there, and within a short space of time he had lost
every penny he possessed, along with every stitch of clothing he
was wearing. Being anxious to recoup his losses, he made his way
back in nothing but his shirt to the room where Angiulieri was
resting, and, perceiving that he was fast asleep, took all the money
from his purse and returned to the gaming-table, where he lost
Angiulieri's money as well.

On waking up, Angiulieri stepped out of bed, put on his clothes,
and made inquiries about Fortarrigo. But as he was nowhere to be
found, he assumed that he had lapsed into his former habits and
fallen asleep somewhere or other in a drunken stupor. He therefore
resolved to abandon him, and having caused his palfrey to be ·
saddled and laden with his luggage, his intention being to procure
another servant at Corsignano,[6] he prepared to set off. But when he
came to pay his bill, only to discover that he hadn't a single penny
in his purse, he made a terrible scene about it and the whole of the
innkeeper's household was thrown into turmoil, with Angiulieri
claiming that he had been robbed on the premises and threatening
to have them all arrested and taken to Siena under escort. At that
very moment, however, Fortarrigo appeared on the scene in his
shirt, having come to take away Angiulieri's clothes as he had taken
his money. And when he saw that Angiulieri was about to take to
the road, he said:

'What's all this, Angiulieri? Do we have to go away already?
Please stay a little longer. I pawned my doublet for thirty-eight

shillings, and the man who has it will be bringing it back here any moment. I'm certain he'll let us have it for thirty-five if we pay him right away.'

A heated discussion then ensued, which was still in full spate when someone interrupted them and made it clear to Angiulieri that Fortarrigo was the person who had taken his money, by informing him exactly how much he had lost, whereupon Angiulieri very nearly threw a fit and would have killed Fortarrigo there and then but for the fact that his fear of the law was greater than his fear of God. So he showered him with abuse, and, threatening to have him hanged by the neck or to see that he was forbidden on pain of death to return to Siena, he mounted his horse.

Fortarrigo's response to this torrent of vituperation was to behave as though it was being directed, not at himself, but at somebody else. And he said:

'Come now, Angiulieri! We shan't get anywhere by throwing these little tantrums. Let's approach the matter sensibly: the fact is that we can have the doublet back for thirty-five shillings if we redeem it now, whereas if we wait for as much as a single day, he'll insist on being paid the full thirty-eight, which is what he gave me for it. His only reason for making me this concession is that I wagered the money on his advice. Come on, now! Why should we turn down an opportunity to save three shillings?'

Angiulieri was now growing positively distraught, especially when he saw that he was being stared at suspiciously by all the people around him, who seemed to be under the impression, not that Fortarrigo had gambled away Angiulieri's money, but that Angiulieri was still holding on to some of Fortarrigo's.

'What the hell do I care about your doublet?' he yelled. 'May you be hanged by the neck. Not only do you rob me and gamble away all my money, but you prevent me from leaving as well. And now you stand there making fun of me.'

Fortarrigo still persisted in acting as though Angiulieri's words were meant for someone else, and said to him:

'Ah, why do you want to make me forfeit the three shillings? Do you think I won't let you have the money back again? Come on now, pay up like a true friend. Why are you in such a hurry? We

FOURTH STORY 667

can still reach Torrenieri[7] quite easily by nightfall. Go and find that purse of yours. I tell you I could never find another doublet that suited me as well as that one, not if I were to ransack the whole of Siena. And to think I let the fellow have it for thirty-eight shillings! It's worth every penny of forty at least; so you're letting me down twice over.'

Distressed beyond all measure that the fellow, after stealing his money, should now have the gall to hold him up with his prattle, Angiulieri offered no reply, but turned his palfrey's head and set off along the road to Torrenieri. But Fortarrigo had thought of a cunning idea, and began to jog along behind him, still clad in nothing more than his shirt. For at least two miles he stuck to his tail, pleading with him over and over again on the subject of his doublet, and just as Angiulieri began to quicken his pace to avoid having to listen, Fortarrigo caught sight of a number of farm-workers in a field bordering the road some distance ahead. So he yelled to them at the top of his voice, saying:

'Stop him! Stop him!'

And so, brandishing their hoes and their spades, they blocked the road and stopped Angiulieri from going any further, supposing him to have robbed the shirt-clad figure who was stumbling along and shouting in his wake. And albeit Angiulieri explained to them how matters stood, and told them who he was, it made very little difference.

But Fortarrigo now arrived at the spot, and fixing Angiulieri with a withering look, he said:

'You miserable sneak-thief! I could just about kill you for running off with my belongings like this.'

Then, turning to the peasants, he said:

'Gentlemen, you can see the sort of state he left me in, sneaking off from the inn as he did, after gambling away everything he possessed! But with God's help and your own, I can say that I've salvaged something at least, and I shall always be grateful to you for your timely assistance.'

Angiulieri gave them an opposite version of what had happened, but they refused to listen. So Fortarrigo, with the help of the peasants, dragged Angiulieri from his palfrey to the ground, stripped

the clothes off his back, and put them on himself. Then he mounted
the horse, and leaving Angiulieri barefoot and naked except for his
shirt, he made his way back to Siena, informing everyone he met
that he had won Angiulieri's palfrey and clothes as the result of a
wager.

Thus, instead of presenting himself as a rich man before the
cardinal in the Marches, as he had intended, Angiulieri returned
penniless to Buonconvento in his shirt. Nor, for the time being, did
he have the courage to return to Siena, but having borrowed a suit
of clothes, he mounted the jade on which Fortarrigo had been
riding, and made his way to Corsignano, where he stayed with
relatives until his father came once more to his assistance.

Although Fortarrigo's cunning upset the well-laid plans of Angiulieri on this occasion, he did not go unpunished, for Angiulieri paid
him back later, when a suitable time and place presented
themselves.

FIFTH STORY

*Calandrino falls in love with a young woman, and Bruno provides him
with a magic scroll, with which he no sooner touches her than she goes off
with him. But on being discovered with the girl by his wife, he finds
himself in very serious trouble.*

Neifile's story was of no great length, and when it drew to a close it
was passed off by the company without much laughter or comment.
The queen now turned to Fiammetta, ordering her to follow.
Fiammetta gaily replied that she would do so with pleasure, and
began:

Noble ladies, as you will doubtless be aware, the more one
returns to any given subject, the greater the pleasure it brings,
provided the person by whom it is broached selects the appropriate
time and place. And since we are assembled here for no other
purpose than to rejoice and be merry, I consider this a suitable time
and a proper place for any subject that will promote our joy and
pleasure; for even if it had been aired a thousand times already, we

could return to it as many times again, and it would still afford delight to us all.

Hence, albeit we have referred many times to the doings of Calandrino, they are invariably so amusing, as Filostrato pointed out a little earlier, that I shall venture to add a further tale to those we have already heard about him. I could easily have told it in some other way, using fictitious names, had I wished to do so; but since by departing from the truth of what actually happened, the storyteller greatly diminishes the pleasure of his listeners, I shall turn for support to my opening remarks, and tell it in its proper form.

Niccolò Cornacchini,[1] a wealthy fellow citizen of ours, owned various lands including a beautiful estate at Camerata,[2] on which he caused a fine and splendid mansion to be built, commissioning Bruno and Buffalmacco to paint it throughout with frescoes. So enormous was the task with which they were confronted that they first enlisted the aid of Nello and Calandrino, then they all got down to work.

Now, albeit one of the rooms contained a bed and other pieces of furniture, nobody was living on the premises except for an elderly housekeeper, and accordingly every so often one of Niccolò's sons, a young bachelor whose name was Filippo, was in the habit of turning up with some young lady or other, who would minister to his pleasures for a day or two and then be sent away.

On one of these visits, he arrived at the mansion with a girl, Niccolosa by name, who was kept by a scoundrelly fellow called Mangione at a house in Camaldoli,[3] whence he let her out on hire. This girl had a beautiful figure, dressed well, and, for a woman of her sort, was very polite and well spoken. And one day, around noon, having emerged from the bedroom in a flimsy white shift, her hair tied up in a bun, she happened to be washing her hands and face at a well in the courtyard when Calandrino came to the well for some water.

He gave her a friendly greeting, which she acknowledged, then she began to stare at him, not because she found him the least bit attractive, but because she was fascinated by his odd appearance.

Calandrino returned her gaze, and on seeing how beautiful she was, began to think of various excuses for not returning with the water to his companions. However, not knowing who she was, he was afraid to address her, and the girl, perceiving that he was still staring at her, mischievously rolled her eyes at him a couple of times and fetched a few little sighs, so that Calandrino instantly fell in love with her and stood rooted to the spot till she was called inside by Filippo.

On returning to his work, Calandrino did nothing but heave one huge sigh after another; and Bruno, who always kept an eye on him because he found him so entertaining, noticed this and said:

'What the devil's the matter, comrade Calandrino? You do nothing but sigh the whole time.'

'Comrade,' said Calandrino, 'if only I had someone to help me, I could be the happiest man alive.'

'What do you mean?' said Bruno.

'Don't tell a soul,' said Calandrino, 'but there's a girl down there who's lovelier than a nymph, and she's so much in love with me that you'd be astonished. I came across her just now when I went to fetch the water.'

'Good heavens!' said Bruno. 'You'd better be careful, in case it's Filippo's wife.'

'That's exactly who I think she is,' said Calandrino, 'for he called to her from the bedroom, and she went in to him. But anyway, what does it matter? For a girl like that, I'd slip one over on Jesus Christ, let alone Filippo. The truth is, comrade, that I'm so wild about her that I can't begin to tell you how I feel.'

Then Bruno said:

'I'll make one or two inquiries for you, comrade, and find out who she is. If she turns out to be Filippo's wife, I'll fix things up for you in a trice, because she happens to be a very close friend of mine. But how are we to prevent Buffalmacco from finding out? I never get a chance to speak to her except when he is with me.'

'I'm not worried about Buffalmacco,' said Calandrino, 'but we must keep it a secret from Nello, because Tessa⁴ is a kinswoman of his and he would ruin everything.'

'That's true,' said Bruno.

Now, Bruno knew perfectly well who she was, for he had seen her arriving at the house, and Filippo had told him in any case. So as soon as Calandrino downed tools for a moment to go and see whether he could catch a glimpse of the girl, Bruno told Nello and Buffalmacco all about Calandrino's sudden infatuation, and together they agreed what they should do about it.

As soon as Calandrino returned, Bruno whispered in his ear:

'Did you see her?'

'Ah, that I did!' Calandrino replied. 'She's struck me all of a heap.'

'I'll just go and see whether she's the one I think she is,' said Bruno, 'in which case you can safely leave everything to me.'

So Bruno went downstairs, and finding Filippo and the girl together, he carefully explained the sort of man that Calandrino was, and told them what he had said. He then arranged with each of them what they should do and say so that they could all have a merry time at Calandrino's expense over this little love-affair of his. And returning to Calandrino, he said:

'Just as I thought: it's Filippo's wife. So we shall have to tread very warily, because if Filippo gets wind of this affair, he'll spill so much of our blood that all the water in the Arno won't wash it away. But what message would you like me to give her, if I should have a chance to speak to her?'

'Faith!' replied Calandrino. 'You're to tell her first and foremost that I wish her a thousand bushels of the sort of love that fattens a girl; then you're to say that I'm her obedient servant, and if there's anything she needs . . . Do you follow me?'

'Indeed I do,' said Bruno. 'Leave everything to me.'

When suppertime came, they all abandoned work for the day and made their way downstairs to the courtyard, where Filippo and Niccolosa stood loitering about for Calandrino's benefit. Fixing his gaze on Niccolosa, Calandrino began to perform a whole series of curious antics, so blatantly obvious that even a blind man would have noticed. As for Niccolosa, in view of what Bruno had told her, she gave Calandrino every encouragement, and took the greatest delight in his eccentricities. And whilst all this was going on,

Filippo was deep in conversation with Buffalmacco and the others, pretending not to notice.

After a while, however, much to Calandrino's annoyance, Filippo and the girl went away; and as they were on their way back to Florence, Bruno said to him:

'There's no doubt about it, Calandrino, you've got her in the palm of your hand. Holy Mother of God, if you were to bring along your rebeck[5] and serenade her with one or two of those love-songs of yours, she'd be so eager to come to you that she'd hurl herself bodily through the window.'

'Do you really think so, comrade?' said Calandrino. 'Do you think I ought to fetch it?'

'I certainly do,' Bruno replied.

Whereupon Calandrino said:

'You wouldn't believe me today, when I told you. But you must admit, comrade, that when it comes to obtaining what I want, I know better than anybody else how to go about it. What other man could have persuaded a lady of her quality to fall in love with him so quickly? Could any of those young gallants have done it, who parade up and down the whole day long, spouting like a tap, and who wouldn't know how to gather three handfuls of nuts in a thousand years? Just wait till you see what I can do with my rebeck: you'll be amazed! You needn't think I'm past the age for this sort of thing, because I'm not, and she knows it. And once I lay my paws on her, she'll know it even better. God's truth! I'll sport with her so merrily that she'll cling to me like a mother besotted with her son.'

'Ah, yes!' said Bruno. 'You'll make a proper meal out of her. I can see you now, in my mind's eye, nibbling her sweet red lips and her rosy cheeks with those lute-peg teeth of yours, and then devouring her whole body, piece by succulent piece.'

On hearing these words, Calandrino felt as though he was already getting down to business, and he skipped and sang, being seized by such a transport of delight that he almost split his hide.

Next day he brought along his rebeck, to the strains of which, much to the delight of all the others, he sang a number of songs. But to cut a long story short, he became so frantically eager to see the girl as often as possible, that he did practically no work at all, for he would be dashing to and fro a thousand times a day, first to the windows, then to the door, then to the courtyard, in the hope of catching a glimpse of her. And for her part, the girl, astutely following Bruno's instructions, gave Calandrino as many opportunities to see her as she possibly could.

But Bruno also played the role of go-between, supplying Calandrino with answers to the messages he sent her, and from time to time delivering a note in Niccolosa's own hand. And whenever she was not actually there, as was more often than not the case, he got her to write letters to Calandrino in which, whilst holding out every hope that his devoted love would soon have its reward, she explained that she was staying at the house of her kinsfolk, where for the present it was impossible for him to see her.

Bruno and Buffalmacco kept a careful watch on the progress of the affair, being hugely entertained by Calandrino's antics; and every so often they persuaded him to hand over various objects which they claimed his lady had requested, such as an ivory comb, a purse, a small dagger, and other such trifles, in return bringing him some worthless little rings, which sent Calandrino into raptures. But apart from this they coaxed one or two good meals out of him, and he showed them various other little favours to encourage them in their efforts on his behalf.

Now, after being kept on tenterhooks in this manner for at least two months without making any further progress, Calandrino, seeing that the work was nearing completion, and realizing that unless he gathered the fruits of his love before the frescoes were finished he would never have another opportunity, began to solicit Bruno's aid with all the power at his command. So when she next came to stay at the house, Bruno made arrangements with Filippo and the girl about what they were to do, then he went to Calandrino and said:

'Look here, comrade, this woman has promised me a thousand times that she would give you what you wanted, but when it comes to the point she does nothing, and I strongly suspect that she's leading us by the nose. So unless you have any objection, as she won't keep her promises, we shall make her keep them whether she wants to or not.'

'Ah yes!' Calandrino replied. 'Let's do that, for the love of God, and do it quickly.'

'Are you bold enough to touch her with a scroll that I shall give you?' asked Bruno.

'Of course I am,' said Calandrino.

'In that case,' said Bruno, 'see that you let me have a small piece of parchment from a stillborn lamb, a live bat, three grains of incense, and a candle that has been blessed, and leave the rest to me.'

Calandrino accordingly spent the whole of that evening attempting by various ingenious means to catch a live bat, which he eventually succeeded in doing, and took it along to Bruno next morning, together with the other items he had specified. Bruno then withdrew to an inner room, filled the parchment with a series of meaningless hieroglyphics, and brought it back to Calandrino, saying:

'Now listen, Calandrino: if you touch her with this parchment, she will immediately come with you and do whatever you want. So if Filippo should go off anywhere today, you must contrive to approach her and touch her with the scroll, then make your way round the side of the house to the barn, which is the ideal spot for your purposes as no one ever goes near it. You'll find that she will follow you, and once she reaches the barn, you know exactly what you have to do.'

Calandrino was overjoyed, and seizing the parchment, he said:

'Just you leave it to me, comrade.'

Nello, against whom Calandrino was constantly on his guard, was enjoying the affair as much as anyone, and was every bit as eager to make a fool of him; so on Bruno's instructions he went down to Florence, called on Calandrino's wife, and said to her:

'You remember the hiding Calandrino gave you, Tessa, for no reason at all, on the day he came home from the Mugnone with all those stones[6]? Well, now's your chance to be even with him, and if you fail to take it, you needn't regard me as your friend or your kinsman ever again. He's fallen in love with some woman up there at Camerata, and she's such a wanton little baggage that she's forever going off with him in private. They've arranged to meet today, as a matter of fact, so I want you to come and see, and punish him as he deserves.'

Monna Tessa was not at all amused by what she had heard, and leaping to her feet, she exclaimed:

'Ah, false villain, so this is how he treats me, is it? By all that's holy, he shan't get away with it, not if I can help it.'

Seizing her cloak, she promptly set forth, accompanied by a maidservant, and made her way up to Camerata with Nello, walking at such a furious pace that he was scarcely able to keep up. However, long before she reached the mansion, Bruno saw her coming and said to Filippo:

'There's our friend coming now.'

Filippo therefore went to the part of the house where Calandrino and the others were working, and said:

'Gentlemen, I have some urgent business to attend to in Florence, so keep up the good work.' And taking his leave of them, he went and concealed himself in a place from which, without being observed, he would be able to see what Calandrino was doing.

As soon as Calandrino imagined Filippo to be well on his way to Florence, he descended to the courtyard, where, finding Niccolosa alone, he engaged her in conversation. She had been carefully briefed on what she was to do, and walking over to Calandrino, she treated him with greater familiarity than usual. Calandrino therefore touched her with the scroll, and immediately directed his steps towards the barn without saying a word. She followed him in, closed the door behind her, and threw her arms about his neck; then she pushed him over on to some straw that was lying on the floor and promptly sat astride his prostrate form, forcing his hands back against his shoulders. And without allowing him to bring his face close to hers, she gazed at him rapturously, saying:

'Oh, my sweet Calandrino, heart of my body, my dearest, my darling, my angel, how long I have been yearning to have you all to myself and hold you in my arms! You've swept me off my feet with your winning ways! You've captured my heart with that rebeck of yours! Is it really possible that I am holding you in my embrace?'

'Alas, my dearest,' said Calandrino, who was scarcely able to move. 'Let me up, so that I may kiss you.'

'Oh, but you are too hasty,' said Niccolosa. 'First let me have a good look at you. Let me feast my eyes upon your dear, sweet face.'

Bruno and Buffalmacco saw and heard everything that passed between them, having meanwhile joined Filippo in his hiding place. And just as Calandrino had freed his arms, and was on the point of kissing Niccolosa, along came Nello with Monna Tessa.

'I swear to God they are in there together,' he said, as they came up to the door of the barn. Fuming with rage, Calandrino's wife applied both her hands to the door and pushed it open. On entering the barn, she saw Calandrino lying there on his back, straddled by Niccolosa, who no sooner caught sight of Monna Tessa than she leapt to her feet and ran off to join Filippo.

Before Calandrino could get up, Monna Tessa pounced upon him and attacked him with her nails, clawing his face all over before seizing him by the hair and dragging him round the floor of the barn, saying:

'You filthy, despicable dog, so you'd do this to me, would you? A curse on all the love I ever bore you, demented old fool that you are. Don't you think you have enough to do, keeping the home fires burning, without going off to stoke up other people's? A fine lover you would make for anyone! Don't you know yourself, villain? Don't you realize, scoundrel, that if they were to squeeze you from head to toe, there wouldn't be enough juice to make a sauce? God's faith, it wasn't your wife who was getting you with child[7] this time. May the Lord make her suffer, whoever she is, for she must surely be a depraved little hussy to take a fancy to a precious jewel like you.'

When he first saw his wife coming in, Calandrino was unsure whether he was dead or alive, and hadn't the courage to defend himself against her furious onslaught. But in the end, all torn and bleeding and dishevelled, he picked up his cape, staggered to his feet, and humbly entreated Monna Tessa not to shout unless she wanted him to be torn to pieces, for the woman who was with him was none other than the wife of the master of the house.

'I don't care who she is,' bawled Monna Tessa. 'May God punish her as she deserves.'

Pretending to have been attracted by all the noise, Bruno and Buffalmacco now appeared on the scene, having laughed themselves silly along with Filippo and Niccolosa as they watched this spectacle; and after much heated discussion, they pacified Monna Tessa and advised Calandrino to return to Florence and never show his face there again in case Filippo came to hear of what had happened and did him some serious mischief.

And so, scratched and torn to ribbons, Calandrino made his way back to Florence feeling all forlorn and dejected; and not having the courage to return to Camerata, he resigned himself to the torrent of strictures and abuse to which he was subjected day and night by Monna Tessa, and made an end to his love for Niccolosa, having supplied a feast of entertainment, not only for his companions, but for Filippo and Niccolosa as well.

SIXTH STORY

Two young men lodge overnight at a cottage, where one of them goes and sleeps with their host's daughter, whilst his wife inadvertently sleeps with the other. The one who was with the daughter clambers into bed beside her father, mistaking him for his companion, and tells him all · about it. A great furore then ensues, and the wife, realizing her mistake, gets into her daughter's bed, whence with a timely explanation she restores the peace.

As on previous occasions, so also on this, the company was heartily amused by Calandrino's doings, which the ladies had no sooner finished debating than the queen called on Panfilo to address them; and he began as follows:

Laudable ladies, the name of Calandrino's lady-love reminds me of a tale about another Niccolosa, which I should now like to relate to you, for as you will see, it shows us how a good woman's presence of mind averted a serious scandal.

★

Not long ago, there lived in the valley of the Mugnone¹ a worthy man who earned an honest penny by supplying food and drink to wayfarers; and although he was poor, and his house was tiny, he would from time to time, in cases of urgent need, offer them a night's lodging, but only if they happened to be people he knew.

Now, this man had a most attractive wife, who had borne him two children, the first being a charming and beautiful girl of about fifteen or sixteen, as yet unmarried, whilst the second was an infant, not yet twelve months old, who was still being nursed at his mother's breast.

The daughter had caught the eye of a lively and handsome young Florentine gentleman who used to spend much of his time in the countryside, and he fell passionately in love with her. Nor was it long before the girl, being highly flattered to have won the affection of so noble a youth, which she strove hard to retain by displaying the greatest affability towards him, fell in love with him. And neither of the pair would have hesitated to consummate their love, but for the fact that Pinuccio (for such was the young man's name) was not prepared to expose the girl or himself to censure.

At length however, his ardour growing daily more intense, Pinuccio was seized with a longing to consort with her, come what may, and it occurred to him that he must find some excuse for lodging with her father overnight, since, being conversant with the layout of the premises, he had good reason to think that he and the girl could be together without anyone ever being any the wiser. And no sooner did this idea enter his head than he promptly took steps to carry it into effect.

Late one afternoon, he and a trusted companion of his called Adriano, who knew of his love for the girl, hired a couple of pack-horses, and having laden them with a pair of saddlebags, filled probably with straw, they set forth from Florence; and after riding round in a wide circle they came to the valley of the Mugnone, some time after nightfall. They then wheeled their horses round to make it look as though they were returning from Romagna, rode up to the cottage of our worthy friend, and knocked at the door. And since the man was well acquainted with both Pinuccio and his companion, he immediately came down to let them in.

'You'll have to put us up for the night,' said Pinuccio. 'We had intended to reach Florence before dark, but as you can see, we've made such slow progress that this is as far as we've come, and it's too late to enter the city at this hour.'

'My dear Pinuccio,' replied the host, 'as you know, I can't exactly offer you a princely sort of lodging. But no matter: since night has fallen and you've nowhere else to go, I shall be glad to put you up as best I can.'

So the two young men dismounted, and having seen that their nags were comfortably stabled, they went into the house, where, since they had brought plenty to eat with them, they made a hearty supper along with their host. Now, their host had only one bedroom, which was very tiny, and into this he had crammed three small beds,[2] leaving so little space that it was almost impossible to move between them. Two of the beds stood alongside one of the bedroom walls, whilst the third was against the wall on the opposite side of the room; and having seen that the least uncomfortable of the three was made ready for his guests, the host invited them to sleep in that for the night. Shortly afterwards, when they appeared to be asleep, though in reality they were wide awake, he settled his daughter in one of the other two beds, whilst he and his wife got into the third; and beside the bed in which she was sleeping, his wife had placed the cradle containing her infant son.

Having made a mental note of all these arrangements, Pinuccio waited until he was sure that everyone was asleep, then quietly left his bed, stole across to the bed in which his lady-love was sleeping, and lay down beside her. Although she was somewhat alarmed, the girl received him joyously in her arms, and they then proceeded to take their fill of that sweet pleasure for which they yearned above all else.

Whilst Pinuccio and the girl were thus employed, a cat, somewhere in the house, happened to knock something over, causing the man's wife to wake up with a start. Being anxious to discover what it was, she got up and groped her way naked in the dark towards that part of the house from which the noise had come.

Meanwhile Adriano also happened to get up, not for the same reason, but in order to obey the call of nature, and as he was groping his way towards the door with this purpose in view, he came in contact with the cradle deposited there by the woman. Being unable to pass without moving it out of his way, he picked it up and set it down beside his own bed; and after doing what he had to do, he returned to his bed and forgot all about it.

Having discovered the cause of the noise and assured herself that nothing important had fallen, the woman swore at the cat, and, without bothering to light a lamp and explore the matter further, returned to the bedroom. Picking her way carefully through the darkness, she went straight to the bed where her husband was lying; but on finding no trace of the cradle, she said to herself: 'How stupid I am! What a fine thing to do! Heavens above, I was just about to step into the bed where my guests are sleeping.' So she walked a little further up the room, found the cradle, and got into bed beside Adriano, thinking him to be her husband.

On perceiving this, Adriano, who was still awake, gave her a most cordial reception; and without a murmur he tacked hard to windward over and over again, much to her delight and satisfaction.

This, then, was how matters stood when Pinuccio, who had gratified his longings to the full and was afraid of falling asleep in the young lady's arms, abandoned her so as to go back and sleep in his own bed. But on reaching the bed to find the cradle lying there, he moved on, thinking he had mistaken his host's bed for his own, and ended up by getting into bed with the host, who was awakened by his coming. And being under the impression that the man who lay beside him was Adriano, Pinuccio said:

'I swear to you that there was never anything so delicious as Niccolosa. By the body of God, no man ever had so much pleasure with any woman as I have been having with her. Since the time I left you, I assure you I've been to the bower of bliss half a dozen times at the very least.'

The host was not exactly pleased to hear Pinuccio's tidings, and having first of all asked himself what the devil the fellow was doing in his bed, he allowed his anger to get the better of his prudence, and exclaimed:

'What villainy is this, Pinuccio? I can't think why you should have played me so scurvy a trick, but by all that's holy, I shall pay you back for it.'

Now, Pinuccio was not the wisest of young men, and on perceiving his error, instead of doing all he could to remedy matters, he said:

'Pay me back? How? What could you do to me?'

Whereupon the host's wife, thinking she was with her husband, said to Adriano:

'Heavens! Just listen to the way those guests of ours are arguing with one another!'

Adriano laughed, and said:

'Let them get on with it, and to hell with them. They had far too much to drink last night.'

The woman had already thought she could detect the angry tones of her husband, and on hearing Adriano's voice, she realized at once whose bed she was sharing. So being a person of some intelligence, she promptly got up without a word, seized her baby's cradle, and having picked her way across the room, which was in total darkness, she set the cradle down beside the bed in which her daughter was sleeping and scrambled in beside her. Then, pretending to have been aroused by the noise her husband was making, she called out to him and demanded to know what he was quarrelling with Pinuccio about. Whereupon her husband replied:

'Don't you hear what he says he has done to Niccolosa this night?'

'He's telling a pack of lies,' said the woman. 'He hasn't been anywhere near Niccolosa, for I've been lying beside her myself the whole time and I haven't managed to sleep a wink. You're a fool to take any notice of him. You men drink so much in the evening that you spend the night dreaming and wandering all over the place in your sleep, and imagine you've performed all sorts of miracles: it's a thousand pities you don't trip over and break your necks! What's Pinuccio doing there anyway? Why isn't he in his own bed?'

At which point, seeing how adroitly the woman was concealing both her own and her daughter's dishonour, Adriano came to her support by saying:

'How many times do I have to tell you, Pinuccio, not to wander about in the middle of the night? You'll land yourself in serious trouble one of these days, with this habit of walking in your sleep, and claiming to have actually done the fantastic things you dream about. Come back to bed, curse you!'

When he heard Adriano confirm what his wife had been saying, the host began to think that Pinuccio really had been dreaming after all; and seizing him by the shoulder, he shook him and yelled at him, saying:

'Wake up, Pinuccio! Go back to your own bed!'

Having taken all of this in, Pinuccio now began to thresh about as though he were dreaming again, causing his host to split his sides with laughter. But in the end, after a thorough shaking, he pretended to wake up; and calling to Adriano, he said:

'Why have you woken me up? Is it morning already?'

'Yes,' said Adriano. 'Come back here.'

Pinuccio kept up the pretence, showing every sign of being extremely drowsy, but in the end he left his host's side and staggered back to bed with Adriano. When they got up next morning, their host began to laugh and make fun of Pinuccio and his dreams. And so, amid a constant stream of merry banter, the two young men saddled and loaded their horses, and after drinking the health of their host, they remounted and rode back to Florence, feeling no less delighted with the manner than with the outcome of the night's activities.

From then on, Pinuccio discovered other ways of consorting with Niccolosa, who meanwhile assured her mother that he had certainly been dreaming. And thus the woman, who retained a vivid memory of Adriano's embraces, was left with the firm conviction that she alone had been awake on the night in question.

SEVENTH STORY

Talano d'Imolese dreams that his wife is savaged all about the throat and the face by a wolf, and tells her to take care; but she ignores his warning, and the dream comes true.

Panfilo's story being now at an end, the woman's presence of mind was applauded by one and all, after which the queen called upon Pampinea to tell hers, and she began as follows:

Delectable ladies, we have talked on previous occasions[1] about the truths embodied in dreams, which many of us refuse to take seriously. But even though this topic has already been aired, I am determined to tell you a pithy little tale showing what happened not long ago to a neighbour of mine through ignoring a dream of her husband's in which she appeared.

I don't know whether you were ever acquainted with Talano d'Imolese,[2] but he was a person of high repute, and was married to a young woman called Margarita, who, though exceedingly beautiful, was the most argumentative, disagreeable and self-willed creature on God's earth, for she would never heed other people's advice and regarded everyone but herself as an incompetent fool. This made life very difficult for Talano, but since he had no choice in the matter, he bore it all philosophically.

Now one night, when Talano happened to be staying with this wife of his at one of their country estates, he dreamt that he saw her wandering through some very beautiful woods, which were situated not far away from the house. As he watched, an enormous and ferocious wolf seemed to emerge from a corner of the woods and hurl itself at Margarita's throat, dragging her to the ground. She struggled to free herself, screaming for help, and when at length she managed to escape from its clutches, the whole of her throat and face appeared to be torn to ribbons. So when Talano got up next morning, he said to his wife:

'Woman, your cussedness has been the bane of my life since the day we were married; but all the same I should be sorry if you came to any harm, and therefore, if you'll take my advice, you won't venture forth from the house today.'

When she asked him the reason, he told her about his dream, whereupon she tossed her head in the air and said:

'Evil wishes beget evil dreams. You pretend to be very anxious for my safety, but you only dream these horrid things about me because you'd like to see them happen. You may rest assured that I shall never give you the satisfaction of seeing me suffer any such fate as the one you describe, whether on this day or any other.'

'I knew you would say that,' said Talano. 'A mangy dog never thanks you for combing its pelt. But you may think whatever you like. I only mentioned it for your own good, and once again I advise you to stay at home today, or at any rate to keep well away from those woods of ours.'

'Very well,' said the woman, 'I'll do as you say.'

But then she began to think to herself: 'Here's a crafty fellow! Do you see how he tries to frighten me out of going near the woods today? He's doubtless made an appointment there with some strumpet or other, and doesn't want me to find him. Ah, he'd do well for himself at a supper for the blind, but knowing him as I do, I should be a great fool to take him at his word. He certainly won't get away with this. I shall find out what business takes him to those woods, even if I have to wait there the whole day.'

No sooner had she reached the end of these deliberations than her husband left the house, whereupon she too left the house by a separate door and made her way to the woods without a moment's delay, keeping out of sight as much as possible. On entering the woods, she concealed herself in the thickest part she could find, and kept a sharp lookout on all sides so that she could see if anyone was coming.

Nothing was further removed from her thoughts than the prospect of seeing any wolves, but all of a sudden, whilst she was standing there in the way we have described, a wolf of terrifying size leapt out from a nearby thicket; on seeing which, she scarcely had time to exclaim 'Lord, deliver me!' before the wolf hurled itself at her throat, seized her firmly in its jaws, and began to carry her off as though she were a new-born lamb.

So tightly was the wolf holding on to her throat that she was unable to scream for help, nor was there anything else she could do; and hence the wolf, as it bore her away, would assuredly have strangled her but for the fact that it ran towards some shepherds, who yelled at the beast and forced it to release her. The poor, unfortunate woman was recognized by the shepherds, who carried her back to her house, and after long and intensive treatment at the hands of various physicians, she recovered. Her recovery was not complete, however, for the whole of her throat and a part of her face were so badly disfigured that whereas she was formerly a beautiful woman, she was thenceforth deformed and utterly loathsome to look upon. Hence she was ashamed to show herself in public, and shed many a bitter tear for her petulant ways and her refusal to give credence, when it would have cost her nothing, to her husband's prophetic dream.

EIGHTH STORY

Biondello plays a trick on Ciacco in regard of a breakfast, whereupon Ciacco discreetly avenges himself, causing Biondello to receive a terrible hiding.

Each and every member of the joyful company maintained that what Talano had seen in his sleep was no dream, but rather a vision, as it corresponded so exactly with what had actually taken place. But when they had all finished talking, the queen called upon Lauretta to follow, and so she began:

Judicious ladies, just as my predecessors today have almost without exception taken their cue from something already said, I too am prompted, by the account Pampinea gave us yesterday of the scholar's bitter vendetta, to tell you of another vendetta, which, whilst it was no laughing matter for its victim, was at the same time rather less brutal.

I would have you know, then, that in Florence there was once a man known to everyone as Ciacco,[1] who was the greatest glutton that ever lived. Since his purse was unequal to the demands made upon it by his gluttony, and since he was also a highly cultivated person, never at a loss for something clever and amusing to say, he built a reputation for himself, not exactly as a jester but rather as a wit, and took to mixing with wealthy people possessing a taste for good food, with whom he regularly supped and breakfasted even when not invited.

In Florence, at the time of which I am speaking, there was a man called Biondello, who was a dapper little fellow, elegant to a fault and neater than a fly, with a coif surmounting a head of long, fair hair, exquisitely arranged so that not a single strand was out of place, and this man practised the same profession as Ciacco.

One morning, during Lent, Biondello was at the fishmarket buying a pair of huge lampreys for Messer Vieri de' Cerchi,[2] when he was observed by Ciacco, who went up to him and said:

'Oho! What have we here?'

To which Biondello replied:

'The other three that were sent to Messer Corso Donati's[3] yesterday evening, along with a sturgeon, were much finer specimens than these. He's invited one or two gentlemen to breakfast, and because he thought there might not be enough to go round, he got me to purchase these other two. Won't you be coming?'

'What a question to ask!' Ciacco replied. 'Of course I shall be coming.'

At what seemed to him an appropriate hour, Ciacco made his way to the house of Messer Corso, whom he found with several of his neighbours waiting to go to breakfast. When Messer Corso asked him the nature of his business, Ciacco replied:

'I have come, sir, in order to breakfast with you and your friends.'

'You are most welcome,' said Messer Corso. 'And since the meal is now ready, let us go and eat.'

So they all sat down at table, and after a first course of tunny and chick-peas they had some fried fish from the Arno, after which the meal came abruptly to an end.

On discovering that Biondello had deceived him, Ciacco was boiling with indignation, and resolved to pay him back in his own coin. A few days later he came across Biondello, who had meanwhile amused a number of people with the tale of his little hoax. No sooner did Biondello catch sight of Ciacco than he greeted him and asked, with a broad grin, what he had thought of Messer Corso's lampreys.

'That is a question,' replied Ciacco, 'which you will be far better able to answer yourself, before another week has passed.'

After leaving Biondello, Ciacco went to work without further ado, and having agreed upon terms with a crafty intermediary, he handed him an enormous wine-bottle, led him to a spot near the Loggia de' Cavicciuli,[4] and pointing out to him a gentleman there called Messer Filippo Argenti[5] – a huge, powerful, muscular-looking fellow, who was as haughty, hot-tempered, and quarrelsome a man as ever drew breath – he said:

'You are to go up to that man over there with this flask in your hand, and say to him: "Sir, I have been sent to you by Biondello, who asks if you will be so kind as to rubify this flask for him with some of your excellent red wine, as he wants to wet his whistle with his comrades." But be very careful not to let him lay his hands on you, otherwise you'll have a thin time of it and my plans will be ruined.'

'Do I have to say anything else?' said the intermediary.

'No,' said Ciacco. 'Now off you go, and when you've said your piece, return here to me with the flask and I shall pay you your fee.'

So the intermediary made his way across to Messer Filippo and delivered the message, which Messer Filippo no sooner heard than he concluded that Biondello, who was no stranger to him, was having a joke at his expense. Not being slow to take offence, he went all red in the face and said:

'Rubify? Wet his whistle? God curse the fellow, and you too!'

Whereupon he leapt to his feet and shot out an arm at the intermediary, intending to take him by the scruff of the neck. But the latter, being on his guard, was too quick for him and took to his heels. He then returned by a roundabout route to Ciacco, who had witnessed the whole scene, and told him what Messer Filippo had said.

Ciacco was delighted, and having paid the man his fee, went off in search of Biondello, never resting for a moment till he found him.

'Have you been to the Loggia de' Cavicciuli lately?' he asked him.

'No, I haven't,' replied Biondello. 'Why do you ask?'

'Because I've heard that Messer Filippo is looking for you,' said Ciacco. 'I couldn't tell you what it is he wants.'

'Good,' said Biondello. 'I'll go over there and converse with him a little.'

Biondello then took his leave, and Ciacco followed him at a discreet distance to see what would happen. Meanwhile Messer Filippo, having failed to catch the intermediary, had been left in a towering rage and was breathing fire and fury, being unable to make any sense of the man's words except that Biondello, at the prompting of some person or other, was making fun of him. And it was whilst he was fuming away in this manner that Biondello arrived on the scene.

No sooner did Messer Filippo set eyes on Biondello than he strode up to him and gave him a tremendous punch in the face.

'Oh alas, sir!' cried Biondello. 'What does this mean?'

'Scoundrel!' yelled Messer Filippo, tearing Biondello's coif to ribbons and hurling his hood to the ground, at the same time raining blows upon him. 'You'll see only too clearly what it means. I'll teach you to send people to me with all this talk of rubifying flasks and wetting your whistle. Do you suppose you can make fun of me as though I were a child?'

And so saying, he pounded Biondello's face with a pair of fists that seemed to be made of iron. Nor was this all, for he disarranged every hair on the poor fellow's head, and having rolled him over in the mud, tore all the clothes he was wearing to shreds. So zealously did he address himself to his task that from the first moment to the last Biondello was unable to utter so much as a single syllable, or to ask him why he was attacking him. He had certainly heard Messer Filippo talk about 'rubifying flasks' and 'wetting whistles', but what these phrases might signify he had no idea.

Having taken an almighty drubbing, he was eventually surrounded by a number of onlookers, who succeeded with the greatest difficulty in removing him, battered and bedraggled, from Messer Filippo's reach. They then explained why Messer Filippo had done it and admonished him for sending such a message, telling him that in future he should remember who Messer Filippo was and that he was not a man to be trifled with.

His eyes full of tears, Biondello protested his innocence, denying that he had ever sent anyone to Messer Filippo for wine. But there was little he could do about it now, and after making himself look a little more presentable he returned home, sorrowful and forlorn, rightly concluding that this was a piece of Ciacco's handiwork. Several days later, when the bruises had faded from his face and he once again began to show himself in public, one of the first people he happened to meet was Ciacco.

'Tell me, Biondello,' he asked, laughing, 'what opinion did you form of Messer Filippo's wine?'

'The same as the one you formed of Messer Corso's lampreys,' he replied.

Then Ciacco said:

'From now on it's up to you: if you should ever try to present me with another of those sumptuous meals, I shall supply you with one of these excellent drinks.'

Knowing it was easier for him to bear ill-will to Ciacco than to do him any actual harm, Biondello bade him a polite good day, and took care never to play any tricks on him again.

NINTH STORY

Two young men ask Solomon's advice, the first as to how he may win people's love, the second as to how he should punish his obstinate wife. Solomon replies by telling the former to love, and the latter to go to Goosebridge.

Not wishing to revoke Dioneo's privilege, the queen saw that she alone remained to tell a story, and when the ladies had finished laughing over the hapless Biondello, she cheerfully thus began:

Lovable ladies, if the order of things is impartially considered, it will quickly be apparent that the vast majority of women are through Nature and custom, as well as in law, subservient to men, by whose opinions their conduct and actions are bound to be governed. It therefore behoves any woman who seeks a calm, contented and untroubled life with her menfolk, to be humble, patient, and obedient, besides being virtuous, a quality that every judicious woman considers her especial and most valued possession.

Even if this lesson were not taught to us by the law, which in all things is directed to the common good, and by usage (or custom as we have called it), Nature proves it to us very plainly, for she has made us soft and fragile of body, timid and fearful of heart, compassionate and benign of disposition, and has furnished us with meagre physical strength, pleasing voices, and gently moving limbs. All of which shows that we need to be governed by others; and it stands to reason that those who need to be aided and governed must be submissive, obedient, and deferential to their benefactors and governors. But who are the governors and benefactors of us women, if they are not our menfolk? Hence we should always submit to men's will, and do them all possible honour, and any woman who behaves differently is worthy, in my opinion, not only of severe censure, but of harsh punishment.

I have expressed views of this kind on previous occasions, and I was confirmed in them a little while ago by what Pampinea told us about Talano's obstinate wife, to whom God sent the punishment that her husband was unable to visit upon her. I repeat, therefore, that in my judgement, all those women should be harshly and rigidly punished, who are other than agreeable, kindly, and compliant, as required by Nature, usage, and law.

Hence I should like to acquaint you with a piece of advice that was once proffered by Solomon,[1] for it is a useful remedy in treating those who are afflicted by the malady of which I have spoken. It should not be thought that his counsel applies to all women, regardless of whether they require such a remedy, although men have a proverb which says: 'For a good horse and a bad, spurs are required; for a good woman and a bad, the rod is required.'[2] Which words, being frivolously interpreted, all women would readily concede to be true; but I suggest that even in their moral sense they are no less admissible.

All women are pliant and yielding by nature, and hence for those who step beyond their permitted bounds the rod is required to punish their transgressions; and in order to sustain the virtue of the others, who practise restraint, the rod is required to encourage and frighten them.

But leaving all preaching aside, and coming to what I propose to tell you, I say that when the fame of Solomon's wisdom, having spread to the four corners of the earth, was at its highest peak, and it was known that he would share it unstintingly with anyone wishing to verify it in person, many people came to him from different parts of the world to ask his advice on matters of great privacy and complexity; and one of those who set out to go and consult him was a young man called Melissus,[3] who was of a noble family and very rich, and was born and bred in the town of Lajazzo.[4]

As he was on his way to Jerusalem, after leaving Antioch he chanced upon another young man, riding in the same direction, whose name was Joseph; and after a while, as is usually the way with travellers, they fell into conversation.

Having learned what manner of man this Joseph was, and whence he had come, he asked him where he was going and for what purpose. To which Joseph replied that he was going to seek Solomon's advice about how he should deal with his wife, who was the most perverse and stubborn woman on earth, and against whose wilfulness all his entreaties, endearments, and everything else had availed him nothing. Then he in turn asked Melissus whence he had come, where he was going, and why; and Melissus replied:

'I come from Lajazzo, and like yourself, I too suffer a misfortune. I am a rich young man, and I spend my substance in banqueting and entertaining my fellow citizens, but the curious thing about it is that despite all this I cannot find a single man who wishes me well. And so I am going where you are going, to seek advice about what I must do to be loved.'

So the two companions journeyed on together, and on reaching Jerusalem, through the good offices of one of Solomon's lords, they were ushered into his presence and Melissus briefly explained the nature of his business. And all that Solomon said by way of reply was: 'Love.'

This said, Melissus was promptly shown the door, and Joseph explained his own reason for coming. But the only answer he received from Solomon was: 'Go to Goosebridge,' and the words were scarcely out of the King's mouth before Joseph, too, was removed from his presence. Outside, he found Melissus waiting for him, and told him about the answer he had been given.

After pondering upon these words without succeeding in extracting a meaning from them, or anything that might help to resolve their problems, the two young men, feeling they had been made to look foolish, began to make their way homewards. After travelling for several days, they came to a fine-looking bridge across a river; and since a lengthy baggage-train of mules and horses happened to be using the bridge, they were forced to wait till all the animals had crossed it.

When all but a few of them had done so, one of the mules took fright, in the way they frequently do, and refused to take another step. So one of the muleteers took hold of a stick and began to beat it, quite gently to begin with, in order to make it go across. But the mule, veering from one side of the road to the other and occasionally turning back, was utterly determined not to go on. This caused the muleteer to lose his temper completely, and he began to beat it with his stick quite unmercifully, raining a series of terrible blows on its head, its flanks, and its hindquarters, but all to no avail.

Melissus and Joseph, who were standing there watching all this, directed a stream of abuse at the muleteer, saying:

'Hey! villain, what are you doing? Do you want to kill the poor beast? Why don't you try talking nicely to him and leading him across gently? He'll come more quickly that way than by beating him as you are doing.'

'You know your horses and I know my mule,' replied the muleteer. 'Just you leave him to me.'

Having said this he began to beat the mule all over again, and administered so many blows to each of its flanks that the mule moved on, and the muleteer's point was made.

As the two young men were about to proceed on their way, Joseph saw a fellow sitting on the farther side of the bridge and asked him what the place was called.

'Sir,' the good man replied, 'this place is called Goosebridge.'

No sooner did Joseph hear the name than he recalled the words of Solomon, and said to Melissus:

'I do declare, my friend, that the advice I had from Solomon may yet turn out to be sound and sensible. For now it's perfectly plain to me that I've never known how to beat my wife properly, and this muleteer has shown me what I must do.'

A few days later they came to Antioch, and Joseph invited Melissus to stay with him and rest for a few days before going on with his journey. Having met with an icy reception from his wife, Joseph told her to see that supper was prepared, taking her instructions from Melissus; and the latter, seeing that Joseph wanted him to do it, briefly explained what he would like to eat. But the woman, true to her old habits, did almost the exact opposite of what Melissus had prescribed; and when Joseph saw what she had done, he rounded on her angrily and said:

'Were you not told about the kind of supper you were to serve?'

The woman turned to him defiantly, and said:

'What are you talking about? Bah! get on with your supper, if you want it. I shall do as I think fit, not as I am told. If you don't like it, you can lump it.'

Melissus was astounded by the woman's reply, and took great exception to it. And Joseph said: 'Woman, you are just the same as ever; but believe me, I shall make you change your ways.' Then, turning to Melissus, he said: 'We shall soon see, my friend, whether Solomon's advice was sound. Pray be good enough to stay and observe what I shall do, and look upon it as a game. If you should be tempted to interfere, remember what the muleteer said to us when we felt so sorry for his mule.'

'Since I am a guest in your house,' said Melissus, 'I have no intention of opposing your wishes.'

Having laid his hands on a good, stout stick of sapling oak, Joseph made his way to his wife's bedroom, to which she had retired, mumbling and muttering angrily to herself, from the supper-table. And grabbing her by the tresses, he flung her to the floor at his feet and began to belabour her cruelly.

The woman first began to shriek and then to threaten; but on finding that Joseph was totally unmoved by all this, she began, bruised and battered from head to toe, to plead with him in God's name to spare her life, saying she would never again do anything to displease him.

None of this had the slightest effect upon Joseph, who on the contrary tanned her hide with ever-increasing fury, dealing her hefty blows about the ribs, the haunches, and the shoulders until eventually he stopped from sheer exhaustion. And to cut a long story short, there was not a bone nor a muscle nor a sinew in the good woman's back that was not rent asunder.

His task completed, Joseph came back to Melissus and said to him:

'Tomorrow we shall see how Solomon's advice to go to Goose-bridge has stood up to the test.' Then, having rested for a while, he washed his hands and supped with Melissus; and in due course they both retired to bed.

Meanwhile his unfortunate wife picked herself up with great difficulty from the floor and collapsed on to her bed, where she slept as best she could till the following morning. And having risen very early, she sent to ask Joseph what he would like for breakfast.

Joseph had a good laugh with Melissus over this, and issued the necessary instructions. And when, in due course, they came down to breakfast, they found an excellent meal awaiting them, precisely as Joseph had ordered. Hence they were both full of praise for the advice which at first they had ill understood.

A few days later, Melissus took his leave of Joseph and returned home, where he told a wise man about what he had heard from Solomon; and the man said:

'He could not have given you a truer or a better piece of advice. You know perfectly well that you love no one, and that you dispense your hospitality and your favours, not because you love other people, but merely for pomp and pride. Love, therefore, as Solomon told you, and you will be loved.'[5]

So that was how the shrew was punished, and how the young man came to be loved through loving others.

TENTH STORY

Father Gianni is prevailed upon by Neighbour Pietro to cast a spell in order to turn his wife into a mare; but when he comes to fasten on the tail, Neighbour Pietro, by saying that he didn't want a tail, completely ruins the spell.

This story of the queen's produced one or two murmurs from the ladies, and one or two laughs from the young men; but when they had quieted down, Dioneo began to address them as follows:

Charming ladies, the beauty of a flock of white doves is better enhanced by a black crow than by a pure white swan; and likewise the presence of a simpleton among a group of intelligent people will sometimes add brilliance and grace to their wisdom, as well as affording pleasure and amusement.

Accordingly, since you are all models of tact and discretion, whereas I am something of a fool, I ought to command a higher place in your affections, by augmenting the light of your excellence through my own shortcomings, than if I were to diminish it by my superior worth. And hence, in telling you the story I am about to relate, I must claim greater licence to present myself in my true colours, and crave your more patient indulgence, than if I were blessed with greater intelligence. I shall tell you a tale, then, of no great length, from which you will learn how carefully one must observe the instructions of those who do things with the aid of magic, and how the slightest failure to do so may ruin all the magician has achieved.

Some years ago, in Barletta, there was a priest called Father Gianni di Barolo,[1] who, because he had a poor living and wished to supplement his income, took to carrying goods, with his mare, round the various fairs of Apulia, and to buying and selling. In the course of his travels, he became very friendly with a man called Pietro da Tresanti,[2] who practised the same trade as his own, but with a donkey, and in token of his friendship and affection he always addressed him, in the Apulian fashion, as Neighbour Pietro.

And whenever Pietro came to Barletta, Father Gianni always invited him to his church, where he shared his quarters with him and entertained him to the best of his ability.

For his own part, Neighbour Pietro was exceedingly poor and had a tiny little house in Tresanti, hardly big enough to accommodate himself, his donkey, and his beautiful young wife. But whenever Father Gianni turned up in Tresanti, he took him to his house and entertained him there as best he could, in appreciation of the latter's hospitality in Barletta. However, when it came to putting him up for the night, Pietro was unable to do as much for him as he would have liked, because he only had one little bed, in which he and his beautiful wife used to sleep. Father Gianni was therefore obliged to bed down on a heap of straw in the stable, alongside his mare and Pietro's donkey.

Pietro's wife, knowing of the hospitality which the priest accorded to her husband in Barletta, had offered on several occasions, when the priest came to stay with them, to go and sleep with a neighbour of hers called Zita Carapresa di Giudice Leo, so that the priest could sleep in the bed with her husband. But the priest wouldn't hear of it, and on one occasion he said to her:

'My dear Gemmata, don't trouble your head over me. I am quite all right, because whenever I choose I can transform this mare³ of mine into a fair young maid and turn in with her. Then when it suits me I turn her back into a mare. And that is why I'd never be without her.'

The young woman was astonished, believed every word of it, and told her husband, adding:

'If he's as good a friend as you say, why don't you get him to teach you the spell, so that you can turn me into a mare and run your business with the mare as well as the donkey? We should earn twice as much money, and when we got home you could turn me back into a woman, as I am now.'

Being more of a simpleton than a sage, Neighbour Pietro believed all this and took her advice to heart; and he began pestering Father Gianni for all he was worth to teach him the secret. Father Gianni did all he could to talk him out of his folly, but without success, and so he said to him:

'Very well, since you insist, tomorrow we shall rise, as usual, before dawn, and I shall show you how it's done. To tell the truth, as you'll see for yourself, the most difficult part of the operation is to fasten on the tail.'

That night, Pietro and Gemmata were looking forward so eagerly to this business that they hardly slept a wink, and as soon as the dawn was approaching, they scrambled out of bed and called Father Gianni, who, having risen in his nightshirt, came to Pietro's tiny little bedroom and said:

'I know of no other person in the world, apart from yourself, for whom I would perform this favour, but as you continue to press me, I shall do it. However, if you want it to work, you must do exactly as I tell you.'

They assured him that they would do as he said. So Father Gianni picked up a lantern, handed it to Neighbour Pietro, and said:

'Watch me closely, and memorize carefully what I say. Unless you want to ruin everything, be sure not to utter a word, no matter what you may see or hear. And pray to God that the tail sticks firmly in place.'

Neighbour Pietro took the lantern and assured him he would do as he had said. Then Father Gianni got Gemmata to remove all her clothes and to stand on all fours like a mare, likewise instructing her not to utter a word whatever happened, after which he began to fondle her face and her head with his hands, saying:

'This be a fine mare's head.'

Then he stroked her hair, saying:

'This be a fine mare's mane.'

And stroking her arms, he said:

'These be fine mare's legs and fine mare's hooves.'

Then he stroked her breasts, which were so round and firm that a certain uninvited guest was roused and stood erect. And he said:

'This be a fine mare's breast.'

He then did the same to her back, her belly, her rump, her thighs and her legs: and finally, having nothing left to attend to except the tail, he lifted his shirt, took hold of the dibber that he did his planting with, and stuck it straight and true in the place made for it, saying:

'And this be a fine mare's tail.'

Until this happened, Neighbour Pietro had been closely observing it all in silence, but he took a poor view of this last bit of business, and exclaimed:

'Oh, Father Gianni, no tail! I don't want a tail!'

The vital sap which all plants need to make them grow had already arrived, when Father Gianni, standing back, said:

'Alas! Neighbour Pietro, what have you done? Didn't I tell you not to say a word no matter what you saw? The mare was just about to materialize, but now you've ruined everything by opening your mouth, and there's no way of ever making another.'

'That suits me,' said Neighbour Pietro. 'I didn't want the tail. Why didn't you ask me to do it? Besides, you stuck it on too low.'

To which Father Gianni replied:

'I didn't ask you because you wouldn't have known how to fasten it on, the first time, as deftly as I.'

The young woman, hearing these words, stood up and said to her husband, in all seriousness:

'Pah! what an idiot you are! Why did you have to ruin everything for the pair of us? Did you ever see a mare without a tail? So help me God, you're as poor as a church mouse already, but you deserve to be a lot poorer.'

Now that it was no longer possible to turn the young woman into a mare because of the words that Neighbour Pietro had uttered, she put on her clothes again, feeling all sad and forlorn. Meanwhile her husband prepared to return to his old trade, with no more than a donkey as usual: then he and Father Gianni went off to the fair at Bitonto[4] together, and he never asked the same favour of him again.

*   *   *

How the ladies laughed to hear this tale, whose meaning they had grasped more readily than Dioneo had intended, may be left to the imagination of those among my fair readers who are laughing at it still. However, the stories were now at an end, the sun's heat had begun to abate, and the queen, knowing that her sovereignty had run its course, rose to her feet and removed her crown. This she placed upon the head of Panfilo, who alone remained to be invested with the honour; and smiling she said:

'My lord, you are left with an arduous task, for since you are the last, you must make up for the failings of myself and my predecessors in the office to which you have now acceded. God grant you grace in this undertaking, as He has granted it to me in crowning you our king.'

Accepting with joy the honour she had bestowed upon him, Panfilo replied:

'Your own excellence, madam, and that of my other subjects, will ensure that my reign is no less worthy of praise than those that have preceded it.' Then, following the example of his predecessors, he made all necessary arrangements with the steward; after which he turned to address the waiting ladies:

'Enamoured ladies,' he said, 'our queen of today, Emilia, prudently left you at liberty to speak on whatever subject you chose, so that you might rest your faculties. But now that you are refreshed, I consider that we should revert to our customary rule, and I therefore want you all to think of something to say, tomorrow, on the subject of *those who have performed liberal or munificent deeds, whether in the cause of love or otherwise.* The telling and the hearing of such things will assuredly fill you with a burning desire, well disposed as you already are in spirit, to comport yourselves valorously. And thus our lives, which cannot be other than brief in these our mortal bodies, will be preserved by the fame of our achievements – a goal which every man who does not simply attend to his belly, like an animal, should not only desire but most zealously pursue and strive to attain.'

The theme proposed by Panfilo was unanimously approved by the joyful company, and by the leave of their new king they all arose from where they were sitting and applied themselves, each according to his taste, to their usual pastimes; and thus they whiled away the time until supper. To this they came in festive mood, and at the end of the meal, which was served with meticulous care and formal propriety, they rose from their places and proceeded to dance as usual. They then sang countless songs, more entertaining for the words than polished in the singing, till finally the king asked

Neifile to sing one on her own account. And without further ado, in
a clear and gladsome voice, she began charmingly to sing, as follows:

> 'I am so young[1] I love to sing
> And take delight in the early spring
> Thanks to the sweet thoughts Love doth bring.
>
> 'I see in green fields as I go
> Yellow and red and white flowers blow,
> Briar-roses and fair lilies grow.
>
> 'And in all these his face I see
> Who has so taken hold of me
> His wish is mine eternally.
>
> 'And when one certain bloom I spy
> Which most recalls him to my eye
> I pluck and greet it lovingly,
>
> 'Kiss it, and thus show that I know
> What my whole soul aspireth to
> And where my heart desires to go:
>
> 'Then, with the rest, I place it there
> Among a posy bound with care
> With my own light and golden hair.
>
> 'That pleasure given by a flower
> To mortal eyes through Nature's power
> Is so bestowed on me that there
>
> 'I fancy my sweet love to be
> Standing himself in front of me,
> Whose person hath so kindled me.
>
> 'Never in words could be expressed
> Its scent's effect upon my breast,
> Of which my sighs are witnesses.
>
> 'They never harsh nor rough breathe forth
> But warm and sweet, of greater worth
> Than other ladies' here on earth,

'And make their way unto my love,
Who when he hears them straight doth move
To bring me bliss just as, in sooth,
I murmur, "Come to me, and prove
I never need despair thy love."'

The king and all the ladies heaped lavish praise upon Neifile's song; after which, since much of the night was already spent, the king decreed that everyone should go and rest until the morning.

Here ends the Ninth Day of the Decameron

TENTH DAY

Here begins the Tenth and Last Day, wherein, under the rule of Panfilo, *the discussion turns upon those who have performed liberal or munificent deeds,*[1] *whether in the cause of love or otherwise.*

One or two cloudlets in the western sky were still suffused with crimson, whilst those in the east, caught in the rays of the approaching sun, were already brightly tipped with gold, when Panfilo got up and caused the ladies and his two companions to be roused. When all were present, he conferred with them and decided upon the place to which they should go to amuse themselves; he then set forth at a leisurely pace, accompanied by Filomena and Fiammetta, and followed by all the rest. For some little time they sauntered gaily along, talking about the lives they intended to lead in the future, and answering each other's questions, until, having walked a considerable distance, they found that the sun was becoming too hot for their comfort, and returned to the palace. Gathering round the fountain, they had some glasses rinsed in its limpid waters, and those among them who were thirsty drank their fill; after which they roamed freely through the garden, savouring its delectable shade, until the hour of breakfast. And when they had eaten and slept, as was their custom, they forgathered in a spot designated by the king, who called upon Neifile to tell the first story; whereupon she cheerfully began, as follows:

FIRST STORY

A worthy knight enters the service of the King of Spain, by whom he feels that he is ill-requited; so the King gives him irrefutable proof that the fault lies, not with himself, but with the knight's own cruel fortune, in the end rewarding him most handsomely.

I account it an especial favour, honourable ladies, that our king should have singled me out to speak first on so weighty a theme as that of munificence, which, even as the sun embellishes and graces the whole of the heavens, is the light and splendour of every other virtue. So I shall tell you a little story, which to my way of thinking is most delightful, and which surely cannot be other than profitable to recall.

You are to know, then, that of the many gallant knights who have graced our city for longer than I can remember, there was one in particular, Messer Ruggieri de' Figiovanni,[1] who was possibly the finest of them all. Being both wealthy and stout of heart, and seeing that, because of the general tenor of Tuscan manners, there would be little or no opportunity for him to prove his worth by remaining in these parts, he made up his mind to spend some time with King Alphonso of Spain,[2] who was better renowned for his prowess than any other ruler of his day. And so he set out with a most impressive array of armour and horses and a large retinue, and made his way to Alphonso's court in Spain, where the King accorded him a gracious welcome.

There accordingly he settled, and because of his princely style of living and the prodigious feats he accomplished in the field, he quickly made his mark as a man of valour.

But the longer he remained at Alphonso's court, the more it seemed to him, through closely observing the ways of the King, that he was granting castles, towns and baronies to one man after another with very little discretion, giving them to people who had done nothing to deserve them. Now, Messer Ruggieri was conscious of his own merits, and since nothing was given to him, he considered that his own standing was thereby greatly diminished. He therefore decided to leave, and went to the King to ask his permission to do so. The King granted his request, and presented him with a most handsome-looking mule, the finest that any man had ever ridden, for which Messer Ruggieri was grateful in view of the long journey ahead of him.

The King then instructed one of his confidential servants to arrange as best he could to accompany Messer Ruggieri throughout the first day of his journey without allowing him to suspect that he had been sent by the King, and to make a mental note of everything Ruggieri said about him, so that he could report it later word for word. And on the second morning he was to order Messer Ruggieri to return to the King.

The servant kept watch, and as soon as Messer Ruggieri left the city, attached himself to his entourage in as natural a manner as possible, giving him the impression that he too was going to Italy.

So they rode along together, with Messer Ruggieri seated astride the mule presented to him by the King, conversing on various topics with his new companion, until at a certain point, just before tierce, he said:

'I suppose we ought to stop and relieve the animals.' So they stopped at a suitable place, where all the animals relieved themselves with the exception of the mule. They then rode on, with the King's servant still listening carefully to the words of the knight, till they came to a watercourse, where, as they were watering their mounts, the mule staled into the river. On seeing this, Messer Ruggieri said:

'Ah! God curse you, beast! you're just like the gentleman who presented you to me.'

The King's servant noted these words, and though he noted many more in the course of their long day's journey together, he heard nothing else from Ruggieri's lips that was other than highly complimentary to the King. Next morning, as soon as they were mounted and about to set off again for Tuscany, the servant delivered the King's order to Messer Ruggieri, who immediately turned back.

Having already been informed of what Messer Ruggieri had said about the mule, the King summoned him to his presence, welcomed him with a broad smile, and asked him why he had compared him to the mule, or rather vice versa.

Messer Ruggieri replied, with the greatest of candour:

'My lord, I compared it to you for this reason, that just as you bestow your gifts where they are inappropriate, and withhold them where they would be justified, so the mule relieved itself, not in the right place, but in the wrong one.'

So the King said:

'Messer Ruggieri, it was not because I failed to recognize in you a most gallant knight, deserving of the highest honours, that I withheld my bounty from you and bestowed it on many others, who were insignificant by comparison with yourself. The blame rests not with me but with your fortune, which has prevented me from giving you your deserts. And I intend to prove to you that I am speaking the truth.'

'My lord,' replied Messer Ruggieri, 'the fact that you have not rewarded me is immaterial, for I never had any desire to multiply my wealth. What distresses me is the absence of any token of your esteem. However, I consider your explanation to be sound and reasonable, and though I am ready to see whatever you wish to show me, I accept your word and there's no need for you to prove it.'

The King then led him into a great hall, where, as he had arranged beforehand, there were two large chests,[3] both of which were padlocked; and in the presence of a large gathering, he said:

'Messer Ruggieri, one of these chests contains my crown, my orb and my royal sceptre, along with many fine brooches, rings and jewelled belts of mine and every other precious stone I possess. The other is filled with earth. Choose whichever one you like, and it shall be yours to keep, and thus you shall see whether it was I or your fortune that failed to acknowledge your worth.'

Seeing that this was what the King desired him to do, Messer Ruggieri chose one of the chests. The King ordered it to be opened, and it was found to be full of earth. Whereupon the King laughed and said:

'As you can see for yourself, Messer Ruggieri, I was telling you the truth about your fortune; but your merits are such that I am bound to oppose her powers. I know that you have little inclination to become a Spaniard, and hence I have no wish to give you either towns or castles in my domain; but in defiance of your fortune, I want you to have the chest of which she deprived you, so that you may take it to your native land and justly boast among your fellow-citizens of your achievements, to which my gifts will bear witness.'

Messer Ruggieri accepted the chest, thanked the King in a manner befitting so generous a gift, and returned with it, well content, to Tuscany.

SECOND STORY

Ghino di Tacco captures the Abbot of Cluny, cures him of a stomach ailment, and then releases him. The Abbot returns to the court of Rome, where he reconciles Ghino with Pope Boniface and creates him a Knight Hospitaller.

After they had finished praising King Alphonso for the munificence he displayed towards the Florentine knight, the king, who had been mightily pleased by Neifile's account, called upon Elissa to tell the next story; and she promptly began, as follows:

Tender ladies, there is no denying that for a king to have acted munificently, and bestowed his munificence upon one who had served him well, is all very fine and commendable. But what are we to think when we are told about a member of the clergy whose munificence was all the more remarkable in that he bestowed it on a person whom no one would have blamed him for treating as his enemy? Surely we can only conclude that whereas the munificence of the King was a virtue, that of the priest was a miracle; for these latter are so incredibly mean that women are positively generous by comparison, and they fight tooth and nail against every charitable instinct. Moreover, whereas all men naturally crave to be avenged for wrongs they have received, we know from experience that the members of the clergy, though they preach submissiveness and warmly commend the pardoning of wrongs, surpass all other men in the zeal with which they conduct their vendettas. But in the story you are about to hear, you will plainly discover how one of their number revealed his munificence.

Ghino di Tacco,[1] whose feats of daring and brigandage brought him great notoriety after being banished from Siena and incurring the enmity of the Counts of Santa Fiora, staged a rebellion in Radicofani against the Church of Rome; and having established himself in the town, he made sure that anyone passing through the surrounding territory was set upon and robbed by his marauders.

Now, the ruling Pope in Rome was Boniface VIII,[2] and to his court there came the Abbot of Cluny,[3] who was reputed to be one of the richest prelates in the world. In the course of his stay there, however, he ruined his stomach, and was advised by the physicians to go to the baths of Siena,[4] where he was certain to recover. And so, having obtained permission from the Pope, he set out for Siena, heedless of the reputation of Ghino, accompanied by a huge and splendid train of goods, baggage, horses and servants.

On learning of his approach, Ghino di Tacco spread out his nets, and without allowing so much as a single page-boy to escape, he cut off the Abbot with the whole of his retinue and belongings in a narrow gorge. This done, he dispatched his ablest lieutenant to the Abbot, suitably escorted, who very politely requested the Abbot, on his master's behalf, to be good enough to make his way to Ghino's fortress and dismount there. On hearing this, the Abbot flew into a terrible rage and replied that he had no intention of doing any such thing, as he had nothing to discuss with Ghino. In short, he was going to continue his journey, and would like to see anyone try to prevent him.

Whereupon Ghino's emissary, speaking in deferential tones, said to him:

'My lord, you have come to a place where except for the power of God we fear nothing, and where excommunications and interdicts are entirely ineffectual. Please be good enough, therefore, to comply with Ghino's wishes in this matter.'

Whilst these words were being exchanged, the whole place had been surrounded by brigands; and so the Abbot, realizing that he and his men were trapped, set off in high dudgeon with Ghino's emissary along the road leading to the fortress, together with all his goods and retinue. Having dismounted at a large house, he was lodged, on Ghino's instructions, in an extremely dark and uncomfortable little room, whereas all the others were given very comfortable quarters, each according to his rank, in various parts of the fortress. And as for the horses and all the Abbot's belongings, these were put in a safe place and left untouched.

Once this was done, Ghino went to the Abbot and said to him:

'My lord, I am sent by Ghino, of whom you are a guest, in order to ask whether you will be so good as to inform him where you were going, and for what reason.'

The Abbot, being a sensible man, had by this time swallowed his pride, and informed him where he was going and why, whereupon Ghino took his leave of him, and resolved to try and cure him without the aid of spa-waters. Having given instructions that the room should be closely guarded and that a large fire should be kept burning in the grate, he left the Abbot alone until the following morning, when he returned bringing him two slices of toasted bread wrapped in a spotless white cloth, together with a large glass of Corniglia[5] wine from the Abbot's own stores. And he addressed the Abbot as follows:

'My lord, when Ghino was younger, he studied medicine, and he claims to have learnt that there is no better cure for the stomach-ache than the one he is about to administer, which begins with these things I have brought you. Take them, then, and be of good cheer.'

His hunger being greater than his appetite for jesting, the Abbot ate the bread and drank the wine, at the same time displaying his indignation. He then became very truculent, asked a number of questions, and issued a lot of advice; and he made a special point of asking to see Ghino.

Since much of what he had said was pointless, Ghino chose to ignore it; but to some of the Abbot's questions he gave polite answers, affirming that Ghino would visit him as soon as he could. Having given him this assurance, he took his leave, and a whole day elapsed before he returned, bringing the same quantity of toasted bread and Corniglia wine as before.

He kept him in this fashion for several days, until he perceived that the Abbot had eaten some dried beans, which he had deliberately left in the room after smuggling them in on an earlier visit.

He therefore asked the Abbot on Ghino's behalf whether his stomach seemed any better, to which the Abbot replied:

'It would seem to be all right, if only I were out of his clutches; and apart from that, my one great longing is to eat, so fully have his remedies restored me to health.'

Ghino therefore made arrangements for the Abbot's servants to furnish a stately chamber with the Abbot's own effects, and gave orders for a great banquet to be prepared, to which a number of the residents and all of the Abbot's retinue were invited. And next morning he went to the Abbot and said:

'My lord, since you are feeling well again, the time has come for you to leave the sick-room.' And taking him by the hand, he led him to the stately chamber and left him there with his own attendants, whilst he went off to make sure that the banquet would be truly magnificent.

The Abbot relaxed for a while in the company of his own folk, and described to them the sort of life he had been living, whereas they on the other hand declared of one accord that Ghino had entertained them lavishly. But the time having now arrived for them to eat, the Abbot and all the others were regaled with a succession of excellent dishes and superb wines, though Ghino still refrained from telling the Abbot who he was.

The Abbot was entertained in this way for several days running, but eventually Ghino gave instructions for all of his effects to be brought to a large room overlooking a courtyard where every one of the Abbot's horses was assembled, down to the most decrepit-looking nag he possessed. He then called on the Abbot and asked him how he was feeling and whether he was strong enough to travel. The Abbot replied that he was as strong as an ox, that he had fully recovered from his stomach ailment, and that once he was out of Ghino's hands, his troubles would be over.

Then Ghino took the Abbot to the room in which his goods and the whole of his retinue were gathered, and, guiding him to a window whence he could see all his horses, he said:

'My lord Abbot, you must realize that gentle birth, exile, poverty, and the desire to defend his life and his nobility against numerous powerful enemies, rather than any instinctive love of evil, have driven Ghino di Tacco, whom you see before you, to become a highway robber and an enemy of the court of Rome. But because you seem a worthy gentleman, and because I have cured you of the malady affecting your stomach, I do not intend to treat you as I would treat any other person who fell into my hands, of whose possessions I would take as large a portion as I pleased. On the contrary, I propose that you yourself, having given due regard to my needs, should decide how much or how little of your property you would care to leave with me. All your goods are set out here before you, and from this window you can see your horses tethered in the courtyard. I therefore bid you take as much or as little as you please, and you are henceforth free to leave whenever you wish.'

The Abbot was astonished and delighted to hear such generous sentiments from the lips of a highway robber, and promptly shed his anger and disdain, being filled instead with a feeling of goodwill towards Ghino, whom he was now disposed to look upon as a bosom friend. And he rushed to embrace him, saying:

'I swear to God that in order to win the friendship of such a man as I now judge you to be, I should willingly endure far greater wrongs than any you appear to have done me hitherto. A curse upon Fortune, that has compelled you to pursue so infamous a calling!'

Then the Abbot singled out an essential minimum of his numerous belongings and his horses, and leaving all the rest to Ghino, he returned to Rome.

The Pope had heard all about the seizure of the Abbot, and took a very serious view of the matter; but the first question he asked on seeing him again was whether the baths had done him any good. To which the Abbot replied, with a smile:

'Holy Father, without going as far as the baths I came across an excellent physician, who cured me completely.' He then described the manner of his cure, much to the pontiff's amusement; and he went on to ask the Pope, under the promptings of his generous instincts, to grant him a certain favour.

The Pope, thinking he would ask for something quite different, readily agreed to grant his request, whereupon the Abbot said:

'Holy Father, the favour I intend to ask of you is that you restore my physician, Ghino di Tacco, to your good graces, for he is assuredly one of the finest and worthiest men I have ever met. As to his wicked ways, I believe them to be more the fault of Fortune than his own; and if you will change his fortune by granting him the wherewithal to live in a style appropriate to his rank, I am convinced that within a short space of time, you will come to share my high opinion of him.'

The Pope was a person of lofty sentiments, always well disposed towards men of excellence, and he said that if Ghino was as fine a man as the Abbot claimed, he would gladly do as he was asked. And he told the Abbot to arrange for Ghino to come to Rome, it being perfectly safe for him to do so.

And so, in accordance with the Abbot's wishes, Ghino came to the papal court under safe conduct. Nor had he been there long before his worth was acknowledged by the Pope, who made peace with him and granted him a large priory in the Order of the Hospitallers,[6] having first created him a Knight of that Order. This position he held for the rest of his days, remaining a friend and servant of Mother Church and the Abbot of Cluny.

THIRD STORY

Mithridanes is filled with envy over Nathan's reputation for courtesy, and sets out to murder him. He comes across Nathan by accident but fails to recognize him, and after learning from Nathan's own lips the best way to carry out his intentions, he finds Nathan in a copse, as arranged. When he realizes who it is, he is filled with shame, and thenceforth becomes Nathan's friend.

The tale they had just been told, about an act of generosity performed by a member of the clergy, was certainly felt by one and all to be something akin to a miracle. But once the ladies had finished debating its novelty, the king called upon Filostrato to proceed, and he forthwith began, as follows:

Noble ladies, great though the munificence of the King of Spain undoubtedly was, and that of the Abbot of Cluny possibly without precedent, you will perhaps be no less amazed to hear of a person who, in order to extend his generosity to another man who was thirsting not only for his blood but for his very life, astutely arranged to give him what he was seeking. Moreover, as I propose to show you in this little story of mine, he would have succeeded therein if his adversary had chosen to accept his offer.

It is quite certain (if the word of various Genoese[1] and of others who have been to those parts may be trusted) that in the region of Cathay[2] there once lived a man of noble lineage, wealthy beyond compare, whose name was Nathan. This man owned a small estate not far from a road along which anyone travelling from the West to the East or vice versa was more or less obliged to pass, and since he was a person of lofty and generous sentiments, who desired to be known by his works, he gathered about him a number of architects and craftsmen, who within a short space of time built for him one of the finest and largest and richest palaces ever seen, and furnished it in excellent taste with all things meet for the reception and entertainment of gentlefolk. There he kept a splendid and numerous retinue of servants, and took pains to ensure that all those people who came and went were received and entertained in a most festive and agreeable manner. To this laudable custom he was so unswervingly attached that before very long his fame had spread, not only throughout the Orient, but to most parts of the western world as well.

When he had arrived at a ripe old age without ever wearying of dispensing his largesse, his reputation chanced to reach the ears of a young man called Mithridanes, who lived in that same part of the world, and who, feeling himself to be no less wealthy than Nathan, grew jealous of Nathan's fame and excellence, and resolved, through a display of greater liberality, either to nullify or darken the old man's name. And so, having built a palace similar to Nathan's, he began to entertain all those who came and went on a more lavish scale than any ever previously known, and there is no doubt that within a short time he became very famous.

Now one day, whilst the young man was sitting all alone in the main courtyard, a woman happened to enter the palace by one of the gates, ask him for alms, and be given them. She then returned by way of a second gate, approached him again, and was given a further sum of money. This happened twelve times in succession, and when she returned for the thirteenth time, Mithridanes said to her:

'My good woman, you are very persistent with this begging of yours.' But he gave her the alms just the same.

On hearing what he had said, the old woman exclaimed:

'Ah, how wonderful is the generosity of Nathan! For his palace has thirty-two gates, just like this one, and I passed through each of them in turn, asked him for alms, and obtained them every time, without his ever so much as hinting that he knew who I was. Yet here I have only to pass through thirteen before I am recognized and given a scolding.' And so saying, she went away and never returned.

Mithridanes took the old woman's words about Nathan as a slight on his own reputation, and flying into a violent rage, he exclaimed:

'Poor fool that I am! How can I ever hope to match Nathan's generosity in greater things, let alone surpass him as I sought, when even in the most trivial affairs I cannot even approach him? All my efforts will be quite futile until he is removed from the face of the earth. He shows no sign of dying from old age, so I shall have to do the job with my own hands, and the sooner the better.'

He then leapt angrily to his feet, and without revealing his intentions to a living soul, set out on horseback with a mere handful of companions; and after the third day he came to the place where Nathan lived. Evening was now approaching, and having bidden his companions to pretend he was a total stranger to them, and find themselves somewhere to stay pending further instructions, he was left to his own devices. Not very far from Nathan's fair palace he came across its owner, all alone and very plainly attired, taking a pleasant stroll in the cool of the evening; and not realizing who it was, he asked him whether he could direct him to Nathan's house.

'My son,' Nathan gaily replied, 'nobody in these parts could show you better than I how to get there. So if you have no objection, I'll take you there myself.'

The young man gladly accepted his offer, but told him that if possible he did not want Nathan to see him or to know that he was there.

'Since you want it to be so,' said Nathan, 'I shall attend to that as well.'

Mithridanes therefore dismounted, and, walking along with Nathan, who was very soon entertaining him with a stream of fine talk, he made his way to the beautiful palace.

On reaching the palace, Nathan got one of his servants to take the young man's horse, and, whispering into the servant's ear, instructed him to pass the word immediately through the entire household that no one was to tell the young man that he himself was Nathan. And this command was carried out.

Once they were inside the palace, he saw that Mithridanes was lodged in an exquisite room, to which no one was admitted except the servants he had deputed to wait upon him. And making the visitor feel completely at home there, Nathan himself kept him company.

Thus they spent the evening together, and although Mithridanes treated Nathan with the deference of a son conversing with a father, he was unable to refrain from asking him who he was.

'I am one of Nathan's menial servants,' replied Nathan, 'and although I have been with him ever since my infancy, he has never raised me above my present station; so that, even if everyone else praises him to the skies, I myself have little to thank him for.'

The old man's words raised hopes in Mithridanes of being able to carry out his evil purpose more safely and discreetly, especially when Nathan went on to ask him very politely to tell him who he was and the nature of his business in that part of the world, offering him all the advice and assistance he could give.

Mithridanes paused for some little time before replying, but eventually decided to take him into his confidence. After much beating about the bush he came to the point; and having sworn him to secrecy he requested his help and advice, revealing exactly who he was, why he was there, and what had prompted him to come.

On hearing Mithridanes speak, and learning of his cruel resolve, Nathan was extremely perturbed. But he was not deficient in courage, and scarcely paused for a moment before replying, without batting an eyelid:

'Your father was a man of excellent worth, Mithridanes, and you are clearly intent upon following his example by this lofty enterprise of yours, wherein you extend a generous hand to all who come to you. Moreover, I warmly commend your envy of Nathan, for if this form of jealousy were more widespread, the world, which is very miserly, would soon become a better place to live in. I shall certainly keep your intentions a secret, but rather than render you any great assistance, I can offer you some useful advice, which is this. Some half a mile from where we stand, you can see a copse where practically every morning Nathan goes for a long walk, entirely alone; it will be a simple matter for you to find him there and deal with him as you please. But if you kill him, and wish to make good your escape, you must leave the copse, not by the way you entered, but along the path you see over there to the left, for although it is a little more difficult, it will lead you home by a shorter and safer route.'

Having imparted this information to Mithridanes, Nathan took his leave, and Mithridanes secretly sent word to his companions, who had likewise found lodging in the palace, about where they were to wait for him on the following day. Meanwhile Nathan had no misgivings about the advice he had offered, and when the next day came, not having changed his mind in the slightest, he set off alone for the copse to meet his doom.

Mithridanes had no other weapons but a sword and a bow, and as soon as he had risen he girded them on, mounted his horse, and rode over to the copse, where from some distance away he espied the solitary figure of Nathan sauntering among the trees. He galloped towards him, but being resolved to see his face and hear him speak before attacking him, he seized him by the turban he was wearing and exclaimed:

'Greybeard, your hour has come!'

By way of answer, all that Nathan said was:

'In that case I have only myself to blame.'

On hearing his voice and observing his features, Mithridanes recognized him at once as the man who had been so hospitable and sociable towards him, and had given him such faithful advice; hence his fury immediately subsided and his anger gave way to a feeling of shame. And having thrown away his sword, which he had already drawn in readiness to strike, he dismounted from his horse and flung himself in tears at Nathan's feet, saying:

'How clearly, dearest father, do I perceive your liberality, seeing the ingenious way in which you have come to offer me the life which without any reason I was eager to take, as you discovered for yourself from my own lips. But God was more heedful than I of my obligations, and in this moment of supreme need He has opened my eyes, which vile envy had kept so tightly sealed. And because you have been so compliant towards my evil design, I am all the more conscious of the debt of penitence that I owe you. Avenge yourself upon me, therefore, in whatever way you think my crime deserves.'

Having helped Mithridanes to his feet, Nathan kissed and embraced him affectionately and said:

'My son, as to your evil design, as you call it, there is no need either to ask or to grant forgiveness, because you pursued it, not out of hatred but in order to be better thought of. Fear me not, then, and rest assured that in view of the loftiness of your motives, no other living person loves you as greatly as I, for you do not devote your energies to the accumulation of riches, as misers do, but to spending what you have amassed. Nor should you feel ashamed for having wanted to kill me to acquire fame, or imagine that I marvel to hear it. In order to extend their dominions, and hence their fame, the mightiest emperors and greatest kings have practised virtually no other art than that of killing, not just one person as you intended, but countless thousands, setting whole provinces ablaze and razing whole cities to the ground. So that if, to enhance your personal fame, it was only me that you wanted to kill, there was nothing marvellous or novel about what you were doing, which on the contrary was very commonplace.'

Without wishing to excuse himself, Mithridanes praised Nathan for presenting his wicked design in so seemly a light, and concluded by expressing his utter astonishment that Nathan had been prepared to supply him not only with the means but also with advice for achieving his object. Whereupon Nathan replied:

'Mithridanes, neither my compliance nor my advice should astonish you, for ever since I became my own master, and began to pursue those same ideals by which you too are now inspired, I have always sought, so far as it lay within my power, to grant the desires of anyone crossing my threshold. You came here with the desire of taking my life, and when I heard what it was that you wanted, so that you would not be the only person ever to leave my house empty-handed, I forthwith resolved to present it to you: and with this purpose in mind, I gave you the advice I considered most apt for taking my life without losing your own. Therefore I repeat: if this is what you want, I implore you to take my life and do whatever you please with it, for I can think of no better way of bestowing it. I have had the use of it now these eighty years, during which it has brought me all the pleasures and joys I could desire; and I realize that, like all other men and nearly everything under the sun, I am subject to the laws of Nature, and have very little of it left. Hence I consider it far preferable to give it away now, just as I have always given away and spent my treasures, than to cling to it until such time as Nature deprives me of it against my will.

'Even if one were to give away a hundred years, it would not amount to much of a gift; and surely it is a much more trivial matter to give away the six or eight years of my life that still remain to me. Take it then, if you want it, I do implore you; for during all the years I have lived here, I have never yet found anyone who wanted it, and if you do not take it, now that you have asked for it, I doubt whether I shall ever find anyone else. But even if I should happen to do so, I realize that the longer I keep it, the less valuable it becomes. Take it therefore, I beg you, before it loses its worth entirely.'

'God forbid,' said Mithridanes, feeling deeply ashamed, 'that I should even contemplate taking so precious a thing as your life, as until just now I was thinking of doing, let alone that I should actually deprive you of it. Far from wanting to shorten its years, I would gladly augment them with some of my own, if such a thing were possible.'

'Supposing it were,' Nathan promptly replied, 'would you really oblige me to accept them, and thus serve you as I have never served another living soul, by taking something of yours, when I have never before taken anything from anyone?'

'Yes,' said Mithridanes, without a moment's hesitation.

'Then do as I suggest,' said Nathan. 'You remain here in my house, young as you are, and assume the name of Nathan, whilst I go to live in yours, and henceforth call myself Mithridanes.'

To which Mithridanes replied:

'If I were able to comport myself so impeccably as you do now, and as you have always done in the past, I should accept your offer without a second thought; but because I feel quite certain that my deeds would only diminish the fame of Nathan, and because I have no intention of impairing another's name for that to which I cannot myself aspire, I am obliged to refuse it.'

After conversing agreeably together on these and many other matters, they returned as Nathan wished to the palace, where for several days on end he entertained Mithridanes in sumptuous style, giving him every encouragement to persevere in his great and noble resolve. And when Mithridanes wanted to return home with his companions, Nathan let him go, having made it abundantly clear that his liberality could never be surpassed.

FOURTH STORY

Messer Gentile de' Carisendi comes from Modena and takes from the tomb the lady he loves, who has been buried for dead. She revives and gives birth to a male child, and later Messer Gentile restores her and the child to Niccoluccio Caccianimico, the lady's husband.

Miraculous indeed did it seem to all those present that anyone should be liberal with his own blood; and everyone agreed that Nathan's generosity had certainly exceeded that of the King of Spain or the Abbot of Cluny. But after they had debated the matter at some length, the king fixed his gaze on Lauretta, thus showing that he wanted her to tell the next story; and Lauretta began forthwith, as follows:

Fair young ladies, so goodly and magnificent are the things we have been told, so fully has the ground already been covered, that those of us who have not yet told our tales would surely be left with no area to explore, unless of course we turn to the deeds of lovers, wherein a most copious supply of tales on any topic is always to be found. For this reason, and also because matters of this sort are especially fascinating for people of our age, I should like to tell you of a generous deed performed by one who was in love. And if it is true that in order to possess the object of their love men will give away whole fortunes, set aside their enmities, and place their lives, their honour, and (what is more important) their reputation in serious jeopardy, then possibly you will conclude, all things considered, that his action was no less striking than some of the ones already described.

In Bologna, then, that illustrious city in the Lombard plain, there once lived a gentleman called Messer Gentile de' Carisendi,[1] distinguished for his valour and noble blood, who whilst still in his youth became enamoured of a gentlewoman, Madonna Catalina by name, who was the wife of a certain Niccoluccio Caccianimico. But because his love for the lady was ill-requited he almost despaired of it and went away to Modena, where he had been appointed to the office of *podestà*.

At the time of which we are speaking, Niccoluccio was absent from Bologna, and his wife, being pregnant, was staying at an estate of his, some three miles distant from the city, where she had the misfortune to contract a sudden and cruel malady, whose effects were so powerful and serious that all sign of life in her was extinguished, and consequently she was adjudged, even by her physicians, to be dead. Since her closest women relatives claimed to have heard from her own lips that she had not been pregnant sufficiently long for the unborn creature to be perfectly formed, they troubled themselves no further on that score, and after shedding many tears, they buried her, just as she was, in a tomb in the local church.

The news of the lady's demise was immediately reported to Messer Gentile by one of his friends, and despite the fact that she had never exactly smothered him with her favours, he was quite overcome with sorrow. But at length he said to himself:

'So, Madonna Catalina, you are dead! You never accorded me so much as a single glance when you were alive; but now that you are dead, and cannot reject my love, I am determined to steal a kiss or two from you.'

Night had already fallen, and having made arrangements to depart in secret, he took horse with one of his servants, riding without pause[2] till he came to the place where the lady was buried. Having opened up the tomb, he made his way cautiously inside, and lying down beside her, he drew his face to hers and kissed her again and again, shedding tears profusely as he did so.

But as every woman knows, no sooner does a man obtain one thing, especially if he happens to be in love, than he wants something else; and just as Messer Gentile had made up his mind to tarry there no longer, he said to himself: 'Ah! why should I not place my hand gently on her breast, now that I am here? I have never touched her before, and I shall never have another opportunity.'

And so, overcome by this sudden longing, he placed his hand on the lady's bosom, and after keeping it there for some little time, he thought he could detect a faint heartbeat. Whereupon, subduing all his fears, he examined her more closely and discovered that she was in fact still alive, though the actual signs of life were minimal and very weak. He then removed her from the tomb as gently as possible with the aid of his servant, and having set her across his saddle-bow, he conveyed her in secret to his house in Bologna.

His mother, a wise and resourceful woman, was living in the house, and on hearing her son's lengthy account of all that had happened she was filled with compassion and skilfully restored Catalina to life by putting her in a warm bath and then setting her in front of a well-stoked fire. On coming to her senses, she cast a deep sigh, and said:

'Alas! where am I now?'

'Don't worry,' the worthy lady replied, 'you are in good hands.'

When she had fully recovered her wits, she looked about her and

discovered to her amazement that she was in totally strange surroundings, with Messer Gentile standing before her. She turned to his
mother and asked her to explain how she came to be there,
whereupon Messer Gentile gave her a faithful account of all that
had happened. At this she began to sob, but eventually she thanked
him as best she could and implored him out of the love he had
borne her and his sense of honour to do nothing to her in his house
that would bring herself or her husband into discredit, and to let her
return home as soon as daylight came.

'My lady,' replied Messer Gentile, 'no matter how deeply I may
have yearned in former times, I have no intention either now or in
the future (since God has granted me this favour of restoring you to
life on account of the love I once bore you) of treating you
otherwise than as a very dear sister, either here or anywhere else.
But the office I performed tonight on your behalf deserves some
kind of reward; and hence I trust you will not deny me the favour I
am about to ask of you.'

The lady graciously signified her willingness to grant him the
favour, provided it lay in her power to do so and there was nothing
improper about it. So Messer Gentile said:

'My lady, all your kinsfolk and all the people in Bologna firmly
believe you to be dead, so that no one in your house is expecting
you. Hence I should like you to be so kind as to stay here quietly
with my mother until I return from Modena, which will be quite
soon. My reason for asking you this is that I propose to make a
precious gift of you to your husband, in a formal ceremony to
which all the leading citizens will be invited.'

The lady was longing to gladden her kinsfolk with the news of
her return from the dead, but since she acknowledged her debt to
Messer Gentile and saw nothing wrong in his request, she resolved
to do as he had asked; and she pledged him her word to that effect.

Scarcely had she finished giving him her answer than she felt the
first indications that she was about to be delivered of her child, and
not long afterwards, with the tender assistance of Messer Gentile's
mother, she gave birth to a handsome boy. This event increased a
thousandfold the happiness both of Messer Gentile and herself; and
after ordering that she should have everything she needed and that

she was to be treated exactly as though she were his own wife, Messer Gentile returned in secret to Modena.

When the period of his office at Modena came to an end and he was on the point of returning to Bologna, he arranged that on the morning of his arrival a great and splendid banquet should be given at his house for a large number of the city's notables, including Niccoluccio Caccianimico. Upon his arrival he dismounted and went to join his guests, having first called on the lady to find that she was looking healthier and lovelier than ever, and that her small son was also fit and well. And then, with matchless cordiality, he showed his guests to the table and saw that they were regally dined and wined.

When the meal was approaching its end, Messer Gentile, having previously told the lady what he intended to do and arranged with her concerning the manner in which she was to comport herself, got up and addressed them as follows:

'Gentlemen, I recall having once been told that in Persia there is a custom,[3] highly agreeable to my way of thinking, whereby when a person wishes to pay the highest honour to a friend, he invites him to his house and shows him the thing he holds most dear, whether it be his wife, his mistress, his daughter, or what you will, at the same time declaring that if it were possible to do so, he would even more readily show him the very heart from his body. And I propose that we should observe this selfsame custom here in Bologna.

'You have been good enough to honour my banquet with your presence, and I now intend to honour you in the Persian style by showing you the most precious thing I possess or am ever likely to possess. But before doing this, I would ask you to give me your opinion upon the problem that I am about to place before you. A certain person has in his house a good and most loyal servant, who suddenly falls seriously ill; the gentleman in question, without waiting for the ailing servant to breathe his last, has him thrown on to the street and takes no further interest in him; then a stranger comes along who, taking pity on the invalid, conveys him to his house, where, with much loving care and at much expense, he restores him to his former state of health. Now what I should like to know is whether, if the second gentleman keeps him and uses his services, the first has any reasonable ground for complaint or regret when he demands to have him back and is refused.'

Messer Gentile's noble guests, having discussed the various pros and cons amongst themselves, all reached the same conclusion; and since Niccoluccio Caccianimico was a gifted and eloquent speaker, they left it to him to deliver their reply.

Niccoluccio began by extolling the Persian custom, then said that he and his fellow guests were of the unanimous opinion that the first gentleman had no legal claim to the servant, because in the instance cited he had not only abandoned him but cast him away; and that on account of the good offices rendered by the second gentleman, it appeared he was entitled to regard the servant as his own, because in refusing to give him up, he was neither causing any trouble, nor offering any insult, nor doing any injury, to the first.

All the others sitting round the tables (and there was many a worthy gentleman among them) chorused their approval of the answer Niccoluccio had given; and Messer Gentile, delighted with this reply and with the fact that it had come from Niccoluccio himself, affirmed that he too shared their opinion. Then he said:

'The time has come for me to do you honour as I promised.' And summoning two of his servants, he sent them to the lady, whom he had caused to be regally attired and adorned, requesting that she be pleased to come and gladden the gentlemen with her presence. Taking her bonny infant in her arms, she descended, accompanied by the two servants, to the hall, where at Messer Gentile's bidding she sat down next to one of the gentlemen; and then he said:

'Gentlemen, this is the jewel that I cherish above all others, and intend to treasure always. See for yourselves whether you think I have good cause.'

The gentlemen paid her eloquent homage and warmly commended her, and having assured their host that he ought indeed to cherish her, they all began to gaze in her direction. Many of those present would have sworn she was the person she actually was, but for the fact that they understood her to be dead. But the one who gazed most intently of all upon her was Niccoluccio, who was dying to know who she was; and no sooner did his host move aside from the lady than his curiosity got the better of him and he asked her whether she was a Bolognese or a foreigner.

On hearing this question being put to her by her own husband, it was something of an effort for the lady to withhold a reply; but faithful to her instructions she remained silent. Another of the gentlemen asked her whether the infant was hers, and yet another inquired whether she was Messer Gentile's wife, but to neither did she offer any answer. However they were now rejoined by Messer Gentile, and one of his guests said to him:

'This jewel of yours is indeed very beautiful, but are we right in thinking she is dumb?'

'Gentlemen,' replied Messer Gentile, 'that she has hitherto remained silent is no small proof of her virtue.'

'You tell us then,' replied the other. 'Who is she?'

'I shall be only too happy to tell you,' he replied, 'provided that you all promise not to move from your places, no matter what I may say, until I have finished speaking.'

They all gave him their promise, and once the tables had been cleared, Messer Gentile took his seat alongside the lady and said:

'Gentlemen, this lady is the faithful and loyal servant to whom I was referring in the question I put to you just now. Being little prized by her own people, she was cast like something vile and useless into the gutter, whence I myself retrieved her, and by dint of my loving care I removed her from death's grasp with my own hands. In recognition of my pure affection for the lady, God has transformed her from a fearsome corpse into the lovely object that you see before you. But so that you may have a better idea of how this came about, I shall briefly explain the circumstances.'

And so, much to the amazement of his hearers, he gave a clear account of all that had happened from the time he had first fallen in love with the lady until that very hour, then added:

'Therefore, unless you have suddenly changed your opinion, and Niccoluccio especially, this lady belongs to me as of right, and no one can lawfully demand her return.'

To this assertion nobody offered any reply, but they all waited to discover what he was going to say next. Niccoluccio, along with one or two others and the lady herself, dissolved into tears; but

Messer Gentile rose to his feet, took the tiny infant in his arms, and, leading the lady by the hand, walked up to Niccoluccio, saying:

'Stand up now, my friend: I shall not restore your wife to you, for she was cast out by your kinsfolk and her own; but I wish to present you with this lady, together with her little child, of whom you are assuredly the father, though I am his godfather, and when I held him at his christening I named him Gentile. Nor should you cherish her any the less for having spent the best part of three months under my roof; for I swear to you in the name of God (who possibly willed that I should fall in love with her so that my love would be the instrument of her deliverance) that she never led a more upright existence with her parents or with you yourself than the life she has lived here in this house under my mother's care.'

He then turned to the lady and said:

'I now release you, my lady, from every promise you gave me, and hereby deliver you to Niccoluccio.' And having left the lady and the child with Niccoluccio, he returned to his place.

Niccoluccio received his wife and son eagerly in his arms, his joy being all the greater for being so totally unexpected, and thanked Messer Gentile to the best of his power and ability. This touching scene moved all the other guests to tears, and they were full of praise for Messer Gentile, as indeed were all those who came to hear of his story.

The lady was welcomed home amid scenes of great rejoicing, and for a long time afterwards the people of Bologna regarded her with awe as someone who had returned from the dead. And as for Messer Gentile, for the rest of his life he remained a close friend of Niccoluccio as well as of the families of both Niccoluccio and his wife.

What are we to conclude then, gentle ladies? Are we to regard a king who gave away his crown and sceptre, an abbot who reconciled an outlaw to the Pope at no cost to himself, or an old man who exposed his throat to the dagger of his adversary, as being in any way comparable to one who performed so noble a deed as Messer Gentile? For here we have the case of a man in the ardent flush of youth, who, believing himself to be legally entitled to that which the negligence of others had discarded and which he had the good fortune to retrieve, not only kept his ardour under decent restraint, but on obtaining the very object which he had coveted with his whole being for so long, generously surrendered it. In all conscience, none of the instances previously cited seems to me comparable to this.

FIFTH STORY

Madonna Dianora asks Messer Ansaldo for a beautiful May garden in the month of January, and Messer Ansaldo fulfils her request after hiring the services of a magician. Her husband then gives her permission to submit to Messer Ansaldo's pleasure, but on hearing of the husband's liberality Messer Ansaldo releases her from her promise, whilst the magician excuses Messer Ansaldo from the payment of any fee.

Every member of the joyful company praised Messer Gentile to the very skies, after which the king called upon Emilia to follow: and with a confident air, as though she were longing to speak, she thus began:

Dainty ladies, no one can seriously deny that Messer Gentile acted munificently, but if anyone should claim that to do more would be impossible, it will not be too difficult to prove that they are wrong, as I propose to show you in this little story of mine.

In the province of Friuli,[1] which is cold but richly endowed with beautiful mountains, numerous rivers, and limpid streams, there is a town called Udine, where once there lived a beautiful noblewoman called Madonna Dianora, who was married to a most agreeable and good-natured man, exceedingly wealthy, whose name was Gilberto. Because of her outstanding worth, this lady attracted the undying love of a great and noble lord called Messer Ansaldo Gradense, a man of high repute, famous throughout the land for his feats of arms and deeds of courtesy. But although he loved her fervently and did everything he possibly could to persuade her to requite his love, sending her numerous messages to this end, all his efforts were unavailing. Eventually the lady grew tired of the knight's entreaties, and seeing that however firmly she rejected his approaches he still persisted in loving and importuning her, she decided to rid herself of him once and for all by requesting him to do something for her that was both bizarre and, as she thought, impossible. So one day, she said to the woman who regularly came to see her on Messer Ansaldo's behalf:

'My good woman, you have repeatedly assured me that Messer Ansaldo loves me above all else, and offered me sumptuous gifts on his behalf, all of which I prefer that he should keep, for they could never induce me to love him or submit to his pleasure. If only I could be certain, however, that he loved me as much as you claim, I should undoubtedly bring myself to love him and do his bidding. So if he will offer me proof of his love by doing what I intend to ask of him, I shall be only too ready to obey his commands.'

'And what is it, ma'am,' the good woman asked, 'that you want him to do?'

'What I want is this,' replied the lady. 'In the month of January that is now approaching, I want a garden, somewhere near the town, that is full of green plants, flowers, and leafy trees, exactly as though it were the month of May. And if he fails to provide it, let him take good care never to send you or anyone else to me again. For if he should provoke me any further, I shall no longer keep this matter a secret as I have until now, but I shall seek to rid myself of his attentions by complaining to my husband and kinsfolk.'

On hearing about the lady's proposition, the gentleman naturally felt that she was asking him to do something very difficult, or rather well-nigh impossible, and realized that her only reason for demanding such a thing was to dash his hopes; but nevertheless he resolved that he would explore every possible means of furnishing her request. He therefore set inquiries afoot in various parts of the world to see whether anyone could be found to advise and assist him in the matter, and eventually got hold of a man who offered to do it by magic, provided he was well-enough paid. So Messer Ansaldo agreed to pay him a huge sum of money, and waited contentedly for the time the lady had appointed. And during the night preceding the calends of January, when the cold was very intense and everything was covered in snow and ice, the magician employed his skills to such good effect that in a beautiful meadow not far from the town, there appeared next morning, as all those who saw it bore witness, one of the fairest gardens that anyone had ever seen, with plants and trees and fruits of every conceivable kind. No sooner did Messer Ansaldo feast his eyes upon this spectacle than he caused a quantity of the finest fruits and flowers to be gathered and secretly presented to his lady, inviting her to come and see the garden she had asked for, so that she would not only realize how much he loved her, but recall the solemn pledge she had given and take steps to keep her word in the manner of a true gentlewoman.

The lady had been hearing many reports of the wonderful garden, and when she saw the flowers and the fruits, she began to repent of her promise. But for all her repentance, being curious to observe so rare a phenomenon, she went with several other ladies of the town to see the garden, and after commending it greatly and betraying no little astonishment, she made her way home in the depths of despair, thinking of what it obliged her to do. So profound was her distress, in fact, that she was unable to conceal it, with the inevitable result that her husband, noticing how melancholy she looked, demanded to know the reason. For some little time she remained silent, being too embarrassed to say anything, but finally he forced her to tell him the whole story from beginning to end.

Gilberto was at first extremely angry, but after mature reflection, bearing in mind the purity of his wife's intentions, he put aside his anger and said:

'Dianora, no wise or virtuous woman should ever pay heed to messages of that sort, nor should she ever barter her chastity with anyone, no matter what terms she may impose. The power of words received by the heart through the ears is greater than many people think, and to those who are in love nearly everything becomes possible.[2] Hence you did wrong, first of all to pay any heed to him and secondly to barter with him. But because I know you were acting from the purest of motives, I shall allow you, so as to be quit of your promise, to do something which possibly no other man would permit, being swayed also by my fear of the magician, whom Messer Ansaldo, if you were to play him false, would perhaps encourage to do us a mischief. I therefore want you to go to him, and endeavour in every way possible to have yourself released from this promise without loss of honour; but if this should prove impossible, just for this once you may give him your body, but not your heart.'

On hearing her husband speak in this way, the lady burst into tears, maintaining that she wanted no such favour from him; but no matter how loudly she protested, Gilberto was adamant. And so next morning, just as dawn was breaking, the lady set out, by no means richly adorned, together with one of her maids, and preceded by two of her husband's retainers she made her way to Messer Ansaldo's house. Messer Ansaldo was astounded to hear that his lady had come, and leaping out of bed he summoned the magician and said to him:

'I want you to see for yourself how great a prize your skill has procured me.'

They then descended to meet her, and Messer Ansaldo greeted her courteously and reverentially, without any show of unbridled passion, after which they all made their way into a splendid apartment where a huge fire was burning. After having offered her somewhere to sit, Messer Ansaldo said:

'My lady, if the love I have so long borne you merits any reward, I beseech you to do me the kindness of telling me truthfully why you have come here at this hour of day with so few people to bear you company.'

To which the lady replied, confused and almost in tears:

'Sir, I am led here, not because I love you or because I pledged you my word, but because I was ordered to come by my husband, who, paying more regard to the labours of your unruly love than to his own or his wife's reputation, has constrained me to call upon you. And by his command I am ready to submit for this once to your every pleasure.'

Great as Messer Ansaldo's astonishment had been when the lady arrived, his astonishment on hearing her words was considerably greater; and because he was deeply moved by Gilberto's liberality, his ardour gradually turned to compassion.

'My lady,' he said, 'since it is as you say, God forbid that I should ever impair the reputation of one who shows compassion for my love. With your consent, therefore, whilst you are under my roof I shall treat you exactly as though you were my sister, and whenever you choose you shall be free to depart, provided that you convey to your husband all the thanks you deem appropriate for the immense courtesy he has shown me, and that you look upon me always in future as your brother and your servant.'

The lady was pleased beyond measure to hear these words.

'Nothing could ever make me believe,' she said, 'in view of your impeccable manners, that my coming to your house would have any other sequel than the one which I see you have made of it, for which I shall always remain in your debt.'

Then, having taken her leave, she returned to Gilberto suitably attended and told him what had happened. And from that day forth, Gilberto and Messer Ansaldo became the closest of loyal friends.

After perceiving how liberally Gilberto had behaved towards Messer Ansaldo, and Messer Ansaldo towards the lady, the magician said to Messer Ansaldo, as the latter was about to present him with his fee:

'Heaven forbid that after observing Gilberto's generosity in respect of his honour, and yours in respect of your love, I should not be equally generous in respect of my reward. And since I know that you can put this sum of money to good use, I intend that you should keep it.'

Messer Ansaldo was thrown into confusion and tried in every way possible to make him accept the whole or part of the money, but his efforts were unavailing; and when the magician, having after the third day removed his garden, signified his intention of leaving, he bade him good luck and God-speed. And now that his heart was purged of the lustful passion he had harboured for the lady, he was thenceforth inspired to regard her with deep and decorous affection.

What is to be our verdict here, fond ladies? Are we to award pride of place to the instance of a lady who was all but dead,[3] and a love already grown lukewarm through loss of expectation, in preference to the liberality of Messer Ansaldo, whose love was more fervent than ever, being as it were inflamed by greater expectation, and who was holding the prize he had so strenuously pursued in the very palm of his hand? In my view it would be quite absurd to suppose that the first of these generous deeds could be compared with the second.

SIXTH STORY

King Charles the Old, victorious in battle, falls in love with a young girl; but later he repents of his foolish fancy, and bestows both her and her sister honourably in marriage.

It would take far too long to recount in full the various discussions that now took place amongst the ladies as to whether Gilberto or Messer Ansaldo or the magician had displayed the greater liberality in the affair of Madonna Dianora. Suffice it to say that after the king had allowed them ample time to debate the question, he looked towards Fiammetta and ordered her to silence their arguments by telling her story, and without further ado she began as follows:

Illustrious ladies, I have always been of the opinion that in a gathering such as ours, we should talk in such general terms that the meaning of what we say should never give rise to argument among us through being too narrowly defined. Such arguments as these are better conducted among scholars in seats of learning than among ourselves, who have quite enough to do in coping with our distaffs and our spindles. And therefore, since the story I was going to tell you is possibly a little ambiguous and I see you squabbling over those we have already heard, I shall abandon it and tell you another, concerning the chivalrous action, not of any insignificant man, but of a valiant king, whose reputation was in no way diminished in consequence.

Now, all of you will frequently have heard mention of King

Charles the Old,[1] or in other words Charles the First, by whose magnificent enterprise, as well as by the glorious victory he later achieved against King Manfred, the Ghibellines were expelled from Florence and the Guelphs returned to the city. Hence it came about that a certain knight, called Messer Neri degli Uberti,[2] left Florence with his entire household and a large fortune, bent upon taking refuge under the very nose of King Charles; and so as to seek a secluded spot, where he might live out his remaining years in peace, he went to Castellammare di Stabia,[3] where, a stone's throw away from the other habitations in the area, amid the olives, hazels, and chestnuts that abound in those parts, he purchased an estate on which he built a fine and comfortable mansion. Beside the mansion he laid out a delectable garden, in the centre of which, there being a goodly supply of fresh water, he constructed a fine, clear fishpond in the Florentine style, which he stocked in his own good time with abundant supplies of fish.

His sole occupation being that of making his garden daily more attractive, it happened that King Charles, in the heat of summer, went to Castellammare to relax for a while, and on hearing of the beauty of Messer Neri's garden, he was anxious to inspect it. But knowing to whom it belonged, he decided that since the knight was a political adversary of his, he would make his visit informal, and sent word that on the following evening he desired to sup with him incognito in his garden, together with four companions.

Messer Neri took very kindly to this proposal, and having made preparations on a truly lavish scale, and arranged with his household what was to be done, he received the King in his fair garden as cordially as he possibly could. After inspecting and admiring the whole of Messer Neri's garden and his house, the King washed and sat down at one of the tables, which had been placed at the side of the pool. He then ordered Count Guy de Montfort,[4] who was one of his four companions, to sit on his right and Messer Neri on his left, and directed the other three to wait upon him, taking their instructions from Messer Neri.

Dainty dishes were set before him, and wines of rare excellence, and the King was warmly appreciative of the way in which everything had been so tastefully and admirably planned, without anyone knowing he was there or making him feel embarrassed.

Whilst he was contentedly addressing his meal, and admiring the solitude of his surroundings, there came into the garden two young girls, each about fourteen years old, who were as fair as threads of gold, their hair a mass of ringlets surmounted by a garland of periwinkle flowers, and looking more like angels than anything else, so fine and delicate were their features. Their bodies were clothed in sheer linen dresses, white as driven snow, with closely fitting bodices and bell-shaped skirts cascading down from their waists to their feet. The girl in front was carrying upon her shoulders a pair of fishnets, which she held with her left hand, whilst in her right she carried a long pole. The girl behind had a frying-pan slung over her left shoulder, a bundle of sticks beneath her left arm, and a trivet in her left hand, whilst in her other hand she held a cruse of oil and a small lighted torch. The sight of these two girls filled the King with surprise, and he waited with interest to see what it might import.

The girls came forward, chaste and modest in their bearing, and curtsied to the King. Then they walked to the edge of the fishpond, where the one with the frying-pan put it down along with all the other things she was carrying and took the pole from her companion, after which they both waded into the pool till the water came up to their breasts.

One of Messer Neri's servants forthwith lit the fire on the bank of the pool, and pouring the oil into the frying-pan, he placed it on the trivet and waited for the girls to throw him out some fish. And whilst one of them poked about in the places where she knew the fish to be hiding, the other wielded her nets to such good purpose that within a short space of time, to the huge delight of the King who was watching their every movement, they caught fish by the score. Some of these they threw to the servant, who tossed them almost before they were dead into the frying-pan; but then they began to pick out some of the finest specimens, as they had been instructed, and to throw them up on the table in front of the King, the Count, and their father.

The sight of these fishes writhing about on the table was marvellously pleasing to the King, who in his turn picked some of them

up and politely tossed them back to the girls. And in this fashion
they sported for some little time until the servant had cooked the
ones he had been given, which at Messer Neri's bidding were
placed before the King, more by way of an entremets than as a
specially choice or delectable dish.

On seeing that the fish had been cooked, the girls emerged from
the pool, their fishing done, with their thin white dresses clinging to
their flesh so as to conceal almost nothing of their dainty bodies.
And having taken up each of the things they had brought with
them, they walked shyly past the King and made their way back
into the house.

The King, the Count, and the others who were waiting upon
him had been eyeing the two girls most attentively, and each of
them had secretly much admired their beauty and shapeliness, as
well as their charm and impeccable manners, but it was upon the
King that they made the deepest impression. Indeed, he had studied
every part of their bodies with such rapt attention as they emerged
from the water, that if anyone had pinched him at that moment he
would not have noticed. The more he thought about them, without
knowing who they were nor how they came to be there, the more
he felt in his heart a burning desire to pleasure them, and because of
this he knew full well that unless he was very careful he would soon
be falling in love; nor could he decide which of the two he
preferred, so closely did they resemble one another in every
particular.

After he had pondered this question for a while, he turned to
Messer Neri and asked him who the two maidens were, and Messer
Neri replied:

'My lord, they are my twin daughters, of whom the one is called
the lovely Ginevra and the other the fair Isotta.' The King heaped
compliments upon them, exhorting him to bestow them in marriage, to which Messer Neri replied apologetically that he no longer
had the wherewithal to do so.

By now the supper was nearly over, with only the fruit remaining
to be served, and the two girls reappeared, clad in gowns of finest
sendal and bearing two huge silver trays, piled high with all the
different fruits that were in season, which they placed upon the

table before the King. This done, they stepped back a little from the table, and began to sing a song beginning:

> The story of my plight, O Love,
> Could not be told in many words,

in such sweet and pleasant tones, that it seemed to the King, as he sat there listening and gazing with rapture upon them, that all nine orders of the angels had come down there to sing. But when their song was finished, they knelt before the King and respectfully asked his permission to withdraw, and although he was loath to see them go, he granted it with a show of cheerfulness.

The supper being now at an end, the King and his companions remounted their horses, and having taken their leave of Messer Neri, they returned, conversing on many different topics, to the royal lodge, where the King continued to harbour his secret passion; nor was he able, however weighty the affairs of state which supervened, to forget the charm and beauty of the lovely Ginevra, for whose sake he also loved the sister who resembled her so closely. Indeed, he could think of practically nothing else, so hopelessly had he become entangled in the snares of love; and in order to see Ginevra, he invented various pretexts for paying frequent visits to the delectable garden of Messer Neri, with whom he formed close ties of friendship.

But eventually, having reached the end of his tether, he became convinced that he was left with no other alternative except to abduct not only Ginevra but both the girls from their father, and disclosed both his love and his intention to Count Guy, who, being a valiant nobleman, said to him:

'My lord, I am greatly astonished by what you have told me, the more so because I feel that I am better acquainted with your ways than any other man alive, having known you intimately ever since you were a child. I do not recall that you were ever infected by any such passion in your youth, when Love should all the more easily have gripped you in its talons; and hence, to hear that you have fallen hopelessly in love now that you are approaching old age is so strange to me, so bizarre, as to seem little short of a miracle. Moreover, if I had the task of reproaching you for it, I know very well what I should say to you, seeing that you are still on a warlike footing in a kingdom newly acquired, among an alien people, full of deceits and treachery, and that you are preoccupied with matters of the gravest importance which prevent you from sitting comfortably upon your throne; yet despite all this you have succumbed to the temptations of love.

'This is not the action of a magnanimous king, but rather of a weak-willed youth. But what is far more serious, you say you have decided that you must abduct his two daughters from this unfortunate knight, who honoured you in his house beyond his means, and in order to honour you the more, displayed them almost naked to you, thus testifying that he trusts you implicitly, and that he firmly believes you to be no ravening wolf, but a king.

'Can you have so soon forgotten that it was Manfred's abuse of his subjects' womenfolk that opened the gates of this realm to you? Was there ever an act of betrayal more deserving of eternal punishment than this, whereby you deprive a man who does you honour, not only of his good name, but of his source of hope and consolation? What will people say of you, if you do such a thing? Perhaps you think it would be a sufficient excuse to say: "I did it because he is a Ghibelline." But is it consistent with the justice of a king that those who look to him for protection, no matter who they may be, should receive this kind of treatment? Let me remind you, my lord, that you covered yourself with glory by conquering Manfred and defeating Conradin.[5] But it is far more glorious to conquer oneself. And therefore, as you have to govern others, conquer these feelings of yours, curb this wanton desire, and do not allow the splendour of your achievements to be dimmed by any such deed as this.'

The Count's words pierced the King to the very core of his being, affecting him all the more deeply because he knew them to be true; and so after unloosing a fervent sigh or two, he said:

'My dear Count, it is certainly true that to the experienced soldier, all other enemies, however powerful, are exceedingly weak and easy to conquer by comparison with his own desires. But although I shall suffer great torment, and the effort required is incalculable, your words have spurred me on to such a degree that I am determined, before many days have elapsed, to show you by my deeds that, just as I can conquer others, I am likewise able to master myself.'

Nor did many days elapse from the time these words were spoken before the King, having meanwhile returned to Naples, resolved to deprive himself of all occasion for straying from the path of virtue, at the same time repaying Messer Neri's hospitality. And this he would do by bestowing the two girls in marriage as though they were his own daughters, even though it was hard for him to let others possess what he so ardently desired for himself. So with Messer Neri's ready consent he supplied them both with splendid dowries and forthwith bestowed them in marriage, giving the lovely Ginevra to Messer Maffeo da Palizzi, and the fair Isotta to Messer Guiglielmo della Magna,[6] who were noble knights and mighty barons both. And after consigning them to their respective husbands, he retired in agonies of despair to Apulia, where by dint of constant effort he mortified his ardent longings to such good and purposeful effect that the chains of Love were shattered, and for as long as he lived he was never a slave to this kind of passion again.

There are doubtless those who will say that it was a trifling matter for a king to bestow two girls in marriage, and I will agree with them. But I say it was no trifle, but a prodigy, if we consider that this action was performed by a king in love, who married off the girls he loved without having taken or gathered a single leaf, flower or fruit from his love.

Thus then did this magnificent king comport himself, richly rewarding the noble knight, commendably honouring the girls he · loved, and firmly subduing his own instinctive feelings.

SEVENTH STORY

On hearing that a young woman called Lisa has fallen ill on account of her fervent love for him, King Peter goes to comfort her, and later on he marries her to a young nobleman; and having kissed her on the brow, he thenceforth always styles himself her knight.

When Fiammetta had reached the end of her tale, and fulsome praise had been accorded to the heroic munificence of King Charles (albeit one of the ladies present, being a Ghibelline, refused to extol him), Pampinea at the king's behest began as follows:

Winsome ladies, no sensible person would disagree with what you have said about good King Charles, unless she had other reasons for disliking him; but since his deed has now reminded me of another, perhaps equally commendable, that was performed by an adversary of his for the sake of yet another young country-woman of ours, I should like to tell you about it.

At the time when the French were driven from Sicily,[1] there was living in Palermo a very rich Florentine apothecary called Bernardo Puccini, whose wife had borne him one child only, an exquisitely beautiful daughter who was now of marriageable age. King Peter of Aragon,[2] having made himself master of the island, was staging a magnificent tournament in Palermo with all his lords, and whilst he was jousting in the Catalan style,[3] it happened that Bernardo's daughter, whose name was Lisa, was viewing the proceedings from a window along with some other ladies. When she saw the King riding in the joust, she was filled with so much admiration that after watching him perform in one or two further contests she fell passionately in love with him. The festivities came to an end, and Lisa went about her father's house, unable to think of anything else but the lofty and splendid love to which she aspired. But that which grieved her most was the knowledge of her lowly con-dition, which left her with scarcely any hope that her love could be brought to a happy conclusion. Nevertheless she would not be deterred from loving the King, though for fear of making things worse for herself, she dared not reveal her love to a single living soul.

The King neither noticed nor cared about any of this, which made her affliction all the more difficult to bear. As her love continued to increase, so also did her melancholy, till eventually, being unable to endure it any longer, the beautiful Lisa fell ill and began to waste visibly away from one day to the next, like snow in the rays of the sun.

Her father and mother, who were heartbroken by the turn that events had taken, assisted her in every way they could, nursing her day and night, calling in various physicians, and plying her with medicines. But it was all to no avail, for the girl, having despaired of her love, had chosen not to go on living. Since, however, her father had offered to supply her every need, she suddenly got it into her head that before she died, if suitable means could be found, she would inform the King of her love and of her resolve to perish. So one day she asked her father to summon Minuccio d'Arezzo[4] to her bedside.

This Minuccio was held to be one of the finest singers and musicians of his day, being always welcome at King Peter's court, and Bernardo, thinking that Lisa wished to hear him sing and play to her, sent him a message to that effect. Being an obliging sort of fellow, he promptly came to see her, and after cheering her up a little with words of tender affection, he played her one or two melodious airs on his viol, then sang her some songs; all of which added fuel to the flames of the young lady's passion, whereas he had meant to comfort her.

The young lady then told Minuccio that she would like a few words with him in private, and when everyone else had withdrawn, she said to him:

'Minuccio, I have chosen you to be the loyal custodian of a secret of mine, trusting in the first place that you will never disclose it to anyone except the person whose name I shall give you; and secondly, that you will do all in your power to render me your assistance. This I beg of you.

'You are to know then, my dear Minuccio, that on the day that our lord King Peter held the great feast celebrating his accession to the throne, fate decreed that I should set my eyes upon him as he was jousting, and such was the fiery passion that he kindled in my soul that I have been brought to the sorry plight in which you see me. Since I know how ill it befits a king to return my love, which I can neither expel from my heart nor even suppress, and which is altogether too much for me to bear, I have chosen to die as the lesser evil, and die I shall.

'But the truth is that nothing would distress me more than to depart this life without first bringing my love to his notice, and since I know of no one better placed than yourself to inform him of my intentions, I wish to charge you with this mission, which I implore you to accept. And when you have carried it out you must let me know, so that I may be freed from these torments and die in peace.'

She then fell silent, having wept continuously as she said all this, and Minuccio, amazed no less by the nobility of her sentiments than by the cruelty of her resolve, which sorely troubled him, immediately thought of an apt way of furnishing her request.

'Lisa,' he said, 'I pledge you my word, by which you may rest assured that you will never be deceived. Moreover I shall offer you my assistance, in token of my admiration for this lofty enterprise wherein you have set your heart upon so mighty a king. And if you will be of good cheer, I hope to take such steps as I think will enable me, before three days have passed, to bring you tidings that will make you exceedingly happy. But so as not to waste any time, I shall go and make a start right away.'

Lisa promised to take a rosier view of the matter, and after repeating her entreaties all over again, she bade him farewell.

Minuccio then went away, and, having called on Mico da Siena,[5] who was a very able versifier of those times, he talked him into composing the following little song:

> Bestir thyself, O Love, go to my lord,
> Recount to him the torments I endure;
> Tell him that death will soon be my reward,
> For I must hide my yearning out of awe.
>
> Visit the place where my lord dwells,
> With clasp'd hands, Love, I thee entreat;
> Tell him that evermore for him
> My heart yearns with a passion sweet.
> Because this fire inflames me so
> I fear that it will stop my breath;
> I know not when my sufferings
> Will bring me through desire to death
> Out of my fear and shame; ah me!
> Go, tell him of my malady.

Love, ever since I fell in love
With him, you always granted me
More fear than courage; wherefore I
Could never show it openly
To him who takes away my breath,
And death is hard as I lie dying.
Perhaps he would not be displeased
If he were conscious of my sighing
And I could find the power to show
To him the measure of my woe.

Since it was not thy pleasure, Love,
That I should ever make so bold
As to lay bare my heart through words
Or looks, or to my lord unfold
My love; I beg you, master sweet,
Go and remind him of that day
I saw him with his shield and lance
With other knights upon the way,
When I first languished for his sake
And when my heart began to break.

For these words Minuccio promptly devised a melody, which had a sweet and sorrowful lilt as befitted the text, and on the third day he turned up at court, where King Peter, who was still at breakfast, asked him to sing a song to the strains of his viol. He thereupon began to sing and play this melody in tones of such sweet harmony that all those present in the regal hall appeared to be spellbound, so silently and raptly did they listen, the King himself being more engrossed, perhaps, than any other.

When Minuccio's song was finished, the King asked him whence it had come, as he could not recall ever having heard it.

'My lord,' replied Minuccio, 'the words were written less than three days ago, and so too was the melody.' And when the King asked him for whom the song had been composed, he replied: 'This I dare not reveal to anyone other than yourself.'

The King was eager to be told, and once the tables were cleared he took Minuccio with him to his chamber, where Minuccio supplied him with a detailed account of all that he had heard. The King was overjoyed, sang the girl's praises, and declared that her fortitude was such as to demand his compassion. Minuccio was therefore to go to her on his behalf, comfort her, and tell her he would visit her that evening without fail, a little before vespers.

Delighted to be the bearer of such pleasant tidings, Minuccio went straightway to the girl with his viol, and as soon as they were alone together, related all that had happened. Then he sang her the song, accompanying himself on his viol.

The girl was so happy and contented by all this that she at once began to show marked signs of improvement, without anyone in the house knowing or suspecting the reason. And she began to count the hours until vespers, when she was to see her lord and master.

Being of a kindly and generous disposition, the King, having reflected at length upon what he had heard from Minuccio, and recalling the girl and her beauty very clearly, was stirred to even greater pity than before. Towards the hour of vespers he mounted his horse, giving the impression he was going on a jaunt, and rode to the place where the house of the apothecary stood. This latter had a very fine garden, and the King, having sent one of his attendants to ask for the gates to be opened, rode into the garden and dismounted. And after conversing with Bernardo for a while, he inquired about his daughter, asking him whether he had yet bestowed her in marriage, to which Bernardo replied:

'My lord, she is not yet married. As a matter of fact she has been very ill, and she still is, though she has taken a miraculous turn for the better this very afternoon.'

The King was quick to realize what this improvement signified, and said:

'In good truth, the world would be the poorer for the untimely loss of so lovely an object. Let us go and call upon her.'

A little while later, attended by Bernardo and only two companions, he made his way to the girl's room, which he no sooner entered than he walked straight up to the bed. The girl was sitting up a little in eager anticipation of his coming, and he took her by the hand, saying:

'What is the meaning of this, my lady? You are young, you should be bringing solace to others, instead of which you take to your sick-bed. We would ask you to be good enough to cheer up, for our sake, so that you may quickly recover.'

On feeling herself being touched by the hands of the person she loved above all else, the girl, albeit a little embarrassed, was filled with so much pleasure that she might have been in Paradise itself; and haltingly she replied:

'My lord, it was only because I was trying to support a burden that was far too heavy for my feeble powers that I succumbed to this malady. But with your kind assistance, you shall soon see me rid of it.'

Only the King was able to grasp the covert meaning of Lisa's words. She rose still higher in his esteem, and several times over he inwardly swore at Fortune for making her the daughter of such a man as Bernardo. But after he had spent some time in her company, and consoled her even further, he took his leave.

The King's considerate gesture was widely commended, being looked upon as a signal honour for the apothecary and his daughter. Nor was any woman ever more contented with her lover than was Lisa with the visit of the King; and within a few days, aided by the renewal of her hopes, she recovered her health and seemed more lovely than ever.

But now that she was well again, the King, having consulted with the Queen[6] as to how he should reward so great a love, took horse one morning with a number of his lords, and rode to the house of the apothecary. Entering the garden, he sent for Bernardo and his daughter, and meanwhile the Queen also arrived there with many fine ladies, who received the girl in their midst with great rejoicing, marvellous to behold.

At length the King, with the Queen at his side, summoned the girl and said to her:

'Worthy young lady, through your great love for us you have won for yourself a great honour, which for our sake we trust you will accept. The honour is this, that since you are as yet unmarried, we desire you to take as your husband the person we shall nominate, it being none the less our intention always to style ourselves your loyal knight, and of all your love we require no more than a single kiss.'

The girl was so embarrassed that the whole of her face turned crimson, and in a low voice, making the King's pleasure her own, she replied:

'My lord, I am quite sure that if it were known that I was in love with you, most people would consider me to be mad, for they would think I had taken leave of my senses and was unaware of the distinction between your rank and mine. But God alone can see inside the hearts of mortals, and He knows that ever since I first became attracted to you, I have known full well that you are a king, that I am the daughter of Bernardo the apothecary, and that it ill becomes me to direct the ardour of my affections towards so lofty a goal. But as you know far better than I, when people fall in love they are guided, not by reason, but by their natural inclinations and desires. These I repeatedly opposed with all my strength until, no longer able to resist, I loved you then as I love you now and as I shall love you forever. And because I was always prepared, from the moment I fell in love with you, to make my wishes accord with your own, not only shall I be willing to accept and treasure the husband you choose to bestow upon me, who will bring me dignity and honour, but if you were to order me to walk through fire, and I thought it would please you, I should do it gladly. As for my having a king as my loyal knight, you know how well it would suit a person of my condition, and hence I will say no more on the subject; nor will I concede the single kiss that you require of my love, without the permission of my lady the Queen. For the great kindness, however, which you and the Queen have displayed towards me, may God give you thanks and reward you on my behalf, since I myself could never repay you.'

She said no more, but the answer she had given was greatly pleasing to the Queen, who was now persuaded that the girl was as wise as the King had affirmed. The King then summoned Lisa's parents, and on learning that they approved of what he was proposing, he sent for a certain young man called Perdicone,[7] who was gently bred but poor, and placing some rings in his hand, induced him to marry the girl without any show of reluctance.

Nor was this all, for apart from the many precious jewels that he and the Queen presented to Lisa, the King forthwith appointed him lord of Cefalù and Caltabellotta,[8] two excellent and very lucrative estates, saying:

'These we grant you by way of dowry for your wife; and as for our intentions with regard to yourself, of these you will learn in due course.'

Then, turning to the girl, he said:

'Now we desire to take the fruit of your love which is our due.' And holding her head between his hands, he kissed her on the brow.

Perdicone, along with Lisa's father and mother, and Lisa herself, well content with what had happened, celebrated the wedding in truly magnificent style, and their marriage was a happy one.

As a good many people affirm, the King was most scrupulous to observe his compact with the girl, for he always styled himself her loyal knight for as long as he lived, and never entered the lists without displaying the favour she had sent him.

By deeds such as these, then, does a sovereign conquer the hearts of his subjects, furnish occasions to others for similar deeds, and acquire eternal renown. But among the rulers of today, there are few if any who train the bowstrings of their minds upon any such objective, most of them having been changed into pitiless tyrants.

EIGHTH STORY

Sophronia, thinking she has married Gisippus, has really married Titus Quintus Fulvius, with whom she goes off to Rome, where Gisippus turns up in abject poverty. Believing that Titus has snubbed him, he confesses to a murder so that he will be put to death. But Titus recognizes him, and claims that he himself has done the murder, in order to secure Gisippus' release. On perceiving this, the real murderer gives himself up, whereupon all three are released by Octavianus. Titus then bestows his sister upon Gisippus in marriage, and shares with him all he possesses.

Pampinea having finished her tale, King Peter was extolled by all the ladies, but more especially by the one who was a Ghibelline;

then Filomena began, at the king's command, as follows:

Magnificent ladies, which of us is not aware that kings, if they be so inclined, can do all sorts of wondrous things, and that they above all others are called upon to display munificence? Those people do well, then, who possess ample means and do all that is expected of them; but we ought neither to marvel thereat, nor laud them to the skies, as we should the person who is equally munificent but of whom, his means being slender, less is expected. So that if you are impressed by the actions of kings, and expend so many words in extolling them, I have no doubt whatsoever that when similar actions to these, or nobler ones, are performed by people like ourselves, your delight will be all the greater, your praises all the more fulsome. And hence I am minded to tell you a story about two private citizens, who were friends, and about the laudable generosity that each of them displayed towards the other.

Now, at the time when Octavianus Caesar,[1] before he was called Augustus, was ruling the Roman Empire in the office known as the triumvirate, there lived in Rome a gentleman called Publius Quintus Fulvius,[2] who had a son called Titus Quintus Fulvius. This latter was exceptionally clever, and his father sent him to study philosophy in Athens,[3] doing all in his power to commend him to a nobleman of that city called Chremes,[4] who was a very old friend of his. Chremes lodged him under his own roof with a son of his called Gisippus, and Titus and Gisippus were both sent by Chremes to study under the guidance of a philosopher named Aristippus.[5]

Being regularly in one another's company, the two young men discovered that they shared many interests in common, and this gave rise to a powerful sense of mutual friendship and brotherliness, which lasted for the rest of their lives. Indeed, it was only when they were together that either Titus or Gisippus could feel happy and relaxed. Having once embarked upon their studies, since both were endowed with equally high intelligence, they scaled the glorious heights of philosophy side by side, amid a hail of marvellous tributes. And in this way of life, to the enormous delight of

Chremes, who treated both alike as his sons, they continued for three whole years, at the end of which it came about that Chremes, already an old man, passed from this world as all things eventually must. Nor were the friends and kinsfolk of Chremes able to decide which of the two deserved greater compassion in this sudden loss, for he had been a father to them both, and both were equally broken-hearted.

A few months later, Gisippus was confronted by a deputation of his friends and relatives, who along with Titus persuaded him to take a wife, and they found him an incredibly lovely Athenian girl of impeccably noble breeding, some fifteen years of age, whose name was Sophronia.

One day, a little before the date appointed for the nuptials, Gisippus asked Titus, since he had not yet set eyes upon the girl, to come with him to see her. So they went to her house, and with the girl sitting between the two of them, Titus began to scrutinize her very closely, as though to form an estimate of the beauty of his friend's future wife. But such was the boundless pleasure he experienced in surveying each part of her body that he was lost in silent admiration, and, though he showed no sign of what he was feeling, he burned with a passion more ardent than any ever kindled by a woman in her lover's breast. However, after spending some little time with her, they took their leave and returned home.

On arriving at the house, Titus retired to his room alone and began to meditate upon the young woman's charms; and the longer he brooded upon her, the fiercer his ardour became. Perceiving the state he was in, he cast many a passionate sigh and began to commune with himself, saying: 'Ah, Titus, what a beggarly way to behave! Where, upon whom, do you set your hopes, your heart and your love? Don't you realize that the hospitality you have received from Chremes and his family, and the perfect friendship that unites you to Gisippus, her future husband, require that you should treat this girl with all the reverence owing to a sister? Will you allow yourself to be carried away by the delusions of love, the specious visions of desire? Open your eyes, you fool, and come to your senses. Make way for reason, bridle your lascivious desires, curb your unwholesome longings, and direct your thoughts elsewhere. Fight against your lust from the outset, and conquer yourself while you still have time. It is wrong for you to want this thing, it is dishonest; and even if you were certain (which you are not) of achieving your object, you would only have to think where the duty of a true friend lies, as you are bound to do in any case, to dismiss the idea from your mind. What will you do, then, Titus? If you want to do what is proper, abandon this unseemly love.'

But then he remembered Sophronia's beauty, and took the opposite viewpoint, rejecting all his previous arguments. And he said to himself: 'The laws of Love are more powerful than any others; they even supplant divine laws, let alone those of friendship. How often in the past have fathers loved their daughters, brothers their sisters, or mothers their stepsons? These are far more reprehensible than the man who loves the wife of his friend, for he is only doing what a thousand others have done before him. Besides, I am young, and youth is entirely subject to the power of Love. So that wherever Love decides to lead me, I am bound to follow. Honesty is all very well for older people, but I can only act in accordance with the dictates of Love. The girl is so beautiful that no one could fail to love her; so that if I, who am young, fall in love with her, who can justly reproach me? It is not because she belongs to Gisippus that I love her, but purely for her own sake, and I should love her no matter to whom she belonged. Here Fortune is at fault for having conceded her to my friend Gisippus rather than to some other man. But if anyone has to love her (as she must be loved, and deservedly so, on account of her beauty), then Gisippus should be all the more pleased to discover that she is loved by me and not by another.'

But then, reproaching himself for being so foolish, he returned to the contrary viewpoint, and for the rest of the day and the ensuing night he veered perpetually back and forth between the two sets of arguments. And after spending several days and nights, gradually wearing himself to a thread over it, and going without food or sleep, he was driven to take to his bed in a state of exhaustion.

Great was the distress of Gisippus when, after observing Titus lost in deep thought for days on end, he now discovered that his friend was ill. Never leaving his side, he attempted to comfort him using all the skill and loving care in his power, and from time to time he earnestly entreated him to disclose the reason for his sickness and melancholy. Titus offered him a series of spurious explanations, none of which satisfied Gisippus, so that in the end, unable to withstand the pressure that Gisippus was continuing to apply upon him, he burst into tears. And heaving many a sigh, he answered him as follows:

'If only the gods had so willed it, Gisippus, I would much rather have died than continued to live, when I think how Fortune has driven me to the point where my virtue had to be put to the test, and where, to my very great shame, you have found it wanting. But I confidently expect to receive, before long, my just reward in the form of my death, and this will be dearer to me than to go on living with the memory of my baseness, which, since there is nothing I either could or should conceal from you, I shall tell you about, though I burn with shame to speak of it.'

And so, starting from the beginning, he explained the cause of his melancholy, describing the conflict that had raged between his contrasting thoughts, which of them had won the day, and how he was wasting away for love of Sophronia. Moreover he declared that since he knew his attitude to be wholly improper, he had resolved that he would die by way of penance, and believed he would shortly achieve this desirable aim.

On hearing what Titus had said, and observing how bitterly he wept, Gisippus was at first somewhat taken aback, for although his own passionate feelings towards the beautiful Sophronia were more restrained, he too was fascinated by her charms. But he instantly decided that his friend's life meant more to him than Sophronia, and being moved to tears by the tears of his comrade, he replied, sobbing continuously:

'If, Titus, you were less in need of reassurance, I should take you severely to task, seeing that you have abused our friendship by not telling me earlier of this overwhelming passion. Even if you felt that your thoughts were improper, that was no reason for concealing them from your friend, any more than if they were proper: for just as a true friend takes a delight in sharing his friend's proper thoughts, so he will attempt to wean him away from those that are improper. But enough of that for the present: let us turn to the question that I take to be the more urgent. The fact that you have fallen violently in love with Sophronia, my promised bride, does not surprise me in the least; indeed I should be most surprised if you hadn't, considering her beauty and your own loftiness of spirit, which renders you all the more susceptible to passionate feelings, the greater the excellence of the object that arouses your liking. And inasmuch as you do right to love Sophronia, at the same time you do wrong to complain about Fortune (though you make no mention of this) for conceding her to me, as though you felt that there would be nothing improper about loving her if she belonged to another. But if you are still as wise as you always were, you should be counting your lucky stars that she was given to me and not to anyone else. For had she belonged to another, no matter how proper your love may have been, he would have preferred to keep her to himself rather than allow you to love her, whereas in my case, if you consider me your friend, as I am, you must hope for a kindlier fate. And the reason is this, that ever since our friendship began, I cannot recall possessing anything that was not as much yours as it was mine.

'Just as I have shared my other possessions with you, so I would share Sophronia, if I were already married to her and no other solution were possible; but as the matter stands at present, I am able to ensure that she is yours alone, and that is what I intend to do. For I should be a poor sort of friend if I were unable to convert you to my own way of thinking when the thing can be so decorously arranged. It is perfectly true that Sophronia is my promised bride, that I love her a great deal, and that I was eagerly looking forward to our marriage; but because your love for her is greater, and because you desire more fervently than I to possess so precious an object, you may rest assured that she shall enter the bridal chamber, not as my wife, but as yours. Fret no more then, cast aside your gloom, retrieve your health, your spirits and your gaiety; and from this time forth, look forward cheerfully to the reward of your love – a love far worthier than mine ever was.'

To hear Gisippus speak in these terms, Titus was at one and the same time delighted and ashamed: delighted on account of the tempting picture Gisippus had drawn, and ashamed because common sense argued that the greater the generosity of his friend, the more unseemly did it appear for him to profit from it. And so, with tears still rolling down his cheeks, he replied with an effort as follows:

'Gisippus, your true and generous friendship shows me very clearly where my duty lies. God forbid that I should ever accept from you as mine the wife that He has given you as a mark of your superior worth. Had He judged that she ought to be mine, neither you nor anyone else can deny that He would never have given her to you. Be content, therefore, that in His infinite wisdom He has chosen you as the recipient of His largesse, and leave me to waste away in the tears of woe He has allotted to one who is unworthy of such bounty; for either I shall conquer my grief, in which case you will be happy, or it will conquer me and I shall be released from my suffering.'

To which Gisippus replied:

'If, Titus, our friendship is such as to enable me to force your acquiescence in any single one of my decisions, or if it can induce you to consent of your own accord, now is the time when I intend to exploit it to the full; and if you are determined to reject my entreaties, I shall use whatever compulsion is necessary to protect the interests of a friend, and to make Sophronia yours. I know the havoc that the powers of Love can inflict, I know they have led, not one, but countless lovers to an unhappy death; and I can see that they have taken so tight a hold upon you that there is no longer any question of your turning back, or of conquering your tears. If you were to go on like this you would perish, in which event there is no doubt that I should speedily follow you. So even if I had no other cause for loving you, your life is precious to me because my own life depends upon it. Sophronia shall be yours, then, for it will not be easy for you to find another that you like nearly so much, whereas I can easily divert my love to some other woman, and then we shall both be satisfied. I should not perhaps be so generous, if wives were so scarce and difficult to find as friends, but since I can

find another wife, but not another friend, with the greatest of ease, I
prefer, rather than to lose you, not to lose her exactly, but as it were
to transfer her. For I shan't lose her by giving her to you, but
simply hand her over to my second self, at the same time changing
her lot for the better. So if my entreaties mean anything to you, I
entreat you here and now to cast aside your sorrows and bring
solace to us both. Take heart, and prepare to enjoy the bliss for
which your ardent love is yearning.'

Titus was reluctant to consent to the idea that Sophronia should
become his wife, and hence refused at first to have anything to do
with it; but being prodded by his love on the one hand, and
propelled by his friend's insistence on the other, he eventually
faltered and said:

'See here, Gisippus, I cannot tell which of us would remain the
more contented if I were to do the thing you implore me to do,
seeing that you claim it would give you so much pleasure. But as
your liberality is such as to disarm my natural shame, I shall do it.
Of this you may be certain, however, that I do it in the knowledge
that you are not only giving me the woman I love, but also saving
my life. Thus does your compassion for my plight exceed my own,
and I pray that the gods may grant me the means whereby I may
yet make you honourable amends and show you how deeply I prize
the blessing you have conferred upon me.'

When Titus had finished speaking, Gisippus said:

'If we want our plans to succeed, Titus, this is what I think we
ought to do. As you know, it was only after long discussions
between Sophronia's kinsfolk and my own that she became my
promised bride, and hence, if I were suddenly to announce that I no
longer wish to marry her, there would be an awful scandal and I
would cause distress to both our families. This would not worry me
in the least, if I could see her being married to you as a result. But if
I were to leave her in the lurch like this, I fear that her kinsfolk
would promptly marry her off to some other fellow, and not
necessarily to you, in which case you will have lost Sophronia and I
shall have gained nothing. So it seems to me that if you are in
agreement I should carry on with what I have begun, fetch her back
here as my wife, and celebrate the nuptials, after which you and

Sophronia, by whatever secret means we shall devise, will sleep together as man and wife. Later on, when the time and the place are appropriate, we shall disclose how matters stand; if they like the idea, all well and good; but if they don't, they'll have to lump it, because by that time the deed will be done and there'll be no way of setting things in reverse.'

Titus agreed to the plan, and so Gisippus went ahead and welcomed Sophronia to his house as his bride, by which time Titus was strong and well again. A great feast was held, and when night had descended, the waiting maids left the new bride in her husband's bed and departed.

Now the rooms of Titus and Gisippus were adjacent, and it was possible to pass freely from the one to the other; so on entering his room, Gisippus extinguished all the lights, betook himself quietly to Titus, and bade him go sleep with his lady.

Titus was overcome with embarrassment, began to have second thoughts, and refused to go. But Gisippus, after remonstrating with him at length, sent him all the same, being no less prepared to do Titus' pleasure than he had claimed.

Having eased himself into the bed, Titus took the girl in his arms, and asked her in a voice no louder than a whisper whether she wanted to be his wife, as though playing some sort of game with her. The girl replied in the affirmative, thinking he was Gisippus, whereupon he placed a fine and precious ring on her finger, saying:

'And I want to be your husband.'

The marriage was then consummated, and thereafter Titus long continued to disport himself amorously with her, neither Sophronia nor anyone else ever suspecting that the person with whom she shared her bed was not Gisippus.

This, then, was where the marriage of Sophronia and Titus stood, when Titus was informed by letter that Publius, his father, had departed this life, and that hence he should return to Rome at once to attend to his affairs. So after consulting with Gisippus, he decided to leave Athens and take Sophronia with him, which he was neither prepared nor easily able to do without explaining everything to Sophronia.

So one day, they called her into the room and took her fully into their confidence, nor could she doubt that their story was true because of numerous things that had passed between Titus and herself. And having cast a withering look, first at one, then at the other, she burst into floods of tears, complaining bitterly of the trick Gisippus had played on her. But before anyone else in the house came to hear of it, she took refuge in the house of her father, to whom, as well as to her mother, she recounted the way in which she and they had been hoodwinked by Gisippus, pointing out that she was married, not to Gisippus as they supposed, but to Titus.

Sophronia's father, who took a very grave view of the matter, complained loud and long to his kinsfolk, as well as to the kinsfolk of Gisippus, and there was a huge palaver, followed in turn by a great deal of gossip. Gisippus incurred the hatred of both Sophronia's kinsfolk and his own, and everyone declared that he deserved to be not only censured but punished most severely. But he maintained that he had acted honourably and in such a way as to merit the gratitude of Sophronia's kinsfolk, inasmuch as he had married her to someone better than himself.

For his part, Titus heard all that was going on, and patiently bore the suffering it caused him. But eventually, knowing the Greeks had a habit of raising an enormous clamour and intensifying their threats until such time as they found someone to answer them back, when they would suddenly become not only humble but positively servile, he decided that their prattle could no longer be allowed to pass without a rejoinder. His Roman heart being wedded to the guile of an Athenian, he skilfully persuaded the kinsfolk of Gisippus and Sophronia to forgather in a temple, to which he came, accompanied only by Gisippus. And he addressed the people waiting there as follows:

'In the opinion of many philosophers, all human actions conform to the will and decree of the immortal gods, and hence there are those who maintain that whatever we mortals do here on earth, either now or in the future, is inevitable and preordained; whereas certain others apply this principle of necessity only to what is already past and done with. Now, if we examine these opinions with a modicum of care, we shall clearly perceive that the person who criticizes that which cannot be changed is behaving exactly as though he wishes to prove himself wiser than the gods, who, to the best of our knowledge and belief, control and govern us, and all things pertaining to us, by a process of eternal and infallible logic. Thus you may very readily perceive the senseless and bestial arrogance of those who criticize their inscrutable ways, just as you will appreciate with what strong and substantial chains those people deserve to be bound, who permit themselves to be carried away by such excess of daring. Among these latter, you yourselves are all, in my opinion, to be numbered, unless I have been misinformed as to what you have been saying, and are still saying, about Sophronia's having become my wife after you had given her to Gisippus; for you overlook the fact that she was destined, *ab aeterno* so to speak, not for Gisippus but for me, as we now know from the sequel. Since however it appears that the secret insight and inscrutable purpose of the gods are a subject too abstruse and difficult for many people to follow, I shall assume that the gods play no part whatever in our affairs, and confine myself to the logic of mortals, in appealing to which I shall be obliged to do two things that are wholly at odds with my nature: for in the first place I must praise myself a little, and in the second I must disparage or humiliate another. But since I have no intention of departing from the truth in either case, and since this is what the present occasion demands, I shall none the less proceed.

'Prompted more by anger than by reason, you complain about Gisippus, whom you abuse, attack and condemn with these perpetual murmurs or rather outcries of yours, simply because he arranged to give to me the wife whom you had arranged to give to him. But in my opinion he deserves the highest praise, for two reasons: first, because he acted in the manner of a true friend, and secondly because his wisdom in so doing was superior to your own. Now, I have no intention of explaining to you, here and now, that which the sacred laws of friendship require that a man should do for his friend, being content simply to have reminded you that the ties of friendship may be much more binding than those of blood or kinship. For our friends are of our own choosing, whereas our kinsfolk are those that Fortune has allotted to us. So if my life was more precious to Gisippus than your goodwill, none of you should marvel thereat, since I am his friend, or regard myself as such.

'But let us turn to the second reason, which, if I am to prove that
he was wiser than you are, I shall have to expound to you at greater
length; for you seem to know nothing of the providence of the
gods, and to know far less about the consequences of friendship. I
say, then, that it was your judgement, your counsel, and your
resolve that Sophronia should be given to Gisippus, a young man
and a philosopher; and Gisippus gave her to a young man and a
philosopher. You wanted her to go to an Athenian, and Gisippus
gave her to a Roman. You gave her to a noble youth, Gisippus to
a nobler; you to a rich young man, Gisippus to a richer; you to a
youth who loved her not, and scarcely even knew her, Gisippus to
a youth who loved her above all other blessings, including life itself.

'But in order to see whether what I say is true, and whether
Gisippus is worthier of greater commendation than yourselves, let
us examine the evidence point by point. That I am a young man
and a philosopher, like Gisippus, my countenance and my condition
will readily attest, without pursuing the matter any further. We are
both of the same age, and we have always kept abreast of one
another in our studies. It is true that he is an Athenian, and I am a
Roman. But should there be any dispute upon the rival merits of
our cities, I would remind you that my own city is free, whilst his
pays tribute; I would remind you that my city rules the entire
world, whilst his is one of her vassals; and I would remind you that
whereas my city is renowned for her soldiers, her statesmen, and
her men of letters, it is only for the last of these that Gisippus can
boast of his.

'Moreover, though you may look upon me here as a very
humble scholar, I was not born of the dregs of the Roman populace.
My private house in Rome, and the places of public resort, are
filled with ancient statues of my ancestors, and you will find that
the annals of the city abound with descriptions of the many triumphs
celebrated on the Capitol by the Quintii. Nor has my family fallen
into decay on account of its antiquity, for on the contrary the glory
of our name shines more resplendently now than at any time in the
past.

'Concerning my wealth, modesty forbids that I should speak,
bearing in mind that poverty with honour has long been regarded

by the noble citizens of Rome as a priceless legacy. But if, after the opinion of the common herd, poverty is to be condemned and riches commended, of these I have abundant store, not out of avarice but out of the kindness of Fortune. And whilst I am fully aware of the value which, quite rightly, you placed upon having Gisippus as your kinsman here in Athens, there is no reason why I should be less of an asset to you in Rome, seeing that you will discover me to be an excellent host to you there, as well as a valuable, solicitous and powerful patron, who will be only too ready to assist you, whether in your public or your personal concerns.

'Who, therefore, having set all prejudice aside and examined the matter dispassionately, would rate your counsels higher than those of my friend Gisippus? No one, to be sure. Thus Sophronia is rightly wedded to Titus Quintus Fulvius, and if anyone deplores or bemoans the fact, he is both misguided and misinformed. Possibly there are those who will say that Sophronia is complaining, not of being wedded to Titus, but of the manner in which she became his wife, secretly, by stealth, and without the knowledge of a single friend or relative. But there is nothing miraculous about this, nor is it the first time that such a thing has happened.

'I gladly leave aside those who have married against the wishes of their fathers; and those who have eloped with their lovers, becoming their mistresses rather than their wives; and those who have divulged their wedded state, not in so many words, but through pregnancy and childbirth, thus leaving their fathers with no alternative but to consent. This was not the case with Sophronia, who on the contrary was bestowed upon Titus by Gisippus in an orderly, discreet, and honourable manner. There are those who will say that Gisippus had no right to bestow her in marriage, but these are merely foolish and womanly scruples, the product of shallow reasoning. This is by no means the first occasion on which Fortune has used strange and wonderful ways to achieve her established aims. What do I care if a cobbler, not to mention a philosopher, manages some affair of mine in his own way, whether openly or furtively, so long as the end result is a good one? If the cobbler has been indiscreet, then admittedly I must take good care not to let him meddle again in my affairs, but at the same time I must thank him for the services he has rendered. So that if Gisippus has married Sophronia well, to complain of the man and his methods is a piece of gratuitous folly; and if you suspect his judgement, thank him for what he has done, and see that he is never given the chance to do it again.

'Nevertheless I must make it clear that I never sought, whether by native cunning or deliberate fraud, to besmirch the honour and the fame of your family in the person of Sophronia. Although I married her in secret, I was no plunderer, intent on despoiling her of her virginity, nor did I wish to possess her on dishonourable terms, like one who was your enemy and who spurned your kinship. I wanted her because I was ardently enamoured of her enchanting beauty and superior worth. Yet I knew that had I sought your formal consent, which you may feel I was obliged to obtain, it would not have been forthcoming, since, loving her deeply as you do, you would have feared that I would take her away to Rome.

'Accordingly I resorted to the secret measures that can now be openly revealed, and I forced Gisippus, for my sake, to fall in with my plans. Moreover, though I was passionately in love with her, it was not as her lover that I conjoined myself to Sophronia, but as her husband. For as she herself can truthfully bear witness, I kept my distance until after I had wedded her by saying the necessary words and placing the ring on her finger, and when I asked her whether she would have me as her husband, she told me that she would. If she feels she was deceived, she should not blame me, but herself, for failing to ask me who I was. So the enormous crime, the terrible sin, the unpardonable wrong committed by Gisippus, my devoted friend, and by myself, her devoted admirer, was simply that Sophronia was married to Titus Quintus in secret; for this reason alone do you tear him to pieces, bombard him with threats, and sharpen your knives against him. What more would you have done, had he given her to a serf, a scoundrel, or a slave? Where would you have found the fetters, the dungeons, or the tortures equal to his offence?

'But of this let us say no more for the present. Something has now occurred which I was not yet expecting, namely, that my father has died and I am obliged to return to Rome; and because I wish to take Sophronia with me, I have revealed to you that which otherwise I might have continued to conceal. If you are wise, you will cheerfully accept it, for had I wished to deceive or offend you, I could have disowned her and left her on your hands. But heaven forbid that the heart of a Roman should ever harbour so cowardly a design.

'Sophronia then is mine, not only by the consent of the gods and the authority of human law, but through the good sense of my friend Gisippus and the skilful manner of my wooing her. But it seems that you disapprove of this, possibly because you think yourselves wiser than the gods and your fellow beings, for you obstinately persist in doing two things that are highly repugnant to me. In the first place you hold on to Sophronia when you have no right to do such a thing without my consent; and secondly you treat Gisippus, to whom you are deeply indebted, as your enemy. It is not my intention to prove to you still further how foolishly you are behaving, being content for the present to offer you some friendly advice: to wit, that you should forget about your grievances, set all your anger aside, and see that Sophronia is restored to me, so that I may depart from Athens in peace, as your kinsman, and live henceforth as one of yourselves. For of this you may be certain, that whether or not you like what has been done, if you fail to heed my advice I shall take Gisippus with me, and once I return to Rome, I shall make quite sure that she who is rightfully mine is restored to me, however much you may object. And you shall learn from experience what havoc can be wrought by the wrath of a Roman, once you have made him your lifelong enemy.'

Having said what he had to say, Titus, his features contorted with anger, rose to his feet; and taking Gisippus by the hand, he led him out of the temple, tossing his head from side to side and looking daggers at all the people present, as if to show how little he was daunted by their numbers.

The people he had left behind in the temple, in part persuaded by the force of his arguments, in part alarmed by his concluding words, decided of one accord that since Gisippus had turned them down, it was better to have Titus as their kinsman than to have lost a kinsman in Gisippus and gained an enemy in Titus.

So they went and sought out Titus, and told him they were willing that Sophronia should be his, adding that they would be glad to have him as a dear kinsman and Gisippus as a good friend. And after celebrating their friendship and kinship in a style suited to the occasion, they went their separate ways. Sophronia was then restored to Titus, and being a sensible girl, she made a virtue of necessity and soon accorded Titus the love she had formerly had for Gisippus. And she went with him to Rome, where she was received with great honour.

Meanwhile Gisippus stayed on in Athens, but could no longer command much esteem among most of his fellow citizens; and not long afterwards, through factional strife in the city, he was driven out of Athens, poor and destitute, and condemned to perpetual exile along with all the members of his family. Now that he was banished, before very long he became not only a pauper but a beggar, and made his way as best he could to Rome, in order to discover whether Titus still remembered him. On learning that Titus was alive and that all the Romans sang his praises, he found out where he was living, then went and stood outside his house. Eventually Titus made his appearance, and though Gisippus would not venture to address him because of his beggarly condition, he endeavoured to let himself be seen so that Titus might recognize and send for him. When, therefore, Titus passed him by without any show of recognition, Gisippus was convinced that he had been deliberately snubbed, and remembering all he had done for Titus in the past, he retreated from the scene in dudgeon and despair.

It was already dark when Gisippus, hungry and penniless, having nowhere to go and heartily wishing he were dead, strayed into a very lonely part of the city where he came across a large cave, into which he crept with the intention of sheltering there for the night. And on the cave's bare floor, ill-apparelled and exhausted by prolonged weeping, he fell fast asleep. Just before dawn, however, a pair of burglars came to this very cave with the proceeds of their night's activities, and having started to quarrel with one another, the more powerful of the two killed his companion and made off.

All of this was seen and heard by Gisippus, who, being himself intent upon dying, felt that he had now discovered a way of achieving his goal without resorting to suicide. So he stayed where he was until the praetorian guards, having quickly got wind of the affair, arrived at the scene of the crime and bundled him off into custody. He was then interrogated and confessed to the murder, adding that he had been unable to find his way out of the cave; whereupon the praetor, whose name was Marcus Varro, sentenced him to death by crucifixion, which in those days was the regular method of execution.

By a singular coincidence, at that very moment Titus turned up at the law court, and on staring the wretched prisoner in the face, having learned the reasons for the sentence, he recognized him at once as Gisippus. Titus wondered how the fortunes of Gisippus could have reached so low an ebb, and how on earth he came to be in Rome; but his chief concern was to assist his friend in his hour of need, and since he could see no other way of saving him except by shifting the blame from Gisippus to himself, he quickly stepped forward and exclaimed:

'Marcus Varro, recall the wretched fellow you have just condemned, for he is innocent. I have already offended the gods enough by striking the blow that killed the person whose body was found by your men this morning, without wishing to offend them now with the death of another innocent.'

Not only was Varro astonished to hear these words, but aggrieved that everyone in court should also have heard them; and since he was · morally obliged to follow the course prescribed by the laws of the land, he had Gisippus brought back and said to him, in the presence of Titus:

'How could you be so foolish as to confess, without being forced, to a crime that you never committed, knowing full well that your life was at stake? You told us that you were the person who killed that fellow in the cave last night, and now this other man comes and says it was he and not you who did the killing.'

Gisippus looked up, saw that it was Titus, and realized at once that he was doing this for his deliverance, out of gratitude for the favour that Gisippus had done him in the past. And so, shedding many a piteous tear, he turned to the praetor and said:

'I assure you, Varro, that it was I who killed him. It is too late now for Titus to concern himself with my deliverance.'

Whereupon Titus for his part said:

'My lord, as you see, this fellow is a foreigner, and when they found him beside the body of the victim, he was unarmed. You have only to look at him to realize that it's his poverty that makes him want to die. Let him go, therefore, and give to me the punishment I deserve.'

Varro, marvelling at the persistence of the two men, was already of the opinion that neither of them was guilty, and just as he was deliberating how best to absolve them, there suddenly stepped forth a youth named Publius Ambustus, who was known to everyone in Rome as a hardened criminal and notorious thief, and who in fact was the real murderer. And knowing that neither of the two was guilty of the crime to which both were confessing, he was so overwhelmed by their innocence that out of pure compassion he went up to Varro and said:

'My lord, fate decrees that I should solve the enigma of these two men, though who the god is that cajoles and compels me from within to expose my iniquitous deed, I know not. Take note, then, that neither of the two is guilty of the crime to which they both confess. It was I, in fact, who killed the man this morning at sunrise, and as I was dividing the spoils of our night's activities with the fellow I murdered, I saw this poor wretch lying asleep in the cave. As for Titus, he has no need of me for a champion: everyone knows him to be an upright citizen, who would never stoop to such a deed as this. Release them therefore, and punish me in the manner prescribed by the laws.'

News of the affair had meanwhile reached the ears of Octavianus, who summoned the three men to his presence and demanded to know why each of them was so eager to be convicted of the murder, whereupon they all explained their motives in turn. And in the end he released all three, the first two because they were innocent, and the third for the sake of the others.

Titus then took hold of his friend Gisippus, and after scolding him severely for treating him so coldly and suspiciously, he made a great fuss of him and led him away to his house, where Sophronia, with tears of compassion, greeted him as a brother. And after Titus had to some extent restored his spirits, and clothed him once again in a manner befitting his nobility and excellence, he not only made him joint owner of all his treasures and possessions, but also presented him with a wife in the person of a young sister of his called Fulvia. Then he said to him:

'It is now up to you to decide, Gisippus, whether you want to stay here with me, or return to Greece with all the things I have given you.'

Prompted on the one hand by the fact that he was exiled from his native city, and on the other by his just regard for the precious friendship of Titus, Gisippus consented to become a citizen of Rome, where they lived long and happily together under the same roof, Gisippus with his Fulvia and Titus with his Sophronia; and if such a thing were conceivable, their friendship gained steadily in strength with every day that passed.

Friendship, then, is a most sacred thing, not only worthy of singular reverence, but eternally to be praised as the deeply discerning mother of probity and munificence, the sister of gratitude and charity, and the foe of hatred and avarice, ever ready, without waiting to be asked, to do virtuously unto others that which it would wish to be done unto itself. But very seldom in this day and age do we find two persons in whom its hallowed effects may be seen, this being the fault of men's shameful and miserly greed, which, being solely concerned with seeking its own advantage, has banished friendship to perpetual exile beyond earth's farthest limits.

Except for the power of friendship, what quantity of love or riches, what kinsman's bond, could have wrought so powerful an effect upon the heart of Gisippus as to persuade him, on witnessing the fervour, the tears, and the sighs of Titus, to concede to him the fair and gracious promised bride with whom he was himself in love? Except for the power of friendship, what laws, what threats, what fear of consequence, could have prevented the youthful arms of Gisippus, in darkened or deserted places, or in the privacy of his own bed, from embracing this delectable girl, occasionally perhaps at her own invitation? Except for the power of friendship, what prospect of superior rank, or rich reward, or material gain, could have made Gisippus so indifferent to the loss of his own and Sophronia's kinsfolk, so indifferent to the slanderous rumours of the populace, so indifferent to the jests and jibes of his fellow men, as to gratify his comrade's desire?

And on the other hand, what other force but friendship would have prompted Titus, eagerly and without vacillation, to place his life in jeopardy in order to save Gisippus from the cross of his own desiring, when no one would have blamed him for turning a blind eye to the affair? What other force but friendship would have prompted Titus promptly and generously to share his extensive wealth with Gisippus, whose own possessions had been seized from him by Fortune? What other force but friendship would have prompted Titus readily and zealously to bestow his own sister in marriage upon Gisippus, when he could see that he was penniless and utterly destitute?

Men may thus continue to desire throngs of relatives, hordes of brothers, and swarms of children, and as their wealth increases, so they may multiply the number of their servants. But what they will fail to perceive is that every one of these, no matter who he may be, is more apprehensive of the tiniest peril to himself than eager to save his father, brother, or master from a great calamity, whereas between two friends, the position is quite the reverse.

NINTH STORY

Messer Torello offers hospitality to Saladin, who is disguised as a merchant. A Crusade is launched, and before setting off Messer Torello instructs his wife that, failing his return, she may remarry by a certain date. He is taken prisoner, but his skill in training hawks brings him to the notice of the Sultan, who recognizes him, reminds him of their previous encounter, and entertains him most lavishly. And when Messer Torello falls ill, he is conveyed by magic in the space of a single night to Pavia, where his wife's second marriage is about to be solemnized. But he is recognized by his wife at the wedding-feast, whence he returns with her to his house.

When Filomena had finished speaking, and fulsome praise had been bestowed by one and all upon Titus for his magnificent gesture of gratitude, the king, wishing to reserve the last place for Dioneo, began to address them as follows:

Enchanting ladies, what Filomena says about friendship is undoubtedly true, and it was not without reason that she complained, in her closing remarks, of the scant regard in which friendship is held by the people of today. If we had come here to rectify or even to condemn the world's shortcomings, I would reinforce her words with a lengthy speech of my own. But since we have another end in view, it occurs to me that I might now acquaint you, in the form of a narrative, lengthy perhaps but agreeable throughout, with one of the munificent deeds performed by Saladin.[1] For even though it may not be possible for any of us, through lack of means, to win the complete friendship of another by emulating the things of which you will hear in my tale, at least we may take a delight in being courteous to people, in the hope that sooner or later our actions will bring their reward.

You are to know, then, that during the reign of the Emperor Frederick I,[2] the Christians launched a great Crusade to recover the Holy Land, and that according to certain reports, Saladin, an outstandingly able ruler who was Sultan of Babylon at that period, having heard about this Crusade some time in advance, resolved to see for himself what preparations the Christian princes were making, the better to defend himself against them. So he settled all his outstanding affairs in Egypt, and, giving the impression he was going on a pilgrimage, set forth in the guise of a merchant, with an escort consisting solely of two very senior and judicious counsellors and three attendants. Their tour of inspection took them through many Christian countries, and one day, in the late afternoon, they were riding through Lombardy before crossing the Alps, when, on the road from Milan to Pavia, they happened to meet a nobleman called Messer Torello, of Strà in the province of Pavia,[3] who, along with his attendants, his dogs, and his falcons, was going to stay at a beautiful estate of his on the banks of the Ticino. As soon as Messer Torello caught sight of these men, he observed that they were foreigners of gentle birth, and desired to do them honour. So

that when Saladin inquired of one of Torello's attendants how far
it was to Pavia, and whether they could reach it by nightfall,
Torello himself replied, before the servant had time to open his
mouth:

'By the time you reach Pavia, gentlemen, it will be too late for
you to enter the city.'

'Then perhaps you will be good enough,' said Saladin, 'since we
are strangers in these parts, to tell us where we may find the best
night's lodging.'

'With pleasure,' said Messer Torello. 'I was just about to send
one of these attendants of mine on an errand to a spot not far from
Pavia. I shall get him to accompany you, and he will take you to a
place where you will lodge in great comfort.'

He then went up to the shrewdest of his attendants, told him
what he had to do, and sent him off with Saladin's party. Meanwhile
he himself rode rapidly on to his country house, where he arranged
for the finest possible supper to be prepared and for tables to be set
in the garden, after which he went and waited at the main gate for
his guests to arrive. The attendant, conversing on many different
subjects with his gently bred companions, led them by a circular
route along various byways and eventually brought them, without
their knowing it, to his master's estate.

As soon as Messer Torello saw them coming, he advanced on
foot to meet them, and laughing heartily he said:

'Gentlemen, I bid you the warmest of welcomes.'

Being of a very astute disposition, Saladin realized that the
worthy knight had not invited them when they first met for fear of
their refusing, and that, so as to make it impossible for them to
deny him their company that evening, he had cleverly beguiled
them into coming to his house. And having returned Messer
Torello's greeting, he said:

'Sir, if it were possible to complain of courteous men, we should
have good cause for complaint against you, for to say nothing
of taking us slightly out of our way, you have more or less
constrained us to accept this handsome gesture of yours, when
all we did to merit your civility was to exchange a single greeting
with you.'

To which the knight, who was no less wise than he was eloquent, replied:

'If I may judge from your appearance, gentlemen, my civility is bound to be a poor thing by comparison with your deserts. But to tell the truth you could not have found a decent place to lodge outside Pavia. Do not be aggrieved, then, to have added a few more miles to your journey for the sake of a little less discomfort.'

As he was speaking, his servants gathered round the visitors, and as soon as they had dismounted, their horses were led away to the stables. Meanwhile Messer Torello conducted the three gentlemen to the rooms that had been prepared for them, where they were helped off with their riding-boots, after which Torello offered them refreshment in the form of deliciously cool wines, and detained them with agreeable talk until it was time to go to supper.

Saladin and his companions and attendants were all conversant with the Italian tongue, so that they had no difficulty in following Messer Torello or in making themselves understood, and they were all of the opinion that this knight was the most agreeable, civilized, and affable gentleman they had so far had occasion to meet.

For his own part, Messer Torello concluded that they were gentlemen of quality, much more distinguished than he had previously thought, and reproached himself for his inability to entertain them in company that evening, with a banquet of greater splendour. He therefore resolved that he would make amends next morning, and having explained to one of his servants what he had in mind, he sent him to Pavia, which never closed its gates[4] and was very close at hand, with a message for his wife, a lady of great intelligence and exceptional spirit. This done, he led his visitors into the garden, and politely asked them who they were, whence they came, and where they were going, to which Saladin replied:

'We are Cypriot merchants, we come from Cyprus, and we are on our way to Paris to conduct certain business of ours.'

'Would to God,' said Messer Torello, 'that this country of ours produced gentlemen of a kind to compare with what I see of the merchants of Cyprus.'

On these and other matters they conversed for a while, until supper was served and Messer Torello invited them to take their places at table; and albeit the meal was impromptu, it was splendidly arranged and they dined exceedingly well. Nor had the tables long been cleared before Messer Torello, observing that his guests were tired, showed them to sumptuous beds in which to lie down and rest, and shortly thereafter he too retired to bed.

The servant he had sent to Pavia delivered the message to his lady, who, in a spirit more worthy of a prince than of a woman, promptly summoned a number of her husband's friends and servants, and set all preparations in train for a sumptuous banquet. And apart from seeing that invitations were delivered, by the light of torches, to many of the city's leading nobles, she laid in a supply of clothes and silks and furs, and carried out all the instructions her husband had sent her, down to the tiniest detail.

Next morning, when the gentlemen had risen, Messer Torello invited them to join him for an expedition on horseback, and having called for his falcons, he took his guests to a nearby stretch of shallow water and showed them how magnificently the birds could fly. But when Saladin inquired whether there was anyone who could take them to Pavia and direct them to the most comfortable inn, Messer Torello said:

'I myself will direct you, for I am obliged to go to Pavia in any case.'

The gentlemen believed him, gladly accepted his offer, and set off with him on the road to Pavia, where they arrived a little after tierce. Thinking they were being directed to the finest of the city's inns, they came with Messer Torello to his mansion, where already some fifty or more of the leading citizens were assembled to greet them, and these immediately gathered round them, seizing their reins and their stirrups. Saladin and his companions no sooner saw this than they realized all too well what it signified, and they said:

'Messer Torello, we did not ask for any such favour as this. You entertained us royally last night, far better than we had any right to expect, and therefore you could easily have left us now to proceed on our way.'

To which Messer Torello replied:

'If, gentlemen, I was able to do you a service last night, for that I was indebted, not so much to yourselves, but rather to Fortune, who overtook you at such an hour on the road that you had no alternative but to come to my humble dwelling; but for the service we shall do you this morning, I and all these gentlemen who surround you are beholden only to you, and if you think it courteous to deny us your company at breakfast, you are at liberty to do so.'

Acknowledging defeat, Saladin and his companions dismounted, and after being welcomed by the gentlemen, they were gaily conveyed to the rooms which had been sumptuously prepared to receive them. They then divested themselves of their travelling attire, and, having taken a little refreshment, made their way to the banqueting hall, where everything was magnificently arranged. Having washed their hands, with all due pomp and ceremony they were ushered to their places at table, where they were plied with numerous dishes, each of them so exquisitely served that if the Emperor himself had been present, it would not have been possible to entertain him more handsomely. And even though Saladin and his two companions were mighty lords, accustomed to extraordinary acts of homage, they none the less marvelled at this one, which, considering the quality of the knight, whom they knew to be no prince, but a private citizen, seemed to them as magnificent as any they had ever seen.

When the meal was over, the tables were cleared and they talked learnedly together until, at Messer Torello's suggestion, it being very hot, all the gentlemen of Pavia went home to take their siesta, leaving him alone with his three visitors. And so that none of his treasures should remain hidden from their eyes, he escorted them into another room and sent for his excellent lady. She was a tall and very beautiful woman, and, decked in sumptuous robes, flanked by her two small children, who looked for all the world like angels, she came before them and charmingly paid her respects. No sooner did she appear than the gentlemen rose to their feet, greeted her with deference, and invited her to sit in their midst, making much ado over her enchanting little children. And after entering upon a pleasant conversation with the three visitors, in the course of which

Messer Torello got up and left them alone together, she graciously inquired whence they had come and whither they were bound, whereupon the gentlemen gave her the answer they had already given to Messer Torello.

The lady smiled, and said:

'Then I see that my woman's instinct may well have its uses, for I want to ask you a special favour, namely, that you will neither refuse nor despise the trifling gift that I shall cause to be brought to you. On the contrary, I beg you to accept it, but you must bear in mind that a woman's heart is not so large as a man's, and her gifts are correspondingly smaller. So I trust you will pay more heed to the donor's good intentions than to the size of the gift.'

She then sent for two pairs of robes for each of the guests, one lined with silk and the other with fur, all of a quality more suited to a prince than to any merchant or private citizen. And these she presented to the gentlemen, along with three silken jackets and small-clothes, saying:

'Take these robes: they are like the ones in which I have arrayed my husband. As for the other things, though they are worth little, you may well find them useful, seeing that you are distant from your womenfolk. You have come a long way and still have far to go, and merchants take a pride in their appearance.'

The gentlemen could scarcely believe their eyes. It was abundantly clear that Messer Torello was bent upon doing them every possible honour, and for a moment they suspected, seeing that the robes were more sumptuous than those of any merchant, that he had seen through their disguise. However, one of them answered the lady as follows:

'These things are so exquisite, madam, that it would be difficult for anyone to accept them. But how are we to refuse, when you press them upon us with so much eloquence?'

Thus her gift was accepted, and since Messer Torello had now returned, the lady took her leave of the three gentlemen and went away to see that their servants were likewise supplied with garments, of a style suited to their condition. Meanwhile, in response to the earnest entreaties of Messer Torello, the gentlemen agreed to spend the rest of the day with him, and after they had taken their siesta, they donned their new robes and toured the city on horseback with their host. And when it was time for supper, they were splendidly dined and wined in the company of numerous eminent citizens.

In due course they retired to bed, and when they rose at daybreak, they found that their tired old nags had been replaced by a trio of sturdy and splendid-looking palfreys, and that fresh, strong horses had also been provided for their servants; on seeing which, Saladin turned to his companions and said:

'I swear to God that there was never a more perfect gentleman than this, nor any more courteous or considerate. And if the kings of Christendom are such excellent princes as this man is a knight, the Sultan of Babylon will be powerless to resist a single one of them, let alone all those we have seen preparing to march against him.' But realizing that Messer Torello would not take no for an answer, they thanked him most politely and mounted their horses.

Messer Torello, together with several of his friends, escorted the gentlemen for a goodly distance along the road leading out of the city. But eventually Saladin begged him to turn back, being unable to tarry any longer, though it grieved him to part company with his host, whom he had come by now to regard with the deepest affection. And albeit Messer Torello was no less loath to part company with his guests, he said:

'Since you want me to leave you, gentlemen, I shall do so. But first I should like to say this: I know not who you are, nor do I wish to know more than you are willing to tell me. But whoever you may be, you cannot persuade me to believe that you are merchants. And with that I bid you farewell.'

To which Saladin, having already taken his leave of Messer Torello's companions, replied as follows:

'We may yet have the chance, sir, of showing you some of our merchandise, and then you shall be persuaded well enough. But meanwhile we bid you adieu.'

Saladin then rode off with his companions, being firmly resolved, if his life were spared and he avoided defeat in the war with which he was faced, to return the hospitality of Messer Torello in full. He talked a great deal to his companions about Messer Torello and his lady, and about all the things he had done for them, waxing more eloquent in his praises on each occasion he returned to the subject. And when, at the cost of no little fatigue, his tour of the West was completed, he returned by sea with his companions to Alexandria, where, now that he was fully apprised of the facts, he drew up his plan of defence. Meanwhile Messer Torello had returned to Pavia, and although he pondered at great length upon who these three men might have been, he never arrived at the truth nor even came anywhere near it.

When the time arrived for the Crusade, and the soldiers were assembling everywhere in large numbers, Messer Torello, undeterred by the tears and entreaties of his lady, firmly made up his mind to go with them. He therefore made all his preparations, and as he was about to ride away, he summoned his wife, whom he loved very deeply, and said to her:

'As you see, my lady, I am joining this Crusade, both for personal renown and the good of my soul. I leave our good name and our possessions in your hands; and since my return is far less certain than my departure, owing to any of a thousand accidents that may befall me, I want you to promise me this: that whatever should be my fate, failing positive news that I live, you will wait for a year and a month and a day before you remarry, beginning from this, the day of my departure.'

'Torello,' she replied, weeping most bitterly, 'how I am to bear all the sorrow into which I am plunged by your going away, I simply cannot tell. But if I am strong enough to survive it, and if anything should happen to you, rest assured that for as long as I live I shall be wedded to Messer Torello and his memory.'

'My lady,' said Messer Torello, 'I am convinced that you will do all in your power to keep such a promise; but you are young and beautiful, you come from a famous family, and as everyone knows, you are a woman of exceptional gifts. Hence I have no doubt that if I am reported as missing, many a fine gentleman will be seeking your hand from your brothers and kinsfolk, who will subject you to so much pressure, that whether you like it or not you will be forced to comply with their wishes. And that is why I do not ask you to wait any longer than the period I have stated.'

'I shall do my utmost to keep my promise,' said the lady. 'And even if I am forced to act differently, at least I shall follow these instructions of yours to the letter. But I pray to God that neither you nor I will be brought to any such extremity.'

Having uttered these words, the lady burst into tears and embraced Messer Torello. Then, taking a ring from her finger, she presented it to him saying:

'If I should happen to die before we meet again, remember me when you look upon this ring.'

Messer Torello accepted the ring, and having mounted his horse, he bade farewell to everyone and proceeded on his way. On arriving with his followers at Genoa, he boarded a galley, and after a prosperous voyage he landed at Acre,[5] where he joined the main body of the Christian host. But almost overnight the army was afflicted by a great and deadly fever, in the course of which, whether through good judgement or good fortune, Saladin captured nearly all the Christians who managed to survive, divided them up, and imprisoned them in various cities of his realm. Among those captured was Messer Torello, who was marched away to prison in Alexandria, where, since no one was aware of his importance and he was afraid to disclose his identity, he was compelled to apply himself to the training of hawks, a science which he had mastered to perfection. And when his prowess came to the notice of Saladin, he had him removed from captivity and appointed him his falconer.

Neither of them recognized the other, and Messer Torello, whom Saladin referred to simply as 'the Christian', constantly had the thought of Pavia at the back of his mind and attempted several times to escape, but without success. So that when a party of Genoese emissaries came to Saladin's court to arrange for the ransom of certain fellow citizens of theirs, he resolved that before they departed he would write to his wife, letting her know he was alive and would return to her as soon as he could, and asking her to wait for him. And having written the letter, he earnestly begged one of the emissaries, whom he knew personally, to see that it was delivered to his uncle, who was the Abbot of San Pietro in Ciel d'Oro,[6] in Pavia.

This being the way matters stood with Messer Torello, it happened that as Saladin was conversing with him one day on the subject of his hawks, Messer Torello began to smile and his mouth assumed a certain expression, of which Saladin had taken particular note when staying at his house in Pavia. Consequently Saladin called Messer Torello to mind, and after peering at the falconer more intently, he was almost sure that this man and Messer Torello were one and the same. So, changing the subject, he said:

'Tell me, Christian, in what part of the West do you live?'

'My lord,' replied Messer Torello, 'I am a Lombard, from a city called Pavia, and I am a poor man of low estate.'

When Saladin heard this, he was virtually certain that his surmise was correct, and gleefully thought to himself: 'God has now given me the chance to show this man how greatly I valued his kindness towards me.' However, he said no more on the subject, but gave orders for all his robes to be laid out on display in one of the rooms of the palace, into which he took Messer Torello, and said to him:

'Take a look at these clothes, Christian, and tell me whether you ever saw any of them before.'

Messer Torello began to inspect them, and albeit he caught sight of the garments his wife had presented to Saladin, it never entered his head that they could be the ones in question. However, he replied:

'My lord, I recognize none of them, though it's true that these two resemble certain robes which I myself once wore, and were also worn by three merchants who came to stay with me.'

Whereupon Saladin, unable to restrain himself any longer, threw his arms affectionately round Messer Torello's neck, saying:

'You are Messer Torello of Strà; I am one of the three merchants to whom your good lady presented these garments, and the time has now come to persuade you of the quality of my merchandise, as I promised you I would, God willing, on the day I departed.'

On hearing this, Messer Torello was delighted and ashamed at one and the same time, for on the one hand he was delighted to have had so eminent a guest beneath his roof, whilst on the other he was ashamed at the thought of having entertained him so frugally. But Saladin continued:

'Messer Torello, now that God has sent you here to me, you

must no longer think of me as your master, but rather as your servant.'

After much rejoicing in each other's company, Saladin caused him to be dressed in regal robes, and having presented him to a gathering of the leading peers of his realm, and spoken at length of Messer Torello's excellence, he commanded that those of them who set any store by his favour should honour the person of Messer Torello as they would his own. And this was precisely what each of them did from that day forth, especially the two gentlemen who had stayed with Saladin in Messer Torello's house.

Messer Torello's sudden elevation to the pinnacle of renown took his mind away for a while from his affairs in Lombardy, the more so because he had every reason to believe that his letter had been safely delivered into the hands of his uncle.

But on the very day that the Christian host fell into Saladin's hands, a Provençal knight of no great repute, whose name was Messer Torello of Digne,[7] had died and was buried in the Christian camp; and since Messer Torello of Strà was famed for his nobility throughout the whole of the army, whenever anyone heard that Messer Torello was dead they at once assumed it was the latter of the two, and not the former, who was meant. Before they had a chance to perceive their mistake Messer Torello was taken prisoner, so that many Italians returned with tidings of his death, and there were those who had the audacity to assert that they had seen his corpse and attended his burial. And when this came to the knowledge of his wife and family, it brought enormous and incalculable sorrow, not only to them but to all who had known him.

We should be hard put to describe in few words the nature and extent of the grief, the sadness, and the heartache experienced by his lady. Suffice it to say that when, after mourning continuously for several months on end, the pangs of her sorrow began to abate, and her hand was being sought by the most powerful men in Lombardy, she was urged by her brothers and the rest of her kinsfolk to remarry. Time after time she refused, bursting into floods of tears whenever the subject was mentioned. Eventually however she was forced to accede to the wishes of her kinsfolk, but only on condition that she should remain unmarried till the period prescribed in her promise to Messer Torello had expired.

This, then, was how matters stood in Pavia with the lady when one day, about a week before she was due to be married, Messer Torello chanced to catch sight in Alexandria of a man he had seen embarking with the Genoese emissaries on the galley that was leaving for Genoa. He therefore sent for him, and asked him what sort of a voyage they had had, and when they had arrived at Genoa.

'My lord,' said the man, 'I left the galley in Crete, where I later heard that her voyage ended in disaster; for as she was approaching Sicily, she ran into a northerly gale which drove her on to the Barbary reefs, and everyone aboard was drowned, including two of my brothers.'

Messer Torello believed every word of this account, which happened to be all too accurate, and when he recalled that less than a week remained of the period he had asked his wife to await his return, and realized that nothing had been heard of him in Pavia, he was convinced that she was by now betrothed to another. So deep was the despair into which he was cast that he lost the desire to eat, took to his bed, and resolved to die.

When Saladin, who greatly loved Messer Torello, heard news of this, he came in person to see him. And having, by dint of earnest and repeated entreaties, discovered the reason for his sorrow and his malady, he censured him severely for not confiding in him earlier, then begged him to take heart, declaring that if Torello would cheer up he would arrange for him to be in Pavia on the date he had prescribed. And he explained how it was to be accomplished.

Messer Torello took Saladin at his word, and since he had frequently heard that this sort of thing was possible and had often been done before, he began to feel more optimistic and to urge Saladin that he should attend to it at once.

Saladin therefore enjoined one of his magicians,[8] with whose skill he was already well acquainted, to seek out a way of transporting Messer Torello on a bed to Pavia, in the space of a single night. The magician replied that this would be done, but that for Torello's own good he must first of all put him to sleep.

This arranged, Saladin returned to Messer Torello, and finding him still entirely resolved to be in Pavia by the date agreed if this were possible, and to die if it were not, he addressed him as follows:

'God knows, Messer Torello, that I cannot blame you in the slightest for loving your wife so dearly and for being so concerned at the thought of losing her to another. For of all the ladies I ever recall having met, she is the one whose way of life, whose manners, and whose demeanour – to say nothing of her beauty, which will fade like the flower – seem to me most precious and commendable. Nothing would have given me greater joy, since Fortune has brought you to Alexandria, than for us to have spent the rest of our lives together here, ruling as equals over the kingdom I now govern. God has willed that these wishes of mine should not be granted, but now that you have taken it into your head to die unless you are back again in Pavia by the date you prescribed, I dearly wish that I had known of all this in time for me to restore you to your home with the dignity, the splendour, and the company that your excellence deserves. Since, however, I am not even allowed to do this, and you are determined to be in Pavia forthwith, I shall do my best to get you there in the manner I have told you of.'

'My lord,' said Messer Torello, 'quite apart from your words, your actions have supplied me with abundant proof of your benevolence towards me, which far exceeds all my deserts, and even if you had said nothing, I should have lived and died in the certain knowledge that what you say is true. But since my mind is made up on the subject, I beg you to act quickly in the manner you have proposed, for after tomorrow I shall no longer be expected.'

Saladin assured him that everything was settled; and on the next day, it being his intention to send him on his way that same evening, he caused a most beautiful and sumptuous bed to be prepared in one of the great halls of his palace. It was a bed fashioned in the style of the East, with mattresses covered all over in velvet and cloth of gold, and Saladin had it bedecked with a quilt, embroidered with enormous pearls and the finest of precious stones, geometrically arranged, which was looked upon later, in these parts, as a priceless treasure. And finally he had two pillows placed upon it, of a quality appropriate to the bed itself. This done, he ordered that Messer Torello, who had now recovered, should be clothed in a robe of the kind that Saracens wear, more opulent and splendid than any that was ever seen, whilst around his head he caused one of his longest turbans to be wound.

It was already late in the evening when Saladin, along with many of his lords, went to Messer Torello's room; and having sat down beside him, he began, almost in tears, to address him as follows:

'Messer Torello, the time is approaching for you to be severed from me, and since I can neither go with you nor send another in my place, being prevented from doing so by the manner of your travelling, I am forced to take my leave of you here and now, which is why I have come. But before bidding you farewell, I implore you in the name of our love and our friendship to remember me. And before our lives are spent, I beg you if possible to settle your affairs in Lombardy and come once more to visit me; for not only will I rejoice to see you, but I shall then be able to repair the omissions which your haste to depart imposes upon me. Until such time as this should come about, let it not weary you to visit me with your letters, and ask of me whatever you please, for you may be sure that there is no other person on earth whose wants I would supply more readily.'

Messer Torello, being unable to control his tears, was prevented from replying at any length. And so in few words he declared it was impossible for him ever to forget Saladin's courteous deeds and sterling worth, and that without fail he would do as Saladin had requested, whenever the opportunity arose. So Saladin enfolded him tenderly in his arms, kissed him, and, weeping copiously, wished him God-speed and withdrew. Then all his nobles took their leave of Messer Torello and accompanied Saladin to the hall where the bed had been set.

But the hour was now late, and the magician being anxious to conduct the affair to a speedy conclusion, a physician came to Messer Torello with a certain potion, which he persuaded him to drink, explaining that it would fortify him for what lay ahead. Soon afterwards he fell asleep, and as he slept he was conveyed on Saladin's orders to the sumptuous bed, upon which Saladin placed a large, beautiful and priceless crown, which he marked in such a way that in due course it was clearly seen to have been sent from Saladin to Messer Torello's wife. Then on Messer Torello's finger he placed a ring containing a large ruby, whose value, since it glowed and glittered like a flaming torch, was well-nigh impossible to assess. He next had Messer Torello girded with a sword, so richly ornamented that it, too, could not easily be valued. Nor was this all, for he pinned a brooch to Messer Torello's breast, studded with pearls whose like were never seen, and many other precious stones besides. And on either side of his sleeping form, he caused an enormous golden bowl, overflowing with doubloons, to be placed, whilst all around him he set numerous rings and belts and strings of pearls and other objects, which would take too long to describe. This done, he kissed Messer Torello once more, and told the magician to make haste, whereupon before his very eyes the bed and Messer Torello suddenly disappeared in their entirety, leaving Saladin behind to converse with his nobles about him.

As he had requested, Messer Torello was deposited, along with all the aforesaid jewels and finery, in the church of San Pietro in Ciel d'Oro in Pavia, where he still lay asleep when the bell was rung for matins and the sexton entered the church carrying a lantern. Being suddenly confronted with the sight of the opulent bed, he could hardly believe his eyes, and such was the terror by which he was seized that he turned on his heel and came running out of the church, much to the amazement of the Abbot and the monks, who demanded to know the reason. Whereupon the sexton told them what he had seen.

'Come now,' said the Abbot, 'it's not as if you were a child any more, or a newcomer to this church, to be frightened so easily. Let's all go and see what has startled you.'

So the Abbot and his monks, having kindled a number of lights, entered the church and saw this amazing and sumptuous bed, with the sleeping knight upon it. And just as they were casting a wary and timorous eye over all the princely jewels, standing well back from the bed, the power of the potion happened to expend itself, Messer Torello stirred, and a great, deep sigh escaped his lips.

On seeing this, the monks, and also the Abbot, were frightened out of their wits, and they all ran away crying 'Lord, deliver us!'

Having opened his eyes and looked about him, Messer Torello

discovered to his great joy that he was in the very place where he had asked to be left. And whereas he had known of the munificence of Saladin in the past, when he sat up now and surveyed, one by one, the objects with which he was surrounded, he was all the more conscious of it and deemed it greater than ever. But meanwhile he could hear the monks running away, and guessing the reason, he began, without stirring any further, to call to the Abbot by name, begging him not to be frightened as it was only Torello, his nephew.

On hearing this, the Abbot's fears increased, since for many months past he had assumed Torello to be dead. But after a while, drawing strength from the power of reason, and continuing to hear his name being called, he crossed himself devoutly and went cautiously up to Torello, who said to him:

'Oh, my father, of what are you afraid? By the grace of God, I am alive, and I have come back here from across the sea.'

Albeit Torello was thickly bearded and dressed in Arabian clothes, the Abbot soon recognized him; and being wholly reassured, he took him by the hand, saying: 'My son, I bid you a hearty welcome.' Then he continued: 'Our alarm ought not to surprise you, for there isn't a man in the whole of Pavia who is not convinced that you are dead. Indeed I may tell you that your wife, Madonna Adalieta,[9] overcome by the threats and entreaties of her kinsfolk, has been forced to remarry. This very morning she is to go to her new husband, and all is made ready for the nuptials and the banquet.'

Messer Torello stepped forth from his sumptuous bed, and after cordially embracing the Abbot and the monks, he begged them one and all to say nothing to anyone of his return until he had attended to a certain affair. He then saw to it that the precious jewels were left in a safe place, after which he gave an account to the Abbot of all that had so far happened to him. The Abbot, delighted with Messer Torello's good fortune, joined with him in giving thanks to God, after which Messer Torello asked the Abbot the name of his wife's second husband; and the Abbot told him.

Then Messer Torello said:

'Before my return is made public, I mean to find out how my

wife comports herself at these nuptials; so although it is not the custom for the religious to attend such a banquet as this, I want you to arrange, for my sake, that we should be present.'

The Abbot readily agreed; and soon after daybreak he sent a message to the bridegroom, saying that he wished to bring a friend to the nuptials, to which the gentleman replied that he would be very glad to see them.

When the hour for the banquet arrived, Messer Torello went with the Abbot, in the clothes in which he was standing, to the bridegroom's house, being stared at in amazement by everyone who saw him, but recognized by none. The Abbot told everyone that Torello was a Saracen whom the Sultan had dispatched to the King of France as his envoy.

Messer Torello was accordingly placed at a table directly facing his lady, whom he gazed upon in rapturous delight, at the same time thinking that she wore a troubled look on account of these nuptials. Every so often, she returned his gaze, not because she had the slightest idea who he was (for his long beard, his strange attire, and her conviction that he was dead made this impossible), but by virtue of the extraordinary clothes he was wearing.

But when he felt that the time had come to put her memory of him to the test, Messer Torello took hold of the ring which the lady had given him on the day of his departure, and, sending for a young man who was waiting upon her, he said to him:

'Tell the bride, with my compliments, that in our country, whenever any stranger such as myself attends a bridal feast such as hers, it is the custom for her to send him the cup from which she is drinking, filled with wine, to signify her pleasure at his coming. When the stranger has consumed his fill, he replaces the lid of the wine-cup, and the bride drinks up the remainder.'

The youth conveyed this message to the lady, who, displaying her wonted tact and courtesy, supposing him to be some great panjandrum, hastened to show him that she held his presence dear. And she ordered that a large golden cup, which stood on the table before her, should be rinsed and filled with wine and taken to the gentleman.

Messer Torello, having meanwhile placed her ring in his mouth, drank in such a way as to let it fall into the cup without anyone having noticed. Leaving no more than a modicum of wine in the cup, he replaced the lid and returned it to the lady. Then the lady took hold of the cup, removed the lid, raised it to her lips to complete the ritual, and caught sight of the ring, which she inspected closely for a while without saying a word. Identifying the ring as the one she had given to Messer Torello at his departure, she picked it up and fixed her gaze upon the so-called stranger. And now that she could see who it was, she overturned the table at which she was sitting, as though she had gone berserk, and cried out:

'This is my lord; this truly is Messer Torello!'

She then ran over to the table where Messer Torello was sitting, and, heedless of the drapery and the other things lying upon it, she flung herself bodily forward and clasped him firmly in her embrace; nor could she be detached from around his neck, no matter what anyone present said or did, until she was told by Messer Torello to curb her feelings a little as she would have all the time in the world to embrace him afterwards.

She accordingly stood up straight, and although by now the wedding-feast was in total disarray, the return of so valiant a knight gave rise to greater rejoicing than ever. But then, at Messer Torello's request, everyone was silent as he narrated the story of all his adventures from the day of his departure, ending up by saying that the gentleman who, believing him to be dead, had married his wife, could hardly take it amiss, since he was really alive, if he claimed her as his own.

The bridegroom, though somewhat embarrassed, freely and amiably replied that Messer Torello was at liberty to dispose in whatever way he pleased of that which was rightfully his own. So the lady restored to the bridegroom the ring and the crown he had given her, and in their place she wore the ring she had taken from the wine-cup, and the crown sent to her by the Sultan. They then went forth from the bridegroom's house, and made their way, with all the pomp of a nuptial procession, to the house of Messer Torello, where there was no end to the rejoicing of his sorrowing friends and relatives and of the townspeople in general, who looked upon his return as nothing short of a miracle.

After giving away some of his precious gems to the gentleman who had borne the expense of the wedding-feast, as well as to the Abbot and to various other people, Messer Torello informed Saladin, through more than a single messenger, of his felicitous return to Pavia, declaring himself to be his friend and servant. And for many years thereafter, he lived with his admirable lady, comporting himself more courteously than ever.

This, then, was how the trials of Messer Torello and his beloved wife were brought to an end, and how they were rewarded for their prompt and cheerful acts of courtesy. Many are those who attempt to perform such deeds, who, though they possess the wherewithal, are so inept in carrying them out that before they are finished they cost the recipient more than they are worth. So that if their deeds do not redound to their credit, neither they nor others should have any reason to marvel.

TENTH STORY

The Marquis of Saluzzo, obliged by the entreaties of his subjects to take a wife, follows his personal whims and marries the daughter of a peasant. She bears him two children, and he gives her the impression that he has put them to death. Later on, pretending that she has incurred his displeasure and that he has remarried, he arranges for his own daughter to return home and passes her off as his bride, having meanwhile turned his wife out of doors in no more than the shift she is wearing. But on finding that she endures it all with patience, he cherishes her all the more deeply, brings her back to his house, shows her their children, who have now grown up, and honours her as the Marchioness, causing others to honour her likewise.

The lengthy tale of the king, which everyone seemed to have greatly enjoyed, being now at an end, Dioneo, laughing gaily, addressed them as follows:

'If the poor fellow, who was looking forward to raising and lowering the werewolf's tail[1] on the very next night, could hear the praises you are heaping on Messer Torello, he wouldn't give you twopence for the lot of them.' Then, knowing that he alone was left to tell his story, he began:

Sweet and gentle ladies, this day has been devoted, so far as I can see, to the doings of kings and sultans and people of that sort; and therefore, so as not to place too great a distance between us, I want to tell you of a marquis, whose actions, even though things turned out well for him in the end, were remarkable not so much for their munificence as for their senseless brutality. Nor do I advise anyone to follow his example, for it was a great pity that the fellow should have drawn any profit from his conduct.

A very long time ago, there succeeded to the marquisate of Saluzzo[2] a young man called Gualtieri, who, having neither wife nor children, spent the whole of his time hunting and hawking, and never even thought about marrying or raising a family, which says a great deal for his intelligence. His followers, however, disapproved of this, and repeatedly begged him to marry so that he should not be left without an heir nor they without a lord. Moreover, they offered to find him a wife whose parentage would be such as to strengthen their expectations and who would make him exceedingly happy.

So Gualtieri answered them as follows:

'My friends, you are pressing me to do something that I had always set my mind firmly against, seeing how difficult it is to find a person who will easily adapt to one's own way of living, how many thousands there are who will do precisely the opposite, and what a miserable life is in store for the man who stumbles upon a woman ill-suited to his own temperament. Moreover it is foolish of you to believe that you can judge the character of daughters from the ways of their fathers and mothers, hence claiming to provide me with a wife who will please me. For I cannot see how you are to know the fathers, or to discover the secrets of the mothers; and even if this were possible, daughters are very often different from either of their parents. Since, however, you are so determined to bind me in chains of this sort, I am ready to do as you ask; but so that I have only myself to blame if it should turn out badly, I must insist on marrying a wife of my own choosing. And I hereby declare that no matter who she may be, if you fail to honour her as your lady you will learn to your great cost how serious a matter it is for you to have urged me to marry against my will.'

To this the gentlemen replied that if only he would bring himself to take a wife, they would be satisfied.

Now, for some little time, Gualtieri had been casting an appreciative eye on the manners of a poor girl from a neighbouring village, and thinking her very beautiful, he considered that a life with her would have much to commend it. So without looking further afield, he resolved to marry the girl; and having summoned her father, who was very poor indeed, he arranged with him that he should take her as his wife.

This done, Gualtieri brought together all his friends from the various parts of his domain, and said to them:

'My friends, since you still persist in wanting me to take a wife, I am prepared to do it, not because I have any desire to marry, but rather in order to gratify your wishes. You will recall the promise you gave me, that no matter whom I should choose, you would rest content and honour her as your lady. The time has now come when I want you to keep that promise, and for me to honour the promise I gave to you. I have found a girl after my own heart, in this very district, and a few days hence I intend to marry her and convey her to my house. See to it, therefore, that the wedding-feast lacks nothing in splendour, and consider how you may honourably receive her, so that all of us may call ourselves contented – I with you for keeping your promise, and you with me for keeping mine.'

As of one voice, the good folk joyously gave him their blessing, and said that whoever she happened to be, they would accept her as their lady and honour her as such in all respects. Then they all prepared to celebrate the wedding in a suitably grand and sumptuous manner, and Gualtieri did the same. A rich and splendid nuptial feast was arranged, to which he invited many of his friends, his kinsfolk, great nobles and other people of the locality; moreover he caused a quantity of fine, rich robes to be tailored to fit a girl whose figure appeared to match that of the young woman he intended to marry; and lastly he laid in a number of rings and ornamental belts, along with a precious and beautiful crown, and everything else that a bride could possibly need.

Early on the morning of the day he had fixed for the nuptials, Gualtieri, his preparations now complete, mounted his horse together with all the people who had come to do him honour, and said:

'Gentlemen, it is time for us to go and fetch the bride.'

He then set forth with the whole of the company in train, and eventually they came to the village and made their way to the house of the girl's father, where they met her as she was returning with water from the fountain, making great haste so that she could go with other women to see Gualtieri's bride arriving. As soon as Gualtieri caught sight of her, he called to her by her name, which was Griselda,[3] and asked her where her father was, to which she blushingly replied:

'My lord, he is at home.'

So Gualtieri dismounted, and having ordered everyone to wait for him outside, he went alone into the humble dwelling, where he found the girl's father, whose name was Giannùcole, and said to him:

'I have come to marry Griselda, but first I want to ask her certain questions in your presence.' He then asked her whether, if he were to marry her, she would always try to please him and never be upset by anything he said or did, whether she would obey him, and many other questions of this sort, to all of which she answered that she would.

Whereupon Gualtieri, having taken her by the hand, led her out of the house, and in the presence of his whole company and of all the other people there he caused her to be stripped naked. Then he called for the clothes and shoes which he had had specially made, and quickly got her to put them on, after which he caused a crown to be placed upon the dishevelled hair of her head. And just as everyone was wondering what this might signify, he said:

'Gentlemen, this is the woman I intend to marry, provided she will have me as her husband.' Then, turning to Griselda, who was so embarrassed that she hardly knew where to look, he said:

'Griselda, will you have me as your wedded husband?'

To which she replied:

'I will, my lord.'

'And I will have you as my wedded wife,' said Gualtieri, and he married her then and there before all the people present. He then helped her mount a palfrey, and led her back, honourably attended, to his house, where the nuptials were as splendid and as sumptuous, and the rejoicing as unrestrained, as if he had married the King of France's daughter.

Along with her new clothes, the young bride appeared to take on a new lease of life, and she seemed a different woman entirely. She was endowed, as we have said, with a fine figure and beautiful features, and lovely as she already was, she now acquired so confident, graceful and decorous a manner that she could have been taken for the daughter, not of the shepherd Giannùcole, but of some great nobleman, and consequently everyone who had known her before her marriage was filled with astonishment. But apart from this, she was so obedient to her husband, and so compliant to his wishes, that he thought himself the happiest and most contented man on earth. At the same time she was so gracious and benign towards her husband's subjects, that each and every one of them was glad to honour her, and accorded her his unselfish devotion, praying for her happiness, prosperity, and greater glory. And whereas they had been wont to say that Gualtieri had shown some lack of discretion in taking this woman as his wife, they now regarded him as the wisest and most discerning man on earth. For no one apart from Gualtieri could ever have perceived the noble qualities that lay concealed beneath her ragged and rustic attire.

In short, she comported herself in such a manner that she quickly earned widespread acclaim for her virtuous deeds and excellent character not only in her husband's domain but also in the world at large; and those who had formerly censured Gualtieri for choosing to marry her were now compelled to reverse their opinion.

Not long after she had gone to live with Gualtieri she conceived a child, and in the fullness of time, to her husband's enormous joy, she bore him a daughter. But shortly thereafter Gualtieri was seized with the strange desire to test Griselda's patience, by subjecting her to constant provocation and making her life unbearable.

At first he lashed her with his tongue, feigning to be angry and claiming that his subjects were thoroughly disgruntled with her on account of her lowly condition, especially now that they saw her bearing children; and he said they were greatly distressed about this infant daughter of theirs, of whom they did nothing but grumble.

The lady betrayed no sign of bitterness on hearing these words, and without changing her expression she said to him:

'My lord, deal with me as you think best[4] for your own good name and peace of mind, for I shall rest content whatever you decide, knowing myself to be their inferior and that I was unworthy of the honour which you so generously bestowed upon me.'

This reply was much to Gualtieri's liking, for it showed him that she had not been puffed with pride by any honour that he or others had paid her.

A little while later, having told his wife in general terms that his subjects could not abide the daughter she had borne him, he gave certain instructions to one of his attendants, whom he sent to Griselda. The man looked very sorrowful, and said:

'My lady, if I do not wish to die, I must do as my lord commands me. He has ordered me to take this daughter of yours, and to . . .' And his voice trailed off into silence.

On hearing these words and perceiving the man's expression, Griselda, recalling what she had been told, concluded that he had been instructed to murder her child. So she quickly picked it up from its cradle, kissed it, gave it her blessing, and albeit she felt that her heart was about to break, placed the child in the arms of the servant without any trace of emotion, saying:

'There: do exactly as your lord, who is my lord too, has instructed you.[5] But do not leave her to be devoured by the beasts and the birds, unless that is what he has ordered you to do.'

The servant took away the little girl and reported Griselda's words to Gualtieri, who, marvelling at her constancy, sent him with the child to a kinswoman of his in Bologna, requesting her to rear and educate her carefully, but without ever making it known whose daughter she was.

Then it came about that his wife once more became pregnant, and in due course she gave birth to a son, which pleased Gualtieri enormously. But not being content with the mischief he had done already, he abused her more viciously than ever, and one day he glowered at her angrily and said:

'Woman, from the day you produced this infant son, the people have made my life a complete misery, so bitterly do they resent the thought of a grandson of Giannùcole succeeding me as their lord. So unless I want to be deposed, I'm afraid I shall be forced to do as I did before, and eventually to leave you and marry someone else.'

His wife listened patiently, and all she replied was:

'My lord, look to your own comfort, see that you fulfil your wishes, and spare no thought for me, since nothing brings me pleasure unless it pleases you also.'

Before many days had elapsed, Gualtieri sent for his son in the same way that he had sent for his daughter, and having likewise pretended to have had the child put to death, he sent him, like the little girl, to Bologna. To all of this his wife reacted no differently, either in her speech or in her looks, than she had on the previous occasion, much to the astonishment of Gualtieri, who told himself that no other woman could have remained so impassive. But for the fact that he had observed her doting upon the children for as long as he allowed her to do so, he would have assumed that she was glad to be rid of them, whereas he knew that she was too judicious to behave in any other way.

His subjects, thinking he had caused the children to be murdered, roundly condemned him and judged him a cruel tyrant, whilst his wife became the object of their deepest compassion. But to the women who offered her their sympathy in the loss of her children, all she ever said was that the decision of their father was good enough for her.

Many years after the birth of his daughter, Gualtieri decided that the time had come to put Griselda's patience to the final test. So he told a number of his men that in no circumstances could he put up with Griselda as his wife any longer, having now come to realize that his marriage was an aberration of his youth. He would therefore do everything in his power to obtain a dispensation from the Pope, enabling him to divorce Griselda and marry someone else. For this

he was chided severely by many worthy men, but his only reply
was that it had to be done.

On learning of her husband's intentions, from which it appeared
she would have to return to her father's house, in order perhaps to
look after the sheep as she had in the past, meanwhile seeing the
man she adored being cherished by some other woman, Griselda
was secretly filled with despair. But she prepared herself to endure
this final blow as stoically as she had borne Fortune's earlier assaults.

Shortly thereafter, Gualtieri arranged for some counterfeit letters
of his to arrive from Rome, and led his subjects to believe that in
these, the Pope had granted him permission to abandon Griselda
and remarry.

He accordingly sent for Griselda, and before a large number of
people he said to her:

'Woman, I have had a dispensation from the Pope, allowing me
to leave you and take another wife. Since my ancestors were great
noblemen and rulers of these lands, whereas yours have always been
peasants, I intend that you shall no longer be my wife, but return to
Giannùcole's house with the dowry you brought me, after which I
shall bring another lady here. I have already chosen her and she is
far better suited to a man of my condition.'

On hearing these words, the lady, with an effort beyond the
power of any normal woman's nature, suppressed her tears and
replied:

'My lord, I have always known that my lowly condition was
totally at odds with your nobility, and that it is to God and to
yourself that I owe whatever standing I possess. Nor have I ever
regarded this as a gift that I might keep and cherish as my own, but
rather as something I have borrowed; and now that you want me to
return it, I must give it back to you with good grace. Here is the
ring with which you married me: take it. As to your ordering me
to take away the dowry that I brought, you will require no
accountant, nor will I need a purse or a pack-horse, for this to be
done. For it has not escaped my memory that you took me naked as
on the day I was born.[6] If you think it proper that the body in
which I have borne your children should be seen by all the people, I
shall go away naked. But in return for my virginity, which I

brought to you and cannot retrieve, I trust you will at least allow me, in addition to my dowry, to take one shift away with me.'

Gualtieri wanted above all else to burst into tears, but maintaining a stern expression he said:

'Very well, you may take a shift.'

All the people present implored Gualtieri to let her have a dress, so that she who had been his wife for thirteen years and more would not have to suffer the indignity of leaving his house in a shift, like a pauper; but their pleas were unavailing. And so Griselda, wearing a shift, barefoot, and with nothing to cover her head, having bidden them farewell, set forth from Gualtieri's house and returned to her father amid the weeping and the wailing of all who set eyes upon her.

Giannùcole, who had never thought it possible that Gualtieri would keep his daughter as his wife, and was daily expecting this to happen, had preserved the clothes she discarded on the morning Gualtieri had married her. So he brought them to her, and Griselda, having put them on, applied herself as before to the menial chores in her father's house, bravely enduring the cruel assault of hostile Fortune.

No sooner did Gualtieri drive Griselda away, than he gave his subjects to understand that he was betrothed to a daughter of one of the Counts of Panago.[7] And having ordered that grandiose preparations were to be made for the nuptials, he sent for Griselda and said to her:

'I am about to fetch home this new bride of mine, and from the moment she sets foot inside the house, I intend to accord her an honourable welcome. As you know, I have no women here who can set the rooms in order for me, or attend to many of the things that a festive occasion of this sort requires. No one knows better than you how to handle these household affairs, so I want you to make all the necessary arrangements. Invite all the ladies you need, and receive them as though you were mistress of the house. And when the nuptials are over, you can go back home to your father.'

Since Griselda was unable to lay aside her love for Gualtieri as readily as she had dispensed with her good fortune, his words pierced her heart like so many knives. But she replied:

'My lord, I am ready to do as you ask.'[8]

And so, in her coarse, thick, woollen garments, Griselda returned to the house she had quitted shortly before in her shift, and started to sweep and tidy the various chambers. On her instructions, the beds were draped with hangings, the benches in the halls were suitably adorned, the kitchen was made ready; and she set her hand, as though she were a petty serving wench, to every conceivable household task, never stopping to draw breath until she had everything prepared and arranged as befitted the occasion.

Having done all this, she caused invitations to be sent, in Gualtieri's name, to all the ladies living in those parts, and began to await the event. And when at last the nuptial day arrived, heedless of her beggarly attire, she bade a cheerful welcome to each of the lady guests, displaying all the warmth and courtesy of a lady of the manor.

Gualtieri's children having meanwhile been carefully reared by his kinswoman in Bologna, who had married into the family of the Counts of Panago, the girl was now twelve years old, the loveliest creature ever seen, whilst the boy had reached the age of six. Gualtieri had sent word to his kinswoman's husband, asking him to do him the kindness of bringing this daughter of his to Saluzzo along with her little brother, to see that she was nobly and honourably escorted, and to tell everyone he met that he was taking her to marry Gualtieri, without revealing who she really was to a living soul.

In accordance with the Marquis's request, the gentleman set forth with the girl and her brother and a noble company, and a few days later, shortly before the hour of breakfast, he arrived at Saluzzo, where he found that all the folk thereabouts, and numerous others from neighbouring parts, were waiting for Gualtieri's latest bride.

After being welcomed by the ladies, she made her way to the hall where the tables were set, and Griselda, just as we have described her, went cordially up to meet her, saying:

'My lady, you are welcome.'

The ladies, who in vain had implored Gualtieri to see that Griselda remained in another room, or to lend her one of the dresses that had once been hers, so that she would not cut such a sorry figure in front of his guests, took their seats at table and addressed themselves to the meal. All eyes were fixed upon the girl, and everyone said that Gualtieri had made a good exchange. But Griselda praised her as warmly as anyone present, speaking no less admiringly of her little brother.

Gualtieri felt that he had now seen all he wished to see of the patience of his lady, for he perceived that no event, however singular, produced the slightest change in her demeanour, and he was certain that this was not because of her obtuseness, as he knew her to be very intelligent. He therefore considered that the time had come for him to free her from the rancour that he judged her to be hiding beneath her tranquil outward expression. And having summoned her to his table, before all the people present he smiled at her and said:

'What do you think of our new bride?'

'My lord,' replied Griselda, 'I think very well of her. And if, as I believe, her wisdom matches her beauty, I have no doubt whatever that your life with her will bring you greater happiness than any gentleman on earth has ever known. But with all my heart I beg you not to inflict those same wounds upon her that you imposed upon her predecessor, for I doubt whether she could withstand them, not only because she is younger, but also because she has had a refined upbringing, whereas the other had to face continual hardship from her infancy.'

On observing that Griselda was firmly convinced that the young lady was to be his wife, and that even so she allowed no hint of resentment to escape her lips, Gualtieri got her to sit down beside him, and said:

'Griselda, the time has come for you to reap the reward of your unfailing patience, and for those who considered me a cruel and bestial tyrant, to know that whatever I have done was done of set purpose, for I wished to show you how to be a wife, to teach these people how to choose and keep a wife, and to guarantee my own peace and quiet for as long as we were living beneath the same roof. When I came to take a wife, I was greatly afraid that this peace would be denied me, and in order to prove otherwise I tormented and provoked you in the ways you have seen. But as I have never known you to oppose my wishes, I now intend, being persuaded that you can offer me all the happiness I desired, to restore to you in a single instant that which I took from you little by little, and delectably assuage the pains I have inflicted upon you. Receive with gladsome heart, then, this girl whom you believe to be my bride, and also her brother. These are our children, whom you and many others have long supposed that I caused to be cruelly murdered; and I am your husband, who loves you above all else, for I think I can boast⁹ that there is no other man on earth whose contentment in his wife exceeds my own.'

Having spoken these words, he embraced and kissed Griselda, who by now was weeping with joy; then they both got up from table and made their way to the place where their daughter sat listening in utter amazement to these tidings. And after they had fondly embraced the girl and her brother, the mystery was unravelled to her, as well as to many of the others who were present.

The ladies rose from table in transports of joy, and escorted Griselda to a chamber, where, with greater assurance of her future happiness, they divested her of her tattered garments and clothed her anew in one of her stately robes. And as their lady and their mistress, a rôle which even in her rags had seemed to be hers, they led her back to the hall, where she and Gualtieri rejoiced with the children in a manner marvellous to behold.

Everyone being delighted with the turn that events had taken, the feasting and the merrymaking were redoubled, and continued unabated for the next few days. Gualtieri was acknowledged to be very wise, though the trials to which he had subjected his lady were regarded as harsh and intolerable, whilst Griselda was accounted the wisest of all.

The Count of Panago returned a few days later to Bologna, and Gualtieri, having removed Giannùcole from his drudgery, set him up in a style befitting his father-in-law, so that he lived in great comfort and honour for the rest of his days. As for Gualtieri himself, having married off his daughter to a gentleman of renown, he lived long and contentedly with Griselda, never failing to honour her to the best of his ability.

What more needs to be said, except that celestial spirits may sometimes descend even into the houses of the poor, whilst there are those in royal palaces who would be better employed as swineherds than as rulers of men? Who else but Griselda could have endured so cheerfully the cruel and unheard of trials that Gualtieri imposed upon her without shedding a tear? For perhaps it would have served him right if he had chanced upon a wife, who, being driven from the house in her shift, had found some other man to shake her skin-coat for her, earning herself a fine new dress in the process.

* * *

Dioneo's story had ended, and the ladies, some taking one side and some another, some finding fault with one of its details and some commending another, had talked about it at length, when the king, having raised his eyes to observe that the sun had already sunk low in the evening sky, began, without getting up, to address them as follows:

'Graceful ladies, the wisdom of mortals consists, as I think you know, not only in remembering the past and apprehending the present, but in being able, through a knowledge of each, to antici- pate the future,[1] which grave men regard as the acme of human intelligence.

'Tomorrow, as you know, a fortnight will have elapsed since the day we departed from Florence to provide for our relaxation, preserve our health and our lives, and escape from the sadness, the suffering and the anguish continuously to be found in our city since this plague first descended upon it. These aims we have achieved, in my judgement, without any loss of decorum. For as far as I have been able to observe, albeit the tales related here have been amusing, perhaps of a sort to stimulate carnal desire, and we have continually partaken of excellent food and drink, played music, and sung many songs, all of which things may encourage unseemly behaviour among those who are feeble of mind, neither in word nor in deed nor in any other respect have I known either you or ourselves to be worthy of censure. On the contrary, from what I have seen and heard, it seems to me that our proceedings have been marked by a constant sense of propriety, an unfailing spirit of harmony, and a continual feeling of brotherly and sisterly amity. All of which pleases me greatly, as it surely redounds to our communal honour and credit.

'Accordingly, lest aught conducive to tedium should arise from a custom too long established, and lest, by protracting our stay, we should cause evil tongues to start wagging, I now think it proper, since we have all in turn had our share of the honour still invested in me, that with your consent we should return whence we came. If, moreover, you consider the matter carefully, our company being known to various others hereabouts, our numbers could increase in such a way as to destroy all our pleasure. And so, if my advice should command your approval, I shall retain the crown that was given me until our departure, which I propose should take effect tomorrow morning. But if you decide otherwise, I already have someone in mind upon whom to bestow the crown for the next day to follow.'

The ladies and the young men, having debated the matter at considerable length, considered the king's advice, in the end, to be sensible and just, and decided to do as he had said. He therefore sent for the steward and conferred with him with regard to the following morning's arrangements, and having dismissed the company till supper-time, he rose to his feet.

The ladies and the other young men followed suit, and turned their attention to various pastimes as usual. When it was time for supper, they disposed of the meal with infinite relish, after which they turned to singing and music and dancing. And while Lauretta was leading a dance, the king called for a song from Fiammetta, who began to sing, most charmingly, as follows:

'If love could come unmixed with jealousy
Then there is not a living woman born
Who could be merrier than I would be.

'If these effects a woman may content:
Deserving virtue and gay youthfulness;
Wisdom; fair conduct; prowess; dauntlessness;
Perfection of address; speech which doth move;

Then I should be that she, whose happiness
Is thus attained in person of my love.

'But other women are as wise as I,
I fear the worst, and tremble with dismay
Seeing those others seek to steal away
Him who has stolen mine own soul, and so
Turning my great bliss into misery
Whereat I sigh aloud and live in woe.

'Felt I his faith as equal to his worth
I would not feel this jealousy and pain.
But such his worth, and such the ways of men
And such the wiles of women who allure,
I fear that each one seeks my love to gain
And, heartsick, I would gladly death endure.

'But, in God's name, let every woman know
Not to attempt such injury on me:
For if there should be one whose flattery
Or words or gestures should entice him hence
Then may I be deformed if bitterly
I do not make her weep for her offence.'

No sooner did Fiammetta end her song, than Dioneo, who was standing beside her, laughed and said to her:

'You would be doing all the others a great kindness, madam, if you were to tell them his name, in case they unwittingly take him away from you, seeing that you are bound to be so angry about it.'

After this song of Fiammetta's, they sang a number of others, and when it was nearly midnight, they all, at the king's behest, retired to bed.

Next morning they arose at the crack of dawn, by which time all their baggage had been sent on ahead by the steward, and with their wise king leading the way they returned to Florence. Having taken their leave of the seven young ladies in Santa Maria Novella, whence they had all set out together, the three young men went off in search of other diversions; and in due course the ladies returned to their homes.

AUTHOR'S EPILOGUE

Noble young ladies, for whose solace I undertook this protracted labour, I believe that with the assistance of divine grace (the bestowal of which I impute to your compassionate prayers rather than to any merit of my own) those objectives which I set forth at the beginning of the present work have now been fully achieved. And so, after giving thanks, firstly to God and then to yourselves, the time has come for me to rest my pen and weary hand. Before conceding this repose, however, since I am fully aware that these tales of mine are no less immune from criticism than any of the other things of this world, and indeed I recall having shown this to be so at the beginning of the Fourth Day, I propose briefly to reply to certain trifling objections which, though remaining unspoken, may possibly have arisen in the minds of my readers, including one or two of yourselves.

There will perhaps be those among you who will say that in writing these stories I have taken too many liberties, in that I have sometimes caused ladies to say, and very often to hear, things which are not very suitable to be heard or said by virtuous women. This I deny, for no story is so unseemly as to prevent anyone from telling it, provided it is told in seemly language; and this I believe I may reasonably claim to have done.

But supposing you are right (for I have no wish to start a dispute with you, knowing I shall finish on the losing side), I still maintain, when you ask me why I did it, that many reasons spring readily to mind. In the first place, if any of the stories is lacking in restraint, this is because of the nature of the story itself, which, as any well-informed and dispassionate observer will readily acknowledge, I could not have related in any other way without distorting it out of all recognition. And even if the stories do, perhaps, contain one or two trifling expressions that are too unbridled for the liking of those prudish ladies who attach more weight to words than to deeds, and are more anxious to seem virtuous than to be virtuous, I assert that it was no more improper for me to have written them than for men and women at large, in their everyday speech, to use such words as *hole*, and *rod*, and *mortar*, and *pestle*, and *crumpet*, and *stuffing*, and any number of others. Besides, no less latitude should be granted to my pen than to the brush of the painter, who without incurring censure, of a justified kind at least, depicts Saint Michael striking the serpent with his sword or his lance,[1] and Saint George transfixing the dragon wherever he pleases; but that is not all, for he makes Christ male and Eve female, and fixes to the Cross, sometimes with a single nail, sometimes with two,[2] the feet of Him who resolved to die thereon for the salvation of mankind.

Furthermore it is made perfectly clear that these stories were told neither in a church, of whose affairs one must speak with a chaste mind and a pure tongue (albeit you will find that many of her chronicles are far more scandalous than any writings of mine), nor in the schools of philosophers, in which, no less than anywhere else, a sense of decorum is required, nor in any place where either churchmen or philosophers were present. They were told in gardens, in a place designed for pleasure, among people who, though young in years, were none the less fully mature and not to be led astray by stories, at a time when even the most respectable people saw nothing unseemly in wearing their breeches over their heads if they thought their lives might thereby be preserved.

Like all other things in this world, stories, whatever their nature, may be harmful or useful, depending upon the listener. Who will deny that wine, as Tosspot and Bibber and a great many others affirm, is an excellent thing for those who are hale and hearty, but harmful to people suffering from a fever? Are we to conclude, because it does harm to the feverish, that therefore it is pernicious? Who will deny that fire is exceedingly useful, not to say vital, to men and women? Are we to conclude, because it burns down houses and villages and whole cities, that therefore it is pernicious? And in the same way, weapons defend the liberty of those who desire to live peaceably, and very often they kill people, not because they are evil in themselves, but because of the evil intentions of those who make use of them.

No word, however pure, was ever wholesomely construed by a mind that was corrupt. And just as seemly language leaves no mark upon a mind that is corrupt, language that is less than seemly cannot contaminate a mind that is well ordered, any more than mud will sully the rays of the sun, or earthly filth the beauties of the heavens.

What other books, what other words, what other letters, are more sacred, more reputable, more worthy of reverence, than those of the Holy Scriptures? And yet there have been many who, by perversely construing them, have led themselves and others to perdition. All things have their own special purpose, but when they are wrongly used a great deal of harm may result, and the same applies to my stories. If anyone should want to extract evil counsel from these tales, or fashion an evil design, there is nothing to prevent him, provided he twists and distorts them sufficiently to find the thing he is seeking. And if anyone should study them for the usefulness and profit they may bring him, he will not be disappointed. Nor will they ever be thought of or described as anything but useful and seemly, if they are read at the proper time by the people for whom they were written. The lady who is forever saying her prayers, or baking pies and cakes for her father confessor, may leave my stories alone: they will not run after anyone demanding to be read, albeit they are no more improper than some of the trifles that self-righteous ladies talk about, or even engage in, if the occasion arises.

There will likewise be those among you who will say that some of the stories included here would far better have been omitted. That is as may be: but I could only transcribe the stories as they were actually told, which means that if the ladies who told them had told them better, I should have written them better. But even if one could assume that I was the inventor as well as the scribe of these stories (which was not the case), I still insist that I would not feel ashamed if some fell short of perfection, for there is no craftsman other than God whose work is whole and faultless in every respect. Even Charlemagne, who first created the Paladins, was unable to produce them in numbers sufficient to form a whole army.

Whenever you have a multitude of things you are bound to find differences of quality. No field was ever so carefully tended that neither nettles nor brambles nor thistles were found in it, along with all the better grass. Besides, in addressing an audience of unaffected young ladies, such as most of you are, it would have been foolish of me to go to the trouble of searching high and low for exquisite tales to relate, and take excessive pains in weighing my words. And the fact remains that anyone perusing these tales is free to ignore the ones that give offence, and read only those that are pleasing. For in order that none of you may be misled, each of the stories bears on its brow the gist of that which it hides in its bosom.

I suppose it will also be said that some of the tales are too long, to which I can only reply that if you have better things to do, it would be foolish to read these tales, even if they were short. Although much time has elapsed from the day I started to write until this moment, in which I am nearing the end of my labours, it has not escaped my memory that I offered these exertions of mine to ladies with time on their hands, not to any others; and for those who read in order to pass the time, nothing can be too long if it serves the purpose for which it is intended.

Brevity is all very well for students, who endeavour to use their time profitably rather than while it away, but not for you, ladies, who have as much time to spare as you fail to consume in the pleasures of love. And besides, since none of you goes to study in Athens, or Bologna, or Paris,[3] you have need of a lengthier form of address than those who have sharpened their wits with the aid of their studies.

Doubtless there are also those among you who will say that the matters I have related are overfilled with jests and quips, of a sort that no man of weight and gravity should have committed to paper. Inasmuch as these ladies, prompted by well-intentioned zeal, show a touching concern for my good name, it behoves me to thank them, and I do so.

But I would answer their objection as follows: I confess that I do have weight, and in my time I have been weighed on numerous occasions; but I assure those ladies who have never weighed me that I have little gravity. On the contrary, I am so light that I float on the surface of water. And considering that the sermons preached by friars to chastise the faults of men are nowadays filled, for the most part, with jests and quips and raillery, I concluded that the same sort of thing would be not out of place in my stories, written to dispel the woes of ladies. But if it should cause them to laugh too much, they can easily find a remedy by turning to the Lament of Jeremiah, the Passion of Our Lord, and the Plaint of the Magdalen.[4]

There may also be those among you who will say that I have an evil and venomous tongue, because in certain places I write the truth about the friars. But who cares? I can readily forgive you for saying such things, for doubtless you are prompted by the purest of motives, friars being decent fellows, who forsake a life of discomfort for the love of God,[5] who do their grinding when the millpond's full,[6] and say no more about it. Except for the fact that they all smell a little of the billy-goat,[7] their company would offer the greatest of pleasure.

I will grant you, however, that the things of this world have no stability, but are subject to constant change, and this may well have happened to my tongue. But not long ago, distrusting my own opinion (which in matters concerning myself I trust as little as possible), I was told by a lady, a neighbour of mine, that I had the finest and sweetest tongue in the world;[8] and this, to tell the truth, was at a time when few of these tales remained to be written. So because the aforementioned ladies are saying these things in order to spite me, I intend that what I have said shall suffice for my answer.

And now I shall leave each lady to say and believe whatever she may please, for the time has come for me to bring all words to an end, and offer my humble thanks to Him who assisted me in my protracted labour and conveyed me to the goal I desired. May His grace and peace, sweet ladies, remain with you always, and if perchance these stories should bring you any profit, remember me.

Here ends the Tenth and last Day of
the book called Decameron,
otherwise known as Prince Galahalt.

NOTES

PROLOGUE

1. *the book called Decameron* Following a practice adopted in several of his earlier works, B. uses a pseudo-Greek title, meaning 'Ten Days', and by a typical ironic twist, he points up the contrast between his own collection of narratives and Saint Ambrose's series of erudite allegorical sermons on the six days of the Creation, the medieval devotional text known as the *Hexaemeron* (Six Days). B.'s subtitle (*Prince Galeotto*, or *Galahalt*) is no less equivocal, being derived from the character who before B.'s own transformation of the Greek Pandarus in his narrative poem, *Filostrato*, was the archetypal go-between of medieval romance.

2. *To take pity* In accordance with one of the rules of medieval rhetoric, '*opus illustrant proverbia*' ('proverbs illustrate the work'), B. opens his book with a proverbial saying.

3. *a most noble and lofty love* Until well into the present century, this was interpreted by B.'s biographers as a reference to Maria d'Aquino, natural daughter of the Angevin ruler of Naples, King Robert, with whom the author was supposed, because of a series of cryptic references in several of his earlier works, to have had an amorous liaison. There is no clear evidence that such a lady ever existed, and it is now generally accepted that in claiming to have loved a woman of royal birth, B. was simply following a well-established precept of medieval Love theorists, in particular Andreas Capellanus.

4. *a hundred stories or fables or parables or histories* The Italian reads '*cento favole o parabole o istorie*', a phrase that happens to summarize the known sources of many of the *Decameron*'s stories: French *fabliaux*, Latin *exempla* and Italian historical chronicles. See Translator's Introduction, p.lviii.

FIRST DAY

(Introduction)

1. *the end of mirth is heaviness* B. is quoting from Proverbs xiv, 13: 'Even in laughter the heart is sorrowful; and the end of that mirth is heaviness.' But the whole of this opening paragraph, with its references to 'an irksome and ponderous opening', 'this grim beginning', and the

'steep and rugged hill, beyond which there lies a beautiful and delectable plain', signals the author's intention to write a work conforming to the rules of a particular literary genre. Dante's visionary journey from the sorrows of Hell to the joys of Paradise had been chronicled in his great epic poem, the *Commedia*. Italian commentators often refer to B.'s work as the Human Comedy, the secular counterpart to Dante's *Divine Comedy*. But the distinction is misleading, implying as it does that Dante's concern with the secular world is less evident, which is patently absurd.

2. *the deadly pestilence*   Nowadays known in Northern Europe as the Black Death, the plague of 1347 to 1351 is thought to have reduced the total population by one third, causing enormous damage to established social institutions. B.'s famous description of its ruinous effects in Florence in 1348, graphic and convincing though it may appear, is not to be read as the eyewitness account he claims it to be. It is in fact based upon earlier plague descriptions, in particular the one found in the eighth-century *Historia Langobardorum* by Paulus Diaconus ('Paul the Deacon'). Confirmation that it should be read as a literary artefact is found in its concluding paragraph ('Ah, how great a number of splendid palaces,' etc., p. 13), where the writing is heavily loaded with rhetorical devices such as anaphora and a variant of the *ubi sunt* motif of classical literature.

3. **Galen, Hippocrates and Aesculapius**   Galen (AD 129–199) was the founder of experimental physiology, whilst Hippocrates (*c.* 460–*c.* 377 BC) is traditionally regarded as the father of medicine. Aesculapius (or Asclepius), on the other hand, was a mythical figure, the Graeco-Roman god of medicine. It was common for the three names to be linked by medieval writers whenever medical authority required to be invoked.

4. *seven young ladies*   The occult significance of numbers, a regular feature of medieval literature, is much in evidence in the *Decameron*. The seven ladies are clearly symbolic, if only because none is married yet all are older than the normal marriageable age of between fourteen and seventeen. The range of their ages ('none was older than twenty-seven or younger than eighteen') is itself significant, both limits being multiples of nine, the so-called golden number. Their unswerving propriety, to which B. refers at regular intervals, makes it probable that he intended the female members of his group of storytellers to represent the four cardinal virtues (Prudence, Justice, Temperance, Fortitude) and the three theological virtues (Faith, Hope, Love).

5. **Santa Maria Novella**   The scene for the beginning of the frame story (in preference, say, to a more centrally located church such as the Florentine

cathedral, or Duomo) was probably selected because of the association of its name with the telling of a story, or *novella*.

6. *man is the head of woman* See Ephesians (v, 23): 'For the husband is the head of the wife.' It has become fashionable in recent years to think of B. as a feminist writer *ante litteram*. At times, however, passages like these suggest that he was no more feminist than Saint Paul.

7. *three young men* No less symbolic numerically than the seven young ladies, whom they complement to make up the perfect number of ten, the three young men possibly represent the tripartite division of the soul into Reason (Panfilo), Anger (Filostrato) and Lust (Dioneo).

8. *the spot in question* On the basis of the details supplied by the writer, scholars have attempted to identify the exact location of the first of the storytellers' country retreats. But the place is imaginary. The seemingly realistic description conceals B.'s expert handling of the literary topos known as the *locus amænus*. Other, more elaborate examples are seen in the Introduction to the Third Day and the Conclusion of the Sixth Day.

9. *Dioneo's manservant, Parmeno* By giving the seven servants names that are associated with the lower social orders in classical literature, more especially in the Hellenistic comedies of Terence and Plautus, B. further heightens the sense of distance separating the world of the frame from that of the narratives.

10. *on the stroke of tierce* Medieval writers generally use one of the canonical hours, such as Matins, Tierce (or Terce), Sext, Nones, Vespers and Compline, to indicate the time of day. Tierce is recited at the third hour after sunrise. At the equinox it corresponds roughly to 9.00 a.m.

11. *shortly after nones* Nones is the canonical office recited at the ninth hour of the day, about 3.00 p.m.

First Story

1. *Musciatto Franzesi* Like many of the other characters in the *Decameron*, those appearing in this first story are based on actual people. Fourteenth-century chroniclers relate that Musciatto, a Florentine financier, made a huge fortune in France, chiefly through advising the French king, Philip the Fair, to counterfeit coinage and fleece Italian merchants. Cepperello Dietaiuti of Prato was one of his business associates. The military expedition into Italy, encouraged by Pope Boniface VIII, of King Philip's brother, Charles of Valois ('Carlo Senzaterra', or Charles Lackland) took place in 1301. One of its most famous consequences was the banishment and exile from Florence of Dante Alighieri.

2. *Ciappelletto*   In order to follow this long-winded explanation of the character's name, the English reader should bear in mind that *-etto*, like *-ello*, is a diminutive suffix, and that B. possibly thought the name Cepperello was derived from *ceppo* ('log' or 'tree-stump'), whereas it was almost certainly a diminutive form of Ciapo, or Jacopo. On the other hand it is possible that a sexual allusion was intended (Cepperello = 'little log' or 'little prick'). Either way, Cepperello was a far more appropriate name for this incorrigible scoundrel than Ciappelletto ('chaplet' or 'garland').

3. *flung into the moat like a dog*   According to the Florentine chronicler Giovanni Villani (*c.* 1275–1348), it was common practice for the bodies of suicides, heretics, and excommunicates to be thrown into the moat surrounding the walls of the city.

4. *these Lombard dogs*   In France, as in England, a Lombard was anyone who came from the northern part of Italy, including Tuscany. Lombard Street in London and the Rue des Lombards in Paris bear witness to the connection between such Italian expatriates and the world of banking and commerce.

5. *Soon after vespers*   Vespers, the sixth of the canonical hours, is recited or sung towards evening.

Second Story

1. *in Paris . . . difficulties?*   Paris in the Middle Ages was considered to be the focal point of all knowledge, especially in the fields of philosophy and theology.

2. *could prevent me from becoming a Christian*   The reasons Abraham gives for becoming a Christian are similar to those found in various earlier accounts of Jews or Saracens unexpectedly converted to the Christian faith.

3. *Nôtre Dame de Paris*   The most famous Gothic cathedral of the Middle Ages, a fitting location for Abraham's conversion and baptism.

Third Story

1. *Melchizedek*   B.'s Melchizedek (literally 'king of justice') became the model for similar figures in later literature, notably the main character in Gotthold Lessing's *Nathan der Weise* (1779). The parable of the wise Jew was a popular subject in medieval literature, as was the story of the three rings, which had appeared in the earlier collection of tales known as *Il novellino*. A notable feature of B.'s version is that, like other stories in the

Decameron (e.g. I, 7 and V, 9) it is emboxed within a narrative already itself emboxed.

2. **Saladin** Of Kurdish origin, the Muslim leader Salah ad-Din (1137–93), popularly known as Saladin, gained enormous respect and popularity in the Christian world for his diplomacy, military genius, scholarliness, and generosity of spirit. The last of these qualities is splendidly celebrated in the *Decameron*'s penultimate narrative (X, 9). In the *Commedia*, Dante had placed Saladin in the area of Limbo reserved for the souls of virtuous Pagans.

Fourth Story

1. **Dioneo** Significantly, the first of the *Decameron*'s salacious tales is told by the most extrovert member of the *brigata*. After the first day, he secures the privilege of telling the tenth and last story each day, invariably choosing a narrative that is to a greater or lesser degree improper. He it is who presides over the seventh day's storytelling, devoted to the ingenious stratagems of adulterous wives.

2. **Lunigiana** A mountainous region of north-west Tuscany, stretching down from the border with Emilia-Romagna to the Ligurian Sea. There is evidence to suggest that in choosing the location for this story, B. may have had in mind the Benedictine priory of Santa Croce del Corvo, north of Lerici.

Fifth Story

1. **Montferrat** A region now in northern Italy, lying south of Turin, on the direct route between France and the major Italian seaport of Genoa. In the Middle Ages, it was an independent march, or marquisate.

2. **a Crusade to the Holy Land** The aim of the Third Crusade (1189–92) was the recapture of Jerusalem, which had fallen to Saladin's armies in 1187. The crusaders failed to achieve their objective. B.'s story is set a few months before March 1191, when King Philippe, en route to the Holy Land, signed a treaty of alliance in Sicily with Richard I ('Lionheart') of England.

3. **Philippe Le Borgne** Philip Augustus II of France ('Le Borgne', or 'one-eyed') embarked at Genoa for the Third Crusade at the end of August 1190. The ruler of Montferrat at that time was Guglielmo il Vecchio, whose wife, Giulia of Austria, already over seventy years old, was unlikely to have stirred Philip's amorous inclinations. Guglielmo died in 1191, to be succeeded by his son Corrado degli Aleramici, who had left for the Holy Land several years earlier, becoming famous for his defence of Jerusalem

and Tyre. Corrado was a widower at the time of his marriage in Constantinople in 1187 to Theodora, the sister of the Emperor. Theodora never set foot in Montferrat. Philip is in any case known to have arrived in Genoa, not by the way of Montferrat, but via the Riviera. The intermingling of fact and fantasy is a recurrent feature of the *Decameron*'s narratives.

Sixth Story

1. *an inquisitor*   The papal Inquisition for the apprehension and trial of heretics has a longer history than is commonly supposed. It was instituted by Pope Gregory IX in 1231. The use of torture to obtain confessions was first authorized by Innocent IV in 1252. Those found guilty of heresy could be sentenced to a wide range of penalties, from simple prayer and fasting to the confiscation of property and imprisonment.

2. *cum gladiis et fustibus*   'with swords and staves'. The phrase is biblical (see Matthew xxvi, 47).

3. *Saint John Golden-Mouth*   Saint John Chrysostom, the fourth-century Archbishop of Constantinople, earned his nickname (Gr. *chrysos* ['gold'] + *stoma* ['mouth']) through the clarity of his preaching. In its italianized form, the name San Giovanni Boccadoro was used by medieval satirists to connote the money-grubbing practices of the clergy.

4. *an Epicurean*   In the medieval mind, Epicurus (341–270 BC) was associated with the denial of the immortality of the soul. Dante's circle of the heretics is a cemetery of flaming tombs, containing the souls of 'Epicurus and all his followers, who make the soul die with the body' ('*con Epicuro tutt' i suoi seguaci, /che l'anima col corpo morta fanno*') (*Inferno*, X, 14–15).

5. *'it was that passage ... hundredfold'*   See Matthew xix, 29: 'And everyone that hath forsaken houses, or brethren, or sisters, or father, or mother, or wife, or children, or lands, for my name's sake, shall receive an hundredfold, and shall inherit everlasting life.'

Seventh Story

1. *Can Grande della Scala*   Lord of Verona from 1311 to 1329, Can Grande was the younger brother of Bartolomeo della Scala, the 'great Lombard' with whom Dante had taken refuge in the early years of his exile. Can Grande is eulogized by Dante (*Paradiso*, XVII, 76–93) for both his military prowess and his outstanding generosity.

2. *Frederick the Second*   King of Sicily (1197–1250), Duke of Swabia (1228–35), German King (1212–50), and Holy Roman Emperor (1220–50),

Frederick II was arguably the most powerful ruler in medieval European history. A patron and practitioner of the arts, he attracted numerous poets and men of letters to his court, which was the focal point of the earliest Italian school of poetry, the so-called Scuola Siciliana. His liberality became a byword among generations of later writers.

3. *Primas*   A canon of Cologne, Primas achieved a wide reputation in the first half of the thirteenth century as a witty and spontaneous Latin versifier. Under the name of Golias he composed a number of popular student songs. He was much in demand as an entertainer of prelates and princes.

4. *Cluny*   The Benedictine abbey at Cluny in Burgundy, founded in 910 by Duke William the Pious of Aquitaine, became legendary in the Middle Ages for its wealth and its patronage of the arts.

Eighth Story

1. *Ermino de' Grimaldi*   The Grimaldis were one of the oldest and most powerful patrician families in the Genoese republic. No Ermino de' Grimaldi is recorded as head of the family in the city's archives. B. seems to have invented the character to illustrate the miserliness of the Genoese in general, which was (and still is) proverbial. In a later story (II, 4) the Genoese are described (p. 93) as 'a rapacious, money-grubbing set of people'.

2. *Guiglielmo Borsiere*   Guiglielmo Borsiere had been named in Dante's *Inferno* (XVI, 70) as a recent newcomer to the circle where punishment is being inflicted on the souls of homosexuals who had gained distinction for military valour and impeccable manners. The reference to Borsiere leads straight into Dante's famous denunciation of the Florentine *nouveaux riches*, who had brought shame upon the city by their arrogance and materialism ('*La gente nova e' subiti guadagni/orgoglio e dismisura han generata,/Fiorenza, in te, si che tu già ten piagni*' – 'Upstarts and quick profits have generated such pride and excess in you, Florence, as to make you weep'). The fiercely admonitory tone of the episode from the *Inferno* doubtless explains B.'s own apparently irrelevant diatribe at this point against the ill manners of his contemporaries.

Ninth Story

1. *the first King of Cyprus*   Guy de Lusignan, dispossessed King of Jerusalem, was installed as the island's first monarch in 1191 by Richard I

'Lionheart', who had conquered the island on his way to the Third Crusade. Guy was a notoriously weak and incapable ruler. So too, however, was Godfrey of Bouillon, who assumed the title of Defender of the Holy Sepulchre (*Advocatus Sancti Sepulchri*) after Jerusalem had fallen a century earlier, in 1090, to the Christian armies of the First Crusade. The anachronistic reference to Godfrey is superfluous to the narrative unless B. intended his story, the shortest in the *Decameron*, to be read as a warning against the consequences of weak government in general.

Tenth Story

1. **Master Alberto**   The character is probably based on a famous Bolognese physician and academic of the time, Alberto de' Zancari, who was born around 1280 and was still alive towards the end of 1348. His second wife was called Margherita, which is the name B. gives to the female protagonist of his tale. A similar theme (the failed attempt of a younger woman to taunt an elderly admirer) is treated in VIII, 7, but whereas here the scholar's reproof is administered with the utmost delicacy, in the later story, violently anti-feminist, the woman is punished with extreme cruelty and vindictiveness.

(Conclusion)

1. **to restrict the matter of our storytelling**   From now on, with the exception of the ninth day, each of the remaining days will be devoted to the narration of stories on a single prescribed topic. Even the stories already told, those of the first day, have certain unifying elements. All depend for their effect on a display of eloquence or quick-wittedness on the part of the main character. All involve the reversal of the outcome that characters (and readers) have been led to anticipate.

SECOND DAY

First Story

1. **Saint Arrigo**   The main characters in the story are fictive reconstructions of actual people. A church chronicler of the period reports that the Blessed Arrigo had led a blameless life working as a porter in Treviso. The same writer claims that when Arrigo died, on 10 June 1315, his body was

taken into the cathedral and that contact with his corpse wrought various miracles, including the healing of a paralytic. His tomb in the cathedral of Treviso still bears an inscription claiming that the cathedral bells rang of their own accord at the moment of his death. Stecchi and Martellino were two notoriously bawdy Florentine travelling clowns, or *buffoni*, who specialized in mimicry and impersonation. The story itself contains obvious echoes of the accounts found in Mark ii, 2 and Luke v, 19 of the man stricken with the palsy who is at first prevented from reaching Jesus by the throng of people surrounding him.

2. *swarming with Germans* Compatriots, presumably, of Arrigo, who had been born in Bolzano, where German was and still is the main vehicle of communication.

3. *out of the frying-pan . . . straight in the fire* The translation is literal. B.'s use of the proverbial saying pre-dates its first recorded English appearance, in Sir Thomas More's treatise on heresy (1528), by nearly two centuries.

Second Story

1. *Saint Julian's paternoster* A popular prayer in the Middle Ages, especially among travellers, Julian being their patron saint. Saint Julian ('Julian the Hospitaller') had his origins in medieval romance rather than historical reality. His story is told in the *Legenda aurea* (*Golden Legend*), a collection of so-called lives of saints compiled by Jacques de Voragine in the thirteenth century, where Julian is described as a nobleman who through a mistake of identity killed his own father and mother. He expiated his unwitting crime by going to live with his wife beside a ford across a river, where they assisted travellers and built a refuge for the poor. As B.'s text makes clear (p. 77), his 'paternoster' included 'reciting an Our Father and a Hail Mary for the souls of Saint Julian's father and mother' and ended with a prayer to God and the saint for a good night's lodging. Implicit within the good night's lodging was the provision of an attractive sleeping companion.

2. *a war in the countryside* Probably an allusion to the struggle between Azzo VIII of Ferrara and his brother Francesco over hereditary rights, brought about by the former's marriage to Beatrice of Anjou in 1305.

3. *as if he had been turned into a stork* The expression, used by Dante (*Inferno*, XXXII, 34–6), occurs again in the story of the scholar and the widow (*Decameron*, VIII, 7). The noise made by storks with their beaks is similar to the sound of chattering teeth.

Third Story

1. *Agolanti*   The Florentine merchant in the previous tale was called Sandro Agolanti. The profession with which the Agolanti family was associated was moneylending.

2. *a totally unexpected war.* Unusually for B., the historical framework of this story is as shaky and improbable as the plot itself. The 'unexpected war' referred to at one point in the narrative is possibly the rebellion against Henry II led by his sons, Henry and Richard, in 1173. But in 1173 the King of Scotland was William I, still only thirty years old, who would hardly fit the pseudo-Abbot's description of him as 'a very old man'. Other features of the tale suggest a period closer to Boccaccio's own day, possibly during the turbulent reign (1307–27) of Edward II, marked by continuous conflicts including his defeat at Bannockburn in 1314. A more plausible candidate as the princess's prospective husband would therefore be Robert the Bruce, who by 1327 was in his early fifties and suffering from the terminal illness, possibly leprosy, which led to his death in 1329.

3. *Bruges*   The main Florentine banking houses, the Bardi and the Peruzzi, had branches in Bruges, which during the fourteenth century established itself as the mercantile metropolis of Europe.

4. *Earl of Cornwall*   The choice of name suggests a possible association between the bestowal by Edward II of this title on his favourite, Piers Gaveston, and the homosexual overtones of the encounter between Alessandro and the Abbot ('The Abbot . . . began to caress him in the manner of a young girl fondling her lover, causing Alessandro to suspect . . . that the youth was possibly in the grip of some impure passion', p. 88).

5. *he later conquered Scotland*   Alexander (*italice* Alessandro) was the name of three Scottish kings, of whom the last, Alexander III, was married when he was ten to the eleven-year-old daughter of the King of England, Henry III. Neither he nor his predecessors was of Italian origin, but the marriage of a later Scottish king, Edward de Balliol, to a niece of King Robert of Naples around 1331 (when B. was moving in Angevin courtly circles there) offers a possible clue to the unravelling of the tale's Scottish connection.

Fourth Story

1. *the Amalfi coast*   In this fond description of the Amalfi coast, south of Naples, there is more than a hint of the nostalgia B. was known to have experienced for the playground of the Neapolitan nobility, with whom he

associated during the years he spent as a young Florentine businessman in
the Angevin capital.

2. *Ravello* A small town in the hills above Amalfi, where B. had a
number of friends including the grammarian Angelo di Ravello. Its cathedral contains an ornate pulpit dedicated to the Rufolo family, who lived
nearby in one of several stately palaces with extensive gardens overlooking
the Amalfi coast. The hero of B.'s tale is based on one Lorenzo Rufolo, who
after losing the favour of the Angevin king turned to piracy before being
captured and imprisoned in a castle in Calabria, where he died in 1291.

3. *the Archipelago* i.e. the Greek Archipelago, in the Aegean.

4. *two large Genoese carracks* Carracks were large merchant ships. It was
usual for them to be heavily armed like the ocean-going galleons of the
fifteenth and sixteenth centuries.

Fifth Story

1. *The Fleshpots* In Italian, *Malpertugio* ('Evil Hole'), a district near the
commercial centre of Naples which took its name from an aperture in
the city walls that provided a shortcut to the harbour. It was notorious in the
thirteenth and fourteenth centuries as the city's red-light quarter.

2. *a supporter of the Guelphs . . . King Charles . . . King Frederick* The
reference is to the struggles between the dynasties of Anjou and Aragon for
control of Naples and Sicily in the late thirteenth and early fourteenth
centuries. Charles I of Anjou, with the support of the papacy, had conquered
Naples and Sicily in the 1260s, putting an end to the last representatives of
the Hohenstaufen dynasty. The uprising known as the Sicilian Vespers
against the harsh rule of Charles I in 1282 led to the expulsion of the French
and their Guelph adherents from the island and the advent of the Aragonese,
who, supported by the Ghibellines, eventually proclaimed Frederick III as
King of Sicily in 1296. B.'s tale is set at a later date, some years after the
treaty of Caltabellotta (1302), under which the King of Naples, Charles II,
agreed to give up his claim to Sicily after a series of abortive attempts to
restore the Angevins to power in the island. It is presumably to one of these
failed conspiracies that the lady's embroidered account of her marriage to a
Guelph-supporting Sicilian relates.

3. *Greek wine* A white wine that was popular in southern Italy.

4. *Madonna Fiordaliso* The name of the Sicilian courtesan ('Fleur-de-lis')
has similar floral associations to that of Madonna Jancofiore, her close
counterpart in a later story (VIII, 10), who is also Sicilian. The two
characters were probably based on a Sicilian lady reported in a document of

1341 as living in a house in the Neapolitan Malpertugio quarter, a certain Madonna Flora, whose acquaintance B. may well have made when relaxing from his duties as a young banking official in the city.

5. *Ruga Catalana*   An important thoroughfare leading from the harbour to the upper part of the city, deriving its name from the numerous Catalan expatriates who occupied influential positions at the Angevin court.

6. *Butch Belchfire*   The Italian reads '*il scarabone Buttafuoco*', literally 'the villain Flingfire'. The surname can still be found in Sicily. A document dated May 1336 from the Neapolitan royal archives records that a Sicilian named Francesco Buttafuoco, recently deceased, had received an income for loyal services to the Angevin cause. Like Madonna Flora, he may possibly have been a prototype for one of B.'s characters in this, the most Neapolitan of his stories.

7. *Filippo Minutolo*   Because the archbishop Minutolo died on 24 October 1301, it is theoretically possible to date the events of the novella with absolute precision. But the stifling heat which had caused Andreuccio to remove all his clothes in the Sicilian lady's bedroom suggests high summer rather than late autumn. The mingling of historical fact with literary fiction is a characteristic of many of B.'s narratives.

Sixth Story

1. *Manfred*   The last of the Hohenstaufen emperors, Manfred was in fact crowned King of Sicily (i.e. the whole of southern Italy, including Naples) in August 1258, eight years after the death of Frederick II. As protector of the Italian Ghibellines, his rule was marked by bitter conflict with the papacy. Pope Clement IV offered the Sicilian throne to Charles of Anjou, who, having sailed for Rome in May 1265, defeated Manfred's armies near Benevento in February 1266. The circumstances of Manfred's death at Benevento are recalled by Dante in a memorably dramatic episode of the *Commedia* (*Purgatorio*, III, 103–45).

2. *Capece . . . Caracciolo*   Two leading families of the Neapolitan aristocracy. History records no Arrighetto Capece, but Corrado Capece was Manfred's governor-general in the island of Sicily up to the time of Manfred's death in 1266. He afterwards led an uprising in Sicily against the Angevin rule, and was captured, defenestrated and hanged in Catania. Contemporary records indicate that his wife was named Biancofiore or Beritola, a lady from a branch of the Caracciolo family, also opposed to Angevin rule.

3. *Lipari . . . Ponza*   Both Lipari and Ponza are the chief islands of a group, the first some twenty-five miles north of the Sicilian coast, the second about seventy-five miles west of the Bay of Naples. In describing Ponza as

uninhabited at the time of his narrative, B. is engaging in poetic licence.

4. **Currado** Conrad II Malaspina, Marquis of Villafranca, who died in 1294, is celebrated by Dante (*Purgatorio*, VIII, 109–39) for his chivalric virtues of liberality and military valour. The Malaspina rulers of the Lunigiana, being supporters of the Ghibelline cause, would naturally have offered refuge to a fugitive from the Angevins, which is why B. weaves them into his charming but unhistorical fiction.

5. **Cavriuola** i.e. doe, or female deer.

6. **Guasparrino d'Oria** The d'Oria or Doria family, prominent in Genoese political, military and economic life from the twelfth century onwards was, like the Malaspina family, Ghibelline in its political sympathies. There is no record of a Guasparrino d'Oria during the period in which the events of the novella are supposed to have occurred. Piracy and slave-trading were common practices among Genoese seafarers.

7. **Dismayed ... by what he saw** The motif of a father discovering his daughter *in flagrante* with a young lover is one that B. exploits elsewhere in the *Decameron*, for instance in the tragic tale of Tancred and Ghismonda (IV, 1) and in the richly humorous account of Caterina's capture of the nightingale (V, 4).

8. **a rebellion in Sicily** Clearly a reference to the Sicilian Vespers, the uprising of March 1282, led by Giovanni da Procida and supported by Peter III of Aragon, that forced the Angevins out of Sicily. The 'fourteen long years' of which Giannotto later speaks to his gaoler should in fact have been sixteen if (as implied earlier in the story) his misfortunes began with Manfred's defeat at Benevento in 1266. But historical accuracy is not one of the tale's strong points.

9. **When the chaste and joyful greetings had been repeated three or four times** A direct quotation from the opening lines of canto VII of Dante's *Purgatorio* ('*Poscia che l'accoglienze oneste e liete/furo iterate tre e quattro volte*'). The text of the *Decameron* contains many such examples of the insertion of familiar quotations from earlier poets, especially Dante, a practice later commended by the stylistic theorists of the Renaissance.

10. **Lerici** A port in Lunigiana near the mouth of the River Magra, where travellers from Genoa and other 'distant' parts were accustomed to disembark en route to Tuscany and Emilia.

Seventh Story

1. **Beminedab** Thought to be based on the biblical Amminadab fleetingly mentioned in the Book of Numbers and in Saint Matthew's Gospel, this fictitious name is used by other medieval writers to indicate an oriental ruler

of an indeterminate epoch. The name has mildly humorous associations.

2. *Alatiel*   Like Beminedab, the name is fictitious, but it happens to be an anagram of La Lieta ('The Happy Woman'), offering a possible clue to the way in which the story is intended to be read.

3. *the King of Algarve*   Algarve, from the Arabic *al-Gharb*, meaning 'the West', was a much more extensive region than the area of that name in modern Portugal. It corresponded roughly to northern Morocco, including a long stretch of the African Mediterranean coast, and the south-western part of the Iberian peninsula. Its wool was greatly prized in European markets. B.'s employers, the Compagnia dei Bardi, imported wool from Algarve via a trading post on the island of Majorca, where Alatiel's sexual odyssey begins.

4. *neither he nor they could understand what the other party was saying*   A recurrent feature of Alatiel's sexual encounters is her inability to communicate verbally with her various abductors. In an absorbing analysis of this particular novella, Guido Almansi argues that 'Alatiel is not "a beautiful woman". She is a superhuman figure; mythic, or at least closely related to a myth. Even her linguistic isolation can be read as an ambivalent sign . . . On the one hand, her complete ignorance of West European languages is convincing from a narrative standpoint, and serves to give special emphasis to the gesticulations of the characters . . . Yet her non-communication is also . . . a sign standing for Alatiel's isolation, which is due to her superhuman features. Any mating with a mythic character must take place in silence, because there can exist no dialogue, no normative vocabulary, for the relationship between man and myth.' (*The Writer as Liar*, p. 124.)

5. *Alexandrian fashion*   Presumably the Egyptian *danse du ventre*, which would explain the boosting of Pericone's expectations.

6. *Corinth in the Pelopponese*   The Italian text reads '*Chiarenza in Romania*'. It was customary to refer to the whole of the Eastern Roman Empire as Romania. Chiarenza is an italianized form of Corinth.

7. *Saint Stiffen-in-the-Hand*   The Italian text reads '*santo Cresci in Man*' ('Saint Grow-in-Hand'), an equivocal phallic metaphor of which the variant '*san Cresci in Val Cava*' ('Saint-Grow-in-Hollow-Vale') turns up towards the end of the story (p. 145) in the false account that Alatiel gives to her father of her wanderings. The latter phrase, in common use among humorous poets, was not invented by them, but was the actual name of a sanctuary in the Mugello, a mountainous region to the north-east of Florence.

8. *Prince of Morea*   Morea, the name given in the fourteenth century to the Peloponnese (that part of the Greek mainland lying south of the Gulf of Corinth), had dynastic ties with the Angevin rulers of Naples. B.'s friend, Niccola Acciaiuoli, spent three years there (1338–41) assisting Catherine of

Valois-Courtenay (a descendant of Baldwin II, the last Latin emperor of Constantinople) to establish her claim to the province of Achaea on the north coast of the Peloponnese.

9. *Duke of Athens*   The title, like that of the Prince of Morea, has encouraged one or two commentators to speculate that the story carries allegorical overtones, Alatiel representing the desirability and impermanence of political power. Walter of Brienne, Duke of Athens, was set up as ruler of Florence in 1342 by the Bardi and Peruzzi banking companies in an attempt to restore their fortunes after making huge losses on loans to Edward III of England and Robert of Naples. He was deposed by the *popolo minuto* (lesser guilds and merchants) in 1343. B. had made Walter's personal acquaintance in Naples when the latter was preparing an expedition to assert his territorial claims in Greece.

10. *Aegina*   The island in the Saronic Gulf, some thirty miles south-west of Athens.

11. *Chios*   Island in the eastern Aegean, five miles from the west coast of Turkey.

12. *Uzbek*   Not, as B. claims, the King of the Turks, but the Khan of the Golden Horde of southern Russia. He reigned from 1313 to 1341, establishing friendly relations with both Islam and Christendom. He encouraged the growth of trade between the Crimea and the Italian maritime republics. Naturally there is no connection, except for the name, between the Russian ruler and the character in the story.

13. *the King of Cappadocia, Basano*   Both the name, Basano, and his title are fictitious. B. probably chose Cappadocia, a strategically important province in Asia Minor, because of its remoteness and its classical literary associations. The name Basano may conceivably reflect that of a chamberlain to King Robert of Naples, Baldon Bassano, who was active at one time on behalf of the Angevins in the eastern Mediterranean.

14. *Aiguesmortes*   A port on the Provençal coast some twenty miles east of Montpelier, Aiguesmortes was a popular trading centre for Italian merchants from Florence and Genoa. The name (literally 'dead waters') stands in marked and significant contrast with the stormy waters over which Alatiel has travelled in her sexual odyssey.

15. *'A kissed mouth ... new again'*   Though the saying (*'Bocca basciata non perde ventura, anzi rinnuova come fa la luna'*) may indeed have become proverbial in Italy, this is its first recorded appearance in literature.

Eighth Story

1. *Roman imperial authority*   The title of Holy Roman Emperor passed

from French into German hands in 962, with the coronation in Rome of Otto I of Saxony. The historical setting of the tale is imprecise, however. There are numerous antecedents in both classical and medieval literature for B.'s account of the vindictiveness of a woman spurned. It is possible, however, that the initial inspiration for his tale came from Dante's reference in *Purgatorio* (VI, 19–24) to the fate of Pierre de la Brosse, whose soul was 'severed from its body' by the 'hatred and envy' of the Lady of Brabant. According to popular tradition, Mary of Brabant, the second wife of Philip III of France, wrongly accused Pierre de la Brosse, the king's surgeon, of attempting to rape her. Pierre was charged with treason and hanged in 1278.

2. *Violante* The name is one that B. gave to one of his own children, born around 1349, whose death at the age of six or seven is tenderly commemorated by the poet in one of his Latin eclogues.

3. *Strangford* Strangford Lough, a sheltered inlet of the Irish Sea on the coast of Ulster, was well known in the Middle Ages as a point of entry into Ireland.

4. *returned to England* More precisely to Wales, but for B., as for most Italians of the present day, Wales (like Scotland and Northern Ireland) forms part of *Inghilterra*. Even Branca describes Wales as 'the western region of England' ('*la regione occidentale dell'Inghilterra*').

5. *the new King reopened hostilities* The imprecision of the tale's historical framework is further underlined by the fact that none of the happenings recorded in this paragraph corresponds with any identifiable historical event.

Ninth Story

1. *they drew up a form of contract* Wagers concerning a wife's fidelity, a commonplace topic in medieval and Renaissance literature, formed what is nowadays known as the '*cycle de la gageure*' ('wager cycle'). The similarities between B.'s story and the sub-plot of Shakespeare's *Cymbeline* are so obvious as to suggest a direct connection between the two. In Shakespeare's play, Posthumus, exiled in Rome, wagers Imogen's chastity against Iachimo's boast that he will seduce her. Iachimo, having hidden in a trunk in Imogen's bedroom, emerges as she sleeps and observes a mole on her breast, memorizes details of the room's furnishings and steals a bracelet. Posthumus, incensed by the apparent evidence of his wife's infidelity, sails for England with the intention of killing her. But it is almost certain that the source of the wager-plot in *Cymbeline* was *Frederyke of Jennen*, a translation from a fifteenth-century German version of B.'s story.

2. *a mole, surrounded by a few strands of fine, golden hair*   Shakespeare transforms this prosaic anatomical detail into 'A mole cinque-spotted, like the crimson drops/I' the bottom of a cowslip' (*Cymbeline*, II, ii).

3. *Albenga*   A harbour on the Ligurian coast a few miles west of Finale Ligure, the town from which Zinevra takes her assumed name of Sicurano da Finale. Branca prefers the reading *Alba*, explaining that this was the old name for Albisola, a harbour slightly north-east of Savona.

Tenth Story

1. *a city where most of the women look as ugly as sin*   The ugliness of Pisan women, like the miserliness of Genoese men (see I, 8), was proverbial among Florentines.

2. *vernaccia*   A white wine, thought to possess medicinal qualities (see X, 2), but here presumably brought into the narrative as a supposed aphrodisiac.

3. *a calendar . . . of the sort that was once in use in Ravenna*   Ravenna was said to have as many churches as the number of days in the year, with the result that the city celebrated an extraordinary number of Saints' days.

4. *the four Ember weeks*   Specifically, the weeks following the first Sunday in Lent, Whitsunday, 14 September, and 13 December.

5. *Montenero*   A promontory some twenty miles south of Pisa.

6. *Monaco*   The principality was a notorious haven for pirates in the fourteenth century. The only other story in the *Decameron* that includes a reference to Monaco is VIII, 10, where the chief character, Salabaetto, claims that one of his ships has been seized by Monegasque pirates.

7. *mortar sin . . . pestle sin*   Bartolomea is deliberately punning on her husband's reference to mortal sin, using a sexual metaphor that reappears in the story of Monna Belcolore (VIII, 2).

8. *There's never any rest for the bar*   The Italian text reads '*Il mal furo non vuol far festa*,' literally 'The wicked hole refuses to take a holiday.' As elsewhere in the story, B. is engaging in gentle mockery of Pisan pronunciation. The sexual pun of the original is made possible because *furo*, the equivalent of Florentine *foro*, can refer both to the vagina and to the bar, or legal profession. The translation exploits the sexual connotation of 'bar' in American English.

(Conclusion)

1. *tomorrow is Friday and the next day is Saturday*   For the reasons spelled out here by Neifile, there is no storytelling on the last two days of

the week. Hence the retreat of the storytellers to the countryside includes
four days of ablutions, rest and prayer as well as the ten days of storytelling.
It should be noted that the 'Sabbath' in fourteenth-century Florence ran
from noon on Saturday to noon on Sunday, noon being taken to mean the
ninth hour of the day after sunrise.

2. *to avoid being joined by others* As at other points in the *Decameron*,
stress is laid upon the need of the group to distance itself from the world
outside.

THIRD DAY

(Introduction)

1. *before tierce was half spent* Less than an hour and a half after sunrise.
2. *a most beautiful and ornate palace* The description of the second *locus
amœnus* differs from that of the first chiefly in the extended account of the
beauties of the walled garden. The connection between the garden and the
earthly paradise, or Garden of Eden, becomes explicit with the writer's
assertion (p.191) that 'if Paradise were constructed on earth, it was inconceivable that it could take any other form.'

First Story

1. *slung an axe over his shoulder* The narrative detail of the axe, repeated
at the end of the story, when read in conjunction with the various
references to Masetto's tending of the nuns' garden, has obvious phallic
overtones.

Second Story

1. *wisdom . . . guile* This story can be read as a caustic commentary on
the concept of honour, with intelligence as a prominent secondary theme.
Emphasis is laid throughout on the wisdom of the king and the cleverness
of the groom. The two men are engaged in a sophisticated game of cat and
mouse, from which both emerge with credit, and with the honour of the
sovereign and his queen finally unimpaired.
2. *Agilulf* Agilulf, Duke of Turin, through his marriage to the Catholic
Bavarian princess Theodelinda, widow of Authari, ascended the Lombard
throne in AD 590. Pavia, some twenty miles south of Milan, had fallen to

the Lombards in 572 and became the seat of the Lombard kings, whose rule extended over all of the main cities in Italy north of the Po. B.'s knowledge of the Lombard Empire was derived from the *Historia Langobardorum*, compiled in the latter part of the eighth century by Paulus Diaconus ('Paul the Deacon'), whose description of Agilulf bears a close resemblance to B.'s own presentation of his character. The assertion, later in the story, that 'in those days, men wore their hair very long' (p. 204) is likewise based on a passage from Paulus Diaconus.

3. *a flaming torch in one hand and a stick in the other* Like Masetto's axe in the previous tale, the torch and the stick are strongly suggestive of the character's intentions.

Third Story

1. *the forty masses of Saint Gregory* Pope Gregory I ('Gregory the Great'), who ordained that the Kyrie Eleison should be repeated nine times, celebrated thirty masses for the liberation of the soul of the monk Justus. The lady's deliberate exaggeration of the number contributes to the vigorously anti-clerical tone of the whole story.

Fourth Story

1. *a tertiary in the Franciscan Order* Tertiaries are so called because they belong, not to the first order (monks) or to the second (nuns), but to a third order consisting of lay members who take simple vows and are allowed to remain outside the monastery and to own property, whilst following a portion of monastic rule. In B.'s day, they were for the most part Franciscans, and were notorious for their excessive piety. Many of them engaged in self-flagellation, a common devotional practice in the thirteenth and fourteenth centuries.

2. *the sermons of Brother Anastasius or the Plaint of the Magdalen* The latter could be a reference to any one of a number of devotional texts bearing some such title, but of the former work there is no record. B. probably invented it himself, furnishing its fictitious author with a name, Anastasius, that was popular in religious orders.

3. *compline* The last of the canonical hours, recited at sunset. Friar Puccio's uncomfortable penance is to coincide with the hours from sunset to sunrise, when the first canonical hour, Matins, is recited.

4. *astride the nag of Saint Benedict or Saint John Gualbert* The colourful metaphor for sexual congress is invoked because the two saints were often

depicted riding a donkey, in this case standing (literally) for the male member.

Fifth Story

1. *the Vergellesi family of Pistoia* A leading family of Pistoia, north of Florence, the Vergellesi were politically active in the early part of the fourteenth century on behalf first of the White Guelphs then of the Ghibellines. Francesco de' Vergellesi is recorded as having undertaken a political mission to the French court in 1313, and around 1326 he was indeed appointed *podestà* (governor) in the province of Lombardy.

Sixth Story

1. *one of those prudes* Nothing in what we are told about Catella merits such a description, with the possible exception of her jealous love for her husband, which is exploited by her admirer in a fashion that can only be thought of as callous and despicable. Possibly the most unpleasant story in the whole collection, this account of the cruel rape of a virtuous wife gives the lie to the claim that the *Decameron* is a feminist work *ante litteram*. Although the story is being narrated by one of the young ladies, Fiammetta, the viewpoint is decidedly masculine and anti-feminist. It is fair to add that the specious arguments presented in B.'s tale by the rapist to his victim are based upon passages from Livy and Valerius Maximus describing Tarquin's rape of Lucretia.

2. *Ricciardo Minutolo* The surname is also that of the dead archbishop in II, 5. Minutolo was the name of a leading Neapolitan patrician family, as also was Sighinolfo, the married name of the lady, Catella, who is the object of Ricciardo's obsessive affection. Both Ricciardo Minutolo and Filippo Sighinolfi were known to B. during his fourteen-year sojourn in Naples, although Sighinolfi's wife was not called Catella, but Mattea. It is unlikely that either family would have approved of B.'s fictive account of their marital arrangements.

3. *to meet in secret at a bagnio* The bagnio (in Italian, *bagno*), or Turkish bath-house, was a favourite meeting-place for adulterous lovers.

Seventh Story

1. *Tedaldo degli Elisei . . . Aldobrandino Palermini* As in the previous tale, the two families involved were among the oldest-established in the

city where the novella is set, but the historical records reveal no trace of either a Tedaldo degli Elisei or an Aldobrandino Palermini.

2. *the devil's mouth at the bottom of the abyss*   It was common for artists to depict the souls of the damned being devoured by demons. In his *Inferno*, Dante reserves this punishment for the three worst sinners of all, Judas Iscariot, Brutus and Cassius. As traitors to the founders of Church and Empire, each is being gnawed by one of the three slavering mouths of the giant Lucifer at the very centre of Hell.

3. *There was once a time . . .*   The lengthy tirade that follows, against the depravity of the religious, was to become a model for later writers engaging in anti-clerical invective. The *Decameron* contains numerous examples of a mocking attitude towards the religious, who along with women were the most popular target for medieval satirists. Bearing in mind the care with which the stories of the *Decameron* were assembled, it is hardly coincidental that the invective of III, 7 is repeated in a more concise and less abrasive form in VII, 3, the story of Friar Rinaldo.

Eighth Story

1. *having seated herself at his feet*   It was the normal practice for the penitent to adopt some such posture of humility before the father confessor. The confessional was of much later origin, being first introduced in the sixteenth century by a decree of the Council of Trent.

2. *no loss of saintliness is involved*   Writing some 150 years later, Machiavelli, in his comedy *Mandragola*, places an identical piece of casuistry in the mouth of Fra Timoteo, a father confessor who has been bribed to persuade a chaste married woman, Lucrezia, to commit adultery with a young admirer.

3. *the Old Man of the Mountain*   Hassan-ben-Sabah, the sheik Al Jebal, and founder of a sect of oriental fanatics, active between the eleventh and thirteenth centuries, was known as the Old Man of the Mountain because the sect migrated to Mount Lebanon and made it their stronghold. The members of the sect were called Assassins (from *hashshashin*, 'hashish smokers') because they were said to take hashish to induce visions of Paradise before setting out on their murderous expeditions. The Abbot drugs Ferondo with the intention of sending him not to Paradise but to Purgatory. The history of the Assassins was first recounted in western Europe by Marco Polo in the latter part of the thirteenth century in *Il Milione*, a popular text that was transcribed in numerous different versions.

4. *This kind of gibberish* Nonsensical statements of the kind just recorded are part of B.'s stock-in-trade in depicting the gullibility of certain of his characters or groups of characters. Further examples are found in the tales of Friar Cipolla (VI, 10), Monna Belcolore (VIII, 2), Calandrino and the heliotrope (VIII, 3), and Master Simone (VIII, 9). As a rule, they include a sprinkling of scatological or (in the case of Cipolla's sermon to the Certaldese) blasphemous elements.

5. *your wife will present you with a son* The passage recalls the angel's words to Zacharias (Luke i, 13): 'Fear not Zacharias: . . . thy wife Elisabeth shall bear thee a son, and thou shalt call his name John.'

6. *the Arse-angel Bagriel* In the original text, the Archangel Gabriel's name emerges from Ferondo's lips as '*Ragnolo Braghiello*', a piece of linguistic burlesque suggestive of spiders and breeches.

Ninth Story

1. *Gilette of Narbonne* Narbonne, at the northern tip of the county of Roussillon, is on the Mediterranean coast, halfway between Montpelier and Perpignan. In Shakespeare's baroque version of B.'s story, *All's Well That Ends Well*, Gilette's name is changed to Helen, and one or two new characters, notably Parolles, are introduced. Shakespeare probably read the tale in Painter's *Palace of Pleasure*, a collection of stories from classical and Italian sources. Those taken by Painter from the *Decameron*, being translated from the French, were twice removed from the original. The bare outlines of B.'s story are traceable to the *Sakuntala* of the fifth-century Sanskrit poet and dramatist Kalidasa.

2. *a fistula* The OED defines a fistula as 'a long, sinuous pipe-like ulcer with a narrow orifice'.

3. *the Florentines were waging war against the Sienese* Florence and Siena were at war with one another at various times in the thirteenth century. The most famous battle between their respective armies took place in 1260 at Montaperti, where the Florentines suffered a humiliating defeat.

4. *Montpelier* An important trading centre, Montpelier was the capital of the county of Roussillon.

Tenth Story

1. *Gafsa* An inland town in Tunisia, known to Italians of B.'s day chiefly for its monastery.

2. *the Sahara* A literal translation of B.'s text here would read 'the

Theban desert'. In the fourteenth century, the region around Thebes, in Upper Egypt, was noted for the large number of hermits who had settled there.

3. *the resurrection of the flesh* The profane sexual metaphor had first appeared in *The Golden Ass*, written in the second century AD by Lucius Apuleius. This paragraph of B.'s text and all subsequent narrative details up to the outbreak of the fire in Gafsa were a notorious stumbling-block to B.'s English translators for over 500 years. Until the end of the nineteenth century, they omitted the story altogether or resorted at this point to either the original Italian or one of the French versions. Pornography, it seemed, was permissible provided it appeared in a language that only a minority of one's readers could understand. Edward Gibbon had used the same device in his autobiography: 'My English text is chaste, and all licentious passages are left in the decent obscurity of a learned language.'

(Conclusion)

1. *the name by which you address me* B. intended that 'Filostrato' (Philostratos) should convey the meaning of 'vanquished by Love', which is why he had chosen that name as the title of his narrative poem on the ill-fated love of Troilus for Cressida, written some twenty years before. Since the poem was dedicated to a lady called Filomena, it is probable that when, a little earlier, Filostrato speaks of 'one of your number', he is referring to the Filomena who appears in the *Decameron* as one of the group of storytellers.

2. *a song about Messer Guiglielmo and the Lady of Vergiù* An Italian version of the thirteenth-century French narrative poem *La Chastelaine de Vergi*.

3. *He who moves the stars and heavens* The Italian text reads '*Colui che move il cielo e ogni stella*', a line that is based on Dante's '*L'Amor che move il sole e l'altre stelle*' ('Love that moves the Sun and the other stars') from *Paradiso*, XXXIII, 145. B. has modified Dante's reference to God's love so as to allude to the Creator himself. Lauretta's lugubrious song is a fitting prelude to the stories of the Fourth Day, concerning those whose love ended unhappily.

4. *in the Milanese fashion* The Milanese had a reputation for their materialism and practical common sense. Their interpretation of Lauretta's song ('a good fat pig [is] better than a comely wench') would be roughly equivalent to the English 'A bird in the hand is worth two in the bush.' It is better, in other words, to have a jealous husband than no husband at all.

FOURTH DAY

(Introduction)

1. ***Envy's fiery and impetuous blast*** The image of a blast of wind striking the highest summits is borrowed from Dante's *Paradiso* (XVII, 133–4): '*Questo tuo grido farà come vento/Che le più alte cime più percuote*' ('This cry of yours will do as does the wind/Which strikes most powerfully upon the highest summits'). In what follows, B. mounts a spirited and reasoned defence of vernacular narrative prose, which before the appearance of the *Decameron* had never achieved recognition as a serious poetic genre. It is unnecessary to surmise that the various errors of which B. claims to have been accused by his critics presuppose that the thirty stories he had written so far were already in circulation, although, being a good storyteller, that is the impression he seeks to create. In effect, he is forestalling the criticism of his possible detractors by assembling all of their possible arguments, then demolishing them one by one, in the process employing the tools of the narrator's craft.

2. ***which bear no title*** The phrase used by B., *senza titolo*, is a technical one. Its explanation is to be found in his commentary on Dante's *Commedia*, where at one point he refers to Ovid's *Amores*, which 'some call *Liber amorum* and others *Sine titulo* ['Without title'] because it does not deal with any continuous body of material from which it can be given a title, but proceeds by way of some lines on one subject and some on another, or what we may therefore describe as single pieces'. The appropriateness to the *Decameron* of such a description is reasonably clear.

3. ***homely and unassuming style*** B. is indulging in false modesty. The style of the *Decameron* is so refined, imposing and elegant that it became a model for all the foremost prose writers of the Italian Renaissance.

4. ***poverty alone is without envy*** The Italian, '*sola la miseria è senza invidia*', is a direct translation from Valerius Maximus: '*Sola miseria caret invidia.*'

5. ***not a complete story*** The tale, of oriental origin, is in fact sufficiently complete for commentators to refer to it as the 101st story of the *Decameron*. In the English translation of 1702, the editors not only dispensed entirely with the frame, but included this story in place of the account of Alibech's incarceration of the Devil (III, 10).

6. ***Filippo Balducci*** Several members of the Balducci family appear in the historical records as agents of the banking firm the Compagnia dei Bardi, which employed B.'s father.

7. **Mount Asinaio**   B. writes *Monte Asinaio*, literally Mount Donkeyman, a corruption for humorous effect of *Monte Senario*, noted for its caves where Florentine hermits traditionally took up residence.

8. **goslings**   A literal translation of the Italian *papere*, but perhaps the contemporary English slang expression, 'birds', would convey the sense more effectively.

9. **the leek's head**   For the sexual connotations of the leek, see also I, 10.

10. **Guido Cavalcanti . . . Dante Alighieri . . . Cino da Pistoia**   All three wrote in the *dolce stil novo* ('sweet new style'), a poetic mode that celebrated womanly beauty as the agency for the understanding of deep philosophical truths. Cavalcanti (*c.* 1259–1300), Dante's close friend, is the protagonist of *Decameron*, VI, 9, where his reputed atheism triggers the events of the narrative. Dante (1265–1321) promised in the concluding chapter of the *Vita nuova* that he would celebrate the beauty of Beatrice in words that had never been said of any other woman, a promise magnificently fulfilled in his great epic, the *Divine Comedy*. Cino da Pistoia (*c.* 1265–1336), the last significant poet of the *dolce stil*, was also one of Italy's leading academic lawyers. B. is known to have attended his lectures on jurisprudence in the University of Naples.

11. **in the words of the Apostle . . . suffer need**   See Philippians iv, 12: '. . . every where and in all things I am instructed . . . both to abound and to suffer need.'

First Story

1. **Tancredi, Prince of Salerno**   None of the characters in the story has any historical counterpart. Salerno was one of the earliest Norman fiefdoms in Italy, and B. gives Norman names both to the Prince and to Ghismonda's lover.

2. **the usual age for taking a husband**   It was normal for girls to be married around the age of fifteen.

3. **Neither you nor I can resist the power of Love**   These, the only words spoken by Guiscardo in the whole of the novella, recall Virgil's *Omnia vincit Amor*, 'Love conquers all' (*Eclogues*, X, 69). The phrase is reminiscent, also, of Francesca da Rimini's claim (*Inferno*, V, 103) that Love is unforgiving to anyone who is loved: '*Amor, che a nessun amato Amor perdona.*'

Second Story

1. *Venice* The only story in the *Decameron* set in Venice is interlaced with uncomplimentary remarks about the city and its inhabitants. It is a place 'where the scum of the earth can always find a welcome' (p. 303). Monna Lisetta, 'being a Venetian', is 'capable of talking the hind leg off a donkey' (p. 304). Friar Alberto is tricked into believing that he will make good his escape, 'which goes to show how far you can trust a Venetian' (p. 311). B.'s low opinion of Venice and the Venetians is doubtless coloured by the rivalry between Florence and one of her most powerful competitors on the European commercial scene.

2. *the most blessed woman on earth* The phrase invites comparison with the words addressed to the Virgin Mary by the Angel Gabriel in Luke i, 28: 'blessed art thou amongst women.' The following paragraph makes it clear that the first part of the story may be read as an irreverent, not to say blasphemous, re-enactment of the Annunciation.

3. *the Rialto district* The business centre of Venice.

Third Story

1. *Candia* Now known as Iráklion (Heraklion), Candia was the largest city on the island of Crete. The island was sold to Venice in 1204, and Candia was the Venetian form of the Arabic 'Khandaq' ('Moat'), by which name the city was known to its former Saracen rulers. The Florentine banking house of Peruzzi had a trading post in Candia's thriving commercial quarter.

Fourth Story

1. *there are many . . . verbal report* The belief that Love is kindled only by the eyes was central to the poetry of the *dolce stil novo*. It has been suggested (by Branca for instance) that Elissa's refutation of the theory in this passage carries polemical undertones, perhaps signalling B.'s attempt to distance himself from the poets of the *dolce stil*. But other stories in the *Decameron*, notably the tale of Cimon (V, 1), point to an opposite conclusion.

2. *William the Second* King of Sicily from 1166 to 1189, William II ('William the Good') had no children, but he was in fact the nephew of Ruggieri and Costanza (Constance), the latter of whom succeeded him on

the Sicilian throne. Needless to add, the impetuous young hero of B.'s
story, Gerbino, is an invention of his own. So, too, is the King of Granada,
to whom the object of Gerbino's passionate love, Gostanza, is promised in
marriage. The kingdom of Granada was not established until the early
thirteenth century.

3. **Barbary**   Usually a term referring to the Saracen countries along the
north coast of Africa, Barbary is here used in a more limited sense for the
part of Africa closest to Sicily. It was only the King of Tunis who was a
tributary to the King of Sicily.

4. **sent him his glove**   The presentation of a glove in token of a word of
honour was a custom of Germanic origin. Later in the story, B. seems to be
mocking the practice when Gerbino tells Gostanza's guardians that since
there are no falcons around, the glove is superfluous.

Fifth Story

1. **a pot of basil**   B.'s story of Lisabetta and the pot of basil has no clear
antecedents. It is the direct source of Keats's celebrated poem on the same
subject, *Isabella, or the Pot of Basil*.

2. **San Gimignano**   A town in Tuscany, roughly midway between
Florence and Siena, famous for its numerous tall towers, originally
seventy-two in number but now reduced to fourteen, which were
built by leading families both as defensive bastions and as ostentatious monuments to their wealth and importance. Merchants from San
Gimignano who set up business in Messina included certain members of the
powerful Ardinghelli family, who, like Lisabetta's brothers in B.'s story but
presumably for different reasons, in the middle of the thirteenth century
transferred their business from Messina to Naples.

3. **Salernitan basil**   Salerno is not especially famous for its basil. The
Italian text ('*bassilico salernetano*') is possibly corrupt at this point, and
B. may well have intended to refer to the basil of Benevento ('*basilico
beneventino*'), which was prized elsewhere for its strong aroma and
vigorous growth. On the other hand it has been suggested by Antonio
Mazzarino that B. may have intended to write *silermontano*, with reference
to an aromatic plant having a tall stem of which the Latin name is *siser
montanum*. Mazzarino also made the intriguing discovery that an Arabic
treatise on plants, current in B's day, lists eleven kinds of basil, including
one called *al-adjamddjami*, a word based on the Arabic term for a skull
or cranium.

Sixth Story

1. **some red and others white** Roses, symbolic of pure love and of regeneration and the resurrection of the dead, lend to this touching narrative of love and death a recurrent leitmotif.

Seventh Story

1. **a poor man's daughter** Simona and her lover, Pasquino, have special significance as the first working-class hero and heroine in the history of European tragic literature. Both are engaged in the manufacture of woollens, the staple industry of medieval Florence and the source of much of its wealth.

2. **the pardoning at San Gallo** According to Franco Sacchetti (c. 1330–1400), it was the custom, on the first Sunday of the month, for Florentines from the poorer classes to go to one of the churches outside the San Gallo gate to receive indulgences and spend the day in the countryside.

3. **sage** The tragic events of the tale are based on a popular superstition, recorded in a document of the early thirteenth century, according to which the leaves of a sage bush could be rendered poisonous through being nibbled by toads.

4. **Guccio Imbratta** A character who turns up again as Friar Cipolla's servant in VI, 10.

Eighth Story

1. **turn a plum into an orange** The Italian text reads '*fare del pruno un melrancio*', literally 'to make an orange-tree out of a plum-tree', implying that what is unremarkable may be transformed into something more desirable. The nearest English equivalent ('to make a silk purse out of a sow's ear') is inappropriate to the particular context.

Ninth Story

1. **Guillaume de Cabestanh** The name is that of an early thirteenth-century Provençal poet, who dedicated two of his compositions to his lord and master, Raimon de Castel-Roussillon. Another Provençal poet narrates the story of Cabestanh's amorous liaison with Raimon's wife, ending in the tragic deaths of the two lovers. B., who was familiar with the Provençal tradition, changed Raimon's name to Guillaume and wove a narrative of his own from various threads including an allegorical episode from Dante's

Vita nuova and the tragedy *Thyestes*, by Seneca. In Chapter III of the *Vita nuova*, Dante describes a dream in which he saw a fearsome-looking figure bearing in his arms a naked woman draped in a blood-stained sheet. In one of his hands, he is holding Dante's heart, which he compels the lady to eat. In Seneca's tragedy, Thyestes is invited to a banquet at which he unwittingly devours the flesh of his own sons.

Tenth Story

1. **Mazzeo della Montagna** Matteo (or Mazzeo) Selvatico, a native of Mantua, was author of a medical encyclopaedia which he dedicated to King Robert of Naples in 1317. The work, written in Latin, adds the adjective '*mantuanus*' ('of Mantua') to the name of its author, which in popular speech became corrupted to '*montanus*' ('of the mountain'), hence Matteo della Montagna. Matteo, one of the most famous physicians at the earliest European medical school at Salerno, died in extreme old age at some time after 1342. B. would certainly have heard of him, and may even have made his acquaintance, during his sojourn in Naples between 1327 and 1341.

2. **Amalfi** About fifteen miles to the west of Salerno.

(Conclusion)

1. **one of the ladies dancing** The reference is almost certainly to Filomena, the name of the dedicatee of the *Filostrato*, which tells the story of the ill-fated love of Troilus for Cressida.

FIFTH DAY

(Introduction)

1. **shortly after nones** Around 3 p.m. See notes to Introduction to First Day (p. 805).

First Story

1. **Cimon** The initial idea for the character of Cimon possibly came from a passage in Valerius Maximus linking the name with imbecility in the popular imagination. Neither he nor the other characters in the story have any historical basis. The transformation of the main character from idiot to

nonpareil by the vision of a beautiful woman is strongly reminiscent of ideas expounded by earlier Italian poets, more especially because of the hypnotic effect produced on Cimon when Iphigenia opens her eyes ('Cimon made no reply, but stood there gazing into her eyes, which seemed to shine with a gentleness that filled him with a feeling of joy such as he had never known before' – p. 369). The story may thus be read as an attempt to translate a major theme of the *dolce stil novo* into narrative terms, pursuing it to its extreme consequences, in this case involving a considerable amount of violence.

2. *the month of May*   The season, together with scenic elements such as the leafy wood and the cool fountain, are conventional ingredients of the rhetorical topos of the *locus amœnus*. The sleeping Iphigenia, and her awakening, carry allegorical overtones of Cimon's newly discovered awareness of his dormant potential for excellence.

Second Story

1. *Lipari*   The island has figured earlier in the story of Madonna Beritola (II, 6). Otherwise relatively unimportant, it was well known as the scene of a naval battle in 1339. It was also a notorious haven for buccaneers, which might explain why B. chose that location for a story whose hero turns to piracy.

2. *Susa*   Unusually for B., whose knowledge of Mediterranean geography is in general surprisingly accurate, the particulars he gives of Gostanza's voyage strain his reader's credulity. The town of Susa indeed lies some hundred miles south of Tunis, but the distance by sea from Lipari, about 300 miles, could hardly have been covered in a single day under a 'wind [that] blew so gently from the north that the sea was barely disturbed' (p. 380). A breeze from that direction would in any case have driven Gostanza's boat eventually on to the north coast of Sicily.

Third Story

1. *Rome – which was once the head . . . of the civilized world*   The narrator is qualifying the inscription '*Roma caput mundi*' ('Rome the head of the world') which appeared on Roman coinage. B.'s tale is set in the early part of the fourteenth century during the so-called 'Babylonian Captivity' (1309–77) of the papacy. The power vacuum resulting from the forced removal of the papal court to Avignon led to a state of lawlessness in Roman territory, which is graphically illustrated in this particular narrative.

2. *Anagni*   A hill-town some thirty miles south-east of Rome, the birth-

place of four popes including Boniface VIII. It lies just off the Via Latina, the conventional route in B.'s day for travellers between Rome and Naples.

3. *the Orsini* One of the oldest and most powerful of Roman princely families, the Orsini were staunch supporters of the Guelph, pro-papal cause in the struggles between Church and Empire in the thirteenth and early fourteenth centuries. Their long-standing rivals for political power in the papal territories were the Colonna family, who traditionally espoused the imperial cause of the Ghibellines. One assumes it is a band of Colonna supporters that has seized Pietro and now threatens to hang him from the branches of an oak.

Fourth Story

1. *Lizio da Valbona* A Guelph nobleman of Bertinoro, in the mountains of the Romagna between Cesena and Forlí, Lizio da Valbona was widely known in the late thirteenth century for his outstandingly noble and generous temperament. Dante refers to him (*Purgatorio*, XIV, 97) in a passage deploring the disappearance of such virtues in the Romagna of his own day. In the same line, he also refers to a Ghibelline nobleman of the Romagna, Arrigo Mainardi, and it is probable that B. had the passage in mind when selecting the names for the two male characters in his story.

Fifth Story

1. *Fano* A town on the Adriatic coast, north of Ancona.
2. *Faenza* The street brawls described in the story may be supposed to have taken place around the year 1254, thirteen years after Faenza, which is situated halfway between Bologna and Rimini, had been captured and plundered by the troops of the Emperor Frederick II.

Sixth Story

1. *Marin Bòlgaro* Still alive in 1341, Marin Bulgaro was held in high esteem in the Angevin court for the assistance he had rendered to the monarchy earlier in the century in planning and building the Neapolitan fleet. He was known personally to B., who records him in glowing terms in *De casibus virorum illustrium*, a series of biographies of famous men, which also contains a flattering account of Giovanni of Procida, who later in the story is described as the 'blood-brother' of Landolfo, the father of the tale's young hero, Gianni.

2. **swimming there and back**   The classical myth of Leander swimming across the Hellespont to join his beloved Hero, as recounted by Virgil in the *Georgics* and by Ovid in the *Heroides*, was clearly in B.'s mind in depicting the strength of Gianni's love for Restituta. The story of their love closely resembles one of the central episodes in an earlier work of B.'s, the *Filocolo*.

3. **King Frederick of Sicily**   Frederick II of Aragon succeeded his older brother James I as King of Sicily in 1296. Their mother was the widow of Peter of Aragon, Constance, who left the island in 1297, accompanied among others by Ruggieri di Loria, the Admiral of the Royal Fleet, who later in the story saves Gianni and Restituta from being burnt at the stake. The narrative is notionally set, therefore, at some time between 1296 and 1297.

4. **La Cuba**   The famous Moorish building in Palermo, built in the twelfth century, which has survived to the present day.

5. **from Cape Minerva to Scalea**   The coastline from Punta Campanella, opposite Capri, to Scalea, in northern Calabria.

6. **a huge, blazing torch**   Clearly symbolic of the king's passionate intentions, the blazing torch recalls a similar narrative detail in the account of King Agilulf's arrival at dead of night at the door leading to his queen's bedroom (II, 2).

7. **Ischia would be lost to you tomorrow**   Despite its proximity to the Angevin capital, Ischia remained under Aragonese rule until 1299.

Seventh Story

1. **King William**   William II, Norman King of Sicily (also referred to in IV, 4), reigned between 1166 and 1189.

2. **Amerigo Abate of Trapani**   For generations, from the Norman to the Aragonese period of Sicilian history, the Abbate family occupied high office in Trapani as *capitani*, or commanders of the local militia. There is no record of an Amerigo Abbate during the Norman period, but Arrigo (Amerigo) Abbate was active as privy counsellor to the Hohenstaufen kings, Frederick II and Manfred, during the thirteenth century. It has been suggested that the various references in the story to historical incidents are a fictional transposition to the twelfth century of events which took place at a much later date.

3. **Genoese pirates**   Piracy and slave-trading were practices with which the Genoese were traditionally associated. It was by Genoese pirates that Beritola's children were seized (II, 6) on the island of Ponza.

4. **supposing him to be a Turk**   Being Armenian, Teodoro was already a Christian.

5. *Violante* Not exactly commonplace, Violante was also the name of the seven-year-old daughter of the Count of Antwerp (II, 8). B.'s own daughter of that name, to whom he was deeply attached, was roughly the same age when she died in 1356.

6. *a series of thunderclaps* The storm from which Violante and Teodoro take refuge, prefacing their experience of 'Love's ultimate delights', is strongly reminiscent of the storm in Book IV of Virgil's *Aeneid* that leads to Dido taking shelter with Aeneas in a cave, with precisely the same consequences.

7. *the Viceroy* The term used by B. is *capitano*, meaning the chief of the local militia. Since he was appointed directly by the royal court in Palermo, he was in effect the king's representative.

8. *ambassadors from the King of Armenia* The kingdom of Armenia, not to be confused with Armenia proper, was originally established as a principality by emigrating Armenians in Cilicia on the south-east coast of Asia Minor in the twelfth century, after Armenia had been overrun by the Seljuqs. Known to historians as Little Armenia or Lesser Armenia, it was an important assembly-point for Christian armies during the Crusades, as well as offering a secure route for Italian merchants trading with the Orient. Trapani, in Sicily, was a regular port of call on the route from the eastern Mediterranean to Rome. The 'Crusade that was about to be launched' was presumably the Third Crusade, which set out in May 1189 under the Emperor Frederick Barbarossa, who was drowned en route the following year. In that case the reference to the King of Armenia is anachronistic, as the principality did not become a kingdom until 1199.

9. *Lajazzo* Located on the coast of Little Armenia, Lajazzo (Ayas) was the easternmost Christian port of call in the Mediterranean. An important trading centre, it was described by Marco Polo in *Il Milione* as a town to which 'all the spices and all the silk and cloth of gold are brought from the interior; and merchants from Venice, Genoa, and everywhere else come here to purchase them'.

Eighth Story

1. *Ravenna* The city of Ravenna, on the Adriatic coast, was well known to B., who stayed there many times between 1346 and 1361–2. Dante had died in Ravenna in 1321, and several features in the tale that follows are clearly inspired by passages from the *Commedia*. The names of the two protagonists, Nastagio degli Onesti and the daughter of Paolo Traversari, recall the line from *Purgatorio* (XIV, 107) where Dante names the Anastagi

and Traversari families as representatives of a tradition of courtesy that has
now disappeared from the Romagna. In describing the Earthly Paradise
(*Purgatorio*, XXVIII, 19–20), Dante likens the breezes among the leaves of
the trees to the sirocco blowing through the pinewoods at Classe, which is
where Nastagio, in B.'s story, experiences his awesome vision. The punishment meted out to the girl in the woods is reminiscent of the fate that
befalls the souls of the Profligate in Dante's Wood of the Suicides (*Inferno*,
XIII), where they are torn apart by fearsome black mastiffs. Finally, Count
Ugolino (*Inferno*, XXXIII) describes a prophetic dream in which he witnessed a wolf and its cubs being chased by hounds, which he saw 'tear open
the flanks of father and children with their sharp teeth'.

2. **towards the beginning of May**   Spring was the time of year associated
by medieval poets with the experience of a vision, the classic example being
Dante's *Commedia*. The tradition of lovers' visions being set in the month of
May was one that continued into the Renaissance period.

Ninth Story

1. **Coppo di Borghese Domenichi**   The eulogy of Coppo (= Jacopo) di
Borghese Domenichi seems an irrelevant digression, but in fact confers
upon the narrative a curiously appropriate sense of chivalrous virtue,
wisdom and authority. In a long career of service to the Florentine republic
dating back to 1308, Coppo had occupied the highest offices of state with
great distinction, attracting the praise not only of B. but of other writers of
the period. B. speaks highly of him elsewhere, notably in his commentary
on the *Commedia* and in a letter he wrote in April 1353 to the companion of
his youth, Zanobi da Strada, where he laments Coppo's recent death. The
qualities attributed by Fiammetta to Coppo as a storyteller ('he excelled all
others, for he was more coherent, possessed a superior memory, and spoke
with greater eloquence') could well apply, of course, to B. himself.

2. **Alberighi**   The Alberighi are listed in Dante's *Paradiso* (XVI, 89) as one
of the oldest Florentine families. They lived in the same quarter of the city
as Dante's own family, the Alighieri.

3. **Campi**   Campi Bisenzio, about ten miles north-west of Florence, on
the road to Prato.

Tenth Story

1. **Perugia**   The tale of the reluctant husband is probably set in Perugia
because of the town's homophile reputation.

2. **to go clogging through the dry**   The Italian text reads '*andare in zoccoli*

per l'asciutto', a proverbial expression for engaging in homosexual practices which has no real equivalent in English. Clogs (*zoccoli*) usually have sodomitic connotations in the literature of the period, a further example in the *Decameron* being found in the sermon of Friar Cipolla (VI, 10). The expression that follows (in Italian *'portare altrui in nave per lo piovoso'*) is perhaps self-explanatory, being partly akin to 'do a wet bottom', which Eric Partridge, in *A Dictionary of Slang and Unconventional English*, defines as '(of women) to have sexual intercourse'.

3. **Saint Verdiana feeding the serpents** According to popular legend, two serpents entered the saint's cell at Castelfiorentino, but realizing that they had been sent to drive her away and lead her into sin, she kept them with her and fed them.

4. **women exist for no other purpose** Outwardly pro-feminist, the *Decameron* contains many such instances of misogynist sentiment. In this case the statement occurs in the context of the old bawd's diatribe, itself a rhetorical exercise on the topos known as *vituperium*, of which the most common targets were women and the religious.

(Conclusion)

1. **'Monna Aldruda . . . tidings I bring'** The first of Dioneo's extensive repertoire of bawdy songs is, like the others, plebeian in origin, and therefore considered by the queen unsuitable for the ears of a company of young patricians. In Chapter XX of his famous book on good manners, *Il Galateo*, Giovanni della Casa in the sixteenth century refers specifically to this passage from the *Decameron*, and counsels against the imitation of Dioneo's 'vulgar and plebeian manners'.

SIXTH DAY

(Introduction)

1. **a song about Troilus and Cressida** The story of Troilus's ill-fated love for Cressida was one that B. himself had told in the verses of the *Filostrato*. Having as its main theme the inconstancy of women, it forms an apt introduction to the account of the dispute between the servants over whether Sicofante's wife went to her husband a virgin.

2. **a great commotion** This is the only point in the whole of the *Decameron* at which the idyllic calm of the storytellers' world is disturbed by an external event. The servants' quarrel serves as a reminder, at the mid-point

of the work, of the mundane happenings of normal everyday existence, as well as offering a pretext for the subject matter of the tales recounted on the seventh day.

3. *Sicofante* The name, like those of the 'mechanicals' in the frame story, is of Greek origin, and means literally 'a displayer of figs', which in Italian could imply one who makes obscene gestures. But B. probably chose the name merely to convey an impression of the character's simple-mindedness.

First Story

1. *Since Pampinea has already spoken at some length on this subject* The reference is to Pampinea's introductory remarks to the story of Master Alberto (I, 10).

2. *he ruined it completely* The story told so ineptly by the knight 'in itself was indeed excellent', and thus presumably on a par with the stories B. himself is in the process of narrating. The tale of Madonna Oretta's tactful dismissal of her incoherent companion may be read as an extended metaphor of the act of storytelling, or what some of B.'s commentators describe as a *metanovella*. By listing the knight's various failings (verbal repetition, recapitulation of the plot, apologies for getting things wrong, and confusing the names of the characters) B. is pointing up by contrast the qualities expected of a good storyteller like himself. It has been suggested that the placing of the story at roughly the halfway point in the hundred tales is also significant, comparisons being drawn with Dante's placing of the discourse on Love (the central theme of the *Commedia*) exactly midway through the poem, in canto XVII of *Purgatorio*. But the analogy is inexact, both because the art of storytelling is not one of B.'s major themes, and because the true halfway point of the *Decameron* (allowance being made for the tale of Filippo Balducci in the Introduction to the Fourth Day) is the last story of the Fifth Day.

Second Story

1. *Geri Spina* The husband of Madonna Oretta, in the previous tale, was a politically active Florentine merchant, named by the chronicler Giovanni Villani as one of the leaders of the Black Guelph faction at the turn of the fourteenth century. He died at some time between 1321 and 1332.

2. *Pope Boniface* The delegation from Pope Boniface VIII, of whom Geri Spina was a leading supporter in Florence, visited the city in 1300 in an abortive attempt to settle disputes between the White and Black Guelphs.

3. *Santa Maria Ughi* A small church near the Palazzo Strozzi, in the

centre of Florence. The Pope's emissaries, who were lodging 'under Messer Geri's roof' near the Santa Trinità bridge, would have had to walk past the Palazzo Strozzi, whether on their way to the houses of the Cerchi or of the Donati, leaders of the White and Black Guelphs respectively.

4. *to the Arno* Cisti is implying that the servant's huge flask would be better filled from the river on which Florence stands.

Third Story

1. *Antonio d'Orso* Bishop of Florence between 1309 and 1322, Antonio d'Orso had a reputation for parsimony. He was also a man of exceptional learning, and in 1310 he was appointed a privy counsellor to Edward II of England.

2. *Dego della Ratta* After coming to Naples in the retinue of Violante of Aragon when she arrived from Spain for her marriage to King Robert, Dego della Ratta served the Angevin court in various capacities, visiting Florence as the King's marshal on three separate occasions, the last in 1317–18.

3. *the feast of St John* 27 December.

4. *the palio* Like its more famous counterpart, still held annually in the main square of Siena, the *palio* in Florence was a race between horses and riders representing the various districts of the city. Porta San Piero, the quarter where Monna Nonna 'had recently been married and set up house', lay on the route followed by the riders.

Fourth Story

1. *Currado Gianfigliazzi* The Gianfigliazzi family was associated with the Florentine banking community, in particular the Peruzzi. Dante (*Inferno*, XVII) claims to have come across the soul of one of them in the circle of Hell where money-lenders are punished. Currado Gianfigliazzi was renowned in early fourteenth-century Florence for his lavish hospitality.

2. *Peretola* The Gianfigliazzi owned various properties in the region of Peretola, a small town in the Florentine countryside.

3. *Chichibio* A common Venetian name, based onomatopoeically on the sound made by the chaffinch. Because the character in B.'s well-known story was simple-minded, the name later acquired derogatory overtones, being applied to persons of low intelligence. A near English equivalent would be 'bird-brain'.

4. *hence a good liar* B.'s profound dislike of the Venetians, already evident from the tale of Monna Lisetta (IV, 2), is further underlined by this aside on their mendacity.

Fifth Story

1. **Forese da Rabatta**   Not only a famous jurist of the first half of the fourteenth century, Forese also took a leading part in the management of Florentine political affairs, occupying the office of *priore* several times between 1320 and 1335, and that of *gonfaloniere* in 1339–40.

2. **Baronci**   The allusion is clarified in the story that follows.

3. **Giotto**   The most important Italian painter of the fourteenth century, Giotto was born in either 1266–7 or 1276, and died in 1337. In a passage concerning the transience of earthly fame, Dante tells us that Giotto has eclipsed Cimabue as the most famous painter of his day (*Purgatorio*, XI, 94– 5). B. probably met him when the painter was working in Naples between 1329 and 1333. The *trompe l'œil* effect that B. attributes to Giotto's realism ('people's eyes are deceived and they mistake the picture for the real thing') reflects the general view of B. and his contemporaries that Giotto was a great innovator in the art of painting.

4. **Mugello**   Both Forese and Giotto had been born in the Mugello, which lies to the north-east of Florence.

Sixth Story

1. **Montughi**   A hillside village a few miles north of Florence. Many wealthy Florentines had country houses in the area.

2. **Uberti ... Lamberti**   Two of the oldest families in Florence. The Uberti are especially well remembered because of the famous episode in the *Commedia* where Dante depicts the proud figure of Farinata degli Uberti rising from a flaming tomb in the circle of the Heretics (*Inferno*, X, 35–6).

3. **Baronci**   As the story shows, the Baronci, a well-to-do family of the Florentine bourgeoisie, were notoriously ill-favoured. But Scalza's explanation (that they were formed when God was learning the rudiments of his craft) caused problems for B.'s post-Tridentine editors, as well as for his English translators. The apparent blasphemy so shocked the 1620 translator that he replaced it with a different tale altogether, whilst in the 1702 translation Scalza is reported as saying that the antiquity of the Baronci 'will be evident by that Prometheus made them in time when he first began to Paint, and made others after he was Master of his Art'. The 1741 translator has Scalza saying: 'You must understand therefore that they were formed when nature was in its infancy, and before she was perfect at her work.' This became the standard way of translating the passage until John Payne set matters right in 1886. He anglicized the Baronci, calling them 'the Cadgers', claiming in a footnote that Baronci is 'the Florentine name

for what we should call professional beggars'. Later in the same footnote, Payne observes, with tongue firmly in cheek, that 'this story has been a prodigious stumbling-block to former translators, not one of whom appears to have had the slightest idea of Boccaccio's meaning'.

Seventh Story

1. *Rinaldo de' Pugliesi* Like the Montagues and Capulets in Verona, the two families named in this story, the Pugliesi and the Guazzalotri, were sworn enemies in the town of Prato, which lies some fifteen miles north-west of Florence.

2. *podestà* In this context, the *podestà* is the chief magistrate. The same title can also indicate a chief executive official appointed by some central authority, as in III, 5, where Francesco Vergellesi is appointed *podestà di Milano* ('governor of Milan').

3. *Throw it to the dogs?* The phrase used by Madonna Filippa recalls Matthew vii, 6: *'Nolite dare sanctum canibus'* ('Give not that which is holy unto the dogs'). *Sanctum* and *sacrum* were colloquial terms in B.'s day for a woman's body.

Eighth Story

1. *Cesca* Diminutive of Francesca. The tale of the disagreeable young woman is unusual in that no precise location is specified, though one assumes that, like most of the other stories in the Sixth Day, it is set in Florence.

2. *in the glass* In medieval literature, the mirror was interpreted as a symbol of truth.

Ninth Story

1. *Betto Brunelleschi* A leading figure in Florentine politics at the turn of the fourteenth century, Betto Brunelleschi, originally a White Guelph, was a friend both of Guido Cavalcanti (the central figure in B.'s story) and of Dante, who dedicated one of his sonnets to him. After the events of 1301 that led to Dante's exile, he became a powerful figure among the ruling Black Guelphs, and brought about the downfall and death of their discredited leader, Corso Donati. He was murdered by two of Corso's young kinsmen in 1311.

2. *Cavalcanti's son, Guido* Affectionately described by Dante as his *primo amico* ('first friend'), Guido Cavalcanti was, after Dante himself, the leading poet of the *dolce stil novo*. He was exiled from Florence in 1300, but

having contracted malaria was allowed to return, and he died in August of the same year. On the evidence of Guido's poems, B.'s complimentary assessment of his gifts as a logician and natural philosopher is well justified, but there is no good reason to suppose that he was an Epicurean in its medieval sense of atheist. The stigma of atheism attaching to his name probably arose because Dante, in the tenth canto of *Inferno*, describes his encounter with the spirit of Guido's father, Cavalcante de' Cavalcanti, in the circle of those who denied the immortality of the soul.

3. ***Orsammichele ... Corso degli Adimari ... San Giovanni ... Santa Reparata*** Orsammichele is a district near the centre of Florence, named after the church of San Michele in Orto. The road linking San Michele with the baptistery of San Giovanni (Corso degli Adimari) is now known as the Via Calzaiuoli. The church of Santa Reparata, alongside the baptistery, was demolished to make way for the cathedral of Florence, Santa Maria del Fiore, on which work began in 1294.

4. ***the tombstones, which were very tall*** P. F. Watson, in an article published in *Studi sul Boccaccio*, XVIII (1989), points out that the '*arche, che grandi erano*' of the original text refers, not to tombstones, but to sarcophagi: 'An *arca di marmo* ... enriches our sense of Guido's plight and Guido's leap ... What lies behind Cavalcanti as Betto's men close in is a row of stone boxes with very thick walls. They are also very large. The sarcophagus now in the Cathedral museum's courtyard and its companion stand over a metre high. Factor in a lid of some thickness, and the sarcophagi now tower over a Fiat 500 and match the height of men six hundred years ago ... No horses can pursue [Cavalcanti] along the narrow passage left between the *arche* and the Baptistery's south-east wall.' Watson's interpretation of the passage is correct, but it is questionable whether a more exact translation would be better suited to the context for an English reader. Later in the same article, Watson makes the novel suggestion that in B.'s tale, Cavalcanti may be seen as '*Mercurius psychopompos*, the god who conducts the souls of the Dead to the Underworld'.

Tenth Story

1. ***friars of Saint Anthony*** The founder of organized monasticism, St Anthony (*c.* 251–356) was one of the most popular saints of the early Middle Ages. The black-robed Hospitallers of Saint Anthony were a familiar sight in the towns and villages of western Europe, ringing small bells as they collected alms. But by the end of the thirteenth century, their greed, like that of their pigs which were allowed by special dispensation to

roam freely through the streets, had become proverbial. Dante writes scathingly (*Paradiso*, XXIX, 124) of Anthony fattening his swine on empty promises ('*Di questo ingrassa il porco sant' Antonio*').

2. **Certaldo** The town where B. spent most of the last thirteen years of his life lies about twenty miles south-west of Florence. He was possibly born there, and in an earlier work he proudly describes himself as one of its citizens.

3. **Cipolla** A *cipolla* is an onion, as may be deduced from the reason B. gives for the character's popularity in and around Certaldo, where an onion is depicted in the town's coat of arms. Like most of what Cipolla later has to say in his famous sermon to his captive audience, his name carries nonsensical and equivocal overtones.

4. **Cicero ... Quintilian** Two of the most famous orators and rhetoricians of ancient Rome.

5. **after nones** After three o'clock in the afternoon.

6. **the citadel** The *castello*, or citadel, situated in the upper part of the town, was the headquarters of the local administration.

7. **Guccio Porco** Balena ('Whale'), Imbratta ('Befoul') and Porco ('Pig'), the nicknames of Cipolla's servant, form the preliminaries to a grotesque caricature, introduced with an unusual amount of supporting detail. The only other character in the *Decameron* to be presented in so prolix a fashion is Ser Ciappelletto (I, 1), where the narrative required a clear initial awareness of the dying man's iniquitous way of life. Here, on the other hand, the verbose description of Guccio and of his wooing of the scullerymaid foreshadow the ludicrous oratorical outpourings of Cipolla himself.

8. **Lippo Topo** Once thought to be a cartoonist of moderate artistic talent specializing in the drawing of comically distorted figures, Lippo Topo seems in fact to have been proverbial for his laziness, but there is no evidence that he was a painter.

9. **Altopascio** The abbey of the Hospitallers, near Lucca, renowned for its generous doles of soup.

10. **the Lord of Chatillon** A fictional title suggesting the possessor of enormous wealth.

11. **Confiteor** Literally 'I confess', the *Confiteor* is a prayer recited at the beginning of the Mass and other church rituals.

12. **those parts where the sun appears** The sun will appear anywhere, but Cipolla is giving his listeners the impression that he has travelled in the Orient. In similar vein, he later claims to have visited 'the mountains of the Basques, where all the waters flow downwards', as though this were a phenomenon that was out of the ordinary.

13. *the privileges of the Porcellana* Probably a veiled reference to the practice of sodomy, a vice to which monks and friars were traditionally susceptible. But Porcellana, like most of the places named in the opening section of Cipolla's sermon, was also the name of a locality in Florence. In the translation, an attempt has been made to preserve the humorous impact of Cipolla's rapid succession of Florentine *doubles entendres*, in many cases replacing them with others having wider European and/or Mediterranean associations.

14. *the land of Abruzzi* Wild and inaccessible, the mountainous Abruzzi region in eastern Italy would have suggested to Cipolla's audience a remote part of the universe. His claim that the inhabitants 'go climbing the hills in clogs' has strong homosexual undertones (see notes to V, 10).

15. *clothe pigs in their own entrails* i.e. 'make sausages', but the phrase probably has obscene connotations, like the reference to their 'carrying bread on staves, and wine in pouches'.

16. *Parsnipindia* The original reads '*India Pastinaca*'. B. is possibly using *pastinaca* ('parsnip') in the same way that *carota* ('carrot') is sometimes used to indicate a cock-and-bull story.

17. *Maso del Saggio* Well known in fourteenth-century Florence as a perpetrator of practical jokes, he appears again in three later stories (VIII, 3, 5 and 6).

18. *Besokindas Tocursemenot* In the original, *Nonmiblasmete Sevoipiace*, a name coined on Old French: '*Ne me blasmez se vos plait.*'

19. *all the holy relics* Like Chaucer's Pardoner, Cipolla is the instrument for a satirical attack on the cult of holy relics, which by the mid-fourteenth century had reached its zenith. B.'s catalogue of relics is more equivocal than Chaucer's, incorporating certain items that are clearly blasphemous, such as the 'straight and firm' finger of the Holy Ghost and 'the Word-made-flash-in-the-pan'. The latter phrase represents the translator's despairing attempt to render B.'s hugely comical '*Verbum-caro-fatti-alle-finestre*' (literally 'Verbum-Caro-get-thee-to-the-windows'), a corruption of *John* i, 14: '*Verbum caro factum est*' ('And the Word was made flesh').

20. *the Rumpiad . . . Capretius* By inviting comparison to the *Iliad* and Lucretius, the translation comes near to conveying the strong homosexual overtones of B.'s *Monte Morello* (a mountain north of Florence whose name also serves as a slang term for the male posterior), and *Caprezio*, based on the Italian name for the Latin poet. A *capro* being a he-goat, the two names suggest the practice of sodomy in both its passive and active forms.

21. *Saint Gherardo da Villamagna's sandals* Saint Gherardo was one of the earliest followers of Saint Francis of Assisi. By claiming he had

presented one of the saint's sandals (*zoccoli*) to Gherardo di Bonsi ('who holds him in the deepest veneration'), Cipolla is implying that the latter was given to homosexual practices. Gherardo di Bonsi was in fact one of the most highly respected members of the Arte della Lana, the Florentine woollen guild, and founder of the hospital of San Gherardo in the Via San Gallo.

22. *the Feast of Saint Lawrence* i.e. 10 August. Popular tradition has it that Saint Lawrence was martyred by being roasted on a gridiron, which is the saint's emblem, but it is more likely that he was beheaded.

23. *they will never be touched by fire without getting burnt* Cipolla's concluding master stroke is to make his hearers believe the opposite of what he actually says.

(Conclusion)

1. *a guilty conscience* Dioneo's suggestion of the possible reason for the ladies' reluctance to discuss the topic he has prescribed, anticipating Freud, reflects B.'s intuitive understanding of the human psyche.

2. *the Valley of the Ladies* The third, and most elaborate, *locus amœnus* in the *Decameron* is a refined and more detailed version of similar locations described in two of B.'s earlier works, the *Caccia di Diana* and *Ninfale fiesolano*. It will become the setting for the tales of adulterous wives recounted on the Seventh Day, where the contrast between the mythical, pre-lapsarian world of the storytellers and the everyday world of the narratives is more than usually pronounced.

3. *carole* A medieval dance in a ring or chain, performed to the singing · of the dancers.

4. *flowers of red and white* Perhaps the flowers associated with wedding rites: roses and lilies.

5. *cornemuse* A kind of bagpipe.

SEVENTH DAY

(Introduction)

1. *Lucifer* The morning star, or the planet Venus as it appears in the sky before sunrise. The oblique reference to Venus may be a signifier of the venereal doings of the chief characters of the day's stories.

First Story

1. **werewolves** The Italian term is *fantasima*, described by B.'s contemporary, Jacopo Passavanti, as 'an animal resembling a satyr, or cat monkey, which goes around at night causing distress to people'.

2. **San Pancrazio** A district named after the Franciscan convent on what is now the Via della Spada. Friar Puccio, the pious and simple-minded husband of III, 4, lived in the same quarter of the city.

3. **the song of Saint Alexis** Possibly the *Ritmo di Sant'Alessio*, one of the earliest specimens of Italian verse, written in the early thirteenth century.

4. **the lament of Saint Bernard** Perhaps a rhyming version of the so-called *Sayings of St Bernard.*

5. **the laud of Lady Matilda** Matilde of Magdeburg, a mystic whose visions were given currency in Italy by the Dominicans, the monastic order that controlled the church of Santa Maria Novella.

6. **Mannuccio dalla Cuculia** The Mannucci were a prominent Florentine family, who lived in the San Frediano quarter, one of whose districts was called Cuculia ('cuckoo') after a chapel containing a painting of the Madonna that included a cuckoo. But the name given by B. to Monna Tessa's father comically prefigures the gulling of her pious husband.

7. **Camerata** A village on the slopes leading up to Fiesole, a few miles north of Florence.

8. **the skull of an ass** The placing of an ass's skull on a stake to protect one's crops was a propitiatory rite going back to the times of the ancient Etruscans. B. has given the custom a secondary purpose.

9. **Te lucis** The hymn attributed to Saint Ambrose in which God's help is invoked against nocturnal spirits. It includes the words '*Procul recedant somnia/Et noctium phantasmata*' ('May dreams and phantoms of the night go far away').

10. **Intemerata** The popular antiphon *O Virgo intemerata* ('O Virgin undefiled') was one of the prayers mockingly listed by the highway robber in the story of Rinaldo d'Asti (II, 2).

11. **have a good spit** According to popular tradition, spitting was an essential part of the exorcizing ritual. In his book on popular Sicilian incantational formulas, Giuseppe Bonomo writes that 'Spitting is a very powerful means of warding off the evil eye' and that 'If you spit three times it is even better.' When Federigo responds to Gianni's spitting by groaning about his teeth, he is giving the impression that the fangs of the werewolf have been well and truly drawn.

12. **this second account** The alternative version is invoked, both to en-

hance the tale's plausibility by giving it the air of an actual event, and to allow the insertion of a second incantation, almost as comical as the first.

Second Story

1. **Peronella**   The tale of Peronella and the tub is derived directly, like that of the homosexual husband (V, 10), from *The Golden Ass* by Apuleius, one of B.'s favourite Latin authors.

2. **Giannello Scrignario**   As usual in B.'s narratives, the character's name is that of an actual person. Giannello is a diminutive of Giovanni, and the Scrignari brothers, Giovanni and Niccolò, are recorded in 1324 as living in or near the Piazza Portanova, near the Avorio district, where the *novella* is set.

3. **the feast of Saint Galeone**   Not the most familiar of saints, Galeone (or Eucalione) had a chapel dedicated to him in that part of Naples where the action of the story takes place.

4. **a Parthian mare**   'One doesn't have to go as far as Parthia to see stallions adopting an approach from behind to mares on heat' (Almansi). That is so, but B. doubtless had in mind that Parthians were famous for turning their backs, as Peronella does to facilitate her lover's access, and he is here employing a modified version of a simile derived from Apuleius and Ovid. Almansi correctly points out that the image forms part in the original text of some splendidly rhythmical and evocative prose.

Third Story

1. **the child's godfather**   In the Middle Ages, the bond between a child's natural parent and its godparent was held to be so sacred that any sexual relationship between the two was considered incestuous.

2. **not the one from Milan**   The saint referred to in the story is not Saint Ambrose, patron saint of Milan, but a Dominican friar of Siena, the Blessed Ambrogio Sansedoni, who was posthumously honoured by the Commune of Siena in 1288 when a chapel was dedicated to his memory.

Fourth Story

1. **Arezzo**   A flourishing commune in fourteenth-century Italy, Arezzo lies some forty-five miles south-east of Florence. Petrarch, B.'s friend and mentor, was born there in 1304. It was (and still is) notable for its many splendid churches and other elegant buildings. It is slightly surprising that

this is the only story in the *Decameron* to be set in so distinctive a city. Typically Aretine are the names of the husband and wife, Tofano and Ghita, diminutives of Cristofano (Cristoforo) and Margherita respectively. The jealousy of husbands was a common theme in medieval popular literature. This particular story appears to be directly derived from one of the *exempla* in Peter Alphonsi's *Disciplina clericalis*, a collection of anecdotes used by preachers as source material for moralizing sermons.

Fifth Story

1. *she seated herself at his feet*   As noted earlier (III, 8, note 1), this was the penitent's normal posture in the presence of the priest confessor. The confessional in its present form was introduced after the Council of Trent in the sixteenth century.

2. *A little before tierce*   Usually interpreted as just before 9 a.m. Strictly speaking, tierce is the third hour after sunrise, which at Christmas time, when the action of the story takes place, would be later in the morning.

Sixth Story

1. *those who naïvely maintain that Love impairs the intellect*   The narrator is probably thinking of various Latin tags claiming that Love and Wisdom were incompatible. A more recent formulation is Samuel Johnson's 'Love is the wisdom of the fool and the folly of the wise.'

Seventh Story

1. *Madonna Beatrice, the wife of Egano de' Galluzzi*   The Galluzzi were a prominent Bologna family, but there is no record of any Egano Galluzzi. The name Beatrice inevitably recalls that of the lady fulsomely described by Dante in the *Vita nuova*, in whose honour he composed the *Divine Comedy*. The Provençal troubadour Jaufré Rudel had been a prominent singer of distant love (*amor de lonh*) in the twelfth century, and the first part of B.'s story is suffused with the motifs of the poetry of courtly love and of early French chivalresque romance. Other examples of *amor de lonh* may be found in the stories of the Marchioness of Montferrat and the King of France (I, 5) and of Gerbino's fateful love for the daughter of the King of Tunis (IV, 4).

2. *to play chess*   The game of chess as the agency for revealing amorous passion was a common topos in the medieval romances. B. had used it in Book IV of his own early prose romance, the *Filocolo*.

3. *the blood of Bologna!* Unlike the ladies of Pisa (II, 10), Venice (IV, 2) and Milan (VIII, 1), those of Bologna are always presented by B. in a favourable light. (See I, 10 and X, 4.)

4. *a sound thrashing* The sadistic pleasure experienced by adulterous lovers in the thrashing of a husband is a common motif in the medieval French narrative poems known as *fabliaux*, from which the plot-outlines of many of B.'s narratives are derived. The second part of B.'s story can be traced to a number of these, among them *De la dame qui fist batre son mari* ('On the Lady who has her Husband Beaten').

Eighth Story

1. *Berlinghieri* The rise to prominence in Florentine commercial and civic affairs of the Berlinghieri family began around the middle of the fourteenth century, at the time when B. was composing his hundred tales. His account of the marriage of Arriguccio Berlinghieri, of whom incidentally there is no historical record, may be read (like III, 3) as a cautionary tale in which a representative of the Florentine *nouveaux riches* gets his just deserts for aspiring to the ranks of the aristocracy. Certain elements of the story, such as the wife's deceiving of her husband by substituting another woman for herself, are originally to be found in oriental narrative collections such as the *Panchatantra*. As in the previous story, there are clear links with certain of the French *fabliaux*, for instance *De la dame qui fist entendant son mari qu'il sonjoit* ('On the Lady who Persuades her Husband that he is Dreaming'). The shearing of the unfaithful wife's hair has a classical antecedent in Tacitus. But B. makes the story characteristically his own by such details as the length of string attached to the wife's toe and his graphic portrayal of life in contemporary Florence.

2. *with a quill sticking out* It was the custom for merchants and notaries to carry a quill and inkpot in a holder, either attached to their belt or carried in the back pocket of their trousers.

Ninth Story

1. *Argos* By setting the story in ancient Greece, B. is attempting to distance himself from his Latin model, where no location is specified. He enhances the Greek flavour of his own version by changing the husband's name from Decius to Nicostratos. The names of the other characters remain unaltered.

2. *Lydia* The name is that of the protagonist of the medieval Latin poem *Comoedia Lydiae* by Matthew of Vendôme, from which this story clearly

derives, and of which there exists a version transcribed by B. himself in a manuscript known (because it is located in the Laurentian Library in Florence) as the *Codice Laurenziano*. There are numerous antecedents in medieval literature of stories involving the humiliation of a husband as proof of an adulterous wife's devotion to her lover.

3. *Lusca*   In the original Latin poem, the author spares no effort to highlight the connotations of the maidservant's name, equivalent to the French *louche*, meaning not only 'squint-eyed', but 'shady' or 'disreputable'.

4. *a beautiful pear-tree*   Pear-trees producing hallucinatory effects of the kind that Lydia convinces her husband he has experienced are found in French *fabliaux* as well as in other medieval collections of narratives. English-speaking readers will possibly be reminded of the more improbable situation recounted by Chaucer in *The Merchant's Tale*, where the husband's blindness is cured when his wife and her lover engage in sexual congress above his head, precariously perched in the pear-tree's branches.

Tenth Story

1. *the extraordinary simplicity of the Sienese*   As in the earlier story (VII, 3) to which Dioneo refers both at the beginning and at the end of his tale of Tingoccio and Meuccio, the proverbial credulity of the Sienese once again becomes a target for B.'s satire. In both stories, their belief in the quasi-sacred bond of *comparatico* (the status accorded to godparents) is seriously undermined.

(Conclusion)

1. *your namesake*   Lauretta is the diminutive of Laura, the name of the woman whose beauty was celebrated by Petrarch in the poems of his *Canzoniere*. The play on words between the name Laura and *lauro* ('laurel'), the shrub associated with poetic fame, is a recurrent feature of Petrarch's poetry.

2. *Palamon and Arcite*   The two aspirants for the love of Emilia in B.'s prolix narrative poem, the *Teseida*, which Chaucer reduced to more readable proportions in his *Knight's Tale*. The story, just ended, of Tingoccio and Meuccio is read by some commentators as a brief self-parody of B.'s epic.

3. *when Neifile was our queen*   See the Conclusion to the Second Day, where Neifile spells out the reasons for desisting from storytelling on Fridays and Saturdays.

EIGHTH DAY

(Introduction)

1. *a nearby chapel* The attendance of the *brigata* at Sunday Mass in a nearby chapel marks the first and only time that their total isolation from the outside world is breached.

First Story

1. *Madonna Ambruogia* The lady's name is the feminine form of the name of Milan's patron saint, Ambrose. Guasparruolo's grasping wife may be taken as personifying the rapacity of the Milanese, a failing earlier alluded to by the phrase 'in the Milanese fashion' in the concluding lines of the Third Day. The story, based on a French *fabliau*, is retold by Chaucer in *The Shipman's Tale*.

Second Story

1. *Avignon* Seat of the Papacy from 1309 to 1377 during its 'Babylonian Captivity'.

2. *Varlungo* A village in the valley of the Arno now forming part of Florence itself.

3. *Monna Belcolore* Similar in plot to the previous tale, the story of Monna Belcolore (literally 'Mistress Finecolour') is set in B.'s home territory, the Florentine *contado*. Like Cipolla's sermon (VI, 10), it is marked throughout by its richly animated effusions of verbal humour. No translation could do proper justice to its high-spirited account of rustic midsummer passion, reinforced in the telling by a constant stream of Florentinisms and double meanings.

4. *Bentivegna del Mazzo* The name (literally 'may you have joy of the rod'), is of course equivocal. It is also distinctively Florentine, like those of a colourful gallery of other characters whom B. has inserted into the story to enhance its comic effect: Ser Bonaccorri da Ginestreto, Lapuccio, Naldino, Biliuzza, Lotto, Buglietto, Binguccio dal Poggio and Nuto Buglietti. None of these has any real function in the narrative. They are personalities who flash momentarily into being and then subside, like sparks from a catherine wheel.

5. *leather thongs* The priest's curious request hints at an interest in bondage.

6. **Douai**   An expensive fabric taking its name from Douai, in Flanders.

Third Story

1. **Calandrino**   Nickname of the Florentine thirteenth/fourteenth-century painter Nozzo di Perino, famous for his simple-mindedness. This is the first of four stories in the *Decameron* in which he appears as the protagonist, the others being VIII, 6, IX, 3 and IX, 5. Of his two companions, Bruno and Buffalmacco, the latter was a painter of some stature, whose frescoes can still be admired in the church of the Badia in Florence and in the cathedral of Arezzo, as well as in the Camposanto of Pisa.

2. **Maso del Saggio**   Fleetingly referred to earlier in Fra Cipolla's sermon (VI, 10), Maso del Saggio was a well-known Florentine prankster, one of whose escapades is recounted later in the tale of the Marchesan judge (VIII, 5). His nonsensical replies to Calandrino's questions are reminiscent of the gibberish used by Cipolla to hoodwink his audience outside the church in Certaldo.

3. **More than a milling, that spends the whole night trilling**   The translation attempts to preserve the rhyming form of the original ('*più di millanta, che tutta notte canta*'), together with a word suggesting a large number ('milling', for *millanta*, which is based on *mille*, 'thousand').

4. **Monte Morello**   As explained in VI, 10, note 19, Monte Morello is a hill north of Florence whose name carried distinct homosexual overtones.

5. **heliotrope**   Old name for bloodstone, a dark-green variety of quartz spotted with red jasper, used as a semi-precious gem. Dante refers to its magical quality of rendering its bearer invisible in *Inferno* (XXIV, 93), where he writes that the souls of the thieves had no hope of any crevice or heliotrope ('*Senza sperar pertugio o elitropia*') to conceal them from the hideous snakes tormenting them.

6. **Mugnone**   A tributary of the Arno entering the main river near Florence.

7. **in the Hainaut style**   i.e. short and narrow-waisted.

8. **all things lose their virtue in the presence of a woman**   An ancient proverb, popular in medieval times. It was probably based on the story of Adam and Eve.

Fourth Story

1. **a provost**   The head of a cathedral or principal church.

2. **a city of great antiquity**   Fiesole lies on a hill overlooking the Arno and Mugnone valleys a few miles north-east of Florence. It was an important

garrison town and commercial centre in Roman times long before Florence itself was established, but declined rapidly after being conquered by barbarians in AD 405.

3. *Senigallia*   A town on the Adriatic coast, now a seaside resort, but notorious in B.'s day for malaria.

4. *Ciutazza*   The name 'Ciuta' in itself has a repulsive ring about it, which is intensified by the pejorative suffix *-azza*. B.'s portrayal of the maidservant here is reminiscent of his earlier description of the kitchenwench, Nuta, in the tale of Friar Cipolla (VI, 10). The probable source for B.'s story about the substitution of a maidservant for her mistress is the French *fabliau* entitled *Du prestre et d'Alison*.

Fifth Story

1. *the Marches*   A province of eastern Italy bordering on the Adriatic from which the chief magistrate (*podestà*) of Florence was frequently recruited during the fourteenth century.

Sixth Story

1. *the bread and cheese test*   A rudimentary form of lie detector, popular in the Middle Ages, in which people suspected of uttering an untruth were invited to consume a bread and cheese confection whilst a magic formula was being recited. Their inability to swallow it was taken as a sign that they were lying.

2. *dog ginger*   Dog ginger is water pepper, a marsh weed having an acrid juice. B. wrote '*quelle del cane*' ('those of the dog'), which until recently was misinterpreted by most of his English translators as 'dog stools' or 'dog turds'.

3. *the time you took us along the Mugnone*   See VIII, 3.

Seventh Story

1. *leaving her a widow*   The sexual magnetism of widows was a common theme in medieval literature. Other examples in the *Decameron* itself are seen in II, 2, IV, 1, VIII, 4, VIII, 7 and IX, 1. In the *questioni d'amore* sequence of the *Filocolo* (Book IV), there is a long discussion on the question, eventually answered in the affirmative, of whether the love of a widow is preferable to that of a virgin. In stressing the attractions of widows, B. was following the precepts of medieval love theorists such as Andreas Capellanus.

2. **Rinieri** The scholar of this tale, the longest in the *Decameron*, is thought by many commentators to be in part a self-portrait, the account of Rinieri's encounter with the widow Elena reflecting some keenly felt personal experience of unrequited love. An interpretation along those lines seems to be strengthened by a later work, *Corbaccio*, in which B. writes a first-person narrative describing how he fell desperately in love with a widow by whom he was heartlessly rejected. He describes a dream in which he meets the soul of the woman's late husband, who provides such a detailed catalogue of her numerous repellent shortcomings that the narrator is cured of his infatuation. The *Corbaccio* is possibly the most violent anti-feminist diatribe in medieval literature. The tale of the scholar and the widow, also strongly misogynist in tone, casts serious doubt upon B.'s oft-repeated claim, in the pages of the *Decameron*, that his purpose is to bring comfort and pleasure to his lady readers. Another important feature of the tale is the cleverly arranged series of retributive measures, exact opposites of his own torments, that are devised by the scholar to avenge his humiliation. One is reminded of Dante's law of *contrapasso*, whereby sinners are punished exactly according to their deserts, in most cases with what would seem excessive force.

3. **turned into a stork** The same expression was used to describe Rinaldo d'Asti in a similar predicament (II, 2).

4. **shake your skin-coat** 'coït' (Partridge). The Italian reads '*scuotere i pilliccioni*,' a phrase repeated by Dioneo in his provocative concluding gloss on the story of Griselda (p. 795).

Eighth Story

1. **Spinelloccio Tavena ... Zeppa di Mino** The names are those of actual people recorded as living in the Camollia district of Siena around the turn of the fourteenth century, but unlike the characters in B.'s story, both were prominent city burghers. As in the previous tale, the events recall Dante's law of *contrapasso*, in this case applied with less severity, and leading (according to the author) to a happy ending for all of the parties concerned.

2. **his dishonour would thereby be increased** Zeppa's reactions to his discovery that he has been cuckolded are precisely the same as those of King Agilulf in III, 2. In the code of honour to which B.'s readers subscribed, keeping up appearances was sometimes more important than acknowledging reality.

Ninth Story

1. *vair*   A fur, usually from a grey and white squirrel, used for trimming doctoral gowns, which were (and still are) traditionally red in colour. Florentine physicians were trained at Bologna, the oldest Italian university. The university at Florence was not founded until 1349.

2. *Via del Cocomero*   Literally 'Water-Melon Street', it now forms part of the Via Ricasoli, near the Mercato Vecchio. In IX, 3, the location of Simone's surgery is given as 'the Mercato Vecchio, at the sign of the pumpkin'. In each case, it is implied that the occupier of the premises was a simpleton.

3. *mentioned twice here today*   See VIII, 3 and VIII, 6.

4. *the Lucifer at San Gallo*   The façade of the hospital of San Gallo, like the Camposanto in Pisa, carried a large fresco of Lucifer with several mouths, each devouring a sinner. The image derives from Dante, who in canto XXXIV of *Inferno* reserves this punishment for the worst of all sinners, those who committed an act of treachery to their lords and benefactors, specifically Judas, Brutus and Cassius. Dante's conception of Lucifer was probably inspired by the iconographical tradition of Doom mosaics and frescoes. Both he and Boccaccio would have been familiar with just such a mosaic on the ceiling of the Baptistery in Florence.

5. *the cross of Montesone*   Montesone, or Montisoni, is a hill not far from Florence surmounted by a large cross.

6. *Michael Scott*   Scottish philosopher who lived at the court of Frederick II of Sicily. He became a legendary figure in the Middle Ages as a master of the occult sciences. Dante places him among the souls of the Sorcerers in the lower depths of Hell, describing him in *Inferno*, XX, 115–16 as one who 'truly knew every trick of the magical arts' (*veramente/delle magiche frode seppe il gioco*'). In more recent literature, he is referred to in Scott's *Lay of the Last Minstrel* as the wizard of Balwearie.

7. *the Skinkymurra of Prester John*   Bruno's hilarious catalogue of apocryphal first ladies concludes with a reference to the supposed consort of Prester John, himself a figure of dubious authenticity, who was said to be the fabulously wealthy pro-Christian ruler of a far-flung eastern empire. Legends concerning Prester John and his determination to drive the Muslims from Jerusalem, brought back to western Europe by the crusaders, were subject to rich embellishment in the thirteenth and fourteenth centuries.

8. *the cumin*   A medicinal herb with aromatic seeds, said to be effective in expelling wind.

9. *a chamber-pot over his front door*   The distinctive sign for a doctor's surgery, urine analysis being the most commonly used method of diagnosing ailments. But like the previous reference to the pounding of cumin, mention of the chamber-pot is also one of a series of signals en route to the tale's scatological ending.

10. **Hippocras and Avicenna**   Hippocras, or Hippocrates (*c.* 460–*c.* 377 BC) is traditionally regarded as the father of medicine. Avicenna (AD 980–1037), the renowned Persian physician, wrote the *Canon of Medicine*, one of the most famous books in the history of medical science.

11. **Peretola**   A small town about three miles west of Florence.

12. **Cacavincigli**   Yet another scatological reference anticipating the conclusion of the narrative, Cacavincigli (literally 'shit-fodder') was the Florentine name for a street or alley inhabited by riff-raff.

13. **Vallecchio**   A village some twenty miles south-west of Florence, now forming part of Castelfiorentino.

14. **Forlimpopoli**   A town between Forlí and Cesena. The farcical associations of its name were exploited four centuries later by Carlo Goldoni for one of his most famous comic creations, the Marchese di Forlimpopoli, in *La locandiera* (1753). The name of the magistrate to whom Master Simone refers, Guasparruolo da Saliceto, is probably based on Guglielmo da Saliceto, a well-known professor of medicine at Bologna at the turn of the fourteenth century.

15. *the great tall God of Passignano*   Passignano lies on the northern shore of Lake Trasimeno. Its main church had a large fresco depicting God the Father.

16. *you were christened on a Sunday*   Buffalmacco is implying that Simone is brainless, because *sale* ('salt', but also 'mother-wit') could not be bought on Sundays.

17. *the Countess of Cesspool*   The original text reads *la Contessa di Civillari*. One of B.'s early commentators explains that Civillari was an alleyway on the outskirts of Florence used as a public lavatory, from which local farmers dug channels to draw off rich fertilizing material for their crops.

18. **Laterina**   An obvious scatological pun on the name of a village in the Arno valley, not far from Arezzo.

19. *the raised tombs*   Most of the sarcophagi outside Santa Maria Novella were erected there in 1314.

20. *a Knight of the Bath*   The Italian text reads *cavalier bagnato*. Like most chivalric orders, the British Order of the Bath, established by King George I in 1725, has antecedents dating from the Middle Ages. Bathing as a

purification ritual for newly created knights was probably introduced as early as the eleventh century.

21. *I was commenced* 'I received my degree.' The verb is still current at degree ceremonies in Trinity College, Dublin, and at Cambridge.

22. *no longer held* The narrator is probably referring to the *Gioco del Veglio* ('Game of the Old Man'), a mummer's dance featuring the impersonation of the Devil, banned in Florence in 1325.

23. *Santa Maria della Scala . . . the nunnery of Ripole* Buffalmacco's route lay along what is now known as the Via della Scala, past the hospital of Santa Maria (later the monastery of San Martino), founded in 1316, towards the nunnery of Sant' Jacopo di Ripoli. According to Vasari and others the latter contained paintings by both Bruno and Buffalmacco.

Tenth Story

1. *dogana* The Italian word for customs or custom-house is Arabic in origin. In the present context, it is one of a series of elements that lend an exotic flavour to the narrative. The opening paragraph is important as the earliest recorded description, based no doubt upon personal experience, of the workings of a bonded warehouse.

2. *Niccolò da Cignano* The Cignano family was very active in Florentine civic affairs. The name Niccolò di Cecco da Cignano appears in the municipal records around the middle of the fourteenth century. He was possibly employed by the Compagnia Scali, which enjoyed special trading privileges in Angevin territories in Naples and Sicily.

3. *Jancofiore* The Sicilian form of Biancofiore, or Blanchefleur, the Saracen heroine of the Old French metrical romance used by B. as the basis for his turgid prose romance, *Filocolo*. There is an obvious parallel between Jancofiore and the scheming Sicilian woman in the story of Andreuccio (II, 5).

4. *Pietro dello Canigiano* A fellow Florentine and contemporary of B., Pietro dello Canigiano was an influential figure in Angevin courtly circles.

5. *Empress of Constantinople* Catherine of Valois–Courtenay (1301–46), a descendant of the last Latin emperor of Constantinople, Baldwin II.

6. *Monegasque pirates* Paganino, the swashbuckling hero of II, 10, also came from Monaco, a notorious haven for pirates.

(Conclusion)

1. *whatever subject he or she may choose* The stories of the ninth day, like those of the first, will not be restricted to a single prescribed topic.

NINTH DAY

(Introduction)

1. *the eighth heaven* In the Ptolemaic system, the heaven of the 'fixed' stars.

First Story

1. *Palermini ... Chiarmontesi* Both families are recorded by Giovanni Villani as being exiled from Florence for political feuding in support of the Ghibellines. The Chiarmontesi later switched their allegiance to the Guelphs.

2. *Francesca de' Lazzari* The de' Lazzari were a powerful Pistoia family, well known for their active support of the guelphs.

3. *she conceived a plan* Stories concerning the stratagems of women to rid themselves of unwanted suitors were commonplace in medieval literature. B. himself narrates another in X, 5.

4. *Scannadio* The nickname itself (literally 'slit the throat of God') suggests a person of uncommon villainy.

Second Story

1. *psalters* Nuns' veils were so called because their triangular shape resembled that of the musical instrument known as a psalter or psaltery.

Third Story

1. *Nello* Nello di Bandino, a close friend of Bruno and Buffalmacco, is portrayed in IX, 5 as being related to Calandrino's wife, Tessa.

2. *Master Simone* See VIII, 9 for an account of the origins of the doctor's 'close friendship' with Bruno and Buffalmacco.

Fourth Story

1. *Angiulieri* Cecco Angiolieri (c. 1260–c. 1312), a contemporary of Dante's, was the leading figure in the school of burlesque realist poetry that flourished in Tuscany at the turn of the fourteenth century.

2. *Fortarrigo*   Cecco di Fortarrigo Piccolomini, to whom one of Angiolieri's sonnets is addressed, was charged with murder in 1293 and found guilty, but the sentence was not carried out.

3. *their hatred of their respective fathers*   A well-known sonnet of Angiolieri's contains the line '*S' i' fosse morte, andarei da mio padre*' ('If I were death, I'd pay a call on my father'). In a later sonnet addressed to Fortarrigo, he announces the death of his own father, at the same time wishing Fortarrigo's equally detested father immortality. It would seem that B. had the two sonnets in mind when composing his narrative, although his description of Angiolieri ('as handsome a man as he was courteous') contradicts the image of the man that emerges from a reading of Angiolieri's poems.

4. *Buonconvento*   A small town about twenty-five miles south of Siena, where the traveller to the Marches would take a left fork.

5. *at the hour of nones*   About 3 o'clock in the afternoon.

6. *Corsignano*   A town some twelve miles east of Buonconvento, later renamed Pienza by Pope Pius II, Aeneas Silvius Piccolomini, who was born there in 1405.

7. *Torrenieri*   Another small town, roughly halfway between Buonconvento and Corsignano.

Fifth Story

1. *Niccolò Cornacchini*   The Cornacchini were merchant bankers, trading in partnership with the better known Compagnia dei Frescobaldi. Their foreign interests included a branch in England.

2. *Camerata*   A location between Florence and Fiesole where many wealthy Florentines owned country villas. Camerata was also the setting for the story of the mysterious werewolf (VII, 1).

3. *Camaldoli*   A street in the San Pier Maggiore quarter.

4. *Tessa*   Calandrino's wife.

5. *rebeck*   A three-stringed musical instrument of the viola family, with a pear-shaped body and slender neck.

6. *with all those stones*   See the story of Calandrino and the heliotrope (VIII, 3).

7. *getting you with child*   Monna Tessa is referring to the explanation Calandrino had given for his supposed pregnancy (IX, 3).

Sixth Story

1. **the Mugnone** The Mugnone valley, where Calandrino went searching for the heliotrope (VIII, 3), runs north from Florence towards the Romagna.

2. **three small beds** The story of the three beds will be familiar to English readers from Chaucer's use of the same narrative material in *The Reeve's Tale*. The tale had originally appeared in two French *fabliaux*: *De Gombert et les deux clers* and *Le meunier et les deux clers*. B.'s version differs from the others in two important respects. Not only does the host's wife, like the first of the youths, occupy all three beds at various points in the narrative, but by ending up in her daughter's bed she is able to weave a fanciful explanation of what has actually happened, convincing her husband that neither she herself nor their daughter has been interfered with. Thus the story reaches a conclusion that is satisfactory to all of the parties concerned.

Seventh Story

1. **on previous occasions** See IV, 5 and IV, 6.

2. **Talano d'Imolese** The name suggests that, though living in Florence, his family came from Imola, in the Romagna. Talano is a shortened form of Catalano, a name which, according to Branca, was not uncommon in Florence at that period. Stories concerning the unpleasant fate of shrewish women who ignored danger signals are found in other literatures, but this tale, like the tale of the scholar and the widow (VIII, 7) and that of Solomon's advice to the hen-pecked husband (IX, 9), strengthens the view that the *Decameron* is not so feminist a work as its author would have us believe.

Eighth Story

1. **Ciacco** The name, probably a diminutive of Giacomo or Jacopo, became synonymous with the sin of gluttony because of a well-known episode in canto VI of Dante's *Inferno*, where the souls of the gluttonous are subjected to an uninterrupted and foul-smelling torrent of hail, snow and polluted rain. The sinners are lying prone, but Ciacco raises himself to a sitting position and supplies Dante with a prophecy of the poet's imminent exile from Florence. There is no actual record that either Ciacco or his antagonist in B.'s story, Biondello, ever existed.

2. **Vieri de' Cerchi** A rich and powerful political leader, head of the

Florentine White Guelphs, Vieri de' Cerchi was exiled in 1301 and died in Arezzo in 1304.

3. *Corso Donati's* Nicknamed 'Il Barone', Corso Donati was the head of the Black Guelphs. He was exiled in 1300, returned to Florence with the support of Charles of Valois in 1301, and was murdered by his political adversaries in 1308.

4. *Loggia de' Cavicciuli* A gallery forming part of the residence of the Cavicciuli-Adimari family on the Corso Adimari, now the Via Calzaiuoli.

5. *Filippo Argenti* Filippo degli Adimari dei Cavicciuli, renowned for his ostentatious displays of wealth, was called Filippo Argenti because he was said to have had his horse shod with silver (*argento*). His irascibility is memorably recorded by Dante in canto VIII of *Inferno*, where his spirit, immersed in the muddy waters of the Styx, attempts to emerge and grab Dante as he is crossing the river with his guide, Virgil.

Ninth Story

1. *Solomon* The son of David and Bathsheba, Solomon died around 930 BC. His legendary wisdom supplies B. with a pretext for recounting yet another strongly anti-feminist narrative (cf. VIII, 7 and IX, 7), this time set in remote antiquity.

2. *the rod is required* 'Yes, but not a wooden one' is the gloss supplied by one of B.'s earliest commentators, Mannelli.

3. *Melissus* The name is that of a Greek philosopher of the fifth century BC, here used anachronistically to enhance the impression of the story's ancient provenance.

4. *Lajazzo* In B.'s day, a flourishing port and trading centre in the eastern Mediterranean. See note to V, 7.

5. *Love ... and you will be loved* The saying appears in numerous contexts in classical and medieval moralistic writings, for example in one of Seneca's letters, where he writes '*Si vis amari, ama*' ('If you want to be loved, love!').

Tenth Story

1. *Barletta ... Barolo* Barletta is a port on the Adriatic about thirty miles north-west of Bari. Both the Bardi and the Peruzzi had trading posts there. Apart from a brief reference to Brindisi and Trani in II, 4, this is the only story in the *Decameron* set in the southern Italian province of Puglia, then a part of the Kingdom of Sicily. Barolo is the italianized form of the town's Latin name, Barduli.

2. **Tresanti** Town 'of the three saints' (*Trium Sanctorum*), lying some thirty-five miles west of Barletta.

3. **I can transform this mare** The adventures of a young man transformed by magic into an ass are recounted by Apuleius in *The Golden Ass*, of which the Latin title is *Metamorphoses*. Similar transformations occur in other works of medieval literature, including Vincent de Beauvais's *Speculum historiale*, Jacques de Vitry's *Exempla* and Jacopo Passavanti's *Specchio della vera penitenza*. The metamorphosis of a young woman into a mare is described in the *Vitae Patrum* ('Lives of the Fathers') from the *Patrologia Latina*.

4. **Bitonto** An inland market town some ten miles west of Bari, famous for its annual fair that was founded in 1316. It was held on All Saints' Day, 1 November, eleven days before a similar fair in Barletta.

(Conclusion)

1. **I am so young** The opening words of Neifile's song ('*Io mi son giovinetta*') recall the beginning of a poem of Dante's, which begins '*I' mi son pargoletta*'. Her song is in fact shot through with echoes of the poets of the *dolce stil novo*, especially Guido Cavalcanti, whose poem beginning '*Perch' io non spero*', written in exile, is recollected in Neifile's concluding words: '*ch' i' non disperi*'.

TENTH DAY

(Introduction)

1. **liberal or munificent deeds** Munificence (*magnificenzia*), the theme of the tenth and last day, was one of the eleven moral virtues of Aristotelian ethics. Dante defines it in the *Convivio* (IV, 17) as 'the moderator of great expenditures, making and supporting them within appropriate limits'.

First Story

1. **Ruggieri de' Figiovanni** The noble Florentine family of the Figiovanni owned houses and an estate near Certaldo. In the preface to his translation of Ovid's *Heroides*, Carlo de' Figiovanni claims that he often called at B.'s house in Certaldo during the writer's later years to ask for his assistance and advice, which were freely given.

2. **Alphonso of Spain**   The reference is probably to Alphonso X of Castile and Leon (1221–84), whose generosity became proverbial among poets and chroniclers of the period.

3. **two large chests**   There are numerous antecedents in both classical and medieval literature for the story's central episode, involving the act of choosing between two or more sealed cases. Portia's three caskets in *The Merchant of Venice* represent a further example of the same narrative device.

Second Story

1. **Ghino di Tacco**   A Sienese nobleman exiled from the city around 1295 for seizing the castle of Santafiora in the Tuscan Maremma belonging to the powerful Aldobrandeschi family. His stronghold of Radicofani was strategically situated on the Via Cassia, the main route between Rome and Siena. Like Robin Hood, he had a reputation as a highwayman who stole from the rich to give to the poor. B. follows the example of contemporary chroniclers in presenting Ghino in a favourable light, but another side of his character was revealed by his murder of a judge who had sentenced two of his close relatives to death in Siena. Disguising himself as a pilgrim, Ghino entered the courtroom in Rome where the judge was sitting, stabbed him, and carried off his head in triumph. Ghino himself met a violent end when he was assassinated in the countryside near Siena a few years later.

2. **Boniface VIII**   Mentioned briefly in I, 1 and VI, 2, Boniface VIII was pope from 1296 to 1303. It was his interference in Florentine political affairs that led to Dante's exile in 1301. Dante never forgave him, and reserved a place for him among the simoniac popes in the lower depths of his *Inferno*. B. expresses no view about his moral character, simply seeing him as an important figure of recent history.

3. **the Abbot of Cluny**   See I, 7, where B. reinforces the popular belief that he was the richest prelate in Christendom.

4. **the baths of Siena**   The southern region of Sienese territory contained several mineral springs, the best known being Chianciano Terme, about ten miles north of Radicofani.

5. **Corniglia**   A dry white wine named after a town in the Cinque Terre on the Ligurian coast, a few miles north-west of La Spezia.

6. **the Order of the Hospitallers**   Presumably the Order of Saint John of Jerusalem, in recognition of Ghino's proven healing powers! One recent commentator (David Wallace) suggests that Ghino is admitted to the Order 'as one who can cure the diseased body of the Church hierarchy'.

Third Story

1. **various Genoese**   B.'s account of Nathan and his palace was almost certainly based on the description of Kublai Khan written by Marco Polo, a Venetian. His antipathy towards Venice (see IV, 2) probably accounts for his reluctance to clarify his real source.

2. **Cathay**   The riches and wonders of Cathay, or northern China, were fulsomely described by Marco Polo in *Il Milione*. Coleridge made use of the same ultimate source for the *locus amœnus* he depicts in the opening lines of *Kubla Khan*: 'In Xanadu did Kubla Khan / A stately pleasure dome decree . . .'

Fourth Story

1. **Gentile de' Carisendi**   Like the Caccianimico family, the Carisendi were among the most powerful patrician families in medieval Bologna. The famous leaning tower, the smaller of the two towers dominating the centre of the city, is named after the Carisendi.

2. **riding without pause**   The distance separating Modena from Bologna is about twenty-five miles.

3. **in Persia there is a custom**   B. is perhaps using Persia loosely for the Saracen world in general. He had already told this same story in the *questioni d'amore* episode of his *Filocolo*, which is coloured throughout by exotic oriental motifs. Interestingly, the description which follows of Carisendi's banquet itself contains a *questione* concerning how a master should treat his servants, and Caccianimico's summing-up, although less wordy, is reminiscent of the judgements pronounced by Fiammetta at the conclusion of each of the thirteen *questioni* in the earlier work.

Fifth Story

1. **Friuli**   By setting the story in the remote north-east corner of Italy, in a region noted for the severity of its winters, B. maximizes the impact of the central episode. Like the previous tale, the story of the magic garden had appeared in an earlier form in the *questioni d'amore* sequence of the *Filocolo*. Chaucer tells the same story in *The Franklin's Tale*, where the persistent suitor, given the task of removing all the rocks from the coast of Brittany, likewise achieves the impossible with the aid of a magician. The story is oriental in origin, but both writers were possibly using a common French source.

2. **to those who are in love . . . possible**   The tag has classical antecedents,

for instance Cicero's '*Nil difficile amanti*' ('Nothing is difficult to the lover')
(*De oratore*, 10).

3. *a lady who was all but dead*   See the previous tale.

Sixth Story

1. *Charles the Old*   Founder of the Angevin dynasty, Charles I was King
of Naples and Sicily from 1266 to 1285. B. depicts him in a favourable light
not only in this tale and in the story of Madonna Beritola (II, 6), but also in
the *Amorosa visione* and *De casibus*. In reality his reign was marked by acts
of cruelty, and he was a notorious womanizer. At the time the story is set,
not long after his 'glorious victory' over Manfred at Benevento in 1266,
Charles was not exactly 'the Old', for he was born in 1226.

2. *Neri degli Uberti*   The Uberti were a powerful Florentine Ghibelline
family, of whom the most famous was Farinata degli Uberti, victor with
the assistance of King Manfred over the Florentine Guelphs at the battle of
Montaperti (1260). Farinata died in Florence in 1264, but other leading
Ghibellines were expelled by the Guelphs in the aftermath of Manfred's
defeat at Benevento. It is unlikely that King Charles, ruthless pursuer of
Ghibellines in the Kingdom, who gave orders for Farinata's children to be
imprisoned and murdered, would have displayed the kind of tolerance and
courtesy that he is reported in B.'s tale to have shown towards the
historically unidentifiable Neri degli Uberti.

3. *Castellammare di Stabia*   A resort in the south-east corner of the Bay of
Naples, noted for its hot mineral springs and baths and for its fine beaches.
The royal villa Domus Sana, of which B. had some personal knowledge,
was built there as a summer residence for the Angevin court in 1310.

4. *Guy de Montfort*   Son of Simon de Montfort, he was the *éminence grise*
of King Charles, who appointed him his vice-regent in Tuscany. In 1270, in
revenge for the killing of his father at Evesham in 1265, he murdered
Prince Henry, nephew to King Henry III of England, during High Mass in
the Cathedral at Viterbo. Dante placed his soul in the Phlegethon, the river
of boiling blood, among the souls of those who committed acts of violence
against their neighbours (*Inferno*, XII, 119–120).

5. *Conradin*   Manfred's nephew (1252–68), also known as Conrad V, was
the last representative of the Hohenstaufen dynasty. He led an expedition
into Italy in 1267 to regain Sicily from Charles I, was unexpectedly
defeated at Tagliacozza on 23 August, and delivered to Charles, who had
him tried for treason in Naples. After being convicted he was beheaded in
the public marketplace in 1268.

6. *Maffeo da Palizzi ... Guiglielmo della Magna*   According to the

chronicler Giovanni Villani, the Palizzi were the most powerful family in
Messina and acknowledged as the leaders of the large Italian community in
the island of Sicily. A Guiglielmo d'Alemagna is recorded in 1306 as one of
the nobles attending the son of Charles II, Raimondo Berengario.

Seventh Story

1. *when the French were driven from Sicily*   The reference is to the
uprising against French rule known as the Sicilian Vespers, which took
place on 31 March 1282.

2. *Peter of Aragon*   Famous for his great stature and physical strength,
Peter III of Aragon invaded Sicily in August 1282 and was proclaimed king
in Palermo. Since he was a supporter of the imperial, Ghibelline cause, this
tale of his magnanimity forms a nice counter-balance to the previous story
concerning Charles I, champion of the Guelphs and the papacy.

3. *in the Catalan style*   That is, according to the rules prescribed for
tournaments held in Catalonia, which was united with Aragon in 1137.

4. *Minuccio d'Arezzo*   B. was thought until fairly recently to have invented the name of the musician to impart a Tuscan flavour to his
narrative, but it has now been established that a troubadour of that name
was active in the Sicilian court in the latter part of the fourteenth century.

5. *Mico da Siena*   There is no record of a versifier of this name. Whether
or not his identity, like that of Minuccio, eventually comes to light, the
author of the verses is B. himself. Mico's song, composed in Sicily for the
benefit of the Tuscan apothecary's daughter, contains certain lexical and
thematic features typical of the poets of the so-called Sicilian school, many
of whom came originally from Tuscany.

6. *the Queen*   The wife of Peter III was Constance, heiress of Manfred,
but she did not accompany her husband on his Sicilian expedition.

7. *Perdicone*   The name, similar to that of the first of Alatiel's lovers,
Pericone (see II, 7), is of Provençal origin.

8. *Cefalù and Caltabellotta*   Now situated in the administrative divisions
of Palermo and Agrigento respectively.

Eighth Story

1. *Octavianus Caesar*   The adoptive son and heir of Julius Caesar, who
governed Rome as one of three triumvirs after Caesar's assassination in
43 BC, the other triumvirs being Mark Antony and Lepidus. After disposing of Lepidus in 32 BC and Mark Antony in 31 BC, he ruled as consul
until 23 BC, when he was proclaimed the first Roman emperor with the

title of Augustus Caesar. He died at Nola, near Naples, on 19 August AD 14.

2. *Publius Quintus Fulvius*   The father's name is an amalgam of three familiar names from Roman history, the second being that of one of the most famous and powerful families of the Roman republic. B. chooses another familiar Roman first name for the son, Titus, but the name of the other main character, the Greek Gisippus, is B.'s own invention, perhaps by analogy with the name of his tutor, Aristippus. The second part of B.'s story is a reworking of the legend of Damon and Pythias, versions of which are found in classical authors with whose writings B. was familiar, for example Cicero and Valerius Maximus. B. possibly derived the first part of the story from a tale in the *Disciplina clericalis* of Peter Alphonsi. But B.'s story is really a refined rhetorical exercise, at times verging on parody, on a topos, friendship, which was extremely popular in medieval schools of rhetoric.

3. *to study philosophy in Athens*   Athens was the recognized finishing school for the sons of the Roman nobility.

4. *Chremes*   The name almost certainly derives from a character in one of B.'s favourite Latin comedies, Terence's *Phormio*.

5. *Aristippus*   The Greek philosopher of that name was born some four centuries before the events recounted in B.'s story. Possibly B. chose him anachronistically as the tutor of Titus and Gisippus because in the story their altruistic actions reflect some of the philosopher's teachings, for instance that the infliction as well as the suffering of pain should be avoided.

Ninth Story

1. *Saladin*   The most powerful and most generous ruler in the Muslim world, Saladin died in 1193. See also the story of the three rings (I, 3).

2. *the Emperor Frederick I*   Frederick I ('Barbarossa') was German king and Holy Roman Emperor from 1152 to 1190, the year in which he drowned while trying to cross the Saleph River during the Third Crusade, launched in the spring of 1189.

3. *Messer Torello, of Strà in the province of Pavia*   The thirteenth-century chronicler Salimbene da Parma records that a 'Torellus de Strata de Papia' served as governor (*podestà*) for Frederick II in several cities of northern Italy and southern France between 1221 and 1237. B. frequently applies the names of known historical figures to his characters, at times anachronistically, to lend an air of authenticity to his narratives. Pavia, the ancient capital of Lombardy, lies on the left bank of the Ticino River, some twenty miles south of Milan.

4. *which never closed its gates*   Torello had earlier implied that Saladin could not arrive in Pavia before the city's gates were closed for the night, his intention being to mislead him into accepting his hospitality.

5. *Acre*   The last Christian stronghold in the Holy Land, lying on the Mediterranean coast, Acre was conquered in 1104 by the Crusaders, who named the city Saint Jean d'Acre. B.'s claim that the Christian armies were defeated there in 1189 through being weakened by illness reflects accounts of the battle found in Giovanni Villani's chronicle, but is unsupported by later historical evidence.

6. *San Pietro in Ciel d'Oro*   The famous cathedral in the centre of Pavia.

7. *Digne*   A town in the Alpes de Haute Provence, once feudatory to the Angevins of Naples.

8. *one of his magicians*   In general (see II, 1, III, 8, VI, 10, VIII, 3, VIII, 7 and VIII, 9) B. adopts a sceptical or derisive attitude towards all forms of magic and superstition, but both in the present story and in X, 5 the resolution of the plot depends on the successful application of the magical arts. The explanation for this apparent inconsistency lies in his treatment of the theme of the Tenth Day's stories. In their attempts to surpass the previous speaker with their own version of a magnanimous deed, the narrators resort to increasingly improbable examples, culminating in the wholly implausible tale of Griselda.

9. *Adalieta*   A name used in patrician families as an affectionate alternative to Adelaide.

Tenth Story

1. *the werewolf's tail*   Dioneo is referring back to the formula used by Lotteringhi's wife for exorcizing the werewolf (VIII, 1). After telling his story, he uses another scurrilous expression ('*scuotere il pilliccione*', 'to shake one's skin-coat') that had appeared earlier in the tale of the scholar and the widow (VIII, 7). It could be argued that the narrator's light-hearted attitude towards his narrative indicates that this, the most problematical story in the whole of the *Decameron*, should be read rather as an elaborate parable on obedience to the Lord's will rather than as a literal, realistic account of a husband's sadistic cruelty. Parallels with the biblical story of the patience of Job are evident, both in the text and in the narrative itself. *The Clerk's Tale*, Chaucer's version of the same story, was almost certainly based on Petrarch's Latin translation of B.'s novella, as can be seen for instance in its bowdlerization of the episode in which Griselda is stripped naked in the presence of all

the bystanders, men and women alike. Both in Petrarch and in Chaucer, she is stripped of her peasant's garb and regally re-clothed in private by the ladies of the court.

2. **Saluzzo** A town at the foot of the Alps about thirty miles south of Turin, the seat of the marquises of Saluzzo from 1142 to 1548.

3. **Griselda** The name appears to be an invention of B.'s own, perhaps constructed from that of a very different character, Criseida (Cressida), the heroine of his narrative poem *Filostrato*, on which Chaucer's *Troilus and Criseyde* is based.

4. **My lord, deal with me as you think best** Griselda's words recall the response of the Virgin Mary to the Angel Gabriel in Luke i, 38: '*Fiat mihi secundum verbum tuum*' ('Be it unto me according to thy word').

5. **do exactly as your lord ... has instructed you** Griselda's apparent sacrifice of her daughter (and later of her son) at her lord's command forms part of a long tradition of such intensely dramatic moments in classical and biblical literature, for instance Agamemnon's sacrifice of his daughter Iphigenia, Idomeneo's sacrifice of his son Idamante and God's command to Abraham (as a test of his obedience) that he sacrifice his only son, Isaac.

6. **naked as on the day I was born** Griselda's submissive reply to her husband's announcement echoes the words of Job: 'Naked came I out of my mother's womb, and naked shall I return thither: the Lord gave, and the Lord hath taken away' (Job i, 21).

7. **Panago** A form taken from popular speech, Panago (i.e. Pànico, near Bologna) was a feudatory of the counts of Alberti.

8. **My lord, I am ready to do as you ask** Yet another biblical echo, this time of the Virgin's '*Ecce ancilla Dei*' ('Behold the handmaid of the Lord') . from Luke i, 38.

9. **I think I can boast** The Italian text reads '*credendomi poter dar vanto*'. Luigi Russo pointed out that the phrase had a precise and solemn meaning in feudal society. It has to do with the 'vaunts' or boasts made by knights, often over the dinner table, concerning some outstanding personal achievement, defying their companions to cite a more worthy deed of their own.

(Conclusion)

1. **the wisdom of mortals ... anticipate the future** For his definition of wisdom, B. is paraphrasing a passage from Dante's *Convivio* (IV, xxvii, 5): 'A person ought, then, to be prudent, or wise. To be so he must have good recollection of the past, good knowledge of the present and good foresight regarding the future.'

AUTHOR'S EPILOGUE

1. **with his sword or his lance** In other words, with his weapon. B. is continuing to cite nouns with equivocal meanings.

2. **sometimes with a single nail, sometimes with two** More phallic imagery, the mildly blasphemous *double entendre* being made possible because *chiodo* ('nail') derives from the Latin *clavus*, from which the Italian verb *chiavare* ('to screw') also derives. The sexual implications of the phrase tend to be overlooked by academic critics, some of whom have recently engaged in erudite debate over the way in which the Crucifixion is represented by medieval artists. Cimabue's frescoes show Christ's feet nailed separately to the cross. Giotto, more economical, followed the practice of northern European painters in transfixing both feet with a single nail.

3. **Athens, or Bologna, or Paris** The most famous centres of learning in the ancient world (Athens) and the world of B.'s own day and age (Bologna and Paris).

4. **Jeremiah ... Magdalen** The references are to the Lamentations of Jeremiah, sung during Holy Week, to any one of several popular poems on the Passion of Christ such as Jacopone's *Pianto della Madonna*, and to the poem already referred to in the story of Friar Puccio (III, 4).

5. **who forsake a life of discomfort for the love of God** Repetition of the deliberately ambiguous phrase used by Friar Cipolla in his impromptu sermon (VI, 10).

6. **do their grinding when the millpond's full** A phrase used by the priest of Varlungo in the story of Monna Belcolore (VIII, 2).

7. **they all smell a little of the billy-goat** A reference to the homosexual proclivities of the religious, hinted at by Friar Cipolla with his veiled allusion to Capretius (VI, 10).

8. **that I had the finest and sweetest tongue in the world** Almost certainly, what is implied here is an act of cunnilingus. The light-hearted comment is offered in the same spirit as the casual reference to masturbation at the end of IX, 2. None of B.'s previous editors has felt it necessary to comment on his mischievous claim to close physical intimacy with his anonymous lady neighbour. The passage is entirely in keeping with the playful, irreverent tone of the rest of the Epilogue.

MAPS

Note: The maps on the following pages show the geographical location of places etc. named in the Introduction and Notes as well as in the text of the *Decameron* itself. Readers may consult the indexes for page-references to the various locations.

1. *Florence and Tuscany*

2. Italy

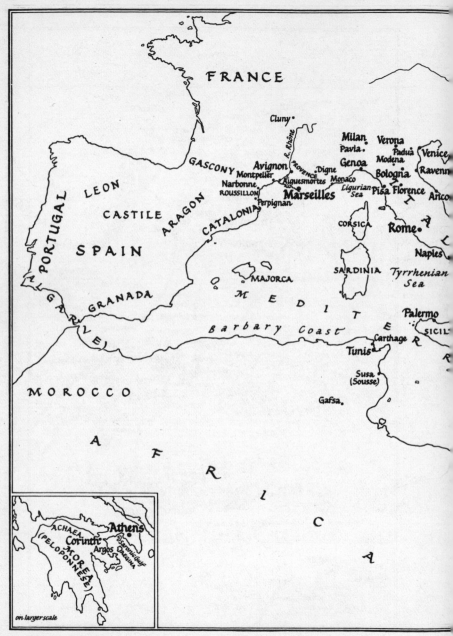

3. *The Mediterranean*

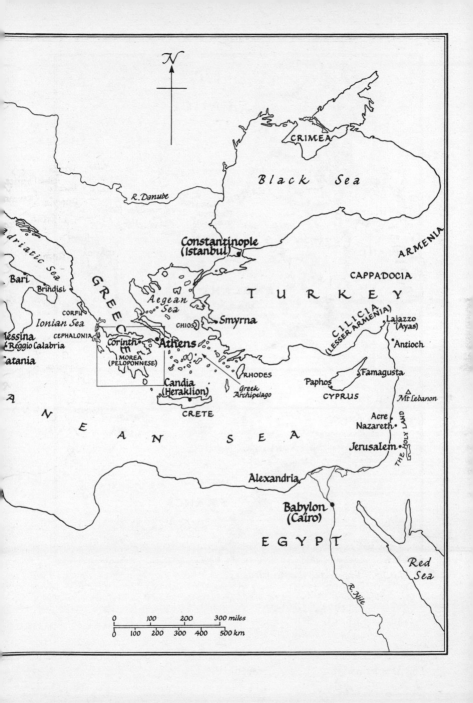

4. *Northern France and the British Isles*

INDEX TO STORIES

878INDEX TO STORIES

INDEX TO TRANSLATOR'S
INTRODUCTION AND NOTES

Other than in the entry under his name, Boccaccio is referred to as B.

READ MORE IN PENGUIN

In every corner of the world, on every subject under the sun, Penguin represents quality and variety – the very best in publishing today.

For complete information about books available from Penguin – including Puffins, Penguin Classics and Arkana – and how to order them, write to us at the appropriate address below. Please note that for copyright reasons the selection of books varies from country to country.

In the United Kingdom: Please write to *Dept. EP, Penguin Books Ltd, Bath Road, Harmondsworth, West Drayton, Middlesex UB7 0DA*

In the United States: Please write to *Consumer Services, Penguin Putnam Inc., 405 Murray Hill Parkway, East Rutherford, New Jersey 07073-2136*. VISA and MasterCard holders call 1-800-631-8571 to order Penguin titles

In Canada: Please write to *Penguin Books Canada Ltd, 10 Alcorn Avenue, Suite 300, Toronto, Ontario M4V 3B2*

In Australia: Please write to *Penguin Books Australia Ltd, 487 Maroondah Highway, Ringwood, Victoria 3134*

In New Zealand: Please write to *Penguin Books (NZ) Ltd, Private Bag 102902, North Shore Mail Centre, Auckland 10*

In India: Please write to *Penguin Books India Pvt Ltd, 11 Community Centre, Panchsheel Park, New Delhi 110017*

In the Netherlands: Please write to *Penguin Books Netherlands bv, Postbus 3507, NL-1001 AH Amsterdam*

In Germany: Please write to *Penguin Books Deutschland GmbH, Metzlerstrasse 26, 60594 Frankfurt am Main*

In Spain: Please write to *Penguin Books S. A., Bravo Murillo 19, 1°B, 28015 Madrid*

In Italy: Please write to *Penguin Italia s.r.l., Via Vittorio Emanuele 45/a, 20094 Corsico, Milano*

In France: Please write to *Penguin France, 12, Rue Prosper Ferradou, 31700 Blagnac*

In Japan: Please write to *Penguin Books Japan Ltd, Iidabashi KM-Bldg, 2-23-9 Koraku, Bunkyo-Ku, Tokyo 112-0004*

In South Africa: Please write to *Penguin Books South Africa (Pty) Ltd, P.O. Box 751093, Gardenview, 2047 Johannesburg*